DEAN KOONTZ

3 Complete Novels

▸   ▸   ▸ Cold Fire

The Key to Midnight

Hideaway

DEAN KOONTZ

3 Complete Novels

▸ ▸ ▸ Cold Fire

The Key to Midnight

Hideaway

G. P. Putnam's Sons ▸▸▸ New York

G. P. Putnam's Sons
Publishers Since 1838
a member of
Penguin Putnam Inc.
375 Hudson Street
New York, NY 10014

Library of Congress Cataloging-in-Publication Data

Koontz, Dean R. (Dean Ray), date.
[Novels. Selections]
Three complete novels / Dean Koontz.
p.   cm.
Contents: Cold fire—The key to midnight—Hideaway.
ISBN 0-399-14626-1
1. Psychological fiction, American.   2. Horror tales,
American.   I. Title.

PS3561.O55 A6   2000   99-087556
813'.54—dc21

Printed in the United States of America

1   3   5   7   9   10   8   6   4   2

BOOK DESIGN BY PATRICE SHERIDAN

Contents

Cold Fire

To Nick and Vicky Page,
who know how to be
good neighbors and friends
—if they would only try.
&
Dick and Pat Karlan,
who are among the few
in "Hollywood"
who own their souls
—and always will.

My life is better for
having known you all.
Weirder, but better!

Part One

The Hero,
The Friend

August 12

Even before the events in the super-market, Jim Ironheart should have known trouble was coming. During the night he dreamed of being pursued across a field by a flock of large blackbirds that shrieked around him in a turbulent flapping of wings and tore at him with hooked beaks as precision-honed as surgical scalpels. When he woke and was unable to breathe, he shuffled onto the balcony in his pajama bottoms to get some fresh air. But at nine-thirty in the morning, the temperature, already ninety degrees, only contributed to the sense of suffocation with which he had awakened.

A long shower and a shave refreshed him.

The refrigerator contained only part of a moldering Sara Lee cake. It resembled a laboratory culture of some new, exquisitely virulent strain of botulinus. He could either starve or go out into the furnace heat.

The August day was so torrid that birds, beyond the boundaries of bad dreams, preferred the bowers of the trees to the sunscorched open spaces of the southern California sky; they sat silently in their leafy shelters, chirruping rarely and without enthusiasm. Dogs padded cat-quick along sidewalks as hot as griddles. No man, woman or child paused to see if an egg would fry on the concrete, taking it as a matter of faith.

After eating a light breakfast at an umbrella-shaded table on the patio of a seaside cafe in Laguna Beach, he was enervated again and sheathed in a dew of perspiration. It was one of those rare occasions when the Pacific could not produce even a dependable mild breeze.

From there he went to the supermarket, which at first seemed to be a sanctuary. He was wearing only white cotton slacks and a blue T-shirt, so the air-conditioning and the chill currents rising off the refrigerated display cases were refreshing.

He was in the cookie department, comparing the ingredients in fudge macaroons to those in pineapple-coconut-almond bars, trying to decide which was the lesser dietary sin, when the fit hit him. On the scale of such things, it was not much of a fit—no convulsions, no violent muscle contractions, no sudden rivers of sweat, no speaking in strange tongues. He just abruptly turned to a woman shopper next to him and said, "Life line."

She was about thirty, wearing shorts and a halter top, goodlooking enough to have experienced a wearying array of come-ons from men, so perhaps she thought he was making a pass at her. She gave him a guarded look. "Excuse me?"

Flow with it, he told himself. Don't be afraid.

He began to shudder, not because of the air-conditioning but because a series of *inner* chills swam through him, like a wriggling school of eels. All the strength went out of his hands, and he dropped the packages of cookies.

Embarrassed but unable to control himself, he repeated: "Life line."

"I don't understand," the woman said.

Although this had happened to him nine times before, he said, "Neither do I."

She clutched a box of vanilla wafers as though she might throw it in his face and run if she decided he was a walking headline (BERSERK MAN SHOOTS SIX IN SUPERMARKET). Nevertheless, she was enough of a good Samaritan to hang in for another exchange: "Are you all right?"

No doubt, he was pale. He felt as if all the blood had drained out of his face. He tried to put on a reassuring smile, knew it was a ghastly grimace, and said, "Gotta go."

Turning away from his shopping cart, Jim walked out of the market, into the searing August heat. The forty-degree temperature change momentarily locked the breath in his lungs. The blacktop in the parking lot was tacky in places. Sun silvered the windshields of the cars and seemed to shatter into dazzling splinters against chrome bumpers and grilles.

He went to his Ford. It had air-conditioning, but even after he had driven across the lot and turned onto Crown Valley Parkway, the draft from the dashboard vents was refreshing only by comparison with the baking-oven atmosphere in the car. He put down his window.

Initially he did not know where he was going. Then he had a vague feeling that he should return home. Rapidly the feeling became a strong hunch, the hunch became a conviction, and the conviction became a compulsion. He absolutely *had* to get home.

He drove too fast, weaving in and out of traffic, taking chances, which was uncharacteristic of him. If a cop had stopped him, he would not have been able to explain his desperate urgency, for he did not understand it himself.

It was as if his every move was orchestrated by someone unseen, controlling him much the way that he controlled the car.

Again he told himself to flow with it, which was easy since he had no choice. He also told himself not to be afraid, but fear was his unshakable companion.

When he pulled into his driveway in Laguna Niguel, the spiky black shadows of palm fronds looked like cracks in the blazing white stucco walls of his small house, as if the structure had dried out and split open in the heat. The red-tile roof appeared to ripple like overlapping waves of flame.

In his bedroom, sunlight acquired a coppery hue as it poured through the tinted windows. It laid a penny-colored glow in stripes across the bed and off-white carpet, alternating with bands of shade from the half-open plantation shutters.

Jim switched on a bedside lamp.

He didn't know he was going to pack for travel until he found himself taking a suitcase from his closet. He gathered up his shaving gear and toiletries first. He didn't know his destination or how long he would be gone, but he included two changes of clothes. These jobs—adventures, missions, whatever in God's name they were—usually didn't require him to be away more than two or three days.

He hesitated, worried that he had not packed enough. But these trips were dangerous; each could be his last, in which case it didn't matter whether he packed too much or too little.

He closed the suitcase and stared at it, not sure what to do next. Then he said, "Gotta fly," and he knew.

The drive to John Wayne Airport, on the southeastern edge of Santa Ana, took less than half an hour. Along the way he saw subtle reminders that southern California had been a desert before the importation of water through aqueducts. A billboard urged water conservation. Gardeners were installing low-maintenance cactus and ice plant in front of a new Southwestern-style apartment building. Between the greenbelts and the neighborhoods of lushly landscaped properties, the vegetation on undeveloped fields and hills was parched and brown, waiting for the kiss of a match in the trembling hand of one of the pyromaniacs contributing to the annual, devastating wildfire season.

In the main terminal at the airport, travelers streamed to and from the boarding gates. The multi-racial crowd belied the lingering myth that Orange County was culturally bland and populated solely by white Anglo-Saxon Protestants. On his way to the bank of TV monitors that displayed a list of arriving and departing PSA flights, Jim heard four languages besides English.

He read the destinations from top to bottom on the monitor. The next to last city—Portland, Oregon—struck a spark of inspiration in him, and he went straight to the ticket counter.

The clerk who served him was a clean-cut young man, as straight-arrow as a Disneyland employee—at first glance.

"The flight to Portland leaving in twenty minutes," Jim said. "Is it full up?"

The clerk checked the computer. "You're in luck, sir. We have three open seats."

While the clerk processed the credit card and issued the ticket, Jim noticed the guy had pierced ears. He wasn't wearing earrings on the job, but the holes in his lobes were visible enough to indicate that he wore them regularly when he was off duty and that he preferred heavy jewelry. When he returned Jim's credit card, his shirtsleeve pulled up far enough on his right wrist to reveal the snarling muzzle of what appeared to be a lavishly detailed, colorful dragon tattoo that extended up his entire arm. The knuckles of that hand were crusted with scabs, as if they had been skinned in a fight.

All the way to the boarding gate, Jim wondered what subculture the clerk swam in after he shed his uniform at the end of the work day and put on street clothes. He had a hunch the guy was nothing as mundane as a biker punk.

The plane took off to the south, with the merciless glare of the sun at the windows on Jim's side. Then it swung to the west and turned north over the ocean, and he could see the sun only as a reflection in the sea below, where its blazing image seemed to transform the water into a vast churning mass of magma erupting from beneath the planet's crust.

Jim realized he was clenching his teeth. He looked down at the armrests of his seat, where his hands were tightly hooked like the talons of an eagle to the rock of a precarious roost.

He tried to relax.

He was not afraid of flying. What he feared was Portland . . . and whatever form of death might be waiting there for him.

2 Holly Thorne was at a private elementary school on the west side of Portland to interview a teacher, Louise Tarvohl, who had sold a book of poetry to a major New York publisher, not an easy feat in an age when most people's knowledge of poetry was limited to the lyrics of pop songs and occasional rhyming television ads for dog food, underarm deodorant, or steel-belted radial tires. Only a few summer classes were under way. Another instructor assumed responsibility for Louise's kids, so she and Holly could talk.

They sat at a redwood picnic table on the playground, after Holly checked the bench to be sure there was no dirt on it that might stain her white cotton dress. A jungle gym was to their left, a swing set to their right. The day was pleasantly warm, and a breeze stirred an agreeable fragrance from some nearby Douglas firs.

"Smell the air!" Louise took a deep button-popping breath. "You can sure tell we're on the edge of five thousand acres of parkland, huh? So little stain of humanity in the air."

Holly had been given an advance copy of the book, *Soughing Cypress and Other Poems*, when Tom Corvey, the editor of the *Press*'s entertainment section, assigned her to the story. She had wanted to like it. She enjoyed seeing people succeed—perhaps because she had not achieved much in her own career as a journalist and needed to be reminded now and then that success was attainable. Unfortunately the poems were jejune, dismally sentimental celebrations of the natural world that read like something written by a Robert Frost manqué, then filtered through the sensibilities of a Hallmark editor in charge of developing saccharine cards for grandma's birthday.

Nevertheless Holly intended to write an uncritical piece. Over the years she had known far too many reporters who, because of envy or bitterness or a misguided sense of moral superiority, got a kick out of slanting and coloring a story to make their subjects look foolish. Except when dealing with exceptionally vile criminals and politicians, she had never been able to work up enough hatred to write that way—which was one reason her career spiral had spun her down through three major newspapers in three large cities to her current position in the more humble offices of the *Portland Press*. Biased journalism was often more colorful than balanced reporting, sold more papers, and was more widely commented upon and admired. But though she rapidly came to dislike Louise Tarvohl even more than the woman's bad poetry, she could work up no enthusiasm for a hatchet job.

"Only in the wilderness am I alive, far from the sights and sounds of civilization, where I can hear the voices of nature in the trees, in the brush, in the lonely ponds, in the dirt."

Voices in the dirt? Holly thought, and almost laughed.

She liked the way Louise looked: hardy, robust, vital, alive. The woman was thirty-five, Holly's senior by two years, although she appeared ten years older. The crow's-feet around her eyes and mouth, her deep laugh lines, and her leathery sun-browned skin pegged her as an outdoors woman. Her sun-bleached hair was pulled back in a ponytail, and she wore jeans and a check-ered blue shirt.

"There is a purity in forest mud," Louise insisted, "that can't be matched in the most thoroughly scrubbed and sterilized hospital surgery." She tilted her face back for a moment to bask in the warm sunfall. "The purity of the natural world cleanses your soul. From that renewed purity of soul comes the sublime vapor of great poetry."

"Sublime vapor?" Holly said, as if she wanted to be sure that her tape recorder would correctly register every golden phrase.

"Sublime vapor," Louise repeated, and smiled.

The inner Louise was the Louise that offended Holly. She had cultivated an otherworldly quality, like a spectral projection, more surface than sub-stance. Her opinions and attitudes were insubstantial, based less on facts and insights than on whims—iron whims, but whims nonetheless—and she ex-pressed them in language that was flamboyant but imprecise, overblown but empty.

Holly was something of an environmentalist herself, and she was dis-mayed to discover that she and Louise fetched up on the same side of some issues. It was unnerving to have allies who struck you as goofy; it made your own opinions seem suspect.

Louise leaned forward on the picnic bench, folding her arms on the red-wood table. "The earth is a living thing. It could talk to us if we were worth talking to, could just open a mouth in any rock or plant or pond and talk as easily as I'm talking to you."

"What an exciting concept," Holly said.

"Human beings are nothing more than lice."

"Lice?"

"Lice crawling over the living earth," Louise said dreamily.

Holly said, "I hadn't thought of it that way."

"God is not only *in* each butterfly—God *is* each butterfly, each bird, each rabbit, every wild thing. I would sacrifice a million human lives—ten million and more!—if it meant saving one innocent family of weasels, because God *is* each of those weasels."

As if moved by the woman's rhetoric, as if she didn't think it was eco-fascism, Holly said, "I give as much as I can every year to the Nature Con-servancy, and I think of myself as an environmentalist, but I see that my consciousness hasn't been raised as far as yours."

The poet did not hear the sarcasm and reached across the table to squeeze Holly's hand. "Don't worry, dear. You'll get there. I sense an aura of great spiritual potentiality around you."

"Help me to understand. . . . God is butterflies and rabbits and every liv-ing thing, and God is rocks and dirt and water—but God isn't us?"

"No. Because of our one *unnatural* quality."

"Which is?"

"Intelligence."

Holly blinked in surprise. "Intelligence is unnatural?"

"A high degree of intelligence, yes. It exists in no other creatures in the natural world. That's why nature shuns us, and why we subconsciously hate her and seek to obliterate her. High intelligence leads to the concept of progress. Progress leads to nuclear weapons, bio-engineering, chaos, and ultimately to annihilation."

"God . . . or natural evolution didn't give us our intelligence?"

"It was an unanticipated mutation. We're mutants, that's all. Monsters."

Holly said, "Then the less intelligence a creature exhibits . . ."

". . . the more natural it is," Louise finished for her.

Holly nodded thoughtfully, as if seriously considering the bizarre proposition that a dumber world was a better world, but she was really thinking that she could not write this story after all. She found Louise Tarvohl so preposterous that she could not compose a favorable article and still hang on to her integrity. At the same time, she had no heart for making a fool of the woman in print. Holly's problem was not her deep and abiding cynicism but her soft heart; no creature on earth was more certain to suffer frustration and dissatisfaction with life than a bitter cynic with a damp wad of compassion at her core.

She put down her pen, for she would be making no notes. All she wanted to do was get away from Louise, off the playground, back into the real world—even though the real world had always struck her as just slightly less screwy than this encounter. But the least she owed Tom Corvey was sixty to ninety minutes of taped interview, which would provide another reporter with enough material to write the piece.

"Louise," she said, "in light of what you've told me, I think you're the most natural person I've ever met."

Louise didn't get it. Perceiving a compliment instead of a slight, she beamed at Holly.

"Trees are sisters to us," Louise said, eager to reveal another facet of her philosophy, evidently having forgotten that human beings were lice, not trees. "Would you cut off the limbs of your sister, cruelly section her flesh, and build your house with pieces of her corpse?"

"No, I wouldn't," Holly said sincerely. "Besides, the city probably wouldn't approve a building permit for such an unconventional structure."

Holly was safe: Louise had no sense of humor—therefore, no capacity to be offended by the wisecrack.

While the woman prattled on, Holly leaned into the picnic table, feigning interest, and did a fast-backward scan of her entire adult life. She decided that she had spent all of that precious time in the company of idiots, fools, and crooks, listening to their harebrained or sociopathic plans and dreams, searching fruitlessly for nuggets of wisdom and interest in their boobish or psychotic stories.

Increasingly miserable, she began to brood about her personal life. She had made no effort to develop close women friends in Portland, perhaps because in her heart she felt that Portland was only one more stop on her peripatetic journalistic journey. Her experiences with men were, if anything, even more disheartening than her professional experiences with interviewees of both sexes. Though she still hoped to meet the right man, get married, have children, and enjoy a fulfilling domestic life, she wondered if anyone nice, sane, intelligent, and genuinely interesting would ever enter her life.

Probably not.

And if someone like that miraculously crossed her path one day, his pleasant demeanor would no doubt prove to be a mask, and under the mask would be a leering serial killer with a chainsaw fetish.

3 Outside the terminal at Portland International Airport, Jim Ironheart got into a taxi operated by something called the New Rose City Cab Company, which sounded like a corporate stepchild of the long-forgotten hippie era, born in the age of love beads and flower power. But the cabbie—Frazier Tooley, according to his displayed license—explained that Portland was called the City of Roses, which bloomed there in multitudes and were meant to be symbols of renewal and growth. "The same way," he said, "that street beggars are symbols of decay and collapse in New York," displaying a curiously charming smugness that Jim sensed was shared by many Portlanders.

Tooley, who looked like an Italian operatic tenor cast from the same mold as Luciano Pavarotti, was not sure he had understood Jim's instructions. "You just want me to drive around for a while?"

"Yeah. I'd like to see some of the city before I check into the hotel. I've never been here before."

The truth was, he didn't know at which hotel he should stay or whether he would be required to do the job soon, tonight, or maybe tomorrow. He hoped that he would learn what was expected of him if he just tried to relax and waited for enlightenment.

Tooley was happy to oblige—not with enlightenment but with a tour of Portland—because a large fare would tick up on the meter, but also because he clearly enjoyed showing off his city. In fact, it was exceptionally attractive. Historic brick structures and nineteenth-century cast-iron-front buildings were carefully preserved among modern glass high rises. Parks full of fountains and trees were so numerous that it sometimes seemed the city was in a forest, and roses were everywhere, not as many blooms as earlier in the summer but radiantly colorful.

After less than half an hour, Jim suddenly was overcome by the feeling that time was running out. He sat forward on the rear seat and heard himself say: "Do you know the McAlbury School?"

"Sure," Tooley said.

"What is it?"

"The way you asked, I thought you knew. Private elementary school over on the west side."

Jim's heart was beating hard and fast. "Take me there."

Frowning at him in the rearview mirror, Tooley said, "Something wrong?"

"I have to be there."

Tooley braked at a red traffic light. He looked over his shoulder. "What's wrong?"

"I just have to be there," Jim said sharply, frustratedly.

"Sure, no sweat."

Fear had rippled through Jim ever since he had spoken the words "life line" to the woman in the supermarket more than four hours ago. Now those ripples swelled into dark waves that carried him toward McAlbury School. With an overwhelming sense of urgency that he could not explain, he said, "I have to be there *in fifteen minutes!*"

"Why didn't you mention it earlier?"

He wanted to say, I didn't *know* earlier. Instead he said, "Can you get me there in time?"

"It'll be tight."

"I'll pay triple the meter."

"Triple?"

"If you make it in time," he said, withdrawing his wallet from his pocket. He extracted a hundred-dollar bill and thrust it at Tooley. "Take this in advance."

"It's that important?"

"It's life and death."

Tooley gave him a look that said: What—are you nuts?

"The light just changed," Jim told him. "Let's move!"

Although Tooley's skeptical frown deepened, he faced front again, hung a left turn at the intersection, and tramped on the accelerator.

Jim kept glancing at his watch all the way, and they arrived at the school with only three minutes to spare. He tossed another bill at Tooley, paying even more than three times the meter, pulled open the door, and scrambled out with his suitcase.

Tooley leaned through his open window. "You want me to wait?"

Slamming the door, Jim said, "No. No, thanks. You can go."

He turned away and heard the taxi drive off as he anxiously studied the front of McAlbury School. The building was actually a rambling white Colonial house with a deep front porch, onto which had been added two single-story wings to provide more classrooms. It was shaded by Douglas firs and huge old sycamores. With its lawn and playground, it occupied the entire length of that short block.

In the house part of the structure directly in front of him, kids were coming out of the double doors, onto the porch, and down the steps. Laughing and chattering, carrying books and large drawing tablets and bright lunchboxes decorated with cartoon characters, they approached him along the school walk, passed through the open gate in the spearpoint iron fence, and turned either uphill or down, moving away from him in both directions.

Two minutes left. He didn't have to look at his watch. His heart was pounding two beats for every second, and he *knew* the time as surely as if he had been a clock.

Sunshine, filtered through the interstices of the arching trees, fell in delicate patterns across the scene and the people in it, as if everything had been draped over with an enormous piece of gossamer lacework stitched from golden thread. That netlike ornamental fabric of light seemed to shimmer in time to the rising and falling music of the children's shouts and laughter, and the moment should have been peaceful, idyllic.

But Death was coming.

Suddenly he knew that Death was coming for one of the children, not for any of the three teachers standing on the porch, just for one child. Not a big catastrophe, not an explosion or fire or a falling airplane that would wipe out a dozen of them. Just one, a small tragedy. But *which* one?

Jim refocused his attention from the scene to the players in it, studying the children as they approached him, seeking the mark of imminent death on one of their fresh young faces. But they all looked as if they would live forever.

"Which one?" he said aloud, speaking neither to himself nor to the children but to. . . . Well, he supposed he was speaking to God. "Which one?"

Some kids went uphill toward the crosswalks at that intersection, and others headed downhill toward the opposite end of the block. In both directions, women crossing guards in bright-orange safety vests, holding big red paddlelike "stop" signs, had begun to shepherd their charges across the streets in small groups. No moving cars or trucks were in sight, so even without the crossing guards there seemed to be little threat from traffic.

One and a half minutes.

Jim scrutinized two yellow vans parked at the curb downhill from him. For the most part, McAlbury seemed to be a neighborhood school, where kids walked to and from their homes, but a few were boarding the vans. The two drivers stood by the doors, smiling and joking with the ebullient, energetic passengers. None of the kids boarding the vans seemed doomed, and the cheery yellow vehicles did not strike him as morgue wagons in bright dress.

But Death was nearer.

It was almost among them.

An ominous change had stolen over the scene, not in reality but in Jim's perception of it. He was now less aware of the golden lacework of light than he was of the shadows within that bright filigree: small shadows the shape of leaves or bristling clusters of evergreen needles; larger shadows the shape of tree trunks or branches; geometric bars of shade from the iron rails of the spearpoint fence. Each blot of darkness seemed to be a potential doorway through which Death might arrive.

One minute.

Frantic, he hurried downhill several steps, among the children, drawing puzzled looks as he glanced at one then another of them, not sure what sort of sign he was searching for, the small suitcase banging against his leg.

Fifty seconds.

The shadows seemed to be growing, spreading, melting together all around Jim.

He stopped, turned, and peered uphill toward the end of the block, where the crossing guard was standing in the intersection, holding up her red "stop" sign, using her free hand to motion the kids across. Five of them were in the street. Another half dozen were approaching the corner and soon to cross.

One of the drivers at the nearby school vans said, "Mister, is something wrong?"

Forty seconds.

Jim dropped the suitcase and ran uphill toward the intersection, still uncertain about what was going to happen and which child was at risk. He was pushed in that direction by the same invisible hand that had made him pack a suitcase and fly to Portland. Startled kids moved out of his way.

At the periphery of his vision, everything had become ink-black. He was aware only of what lay directly ahead of him. From one curb to the other, the intersection appeared to be a scene revealed by a spotlight on an otherwise night-dark stage.

Half a minute.

Two women looked up in surprise and failed to get out of his way fast enough. He tried to dodge them, but he brushed against a blonde in a summery white dress, almost knocking her down. He kept going because he could feel Death among them now, a cold presence.

He reached the intersection, stepped off the curb, and stopped. Four kids in the street. One was going to be a victim. But which of the four? And a victim of what?

Twenty seconds.

The crossing guard was staring at him.

All but one of the kids were nearing the curb, and Jim sensed that the sidewalks were safe territory. The street would be the killing ground.

He moved toward the dawdler, a little red-haired girl, who turned and blinked at him in surprise.

Fifteen seconds.

Not the girl. He looked into her jade-green eyes and knew she was safe. Just *knew* it somehow.

All the other kids had reached the sidewalk.

Fourteen seconds.

Jim spun around and looked back toward the far curb. Four more children had entered the street behind him.

Thirteen seconds.

The four new kids started to arc around him, giving him wary sidelong looks. He knew he appeared to be a little deranged, standing in the street, wide-eyed, gaping at them, his face distorted by fear.

Eleven seconds.

No cars in sight. But the brow of the hill was little more than a hundred yards above the intersection, and maybe some reckless fool was rocketing up the far side with the accelerator jammed to the floorboard. As soon as that image flashed through his mind, Jim knew it was a prophetic glimpse of the instrument Death would use: a drunk driver.

Eight seconds.

He wanted to shout, tell them to run, but maybe he would only panic them and cause the marked child to bolt straight *into* danger rather than away from it.

Seven seconds.

He heard the muffled growl of an engine, which instantly changed to a loud roar, then a piston-shattering scream. A pickup truck shot over the brow of the hill. It actually took flight for an instant, afternoon sun flashing off its windshield and coruscating across its chromework, as if it were a flaming chariot descending from the heavens on judgment day. With a shrill bark of rubber against blacktop, the front tires met the pavement again, and the rear of the truck slammed down with a jarring crash.

Five seconds.

The kids in the street scattered—except for a sandy-haired boy with violet eyes the shade of faded rose petals. He just stood there, holding a lunchbox covered with brightly colored cartoon figures, one tennis shoe untied, watching the truck bear down on him, unable to move, as if he sensed that it wasn't just a truck rushing to meet him but his destiny, inescapable. He was an eight- or nine-year-old boy with nowhere to go but to the grave.

Two seconds.

Leaping directly into the path of the oncoming pickup, Jim grabbed the kid. In what felt like a dream-slow swan dive off a high cliff, he carried the boy with him in a smooth arc to the pavement, rolling toward the leaf-littered gutter, feeling nothing from his impact with the street, his nerves so numbed by terror and adrenaline that he might as well have been tumbling across a field of lush grass and soft loam.

The roar of the truck was the loudest thing he had ever heard, as if it were a thunder *within* him, and he felt something strike his left foot, hard as a hammer blow. In the same instant a terrible wrenching force seemed to wring his ankle as if it were a rag. A white-hot current of pain crackled up his leg, sizzling into his hip joint, exploding in that socket of bone like a Fourth of July bottle rocket bursting in a night sky.

HOLLY STARTED AFTER the man who had collided with her, angry and intending to tell him off. But before she reached the intersection, a gray-and-red pickup erupted over the brow of the hill, as if fired out of a giant sling-shot. She halted at the curb.

The scream of the truck engine was a magic incantation that slowed the flow of time, stretching each second into what seemed to be a minute. From the curb, she saw the stranger sweep the boy out of the path of the pickup, executing the rescue with such singular agility and grace that he almost appeared to be performing a mad, slow-motion ballet in the street. She saw the bumper of the truck strike his left foot, and watched in hor-ror as his shoe was torn off and tossed high into the air, tumbling end over end. Peripherally, she was aware of the man and boy rolling toward the gutter, the truck swerving sharply to the right, the startled crossing guard dropping the paddlelike "stop" sign, the truck ricocheting off a parked car across the street, the man and boy coming to rest against the curb, the truck tipping onto its side and sliding downhill in cascades of yellow and blue sparks—but all the while her attention was focused pri-marily on that shoe tumbling up, up, into the air, silhouetted against the blue sky, hanging at the apex of its flight for what seemed like an hour, then tumbling slowly, slowly down again. She couldn't look away from it, was mesmerized by it, because she had the macabre feeling that the foot was still in the shoe, torn off at the ankle, bristling with splinters of bone, trailing shorn ribbons of arteries and veins. Down it came, down, down, straight toward her, and she felt a scream swelling in the back of her throat.

Down . . . down . . .

The battered shoe—a Reebok—plopped into the gutter in front of her, and she lowered her eyes to it the way she always looked into the face of the monster in a nightmare, not wanting to see but unable to turn away, equally repelled by and attracted to the unthinkable. The shoe was empty. No severed foot. Not even any blood.

She swallowed the unreleased scream. She tasted vomit in the back of her throat, and swallowed that too.

As the pickup came to rest on its side more than half a block down the hill, Holly turned the other way and ran to the man and boy. She was the first to reach them as they started to sit up on the blacktop.

Except for a scraped palm and a small abrasion on his chin, the child appeared to be unhurt. He was not even crying.

She dropped to her knees in front of him. "Are you okay, honey?"

Though dazed, the boy understood and nodded. "Yeah. My hand hurts a little, that's all."

The man in the white slacks and blue T-shirt was sitting up. He had rolled his sock halfway off his foot and was gingerly kneading his left ankle. Though the ankle was swollen and already enflamed, Holly was still sur-prised by the absence of blood.

The crossing guard, a couple of teachers, and other kids gathered around, and a babble of excited voices rose on all sides. The boy was helped up and drawn into a teacher's arms.

Wincing in pain as he continued to massage his ankle, the injured man raised his head and met Holly's gaze. His eyes were searingly blue and, for an instant, appeared as cold as if they were not human eyes at all but the visual receptors of a machine.

Then he smiled. In a blink, the initial impression of coldness was replaced by one of warmth. In fact Holly was overwhelmed by the clarity, morning-sky color, and beauty of his eyes; she felt as if she were peering through them into a gentle soul. She was a cynic who would equally distrust a nun and Mafia boss on first encounter, so her instant attraction to this man was jolting. Though words were her first love and her trade, she was at a loss for them.

"Close call," he said, and his smile elicited one from her.

4 Holly waited for Jim Ironheart in the school hallway, outside the boys' restroom. All of the children and teachers had at last gone home. The building was silent, except for the periodic muffled hum of the maintenance man's electric buffer as he polished the vinyl tile up on the second floor. The air was laced with a faint perfume of chalk dust, craft paste, and pine-scented disinfectant wax.

Outside in the street, the police probably were still overseeing a couple of towing-company employees who were righting the overturned truck in order to haul it away. The driver had been drunk. At the moment he was in the hospital, where physicians were attending to his broken leg, lacerations, abrasions, and contusions.

Holly had gotten nearly everything she required to write the story: background on the boy—Billy Jenkins—who had nearly been killed, the facts of the event, the reactions of the eye-witnesses, a response from the police, and slurred expressions of regret mixed with self-pity from the inebriated driver of the truck. She lacked only one element, but it was the most important—information about Jim Ironheart, the hero of the whole affair. Newspaper readers would want to know everything about him. But at the moment all she could have told them was the guy's name and that he was from southern California.

His brown suitcase stood against the wall beside her, and she kept eyeing it. She had the urge to pop the latches and explore the contents of the bag, though at first she didn't know why. Then she realized it was unusual for a man to be carrying luggage through a residential neighborhood; a reporter was trained—if not genetically compelled—to be curious about anything out of the ordinary.

When Ironheart came out of the restroom, Holly was still staring at the suitcase. She twitched guiltily, as if caught pawing through the contents of the bag.

"How're you feeling?" she asked.

"Fine." He was limping. "But I told you—I'd rather not to interviewed."

He had combed his thick brown hair and blotted the worst of the dirt off his white cotton pants. He was wearing both shoes again, although the left was torn in one spot and battered.

She said, "I won't take much of your time."

"Definitely," he agreed, smiling.

"Oh, come on, be a good guy."

"Sorry, but I'd make dull copy anyway."

"You just saved a child's life!"

"Other than that, I'm boring."

Something about him belied his claim to dullness, although at first Holly could not pinpoint the reason for his strong appeal. He was about thirty-five, an inch or two under six feet, lean but well-muscled. Though he was attractive enough, he didn't have the looks that made her think of movie stars. His eyes were beautiful, yes, but she was never drawn to a man merely because of his looks and certainly not because of one exceptional feature.

He picked up his suitcase and began to limp along the corridor.

"You should see a doctor," she said, falling in at his side.

"At worst, it's sprained."

"It still should be treated."

"Well, I'll buy an Ace bandage at the airport, or when I get back home."

Maybe his manner was what she found so appealing. He spoke softly, smiled easily, rather like a Southern gentleman, though he had no accent. He also moved with unusual grace even when he was limping. She remembered how she had been reminded of ballet when, with the fluidity of a dancer, he had swept the little boy out of the path of the hurtling truck. Exceptional physical grace and an unforced gentility were appealing in a man. But neither of those qualities was what fascinated her. Something else. Something more elusive.

As they reached the front door, she said, "If you're really intent on going home again, I can give you a ride to the airport."

"Thank you. That's very kind, but I don't need a ride."

She followed him onto the porch. "It's a damned long walk."

He stopped, and frowned. "Oh. Yeah. Well . . . there's got to be a phone here. I'll call a cab."

"Come on, you don't have to be afraid of me. I'm not a serial killer. I don't keep a chainsaw in my car."

He stared at her a beat, then grinned disarmingly. "Actually, you look more like the type who favors bludgeoning with a blunt instrument."

"I'm a reporter. We use switchblades. But I haven't killed anyone this week."

"Last week?"

"Two. But they were both door-to-door salesmen."

"It's still homicide."

"Justifiable, though."

"Okay, I accept your offer."

Her blue Toyota was at the far curb, two back from the parked car into which the drunk driver had slammed. Downhill, the tow truck was just hauling away the totaled pickup, and the last of the policemen was getting into a patrol car. A few overlooked splinters of tempered glass from the truck's broken windows still glimmered on the blacktop in the late-afternoon sunshine.

They rode for a block or so in silence.

Then Holly said, "You have friends in Portland?"

"Yeah. From college."

"That's who you were staying with?"

"Yeah."

"They couldn't take you to the airport?"

"They could've if it was a morning flight, but this afternoon they were both at work."

"Ah," she said. She commented on clusters of brilliant yellow roses that hung from vines entwining a split-rail fence at a house they passed, and asked if he knew that Portland called itself the City of Roses, which he did. After another silence, she returned to the *real* conversation: "Their phone wasn't working, huh?"

"Excuse me?"

"Your friends." She shrugged. "I just wondered why you didn't call a cab from their place."

"I intended to walk."

"To the airport?"

"My ankle was fine then."

"It's still a long walk."

"Oh, but I'm a fitness nut."

"Very long walk—especially with a suitcase."

"It's not that heavy. When I'm exercising, I usually walk with hand-weights to get an upper-body workout."

"I'm a walker myself," she said, braking for a red light. "I used to run every morning, but my knees started hurting."

"Mine too, so I switched to walking. Gives your heart the same workout if you keep up your pace."

For a couple of miles, while she drove as slowly as she dared in order to extend the time she had with him, they chatted about physical fitness and fat-free foods. Eventually he said something that allowed her to ask, with complete naturalness, the names of his friends there in Portland.

"No," he said.

"No what?"

"No, I'm not giving you their names. They're private people, nice people, I don't want them being pestered."

"I've never been called a pest before," she said.

"No offense, Miss Thorne, but I just wouldn't want them to have to be in the paper and everything, have their lives disrupted."

"Lots of people *like* seeing their names in the newspaper."

"Lots don't."

"They might enjoy talking about their friend, the big hero."

"Sorry," he said affably, and smiled.

She was beginning to understand why she found him so appealing: his unshakable poise was irresistible. Having worked for two years in Los Angeles, Holly had known a lot of men who styled themselves as laid-back Californians; each portrayed himself as the epitome of self-possession, Mr. Mellow—*rely on me, baby, and the world can never touch either of us; we are beyond the reach of fate*—but none actually possessed the cool nerves and unflappable temperament to which he pretended. A Bruce Willis wardrobe, perfect tan, and studied insouciance did not a Bruce Willis make. Self-confidence could be gained through experience, but real aplomb was something you were either born with or learned to imitate—and the imitation was never convincing to the observant eye. However, Jim Ironheart had been born with enough aplomb, if rationed equally to all the men in Rhode Island, to produce an entire state of cool, unflappable types. He faced hurtling trucks and a reporter's questions with the same degree of equanimity. Just being in his company was oddly relaxing and reassuring.

She said, "That's an interesting name you have."

"Jim?"

He was having fun with her.

"Ironheart," she said. "Sounds like an American Indian name."

"Wouldn't mind having a little Chippewa or Apache blood, make me less dull, a little bit exotic, mysterious. But it's just the Anglicized version of the family's original German name—Eisenherz."

By the time they were on the East Portland Freeway, rapidly approaching the Killingsworth Street exit, Holly was dismayed at the prospect of dropping him at the airline terminal. As a reporter, she still had a lot of unanswered questions. More important, as a woman, she was more intrigued by him than she had been by any man in ages. She briefly considered taking a far more circuitous route to the airport; his lack of familiarity with the city might disguise her deception. Then she realized that the freeway signs were already announcing the upcoming exit to Portland International; even if he had not been reading them, he could not have failed to notice the steady air traffic in the deep-blue eastern sky ahead of them.

She said, "What do you do down there in California?"

"Enjoy life."

"I meant—what do you do for a living?"

"What's your guess?" he asked.

"Well . . . one thing for sure: you're not a librarian."

"Why do you say that?"

"You have a sense of mystery about you."

"Can't a librarian be mysterious?"

"I've never known one who was." Reluctantly she turned onto the airport exit ramp. "Maybe you're a cop of some kind."

"What gives you that idea?"

"Really good cops are unflappable, cool."

"Gee, I think of myself as a warm sort of guy, open and easy. You think I'm cool?"

Traffic was moderately heavy on the airport approach road. She let it slow her even further.

"I mean," she said, "that you're very self-possessed."

"How long have you been a reporter?"

"Twelve years."

"All of it in Portland?"

"No. I've been here a year."

"Where'd you work before?"

"Chicago . . . Los Angeles . . . Seattle."

"You like journalism?"

Realizing that she had lost control of the conversation, Holly said, "This isn't a game of twenty questions, you know."

"Oh," he said, clearly amused, "that's exactly what I thought it was."

She was frustrated by the impenetrable wall he had erected around himself, irritated by his stubbornness. She was not used to having her will thwarted. But he had no meanness in him, as far as she could see, and no great talent for deception; he was just determined to preserve his privacy. As a reporter who had ever-increasing doubts about a journalist's right to intrude in the lives of others, Holly sympathized with his reticence. When she glanced at him, she could only laugh softly. "You're good."

"So are you."

As she stopped at the curb in front of the terminal, Holly said, "No, if I were good, by now I'd at least have found out what the hell you do for a living."

He had a charming smile. And those *eyes*. "I didn't say you were as good as I am—just that you were good." He got out and retrieved his suitcase from the back seat, then returned to the open front door. "Look, I just happened to be in the right place at the right time. By sheer chance, I was able to save that boy. It wouldn't be fair to have my whole life turned upside down by the media just because I did a good deed."

"No, it wouldn't," she agreed.

With a look of relief, he said, "Thank you."

"But I gotta say—your modesty's refreshing."

He looked at her for a long beat, fixed her with his exceptional blue eyes. "So are you, Miss Thorne."

Then he closed the door, turned away, and entered the terminal.

Their last exchange played again in her mind:

Your modesty's refreshing.

So are you, Miss Thorne.

She stared at the terminal door through which he had disappeared, and he seemed too good to have been real, as if she had given a ride to a hitch-hiking spirit. A thin haze filtered flecks of color from the late-afternoon sunlight, so the air had a vague golden cast of the kind that sometimes hung for an instant in the wake of a vanishing revenant in an old movie about ghosts.

A hard, hollow rapping noise startled her.

She snapped her head around and saw an airport security guard tapping with his knuckles on the hood of her car. When he had her attention, he pointed to a sign: LOADING ZONE.

Wondering how long she had sat there, mesmerized by thoughts of Jim Ironheart, Holly released the emergency brake and slipped the car in gear. She drove away from the terminal.

Your modesty's refreshing.

So are you, Miss Thorne.

All the way back into Portland, a sense of the uncanny lay upon her, a perception that someone preternaturally special had passed through her life. She was unsettled by the discovery that a man could so affect her, and she felt uncomfortably girlish, even foolish. At the same time, she enjoyed that pleasantly eerie mood and did not want it to fade.

So are you, Miss Thorne.

5

That evening, in her third-floor apartment overlooking Council Crest Park, as she was cooking a dinner of angel-hair pasta with pesto sauce, pine nuts, fresh garlic, and chopped tomatoes, Holly suddenly wondered how Jim Ironheart could have known the young Billy Jenkins was in danger even before the drunken driver in the pickup truck had appeared over the crest of the hill.

She stopped chopping in the middle of a tomato and looked out the kitchen window. Purple-red twilight was settling over the greensward below. Among the trees, the park lamps cast pool of warm amber light on the grass-flanked walkways.

When Ironheart had charged up the sidewalk in front of McAlbury School, colliding with her and nearly knocking her down, Holly started after him, intending to tell him off. By the time she reached the intersection, he was already in the street, turning right then left, looking a little agitated . . . wild. In fact he seemed so strange, the kids moved around him in a wide arc. She had registered his panicked expression and the kids' reaction to him a second or two *before* the truck had erupted over the crest like a daredevil's car flying off the top of a stunt ramp. Only then had Ironheart focused on Billy Jenkins, scooping the boy out of the path of the truck.

Perhaps he had heard the roar of the engine, realized something was approaching the intersection at reckless speed, and acted out of an instinctive perception of danger. Holly tried to remember if she had been aware of the racing engine as early as when Ironheart had collided with her, but she could not recall. Maybe she had heard it but had not been as alert to its meaning as he had. Or perhaps she hadn't heard it at all because she had been trying to shake off the indefatigable Louise Tarvohl, who had insisted on walking with her to her car; she had felt that she'd go stark raving mad if she were forced to listen to even another minute of the poet's chatter, and she had been distracted by the desperate need to escape.

Now, in her kitchen, she was conscious of only one sound: the vigorously boiling water in the big pot on the stove. She should turn the gas down, put in the pasta, set the timer. . . . Instead she stood at the cutting board, tomato in one hand and knife in the other, staring out at the park but seeing the fateful intersection near the McAlbury School.

Even if Ironheart had heard the approaching engine from halfway down the block, how could he so quickly determine the direction from which the truck was approaching, that its driver was out of control, and that the children were consequently in danger? The crossing guard, initially much closer to the sound than Ironheart, had been taken by surprise, as had the kids themselves.

Okay, well, some people had sharper senses than others—which was why composers of symphonies could hear more complex harmonies and rhythms in music than could the average concertgoer, why some baseball players could see a pop fly against a glary sky sooner than others, and why a master viniculturist could appreciate subtler qualities of a rare vintage than could a stoned-blind wino who was only concerned with the effect. Likewise, some people had far quicker reflexes than others, which was part of what made Wayne Gretzky worth millions a year to a professional ice-hockey team. She had seen that Ironheart had the lightning reflexes of an athlete. No doubt he was also blessed with especially keen hearing. Most people with a notable physical advantage also had other gifts: it was all a matter of good genes. That was the explanation. Simple enough. Nothing unusual. Nothing mysterious. Certainly nothing supernatural. Just good genes.

Outside in the park, the shadows grew deeper. Except at those places where lamplight was shed upon it, the pathway disappeared into gathering darkness. The trees seemed to crowd together.

Holly put down the knife and went to the stove. She lowered the gas flame under the big pot, and the vigorously bubbling water fell to a slow boil. She put the pasta in to cook.

Back at the cutting board, as she picked up the knife, she looked out the window again. Stars began to appear in the sky as the purple light of dusk faded to black and as the crimson smear on the horizon darkened to burgundy. Below, more of the park walkway lay in shadow than in lamplight.

Suddenly she was gripped by the peculiar conviction that Jim Ironheart was going to walk out of darkness into a pool of amber light on the pathway, that he was going to raise his head and look directly up at her window, that somehow he knew where she lived and had come back for her. It was a ridiculous notion. But a chill quivered along her spine, tightening each knotted vertebra.

LATER, NEAR MIDNIGHT, when Holly sat on the edge of her bed and switched off the nightstand lamp, she glanced at her bedroom window, through which she also had a view of the park, and again a chill ran up her back. She started to lie down, hesitated, and got up instead. In panties and T-shirt, her usual sleeping attire, she moved through the dark room to the window, where she parted the sheers between the drapes.

He was not down there. She waited a minute, then another. He did not appear. Feeling foolish and confused, she returned to bed.

SHE WOKE IN the dead hours of the night, shuddering. All she could remember of the dream were blue eyes, intensely blue, with a gaze that penetrated her as completely as a sharp knife slicing through soft butter.

She got up and went into the bathroom, guided only by the thin wash of moonglow that filtered through the sheers over the window. In the bathroom she did not turn on the light. After she peed, she washed her hands and stood for a while just looking at her dim, amorphous reflection in the silvery-black mirror. She washed her hands. She got a drink of cold water. She realized that she was delaying her return to the bedroom because she was afraid she would be drawn to the window again.

This is ridiculous, she told herself. What's gotten into you?

She reentered the bedroom and found herself approaching the window instead of the bed. She parted the sheers.

He was not out there.

Holly felt as much disappointment as relief. As she stared into the night-swaddled reaches of Council Crest Park, an extended chill quivered through her again, and she realized that only half of it was generated by a nameless fear. A strange excitement coursed through her, as well, a pleasant anticipation of . . .

Of what?

She didn't know.

Jim Ironheart's effect on her was profound and lingering. She had never experienced anything like it. Although she struggled to understand what she was feeling, enlightenment eluded her. Mere sexual attraction was not the explanation. She was long past puberty, and neither the tidal pull of hormones nor the girlish desire for romance could affect her like this.

At last she returned to bed. She was certain that she would lie awake for the rest of the night, but to her surprise she soon drifted off again. As she trembled on the wire of consciousness, she heard herself mumble, *those eyes,*" then fell into the yawning void.

IN HIS OWN bed in Laguna Niguel, Jim woke just before dawn. His heart was pounding. Though the room was cool, he was bathed in sweat. He'd been having one of his frequent nightmares, but all he could recall of it was that something relentless, powerful, and vicious had been pursuing him . . .

His sense of onrushing death was so powerful that he had to turn on the lights to be certain that something inhuman and murderous was not actually in the room with him. He was alone.

"But not for long," he said aloud.

He wondered what he meant by that.

August 20 through August 22

1 Jim Ironheart peered anxiously through the dirty windshield of the stolen Camaro. The sun was a white ball, and the light it shed was as white and bitter as powdered lime. Even with sunglasses, he had to squint. Rising off sun-scorched blacktop, currents of superheated air formed into mirages of people and cars and lakes of water.

He was tired, and his eyes felt abraded. The heat illusions combined with occasional dust devils to hamper visibility. The endless vistas of the Mojave Desert made it difficult to maintain an accurate perception of speed; he didn't *feel* as if the car was streaking along at nearly a hundred miles an hour, but it was. In his condition, he should have been driving a lot slower.

But he was filled with a growing conviction that he was too late, that he was going to screw up. Someone was going to die because he had not been quick enough.

He glanced at the loaded shotgun angled in front of the other bucket seat, its butt on the floor, barrels pointed away from him. A full box of shells was on the seat.

Half sick with dread, he pressed the accelerator even closer to the floorboard. The needle on the speedometer dial shivered past the hundred mark.

He topped a long, gradual rise. Below lay a bowl-shaped valley twenty or thirty miles in diameter, so alkaline that it was mostly white, barren but for a few gray tumbleweeds and a stubble of desert scrub. It might have been formed by an asteroid impact eons ago, its outlines considerably softened by the passage of millennia but otherwise still as primeval as any place on earth.

The valley was bisected by the black highway on which mirages of water glistened. Along the shoulders, heat phantoms shimmered and writhed languorously.

He saw the car first, a station wagon. It was pulled off to the right of the roadway, approximately a mile ahead, near a drainage culvert where no water flowed except during rare storms and flash floods.

His heart began to pound harder, and in spite of the rush of cool air coming out of the dashboard vents, he broke into a sweat. *This* was the place.

Then he spotted the motor home, too, half a mile beyond the car, surfacing out of one of the deeper water mirages. It was lumbering away from him, toward the distant wall of the valley, where the highway sloped up between treeless, red-rock mountains.

Jim slowed as he approached the station wagon, not sure where his help was needed. His attention was drawn equally to the wagon and the motor home.

As the speedometer needle fell back across the gauge, he waited for a clearer understanding of his purpose. It didn't come. Usually he was compelled to act, as if by an inner voice that spoke to him only on a subconscious level, or as if he were a machine responding to a pre-programmed course of action. Not this time. Nothing.

With growing desperation, he braked hard and fishtailed to a full stop next to the Chevy station wagon. He didn't bother to pull onto the shoulder. He glanced at the shotgun beside him, but he knew somehow that he did not need it. Yet.

He got out of the Camaro and hurried toward the station wagon. Luggage was piled in the rear cargo area. When he looked through the side window, he saw a man sprawled on the front seat. He pulled open the door—and flinched. So much blood.

The guy was dying but not dead. He had been shot twice in the chest. His head lay at an angle against the passenger-side door, reminding Jim of Christ's head tilted to one side as he hung upon the cross. His eyes cleared briefly as he struggled to focus on Jim.

In a voice as frantic as it was fragile, he said, "Lisa . . . Susie . . . My wife, daughter . . ."

Then his tortured eyes slipped out of focus. A thin wheeze of breath escaped him, his head lolled to one side, and he was gone.

Sick, stricken by an almost disabling sense of responsibility for the stranger's death, Jim stepped back from the open door of the station wagon and stood for a moment on the black pavement under the searing white sun. If he had driven faster, harder, he might have been there a few minutes sooner, might have stopped what had happened.

A sound of anguish, low and primitive, rose from him. It was almost a whisper at first, swelling into a soft moan. But when he turned away from the dead man and looked down the highway toward the dwindling motor home, his cry quickly became a shout of rage because suddenly he knew what had happened.

And he knew what he must do.

In the Camaro again, he filled the roomy pockets of his blue cotton slacks with shotgun shells. Already loaded, the short-barreled pump-action 12-gauge was within easy reach.

He checked the rearview mirror. On this Monday morning, the desert highway was empty. No help in sight. It was all up to him.

Far ahead, the motor home vanished through shimmering thermal currents like undulant curtains of glass beads.

He threw the Camaro in gear. The tires spun in place for an instant, then skidded on the clutching sun-softened blacktop, issuing a scream that echoed eerily across the desert vastness. Jim wondered how the stranger and his family had screamed when he'd been shot point-blank in the chest. Abruptly the Camaro overcame all resistance and rocketed forward.

Tramping the accelerator to the floor, he squinted ahead to catch a glimpse of his quarry. In seconds the curtains of heat parted, and the big vehicle hove into view as if it were a sailing ship somehow making way on that dry sea.

The motor home couldn't compete with the Camaro, and Jim was soon riding its bumper. It was an old thirty-foot Roadking that had seen a lot of miles. Its white aluminum siding was caked with dirt, dented, and rust-spotted. The windows were covered with yellow curtains that had no doubt once been white. It looked like nothing more than the home of a couple of travel-loving retirees living on dwindling Social Security assets, unable to maintain it with the pride they had when it had been new.

Except for the motorcycle. A Harley was chained to a wrought-iron rack to the left of the roof-service ladder on the back of the motor home. It wasn't the biggest bike made, but it was powerful—and not something that a pair of retirees typically tooled around on.

In spite of the cycle, nothing about the Roadking was suspicious. Yet in its wake Jim Ironheart was overcome by a sense of evil so strong that it might as well have been a black tide washing over him with all the power of the sea behind it. He gagged as if he could smell the corruption of those to whom the motor home belonged.

At first he hesitated, afraid that any action he took might jeopardize the woman and child who were evidently being held captive. But the riskiest thing he could do was delay. The longer the mother and daughter were in the hands of the people in the Roadking, the less chance they had of coming out of it alive.

He swung into the passing lane. He intended to get a couple of miles ahead of them and block the road with his car.

In the Roadking's rearview mirror, the driver must have seen Jim stop at the station wagon and get out to inspect it. Now he let the Camaro pull almost even before swinging the motor home sharply left, bashing it against the side of the car.

Metal shrieked against metal, and the car shuddered.

The steering wheel spun in Jim's hands. He fought for control and kept it.

The Roadking pulled away, then swerved back and bashed him again, driving him off the blacktop and onto the unpaved shoulder. For a few hundred yards they rattled forward at high speed in those positions: the Roadking in the wrong lane, risking a head-on collision with any oncoming traffic that might be masked by the curtains of heat and sun glare; the Camaro casting up huge clouds of dust behind it, speeding precariously along the brink of the two-foot drop-off that separated the raised roadbed from the desert floor beyond.

Even a light touch of the brakes might pull the car a few inches to the left, causing it to drop and roll. He only dared to ease up on the accelerator and let his speed fall gradually.

The driver of the Roadking reacted, reducing his speed, too, hanging at Jim's side. Then the motor home moved inexorably to the left, inch by inch, edging relentlessly onto the dirt shoulder.

Being much the smaller and less powerful of the two vehicles, the Camaro could not resist the pressure. It was pushed leftward in spite of Jim's efforts to hold it steady. The front tire found the brink first, and that corner of the car dropped. He hit the brakes; it didn't matter anymore. Even as he jammed his foot down on the pedal, the rear wheel followed the front end into empty space. The Camaro tipped and rolled to the left.

Using a safety harness was a habit with him, so he was thrown sideways and forward, and his sunglasses flew off, but he didn't crack his face against the window post or shatter his breastbone against the steering wheel. Webs of cracks, like the work of a spider on Benzedrine, spread across the windshield. He squeezed his eyes shut, and gummy bits of tempered glass imploded over him. The car rolled again, then started to roll a third time but only made it halfway, coming to rest on its roof.

Hanging upside down in the harness, he was unhurt but badly shaken. He choked on the clouds of white dust that poured in through the shattered windshield.

They'll be coming for me.

He fumbled frantically for the harness release, found it, and dropped the last few inches onto the ceiling of the overturned car. He was curled on top of the shotgun. He had been damn lucky the weapon hadn't discharged as it slammed around inside the tumbling Camaro.

Coming for me.

Disoriented, he needed a moment to find the door handle, which was over his head. He reached up, released it. At first the door would not open. Then it swung outward with a metallic popping and squeaking.

He crawled off the ceiling, out onto the floor of the desert, feeling as if he had become trapped in a surreal Daliesque world of weird perspectives. He reached back in for the shotgun.

Though the ash-fine dust was beginning to settle, he was still coughing it out of his lungs. Clenching his teeth, he tried to swallow each cough. He needed to be quiet if he were to survive.

Neither as quick nor as inconspicuous as the small desert lizards that scooted across his path, Jim stayed low and dashed to a nearby arroyo. When he arrived at the edge of that natural drainage channel, he discovered it was only about four feet deep. He slid over the lip, and his feet made a soft slapping sound as they hit the hard-packed bottom.

Crouching in that shallow declivity, he raised his head slowly to ground level and looked across the desert floor toward the overturned Camaro, around which the haze of alkaline dust had not yet entirely dissipated. On the highway, the Roadking finished reversing along the pavement and halted parallel to the wrecked car.

The door opened, and a man climbed out. Another man, having exited from the far side, hurried around the front of the motor home to join his companion. Neither of them was the kindly-retiree-on-a-budget that one might have imagined behind the wheel of that aging caravan. They appeared to be in their early thirties and as hard as heat-tempered desert rock. One of them wore his dark hair pulled back and knotted into a redoubled ponytail—the passé style that kids now called a "dork knob." The other had short spiky hair on top, but his head was shaved on the sides—as if he thought he was in one of those old Mad Max movies. Both wore sleeveless T-shirts, jeans, and cowboy boots, and both carried handguns. They headed cautiously toward the Camaro, splitting up to approach it from opposite ends.

Jim drew down below the top of the arroyo, turned right—which was approximately west—and hurried in a crouch along the shallow channel. He glanced back to see if he was leaving a trail, but the silt, baked under months of fierce sun since the last rain, did not take footprints. After about fifty feet, the arroyo abruptly angled to the south, left. Sixty feet thereafter, it disappeared into a culvert that led under the highway.

Hope swept through him but did not still the tremors of fear that had shaken him continuously since he had found the dying man in the station wagon. He felt as if he was going to puke. But he had not eaten breakfast and had nothing to toss up. No matter what the nutritionists said, sometimes it paid to skip a meal.

Full of deep shade, the concrete culvert was comparatively cool. He was tempted to stop and hide there—and hope they would give up, go away.

He couldn't do that, of course. He wasn't a coward. But even if his conscience had allowed him to buy into a little cowardice this time, the mysterious force driving him would not permit him to cut and run. To some extent, he was a marionette on strings invisible, at the mercy of a puppeteer unseen, in a puppet-theater play with a plot he could not understand and a theme that eluded him.

A few tumbleweeds had found their way into the culvert, and their brittle spines raked him as he shoved through the barrier they had formed. He came out on the other side of the highway, into another arm of the arroyo, and scrambled up the wall of that parched channel.

Lying belly-flat on the desert floor, he slithered to the edge of the elevated roadbed and eased up to look across the pavement, east toward the motor home. Beyond the Roadking, he could see the Camaro like a dead roach on its back. The two men were standing near it, together now. Evidently, they had just checked the car and knew he was not in it.

They were talking animatedly, but they were too far away for Jim to hear what they were saying. A couple of words carried to him, but they were faded by distance and distorted by the furnace-dry air.

Sweat kept trickling into his eyes, blurring his vision. He blotted his face with his sleeve and squinted at the men again.

They were moving slowly away from the Camaro now, deeper into the desert. One of them was wary, swiveling his head from side to side, and the other studied the ground as they moved, no doubt searching for signs of Jim's passage. Just his luck, one of them would turn out to have been raised by Indian scouts, and they'd be all over him faster than an iguana on a sand beetle.

From the west came the sound of an engine, low at first but growing rapidly louder even as Jim turned his head to look in that direction. Out of a waterfall mirage came a Peterbilt. From Jim's low vantage point, the truck looked so huge that it didn't even seem like a truck but like some futuristic war machine that had traveled backward in time from the twenty-second century.

The driver of the Peterbilt would see the overturned Camaro. In the traditional Samaritan spirit that most truckers showed on the road, he would stop to offer assistance. His arrival would rattle the two killers, and while they were distracted, Jim would get the drop on them.

He had it all figured out—except it didn't work that way. The Peterbilt didn't slow as it approached, and Jim realized he was going to have to flag it down. But before he could even rise up, the big truck swept past with a dragon roar and a blast of hot wind, breaking the speed limit by a Guinness margin, as if it were a judgment wagon driven by a demon and loaded with souls that the devil wanted in hell *right now.*

Jim fought the urge to leap up and yell after it: Where's your traditional Samaritan spirit, you shithead?

Silence returned to the hot day.

On the far side of the road, the two killers looked after the Peterbilt for a moment, then continued their search for Jim.

Furious and scared, he eased back from the shoulder of the highway, flattened out again, and belly-crawled eastward toward the motor home, dragging the shotgun with him. The elevated roadbed was between him and them; they could not possibly see him, yet he more than half expected them to sprint across the blacktop and pump half a dozen rounds into him.

When he dared look up again, he was directly opposite the parked Roadking, which blocked the two men from his view. If he couldn't see them, they couldn't see him. He scrambled to his feet and crossed the pavement to the passenger side of the motor home.

The door on that flank was a third of the way from the front bumper to the rear, not opposite the driver's door. It was ajar.

He took hold of the handle. Then he realized that a third man might have stayed inside with the woman and girl. He couldn't risk going in there until he had dealt with the two outside, for he might be trapped between gunmen.

He moved to the front of the Roadking, and just as he reached the corner, he heard voices approaching. He froze, waiting for the guy with the weird haircut to come around the front bumper. But they stopped on the other side.

"—who gives a shit—"

"—but he mighta seen our license number—"

"—chances are, he's bad hurt—"

"—wasn't no blood in the car—"

Jim sank to one knee by the tire, looked under the vehicle. They were standing on the other side, near the driver's door.

"—we just take the next southbound—"

"—with cops on our tail—"

"—by the time he gets to any cops, we'll be in Arizona—"

"—you hope—"

"—I *know*—"

Rising, moving cautiously, Jim slipped around the front corner of the Roadking. He eased past the first pair of headlights and the engine hatch.

"—cut across Arizona into New Mexico—"

"—they got cops, too—"

"—into Texas, put a few states between us, drive all night if we have to—"

Jim was grateful that the shoulder of the highway was dirt rather than loose gravel. He crept silently across it to the driver's-side headlights, staying low.

"—you know what piss-poor cooperation they got across state lines—"

"—he's out there somewhere, damn it—"

"—so're a million scorpions and rattlesnakes—"

Jim stepped around to their side of the motor home, covering them with the shotgun. "Don't move!"

For an instant they gaped at him the way *he* might have stared at a three-eyed Martian with a mouth in its forehead. They were only about eight feet away, close enough to spit on, which they looked like they deserved. At a distance they had appeared as dangerous as snakes with legs, and they still looked deadlier than anything that slithered in the desert.

They were holding their handguns, pointed at the ground. Jim thrust the shotgun at them and shouted, "Drop 'em, damn it!"

Either they were the hardest of hard cases or they were nuts—probably both—because they didn't freeze at the sight of the shotgun. The guy with the redoubled ponytail flung himself to the ground and rolled. Simultaneously, the refugee from *Road Warrior* brought up his pistol, and Jim pumped a round into the guy's chest at point-blank range, blowing him backward and down and all the way to hell.

The survivor's feet vanished as he wriggled under the Roadking.

To avoid being shot in the foot and ankle, Jim grabbed the open door and jumped onto the step beside the driver's seat. Even as his feet left the ground, two shots boomed from under the motor home, and one of them punctured the tire beside which he'd been standing.

Instead of retreating into the Roadking, he dropped back to the ground, fell flat, and shoved the shotgun under the vehicle, figuring to take his adversary by surprise. But the guy was already out from under on the other side. Jim could see only the black cowboy boots hurrying toward the rear of the motor home. The guy turned the corner—and vanished.

The ladder. At the right rear corner. Next to the racked motorcycle.

The bastard was going onto the roof.

Jim hustled all the way under the Roadking before the killer could look over the edge of the roof, spot him, and fire down. It was no cooler beneath the vehicle, because the sun-scorched earthen shoulder radiated the heat it had been storing up since dawn.

Two cars roared by on the highway, one close after the other. He hadn't heard them coming, maybe because his heart was beating so hard that he felt as if he were inside a kettle drum. He cursed the motorists under his breath, then realized they couldn't be expected to stop when they saw a guy like Dork Knob prowling the top of the motor home with a handgun.

He had a better chance of winning if he continued to do the unexpected, so he immediately crawled on his belly, fast as a marine under fire, to the rear of the Roadking. He twisted onto his back, eased his head out past the rear bumper, and peered up across the Harley, at the ascending rungs that appeared to dwindle into blazing white sun.

The ladder was empty. The killer was already on the roof. He might think that he had temporarily mystified his pursuer with his vanishing act, and in any case he wouldn't expect to be followed with utter recklessness.

Jim slid all the way into the open and went up the ladder. He gripped the hot siderail with one hand, holding the compact shotgun with the other, trying to ascend as soundlessly as possible. His adversary was surprisingly quiet on the aluminum surface above, making barely enough noises of his own to cover an occasional pop and squeak from the aged rungs under Jim's feet.

At the top, Jim cautiously raised his head and squinted across the roof. The killer was two-thirds of the way toward the front of the Roadking, at the right side, looking down. He was moving along on hands and knees, which must have hurt; although the time-stained white paint reflected a lot of the sun, it had stored sufficient heat to sting even well-callused hands and to penetrate blue denim. But if the guy was in pain, he didn't show it; he was evidently as suicidally macho as his dead buddy had been.

Jim eased up another rung.

The killer actually lowered himself onto his belly, though the roof must have scorched instantly through his thin T-shirt. He was trying to maintain as low a profile as possible, waiting for Jim to appear below.

Jim eased up one more rung. The roof now met him at mid-torso. He turned sideways on the ladder and jammed one knee behind the outer upright, wedging himself in place so he would have both hands for the shotgun and so the recoil would not knock him backward to the ground.

If the guy on the roof didn't have a sixth sense, then he was just damned lucky. Jim had not made a sound, but the creep suddenly glanced back over his shoulder and spotted him.

Cursing, Jim swung the shotgun around.

The killer flung himself sideways, off the roof.

Without getting in a shot, Jim pulled his knee from behind the upright and jumped from the ladder. He hit the ground hard but kept his balance, stepped around the corner of the motor home, and squeezed off one round.

But the creep was already bolting through the side door. At worst, he caught a few pellets in one leg. Probably not even that.

He was going after the woman and child.

Hostages.

Or maybe he just wanted to slaughter them before he was cut down himself. The past couple of decades had seen the rise of the vagabond sociopath, roaming the country, looking for easy prey, racking up long lists of victims, attaining sexual release as much from brutal murder as from rape.

In his mind, Jim heard the anguished voice of the dying man in the station wagon: *Lisa . . . Susie . . . My wife, daughter . . .*

With no time for caution, his anger having grown greater than his fear, he raced after the killer, through the door, into the Roadking, entering aft of the cockpit. His sun-dazzled eyes couldn't handle the comparative gloom of the motor home's interior, but he was able to see the psychotic sonofabitch heading toward the rear of the motor home, past the lounge area and into the galley.

A shadowy figure now, with just a dark oval for a face, the killer turned and fired. The slug tore a chunk out of a wall-hung storage cabinet to the left of Jim, showering him with splinters of Formica and smoking particle board.

He didn't know where the woman and child were. He was afraid of hitting them. A shotgun wasn't a precise weapon.

The killer fired again. The second bullet passed so close to Jim's face that it left a wake of stinging-hot wind, like a kiss of fire burning across his right cheek.

He pumped out one round, and the blast shook the tinny walls. The killer screamed and was flung hard against the kitchen sink. Jim fired again, reflexively, half-deafened by the double explosion. The guy was virtually lifted off his feet, hurled backward, slammed against the rear wall, beside a closed door that separated the main living area from the bedroom. Then he dropped.

Grabbing a couple of shells from his pants pocket, reloading the shotgun magazine, Jim moved deeper into the Roadking, past a tattered and sagging sofa.

He knew the man had to be dead, but he could not see well enough to be certain of anything. Though shafts of the Mojave sun shoved in like hot branding irons through the windshield and the open doors, the heavily draped side windows insured that the rear of the Roadking was filled with shadows, and there was a thin acrid haze of smoke from all the gunfire.

When he reached the end of the narrow chamber and looked down, he had no doubt that the man crumpled on the floor was dead. Bloody human garbage. Garbage alive, now garbage dead.

At the sight of the torn and battered corpse, a savage elation gripped him, a furious righteousness that was both thrilling and frightening. He wanted to be sickened by what he had done, even if the dead man had deserved to die, but although the carnage nauseated him, he was not morally repulsed. He had encountered purest evil in human form. Both these bastards deserved worse than he had been able to do to them, deserved long and slow deaths with great suffering, much terror. He felt like an avenging angel, come to judgment, filled with a holy rage. He knew he was teetering on the edge of a psychosis of his own, knew that only the insane were unreservedly certain of the virtue of even their most outrageous acts, but he could find no doubt within him. In fact his anger swelled as if he were God's avatar into whom flowed a direct current of the Almighty's apocalyptic wrath.

He turned to the closed door.

The bedroom lay beyond.

The mother and child had to be in there.

Lisa . . . Susie . . .

But who else?

Sociopathic killers usually operated alone, but sometimes they paired up as these two had done. Larger alliances, however, were rare. Charles Manson and his "family," of course. There were other examples. He couldn't rule anything out, not in a world where the trendiest professors of philosophy taught that ethics were always situational and that everyone's point of view was equally right and valuable, regardless of its logic or hate quotient. It was a world that bred monsters, and this beast might be hydra-headed.

He knew caution was called for, but the exhilarating righteous wrath that filled him also gave him a sense of invulnerability. He stepped to the bedroom door, kicked it open, and shouldered through, knowing he might be gut-shot, not giving a damn, shotgun in front of him, ready to kill and be killed.

The woman and child were alone. On the filthy bed. Bound at wrists and ankles with sturdy strapping tape. Tape across their mouths.

The woman, Lisa, was about thirty, slim, an unusually attractive blonde. But the daughter, Susie, was remarkably more beautiful than her mother, ethereally beautiful: about ten years old, with luminous green eyes, delicate features, and skin as flawless as the membranous interior surface of an eggshell. The girl seemed, to Jim, to be an embodiment of innocence, goodness, and purity—an angel cast down into a cesspool. New power informed his rage at the sight of her bound and gagged in the bedroom's squalor.

Tears streamed down the child's face, and she choked on muffled sobs of terror behind the tape that sealed her lips. The mother was not crying, though grief and fear haunted her eyes. Her sense of responsibility to her daughter—and a visible rage not unlike Jim's—seemed to keep her from falling over the brink of hysteria.

He realized they were afraid of him. As far as they knew, he was in league with the men who had abducted them.

As he propped the shotgun against the built-in dresser, he said, "It's all right. It's over now. I killed them. I killed them both."

The mother stared at him wide-eyed, disbelieving.

He didn't blame her for doubting her. His voice sounded strange: full of fury, cracking on every third or fourth word, tremulous, going from a whisper to a hard bark to a whisper again.

He looked around for something with which to cut them free. A roll of the strapping tape and a pair of scissors lay on the dresser.

Grabbing the scissors, he noticed X-rated videotapes also stacked on the dresser. Suddenly he realized that the walls and ceiling of the small room were papered with obscene photographs torn from the pages of sex magazines, and with a jolt he saw it was filth with a twisted difference: child pornography. There were grown men in the photos, their faces always concealed, but there were no grown women, only young girls and boys, most of them as young as Susie, many of them younger, being brutalized in every way imaginable.

The men he had killed would have used the mother only briefly, would have raped and tortured and broken her only as an example to the child. Then they would have cut her throat or blown her brains out on some desolate dirt road out in the desert, leaving her body for the delectation of lizards and ants and vultures. It was the child they really wanted, and for whom they would have made the next few months or years a living hell.

His anger metastasized into something beyond mere rage, far beyond wrath. A terrible darkness rose inside of him like black crude oil gushing up from a wellhead.

He was furious that the child had seen those photographs, had been forced to lie in those stained and foul-smelling bedclothes with unspeakable obscenity on every side of her. He had the crazy urge to pick up the shotgun and empty a few more rounds into each of the dead men.

They had not touched her. Thank God for that. They hadn't had time to touch her.

But the room. Oh, Jesus, she had suffered an assault just by being in that room.

He was shaking.

He saw that the mother was shaking, too.

After a moment he realized that her tremors were not of rage, like his, but of fear. Fear of *him*. She was terrified of him, more so now than when he had come into the room.

He was glad there was no mirror. He would not have wanted to see his own face. Right now there must be some kind of madness in it.

He had to get a grip on himself.

"It's all right," he assured her again. "I came to help you."

Eager to free them, anxious to quiet their terror, he dropped to his knees beside the bed and cut the tape that was wound around the woman's ankles, tore it away. He snipped the tape around her wrists, as well, then left her to finish freeing herself.

When he cut the bindings from Susie's wrists, she hugged herself defensively. When he freed her ankles, she kicked at him and squirmed away across the gray and mottled sheets. He didn't reach for her, but backed off instead.

Lisa peeled the tape off her lips and pulled a rag out of her mouth, choking and gagging. She spoke in a raspy voice that was somehow simultaneously frantic and resigned: "My husband, back at the car, my husband!"

Jim looked at her and said nothing, unable to put such bleak news into words in front of the child.

The woman saw the truth in his eyes, and for a moment her lovely face was wrenched into a mask of grief and agony. But for the sake of her daughter, she fought down the sob, swallowed it along with her anguish.

She said only, "Oh, my God," and each word reverberated with her loss. "Can you carry Susie?"

Her mind was on her dead husband.

He said, "Can you carry Susie?"

She blinked in confusion. "How do you know her name?"

"Your husband told me."

"But—"

"Before," he said sharply, meaning *before he died*, not wanting to give false hope. "Can you carry her out of here?"

"Yeah, I think so, maybe."

He could have carried the girl himself, but he didn't believe that he should touch her. Though it was irrational and emotional, he felt that what those two men had done to her—and what they *would* have done to her, given a chance—was somehow the responsibility of all men, and that at least a small stain of guilt was his as well.

Right now, the only man in the world who should touch that child was her father. And he was dead.

Jim rose from his knees and edged away from the bed. He backed into a narrow closet door that sprang open as he stepped aside of it.

On the bed, the weeping girl squirmed away from her mother, so traumatized that she did not at first recognize the benign intention of even those familiar loving hands. Then abruptly she shattered the chains of terror and flew into her mother's arms. Lisa spoke softly and reassuringly to her daughter, stroked her hair, held her tight.

The air-conditioning had been off ever since the killers had parked and gone to check the wrecked Camaro. The bedroom was growing hotter by the second, and it stank. He smelled stale beer, sweat, what might have been the lingering odor of dried blood rising from dark maroon stains on the carpet, and other foul odors that he dared not even try to identify.

"Come on, let's get out of here."

Lisa did not appear to be a strong woman, but she lifted her daughter as effortlessly as she would have lifted a pillow. With the girl cradled in her arms, she moved toward the door.

"Don't let her look to the left when you go out," he said. "One of them's dead just beside the door. It isn't pretty."

Lisa nodded once, with evident gratitude for the warning.

As he started to follow her through the doorway, he saw the contents of the narrow closet that had come open when he'd backed against it: shelves of homemade videotapes. On the spines were titles hand-printed on strips of white adhesive tape. Names. The titles were all names. CINDY, TIFFANY. JOEY. CISSY TOMMY. KEVIN. Two were labeled SALLY. Three were labeled WENDY. More names. Maybe thirty in all. He knew what he was looking at, but he didn't want to believe it. Memories of savagery. Mementoes of perversion. Victims.

The bitter blackness welled higher in him.

He followed Lisa through the motor home to the door, and out into the blazing desert sun.

2 Lisa stood in the white-gold sunshine on the shoulder of the highway, behind the motor home. Her daughter stood at her side, clung to her. Light had an affinity for them: it slipped in scintillant currents through their flaxen hair, accented the color of their eyes much the way a jeweler's display lamp enhanced the beauty of emeralds on velvet, and lent an almost mystical luminosity to their skin. Looking at them, it was difficult to believe that the light around them was not within them, too, and that a darkness had entered their lives and filled them as completely as night filled the world in the wake of dusk.

Jim could barely endure their presence. Each time he glanced at them, he thought of the dead man in the station wagon, and sympathetic grief twisted through him, as painful as any physical illness he had ever known.

Using a key that he found on a ring with the motor home ignition key, he unlocked the iron rack that held the Harley-Davidson. It was an FXRS-SP with a 1340cc. single-carburetor, two-valve, push-rod V-twin with a five-speed transmission that powered the rear wheel through a toothed belt instead of a greasy chain. He'd ridden fancier and more powerful machines. This one was standard, about as plain as a Harley could get. But all he wanted from the bike was speed and easy handling; and if it was in good repair, the SP would provide him with both.

Lisa spoke worriedly to him as he unracked the Harley and looked it over. "Three of us can't ride out of here on that."

"No," he said. "Just me."

"Please don't leave us alone."

"Someone'll stop for you before I go."

A car approached. The three occupants gawked at them. The driver put on more speed.

"None of them stop," she said miserably.

"Someone will. I'll wait until they do."

She was silent a moment. Then: "I don't want to get into a car with strangers."

"We'll see who stops."

She shook her head violently.

He said, "I'll know if they're trustworthy."

"I don't . . ." Her voice broke. She hesitated, regained control. "I don't trust anyone."

"There are good people in the world. In fact, most of them are good. Anyway, when they stop, I'll know if they're okay."

"How? How in God's name can you know?"

"I'll know." But he could not explain the *how* of it any more than he could explain how he had known that she and her daughter needed him out here in this sere and blistered wasteland.

He straddled the Harley and pressed the starter button. The engine kicked in at once. He revved it a little, then shut it off.

The woman said, "Who are you?"

"I can't tell you that."

"But why not?"

"This one's too sensational. It'll make nationwide headlines."

"I don't understand."

"They'd splash my picture everywhere. I like my privacy."

A small utility rack was bolted to the back of the Harley. Jim used his belt to strap the shotgun to it.

With a tremor of vulnerability in her voice that broke his heart, Lisa said, "We owe you so much."

He looked at her, then at Susie. The girl had one slender arm around her mother, clinging tightly. She was not listening to their conversation. Her eyes were out of focus, blank—and her mind seemed far away. Her free hand was at her mouth, and she was chewing on her knuckle; she had actually broken the skin and drawn her own blood.

He averted his eyes and stared down at the cycle again.

"You don't owe me anything," he said.

"But you saved—"

"Not everyone," he said quickly. "Not everyone I *should* have."

The distant growl of an approaching car drew their attention to the east. They watched a souped-up black Trans Am swim out of the water mirages. With a screech of brakes, it stopped in front of them. Red flames were painted on the fender back of the front wheel, and the rims of both the wheel wells were protected with fancy chrome trim. Fat twin chrome tailpipes glistered like liquid mercury in the fierce desert sun.

The driver got out. He was about thirty. His thick black hair was combed away from his face, full on the sides, a ducktail in back. He was wearing jeans and a white T-shirt with the sleeves rolled up to reveal tattoos on both biceps.

"Somethin' wrong here?" he asked across the car.

Jim stared at him for a beat, then said, "These people need a ride to the nearest town."

As the man came around the Trans Am, the passenger door opened, and a woman got out. She was a couple of years younger than her companion, dressed in baggy tan shorts, a white halter top, and a white bandana. Unruly dyed-blond hair sprayed out around that piece of headgear, framing a face so heavily made up that it looked like a testing ground for Max Factor. She wore too much clunky costume jewelry, as well: big dangling silver earrings; three strands of glass beads in different shades of red; two bracelets on each wrist, a watch, and four rings. On the upper slope of her left breast was a blue and pink butterfly tattoo.

"You break down?" she asked.

Jim said, "The motor home has a flat."

"I'm Frank," the guy said. "This is Verna." He was chewing gum. "I'll help you fix the tire."

Jim shook his head. "We can't use the motor home anyway. There's a dead man in it."

"Dead man?"

"And another one over there," Jim said, gesturing beyond the Roadking.

Verna was wide-eyed.

Frank stopped chewing his gum for a beat, glanced at the shotgun on the Harley rack, then looked at Jim again. "You kill them?"

"Yeah. Because they kidnapped this woman and her child."

Frank studied him a moment, then glanced at Lisa. "That true?" he asked her.

She nodded.

"Jesus jumpin' catfish," Verna said.

Jim glanced at Susie. She was in another world, and she would need some professional help to reenter this one. He was certain she couldn't hear a thing they said.

Curiously, he felt as detached as the child looked. He was still sinking into that internal darkness, and before long it would swallow him completely. He told Frank: "These guys I killed—they wasted the husband . . . the father. His body's in a station wagon a couple of miles west of here."

"Oh, shit," Frank said, "that's a rough one."

Verna drew against Frank's side and shuddered.

"I want you to take them to the nearest town, fast as you can. Get medical attention for them. Then contact the state police, get them out here."

"Sure," Frank said.

But Lisa said, "Wait . . . no . . . I can't . . ." Jim went to her, and she whispered to him: "They look like . . . I can't . . . I'm just afraid . . ."

Jim put a hand on her shoulder, stared directly into her eyes. "Things aren't always what they appear to be. Frank and Verna are okay. You trust me?"

"Yes. Now. Of course."

"Then believe me. You can trust them."

"But how can you know?" she asked, her voice breaking.

"I *know*," he said firmly.

She continued to meet his eyes for a few seconds, then nodded and said, "All right."

The rest was easy. As docile as if she had been drugged, Susie allowed herself to be lifted into the back seat. Her mother joined her there, cuddled her. When Frank was behind the wheel again and Verna at his side, Jim gratefully accepted a can of root beer from their ice chest. Then he closed Verna's door, leaned down to the open window, and thanked her and Frank.

"You're not waitin' here for the cops, are you?" Frank asked.

"No."

"You're not in trouble, you know. You're the hero here."

"I know. But I'm not waiting."

Frank nodded. "You got your reasons, I guess. You want us to say you was a bald guy with dark eyes, hitched a ride with a trucker going east?"

"No. Don't lie. Don't lie for me."

"Whatever you want," Frank said.

Verna said, "Don't worry. We'll take good care of them."

"I know you will," Jim said.

He drank the root beer and watched the Trans Am until it had driven out of sight.

He climbed on the Harley, thumbed the starter button, used the long heavy shift to slide the gearwheel into place, rolled in a little throttle, released the clutch, and rode across the highway. He went off the shoulder, down the slight incline, onto the floor of the desert, and headed directly south into the immense and inhospitable Mojave.

For a while he rode at over seventy miles an hour, though he had no protection from the wind because the SP had no fairing. He was badly buffeted, and his eyes filled repeatedly with tears that he tried to blame entirely on the raw, hot air that assaulted him.

Strangely, he did not mind the heat. In fact he didn't even feel it. He was sweating, yet he felt cool.

He lost track of time. Perhaps an hour had passed when he realized that he had left the plains and was moving across barren hills the color of rust. He reduced his speed. His route was now filled with twists and turns between rocky outcroppings, but the SP was the machine for it. It had two inches more suspension travel fore and aft than did the regular FXRS, with compatible spring and shock rates, plus twin disc brakes on the front—which meant he could corner like a stunt rider when the terrain threw surprises at him.

After a while he was no longer cool. He was *cold*.

The sun seemed to be fading, though he knew it was still early afternoon. Darkness was closing on him from within.

Eventually he stopped in the shadow of a rock monolith about a quarter of a mile long and three hundred feet high. Weathered into eerie shapes by ages of wind and sun and by the rare but torrential rains that swept the Mojave, the formation thrust out of the desert floor like the ruins of an ancient temple now half-buried in sand.

He propped the Harley on its kickstand.

He sat down on the shaded earth.

After a moment he stretched out on his side. He drew up his knees. He folded his arms across his chest.

He had stopped not a moment too soon. The darkness filled him completely, and he fell away into an abyss of despair.

3 Later, in the last hour of daylight, he found himself on the Harley again, riding across gray and rose-colored flats where clumps of mesquite bristled. Dead, sun-blackened tumbleweed chased him in a breeze that smelled like powdered iron and salt.

He vaguely remembered breaking open a cactus and sucking the moisture out of the water-heavy pulp at the core of the plant, but he was dry again. Desperately thirsty.

As he came over a gentle rise and throttled down a little, he saw a small town about two miles ahead, buildings clustered along a highway. A scattering of trees looked supernaturally lush after the desolation—physical and spiritual—through which he had traveled for the past several hours. Half convinced that the town was only an apparition, he angled toward it nevertheless.

Suddenly, silhouetted against a sky that was growing purple and red with the onset of twilight, the spire of a church appeared, a cross at its pinnacle. Though he realized that he was to some extent delirious and that his delirium was at least partly related to serious dehydration, Jim turned at once toward the church. He felt as if he needed the solace of its interior spaces more than he needed water.

Half a mile from the town, he rode the Harley into an arroyo and left it there on its side. The soft sand walls of the channel gave way easily under his hands, and he quickly covered the bike.

He had assumed he could walk the last half mile with relative ease. But he was worse off than he had realized. His vision swam in and out of focus. His lips burned, his tongue stuck to the roof of his dry mouth, and his throat was sore—as if he were in the grip of a virulent fever. The muscles in his legs began to cramp and throb, and each foot seemed to be encased in a concrete boot.

He must have blacked out on his feet, because the next thing he knew, he was on the brick steps of the white clapboard church, with no recollection of the last few hundred yards of his journey. The words OUR LADY OF THE DESERT were on a brass plaque beside the double doors.

He had been a Catholic once. In a part of his heart, he still was a Catholic. He had been many things—Methodist, Jew, Buddhist, Baptist, Moslem, Hindu, Taoist, more—and although he was no longer any of them in practice, he was still all of them in experience.

Though the door seemed to weigh more than the boulder that had covered the mouth of Christ's tomb, he managed to pull it open. He went inside.

The church was much cooler than the twilit Mojave, but not really cool. It smelled of myrrh and spikenard and the slightly sweetish odor of burning votive candles, causing memories of his Catholic days to flood back to him, making him feel at home.

At the doorway between narthex and nave, he dipped two fingers in the holy-water font and crossed himself. He cupped his hands in the cool liquid, brought them to his mouth, and drank. The water tasted like blood. He looked into the white marble basin in horror, certain that it was brimming with gore, but he saw only water and the dim, shimmering reflection of his own face.

He realized that his parched and stinging lips were split. He licked them. The blood was his own.

Then he found himself on his knees at the front of the nave, leaning against the sanctuary railing, praying, and he did not know how he had gotten there. Must have blacked out again.

The last of the day had blown away as if it were a pale skin of dust, and a hot night wind pressed at the church windows. The only illumination was from a bulb in the narthex, the flickering flames of half a dozen votive candles in red-glass containers, and a small spotlight shining down on the crucifix.

Jim saw that his own face was painted on the figure of Christ. He blinked his burning eyes and looked again. This time he saw the face of the dead man in the station wagon. The sacred countenance metamorphosed into the face of Jim's mother, his father, the child named Susie, Lisa—and then it was no face at all, just a black oval, as the killer's face had been a black oval when he had turned to shoot at Jim inside the shadow-filled Roadking.

Indeed, it wasn't Christ on the cross now, it *was* the killer. He opened his eyes, looked at Jim, and smiled. He jerked his feet free of the vertical support, a nail still bristling from one of them, a black nail hole in the other. He wrenched his hands free, too, a spike still piercing each palm, and he just *drifted* down to the floor, as if gravity had no claim on him except what he chose to allow it. He started across the altar platform toward the railing, toward Jim.

Jim's heart was racing, but he told himself that what he saw was only a delusion. The product of a fevered mind. Nothing more.

The killer reached him. Touched his face. The hand was as soft as rotting meat and as cold as a liquid gas.

Like a true believer in a tent revival, collapsing under the empowered hand of a faith healer, Jim shivered and fell away into darkness.

4

A white-walled room.

A narrow bed.

Spare and humble furnishings.

Night at the windows.

He drifted in and out of bad dreams. Each time that he regained consciousness, which was never for longer than a minute or two, he saw the same man hovering over him: about fifty, balding, slightly plump, with thick eyebrows and a squashed nose.

Sometimes the stranger gently worked an ointment into Jim's face, and sometimes he applied compresses soaked in ice water. He lifted Jim's head off the pillows and encouraged him to drink cool water through a straw. Because the man's eyes were marked by concern and kindness, Jim did not protest.

Besides, he had neither the voice nor the energy to protest. His throat felt as if he had swallowed kerosene and then a match. He did not have the strength even to lift a hand an inch off the sheets.

"Just rest," the stranger said. "You're suffering heatstroke and a bad sunburn."

Windburn. That's the worst of it, Jim thought, remembering the Harley SP, which had not been equipped with a Plexiglas fairing for weather protection.

LIGHT AT THE windows. A new day.

His eyes were sore.

His face felt worse than ever. Swollen.

The stranger was wearing a clerical collar.

"Priest," Jim said in a coarse and whispery voice that didn't sound like his own.

"I found you in the church, unconscious."

"Our Lady of the Desert."

Lifting Jim off the pillows again, he said, "That's right. I'm Father Geary. Leo Geary."

Jim was able to help himself a little this time. The water tasted sweet.

Father Geary said, "What were you doing in the desert?"

"Wandering."

"Why?"

Jim didn't answer.

"Where did you come from?"

Jim said nothing.

"What is your name?"

"Jim."

"You're not carrying any ID."

"Not this time, no."

"What do you mean by that?"

Jim was silent.

The priest said, "There was three thousand dollars in cash in your pockets."

"Take what you need."

The priest stared at him, then smiled. "Better be careful what you offer, son. This is a poor church. We need all we can get."

LATER STILL, JIM woke again. The priest was not there. The house was silent. Once in a while a rafter creaked and a window rattled softly as desert wind stirred fitfully outside.

When the priest returned, Jim said, "A question, Father."

"What's that?"

His voice was still raspy, but he sounded a bit more like himself. "If there's a God, why does He allow suffering?"

Alarmed, Father Geary said, "Are you feeling worse?"

"No, no. Better. I don't mean my suffering. Just . . . why does He allow suffering in general?"

"To test us," the priest said.

"Why do we have to be tested?"

"To determine if we're worthy."

"Worthy of what?"

"Worthy of heaven, of course. Salvation. Eternal life."

"Why didn't God *make* us worthy?"

"Yes, he made us perfect, without sin. But then we sinned, and fell from grace."

"How could we sin if we were perfect?"

"Because we have free will."

"I don't understand."

Father Geary frowned. "I'm not a nimble theologian. Just an ordinary priest. All I can tell you is that it's part of the divine mystery. We fell from grace, and now heaven must be earned."

"I need to pee," Jim said.

"All right."

"Not the bedpan this time. I think I can make it to the bathroom with your help."

"I think maybe you can, too. You're really coming around nicely, thank God."

"Free will," Jim said.

The priest frowned.

BY LATE AFTERNOON, nearly twenty-four hours after Jim stumbled into the church, his fever registered only three-tenths of a degree on the thermometer. His muscles were no longer spasming, his joints did not hurt any more, he was not dizzy, and his chest did not ache when he drew a deep breath. Pain still flared across his face periodically. When he spoke he did so without moving his facial muscles more than absolutely necessary, because the cracks in his lips and in the corners of his mouth reopened easily in spite of the prescription cortisone cream that Father Geary applied every few hours.

He could sit up in bed of his own volition and move about the room with only minimal help. When his appetite returned, as well, Father Geary gave him chicken soup, then vanilla ice cream. He ate carefully, mindful of his split lips, trying to avoid tainting the food with the taste of his own blood.

"I'm still hungry," Jim said when he finished.

"Let's see if you can keep that down first."

"I'm fine. It was only sunstroke, dehydration."

"Sunstroke can kill, son. You need more rest."

When the priest relented a while later and brought him more ice cream, Jim spoke through half-clenched teeth and frozen lips: "Why are some people killers? Not cops, I mean. Not soldiers. Not those who kill in self-defense. The other kind, the murderers. Why do they kill?"

Settling into a straight-backed rocker near the bed, the priest regarded him with one raised eyebrow. "That's a peculiar question."

"Is it? Maybe. Do you have an answer?"

"The simple one is—because there's evil in them."

They sat in mutual silence for a minute or so. Jim ate ice cream, and the stocky priest rocked in his chair. Another twilight crept across the sky beyond the windows.

Finally Jim said, "Murder, accidents, disease, old age . . . Why did God make us mortal in the first place? Why do we have to die?"

"Death's not the end. Or at least that's what I believe. Death is only our means of passage, only the train that conveys us to our reward."

"Heaven, you mean."

The priest hesitated. "Or the other."

Jim slept for a couple of hours. When he woke, he saw the priest standing at the foot of the bed, watching him intently.

"You were talking in your sleep."

Jim sat up in bed. "Was I? What'd I say?"

" 'There is an enemy.' "

"That's all I said?"

"Then you said, 'It's coming. It'll kill us all.' "

A shiver of dread passed through Jim, not because the words had any power of themselves, and not because he understood them, but because he sensed that on a subconscious level he knew all too well what he had meant.

He said, "A dream, I guess. A bad dream. That's all."

But shortly past three o'clock in the morning, during that second night in the rectory, he thrashed awake, sat straight up in bed, and heard the words escaping him again, *"It'll kill us all."*

The room was lightless.

He fumbled for the lamp, switched it on.

He was alone.

He looked at the windows. Darkness beyond.

He had the bizarre but unshakable feeling that something hideous and merciless had been hovering near, something infinitely more savage and strange than anyone in recorded history had ever seen, dreamed, or imagined. Trembling, he got out of bed. He was wearing an ill-fitting pair of the priest's pajamas. For a moment he just stood there, not sure what to do.

Then he switched off the light and, barefoot, went to one window, then the other. He was on the second floor. The night was silent, deep, and peaceful. If something had been out there, it was gone now.

5 The following morning, he dressed in his own clothes, which Father Geary had laundered for him. He spent most of the day in the living room, in a big easy chair, his feet propped on a hassock, reading magazines and dozing, while the priest tended to parish business.

Jim's sunburnt and wind-abraded face was stiffening. Like a mask.

That evening, they prepared dinner together. At the kitchen sink, Father Geary cleaned lettuce, celery, and tomatoes for a salad. Jim set the table, opened a bottle of cheap Chianti to let it breathe, then sliced canned mushrooms into a pot of spaghetti sauce on the stove.

They worked in a comfortable mutual silence, and Jim wondered about the curious relationship that had evolved between them. There had been a dreamlike quality to the past couple of days, as if he had not merely found refuge in a small desert town but in a place of peace outside the real world, a town in the Twilight Zone. The priest had stopped asking questions. In fact, it now seemed to Jim that Father Geary had never been half as probing or insistent as the circumstances warranted. And he suspected that the priest's Christian hospitality did not usually extend to the boarding of injured and suspicious strangers. Why he should receive special consideration at Geary's hands was a mystery to him, but he was grateful for it.

When he had sliced half the mushrooms in the can, he suddenly said, "Life line."

Father Geary turned from the sink, a stalk of celery in hand. "Pardon me?"

A chill swept through Jim, and he almost dropped the knife into the sauce. He put it on the counter.

"Jim?"

Shivering, he turned to the priest and said, "I've got to get to an airport."

"An airport?"

"Right away, Father."

The priest's plump face dimpled with perplexion, wrinkling his tanned forehead far past his long-vanished hairline. "But there's no airport here."

"How far to the nearest one?" Jim asked urgently.

"Well . . . two hours by car. All the way to Las Vegas."

"You've got to drive me there."

"What? Now?"

"Right now," Jim said.

"But—"

"I have to get to Boston."

"But you've been ill—"

"I'm better now."

"Your face—"

"It hurts, and it looks like hell, but it's not fatal. Father, I *have* to get to Boston."

"Why?"

He hesitated, then decided on a degree of revelation. "If I don't get to Boston, someone there is going to be killed. Someone who shouldn't die."

"Who? Who's going to die?"

Jim licked his peeling lips. "I don't know."

"You don't know?"

"But I will when I get there."

Father Geary stared at him for a long time. At last he said, "Jim, you're the strangest man I've ever known."

Jim nodded. "I'm the strangest man *I've* ever known."

WHEN THEY SET out from the rectory in the priest's six-year-old Toyota, an hour of light remained in the long August day, although the sun was hidden behind clouds the color of fresh bruises.

They had been on the road only half an hour when lightning shattered the bleak sky and danced on jagged legs across the somber desert horizon. Flash after flash erupted, sharper and brighter in the pure Mojave air than Jim had ever seen lightning elsewhere. Ten minutes later, the sky grew darker and lower, and rain fell in silvery cataracts the equal of anything that Noah had witnessed while hurrying to complete his ark.

"Summer storms are rare here," Father Geary said, switching on the windshield wipers.

"We can't let it delay us," Jim said worriedly.

"I'll get you there," the priest assured him.

"There can't be that many flights east from Vegas at night. They'd mostly leave during the day. I can't miss out and wait till morning. I've got to be in Boston *tomorrow*."

The parched sand soaked up the deluge. But some areas were rocky or hard-packed from months of blistering sun, and in those places the water spilled off slopes, forming rivulets in every shallow declivity. Rivulets became streams, and streams grew swiftly into rivers, until every bridged arroyo they passed over was soon filled with roiling, churning torrents on which were borne clumps of uprooted desert bunch-grass, fragments of dead tumbleweed, driftwood, and dirty white foam.

Father Geary had two favorite cassette tapes, which he kept in the car: a collection of rock-'n'-roll golden oldies, and an Elton John best-of. He put on Elton. They moved through the storm-hammered day then through the rainswept night to the melodies of "Funeral for a Friend," "Daniel," and "Benny and the Jets."

The blacktop glimmered with quicksilver puddles. To Jim, it was eerie that the water mirages on the highway a few days ago had now become real.

He grew more tense by the minute. Boston called to him, but it was far away, and few things were darker or more treacherous than a blacktop highway through a storm-wracked desert at night. Unless, perhaps, the human heart.

The priest hunched over the wheel as he drove. He studied the highway intently while singing along softly with Elton.

After a while Jim said, "Father, wasn't there a doctor in town?"

"Yes."

"But you didn't call him."

"I got the cortisone prescription from him."

"I saw the tube. It was a prescription for you, made out three months ago."

"Well . . . I've seen sunstroke before. I knew I could treat you."

"But you seemed awfully worried there at first."

The priest was silent for a few miles. Then he said, "I don't know who you are, where you come from, or why you really need to get to Boston. But I do know you're a man in trouble, maybe deep trouble, as deep as it ever gets. And I know . . . at least, I *think* I know that you're a good man at heart. Anyway, it seemed to me that a man in trouble would want to keep a low profile."

"Thanks. I do."

A couple of miles farther, the rain came down hard enough to overwhelm the windshield wipers and force Geary to reduce speed.

The priest said, "You're the one who saved that woman and her little girl."

Jim tensed but did not respond.

"You fit the description on TV," the priest said.

They were silent for a few more miles.

Father Geary said, "I'm not a sucker for miracles."

Jim was baffled by that statement.

Father Geary switched off Elton John. The only sounds were the swish-hum of the tires on the wet pavement and the metronomic thump of the windshield wipers.

"I believe that the miracles of the Bible happened, yes, I accept all of that as real history," the priest said, keeping his eyes on the road. "But I'm reluctant to believe that some statue of the Holy Mother wept real tears in a church in Cincinnati or Peoria or Teaneck last week after the Wednesday-night bingo games, witnessed only by two teenagers and the parish cleaning lady. And I'm not ready to believe that a shadow resembling Jesus, cast on someone's garage wall by a yellow bug light, is a sign of impending apocalypse. God works in mysterious ways, but not with bug lights and garage walls."

The priest fell silent again, and Jim waited, wondering where all this was leading.

"When I found you in the church, lying by the sanctuary railing," Geary said in a voice that grew more haunted word by word, "you were marked by the stigmata of Christ. There was a nail hole in each of your hands—"

Jim looked at his hands and saw no wounds.

"—and your forehead was scratched and prickled with what might have been punctures from a crown of thorns."

His face was still such a mess from the punishment of sun and wind that it was no use searching in the rearview mirror for the minor injuries the priest had described.

Geary said, "I was . . . frightened, I guess. But fascinated, too."

They came to a forty-foot-long concrete bridge at an arroyo where the runoff had overflowed the banks. A dark lake had formed and risen above the edge of the elevated roadbed. Geary bulled forward. Plumes of water, reflecting the car's lights, unfurled on both sides like great white wings.

"I'd never seen stigmata," Geary continued when they were out of the flooded area, "though I'd heard of the phenomenon. I pulled up your shirt . . . looked at your side . . . and found the enflamed scar of what might have been a spear wound."

The events of recent months had been so filled with surprises and amazements that the threshold on Jim's sense of wonder had been raised repeatedly. But the priest's story leaped across it, got to him, and sent a chill of awe along his spine.

Geary's voice had fallen to little more than a whisper. "By the time I got you back to the rectory and into bed, those signs were gone. But I knew I hadn't imagined them. I'd seen them, they'd been real, and I knew there was something special about you."

The lightning had fizzled out long ago; the black sky was no longer adorned by bright, jagged necklaces of electricity. Now the rain began to abate, as well, and Father Geary was able to reduce the speed of the wind-shield wipers even as he increased that of the aging Toyota.

For a while neither of them seemed to know what to say. Finally the priest cleared his throat. "Have you experienced this before—these stigmata?"

"No. Not that I'm aware of. But then, of course, I wasn't aware this time until you told me."

"You didn't notice the marks on your hands before you passed out at the sanctuary railing?"

"No."

"But this isn't the only unusual thing that's been happening to you lately."

Jim's soft laugh was wrenched from him less by amusement than by a sense of dark irony. "Definitely not the only unusual thing."

"Do you want to tell me?"

Jim thought about it awhile before replying. "Yes, but I can't."

"I'm a priest. I respect all confidences. Even the police have no power over me."

"Oh, I trust you, Father. And I'm not particularly worried about the police."

"Then?"

"If I tell you . . . the enemy will come," Jim said, and frowned as he heard himself speaking those words. The statement seemed to have come *through* him rather than from him.

"What enemy?"

He stared out at the vast, lightless expanse of desert. "I don't know."

"The enemy you spoke of in your sleep last night?"

"Maybe."

"You said it would kill us all."

"And it will." He went on, perhaps even more interested in what he said than the priest was, for he had no idea what words he would speak until he heard them. "If it finds out about me, if it discovers that I'm saving lives, special lives, then it'll come to stop me."

The priest glanced at him. "Special lives? Exactly what do you mean by that?"

"I don't know."

"If you tell me about yourself, I'll never repeat to another soul a word of what you say. So whatever this enemy is—how could it find out about you just because you confide in me?"

"I don't know."

"You don't know."

"That's right."

The priest sighed in frustration.

"Father, I'm really not playing games or being purposefully obscure." He shifted in his seat and adjusted the safety harness, trying to get more comfortable; however, his discomfort was less physical than spiritual, and not easily remedied. "Have you heard the term 'automatic writing'?"

Glowering at the road ahead, Geary said, "Psychics and mediums talk about it. Superstitious claptrap. A spirit supposedly seizes control of the medium's hand, while he's in a trance, and writes out messages from Beyond." He made a wordless sound of disgust. "The same people who scoff at the idea of speaking with God—or even at the mere idea of God's existence—naively embrace any con-artist's claim to be a channeler for the spirits of the dead."

"Well, nevertheless, what happens to me sometimes is that someone or something else seems to speak through me, an oral form of automatic writing. I know what I'm saying only because I listen to myself saying it."

"You're not in a trance."

"No."

"You claim to be a medium, a psychic?"

"No. I'm sure I'm not."

"You think the dead are speaking through you?"

"No. Not that."

"Then who?"

"I don't know."

"God?"

"Maybe."

"But you don't know," Geary said exasperatedly.

"I don't know."

"You're not only the strangest man I've ever met, Jim. You're also the most frustrating."

THEY ARRIVED AT McCarran International in Las Vegas at ten o'clock that night. Only a couple of taxis were on the approach road to the airport. The rain had stopped. The palm trees stirred in a mild breeze, and everything looked as if it had been scrubbed and polished.

Jim opened the door of the Toyota even as Father Geary braked in front of the terminal. He got out, turned, and leaned back in for a last word with the priest.

"Thank you, Father. You probably saved my life."

"Nothing that dramatic."

"I'd like to give Our Lady of the Desert some of the three thousand I'm carrying, but I might need it all. I just don't know what's going to happen in Boston, what I might have to spend it for."

The priest shook his head. "I don't expect anything."

"When I get home again, I'll send some money. It'll be cash in an envelope, no return address, but it's honest money in spite of that. You can accept it in good conscience."

"It's not necessary, Jim. It was enough just to meet you. Maybe you should know . . . you brought a sense of the mystical back into the life of a weary priest who had sometimes begun to doubt his calling—but who'll never doubt again."

They regarded each other with a mutual affection that clearly surprised them both. Jim leaned into the car, Geary reached across the seat, and they shook hands. The priest had a firm, dry grip.

"Go with God," Geary said.

"I hope so."

August 24 through August 26

1 Sitting at her desk in the *Press* newsroom in the post-midnight hours of Friday morning, staring at her blank computer screen, Holly had sunk so low psychologically that she just wanted to go home, get into bed, and pull the covers over her head for a few days. She despised people who were always feeling sorry for themselves. She tried to shame herself out of her funk, but she began to pity herself for having descended to self-pity. Of course, it was impossible not to see the humor in that situation, but she was unable to manage a smile at her own expense; instead, she pitied herself for being such a silly and amusing figure.

She was glad that tomorrow morning's edition had been put to bed and that the newsroom was almost deserted, so none of her colleagues could see her in such a debased condition. The only other people in sight were Tommy Weeks—a lanky maintenance man who was emptying wastecans and sweeping up—and George Fintel.

George, who was on the city-government beat, was at his desk at the far end of the big room, slumped forward, head on his folded arms, asleep. Occasionally he snored loud enough for the sound to carry all the way to Holly. When the bars closed, George sometimes returned to the newsroom instead of to his apartment, just as an old dray horse, when left on slack reins, will haul its cart back along a familiar route to the place it thinks of as home. He would wake sometime during the night, realize where he was, and wearily weave off to bed at last. "Politicians," George often said, "are the lowest form of life, having undergone devolution from that first slimy beast that crawled out of the primordial sea." At fifty-seven, he was too burnt-out to start over, so he continued to spend his days writing about public officials whom he privately reviled, and in the process he had come to hate himself, as well, and to seek solace in a prodigious daily intake of vodka martinis.

If she'd had any tolerance for liquor, Holly would have worried about winding up like George Fintel. But one drink gave her a nice buzz, two made her tipsy, and three put her to sleep.

I hate my life, she thought.

"You self-pitying wretch," she said aloud.

Well, I do. I hate it, everything's so hopeless.

"You nauseating despair junkie," she said softly but with genuine disgust.

"You talking to me?" Tommy Weeks said, piloting a push broom along the aisle in front of her desk.

"No, Tommy. Talking to myself."

"You? Gee, what've you got to be unhappy about?"

"My life."

He stopped and leaned on his broom, crossing one long leg in front of the other. With his broad freckled face, jug ears, and mop of carroty hair, he looked sweet, innocent, kind. "Things haven't turned out like you planned?"

Holly picked up a half-empty bag of M & Ms, tossed a few pieces of candy into her mouth, and leaned back in her chair. "When I left the University of Missouri with a journalism degree, I was gonna shake up the world, break big stories, collect Pulitzers for doorstops—and now look at me. You know what I did this evening?"

"Whatever it was, I can tell you didn't enjoy it."

"I was down at the Hilton for the annual banquet of the Greater Portland Lumber Products Association, interviewing manufacturers of prefab pullmans, plyboard salesmen, and redwood-decking distributors. They gave out the Timber Trophy—that's what they call it—for the 'lumber-products man of the year.' I got to interview him, too. Rushed back here to get it all written up in time for the morning edition. Hot stuff like that, you don't want to let the bastards at *The New York Times* scoop you on it."

"I thought you were arts and leisure."

"Got sick of it. Let me tell you, Tommy, the wrong poet can turn you off the arts for maybe a decade."

She tossed more chocolate morsels in her mouth. She usually didn't eat candy because she was determined not to wind up with a weight problem like the one that had always plagued her mother, and she was gobbling M & Ms now just to make herself feel more miserable and worthless. She was in a bad downward spiral.

She said, "TV and movies, they make journalism look so glamorous and exciting. It's all lies."

"Me," Tommy said, "I haven't had the life I planned on, either. You think I figured to wind up head of maintenance for the *Press*, just a glorified janitor?"

"I guess not," she said, feeling small and self-centered for whining at him when his lot in life was not as desirable as her own.

"Hell, no. From the time I was a little kid, I *knew* I was gonna grow up to drive one of those big damn old sanitation trucks, up there in that high cab, pushin' the buttons to operate the hydraulic-ram compactor." His voice became wistful. "Ridin' above the world, all that powerful machinery at my command. It was my dream, and I went for it, but I couldn't pass the city physical. Have this kidney problem, see. Nothin' serious but enough for the city's health insurers to disqualify me."

He leaned on his broom, gazing off into the distance, smiling faintly, probably visualizing himself ensconced in the kingly driver's seat of a garbage truck.

Staring at him in disbelief, Holly decided that his broad face did not, after all, look sweet and innocent and kind. She had misread the meaning of its lines and planes. It was a *stupid* face.

She wanted to say, You idiot! I dreamed of winning Pulitzers, and now I'm a hack writing industry puff pieces about the damn Timber Trophy! *That* is tragedy. You think having to settle for being a janitor instead of a garbage collector is in any way comparable?

But she didn't say anything because she realized that they *were* comparable. An unfulfilled dream, regardless of whether it was lofty or humble, was still a tragedy to the dreamer who had given up hope. Pulitzers never won and sanitation trucks never driven were equally capable of inducing despair and insomnia. And that was the most depressing thought she'd had yet.

Tommy's eyes swam into focus again. "You gotta not dwell on it, Miss Thorne. Life . . . it's like gettin' a blueberry muffin in a coffeeshop when what you ordered was the apricot-nut. There aren't any apricots or nuts in it, and you can get tied up in knots just thinkin' about what you're missin', when the smarter thing to do is realize that blueberries have a nice taste, too."

Across the room, George Fintel farted in his sleep. It was a window-rattler. If the *Press* had been a big newspaper, with reporters hanging around who'd just returned from Beirut or some war zone, they'd have all dived for cover.

My God, Holly thought, my life's nothing but a bad imitation of a Damon Runyon story. Sleazy newsrooms after midnight. Half-baked philosopher-janitors. Hard-drinking reporters who sleep at their desks. But it was Runyon as revised by an absurdist writer in collaboration with a bleak existentialist.

"I feel better just having talked to you," Holly lied. "Thanks, Tommy."

"Anytime, Miss Thorne."

As Tommy set to work with his push broom again and moved on down the aisle, Holly tossed some more candy into her mouth and wondered if she would be able to pass the physical required of potential sanitation-truck drivers. On the positive side, the work would be different from journalism as she knew it—collecting garbage instead of dispensing it—and she would have the satisfaction of knowing that at least one person in Portland would desperately envy her.

She looked at the wall clock. One-thirty in the morning. She wasn't sleepy. She didn't want to go home and lie awake, staring at the ceiling, with nothing to do but indulge in more self-examination and self-pity. Well, actually, that *is* what she wanted, because she was in a wallowing mood, but she knew it wasn't a healthy thing to do. Unfortunately, she was without alternatives: weekday, wee-hour nightlife in Portland was a twenty-four-hour doughnut shop.

She was less than a day away from the start of her vacation, and she desperately needed it. She had made no plans. She was just going to relax, hang out, never once look at a newspaper. Maybe see some movies. Maybe read a few books. Maybe go to the Betty Ford Center to take the self-pity detox program.

She had reached that dangerous state in which she began to brood about her name. Holly Thorne. Cute. Real cute. What in God's name had possessed her parents to hang that one on her? Was it possible to imagine the Pulitzer committee giving that grand prize to a woman with a name more suitable to a cartoon character? Sometimes—always in the still heart of the night, of course—she was tempted to call her folks and demand to know whether this name thing had been just bad taste, a misfired joke, or conscious cruelty.

But her parents were salt-of-the-earth working-class people who had denied themselves many pleasures in order to give her a first-rate education, and they wanted nothing but the best for her. They would be devastated to hear that she loathed her name, when they no doubt thought it was clever and even sophisticated. She loved them fiercely, and she had to be in the deepest trenches of depression before she had the gall to blame them for her shortcomings.

Half afraid that she would pick up the phone and call them, she quickly turned to her computer again and accessed the current-edition file. The *Press*'s data-retrieval system made it possible for any reporter on staff to follow any story through editing, typesetting, and production. Now that tomorrow's edition had been formatted, locked down, and sent to press, she could actually call up an image of each page on her screen. Only the headlines were big enough to read, but any portion of the image could be enlarged to fill the screen. Sometimes she could cheer herself a little by reading a big story before the newspaper hit the street; it sparked in her at least a dim glimmer of the feeling of being an insider, which was one aspect of the job that attracted every dream-besotted young person to a vocation in journalism.

But as she scanned the headlines on the first few pages, looking for an interesting story to enlarge, her gloom deepened. A big fire in St. Louis, nine people dead. Presentiments of war in the Mid-East. An oil spill off Japan. A huge storm and flood in India, tens of thousands homeless. The federal government was raising taxes again. She had always known that the news industry flourished on gloom, disaster, scandal, mindless violence, and strife. But suddenly it seemed to be a singularly ghoulish business, and Holly realized that she no longer *wanted* to be an insider, among the first to know this dreadful stuff.

Then, just as she was about to close the file and switch off the computer, a headline arrested her: MYSTERIOUS STRANGER SAVES BOY. The events at McAlbury School were not quite twelve days in the past, and those four words had a special association for her. Curiosity triggered, she instructed the computer to enlarge the quadrant in which the story began.

The dateline was Boston, and the story was accompanied by a photograph. The picture was still blurry and dark, but the scale was now large enough to allow her to read the text, although not comfortably. She instructed the computer to further enlarge one of the already enlarged quadrants, pulling up the first column of the article so she could read it without strain.

The opening line made Holly sit up straighter in her chair: *A courageous bystander, who would say only that his name was Jim, saved the life of Nicholas O'Conner, 6, when a New England Power and Light Company vault exploded under a sidewalk in a Boston residential area Thursday evening.*

Softly, she said, "What the hell . . . ?"

She tapped the keys, instructing the computer to shift the field of display rightward on the page to show her the multiply enhanced photo that accompanied the piece. She went to a bigger scale, then to a still bigger one, until the face filled the screen.

Jim Ironheart.

Briefly she sat in stunned disbelief, immobilized. Then she was stricken by a need to know more—not only an intellectual but a genuinely physical need that felt not unlike a sudden and intense pang of hunger.

She returned to the text of the story and read it through, then read it again. The O'Conner boy had been sitting on the sidewalk in front of his home, directly on the two-by-three-foot concrete lid that covered the entrance to the power company's vault, which was spacious enough for four men to work together within its subterranean confines. The kid had been playing with toy trucks. His parents had been within sight of him on the front porch of their house, when a stranger had sprinted along the street. "He comes right at Nicky," the boy's father was quoted, "snatches him, so I thought sure he was a nutcase child molester going to steal my son." Carrying the screaming child, the stranger leaped over a low picket fence, onto the O'Conners' lawn, just as a 17,000-volt line in the vault exploded behind him. The blast flipped the concrete lid high into the air, as if it were a penny, and a bright ball of fire roared up in its wake. Embarrassed by the effusive praise heaped on him by Nicky's grateful parents and by the neighbors who had witnessed his heroism, the stranger claimed that he had smelled burning insulation, heard a hissing coming from the vault, and knew what was about to happen because he had "once worked for a power company." Annoyed that a witness had taken his photograph, he insisted on leaving before the media arrived because, as he put it, "I place a high value on my privacy."

That hair's-breadth rescue had occurred at 7:40 Thursday evening in Boston—or 4:40 Portland time yesterday afternoon. Holly looked at the office wall clock. It was now 2:02 Friday morning. Nicky O'Conner had been plucked off that vault cover not quite nine and a half hours ago.

The trail was still fresh.

She had questions to ask the *Globe* reporter who had written the piece. But it was only a little after five in the morning in Boston. He wouldn't be at work yet.

She closed out the *Press*'s current-edition data file. On the computer screen, the standard menu replaced the enlarged newspaper text.

Through a modem she accessed the vast network of data services to which the *Press* subscribed. She instructed the Newsweb service to scan all the stories that had been carried by the wire services and published in the major U.S. newspapers during the past three months, looking for instances in which the name "Jim" had been used within ten words of either "rescue" or the phrase "saved the life." She asked for a printout of every article, if there should be any, but asked to be spared multiples of the same incident.

While Newsweb was fulfilling her request, she snatched up the phone on her desk and called long-distance information for area code 818, then 213, then 714, and 619, seeking a listing for Jim Ironheart in Los Angeles, Orange, Riverside, San Bernardino, and San Diego counties. None of the operators was able to help her. If he actually lived in southern California, as he had told her he did, his phone was unlisted.

The laser printer that she shared with three other workstations was humming softly. The first of Newsweb's finds was sliding into the receiving tray.

She wanted to hurry to the cabinet on which the printer stood, grab the first printout, and read it at once; but she restrained herself, focusing her attention on the telephone instead, trying to think of another way to locate Jim Ironheart down there in the part of California that locals called "the Southland."

A few years ago, she simply could have accessed the California Department of Motor Vehicles computer and, for a small fee, received the street address of anyone holding a valid driver's license in the state. But after the actress Rebecca Schaeffer had been murdered by an obsessed fan who had tracked her down in that fashion, a new law had imposed restrictions on DMV records.

If she had been an accomplished computer hacker, steeped in their arcane knowledge, she no doubt could have finessed entrance to the DMV records in spite of their new safeguards, or perhaps she could have pried into credit-agency databanks to search for a file on Ironheart. She had known reporters who honed their computer skills for just that purpose, but she had always sought her sources and information in a strictly legitimate fashion, without deception.

Which is why you're writing about such thrilling stuff as the Timber Trophy, she thought sourly.

While she puzzled over a solution to the problem, she hurried to the vending room and got a cup of coffee from the coin-operated brewer. It tasted like yak bile. She drank it anyway, because she was going to need the caffeine before the night was through. She bought another cup and returned with it to the newsroom.

The laser printer was silent. She grabbed the pages from its tray and sat down at her desk.

Newsweb had turned up a thick stack of stories from the national press in which the name "Jim" was used within ten words of "rescue" or "saved the life." She counted them quickly. Twenty-nine.

The first was a human-interest piece from the *Chicago Sun-times,* and

Holly read the opening sentence aloud: "Jim Foster, of Oak Park, has rescued over one hundred stranded cats from—"

She dropped that printout in her wastecan and looked at the next one. It was from the *Philadelphia Inquirer*: "Jim Pilsbury, pitching for the Phillies, rescued his club from a humiliating defeat—"

Throwing that one aside, as well, she looked at the third. It was a movie review, so she didn't bother searching for the mention of Jim. The fourth was a reference to Jim Harrison, the novelist. The fifth was a story about a New Jersey politician who used the Heimlich maneuver to save the life of a Mafia boss in a barroom, where they were having a couple of beers together, when the *padrone* began to choke to death on a chunk of peppery-hot Slim Jim sausage.

She was beginning to worry that she would come up empty-handed by the bottom of the stack, but the sixth article, from the *Houston Chronicle*, opened her eyes wider than the vile coffee had. WOMAN SAVED FROM VENGEFUL HUSBAND. On July 14, after winning both financial and child-custody issues in a bitter divorce suit, Amanda Cutter had nearly been shot by her enraged husband, Cosmo, outside her home in the wealthy River Oaks district of the city. After Cosmo missed her with the first two shots, she had been saved by a man who "appeared out of nowhere," wrestled her maddened spouse to the ground, and disarmed him. Her savior had identified himself only as "Jim," and had walked off into the humid Houston afternoon before the police arrived. The thirty-year-old divorcée had clearly been smitten, for she described him as "handsome, sort of muscular, like a superhero right out of a movie, with the dreamiest blue eyes."

Holly could still picture Jim Ironheart's intensely blue eyes. She was not the kind of woman who would refer to them as "dreamy," although they were certainly the clearest and most arresting eyes she'd ever . . . Oh, hell, yes, they *were* dreamy. She was reluctant to admit to the adolescent reaction that he had inspired in her, but she was not any better at deceiving herself than she was at deceiving other people. She recalled an initial eerie impression of inhuman coldness, upon first meeting his gaze, but that passed and never returned from the moment he smiled.

The seventh article was about another modest Jim who had not hung around to accept thanks and praise—or media attention—after rescuing Carmen Diaz, thirty, from a burning apartment house in Miami on the fifth of July. He had blue eyes.

Poring through the remaining twenty-two articles, Holly found two more about Ironheart, though only his first name was mentioned. On June 21, Thaddeus Johnson, twelve, had almost been pitched off the roof of an eight-story Harlem tenement by four members of a neighborhood youth gang who had not responded well to his disdainful rejection of an invitation to join their drug-peddling fraternity. He was rescued by a blue-eyed man who incapacitated the four thugs with a dazzling series of Tae Kwon Do kicks, chops, thrusts, and throws. "He was like Batman without the funny clothes," Thaddeus had told the *Daily News* reporter. Two weeks prior to that, on

June 7, another blue-eyed Jim "just seemed to materialize" on the property of Louis Andretti, twenty-eight, of Corona, California, in time to warn the homeowner not to enter a crawlspace under his house to repair a plumbing leak. "He told me a family of rattlers had settled in there," Andretti told the reporter. Later, when agents from the county's Vector Control inspected the crawlspace from the perimeter, with the aid of a halogen lamp, they saw not just a nest but "something out of a nightmare," and eventually extracted forty-one snakes from beneath the structure. "What I don't understand," Andretti said, "is how that guy knew the rattlers were there, when I *live* in the house and never had a clue."

Now Holly had four linked incidents to add to the rescue of Nicky O'Conner in Boston and Billy Jenkins in Portland, all since the first of June. She typed in new instructions to Newsweb, asking for the same search to be made for the months of March, April, and May.

She needed more coffee, and when she got up to go to the vending room, she saw that George Fintel had evidently awakened and staggered home. She hadn't heard him leave. Tommy was gone, as well. She was alone.

She got another cup of coffee, and it didn't taste as bad as it had before. The brew hadn't improved; her sense of taste had just been temporarily damaged by the first two cups.

Eventually Newsweb located eleven stories in March through May that fit her parameters. After examining the printouts, Holly found only one of them of interest.

On May 15, in Atlanta, Georgia, a blue-eyed Jim had entered a convenience store during an armed robbery. He shot and killed the perpetrator, Norman Rink, who had been about to kill two customers—Sam Newsome, twenty-five, and his five-year-old daughter Emily. Flying high on a cocaine, Ice, and methamphetamine cocktail—Rink had already killed the clerk and two other customers merely for the fun of it. After wasting Rink and assuring himself that the Newsomes were unhurt, Jim had slipped away before the police arrived.

The store security camera had provided a blurry photograph of the heroic intruder. It was only the second photo Holly had found in all the articles. The image was poor. But she immediately recognized Jim Ironheart.

Some details of the incident unnerved her. If Ironheart had an amazing ability—psychic power, whatever—to foresee fatal moments in the lives of strangers and arrive in time to thwart fate, why hadn't he gotten to that convenience store a few minutes sooner, early enough to prevent the deaths of the clerk and other customers? Why had he saved the Newsomes and let the rest die?

She was further chilled by the description of his attack on Rink. He had pumped four rounds from a 12-gauge pistol-grip shotgun into the madman. Then, although Rink was indisputably dead, Jim reloaded and fired another four rounds. "He was in such a rage," Sam Newsome said, "his face red, and he was sweating, you could see the arteries pounding in his temples, across his forehead. He was crying a little, too, but the tears . . . they didn't make him seem any less angry." When done, Jim had expressed regret for cutting Rink down so violently in front of little Emily. He'd explained that men like Rink, who killed innocent people, brought out "a little madness of my own." Newsome told the reporter, "He saved our lives, yeah, but I gotta say the guy was *scary,* almost as scary as Rink."

Realizing that Ironheart might not have revealed even his first name on some occasions, Holly instructed Newsweb to search the past six months for stories in which "rescue" and "saved the life" were within ten words of "blue." She had noticed that some witnesses were vague about his physical description, but that most remembered his singularly blue eyes.

She went to the john, got more coffee, then stood by the printer. As each find was transferred to hard copy, she snatched it up, scanned it, tossed it in the wastecan if it was of no interest or read it with excitement if it was about another nick-of-time rescue. Newsweb turned up four more cases that indisputably belonged in the Ironheart file, even though neither his first nor last name was used.

At her desk again, she instructed Newsweb to search the past six months for the name "Ironheart" in the national media.

While she waited for a response, she put the pertinent printouts in order, then made a chronological list of the people whose lives Jim Ironheart had saved, incorporating the four new cases. She included their names, ages, the location of each incident, and the type of death from which each person had been spared.

She studied that compilation, noting some patterns with interest. But she put it aside when Newsweb completed its latest task.

As she rose from her chair to go to the laser printer, she froze, surprised to discover she was no longer alone in the newsroom. Three reporters and an editor were at their desks, all guys with reputations as early birds, including Hank Hawkins, editor of the business pages, who liked to be at work when the financial markets opened on the East Coast. She hadn't been aware of them coming in. Two of them were sharing a joke, laughing loudly, and Hawkins was talking on the phone, but Holly hadn't heard them until after she'd seen them. She looked at the clock: 6:10. Opalescent early-morning light played at the windows, though she had not realized that the tide of night had been receding. She glanced down at her desk and saw two more paper coffee cups than she remembered getting from the vending machine.

She realized that she was no longer wallowing in despair. She felt better than she had felt in days. Weeks. *Years.* She was a reporter again, for real.

She went to the laser printer, emptied the receiving tray, and returned with the pages to her desk. Ironhearts evidently were not newsmakers. There were only five stories involving people with that surname in the past six months.

Kevin Ironheart—Buffalo, New York. State senator. Announced his intention to run for governor.

Anna Denise Ironheart—Boca Raton, Florida. Found a live alligator in her family room.

Lori Ironheart—Los Angeles, California. Songwriter. Nominated for the Academy Award for best song of the year.

Valerie Ironheart—Cedar Rapids, Iowa. Gave birth to healthy quadruplets.

The last of the five was James Ironheart.

She looked at the heading. The story came from the Orange County *Register*, April 10, and was one of scores of pieces on the same story that had been published statewide. Because of her instructions, the computer had printed out only this single instance, sparing her sheafs of similar articles on the same event.

She checked the dateline. Laguna Niguel. California. *Southern* California. The Southland.

The piece was not accompanied by a photograph, but the reporter's description of the man included a reference to blue eyes and thick brown hair. She was sure he was *her* James Ironheart.

She was not surprised to have found him. She had known that with determined effort she would locate him sooner or later. What surprised her was the subject of the piece in which his full name appeared at last. She expected it to be yet one more story about snatching someone out of death's grasp, and she was not prepared for the headline: LAGUNA NIGUEL MAN WINS SIX MILLION LOTTO JACKPOT.

2

Having followed the rescue of Nicholas O'Conner with his first untroubled night of sleep in the last four, Jim departed Boston on Friday afternoon, August 24. Gaining three hours on the cross-country trip, he arrived at John Wayne Airport by 3:10 P.M. and was home half an hour later.

He went straight into his den and lifted the flap of carpet that revealed the safe built into the floor of the closet. He dialed the combination, opened the lid, and removed five thousand dollars, ten percent of the cash he kept there.

At his desk, he packed the hundred-dollar bills into a padded Jiffy envelope and stapled it shut. He typed a label to Father Leo Geary at Our Lady of the Desert, and affixed sufficient postage. He would mail it first thing in the morning.

He went into the family room and switched on the TV. He tried several movies on cable, but none held his interest. He watched the news for a while, but his mind wandered. After he heated a microwave pizza and popped open a beer, he settled down with a good book—which bored him. He paged through a stack of unread magazines, but none of the articles was intriguing.

Near twilight he went outside with another beer and sat on the patio.

The palm fronds rustled in a light breeze. A sweet fragrance rose from the star jasmine along the property wall. Red, purple, and pink impatiens shone with almost Day-Glo radiance in the dwindling light; and as the sun finished setting, they faded as if they were hundreds of small lightbulbs on a rheostat. Night floated down like a great tossed cape of almost weightless black silk.

Although the scene was peaceful, he was restless. Day by day, week by week, since he had saved the lives of Sam Newsome and his daughter Emily on May 15, Jim had found it increasingly difficult to involve himself in the ordinary routines and pleasures of life. He was unable to relax. He kept thinking of all the good he could do, all the lives he could save, the destinies he could alter, if only the call would come again: "Life line." Other endeavors seemed frivolous by comparison.

Having been the instrument of a higher power, he now found it difficult to settle for being anything less.

AFTER SPENDING THE day collecting what information she could find on James Madison Ironheart, with only a two-hour nap to compensate for the night of sleep she had lost, Holly launched her long-anticipated vacation with a flight to Orange County. On arrival, she drove her rental car south from the airport to the Laguna Hills Motor Inn, where she had reserved a motel room.

Laguna Hills was inland, and not a resort area. But in Laguna Beach, Laguna Niguel, and other coastal towns during the summer, rooms had been booked far in advance. She didn't intend to swim or sunbathe anyway. Ordinarily, she was as enthusiastic a pursuer of skin cancer as anyone, but this had become a working vacation.

By the time she arrived at the motel, she felt as if her eyes were full of sand. When she carried her suitcase into her room, gravity played a cruel trick, pulling her down with five times the usual force.

The room was simple and clean, with enough air-conditioning to re-create the environment of Alaska, in case it was ever occupied by an Eskimo who got homesick.

From vending machines in the breezeway, she purchased a packet of peanut-butter-and-cheese crackers and a can of diet Dr Pepper, and satisfied her hunger while sitting in bed. She was so tired that she felt numb. All of her senses were dulled by exhaustion, including her sense of taste. She might as well have been eating Styrofoam and washing it down with mule sweat.

As if the contact of head and pillow tripped a switch, she fell instantly asleep.

During the night, she began to dream. It was an odd dream, for it took place in absolute darkness, with no images, just sounds and smells and tactile sensations, perhaps the way people dreamed when they had been blind since birth. She was in a dank cool place that smelled vaguely of lime. At first she was not afraid, just confused, carefully feeling her way along the walls of the chamber. They were constructed from blocks of stone with tight mortar joints. After a little exploration she realized there was actually just one wall, a single continuous sweep of stone, because the room was circular. The only sounds were those she made—and the background hiss and tick of rain drumming on a slate roof overhead.

In the dream, she moved away from the wall, across a solid wood floor, hands held out in front of her. Although she encountered nothing, her curiosity suddenly began to turn to fear. She stopped moving, stood perfectly still, certain that she had heard something sinister.

A subtle sound. Masked by the soft but insistent rattle of the rain. It came again. A squeak.

For an instant she thought of a rat, fat and sleek, but the sound was too protracted and of too odd a character to have been made by a rat. More of a creak than a squeak, but not the creak of a floorboard underfoot, either. It faded . . . came again a few seconds later . . . faded . . . came again . . . rhythmically.

When Holly realized that she was listening to the protest of an unoiled mechanism of some kind, she should have been relieved. Instead, standing in that tenebrous room, straining to imagine what machine it might be, she felt her heartbeat accelerate. The creaking grew only slightly louder, but it speeded up a lot; instead of one creak every five or six seconds, the sound came every three or four seconds, then every two or three, then once per second.

Suddenly a strange rhythmic *whoosh, whoosh, whoosh* struck up, as well, in syncopation with the creaking. It was the sound of a wide flat object cutting the air.

Whoosh.

It was close. Yet she felt no draft.

Whoosh.

She had the crazy idea that it was a blade.

Whoosh.

A large blade. Sharp. Cutting the air. Enormous.

Whoosh.

She sensed that something terrible was approaching, an entity so strange that even light—and the full sight of the thing—would not provide understanding. Although she was aware that she was dreaming, she knew she had to get out of that dark and stony place quickly—or die. A nightmare couldn't be escaped just by running from it, so she had to wake up, but she could not, she was too tired, unable to break the bonds of sleep. Then the lightless room seemed to be spinning, she had a sense of some great structure turning around and around (*creak, whoosh*), thrusting up into the rainy night (*creak, whoosh*) and turning (*creak, whoosh*), cutting the air (*creak, whoosh*), she was trying to scream (*creak, whoosh*), but she couldn't force a sound from herself (*whoosh, whoosh, whoosh*), couldn't awaken and couldn't scream for help. *WHOOSH!*

"NO!"

Jim sat up in bed as he shouted the one-world denial. He was clammy and trembling violently.

He had fallen fast asleep with the lamp on, which he frequently did, usually not by accident but by design. For more than a year, his sleep had been troubled by nightmares with a variety of plots and a panoply of boog-eymen, only some of which he could recall when he woke. The nameless, formless creature that he called "the enemy," and of which he had dreamed while recuperating at Our Lady of the Desert rectory, was the most fright-ening figure in his dreamscapes, though not the only monster.

This time, however, the focus of the terror had not been a person or creature. It was a *place*. The windmill.

He looked at the bedside clock. Three-forty-five in the morning.

In just his pajama bottoms, he got out of bed and padded into the kitchen.

The fluorescent light seared his eyes. Good. He wanted to evaporate what residue of sleep still clung to him.

The damn windmill.

He plugged in the coffeemaker and brewed a strong Colombian blend. He sipped half the first cup while standing at the counter, then refilled it and sat down at the breakfast table. He intended to empty the pot because he could not risk going back to bed and having that dream again.

Every nightmare detracted from the quality of rest that sleep provided, but the windmill dream actually took a real physical toll. Whenever he woke from it, his chest always ached, as though his heart had been bruised from hammering too hard against his breastbone. Sometimes the shakes took hours to fade away completely, and he often had headaches that, like now, arced across the top of his skull and throbbed with such power that it seemed as if an alien presence was trying to burst out of him. He knew that if he looked in a mirror, his face would be unnervingly pale and haggard, with blue-black circles around the eyes, like the face of a terminal cancer patient from whom disease had sucked the juice of life.

The windmill dream was not the most frequent of those that plagued him, and in fact it haunted his sleep only one or two nights a month. But it was by far the worst.

Curiously, nothing much happened in it. He was ten years old again, sitting on the dusty wooden floor of the smaller upper chamber, above the main room that held the ancient millstones, with only the flickering light of a fat yellow candle. Night pressed at the narrow windows, which were al-most like castle embrasures in the limestone walls. Rain tapped against the glass. Suddenly, with a creak of unoiled and half-rusted machinery, the four great wooden sails of the mill began to turn outside, faster and faster, cutting like giant scythes through the damp air. The upright shaft, which came out of the ceiling and vanished through a bore in the center of the floor, also began to turn, briefly creating the illusion that the round floor itself were rotating in the manner of a carousel. One level below, the ancient millstones started to roll against each other, producing a soft rumble like distant thunder.

Just that. Nothing more. Yet it scared the hell out of him.

He took a long pull of his coffee.

Stranger still: in real life, the windmill had been a good place, never the scene of pain or terror. It had stood between a pond and a cornfield on his grandparents' farm. To a young boy born and raised in the city, the big mill had been an exotic and mysterious structure, a perfect place to play and fantasize, a refuge in a time of trouble. He could not understand why he was having nightmares about a place that held only good memories for him.

AFTER THE FRIGHTENING dream passed without waking her, Holly Thorne slept peacefully for the rest of the night, as still as a stone on the floor of the sea.

3 Saturday morning, Holly ate breakfast in a booth at the motel coffeeshop. Most of the other customers were obviously vacationers: families dressed almost as if in uniforms of shorts or white slacks and brightly colored shirts. Some of the kids wore caps and T-shirts that advertised Sea World or Disneyland or Knott's Berry Farm. Parents huddled over maps and brochures while they ate, planning routes that would take them to one of the tourist attractions that California offered in such plenitude. There were so many colorful Polo shirts or Polo-shirt knockoffs in the restaurant that a visitor from another planet might have assumed that Ralph Lauren was either the deity of a major religion or dictator of the world.

As she ate blueberry pancakes, Holly studied her list of people who had been spared from death by Jim Ironheart's timely intervention:

MAY 15
  Sam (25) and Emily (5) Newsome—Atlanta, Georgia (murder)

JUNE 7
  Louis Andretti (28)—Corona, California (snakebite)

JUNE 21
  Thaddeus Johnson (12)—New York, New York (murder)

JUNE 30
  Rachael Steinberg (23)—San Francisco, California (murder)

JULY 5
Carmen Diaz (30)—Miami, Florida (fire)

JULY 14
Amanda Cutter (30)—Houston, Texas (murder)

JULY 20
Steven Aimes (57)—Birmingham, Alabama (murder)

AUGUST 1
Laura Lenaskian (28)—Seattle, Washington (drowning)

AUGUST 8
Doogie Burkette (11)—Peoria, Illinois (drowning)

AUGUST 12
Billy Jenkins (8)—Portland, Oregon (traffic fatality)

AUGUST 20
Lisa (30) and Susan (10) Jawolski—Mojave desert (murder)

AUGUST 23
Nicholas O'Conner (6)—Boston, Massachusetts (explosion)

Certain patterns were obvious. Of the fourteen people saved, six were children. Seven others were between the ages of twenty-three and thirty. Only one was older—Steven Aimes, who was fifty-seven. Ironheart favored the young. And there was some evidence that his activities were increasing in frequency: one episode in May; three in June; three in July; and now five already in August with a full week of the month remaining.

Holly was particularly intrigued by the number of people on the list who would have been *murdered* without Ironheart's intervention. Far more people died each year in accidents than at the hands of others. Traffic fatalities alone were more numerous than murders. Yet Jim Ironheart intervened in a considerably greater number of homicides than accidents: eight of the fourteen people on the list had been spared from the malevolent intentions of murderers, over sixty percent.

Perhaps his premonitions more often related to murder than to other forms of death because human violence generated stronger psychic vibrations than accidents . . .

Holly stopped chewing and her hand froze halfway to her mouth with another forkful of blueberry pancake, as she realized just *how* strange this story was. She had been operating at a breathless pace, driven by reportorial ambition and curiosity. Her excitement, then her exhaustion, had prevented her from fully considering all of the implications and ramifications of Ironheart's activities. She put down her fork and stared at her plate, as if she could glean answers and explanations from the crumb patterns and smears in the same way that gypsies read tea leaves and palms.

What the hell *was* Jim Ironheart? A psychic?

She'd never had much interest in extrasensory perception and strange mental powers. She knew there were people who claimed to be able to "see" a murderer just by touching the clothes his victim wore, who sometimes helped police find the bodies of missing persons, who were paid well by the *National Enquirer* to foresee world events and forthcoming developments in the lives of celebrities, who said they could channel the voices of the dead to the living. But her interest in the supernatural was so minimal that she had never really formed an opinion of the validity of such claims. She didn't necessarily believe that all those people were frauds; the whole subject had bored her too much to bother thinking about it at all.

She supposed that her dogged rationality—and cynicism—could bend far enough to encompass the idea that now and then a psychic actually possessed real power, but she wasn't sure that "psychic" was an adequate description of Jim Ironheart. This guy wasn't just going out on a limb in some cheap tabloid to predict that Steven Spielberg would make another hit picture next year (surprise!), or that Schwarzenegger would still speak English with an accent, or that Tom Cruise would dump his current girlfriend, or that Eddie Murphy would still be black for the foreseeable future. *This* guy knew the precise facts of each of those impending deaths—who, when, where, how— far enough in advance to derail fate. He wasn't bending spoons with the power of his mind, wasn't speaking in the gravelly voice of an ancient spirit named Rama-Lama-Dingdong, wasn't reading futures in entrails or wax drippings or Tarot cards. He was *saving lives*, for God's sake, altering destinies, having a profound impact not only on those he saved from death but on the lives of the friends and families who would have been left shattered and bereaved. And the reach of his power extended three thousand miles from Laguna Niguel to Boston!

In fact, maybe his heroics were not confined to the borders of the continental United States. She had not researched the international media for the past six months. Perhaps he had saved lives in Italy, France, Germany, Japan, Sweden, or in Pago Pago for all she knew.

The word "psychic" definitely was inadequate. Holly couldn't even think of a suitable one-word description of his powers.

To her surprise, a sense of wonder had possessed her, like nothing she had felt since she was a kid. Now, an element of awe stole over her as well, and she shivered.

Who was this man? *What* was he?

Little more than thirty hours ago, when she had seen the story about young Nicholas O'Conner in Boston, Holly had known she was on to a big story. By the time she examined the material that Newsweb found for her, she felt it might be the biggest story of her career, regardless of how long she worked as a reporter. Now she had begun to suspect that it might grow into the biggest story of this decade.

"Everything okay?"

Holly said, "Everything's weird," before she realized that she had not asked the question of herself.

The waitress—Bernice, according to the name embroidered on her uniform blouse—was standing beside the table, looking concerned. Holly realized that she had been staring intently at her plate while she'd been thinking about Jim Ironheart, and she had not taken a bite in some time. Bernice had noticed and thought something was wrong.

"Weird?" Bernice said, frowning.

"Uh, yeah—it's weird that I should come into what looks like an ordinary coffeeshop and get the best blueberry pancakes I've ever eaten."

Bernice hesitated, perhaps trying to decide if Holly was putting her on. "You . . . you really like 'em?"

"Love them," Holly said, forking up a mouthful and chewing the cold, sodden pancakes with enthusiasm.

"That's nice! You want anything else?"

"Just the check," Holly said.

She continued to eat the pancakes after Bernice left, because she was hungry and they were there.

As she ate, Holly looked around the restaurant at the colorfully decked-out vacationers who were absorbed in discussions of amusements experienced and amusements yet to come, and the thrill of being an insider coursed through her for the first time in years. She knew something they did not. She was a reporter with a carefully husbanded secret. When fully researched, when written up in crystalline prose as direct and yet evocative as Hemingway's best journalism (well, she was going to *try* for that, anyway), the story would earn front-page, top-of-the-page exposure in every major newspaper in the country, in the world. And what made it so good, what made her tingle, was that her secret had nothing to do with a political scandal, toxic dumping, or the other myriad forms of terror and tragedy that fueled the engine of modern news media. Her story would be one of amazement and wonder, courage and hope, a story of tragedy avoided, lives spared, death thwarted.

Life is *so* good, she thought, unable to stop grinning at her fellow diners.

FIRST THING AFTER breakfast, with the aid of a book of street maps called the *Thomas Guide*, Holly located Jim Ironheart's house in Laguna Niguel. She had tracked down the address via computer from Portland, by checking the public records of real estate transactions in Orange County since the first of the year. She had assumed that anyone winning six million dollars in a lottery might spend some of it on a new house, and she had assumed correctly. He hit the jackpot—presumably thanks to his clairvoyance—in early January. On May 3, he finalized the purchase of a house on Bougainvillea Way. Since the records did not show that he had sold any property, he apparently had been renting before his windfall.

She was somewhat surprised to find him living in such a modest house. The neighborhood was new, just off Crown Valley Parkway, and in the neat, well-landscaped, precision-planned tradition of south Orange County. The streets were wide, gracefully curved, lined with young palms and melaleucas, and the houses were all of compatible Mediterranean styles with roofs in different shades of red and sand and peach tiles. But even in such a desirable south-county city as Laguna Niguel, where the per-square-foot cost of a tract home could rival that of a Manhattan penthouse, Ironheart could easily have afforded better than he had purchased: It looked like a little more than two thousand square feet, the smallest model in the neighborhood; creamy-white stucco; large-pane French windows but no other apparent custom features; a lush green lawn, but small, with azaleas and impatiens and a pair of willowy queen palms that cast lacy shadows on the walls in the temperate morning sun.

She drove by slowly, giving the house a thorough looking over. No car stood in the driveway. The drapes were drawn at the windows. She had no way of knowing if Ironheart was home—short of going up to his front door and ringing the bell. Eventually, she would do just that. But not yet.

At the end of the block, she turned around and drove past the house again. The place was attractive, pleasant, but so *ordinary*. It was hard to believe that an exceptional man, with astonishing secrets, lived behind those walls.

VIOLA MORENO'S TOWNHOUSE in Irvine was in one of those parklike communities the Irvine Company had built in the sixties and seventies, where the plum-thorn hedges had entered woody maturity and the red-gum eucalyptuses and Indian laurels towered high enough to spread a wealth of shade on even the brightest and most cloudless of summer days. It was furnished with an eye to comfort rather than style: an overstuffed sofa, commodious armchairs, and plump footstools, everything in earth tones, with traditional landscape paintings meant to soothe rather than challenge the eye and mind. Stacks of magazines and shelves of books were everywhere at hand. Holly felt at home the moment she crossed the threshold.

Viola was as welcoming and easy to like as her home. She was about fifty, Mexican-American, with flawless skin the shade of lightly tarnished copper and eyes that were merry in spite of being as liquid-black as squid ink. Though she was on the short side and had broadened a little with age, it was easy to see that her looks would once have turned men's heads hard enough to crack vertebrae; she was still a lovely woman. She took Holly's hand at the door, then linked arms with her to lead her through the small house and out to the patio, as if they were old friends and had not just spoken for the first time on the phone the previous day.

On the patio, which overlooked a common greensward, a pitcher of icy lemonade and two glasses stood on a glass-topped table. The rattan chairs were padded with thick yellow cushions.

"I spend a lot of my summer out here," Viola said as they settled into chairs. The day was not too hot, the air dry and clean. "It's a beautiful little corner of the world, isn't it?"

The broad but shallow green vale separated this row of townhouses from the next, shaded by tall trees and decorated with a couple of circular beds of red and purple impatiens. Two squirrels scampered down a gentle slope and across a meandering walkway.

"Quite beautiful," Holly agreed as Viola poured lemonade into their glasses.

"My husband and I bought it when the trees were just sticks and the Hydroseeded greenbelt was still patchy. But we could visualize what it would be like one day, and we were patient people, even when we were young." She sighed. "Sometimes I have bad moments, I get bitter about his dying so young and never having a chance to see what this all grew up into. But mostly I just enjoy it, knowing Joe is somewhere better than this world and that somehow he takes pleasure in my enjoyment."

"I'm sorry," Holly said, "I didn't know you'd been widowed."

"Of course you didn't, dear. How could you know? Anyway, it was a long time ago, back in 1969, when I was just thirty and he was thirty-two. My husband was a career Marine, proud of it, and so was I. So *am* I, still, though he died in Vietnam."

Holly was startled to realize that many of the early victims of that conflict would now have been past middle-age. The wives they left behind had now lived far more years without them than with them. How long until Vietnam seemed as ancient as the crusades of Richard the Lionheart or the Peloponnesian Wars?

"Such a waste," Viola said with an edge to her voice. But the edge was gone an instant later when she said, "So long ago . . ."

The life Holly had imagined for this woman—a calm and peaceful journey of small pleasures, warm and cozy, with perhaps more than its share of laughter—was clearly less than half the story. The firm and loving tone Viola used when she referred to Joe as "my husband" made it clear that no amount of time elapsed could fade his memory in her mind, and that there had been no other man since him. Her life had been profoundly changed and constricted by his death. Although she was obviously an optimistic soul and outgoing by nature, there was a shadow of tragedy on her heart.

One basic lesson that every good journalist learned early in his career was that people were seldom only what they seemed to be—and never less complex than the mystery of life itself.

Viola sipped her lemonade. "Too sweet. I always add too much sugar. Sorry." She put her glass down. "Now tell me about this brother you're searching for. You have me quite intrigued."

"As I told you when I called from Portland, I was an adopted child. The people who took me in were wonderful parents, I have no less love for them than I would for my real parents, but . . . well . . ."

"Naturally, you have a desire to know your real parents."

"It's as if . . . there's an emptiness in me, a dark place in my heart," Holly said, trying not to trowel it on too thick.

She was not surprised by the ease with which she lied, but by how well she did it. Deception was a handy tool with which to elicit information from a source who might otherwise be reluctant to talk. Journalists as highly praised as Joe McGinniss, Joseph Wambaugh, Bob Woodward, and Carl Bernstein had at one time or another argued the necessity of this ingenuity in dealing with interviewees, all in the service of getting at the truth. But Holly had never been this skillful at it. At least she had the good grace to be dismayed and embarrassed by her lies—two feelings that she hid well from Viola Moreno.

"Though the adoption agency's records were barely adequate, I've learned that my real parents, my biological parents, died twenty-five years ago, when I was only eight." Actually, it was Jim Ironheart's parents who had died twenty-five years ago, when he was ten, a fact she had turned up in stories about his lottery win. "So I'll never have a chance to know them."

"What a terrible thing. Now it's *my* turn to be sorry for *you*," Viola said with a note of genuine sympathy in her soft voice.

Holly felt like a heel. By concocting this false personal tragedy, she seemed to be mocking Viola's very real loss. She went on anyway: "But it's not as bleak as it might've been, because I've discovered I have a brother, as I told you on the phone."

Leaning forward with her arms on the table, Viola was eager to hear the details and learn how she could help. "And there's something I can do to help you find your brother?"

"Not exactly. You see, I've already found him."

"How wonderful!"

"But . . . I'm afraid to approach him."

"Afraid? But why?"

Holly looked out at the greensward and swallowed hard a couple of times, as if choking on emotion and struggling to maintain control of herself. She was good. Academy Award stuff. She loathed herself for it. When she spoke, she managed to get a subtle and convincing tremor in her voice: "As far as I know, he's the only blood relative I have in the world, and my only link to the mother and father I'll never know. He's my brother, Mrs. Moreno, and I love him. Even though I've never met him, I love him. But what if I approach him, open my heart to him . . . and he wishes I'd never shown up, doesn't like me or something?"

"Good heavens, of course he'll like you! Why wouldn't he like a nice young woman like you? Why wouldn't he be *delighted* to have someone as sweet as you for a sister?"

I'm going to rot in hell for this, Holly thought miserably.

She said, "Well, it may sound silly to you, but I'm worried about it. I've never made good first impressions with people—"

"You've made an excellent one with me, dear."

Grind my face under your heel, why don't you? Holly thought.

She said, "I want to be careful. I want to know as much as possible about him before I knock on his door. I want to know what he likes, what he doesn't like, how he feels about . . . oh, about all sorts of things. God, Mrs. Moreno, I don't want to blow this."

Viola nodded. "I assume you've come to me because I know your brother, probably had him years ago in one of my classes?"

"You do teach history at a junior high school here in Irvine—"

"That's right. I've worked there since before Joe died."

"Well, my brother wasn't one of your students. He was an English instructor in the same school. I traced him there, and learned you'd taught in the room next to his for ten years, you knew him well."

Viola's face brightened into a smile. "You mean Jim Ironheart!"

"That's right. My brother."

"This is lovely, wonderful, this is *perfect!*" Viola enthused.

The woman's reaction was so excessive that Holly blinked in surprise and didn't know quite what to say next.

"He's a good man," Viola said with genuine affection. "I'd have liked nothing better than to've had a son like him. He comes around now and then for dinner, not as often as he used to, and I cook for him, mother him. I can't tell you how much pleasure that gives me." A wistful expression had settled on her, and she was silent a moment. "Anyway . . . you couldn't have asked for a better brother, dear. He's one of the nicest people I've ever known, a dedicated teacher, so gentle and kind and patient."

Holly thought of Norman Rink, the psychopath who had killed a clerk and two customers in that Atlanta convenience store last May, and who had been killed in turn by gentle, kind Jim Ironheart. Eight rounds from a shotgun at point-blank range. Four rounds fired into the corpse after Rink was obviously dead. Viola Moreno might know the man well, but she clearly had no concept of the rage that he could tap when he needed it.

"I've known good teachers in my time, but none as concerned about his students as Jim Ironheart was. He sincerely cared about them, as if they were his own kids." She leaned back in her chair and shook her head, remembering. "He gave so much to them, wanted so much to make their lives better, and all but the worst-case misfits responded to him. He had a rapport with his students that other teachers would sell their souls for, yet he didn't have to surrender a proper student-teacher relationship to get it. So many of them try to be pals with their students, you see, and that never really works."

"Why did he quit teaching?"

Viola hesitated, smile fading. "Partly, it was the lottery."

"What lottery?"

"You don't know about that?"

Holly frowned and shook her head.

Viola said, "He won six million dollars in January."

"Holysmoke!"

"The first time he ever bought a ticket."

Allowing her initial surprise to metamorphose into a look of worry, Holly said, "Oh, God, now he's going to think I only came around because he's suddenly rich."

"No, no," Viola hastened to assure her. "Jim would never think the worst of anyone."

"I've done well myself," Holly lied. "I don't need his money, I wouldn't take it if he tried to give it to me. My adoptive parents are doctors, not wealthy but well-to-do, and I'm an attorney with a nice practice."

Okay, okay, you really *don't* want his money, Holly thought with self-disgust as caustic as acid, but you're still a mean little lying bitch with a frightening talent for invented detail, and you'll spend eternity standing hip-deep in dung, polishing Satan's boots.

Her mood changing, Viola pushed her chair back from the table, got up, and stepped to the edge of the patio. She plucked a weed from a large terra-cotta pot full of begonias, baby's breath, and copper-yellow marigolds. Absentmindedly rolling the slender weed into a ball between the thumb and forefinger of her right hand, she stared thoughtfully out at the parklike grounds.

The woman was silent for a long time.

Holly worried that she had said something wrong, unwittingly revealing her duplicity. Second by second, she became more nervous, and she found herself wanting to blurt out an apology for all the lies she'd told.

Squirrels capered on the grass. A butterfly swooped under the patio cover, perched on the edge of the lemonade pitcher for a moment, then flew away.

Finally, with a tremor in her voice that was real this time, Holly said, "Mrs. Moreno? Is something wrong?"

Viola flicked the balled-up weed out onto the grass. "I'm just having trouble deciding how to put this."

"Put what?" Holly asked nervously.

Turning to her again, approaching the table, Viola said, "You asked me why Jim . . . why your brother quit teaching. I said it was because he won the lottery, but that really isn't true. If he'd still loved teaching as much as he did a few years ago or even *one* year ago, he would've kept working even if he'd won a hundred million."

Holly almost breathed a sigh of relief that her cover had not been penetrated. "What soured him on it?"

"He lost a student."

"Lost?"

"An eighth-grader named Larry Kakonis. A very bright boy with a good heart—but disturbed. From a troubled family. His father beat his mother, had been beating her as long as Larry could remember, and Larry felt as if he should be able to stop it, but he couldn't. He felt responsible, though he shouldn't have. That was the kind of kid he was, a real strong sense of responsibility."

Viola picked up her glass of lemonade, returned to the edge of the patio, and stared out at the greensward again. She was silent once more.

Holly waited.

Eventually the woman said, "The mother was a co-dependent type, a victim of the father but a collaborator in her own victimization. As troubled in her own way as the father. Larry couldn't reconcile his love for his mother and his respect for her with his growing understanding that, on some level, she liked and *needed* to be beaten."

Suddenly Holly knew where this was going, and she did not want to hear the rest of it. However, she had no choice but to listen.

"Jim had worked so hard with the boy. I don't mean just on his English lessons, not just academically. Larry had opened up to him in a way he'd never been able to open to anyone else, and Jim had been counseling him with the help of Dr. Lansing, a psychologist who works part-time for the school district. Larry seemed to be coming around, struggling to understand his mother and himself—and to some extent succeeding. Then one night, May fifteenth of last year—over fifteen months ago, though it's hard to believe it's been that long—Larry Kakonis took a gun from his father's collection, loaded it, put the barrel in his mouth . . . and fired one bullet up into his brain."

Holly flinched as if struck. In fact she *had* been struck, though the blows—two of them—were not physical. She was jolted, first by the thought of a thirteen-year-old committing suicide when the best of life lay ahead of him. A small problem could seem like a large one at that age, and a genuinely serious problem could seem catastrophic and hopeless. Holly felt a pang of grief for Larry Kakonis, and an undirected anger because the kid had not been given time enough to learn that all horrors can be dealt with and that, on balance, life offered far more joy than despair. But she was equally rattled by the date on which the boy had killed himself: May 15.

One year later, this past May 15, Jim Ironheart had performed his first miraculous rescue. Sam and Emily Newsome. Atlanta, Georgia. Saved from murder at the hands of a sociopathic holdup man named Norman Rink.

Holly could sit still no longer. She got up and joined Viola at the edge of the patio. They watched the squirrels.

"Jim blamed himself," Viola said.

"For Larry Kakonis? But he wasn't responsible."

"He blamed himself anyway. That's how he is. But his reaction seemed excessive, even for Jim. After Larry's death, he lost interest in teaching. He stopped believing he could make a difference. He'd had so many successes, more than any teacher I've ever known, but that one failure was too much for him."

Holly remembered the boldness with which Ironheart had scooped Billy Jenkins out of the path of the hurtling pickup truck. *That* certainly had not been a failure.

"He just sort of spiraled down into gloom," Viola said, "couldn't pull himself out of it."

The man Holly had met in Portland had not seemed depressive. Mysterious, yes, and self-contained. But he'd had a good sense of humor, and he'd been quick to smile.

Viola took a sip of her lemonade. "Funny, it tastes too sour now." She set the glass down on the concrete near her feet and wiped her damp hand on her slacks. She started to speak again, hesitated, but finally said, "Then . . . he got a little strange."

"Strange? In what way?"

"Withdrawn. Quiet. He started taking martial-arts training. Tae Kwon Do. Lots of people are interested in that sort of thing, I guess, but it seemed so out of character for Jim."

It didn't seem out of character for the Jim Ironheart that Holly knew.

Viola said, "It wasn't casual with him, either. Every day after school he went for a lesson at a place in Newport Beach. He became obsessive. I worried about him. So in January, when he won the lottery, I was happy. Six million dollars! That's such a good thing, such *big* luck, it seemed like it would have to turn his life around, bring him out of his depression."

"But it didn't?"

"No. He didn't seem all that surprised or pleased by it. He quit teaching, moved out of his apartment into a house . . . and pulled back even further from his friends." She turned to Holly and smiled. It was the first smile she had managed for a while. "That's why I was so excited when you told me you were his sister, a sister he doesn't even know he has. Because maybe *you* can do for him what winning six million dollars couldn't do."

Guilt over her deception suffused Holly again, bringing a hot blush to her face. She hoped Viola would mistake it for a blush of pleasure or excitement. "It would be wonderful if I could."

"You can, I'm sure. He's alone, or feels that he is. That's part of his problem. With a sister, he won't be alone any more. Go see him today, right now."

Holly shook her head. "Soon. But not yet. I need to . . . build my confidence. You won't tell him about me, will you?"

"Of course not, dear. You should have all the fun of telling him, and what a wonderful moment that'll be."

Holly's smile felt like a pair of rigid plastic lips glued to her face, as false as part of a Halloween costume.

A few minutes later, at the front door, as Holly was leaving Viola put a hand on her arm and said, "I don't want to give you the wrong idea. It won't be *easy* lifting his spirits, getting him back on track. As long as I've known Jim, I've felt there's a sadness deep down in him, like a stain that won't come out which isn't such a surprise, really, when you consider what happened to his parents—his being orphaned when he was only ten, all of that."

Holly nodded. "Thanks. You've been a real help."

Viola impulsively hugged her, planted a kiss on her cheek, and said, "I want to have both you and Jim to dinner as soon as possible. Homemade green-corn tamales, black beans, and jalapeño rice so hot it'll melt your dental fillings!"

Holly was simultaneously pleased and dismayed: pleased to have met this woman, who so quickly seemed to be a favorite aunt of long acquaintance; dismayed because she had met her and been accepted by her under false pretenses.

All the way back to her rental car, Holly fiercely berated herself under her breath. She was at no loss for ugly words and clever damning phrases. Twelve years in newsrooms, in the company of reporters, had acquainted her with enough obscene language to insure her the trophy in a cursing contest with even the most foul-mouthed victim of Tourette's syndrome.

THE YELLOW PAGES listed only one Tae Kwon Do school in Newport Beach. It was in a shopping center off Newport Boulevard, between a custom window-covering store and a bakery.

The place was called Dojo, the Japanese word for a martial-arts practice hall, which was like naming a restaurant "Restaurant" or a dress shop "Dress Shop." Holly was surprised by the generic name, because Asian businessmen often brought a poetic sensibility to the titling of their enterprises.

Three people were standing on the sidewalk in front of Dojo's big window, eating éclairs and awash in the delicious aromas wafting from the adjacent bakery, watching a class of six students go through their routines with a squat but exceptionally limber Korean instructor in black pajamas. When the teacher threw a pupil to the mat inside, the plate-glass window vibrated.

Entering, Holly passed out of the chocolate-, cinnamon-, sugar-, yeast-scented air into an acidic environment of stale incense laced with a vague perspiration odor. Because of a story she'd written about a Portland teenager who won a medal in a national competition, she knew Tae Kwon Do was an aggressive Korean form of karate, using fierce punches, lightning-quick jabs, chops, blocks, chokeholds, and devastatingly powerful, leaping kicks. The teacher was pulling his blows, but there were still a lot of grunts, wheezes, guttural exclamations, and jarring thuds as students slammed to the mat.

In the far right corner of the room, a brunette sat on a stool behind a counter, doing paperwork. Every aspect and detail of her dress and grooming were advertisements for her sexuality. Her tight red T-shirt emphasized her ample chest and outlined nipples as large as cherries. With a touseled mane of chestnut hair given luster by artfully applied blond highlights, eyes subtly but exotically shadowed, mouth too lushly painted with d p-coral lipstick, a just-right tan, disablingly long fingernails painted to match the lipstick, and enough silvery costume jewelry to stock a display case, she would have been the perfect advertisement if women had been a product for sale in every local market.

"Does this thudding and grunting go on all day?" Holly asked.

"Most of the day, yeah."

"Doesn't it get to you?"

"Oh, yeah," the brunette said with a lascivious wink, "I know what you mean. They're like a bunch of bulls ramming at each other. I'm not here an hour every day till I'm so horny I can't stand it."

That was not what Holly had meant. She was suggesting that the noise was headache-inducing, not arousing. But she winked back, girl-to-girl, and said, "The boss in?"

"Eddie? He's doing a couple hundred flights of stairs," the woman said cryptically. "What'd you want?"

Holly explained that she was a reporter, working on a story that had a connection with Dojo.

The receptionist, if that's what she was, brightened at this news instead of glowering, as was often the case. Eddie, she said, was always looking to get publicity for the business. She rose from her stool and stepped to a door behind the counter, revealing that she was wearing high-heeled sandals and tight white shorts that clung to her butt as snugly as a coat of paint.

Holly was beginning to feel like a boy.

As the brunette had indicated, Eddie was delighted to hear that Dojo would be mentioned in a newspaper piece, even if tangentially, but he wanted her to interview him while he continued to do stairs. He was not an Asian, which perhaps explained the unimaginative generic name of his business. Tall, blond, shaggy-haired, blue-eyed, he was dressed only in muscles and a pair of black spandex cyclist's shorts. He was on a StairMaster exercise machine, climbing briskly to nowhere.

"It's great," he said, pumping his exquisitely developed legs. "Six more flights, and I'll be at the top of the Washington monument."

He was breathing hard but not as hard as Holly would have been breathing after running up six flights to her third-floor apartment in Portland.

She sat in a chair he had indicated, which put the StairMaster directly in front of her, giving her a full side view of him. His sun-bronzed skin glistened with sweat, which also darkened the hair at the nape of his thick neck. The spandex embraced him as intimately as the white shorts had clung to the receptionist. It almost seemed as if he had known Holly was coming and had carefully arranged the StairMaster and her chair to display himself to his best advantage.

Although she was plunging into deception again, Holly did not feel as bad about lying to Eddie as she had felt when lying to Viola Moreno. For one thing, her cover story this time was somewhat less fanciful: that she was doing a multipart, in-depth piece about James Ironheart (the truth), focusing on the effect that winning a lottery had upon his life (a lie), all with his approval (a lie). A veracity percentage as high as thirty-three percent was enough to salve her guilt, which she supposed didn't say much for the quality of her conscience.

"Just so you spell Dojo right," Eddie said. Looking back and down at his right leg, he added happily, "Look at that calf, hard as rock."

As if she hadn't been looking at it all along.

"The fat layer between my skin and the muscle underneath, it's hardly there, burned it all away."

Another reason she didn't mind lying to Eddie was because he was a vain, self-involved jerk.

"Three more flights to the top of the monument," he said. The rhythm of his speech was tied to the pattern of his breathing, the words rising and falling with each inhalation and exhalation.

"Just three? Then I'll wait."

"No, no. Ask your questions. I won't stop at the top. I'm gonna see how much of the Empire State Building I can climb next."

"Ironheart was a student of yours."

"Yeah. Taught him myself."

"He came to you long before he won the lottery."

"Yeah. More than a year ago."

"May of last year, I think."

"Mighta been."

"Did he tell you why he wanted to learn Tae Kwon Do?"

"Nope. But he had a passion." He almost shouted his next words, as if he'd triumphantly completed a real climb: "Top of the monument!" He increased his pace instead of slacking off.

"Did you think it was odd?"

"Why?"

"Him being a schoolteacher, I mean."

"We get schoolteachers. We get all kinds. Everyone wants to kick ass." He sucked in a very deep breath, blew it out, and said, "In the Empire State now, going up."

"Was Ironheart good?"

"Excellent! Coulda been a competitor."

"Could've been? You mean he dropped out?"

Breathing a little harder than before, the words coming in a quicker though similar rhythm, he said: "Hung in there seven or eight months. Every day. He was a real glutton for punishment. Pumping iron and doing aerobics *plus* martial arts. Ate his way through the pain. Man was getting tough enough to fuck a rock. Sorry. But he was. Then he quit. Two weeks after he won the bucks."

"Ah, I see."

"Don't get me wrong. Wasn't the money that made him quit."

"Then what?"

"He said I'd given him what he needed, he didn't want any more."

"What he needed?" she asked.

"Enough Tae Kwon Do for what he wanted to do."

"Did he say what he wanted to do?"

"Nope. Kick someone's ass, I guess."

Eddie was really pushing himself now, ramming his feet down on the StairMaster, pumping and pumping, so much sweat on his body that he appeared to be coated in oil, droplets spraying off his hair when he shook his head, the muscles in his arms and across his broad back bulging almost as fiercely as those in his thighs and calves.

Sitting in the chair about eight feet from the man, Holly felt as if she were ringside at some sleazy strip club where the gender roles had been reversed. She got up.

Eddie was staring straight ahead at the wall. His face was creased by lines of strain, but he had a dreamy, faraway look in his eyes. Maybe, instead of the wall, he saw the endless stairwell in the Empire State Building.

"Anything else he ever told you that seemed . . . interesting, unusual?" she asked.

Eddie didn't answer. He was concentrating on the climb. The arteries in his neck had swelled and were throbbing as if evenly spaced, small, fat fish were schooling through his bloodstream.

As Holly reached the door, Eddie said, "Three things."

She turned to him again. "Yeah?"

Without looking at her, his eyes still out of focus, not for an instant slackening his pace, speaking to her from the stairwell of that skyscraper in distant Manhattan, he said, "Ironheart's the only guy I ever met who can obsess better than I can."

Frowning, Holly thought about that. "What else?"

"The only lessons he missed were two weeks in September. Went up north, Marin County somewhere, to take a course in aggressive driving."

"What's that?"

"Mostly they teach chauffeurs for politicians, diplomats, rich businessmen how to handle a car like James Bond, escape terrorist traps, kidnappers, shit like that."

"He talk about why he needed that kind of training?"

"Just said it sounded like fun."

"That's two things."

He shook his head. Sweat flew, spattered the surrounding carpet and furniture. Holly was just out of range. He still didn't look at her. "Number three—after he figured he had enough Tae Kwon Do, the next thing he wanted was to learn guns."

"Learn guns?"

"Asked me if I knew anyone could teach him marksmanship, all about weapons. Revolver, pistols, rifles, shotguns . . ."

"Who'd you send him to?"

He was panting now but still able to speak clearly between each gasping breath: "Nobody. Guns aren't my thing. But you know what I think? I think he was one of these guys reads *Soldier of Fortune*. Gets caught up in the fantasy. Wants to be a mercenary. He sure was preparing for a war."

"Didn't it worry you to be helping someone like that?"

"Not as long as he paid for his lessons."

She opened the door, hesitated, watching him. "You have a counter on that contraption?"

"Yeah."

"What floor are you on?"

"Tenth," Eddie said, the word distorted as he spoke it on a deep exhalation. The next time he breathed out, he also issued a whoop of pleasure along with his wind. "Jesus, I have legs of stone, fuckin' granite, I think I could get a man in a scissor hold, crack him in half with my legs. You put that in your article, okay? I could crack a guy clean in half."

Holly left, closing the door softly behind her.

In the main room, the martial-arts class was even more active than when she had entered. The current exercise involved a group attempt to gang up on their Korean instructor, but he was blocking and throwing and whirling and leaping like a dervish, dealing with them as fast as they came at him.

The brunette had removed her silvery jewelry. She had changed into Reeboks, looser shorts, a different T-shirt, and a bra. Now she was doing stretching exercises in front of the reception counter.

"One o'clock," she explained to Holly. "My lunch hour. I always run four or five miles instead of eating. Bye." She jogged to the door, pushed through it into the warm August day, and sprinted out of sight along the front of the shopping center.

Holly went outside, too, and stood for a moment in the lovely sunshine, newly aware of how many of the shoppers, coming to and going from their cars, were in good physical shape. Having moved to the northwest almost a year and a half ago, she had forgotten how health conscious many southern Californians were—and how aware of their appearance. Per capita, Orange County had a lot fewer jowls, love handles, spare tires, pot guts, and pear-shaped bottoms than Portland.

Looking good and feeling good were imperatives of the southern-California lifestyle. It was one of the things she loved about the place. It was also one of the things she hated about it.

She went next door to the bakery for lunch. From the display cases, she selected a chocolate éclair, a crème brûlée tart with kiwi on top, a piece of white-chocolate macadamia-nut cheesecake with Oreo-crumb crust, a cinnamon wheel, and a slice of orange roulade. "And a diet Coke," she told the clerk.

She carried her tray to a table near a window, where she could watch the passing parade of taut, tanned bodies in summer gear. The pastries were wonderful. She ate a little of this, now a little of that, savoring each bite, intending to polish off every crumb.

After a while she realized someone was watching her. Two tables away, a heavyset woman, about thirty-five, was staring with a mixture of disbelief and envy; she only had one miserable fruit tart, a bakery junkie's equivalent of a Nutri/System multigrain cracker.

Feeling both a need to explain herself and a certain sympathy, Holly said, "I wish I wasn't doing this, but I can't help it. If I can't do anything else, then I always binge when I'm horny."

The heavyset woman nodded. "Me, too."

SHE DROVE TO Ironheart's place on Bougainvillea Way. She knew enough about him now to risk approaching him, and that was what she intended to do. But instead of pulling into his driveway, she cruised slowly past the house again.

Instinct told her that the time was not right. The portrait of him that she had constructed only *seemed* to be complete. There was a hole in it somewhere. She sensed that it would be dangerous to proceed before that hole had been painted in.

She returned to the motel and spent the rest of the afternoon and early evening sitting by the window in her room, drinking Alka-Seltzer, then diet 7-Up, staring out at the jewel-blue pool in the middle of the lushly landscaped courtyard, and thinking. Thinking.

Okay, she told herself, the story to date. Ironheart is a man with a sadness at his core, probably because of being orphaned when he was only ten. Let's say he's spent a lot of his life brooding about death, especially about the injustice of premature death. He dedicates his life to teaching and helping kids, maybe because no one was there for *him* when he was a boy and had to cope with the deaths of his mother and father. Then Larry Kakonis commits suicide. Ironheart is shattered, feels he should have been able to prevent it. The boy's death brings to the surface all of Ironheart's buried rage: rage at fate, destiny, the biological fragility of the human species—rage at God. In a state of severe mental distress bordering on outright imbalance, he decides to make himself over into Rambo and *do* something to fight back at fate, which is a weird response at best, absolutely nuts at worst. With weight lifting, aerobic endurance training, and Tae Kwon Do, he turns himself into a fighting machine. He learns to drive like a stuntman. He becomes knowledgeable in the use of all manner of guns. He's ready. Just one more thing. He teaches himself to be a clairvoyant, so he can win the lottery and be independently wealthy, making it possible to devote himself to his crusade—and so he can know just *when* a premature death is about to occur.

That was where it all fell apart. You could go to a place like Dojo to learn martial arts, but the Yellow Pages had no listing for schools of clairvoyance. Where the hell had he gotten his psychic power?

She considered the question from every imaginable angle. She wasn't trying to brainstorm an answer, only figure out an approach to researching possible explanations. But magic was magic. There was no way to research it.

She began to feel as though she was employed by a sleazy tabloid, not as a reporter but as a concocter of pieces about space aliens living under Cleveland, half-gorilla and half-human babies born to amoral female zookeepers, and inexplicable rains of frogs and chickens in Tajikistan. But, damn it, the hard facts were that Jim Ironheart had saved fourteen people from death, in every corner of the country, always at the penultimate moment, with miraculous foresight.

By eight o'clock, she had the urge to pound her head against the table, the wall, the concrete decking around the pool outside, against anything hard enough to crack her mental block and drive understanding into her. She decided that it was time to stop thinking, and go to dinner.

She ate in the motel coffeeshop again—just broiled chicken and a salad to atone for lunch at the bakery. She tried to be interested in the other customers, do a little people-watching. But she could not stop thinking about Ironheart and his sorcery.

He dominated her thoughts later, as well, when she was lying in bed, trying to sleep. Staring at the shadows on the ceiling, cast by the landscape lighting outside and the half-open Levolor blinds on the window, she was honest enough with herself to admit he fascinated her on other than professional levels. He was the most important story of her career, yes, true. And, yes, he was so mysterious that he would have intrigued anyone, reporter or not. But she was also drawn to him because she had been alone a long time, loneliness had carved an emptiness in her, and Jim Ironheart was the most appealing man she had met in ages.

Which was insane.

Because maybe *he* was insane.

She was not one of those women who chased after men who were all wrong for her, subconsciously seeking to be used, hurt, and abandoned. She was picky when it came to men. That was why she was alone, for God's sake. Few men measured up to her standards.

Sure. Picky, she thought sarcastically. That's why you've got this lech for a guy who has delusions of being Superman without the tights and cape. Get real, Thorne. Jesus.

Entertaining romantic fantasies about James Ironheart was short-sighted, irresponsible, futile, and just plain stupid.

But those *eyes*.

Holly fell asleep with an image of his face drifting in her mind, watching over her as if it were a portrait on a giant banner, rippling gently against a cerulean sky. His eyes were even bluer than that celestial backdrop.

In time she found herself in the dream of blindness again. The circular room. Wooden floor. Scent of damp limestone. Rain drumming on the roof. Rhythmic creaking. *Whoosh*. Something was coming for her, a part of the darkness that had somehow come alive, a monstrous presence that she could neither hear nor see but could feel. The Enemy. *Whoosh*. It was closing in relentlessly, hostile and savage, radiating cold the way a furnace radiated heat. *Whoosh*. She was grateful that she was blind, because she knew the thing's appearance was so alien, so terrifying, that just the sight of it would kill her. *Whoosh*. Something touched her. A moist, icy tendril. At the base of her neck. A pencil-thin tentacle. She cried out, and the tip of the probe bored into her neck, pierced the base of her skull—

Whoosh.

With a soft cry of terror, she woke. No disorientation. She knew immediately where she was: the motel, Laguna Hills.

Whoosh.

The sound of the dream was still with her. A great blade slicing through the air. But it was not a dream sound. It was real. And the room was as cold as the pitch-black place in the nightmare. As if weighted down by a heart swollen with terror, she tried to move, could not. She smelled damp limestone. From below her, as if there were vast rooms under the motel, came a soft rumbling sound of—she somehow knew—large stone wheels grinding against each other.

Whoosh.

Something unspeakable was still squirming along the back of her neck, writhing sinuously within her skull, a hideous parasite that had chosen her for a host, worming its way into her, going to lay its eggs in her brain. But she could not move.

Whoosh.

She could see nothing but bars of pale, pale light against part of the black ceiling, where the moonsoft glow of landscape lighting projected the image of the windowblind slats. She desperately wanted more light.

Whoosh.

She was making pathetic whimpers of terror, and she so thoroughly despised herself for her weakness that she was finally able to shatter her paralysis. Gasping, she sat up. Clawed at the back of her neck, trying to tear off the oily, frigid, wormlike probe. Nothing there. Nothing. Swung her legs over the edge of the bed. Fumbled for the lamp. Almost knocked it over. Found the switch. Light.

Whoosh.

She sprang off the bed. Felt the back of her head again. Her neck. Between her shoulder blades. Nothing. Nothing there. Yet she *felt* it.

Whoosh.

She was over the edge of hysteria and unable to return, making queer little animal sounds of fear and desperation. Out of the corner of her eye, she saw movement. Swung around. The wall behind the bed. Sweating. Glistening. The entire wall bulged toward her, as if it were a membrane against which a great and terrible mass was pressing insistently. It throbbed repulsively, like an enormous internal organ in the exposed and steaming guts of a prehistoric behemoth.

Whoosh.

She backed away from the wet, malignantly animated wall. Turned. Ran. Had to get out. Fast. The Enemy. It was coming. Had followed her. Out of the dream. The door. Locked. Deadbolt. Disengaged it. Hands shaking. The Enemy. Coming. Brass security chain. Rattled it free. Door. Jerked it open. Something was on the threshold, filling the doorway, bigger than she was, something beyond human experience, simultaneously insectile and arachnoid and reptilian, squirming and jittering, a tangled mass of spider legs and antennae and serpentine coils and roachlike mandibles and multifaceted eyes and rattlesnake fangs and claws, a thousand nightmares rolled into one, but she was *awake*. It burst through the door, seized her, pain exploding from her sides where its talons tore at her, and she screamed——a night breeze.

That was the only thing coming through the open door. A soft, summery night breeze.

Holly stood in the doorway, shuddering and gasping for breath, looking out in astonishment at the concrete promenade of the motel. Lacy queen palms, Australian tree ferns, and other greenery swayed sensuously under the caress of the tropical zephyr. The surface of the swimming pool rippled gently, creating countless ever-changing facets, refracting the pool-bottom lights, so it seemed as if there was not a body of water in the middle of the courtyard but a hole filled with a pirate's treasure of polished sapphires.

The creature that had attacked her was gone as if it had never existed. It had not scuttled away or scurried up some web; it had simply evaporated in an instant.

She no longer felt the icy, squirming tendril on the back of her neck or inside her skull.

A couple of other guests had come out of rooms farther along the promenade, evidently to investigate her scream.

Holly stepped back from the threshold. She did not want to attract their attention now.

She glanced over her shoulder. The wall behind the bed was only a wall again.

The clock built into the nightstand showed 5:08 A.M.

She eased the door shut, and suddenly she had to lean against it, because all the strength went out of her legs.

Instead of being relieved that the strange ordeal had ended, she was shattered. She hugged herself and shivered so hard, her teeth chattered. She began to cry softly, not from fear of the experience, concern for her current safety, or concern about her sanity, but from a profound sense of having been totally violated. Briefly but for too long, she had been helpless, victimized, enslaved by terror, controlled by an entity beyond her understanding. She'd been psychologically raped. Something needful had overpowered her, forced its way into her, denying her free will; though gone now, it had left traces of itself within her, a residue that stained her mind, her soul.

Just a dream, she told herself encouragingly.

But it had not been a dream when she sat up in bed and snapped on the lamp. The nightmare had followed her into the waking world.

Just a dream, don't make so much of it, get control of yourself, she thought, struggling to regain her equanimity. You dreamed you were in that lightless place, then you *dreamed* that you sat up in bed and turned on the light, then in your *dream* you saw the wall bulging and ran for the door. But you were only sleepwalking, you were still asleep when you pulled the door open, still asleep when you saw the boogeyman and screamed, which was when you finally woke up for real, screamed yourself awake.

She wanted to believe that explanation, but it was too pat to be credible. No nightmare she'd ever known had been that elaborate in its texture and detail. Besides, she never sleepwalked.

Something real had been reaching for her. Maybe not the insect-reptile-spider thing in the doorway. Maybe that was only an image in which another entity clad itself to frighten her. But something had been pushing through to this world from . . .

From where?

It didn't matter where. From out there. From beyond. And it almost got her.

No. That was ridiculous. Tabloid stuff. Even the *National Enquirer* didn't publish trash that trashy anymore. I WAS MIND-RAPED BY A BEAST FROM BEYOND. Crap like that was three steps below CHER ADMITS BEING SPACE ALIEN, two steps below JESUS SPEAKS TO NUN FROM INSIDE A MICROWAVE, and even a full step below ELVIS HAD BRAIN TRANSPLANTED, LIVES NOW AS ROSEANNE BARR.

The more foolish she felt for entertaining such thoughts, the calmer she became. Dealing with the experience was easier if she could believe that it was all a product of her overactive imagination, which had been unreasonably stimulated by the admittedly fantastic Ironheart case.

Finally she was able to stand on her own, without leaning on the door. She relocked the deadbolt, reengaged the security chain.

As she stepped away from the door, she became aware of a hot, stinging pain in her left side. It wasn't serious, but it made her wince, and she realized that a similar but lesser pain sizzled in her right side as well.

She took hold of her T-shirt to lift it and look at herself—and discovered that the fabric was slashed. Three places on the left side. Two on the right. It was spotted with blood.

With renewed dread, Holly went into the bathroom and switched on the harsh fluorescent light. She stood in front of the mirror, hesitated, then pulled the torn T-shirt over her head.

A thin flow of blood seeped down her left flank from three shallow gashes. The first laceration was just under her breast, and the others were spaced at two-inch intervals. Two scratches blazed on her right side, though they were not as deep as those on the left and were not bleeding freely.

The claws.

JIM THREW UP in the toilet, flushed, then rinsed his mouth twice with mint-flavored Listerine.

The face in the mirror was the most troubled he had ever seen. He had to look away from the reflection of his own eyes.

He leaned against the sink. For at least the thousandth time in the past year, he wondered what in God's name was happening to him.

In his sleep he had gone to the windmill again. Never before had the same nightmare troubled him two nights in a row. Usually, weeks passed between reoccurrences.

Worse, there had been an unsettling new element—more than just the rain on the narrow windows, the lambent flame of the candle and the dancing shadows it produced, the sound of the big sails turning outside, the low rumble of the millstones below, and an inexplicable pall of fear. This time he'd been aware of a malevolent presence, out of sight but drawing nearer by the second, something so evil and alien that he could not even imagine its form or full intentions. He had expected it to burst out of the limestone wall, erupt through the plank floor, or explode in upon him from the heavy timbered door at the head of the mill stairs. He had been unable to decide which way to run. Finally he had yanked open the door—and awakened with a scream. If anything had been there, he could not remember what it had looked like.

Regardless of the appearance it might have had, Jim knew what to call it: the enemy. Except that now he thought of it with a capital "T" and a capital "E." The Enemy. The amorphous beast that haunted many of his other nightmares had found its way into the windmill dream, where it had never terrorized him before.

Crazy as it seemed, he sensed that the creature was not merely a fantasy spawned by his subconscious while he slept. It was as real as he was himself. Sooner or later it would cross the barrier between the world of dreams and the waking world as easily as it had crossed the barrier between different nightmares.

4

Holly never considered going back to bed. She knew she would not sleep again for many hours, until she was so exhausted that she would be unable to keep her eyes open no matter how much strong black coffee she drank. Sleep had ceased to be a sanctuary. It was, instead, a source of danger, a highway to hell or somewhere worse, along which she might encounter an inhuman traveler.

That made her angry. Everyone needed and deserved the refuge of sleep.

As dawn came, she took a long shower, carefully but diligently scrubbing the shallow lacerations on her sides, although the soap and hot water stung the open flesh. She worried that she would develop an infection as strange as the briefly glimpsed monstrosity that had inflicted her wounds.

That sharpened her anger.

By nature, she was a good Girl Scout, always prepared for any eventuality. When traveling, she carried a few first-aid supplies in the same kit with her Lady Remington shaver: iodine, gauze pads, adhesive tape, Band-Aids, a small aerosol can of Bactine, and a tube of ointment that was useful for soothing minor burns. After toweling off from the shower, she sat naked on the edge of the bed, sprayed Bactine on her wounds, then daubed at them with iodine.

She had become a reporter, in part, because as a younger woman she had believed that journalism had the power to explain the world, to make sense of events that sometimes seemed chaotic and meaningless. More than a decade of newspaper employment had shaken her conviction that the human experience *could* be explained all or even most of the time. But she still kept a well-ordered desk, meticulously arranged files, and neat story notes. In her closets at home, her clothes were arranged according to season, then according to the occasion (formal, semi-formal, informal), then by color. If life insisted on being chaotic, and if journalism had failed her as a tool for bringing order to the world, at least she could depend on routine and habit to create a personal pocket universe of stability, however fragile, beyond which the disorder and tumult of life were kept at bay.

The iodine stung.

She was angrier. Seething.

The shower disturbed the clots that had coagulated in the deeper scratches on her left side. She was bleeding slightly again. She sat quietly on the edge of the bed for a while, holding a wad of Kleenex against the wounds, until the lacerations were no longer oozing.

By the time Holly had dressed in tan jeans and an emerald-green blouse, it was seven-thirty.

She already knew how she was going to start the day, and nothing could distract her from her plans. She had no appetite whatsoever for breakfast. When she stepped outside, she discovered that the morning was cloudless and unusually temperate even for Orange County, but the sublime weather had no mellowing influence on her and did not tempt her to pause even for a moment to relish the early sun on her face. She drove the rental car across the parking lot, out to the street, and headed toward Laguna Niguel. She was going to ring James Ironheart's doorbell and demand a lot of answers.

She wanted his full story, the explanation of how he could know when people were about to die and why he took such extreme risks to save total strangers. But she also wanted to know why last night's bad dream had become real, how and why her bedroom wall had begun to glisten and throb like flesh, and what manner of creature had popped out of her nightmare and seized her in talons formed of something more substantial than dreamstuff.

She was convinced that he would have the answers. Last night, for only the second time in her thirty-three years, she'd encountered the unknown, been sideswiped by the supernatural. The first time had been on August 12, when Ironheart had miraculously saved Billy Jenkins from being mowed down by a truck in front of the McAlbury School—although she hadn't realized until later that he had stepped right out of the Twilight Zone. Though she was willing to cop to a lot of faults, stupidity was not one of them. Anyone but a fool could see that both collisions with the paranormal, Ironheart and the nightmare-made-real, were related.

She was more than merely angry. She was pissed.

As she cruised down Crown Valley Parkway, she realized that her anger sprang, in part, from the discovery that her big, career-making story was turning out not to be strictly about amazement and wonder and courage and hope and triumph, as she had anticipated. Like the vast majority of articles that had appeared on the front pages of newspapers since the invention of the printing press, this story had a dark side.

JIM HAD SHOWERED and dressed for church. He did not regularly attend Sunday Mass anymore, or the services of any other of the religions to which he had been sporadically committed over the years. But having been in the control of a higher power since at least last May, when he had flown to Florida to save the lives of Sam and Emily Newsome, he was disposed to think about God more than usual. And since Father Geary had told him about the stigmata that had marked his body while he lay unconscious on the floor of Our Lady of the Desert, less than a week ago, he had felt the tidal pull of Catholicism for the first time in a couple of years. He didn't actually expect that the mystery of recent events would be cleared up by answers he would find in church—but he could hope.

As he plucked his car keys off the pegboard on the kitchen wall beside the door to the garage, he heard himself say, "Life line." Immediately, his plans for the day were changed. He froze, not sure what to do. Then the familiar feeling of being a marionette overcame him, and he hung the keys back on the pegboard.

He returned to the bedroom and stripped out of his loafers, gray slacks, dark-blue sportcoat, and white shirt. He dressed in chinos and a blousy Hawaiian shirt, which he wore over his pants in order to be as unhampered as possible by his clothing.

He needed to stay loose, flexible. He had no idea *why* looseness and flexibility were desirable for what lay ahead, but he felt the need just the same.

Sitting on the floor in front of the closet, he selected a pair of shoes—the most comfortable, broken-in pair of Rockports that he owned. He tied them securely but not too tightly. He stood up and tested the fit. Good.

He reached for the suitcase on the top shelf, then hesitated. He was not sure that he would require luggage. A few seconds later, he *knew* that he would be traveling light. He slid the closet door shut without taking down the bag.

No luggage usually meant that his destination would be within driving distance and that the round-trip, including the time needed to perform whatever work was expected of him, would take no more than twenty-four hours. But as he turned away from the closet, he surprised himself by saying, "Airport." Of course, there were a lot of places to which he could fly round-trip in a single day.

He picked his wallet off the dresser, waited to see if he felt compelled to put it down again, and finally slipped it into his hip pocket. Evidently he would need not only money but ID—or at least he would not risk exposure by carrying it.

As he walked to the kitchen again and took the car keys off the pegboard, fear played through him, although not as strongly as it had the last time he had left his house on a mission. That day he had been "told" to steal a car so it could not be traced to him, and to drive into the Mojave Desert. This time he might encounter adversaries even more formidable than the two men in the Roadking, but he was not as worried as he'd been before. He knew he could die. Being the instrument of a higher power came with no guarantees of immortality; he was still only a man whose flesh could be torn, whose bones could be broken, and whose heart could be stopped instantly with a well-placed bullet. The amelioration of his fear was attributable solely to his somewhat mystical journey on the Harley, two days with Father Geary, the report of the stigmata that had appeared on him, and the resulting conviction that a divine hand was at work in all of this.

HOLLY WAS ON Bougainvillea Way, a block from Ironheart's house, when a dark-green Ford backed out of his driveway. She did not know what kind of car he drove, but since he lived alone, she assumed the Ford had to be his.

She speeded up, half intending to swing around him, angle across his bow, force him to stop, and confront him right in the street. Then she slowed down again, figuring discretion was seldom a fatal error. She might as well see where he was going, what he was up to.

As she passed his house, the automatic garage door was rolling down. Just before it closed, she was able to see that no other car was in there. The man in the Ford had to be Ironheart.

Because she had never been assigned to stories about paranoid drug lords or bent politicians or corrupt businessmen, Holly was not expert at tailing a surveillance subject through traffic. The skills and techniques of clandestine operations were not necessary when you wrote exclusively about Timber Trophies, performance artists in radiation suits who juggled live mice on the steps of city hall and called it "art," and pie-eating contests. She was also mindful of the fact that Ironheart had taken a two-week course in aggressive driving at a special school in Marin County; if he knew how to handle a car well enough to shake off pursuing terrorists, he would leave her in the dust about thirty seconds after he realized she was following him.

She hung as far back as she dared. Fortunately, the Sunday-morning traffic was heavy enough to allow her to hide behind other cars. But it was light enough so she didn't have to worry that the lanes would suddenly clog up between her and Ironheart, cutting her off until he disappeared from sight.

He drove east on Crown Valley Parkway to Interstate 5, then north toward Los Angeles on 405.

By the time they had passed the clustered high rises around South Coast Plaza, the primary shopping and office center for the two million people in the Orange County metroplex, Holly's mood was better than it had been. She was proving to be adept at mobile surveillance, staying from two to six cars in back of Ironheart but always close enough to follow if he abruptly swung onto an exit ramp. Her anger was tempered by the pleasure she took in her skillful pursuit. Now and then she even found herself admiring the clarity of the blue sky and the profusely flowering pink and white oleanders that flanked the freeway at some places.

Passing Long Beach, however, she began to worry that she was going to spend the whole day on the road with him, only to discover that wherever he was going had nothing to do with the enigma that concerned her. Even a self-appointed superhero with clairvoyant powers might just spend a day taking in a theater matinee, doing nothing more dangerous than eating Szechuan Chinese with the chef's hottest mustard.

She began to wonder, as well, if he might become aware of her through his psychic powers. Sensing her a few cars back seemed a lot easier than foreseeing the approaching death of a small boy in Boston. On the other hand, maybe clairvoyance was an inconstant power, something he could not turn on and off at will, and maybe it only worked on the big things, zapping him with either visions of danger and destruction and death—or no visions at all. Which made sense in a way. It would probably drive you insane to have psychic visions that told you in advance whether you were going to enjoy a particular movie, have a good dinner, or get a bad case of gas and the bloats from that garlicky angel-hair pasta that you were enjoying so much. Nevertheless, she dropped back a little farther, putting one more car between them.

When Ironheart left the freeway at the exit for Los Angeles International Airport, Holly became excited. Perhaps he was only meeting someone on an incoming flight. But it was more likely that he was catching a plane out, embarking on one of his timely rescue missions, just as he had flown to Portland on August 12, nearly two weeks ago. Holly was not prepared to travel; she didn't even have a change of clothes. However, she had cash and credit cards to handle expenses, and she could buy a fresh blouse anywhere. The prospect of tailing him all the way to the scene of the action tantalized her. Ultimately, when she wrote about him, she would be able to do so with more authority if she had been an eye-witness at *two* of his rescues.

She almost lost her nerve when he swung off the airport service loop into a parking garage, because there was no longer a convenient car between them to mask her presence. But the alternative was to drive on, park in another garage, and lose him. She hung back only as far as she dared and took a ticket from the dispenser seconds after he did.

Ironheart found an empty slot halfway along a row on the third level, and Holly pulled in ten spaces past him. She slumped down in her seat a little and remained in her car, giving him a headstart so there was less of a chance of him glancing back and seeing her.

She almost waited too long. When she got out of her car, she was barely in time to glimpse him as he turned right and disappeared around a wall at the bottom of the ramp.

She hurried after him. The soft, flat *slap-slap* of her footsteps echoed hollowly off the low concrete ceiling. At the base of the ramp, when she turned the corner, she saw him enter a stairwell. By the time she passed through that door after him, she heard him descend the final flight and open the door below.

Thanks to his colorful Hawaiian shirt, she was able to stay well behind him, mingling with other travelers, as he crossed the service road and entered the United Airlines terminal. She hoped they weren't going to Hawaii. Researching a story without the financial backing of the newspaper was expensive enough. If Ironheart was going to save someone's life today, she hoped he would do it in San Diego instead of Honolulu.

In the terminal, she hung back behind a group of tall Swedes, using them for cover, while Ironheart stood for a while at a bank of monitors, studying the schedule of upcoming departures. Judging by the frown on his face, he didn't see the flight he wanted. Or maybe he simply didn't yet *know* which flight he wanted. Perhaps his premonitions did not come to him full-blown; he might have to work at them, nurse them along, and he might not know exactly where he was going or whose life he would be saving until he got there.

After a few minutes, he turned from the monitors and strode along the concourse to the ticket counter. Holly continued to stay well back of him, watching from a distance, until she realized that she would not know his destination unless she was close enough to hear him give it to the clerk. Reluctantly she closed the gap.

She could wait until he had bought the ticket, of course, follow him to see which gate he waited at, then book herself on the same flight. But what if the plane took off while she was dashing through the endless hallways of the terminal? She could also try to cajole the clerk into telling her what flight Ironheart had taken by claiming to have picked up a credit card he'd dropped. But the airline might offer to return it to him; or if they found her story suspicious, they might even call security guards.

In the line at the ticket counter, she dared to close within one person of Ironheart. The only traveler between them was a burly, big-bellied man who looked like an NFL linebacker gone to seed; he had mildly offensive body odor, but he provided considerable cover, for which she was grateful.

The short line moved quickly. When Ironheart stepped up to the counter, Holly eased out around the fat man and strained forward to hear whatever destination was mentioned.

The public-address system inconveniently brought forth a woman's soft, sensuous, yet zombielike voice, announcing the discovery of a lost child. At the same time, a noisy group of New Yorkers went past, complaining about the perceived phoniness of California's have-a-nice-day service ethic, apparently homesick for hostility. Ironheart's words were drowned out.

Holly inched nearer to him.

The fat man frowned down at her, evidently suspecting her of attempted line-jumping. She smiled at him in such a way as to assure him that she had no evil intentions and that she knew he was large enough to squash her like a bug.

If Ironheart glanced back now, he would look directly into her face. She held her breath, heard the clerk say, ". . . O'Hare Airport in Chicago, leaving in twenty minutes . . . ," and slipped back behind the fat man, who looked over his shoulder to frown down at her again.

She wondered why they had come to LAX for a flight to Chicago. She was pretty sure there were plenty of connections to O'Hare from John Wayne in Orange County. Well . . . though Chicago was farther than San Diego, it was preferable to—and cheaper than—Hawaii.

Ironheart paid for his ticket and hurried off in search of his gate without glancing in Holly's direction.

Some psychic, she thought.

She was pleased with herself.

When she reached the counter, she presented a credit card and asked for a seat on the same flight to Chicago. For a moment she had the terrible feeling that the clerk would say the plane was fully booked. But there were seats left, and she got her ticket.

The departure lounge at the gate was nearly empty. Boarding of the flight had virtually been completed. Ironheart was nowhere in sight.

On the way along the tunnel-like boarding gate to the door of the aircraft, she began to worry that he would see her when she had to walk back the aisle to her seat. She could pretend not to notice him, or pretend not to recognize him if he approached her. But she doubted that he would believe her presence on his flight was sheer coincidence. An hour and a half ago, she'd been in a rush to confront him. Now she wanted nothing more than to *avoid* confrontation. If he saw her, he would abort his trip; she might never get another chance to be present at one of his last-minute rescues.

The plane was a wide-body DC-10 with two aisles. Each row of nine seats was divided into three sections: two by the window on the port side, five down the center, two by the window on the starboard side. Holly was assigned to row twenty-three, seat H, which was on the starboard flank, one seat removed from the window. As she headed back the aisle, she scanned the faces of her fellow passengers, hoping she wouldn't lock eyes with Jim Ironheart. In fact, she would rather not see him at all during the flight, and worry about catching sight of him again at O'Hare. The DC-10 was an immense aircraft. Though a number of seats were empty, more than two hundred and fifty people were onboard. She and Ironheart might very well fly around the world together without bumping into each other; getting through the few hours to Chicago should be a cinch.

Then she saw him. He was sitting in the five-wide middle section of row sixteen, the port-aisle seat, on the other side of the plane. He was paging through an issue of the airline's magazine, and she prayed that he would not look up until she was past him. Though she had to step aside for a flight attendant escorting a small boy who was flying alone, her prayer was answered. Ironheart's head remained bowed over the publication until she was past him. She reached 23-H and sat down, sighing with relief. Even if he went to the restroom, or just got up to stretch his legs, he would probably never have any reason to come around to the starboard aisle. Perfect.

She glanced at the man in the window seat beside her. He was in his early thirties, tanned, fit, and intense. He was wearing a dark-blue business suit, white shirt, and tie even on a Sunday flight. His brow was as furrowed as his suit was well-pressed, and he was working on a laptop computer. He was wearing headphones, listening to music or pretending to, in order to discourage conversation, and he gave her a cool smile calculated to do the same.

That was fine with her. Like a lot of reporters, she was not garrulous by nature. Her job required her to be a good listener, not necessarily a good talker. She was content to pass the trip with the airline's magazine and her own Byzantine thoughts.

TWO HOURS INTO the flight, Jim still had no idea where he was expected to go when he got off the plane at O'Hare. He was not concerned about it, however, because he had learned to be patient. The revelation always came, sooner or later.

Nothing in the airline's magazine was of interest to him, and the in-flight movie sounded as if it were about as much fun as a vacation in a Soviet prison. The two seats to the right of him were empty, so he was not required to make nice with a stranger. He tilted his seat slightly, folded his hands on his stomach, closed his eyes, and passed the time—between the flight attendants' inquiries about his appetite and comfort—by brooding about the windmill dream, puzzling out what significance it had, if any.

That was what he *tried* to brood about, anyway. But for some curious reason, his mind wandered to Holly Thorne, the reporter.

Hell, now he was being disingenuous, because he knew perfectly well why she had been drifting in and out of his thoughts ever since he had met her. She was a treat for the eyes. She was intelligent, too; one look at her, and you knew about a million gears were spinning in her head, all meshing perfectly, well-oiled, quiet and productive.

And she had a sense of humor. He would give anything to share his days and his long, dream-troubled nights with a woman like that. Laughter was usually a function of sharing—an observation, a joke, a moment. You didn't laugh a lot when you were always alone; and if you did, that probably meant you should make arrangements for a long stay in a resort with padded walls.

He had never been smooth with women, so he had often been without them. And he had to admit, even before this recent strangeness had begun, he was sometimes difficult to live with. Not depressive exactly but too aware that death was life's companion. Too inclined to brood about the coming darkness. Too slow to seize the moment and succumb to pleasure. If—

He opened his eyes and sat up straighter in his seat, because suddenly he received the revelation that he had been expecting. Or part of it, at least. He still did not know what was going to happen in Chicago, but he knew the names of the people whose lives he was expected to save: Christine and Casey Dubrovek.

To his surprise, he realized they were on this plane with him—which led him to suspect that the trouble might come in the terminal at O'Hare, or at least soon after touchdown. Otherwise he would not have crossed their path so early. Usually, he encountered the people he saved only minutes before their lives were thrown into jeopardy.

Compelled by those forces that had been guiding him periodically since last May, he got up, headed to the front of the plane, crossed over to the starboard side, and started back that aisle. He had no idea what he was doing until he stopped at row twenty-two and looked down at the mother and child in seats H and I. The woman was in her late twenties; she had a sweet face, not beautiful but gentle and pretty. The child was five or six years old.

The woman looked up at him curiously, and Jim heard himself say, "Mrs. Dubrovek?"

She blinked in surprise. "I'm sorry . . . do I know you?"

"No, but Ed told me you were taking this flight and asked me to look you up." When he spoke that name, he knew Ed was her husband, though he had no idea where that knowledge had come from. He squatted down beside her seat and gave her his best smile. "I'm Steve Harkman. Ed's in sales, I'm in advertising, so we drive each other nuts in about a dozen meetings a week."

Christine Dubrovek's madonna face brightened. "Oh, yes, he's spoken about you. You only joined the company, what, a month ago?"

"Six weeks now," Jim said, flowing with it, confident the right answers would pour out of him even if he didn't know what in the hell they were. "And this must be Casey."

The little girl was in the seat by the window. She raised her head, shifting her attention from a pop-up storybook. "I'm gonna be six tomorrow, it's my birthday, and we're gonna visit grandpop and grandma. They're real old, but they're nice."

He laughed and said, "I'll bet they're sure proud to have a granddaughter cute as you."

WHEN HOLLY SAW him coming along the starboard aisle, she was so startled that she almost popped out of her seat. At first she thought he was looking straight at her. She had the urge to start blurting out a confession—"Yes, all right, I've been following you, checking up on you, invading your privacy with a vengeance"—even before he reached her. She knew precious few other reporters who would have felt guilty about probing into his life, but she couldn't seem to eliminate that streak of decency that had interfered with her career advancement ever since she'd gotten her journalism degree. It almost wrecked everything for her again—until she realized he was looking not at her but at the brunette immediately in front of her. Holly swallowed hard, and slid down a few inches in her seat instead of leaping up in a frenzy of confession. She picked up the airline's magazine, which she'd previously discarded; slowly, deliberately she opened it to cover her face, afraid that too quick a move would draw his attention before she had concealed herself behind those glossy pages.

The magazine blocked her view of him, but she could hear every word he was saying and most of the woman's responses. She listened to him identify himself as Steve Harkman, a company ad executive, and wondered what his charade was all about.

She dared to tilt her head far enough to peek around the magazine with one eye. Ironheart was hunkered down in the aisle beside the woman's seat, so close that Holly could have spit on him, although she was no more practiced at target-spitting than she was at clandestine surveillance.

She realized her hands were trembling, making the magazine rattle softly. She untilted her head, stared at the pages in front of her, and concentrated on being calm.

"HOW ON EARTH did you recognize me?" Christine Dubrovek asked.

"Well, Ed doesn't *quite* paper his office with pictures of you two," Jim said.

"Oh, that's right," she said.

"Listen, Mrs. Dubrovek—"

"Call me Christine."

"Thank you. Christine . . . I've got an ulterior motive for coming over here and pestering you like this. According to Ed, you've got a knack for matchmaking."

That must have been the right thing to say. Already aglow, her sweet face brightened further. "Well, I do like getting people together if I think they're right for each other, and I've got to admit I've had more than a little success at it."

"You make matches, Mommy?" Casey Dubrovek asked.

Uncannily in synch with the workings of her six-year-old's mind, Christine said, "Not the cigarette kind, honey."

"Oh. Good," Casey said, then returned to her pop-up storybook.

"The thing is," Jim said, "I'm new in Los Angeles, been there only eight weeks, and I'm your classic, original lonely guy. I don't like singles' bars, don't want to buy a gym membership just to meet women, and figure anybody I'd connect with through a computer service has to be as desperate and messed up as I am."

She laughed. "You don't look desperate or messed up to me."

"Excuse me, sir," a stewardess said with friendly firmness, touching Jim's shoulder, "but I can't allow you to block the aisle."

"Oh, sure, yeah," he said, standing up. "Just give me a minute." Then to Christine: "Listen, this is embarrassing, but I'd really like to talk to you, tell you about myself, what I'm looking for in a woman, and see if maybe you know someone . . . ?"

"Sure, I'd love that," Christine said with such enthusiasm that she was surely the reincarnation of either some hillbilly woman who had been a much sought-after troth-finder or a successful *schatchen* from Brooklyn.

"Hey, you know, the two seats next to mine are empty," he said. "Maybe you could sit with me the rest of the way. . . ."

He expected her to be reluctant to give up window seats, and an inexplicable twist of anxiety knotted his stomach while he waited for her response.

But she hesitated for only a second or two. "Yes, why not."

The stewardess, still hovering near them, nodded her approval.

To Jim, Christine said, "I thought Casey would like the scenery from way up here, but she doesn't seem to care much. Besides, we're almost at the back of the wing, and it blocks a lot of our view."

Jim did not understand the reason for the wave of relief that swept through him when he secured her agreement to move, but a lot of things mystified him these days. "Good, great. Thank you, Christine."

As he stepped back to let Christine Dubrovek get up, he noticed the passenger in the seat behind her. The poor woman was evidently terrified of flying. She was holding a copy of *Vis à Vis* in front of her face, trying to take her mind off her fears with a little reading, but her hands were shaking so badly that the magazine rattled continuously.

"Where are you sitting?" Christine asked.

"The other aisle, row sixteen. Come on, I'll show you."

He lifted her single piece of carry-on luggage while she and Casey gathered up a few other small items, then he led them to the front of the plane and around to the port aisle. Casey entered row sixteen, and her mother followed.

Before Jim settled down himself, something impelled him to look back across the wide-bodied plane to the aerophobic woman whom they had left behind in row twenty-three. She had lowered the magazine. She was watching him. He knew her.

Holly Thorne.

He was stunned.

Christine Dubrovek said, "Steve?"

Across the plane, the reporter realized that Jim had seen her. She was wide-eyed, frozen. Like a deer caught in car headlights.

"Steve?"

He looked down at Christine and said, "Uh, excuse me a minute, Christine. Just a minute. I'll be right back. Wait here. Okay? Wait right here."

He went forward and across to the starboard aisle again.

His heart was hammering. His throat was tight with fear. But he didn't know why. He was not afraid of Holly Thorne. He knew at once that her presence was no coincidence, that she had tumbled to his secret and had been following him. But right now he didn't care. Discovery, being unmasked—that was not what frightened him. He had no idea what *was* cranking up his anxiety, but it was escalating to a level at which adrenaline would soon start to squirt out his ears.

As he made his way back the aisle toward the reporter, she started to get up. Then a look of resignation slid across her face, and she sat down again. She was as easy to look at as he remembered, though the skin around her eyes was slightly dark, as if from lack of sleep.

When he arrived at row twenty-three, he said, "Come on." He reached for her hand.

She did not give it to him.

"We've got to talk," he said.

"We can talk here."

"No, we can't."

The stewardess who had warned him about blocking the aisle was approaching again.

When Holly would not take his hand, he gripped her by the arm and urged her to get up, hoping she would not force him to yank her out of the seat. The stewardess probably already thought he was some pervert Svengali who was herding up the best-looking women on the flight to surround himself with a harem over there on the port side. Happily, the reporter rose without further protest.

He led her back through the plane to a restroom. It was not occupied, so he pushed her inside. He glanced back, expecting to see the stewardess watching him, but she was attending to another passenger. He followed Holly into the tiny cubicle and pulled the door shut.

She squeezed into the corner, trying to stay as far away from him as possible, but they were still virtually nose to nose.

"I'm not afraid of you," she said.

"Good. There's no reason to be."

Vibrations were conducted well by the burnished-steel walls of the lavatory. The deep drone of the engines was somewhat louder there than in the main cabin.

She said, "What do you want?"

"You've got to do exactly what I tell you."

She frowned. "Listen, I—"

"*Exactly* what I tell you, and no arguments, there's no time for arguments," he said sharply, wondering what the hell he was talking about.

"I know all about your—"

"I don't care what you know. That's not important now."

She frowned. "You're shaking like a leaf."

He was not only shaking but sweating. The lavatory was cool enough, but he could feel beads of sweat forming across his forehead. A thin trickle coursed down his right temple and past the corner of his eye.

Speaking rapidly, he said, "I want you to come forward in the plane, sit farther front near me, there're a couple of empty seats in that area."

"But I—"

"You can't stay where you are, back there in row twenty-three, no way."

She was not a docile woman. She knew her own mind, and she was not used to being told what to do. "That's my seat. Twenty-three H. You can't strongarm me—"

Impatiently, he said, "If you sit there, you're going to die."

She looked no more surprised than he felt—which was plenty damn surprised. "Die? What do you mean?"

"I don't know." But then unwanted knowledge came to him. "Oh, Jesus. Oh, my God. We're going down."

"What?"

"The plane." Now his heart was racing faster than the turbine blades in the great engines that were keeping them aloft. "Down. All the way down."

He saw her incomprehension give way to a dreadful understanding. "Crash?"

"Yes."

"When?"

"I don't know. Soon. Beyond row twenty, almost nobody's going to survive." He did not know what he was going to say until he said it, and as he listened to his own words he was horrified by them. "There'll be a better survival rate in the first nine rows, but not good, not good at all. You've got to move into my section."

The aircraft shuddered.

Holly stiffened and looked around fearfully, as if she expected the lavatory walls to crumple in on them.

"Turbulence," he said. "Just turbulence. We've got . . . a few minutes yet."

Evidently she had learned enough about him to have faith in his prediction. She did not express any doubt. "I don't want to die."

With an increasing sense of urgency, Jim gripped her by the shoulders. "That's why you've got to come forward, sit near me. Nobody's going to be killed in rows ten through twenty. There'll be injuries, a few of them serious, but nobody's going to die in that section, and a lot of them are going to walk out of it unhurt. Now, for God's sake, come on."

He reached for the door handle.

"Wait. You've got to tell the pilot."

He shook his head. "It wouldn't help."

"But maybe there's something he can do, stop it from happening."

"He wouldn't believe me, and even if he did . . . I don't know what to tell him. We're going down, yeah, but I don't know why. Maybe a mid-air collision, maybe structural failure, maybe there's a bomb aboard—it could be anything."

"But you're a psychic, you must be able to see more details if you try."

"If you believe I'm a psychic, you know less about me than you think you do."

"You've got to try."

"Oh, lady, I'd try, I'd try like a sonofabitch if it would do any good. But it won't."

Terror and curiosity fought for control of her face. "If you're not a psychic—what are you?"

"A tool."

"Tool?"

"Someone or something uses me."

The DC-10 shuddered again. They froze, but the aircraft did not take a sudden plunge. It went on as before, its three big engines droning. Just more turbulence.

She grabbed his arm. "You can't let all those people die!"

A rope of guilt constricted his chest and knotted his stomach at the implication that the deaths of the others aboard would somehow be his fault.

He said, "I'm here to save the woman and the girl, no one else."

"That's horrible."

Opening the lavatory door, he said, "I don't like it any more than you do, but that's the way it is."

She did not let go of his arm but jerked at it angrily. Her green eyes were haunted, probably with her own visions of battered bodies strewn across the earth among smoking chunks of wreckage. She repeated herself, whispering fiercely this time: "You can't let all those people die."

Impatiently, he said, "Either come with me, or die with the rest of them."

He stepped out of the lavatory, and she followed him, but he did not know whether she was going to accompany him back to his section. He hoped to God she would. He really could not be held responsible for all the other people who would perish, because they would have died even if he had not come aboard; that was their fate, and he had not been sent to alter *their* destinies. He could not save the whole world, and he had to rely on the wisdom of whatever higher power was guiding him. But he most definitely would be responsible for Holly Thorne's death, because she would never have taken the flight if, unwittingly, he had not led her onto it.

As he moved forward along the port aisle, he glanced to his left at the portholes and clear blue sky beyond. He had a too vivid sense of the yawning void under his feet, and his stomach flopped.

When he reached his seat in row sixteen, he dared to look back. Relief flooded through him at the sight of Holly trailing close.

He pointed to a pair of empty seats immediately behind his and Christine's.

Holly shook her head. "Only if you'll sit down with me. We have to talk."

He glanced down at Christine, then at Holly. He was acutely aware of time slipping away like water swirling down a drain. The awful moment of impact was drawing closer. He wanted to pick the reporter up, stuff her into the seat, engage her seatbelt, and lock her in place. But seatbelts didn't have locks.

Unable to conceal his extreme frustration, he spoke to her through gritted teeth. "My place is with them," he said, meaning with Christine and Casey Dubrovek.

He had spoken quietly, as had Holly, but other passengers were beginning to look at them.

Christine frowned up at him, craned her neck to look back at Holly, and said, "Is something wrong, Steve?"

"No. Everything's fine," he lied.

He glanced at the portholes again. Blue sky. Vast. Empty. How many miles to the earth below?

"You don't look well," Christine said.

He realized that his face was still sheathed in a greasy film of sweat. "Just a little warm. Uh, look, I ran into an old friend. Gimme five minutes?"

Christine smiled. "Sure, sure. I'm still going over a mental list of the most-eligible."

For a moment he had no idea what the hell she was talking about. Then he remembered that he had asked her to play matchmaker for him. "Good," he said. "Great. I'll be right back, we'll talk."

He ushered Holly into row seventeen. He took the aisle seat next to her.

On the other side of Holly was a grandmotherly tub of a woman in a flower-print dress, with blue-tinted gray hair in a mass of tight curls. She was sound asleep, snoring softly. A pair of gold-framed eyeglasses, suspended around her neck on a bead chain, rested on her matronly bosom, rising and falling with her steady breathing.

Leaning close to him, keeping her voice so low it could not even carry across the narrow aisle, but speaking with the conviction of an impassioned political orator, Holly said, "You can't let all those people die."

"We've been through this," he said restively, matching her nearly inaudible pitch.

"It's your responsibility—"

"I'm just one man!"

"But one very special man."

"I'm not God," he said plaintively.

"Talk to the pilot."

"Jesus, you're relentless."

"Warn the pilot," she whispered.

"He won't believe me."

"Then warn the passengers."

"There aren't enough empty seats in this section for all of them to move here."

She was furious with him, quiet but so intense that he could not look away from her or dismiss what she was saying. She put a hand on his arm, gripping him so tightly that it hurt. "Damn it, maybe they could do *something* to save themselves."

"I'd only cause a panic."

"If you can save more, but you let them die, it's murder," she whispered insistently, anger flashing in her eyes.

That accusation hit him hard and had something of the effect of a hammer blow to the chest. For a moment he could not draw his breath. When he could speak, his voice broke repeatedly: "I hate death, people dying, I *hate* it. I want to save people, stop all the suffering, be on the side of life, but I can only do what I can do."

"Murder," she repeated.

What she was doing to him was outrageous. He could not carry the load of responsibility she wanted to pile on his shoulders. If he could save the Dubroveks, he would be working two miracles, mother and child spared from the early graves that had been their destinies. But Holly Thorne, in her ignorance about his abilities, was not satisfied with two miracles; she wanted three, four, five, ten, a hundred. He felt as if an enormous weight was bearing down on him, the weight of the whole damned airplane, crushing him into the ground. It was not right of her to put the blame on him; it wasn't fair. If she wanted to blame someone, she should cast her accusations at God, who worked in such mysterious ways that He had ordained the necessity of the plane crash in the first place.

"Murder." She dug her fingers into his arm even harder.

He could feel anger radiating from her like the heat of the sun reflected off a metal surface. Reflected. Suddenly, he realized that image was too apt to be anything less than Freudian. Her anger over his unwillingness to save everyone on the plane was no greater than his own anger over his inability to do so; her rage was a reflection of his own.

"Murder," she repeated, evidently aware of the profound affect that accusation had on him.

He looked into her beautiful eyes, and he wanted to hit her, punch her in the face, smash her with all of his strength, knock her unconscious, so she wouldn't put his own thoughts into words. She was too perceptive. He hated her for being *right*.

Instead of hitting her, he got up.

"Where are you going?" she demanded.

"To talk to a flight attendant."

"About what?"

"You win, okay? You win."

Making his way toward the back of the plane, Jim looked at the people he passed, chilled by the knowledge that many of them would be dead soon.

As his desperation intensified, so did his imagination, and he saw skulls beneath their skin, the glowing images of bones shining through their flesh, for they were the living dead. He was nauseous with fear, not for himself but for them.

The plane bucked and shimmied as if it had driven over a pothole in the sky. He grabbed at the back of a seat to steady himself. But this was not the big one.

The flight attendants were gathered farther back in the plane, in their work area, preparing to serve the lunch trays that had just come up from the galley. They were a mixed group, men and women, a couple in their twenties and the others as old as fifty-something.

Jim approached the oldest of them. According to the tag she wore, her name was Evelyn.

"I've got to talk to the pilot," he said, keeping his voice low, although the nearest passengers were well forward of them.

If Evelyn was surprised by his request, she didn't show it. She smiled just as she had been trained to smile. "I'm sorry, sir, but that isn't possible. Whatever the problem is, I'm sure I can help—"

"Listen, I was in the lavatory, and I heard something, a *wrong* sound," he lied, "not the right kind of engine noise."

Her smile became a little wider but less sincere, and she went into her reassure-the-nervous-traveler mode. "Well, you see, during flight it's perfectly normal for the pitch of the engines to change as the pilot alters airspeed and—"

"I know that." He tried to sound like a reasonable man to whom she ought to listen. "I've flown a lot. This was different." He lied again: "I know aircraft engines, I work for McDonnell Douglas. We designed and built the DC-10. I *know* this plane, and what I heard in the lav was *wrong*."

Her smile faltered, most likely not because she was starting to take his warning seriously but merely because she considered him to be a more inventive aerophobe than most who panicked in mid-flight.

The other flight attendants had paused in their lunch-service preparations and were staring at him, no doubt wondering if he was going to be a problem.

Evelyn said carefully, "Well, really, everything's functioning well. Aside from some turbulence—"

"It's the tail engine," he said. That was not another lie. He was receiving a revelation, and he was letting the unknown source of that revelation speak through him. "The fan assembly is starting to break apart. If the blades tear loose, that's one thing, the pieces can be contained, but if the entire fan-blade assembly shatters, God knows what could happen."

Because of the specificity of his fear, he did not sound like a typical aerophobic passenger, and all of the flight attendants were staring at him with, if not respect, at least a wary thoughtfulness.

"Everything's fine," Evelyn said, per training. "But even if we lost an engine, we can fly on two."

Jim was excited that the higher power guiding him had evidently decided to give him what he needed to convince these people. Maybe something *could* be done to save everyone on the flight.

Striving to remain calm and impressive, he heard himself saying, "That engine has forty thousand pounds of thrust, it's a real monster, and if it blows up, it's like a bomb going off. The compressors can back-vent, and those thirty-eight titanium blades, the fan assembly, even pieces of the rotor can explode outward like shrapnel, punching holes in the tail, screwing up the rudders and elevators . . . The whole tail of the plane could disintegrate."

One of the flight attendants said, "Maybe somebody should just mention this to Captain Delbaugh."

Evelyn did not instantly object.

"I know these engines," Jim said. "I can explain it to him. You don't have to take me on the flight deck, just let me speak to him on the intercom."

Evelyn said, "McDonnell Douglas?"

"Yeah. I've been an engineer there for twelve years," he lied.

She was now full of doubt about the wisdom of the standard response she had learned in training. She was almost won over.

With hope blossoming, Jim said, "Your captain's got to shut down engine number two. If he shuts it down and goes the rest of the way on one and three, we'll make it, all of us, we'll make it alive."

Evelyn looked at the other flight attendants, and a couple of them nodded. "I guess it wouldn't hurt if . . ."

"Come on," Jim said urgently. "We might not have much time."

He followed Evelyn out of the attendants' work area and into the starboard aisle in the economy-class section, heading forward.

The plane was rocked by an explosion.

Evelyn was thrown hard to the deck. Jim pitched forward, too, grabbed at a seat to avoid falling atop the woman, overcompensated and fell to one side instead, against a passenger, then to the floor, as the plane started to shimmy. He heard lunch trays still crashing to the deck behind him, people crying out in surprise and alarm, and one thin short scream. As he tried to scramble to his feet, the aircraft nosed down, and they started to lose altitude.

HOLLY MOVED FORWARD from row seventeen, sat beside Christine Dubrovek, introduced herself as a friend of Steve Harkman's, and was nearly thrown out of her seat when a sickening shockwave pumped through the aircraft. It was followed a fraction of a second later by a solid *thump*, as if they had been struck by something.

"Mommy!" Casey had been belted in her seat, even though the seatbelt signs were not on. She was not thrown forward, but the storybooks on her lap clattered to the deck. Her eyes were huge with fear.

The plane started to lose altitude.

"Mommy?"

"It's okay," Christine said, obviously struggling to conceal her own fear from her daughter. "Just turbulence, an air pocket."

They were dropping fast.

"You're gonna be okay," Holly told them, leaning past Christine to make sure the little girl heard her reassurances. "Both of you are going to be okay if you just stay here, don't move, stay right in these seats."

Knifing down . . . a thousand feet . . . two thousand . . .

Holly frantically belted herself in her seat.

. . . three thousand . . . four thousand . . .

An initial wave of horror and panic gripped the passengers. But that was followed quickly by a breathless silence, as they all clung to the arms of their seats and waited to see if the damaged aircraft was going to pull up in time— or tip downward at an even more severe angle.

To Holly's surprise, the nose slowly came up. The plane leveled off again.

A communal sigh of relief and a smattering of applause swept through the cabin.

She turned and grinned at Christine and Casey. "We're going to be all right. We're all going to make it."

The captain came on the loudspeaker and explained that they had lost one of their engines. They could still fly just fine on the remaining two, he assured them, though he suggested they might need to divert to a suitable airfield closer than O'Hare, only to be safe. He sounded calm and confident, and he thanked the passengers for their patience, implying that the worst they would suffer was inconvenience.

A moment later Jim Ironheart appeared in the aisle, and squatted beside Holly. A spot of blood glimmered at the corner of his mouth; he had evidently been tossed around a little.

She was so exhilarated, she wanted to kiss him, but she just said, "You did it, you changed it, you made a difference somehow."

He looked grim. "No." He leaned close to her, put his face almost against hers, so they could talk in whispers as before, though she thought Christine Dubrovek must be hearing some of it. He said, "It's too late."

Holly felt as if he had punched her in the stomach. "But we leveled off."

"Pieces of the exploding engine tore holes in the tail. Severed most of the hydraulic lines. Punctured the others. Soon they won't be able to steer the airplane."

Her fear had melted. Now it came back like ice crystals forming and linking together across the gray surface of a winter pond.

They were going down.

She said, "You know *exactly* what happened, you should be with the captain, not here."

"It's over. I was too late."

"No. Never—"

"Nothing I can do now."

"But—"

A flight attendant appeared, looking shaken but sounding calm. "Sir, please return to your seat."

"All right, I will," Jim said. He took Holly's hand first, and squeezed it. "Don't be afraid." He looked past her at Christine, then at Casey. "You'll be all right."

He moved back to row seventeen, the seat immediately behind Holly. She was loath to lose sight of him. He helped her confidence just by being within view.

FOR TWENTY-SIX YEARS, Captain Sleighton Delbaugh had earned his living in the cockpits of commercial airliners, the last eighteen as a pilot. He had encountered and successfully dealt with a daunting variety of problems, a few of them serious enough to be called crises, and he had benefited from United's rigorous program of continuous instruction and periodic recertification. He felt he was prepared for anything that could happen in a modern aircraft, but he found it difficult to believe what *had* happened to Flight 246.

After engine number two failed, the bird went into an unplanned descent, and the controls stiffened. They managed to correct its attitude, however, and dramatically slow its descent. But losing eleven thousand feet of altitude was the least of their problems.

"We're turning right," Bob Anilov said. He was Delbaugh's first officer, forty-three, and an excellent pilot. "Still turning right. It's locking up, Slay."

"We've got partial hydraulic failure," said Chris Lodden, their flight engineer. He was the youngest of the three and a favorite of virtually every female flight attendant who met him, partly because he was good-looking in a fresh-faced farmboy way, but largely because he was a little shy, which made him a novelty among the cocksure men on most flight crews. Chris was seated behind Anilov and in charge of monitoring the mechanical systems.

"It's going harder right," Anilov said.

Already Delbaugh was pulling the yoke full aft, left wheel. "Damn."

Anilov said, "No response."

"It's worse than a partial loss," Chris Lodden said, tapping and adjusting his instruments as if he was having trouble believing what they were telling him. "How can this be right?"

The DC-10 had three hydraulic systems, well-designed backup. They couldn't have lost everything. But they had.

Pete Yankowski—a balding, red-mustached flight instructor from the company's training facility in Denver—was riding with the crew on his way to visit his brother in Chicago. As an OMC—observing member of crew— he was in the fold-down jumpseat immediately behind Delbaugh, virtually peering over the captain's shoulder. He said, "I'll go have a look at the tail, assess the damage."

As Yankowski left, Lodden said, "The only control we've got is engine thrust."

Captain Delbaugh had already begun to use it, cutting the power to the engine on the right, increasing it to the other—the port—engine in order to pull them to the left and out of their unwanted turn. When they began to swing too far to the left, he would have to increase the power to the starboard engine again and bring them around that way a little.

With the flight engineer's assistance, Delbaugh determined that the outboard and inboard elevators on the tail were gone, dead, useless. The inboard ailerons on the wings were dead. The outboard ailerons were dead. Same for the flaps and spoilers.

The DC-10 had a wingspan of over one hundred and fifty-five feet. Its fuselage was a hundred and seventy feet long. It was more than just an airplane. It was literally a ship that sailed the sky, the very definition of a "jumbo jet," and virtually the only way they now had to steer it was with the two General Electric/Pratt & Whitney engines. Which was only a little better than a driver trying to steer a runaway automobile by leaning to one side and then to the other, desperately struggling to influence its course with his shifting weight.

A FEW MINUTES had passed since the tail engine exploded, and they were still aloft.

Holly believed in a god, not due to any life-altering spiritual experience, but largely because the alternative to belief was simply too grim. Although she had been raised a Methodist and for a while toyed with the idea of conversion to Catholicism, she had never made up her mind what sort of god she preferred, whether one of the gray-suited Protestant varieties or the more passionate Catholic divinity or something else altogether. In her daily life she did not turn to heaven for help with her problems, and she only said grace before meals when she was visiting her parents in Philadelphia. She would have felt like a hypocrite if she had fallen into prayer now, but she nevertheless hoped that God was in a merciful mood and watching over the DC-10, whatever His or Her gender might be and regardless of His or Her preference in worshipers.

Christine was reading one of the pop-up storybooks with Casey, adding her own amusing commentary to the adventures of the animal characters, trying to distract her daughter from the memory of the muffled explosion and subsequent plunge. The intensity of her focus on the child was a giveaway of her true inner feelings: she was scared, and she knew that the worst had not yet passed.

Minute by minute, Holly slipped deeper into a state of denial, unwilling to accept what Jim Ironheart had told her. It was not her own survival, or his, or that of the Dubroveks that she doubted. He had proven himself to be singularly successful when he entered combat with fate; and she was reasonably confident that their lives were secure in the forward section of the economy-class seats, as he had promised. What she wanted to deny, *had* to deny, was that so many others on the flight were going to die. It was intolerable to think that the old and young, men and women, innocent and guilty, moral and immoral, the kind and the mean-spirited were going to die in the same event, compacted together against some rocky escarpment or on a field of wildflowers set afire by burning jet fuel, with no favor given to those who had led their lives with dignity and respect for others.

OVER IOWA, FLIGHT 246 passed out of Minneapolis Center, the air-traffic-control jurisdiction after Denver Center, and now responded only to Chicago Center. Unable to regain hydraulics, Captain Delbaugh requested and received permission from United's dispatcher and from Chicago to divert from O'Hare to the nearest major airport, which was Dubuque, Iowa. He relinquished control of the plane to Anilov, so he and Chris Lodden would be able to concentrate on finding a way through their crisis.

As a first step, Delbaugh radioed System Aircraft Maintenance (SAM) at San Francisco International Airport. SAM was United's central maintenance base, an enormous state-of-the-art complex with a staff of over ten thousand.

"We have a situation here," Delbaugh told them calmly. "Complete hydraulic failure. We can stay up awhile, but we can't manuever."

At SAM, in addition to United's own employees, experts were also on duty twenty-four hours a day from suppliers of every model of aircraft currently in operation by the airline—including a man from General Electric, where the CF-6 engines had been built, and another from McDonnell Douglas, which had designed and manufactured the DC-10. Manuals, books, and a massive amount of computer-accessible data about each airplane type was available to staff at SAM, in addition to an exhaustively detailed maintenance history of every craft in the United fleet. They could tell Delbaugh and Lodden about every mechanical problem their particular plane had experienced during its lifetime, exactly what had been done to it during its most recently scheduled maintenance, and even when upholstery damage had been repaired—virtually everything except how much loose change had fallen into its seats from passengers' pockets and been left behind during the past twelve months.

Delbaugh also hoped they could tell him how the hell he was supposed to fly an aircraft as large as an apartment building without the aid of elevators, rudders, ailerons, and other equipment that allowed him to maneuver. Even the best flight training programs were structured under the assumption that a pilot would retain *some* degree of control in a catastrophic incident, thanks to redundant systems provided by the designers. Initially, the people at SAM had trouble accepting that he had lost all hydraulics, assuming he meant he'd had a fractional loss. He finally had to snap at them to make them understand, which he deeply regretted not only because he wanted to uphold the tradition of quiet professionalism that pilots before him had established in dire circumstances, but also because he was seriously spooked by the sound of his own angry voice and thereafter found it more difficult to deceive himself that he actually felt as calm as he was pretending to be.

Pete Yankowski, the flight instructor from Denver, returned from his trip to the rear of the plane and reported that through a window he had spotted an eighteen-inch hole in the horizontal part of the tail. "There's probably more damage I couldn't see. Figure shrapnel ripped up the rear section behind the aft bulkhead, where all the hydraulic systems pass through. At least we didn't depressurize."

Dismayed at the rippling sensation that quivered through his bowels, achingly aware that two hundred and fifty-three passengers and ten other crew members were depending on him to bring them home alive, Delbaugh conveyed Yankowski's information to SAM. Then he asked for assistance in determining how to fly the severely disabled aircraft. He was not surprised when, after an urgent consultation, the experts in San Francisco could come up with no recommendations. He was asking them to do the impossible, tell him how to remain the master of this behemoth with no substantial controls other than the throttles—the same unfair request that God was making of him.

He stayed in touch with United's dispatcher office, as well, which tracked the progress of all the company's hardware in the air. In addition, both channels—the dispatcher and SAM—were patched in to United's headquarters near O'Hare International in Chicago. A lot of interested and anxious people were tied to Delbaugh by radio, but they were all as much at a loss for good suggestions as were the experts in San Francisco.

To Yankowski, Delbaugh said, "Ask Evelyn to find that guy from McDonnell Douglas she told us about. Get him up here quick."

As Pete left the flight deck again, and as Anilov struggled with his control wheel in a determined if vain attempt to get at least some response from the craft, Delbaugh told the shift manager at SAM that a McDonnell Douglas engineer was aboard. "He warned us something was wrong with the tail engine just before it exploded. He could tell from the sound of it, I guess, so we'll get him in here, see if he can help."

At SAM, the General Electric expert on CF-6 turbofan engines came back at him: "What do you mean, he could tell by the sound? How could he tell by the sound? What did it sound like?"

"I don't know," Delbaugh replied. "We didn't notice any unusual noises or unexpected changes in pitch, and neither did the flight attendants."

The voice in Delbaugh's headset crackled in response: "That doesn't make sense."

McDonnell Douglas's DC-10 specialist at SAM sounded equally baffled: "What's this guy's name?"

"We'll find out. All we know right now is his first name," Sleighton Delbaugh said. "It's Jim."

AS THE CAPTAIN announced to the passengers that they would be landing in Dubuque as a result of mechanical problems, Jim watched Evelyn approach him along the port aisle, weaving because the plane was no longer as steady as it had been. He wished she would not ask him what he knew she had to ask.

". . . and it might be a little rough," the captain concluded.

As the pilots reduced power to one engine and increased it to the other, the wings wobbled, and the plane wallowed like a boat in a swelling sea. Each time it happened, they recovered quickly, but between those desperate course corrections, when they were unlucky enough to hit air turbulence, the DC-10 did not ride through it as confidently as it had done all the way out from LAX.

"Captain Delbaugh would like you to come forward if you could," Evelyn said when she reached him, soft-voiced and smiling as if delivering an invitation to a pleasant little luncheon of tea and finger sandwiches.

He wanted to refuse. He was not entirely sure that Christine and Casey—or Holly, for that matter—would live through the crash and its immediate aftermath without him at their side. He knew that on impact a ten-row chunk of the fuselage aft of first-class would crack loose from the rest of the plane, and that less damage would be done to it than to the forward and rear sections. Before he had intervened in the fate of Flight 246, all of the passengers in those favored seats had been destined to come out of the crash with comparatively minor injuries or no injuries at all. He was sure that all of those marked for life were still going to live, but he was not certain that merely moving the Dubroveks into the middle of the safety zone was sufficient to alter their fate and insure their survival. Perhaps, after impact, he would have to be there to get them through the fire and out of the wreckage—which he could not do if he was with the flight crew.

Besides, he had no idea whether the crew was going to survive. If he was with them in the cockpit on impact . . .

He went with Evelyn anyway. He had no choice—at least not since Holly Thorne had insisted that he might be able to do more than save one woman and one child, might thwart fate on a large scale instead of a small one. He remembered too clearly the dying man in the station wagon out on the Mojave Desert and the three murdered innocents in the Atlanta convenience store last May, people who could have been spared along with others if he had been allowed to arrive in time to save them.

As he went by row sixteen, he checked out the Dubroveks, who were huddled over a storybook, then he met Holly's eyes. Her anxiety was palpable.

Following Evelyn forward, Jim was aware of the passengers looking at him speculatively. He was one of their own, elevated to special status by their predicament, which they were beginning to suspect was worse than they were being told. They were clearly wondering what special knowledge he possessed that made his presence in the cockpit desirable. If only they knew.

The plane was wallowing again.

Jim picked up a trick from Evelyn. She did not just weave where the tilting deck forced her to go, but attempted to anticipate its movement and lean in the opposite direction, shifting her point of gravity to maintain her balance.

A couple of the passengers were discreetly puking into airsickness bags. Many others, though able to control their nausea, were gray-faced.

When Jim entered the cramped, instrument-packed cockpit, he was appalled by what he saw. The flight engineer was paging through a manual, a look of quiet desperation on his face. The two pilots—Delbaugh and First. Officer Anilov, according to the flight attendant who had not entered with Jim—were struggling with the controls, trying to wrench the right-tending jumbo jet back onto course. To free them to concentrate on that task, a red-haired balding man was on his knees between the two pilots, operating the throttles at the captain's direction, using the thrust of the remaining two engines to provide what steering they had.

Anilov said, "We're losing altitude again."

"Not serious," Delbaugh said. Aware that someone had entered, Delbaugh glanced back at Jim. In the captain's position, Jim would have been sweating like a race-lathered horse, but Delbaugh's face glistened with only a fine sheen of perspiration, as if someone had spritzed him with a plant mister. His voice was steady: "You're him?"

"Yeah," Jim said.

Delbaugh looked forward again. "We're coming around," he said to Anilov, and the co-pilot nodded. Delbaugh ordered a throttle change, and the man on the floor complied. Then, speaking to Jim without looking at him, the captain said, "You knew it was going to happen."

"Yeah."

"So what else can you tell me?"

Bracing himself against a bulkhead as the plane shuddered and wallowed again, Jim said, "Total hydraulic failure."

"I mean, something I don't know," Delbaugh replied with cool sarcasm. It justifiably could have been an angry snarl, but he was admirably in command of himself. Then he spoke to approach control, obtaining new instructions.

Listening, Jim realized that the Dubuque tower was going to bring in Flight 246 by way of a series of 360-degree turns, in an attempt to line it up with one of the runways. The pilots could not easily guide the plane into a straight approach, as usual, because they had no real control. The disabled craft's maddening tendency to turn endlessly to the right was now to be incorporated into a breathtakingly conceived plan that would let it find its way into the barn like a stubborn bull determined to resist the herder and follow its own route home. If the radius of each turn was carefully calculated and matched to an equally precise rate of descent, they might eventually be able to bring 246 head-on to a runway and all the way in.

Impact in five minutes.

Jim twitched in shock and almost spoke those four words aloud when they came to him.

Instead, when the captain finished talking to the tower, Jim said, "Is your landing gear operable?"

"We got it down and locked," Delbaugh confirmed.

"Then we might make it."

"We *will* make it," Delbaugh said. "Unless there's another surprise waiting for us."

"There is," Jim said.

The captain glanced worriedly at him again. "What?"

Impact in four minutes.

"For one thing, there'll be a sudden windshear as you're going in, oblique to you, so it won't drive you into the ground. But the reflected updraft from it will give you a couple bad moments. It'll be like you're flying over a washboard."

"What're you talking about?" Anilov demanded.

"When you're making your final approach, a few hundred feet from the end of the runway, you'll still be at an angle," Jim said, once more allowing some omniscient higher power to speak through him, "but you'll have to go for it anyway, no other choice."

"How can you know that?" the flight engineer demanded.

Ignoring the question, Jim went on, and the words came in a rush: "The plane'll suddenly drop to the right, the wing'll hit the ground, and you'll cartwheel down the runway, end over end, off it, into a field. The whole damn plane'll come apart and burn."

The red-haired man in civilian clothes, operating the throttles, looked back at Jim in disbelief. "What crock of shit is this, who the hell do you think you are?"

"He knew about engine number two before it blew up," Delbaugh said coolly.

Aware that they were entering the second of the trio of planned 360-degree turns and that time was swiftly running out, Jim said, "None of you in the cockpit will die, but you'll lose a hundred and forty-seven passengers, plus four flight attendants."

"Oh my God," Delbaugh said softly.

"He can't *know* this," Anilov objected.

Impact in three minutes.

Delbaugh gave additional instructions to the red-haired man, who manipulated the throttles. One engine grew louder, the other softer, and the big craft began its second turn, shedding some altitude as it went.

Jim said, "But there's a warning, just before the plane tips to the right."

"What?" Delbaugh said, still unable to look at him, straining to get what response he could from the wheel.

"You won't recognize what it means, it's a strange sound, like nothing you've heard before, because it's a structural failure in the wing coupling, where it's fixed to the fuselage. A sharp twang, like a giant steel-guitar string. When you hear it, if you increase power to the port engine immediately, compensating to the left, you'll keep her from cartwheeling."

Anilov had lost his patience. "This is nuts. Slay, I can't *think* with this guy here."

Jim knew Anilov was right. Both System Aircraft Maintenance in San Francisco and the dispatcher had been silent for a while, hesitant to interfere with the crew's concentration. If he stayed there, even without saying another word, he might unintentionally distract them at a crucial moment. Besides, he sensed that there was nothing more of value that he would be given to tell them.

He left the flight deck and moved as quickly as possible toward row sixteen.

Impact in two minutes.

HOLLY KEPT WATCHING for Jim Ironheart, hoping he would rejoin them. She wanted him nearby when the worst happened. She had not forgotten the bizarre dream from last night, the monstrous creature that had seemed to come out of her nightmare and into her motel room; neither had she forgotten how many people he had killed in his quest to protect the lives of the innocent, nor how savagely he slaughtered Norman Rink in that Atlanta convenience store. But the dark side of him was outweighed by the light. Though an aura of danger surrounded him, she also felt curiously safe in his company, as if within the protective nimbus of a guardian angel.

Through the public-address system, one of the flight attendants was instructing them on emergency procedures. Other attendants were positioned throughout the plane, making sure everyone was following directions.

The DC-10 was wallowing and shimmying again. Worse, although without a wooden timber anywhere in its structure, it was creaking like a sailing ship on a storm-tossed sea. The sky was blue beyond the portholes, but evidently the air was more than blustery; it was raging, tumultuous.

None of the passengers had any illusions now. They knew they were going in for a landing under the worst conditions, and that it would be rough. Maybe fatal. Throughout the enormous plane, people were surprisingly quiet, as if they were in a cathedral during a solemn service. Perhaps, in their minds' eyes, they were experiencing their own funerals.

Jim appeared out of the first-class section and approached along the port aisle. Holly was immensely relieved to see him. He paused only to smile encouragingly at the Dubroveks, and to put his hand on Holly's shoulder and give her a gentle squeeze of reassurance. Then he settled into the seat behind her.

The plane hit a patch of turbulence worse than anything before. She was half convinced that they were no longer flying but sledding across corrugated steel.

Christine took Holly's hand and held it briefly, as if they were old friends—which, in a curious way, they were, thanks to the imminence of death, which had a bonding effect on people.

"Good luck, Holly."

"You, too," Holly said.

Beyond her mother, little Casey looked so small.

Even the flight attendants were seated now, and in the position they had instructed the passengers to take. Finally Holly followed their example and assumed the posture that contributed to the best chance of survival in a crash: belted securely in the seat, bent forward, head tucked between her knees, gripping her ankles with her hands.

The plane came out of the shattered air, slipping down glass-smooth for a moment. But before Holly had time to feel any relief, the whole sky seemed to be shaking as though gremlins were standing at the four corners and snapping it like a blanket.

Overhead storage compartments popped open. Traincases, valises, jackets, and personal items flew out and rained down on the seats. Something struck the center of Holly's bowed back, bouncing off her. It was not heavy, hardly hurt at all, but she suddenly worried that a traincase, laden with some woman's makeup and jars of face cream, would drop at precisely the right angle to crack her spine.

CAPTAIN SLEIGHTON DELBAUGH called out instructions to Yankowski, who continued to kneel between the pilots, operating the throttles while they were preoccupied with maintaining what little control they had left. He was braced, but a hard landing was not going to be kind to him.

They were coming out of the third and final 360-degree turn. The runway was ahead of them, but not straight-on, just as Jim—damn, he'd never gotten the guy's last name—had predicted.

Also as the stranger had foreseen, they were descending through exceptional turbulence, bucking and shuddering as if they were in a big old bus with a couple of bent axles, thundering down a steep and rugged mountain road. Delbaugh had never seen anything like it; even if the plane had been intact, he'd have been concerned about landing in those treacherous crosswinds and powerful rising thermals.

But he could not pull up and go on, hoping for better conditions at another airport or on another pass at this one. They had kept the jumbo jet in the air for thirty-three minutes since the tail-engine explosion. That was a feat of which they could be proud, but skill and cleverness and intelligence and nerve were not enough to carry them much farther. Minute by minute, and now second by second, keeping the stricken DC-10 in the air was increasingly like trying to fly a massive rock.

They were about two thousand meters from the end of the runway and closing fast.

Delbaugh thought of his wife and seventeen-year-old son at home in Westlake Village, north of Los Angeles, and he thought of his other son, Tom, who was already on his way to Willamette to get ready for his junior year. He longed to touch their faces and hold them close.

He was not afraid for himself. Well, not much. His relatively mild concern for his own safety was not a result of the stranger's prediction that the flight crew would survive, because he didn't know if the guy's premonitions were always correct. In part, it was just that he didn't have *time* to be concerned about himself.

Fifteen hundred meters.

Mainly, he was worried about his passengers and crew, who trusted him with their lives. If any part of the crash was his fault, due to a lack of resolve or nerve or quickness, all the good he had done and tried to do in his life would not compensate for this one catastrophic failure. Perhaps that attitude proved that he was, as some friends suggested, too hard on himself, but he knew that many pilots worked under no less heavy a sense of responsibility.

He remembered what the stranger had said: "*. . . you'll lose a hundred and forty-seven passengers . . .*"

His hands throbbed with pain as he kept a tight grip on the yoke, which vibrated violently.

"*. . . plus four flight attendants . . .*"

Twelve hundred meters.

"She wants to come right," Delbaugh said.

"Hold her!" Anilov said, for at this low altitude and on an approach, it was all in Delbaugh's hands.

One hundred and fifty-one dead, all those families bereaved, countless other lives altered by a single tragedy.

Eleven hundred meters.

But how the hell could that guy know how many would die? Not possible. Was he trying to say he was clairvoyant or what? It was all a crock, as Yankowski had said. Yeah, but he knew about the engine before it exploded, he knew about the washboard turbulence, and only an idiot would discount all of that.

A thousand meters.

"Here we go," Delbaugh heard himself say.

BENT FORWARD IN his seat, head between his knees, gripping his ankles, Jim Ironheart thought of the punchline to an old joke: kiss your ass goodbye.

He prayed that by his own actions he had not disrupted the river of fate to such an extent that he would wash away not only himself and the Dubroveks but other people on Flight 246 who had never been meant to die in the crash. Because of what he had told the pilot, he had potentially altered the future, and now what happened might be worse, not better, than what had been *meant* to happen.

The higher power working through him had seemed, ultimately, to approve of his attempt to save more lives than just those of Christine and Casey. On the other hand, the nature and identity of that power was so enigmatic that only a fool would presume to understand its motives or intentions.

The plane shivered and shook. The scream of the engines seemed to grow ever more shrill.

He stared at the deck beneath his feet, expecting it to burst open in his face.

More than anything, he was afraid for Holly Thorne. Her presence on the flight was a profound deviation from the script that fate had originally written. He was eaten by a fear that he might save the lives of more people on the plane than he'd at first intended—but that Holly would be broken in half by the impact.

AS THE DC-10 quaked and rattled its way toward the earth, Holly squeezed herself into as tight a package as she could, and closed her eyes. In her private darkness, faces swam through her mind: her mom and dad, which was to be expected; Lenny Callaway, the first boy she had ever loved, which was not expected, because she had not seen him since they were both sixteen; Mrs. Rooney, a high-school teacher who had taken a special interest in her; Lori Clugar, her best friend all through high school and half of college, before life had carried them to different corners of the country and out of touch; and more than a dozen others, all of whom she had loved and still loved. No one person could have occupied her thoughts for more than a fraction of a second, yet the nearness of death seemed to distort time, so she felt as if she were lingering with each beloved face. What flashed before her was not her life, but the special people in it—though in a way that was the same thing.

Even above the creak-rumble-shriek of the jet, and in spite of her focus on the faces in her mind, she heard Christine Dubrovek speak to her daughter in the last moments of their shaky descent: "I love you, Casey."

Holly began to cry.

THREE HUNDRED METERS.
Delbaugh had the nose up.

Everything looked good. As good as it *could* look under the circumstances.

They were at a slight angle to the runway, but he might be able to realign the aircraft once they were on the ground. If he couldn't bring it around to any useful degree, they would roll three thousand or maybe even four thousand feet before their angle of approach carried them off the edge of the pavement and into a field where it appeared that a crop of some kind had been harvested recently. That was not a desirable termination point, but at least by then a lot of their momentum would have been lost; the plane might still break up, depending on the nature of the bare earth under its wheels, but there was little chance that it would disintegrate catastrophically.

Two hundred meters.

Turbulence gone.

Floating. Like a feather.

"All right," Anilov said, just as Delbaugh said, "Easy, easy," and they both meant the same thing: it looked good, they were going to make it.

One hundred meters.

Nose still up.

Perfect, perfect.

Touchdown and—

TWANG!

—the tires barked on the blacktop simultaneously with the queer sound. Delbaugh remembered the stranger's warning, so he said, "Power number one!" and pulled hard to the left. Yankowski remembered as well, though he had said it was all a crock, and he responded to Delbaugh's throttle command even as it was being given. The right wing dipped, just as they had been told it would, but their quick action pulled the plane left, and the right wing came back up. There was a danger of overcompensation, so Delbaugh issued a new throttle command while still trying to hold the craft to the left. They were rolling along, rolling along, the plane shaking, and he gave the order to reverse engines because they couldn't, for God's sake, continue to accelerate, they were in mortal danger as long as they were moving at high speed, rolling, rolling, moving inexorably at an angle on the runway, rolling and slowing now, but rolling. And the right wing was tipping down again, accompanied by hellish popping and metallic tearing noises as age-fatigued steel—trouble in the joining of wing and fuselage, Jim had said—succumbed to the stress of their wildly erratic flight and once-in-a-century crosswinds. Rolling, rolling, but Delbaugh couldn't do a damn thing about a structural failure, couldn't get out there and reweld the joints or hold the damn rivets in place. Rolling, rolling, their momentum dropping, but the right wing still going down, none of his countermeasures working any longer, the wing down, and down, oh God, the wing—

———

Holly felt the plane tipping farther to the right than before. She held her breath—or thought she did, but at the same time she heard herself gasping frantically.

The creaks and squeals of tortured metal, which had been echoing eerily through the fuselage for a couple of minutes, suddenly grew much louder. The aircraft tipped farther to the right. A sound like a cannonshot boomed through the passenger compartment, and the plane bounced up, came down hard. The landing gear collapsed.

They were sliding along the runway, rocking and jolting, then the plane began to turn as it slid, making Holly's heart clutch up and her stomach knot. It was the biggest carnival ride in the world, except it wasn't any fun at all; her seatbelt was like a blade against her midriff, cutting her in half, and if there had been a carny ticket-taker, she knew he would have had the ghastly face of a rotting corpse and a rictus for a smile.

The noise was intolerable, though the passengers' screaming was not the worst of it. For the most part their voices were drowned out by the scream of the aircraft itself as its belly dissolved against the pavement and other pieces of it were torn loose. Maybe dinosaurs, sinking into Mesozoic pits of tar, had equaled the volume of that dying cry, but nothing on the face of the earth since that era had protested its demise at such a piercing pitch and thunderous volume. It wasn't purely a machine sound; it was metallic but somehow alive, and it was so eerie and chilling that it might have been the combined, tortured cries of all the denizens of hell, hundreds of millions of despairing souls wailing at once. She was sure her eardrums would burst.

Disregarding the instructions she had been given, she raised her head and looked quickly around. Cascades of white, yellow, and turquoise sparks foamed past the portholes, as if the airplane was passing through an extravagant fireworks display. Six or seven rows ahead, the fuselage cracked open like an eggshell rapped against the edge of a ceramic bowl.

She had seen enough, too much. She tucked her head between her knees again.

She heard herself chanting at the deck in front of her, but she was caught in such a whirlpool of horror that the only way she could discover what she was saying was to strain to hear herself above the cacophony of the crash: "Don't, don't, don't, don't, don't, don't . . ."

Maybe she passed out for a few seconds, or maybe her senses shut down briefly due to extreme overload, but in a wink everything was still. The air was filled with acrid odors that her recovering senses could not identify. The ordeal was over, but she could not recall the plane coming to rest.

She was alive.

Intense joy swept through her. She raised her head, sat up, ready to whoop with the uncontainable thrill of survival—and saw the fire.

The DC-10 had not cartwheeled. The warning to Captain Delbaugh had paid off.

But as Jim had feared, the chaotic aftermath of the crash held as many dangers as the impact itself.

Along the entire starboard side of the plane, where jet fuel had spilled, orange flames churned at the windows. It appeared as if he was voyaging aboard a submarine in a sea of fire on an alien world. Some of the windows had shattered on impact, and flames were spouting through those apertures, as well as through the ragged tear in the fuselage that now separated economy class from the forward section of the airliner.

Even as Jim uncoupled his seatbelt and got shakily to his feet, he saw seats catching afire on the starboard side. Passengers over there were crouching or dropping down on their hands and knees to scramble under the spreading flames.

He stepped into the aisle, grabbed Holly, and hugged her as she struggled to her feet. He looked past her at the Dubroveks. Mother and child were uninjured, though Casey was crying.

Holding Holly by the hand, searching for the quickest way out, Jim turned toward the back of the aircraft and for a moment could not understand what he was seeing. Like a voracious blob out of an old horror movie, an amorphous mass churned toward them from the hideously gouged and crumpled rear of the DC-10, black and billowy, devouring everything over which it rolled. Smoke. He hadn't instantly realized it was smoke because it was so thick that it appeared to have the substance of a wall of oil or mud.

Death by suffocation, or worse, lay behind them. They would have to go forward in spite of the fire ahead. Flames licked around the torn edge of fuselage on the starboard side, reaching well into the cabin, fanning across more than half the diameter of the sliced-open aircraft. But they should be able to exit toward the port side, where no fire was yet visible.

"Quick," he said, turning to Christine and Casey as they came out of row sixteen. "Forward, fast as you can, go, go!"

However, other passengers from the first six rows of the economy section were in the aisle ahead of them. Everyone was trying to get out fast. A valiant young flight attendant was doing what she could to help, but progress was not easy. The aisle was littered with carry-on luggage, purses, paperback books, and other items that had fallen out of the overhead storage compartments, and within a few shuffling steps, Jim's feet had become entangled in debris.

The churning smoke reached them from behind, enfolded them, so pungent that his eyes teared at once. He not only choked on the first whiff of fumes but gagged with revulsion, and he did not want to think about what might be burning behind him in addition to upholstery, foam seat cushions, carpet, and other elements of the aircraft's interior decor.

As the thick oily cloud poured past him and engulfed the forward section, the passengers ahead began to vanish. They appeared to be stepping through the folds of a black velvet curtain.

Before visibility dropped to a couple of inches, Jim let go of Holly and touched Christine's shoulder. "Let me take her," he said, and scooped Casey into his arms.

A paper bag from an LAX giftshop was in the aisle at his feet. It had burst open as people tramped across it. He saw a white T-shirt—I LOVE L.A.—with pink and peach and pale-green palm trees.

He snatched up the shirt and pushed it into Casey's small hands. Coughing, as was everyone around him, he said, "Hold it over your face, honey, breathe through it!"

Then he was blind. The foul cloud around him was so dark that he could not even see the child he was carrying. Indeed, he could not actually perceive the churning currents of the cloud itself. The blackness was deeper than what he saw when he closed his eyes, for behind his lids, pinpoint bursts of color formed ghostly patterns that lit his inner world.

They were maybe twenty feet from the open end of fuselage. He was not in danger of getting lost, for the aisle was the only route he could follow.

He tried not to breathe. He could hold his breath for a minute, anyway, which ought to be long enough. The only problem was that he had already inhaled some of the bitter smoke, and it was caustic, burning his throat as if he had swallowed acid. His lungs heaved and his esophagus spasmed, forcing him to cough, and every cough ended in an involuntary though thankfully shallow inhalation.

Probably less than fifteen feet to go.

He wanted to scream at the people in front of him: *move, damn you, move!* He knew they were stumbling forward as fast as they could, every bit as eager to get out as he was, but he wanted to shout at them anyway, felt a shriek of rage building in him, and he realized he was teetering on the brink of hysteria.

He stepped on several small, cylindrical objects, floundering like a man walking on marbles. But he kept his balance.

Casey was wracked by violent coughs. He could not hear her, but holding her against his chest, he could feel each twitch and flex and contraction of her small body as she struggled desperately to draw half-filtered breaths through the I LOVE L.A. shirt.

Less than a minute had passed since he had started forward, maybe only thirty seconds since he had scooped up the girl. But it seemed like a long journey down an endless tunnel.

Although fear and fury had thrown his mind into a turmoil, he was thinking clearly enough to remember reading somewhere that smoke rose in a burning room and hung near the ceiling. If they didn't reach safety within a few seconds, he would have to drop to the deck and crawl in the hope that he would escape the toxic gases and find at least marginally cleaner air down there.

Sudden heat coalesced around him.

He imagined himself stepping into a furnace, his skin peeling off in an instant, flesh blistering and smoking. His heart already thudded like a wild thing throwing itself against the bars of a cage, but it began to beat harder, faster.

Certain that they had to be within a few steps of the hole in the fuselage that he had glimpsed earlier, Jim opened his eyes, which stung and watered copiously. Perfect blackness had given way to a charcoal-gray swirl of fumes through which throbbed blood-red pulses of light. The pulses were flames shrouded by smoke and seen only as reflections bouncing off millions of swirling particles of ash. At any moment the fire could burst upon him from out of the smoke and sear him to the bone.

He was not going to make it.

No breathable air.

Fire seeking him on all sides.

He was going to ignite. Burn like a living tallow candle. In a vision sparked by terror rather than by a higher power, he saw himself dropping to his knees in defeat. The child in his arms. Fusing with her in a steel-melting inferno . . .

A sudden wind pulled at him. The smoke was sucked away toward his left.

He saw daylight, cool and gray and easily differentiated from the deadly glow of burning jet fuel.

Propelled by a gruesome image of himself and the child fried by a flash fire on the very brink of safety, he threw himself toward the grayness and fell out of the airliner. No portable stairs were waiting, of course, no emergency chute, just bare earth. Fortunately a crop had recently been harvested, and the stubble had been plowed under for mulch. The newly tilled earth was hard enough to knock the wind out of him but far too soft to break his bones.

He clung fiercely to Casey, gasping for breath. He rolled onto his knees, got up, still holding her in his arms, and staggered out of the corona of heat that radiated from the blazing plane.

Some of the survivors were running away, as if they thought the DC-10 had been loaded with dynamite and was going to blow half the state of Iowa to smithereens any second now. Others were wandering aimlessly in shock. Still others were lying on the ground: some too stunned to go another inch; some injured; and perhaps some of them were dead.

Grateful for the clean air, coughing out sour fumes from his soiled lungs, Jim looked for Christine Dubrovek among the people in the field. He turned this way and that, calling her name, but he couldn't see her. He began to think that she had perished in the airplane, that he might not have been treading over only passengers' possessions in the port aisle but also over a couple of the passengers themselves.

Perhaps sensing what Jim was thinking, Casey let the palm tree-decorated

T-shirt fall from her grasp. Clinging to him, coughing out the last of the smoke, she began to ask for her mother in a fearful tone of voice that indicated she expected the worst.

A burgeoning sense of triumph had taken hold of him. But now a new fear rattled in him like ice cubes in a tall glass. Suddenly the warm August sun over the Iowa field and the waves of heat pouring off the DC-10 did not touch him, and he felt as though he was standing on an arctic plain.

"Steve?"

At first he did not react to the name.

"Steve?"

Then he remembered that he had been Steve Harkman to her—which she and her husband and the *real* Steve Harkman would probably puzzle about for the rest of their lives—and he turned toward the voice. Christine was there, stumbling through the freshly tilled earth, her face and clothes stained from the oily smoke, shoeless, arms out to receive her little girl.

Jim gave the child to her.

Mother and daughter hugged each other fiercely.

Weeping, looking across Casey's shoulder at Jim, Christine said, "Thank you, thank you for getting her out of there, my God, Steve, I can't ever thank you enough."

He did not want thanks. All he wanted was Holly Thorne, alive and uninjured.

"Have you seen Holly?" he asked worriedly.

"Yes. She heard a child crying for help, she thought maybe it was Casey." Christine was shaking and frantic, as if she was not in the least convinced their ordeal was over, as if she thought the earth might crack open and hot lava spew out, beginning a new chapter of the nightmare. "How did we get separated? We were behind one another, then we were outside, and in the turmoil, somehow you and Casey just weren't there."

"Holly," he said impatiently. "Where'd she go?"

"She wanted to go back inside for Casey, but then she realized the cry was coming from the forward section." Christine held up a purse and chattered on: "She carried her purse out of there without realizing she did it, so she gave it to me and went back, she knew it couldn't be Casey, but she went anyway."

Christine pointed, and for the first time Jim saw that the front of the DC-10, all the way back through the first-class section, had completely torn free from the portion in which they had been riding. It was two hundred feet farther along the field. Though it was burning less vigorously than the larger mid-section, it was considerably more mangled than the rest of the craft, including the badly battered rear quarter.

He was appalled to hear that Holly had reentered *any* part of the smoldering wreckage. The cockpit and forward section rested in that Iowa field like a monolith in an alien graveyard on a faraway world, wildly out of place here, and therefore infinitely strange, huge and looming, thoroughly ominous.

He ran toward it, calling Holly's name.

THOUGH SHE KNEW it was the very plane in which she had departed Los Angeles a few hours ago, Holly could barely believe that the forward section of the DC-10 had actually once been part of a whole and functioning aircraft. It seemed more like a deeply disturbed sculptor's interpretation of a DC-10, welded together from parts of real airliners but also from junk of every description, from pie pans and cake tins and garbage cans and old lengths of pipe, from auto fenders and scrap wire and aluminum siding and pieces of a wrought-iron fence. Rivets had popped; glass had dissolved; seats had torn loose and piled up like broken and unwanted armchairs in the corner of an auction barn; metal had bent and twisted, and in places it had shattered as completely as crystal met by a hammer. Interior fuselage panels had peeled back, and heavy structural beams had burst inward. The floor had erupted upward in places, either from the impact or from an explosion below. Everywhere jagged, gnarled metal objects bristled in profusion, and it looked like nothing so much as a junkyard for old machines just after a tornado had passed through.

Trying to track down what sounded like the cries of a frightened child, Holly could not always proceed erect. She had to crouch and squirm through pinched spaces, pushing things aside when she could, going over or around or under whenever an obstacle proved to be immovable. The neat rows and aisles of the plane had been pulled and hammered into a maze.

She was shaken when she spotted yellow and red flickers of flame along the perimeter of the deck and in the starboard front corner by the bulkhead that separated the passenger cabin from the cockpit. But the fire was fitful, unlike the blistering conflagration that she had fled moments ago. It might abruptly flare up, of course, consuming everything in its path, although currently it seemed unable to find sufficiently combustible material or oxygen to do more than barely sustain itself.

Smoke curled around her in sinuous tendrils, but it was more annoying than threatening. Breathable air was in good supply, and she didn't even cough much.

More than anything, the corpses were what unnerved her. Though the crash apparently had been somewhat less severe than it would have been without Jim Ironheart's intervention, not everyone had survived, and a number of fatalities had occurred in the first-class section. She saw a man pinned to his seat by a foot-long, inch-diameter steel tube that had pierced his throat; his sightless eyes were wide open in a final expression of surprise. A woman, nearly decapitated, was on her side, still belted into her seat, which had torn free of the deck plates to which it had been bolted. Where other seats had broken free and slammed together, she saw injured passengers and cadavers heaped on one another, and the only way to tell the quick from the dead was to listen closely to determine which of them was groaning.

She blanked out the horror. She was aware of the blood, but she looked through it rather than at it. She averted her eyes from the most grievous wounds, refused to dwell on the nightmare images of the shattered passengers whom she kept confronting. Human bodies became abstract forms to her, as if they were not real but only blocks of shape and color put down on canvas by a cubist imitating Picasso. If she allowed herself to think about what she was seeing, she would either have to retrace the route she had taken and get out, or curl into a fetal ball and weep.

She encountered a dozen people who needed to be extracted from the wreckage and given immediate medical treatment, but they were all either too large or too tightly wedged in the rubble for her to be of any assistance. Besides, she was drawn forward by the haunting cries of the child, driven by that instinctive understanding that children were always to be saved first: one of the major clauses of nature's genetically programmed triage policy.

Sirens rose in the distance. She had never paused to think that professional rescuers would be on their way. It didn't matter. She couldn't go back and wait for them to handle this. What if reaching the child a minute or two sooner made all the difference between death and survival?

As Holly inched forward, now and then glimpsing anemic but worrisome flames through gaps in the web of destruction, she heard Jim Ironheart behind her, calling her name at the opening where the forward part of the plane had been amputated from the rest of it. In the chaos after falling from the mid-section of the DC-10, they had apparently emerged from the smoke at different places, heading in opposite directions, for she had not been able to find him even though he should have been right behind her. She had been pretty sure that he and Casey had survived, if only because he obviously had a talent for survival; but it was good to hear his voice.

"In here!" she shouted, although the tangle of devastation prevented her from seeing him.

"What're you doing?"

"Looking for a little boy," she called back. "I hear him, I'm getting closer, but I can't see him yet."

"Get out of there!" he shouted above the increasingly loud wail of approaching emergency vehicles. "Paramedics are on the way, they're trained for this."

"Come on," she said, pushing forward. "There're other people in here who need help *now!*"

Holly was nearing the front of the first-class section, where the steel ribs of the fuselage had broken inward but not in such profusion as in the area behind her. Detached seats, carry-on luggage, and other detritus had flown forward on impact, however, piling up deeper there than anywhere else. More people had wound up in that pile, too, both dead and alive.

When she shoved a broken and empty seat out of her way and paused to get her breath, she heard Jim clawing into the wreckage behind her.

Lying on her side, she squirmed through a narrow passage and into a pocket of open space, coming face to face with the boy whose cries she had been following. He was about five years old, with enormous dark eyes. He blinked at her in amazement and swallowed a sob, as if he had never really expected anyone to reach him.

He was under an inverted bank of five seats, in a peaked space formed by the seats themselves, as if in a tent. He was lying on his belly, looking out, and it seemed as if he ought to be able to slither into the open easy enough.

"Something's got my foot," he said. He was still afraid, but manageably so. He had cast off the greater part of his terror the moment he had seen her. Whether you were five years old or fifty, the worst thing always was being alone. "Got my foot, won't let go."

Coughing, she said, "I'll get you out, honey. You'll be okay."

Holly looked up and saw another row of seats piled atop the lower bank. Both were wedged in by a mass of twisted steel pressing down from the caved-in ceiling, and she wondered if the forward section had rolled once before coming to rest right-side up.

With her fingertips she wiped the tears off his cheeks. "What's your name, honey?"

"Norwood. Kids call me Norby. It don't hurt. My foot, I mean."

She was glad to hear that.

But then, as she studied the wreckage around him and tried to figure out what to do, he said, "I can't feel it."

"Feel what, Norby?"

"My foot. It's funny, like something's holding it, 'cause I can't get loose, but then I can't *feel* my foot—you know?—like it maybe isn't there."

Her stomach twisted at the image his words conjured in her mind. Maybe it wasn't that bad. Maybe his foot was only pinched between two surfaces, just numb, but she had to think fast and move fast because he might be losing blood at an alarming rate.

The space in which he lay was too cramped for her to squeeze in past him, find his foot, and disentangle it. Instead, she rolled onto her back, bent her legs, and braced the soles of her shoes against the seats that peaked over him.

"Okay, honey, I'm going to straighten my legs, try to shove this up a little, just a couple inches. When it starts lifting, try to pull your foot out of there."

As a snake of thin gray smoke slipped from the dark space behind Norby and coiled in front of his face, he wheezed and said, "There's d-d-dead people in here with me."

"That's okay, baby," she said, tensing her legs, flexing them a little to test the weight she was trying to lever off him. "You won't be there for long, not for long."

"My seat, then an empty seat, then dead people," Norby said shakily.

She wondered how long the trauma of this experience would shape his nightmares and bend the course of his life.

"Here goes," she said.

She pressed upward with both feet. The pile of seats and junk and bodies was heavy enough, but the half-collapsed section of the ceiling, pushing down on everything else, did not seem to have any give in it. Holly strained harder until the steel deck, covered with only a thin carpet, pressed painfully into her back. She let out an involuntary sob of agony. Then she strained even harder, harder, angry that she could not move it, *furious*, and—

—it moved.

Only a fraction of an inch.

But it moved.

Holly put even more into it, found reserves she did not know she possessed, forced her feet upward until the pain throbbing in her legs was markedly worse than that in her back. The intruding tangle of ceiling plates and struts creaked and bent back an inch, two inches; the seats shoved up just that far.

"It's still got me," the boy said.

More smoke was oozing out of the lightless space around him. It was not pale-gray but darker than before, sootier, oilier, and with a new foul stench. She hoped to God the desultory flames had not, at last, ignited the upholstery and foam padding that formed the cocoon from which the boy was struggling to emerge.

The muscles in her legs were quivering. The pain in her back had seeped all the way through to her chest; each heartbeat was an aching thud, each inhalation was a torment.

She did not think she could hold the weight any longer, let alone lift it higher. But abruptly it jolted up another inch, then slightly more.

Norby issued a cry of pain and excitement. He wriggled forward. "I got away, it let go of me."

Relaxing her legs and easing the load back into place, Holly realized that the boy had thought what she, too, might have thought if she'd been a five-year-old in that hellish position: that his ankle had been clenched in the cold and iron-strong hand of one of the dead people in there with him.

She slid aside, giving Norby room to pull himself out of the hollow under the seats. He joined her in the pocket of empty space amidst the rubble and snuggled against her for comforting.

From farther back in the plane, Jim shouted: "Holly!"

"I found him!"

"I've got a woman here, I'm getting her out."

"Great!" she shouted.

Outside, the pitch of the sirens spiraled lower and finally down into silence as the rescue teams arrived.

Although more blackish smoke was drifting out of the dark space from which Norby had escaped, Holly took the time to examine his foot. It flopped to one side, sickeningly loose, like the foot of an old rag doll. It was broken at the ankle. She tore his sneaker off his rapidly swelling foot. Blood darkened his white sock, but when she looked at the flesh beneath, she discovered that it was only abraded and scored by a few shallow cuts. He was not going to bleed to death, but soon he was going to become aware of the excruciating pain of the broken ankle.

"Let's go, let's get out," she said.

She intended to take him back the way she had come, but when she glanced to her left, she saw another crack in the fuselage. This one was immediately aft of the cockpit bulkhead, only a few feet away. It extended up the entire curve of the wall but did not continue onto the ceiling. A section of interior paneling, the insulation beneath it, structural beamwork, and exterior plating had either blown inward among the other debris or been wrenched out into the field. The resultant hole was not large, but it was plenty big enough for her to squeeze through with the boy.

As they balanced on the rim of the ravaged hull, a rescue worker appeared in the plowed field about twelve feet below them. He held his arms out for the boy.

Norby jumped. The man caught him, moved back.

Holly jumped, landed on her feet.

"You his mother?" the man asked.

"No. I just heard him crying, went in after him. He's got a broken ankle there."

"I was with my Uncle Frank," Norby said.

"Okay," the rescue worker said, trying to strike a cheerful note, "then let's find Uncle Frank."

Norby said flatly, "Uncle Frank's dead."

The man looked at Holly, as if she might know what to say.

Holly was mute and shaken, filled with despair that a boy of five should have to experience such an ordeal. She wanted to hold him, rock him in her arms, and tell him that everything would be right with the world.

But nothing is right with the world, she thought, because Death is part of it. Adam disobeyed and ate the apple, gobbled up the fruit of knowledge, so God decided to let him know all sorts of things, both light and dark. Adam's children learned to hunt, to farm, to thwart the winter and cook their food with fire, make tools, build shelters. And God, wanting to give them a *well-rounded* education, let them learn, oh, maybe a million ways to suffer and die. He encouraged them to learn language, reading and writing, biology, chemistry, physics, the secrets of the genetic code. And He taught them the exquisite horrors of brain tumors, muscular dystrophy, bubonic plague, cancer run amok in their bodies—and not least of all airplane crashes. You wanted knowledge, God was happy to oblige, He was an enthusiastic teacher, a *demon* for knowledge, piling it on in such weight and exotic detail that sometimes you felt you were going to be crushed under it.

By the time the rescue worker turned away and carried Norby across the field toward a white ambulance parked on the edge of the runway, Holly had gone from despair to anger. It was a useless rage, for there was no one but God against whom she could direct it, and the expression of it could change nothing. God would not free the human race from the curse of death just because Holly Thorne thought it was a gross injustice.

She realized that she was in the grip of a fury not unlike that which seemed to motivate Jim Ironheart. She remembered what he had said during their whispered conversation in row seventeen, when she had tried to bully him into saving not just the Dubroveks but everyone aboard Flight 246: "*I hate death, people dying, I hate it!*" Some of the people he saved had quoted him making similar remarks, and Holly remembered what Viola Moreno had said about the deep and quiet sadness in him that perhaps grew out of being an orphan at the age of ten. He quit teaching, walked away from his career, because Larry Kakonis's suicide had made all his effort and concern seem pointless. That reaction at first appeared extreme to Holly, but now she understood it perfectly. She felt the same urge to cast aside a mundane life and do something more meaningful, to crack the rule of fate, to wrench the very fabric of the universe into a shape other than what God seemed to prefer for it.

For a fragile moment, standing in that Iowa field with the wind blowing the stink of death to her, watching the rescue worker walk away with the little boy who had almost died, Holly felt closer to Jim Ironheart than she had ever been to another human being.

She went looking for him.

The scene around the broken DC-10 had become more chaotic than it had been immediately after the crash. Fire trucks had driven onto the plowed field. Streams of rich white foam arced over the broken plane, frosted the fuselage in whipped-creamlike gobs, and damped the flames on the surrounding fuelsoaked earth. Smoke still churned out of the mid-section, plumed from every rent and shattered window; shifting to the whims of the wind, a black canopy spread over them and cast eerie, constantly changing shadows as it filtered the afternoon sunshine, raising in her mind the image of a grim kaleidoscope in which all the pieces of glass were either black or gray. Rescue workers and paramedics swarmed over the wreckage, searching for survivors, and their numbers were so unequal to the awesome task that some of the more fortunate passengers pitched in to help. Other passengers—some so untouched by the experience that they appeared freshly showered and dressed, others filthy and disheveled—stood alone or in small groups, waiting for the minibuses that would take them to the Dubuque terminal, chattering nervously or stunned into silence. The only things threading the crash scene together and providing it with some coherence were the static-filled voices crackling on shortwave radios and walkie-talkies.

Though Holly was searching for Jim Ironheart, she found instead a young woman in a yellow shirtwaist dress. The stranger was in her early twenties, slender, auburn-haired, with a porcelain face; and though uninjured she badly needed help. She was standing back from the still-smoking rear section of the airliner, shouting a name over and over again: "Kenny! Kenny! Kenny!" She had shouted it so often that her voice was hoarse.

Holly put a hand on the woman's shoulder and said, "Who is he?"

The stranger's eyes were the precise blue of wisteria—and glazed. "Have you seen Kenny?"

"Who is he, dear?"

"My husband."

"What does he look like?"

Dazed, she said, "We were on our honeymoon."

"I'll help you look for him."

"No."

"Come on, kid, it'll be all right."

"I don't want to look for him," the woman said, allowing Holly to turn her away from the plane and lead her toward the ambulances. "I don't want to see him. Not the way he'll be. All dead. All broken up and burned and dead."

They walked together through the soft, tilled earth, where a new crop would be planted in late winter and sprout up green and tender in the spring, by which time all signs of death would have been eradicated and nature's illusion of life-everlasting restored.

5

Something was happening to Holly. A fundamental change was taking place in her. She didn't understand what it was yet, didn't know what it would mean or how different a person she would be when it was complete, but she was aware of profound movement in the bedrock of her heart, her mind.

Because her inner world was in such turmoil, she had no spare energy to cope with the outer world, so she placidly followed the standard post-crash program with her fellow passengers.

She was impressed by the web of emotional, psychological, and practical support provided to survivors of Flight 246. Dubuque's medical and civil-defense community—which obviously had planned for such an emergency—responded swiftly and effectively. In addition psychologists, counselors, ministers, priests, and a rabbi were available to the uninjured passengers within minutes of their arrival at the terminal. A large VIP lounge—with mahogany tables and comfortable chairs upholstered in nubby blue fabric—had been set aside for their use, ten or twelve telephone lines sequestered from normal airport operations, and nurses provided to monitor them for signs of delayed shock.

United's employees were especially solicitous, assisting with local overnight accommodations and new travel arrangements, as quickly as possible reuniting the uninjured with friends or relatives who had been transported to various hospitals, and compassionately conveying word of loved ones' deaths. Their horror and grief seemed as deep as that of the passengers, and they were shaken and remorseful that such a thing could happen with one of their planes. Holly saw a young woman in a United jacket turn suddenly and leave the room in tears, and all the others, men and women alike, were pale and shaky. She found herself wanting to console *them*, put an arm around them and tell them that even the best-built and best-maintained machines were doomed to fail sooner or later because human knowledge was imperfect and darkness was loose in the world.

Courage, dignity, and compassion were so universally in evidence under such trying circumstances that Holly was dismayed by the full-scale arrival of the media. She knew that dignity, at least, would be an early victim of their assault. To be fair, they were only doing their job, the problems and pressures of which she knew too well. But the percentage of reporters who could perform their work properly was no greater than the percentage of plumbers who were competent or the percentage of carpenters who could miter a doorframe perfectly every time. The difference was that unfeeling, inept, or downright hostile reporters could cause their subjects considerable embarrassment and, in some cases, malign the innocent and permanently damage reputations, which was a lot worse than a backed-up drain or mismatched pieces of wood molding.

The whole spectrum of TV, radio, and print journalists swarmed into the airport and soon penetrated even those areas where their presence was officially restricted. Some were respectful of the survivors' emotional and mental condition, but most of them badgered the United employees about "responsibility" and "moral obligation," or hounded the survivors to reveal their innermost fears and relive the recent horror for the delectation of news consumers. Though Holly knew the drill and was expert at fending them off, she was asked the same question half a dozen times by four different reporters within fifteen minutes: "How did you feel?" How did you feel when you heard it might be a crash landing? How did you *feel* when you thought you were going to die? How did you feel when you saw that some of those around you *had* died?

Finally, cornered near a large observation window that looked out on arriving and departing flights, she blew up at an eager and expensively coiffured CNN reporter named Anlock, who simply could not understand that she was unflattered by his attentions. "Ask me what I saw, or ask me what I think," she told him. "Ask me who, what, where, why, and how, but for God's sake don't ask me how I feel, because if you're a human being you've got to *know* how I feel. If you have any empathy at all for the human condition, you've got to know."

Anlock and his cameraman tried to back off, move on to other prey. She was aware that most of the people in the crowded room had turned to see what the commotion was about, but she didn't care. She was not going to let Anlock off that easily. She stayed with him:

"You don't want facts, you just want drama, you want blood and thunder, you want people to bare their souls to you, then you edit what they say, change it, misreport it, get it all wrong most of the time, and that's a kind of rape, damn it."

She realized that she was in the grip of the same rage she had experienced at the crash site, and that she was not half as angry at Anlock as she was at God, futile as that might be. The reporter was just a more convenient target than the Almighty, who could stay hidden in some shadowy corner of His heaven. She'd thought her anger had subsided; she was disconcerted to find that same black fury welling high within her again.

She was over the top, out of control, and she didn't care—until she realized CNN was on the air live. A predatory glint in Anlock's eyes and a twist of irony in his expression alerted her that he was not entirely dismayed by her outburst. She was giving him good color, first-rate drama, and he could not resist using it even if he was the object of her abuse. Later, of course, he would magnanimously excuse her behavior to viewers, insincerely sympathizing with the emotional trauma she had endured, thus coming off as a fearless reporter *and* a compassionate guy.

Furious with herself for playing into his game when she should have known that only the reporter ever wins, Holly turned from the camera. Even as she walked away, she heard Anlock saying, ". . . quite understandable, of course, given what the poor woman has just been through . . ."

She wanted to go back and smash him in the face. And wouldn't *that* please him!

What's wrong with you, Thorne? she demanded of herself. You never lose it. Not like this. You never lose it, but now you're definitely, absolutely losing it.

Trying to ignore the reporters and suppress her sudden interest in self-analysis, she went looking for Jim Ironheart again but still had no luck locating him. He was not among the latest group arriving from the crash site. None of the United employees could find his name on the passenger roster, which did not exactly surprise Holly.

She figured he was still in the field, assisting the search-and-rescue team in whatever way he could. She was eager to speak with him, but she would have to be patient.

Although some of the reporters were wary of her after the way she verbally assaulted Anlock, she knew how to manipulate her own kind. Sipping from a Styrofoam cup of bitter black coffee—as if she needed caffeine to improve her edge—she drifted around the room and into the hall outside, pumping them without revealing that she was one of them, and she was able to obtain bits of interesting information. Among other things, she discovered that two hundred survivors were already accounted for, and that the death toll was unlikely to exceed fifty, a miraculously low number of fatalities, considering the breakup of the plane and the subsequent fire. She should have been exhilarated by that good news, for it meant Jim's intervention had permitted the captain to save many more lives than fate had intended; but instead of rejoicing, she brooded about those who, in spite of everything, had been lost.

She also learned that members of the flight crew, all of whom survived, were hoping to find a passenger who had been a great help to them, a man described as "Jim Something, sort-of-a-Kevin-Costner-lookalike with very blue eyes." Because the first federal officials to arrive on the scene were also eager to talk to Jim Something, the media began looking for him as well.

Gradually Holly realized that Jim would not be putting in an appearance. He would fade, just as he always did after one of his exploits, moving quickly beyond the reach of reporters and officialdom of all stripes. Jim was the only name for him that they would ever have.

Holly was the first person, at the site of one of his rescues, to whom he had given his full name. She frowned, wondering why he had chosen to reveal more to her than to anyone else.

Outside the door of the nearest women's restroom, she encountered Christine Dubrovek, who returned her purse and asked about Steve Harkman, never realizing that he was the mysterious Jim after whom everyone else was inquiring.

"He had to be in Chicago this evening, no matter what, so he's already rented a car and left," Holly lied.

"I wanted to thank him again," Christine said. "But I guess I'll have to wait until we're both back in Los Angeles. He works in the same company as my husband, you know."

Casey, close at her mother's side, had scrubbed the soot off her face and combed her hair. She was eating a chocolate bar, but she did not appear to be enjoying it.

As soon as she could, Holly excused herself and returned to the emergency-assistance center that United had established in a corner of the VIP lounge. She tried to arrange for a flight that, regardless of the number of connections, would return her to Los Angeles that night. But Dubuque was not exactly the hub of the universe, and all seats to anywhere in southern California were already booked. The best she could do was a flight to Denver in the morning, followed by a noon flight from Denver to LAX.

United arranged overnight lodging for her, and at six o'clock, Holly found herself alone in a clean but cheerless room at the Best Western Midway Motor Lodge. Maybe it was not really so cheerless; in her current state of mind, she would not have been capable of appreciating a suite at the Ritz.

She called her parents in Philadelphia to let them know she was safe, in case they had seen her on CNN or spotted her name among a list of Flight 246 survivors in tomorrow's newspaper. They were happily unaware of her close call, but they insisted on whipping up a prime case of retrospective fright. She found herself consoling them, instead of the other way around, which was touching because it confirmed how much they loved her. "I don't care how important this story is you're working on," her mother said, "you can take a bus the rest of the way, and a bus home."

Knowing she was loved did not improve Holly's mood.

Though her hair was a tangled mess and she smelled of smoke, she walked to a nearby shopping center, where she used her Visa card to purchase a change of clothes: socks, underwear, blue jeans, a white blouse, and a lightweight denim jacket. She bought new Reeboks, too, because she could not shake the suspicion that the discolorations on her old pair were bloodstains.

In her room again, she took the longest shower of her life, lathering and relathering herself until one entire complimentary motel-size bar of soap had been reduced to a crumbling sliver. She still did not feel clean, but she finally turned the water off when she realized that she was trying to scrub away something that was inside of her.

She ordered a sandwich, salad, and fruit from room service. When it came, she could not eat it.

She sat for a while, just staring at the wall.

She dared not turn on the television. She didn't want to risk catching a news report about the crash of Flight 246.

If she could have called Jim Ironheart, she would have done so at once. She would have called him every ten minutes, hour after hour, until he arrived home and answered. But she already knew that his number was not listed.

Eventually she went down to the cocktail lounge, sat at the bar, and ordered a beer—a dangerous move for someone with her pathetic tolerance for alcohol. Without food to accompany it, one bottle of Beck's would probably knock her unconscious for the rest of the night.

A traveling salesman from Omaha tried to strike up a conversation with her. He was in his mid-forties, not unattractive, and seemed nice enough, but she didn't want to lead him on. She told him, as nicely as she could, that she was not looking to get picked up.

"Me neither," he said, and smiled. "All I want is someone to talk to."

She believed him, and her instincts proved reliable. They sat at the bar together for a couple of hours, chatting about movies and television shows, comedians and singers, weather and food, never touching on politics, plane crashes, or the cares of the world. To her surprise, she drank three beers and felt nothing but a light buzz.

"Howie," she said quite seriously when she left him, "I'll be grateful to you for the rest of my life."

She returned to her room alone, undressed, slid under the sheets, and felt sleep stealing over her even as she put her head on the pillow. Pulling the covers around her to ward off the chill of the air conditioner, she spoke in a voice slurred more by exhaustion than by beer: "Snuggle down in my cocoon, be a butterfly soon." Wondering where *that* had come from and what she meant by it, she fell asleep.

Whoosh, whoosh, whoosh, whoosh, whoosh . . .

Though she was in the stone-walled room again, the dream was different in many ways from what it had been previously. For one thing, she was not blind. A fat yellow candle stood in a blue dish, and its dancing orange flame revealed stone walls, windows as narrow as embrasures, a wooden floor, a turning shaft that came through the ceiling above and disappeared through a hole into the room below, and a heavy door of iron-bound timbers. Somehow she knew that she was in the upper chamber of an old windmill, that the sound—*whoosh, whoosh, whoosh*—was produced by the mill's giant sails cutting the turbulent night wind, and that beyond the door lay curved limestone steps that led down to the milling room. Though she was standing when the dream began, circumstances changed with a ripple, and she was suddenly sitting, though not in an ordinary chair. She was in an airline seat, belted in place, and when she turned her head to the left, she saw Jim Iron-heart seated beside her. "This old mill won't make it to Chicago," he said solemnly. And it seemed quite logical that they were flying in that stone structure, lifted by its four giant wood-slat sails the way an airliner was kept aloft by its jets or propellers. "We'll survive, though—won't we?" she asked. Before her eyes, Jim faded and was replaced by a ten-year-old boy. She marveled at this magic. Then she decided that the boy's thick brown hair and electric-blue eyes meant he was Jim from another time. According to the liberal rules of dreams, that made his transformation less magical and, in fact, altogether logical. The boy said, "We'll survive if *it* doesn't come." And she said, "What is *it*?" And he said, "The Enemy." Around them the mill seemed to respond to his last two words, flexing and contracting, pulsing like flesh, just as her motel-room wall in Laguna Hills had bulged with ma-levolent life last night. She thought she glimpsed a monstrous face and form taking its substance from the very limestone. "We'll die here," the boy said, "we'll all die here," and he seemed almost to welcome the creature that was trying to come out of the wall. *WHOOSH!*

Holly came awake with a start, as she had at some point during each of the past three nights. But this time no element of the dream followed her into the real world, and she was not terrified as she had been before. Afraid, yes. But it was a low-grade fear, more akin to disquiet than to hysteria.

More important, she rose from the dream with a buoyant sense of liber-ation. Instantly awake, she sat up in bed, leaned back against the headboard, and folded her arms across her bare breasts. She was shivering neither with fear nor because of a chill, but with excitement.

Earlier in the night, tongue lubricated by beer, she had spoken a truth as she had slipped off the precipice of sleep: *"Snuggle down in my cocoon, be a butterfly soon."* Now she knew what she had meant, and she understood the changes that she had been going through ever since she had tumbled to Ironheart's secret, changes that she had only begun to realize were under way when she had been in the VIP lounge at the airport after the crash.

She was never going back to the *Portland Press*.

She was never going to work on a newspaper again.

She was finished as a reporter.

That was why she had overreacted to Anlock, the CNN reporter at the airport. Loathing him, she was nevertheless eaten by guilt on a subconscious level because he was chasing a major story that she was ignoring even though she was a *part* of it. If she was a reporter, she should have been interviewing her fellow survivors and rushing to write it up for the *Press*. No such desire touched her, however, not even for a fleeting moment, so she took the raw cloth of her subconscious self-disgust and tailored a suit of rage with enormous shoulders and wide, wide lapels; then she dressed herself in it and strutted and seethed for the CNN camera, all in a frantic attempt to deny that she didn't care about journalism anymore and that she was going to walk away from a career and a commitment that she had once thought would last all her life.

Now she got out of bed and paced, too excited to sit still.

She was finished as a reporter.

Finished.

She was free. As a working-class kid from a powerless family, she had been obsessed by a lifelong need to feel important, included, a real insider. As a bright child who grew into a brighter woman, she had been puzzled by the apparent disorderliness of life, and she had been compelled to explain it as best she could with the inadequate tools of journalism. Ironically, the dual quest for acceptance and explanations—which had driven her to work and study seventy-and eighty-hour weeks for as long as she could remember—had left her rootless, with no significant lover, no children, no real friends, and no more answers to the difficult questions of life than those with which she had started. Now she was suddenly free of those needs and obsessions, no longer concerned about belonging to any elite club or explaining human behavior.

She had thought she hated journalism. She didn't. What she hated was her failure at it; and she had failed because journalism had never been the right thing for her.

To understand herself and break the bonds of habit, all she had needed was to meet a man who could work miracles, and survive a devastating airline tragedy.

"Such a *flexible* woman, Thorne," she said aloud, mocking herself. "So insightful."

Why, good heavens, if meeting Jim Ironheart and walking away from a plane crash hadn't made her see the light, then surely she'd have figured it out just as soon as Jiminy Cricket rang her doorbell and sang a cleverly rhymed lesson-teaching song about the differences between wise and stupid choices in life.

She laughed. She pulled a blanket off the bed, wound it around her nude body, sat in one of the two armchairs, drew her legs up under her, and laughed as she had not laughed since she had been a giddy teenager.

No, that was where the problem began: she had *never* been giddy. She had been a serious-minded teenager, already hooked on current events, worried about World War III because they told her she was likely to die in a nuclear holocaust before she graduated from high school; worried about overpopulation because they told her that famine would claim one and a half billion lives by 1990, cutting the world population in half, decimating even the United States; worried because man-made pollution was causing the planet to cool down drastically, insuring another ice age that would destroy civilization *within her own lifetime!!!!*, which was front-page news in the late seventies, before the Greenhouse Effect and worries about planetary warming. She had spent her adolescence and early adulthood worrying too much and enjoying too little. Without joy, she had lost perspective and had allowed every news sensation—some based on genuine problems, some entirely fraudulent—to consume her.

Now she laughed like a kid. Until they hit puberty and a tide of hormones washed them into a new existence, kids knew that life was scary, yeah, dark and strange, but they also knew that it was silly, that it was meant to be fun, that it was an adventurous journey down a long road of time to an unknown destination in a far and wondrous place.

Holly Thorne, who suddenly liked her name, knew where she was going and why.

She knew what she hoped to get from Jim Ironheart—and it was not a good story, journalistic accolades, a Pulitzer. What she wanted from him was better than that, more rewarding and enduring, and she was eager to confront him with her request.

The funny thing was, if he agreed and gave her what she wanted, she might be buying into more than excitement, joy, and a meaningful existence. She knew there was danger in it, as well. If she got what she asked from him, she might be dead a year from now, a month from now—or next week. But for the moment, at least, she focused on the prospect of joy and was not deterred by the possibility of early death and endless darkness.

Part Two

The Windmill

August 27 into August 29

1 Holly changed planes in Denver, gained two time zones traveling west, and arrived at Los Angeles International at eleven o'clock Monday morning. Unencumbered by luggage, she retrieved her rental car from the parking garage, drove south along the coast to Laguna Niguel, and reached Jim Ironheart's house by twelve-thirty.

She parked in front of his garage, followed the tile-trimmed walkway directly to his front door, and rang the bell. He did not answer. She rang it again. He still did not answer. She rang it repeatedly, until a reddish impression of the button marked the pad of her right thumb.

Stepping back, she studied the first- and second-floor windows. Plantation shutters were closed over all of them. She could see the wide slats through the glass.

"I know you're in there," she said quietly.

She returned to her car, put the windows down, and sat behind the steering wheel, waiting for him to come out. Sooner or later he would need food, or laundry detergent, or medical attention, or toilet paper, *something*, and then she would have him.

Unfortunately, the weather was not conducive to a long stakeout. The past few days had been warm but mild. Now the August heat had returned like a bad dragon in a storybook: scorching the land with its fiery breath. The palm trees drooped and the flowers began to wilt in the blistering sun. Behind all of the elaborate watering systems that maintained the lush landscaping, the dispossessed desert waited to reassert itself.

Baking as swiftly and evenly as a muffin in a convection oven, Holly finally put up the windows, started the car, and switched on the air conditioner. The cold draft was heavenly, but before long the car began to overheat; the needle rose swiftly toward the red section of the arc on the temperature gauge.

At one-fifteen, just three-quarters of an hour after she had arrived, Holly threw the car in reverse, backed out of the driveway, and returned to the Laguna Hills Motor Inn. She changed into tan shorts and a canary-yellow calypso blouse that left her belly bare. She put on her new running shoes, but without socks this time. At a nearby Sav-on drugstore, she bought a vinyl-strap folding lounge chair, beach towel, tube of tanning cream, picnic cooler, bag of ice, six-pack of diet soda, and a Travis McGee paperback by John D. MacDonald. She already had sunglasses.

She was back at Ironheart's house on Bougainvillea Way before two-thirty. She tried the doorbell again. He refused to answer.

Somehow she knew he was in there. Maybe *she* was a little psychic.

She carried the ice chest, folding lounger, and other items around the side of the house to the lawn in back. She set up the chair on the grass, just beyond the redwood-covered patio. In a few minutes, she was comfy.

In the MacDonald novel, Travis McGee was sweltering down there in Fort Lauderdale, where they were having a heatwave so intense it even took the bounce out of the beach bunnies. Holly had read the book before; she chose to reread it now because she had remembered that the plot unfolded against a background of tropical heat and humidity. Steamy Florida, rendered in MacDonald's vivid prose, made the dry air of Laguna Niguel seem less torrid by comparison, even though it had to be well over ninety degrees.

After about half an hour, she glanced at the house and saw Jim Ironheart standing at the big kitchen window. He was watching her.

She waved.

He did not wave back at her.

He walked away from the window but did not come outside.

Opening a diet soda, returning to the novel, she relished the feel of the sun on her bare legs. She was not worried about a burn. She already had a little tan. Besides, though blond and fair-skinned, she had a tanning gene that insured against a burn as long as she didn't indulge in marathon sun-bathing.

After a while, when she got up to readjust the lounger so she could lie on her stomach, she saw Jim Ironheart standing on the patio, just outside the sliding glass door of his family room. He was in rumpled slacks and a wrinkled T-shirt, unshaven. His hair was lank and oily. He didn't look well.

He was about fifteen feet away, so his voice carried easily to her: "What do you think you're doing?"

"Bronzing up a little."

"Please leave, Miss Thorne."

"I need to talk to you."

"We have nothing to talk about."

"Hah!"

He went back inside and slid the door shut. She heard the latch click.

After lying on her stomach for almost an hour, dozing instead of reading, she decided she'd had enough sun. Besides, at three-thirty in the afternoon, the best tanning rays were past.

She moved the lounger, cooler, and the rest of her paraphernalia onto the shaded patio. She opened a second diet soda and picked up the MacDonald novel again.

At four o'clock she heard the family-room door sliding open again. His footsteps approached and stopped behind her. He stood there for a while, evidently looking down at her. Neither of them spoke, and she pretended to keep reading.

His continued silence was eerie. She began to think about his dark side—the eight shotgun rounds he had pumped into Norman Rink in Atlanta, for one thing—and she grew increasingly nervous until she decided that he was *trying* to spook her.

When Holly picked up her can of soda from the top of the cooler, took a sip, sighed with pleasure at the taste, and put the can down again all without letting her hand tremble even once, Ironheart at last came around the lounge chair and stood where she could see him. He was still slovenly and unshaven. Dark circles ringed his eyes. He had an unhealthy pallor.

"What do you want from me?" he asked.

"That'll take a while to explain."

"I don't have a while."

"How long do you have?"

"One minute," he said.

She hesitated, then shook her head. "Can't do it in a minute. I'll just wait here till you've got more time."

He stared at her intimidatingly.

She found her place in the novel.

He said, "I could call the police, have you put off my property."

"Why don't you do that?" she said.

He stood there a few seconds longer, impatient and uncertain, then reentered the house. Slid the door shut. Locked it.

"Don't take forever," Holly muttered. "In about another hour, I'm gonna have to use your bathroom."

Around her, two hummingbirds drew nectar from the flowers, the shadows lengthened, and exploding bubbles made hollow ticking sounds inside her open can of soda.

Down in Florida, there were also hummingbirds and cool shadows, icy bottles of Dos Equis instead of diet cola, and Travis McGee was getting into deeper trouble by the paragraph.

Her stomach began to grumble. She had eaten breakfast at the airport in Dubuque, surprised that her appetite had not been suppressed forever by the macabre images burned into her mind at the crash scene. She had missed lunch, thanks to the stakeout; now she was famished. Life goes on.

Fifteen minutes ahead of Holly's bathroom deadline, Ironheart returned. He had showered and shaved. He was dressed in a blue boatneck shirt, white cotton slacks, and white canvas Top-Siders.

She was flattered by his desire to make a better appearance.

"Okay," he said, "what do you want?"

"I need to use your facilities first."

A long-suffering look lengthened his face. "Okay, okay, but then we talk, get it over with, and you go."

She followed him into the family room, which was adjacent to an open breakfast area, which was adjacent to an open kitchen. The mismatched furniture appeared to have been purchased on the cheap at a warehouse clearance sale immediately after he had graduated from college and taken his first teaching job. It was clean but well worn. Hundreds of paperback books filled free-standing cases. But there was no artwork of any kind on the walls, and no decor pieces such as vases or bowls or sculptures or potted plants lent warmth to the room.

He showed her the powder room off the main entrance foyer. No wallpaper, white paint. No designer soaps shaped like rosebuds, just a bar of Ivory. No colorful or embroidered handtowels, just a roll of Bounty standing on the counter.

As she closed the door, she looked back at him and said, "Maybe we could talk over an early supper. I'm starved."

When she finished in the bathroom, she peeked in his living room. It was decorated—to use the word as loosely as the language police would allow—in a style best described as Early Garage Sale, though it was even more Spartan than the family room. His house was surprisingly modest for a man who had won six million in the state lottery, but his furniture made the house seem Rockefellerian by comparison.

She went out to the kitchen and found him waiting at the round breakfast table.

"I thought you'd be cooking something," she said, pulling out a chair and sitting opposite him.

He was not amused. "What do you want?"

"Let me start by telling you what I *don't* want," she said. "I don't want to write about you, I've given up reporting, I've had it with journalism. Now, you believe that or not, but it's true. The good work you're doing can only be hampered if you're being hounded by media types, and lives will be lost that you might otherwise save. I see that now."

"Good."

"And I don't want to blackmail you. Anyway, judging by the unconscionably lavish style in which you live, I doubt you've got more than eighteen bucks left."

He did not smile. He just stared at her with those gas flame–blue eyes.

She said, "I don't want to inhibit your work or compromise it in any way. I don't want to venerate you as the Second Coming, marry you, bear your children, or extract from you the meaning of life. Anyway, only Elvis Presley knows the meaning of life, and he's in a state of suspended animation in an alien vault in a cave on Mars."

His face remained as immobile as stone. He was *tough*.

"What I want," Holly said, "is to satisfy my curiosity, learn how you do what you do, and why you do it." She hesitated. She took a deep breath. Here came the big one: "And I want to be part of it all."

"What do you mean?"

She spoke fast, running sentences together, afraid he would interrupt her before she got it all out, and never give her another chance to explain herself. "I want to work with you, help you, contribute to your mission, or whatever you call it, however you think of it, I want to save people, at least help *you* save them."

"There's nothing you could do."

"There must be something," she insisted.

"You'd only be in the way."

"Listen, I'm intelligent—"

"So what?"

"—well-educated—"

"So am I."

"—gutsy—"

"But I don't need you."

"—competent, efficient—"

"Sorry."

"Damn it!" she said, more frustrated than angry. "Let me be your secretary, even if you don't need one. Let me be your girl Friday, your good right hand—at least your *friend*."

He seemed unmoved by her plea. He stared at her for so long that she became uncomfortable, but she would not look away from him. She sensed that he used his singularly penetrating gaze as an instrument of control and intimidation, but she was not easily manipulated. She was determined not to let him shape this encounter before it had begun.

At last he said, "So you want to be my Lois Lane."

For a moment she had no idea what he was talking about. Then she remembered: Metropolis, the *Daily Planet*, Jimmy Olsen, Perry White, Lois Lane, Clark Kent, Superman.

Holly knew he was trying to irritate her. Making her angry was another way of manipulating her; if she became abrasive, he would have an excuse to turn her away. She was determined to remain calm and reasonably congenial in order to keep the door open between them.

But she could not sit still and control her temper at the same time. She needed to work off some of the energy of anger that was overcharging her batteries. She pushed her chair back, got up, and paced as she responded to him: "No, that's exactly what I *don't* want to be. I don't want to be your chronicler, intrepid girl reporter. I'm sick of journalism." Succinctly, she told him why. "I don't want to be your swooning admirer, either, or that well-meaning but bumbling gal who gets herself in trouble all the time and has to rely on you to save her from the evil clutches of Lex Luthor. Something amazing is happening here, and I want to be part of it. It's also dangerous, yeah, but I still want to be a part of it, because what you're doing is so . . . so meaningful. I want to contribute any way I can, do something more worthwhile with my life than I've done so far."

"Do-gooders are usually so full of themselves, so unconsciously arrogant, they do more damage than good," he said.

"I'm not a do-gooder. That's not how I see myself. I'm not at all interested in being praised for my generosity and self-sacrifice. I don't need to feel morally superior. Just *useful*."

"The world is full of do-gooders," he said, refusing to relent. "If I needed an assistant, which I don't, why would I choose you over all the *other* do-gooders out there?"

He was an impossible man. She wanted to smack him.

Instead she kept moving back and forth as she said, "Yesterday, when I crawled back into the plane for that little boy, for Norby, I just . . . well, I amazed myself. I didn't know I had anything like that in me. I wasn't brave, I was scared to death the whole time, but I got him out of there, and I never felt better about myself."

"You like the way people look at you when they know you're a hero," he said flatly.

She shook her head. "No, that's not it. Aside from one rescue worker, no one *knew* I'd pulled Norby out of there. I liked the way *I* looked at me after I'd done it, that's all."

"So you're hooked on risk, heroism, you're a courage junkie."

Now she wanted to smack him twice. In the face. *Crack, crack.* Hard enough to set his eyes spinning. It would make her feel so good.

She restrained herself. "Okay, fine, if that's the way you want to see it, then I'm a courage junkie."

He did not apologize. He just stared at her.

She said, "But that's better than inhaling a pound of cocaine up my nose every day, don't you think?"

He did not respond.

Getting desperate but trying not to show it, Holly said, "When it was all over yesterday, after I handed Norby to that rescue worker, you know what I felt? More than anything else? Not elation at saving him—that too, but not mainly that. And not pride or the thrill of defeating death myself. Mostly I felt *rage*. It surprised me, even scared me. I was so furious that a little boy almost died, that his uncle had died beside him, that he'd been trapped under those seats with corpses, that all of his innocence had been blown away and that he couldn't ever again just enjoy life the way a kid ought to be able to. I wanted to punch somebody, wanted to make somebody apologize to him for what he'd been through. But fate isn't a sleazeball in a cheap suit, you can't put the arm on fate and make it say it's sorry, all you can do is stew in your anger."

Her voice was not rising, but it was increasingly intense. She paced faster, more agitatedly. She was getting passionate instead of angry, which was even more certain to reveal the degree of her desperation. But she couldn't stop herself:

"Just stew in anger. Unless you're Jim Ironheart. *You* can do something about it, make a difference in a way nobody ever made a difference before. And now that I know about you, I can't just get on with my life, can't just shrug my shoulders and walk away, because you've given me a chance to find a strength in myself I didn't know I had, you've given me hope when I didn't even realize I was longing for it, you've shown me a way to satisfy a need that, until yesterday, I didn't even know I had, a need to fight back, to spit in Death's face. Damn it, you can't just close the door now and leave me standing out in the cold!"

He stared at her.

Congratulations, Thorne, she told herself scornfully. You were a monument to composure and restraint, a towering example of self-control.

He just stared at her.

She had met his cool demeanor with heat, had answered his highly effective silences with an ever greater cascade of words. One chance, that was all she'd had, and she'd blown it.

Miserable, suddenly drained of energy instead of overflowing with it, she sat down again. She propped her elbows on the table and put her face in her hands, not sure if she was going to cry or scream. She didn't do either. She just sighed wearily.

"Want a beer?" he asked.

"God, yes."

LIKE A BRUSH of flame, the westering sun slanted through the tilted plantation shutters on the breakfast-nook window, slathering bands of copper-gold fire on the ceiling. Holly slumped in her chair, and Jim leaned forward in his. She stared at him while he stared at his half-finished bottle of Corona.

"Like I told you on the plane, I'm not a psychic," he insisted. "I can't foresee things just because I want to. I don't have visions. It's a higher power working through me."

"You want to define that a little?"

He shrugged. "God."

"God's talking to you?"

"Not talking. I don't hear voices, His or anybody else's. Now and then I'm compelled to be in a certain place at a certain time . . ."

As best he could, he tried to explain how he had ended up at the Mc-Albury School in Portland and at the sites of the other miraculous rescues he had performed. He also told her about Father Geary finding him on the floor of the church, by the sanctuary railing, with the stigmata of Christ marking his brow, hands, and side.

It was off-the-wall stuff, a weird brand of mysticism that might have been concocted by an heretical Catholic and peyote-inspired Indian medicine man in association with a no-nonsense, Clint Eastwood-style cop. Holly was fascinated. But she said, "I can't honestly tell you I see God's big hand in this."

"I do," he said quietly, making it clear that his conviction was solid and in no need of her approval.

Nevertheless she said, "Sometimes you've had to be pretty damned violent, like with those guys who kidnapped Susie and her mother in the desert."

"They got what they deserved," he said flatly. "There's too much darkness in some people, corruption that could never be cleaned out in five lifetimes of rehabilitation. Evil is real, it walks the earth. Sometimes the devil works by persuasion. Sometimes he just sets loose these sociopaths who don't have a gene for empathy or one for compassion."

"I'm not saying you didn't *have* to be violent in some of these situations. Far as I can see, you had no choice. I just meant—it's hard to see God encouraging his messenger to pick up a shotgun."

He drank some beer. "You ever read the Bible?"

"Sure."

"Says in there that God wiped out the evil people in Sodom and Gomorrah with volcanoes, earthquakes, rains of fire. Flooded the whole world once, didn't He? Made the Red Sea wash over the pharaoh's soldiers, drowned them all. I don't think He's going to be skittish about a little old shotgun."

"I guess I was thinking about the God of the New Testament. Maybe you heard about Him—understanding, compassionate, merciful."

He fixed her with those eyes again, which could be so appealing that they made her knees weak or so cold they made her shiver. A moment ago they had been warm; now they were icy. If she'd had any doubt, she knew from his frigid response that he had not yet decided to welcome her into his life. "I've met up with some people who're such walking scum, it'd be an insult to animals to call them animals. If I thought God always dealt mercifully with their kind, I wouldn't want anything to do with God."

HOLLY STOOD AT the kitchen sink, cleaning mushrooms and slicing tomatoes, while Jim separated egg whites from yolks to make a pair of comparatively low-calorie omelettes.

"All the time, people are dying conveniently, right in your own backyard. But often you go clear across the country to save them."

"Once to France," he said, confirming her suspicion that he had ventured out of the country on his missions. "Once to Germany, twice to Japan, once to England."

"Why doesn't this higher power give you only local work?"

"I don't know."

"Have you ever wondered what's so special about the people you save? I mean—why them and not others?"

"Yeah. I've wondered about it. I see stories on the news every week about innocent people being murdered or dying in accidents right here in southern California, and I wonder why He didn't choose to save them instead of some boy in Boston. I just figure the boy in Boston—the devil was conspiring to take him before his time, and God used me to prevent that."

"So many of them are young."

"I've noticed that."

"But you don't know why?"

"Not a clue."

THE KITCHEN WAS redolent of cooking eggs, onions, mushrooms, and green peppers. Jim made one big omelette in a single pan, planning to cut it in half when it was done.

While Holly monitored the progress of the whole-wheat bread in the toaster, she said, "Why would God want you to save Susie and her mother out there in the desert—but not the girl's father?"

"I don't know."

"The father wasn't a bad man, was he?"

"No. Didn't seem to be."

"So why not save them all?"

"If He wants me to know, He'll tell me."

Jim's certainty about being in God's good grace and under His guidance, and his easy acceptance that God *wanted* some people to die and not others, made Holly uneasy.

On the other hand, how could he react to his extraordinary experience in any other way? No point in arguing with God.

She recalled an old saying, a real chestnut that had become a cliché in the hands of the pop psych crowd: God grant me the courage to change those things I can't accept, to accept those things I can't change, and the wisdom to know the difference. Cliché or not, that was an eminently sane attitude.

When the two pieces of bread popped up, she plucked them from the toaster. As she toasted two more, she said, "If God wanted to save Nicholas O'Conner from being fried when that power-company vault went up, why didn't He just prevent it from exploding in the first place?"

"I don't know."

"Doesn't it seem odd to you that God has to use you, run you clear across the country, throw you at the O'Conner boy an instant before that 17,000-volt line blows up? Why couldn't He just . . . oh, I don't know . . . just spit on the cable or something, fix it up with a little divine saliva before it went blooey? Or instead of sending you all the way to Atlanta to kill Norman Rink in that convenience store, why didn't God just tweak Norman's brain a little, give him a timely stroke?"

Jim artfully tilted the pan to turn over the omelette. "Why did He make mice to torment people and cats to kill the mice? Why did He create aphids that kill plants, then ladybugs to eat the aphids? And why didn't He give us eyes in the back of our head—when He gave us so many reasons to need them there?"

She finished lightly buttering the first two slices of toast. "I see what you're saying. God works in mysterious ways."

"Very."

THEY ATE AT the breakfast table. In addition to toast, they had sliced tomatoes and cold bottles of Corona with the omelettes.

The purple cloth of twilight slid across the world outside, and the undraped form of night began to reveal itself.

Holly said, "You aren't entirely a puppet in these situations."

"Yes, I am."

"You have some power to determine the outcome."

"None."

"Well, God sent you on Flight Two forty-six to save just the Dubroveks."

"That's right."

"But then you took matters into your own hands and saved more than just Christine and Casey. How many were supposed to die?"

"A hundred and fifty-one."

"And how many actually died?"

"Forty-seven."

"Okay, so you saved a hundred and two more lives than He sent you to save."

"A hundred and three, counting yours—but only because He allowed me to do it, helped me to do it."

"What—you're saying God wanted you to save just the Dubroveks, but then He changed His mind?"

"I guess so."

"God isn't sure what He wants?"

"I don't know."

"God is sometimes confused?"

"I don't know."

"God is a waffler?"

"Holly, I just don't know."

"Good omelette."

"Thank you."

"I have trouble understanding why God would ever change His mind about anything. After all, He's infallible, right? So He can't have made the wrong decision the first time."

"I don't concern myself with questions like that. I just don't think about it."

"Obviously," she said.

He glared at her, and she felt the full effect of his eyes in their arctic mode. Then focusing on his food and beer, he refused to respond to Holly's next few conversational gambits.

She realized that she was no closer to winning his trust than she had been when he had reluctantly invited her in from the patio. He was still judging her, and on points she was probably losing. What she needed was a solid knockout punch, and she thought she knew what it was, but she didn't want to use it until the right moment.

When Jim finished eating, he looked up from his empty plate and said, "Okay, I've listened to your pitch, I've fed you, and now I want you to go."

"No, you don't."

He blinked. "Miss Thorne—"

"You called me Holly before."

"Miss Thorne, please don't make me *throw* you out."

"You don't want me to go," Holly said, striving to sound more confident than she felt. "At all the scenes of these rescues, you've given only your first name. No one's learned anything more about you. Except me. You told me you lived in southern California. You told me your last name was Ironheart."

"I never said you were a bad reporter. You're good at prying information—"

"I didn't pry. You gave it. And if it wasn't something you wanted to give, a grizzly bear with an engineering degree and crowbar couldn't pry it out of you. I want another beer."

"I asked you to go."

"Don't stir yourself. I know where you keep the suds."

She got up, stepped to the refrigerator, and withdrew another bottle of Corona. She was walking on the wild side now, at least for her, but a third beer gave her an excuse—even if a flimsy one—to stay and argue with him. She had downed three bottles last night, at the motel cocktail lounge in Dubuque. But then she had still been saturated with adrenaline, as superalert and edgy as a Siamese cat on Benzedrine, which canceled out the alcohol as fast as it entered her bloodstream. Even so, she had hit the bed as hard as a lumberjack who'd downed a dozen boilermakers. If she passed out on

Ironheart, she'd no doubt wake up in her car, out in the street, and she would never get inside his house again. She opened the beer and returned to the table with it.

"You *wanted* me to find you," she said as she sat down.

He regarded her with all the warmth of a dead penguin frozen to an ice floe. "I did, huh?"

"Absolutely. That's why you told me your last name and where I could find you."

He said nothing.

"And you remember your last words to me at the airport in Portland?"

"No."

"It was the best come-on line any guy's ever dropped on me."

He waited.

She made him wait a little longer while she took a sip of beer straight from the bottle. "Just before you closed the car door and went into the terminal, you said, 'So are you, Miss Thorne.' "

"Doesn't sound like much of a come-on line to me."

"It was romantic as hell."

" 'So are you, Miss Thorne.' And what had you just said to me. 'You're an asshole, Mr. Ironheart'?"

"Ho, ho, ho," she said. "Try to spoil it, go ahead, but you can't. I'd told you that your modesty was refreshing, and you said, 'So are you, Miss Thorne.' My heart just now went pitty-pat-pitty-pat again, remembering it. Oh, you knew just what you were doing, you smoothie. Told me your name, told me where you lived, gave me a lot of those eyes, those damned eyes, played coy, then hit me with 'So are you, Miss Thorne,' and walked away like Bogart."

"I don't think you should have any more of that beer."

"Yeah? Well, I think I'll sit here all night, drinking one of 'em after another."

He sighed. "In that case, I'd better have another one myself."

He got another beer and sat down again.

Holly figured she was making progress.

Or maybe he was setting her up. Maybe getting cozy over Corona was a trick of some kind. He was clever, all right. Maybe he was going to try to drink her under the table. Well, he'd lose *that* one, because she'd be under the table long before him!

"You wanted me to find you," she told him.

He said nothing.

"You know why you wanted me to find you?"

He said nothing.

"You wanted me to find you because you really did think I was refreshing, and you're the loneliest, sorriest guy between here and Hardrock, Missouri."

He said nothing. He was good at that. He was the best guy in the world at saying nothing at just the right time.

She said, "You make me want to smack you."

He said nothing.

Whatever confidence the Corona had given her suddenly began to drain away. She sensed that she was losing again. For a couple of rounds, there, she had definitely been winning on points, but now she was being beaten back by his silence.

"Why are all these boxing metaphors running through my head?" she asked him. "I hate boxing."

He slugged down some of his Corona and, with a nod, indicated her bottle, from which she had drunk only a third. "You really insist on finishing that?"

"Hell, yes." She was aware that the brewski was beginning to affect her, perhaps dangerously, but she was still plenty sober enough to recognize that the moment had come for her knockout punch. "If you don't tell me about that place, I'm going to sit here and drink myself into a fat, slovenly, alcoholic old crone. I'm going to die here at the age of eighty-two, with a liver the size of Vermont."

"Place?" He looked baffled. "What place?"

Now. She chose a soft but clear whisper in which to deliver the punch: "The windmill."

He didn't exactly fall to the canvas, and no cartoon stars swarmed around his head, but Holly could see that he had been rocked.

"You've been to the windmill?" he asked.

"No. You mean it's a real place?"

"If you don't know that much, then how could you know about it at all?"

"Dreams. Windmill dreams. Each of the last three nights."

He paled. The overhead light was not on. They were sitting in shadows, illuminated only by the secondhand glow of the range-hood and sink lights in the kitchen and by a table lamp in the adjacent family room, but Holly saw him go pale under his tan. His face seemed to hover before her in the gloom like the face-shaped wing configuration of a big snow-white moth.

The extraordinary vividness and unusual nature of the nightmare—and the fact that the effects of the dream had continued after she had awakened in her motel room—had encouraged her to believe that it was somehow connected with Jim Ironheart. Two encounters with the paranormal in such close succession *had* to be linked. But she was relieved, all the same, when his stunned reaction confirmed her suspicion.

"Limestone walls," she said. "Wooden floor. A heavy wooden door, banded in iron, that opens on some limestone steps. A yellow candle in a blue dish."

"I've dreamed about it for years," he said softly. "Once or twice a month. Never more often than that. Until the last three nights. But how can we be having the same dream?"

"Where's the real windmill?"

"On my grandparents' farm. North of Santa Barbara. In the Santa Ynez Valley."

"Did something terrible happen to you there, or what?"

He shook his head. "No. Not at all. I loved that place. It was . . . a sanctuary."

"Then why did you go pale when I mentioned it?"

"Did I?"

"Picture an albino cat chasing a mouse around a corner and running into a Doberman. That pale."

"Well, when I dream of the mill, it's always frightening—"

"Don't I know it. But if it was a good place in your life, a sanctuary like you say, then why does it feature in nightmares?"

"I don't know."

"Here we go again."

"I really don't," he insisted. "Why did *you* dream about it, if you've never even been there?"

She drank more beer, which did not clarify her thinking. "Maybe because you're projecting your dream at me. As a way to sort of make a connection between us, draw me to you."

"Why would I want to draw you to me?"

"Thanks a lot."

"Anyway, like I told you before, I'm no psychic, I don't have abilities like that. I'm just an instrument."

"Then it's this higher power of yours," she said. "It's sending me the same dream because it wants us to connect."

He wiped one hand down his face. "This is too much for me right now. I'm so damned tired."

"Me, too. But it's only nine-thirty, and we've still got a lot to talk about."

"I only slept about an hour last night," he said.

He really did look exhausted. A shave and a shower had made him presentable, but the bruise-dark rings around his eyes were getting darker; and he had not regained color in his face after turning pale at the mention of her windmill dreams.

He said, "We can pick this up in the morning."

She frowned. "No way. I'll come back in the morning, and you won't let me in."

"I'll let you in."

"That's what you say now."

"If you're having that dream, then you're part of this whether I like it or not."

His tone of voice had gone from cool to cold again, and it was clear that what he meant by "whether I like it or not" was really "even though I don't like it."

He was a loner, evidently always had been. Viola Moreno, who had great affection for him, claimed he was well-liked by his students and colleagues. She'd spoken of a fundamental sadness in him, however, that separated him from other people, and since quitting his teaching position, he had seen little of Viola or his other friends from that life. Though intrigued by the news that he and Holly were sharing a dream, though he had called her "refreshing," though he was to some degree attracted to her, he obviously resented her intrusion into his solitude.

Holly said, "No good. You'll be gone when I get here in the morning, I won't know where you went, maybe you'll never come back."

He had no energy for resistance. "Then stay the night."

"You have a spare bedroom?"

"Yeah. But there's no spare bed. You can sleep on the family room couch, I guess, but it's damned old and not too comfortable."

She carried her half-empty beer into the adjacent family room, and tested the sagging, brown sofa. "It'll be good enough."

"Whatever you want." He seemed indifferent, but she sensed that his indifference was a pretense.

"You have any spare pajamas?"

"Jesus."

"Well, I'm sorry, but I didn't bring any."

"Mine'll be too big for you."

"Just makes them more comfortable. I'd like to shower, too. I'm sticky from tanning lotion and being in the sun all afternoon."

With the put-upon air of a man who had found his least favorite relative standing on his doorstep unannounced, he took her upstairs, showed her the guest bath, and got a pair of pajamas and a set of towels for her.

"Try to be quiet," he said. "I plan to be sound asleep in five minutes."

LUXURIATING IN THE fall of hot water and clouds of steam, Holly was pleased that the shower did not take the edge off her beer buzz. Though she had slept better last night than Ironheart claimed to have, she had not gotten a solid eight hours in the past few days, and she was looking forward to a Corona-induced sleep even on the worn and lumpy sofa.

At the same time, she was uneasy about the continued fuzziness of her mind. She needed to keep her wits about her. After all, she was in the house of an undeniably strange man who was largely a cipher to her, a walking mystery. She understood little of what was in his heart, which pumped secrets and shadows in greater quantity than blood. For all his coolness toward her, he seemed basically a good man with benign intentions, and it was difficult to believe that he was a threat to her. On the other hand, it was not unusual to see a news story about a berserk mass murderer who—after brutally slaying his friends, family, and coworkers—was described by his astonished neighbors as "a really nice guy." For all she knew, in spite of his claim to be the avatar of God, by day Jim Ironheart heroically risked his own life to save the lives of strangers—and, by night, tortured kittens with maniacal glee.

Nevertheless, after she dried off on the clean-smelling, fluffy bath towel, she took another long swallow of her Corona. She decided that a full night of deep and dreamless sleep was worth the risk of being butchered in her bed.

She put on his pajamas, rolled up the cuffs of the pants and the sleeves.

Carrying her bottle of Corona, which still contained a swallow or two, she quietly opened the bathroom door and stepped into the second-floor hallway. The house was eerily silent.

Heading toward the stairs, she passed the open door of the master bedroom and glanced inside. Extension-arm brass reading lamps were mounted on the wall on both sides of the bed, and one of them cast a narrow wedge of amber light on the rumpled sheets. Jim was lying on his back in bed, his arms folded on the two pillows under his head, and he seemed to be awake.

She hesitated, then stepped into the open doorway. "Thanks," she said, speaking softly in case he was asleep, "I feel a lot better."

"Good for you."

Holly entered the room and moved close enough to the bed to see his blue eyes shining in the backsplash of the lamp. The covers were pulled up past his navel, but he was not wearing pajama tops. His chest and arms were lean but well-muscled.

She said, "Thought you'd be asleep by now."

"Want to be, need to be, but I can't shut my mind off."

Looking down at him, she said, "Viola Moreno says there's a deep sadness in you."

"Been busy, haven't you?"

She took a small swallow of Corona. One left. She sat down on the edge of the bed. "Do your grandparents still have the farm with the windmill?"

"They're dead."

"I'm sorry."

"Grandma died five years ago, Grandpa eight months later—as if he really didn't want to go on without her. They had good, full lives. But I miss them."

"You have anybody?"

"Two cousins in Akron," he said.

"You stay in touch?"

"Haven't seen them in twenty years."

She drank the last of the Corona. She put the empty bottle on the nightstand.

For a few minutes neither of them spoke. The silence was not awkward. Indeed, it was comfortable.

She got up and went around to the other side of the bed. She pulled back the covers, stretched out beside him, and put her head on the other two pillows.

Apparently, he was not surprised. Neither was she.

After a while, they held hands, lying side by side, staring at the ceiling.

She said, "Must've been hard, losing your parents when you were just ten."

"Real bad."

"What happened to them?"

He hesitated. "A traffic accident."

"And you went to live with your grandparents?"

"Yeah. The first year was the hardest. I was . . . in bad shape. I spent a lot of time in the windmill. It was my special place, where I went to play . . . to be alone."

"I wish we'd been kids together," she said.

"Why?"

She thought of Norby, the boy she had pulled from the sarcophagus under the DC-10's overturned seats. "So I could've known you before your parents died, what you were like then, untouched."

Another stretch of time passed in silence.

When he spoke, his voice was so low that Holly could barely hear it above the thumping of her own heart: "Viola has a sadness in her, too. She looks like the happiest lady in the world, but she lost her husband in Vietnam, never got over it. Father Geary, the priest I told you about, he looks like every devout parish rector from every old sentimental Catholic movie ever made in the thirties and forties, but when I met him he was weary and unsure of his calling. And you . . . well, you're pretty and amusing, and you have an air of efficiency about you, but I'd never have guessed that you could be as relentless as you are. You give the impression of a woman who moves easy through life, interested in life and in her work, but never moving against a current, always with it, easy. Yet you're really like a bulldog when you get your teeth in something."

Staring at the dapple of light and shadow on the ceiling, holding his strong hand, Holly considered his statement for a while. Finally she said, "What's your point?"

"People are always more . . . complex than you figure."

"Is that just an observation . . . or a warning?"

He seemed surprised by her question. "Warning?"

"Maybe you're warning me that you're not what you seem to be."

After another long pause, he said, "Maybe."

She matched his silence. Then she said, "I guess I don't care."

He turned toward her. She moved against him with a shyness that she had not felt in many years. His first kiss was gentle, and more intoxicating than three bottles or three cases of Corona.

Holly realized she'd been deceiving herself. She had needed the beer not to soothe her nerves, not to insure an uninterrupted night of sleep, but to give her the courage to seduce him—or to be seduced. She had sensed that he was abysmally lonely, and she had told him so. Now she understood that her loneliness had exceeded his, and that only the smallest part of her desolation of spirit had resulted from her disenchantment with journalism; most of it was simply the result of being alone, for the most part, all of her adult life.

Two pajama bottoms and one top seemed to dissolve between them like clothes sometimes evaporate in erotic dreams. She moved her hands over him with increasing excitement, marveling that the sense of touch could convey such intricacies of shape and texture, or give rise to such exquisite longings.

She had a ridiculously romantic idea of what it would be like to make love to him, a dreamy-eyed girl's fantasy of unmatched passion, of sweet tenderness and pure hot sex in perfect balance, every muscle in both of them flexing and contracting in sublime harmony or, at times, in breathless counterpoint, each invasive stroke a testament to mutual surrender, two becoming one, the outer world of reason overwhelmed by the inner world of feeling, no wrong word spoken, no sigh mistimed, bodies moving and meshing in precisely the same mysterious rhythms by which the great invisible tidal forces of the universe ebbed and flowed, elevating the act above mere biology and making of it a mystical experience. Her expectations proved, of course, to be ridiculous. In reality, it was more tender, more fierce, and far better than her fantasy.

THEY FELL ASLEEP like spoons in a drawer, her belly against his back, her loins against his warm bottom. Hours later, in those reaches of the night that were usually—but no longer—the loneliest of all, they woke to the same quiet alarm of renewed desire. He turned to her, she welcomed him, and this time they moved together with an even greater urgency, as if the first time had not taken the edge off their need but had sharpened it the way one dose of heroin only increases the addict's desire for the next.

At first, looking up into Jim's beautiful eyes, Holly felt as if she were gazing into the pure fire of his soul. Then he gripped her by the sides, half lifting her off the mattress as he eased deep into her, and she felt the scratches burning in her flanks and remembered the claws of the thing that had stepped magically out of a dream. For an instant, with pain flashing in her shallow wounds, her perception shifted, and she had the queer feeling that it was a cold blue fire into which she gazed, burning without heat. But that was only a reaction to the stinging scratches and the pain-engendered memory of the nightmare. When he slid his hands off her sides and under her, lifting, she rose to meet him, and he was all warmth now, not the faintest chill about him. Together they generated enough heat to sear away that brief image of a soul on ice.

THE FROST-PALE GLOW of the unseen moon backlit banks of coaly clouds that churned across the night sky.

Unlike in other recent dreams, Holly was standing outside on a graveled path that led between a pond and a cornfield toward the door in the base of the old windmill. The limestone structure rose above her at a severe angle, recognizably a mill but nonetheless an alien place, unearthly.

The huge sails, ragged with scores of broken or missing vanes, were silhouetted against the foreboding sky and angled like a tilted cross. Although a blustery wind sent moon-silvered ripples across the ink-dark pond and rattled the nearby cornstalks, the sails were still. The mill obviously had been inoperable for many years, and the mechanisms were most likely too rusted to allow the sails to turn.

A spectral muddy-yellow light flickered at the narrow windows of the upper room. Beyond the glass, strange shadows moved across the interior limestone walls of that high chamber.

She didn't want to get any closer to the building, had never been more frightened of a place in her life, but she was unable to halt herself. She was drawn forward as if she were the spellbound thrall of some powerful sorcerer.

In the pond to her left, something was wrong with the mooncast reflection of the windmill, and she turned to look at it. The pattern of light and shade on the water was reversed from what it should have been. The mill shadow was not a dark geometric form imposed on the water over the filigree of moonlight; instead, the image of the mill was brighter than the surface of the pond around it, as if the mill were luminous, the brightest object in the night, when in fact its stones rose in an ebony and forbidding pile. Where the high windows were filled with lambent light in the real mill, black rectangles floated in the impossible reflection, like the empty eyeholes in a fleshless skull.

Creak . . . creak . . . creak . . .

She looked up.

The massive sails were trembling in the wind and beginning to move. They forced the corroded gears that drove the windshaft and, in turn, the grinding stones in the millroom at its base.

Wanting only to wake up or, failing that, to flee back along the gravel path over which she had come, Holly drifted inexorably forward. The giant sails began to turn clockwise, gaining speed, producing less creaking as the gears unfroze. It seemed to her that they were like the fingers of a monstrous hand, and the jagged end of every broken vane was a claw.

She reached the door.

She did not want to go inside. She knew that within lay a hell of some kind, as bad as the pits of torture described by any fire-and-brimstone preacher who had ever thundered a sermon in old Salem. If she went in there, she would never come out alive.

The sails swooped down at her, passing just a couple of feet over her head, the splintered wood reaching for her: *Whoosh, whoosh, whoosh, whoosh.*

In the grip of a trance even more commanding than her terror, she opened the door. She stepped across the threshold. With the malevolent animation that objects possessed only in dreams, the door pulled out of her hand, slammed shut behind her.

Ahead lay the lightless lower room of the mill, in which the worn stone wheels ground against each other.

To her left, barely visible in the gloom, stairs led up. Ululant squeals and haunting cries echoed from above, like the night concert performed by the wildlife in a jungle, except none of these voices was quite that of a panther or monkey or bird or hyena. Electronic sounds were part of the mix, and what seemed to be the brittle shrieks of insects passed through a stereo amplifier. Underlying the cacophony was a monotonous, throbbing, three-note bass refrain that reverberated in the stone walls of the stairwell and, before she had climbed halfway to the second floor, in Holly's bones as well.

She passed a narrow window on her left. An extended series of lightning bolts crackled across the vault of the night, and at the foot of the mill, like a trick mirror in a funhouse, the dark pond turned transparent. Its depths were revealed, as though the lightning came from under the water, and Holly saw an infinitely strange shape resting on the bottom. She squinted, trying to get a better look at the object, but the lightning sputtered out.

The merest glimpse of the thing, however, sent a cold wind through the hollows of her bones.

She waited, hoping for more lightning, but the night remained as opaque as tar, and black rain suddenly spattered against the window. Because she was halfway to the second floor of the mill, more muddy-orange and yellow light flickered around her than had reached her at the foot of the stairs. The window glass, backed by utter darkness now and painted with sufficient luminescence to serve as a dim mirror, presented her reflection.

But the face she possessed in this dream was not her own. It belonged to a woman twenty years older than Holly, to whom she bore no resemblance.

She'd never before had a dream in which she occupied the body of another person. But now she understood why she had been unable to turn back from the mill when she'd been outside, and why she was unable to stop herself from climbing to the high room even though, on one level, she knew she was dreaming. Her lack of control was not the usual helplessness that transformed dreams into nightmares, but the result of sharing the body of a stranger.

The woman turned from the window and continued upward toward the unearthly shrieks, cries, and whispers that echoed down to her with the fluctuant light. Around her the limestone walls pounded with the tripartite bass beat, as if the mill were alive and had a massive three-chambered heart.

Stop, turn back, you're going to die up there, Holly shouted, but the woman could not hear her. Holly was only an observer in her own dream, not an active participant, unable to influence events.

Step by step. Higher.

The iron-bound timber door stood open.

She crossed the threshold. Into the high room.

The first thing she saw was the boy. He was standing in the middle of the room, terrified. His small hands, curled in fists, were at his sides. A three-inch-diameter decorative candle stood in a blue dish at his feet. A hardcover book lay beside the dish, and she glimpsed the word "mill" on the colorful dustjacket.

Turning to look at her, his beautiful blue eyes darkened by terror, the boy said, "I'm scared, help me, the walls, the *walls!*"

She realized that the single candle was not producing all of the peculiar glow suffusing the room. Other light glimmered in the walls, as if they were not made of solid limestone but of semitransparent and magically radiant quartz in shades of amber. At once she saw that something was alive *within* the stone, something luminous which could move through solid matter as easily as a swimmer could move through water.

The wall swelled and throbbed.

"It's coming," the boy said with evident fear but also with what might have been a perverse excitement, "and nobody can stop it!"

Suddenly it was born out of the wall. The curve of mortared blocks split like the spongy membrane of an insect's egg. And taking shape from a core of foul muck where limestone should have been—

"No!"

Choking on a scream, Holly woke.

She sat up in bed, something touched her, and she wrenched away from it. Because the room was awash in morning light, she saw that it was only Jim.

A dream. Just a dream.

As had happened two nights ago in the Laguna Hills Motor Inn, however, the creature of the dream was trying to force its way into the waking world. It was not coming through a wall this time. The ceiling. Directly over the bed. The white-painted drywall was no longer white or dry, but mottled amber and brown, semitransparent and luminous as the stone in the dream had been, oozing a noxious mucus, bulging as some shadowy entity struggled to be born into the bedroom.

The dream-thing's thunderous three-part heartbeat—*lub-dub-DUB, lub-dub-DUB*—shuddered through the house.

Jim rolled off the bed and onto his feet. He had slipped into his pajama bottoms again during the night, just as Holly had slipped into the roomy top which hung halfway to her knees. She scrambled to his side. They stared up in horror at the pulsing birth sac which the ceiling had become, and at the shadowy writhing form struggling to breach that containing membrane.

Most frightening of all—this apparition was in daylight. The plantation shutters had not been completely closed over the windows, and slats of morning sunshine banded the room. When something from Beyond found you in the dead hours of the night, you half expected it. But sunshine was supposed to banish all monsters.

Jim put a hand against Holly's back, pushed her toward the open door to the hallway. "Go, get out!"

She took only two steps in that direction before the door slammed shut of its own accord. As if an exceptionally powerful poltergeist were at work, a mahogany highboy, as old and well-used as everything in the house, erupted away from the wall beside her, almost knocking her down. It flew across the bedroom, slammed into the door. A dresser and a chair followed that tall chest of drawers, effectively barricading the only exit.

The windows in the far wall presented an avenue of escape, but they would have to crouch to slip under the increasingly distended central portion of the ceiling. Having accepted the illogic of the waking nightmare, Holly was now loath to press past that greasy and obscenely throbbing pouch, for fear that it would split open as she moved under it, and that the creature within would seize her.

Jim pulled her back with him into the adjoining bathroom. He kicked the door shut.

Holly swung around, searching. The only window was set high and was too small to provide a way out.

The bathroom walls were untainted by the organic transformation that had overcome the bedroom, but they still shook with the triple bass thud of the inhuman heartbeat.

"What the hell is that?" he demanded.

"The Enemy," she said at once, surprised that he didn't know. "The Enemy, from the dream."

Above them, starting from the partition that the bath shared with the bedroom, the white ceiling began to discolor as if abruptly saturated with red blood, brown bile. The sheen of semigloss paint on drywall metamorphosed into a biological surface and began to throb in time with the thunderous heartbeat.

Jim pulled her into a corner by the vanity, and she huddled helplessly against him. Beyond the pregnant droop of the lowering ceiling, she saw repulsive movement like the frenzied squirming of a million maggots.

The thudding heartbeat increased in volume, booming around them.

She heard a wet, tearing sound. None of this could be happening, yet it was, and that sound made it more real than the things she was seeing with her own eyes, because it was such a filthy sound and so hideously intimate, too *real* for a delusion or a dream.

The door crashed open, and the ceiling burst overhead, showering them with debris.

But with that implosion, the power of the lingering nightmare was exhausted, and reality finally, fully reasserted itself. Nothing monstrous surged through the open door; only the sun-filled bedroom lay beyond. Although the ceiling had looked entirely organic when it had burst in upon them, no trace of its transformed state remained; it was only a ceiling again. The rain of debris included chunks of wallboard, flaked and powdered drywall paste, splinters of wood, and wads of fluffy Fiberglas insulation—but nothing alive.

The hole itself was astonishing enough to Holly.

Two nights ago, in the motel, though the wall had bulged and rippled as if alive, it had returned to its true composition without a crack. No evidence of the dream-creature's intrusion had been left behind except the scratches in her sides, which a psychologist might have said were self-inflicted. When the dust settled, everything might have been just a fantastically detailed delusion.

But the mess in which they were now standing was no delusion. The pall of white dust in the air was real.

In a state of shock, Jim took her hand and led her out of the bathroom. The bedroom ceiling had not crashed down. It was as it had been last night: smooth, white. But the furniture was piled up against the door as if washed there by a flood.

Madness favored darkness, but light was the kingdom of reason. If the waking world provided no sanctuary from nightmares, if daylight offered no sanctuary from unreason, then there was no sanctuary anywhere, anytime, for anyone.

2 The attic light, a single sixty-watt bulb dangling from a beam, did not illuminate every corner of that cramped and dusty space. Jim probed into the many recesses with a flashlight, edged around heating ducts, peered behind each of the two fireplace chimneys, searching for . . . whatever had torn apart the bathroom ceiling. He had no idea what he expected to find. Besides the flashlight, he carried a loaded revolver. The thing that destroyed the ceiling had not descended into the bathroom, so it had to be in the attic above. However, because he lived with a minimum of possessions, Jim had nothing to store up there under the roof, which left few possible hiding places. He was soon satisfied that those high reaches of his house were untenanted except by spiders and by a small colony of wasps that had constructed a nest in a junction of rafters.

Nothing could have escaped those confines, either. Aside from the trapdoor by which he had entered, the only exits from the attic were the ventilation cut-outs in opposing eaves. Each was about two feet long and twelve inches high, covered with tightly fitted screens that could be removed only with a screwdriver. Both screens were secure.

Part of that space had plank flooring, but in some places nothing but insulation lay between the exposed floor studs, which were also the ceiling studs of the rooms below. Duck-walking on those parallel supports, Jim cautiously approached the rupture above the master bathroom. He peered down at the debris-strewn floor where he and Holly had been standing.

What in the hell had happened?

At last conceding that he would find no answers up there, he returned to the open access and climbed down into the second-floor linen closet. He folded up the accordion ladder into the closet ceiling, which neatly closed off the attic entrance.

Holly was waiting for him in the hallway. "Well?"

"Nothing," he said.

"I knew there wouldn't be."

"What happened here?"

"It's like in the dream."

"What dream?" he demanded.

"You said you've had the windmill dreams, too."

"I do."

"Then you know about the heartbeat in the walls."

"No."

"And the way the walls change."

"No, none of that, for Christ's sake! In my dream, I'm in the high room of the windmill, there's a candle, rain at the windows."

She remembered how surprised he had been at the sight of the bedroom ceiling distended and strange above them.

He said, "In the dream, I have a sense that something's coming, something frightening and terrible—"

"The Enemy," she said.

"Yes! Whatever that might be. But it never comes, not in *my* dreams. I always wake up before it comes."

He stalked down the hall and into the master bedroom, and she followed him. Standing beside the battered furniture that he had shoved away from the door, he stared up in consternation at the undamaged ceiling.

"I saw it," he said, as if she had called him a liar.

"I know you did," she said. "I saw it, too."

He turned to her, looking more desperate than she had seen him even aboard the doomed DC-10. "Tell me about your dreams, I want to hear all of them, every detail."

"Later, I'll tell you everything. First let's shower and get dressed. I want out of this place."

"Yeah, okay, me too."

"I guess you realize where we've got to go."

He hesitated.

She answered for him, "The windmill."

He nodded.

They showered together in the guest bathroom, only to save time—and because both of them were too edgy to be alone at the moment. She supposed that, in a different mood, she would have found the experience pleasantly erotic. But it was surprisingly platonic, considering the fierce passion of the night just passed.

He touched her only when they had stepped out of the shower and were hurriedly toweling dry. He leaned close, kissed the corner of her mouth, and said, "What have I gotten you into, Holly Thorne?"

LATER, WHILE JIM hurriedly packed a suitcase, Holly wandered only as far as the upstairs study, which was next to his bedroom. The place had a disused look. A thin layer of dust covered the top of the desk.

Like the rest of the house, his study was humble. The cheap desk had probably been purchased at a cut-rate office-supplies warehouse. The other furniture included just two lamps, an armchair on a wheel-and-swivel base, two free-standing bookcases overflowing with worn volumes, and a worktable as bare as the long-unused desk.

All of the two hundred or more books were about religion: fat histories of Islam, Judaism, Buddhism, Zen Buddhism, Christianity, Hinduism, Taoism, Shintoism, and others; the collected works of St. Thomas Aquinas, Martin Luther; *Scientists and Their Gods*; the Bible in several versions—Douay, King James, American Standard; the Koran; the Torah, including the Old Testament and the Talmud; the Tripitaka of Buddhism, the Agama of Hinduism, the Zend-Avesta of Zoroastrianism, and the Veda of Brahmanism.

In spite of the curious completeness of that part of his personal library, the most interesting thing in the room was the gallery of photographs that occupied two walls. Of the thirty-some 8 × 10 prints, a few were in color but most were black and white. The same three people featured in all of them: a strikingly lovely brunette, a good-looking man with bold features and thinning hair, and a child who could be no one but Jim Ironheart. Those eyes. One photograph showed Jim with the couple—obviously his parents—when he was only an infant swaddled in a blanket, but in the others he was not much younger than four and never older than about ten.

When he'd been ten, of course, his parents had died.

Some photos showed young Jim with his dad, some with his mom, and Holly assumed the missing parent had always been the one with the camera. A handful included all three Ironhearts. Over the years, the mother only grew more striking; the father's hair continued to thin, but he appeared to be happier as time passed; and Jim, taking a lesson from his mother, became steadily better looking.

Often the backdrop of the picture was a famous landmark or the sign for one. Jim and both parents in front of Radio City Music Hall when he'd been about six. Jim and his father on the boardwalk at Atlantic City when Jim was four or five. Jim and his mother at a sign for Grand Canyon National Park, with a panoramic vista behind them. All three Ironhearts in front of Sleeping Beauty Castle in the heart of Disneyland, when Jim was only seven or eight. Beale Street in Memphis. The sun-splashed Fontainebleau Hotel in Miami Beach. An observation deck overlooking the faces of Mount Rushmore. Buckingham Palace in London. The Eiffel Tower. The Tropicana Hotel, Las Vegas. Niagara Falls. They seemed to have been everywhere.

In every case, no matter who was holding the camera or where they were, those in the shot looked genuinely happy. Not one face in one print was frozen in an insincere smile, or caught with one of those snap-the-damn-picture expressions of impatience that could be found in abundance in most family photo albums. Often, they were laughing instead of merely smiling, and in several instances they were caught in the middle of horseplay of one kind or another. All three were touchers, too, not simply standing side by side or in brittle poses. They were usually shown with their arms around one another, sometimes hugging, occasionally kissing one another on the cheek or casually expressing affection in some fashion.

The boy in the photographs revealed no hint of the sometimes moody adult he would become, and Holly could see that the untimely death of his parents had changed him profoundly. The carefree, grinning boy in the photographs had been lost forever.

One black-and-white particularly arrested her. It showed Mr. Ironheart sitting on a straight-backed chair. Jim, maybe seven years old, was on his father's lap. They were in tuxedos. Mrs. Ironheart stood behind her husband, her hand on his shoulder, wearing a slinky sequined cocktail dress that emphasized her wonderful figure. They faced the camera directly. Unlike the other shots, this one was carefully posed, with nothing but a piece of artfully draped cloth as a backdrop, obviously set up by a professional photographer.

"They were wonderful," Jim said from the doorway. She had not heard him approaching. "No kid ever had better folks than them."

"You traveled a lot."

"Yeah. They were always going somewhere. They loved to show me new places, teach me things firsthand. They would've made wonderful schoolteachers, let me tell you."

"What work did they do?"

"My dad was an accountant at Warner Brothers."

"The movie studio?"

"Yeah." Jim smiled. "We lived in L.A. Mom—she wanted to be an actress, but she never got a lot of jobs. So mostly she was a hostess at a restaurant on Melrose Avenue, not far from the Paramount lot."

"You were happy, weren't you?"

"Always."

She pointed to the photo in which the three of them were dressed with glittery formality. "Special occasion?"

"Times just the two of them should have celebrated, like wedding anniversaries, they insisted on including me. They always made me feel special, wanted, loved. I was seven years old when that photo was taken, and I remember them making big plans that night. They were going to be married a hundred years, they said, and be happier each year than the one before, have lots more children, own a big house, see every corner of the world before they died together in their sleep. But just three years later they were . . . gone."

"I'm sorry, Jim."

He shrugged. "It's a long time ago. Twenty-five years." He looked at his wristwatch. "Come on, let's go. It'll take us four hours to reach the farm, and it's already nine o'clock."

AT THE LAGUNA Hills Motor Inn, Holly quickly changed into jeans and a blue-checkered blouse, then packed the rest of her belongings. Jim put her suitcase in the trunk of his car.

While she returned her room key and paid her bill at the front desk in the motel office, she was aware of him watching her from behind the wheel of his Ford. She would have been disappointed, of course, if he had not liked to watch her. But every time she looked through the plate-glass window at him, he was so motionless, so cool and expressionless behind his heavily tinted sunglasses, that his undivided attention was disconcerting.

She wondered if she was doing the right thing by going with him to the Santa Ynez Valley. When she walked out of the office and got in the car with him, he would be the only person in the world who knew where she was. All of her notes about him were in her suitcase; they could disappear with her. Then she would be just a woman, alone, who had vanished while on vacation.

As the clerk finished filling out the credit-card form, Holly considered phoning her parents in Philadelphia to let them know where she was going and with whom. But she would only alarm them and be on the phone half an hour trying to reassure them that she was going to be just fine.

Besides, she had already decided that the darkness in Jim was less important than the light, and she had made a commitment to him. If he occasionally made her uneasy . . . well, that was part of what had drawn her to him in the first place. A sense of danger sharpened the edge of his appeal. At heart, he was a good man.

It was foolish to worry about her safety after she had already made love to him. For a woman, in a way that could never be true for a man, the first night of sexual surrender involved one of the moments of greatest vulnerability in a relationship. Assuming, of course, that she had surrendered not solely because of physical need but because she loved him. And Holly loved him.

"I'm in love with him," she said aloud, surprised because she had convinced herself that his appeal was largely the result of his exceptional male grace, animal magnetism, and mystery.

The clerk, ten years younger than Holly and therefore more inclined to think that love was everywhere and inevitable, grinned at her. "It's great, isn't it?"

Signing the charge slip, Holly said, "Do you believe in love at first sight?"
"Why not?"

"Well, it's not first sight, really. I've known the guy since August twelfth, which is . . . sixteen days."

"And you're not married yet?" the clerk joked.

When Holly went out to the Ford and got in beside Jim, she said, "When we get where we're going, you won't carve me up with a chainsaw and bury me under the windmill, will you?"

Apparently he understood her sense of vulnerability and took no offense, for he said with mock solemnity, "Oh, no. It's full-up under the mill. I'll have to bury pieces of you all over the farm."

She laughed. She was an idiot for fearing him.

He leaned over and kissed her. It was a lovely, lingering kiss.

When they parted, he said, "I'm taking as big a risk as you are."

"Let me assure you, I've never hacked anyone to bits with an ax."

"I mean it. I haven't been lucky in love."

"Me neither."

"This time will be different for both of us."

He gave her another kiss, shorter and sweeter than the first one, then started the car and backed out of the parking space.

In a determined attempt to keep the dying cynic in her alive, Holly reminded herself that he had not actually said he loved her. His commitment had been carefully and indirectly phrased. He might be no more reliable than other men she had trusted over the years.

On the other hand, she had not actually said that she loved him, either. Her commitment had been no more effusively stated than his. Perhaps because she still felt the need to protect herself to some extent, she had found it easier to reveal her heart to the motel clerk than to Jim.

WASHING DOWN BLUEBERRY muffins with black coffee, for which they had stopped at a convenience store, they traveled north on the San Diego Freeway. The Tuesday-morning rush hour had passed, but at some places traffic still clogged all lanes and moved like a snail herd being driven toward a gourmet restaurant.

Comfortably ensconced in the passenger seat, Holly told Jim about her four nightmares, as promised. She started with the initial dream of blindness on Friday night, concluding with last night's spookshow, which had been the most bizarre and fearful of all.

He was clearly fascinated that she had dreamed about the mill without even knowing of its existence. And on Sunday night, after surviving the crash of Flight 246, she had dreamed of him at the mill *as a ten-year-old boy*, when she could not yet have known either that the mill was a familiar place to him or that he had spent a lot of time there when he was ten.

But the majority of his questions related to her most recent nightmare. Keeping his eyes on the traffic ahead, he said, "Who was the woman in the dream if she wasn't you?"

"I don't know," Holly said, finishing the final bite of the last muffin. "I had no sense of her identity."

"Can you describe her?"

"I only saw her reflection in that window, so I can't tell you much, I'm afraid." She drank the last of the coffee from her big Styrofoam cup, and thought a moment. It was easier to visualize the scenes of that dream than it should have been, for dreams were usually quick to fade from memory. Images from that one returned to her quite vividly, however, as if she had not dreamed them but experienced them in real life. "She had a broad clear face, more handsome in a womanly way than pretty. Wide-set eyes, full mouth. A beauty mark high on her right cheek, I don't think it could've been a spot on the glass, just a little round dot. Curly hair. Do you recognize her?"

"No," he replied. "Can't say that I do. Tell me what you saw at the bottom of the pond when the lightning flashed."

"I'm not sure what it was."

"Describe it as best you can."

She pondered for a moment, then shook her head. "I can't. The woman's face was fairly easy to recall because when I saw it in the dream I knew what it was, a face, a human face. But whatever was lying at the bottom of the pond . . . that was strange, like nothing I'd ever seen before. I didn't know what I was looking at, and I had such a brief glimpse of it and . . . well, now it's just gone. Is there really something peculiar under that pond?"

"Not that I know of," he said. "Could it've been a sunken boat, a row-boat, anything like that?"

"No," she said. "Nothing at all like that. Much bigger. Did a boat sink in the pond once?"

"I never heard of it, if one did. It's a deceptive-looking bit of water, though. You expect a millpond to be shallow, but this one is deep, forty or fifty feet to-ward the center. It never dries out, and it doesn't shrink during dry years, ei-ther, because it's formed over an artesian well, not just an aquifer."

"What's the difference?"

"An aquifer is what you drill into when you're sinking a well, it's sort of a reservoir or stream of underground water. Artesian wells are rarer. You don't drill into one to find water, 'cause the water is already coming to the surface under pressure. You'd have the devil's own time trying to *stop* the stuff from percolating up."

The snarl of traffic began to loosen, but Jim did not take full advantage of opportunities to change lanes and swing around slower-moving vehicles. He was more interested in her answers than in making better time.

He said, "And in the dream, when you got to the top of the stairs—or when this woman got to the top of the stairs—you saw a ten-year-old boy standing there, and somehow you knew he was me."

"Yes."

"I don't look much like I looked when I was ten, so how'd you recognize me?"

"Mostly it was your eyes," Holly said. "They haven't changed much in all these years. They're unmistakable."

"Lots of people have blue eyes."

"Are you serious? Honey, your blue eyes are to other blue eyes what Sinatra's voice is to Donald Duck's."

"You're prejudiced. What did you see in the wall?"

She described it again.

"Alive in the stone? This just gets stranger and stranger."

"I haven't been bored in days," she agreed.

Beyond the junction with Interstate 10, traffic on the San Diego Freeway became even lighter, and finally Jim began to put some of his driving skills to use. He handled the car the way a first-rate jockey handled a thorough-bred horse, finessing from it that extra degree of performance that won races. The Ford was only a stock model with no modification, but it responded to him as if it wanted to be a Porsche.

After a while Holly began to ask questions of her own. "How come you're a millionaire but you live relatively cheap?"

"Bought a house, moved out of my apartment. Quit my job."

"Yeah, but a modest house. And your furniture's falling apart."

"I needed the privacy of my own house to meditate and rest between . . . assignments. But I didn't need fancy furniture."

Following a few minutes of mutual silence, she said, "Did I catch your eye the way you caught mine, right off the bat, up in Portland?"

He smiled but didn't look away from the highway. " 'So are you, Miss Thorne.' "

"So you admit it!" Holly said, pleased. "It *was* a come-on line."

They made excellent time from the west side of Los Angeles all the way to Ventura, but then Jim began to slack off again. Mile by mile, he drove with less aggression.

Initially Holly thought he was lulled by the view. Past Ventura, Route 101 hugged beautiful stretches of coastline. They passed Pitas Point, then Rincon Point, and the beaches of Carpinteria. The blue sea rose, the blue sky fell, the golden land wedged itself between them, and the only visible turbulence in the serene summer day was the white-capped surf, which slipped to the shore in low combers and broke with a light, foamy spray.

But there was a turbulence in Jim Ironheart, too, and Holly only became aware of his new edginess when she realized that he was not paying any attention to the scenery. He had slowed down not to enjoy the view but, she suspected, to delay their arrival at the farm.

By the time they left the superhighway, turned inland at Santa Barbara, crossed the city, and headed into the Santa Ynez Mountains, Jim's mood was undeniably darker. His responses to her conversational sallies grew shorter, more distracted.

State Route 154 led out of the mountains into an appealing land of low hills and fields painted gold by dry summer grass, clusters of California live oaks, and horse ranches with neat white fencing. This was not the farming-intense, agribusiness atmosphere of the San Joaquin and certain other val-leys; there were serious vineyards here and there, but the occasional farms appeared to be, as often as not, gentlemen's operations maintained as get-aways for rich men in Los Angeles, more concerned with cultivating a pic-turesque alternate lifestyle than with real crops.

"We'll need to stop in New Svenborg to get a few things before we head out to the farm," Jim said.

"What things?"

"I don't know. But when we stop . . . I'll know what we need."

Lake Cachuma came and went to the east. They passed the road to Solvang on the west, then skirted Santa Ynez itself. Before Los Olivos, they headed east on another state route, and finally into New Svenborg, the closest town to Ironheart Farm.

In the early nineteen hundreds, groups of Danish-Americans from the Midwest had settled in the Santa Ynez Valley, many of them with the intention of establishing communities that would preserve Danish folk arts and customs and, in general, the ways of Danish life. The most successful of these settlements was Solvang, about which Holly had once written a story; it had become a major tourist attraction because of its quaint Danish architecture, shops, and restaurants.

New Svenborg, with a population of fewer than two thousand, was not as elaborately, thoroughly, authentically, *insistently* Danish as Solvang. Depressing desert-style stucco buildings with white-rock roofs, weathered clapboard buildings with unpainted front porches that reminded Holly of parts of rural Texas, Craftsman bungalows, and white Victorian houses with lots of gingerbread and wide front porches stood beside structures that were distinctly Danish with half-timbered walls and thatched roofs and leaded-glass windows. Half a dozen windmills dotted the town, their vanes silhouetted against the August sky. All in all, it was one of those singular California mixes that sometimes resulted in delightful and unexpected harmonies; but in New Svenborg, the mix did not work, and the mood was discordancy.

"I spent the end of my childhood and my entire adolescence here," Jim said as he drove slowly down the quiet, shadowy main street.

She figured that his moodiness could be attributed as much to New Svenborg as to his tragic family history.

To an extent, that was unfair. The streets were lined with big trees, the charming streetlamps appeared to have been imported from the Old Country, and most of the sidewalks were gracefully curved and time-hoved ribbons of well-worn brick. About twenty percent of the town came straight from the nostalgic Midwest of a Bradbury novel, but the rest of it still belonged in a David Lynch film.

"Let's take a little tour of the old place," he said.

"We should be getting to the farm."

"It's only a mile north of town, just a few minutes away."

That was all the more reason to get there, as far as Holly was concerned. She was tired of being on the road.

But she sensed that for some reason he wanted to show her the town—and not merely to delay their arrival at Ironheart Farm. Holly acquiesced. In fact she listened with interest to what he had to tell her. She had learned that he found it difficult to talk about himself and that he sometimes made personal revelations in an indirect or even casual manner.

He drove past Handahl's Pharmacy on the east end of Main Street, where locals went to get a prescription filled, unless they preferred to drive twenty miles to Solvang. Handahl's was also one of only two restaurants in town, with (according to Jim) "the best soda fountain this side of 1955." It was also the post office and only newsstand. With its multiply peaked roof, verdigris-copper cupola, and beveled-glass windows, it was an appealing enterprise.

Without shutting the engine off, Jim parked across the street from the library on Copenhagen Lane, which was quartered in one of the smaller Victorian houses with considerably less gingerbread than most. The building was freshly painted, with well-tended shrubbery, and both the United States and California flags fluttered softly on a tall brass pole along the front walkway. It looked like a small and sorry library nonetheless.

"A town this size, it's amazing to find a library at all," Jim said. "And thank God for it. I rode my bike to the library so often . . . if you added up all the miles, I probably pedaled halfway around the world. After my folks died, books were my friends, counselors, psychiatrists. Books kept me sane. Mrs. Glynn, the librarian, was a great lady, she knew just how to talk to a shy, mixed-up kid without talking *down* to him. She was my guide to the most exotic regions of the world and distant times—all without leaving her aisles of books."

Holly had never heard him speak so lovingly or half so lyrically of anything before. The Svenborg library and Mrs. Glynn had clearly been lasting and favorable influences on his life.

"Why don't we go in and say hello to her?" Holly suggested.

Jim frowned. "Oh, I'm sure she's not the librarian any more, most likely not even alive. That was twenty-five years ago when I started coming here, eighteen years ago when I left town to go to college. Never saw her after that."

"How old was she?"

He hesitated. "Quite old," he said, and put an end to the talk of a nostalgic visit by slipping the Ford into gear and driving away from there.

They cruised by Tivoli Gardens, a small park at the corner of Main and Copenhagen, which fell laughably short of its namesake. No fountains, no musicians, no dancing, no games, no beer gardens. There were just some roses, a few beds of late-summer flowers, patchy grass, two park benches, and a well-maintained windmill in the far corner.

"Why aren't the sails moving?" she asked. "There's some wind."

"None of the mills actually pumps water or grinds grain any more," he explained. "And since they're largely decorative, no sense in having to live with the noise they make. Brakes were put on the mechanisms long ago." As they turned the corner at the end of the park, he added: "They made a movie here once."

"Who did?"

"One of the studios."

"Hollywood studio?"

"I forget which."

"What was it called?"

"Don't remember."

"Who starred in it?"

"Nobody famous."

Holly made a mental note about the movie, suspecting that it was more important to Jim and to the town than he had said. Something in the off-handed way he'd mentioned it, and his terse responses to her subsequent questions, alerted her to an unspoken subtext.

Last of all, at the southeast corner of Svenborg, he drove slowly past Zacca's Garage, a large corrugated-steel Quonset hut perched on a cement-block foundation, in front of which stood two dusty cars. Though the building had been painted several times during its history, no brush had touched it in many years. Its numerous coats of paint were worn in a random patch-work and marked by liberal encrustations of rust, which created an unin-tended camouflage finish. The cracked blacktop in front of the place was pitted with potholes that had been filled with loose gravel, and the surround-ing lot bristled with dry grass and weeds.

"I went to school with Ned Zacca," Jim said. "His dad, Vernon, had the garage then. It was never a business to make a man rich, but it looked better than it does now."

The big airplane hangar-style roll-aside doors were open, and the interior was clotted with shadows. The rear bumper of an old Chevy gleamed dully in the gloom. Although the garage was seedy, nothing about it suggested danger. Yet the queerest chill came over Holly as she peered through the hangar doors into the murky depths of the place.

"Ned was one mean sonofabitch, the school bully," Jim said. "He could sure make a kid's life hell when he wanted to. I lived in fear of him."

"Too bad you didn't know Tae Kwon Do then, you could've kicked his ass."

He did not smile, just stared past her at the garage. His expression was odd and unsettling. "Yeah. Too bad."

When she glanced at the building again, she saw a man in jeans and a T-shirt step out of the deepest darkness into gray half-light, moving slowly past the back of the Chevy, wiping his hands on a rag. He was just beyond the infall of sunshine, so she could not see what he looked like. In a few steps he rounded the car, fading into the gloom again, hardly more material than a specter glimpsed in a moonlit graveyard.

Somehow, she knew the ghostly presence in the Quonset was Ned Zacca. Curiously, though he had been a menacing figure to Jim, not to her, Holly felt her stomach twist and her palms turn damp.

Then Jim touched the accelerator, and they were past the garage, heading back into town.

"What did Zacca do to you exactly?"

"Anything he could think of. He was a regular little sadist. He's been in prison a couple of times since those days. But I figured he was back."

"Figured? How?"

He shrugged. "I just sensed it. Besides, he's one of those guys who never gets caught at the big stuff. Devil's luck. He might do a fall every great once in a while, but always for something small-time. He's dumb but he's clever."

"Why'd you want to go there?"

"Memories."

"Most people, when they want a little nostalgia, they're only interested in good memories."

Jim did not reply to that. Even before they arrived in Svenborg, he had settled into himself like a turtle gradually withdrawing into its shell. Now he was almost back into that brooding, distant mood in which she had found him yesterday afternoon.

The brief tour had given her not a comfortable feeling of small-town security and friendliness, but a sense of being cut off at the back end of nowhere. She was still in California, the most populous state in the union, not much farther than sixty miles from the city of Santa Barbara. Svenborg had almost two thousand people of its own, which made it bigger than a lot of gas-and-graze stops along the interstate highways. The sense of isolation was more psychological than real, but it hovered over her.

Jim stopped at The Central, a prospering operation that included a service station selling generic gasoline, a small sporting-goods outlet peddling supplies to fishermen and campers, and a well-stocked convenience store with groceries, beer, and wine. Holly filled the Ford's tank at the self-service pump, then joined Jim in the sporting-goods shop.

The store was cluttered with merchandise, which overflowed the shelves, hung from the ceiling, and was stacked on the linoleum floor. Wall-eyed fishing lures dangled on a rack near the door. The air smelled of rubber boots.

At the check-out counter, Jim already had piled up a pair of high-quality summerweight sleeping bags with air-mattress liners, a Coleman lantern with a can of fuel, a sizable Thermos ice chest, two big flashlights, packages of batteries for the flashes, and a few other items. At the cash register, farther along the counter from Jim, a bearded man in spectacles as thick as bottle glass was ringing up the sale, and Jim was waiting with an open wallet.

"I thought we were going to the mill," Holly said.

"We are," Jim said. "But unless you want to sleep on a wooden floor without benefit of *any* conveniences, we need this stuff."

"I didn't realize we were staying overnight."

"Neither did I. Until I walked in here and heard myself asking for these things."

"Couldn't we stay at a motel?"

"Nearest one's clear over to Santa Ynez."

"It's a pretty drive," she said, much preferring the commute to spending a night in the mill.

Her reluctance arose only in part from the fact that the old mill promised to be uncomfortable. The place was, after all, the locus of both their nightmares. Besides, since arriving in Svenborg, she had felt vaguely . . . threatened.

"But something's going to happen," he said. "I don't know what. Just . . . something. At the mill. I feel it. We're going to . . . get some answers. But it might take a little time. We've got to be ready to wait, be patient."

Though Holly was the one who had suggested going to the mill, she suddenly didn't *want* answers. In a dim premonition of her own, she perceived an undefined but oncoming tragedy, blood, death, and darkness.

Jim, on the other hand, seemed to shed the lead weight of his previous apprehension and take on a new buoyancy. "It's good—what we're doing, where we're going. I *sense* that, Holly. You know what I mean? I'm being told we made the right move in coming here, that there's something frightening ahead of us, yes, something that's going to shock the hell out of us, maybe very real danger, but there's also something that's going to lift us up." His eyes were shining and he was excited. She had never seen him like this, not even when they had been making love. In whatever obscure way it touched him, this higher power of his was in contact with him now. She could see his quiet rapture. "I feel a . . . a strange sort of jubilation coming, a wonderful discovery, revelations . . ."

The bespectacled clerk had stepped away from the cash register to show them the total on the tape. Grinning, he said, "Newlyweds?"

At the convenience store next door, they bought ice for the chest, then orange juice, diet soda, bread, mustard, bologna-olive loaf, and prepackaged cheese slices.

"Olive loaf," Holly said wonderingly. "I haven't eaten this stuff since I was maybe fourteen and I learned I had arteries."

"And how about these," he said, snatching a box of chocolate-covered doughnuts off a shelf, adding it to the market basket that he was carrying. "Bologna sandwiches, chocolate doughnuts . . . and potato chips, of course. Wouldn't be a picnic without chips. The crinkled kind, okay? Some cheese twists, too. Chips and cheese twists, they go together."

Holly had never seen him like this: almost boyish, with no apparent weight on his shoulders. He might have been setting out on a camping trip with friends, a little adventure.

She wondered if her own apprehension was justified. Jim was, after all, the one whose presentiments had proven to be accurate. Maybe they *were* going to discover something wonderful at the mill, unravel the mystery behind the last-minute rescues he had performed, maybe even encounter this higher power to which he referred. Perhaps The Enemy, in spite of its ability to reach out of a dream into the real world, was not as formidable as it seemed.

At the cash register, after the clerk finished bagging their purchases and was making change, Jim said, "Wait a minute, one more thing," and hurried to the rear of the store. When he returned, he was carrying two lined yellow tablets and one black, fine-point felt-tip pen. To Holly, he said, "We'll be needing these tonight."

When they had loaded the car and pulled out of the parking lot at The Central, heading for the Ironheart farm, Holly indicated the pen and tablets, which she was holding in a separate bag. "What'll we be needing these for?"

"I haven't the slightest idea. I just suddenly knew we have to have them."

"That's just like God," she said, "always being mysterious and obscure."

After a silence, he said, "I'm not so sure any more that it's God talking to me."

"Oh? What changed your mind?"

"Well, the issues you raised last evening, for one thing. If God didn't want little Nick O'Conner to die up there in Boston, why didn't He just stop that vault from exploding? Why chase me clear across the country and 'throw' me at the boy, as you put it?

"And why would He up and change His mind about the people on the airliner, let more of them live, just because I decided they should? They were all questions I'd asked myself, but you weren't willing to settle for the easy answers that satisfied me." He looked away from the street for a moment as they reached the edge of town, smiled at her, and repeated one of the questions she had asked him yesterday when she had been needling him: "Is God a waffler?"

"I would've expected . . ."

"What?"

"Well, you were so sure you could see a divine hand in this, it must be a bit of a letdown to consider less exalted possibilities. I'd expect you to be a little bummed out."

He shook his head. "I'm not. You know, I always had trouble accepting that it was God working through me, it seemed like such a crazy idea, but I lived with it just because there wasn't any better explanation. There still *isn't* a better explanation, I guess, but another possibility has occurred to me, and it's something so strange and wonderful in its way that I don't mind losing God from the team."

"What other possibility?"

"I don't want to talk about it just yet," he said as sunlight and tree shadows dappled the dusty windshield and played across his face. "I want to think it through, be sure it makes sense, before I lay it out for you, 'cause I know now you're a hard judge to convince."

He seemed happy. Really happy. Holly had liked him pretty much since she had first seen him, regardless of his moodiness. She had perceived a hopefulness beneath his glower, a tenderness beneath his gruffness, a better man beneath the exterior of a lesser one, but in his current buoyant mood, she found him easier than ever to like.

She playfully pinched his cheek.

"What?" he said.

"You're cute."

As they drove out of Svenborg, it occurred to Holly that the distribution pattern of the houses and other buildings was more like a pioneer settlement than like a modern community. In most towns, buildings were concentrated more densely in the center, with larger lots and increasing open space toward the perimeter, until finally the last structures gave way to rural precincts. But when they came to the city limits of Svenborg, the delineation between town and country was almost ruler-straight and unmistakable. Houses stopped and brushland began, with only an intervening firebreak, and Holly could not help but think of pioneers in the Old West constructing their outposts with a wary eye toward the threats that might arise out of the lawless badlands all around them.

Inside its boundaries, the town seemed ominous and full of dark secrets. Seen from the outside—and Holly turned to stare back at it as the road rose toward the brow of a gentle hill—it looked not threatening but threatened, as if its residents knew, in their bones, that something frightful in the golden land around them was waiting to claim them all.

Perhaps fire was all they feared. Like much of California, the land was parched where human endeavor had not brought water to it.

Nestled between the Santa Ynez Mountains to the west and the San Rafael Mountains to the east, the valley was so broad and deep that it contained more geographical variety than some entire states back East—though at this time of year, untouched by rain since early spring, most of it was brown and crisp. They traveled across rounded golden hills, brown meadows. The better vantage points on their two-mile route revealed vistas of higher hills overgrown with chaparral, valleys within the valley where groves of California live oaks flourished, and small green vineyards encircled by vast sere fields.

"It's beautiful," Holly said, taking in the pale hills, shining-gold meadows, and oily chaparral. Even the oaks, whose clusters indicated areas with a comparatively high water table, were not lush but a half-parched silver-green. "Beautiful, but a tinderbox. How would they cope with a fire out here?"

Even as she posed that question, they came around a bend in the road and saw a stretch of blackened land to the right of the two-lane county road. Brush and grass had been reduced to veins of gray-white ash in coal-black soot. The fire had taken place within the past couple of days, for it was still recent enough to lend a burnt odor to the August air.

"That one didn't get far," he said. "Looks like ten acres burned at most. They're quick around here, they jump at the first sign of smoke. There's a good volunteer group in town, plus a Department of Forestry station in the valley, lookout posts. If you live here, you don't forget the threat—you just realize after a while that it can be dealt with."

Jim sounded confident enough, and he had lived there for seven or eight years, so Holly tried to suppress her pyrophobia. Nevertheless, even after they had passed the charred land and could no longer smell the scorched brush, Holly had an image in her mind of the huge valley at night, aflame from end to end, vortexes of red-orange-white fire whirling like tornadoes and consuming everything that lay between the ramparts of the two mountain ranges.

"Ironheart Farm," he said, startling her.

As Jim slowed the Ford, Holly looked to the left of the blacktop county route.

A farmhouse stood a hundred feet back from the road, behind a withered lawn. It was of no particular architectural style, just a plain but cozy-looking two-story farmhouse with white aluminum siding, a red-shingle roof, and a commodious front porch. It might have been lifted off its foundation anywhere in the Midwest and plunked down on new footings here, for there were thousands like it in those cornbelt states.

Maybe a hundred yards to the left of the house, a red barn rose to a tarnished horse-and-carriage weather vane at the pinnacle of its peaked roof. It was not huge, only half again as large as the unimposing house.

Behind the house and barn, visible between them, was the pond, and the structure at its far side was the most arresting sight on the farm. The windmill.

3 Jim stopped in the driveway turnaround between house and barn, and got out of the Ford. He *had* to get out because the sight of the old place hit him harder than he had expected, simultaneously bringing a chill to the pit of his stomach and a flush of heat to his face. In spite of the cool draft from the dashboard vents, the air in the car seemed warm and stale, too low in oxygen content to sustain him. He stood in the fresh summer air, drawing deep breaths, and tried not to lose control of himself.

The blank-windowed house held little power over him. When he looked at it, he felt only a sweet melancholy that might, given time, deepen into a more disturbing sadness or even despair. But he could stare at it, draw his breath normally, and turn away from it without being seized by a powerful urge to look at it again.

The barn exerted no emotional pull on him whatsoever, but the windmill was another story. When he turned his gaze on that cone of limestone beyond the wide pond, he felt as though he were being transformed into stone himself, as had been the luckless victims of the mythological serpent-haired Medusa when they had seen her snake-ringed face.

He'd read about Medusa years ago. In one of Mrs. Glynn's books. That was in the days when he wished with all his heart that he, too, could see the snake-haired woman and be transformed into unfeeling rock. . . .

"Jim?" Holly said from the other side of the car. "You okay?"

With its high-ceilinged rooms—highest on the first floor—the two-story mill was actually four stories in height. But to Jim, at that moment, it looked far taller, as imposing as a twenty-story tower. Its once-pale stones had been darkened by a century of grime. Climbing ivy, roots nurtured by the pond that abutted one flank of the mill, twined up the rough stone face, finding easy purchase in deep-mortared joints. With no one to perform needed maintenance, the plant had covered half the structure, and had grown entirely over a narrow first-floor window near the timbered door. The wooden sails looked rotten. Each of those four arms was about thirty feet in length, making a sixty-foot spread across adjoining spans, and each was five feet wide with three rows of vanes. Since he had last seen the mill, more vanes had cracked or fallen away altogether. The time-frozen sails were stopped not in a cruciform but in an X, two arms reaching toward the pond and two toward the heavens. Even in hot bright daylight, the windmill struck Jim as menacing and seemed like a monstrous, ragged-armed scarecrow clawing at the sky with skeletal hands.

"Jim?" Holly said, touching his arm.

He jumped as if he had not known who she was. In fact, for an instant, as he looked down at her, he saw not only Holly but a long-dead face, the face of . . .

But the moment of disorientation passed. She was only Holly now, her identity no longer entwined with that of another woman as it had been in her dream last night.

"You okay?" she asked again.

"Yeah, sure, just . . . memories."

Jim was grateful when Holly directed his attention from the mill to the farmhouse. She said, "Were you happy with your grandparents?"

"Lena and Henry Ironheart. Wonderful people. They took me in. They suffered so much for me."

"Suffered?" she said.

He realized that it was too strong a word, and he wondered why he had used it. "Sacrificed, I mean. In lots of ways, little things, but they added up."

"Taking on the support of a ten-year-old boy isn't something anyone does lightly," Holly said. "But unless you demanded caviar and champagne, I wouldn't think you'd have been much of a hardship to them."

"After what happened to my folks, I was . . . withdrawn, in bad shape, uncommunicative. They put in a lot of time with me, a lot of love, trying to bring me back . . . from the edge."

"Who lives here these days?"

"Nobody."

"But didn't you say your grandparents died five years ago?"

"The place wasn't sold. No buyers."

"Who owns it now?"

"I do. I inherited it."

She surveyed the property with evident bewilderment. "But it's lovely here. If the lawn was being watered and kept green, the weeds cut down, it would be charming. Why would it be so hard to sell?"

"Well, for one thing, it's a damned quiet life out here, and even most of the back-to-nature types who dream of living on a farm really mean a farm close to a choice of movie theaters, bookstores, good restaurants, and dependable European-car mechanics."

She laughed at that. "Baby, there's an amusing little cynic lurking in you."

"Besides, it's hardscrabble all the way, trying to earn a living on a place like this. It's just a little old hundred-acre farm, not big enough to make it with milk cows or a beef herd—or any one crop. My grandpa and grandma kept chickens, sold the eggs. And thanks to the mild weather, they could get two crops. Strawberries came into fruit in February and all the way into May. That was the money crop—berries. Then came corn, tomatoes—*real* tomatoes, not the plastic ones they sell in the markets."

He saw that Holly was still enamored of the place. She stood with her hands on her hips, looking around as if she might buy it herself.

She said, "But aren't there people who work at other things, not farmers, would just like to live here for the peace and quiet?"

"This isn't a real affluent area, not like Newport Beach, Beverly Hills. Locals around here don't have extra money just to spend on lifestyle. The best hope of selling a property like this is to find some rich movie producer or recording executive in L.A. who wants to buy it for the land, tear it down, and put up a showplace, so he can say he has a getaway in the Santa Ynez Valley, which is the trendy thing to have these days."

As they talked, he grew increasingly uneasy. It was three o'clock. Plenty of daylight left. But suddenly he dreaded nightfall.

Holly kicked at some wiry weeds that had pushed up through one of the many cracks in the blacktop driveway. "It needs a little cleanup, but everything looks pretty good. Five years since they died? But the house and barn are in decent shape, like they were painted only a year or two ago."

"They were."

"Keep the place marketable, huh?"

"Sure. Why not?"

The high mountains to the west would eat the sun sooner than the ocean swallowed it down in Laguna Niguel. Twilight would come earlier here than there, although it would be prolonged. Jim found himself studying the lengthening purple shadows with the fearfulness of a man in a vampire movie hastening toward shelter before the coffin lids banged open.

What's wrong with me? he wondered.

Holly said, "You think you'd ever want to live here yourself?"

"Never!" he said so sharply and explosively that he startled not only Holly but himself. As if overcome by a dark magnetic attraction, he looked at the windmill again. A shudder swept through him.

He was aware that she was staring at him.

"Jim," she said softly, "what happened to you here? What in the name of God happened twenty-five years ago in that mill?"

"I don't know," he said shakily. He wiped one hand down his face. His hand felt warm, his face cold. "I can't remember anything special, anything odd. It was where I played. It was . . . cool and quiet . . . a nice place. Nothing happened there. Nothing."

"Something," she insisted. "Something happened."

HOLLY HAD NOT been close to him long enough to know if he was frequently on an emotional roller coaster as he had been since they had left Orange County, or if his recent rapid swings in mood were abnormal. In The Central, buying food for a picnic, he'd soared out of the gloom that had settled over him when they crossed the Santa Ynez Mountains, and he'd been almost jubilant. Then the sight of the farm was like a plunge into cold water for him, and the windmill was the equivalent of a drop into an ice chasm.

He seemed as troubled as he was gifted, and she wished that she could do something to ease his mind. She wondered if urging him to come to the farm had been wise. Even a failed career in journalism had taught her to leap into the middle of unfolding events, seize the moment, and run with it. But perhaps this situation demanded greater caution, restraint, thought, and planning.

They got back into the Ford and drove between the house and barn, around the big pond. The graveled path, which she remembered from last night's dream, had been made wide enough for horses and wagons in another era. It easily accommodated the Ford, allowing them to park at the base of the windmill.

When she stepped from the car again, she was beside a cornfield. Only a few parched wild stalks thrust up from that abandoned plot of earth beyond the split-rail fence. She walked around the back of the car, across the gravel, and joined Jim where he stood on the bank of the pond.

Mottled blue-green-gray, the water resembled a slab of slate two hundred feet in diameter. It was almost as still as a piece of slate, as well. Dragonflies and other insects, alighting briefly on the surface, caused occasional dimples. Languid currents, far too subtle to produce ripples, made the water shimmer almost imperceptibly near the shore, where green weeds and a few clusters of white-plumed pampas grass thrived.

"Still can't remember quite what you saw in that dream?" Jim asked.

"No. It probably doesn't matter anyway. Not everything in a dream is significant."

In a low voice, almost as if speaking to himself, he said, "It was significant."

Without turbulence to stir up sediment, the water was not muddy, but neither was it clear. Holly figured she could see only a few feet below the surface. If it actually was fifty or sixty feet deep at the center, as Jim had said, that left a lot of volume in which something could remain hidden.

"Let's have a look in the mill," she said.

Jim got one of the new flashlights from the car and put batteries in it. "Even in daylight, it can be kind of dark in there."

The door was in an antechamber appended to the base of the conical main structure of the mill, much like the entrance to an Eskimo igloo. Although unlocked, the door was warped, and the hinges were rusted. For a moment it resisted Jim, then swung inward with a screech and a brittle splintering sound.

The short, arched antechamber opened onto the main room of the mill, which was approximately forty feet in diameter. Four windows, evenly spaced around the circumference, filtered sunlight through filthy panes, leeching the summer-yellow cheer from it and imparting a wintry gray tint that did little to alleviate the gloom. Jim's big flashlight revealed dust- and cobweb-shrouded machinery that could not have appeared more exotic to Holly if it had been the turbine room of a nuclear submarine. It was the cumbersome low technology of another century—massive wooden gears, cogs, shafts, grinding stones, pulleys, old rotting lengths of rope—so oversized and complicated that it all seemed like the work not merely of human beings from another age but of a different and less evolved species altogether.

Because he had grown up around mills, even though they had not been in use since before his birth, Jim knew the names of everything. Pointing with the flashlight beam, he tried to explain how the mill had functioned, talking about the spurwheel and the quant, the mace and the rynd, the runner stone and the bed stone. "Ordinarily you couldn't look up through the mechanisms quite like this. But, see, the floor of the spurwheel loft is rotted out, not much of it left, and the bridge floor gave way when those huge stones broke loose and fell."

Though he had regarded the mill with fear when they had stood outside, his mood had begun to change after they entered it. To Holly's surprise, as Jim tried to explain the millworks to her, he began to exhibit some of that boyish enthusiasm that she had first seen when they had been grocery shopping at The Central in Svenborg. He was pleased by his knowledge, and he wanted to show it off a little, the way a bookish kid was always happy to demonstrate what he had learned at the library while others his age were out playing baseball.

He turned to the limestone stairs on their left and climbed without hesitation, running one hand lightly along the curved wall as he went. There was a half-smile on his face as he looked around, as if only the good memories were flooding in on him now.

Puzzled by his extremely mercurial mood, trying to imagine how the mill could frighten and delight him simultaneously, Holly somewhat reluctantly followed him up toward what he had called "the high room." She had no good memories to associate with the mill, only the fearful images of her nightmares, and those returned to her as she ascended behind Jim. Thanks to her dream, the narrow twist of stairs was familiar to her, though she was climbing it for the first time—which was an uncanny feeling, far eerier than mere *déjà vu*.

Halfway up the stairs, she stopped at the window that overlooked the pond. The glass was frosted with dust. She used her hand to wipe one pane, and squinted at the water below. For an instant she thought she saw something strange beneath the placid surface—then realized she was seeing only the reflection of a cloud drifting across the sky.

"What is it?" Jim asked with boyish eagerness. He had stopped a few steps above her.

"Nothing. A shadow."

They continued all the way to the upper chamber, which proved to be an unremarkable room, about twelve or fourteen feet in diameter, less than fifteen feet high at its apex. The curved limestone wall wrapped around to meet itself, and curved up to form the ceiling, so it seemed as if they were standing inside the domed nose cone of a rocket. The stone was not semi-transparent as it had been in her dream, and no strange amber lights played within it. An arcane mechanism was offset in the dome, through which the motion of the wind-turned sails outside was translated into horizontal movement to crank a vertical wood shaft. The thick shaft disappeared through a hole in the center of the floor.

Remembering how they had stood downstairs and looked up through the buckled and broken decks within the multi-level millworks, Holly gingerly tested the wood floor. No rot was visible. The planks and the joists under them seemed sturdy.

"Lots of dust," Jim said, as their feet stirred up little clouds with each step.

"And spiders," Holly noted.

Wrinkling her face in disgust, she peered up at the husks of sucked-dry insects dangling in the elaborate webs that had been spun around the long-stilled mechanism overhead. She didn't fear spiders, but she didn't like them either.

"We need to do some cleaning before we set up camp," he said.

"Should've bought a broom and a few other things while we were in town."

"There're cleaning materials at the house. I'll bring them here while you start unloading the car."

"The house!" Holly was exhilarated by a lovely inspiration. "When we set out for the mill, I didn't realize this property was still yours, no one living here. We can put the sleeping bags in the house, stay there, and visit this room as often as we need to."

"Nice thought," Jim said, "but it's not that easy. Something's going to happen here, Holly, something that'll give us answers or put us on the road to finding them. I feel it. I know it . . . well, just the way I know these things. But we can't pick the time for the revelation. It doesn't work that way. We can't ask God—or whatever is behind this—to punch a time clock and deliver revelations only between regular business hours. We have to stay here and be patient."

She sighed. "Okay, yeah, if you—"

Bells interrupted her.

It was a sweet silvery ringing, neither heavy nor clangorous, lasting only two or three seconds, pleasingly musical. It was so light and gay, in fact, that it should have seemed a frivolous sound against the backdrop of that ponderous stone structure. It was not in the least frivolous, however, because inexplicably it triggered in Holly serious associations—thoughts of sin and penitence and redemption.

The trilling faded even as she turned in search of the source. But before she could ask Jim what it had been, it came again.

This time, Holly understood why she associated the sound with issues of spirituality. It was the precise tone of the bells that an altarboy rang during Mass. The sweet ringing brought back to her the smell of spikenard and myrrh from her college days when she had toyed with the idea of converting to Catholicism.

The bells faded again.

She turned to Jim and saw him grinning.

"What is it?" she asked.

"I forgot all about this," he said wonderingly. "How could I have forgotten all about this?"

The bells tinkled again, silvery and pure.

"Forgot what?" she asked. "What're those bells?"

"Not bells," he said as they faded. He hesitated, and as the sound returned a fourth time, he finally said, "The ringing is in the stone."

"Ringing stone?" she said in bewilderment.

As the bells sounded twice again, she circled the room, cocking her head this way and that, until it seemed to her that the music did, indeed, originate from the limestone wall, pealing out not from any single location but equally from every block of that curved surface, no louder at one point than another.

She told herself that stone could not ring, certainly not in such a dulcet voice. A windmill was an unusual structure and could have tricky acoustics. From a high-school class trip to Washington, she remembered a tourguide showing them a spot in the Capitol's rotunda from which even a whispered conversation was picked up and, by a quirk of architecture, transmitted across the huge dome to the far side of that great space, where eavesdroppers could hear it with perfect clarity. Perhaps something similar was at work here. If bells were rung or other sounds made at a particular place in a far corner of the first floor of the mill, a peculiarity of acoustics might transmit it in equal volume along all the walls on every floor. That explanation was more logical than the concept of magical, ringing stone—until she tried to imagine who would be secretly ringing the bell, and why.

She put one hand against the wall.

The limestone was cool. She detected faint vibrations in it.

The bell fell silent.

The vibrations in the wall subsided.

They waited.

When it was clear that the ringing would not resume, Holly said, "When did you hear it before?"

"When I was ten."

"And what happened after the ringing, what did it signify?"

"I don't know."

"But you said you just remembered it."

His eyes were shining with excitement. "Yeah. I remember the ringing. But not what caused it or what followed it. Though I think . . . it's a good sign, Holly." A note of rapture entered his voice. "It means something very fine is going to happen, something . . . wonderful."

Holly was frustrated. In spite of the mystical aspect of Jim's life-saving missions—and in spite her own paranormal experiences with dreams and the creatures in them—she had come to the farm with the hope of finding logical answers to all that had transpired. She had no idea what those answers could be. But she'd had an unspoken faith in the scientific method. Rigorous investigative procedures combined with careful thought, the use of deductive and inductive reasoning as needed, would lead to solutions. But now it seemed that logic was out the window. She was perturbed by Jim's taste for mysticism, though she had to admit that he had embraced illogic from the start, with all his talk of God, and had taken no pains to conceal it.

She said, "But, Jim, how could you have forgotten anything as weird as ringing stones or any of the rest of whatever happened to you here?"

"I don't think I just forgot. I think I was *made* to forget."

"By whom?"

"By whomever or whatever just made the stone ring again, by whatever's behind all these recent events." He moved toward the open door. "Come on, let's get this place cleaned up, move in. We want to be ready for whatever's going to happen next."

She followed him to the head of the steps but stopped there and watched him descend two at a time, with the air of a kid excited by the prospect of adventure. All of his misgivings about the mill and his fear of The Enemy seemed to have evaporated like a few beads of water on a red-hot griddle. His emotional roller coaster was cresting the highest point on the track thus far.

Sensing something above her head, Holly looked up. A large web had been spun above the door, across the curve where the wall became the ceiling. A fat spider, its body as big around as her thumbnail and its spindly legs almost as long as her little finger, greasy as a dollop of wax and dark as a drop of blood, was feeding greedily on the pale quivering body of a snared moth.

4 With a broom, dustpan, bucket of water, mop, and a few rags, they made the small upper chamber livable in short order. Jim even brought some Windex and paper towels from the store of cleaning supplies at the house, so they could scrub the grime off the windows, letting in a lot more light. Holly chased down and killed not only the spider above the door but seven others, checking darker corners with one of the flashlights until she was sure she had found them all.

Of course the mill below them was surely crawling with countless other spiders. She decided not to think about that.

By six o'clock, the day was waning but the room was bright enough without the Coleman lantern. They were sitting Indian fashion on their inflatable-mattress sleeping bags, with the big cooler between them. Using the closed lid as a table, they made thick sandwiches, opened the potato chips and cheese twists, and popped the tops off cans of root beer. Though she had missed lunch, Holly had not thought about food until they'd begun to prepare it. Now she was hungrier than she would have expected under the circumstances. Everything was delicious, better than gourmet fare. Olive loaf and cheese on white bread, with mustard, recalled for her the appetites of childhood, the intense flavors and forgotten innocent sensuality of youth.

They did not talk much as they ate. Silences did not make either of them feel awkward, and they were taking such primal pleasure from the meal that no conversation, regardless of how witty, could have improved the moment. But that was only part of the reason for their mutual reticence. Holly, at least, was also unable to think *what* to say under these bizarre circumstances, sitting in the high room of a crumbling old mill, waiting for an encounter with something supernatural. No small talk of any kind felt adequate to the moment, and a serious discussion of just about anything would seem ludicrous.

"I feel sort of foolish," she said eventually.

"Me, too," he admitted. "Just a little."

At seven o'clock, when she was opening the box of chocolate-covered doughnuts, she suddenly realized the mill had no lavatory. "What about a bathroom?"

He picked up his ring of keys from the floor and handed them to her. "Go on over to the house. The plumbing works. There's a half-bath right off the kitchen."

She realized the room was filling with shadows, and when she glanced at the window, she saw that twilight had arrived. Putting the doughnuts aside, she said, "I want to zip over there and get back before dark."

"Go ahead." Jim raised one hand as if pledging allegiance to the flag. "I swear on all that I hold sacred, I'll leave you at least one doughnut."

"Half the box better be there when I get back," she said, "or I'll kick your butt all the way into Svenborg to buy more."

"You take your doughnuts seriously."

"Damn right."

He smiled. "I like that in a woman."

Taking a flashlight to negotiate the mill below, she rose and went to the door. "Better start up the Coleman."

"Sure thing. When you get back, it'll be a right cozy little campsite."

Descending the narrow stairs, Holly began to worry about being separated from Jim, and step by step her anxiety increased. She was not afraid of being alone. What bothered her was leaving him by himself. Which was ridiculous. He was a grown man and far more capable of effective self-defense than was the average person.

The lower floor of the mill was much darker than when she had first seen it. Curtained with cobwebs, the dirty windows admitted almost none of the weak light of dusk.

As she crossed toward the arched opening to the antechamber, she was overcome by a creepy sense of being watched. She knew they were alone in the mill, and she chided herself for being such a ninny. But by the time she reached the archway, her apprehension had swelled until she could not resist the urge to turn and shine the flashlight into the chamber behind her. Shadows were draped across the old machinery as copiously as black crepe in an amusement-park haunted house; they slid aside when the flashlight beam touched them, fell softly back into place as the beam moved on. Each corner, undraped, revealed no spy. Someone could be sheltering behind one part of the millworks or another, and she considered prowling through the ruins in search of an intruder.

But abruptly she felt foolish, too easily spooked. Wondering what had happened to the intrepid reporter she had once been, Holly left the mill.

The sun was beyond the mountains. The sky was purple and that deep iridescent blue seen in old Maxfield Parrish paintings. A few toads were croaking from their shadowy niches along the banks of the pond.

All the way around the water, past the barn, to the back door of the house, Holly continued to feel watched. However, though it was possible that someone might be lurking in the mill, it was not too likely that a virtual platoon of spies had taken up positions in the barn, the surrounding fields, and the distant hills, intent on observing her every move.

"Idiot," she said self-mockingly as she used one of Jim's keys to open the back door.

Though she had the flashlight, she tried the wall switch unthinkingly. She was surprised to discover that the electrical service was still connected.

She was more surprised, however, by what the light revealed: a fully furnished kitchen. A breakfast table and four chairs stood by the window. Copper pots and pans dangled from a ceiling fixture, and twin racks of knives and other utensils hung on the wall near the cooktop. A toaster, toaster oven, and blender stood on the counters. A shopping list of about fifteen items was affixed to the refrigerator with a magnet in the shape of a can of Budweiser.

Hadn't Jim gotten rid of his grandparents' belongings when they had died five years ago?

Holly ran a finger along one of the counters, drawing a line through the thin coat of dust. But it was, at most, a three-month accumulation, not five years' worth of dirt.

After she used the bathroom adjacent to the kitchen, she wandered along the hallway, through the dining room and living room, where a full complement of furniture also stood under a light shroud of dust. Some of the paintings hung aslant. Crocheted antimacassars protected the backs and arms of the chairs and sofas. Long unwound, the tall grandfather clock was not ticking. In the living room, the magazine rack beside the La-Z-Boy recliner was crammed full of publications, and inside a mahogany display case, bibelots gleamed dully beneath their own skin of dust.

Her first thought was that Jim had left the house furnished in order to be able to rent it out while searching for a buyer. But on one wall of the living room were framed 8 × 10 photographs that would not have been left to the mercy of a tenant: Jim's father as a young man of about twenty-one; Jim's father and mother in their wedding finery; Jim at the age of five or six, with both parents.

The fourth and final picture was a two-shot, head and shoulders, of a pleasant-looking couple in their early fifties. The man was on the burly side, with bold square features, yet recognizably an Ironheart; the woman was more handsome, in a female way, than pretty, and elements of her face could also be seen in Jim and his father. Holly had no doubt that they were Jim's paternal grandparents, Lena and Henry Ironheart.

Lena Ironheart was the woman in whose body Holly had ridden like a spirit during last night's dream. Broad, clear face. Wide-set eyes. Full mouth. Curly hair. A natural beauty spot, just a little round dot of skin discoloration, marked the high curve of her right cheek.

Though Holly had described this woman accurately to Jim, he had not recognized her. Maybe he didn't think of her eyes as being wide-set or her mouth as being full. Maybe her hair had been curly only during part of her life, due to the attentions of a beautician. But the beauty spot had to have clicked a switch in his memory, even five years after his grandmother's death.

The sense of being watched had not entirely left Holly even after she had entered the house. Now, as she stared at Lena Ironheart's face in the photograph, the feeling of being under observation grew so acute that she abruptly wheeled around and looked back across the living room.

She was alone.

She stepped quickly to the archway and through it into the front hall. Deserted.

A dark mahogany staircase led up to the second floor. The dust on the newel post and bannister was undisturbed: no palm marks, no fingerprints.

Looking up the first flight, she said, "Hello?" Her voice sounded queerly flat in the empty house.

No one responded to her.

Hesitantly, she started to climb the stairs.

"Who's there?" she called.

Only silence answered her.

Frowning, she stopped on the third step. She glanced down into the front hall, then up toward the landing again.

The silence was too deep, unnatural. Even a deserted house had some noise in it, occasional creaks and ticks and pops from old wood swelling or contracting, a rattle from a loose windowpane tapped by a finger of wind.

But the Ironheart house was so hushed, Holly might have thought that she'd gone deaf, except that she could hear the sounds she made herself.

She climbed two more steps. Stopped again.

She *still* felt she was under observation. It was as if the old house itself watched her with malevolent interest, alive and sentient, possessed of a thousand eyes hidden in the wood moldings and in the pattern of the wallpaper.

Dust motes drifted in the rays of the landing light above.

Twilight pressed its purple face to the windows.

Standing just four steps below the landing, partly under the second flight that led into the unseen upstairs hallway, she became convinced that something was waiting for her on the second floor. It was not necessarily The Enemy up there, not even anything alive and hostile—but something horrible, the discovery of which would shatter her.

Her heart was hammering. When she swallowed, she found a lump in her throat. She drew breath with a startling, ragged sound.

The feeling of being watched and of trembling on the brink of a monstrous revelation became so overpowering that she turned and hurried down the steps. She did not flee pell-mell out of the house; she retraced her path and turned off all the lights as she went; but she did not dally, either.

Outside, the sky was purple-black where it met the mountains in the east, purplish-red where it touched the mountains in the west, and sapphire-blue between. The golden fields and hills had changed to pale gray, fading to charcoal, as if a fire had swept them while she was in the house.

As she crossed the yard and moved past the barn, the conviction that she was under observation only grew more intense. She glanced apprehensively at the open black square of the hay loft, the windows on either side of the big red double doors. It was a gut-clenching sensation of such primitive power that it transcended mere instinct. She felt as if she were a guinea pig in a laboratory experiment, with wires hooked into her brain, while scientists sent pulses of current directly into the raw cerebral tissues that controlled the fear reflex and generated paranoid delusions. She had never experienced anything like it, knew that she was teetering on the thin edge of panic, and struggled to get a grip on herself.

By the time she reached the graveled drive that curved around the pond, she was running. She held the extinguished flashlight like a club, prepared to swing it hard at anything that darted toward her.

The bells rang. Even above her frantic breathing, she heard the pure, silvery trilling of clappers rapidly striking the inner curves of perfectly tuned bells.

For an instant she was amazed that the phenomenon was audible outside the windmill and at a distance, as the building was halfway around the pond from her. Then something flickered in her peripheral vision even before the first spell of ringing ended, and she looked away from the mill, toward the water.

Pulses of blood-red light, originating at the center of the pond, spread outward toward the banks in tight concentric circles, like the measured ripples that radiated from the point at which a dropped stone struck deep water. That sight brought Holly to a stumbling halt; she almost went to her knees as gravel rolled under her feet.

When the bells fell silent, the crimson light in the pond was immediately snuffed out. The water was much darker now than when she had first seen it in mid-afternoon. It no longer had all the somber hues of slate, but was as black as a polished slab of obsidian.

The bells rang again, and the crimson light pulsed from the heart of the pond, radiating outward. She could see that each new bright blossom was not born on the surface of the water but in its depths, dim at first but swiftly rising, almost bursting like an overheated incandescent bulb when it neared the surface, casting waves of light toward the shore.

The ringing ceased.

The water darkened.

The toads along the shoreline were not croaking any more. The ever-murmuring world of nature had fallen as silent as the interior of the Ironheart farmhouse. No coyote howl, no insect cry, no owl hoot, no bat shriek or flap of wing, no rustling in the grass.

The bells sounded again, and the light returned, but this time it was not as red as gore, more of an orange-red, though it was brighter than before. At the water's edge, the feathery white panicles of the pampas grass caught the curious radiance and glowed like plumes of iridescent gas.

Something was rising from the bottom of the pond.

As the throbbing luminescence faded with the next cessation of the bells, Holly stood in the grip of awe and fear, knowing she should run but unable to move.

Ringing.

Light. Muddy-orange this time. No red tint at all. Brighter than ever.

Holly broke the chains of fear and sprinted toward the windmill.

On all sides, the palpitant light enlivened the dreary dusk. Shadows leapt rhythmically like Apaches dancing around a war fire. Beyond the fence, dead cornstalks bristled as repulsively as the spiny legs and plated torsos of praying mantises. The windmill appeared to be in the process of changing magically from stone to copper or even to gold.

The ringing stopped and the light went out as she reached the open door of the mill.

She raced across the threshold, then skidded to a stop in the darkness, on the brink of the lower chamber. No light at all came through the windows now. The blackness was tarry, cloying. As she fumbled for the switch on the flashlight, she found it hard to draw breath, as if the darkness itself had begun flowing into her lungs, suffocating her.

The flashlight came on just as the bells began to ring again. She slashed the beam across the room and back, to be sure nothing was there in the gloom, reaching for her. Then she found the stairs to her left and hurried toward the high room.

When she reached the window at the halfway point, she put her face to the pane of glass that she had wiped clean with her hand earlier in the day. In the pond below, the rippling bull's-eye of light was brighter still, now amber instead of orange.

Calling for Jim, Holly ran up the remaining stairs.

As she went, lines of Edgar Allan Poe's poetry, studied an age ago in junior high school and thought forgotten, rang crazily through her mind:

> Keeping time, time, time,
> In a sort of Runic rhyme,
> To the tintinnabulation that so musically wells
> From the bells, bells, bells, bells,
> Bells, bells, bells—

She burst into the high room, where Jim stood in the soft winter-white glow of the Coleman gas lantern. He was smiling, turning in a circle and looking expectantly at the walls around him.

As the bells died away, she said, "Jim, come look, come quick, something's in the lake."

She dashed to the nearest window, but it was just far enough around the wall from the pond to prevent her seeing the water. The other two windows were even more out of line with the desired view, so she did not even try them.

"The ringing in the stone," Jim said dreamily.

Holly returned to the head of the stairs as the bells began to ring again. She paused and looked back just long enough to be sure that Jim was following her, for he seemed in something of a daze.

Hurrying down the stairs, she heard more lines of Poe's poem reverberating in her mind:

> Hear the loud alarum bells—
> Brazen bells!
> What a tale of terror, now, their turbulency tells!

She had never been the kind of woman to whom sprang lines of verse appropriate to the moment. She couldn't recall quoting a line of poetry or even reading any—other than Louise Tarvohl's treacle!—since college.

When she reached the window, she scrubbed frantically at another pane with the palm of her hand, to give them a better view of the spectacle below. She saw that the light was blood-red again and dimmer, as if whatever had been rising through the water was now sinking again.

> Oh, the bells, bells bell!
> What a tale their terror tells—

It seemed crazy to be mentally reciting poetry in the midst of these wondrous and frightening events, but she had never been under such stress before. Maybe this was the way the mind worked—giddily dredging up long-forgotten knowledge—when you were about to meet a higher power. Because that's just what she felt was about to happen, an encounter with a higher power, perhaps God but most likely not. She didn't really think God lived in a pond, although any minister or priest would probably tell her that God lived everywhere, in all things. God was like the eight-hundred-pound gorilla who could live anywhere he wanted.

Just as Jim reached her, the ringing stopped, and the crimson light in the pond quickly faded. He squeezed in beside her and put his face to the glass.

They waited.

Two seconds ticked by. Two more.

"No," she said. "Damn it, I wanted you to see."

But the ringing did not resume, and the pond remained dark out there in the steadily dimming twilight. Night would be upon them within a few minutes.

"What was it?" Jim asked, leaning back from the window.

"Like something in a Spielberg film," she said excitedly, "rising up out of the water, from deep under the pond, light throbbing in time with the bells. I think that's where the ringing originates, from the thing in the pond, and somehow it's transmitted through the walls of the mill."

"Spielberg film?" He looked puzzled.

She tried to explain: "Wonderful and terrifying, awesome and strange, scary and damned exciting all at once."

"You mean like in *Close Encounters?* Are you talking a starship or something?"

"Yes. No. I'm not sure. I don't know. Maybe something weirder than that."

"Weirder than a starship?"

Her wonder, and even her fear, subsided in favor of frustration. She was not accustomed to finding herself at a complete loss for words to describe things that she had felt or seen. But with this man and the incomparable experiences in which he became entangled, even her sophisticated vocabulary and talent for supple phrase-making failed her miserably.

"Shit, yes!" she said at last. "Weirder than a starship. At least weirder than the way they show them in the movies."

"Come on," he said, ascending the stairs again, "let's get back up there." When she lingered at the window, he returned to her and took her hand. "It isn't over yet. I think it's just beginning. And the place for us to be is the upper room. I *know* it's the place. Come on, Holly."

5 They sat on the inflatable-mattress sleeping bags again.

The lantern cast a pearly-silver glow, whitewashing the yellow-beige blocks of limestone. In the baglike wicks inside the glass chimney of the lamp, the gas burned with a faint hiss, so it seemed as if whispering voices were rising through the floorboards of that high room.

Jim was poised at the apex of his emotional roller coaster, full of childlike delight and anticipation, and this time Holly was right there with him. The light in the pond had terrified her, but it had also touched her in other ways, sparking deep psychological responses on a primitive sub-subconscious level, igniting fuses of wonder and hope which were fizzing-burning unquenchably toward some much-desired explosion of faith, emotional catharsis.

She had accepted that Jim was not the only troubled person in the room. His heart might contain more turmoil than hers, but she was as empty, in her own way, as he was in his. When they'd met in Portland, she had been a burnt-out cynic, going through the motions of a life, not even trying to identify and fill the empty spaces in her heart. She had not experienced the tragedy and grief that he had known, but now she realized that leading a life equally devoid of tragedy *and* joy could breed despair. Passing days and weeks and years in the pursuit of goals that had not really mattered to her, driven by a purpose she had not truly embraced, with no one to whom she was profoundly committed, she had been eaten by a dry-rot of the soul. She and Jim were the two pieces of a yin-yang puzzle, each shaped to fill the hollowness in the other, healing each other merely by their contact. They fit together astonishingly well, and the match seemed inevitable; but the puzzle might never have been solved if the halves of it had not been brought together in the same place at the same time.

Now she waited with nervous excitement for contact with the power that had led Jim to her. She was ready for God or for something quite different but equally benign. She could not believe that what she had seen in the pond was The Enemy. That creature was apart from this, connected somehow but different. Even if Jim had not told her that something fine and good was coming, she eventually would have sensed, on her own, that the light in the water and the ringing in the stone heralded not blood and death but rapture.

They spoke tersely at first, afraid that voluble conversation would inhibit that higher power from initiating the next stage of contact.

"How long has the pond been here?" she asked.

"A long time."

"Before the Ironhearts?"

"Yeah."

"Before the farm itself?"

"I'm sure it was."

"Possibly forever?"

"Possibly."

"Any local legends about it?"

"What do you mean?"

"Ghost stories, Loch Ness, that kind of stuff."

"No. Not that I've ever heard."

They were silent. Waiting.

Finally Holly said, "What's your theory?"

"Huh?"

"Earlier today you said you had a theory, something strange and wonderful, but you didn't want to talk about it till you'd thought it through."

"Oh, right. Now maybe it's more than a theory. When you said you'd seen something under the pond in your dream . . . well, I don't know why, but I started thinking about an encounter. . . ."

"Encounter?"

"Yeah. Like what you said. Something . . . alien."

"Not of this world," Holly said, remembering the sound of the bells and the light in the pond.

"They're out there in the universe somewhere," he said with quiet enthusiasm. "It's too big for them not to be out there. And someday they'll be coming. Someone will encounter them. So why not me, why not you?"

"But it must've been there under the pond when you were ten."

"Maybe."

"Why would it be there all this time?"

"I don't know. Maybe it's been there a lot longer. Hundreds of years. Thousands."

"But why a starship at the bottom of a pond?"

"Maybe it's an observation station, a place where they monitor human civilization, like an outpost we might set up in Antarctica to study things there."

Holly realized they sounded like kids sitting under the stars on a summer night, drawn like all kids to the contemplation of the unknown and to fantasies of exotic adventure. On one level she found their musings absurd, even laughable, and she was unable to believe that recent events could have such a neat yet fanciful explanation. But on another level, where she was still a child and always would be, she desperately wanted the fantasy to be made real.

Twenty minutes passed without a new development, and gradually Holly began to settle down from the heights of excitement and nervous agitation to which the lights in the pond had catapulted her. Still filled with wonder but no longer mentally numbed by it, she remembered what had happened to her just prior to the appearance of the radiant presence in the millpond: the overwhelming, preternatural, almost panic-inducing awareness of being watched. She was about to mention it to Jim when she recalled the *other* strange things she had found at the farmhouse.

"It's completely furnished," she said. "You never cleaned the house out after your grandfather died."

"I left it furnished in case I was able to rent it while waiting for a buyer."

Those were virtually the same words she had used, standing in the house, to explain the curious situation to herself. "But you left all their personal belongings there, too."

He did not look at her but at the walls, waiting for some sign of a superhuman presence. "I'd have taken that stuff away if I'd ever found a renter."

"You've left it there for almost five years?"

He shrugged.

She said, "It's been cleaned more or less regularly since then, though not recently."

"A renter might always show up."

"It's sort of creepy, Jim."

Finally he looked at her. "How so?"

"It's like a mausoleum."

His blue eyes were utterly unreadable, but Holly had the feeling she was annoying him, perhaps because this mundane talk of renters and house cleaning and real estate was pulling him away from the more pleasurable contemplation of alien encounters.

He sighed and said, "Yeah, it is creepy, a little."

"Then why . . . ?"

He slowly twisted the lantern control, reducing the flow of gas to the wicks. The hard white light softened to a moon-pale glow, and the shadows eased closer. "To tell you the truth, I couldn't bear to pack up my granddad's things. Together, we'd sorted through grandma's belongings only eight months earlier, when she'd died, and that had been hard enough. When he . . . passed away so soon after her, it was too much for me. For so long, they'd been all I had. Then suddenly I didn't even have them."

A tortured expression darkened the blue of his eyes.

As a flood of sympathy washed through Holly, she reached across the ice chest and took his hand.

He said, "I procrastinated, kept procrastinating, and the longer I delayed sorting through his things, the harder it became to *ever* do it." He sighed again. "If I'd have found a renter or a buyer, that would have forced me to put things in order, no matter how unpleasant the job. But this old farm is about as marketable as a truckload of sand in the middle of the Mojave."

Closing the house upon the death of his grandfather, touching nothing in it for four years and four months, except to clean it once in a while—that was eccentric. Holly couldn't see it any other way. At the same time, however, it was an eccentricity that touched her, moved her. As she had sensed from the start, he was a gentle man beneath his rage, beneath his steely superhero identity, and she liked the soft-hearted part of him, too.

"We'll do it together," Holly said. "When we've figured out what the hell is happening to us, wherever and however we go on from here, there'll be time for us to sort through your grandfather's things. It won't be so difficult if we do it together."

He smiled at her and squeezed her hand.

She remembered something else. "Jim, you recall the description I gave you of the woman in my dream last night, the woman who came up the mill stairs?"

"Sort of."

"You said you didn't recognize her."

"So?"

"But there's a photo of her in the house."

"There is?"

"In the living room, that photograph of a couple in their early fifties—are they your grandparents, Lena and Henry?"

"Yeah. That's right."

"Lena was the woman in my dream."

He frowned. "Isn't that odd . . . ?"

"Well, maybe. But what's odder is, you didn't recognize her."

"I guess your description wasn't that good."

"But didn't you hear me say she had a beauty mark—"

His eyes narrowed, and his hand tightened around hers. "Quick, the tablets."

Confused, she said, "What?"

"Something's about to happen, I feel it, and we need the tablets we bought at The Center."

He let go of her hand, and she withdrew the two yellow, lined tablets and felt-tip pen from the plastic bag at her side. He took them from her, hesitated, looking around at the walls and at the shadows above them, as if waiting to be told what to do next.

The bells rang.

THAT MUSICAL TINTINNABULATION sent a thrill through Jim. He knew that he was on the verge of discovering the meaning not merely of the events of the past year but of the last two and a half decades. And not just that, either. More. Much more. The ringing heralded the revelation of even greater understanding, transcendental truths, an explanation of the fundamental meaning of his entire life, past and future, origins and destiny, and of the meaning of existence itself. Grandiose as such a notion might be, he sensed that the secrets of creation would be revealed to him before he left the windmill, and that he would reach the state of enlightenment he had sought—and failed to find—in a score of religions.

As the second spell of ringing began, Holly started to get up.

Jim figured she intended to descend to the window on the stairs and look into the pond. He said, "No, wait. It's going to happen *here* this time."

She hesitated, then sat down.

As the ringing stopped again, Jim felt compelled to push the ice chest out of the way and put one of the yellow, lined tablets on the floor between him and Holly. He was not sure what he was expected to do with the other tablet and the pen, but after a brief moment of indecision, he held on to them.

When the melodic ringing began a third time, it was accompanied by an impossible pulse of light within the limestone walls. The red glow seemed to well up from inside the stone at a point directly in front of them, then suddenly raced around the room, encircling them with a throbbing band of luminescence.

Even as the strange flare whipped around them, Holly issued a wordless sound of fear, and Jim remembered what she had told him of her dream last night. The woman—whether it had been his grandmother or not—had climbed the stairs into the high room, had seen an amber emanation within the walls, as if the mill was made of colored glass, and had witnessed something unimaginably hostile being born out of those mortared blocks.

"It's okay." He was eager to reassure her. "This isn't The Enemy. It's something else. There's no danger here. This is a different light."

He was only sharing with her the reassurances that were flooding into him from a higher power. He hoped to God that he was correct, that no threat was imminent, for he remembered too well the hideous biological transformation of his own bedroom ceiling in Laguna Niguel little more than twelve hours ago. Light had pulsed within the oily, insectile birth sac that had blistered out of ordinary drywall, and the shadowy form within, writhing and twitching, had been nothing he would ever want to see more directly.

During two more bursts of melodic ringing, the color of the light changed to amber. But otherwise it in no way resembled the menacing radiance in his bedroom ceiling, which had been a different shade of amber altogether— the vile yellow of putrescent matter or of rich dark pus—and which had throbbed in sympathy with an ominous tripartite heartbeat that was not audible now.

Holly looked scared nonetheless.

He wished he could pull her close, put his arm around her. But he needed to give his undivided attention to the higher power that was striving to reach him.

The ringing stopped, but the light did not fade. It quivered, shimmered, dimmed, and brightened. It moved through the otherwise dark wall in scores of separate amoeba-like forms that constantly flowed together and separated into new shapes; it was like a one-dimensional representation of the kaleidoscopic display in one of those old Lava lamps. The ever-changing patterns evolved on all sides of them, from the base of the wall to the apex of the domed ceiling.

"I feel like we're in a bathysphere, all glass, suspended far, far down in the ocean," Holly said. "And great schools of luminescent fish are diving and soaring and swirling past us on all sides, through the deep black water."

He loved her for putting the experience into better words than he could summon, words that would not let him forget the images they described, even if he lived a hundred years.

Unquestionably, the ghostly luminosity lay within the stone, not merely on the surface of it. He could see *into* that now-translucent substance, as if it had been alchemized into a dark but well-clarified quartz. The amber radiance brightened the room more than did the lantern, which he had turned low. His trembling hands looked golden, as did Holly's face.

But pockets of darkness remained, and the constantly moving light enlivened the shadows as well.

"What now?" Holly asked softly.

Jim noticed that something had happened to the yellow tablet on the floor between them. "Look."

Words had appeared on the top third of the first page. They looked as if they had been formed by a finger dipped in ink:

I AM WITH YOU.

6

Holly had been distracted—to say the least!—by the lightshow, but she did not think that Jim could have leaned to the tablet and printed the words with the felt-tip pen or any other instrument without drawing her attention. Yet she found it hard to believe that some disembodied presence had conveyed the message.

"I think we're being encouraged to ask questions," Jim said.

"Then ask it what it is," she said at once.

He wrote a question on the second tablet, which he was holding, and showed it to her:

Who are you?

As they watched, the answer appeared on the first tablet, which lay between and slightly in front of them at such an angle that they could both read it. The words were not burnt onto the paper and were not formed by ink that dripped magically from the air. Instead, the irregular, wavery letters appeared as dim gray shapes and grew darker as they seemed to float up out of the paper, as though a page of the tablet were not one-five-hundredth of an inch thick but a pool of liquid many feet deep. She recognized immediately that this was similar to the effect she had seen earlier when the balls of light had risen to the center of the pond before bursting and casting concentric rings of illumination outward through the water; this was, as well, how the light had first welled up in the limestone walls before the blocks had become thoroughly translucent.

THE FRIEND.

Who are you? The Friend.

It seemed to be an odd self-description. Not "your friend" or "a friend" but *The* Friend.

For an alien intelligence, if indeed that's all it was, the name had curious spiritual implications, connotations of divinity. Men had given God many names—Jehovah, Allah, Brahma, Zeus, Aesir—but even more titles. God was The Almighty, The Eternal Being, The Infinite, The Father, The Savior, The Creator, The Light. The Friend seemed to fit right into that list.

Jim quickly wrote another question and showed it to Holly: *Where do you come from?*

ANOTHER WORLD.

Which could mean anything from heaven to Mars.

Do you mean another planet?

YES.

"My God," Holly said, awed in spite of herself.

So much for the great hereafter.

She looked up from the tablet and met Jim's eyes. They seemed to shine brighter than ever, although the chrome-yellow light had imparted to them an exceptional green tint.

Restless with excitement, she rose onto her knees, then eased back again, sitting on her calves. The top tablet page was filled with the entity's responses. Holly equivocated only briefly, then tore it off and set it aside, so they could see the second page. She glanced back and forth between Jim's questions and the rapidly appearing answers.

From another solar system?

YES.

From another galaxy?

YES.

Is it your vessel we've seen in the pond?

YES.

How long have you been here?

10,000 YEARS.

As she stared at that figure, it seemed to Holly that this moment was more like a dream than some of the actual dreams she'd been having lately. After so much mystery, there were answers—but they seemed to be coming too easily. She did not know what she had expected, but she had not imagined that the murkiness in which they had been operating would clear as quickly as if a drop of a magical universal detergent had been dropped into it.

"Ask her why she's here," Holly said, tearing off the second sheet and putting it with the first.

Jim was surprised. *"She?"*

"Why not?"

He brightened. "Why not?" he agreed.

He turned to a new page in his own tablet and wrote her question: *Why are you here?*

Floating up through the paper to the surface: TO OBSERVE, TO STUDY, TO HELP MANKIND.

"You know what this is like?" Holly said.

"What's it like?"

"An episode of *Outer Limits*."

"The old TV show?"

"Yeah."

"Wasn't that before your time?"

"It's on cable."

"But what do you mean it's like an episode of *Outer Limits*?"

She frowned at TO OBSERVE, TO STUDY, TO HELP MANKIND and said, "Don't you think it's a little . . . trite?"

"Trite?" He was irritated. "No, I don't. Because I haven't any idea what alien contact *should* be like. I haven't had a whole lot of experience with it, certainly not enough to have expectations or be jaded."

"I'm sorry. I don't know . . . it's just . . . okay, let's see where this leads."

She had to admit that she was no less awed than she had been when the light had first appeared in the walls. Her heart continued to thud hard and fast, and she was still unable to draw a really deep breath. She still felt that they were in the presence of something superhuman, maybe even a higher power by one definition or another, and she was humbled by it. Considering what she had seen in the pond, the pulsing luminescence even now swimming through the wall, and the words that kept shimmering into view on the tablet, she would have been hopelessly stupid if she had *not* been awed.

Undeniably, however, her sense of wonder was dulled by the feeling that this entity was structuring the encounter like an old movie or TV script. With a sarcastic note in his voice, Jim had said that he had too little experience with alien contact to have developed any expectations that could be disappointed. But that was not true. Having grown up in the sixties and seventies, he had been as media-saturated as she had been. They'd been exposed to the same TV shows and movies, magazines and books; science fiction had been a major influence in popular culture all their lives. He had acquired plenty of detailed expectations about what alien contact would be like—and the entity in the wall was playing to all of them. Holly's only conscious expectation had been that a *real* close encounter of the third kind would be like nothing the novelists and screenwriters imagined in all their wildest flights of fantasy, because when referring to life from another world, alien *meant* alien, different, beyond easy comparison or comprehension.

"Okay," she said, "maybe familiarity is the point. I mean, maybe it's using our modern myths as a convenient way to present itself to us, a way to make itself comprehensible to us. Because it's probably so radically different from us that we could never understand its true nature or appearance."

"Exactly," Jim said. He wrote another question: *What is the light we see in the walls*?

THE LIGHT IS ME.

Holly didn't wait for Jim to write the next question. She addressed the entity directly: "How can you move through a wall?"

Because the alien seemed such a stickler about form, she was somewhat surprised when it did not insist on hewing to the written question-reply format. It answered her at once: I CAN BECOME PART OF ANYTHING, MOVE WITHIN IT, TAKE SHAPE FROM IT WHENEVER I CHOOSE.

"Sounds a little like bragging," she said.

"I can't believe you can be sarcastic at a time like this," Jim said impatiently.

"I'm not being sarcastic," she explained. "I'm just trying to understand."

He looked doubtful.

To the alien presence, she said, "You understand the problems I'm having with this, don't you?"

On the tablet: YES.

She ripped away that page, revealing a fresh one. Increasingly restless and nervous, but not entirely sure why, Holly got to her feet and turned in a circle, looking at the play of light in the walls as she formulated her next question. "Why is your approach marked by the sound of bells?"

No answer appeared on the tablet.

She repeated the question.

The tablet remained blank.

Holly said, "Trade secret, I guess."

She felt a bead of cold sweat trickle out of her right armpit and down her side, under her blouse. A childlike wonder still worked in her, but fear was on the rise again. Something was wrong. Something more than the cliched nature of the story the entity was giving them. She couldn't quite put her finger on what spooked her.

On his own tablet, Jim quickly wrote another question, and Holly leaned down to read it: *Did you appear to me in this room when I was ten years old?*

YES. OFTEN.

Did you make me forget it?

YES.

"Don't bother writing your questions," Holly said. "Just ask them like I do."

Jim was clearly startled by her suggestion, and she was surprised that he had persisted with his pen and tablet even after seeing that the questions she asked aloud were answered. He seemed reluctant to put aside the felt-tip and the paper, but at last he did. "Why did you make me forget?"

Even standing, Holly could easily read the bold words that appeared on the yellow tablet:

YOU WERE NOT READY TO REMEMBER.

"Unnecessarily cryptic," she muttered. "You're right. It must be male."

Jim tore off the used page, put it with the others, and paused, chewing his lip, evidently not sure what to ask next. Finally he said, "Are you male or female?"

I AM MALE.

"More likely," Holly said, "it's neither. It's *alien*, after all, and it's as likely to reproduce by parthenogenesis."

I AM MALE, it repeated.

Jim remained seated, legs folded, an undiminished look of wonder on his face, more boylike now than ever.

Holly did not understand why her anxiety level was soaring while Jim continued to bounce up and down—well, virtually—with enthusiasm and delight.

He said, "What do you look like?"

WHATEVER I CHOOSE TO LOOK LIKE.

"Could you appear to us as a man or woman?" Jim asked.

YES.

"As a dog?"

YES.

"As a cat?"

YES.

"As a beetle?"

YES.

Without the security of his pen and tablet, Jim seemed to have been reduced to inane questions. Holly half expected him to ask the entity what its favorite color was, whether it preferred Coke or Pepsi, and if it liked Barry Manilow music.

But he said, "How old are you?"

I AM A CHILD.

"A child?" Jim responded. "But you told us you've been on our world for ten thousand years."

I AM STILL A CHILD.

Jim said, "Then is your species very long-lived?"

WE ARE IMMORTAL.

"Wow."

"It's lying," Holly told him.

Appalled by her effrontery, he said, "Jesus, Holly!"

"Well, it is."

And *that* was the source of her renewed fear—the fact that it was not being straight with them, was playing games, deceiving. She had a sense that it regarded them with enormous contempt. In which case, she probably should have shut up, been meekly adoring before its power, and tried not to anger it.

Instead she said, "If it were really immortal, it wouldn't think of itself as a child. It *couldn't* think that way about itself. Infancy, childhood, adolescence, adulthood—those are age categories a species concerns itself with if it has a finite lifespan. If you're immortal, you might be born innocent, ignorant, uneducated, but you aren't born young because you're never really going to get old."

"Aren't you splitting hairs?" Jim asked almost petulantly.

"I don't think so. It's lying to us."

"Maybe its use of the word 'child' was just another way it was trying to make its alien nature more understandable."

YES.

"Bullshit," Holly said.

"Damn it, Holly!"

As Jim removed another page from the tablet, detaching it neatly along its edge, Holly moved to the wall and studied the patterns of light churning through it. Seen close up, they were quite beautiful and strange, not like a smooth-flowing phosphorescent fluid or fiery streams of lava, but like scintillant swarms of fireflies, millions of spangled points not unlike her analogy of luminous, schooling fish.

Holly half expected the wall in front of her to bulge suddenly. Split open. Give birth to a monstrous form.

She wanted to step back. Instead she moved closer. Her nose was only an inch from the transmuted stone. Viewed this intimately, the surge and flux and whirl of the millions of bright cells was dizzying. There was no heat from it, but she imagined she could feel the flicker of light and shadow across her face.

"Why is your approach marked by the sound of bells?" she asked.

After a few seconds, Jim spoke from behind her: "No answer."

The question seemed innocent enough, and one that they should logically be expected to ask. The entity's unwillingness to answer alerted her that the ringing must be somehow vitally important. Understanding the bells might be the first step toward learning something real and true about this creature.

"Why is your approach marked by the sound of bells?"

Jim reported: "No answer. I don't think you should ask that question again, Holly. It obviously doesn't want to answer, and there's nothing to be gained by aggravating it. This isn't The Enemy, this is—"

"Yeah, I know. It's The Friend."

She remained at the wall and felt herself to be face-to-face with an alien presence, though it had nothing that corresponded to a face. It was focused on her now. It was right *there*.

Again she said, "Why is your approach marked by the sound of bells?"

Instinctively she knew that her innocent question and her not-so-innocent repetition of it had put her in great danger. Her heart was thudding so loud that she wondered if Jim could hear it. She figured The Friend, with all its powers, could not only hear her hammering heart but see it jumping like a panicked rabbit within the cage of her chest. It knew she was afraid, all right. Hell, it might even be able to read her mind. She had to show it that she would not allow fear to deter her.

She put one hand on the light-filled stone. If those luminous clouds were not merely a projection of the creature's consciousness, not just an illusion or representation for their benefit, if the thing was, as it claimed, actually alive in the wall, then the stone was now its flesh. Her hand was upon its body.

Faint vibrations passed across the wall in distinctive, whirling vortexes. That was all she felt. No heat. The fire within the stone was evidently cold.

"Why is your approach marked by the sound of bells?"

"Holly, don't," Jim said. Worry tainted his voice for the first time. Perhaps he, too, had begun to sense that The Friend was not entirely a friend.

But she was driven by a suspicion that willpower mattered in this confrontation, and that a demonstration of unflinching will would set a new tone in their relationship with The Friend. She could not have explained why she felt so strongly about it. Just instinct—not a woman's but an ex-reporter's.

"Why is your approach marked by the sound of bells?"

She thought she detected a slight change in the vibrations that tingled across her palm, but she might have imagined it, for they were barely perceptible in the first place. Through her mind flickered an image of the stone cracking open in a jagged mouth and biting off her hand, blood spurting, white bone bristling from the ragged stump of her wrist.

Though she was shaking uncontrollably, she did not step back or lift her hand off the wall.

She wondered if The Friend had sent her that horrifying image.

"Why is your approach marked by the sound of bells?"

"Holly, for Christ's sake—" Jim broke off, then said, "Wait, an answer's coming."

Willpower *did* matter. But for God's sake, why? Why should an all-powerful alien force from another galaxy be intimidated by her unwavering resolution?

Jim reported the response: "It says . . . 'For drama?' "

"For drama?" she repeated.

"Yeah. F-O-R, then D-R-A-M-A, then a question mark."

To the thing in the wall, she said, "Are you telling me the bells are just a bit of theater to dramatize your apparitions?"

After a few seconds, Jim said, "No answer."

"And why the question mark?" she asked The Friend. "Don't you know what the bells mean yourself, where the sound comes from, what makes it, why? Are you only guessing when you say 'for drama'? How can you not know what it is if it always accompanies you?"

"Nothing," Jim told her.

She stared into the wall. The churning, schooling cells of light were increasingly disorienting her, but she did not close her eyes.

"A new message," Jim said. " 'I am going.' "

"Chicken," Holly said softly into the amorphous face of the thing in the wall. But she was sheathed in cold sweat now.

The amber light began to darken, turn orange.

Stepping away from the wall at last, Holly swayed and almost fell. She moved back to her bedroll and dropped to her knee.

New words appeared on the tablet: I WILL BE BACK.

"When?" Jim asked.

WHEN THE TIDE IS MINE.

"What tide?"

THERE IS A TIDE IN THE VESSEL, AN EBB AND FLOW, DARKNESS AND LIGHT. I RISE WITH THE LIGHT TIDE, BUT HE RISES WITH THE DARK.

"He?" Holly asked.

THE ENEMY.

The light in the walls was red-orange now, dimmer, but still ceaselessly changing patterns around them.

Jim said, "Two of you share the starship?"

YES. TWO FORCES. TWO ENTITIES.

It's lying, Holly thought. This, like all the rest of its story, is just like the bells: good theater.

WAIT FOR MY RETURN.

"We'll wait," Jim said.

DO NOT SLEEP.

"Why can't we sleep?" Holly asked, playing along.

YOU MIGHT DREAM.

The page was full. Jim ripped it off and stacked it with the others.

The light in the walls was blood-red now, steadily fading.

DREAMS ARE DOORWAYS.

"What are you telling us?"

The same three words again: DREAMS ARE DOORWAYS.

"It's a warning," Jim said.

DREAMS ARE DOORWAYS.

No, Holly thought, it's a threat.

7

The windmill was just a windmill again. Stones and timbers. Mortar and nails. Dust sifting, wood rotting, iron rusting, spiders spinning in secret lairs.

Holly sat directly in front of Jim, in powwow position, their knees touching. She held both his hands, partly because she drew strength from his touch, and partly because she wanted to reassure him and take the sting out of what she was about to say.

"Listen, babe, you're the most interesting man I've ever known, the sexiest, for sure, and I think, at heart, the kindest. But you do a lousy interview. For the most part, your questions aren't well-thought-out, you don't get at the meat of an issue, you follow up on irrelevancies but generally fail to follow up on the really important answers. And you're a naive enough reporter to think that the subject is always being straight with you, when they're almost never straight with an interviewer, so you don't *probe* the way you should."

He did not seem offended. He smiled and said, "I didn't think of myself as a reporter doing an interview."

"Well, kiddo, that's exactly what the situation was. The Friend, as he calls himself, has information, and we need information to know where we stand, to do our job."

"I thought of it more as . . . I don't know . . . as an epiphany. When God came to Moses with the Ten Commandments, I figure He just told Moses what they were, and if Moses had other questions he didn't feel he had to grill the Big Guy."

"This wasn't God in the walls."

"I know that. I'm past that idea now. But it was an alien intelligence so superior to us that it almost might as well *be* God."

"We don't know that," she said patiently.

"Sure we do. When you consider the high degree of intelligence and the millennia needed to build a civilization capable of traveling across galaxies—good heavens, we're only monkeys by comparison!"

"There, you see, that's what I'm talking about. How do you know it's from another galaxy? Because you believe what it told you. How do you know there's a spaceship under the pond? Because you believe what it told you."

Jim was getting impatient now. "Why would it lie to us, what would it have to gain from lies?"

"I don't know. But we can't be sure that it isn't manipulating us. And when it comes back, like it promised, I want to be ready for it. I want to spend the next hour or two or three—however long we've got—making a list of questions, so we can put it through a carefully planned inquisition. We've got to have a strategy for squeezing *real* information from it, facts not fantasies, and our questions have to support that strategy." When he frowned, she hastened on before he could interrupt. "Okay, all right, maybe it's incapable of lying, maybe it's noble and pure, maybe everything it's told us is the gospel truth. But listen, Jim, this is not an epiphany. The Friend set the rules by influencing you to buy the tablets and pen. It established the question-and-answer format. If it didn't want us to make the best of that format, it would've just told you to shut up and would've blabbered at you from a burning bush!"

He stared at her. He chewed his lip thoughtfully.

He shifted his gaze to the walls where the creature of light had swum in the stone.

Pressing her point, Holly said, "You never even asked it why it wants you to save people's lives, or why some people and not others."

He looked at her again, obviously surprised to realize that he had not pursued the answer to the most important question of all. In the lactescent glow of the softly hissing gas lantern, his eyes were blue again, not green as the amber light had temporarily made them. And troubled.

"Okay," he said. "You're right. I guess I was just swept away by it all. I mean, Holly, whatever the hell it is—it's astounding."

"It's astounding," she acknowledged.

"We'll do what you want, make up a list of carefully thought-out questions. And when it comes back, you should be the one to ask all of them, 'cause you'll be better at ad-libbing other questions if it says anything that needs follow-up."

"I agree," she said, relieved that he had suggested it without being pressured.

She was better schooled at interviewing than he was, but she was also more trustworthy in this particular situation than Jim could ever be. The Friend had a long past relationship with him and had, admittedly, already messed with his memory by making him forget about the encounters they'd had twenty-five years ago. Holly had to assume that Jim was co-opted, to one degree or another corrupted, though he could not realize it. The Friend had been *in his mind,* perhaps on scores or hundreds of occasions, when he had been at a formative age, and when he had been particularly vulnerable due to the loss of his parents, therefore even more susceptible to manipulation and control than most ten-year-old boys. On a subconscious level, Jim Ironheart might be programmed to protect The Friend's secrets rather than help to reveal them.

Holly knew she was walking a thread-thin line between judicious precaution and paranoia, might even be treading more on the side of the latter than the former. Under the circumstances, a little paranoia was a prescription for survival.

When he said he was going outside to relieve himself, however, she much preferred to be with him than alone in the high room. She followed him downstairs and stood by the Ford with her back to him while he peed against the split-rail fence beside the cornfield.

She stared out at the deep black pond.

She listened to the toads, which were singing again. So were the cicadas. The events of the day had rattled her. Now even the sounds of nature seemed malevolent.

She wondered if they had come up against something too strange and too powerful to be dealt with by just a failed reporter and an ex-schoolteacher. She wondered if they ought to leave the farm right away. She wondered if they would be allowed to leave.

Since the departure of The Friend, Holly's fear had not abated. If anything, it had increased. She felt as if they were living under a thousand-ton weight that was magically suspended by a single human hair, but the magic was weakening and the hair was stretched as taut and brittle as a filament of glass.

BY MIDNIGHT, THEY had eaten six chocolate doughnuts and composed seven pages of questions for The Friend. Sugar was an energizer and a consolation in times of trouble, but it was no help to already-frayed nerves. Holly's anxiety had a sharp refined-sugar edge to it now, like a well-stropped razor.

Pacing with the tablet in her hand, Holly said, "And we're not going to let it get away with written answers this time. That just slows down the give and take between interviewer and interviewee. We're going to insist that it talk to us."

Jim was lying on his back, his hands folded behind his head. "It can't talk."

"How do you know that?"

"Well, I'm assuming it can't, or otherwise it would've talked right from the start."

"Don't assume anything," she said. "If it can mix its molecules with the wall, swim through stone—through *anything*, if it's to be believed—and if it can assume any form it wishes, then it can sure as hell form a mouth and vocal cords and talk like any self-respecting higher power."

"I guess you're right," he said uneasily.

"It already said that it could appear to us as a man or woman if it wanted, didn't it?"

"Well, yeah."

"I'm not even asking for a flashy materialization. Just a voice, a disembodied voice, a little sound with the old lightshow."

Listening to herself as she talked, Holly realized that she was using her edginess to pump herself, to establish an aggressive tone that would serve her well when The Friend returned. It was an old trick she had learned when she had interviewed people whom she found imposing or intimidating.

Jim sat up. "Okay, it could talk if it wanted to, but maybe it doesn't want to."

"We already decided we can't let it set all the rules, Jim."

"But I don't understand why we have to antagonize it."

"I'm not antagonizing it."

"I think we should be at least a little respectful."

"Oh, I respect the hell out of it."

"You don't seem to."

"I'm convinced it could squash us like bugs if it wanted to, and that gives me tremendous respect for it."

"That's not the kind of respect I mean."

"That's the only kind of respect it's earned from me so far," she said, pacing around him now instead of back and forth. "When it stops trying to manipulate me, stops trying to scare the crap out of me, starts giving me answers that ring true, then maybe I'll respect it for other reasons."

"You're getting a little spooky," he said.

"*Me?*"

"You're so hostile."

"I am not."

He was frowning at her. "Looks like blind hostility to me."

"It's adversarial journalism. It's the modern reporter's tone and theme. You don't question your subject and later explain him to readers, you *attack* him. You have an agenda, a version of the truth you want to report regardless of the full truth, and you fulfill it. I never approved of it, never indulged in it, which is why I was always losing out on stories and promotions to other reporters. Now, here, tonight, I'm all for the attack part. The big difference is, I *do* care about getting to the truth, not shaping it, and I just want to twist and yank some real facts out of this alien of ours."

"Maybe he won't show up."

"He said he would."

Jim shook his head. "But why should he if you're going to be like this?"

"You're saying he might be *afraid* of me? What kind of higher power is that?"

The bells rang, and she jumped in alarm.

Jim got to his feet. "Just take it easy."

The bells fell silent, rang again, fell silent. When they rang a third time, a sullen red light appeared at one point in the wall. It grew more intense, assumed a brighter shade, then suddenly burst across the domed room like a blazing fireworks display, after which the bells stopped ringing and the multitude of sparks coalesced into the pulsing, constantly moving amoeba-like forms that they had seen before.

"Very dramatic," Holly said. As the light swiftly progressed from red through orange to amber, she seized the initiative. "We would like you to dispense with the cumbersome way you answered our questions previously and simply speak to us directly."

The Friend did not reply.

"Will you speak to us directly?"

No response.

Consulting the tablet that she held in one hand, she read the first question. "Are you the higher power that has been sending Jim on life-saving missions?"

She waited.

Silence.

She tried again.

Silence.

Stubbornly, she repeated the question.

The Friend did not speak, but Jim said, "Holly, look at this."

She turned and saw him examining the other tablet. He held it toward her, flipping through the first ten or twelve pages. The eerie and inconstant light from the stone was bright enough to show her that the pages were filled with The Friend's familiar printing.

Taking the tablet from him, she looked at the first line on the top page: YES. I AM THAT POWER.

Jim said, "He's already answered every one of the questions we've prepared."

Holly threw the tablet across the room. It hit the far window without breaking the glass, and clattered to the floor.

"Holly, you can't—"

She cut him off with a sharp look.

The light moved through the transmuted limestone with greater agitation than before.

To The Friend, Holly said, "God gave Moses the Ten Commandments on tablets of stone, yeah, but He also had the courtesy to talk to him. If God can humble Himself to speak directly with human beings, then so can you."

She did not look to see how Jim was reacting to her adversarial tact. All she cared about was that he not interrupt her.

When The Friend remained silent, she repeated the first question on her list. "Are you the higher power that has been sending Jim on life-saving missions?"

"*Yes. I am that power.*" The voice was a soft, mellifluous baritone. Like the ringing of the bells, it seemed to come from all sides of them. The Friend did not materialize out of the wall in human form, did not sculpt a face from the limestone, but merely produced its voice out of thin air.

She asked the second question on her list. "How can you know these people are about to die?"

"*I am an entity that lives in all aspects of time.*"

"What do you mean by that?"

"*Past, present, and future.*"

"You can foresee the future?"

"*I live in the future as well as in the past and present.*"

The light was coruscating through the walls with less agitation now, as if the alien presence had accepted her conditions and was mellow again.

Jim moved to her side. He put a hand on her arm and squeezed gently, as if to say "good work."

She decided not to ask for any more clarification on the issue of its ability to see the future, for fear they would be off on a tangent and never get back on track before the creature next announced that it was departing. She returned to the prepared questions. "Why do you want these particular people saved?"

"*To help mankind,*" it said sonorously. There might have been a note of pomposity in it, too, but that was hard to tell because the voice was so evenly modulated, almost machinelike.

"But when so many people are dying every day—and *most* of them are innocents—why have you singled out these particular people to be rescued?"

"*They are special people.*"

"In what way are they special?"

"*If allowed to live, each of them will make a major contribution to the betterment of mankind.*"

Jim said, "I'll be damned."

Holly had not been expecting that answer. It had the virtue of being fresh. But she was not sure she believed it. For one thing, she was bothered that The Friend's voice was increasingly familiar to her. She was sure she had heard it before, and in a context that undermined its credibility now, in spite of its deep and authoritative tone. "Are you saying you not only see the future as it will be but as it *might* have been?"

"*Yes.*"

"Aren't we back to your being God now?"

"*No. I do not see as clearly as God. But I see.*"

In his boyish best humor again, Jim smiled at the kaleidoscopic patterns of light, obviously excited and pleased by all that he was hearing.

Holly turned away from the wall, crossed the room, squatted beside her suitcase, and opened it.

Jim loomed over her. "What're you doing?"

"Looking for this," she said, producing the notebook in which she had chronicled the discoveries she'd made while researching him. She got up, opened the notebook, and paged to the list of people whose lives he had saved prior to Flight 246. Addressing the entity throbbing through the limestone, she said, "May fifteenth. Atlanta, Georgia. Sam Newsome and his five-year-old daughter Emily. What are they going to contribute to humanity that makes them more important than all the other people who died that day?"

No answer was forthcoming.

"Well?" she demanded.

"*Emily will become a great scientist and discover a cure for a major disease.*" Definitely a note of pomposity this time.

"What disease?"

"*Why do you not believe me, Miss Thorne?*" The Friend spoke as formally as an English butler on duty, yet in that response, Holly felt she heard the subtle pouting tone of a child under the dignified, reserved surface.

She said, "Tell me what disease, and maybe I'll believe you."

"*Cancer.*"

"Which cancer? There are all types of cancer."

"*All cancers.*"

She referred to her notebook again. "June seventh. Corona, California. Louis Andretti."

"*He will father a child who will grow up to become a great diplomat.*"

Better than dying of multiple rattlesnake bites, she thought.

She said, "June twenty-first. New York City. Thaddeus—"

"*He will become a great artist whose work will give millions of people hope.*"

"He seemed like a nice kid," Jim said happily, buying into the whole thing. "I liked him."

Ignoring him, Holly said, "June thirtieth. San Francisco—"

"*Rachael Steinberg will give birth to a child who will become a great spiritual leader.*"

That voice was bugging her. She knew she had heard it before. But where?

"July fifth—"

"*Miami, Florida. Carmen Diaz. She will give birth to a child who will become president of the United States.*"

Holly fanned herself with the notebook and said, "Why not president of the world?"

"July fourteenth. Houston, Texas. Amanda Cutter. She will give birth to a child who will be a great peacemaker."

"Why not the Second Coming?" Holly asked.

Jim had moved away from her. He was leaning against the wall between two windows, the display of light quietly exploding around him. "What's the matter with you?" he asked.

"It's all too much," she said.

"What is?"

"Okay, it says it wants you to save special people."

"To help mankind."

"Sure, sure," Holly said to the wall.

To Jim she said, "But these people are all just too special, don't you think? Maybe it's me, but it all seems overblown, it's gotten trite again. Nobody's growing up to be just a damned good doctor, or a businessman who creates a new industry and maybe ten thousand jobs, or an honest and courageous cop, or a terrific nurse. No, they're great diplomats, great scientists, great politicians, great peacemakers. Great, great, great!"

"Is this adversarial journalism?"

"Damn right."

He pushed away from the wall, used both hands to smooth his thick hair back from his forehead, and cocked his head at her. "I see your point, why it's starting to sound like another episode of *Outer Limits* to you, but let's think about this. It's a crazy, extravagant situation. A being from another world, with powers that seem godlike to us, decides to use me to better the chances of the human race. Isn't it logical that he'd send me out to save special, *really* special people instead of your theoretical business tycoon?"

"Oh, it's logical," she said. "It just doesn't ring true to me, and I've got a fairly well-developed nose for deception."

"Is that why you were a great success as a reporter?"

She might have laughed at the image of an alien, vastly superior to human beings, stooping to engage in a bickering match. But the impatience and poutiness she'd thought she detected as an undercurrent in some of its previous answers was now unmistakable, and the concept of a hypersensitive, resentful creature with godlike power was too unnerving to be funny at the moment.

"How's that for a higher power?" she asked Jim. "Any second now, he's going to call me a bitch."

The Friend said nothing.

Consulting her notebook again, she said, "July twentieth. Steven Aimes. Birmingham, Alabama."

Schools of light swam through the walls. The patterns were less graceful and less sensuous than before; if the lightshow had been the visual equivalent of one of Brahms's most pacific symphonies, it was now more like the discordant wailing of bad progressive jazz.

"What about Steven Aimes?" she demanded, scared but remembering how an exertion of will had been met with respect before.

"*I am going now.*"

"That was a short tide," she said.

The amber light began to darken.

"*The tides in the vessel are not regular or of equal duration. But I will return.*"

"What about Steven Aimes? He was fifty-seven, still capable of siring a great something-or-other, though maybe a little long in the tooth. Why did you save Steve?"

The voice grew somewhat deeper, slipping from baritone toward bass, and it hardened. "*It would not be wise for you to attempt to leave.*"

She had been waiting for that. As soon as she heard the words, she knew she had been tensed in expectation of them.

Jim, however, was stunned. He turned, looking around at the dark-amber forms swirling and melding and splitting apart again, as if trying to figure out the biological geography of the thing, so he could look it in the eyes. "What do you mean by that? We'll leave any time we want."

"*You must wait for my return. You will die if you attempt to leave.*"

"Don't you want to help mankind any more?" Holly asked sharply.

"*Do not sleep.*"

Jim moved to Holly's side. Whatever estrangement she had caused between her and Jim, by taking an aggressive stance with The Friend, was apparently behind them. He put an arm around her protectively.

"*You dare not sleep.*"

The limestone was mottled with a deep red glow.

"*Dreams are doorways.*"

The bloody light went out.

The lantern provided the only illumination. And in the deeper darkness that followed The Friend's departure, the quiet hiss of the burning gas was the only sound.

8 Holly stood at the head of the stairs, shining a flashlight into the gloom below. Jim supposed she was trying to make up her mind whether they really would be prevented from leaving the mill—and if so, how violently.

Watching her from where he sat on his sleeping bag, he could not understand why it was all turning sour.

He had come to the windmill because the bizarre and frightening events in his bedroom in Laguna Niguel, over eighteen hours ago, had made it impossible to continue ignoring the dark side to the mystery in which he had become enwrapped. Prior to that, he had been willing to drift along, doing what he was compelled to do, pulling people out of the fire at the last minute, a bemused but game superhero who had to rely on airplanes when he wanted to fly and who had to do his own laundry. But the increasing intrusion of

The Enemy—whatever the hell it was—its undeniable evil and fierce hostility, no longer allowed Jim the luxury of ignorance. The Enemy was struggling to break through from some other place, another dimension perhaps, and it seemed to be getting closer on each attempt. Learning the truth about the higher power behind his activities had not been at the top of his agenda, because he had felt that enlightenment would be granted to him in time, but learning about The Enemy had come to seem urgently necessary for his survival—and Holly's.

Nevertheless, he had traveled to the farm with the expectation that he would encounter good as well as evil, experience joy as well as fear. Whatever he learned by plunging into the unknown should at least leave him with a greater understanding of his sacred life-saving mission and the supernatural forces behind it. But now he was more confused than before he'd come. Some developments *had* filled him with the wonder and joy for which he longed: the ringing in the stone, for one; and the beautiful, almost divine, light that was the essence of The Friend. He had been moved to rapture by the revelation that he was not merely saving lives but saving people so special that their survival would improve the fate of the entire human race. But that spiritual bliss had been snatched away from him by the growing realization that The Friend was either not telling them the whole truth or, worst case, was not telling them anything true at all. The childish petulance of the creature was unnerving in the extreme, and now Jim was not sure that *anything* he had done since saving the Newsomes last May was in the service of good rather than evil.

Yet his fear was still tempered by hope. Though a splinter of despair had lodged in his heart and begun to fester, that spiritual infection was held in check by the core of optimism, however fragile, that had always been at the center of him.

Holly switched off the flashlight, returned from the open door, and sat down on her mattress. "I don't know, maybe it was an empty threat, but there's no way of telling till we try to leave."

"You want to?"

She shook her head. "What's the point in getting off the farm anyway? From everything we know, it can reach out to us anywhere we go. Right? I mean it reached you in Laguna Niguel, sent you on these missions, reached you out there in Nevada and sent you on to Boston to rescue Nicholas O'Conner."

"I've felt it with me, at times, no matter where I've gone. In Houston, in Florida, in France, in England—it guided me, let me know what was coming, so I could do the job it wanted done."

Holly looked exhausted. She was drawn and paler than the eerie glow of the gas lantern could account for, and her eyes were shadowed with rings of weariness. She closed her eyes for a moment and pinched the bridge of her nose with thumb and forefinger, a strained look on her face, as if she was trying to suppress a headache.

With all his heart, Jim regretted that she had been drawn into this. But like his fear and despair, his regret was impure, tempered by the deep pleasure he took in her very presence. Though it was a selfish attitude, he was glad that she was with him, no matter where this strange night led them. He was no longer alone.

Still pinching the bridge of her nose, the lines in her forehead carved deep by her scowl, Holly said, "This creature isn't restricted to the area near the pond, or just to psychic contact across great distances. It can manifest itself anywhere, judging by the scratches it left in my sides and the way it entered the ceiling of your bedroom this morning."

"Well, now wait," he said, "we know The Enemy can materialize over considerable distance, yes, but we don't know that The Friend has that ability. It was The Enemy that came out of your dream and The Enemy that tried to reach us this morning."

Holly opened her eyes and lowered her hand from her face. Her expression was bleak. "I think they're one and the same."

"What?"

"The Enemy and The Friend. I don't believe two entities are living under the pond, in that starship, if there *is* a starship, which I guess there is. I think there's only a single entity. The Friend and The Enemy are nothing more than different aspects of it."

Holly's implication was clear, but it was too frightening for Jim to accept immediately. He said, "You can't be serious? You might as well be saying . . . it's insane."

"That *is* what I'm saying. It's suffering the alien equivalent of a split personality. It's acting out both personalities, but isn't consciously aware of what it's doing." Jim's almost desperate need to believe in The Friend as a separate and purely benign creature must have been evident in his face, for Holly took his right hand, held it in both hers, and hurried on before he could interrupt: "The childish petulance, the grandiosity of its claim to be reshaping the entire destiny of our species, the flamboyance of its apparitions, its sudden fluctuations between an attitude of syrupy goodwill and sullen anger, the way it lies so damned transparently yet deludes itself into believing it's clever, its secretiveness about some issues when there is no apparent reason to be secretive—all of that makes sense if you figure we're dealing with an unbalanced mind."

He looked for flaws in her reasoning, and found one. "But you can't believe an insane person, an insane alien individual, could pilot an unimaginably complex spacecraft across lightyears through countless dangers, while completely out of its mind."

"It doesn't have to be like that. Maybe the insanity set in *after* it got here. Or maybe it didn't have to pilot the ship, maybe the ship is essentially automatic, an entirely robotic mechanism. Or maybe there were others of its kind aboard who piloted it, and maybe they're all dead now. Jim, it's never mentioned a crew, only The Enemy. And assuming you buy its extraterrestrial origins, does it really ring true that only two individuals would set out on an intergalactic exploration? Maybe it killed the others."

Everything she was theorizing could be true, but then *anything* she theorized could be true. They were dealing with the Unknown, capital "U," and the possibilities in an infinite universe were infinite in number. He remembered reading somewhere—even many scientists believed that anything the human imagination conceived, regardless of how fanciful, could conceivably exist somewhere in the universe, because the infinite nature of creation meant that it was no less fluid, no less fertile than any man's or woman's dreams.

Jim expressed that thought to Holly, then said, "But what bothers me is that you're doing now what you rejected earlier. You're trying hard to explain it in human terms, when it may be too alien for us to understand it at all. How can you assume that an alien species can even suffer insanity the way we can, or that it's capable of multiple personalities? These are all strictly human concepts."

She nodded. "You're right, of course. But at the moment, this theory's the only one that makes sense to me. Until something happens to disprove it, I've got to operate on the assumption that we're not dealing with a rational being."

With his free hand, he reached out and increased the gas flow to the wicks in the Coleman lantern, providing more light. "Jesus, I've got a bad case of the creeps," he said, shivering.

"Join the club."

"If it is schizo, and if it slips into the identity of The Enemy and can't get back out . . . what might it do to us?"

"I don't even want to think about that," Holly said. "If it's as intellectually superior to us as it seems to be, if it's from a long-lived race with experience and knowledge that makes the whole of the human experience seem like a short story compared to the Great Books of the Western World, then it sure as hell knows some tortures and cruelties that would make Hitler and Stalin and Pol Pot look like Sunday-school teachers."

He thought about that for a moment, even though he tried not to. The chocolate doughnuts he had eaten lay in an undigested, burning wad in his stomach.

Holly said, "When it comes back—"

"For God's sake," he interrupted, "no more adversarial tactics!"

"I screwed up," she admitted. "But the adversarial approach was the correct one, I just carried it too far. I pushed too hard. When it comes back, I'll modify my technique."

He supposed he had more fully accepted her insanity theory than he was willing to acknowledge. He was now in a cold sweat about what The Friend might do if their behavior tipped it into its other, darker identity. "Why don't we jettison confrontation altogether, play along with it, stroke its ego, keep it as happy as we—"

"That's no good. You can't control madness by indulging it. That only creates more and deeper madness. I suspect any nurse in a mental institution would tell you the best way to deal with potentially violent paranoid is to be nice, respectful, but *firm*."

He withdrew his hand from hers because his palms were clammy. He blotted them on his shirt.

The mill seemed unnaturally silent, as if it were in a vacuum where sound could not travel, sealed in an immense bell jar, on display in a museum in a land of giants. At another time Jim might have found the silence disturbing, but now he embraced it because it probably meant The Friend was sleeping or at least preoccupied with concerns other than them.

"It *wants* to do good," he said. "It might be insane, and it might be violent and even evil in its second identity, a regular Dr. Jekyll and Mr. Hyde. But like Dr. Jekyll it really wants to do good. At least we've got that going for us."

She thought about it a moment. "Okay, I'll give you that one. And when it comes back, I'll try to pry some truth out of it."

"What scares me most—is there really anything we can learn from it that could help us? Even if it tells us the whole truth about everything, if it's insane it's going to turn to irrational violence sooner or later."

She nodded. "But we gotta try."

They settled into an uneasy silence.

When he looked at his watch, Jim saw that it was ten minutes past one in the morning. He was not sleepy. He didn't have to worry about drifting off and dreaming and thereby opening a doorway, but he was physically drained. Though he had not done anything but sit in a car and drive, then sit or stand in the high room waiting for revelations, his muscles ached as if he had put in ten hours of heavy manual labor. His face felt slack with weariness, and his eyes were hot and grainy. Extreme stress could be every bit as debilitating as strenuous physical activity.

He found himself wishing The Friend would never return, wishing not in an idle way but with the wholehearted commitment of a young boy wishing that an upcoming visit to the dentist would not transpire. He put every fiber of his being into the wish, as if convinced, the way a kid sometimes could be, that wishes really did now and then come true.

He remembered a quote from Chazal, which he had used when teaching a literature unit on the supernatural fiction of Poe and Hawthorne: *Extreme terror gives us back the gestures of our childhood.* If he ever went back into the classroom, he would be able to teach that unit a hell of a lot better, thanks to what had happened to him in the old windmill.

At 1:25 The Friend disproved the value of wishing by putting in a sudden appearance. This time no bells heralded its approach. Red light blossomed in the wall, like a burst of crimson paint in clear water.

Holly scrambled to her feet.

So did Jim. He could no longer sit relaxed in the presence of this mysterious being, because he was now more than half-convinced that at any moment it might strike at them with merciless brutality.

The light separated into many swarms, surged all the way around the room, then began to change from red to amber.

The Friend spoke without waiting for a question: *"August first. Seattle, Washington. Laura Lenaskian, saved from drowning. She will give birth to a child who will become a great composer and whose music will give solace to many people in times of trouble. August eighth. Peoria, Illinois. Doogie Burkette. He will grow up to be a paramedic in Chicago, where he will do much good and save many lives. August twelfth. Portland, Oregon. Billy Jenkins. He will grow up to be a brilliant medical technologist whose inventions will revolutionize medical care—"*

Jim met Holly's eyes and did not even have to wonder what she was thinking: the same thing he was thinking. The Friend was in its testy, I'll-show-you mode, and it was providing details which it expected would lend credibility to its extravagant claim to be altering human destiny. But it was impossible to know if what it said was true—or merely fantasies that it had worked up to support its story. The important thing, perhaps, was that it seemed to care deeply that they believe it. Jim had no idea why his or Holly's opinion should matter at all to a being as intellectually superior to them as they were to a field mouse, but the fact that it *did* evidently matter seemed to be to their advantage.

"—August twentieth. The Mojave Desert, Nevada. Lisa and Susan Jawolski. Lisa will provide her daughter with the love, affection, and counseling that will make it possible for the girl eventually to overcome the severe psychological trauma of her father's murder and grow up to be the greatest woman statesman in the entire history of the world, a force for enlightenment and compassionate government policies. August twenty-third. Boston, Massachusetts. Nicholas O'Connor, saved from an electrical-vault explosion. He will grow up to become a priest who will dedicate his life to caring for the poor in the slums of India—"

The Friend's attempt to answer Holly's criticism and present a less grandiose version of its work was childishly transparent. The Burkette boy was not going to save the world, just be a damned good paramedic, and Nicholas O'Conner was going to be a humble man leading a self-effacing existence among the needy—but the rest of them were still great or brilliant or staggeringly talented in one way or another. The entity now recognized the need for credibility in its tale of grandeur, but it could not bring itself to significantly water down its professed accomplishments.

And something else was bothering Jim: that voice. The longer he listened to it, the more he became convinced that he had heard it before, not in this room twenty-five years ago, not within its current context at all. The voice had to be appropriated, of course, because in its natural condition the alien almost certainly did not possess anything similar to human vocal cords; its biology would be inhuman. The voice it was imitating, as if it were an impersonator performing in a cosmic cocktail lounge, was that of a person Jim had once known. He could not quite identify it.

"*—August twenty-sixth. Dubuque, Iowa. Christine and Casey Dubrovek. Christine will give birth to another child who will grow up to be the greatest geneticist of the next century. Casey will become an exceptional schoolteacher who will tremendously influence the lives of her students, and who will never fail one of them to the extent that a suicide results.*"

Jim felt as if he had been hit in the chest with a hammer. That insulting accusation, directed at him and referring to Larry Kakonis, shook his remaining faith in The Friend's basic desire to do good.

Holly said, "Shit, that was low."

The entity's pettiness sickened Jim, because he wanted so badly to believe in its stated purpose and goodness.

The scintillant amber light swooped and swirled through the walls, as if The Friend was delighted by the effect of the blow it had struck.

Despair welled so high in Jim that for a moment he even dared to consider that the entity under the pond was not good at all but purely evil. Maybe the people he had saved since May fifteenth were not destined to elevate the human condition but debase it. Maybe Nicholas O'Conner was really going to grow up to be a serial killer. Maybe Billy Jenkins was going to be a bomber pilot who went rogue and found a way to override all the safeguards in the system in order to drop a few nuclear weapons on a major metropolitan area; and maybe instead of being the greatest woman statesman in the history of the world, Susie Jawolski was going to be a radical activist who planted bombs in corporate boardrooms and machine-gunned those with whom she disagreed.

But as he swayed precariously on the rim of that black chasm, Jim saw in memory the face of young Susie Jawolski, which had seemed to be the essence of innocence. He could not believe that she would be anything less than a positive force in the lives of her family and neighbors. He *had* done good works; therefore The Friend had done good works, whether or not it was insane, and even though it had the capacity to be cruel.

Holly addressed the entity within the wall: "We have more questions."

"*Ask them, ask them.*"

Holly glanced at her tablet, and Jim hoped she would remember to be less aggressive. He sensed that The Friend was more unstable than at any previous point during the night.

She said, "Why did you choose Jim to be your instrument?"

"*He was convenient.*"

"You mean because he lived on the farm?"

"*Yes.*"

"Have you ever worked through anyone else the way you've been working through Jim?"

"*No.*"

"Not in all these ten thousand years?"

"*Is this a trick question? Do you think you can trick me? Do you still not believe me when I tell you the truth?*"

Holly looked at Jim, and he shook his head, meaning that this was no time to be argumentative, that discretion was not only the better part of valor but their best hope of survival.

Then he wondered if this entity could read his mind as well as intrude into it and implant directives. Probably not. If it could do that, it would flare into anger now, incensed that they still thought it insane and were patronizing it.

"I'm sorry," Holly said. "It wasn't a trick question, not at all. We just want to know about you. We're fascinated by you. If we ask questions that you find offensive, please understand that we do so unintentionally, out of ignorance."

The Friend did not reply.

The light pulsed more slowly through the limestone, and though Jim knew the danger of interpreting alien actions in human terms, he felt that the changed patterns and tempo of the radiance indicated The Friend was in a contemplative mood. It was chewing over what Holly had just said, deciding whether or not she was sincere.

Finally the voice came again, more mellow than it had been in a while: *"Ask your questions."*

Consulting her tablet again, Holly said, "Will you ever release Jim from this work?"

"Does he want to be released?"

Holly looked at Jim inquiringly.

Considering what he had been through in the past few months, Jim was a bit surprised by his answer: "Not if I'm actually doing good."

"You are. How can you doubt it? But regardless of whether you believe my intentions to be good or evil, I would never release you."

The ominous tone of that last statement mitigated the relief Jim felt at the reassurance that he had not saved the lives of future murderers and thieves.

Holly said, "Why have you—"

The Friend interrupted. *"There is one other reason that I chose Jim Iron-heart for this work."*

"What's that?" Jim asked.

"You needed it."

"I did?"

"Purpose."

Jim understood. His fear of The Friend was as great as ever, but he was moved by the implication that it had wanted to salvage him. By giving meaning to his broken and empty life, it had redeemed him just as surely as it had saved Billy Jenkins, Susie Jawolski, and all the others, though they had been rescued from more immediate deaths than the death of the soul that had threatened Jim. The Friend's statement seemed to reveal a capacity for pity. And Jim knew he'd deserved pity after the suicide of Larry Kakonis, when he had spiraled into an unreasonable depression. This compassion, even if it was another lie, affected Jim more strongly than he would have expected, and a shimmer of tears came to his eyes.

Holly said, "Why have you waited ten thousand years to decide to use someone like Jim to shape human destinies?"

"I had to study the situation first, collect data, analyze it, and then decide if my intervention was wise."

"It took ten thousand years to make that decision? Why? That's longer than recorded history."

No reply.

She tried the question again.

At last The Friend said, *"I am going now."* Then, as if it did not want them to interpret its recent display of compassion as a sign of weakness, it added: *"If you attempt to leave, you will die."*

"When will you be back?" Holly asked.

"Do not sleep."

"We're going to have to sleep sooner or later," Holly said as the amber light turned red and the room seemed to be washed in blood.

"Do not sleep."

"It's two in the morning," she said.

"Dreams are doorways."

Holly flared up: "We can't stay awake forever, damn it!"

The light in the limestone was snuffed out.

The Friend was gone.

SOMEWHERE PEOPLE LAUGHED. Somewhere music played and dancers danced, and somewhere lovers strained toward ecstasy.

But in the high room of the mill, designed for storage and now stacked to the ceiling with an anticipation of violence, the mood was decidedly grim.

Holly loathed being so helpless. Throughout her life she had been a woman of action, even if the actions she took were usually destructive rather than constructive. When a job turned out to be less satisfying than she had hoped, she never hesitated to resign, move on. When a relationship soured or just proved uninteresting, she was always quick to terminate it. If she had often retreated from problems—from the responsibilities of being a conscientious journalist when she had seen that journalism was as corrupt as anything else, from the prospect of love, from putting down roots and committing to one place—well, at least retreat was a form of action. Now she was denied even that.

The Friend had that one good effect on her. It was not going to let her retreat from *this* problem.

For a while she and Jim discussed the latest visitation and went over the remaining questions on her list, to which they made changes and additions. The most recent portion of her ongoing interview with The Friend had resulted in some interesting and potentially useful information. It was only *potentially* useful, however, because they both still felt that nothing The Friend said could be relied upon to be true.

By 3:15 in the morning, they were too weary to stand and too bottom-sore to continue sitting. They pulled their sleeping bags together and stretched out side by side, on their backs, staring at the doomed ceiling.

To help guard against sleep, they left the gas lantern at its brightest setting. As they waited for The Friend to return, they kept talking, not about anything of importance, small talk of every kind, anything to keep their minds occupied. It was difficult to doze off in the middle of a conversation; and if one did slip away, the other would know it by the lack of a response. They also held hands, her right in his left—the logic being that even during a brief pause in the conversation, if one of them started to take a nap, the other would be warned by the sudden relaxation of the sleeper's grip.

Holly did not expect to have difficulty staying awake. In her university days she had pulled all-nighters before exams or when papers were due, and had stayed awake for thirty-six hours without much of a struggle. During her early years as a reporter, when she'd still believed that journalism mattered to her, she had labored away all night on a story, poring over research or listening yet again to interview tapes or sweating over the wording of a paragraph. She had missed nights of sleep in recent years, as well, if only because she was occasionally plagued by insomnia. She was a night owl by nature anyway. Piece of cake.

But though she had not yet been awake twenty-four hours since bolting out of bed in Laguna Niguel yesterday morning she felt the sandman sliding up against her, whispering his subliminal message of sleep, sleep, sleep. The past few days had been a blur of activity and personal change, both of which could be expected to take a toll of her resources. And some nights she had gotten too little rest, only in part because of the dream *Dreams are doorways.* Sleep was dangerous, she had to stay awake. Damn it, she shouldn't need sleep this badly yet, no matter how much stress she had been under lately. She struggled to keep up her end of the conversation with Jim, even though at times she realized that she was not sure what they were talking about and did not fully understand the words that came out of her own mouth. *Dreams are doorways.* It was almost as if she had been drugged, or as if The Friend, after warning them against sleep, was secretly exerting pressure on a narcoleptic button in her brain. *Dreams are doorways.* She fought against the descending oblivion, but she found that she did not possess the strength or will to sit up ... or to open her eyes. Her eyes were closed. She had not realized that her eyes were closed. *Dreams are doorways.* Panic could not arouse her. She continued to drift deeper under the sandman's spell even as she heard her heart pound harder and faster. She felt her hand loosening its grip on Jim's hand, and she knew he would respond to that warning, would keep her awake, but she felt *his* grip loosening on her hand, and she realized they were succumbing to the sandman simultaneously.

She drifted in darkness.

She felt that she was being watched.

It was both a reassuring and a frightening feeling.

Something was going to happen. She sensed it.

For a while, however, nothing happened. Except darkness.

Then she became aware that she had a mission to perform.

But that couldn't be right. Jim was the one who was sent on missions, not her.

A mission. *Her* mission. She would be sent on a mission of her own. It was vitally important. Her life depended on how well she performed. Jim's life depended on it as well. The whole world's continued existence depended on it.

But the darkness remained.

She just drifted. It felt nice.

She slept and slept.

At some point during the night, she dreamed. As nightmares went, this one was a lulu, all the stops pulled out, but it was nothing like her recent dreams of the mill and The Enemy. It was worse than those because it was painted in excruciating detail and because throughout the experience she was in the grip of anguish and terror so intense that nothing in her experience prepared her for it, not even the crash of Flight 246.

Lying on a tile floor, under a table. On her side. Peering out at floor level. Directly ahead is a chair, tubular metal and orange plastic, under the chair a scattering of golden french fries and a cheeseburger, the meat having slid halfway out of the bun on a skid of ketchup-greased lettuce. Then a woman, an old lady, also lying on the floor, head turned toward Holly. Looking through the tubular legs of the chair, across the fries and disarranged burger, the lady stares at her, a look of surprise, stares and stares, never blinking, and then Holly sees that the lady's eye nearest the floor isn't there anymore, an empty hole, blood leaking out. Oh, lady. Oh, lady, I'm sorry, I'm so sorry. Holly hears a terrible sound, *chuda-chuda-chuda-chuda-chuda-chuda-chuda*, doesn't recognize it, hears people screaming, a lot of people, *chuda-chuda-chuda-chuda*, still screaming but not as much as before, glass shattering, wood breaking, a man shouting like a bear, roaring, very angry and roaring, *chuda-chuda-chuda-chuda-chuda-chuda-chuda-chuda*. She knows now that it's gunfire, the heavy rhythmic pounding of an automatic weapon, and she wants to get out of there. So she turns in the opposite direction from which she's been facing because she doesn't want to—can't, just can't!—crawl by the old lady whose eye has been shot out. But behind her is a little girl, about eight, lying on the floor in a pink dress with black patent-leather shoes and white socks, a little girl with white-blond hair, a little girl with, a little girl with, a little girl with patent-leather shoes, a little girl with, a little girl with, a little girl with white socks, a little girl with, a little girl with with with with *with half her face shot off*! A red smile. Broken white teeth in a red, lopsided smile. Sobbing, screaming, and still more *chuda-chuda-chuda-chuda*, it's never going to stop, it's going to go on forever, that terrible sound, *chuda-chuda-chuda*. Then Holly's moving, scrambling on her hands and knees, away from both the old lady and the little girl with half a face. Unavoidably her hands slap-skip-skid-slide through warm french fries, a hot fish sandwich, a puddle of mustard, as she moves, moves, staying under the tables, between the chairs, then she puts her hand down in the icy slush of a spilled Coke, and when she sees the image of Dixie Duck on the large paper cup from which the soda has spilled, she knows where she is, she's in a Dixie Duck Burger Palace, one of her favorite places in the world. Nobody's screaming now, maybe they realize that a Dixie Duck is not a place you should scream, but somebody is sobbing and groaning, and somebody else is saying please-please-please-please over and over again. Holly starts to crawl out from under another table, and she sees a man in a costume standing a few feet from her, turned half away from her, and she thinks maybe this is all just a trick, trick-or-treat, a Halloween performance. But it isn't Halloween. Yet the man is in a *costume*, he's wearing combat boots like G. I. Joe and camouflage pants and a black T-shirt and a beret, like the Green Berets wear, only this one is black, and it must be a costume because he isn't really a soldier, can't be a soldier with that big sloppy belly overhanging his pants, and he hasn't shaved in maybe a week, soldiers have to shave, so he's only wearing soldier stuff. This girl is kneeling on the floor in front of him, one of the teenagers who works at Dixie Duck, the pretty one with the red hair, she winked at Holly when she took her order, now she's kneeling in front of the guy in the soldier costume, with her head bowed like she's praying, except what she's saying is please-please-please-please. The guy is shouting at her about the CIA and mind control and secret spy networks operated out of the Dixie Duck storeroom. Then the guy stops shouting and he looks at the red-haired girl awhile, just looks down at her, and then he says look-at-me, and she says please-please-don't, and he says look-at-me again, so she raises her head and looks at him, and he says what-do-you-think-I-am-stupid? The girl is so scared, she is just so scared, and she says no-please-I-don't-know-anything-about-this, and he says like-shit-you-don't, and he lowers the big gun, he puts the big gun right there in her face, just maybe an inch or two from her face. She says oh-my-god-oh-my-god, and he says you're-one-of-the-rat-people, and Holly is sure the guy will now throw the gun aside and laugh, and everyone playing dead people will get up and laugh, too, and the manager will come out and take bows for the Halloween performance, except it isn't Halloween. Then the guy pulls the trigger, *chuda-chuda-chuda-chuda-chuda*, and the red-haired girl dissolves. Holly eels around and heads back the way she came, moving so fast, trying to get away from him before he sees her, because he's crazy, that's what he is, he's a crazyman. Holly is splashing through the same spilled food and drinks that she splashed through before, past the little girl in the pink dress and right through the girl's blood, praying the crazyman can't hear her scuttling away from him. *CHUDA-CHUDA-CHUDA-CHUDA-CHUDA-CHUDA!* But he must be shooting the other direction, because no bullets are smashing into anything around her, so she keeps going, right across a dead man with his insides coming out, hearing sirens now, sirens wailing outside, the cops'll get this crazyman. Then she hears a crash behind her, a table being overturned, and it sounds so close, she looks back, she sees him, the crazyman, he's coming straight toward her, pushing tables out of his way, kicking aside chairs, he sees her. She clambers over another dead woman and then she's in a corner, on top of a dead man who's slumped in the corner, she's in the lap of the dead man, in the arms of the dead man, and no way to get out of there because the crazyman is coming. The crazyman looks so scary, so bad and scary, that she can't watch him coming, doesn't want to see the gun in her face the way the red-haired girl saw it, so she turns her head away, turns her face to the dead man—

She woke from the dream as she had never awakened from another, not screaming, not even with an unvoiced cry caught in her throat, but gagging. She was curled into a tight ball, hugging herself, dry-heaving, choking not on anything she had eaten but on sheer throat-clogging repulsion.

Jim was turned away from her, lying on his side. His knees were drawn up slightly in a modified fetal position. He was still sound asleep.

When she could get her breath, she sat up. She was not merely shaking, she was rattling. She was convinced she could hear her bones clattering against one another.

She was glad that she had not eaten anything after the doughnuts last evening. They had passed through her stomach hours ago. If she had eaten anything else, she'd be wearing it now.

She hunched forward and put her face in her hands. She sat like that until the rattling quieted to a shudder and the shudder faded to spasms of shivering.

When she raised her face from her hands, the first thing she noticed was daylight at the narrow windows of the high room. It was opalescent gray-pink, a weak glow rather than a sunny-blue glare, but daylight nonetheless. Seeing it, she realized that she had not been convinced she would ever see daylight again.

She looked at her wristwatch. 6:10. Dawn must have broken only a short while ago. She could have been asleep only two to two and a half hours. It had been worse than no sleep at all; she did not feel in the least rested.

The dream. She suspected that The Friend had used its telepathic power to push her down into sleep against her will. And because of the unusually intense nature of the nightmare, she was convinced it had sent her that gruesome reel of mind-film.

But why?

Jim murmured and stirred, then grew still again, breathing deeply but quietly. His dream must not be the same one she'd had; if it was, he would be writhing and crying out like a man on the rack.

She sat for a while, considering the dream, wondering if she had been shown a prophetic vision. Was The Friend warning her that she was going to wind up in a Dixie Duck Burger Palace scrambling for her life through food and blood, stalked by a raving maniac with an automatic carbine? She had never even heard of Dixie Duck, and she couldn't imagine a more ludicrous place to die.

She was living in a society where the streets were crawling with casualties of the drug wars, some of them so brain-blasted that they might well pick up a gun and go looking for the rat people who were working with the CIA, running spy networks out of burger restaurants. She had worked on newspapers all her adult life. She had seen stories no less tragic, no more strange.

After about fifteen minutes, she couldn't bear to think about the nightmare anymore, not for a while. Instead of getting a handle on it through analysis, she became more confused and distressed the longer she dwelt on it. In memory, the images of slaughter did not fade, as was usually the case with a dream, but became more vivid. She didn't need to puzzle it out right now.

Jim was sleeping, and she considered waking him. But he needed his rest as much as she did. There was no sign of The Enemy making use of a dream doorway, no change in the limestone walls or the oak-plank floor, so she let Jim sleep.

As she had looked around the room, studying the walls, she had noticed the yellow tablet lying on the floor under the far window. She had pitched it aside last evening when The Friend had resisted vocalizing its answers and had tried, instead, to present her with responses to all her written questions at once, before she was able to read them aloud. She'd never had a chance to ask it all of the questions on her list, and now she wondered what might be on that answer-tablet.

She eased off her bedding as quietly as possible, rose, and walked carefully across the room. She tested the floorboards as she went to make sure they weren't going to squeak when she put her full weight on them.

As she stooped to pick up the tablet, she heard a sound that froze her. Like a heartbeat with an extra thump in it.

She looked around at the walls, up at the dome. The light from the high-burning lantern and the windows was sufficient to be certain that the limestone was only limestone, the wood only wood.

Lub-dub-DUB, lub-dub-DUB . . .

It was faint, as if someone was tapping the rhythm out on a drum far away, outside the mill, somewhere up in the dry brown hills.

But she knew what it was. No drum. It was the tripartite beat that always preceded the materialization of The Enemy. Just as the bells had, until its final visit, preceded the arrival of The Friend.

As she listened, it faded away.

She strained to hear it.

Gone.

Relieved but still trembling, she picked up the tablet. The pages were rumpled, and they made some noise falling into place.

Jim's steady breathing continued to echo softly around the room, with no change of rhythm or pitch.

Holly read the answers on the first page, then the second. She saw that they were the same responses The Friend had vocalized—although without the spur-of-the-moment questions that she had not written down on the question-tablet. She skimmed down the third and fourth pages, on which it had listed the people Jim had saved—Carmen Diaz, Amanda Cutter, Steven Aimes, Laura Lenaskian—explaining what great things each of them was destined to achieve.

Lub-dub-DUB, lub-dub-DUB, lub-dub-DUB . . .

She snapped her head up.

The sound was still distant, no louder than before.

Jim groaned in his sleep.

Holly took a step away from the window, intending to wake him, but the dreaded sound faded away again. Evidently The Enemy was in the neighborhood, but it had not found a doorway in Jim's dream. He *had* to get his sleep, he couldn't function without it. She decided to let him alone.

Easing back to the window again, Holly held the answer-tablet up to the light. She turned to the fifth page—and felt the flesh on the nape of her neck go as cold and nubbly as frozen turkey skin.

Peeling the pages back with great delicacy, so as not to rustle them more than absolutely necessary, she checked the sixth page, the seventh, the eighth. They were all the same. Messages were printed on them in the wavery hand that The Friend had used when pulling its little words-rising-as-if-through-water trick. But they were not answers to her questions. They were two alternating statements, unpunctuated, each repeated three times per page:

HE LOVES YOU HOLLY
HE WILL KILL YOU HOLLY
HE LOVES YOU HOLLY
HE WILL KILL YOU HOLLY
HE LOVES YOU HOLLY
HE WILL KILL YOU HOLLY

Staring at those obsessively repeated statements, she knew that "he" could be no one but Jim. She focused only on the five hateful words, trying to understand.

And suddenly she thought that she did. The Friend was warning her that in its madness it would act against her, perhaps because it hated her for bringing Jim to the mill, for making him seek answers, and for being a distraction from his mission. If The Friend, which was the sane half of the alien consciousness, could reach into Jim's mind and compel him to undertake life-saving missions, was it possible that The Enemy, the dark half, could reach into his mind and compel him to kill? Instead of the insane personality materializing in monstrous form as it had done for an instant at the motel Friday night and as it attempted to do in Jim's bedroom yesterday, might it choose to use Jim against her, take command of him to a greater extent than The Friend had ever done, and turn him into a killing machine? That might perversely delight the mad-child aspect of the entity.

She shook herself as if casting off a pestering wasp.

No. It was impossible. All right, Jim could kill in the defense of innocent people. But he was incapable of killing someone innocent. No alien consciousness, no matter how powerful, could override his true nature. In his heart he was good and kind and caring. His love for her could not be subverted by this alien force, no matter how strong it was.

But how did she know that? She was engaging in wishful thinking. For all she knew, The Enemy's powers of mental control were so awesome that it could reach into her brain right now and tell her to drown herself in the pond, and she would do as told.

She remembered Norman Rink. The Atlanta convenience store. Jim had pumped eight rounds from a shotgun into the guy, blasting at him again and again, long after he was dead.

Lub-dub-DUB, lub-dub-DUB . . .

Still far away.

Jim groaned softly.

She moved away from the window again, intent on waking him, and almost called out his name, before she realized that The Enemy might be in him already. Dreams are doorways. She didn't have a clue as to what The Friend meant by that, or if it was anything more than stage dressing like the bells. But maybe what it had meant was that The Enemy could enter the dreamer's dream and thus the dreamer's mind. Maybe this time The Enemy did not intend to materialize from the wall but from Jim, in the person of Jim, in total control of Jim, just for a murderous little lark.

Lub-dub-DUB, lub-dub-DUB, lub-dub-DUB . . .

A little louder, a little closer?

Holly felt that she was losing her mind. Paranoid, schizoid, flat-out crazy. No better than The Friend and his other half. She was frantically trying to understand a totally alien consciousness, and the more she pondered the possibilities, the stranger and more varied the possibilities became. In an infinite universe, anything can happen, any nightmare can be made flesh. In an infinite universe, life was therefore essentially the same as a dream. Contemplation of *that*, under the stress of a life-or-death situation, was guaranteed to drive you bugshit.

Lub-dub-DUB, lub-dub-DUB . . .

She could not move.

She could only wait.

The tripartite beat faded again.

Letting her breath out in a rush, she backed up against the wall beside the window, less afraid of the limestone now than she was of Jim Ironheart. She wondered if it was all right to wake him when the three-note heartbeat was not audible. Maybe The Enemy was only in his dream—and therefore in him—when that triple thud could be heard.

Afraid to act and afraid not to act, she glanced down at the tablet in her hand. Some of the pages had fallen shut, and she was no longer looking at the HE LOVES YOU HOLLY/HE WILL KILL YOU HOLLY litany. Before her eyes, instead, was the list of people who had been saved by Jim, along with The Friend's grandiose explanations of their importance.

She saw "Steven Aimes" and realized at once that he was the only one on the list whose fate The Friend had not vocalized during one or another of their conversations last night. She remembered him because he was the only older person on the list, fifty-seven. She read the words under his name, and the chill that had touched her nape earlier was nothing compared to the spike of ice that drove through it now and pierced her spine.

Steven Aimes had not been saved because he would father a child who would be a great diplomat or a great artist or a great healer. He had not been saved because he would make an enduring contribution to the welfare of mankind. The reason for his salvation was expressed in just eleven words, the most horrifying eleven words that Holly had ever read or hoped to read: BECAUSE HE LOOKS LIKE MY FATHER WHOM I FAILED TO SAVE. Not "like *Jim's* father" which The Friend would have said. Not "whom *he* failed to save," as the alien would surely have put it. MY FATHER. I FAILED. MY. I.

The infinite universe just kept expanding, and now an entirely new possibility presented itself to her, revealed in the telling words about Steven Aimes. No starship rested under the pond. No alien had been in hiding on the farm for ten thousand years, ten years, or ten days. The Friend and The Enemy were real enough: they were thirds, not halves, of the same personality, three in one entity, an entity with enormous and wonderful and terrifying powers, an entity both godlike and yet as human as Holly was. Jim Ironheart. Who had been shattered by tragedy when he was ten years old. Who had painstakingly put himself together again with the help of a complex fantasy about star-traveling gods. Who was as insane and dangerous as he was sane and loving.

She did not understand where he had gotten the power that he so obviously possessed, or why he was not aware whatsoever that the power was within him rather than coming from some imaginary alien presence. The realization that he was everything, that the end and beginning of this mystery lay solely in him and not beneath the pond, raised more questions than it answered. She didn't understand how such a thing could be true, but she knew it was, at last, the truth. Later, if she survived, she might have the time to seek a better understanding.

Lub-dub-DUB, lub-dub-DUB . . .

Closer but not close.

Holly held her breath, waiting for the sound to get louder.

Lub-dub-DUB, lub-dub-DUB . . .

Jim shifted in his sleep. He snorted softly and smacked his lips, just like any ordinary dreamer.

But he was three personalities in one, and at least two of them possessed incredible power, and at least one of them was deadly. And it was coming.

Lub-dub-DUB . . .

Holly pressed back against the limestone. Her heart was pounding so hard that it seemed to have hammered her throat half shut; she had trouble swallowing.

The tripartite beat faded.

Silence.

She moved along the curved wall. Easy little steps. Sideways. Toward the timbered, ironbound door. She eased away from the wall just far enough to reach out and snare her purse by its straps.

The closer she got to the head of the stairs, the more certain she became that the door was going to slam shut before she reached it, that Jim was going to sit up and turn to her. His blue eyes would not be beautiful but cold, as she had twice glimpsed them, filled with rage but cold.

She reached the door, eased through it backward onto the first step, not wanting to take her eyes off Jim. But if she tried to back down those narrow stairs without a handrail, she would fall, break an arm or leg. So she turned away from the high room and hurried toward the bottom as quickly as she dared, as quietly as she could.

Though the velvety-gray morning light outlined the windows, the lower chamber was treacherously dark. She had no flashlight, only the extra edge of an adrenaline rush. Unable to remember if any rubble was stacked along the wall that might set up a clatter when she knocked it over, she moved slowly along that limestone curve, her back to it, edging sideways again. The antechamber archway was somewhere ahead on her right. When she looked to her left, she could barely see the foot of the stairs down which she had just descended.

Feeling the wall ahead of her with her right hand, she discovered the corner. She stepped through the archway and into the antechamber. Though that space had been blind-dark last night, it was dimly lit now by the pale post-dawn glow that lay beyond the open outside door.

The morning was overcast. Pleasantly cool for August.

The pond was still and gray.

Morning insects issued a thin, almost inaudible background buzz, like faint static on a radio with the volume turned nearly off.

She hurried to the Ford and stealthily opened the door.

Another panic hit her as she thought of the keys. Then she felt them in a pocket of her jeans, where she had slipped them last night after using the bathroom at the farmhouse. One key for the farmhouse, one key for his house in Laguna Niguel, two keys for the car, all on a simple brass-bead chain.

She threw the purse and tablet into the back seat and got behind the wheel, but didn't close the door for fear the sound would wake him. She was not home free yet. He might burst out of the windmill, The Enemy in charge of him, leap across the short expanse of gravel, and drag her from the car.

Her hands shook as she fumbled with the keys. She had trouble inserting the right one in the ignition. But then she got it in, twisted it, put her foot on the accelerator, and almost sobbed with relief when the engine turned over with a roar.

She yanked the door shut, threw the Ford in reverse, and backed along the gravel path that circled the pond. The wheels spun up a hail of gravel, which rattled against the back of the car as she reversed into it.

When she reached the area between the barn and the house, where she could turn around and head out of the driveway front-first, she jammed on the brakes instead. She stared at the windmill, which was now on the far side of the water.

She had nowhere to run. Wherever she went, he would find her. He could see the future, at least to some extent, if not as vividly or in as much detail as The Friend had claimed. He could transform drywall into a monstrous living organism, change limestone into a transparent substance filled with whirling light, project a beast of hideous design into her dreams and into the doorway of her motel, track her, find her, trap her. He had drawn her into his mad fantasy and most likely still wanted her to play out her role in it. The Friend in Jim—and Jim himself—might let her go. But the third personality—the murderous part of him, The Enemy—would want her blood. Maybe she would be fortunate, and maybe the two benign thirds of him would prevent the other third from taking control and coming after her. But she doubted it. Besides, she could not spend the rest of her life waiting for a wall to bulge outward unexpectedly, form into a mouth, and bite her hand off.

And there was one other problem.

She could not abandon him. He needed her.

From childhood's hour
I have not been
As others were—
I have not seen
As others saw.

—*Alone*, EDGAR ALLAN POE

❱ ❱ ❱

Vibrations in a wire.
Ice crystals in a beating heart.
Cold fire.

A mind's frigidity: frozen steel,
dark rage, morbidity.
Cold fire.

Defense against a cruel life
death and strife:
Cold fire.

—THE BOOK OF COUNTED SORROWS

Part Three

The Enemy

The Rest of August 29

Holly sat in the Ford, staring at the old windmill, scared and exhilarated. The exhilaration surprised her. Maybe she felt upbeat because for the first time in her life she had found something to which she was willing to commit herself. Not a casual commitment, either. Not an until-I-get-bored commitment. She was willing to put her life on the line for this, for Jim and what he could become if he could be healed, for what they could become together.

Even if he had told her she could go, and even if she had felt that his release of her was sincere, she would not have abandoned him. He was her salvation. And she was his.

The mill stood sentinel against the ashen sky. Jim had not appeared at the door. Perhaps he had not yet awakened.

There were still many mysteries within

this mystery, but so much was painfully obvious now. He sometimes failed to save people—like Susie Jawolski's father—because he was not really operating on behalf of an infallible god or a prescient alien; he was acting on his own phenomenal but imperfect visions; he was just a man, special but only a man, and even the best of men had limits. He evidently felt that he had failed his parents somehow. Their deaths weighed heavily on his conscience, and he was trying to redeem himself by saving the lives of others: HE LOOKED LIKE MY FATHER, WHOM I FAILED TO SAVE.

It was now obvious, as well, why The Enemy broke through only when Jim was asleep: he was terrified of that dark aspect of himself, that embodiment of his rage, and he strenuously repressed it when he was awake. At his place in Laguna, The Enemy had materialized in the bedroom while Jim was sleeping and actually had been sustained for a while after Jim had awakened, but when it had crashed through the bathroom ceiling, it had simply evaporated like the lingering dream it was. Dreams are doorways, The Friend had warned, which had been a warning from Jim himself. Dreams were doorways, yes, but not for evil, mind-invading alien monsters; dreams were doorways to the subconscious, and what came out of them was all too human.

She had other pieces of the puzzle, too. She just didn't know how they fit together.

Holly was angry with herself for not having asked the correct questions on Monday, when Jim had finally opened his patio door and let her into his life. He'd insisted that he was only an instrument, that he had no powers of his own. She'd bought it too quickly. She should have probed harder, asked tougher questions. She was as guilty of amateurish interviewing technique as Jim had been when The Friend had first appeared to them.

She had been annoyed by his willingness to accept what The Friend said at face value. Now she understood that he had created The Friend for the same reason that other victims of multiple-personality syndrome generated splinter personalities: to cope in a world that confused and frightened them. Alone and afraid at the age of ten, he had taken refuge in fantasy. He created The Friend, a magical being, as a source of solace and hope. When Holly pressed The Friend to explain itself logically, Jim resisted her because her probing threatened a fantasy which he desperately needed to sustain himself.

For similar reasons of her own, she had not questioned him as toughly as she should have on Monday evening. *He* was *her* sustaining dream. He had come into her life like a heroic figure in a dream, saving Billy Jenkins with dreamlike grace and panache. Until she had seen him, she had not realized how much she needed someone like him. And instead of probing deeply at him as any good reporter would have done, she had let him be what he wanted to pretend to be, for she had been reluctant to lose him.

Now their only hope was to press hard for the whole truth. He could not be healed until they understood why this particular and bizarre fantasy of his had evolved and how in the name of God he had developed the superhuman powers to support it.

She sat with her hands on the steering wheel, prepared to act but with no idea what to do. There seemed to be no one to whom she could turn for help. She needed answers that were to be found only in the past or in Jim's subconscious mind, two terrains that at the moment were equally inaccessible.

Then, hit by a thunderbolt of insight, she realized Jim already had given her a set of keys to unlock his remaining mysteries. When they had driven into New Svenborg, he had taken her on a tour of the town which, at the time, seemed like a tactic to delay their arrival at the farm. But she realized now that the tour had contained the most important revelations he had made to her. Each nostalgic landmark was a key to the past and to the remaining mysteries that, once unlocked, would make it possible for her to help him.

He wanted help. A part of him understood that he was sick, trapped in a schizophrenic fantasy, and he wanted out. She just hoped that he would suppress The Enemy until they had time to learn what they needed to know. That darkest splinter of his mind did not want her to succeed; her success would be its death, and to save itself, it would destroy her if it got the chance.

If she and Jim were to have a life together, or any life at all, their future lay in the past, and the past lay in New Svenborg.

She swung the wheel hard right, began to turn around to head out of the driveway to the county road—then stopped. She looked at the windmill again.

Jim had to be part of his own cure. She could not track down the truth and *make* him believe it. He had to see it himself.

She loved him.

She was afraid of him.

She couldn't do anything about the love; that was just part of her now, like blood or bone or sinew. But almost any fear could be overcome by confronting the cause of it.

Wondering at her own courage, she drove back along the graveled path to the foot of the windmill. She pumped three long blasts from the horn, then three more, waited a few seconds and hit it again, again.

Jim appeared in the doorway. He came out into the gray morning light, squinting at her.

Holly opened her door and stepped out of the car. "You awake?"

"Do I look like I'm sleepwalking?" he asked as he approached her. "What's going on?"

"I want to be damn sure you're awake, *fully* awake."

He stopped a few feet away. "Why don't we open the hood, I'll put my head under it, then you can let out maybe a two-minute blast, just to be sure. Holly, what's going on?"

"We have to talk. Get in."

Frowning, he went around to the passenger's side and got into the Ford with her.

When he settled into the passenger's seat, he said, "This isn't going to be pleasant, is it?"

"No. Not especially."

In front of them, the sails of the windmill stuttered. They began to turn slowly, with much clattering and creaking, shedding chunks and splinters of rotten vanes.

"Stop it," she said to Jim, afraid that the turning sails were only a prelude to a manifestation of The Enemy. "I know you don't want to hear what I have to say, but don't try to distract me, don't try to stop me."

He did not respond. He stared with fascination at the mill, as if he had not heard her.

The speed of the sails increased.

"Jim, damn it!"

At last he looked at her, genuinely baffled by the anger underlying her fear. "What?"

Around, around, around-around-around, aroundaroundaround. It turned like a haunted Ferris wheel in a carnival of the damned.

"Shit!" she said, her fear accelerating with the pace of the windmill sails. She put the car in reverse, looked over her shoulder, and backed at high speed around the pond.

"Where are we going?" he asked.

"Not far."

Since the windmill lay at the center of Jim's delusion, Holly thought it was a good idea to put it out of sight while they talked. She swung the car around, drove to the end of the driveway, and parked facing out toward the county road.

She cranked down her window, and he followed suit.

Switching off the engine, she turned more directly toward him. In spite of everything she now knew—or suspected—about him, she wanted to touch his face, smooth his hair, hold him. He elicited a mothering urge from her of which she hadn't even known she'd been capable—just as he engendered in her an erotic response and passion that were beyond anything she had experienced before.

Yeah, she thought, and evidently he engenders in you a suicidal tendency. Jesus, Thorne, the guy as much as said he'll kill you!

But he also had said he loved her.

Why wasn't *anything* easy?

She said, "Before I get into it . . . I want you to understand that I love you, Jim." It was the dumbest line in the world. It sounded so insincere. Words were inadequate to describe the real thing, partly because the feeling ran deeper than she had ever imagined it would, and partly because it was not a single emotion but was mixed up with other things like anxiety and hope. She said it again anyway: "I really do love you."

He reached for her hand, smiling at her with obvious pleasure. "You're wonderful, Holly."

Which was not exactly I-love-you-too-Holly, but that was okay. She didn't harbor romance-novel expectations. It was not going to be that simple. Being in love with Jim Ironheart was like being in love simultaneously with the tortured Max de Winter from *Rebecca*, Superman, and Jack Nicholson in any role he'd ever played. Though it wasn't easy, it wasn't dull either.

"The thing is, when I was paying my motel bill yesterday morning and you were sitting in the car watching me, I realized you hadn't said you loved me. I was going off with you, putting myself in your hands, and you hadn't said the words. But then I realized I hadn't said them either, I was playing it just as cool, holding back and protecting myself. Well, I'm not holding back any more, I'm walking out on that highwire with no net below—and largely because you told me you loved me last night. So you better have meant it."

A quizzical expression overtook him.

She said, "I know you don't remember saying it, but you did. You have problems with the 'L' word. Maybe because you lost your folks when you were so young, you're afraid to get close to anyone for fear of losing them, too. Instant analysis. Holly Freud. Anyway, you did tell me you loved me, and I'll prove it in a little while, but right now, before I get into this mess, I want you to know I never imagined I could feel about anyone the way I feel about you. So if whatever I say to you in the next few minutes is hard to take, even *impossible* to take, just know where it comes from, only from love, from nothing else."

He stared at her. "Yeah, all right. But Holly, this—"

"You'll get your turn." She leaned across the seat, kissed him, then pulled back. "Right now, you've got to listen."

She told him everything she had theorized, why she had crept out of the mill while he'd been asleep—and why she had returned. He listened with growing disbelief, and she repeatedly cut off his protests by lightly squeezing his hand, putting a hand to his lips, or giving him a quick kiss. The answer-tablet, which she produced from the back seat, stunned him and rendered his objections less vehement. BECAUSE HE LOOKS LIKE MY FATHER WHOM I FAILED TO SAVE. His hands shook as he held the tablet and stared at that incredible line. He turned back to the other surprising messages, repeated page after page—HE LOVES YOU HOLLY/HE WILL KILL YOU HOLLY—and the tremors in his hands became even more severe.

"I would never harm you," he said shakily, staring down at the tablet. "Never."

"I know you'd never want to."

Dr. Jekyll had never wanted to be the murderous Mr. Hyde.

"But you think I sent you this, not The Friend."

"I know you did, Jim. It feels right."

"So if The Friend sent it but the The Friend is me, a part of me, then you believe it really says 'I love you Holly.' "

"Yes," she said softly.

He looked up from the tablet, met her eyes. "If you believe the I-love-you part, why don't you believe the I-will-kill-you part?"

"Well, that's the thing. I do believe a small, dark part of you wants to kill me, yes."

He flinched as if she had struck him.

She said, "The Enemy wants me dead, it wants me dead real bad, because I've made you face up to what's behind these recent events, brought you back here, forced you to confront the source of your fantasy."

He started to shake his head in denial.

But she went on: "Which is what you *wanted* me to do. It's why you drew me to you in the first place."

"No. I didn't—"

"Yes, you did." Pushing him toward enlightenment was extremely dangerous. But that was her only hope of saving him. "Jim, if you can just understand what's happened, accept the existence of two other personalities, even the possibility of their existence, maybe that'll be the beginning of the end of The Friend and The Enemy."

Still shaking his head, he said, "The Enemy won't go peacefully," and immediately blinked in surprise at the words he had spoken and the implication that they conveyed.

"Damn," Holly said, and a thrill coursed through her, not merely because he had just confirmed her entire theory, whether he could admit it or not, but because the five words he had spoken were proof that he wanted out of the Byzantine fantasy in which he had taken refuge.

He was as pale as a man who had just been told that a cancer was growing in him. In fact a malignancy *did* reside within him, but it was mental rather than physical.

A breeze wafted through the open car windows, and it seemed to wash new hope into Holly.

That buoyant feeling was short-lived, however, because new words suddenly appeared on the tablet in Jim's hands: YOU DIE.

"This isn't me," he told her earnestly, in spite of the subtle admission he had made a moment ago. "Holly, this can't be me."

On the tablet, more words appeared: I AM COMING. YOU DIE.

Holly felt as if the world had become a carnival funhouse, full of ghouls and ghosts. Every turn, any moment, without warning, something might spring at her from out of a shadow—or from broad daylight, for that matter. But unlike a carnival monster, this one would inflict real pain, draw blood, kill her if it could.

In hopes that The Enemy, like The Friend, would respond well to firmness, Holly grabbed the tablet from Jim's hand and threw it out the window. "To hell with that. I won't read that crap. Listen to me, Jim. If I'm right, The Enemy is the embodiment of your rage over the deaths of your parents. Your fury was so great, at ten, it terrified you, so you pushed it outside yourself, into this other identity. But you're a unique victim of multiple-personality syndrome because your power allows you to create physical existences for your other identities."

Though acceptance had a toehold in him, he was still struggling to deny the truth. "What're we saying here? That I'm insane, that I'm some sort of socially functional lunatic, for Christ's sake?"

"Not insane," she said quickly. "Let's say disturbed, troubled. You're locked in a psychological box that you built for yourself, and you want out, but you can't find the key to the lock."

He shook his head. Fine beads of sweat had broken out along his hairline, and he was into whiter shades of pale. "No, that's putting too good a face on it. If what you think is true, then I'm all the way off the deep end, Holly, I should be in some damned rubber room, pumped full of Thorazine."

She took both of his hands again, held them tight. "No. Stop that. You can find your way out of this, you can do it, you can make yourself whole again, I know you can."

"How can you know? Jesus, Holly, I—"

"Because you're not an ordinary man, you're special," she said sharply. "You have this power, this incredible force inside you, and you can do such good with it if you want. The power is something you can draw on that ordinary people don't have, it can be a *healing* power. Don't you see? If you can cause ringing bells and alien heartbeats and voices to come out of thin air, if you can turn walls into flesh, project images into my dreams, see into the future to save lives, then you can make yourself whole and right again."

Determined disbelief lined his face. "How could any man have the power you're talking about?"

"I don't know, but you've got it."

"It has to come from a higher being. For God's sake, I'm not Superman."

Holly pounded a fist against the horn ring and said, "You're telepathic, telekinetic, tele-fucking-everything! All right, you can't fly, you don't have X-ray vision, you can't bend steel with your bare hands, and you can't race faster than a speeding bullet. But you're as close to Superman as any man's likely to get. In fact, in some ways you've got him beat because you can see into the future. Maybe you see only bits and pieces of it, and only random visions when you aren't trying for them, but you *can* see the future."

He was shaken by her conviction. "So where'd I get all this magic?"

"I don't know."

"That's where it falls apart."

"It doesn't fall apart just because I don't know," she said frustratedly. "Yellow doesn't stop being yellow just because I don't know anything about why the eye sees different colors. You *have* the power. You *are* the power, not God or some alien under the millpond."

He pulled his hands from hers and looked out the windshield toward the county road and the dry fields beyond. He seemed afraid to face up to the tremendous power he possessed—maybe because it carried with it responsibilities that he was not sure he could shoulder.

She sensed that he was also shamed by the prospect of his own mental illness, and unable to meet her eyes any longer. He was so stoic, so strong, so proud of his strength that he could not accept this suggested weakness in himself. He had built a life that placed a high value on self-control and self-reliance, that made a singular virtue out of self-imposed solitude, in the manner of a monk who needed no one but himself and God. Now she was telling him that his decision to become an iron man and a loner was not a well-considered choice, that it was a desperate attempt to deal with emotional turmoil that had threatened to destroy him, and that his need for self-control had carried him over the line of rational behavior.

She thought of the words on the tablet: I AM COMING. YOU DIE.

She switched on the engine.

He said, "Where are we going?"

As she put the car in gear, pulled out onto the county road, and turned right toward New Svenborg, she did not answer him. Instead, "Was there anything special about you as a boy?"

"No," he said a little too quickly, too sharply.

"Never any indication that you were gifted or—"

"No, hell, nothing like that."

Jim's sudden nervous agitation, betrayed by his restless movement and his trembling hands, convinced Holly that she had touched on a truth. He *had* been special in some way, a gifted child. Now that she had reminded him of it, he saw in that early gift the seeds of the powers that had grown in him. But he didn't want to face it. Denial was his shield.

"What have you just remembered?"

"Nothing."

"Come on, Jim."

"Nothing, really."

She didn't know where to go with that line of questioning, so she could only say, "It's true. You're gifted. No aliens, only you."

Because of whatever he had just remembered and was not willing to share with her, his adamancy had begun to dissolve. "I don't know."

"It's true."

"Maybe."

"It's true. Remember last night when The Friend told us it was a child by the standards of its species? Well, that's because it *is* a child, a perpetual child, forever the age at which you created it—ten years old. Which explains its childlike behavior, its need to brag, its poutiness. Jim, The Friend didn't behave like a ten-thousand-year-old alien child, it just behaved like a ten-year-old human being."

He closed his eyes and leaned back, as if it was exhausting to consider what she was telling him. But his inner tension remained at a peak, revealed by his hands, which were fisted in his lap.

"Where are we going, Holly?"

"For a little ride." As they passed through the golden fields and hills, she kept up a gentle attack: "That's why the manifestation of The Enemy is like a combination of every movie monster that ever frightened a ten-year-old boy. The thing I caught a glimpse of in my motel-room doorway wasn't a *real* creature, I see that now. It didn't have a biological structure that made sense, it wasn't even alien. It was too familiar, a ten-year-old boy's hodge-podge of boogeymen."

He did not respond.

She glanced at him. "Jim?"

His eyes were still closed.

Her heart began to pound. "Jim!"

At the note of alarm in her voice, he sat up straighter and opened his eyes. "What?"

"For God's sake, don't close your eyes that long. You might've been asleep, and I wouldn't have realized it until—"

"You think I can sleep with *this* on my mind?"

"I don't know. I don't want to take the chance. Keep your eyes open, okay? You obviously suppress The Enemy when you're awake, it only comes through all the way when you're asleep."

In the windshield glass, like a computer readout in a fighter-plane cockpit, words began to appear from left to right, in letters about one inch high: DEAD DEAD DEAD DEAD DEAD DEAD.

Scared but unwilling to show it, she said, "To hell with that," and switched on the windshield wipers, as if the threat was dirt that could be scrubbed away. But the words remained, and Jim stared at them with evident dread.

As they passed a small ranch, the scent of new-mown hay entered with the wind through the windows.

"Where are we going?" he asked again.

"Exploring."

"Exploring what?"

"The past."

Distressed, he said, "I haven't bought this scenario yet. I can't. How the hell can I? And how can we ever prove it's true or isn't?"

"We go to town," she said. "We take that tour again, the one you took me on yesterday. Svenborg—port of mystery and romance. What a dump. But it's got *something*. You wanted me to see those places, your subconscious was telling me answers can be found in Svenborg. So let's go find them together."

New words appeared under the first six: DEAD DEAD DEAD DEAD DEAD DEAD.

Holly knew that time was running out. The Enemy wanted through, wanted to gut her, dismember her, leave her in a steaming heap of her own entrails before she had a chance to convince Jim of her theory—and it did not want to wait until Jim was asleep. She was not certain that he could repress that dark aspect of himself as she pushed him closer to a confrontation with the truth. His self-control might crack, and his benign personalities might sink under the rising dark force.

"Holly, if I had this bizarre multiple personality, wouldn't I be cured as soon as you explained it to me, wouldn't the scales immediately fall off my eyes?"

"No. You have to *believe* it before you can hope to deal with it. Believing that you suffer an abnormal mental condition is the first step toward an understanding of it, and understanding is only the first painful step toward a cure."

"Don't talk at me like a psychiatrist, you're no psychiatrist."

He was taking refuge in anger, in that arctic glare, trying to intimidate her as he had tried on previous occasions when he'd not wanted her to get any closer. Hadn't worked then, wouldn't work now. Sometimes men could be so dense.

She said, "I interviewed a psychiatrist once."

"Oh, terrific, that makes you a qualified therapist."

"Maybe it does. The psychiatrist I interviewed was crazy as a loon himself, so what does a university degree matter?"

He took a deep breath and let it out with a shudder. "Okay, suppose you're right and somehow we do turn up undeniable proof that *I'm* crazy as a loon—"

"You aren't crazy, you're—"

"Yeah, yeah, I'm disturbed, troubled, in a psychological box. Call it whatever you want. If we find proof somehow—and I can't imagine how—then what happens to me? Maybe I just smile and say, 'Oh, yes, of course, I made it all up, I was living in a delusion, I'm ever so much better now, let's have lunch.' But I don't think so. I think what happens is . . . I blow apart, into a million pieces."

"I can't promise you that the truth, if we find it, will be any sort of salvation, because so far I think you've found your salvation in fantasy, not in truth. But we can't go on like this because The Enemy resents me, and sooner or later it'll kill me. You warned me yourself."

He looked at the words on the windshield, and said nothing. He was running out of arguments, if not resistance.

The words quickly faded, then vanished.

Maybe that was a good sign, an indication of his subconscious accommodation to her theory. Or maybe The Enemy had decided that she could not be intimidated with threats—and was struggling to burst through and savage her.

She said, "When it's killed me, you'll realize it *is* part of you. And if you love me, like you told me you did through The Friend last night, then what's that going to do to you? Isn't that going to destroy the Jim I love? Isn't that going to leave you with just one personality—the dark one, The Enemy? I think it's a damned good bet. So we're talking your survival here as well as mine. If you want to have a future, then let's dig to the bottom of this."

"Maybe we dig and dig—but there is no bottom. Then what?"

"Then we dig a little deeper."

AS THEY WERE entering town, making the abrupt transition from dead-brown land to tightly grouped pioneer settlement, Holly suddenly said aloud: "Robert Vaughn."

Jim twitched with surprise, not because she had said something mystifying but because that name made an immediate connection for him.

"My God," he said, "that was the voice."

"The voice of The Friend," she said, glancing at him. "So you realized it was familiar, too."

Robert Vaughn, the wonderful actor, had been the hero of television's *The Man from U.N.C.L.E.* and exquisitely oily villain of countless films. He possessed one of those voices with such a rich timbre and range that it could be as threatening, or as fatherly and reassuring, as he chose to make it.

"Robert Vaughn," Holly said. "But why? Why not Orson Welles or Paul Newman or Sean Connery or Fred Flintstone? It's too quirky a choice not to be meaningful."

"I don't know," Jim said thoughtfully, but he had the unnerving feeling he *should* know. The explanation was within his grasp.

Holly said, "Do you still think it's an alien? Wouldn't an alien just manufacture a nondescript voice? Why would it imitate any one particular actor?"

"I saw Robert Vaughn once," Jim said, surprised by a dim memory stirring within him. "I mean, not on TV or in the movies, but for real, up close. A long time ago."

"Where, when?"

"I can't . . . it won't . . . won't come to me."

Jim felt as if he were standing on a narrow spine of land between two precipices, with safety to neither side. On the one hand was the life he had been living, filled with torment and despair that he had tried to deny but that had overwhelmed him at times, as when he had taken his spiritual journey on the Harley into the Mojave Desert, looking for a way out even if the way was death. On the other hand lay an uncertain future that Holly was trying to paint in for him, a future that she insisted was one of hope but which looked to him like chaos and madness. And the narrow spine on which he stood was crumbling by the minute.

He remembered an exchange they'd had as they lay side by side in his bed two nights ago, before they had made love for the first time. He'd said, *People are always more . . . complex than you figure.*

Is that just an observation . . . or a warning?

Warning?

Maybe you're warning me that you're not what you seem to be.

After a long pause, he had said, *Maybe.*

And after her own long pause, she had said, *I guess I don't care.*

He was sure, now, that he had been warning her. A small voice within told him that she was right in her analysis, that the entities at the mill had only been different aspects of him. But if he was a victim of multiple-personality syndrome, he did not believe that his condition could be casually described as a mere mental disturbance or a troubled state of mind, as she had tried to portray it. Madness was the only word that did it justice.

They entered Main Street. The town looked strangely dark and threatening—perhaps because it held the truth that would force him to step off his narrow mental perch into one world of chaos or another.

He remembered reading somewhere that only mad people were dead-certain of their sanity. He was dead-certain of nothing, but he took no comfort from that. Madness was, he suspected, the very essence of uncertainty, a frantic but fruitless search for answers, for solid ground. Sanity was that place of certainty above the whirling chaos.

Holly pulled to the curb in front of Handahl's Pharmacy at the east end of Main Street. "Let's start here."

"Why?"

"Because it's the first stop we made when you were pointing out places that had meant something to you as a kid."

He stepped out of the Ford under the canopy of a Wilson magnolia, one of several interspersed with other trees along both sides of the street. That landscaping softened the hard edges but contributed to the unnatural look and discordant feeling of the town.

When Holly pushed open the front door of the Danish-style building, its glass panes glimmered like jewels along their beveled edges, and a bell tinkled overhead. They went inside together.

Jim's heart was hammering. Not because the pharmacy seemed likely to be a place where anything significant had happened to him in his childhood, but because he sensed it was the first stone on a path to the truth.

The cafe and soda fountain were to the left, and through the archway Jim saw a few people at breakfast. Immediately inside the door was the small newsstand, where morning papers were stacked high, mostly the Santa Barbara daily; there were also magazines, and to one side a revolving wire rack filled with paperback books.

"I used to buy paperbacks here," he said. "I loved books even back then, couldn't get enough of them."

The pharmacy was through another archway to the right. It resembled any modern American pharmacy in that it stocked more cosmetics, beauty aids, and hair-care products than patent medicines. Otherwise, it was pleasantly quaint: wood shelves instead of metal or fiberboard; polished-granite counters; an appealing aroma composed of Bayberry candles, nickle candy, cigar-tobacco effluvium filtering from the humidified case behind the cash register, faint traces of ethyl alcohol, and sundry pharmaceuticals.

Though the hour was early, the pharmacist was on duty, serving as his own checkout clerk. It was Corbett Handahl himself, a heavy wide-shouldered man with a white mustache and white hair, wearing a crisp blue shirt under his starched white lab jacket.

He looked up and said, "Jim Ironheart, bless my soul. How long's it been—at least three, four years?"

They shook hands.

"Four years and four months," Jim said. He almost added, *since grandpa died*, but checked himself without quite knowing why.

Spritzing the granite prescription-service counter with Windex, Corbett wiped it with paper towels. He smiled at Holly. "And *whoever* you are, I am eternally grateful to you for bringing beauty into this gray morning."

Corbett was the perfect smalltown pharmacist: just jovial enough to seem like ordinary folks in spite of being placed in the town's upper social class by virtue of his occupation, enough of a tease to be something of a local character, but with an unmistakable air of competence and probity that made you feel the medicines he compounded would always be safe. Townfolk stopped in just to say hello, not only when they needed some thing, and his genuine interest in people served his commerce. He had been working at the pharmacy for thirty-three years and had been the owner since his father's death twenty-seven years ago.

Handahl was the least threatening of men, yet Jim suddenly felt threatened by him. He wanted to get out of the pharmacy before . . .

Before what?

Before Handahl said the wrong thing, revealed too much.

But what could he reveal?

"I'm Jim's fiancée," Holly said, somewhat to Jim's surprise.

"Congratulations, Jim," Handahl said. "You're a lucky man. Young lady, I just hope you know, the family changed its name from Ironhead, which was more descriptive. Stubborn group." He winked and laughed.

Holly said, "Jim's taking me around town; showing me favorite places. Sentimental journey, I suppose you'd call it."

Frowning at Jim, Handahl said, "Didn't think you ever liked this town well enough to feel sentimental about it."

Jim shrugged. "Attitudes change."

"Glad to hear it." Handahl turned to Holly again. "He started coming in here soon after he moved in with his grandfolks, every Tuesday and Friday when new books and magazines arrived from the distributor in Santa Barbara." He had put aside the Windex. He was arranging counter displays of chewing gum, breath mints, disposable lighters, and pocket combs. "Jim was a real reader then. You still a real reader?"

"Still am," Jim said with growing uneasiness, terrified of what Handahl might say next. Yet for the life of him, he did not know what the man could say that would matter so much.

"Your tastes were kinda narrow, I remember." To Holly: "Used to spend his allowance buying most every science fiction or spook-'em paperback that came in the door. Course, in those days, a two-dollar-a-week allowance went pretty far, if you remember that a book was about forty-five or fifty cents."

Claustrophobia settled over Jim, thick as a heavy shroud. The pharmacy began to seem frighteningly small, crowded with merchandise, and he wanted to get out of there.

It's coming, he thought, with a sudden quickening of anxiety. It's coming.

Handahl said, "I suppose maybe he got his interest in weird fiction from his mom and dad."

Frowning, Holly said, "How's that?"

"I didn't know Jamie, Jim's dad, all that well, but I was only one year behind him at county high school. No offense, Jim, but your dad had some exotic interests—though the way the world's changed, they probably wouldn't seem as exotic now as back in the early fifties."

"Exotic interests?" Holly prodded.

Jim looked around the pharmacy, wondering where it would come from, which route of escape might be blocked and which might remain open. He was swinging between tentative acceptance of Holly's theory and rejection of it, and right now, he was sure she had to be wrong. It wasn't a force inside him. It was entirely a separate being, just as The Friend was. It was an evil alien, just as The Friend was good, and it could go anywhere, come out of anything, at any second, and it *was* coming, he knew it was coming, it wanted to kill them all.

"Well," Handahl said, "when he was a kid, Jamie used to come in here— it was my dad's store then—and buy those old pulp magazines with robots, monsters, and scanty-clad women on the covers. He used to talk a lot about how we'd put men on the moon someday, and everyone thought he was a little strange for that, but I guess he was right after all. Didn't surprise me when I heard he'd given up being an accountant, found a showbiz wife, and was making his living doing a mentalist act."

"Mentalist act?" Holly said, glancing at Jim. "I thought your dad was an accountant, your mom was an actress."

"They were," he said thinly. "That's what they were—before they put together the act."

He had almost forgotten about the act, which surprised him. How could he have forgotten the act? He had all the photographs from the tours, so many of them on his walls; he looked at them everyday, yet he'd pretty much forgotten that they had been taken during travels between performances.

It was coming very fast now.

Close. It was very close.

He wanted to warn Holly. He couldn't speak.

Something seemed to have stolen his tongue, locked his jaws.

It was coming.

It didn't want him to warn her. It wanted to take her by surprise.

Arranging the last of the counter displays, Handahl said, "It was a trag-edy, what happened to them, all right. Jim, when you first came to town to stay with your grandfolks, you were withdrawn, nobody could get two words out of you."

Holly was watching Jim rather than Handahl. She seemed to sense that he was in grave distress.

"Second year, after Lena died," Handahl said, "Jim pretty much clammed up altogether, totally mute, like he was never going to talk another word as long as he lived. You remember that, Jim?"

In astonishment, Holly turned to Jim and said, "Your grandmother died the second year you were here, when you were only eleven?"

I told her five years ago, Jim thought. Why did I tell her five years ago when the truth is twenty-four?

It was coming.

He sensed it.

Coming.

The Enemy.

He said, "Excuse me, gotta get some fresh air." He hurried outside and stood by the car, gasping for breath.

Looking back, he discovered that Holly had not followed him. He could see her through a pharmacy window, talking to Handahl.

It was coming.

Holly, don't talk to him, Jim thought. Don't listen to him, get out of there.

It was coming.

Leaning against the car, he thought: the only reason I fear Corbett Handahl is because he knows more about my life in Svenborg than I remember myself.

Lub-dub-DUB.

It was here.

HANDAHL STARED CURIOUSLY after Jim.

Holly said, "I think he's never gotten over what happened to his parents . . . or to Lena."

Handahl nodded. "Who could get over a horrible thing like that? He was such a nice little kid, it broke your heart." Before Holly could ask anything more about Lena, Handahl said, "Are you two moving into the farmhouse?"

"No. Just staying for a couple of days."

"None of my business, really, but it's a shame that land isn't being farmed."

"Well, Jim's not a farmer himself," she said, "and with nobody willing to buy the place—"

"Nobody willing to buy it? Why, young lady, they'd stand twenty deep to buy it if Jim would put it on the market."

She blinked at him.

He went on: "You have a real good artesian well on that property, which means you always have water in a county that's usually short of it." He leaned against the granite counter and folded his arms across his chest. "The way it works—when that big old pond is full up, the weight of all that water puts pressure on the natural wellhead and slows the inflow of new water. But you start pumping it out of there to irrigate crops, and the flow picks up, and the pond is pretty much always full, like the magic pitcher in that old fairytale." He tilted his head and squinted at her. "Jim tell you he couldn't sell it?"

"Well, I assumed—"

"Tell you what," Handahl said, "maybe that man of yours *is* more sentimental than I'd thought. Maybe he doesn't want to sell the farm because it has too many memories for him."

"Maybe," she said. "But there're bad as well as good memories out there."

"You're right about that."

"Like his grandmother dying," she noodged, trying to get him back on that subject. "That was—"

A rattling sound interrupted her. She turned and saw bottles of shampoo, hairspray, vitamins, and cold medicines jiggling on their shelves.

"Earthquake," Handahl said, looking up worriedly at the ceiling, as if he thought it might tumble in on them.

The containers rattled more violently than ever, and Holly knew they were disturbed by something worse than an earthquake. She was being warned not to ask Handahl any more questions.

Lub-dub-DUB, lub-dub-DUB.

The cozy world of the quaint pharmacy started coming apart. The bottles exploded off the shelves, straight at her. She swung away, drew her arms over her head. The containers hammered her, flew past her and pelted Handahl. The humidor, which stood behind the counter, was vibrating. Instinctively Holly dropped to the floor. Even as she went down, the glass door of that case blew outward. Glass shrapnel cut the air where she had been standing. She scrambled toward the exit as glittering shards rained to the floor. Behind her the heavy cash register crashed off the granite counter, missing her by inches, barely sparing her a broken spine. Before the walls could begin to blister and pulse and bring forth an alien form, she reached the door, fled through the newsstand, and went into the street, leaving Handahl in what he no doubt assumed was earthquake rubble.

The tripartite beat was throbbing up from the brick walkway beneath her feet.

She found Jim leaning against the car, shuddering and whey-faced, with the expression of a man standing on a precipice, peering into a gulf—longing to jump. He did not respond to her when she said his name. He seemed on the verge of surrendering to the dark force that he'd held within—and nurtured—all these years and that now wanted its freedom.

She jerked him away from the car, put her arms around him, held him tight, tighter, repeating his name, expecting the sidewalk to erupt in geysers of brick, expecting to be seized by serrated pincers, tentacles, or cold damp hands of inhuman design. But the triple-thud heartbeat faded, and after a while Jim raised his arms and put them around her.

The Enemy had passed.

But it was only a temporary reprieve.

SVENBORG MEMORIAL PARK was adjacent to Tivoli Gardens. The cemetery was separated from the park by a spearpoint wrought-iron fence and a mix of trees—mostly white cedars and spreading California Peppers.

Jim drove slowly along the service road that looped through the graveyard. "Here." He pulled to the side and stopped.

When he got out of the Ford, he felt almost as claustrophobic as he had in the pharmacy, even though he was standing in the open air. The slate-dark sky seemed to press down toward the gray granite monuments, while those rectangles and squares and spires strained up like the knobs of ancient time-stained bones half buried in the earth. In that dreary light, the grass looked gray-green. The trees were gray-green, too, and seemed to loom precariously, as if about to topple on him.

Going around the car to Holly's side, he pointed north. "There."

She took his hand. He was grateful to her for that.

Together they walked to his grandparents' gravesite. It was on a slight rise in the generally flat cemetery. A single rectangular granite marker served both plots.

Jim's heart was beating hard, and he had difficulty swallowing.

Her name was chiseled into the right-hand side of the monument. LENA LOUISE IRONHEART.

Reluctantly he looked at the dates of her birth and death. She had been fifty-three when she died. And she had been dead twenty-four years.

This must be what it felt like to have been brainwashed, to have had one's memory painted over, false memories airbrushed into the blanks. His past seemed like a fogbound landscape revealed only by the eerie and inconstant luminescent face of a cloud-shrouded moon. He suddenly could not see back through the years with the same clarity he had enjoyed an hour ago, and he could not trust the reality of what he still did see; clear recollections might prove to be nothing more than tricks of fog and shadow when he was forced to confront them closely.

Disoriented and afraid, he held fast to Holly's hand.

"Why did you lie to me about this, why did you say five years?" she asked gently.

"I didn't lie. At least . . . I didn't realize I was lying." He stared at the granite as if its polished surface was a window into the past, and he struggled to remember. "I can recall waking up one morning and knowing that my grandmother was dead. Five years ago. I was living in the apartment then, down in Irvine." He listened to his own voice as if it belonged to someone else, and the haunted tone of it gave him a chill. "I dressed . . . drove north . . . bought flowers in town . . . then came here . . ."

After a while, when he did not continue, Holly said, "Do you remember a funeral that day?"

"No."

"Other mourners?"

"No."

"Other flowers on the grave?"

"No. All I remember is . . . kneeling at the headstone with the flowers I'd brought for her . . . crying . . . I cried for a long time, couldn't stop crying."

Passing him on the way to other graves, people had looked at him with sympathy, then with embarrassment as they had realized the extent of his emotional collapse, then with uneasiness as they had seen a grief in him so wild that it made him seem unbalanced. He could even now remember how wild he had felt that day, glaring back at those who stared at him, wanting nothing more than to claw his way down into the earth and pull it over him as if it were a blanket, taking rest in the same hole as his grandmother. But he could not remember *why* he had felt that way or why he was beginning to feel that way again.

He looked at the date of her death once more—September 25—and he was too frightened now to cry.

"What is it? Tell me," Holly urged.

"That's when I came with the flowers, the only other time I've ever come, the day I remember as the day she died. September twenty-fifth . . . but five years ago, not twenty-four. It was the nineteenth anniversary of her death . . . but at the time it seemed to me, and always has, that she'd only just then died."

They were both silent.

Two large blackbirds wheeled across the somber sky, shrieking, and disappeared over the treetops.

Finally Holly said, "Could it be, you denied her death, refused to accept it when it really happened, twenty-four years ago? Maybe you were only able to accept it nineteen years later . . . the day you came here with the flowers. That's why you remember her dying so much more recently than she did. You date her death from the day you finally accepted it."

He knew at once that she had hit upon the truth, but the answer did not make him feel better. "But Holly, my God, that *is* madness."

"No," she said calmly. "It's self-defense, part of the same defenses you erected to hide so much of that year when you were ten." She paused, took a deep breath, and said, "Jim, how did your grandma die?"

"She . . ." He was surprised to realize that he could not recall the cause of Lena Ironheart's death. One more fog-filled blank. "I don't know."

"I think she died in the mill."

He looked away from the tombstone, at Holly. He tensed with alarm, although he did not know why. "In the windmill? How? What happened? How can you know?"

"The dream I told you about. Climbing the mill stairs, looking through the window at the pond below, and seeing another woman's face reflected in the glass, your grandmother's face."

"It was only a dream."

Holly shook her head. "No, I think it was a memory, your memory, which you projected from your sleep into mine."

His heart fluttered with panic for reasons he could not quite discern. "How can it have been my memory if I don't have it now?"

"You have it."

He frowned. "No. Nothing like that."

"It's locked down in your subconscious, where you can access it only when you're dreaming, but it's there, all right."

If she had told him that the entire cemetery was mounted on a carousel, and that they were slowly spinning around under the bleak gun-metal sky, he would have accepted what she said more easily than he could accept the memory toward which she was leading him. He felt as if he were spinning through light and darkness, light and darkness, fear and rage. . . .

With great effort, he said, "But in your dream . . . I was in the high room when grandma got there."

"Yes."

"And if she died there . . ."

"You witnessed her death."

He shook his head adamantly. "No. My God, I'd remember that, don't you think?"

"No. I think that's why you needed nineteen years even to admit to yourself that she died. I think you saw her die, and it was such a shock that it threw you into long-term amnesia, which you overlaid with fantasies, always more fantasies."

A breeze stirred, and something crackled around his feet. He was sure it was the bony hands of his grandmother clawing out of the earth to seize him, but when he looked down he saw only withered leaves rattling against one another as they blew across the grass.

With each heartbeat now like a fist slamming into a punching bag, Jim turned away from the grave, eager to get back to the car.

Holly put a hand on his arm. "Wait."

He tore loose of her, almost shoved her away. He glared at her and said, "I want to get out of here."

Undeterred, she grabbed and halted him again. "Jim, where is your grandfather? Where is he buried?"

Jim pointed to the plot beside his grandmother's. "He's there, of course, with her."

Then he saw the left half of the granite monument. He had been so intently focused on the right half, on the impossible date of his grandmother's death, that he had not noticed what was missing from the left side. His grandfather's name was there, as it should be, engraved at the same time that Lena's had been: HENRY JAMES IRONHEART. And the date of his birth. But that was all. The date of his death had never been chiseled into the stone.

The iron sky was pressing lower.

The trees seemed to be leaning closer, arching over him.

Holly said, "Didn't you say he died eight months after Lena?"

His mouth was dry. He could hardly work up enough spit to speak, and the words came out in dry whispers like susurrant bursts of sand blown against desert stone. "What the hell do you want from me? I told you . . . eight months . . . May twenty-fourth of the next year. . . ."

"How did he die?"

"I . . . I don't . . . I don't remember."

"Illness?"

Shut up, shut up!

"I don't know."

"An accident?"

"I . . . just . . . I think . . . I think it was a stroke."

Large parts of the past were mists within a mist. He realized now that he rarely thought about the past. He lived totally in the present. He had never realized there were huge holes in his memories simply because there were so many things he had never before *tried* to remember.

"Weren't you your grandfather's nearest relative?" Holly asked.

"Yes."

"Didn't you attend to the details of his funeral?"

He hesitated, frowning. "I think . . . yes . . ."

"Then did you just forget to have the date of his death added to the headstone?"

He stared at the blank spot in the granite, frantically searching an equally blank spot in his memory, unable to answer her. He felt sick. He wanted to curl up and close his eyes and sleep and never wake up, let something else wake up in his place. . . .

She said, "Or did you bury him somewhere else?"

Across the ashes of the burnt-out sky, the shrieking blackbirds swooped again, slashing calligraphic messages with their wings, their meaning no more decipherable than the elusive memories darting through the deeper grayness of Jim's mind.

HOLLY DROVE THEM around the corner to Tivoli Gardens.

When they had left the pharmacy, Jim had wanted to drive to the cemetery, worried about what he would find there but at the same time eager to confront his misremembered past and wrench his recollections into line with the truth. The experience at the gravesite had shaken him, however, and now he was no longer in a rush to find out what additional surprises awaited him. He was content to let Holly drive, and she suspected that he would be happier if she just drove out of town, turned south, and never spoke to him of New Svenborg again.

The park was too small to have a service road. They left the car at the street and walked in.

Holly decided that Tivoli Gardens was even less inviting close up than it had been when glimpsed from a moving car yesterday. The dreary impression it made could not be blamed solely on the overcast sky. The grass was half parched from weeks of summer sun, which could be quite intense in any central California valley. Leggy runners had sprouted unchecked from the rose bushes; the few remaining blooms were faded and dropping petals in the thorny sprawl. The other flowers looked wilted, and the two benches needed painting.

Only the windmill was well maintained. It was a bigger, more imposing mill than the one at the farm, twenty feet higher, with an encircling deck about a third of the way up.

"Why are we here?" she asked.

"Don't ask me. You're the one who wanted to come."

"Don't be thick, babe," she said.

She knew that pushing him was like kicking a package of unstable dynamite, but she had no choice. He was going to blow anyway, sooner or later. Her only hope of survival was to force him to acknowledge that he was The Enemy before that personality seized control of him permanently. She sensed that she was running out of time.

She said, "You're the one who put it on the itinerary yesterday. You said they'd made a movie here once." She was jolted by what she had just said. "Wait a sec—is *this* where you saw Robert Vaughn? Was he in the movie they made here?"

With a bewildered expression that slowly gave way to a frown, Jim turned in place, surveying the small park. At last he headed toward the windmill, and she followed him.

Two historical-marker lecterns flanked the flagstone path in front of the mill door. They were all-weather stone stands. The reading material on the slanted tops was protected behind sheets of Plexiglas in watertight frames. The lectern on the left, to which they stepped first, provided background information about the use of windmills for grain milling, water pumping, and electricity production in the Santa Ynez Valley from the 1800s until well into the twentieth century, followed by a history of the preserved mill in front of them, which was called, rather aptly, the New Svenborg Mill.

That material was as dull as dirt, and Holly turned to the second lectern only because she still had some of the doggedness and appetite for facts that had made her a passable journalist. Her interest was instantly piqued by the title at the top of the second plaque—THE BLACK WINDMILL: BOOK AND MOVIE.

"Jim, look at this."

He joined her by the second marker.

There was a photograph of the jacket of a young-adult novel—*The Black Windmill* by Arthur J. Willott, and the illustration on it was obviously based on the New Svenborg Mill. Holly read the lectern text with growing astonishment. Willott, a resident of the Santa Ynez Valley—Solvang, not Svenborg—had been a successful author of novels for young adults, turning out fifty-two titles before his death in 1982, at the age of eighty. His most popular and enduring book, by far, had been a fantasy-adventure about a haunted old mill and a boy who discovered that the ghosts were actually aliens from another world and that under the millpond was a spaceship which had been there for ten thousand years.

"No," Jim said softly but with some anger, "no, this makes no sense, this can't be right."

Holly recalled a moment from the dream in which she had been in Lena Ironheart's body, climbing the mill stairs. When she had reached the top, she had found ten-year-old Jim standing with his hands fisted at his sides, and he had turned to her and said, "I'm scared, help me, the walls, the *walls!*" At his feet had been a yellow candle in a blue dish. Until now she'd forgotten that beside the dish lay a hardcover book in a colorful dustjacket. It was the same dustjacket reproduced on the lectern: *The Black Windmill.*

"No," Jim said again, and he turned away from the plaque. He stared around worriedly at the breeze-ruffled trees.

Holly read on and discovered that twenty-five years ago, the very year that ten-year-old Jim Ironheart had come to town, *The Black Windmill* had been made into a motion picture. The New Svenborg Mill had served as the primary location. The motion-picture company had created a shallow but convincing millpond around it, then paid to restore the land after filming and to establish the current pocket park.

Still turning slowly around, frowning at the trees and shrubs, at the gloom beneath them that the overcast day could not dispel, Jim said, "Something's coming."

Holly could see nothing coming, and she believed that he was just trying to distract her from the plaque. He did not want to accept the implications of the information on it, so he was trying to make her turn away from it with him.

The movie must have been a dog, because Holly had never heard of it. It appeared to have been the kind of production that was big news nowhere but in New Svenborg and, even there, only because it was based on a book by a valley resident. On the historical marker, the last paragraph of copy listed, among other details of the production, the names of the five most important members of the cast. No big box-office draws had appeared in the flick. Of the first four names, she recognized only M. Emmet Walsh, who was a personal favorite of hers. The fifth cast member was a young and then-unknown Robert Vaughn.

She looked up at the looming mill.

"What is happening here?" she said aloud. She lifted her gaze to the dismal sky, then lowered it to the photo of the dustjacket for Willott's book. "What the *hell* is happening here?"

In a voice quaking with fear but also with an eerie note of desire, Jim said, "It's coming!"

She looked where he was staring, and saw a disturbance in the earth at the far end of the small park, as if something was burrowing toward them, pushing up a yard-wide hump of dirt and sod to mark its tunnel, moving fast, straight at them.

She whirled on Jim, grabbed him. "Stop it!"

"It's coming," he said, wide-eyed.

"Jim, it's you, it's only you."

"No . . . not me . . . The Enemy." He sounded half in a trance.

Holly glanced back and saw the thing passing under the concrete walkway, which cracked and heaved up in its wake.

"Jim, damn it!"

He was staring at the approaching killer with horror but also with, she thought, a sort of longing.

One of the park benches was knocked over as the earth bulged then sank under it.

The Enemy was only forty feet from them, coming fast.

She grabbed Jim by the shirt, shook him, tried to make him look at her. "I saw this movie when I was a kid. What was it called, huh? Wasn't it *Invaders from Mars*, something like that, where the aliens open doors in the sand and suck you down?"

She glanced back. It was thirty feet from them.

"Is that what's going to kill us, Jim? Something that opens a door in the sand, sucks us down, something from a movie to give ten-year-old boys nightmares?"

Twenty feet away.

Jim was sweating, shuddering. He seemed to be beyond hearing anything Holly said.

She shouted in his face anyway: "Are you going to kill me *and* yourself, suicide like Larry Kakonis, just stop being strong and put an end to it, let one of your own nightmares pull you in the ground?"

Ten feet.

Eight.

"Jim!"

Six.

Four.

Hearing a monstrous grinding of jaws in the ground under them, she raised her foot, rammed the heel of her shoe down across the front of his shin, as hard as she could, to make him feel it through his sock. Jim cried out in pain as the ground shifted under them, and Holly looked down in horror at the rupturing earth. But the burrowing stopped simultaneously with his sharp cry. The ground didn't open. Nothing erupted from it or sucked them down.

Shaking, Holly stepped back from the ripped sod and cracked earth on which she had been standing.

Jim looked at her, aghast. "It wasn't me. It can't have been."

BACK IN THE car, Jim slumped in his seat.

Holly folded her arms on the steering wheel, put her forehead on her arms.

He looked out the side window at the park. The giant mole trail was still there. The sidewalk was cracked and tumbled. The bench lay on its side.

He just couldn't believe that the thing beneath the park had been only a figment of his imagination, empowered only by his mind. He had been in control of himself all his life, living a Spartan existence of books and work, with no vices or indulgences. (Except a frighteningly convenient forgetfulness, he thought sourly.) Nothing about Holly's theory was harder for him to accept than that a wild and savage part of him, beyond his conscious control, was the only real danger that they faced.

He was beyond ordinary fear now. He was no longer perspiring or shivering. He was in the grip of a primal terror that left him rigid and Dry-Ice dry.

"It wasn't me," he repeated.

"Yes, it was." Considering that she believed he'd almost killed her, Holly was surprisingly gentle with him. She did not raise her voice; it was softened by a note of great tenderness.

He said, "You're still on this split-personality kick."

"Yes."

"So it was my dark side."

"Yes."

"Embodied in a giant worm or something," he said, trying to hone a sharp edge on his sarcasm, failing. "But you said The Enemy only broke through when I was sleeping, and I wasn't sleeping, so even if I *am* The Enemy, how could I have been that thing in the park?"

"New rules. Subconsciously, you're getting desperate. You're not able to control that personality as easily as before. The closer you're forced to the truth, the more aggressive The Enemy's going to become in order to defend itself."

"If it was me, why wasn't there an alien heartbeat like before?"

"That's always just been a dramatic effect, like the bells ringing before The Friend put in an appearance." She raised her head from her arms and looked at him. "You dropped it because there wasn't time for it. I was reading that plaque, and you wanted to stop me as fast as you could. You needed a distraction. Let me tell you, babe, it was a lulu."

He looked out the window again, toward the windmill and the lectern that held the information about *The Black Windmill*.

Holly put a hand on his shoulder. "You were in a black despair after your parents died. You needed to escape. Evidently a writer named Arthur Willott provided you with a fantasy that fit your needs perfectly. To one extent or another, you've been living in it ever since."

Though he could not admit it to her, he had to admit to himself that he *was* groping toward understanding, that he was on the brink of seeing his past from a new perspective that would make all of the mysterious lines and angles fall into a new and comprehensible shape. If selective amnesia, carefully constructed false memories, and even multiple personalities were not indications of madness but only the hooks he had used to hold on to sanity—

as Holly insisted—then what would happen to him if he let go of those hooks? If he dug up the truth about his past, faced the things he had refused to face when he had turned to fantasy as a child, would the truth drive him mad *this* time? What was he hiding from?

"Listen," she said, "the important thing is that you shut it down before it reached us, before it did any harm."

"My shin hurts like hell," he said, wincing.

"Good," she said brightly.

She started the engine.

"Where are we going now?" he asked.

"Where else? The library."

HOLLY PARKED ON Copenhagen Lane in front of the small Victorian house that served as the New Svenborg library.

She was pleased that her hands were not shaking, that her voice was level and calm, and that she had been able to drive from Tivoli Gardens without weaving all over the road. After the incident in the park, she was amazed that her pants were still clean. She had been reduced to raw terror—a pure, intense emotion untainted by any other. Diluted now, it was still with her, and she knew it would remain with her until they were out of these spooky old woods—or dead. But she was determined not to reveal the depth of her fear to Jim, because he had to be worse off than she was. After all, it was *his* life that was turning out to be a collage of flimsy lies. He needed to lean on her.

As she and Jim went up the front walk to the porch (Jim limping), Holly noticed he was studying the lawn around him, as if he thought something might start burrowing toward them.

Better not, she thought, or you'll have *two* bleeding shins.

But as she went through the front door, she wondered if a jolt of pain would work a second time.

In the paneled foyer, a sign announced NONFICTION SECOND FLOOR. An arrow pointed to a staircase on her right.

The foyer funneled into a first-floor hallway off which lay two large rooms. Both were filled with bookshelves. The chamber on the left also contained reading tables with chairs and a large oak desk.

The woman at the desk was a good advertisement for country living: flawless complexion, lustrous chestnut hair, clear hazel eyes. She looked thirty-five but was probably twelve years older.

The nameplate in front of her said ELOISE GLYNN.

Yesterday, when Holly had wanted to come into the library to see if the much-admired Mrs. Glynn was there, Jim had insisted that she would be retired, that she had been "quite old" twenty-five years ago, when in fact she obviously had been fresh out of college and starting her first job.

By comparison with previous discoveries, this was only a minor surprise.

Jim hadn't wanted Holly to come into the library yesterday, so he'd simply lied. And from the look on his face now, it was clear that Eloise Glynn's youth was no surprise to him either; he had known, yesterday, that he was not telling the truth, though perhaps he had not understood *why* he was lying.

The librarian did not recognize Jim. Either he had been one of those kids who left little impression or, more likely, he had been telling the truth when he'd said he had not been to the library since he'd left for college eighteen years ago.

Eloise Glynn had the bouncy manner and attitude of a girls' sports coach that Holly remembered from high school. "Willott?" she said in answer to Holly's question. "Oh, yes, we've got a truckload of Willott." She bounced up from her chair. "I can show you right where he's at." She came around her desk, stepping briskly, and led Holly and Jim across the hall to the other large room. "He was local, as I'm sure you know. Died a decade ago, but two-thirds of his books are still in print." She stopped in front of the young-adult section and made a sweeping gesture with one hand to indicate two three-foot shelves of Willott titles. "He was a productive man, Artie Willott, so busy that beavers hung their heads in shame when he walked by."

She grinned at Holly, and it was infectious. Holly grinned back at her. "We're looking for *The Black Windmill.*"

"That's one of his most popular titles, never met a kid didn't love it." Mrs. Glynn plucked the book off the shelf almost without looking to see where it was, handed it to Holly. "This for your kid?"

"Actually for me. I read about it on the plaque over in Tivoli Gardens."

"I've read the book," Jim said. "But she's curious."

With Jim, Holly returned to the main room and sat at the table farthest from the desk. With the book between them, they read the first two chapters.

She kept touching him—his hand, shoulder, knee—gentling him. Somehow she had to hold him together long enough for him to learn the truth and be healed by it, and the only glue she could think of was love. She had convinced herself that each small expression of love—each touch, smile, affectionate look or word—was a bonding agent that prevented him from shattering completely.

The novel was well and engagingly written. But what it revealed about Jim Ironheart's life was so astonishing that Holly began to skim and spot read, whispering passages to him, urgently seeking the next startling revelation.

The lead character was named Jim, not Ironheart but Jamison. Jim Jamison lived on a farm that had a pond and an old windmill. The mill was supposedly haunted, but after witnessing a number of spooky incidents, Jim discovered that an alien presence, not a spirit, was quartered in a spacecraft under the pond and was manifesting itself in the mill. It revealed itself to Jim as a soft light that glowed within the mill walls. Communication between Jim and the alien was achieved with the use of two lined, yellow tablets—one for Jim's questions, and one for the alien's answers, which appeared as if by magic. According to the extraterrestrial, it was a being of pure energy and was on earth "TO OBSERVE, TO STUDY, TO HELP MANKIND." It referred to itself as THE FRIEND.

Marking her place with a finger, Holly flipped through the rest of the book to see if The Friend continued to use the awkward tablets for communication all the way to the end. It did. In the story on which Jim Ironheart had based his fantasy, the alien never vocalized.

"Which is why you doubted that *your* alien could vocalize and why you resisted my suggestion that we refuse to play along with the tablet system."

Jim was beyond denial now. He stared at the book with wonder.

His response gave Holly hope for him. In the cemetery, he had been in such distress, his eyes so cold and bleak, that she had begun to doubt if, indeed, he could turn his phenomenal power inward to heal himself. And in the park, for one terrible moment, she had thought that his fragile shell of sanity would crack and spill the yolk of madness. But he had held together, and now his curiosity seemed to be overcoming his fear.

Mrs. Glynn had gone off to work in the stacks. No other patrons had come in to browse.

Holly returned to the story, skim-reading. At the midpoint of the tale, just after Jim Jamison and the alien had their second encounter, the ET explained that it was an entity that lived "IN ALL ASPECTS OF TIME," could perceive the future, and wanted to save the life of a man who was fated to die.

"I'll be damned," Jim said softly.

Without warning, a vision burst in Holly's mind with such force and brilliance that the library vanished for a moment and her inner world became the only reality: she saw herself naked and nailed to a wall in an obscene parody of a crucifix, blood streaming from her hands and feet (a voice whispering: *die, die, die*), and she opened her mouth to scream but, instead of sound swarms of cockroaches poured out between her lips, and she realized she was already dead (*die, die, die*), her putrid innards crawling with pests and vermin—

The hateful phantasm flickered off the screen of her mind as suddenly as it had appeared, and she snapped back into the library with a jolt.

"Holly?" Jim was looking at her worriedly.

A part of him had sent the vision to her, no question about that. But the Jim she was looking at now was not the Jim who had done it. The dark child within him, The Enemy, hate-filled and murderous, was striking at her with a new weapon.

She said, "It's okay. It's all right."

But she didn't feel all right. The vision had left her nauseous and somewhat disoriented.

She had to struggle to refocus on *The Black Windmill*:

The man Jim Jamison had to save, The Friend explained, was a candidate for the United States Presidency, soon to pass through Jim's hometown, where he was going to be assassinated. The alien wanted him to live, instead, because "HE IS GOING TO BE A GREAT STATESMAN AND PEACE-MAKER WHO WILL SAVE THE WORLD FROM A GREAT WAR." Because it had to keep its presence on earth a secret, The Friend wanted to work through Jim Jamison to thwart the assassins: "YOU WILL THROW HIM A LIFE LINE, JIM."

The novel did not include an evil alien. The Enemy had been entirely Jim Ironheart's embellishment, an embodiment of his own rage and self-hatred, which he had needed to separate from himself and control.

With a crackle of inner static, another vision burst across her mind-screen, so intense that it blotted out the real world: she was in a coffin, dead but somehow still in possession of all her senses she could feel worms churning in her (*die, die, die, die*), could smell the vile stench of her own decaying body, could see her rotted face reflected on the inside of the coffin lid as if it was lit and mirrored. She raised skeletal fists and beat on the lid, heard the blows reverberating into the yards of compacted earth above her—

The library again.

"Holly, for God's sake, what's happening?"

"Nothing."

"Holly?"

"Nothing," she said, sensing that it would be a mistake to admit that The Enemy was rattling her.

She finished skimming *The Black Windmill*:

At the end of the novel, when Jim Jamison had saved the future president, The Friend had subsided into quiescence under the pond, instructing Jim to forget that their encounter had ever taken place, and to remember only that he had saved the politician on his own initiative. If a repressed memory of the alien ever surfaced in Jim's mind, he was told that he would "REMEMBER ME ONLY AS A DREAM, AN ENTITY IN A DREAM YOU ONCE HAD." When the alien light faded out of the wall for the last time, the messages on the tablet vanished, leaving no trace of the contact.

Holly closed the book.

She and Jim sat for a while, staring at the dustjacket.

Around her, thousands of times and places, people and worlds, from Mars to Egypt to Yoknapatawpha County, were closed up in the bindings of books like the shine trapped under the tarnished veneer of a brass lamp. She could almost feel them waiting to dazzle with the first turn of a page, come alive with brilliant colors and pungent odors and delicious aromas, with laughter and sobbing and cries and whispers. Books were packaged dreams.

"Dreams are doorways," she told Jim, "and the story in any novel is a kind of dream. Through Arthur Willott's dream of alien contact and adventure, you found a doorway out of your despair, an escape from a crushing sense of having failed your mother and father."

He had been unrelievedly pale since she had shown him the tablet with The Friend's answers. HE LOVES YOU HOLLY/HE WILL KILL YOU HOLLY. Now some color had returned to his face. His eyes were still ghost-ridden, and worry clung to him like shadows to the night, but he seemed to be feeling his way toward an accommodation with all the lies that were his life.

Which was what frightened The Enemy in him. And made it desperate.

Mrs. Glynn had returned from the stacks. She was working at her desk.

Lowering her voice even further, Holly said to Jim, "But why would you hold yourself to blame for the traffic accident that killed them? And how could any kid that age have such a tremendously heavy sense of responsibility?"

He shook his head. "I don't know."

Remembering what Corbett Handahl had told her, Holly put a hand on Jim's knee and said, "Think, honey. Did the accident happen when they were on the road with this mentalist act of theirs?"

He hesitated, frowned. "Yes . . . on the road."

"You traveled with them, didn't you?"

He nodded.

Recalling the photograph of his mother in a glittery gown, Jim and his father in tuxedos, Holly said, "You were part of the act."

Some of his memories apparently were rising like the rings of light had risen in the pond. The play of emotions in his face could not have been faked; he was genuinely astonished to be moving out of a life of darkness.

Holly felt her own excitement growing with his. She said, "What did you do in the act?"

"It was . . . a form of stage magic. My mom would take objects from people in the audience. My dad would work with me, and we would . . . I would hold the objects and pretend to have psychic impressions, tell the people things about themselves that I couldn't know."

"Pretend?" she asked.

He blinked. "Maybe not. It's so strange . . . how little I remember even when I try."

"It wasn't a trick. You could really do it. That's why your folks put together the act in the first place. You *were* a gifted child."

He ran his fingers down the Bro Dart-protected jacket of *The Black Windmill*. "But . . ."

"But?"

"There's so much I still don't understand. . . ."

"Oh, me too, kiddo. But we're getting closer, and I have to believe that's a good thing."

A shadow, cast from within, stole across his face again.

Not wanting to see him slip back into a darker mood, Holly said, "Come on." She picked up the book and took it to the librarian's desk. Jim followed her.

The energetic Mrs. Glynn was drawing on posterboard with a rainbow of colored pencils and magic markers. The colorful images were of well-rendered boys and girls dressed as spacemen, spelunkers, sailors, acrobats, and jungle explorers. She had penciled in but not yet colored the message: THIS IS A LIBRARY. KIDS AND ADVENTURERS WELCOME. ALL OTHERS STAY OUT!

"Nice," Holly said sincerely, indicating the poster. "You really put yourself into this job."

"Keeps me out of barrooms," Mrs. Glynn said, with a grin that made it clear why any kid would like her.

Holly said, "My fiancée here has spoken so highly of you. Maybe you don't remember him after twenty-five years."

Mrs. Glynn looked speculatively at Jim.

He said, "I'm Jim Ironheart, Mrs. Glynn."

"Of course I remember you! You were the most special little boy." She got up, leaned across the desk, and insisted on getting a hug from Jim. Releasing him, turning to Holly, she said, "So you're going to be marrying my Jimmy. That's wonderful! A lot of kids have passed through here since I've been running the place, even for a town this small, and I can't pretend I'd remember all of them. But Jimmy was special. He was a very special boy."

Holly heard, again, how Jim had had an insatiable appetite for fantasy fiction, how he'd been so terribly quiet his first year in town, and how he'd been totally mute during his second year, after the sudden death of his grandmother.

Holly seized that opening: "You know, Mrs. Glynn, one of the reasons Jim brought me back here was to see if we might like to live in the farmhouse, at least for a while—"

"It's a nicer town than it looks," Mrs. Glynn said. "You'd be happy here, I'll guarantee it. In fact, let me issue you a couple of library cards!" She sat down and pulled open a desk drawer.

As the librarian withdrew two cards from the drawer and picked up a pen, Holly said, "Well, the thing is . . . there're as many bad memories for him as good, and Lena's death is one of the worst."

"And the thing is," Jim picked up, "I was only ten when she died—well, almost eleven—and I guess maybe I made myself forget some of what happened. I'm not too clear on how she died, the details, and I was wondering if you remember . . ."

Holly decided that he might make a decent interviewer after all.

Mrs. Glynn said, "I can't say I recall the details of it. And I guess nobody'll ever know what on earth she was doing out in that old mill in the middle of the night. Henry, your grandpa, said she sometimes went there just to get away from things. It was peaceful and cool, a place she could do a little knitting and sort of meditate. And, of course, in those days it wasn't quite the ruin it's become. Still . . . it seemed odd she'd be out there knitting at two o'clock in the morning."

As the librarian recounted what she could recall of Lena's death, confirming that Holly's dream had really been Jim's memory, Holly was touched by both dread and nausea. What Eloise Glynn did not seem to know, what perhaps no one knew, was that Lena had not been in that mill alone.

Jim had been there, too.

And only Jim had come out of it alive.

Holly glanced at him and saw that he had lost all color in his face again. He was not merely pale now. He was as gray as the sky outside.

Mrs. Glynn asked Holly for her driver's license, to complete the library card, and even though Holly didn't want the card, she produced the license.

The librarian said, "Jim, I think what got you through all that pain and loss, more than anything, was books. You pulled way into yourself, read *all* the time, and I think you used fantasy as sort of a painkiller." She handed Holly the license and library card, and said to her: "Jim was an awfully bright boy. He could get totally *into* a book, it became real for him."

Yeah, Holly thought, did it ever.

"When he first came to town and I heard he'd never been to a real school before, been educated by his parents, I thought that was just terrible, even if they did have to travel all the time with that nightclub act of theirs—"

Holly recalled the gallery of photographs on Jim's study walls in Laguna Niguel: Miami, Atlantic City, New York, London, Chicago, Las Vegas . . .

"—but they'd actually done a pretty fine job. At least they'd turned him into a booklover, and that served him well later." She turned to Jim. "I suppose you haven't asked your grandpa about Lena's death because you figure it might upset him to talk about it. But I think he's not as fragile as you imagine, and he'd know more about it than anyone, of course." Mrs. Glynn addressed Holly again: "Is something wrong, dear?"

Holly realized she was standing with the blue library card in her hand, statue-still, like one of those waiting-to-be-reanimated people in the worlds within the books upon the shelves within these rooms. For a moment she could not respond to the woman's question.

Jim looked too stunned to pick up the ball this time. His grandfather was alive somewhere. But where?

"No," Holly said, "nothing's wrong. I just realized how late it's getting—"

A shatter of static, a vision: her severed head screaming, her severed hands crawling like spiders across a floor, her decapitated body writhing and twisting in agony; she was dismembered but not dead, impossibly alive, in a thrall of horror beyond endurance—

Holly cleared her throat, blinked at Mrs. Glynn, who was staring at her curiously. "Uh, yeah, quite late. And we're supposed to go see Henry before lunch. It's already ten. I've never met him." She was babbling now, couldn't stop. "I'm really looking forward to it."

Unless he really *did* die over four years ago, like Jim had told her, in which case she wasn't looking forward to it at all. But Mrs. Glynn did not appear to be a spiritualist who would blithely suggest conjuring up the dead for a little chat.

"He's a nice man," Eloise Glynn said. "I know he must've hated having to move off the farm after his stroke, but he can be thankful it didn't leave him worse than he is. My mother, God rest her soul, had a stroke, left her unable to walk, talk, blind in one eye, and so confused she couldn't always recognize her own children. At least poor Henry has his wits about him, as I understand it. He can talk, and I hear he's the leader of the wheelchair pack over there at Fair Haven."

"Yes," Jim said, sounding as wooden as a talking post, "that's what I hear."

"Fair Haven's such a nice place," Mrs. Glynn said, "it's good of you to keep him there, Jim. It's not a snakepit like so many nursing homes these days."

THE YELLOW PAGES at a public phone booth provided an address for Fair Haven on the edge of Solvang. Holly drove south and west across the valley.

"I remember he had a stroke," Jim said. "I was in the hospital with him, came up from Orange County, he was in the intensive-care unit. I hadn't . . . hadn't seen him in thirteen years or more."

Holly was surprised by that, and her look generated a hot wave of shame that withered Jim. "You hadn't seen your own grandfather in thirteen years?"

"There was a reason. . . ."

"What?"

He stared at the road ahead for a while, then let out a guttural sound of frustration and disgust. "I don't know. There was a reason, but I can't remember it. Anyway, I came back when he had his stroke, when he was dying in the hospital. And I remember him dead, damn it."

"Clearly remember it?"

"Yes."

She said, "You remember the sight of him dead in the hospital bed, all his monitor lines flat?"

He frowned. "No."

"Remember a doctor telling you he'd passed away?"

"No."

"Remember making arrangements for his burial?"

"No."

"Then what's so clear about this memory of him being dead?"

Jim brooded about that awhile as she whipped the Ford around the curving roads, between gentle hills on which scattered houses stood, past white-fenced horse pastures green as pictures of Kentucky. This part of the valley was lusher than the area around New Svenborg. But the sky had become a more somber gray, with a hint of blue-black in the clouds—bruised.

At last he said, "It isn't clear at all, now that I look close at it. Just a muddy impression . . . not a real memory."

"Are you paying to keep Henry at Fair Haven?"

"No."

"Did you inherit his property?"

"How could I inherit if he's alive?"

"A conservatorship then?"

He was about to deny that, as well, when he suddenly remembered a hearing room, a judge. The testimony of a doctor. His granddad's counsel, appearing on the old man's behalf to testify that Henry was of sound mind and wanted his grandson to manage his property.

"Good heavens, yes," Jim said, shocked that he was capable not only of forgetting events from the distant past but from as recently as four years ago. As Holly swung around a slow-moving farm truck and accelerated along a straight stretch of road, Jim told her what he had just remembered, dim as the recollection was. "How can I do this, live this way? How can I totally rewrite my past when it suits me?"

"Self-defense," she said, as she had said before. She swung in front of the truck. "I'd bet that you remember a tremendous amount of precise detail about your work as a teacher, about your students over the years, colleagues you've taught with—"

It was true. As she spoke, he could flash back, at will, through his years in the classroom, which seemed so vivid that those thousands of days might have occurred concurrently only yesterday.

"—because that life held no threat for you, it was filled with purpose and peace. The only things you forget, push relentlessly down into the deepest wells of memory, are those things having to do with the death of your parents, the death of Lena Ironheart, and your years in New Svenborg. Henry Ironheart is part of that, so you continue to wipe him from your mind."

The sky was contusive.

He saw blackbirds wheeling across the clouds, more of them now than he had seen in the cemetery. Four, six, eight. They seemed to be paralleling the car, following it to Solvang.

Strangely, he recalled the dream with which he had awakened on the morning that he had gone to Portland, saved Billy Jenkins, and met Holly. In the nightmare, a flock of large blackbirds shrieked around him in a turbulent flapping of wings and tore at him with hooked beaks as precision-honed as surgical instruments.

"The worst is yet to come," he said.

"What do you mean?"

"I don't know."

"You mean what we learn at Fair Haven?"

Above, the blackbirds swam through the high, cold currents.

Without having a clue as to what he meant, Jim said, "Something very dark is coming."

2 Fair Haven was housed in a large, U-shaped, single-story building outside the town limits of Solvang, with no trace of Danish influence in its architecture. It was strictly off-the-rack design, functional and no prettier than it had to be: cream-tinted stucco, concrete-tile roof, boxy, flat-walled, without detail. But it was freshly painted and in good repair; the hedges were neatly trimmed, the lawn recently mown, and the sidewalks swept clean.

Holly liked the place. She almost wished she lived there, was maybe eighty, watching some TV every day, playing some checkers, with no worry bigger than trying to figure out where she had put her false teeth when she'd taken them out last night.

Inside, the hallways were wide and airy, with yellow vinyl-tile floors. Unlike in many nursing homes, the air was neither tainted with the stench of incontinent patients left unclean by inattentive staff nor with a heavy aerosol deodorant meant to eliminate or mask that stench. The rooms she and Jim passed looked attractive, with big windows opening to valley views or a garden courtyard. Some of the patients lay in their beds or slumped in their wheelchairs with vacant or mournful expressions on their faces, but they were the unfortunate victims of major strokes or late-stage Alzheimer's disease, locked away in memories or torment, largely unconnected to the world around them. Everyone else appeared happy; and patients' laughter actually could be heard, a rarity in such places.

According to the supervisor on duty at the nurses' station, Henry Ironheart had been a resident of Fair Haven for over four years.

Mrs. Danforth, the administrator into whose office they were shown, was new since Henry Ironheart had been checked in. She had the slightly plump, well-groomed, and inoffensively self-satisfied look of a minister's wife in a prosperous parish. Though she could not understand why they needed her to verify something that Jim knew already, she checked her records and showed them that, indeed, Henry Ironheart's monthly bill was always promptly paid by James Ironheart, of Laguna Niguel, by check.

"I'm glad you've come to visit at last, and I hope you'll have a pleasant time," Mrs. Danforth said, with genteel reproach meant to make him feel guilty for not visiting his grandfather more often while at the same time not directly offending him.

After they left Mrs. Danforth, they stood in a corner of the main hallway, out of the bustle of nurses and wheelchair-bound patients.

"I can't just walk in on him," Jim said adamantly. "Not after all this time. I feel . . . my stomach's clutched up, cramped. Holly, I'm afraid of him."

"Why?"

"I'm not sure." Desperation, bordering on panic, made his eyes so disquieting that she did not want to look into them.

"When you were little, did he ever harm you?"

"I don't think so." He strained to see back through the clouds of memory, then shook his head. "I don't know."

Largely because she was afraid to leave Jim alone, Holly tried to convince him that it would be better for them to meet the old man together.

But he insisted she go first. "Ask him most of what we need to know, so when I come into it, we won't have to stay much longer if we don't want to . . . in case it goes bad, gets awkward, unpleasant. Prepare him for seeing me, Holly. Please."

Because he appeared ready to bolt if she did not play things his way, Holly finally agreed. But watching Jim walk into the courtyard to wait there, she already regretted letting him move out of her sight. If he started to lose control again, if The Enemy began to break through, nobody would be with him to encourage him to resist the onslaught.

A friendly nurse helped Holly find Henry Ironheart when he proved not to be in his room. She pointed him out at a card table in the cheery recreation center, at the other end of which a half-dozen residents were watching a game show on television.

Henry was playing poker with his cronies. Four of them were at a table designed to accommodate wheelchairs, and none wore the standard nursing-home attire of pajamas or sweatsuits. Besides Henry, there were two fragile-looking elderly men—one in slacks and a red polo shirt; the other in slacks, white shirt, and bow tie—and a birdlike woman with snow-white hair, who was in a bright-pink pantsuit. They were halfway through a hotly contested hand, with a substantial pile of blue plastic chips in the pot, and Holly waited to one side, reluctant to interrupt them. Then one by one, exhibiting a flair for drama, they revealed their cards, and with a whoop of delight the woman—Thelma, her name was—raked in her winnings, theatrically gloating as the men goodnaturedly questioned her honesty.

Finally intruding into their banter, Holly introduced herself to Henry Ironheart, though without identifying herself as Jim's fiancée. "I'd like to have a few minutes to talk with you about something if I could."

"Jesus, Henry," the man in the polo shirt said, "she's less than half your age!"

"He always was an old pervert," said the guy in the bow tie.

"Oh, get a life, Stewart," Thelma said, speaking to Mr. Bow Tie. "Henry's a gentleman, and he's never been anything else."

"Jesus, Henry, you're gonna be married for sure before you get out of this room today!"

"Which *you* certainly won't be, George," Thelma continued. "And as far as I'm concerned"—she winked—"if it's Henry, marriage doesn't have to be part of it."

They all roared at that, and Holly said, "I can see I'm going to be aced out of this one."

George said, "Thelma gets what she's after more often than not."

Noticing that Stewart had gathered the cards up and was shuffling the deck, Holly said, "I don't mean to interrupt your game."

"Oh, don't worry yourself," Henry said. His words were slightly slurred as a result of his stroke, but he was quite intelligible. "We'll just take a bathroom break."

"At our age," George said, "if we didn't coordinate our bathroom breaks, there'd never be more than two of us at the card table at any one time!"

The others wheeled away, and Holly pulled up a chair to sit near Henry Ironheart.

He was not the vital-looking, square-faced man she had seen in the photograph on the living-room wall of the farmhouse last evening, and without help Holly might not have recognized him. His stroke had left his right side weak, though not paralyzed, and a lot of the time he held that arm curled against his chest, the way an injured animal might favor a paw. He had lost a lot of weight and was no longer a burly man. His face was not gaunt but nearly so, though his skin had good color; the facial muscles on the right side were unnaturally relaxed, allowing his features to droop a little.

His appearance, combined with the slur that thickened every word he spoke, might have sent Holly into a depression over the inevitable direction of every human life—if not for his eyes, which revealed an unbowed soul. And his conversation, though slowed somewhat by his impediment, was that of a bright and humorous man who would not give the fates the satisfaction of his despair; his treacherous body was to be cursed, if at all, in private.

"I'm a friend of Jim's," she told him.

He made a lopsided "O" of his mouth, which she decided was an expression of surprise. At first he did not seem to know what to say, but then he asked, "How is Jim?"

Deciding to opt for the truth, she said, "Not so good, Henry. He's a very troubled man."

He looked away from her, at the pile of poker chips on the table. "Yes," he said softly.

Holly had half expected him to be a child-abusing monster who had been at least in part responsible for Jim's withdrawal from reality. He seemed anything but that.

"Henry, I wanted to meet you, talk to you, because Jim and I are more than friends. I love him, and he's said that he loves me, and it's my hope that we're going to be together a long, long time."

To her surprise, tears brimmed up and slipped from Henry's eyes, forming bright beads in the soft folds of his aged face.

She said, "I'm sorry, have I upset you?"

"No, no, good lord, no," he said, wiping at his eyes with his left hand. "Excuse me for being an old fool."

"I can tell you're anything but that."

"It's just, I never thought . . . Well, I figured Jim was going to spend his life alone."

"Why did you think that?"

"Well . . ."

He seemed distressed at having to say anything negative about his grandson, completely dispelling her lingering expectations that he would be a tyrant of some kind.

Holly helped him. "He does have a way of keeping people at arm's length. Is that what you mean?"

Nodding, he said, "Even me. I've loved him with all my heart, all these years, and I know he loves me in his way, though he's always had real trouble showing it, and he could *never* say it." As Holly was about to ask him a question, he suddenly shook his head violently and wrenched his distorted face into an expression of anguish so severe that for an instant she thought he was having another stroke. "It's not all him. God knows, it's not." The slur in his voice thickened when he grew more emotional. "I've got to face it—part of the distance between us is me, my fault, the blame I put on him that I never should've."

"Blame?"

"For Lena."

A shadow of fear passed across her heart and induced a quiver of angina-like pain.

She glanced at the window that looked out on a corner of the courtyard. It was not the corner to which Jim had gone. She wondered where he was, how he was . . . *who* he was.

"For Lena? I don't understand," she said, though she was afraid that she did.

"It seems unforgivable to me now, what I did, what I allowed myself to think." He paused, looking not at her but through her now, toward a distant time and place. "But he was just so strange in those days, not the child he had been. Before you can even hope to understand what I did, you have to know that, after Atlanta, he was so very strange, all locked up inside."

Immediately Holly thought of Sam and Emily Newsome, whose lives Jim had saved in an Atlanta convenience store—and Norman Rink, into whom he had pumped eight rounds from a shotgun in a blind rage. But Henry obviously was not talking about a recent event in Atlanta; he was referring to some previous incident, much further in the past.

"You don't know about Atlanta?" he asked, reacting to her evident mystification.

A queer sound chittered through the room, alarming Holly. For an instant she could not identify the noise, then realized it was several birds shrieking the way they did when protecting their nests. No birds were in the room, and she supposed their cries were echoing down the fireplace chimney from the roof. Just birds. Their chatter faded.

She turned to Henry Ironheart again. "Atlanta? No, I guess don't know about that."

"I didn't think you did. I'd be surprised if he talked about it even to you, even if he loves you. He just doesn't talk about it."

"What happened in Atlanta?"

"It was a place called the Dixie Duck—"

"Oh, my God," she whispered. She had *been* there in the dream.

"Then you do know some of it," he said. His eyes were pools of sorrow.

She felt her face crumple in grief, not for Jim's parents, whom she had never known, and not even for Henry, who presumably had loved them, but for Jim. "Oh, my God." And then she couldn't say any more because her words backed up behind her own tears.

Henry reached out to her with one liver-spotted hand, and she took it, held it, waiting until she could speak again.

At the other end of the room, bells were ringing, horns blaring on the TV game show.

No traffic accident had killed Jim's parents. That story was his way of avoiding a recounting of the terrible truth.

She had known. She had known, and refused to know.

Her latest dream had not been a warning prophecy but another memory that Jim had projected into her mind as they had both slept. She had not been herself in the dream. She had been Jim. Just as she had been Lena in a dream two nights ago. If a mirror had given her a look at her face, she would have seen Jim's countenance instead of her own, as she had seen Lena's in the windmill window. The horror of the blood-drenched restaurant returned to her now in vivid images that she could not block from memory, and she shuddered violently.

She looked toward the window, the courtyard, frightened for him.

"They were performing for a week at a club in Atlanta," Henry said. "They went out for lunch to Jimmy's favorite place, which he remembered from the last time they'd played Atlanta."

Voice trembling, Holly said, "Who was the gunman?"

"Just a nut. That's what made it so hard. No meaning to it. Just a crazy man."

"How many people died?"

"A lot."

"How many, Henry?"

"Twenty-four."

She thought of young Jim Ironheart in that holocaust, scrambling for his life through the shattered bodies of the other customers, the room filled with cries of pain and terror, reeking with the stench of blood and vomit, bile and urine from the slaughtered corpses. She heard the heavy sound of the automatic weapon again, *chuda-chuda-chuda-chuda-chuda-chuda*, and the please-please-please-please of the terrified young waitress. Even as a dream, it had been almost beyond endurance, all the random horror of existence and all the cruelty of humankind boiled down to one devastating experience, a savage ordeal from which full psychological recovery, even for an adult, would take a lifetime of struggle. For a ten-year-old boy, recovery might seem impossible, reality intolerable, denial necessary, and fantasy the only tool with which to hold on to a shred of sanity.

"Jimmy was the only survivor," Henry said. "If the police had gotten there a few seconds later, Jimmy wouldn't have made it either. They shot the man down." Henry's grip tightened slightly on Holly's hand. "They found Jim in a corner, in Jamie's lap, in his daddy's lap, his daddy's arms, all covered with . . . with his daddy's blood."

Holly remembered the end of the dream—

—the crazyman is coming straight at her, knocking tables and chairs aside, so she scrambles away and into a corner, on top of a dead body, and the crazyman is coming closer, closer, raising his gun, she can't bear to look at him the way the waitress looked at him and then died, so she turns her face to the corpse—

—and she remembered awakening with a jolt, gagging in revulsion.

If she'd had time to look into the face of the corpse, she would have seen Jim's father.

The avian shriek shrilled through the recreation room again. It was louder this time. A couple of the ambulatory residents went to the fireplace to see if any birds were caught behind the damper in the chimney.

"In his daddy's blood," Henry repeated softly. It was clear that, even after all these years, the consideration of that moment was intolerably painful to him.

The boy had not only been in his dead father's arms but surely had known that his mother lay dead among the ruins, and that he was orphaned, alone.

JIM SAT ON a redwood bench in the Fair Haven courtyard. He was alone.

For a day late in August, when the seasonal drought should have been at its peak, the sky was unusually heavy with unshed moisture, yet it looked like an inverted bowl of ashes. Mixes of late-summer flowers, cascading from planting beds onto the wide concrete walkways, were missing half their color without the enhancement of sunshine. The trees shivered as if chilled by the mild August breeze.

Something was coming. Something bad was coming.

He clung to Holly's theory, told himself that nothing would come unless he caused it to appear. He only had to control himself, and they would all survive.

But he still felt it coming.

Something.

He heard the screaky cries of birds.

THE BIRDS HAD fallen silent.

After a while Holly let go of Henry Ironheart's hand, took some Kleenex from her purse, blew her nose, and blotted her eyes. When she could speak, she said, "He blames himself for what happened to his mom and dad."

"I know. He always did. He'd never talk about it, but there were ways it showed, how he blamed himself, how he thought he should have saved them."

"But why? He was only ten years old, a small boy. He couldn't have done anything about a grown man with a submachine gun. For God's sake, how could he feel responsible?"

For the moment, the brightness had gone out of Henry's eyes. His poor lopsided face, already pulled down to the right, was pulled down farther by an inexpressible sadness.

At last he said, "I talked to him about it lots of times, took him on my lap and held him and talked about it, like Lena did, too, but he was so much locked in himself, wouldn't open up, wouldn't say why he blamed himself—hated himself."

Holly looked at her watch.

She had left Jim alone too long.

But she could not interrupt Henry Ironheart in the middle of the revelations that she had come to hear.

"I've thought about it all these long years," Henry continued, "and maybe I figured it out a little. But by the time I started to understand, Jim was grown up, and we'd stopped talking about Atlanta so many years ago. To be completely honest, we'd stopped talking about everything by then."

"So what is it you figured out?"

Henry put his weak right hand in his strong left and stared down at the gnarled lumps that his knuckles made within his time-thinned skin. From the old man's attitude, Holly sensed that he was not sure he should reveal what he needed and wanted to reveal.

"I love him, Henry."

He looked up and met her eyes.

She said, "Earlier you said I'd come here to learn about Atlanta because Jim wouldn't talk about it, and in a way you were right. I came to find out a number of things, because he's frozen me out of some areas of his life. He really loves me, Henry, I've no doubt of that, but he's clenched up like a fist, he can't let loose of certain things. If I'm going to marry him, if it's going to come to that, then I've got to know all about him—or we'll never have a chance to be happy. You can't build a life together on mysteries."

"Of course, you're right."

"Tell me why Jim blames himself. It's killing him, Henry. If I have any hope of helping him, I've got to know what you know."

He sighed and made up his mind. "What I've got to say will sound like superstitious nonsense, but it isn't. I'll make it simple and short, 'cause it sounds even screwier if I dress it up at all. My wife, Lena, had a power. Presentiment, you'd call it, I guess. Not that she could see the future, tell you who would win a horserace or where you'd be a year from now or anything like that. But sometimes . . . well, you might invite her to a picnic

Sunday a week, and without thinking, she'd say it was going to rain like-for-Noah come Sunday a week. And by God it would. Or some neighbor would be pregnant, and Lena would start referring to the baby as either a 'he' or a 'she,' when there was no way for her to know which it would be—and she was always right."

Holly sensed some of the last pieces of the puzzle falling into place. When Henry gave her a maybe-you-think-I'm-an-old-fool look, she took his bad hand and held it reassuringly.

After studying her a moment, he said, "You've seen something special Jim did, haven't you, something like magic?"

"Yes."

"So you maybe know where this is going."

"Maybe."

The unseen birds began to screech again. The residents at the television set turned the sound off and looked around, trying to identify the source of the squealing.

Holly looked toward the courtyard window. No birds there. But she knew why their cries made the hair stand up on the back of her neck: they were somehow connected with Jim. She remembered the way he had looked up at them in the graveyard and how he had studied them in the sky during the drive to Solvang.

"Jamie, our son, was like his mother," Henry said, as if he did not even hear the birds. "He just sometimes *knew* things. Fact is, he was a little more gifted than Lena. And after Jamie had been married to Cara for a while, when she got pregnant, Lena just one day up and said, 'The baby's going to be special, he's going to be a real mage.' "

"Mage?"

"Country talk for someone with a power, with something special about him the way Lena had something special and Jamie, too. Only she meant *real* special. So Jim was born, and by the time he was four . . . well, he was doing things. Like once he touched my pocket comb, which I'd bought at the local barbershop here, and he started talking about things that were in the shop, though he'd never been in there in his life 'cause he lived with Jamie and Cara down in Los Angeles."

He paused and took a few deep breaths. The slur in his voice had begun to thicken. His right eyelid drooped. Talking seemed to tire him as if it were a physical labor.

A male nurse with a flashlight was at the fireplace. He was squinting up into the flue, past the cracks around the damper, trying to see if any birds were trapped up in there.

The shrieking was now overlaid by the frenzied flapping of wings.

"Jimmy would touch an item and *know* where it'd been, bits and pieces about who owned it. Not everything about them, mind you. He just knew whatever he knew, that was it. Maybe he'd touch a personal item of yours and know the names of your parents, what you did for a living. Then he'd touch a personal item from someone else and only know where they'd gone to school, names of their children. Always different things, he couldn't control it. But he always came up with *something* when he tried."

The nurse, trailed by three patients offering advice, had moved away from the fireplace and was frowning up at the air-conditioning vents. The quarrelsome sound of birds still echoed through the room.

"Let's go out to the courtyard," Holly said, getting up.

"Wait," Henry said with some distress, "let me finish this, let me tell you."

Jim, for God's sake, Holly thought, hold on another minute, just another minute or two.

Reluctantly she sat down.

Henry said, "Jim's specialness was a family secret, like Lena's and Jamie's. We didn't want the world to know, come snooping around, call us freaks and God knows what. But Cara, she always wanted so bad to be in show business. Jamie worked down there at Warner Brothers, which was where'd he'd met her, and he wanted what Cara wanted. They decided they could form an act with Jimmy, call him the boy-wonder mentalist, but nobody would ever suspect he really had a power. They played it as a trick, lots of winking at the audience, daring them to figure out just how it was all done— when all the time it was *real*. They made a good living at it, too, and it was good for them as a family, kept them together every day. They'd been so close before the act, but they were closer than ever after they went on the road. No parents ever loved their child more than they loved Jim—or ever got more love given back to them. They were so close . . . it was impossible to think of them ever being apart."

BLACKBIRDS STREAKED ACROSS the bleak sky.

Sitting on the redwood bench, Jim stared up at them.

They almost vanished into the eastern clouds, then turned sharply and came back.

For a while they kited overhead.

Those dark, jagged forms against the sere sky composed an image that might have come from some poem by Edgar Allan Poe. As a kid he'd had a passion for Poe and had memorized all of the more macabre pieces of his poetry. Morbidity had its fascination.

THE BIRD SHRIEKS suddenly stopped. The resulting quiet was a blessing, but Holly was, oddly, more frightened by the cessation of the cries than she had been by the eerie sound of them.

"And the power grew," Henry Ironheart said softly, thickly. He shifted in his wheelchair, and his right side resisted settling into a new position. For the first time he showed some frustration at the limitations of his stroke-altered body. "By the time Jim was six, you could put a penny on the table, and he could move it just by *wanting* it to move, slide it back and forth, make it stand on end. By the time he was eight, he could pitch it in the air, float it there. By the time he was ten, he could do the same with a quarter, a phonograph record, a cake tin. It was the most amazing thing you ever saw."

You should see what he can do at thirty-five, Holly thought.

"They never used any of that in their act," Henry said, "they just stuck to the mentalism, taking personal items from members of the audience, so Jim could tell them things about themselves that just, you know, astonished them. Jamie and Cara figured to include some of his levitations eventually, but they just hadn't figured out how to do it yet without giving the truth away. Then they went to the Dixie Duck down in Atlanta . . . and that was the end of everything."

Not the end of everything. It was the end of one thing, the dark beginning of another.

She realized why the absence of the birds' screams was more disturbing than the sound itself. The cries had been like the hiss of a sparking fuse as it burned down toward an explosive charge. As long as she could hear the sound, the explosion was still preventable.

"And *that's* why I figure Jim thought he should've been able to save them," Henry said. "Because he could do those little things with his mind, float and move things, he thought he should've been able maybe to jam the bullets in that crazy man's gun, freeze the trigger, lock the safety in place, something, something . . ."

"Could he have done that?"

"Yeah, maybe. But he was just a scared little boy. To do those things with pennies and records and cake tins, he had to concentrate. No time to concentrate when the bullets started flying that day."

Holly remembered the murderous sound: *chuda-chuda-chuda-chuda* . . .

"So when we brought him back from Atlanta, he would hardly talk, just a word or two now and then. Wouldn't meet your eyes. Something died in him when Jamie and Cara died, and we could never bring it back again, no matter how much we loved him and how hard we tried. His power died, too. Or seemed to. He never did one of his tricks again, and after a lot of years it was sometimes hard to believe he'd ever done those strange things when he was little."

In spite of his good spirits, Henry Ironheart had looked every one of his eighty years. Now he appeared to be far older, ancient.

He said, "Jimmy was so strange after Atlanta, so unreachable and full of rage . . . sometimes it was possible to love him and still be a little afraid of him. Later, God forgive me, I suspected him of . . ."

"I know," Holly said.

His slack features tightened, and he looked sharply at her.

"Your wife," she said. "Lena. The way she died."

More thickly than usual, he said, "You know so much."

"Too much," she said. "Which is funny. Because all my life I've known too little."

Henry looked down at his culpable hands again. "How could I believe that a boy of ten, even a disturbed boy, could've shoved her down the mill stairs when he loved her so much? Too many years later, I saw that I'd been so damned cruel to him, so unfeeling, so damned stupid. By then, he wouldn't give me the chance to apologize for what I'd done . . . what I'd thought. After he left for college, he never came back. Not once in more than thirteen years, until I had my stroke."

He came back once, Holly thought, nineteen years after Lena's death, to face up to it and put flowers on her grave.

Henry said, "If there was some way I could explain to him, if he'd just give me one chance. . . ."

"He's here now," Holly said, getting up again.

The weight of fear that pulled on the old man's face made him appear even more gaunt than he had been. "Here?"

"He's come to give you that chance," was all that Holly could say. "Do you want me to take you to him?"

THE BLACKBIRDS WERE flocking. Eight of them had gathered now in the sky above, circling.

Once upon a midnight dreary, while I pondered, weak and weary
Over many a quaint and curious volume of forgotten lore—
While I nodded, nearly napping, suddenly there came a tapping,
As of some one gently rapping, rapping at my chamber door.

To the real birds above, Jim whispered, " 'Quoth the Raven, *Nevermore.*' "

He heard a soft rhythmic creaking, as of a wheel going around and around, and footsteps. When he looked up, he saw Holly pushing his wheelchair-bound grandfather along the walkway toward the bench.

Eighteen years had passed since he had gone away to school, and he had seen Henry only once before in all this time. Initially, there had been a few telephone calls, but soon Jim stopped making those and, eventually, stopped accepting them as well. When letters came, he threw them away unopened. He remembered all of that now—and he was beginning to remember why.

He began to rise. His legs would not support him. He remained on the bench.

HOLLY PARKED THE wheelchair facing Jim, then sat beside him. "How you doing?"

Nodding dumbly, he glanced up at the birds circling against the ashen clouds, rather than face his grandfather.

The old man could not look at Jim, either. He studied the beds of flowers intently, as if he had been in a great rush to get outside and have a look at those blooms and nothing else.

Holly knew this was not going to be easy. She was sympathetic toward each of the men and wanted to do her best to bring them together at last.

First, she had to burn away the tangled weeds of one last lie that Jim had told her and that, consciously if not subconsciously, he had successfully told himself. "There was no traffic accident, honey," she said, putting a hand on his knee. "That isn't how it happened."

Jim lowered his eyes from the blackbirds and regarded her with nervous expectation. She could see that he longed to know the truth and dreaded hearing it.

"It happened in a restaurant—"

Jim slowly shook his head in denial.

"—down in Atlanta, Georgia—"

He was still shaking his head, but his eyes were widening.

"—you were with them—"

He stopped denying, and a terrible expression stained his face.

"—it was called the Dixie Duck," she said.

When the memory exploded back to him with pile-driver force, he hunched forward on the bench as if he might vomit, but he did not. He curled his hands into fists on his knees, and his face tightened into a clench of pain, and he made small inarticulate sounds that were beyond grief and horror.

She put an arm around his bent shoulders.

Henry Ironheart looked at her and said, "Oh, my God," as he began to realize the extremity of denial to which his grandson had been driven. "Oh, my God." As Jim's strangled gasps of pain changed into quiet sobs, Henry Ironheart looked at the flowers again, then at his aged hands, then at his feet on the tilted braces of the wheelchair, everywhere he could think to look to avoid Jim and Holly, but at last he met Holly's eyes again. "He had therapy," he said, trying hard to expiate his guilt. "We knew he might need therapy. We took him to a psychiatrist in Santa Barbara. Took him there several times. We did what we could. But the psychiatrist—Hemphill, his name was—he said Jim was all right, he said there was no reason to bring him any more, just after six visits, he said Jim was all right."

Holly said, "What do they ever know? What could Hemphill have done when he didn't really know the boy, didn't love him?"

Henry Ironheart flinched as if she had struck him, though she had not meant her comment to be a condemnation of him.

"No," she said quickly, hoping he would believe her, "what I meant was, there's no mystery why I've gotten farther than Hemphill ever could. It's just because I love him. It's the only thing that ever leads to healing." Stroking Jim's hair, she said, "You couldn't have saved them, baby. You didn't have the power then, not like you have it now. You were lucky to get out alive. Believe me, honey, listen and believe me."

For a moment they sat unspeaking, all of them in pain.

Holly noticed more blackbirds had gathered in the sky. Maybe a dozen of them now. She didn't know how Jim was drawing them there—or why—but she knew that he was, and regarded them with growing dread.

She put a hand over one of Jim's hands, encouraging him to relax it. Though he slowly stopped crying, he kept his fist as tight as a fist of sculpted stone.

To Henry, she said, "Now. This is your chance. Explain why you turned away from him, why you did . . . whatever you did to him."

Clearing his throat, wiping nervously at his mouth with his weak right hand, Henry spoke at first without looking at either of them. "Well . . . you have to know . . . how it was. A few months after he came back from Atlanta, there was this film company in town, shooting a movie—"

"The Black Windmill," Holly said.

"Yeah. He was reading all the time. . . ." Henry stopped, closed his eyes as if to gather strength. When he opened them, he stared at Jim's bowed head and seemed prepared to meet his eyes if he looked up. "You was reading all the time, going through the library shelf by shelf, and because of the film you read the Willott book. For a while it became . . . hell, I don't know . . . I guess maybe you'd have to say it was an obsession with you, Jim. It was the only thing that brought you out of your shell, talking about that book, so we encouraged you to go watch them shoot the picture. Remember? After a while, you started telling us an alien was in our pond and windmill, just like in the book and movie. At first we thought you was just play-acting."

He paused.

The silence lengthened.

About twenty birds in the sky above.

Circling. Silent.

To Henry, Holly said, "Then it began to worry you."

Henry wiped one shaky hand down his deeply lined face, not so much as if he was trying to scrub away his weariness but as if he was trying to slough off the years and bring that lost time closer. "You spent more and more hours in the mill, Jim. Sometimes you'd be out there all day. And evenings, too. Sometimes we'd get up in the middle of the night to use the john, and we'd see a light out there in the mill, two or three or four o'clock in the morning. And you wouldn't be in your room."

Henry paused more often. He wasn't tired. He just didn't want to dig into this part of the long-buried past.

"If it was the middle of the night, we'd go out there to the mill and bring you in, either me or Lena. And you'd be telling us about The Friend in the mill. You started spooking us, we didn't know what to do . . . so I guess . . . we didn't do anything. Anyway, that night . . . the night she died . . . a storm was coming up—"

Holly recalled the dream:

 . . . a fresh wind blows as she hurries along the gravel path . . .

"—and Lena didn't wake me. She went out there by herself and up to the high room—"

 . . . she climbs the limestone stairs . . .

"—pretty good thunderstorm, but I used to be able to sleep through anything—"

 . . . the heavens flash as she passes the stairwell window, and through the glass she sees an object in the pond below . . .

"—I guess, Jim, you was just doing what we always found you doing out there at night, reading that book by candlelight—"

 . . . inhuman sounds from above quicken her heart, and she climbs to the high room, afraid, but also curious and concerned for Jim . . .

"—a crash of thunder finally woke me—"

 . . . she reaches the top of the stairs and sees him standing, hands fisted at his sides, a yellow candle in a blue dish on the floor, a book beside the candle . . .

"—I realized Lena was gone, looked out the bedroom window, and saw that dim light in the mill—"

 . . . the boy turns to her and cries out, *I'm scared, help me, the walls, the walls!* . . .

"—and I couldn't believe my eyes because the sails of the mill were turning, and even in those days the sails hadn't turned in ten or fifteen years, been frozen up—"

 . . . she sees an amber light within the walls, the sour shades of pus and bile; the limestone bulges, and she realizes something is impossibly *alive* in the stone . . .

"—but they were spinning like airplane propellers, so I pulled on my pants, and hurried downstairs—"

 . . . with fear but also with perverse excitement, the boy says, *It's coming, and nobody can stop it!* . . .

"—I grabbed a flashlight and ran out into the rain—"

 . . . the curve of mortared blocks splits like the spongy membrane of an insect's egg; taking shape from a core of foul muck, where limestone should have been, is the embodiment of the boy's black rage at the world and its injustice, his self-hatred made flesh, his own death-wish given a vicious and brutal form so solid that it is an entity itself, quite separate from him . . .

"—I reached the mill, couldn't believe how those old sails were spinning, whoosh, whoosh, whoosh!—"

Holly's dream had ended there, but her imagination too easily supplied a version of what might have happened thereafter. Horrified at the materialization of The Enemy, stunned that the boy's wild tales of aliens in the mill were true, Lena had stumbled backward and fallen down the winding stone stairs, unable to arrest her fall because there was no handrail at which to grab. Somewhere along the way she broke her neck.

"—went inside the mill . . . found her at the bottom of the stairs all busted up, neck twisted . . . dead."

Henry paused for the first time in a while and swallowed hard. He had not looked at Holly once throughout his account of that stormy night, only at Jim's bowed head. With less of a slur in his voice, as if it were vitally important to him to tell the rest of it as clearly as he could, he said:

"I went up the steps and found you in the high room, Jimmy. Do you remember that? Sitting by the candle, holding the book in your hands so tight it couldn't be taken from you till hours later. You wouldn't speak." The old man's voice quavered now. "God forgive me, but all I could think about was Lena being dead, my dear Lena gone, and you being such a strange child all year, and still strange even at that moment, with your book, refusing to talk to me. I guess . . . I guess I went a little mad right then, for a while. I thought you might've pushed her, Jimmy. I thought you might've been in one of your . . . upsets . . . and maybe you pushed her."

As if it had become too much for him to address himself to his grandson any longer, Henry shifted his gaze to Holly. "That year after Atlanta, he'd been a strange boy . . . almost like a boy we didn't know. He was quiet, like I said, but there was rage in him, too, a fury like no child should ever have. It sometimes scared us. The only time he ever showed it was in his sleep . . . dreaming . . . we'd hear him screeching, and we'd go down the hall to his room . . . and he'd be kicking and punching at the mattress, the pillows, clawing at the sheets, furious, taking it all out on something in his dreams, and we'd have to wake him."

Henry paused and looked away from Holly, down at his bent right hand, which lay half useless in his lap.

Jim's fist, under Holly's hand, remained vise-tight.

"You never struck out at Lena or me, Jimmy, you was a good boy, never gave us that kind of trouble. But in the mill that night, I grabbed you and shook you, Jimmy, tried to make you admit how you'd pushed her down the stairs. There was no excuse for what I did, how I behaved . . . except I was grief-crazy over Jamie and Cara, and now over Lena, everyone dying around me, and there was only you, and you were so strange, so strange and locked up in yourself that you scared me, so I turned on you when I should have been taking you in my arms. Turned on you that night . . . and didn't realize what I'd done until a lot of years later . . . too late."

The birds were in a tighter circle now. Directly overhead.

"Don't," she said softly to Jim. "Please don't."

Until Jim responded, Holly could not know if these revelations were for better or worse. If he had blamed himself for his grandma's death merely because Henry had instilled the guilt in him, then he would get past this. If he had blamed himself because Lena had come into the high room, had seen The Enemy materializing from the wall, and had stumbled backward down the stairs in terror, he might still overcome the past. But if The Enemy had torn itself free of the wall and *pushed* her . . .

"I treated you like a murderer for the next six years, until you went away to school," Henry said. "When you was gone . . . well, in time, I started to think about it with a clearer head, and I knew what I'd done. You'd had nowhere to turn for comfort. Your mom and dad were gone, your grandma. You went into town to get books, but you couldn't join in with other kids because that little Zacca bastard, Ned Zacca, he was twice your size and wouldn't ever let you alone. You had no peace except in books. I tried to call you, but you wouldn't take the calls. I wrote but I think you never read the letters."

Jim sat unmoving.

Henry Ironheart shifted his attention to Holly. "He came back at last when I had my stroke. He sat beside me when I was in intensive care. I couldn't speak right, couldn't say what I tried to say, the wrong words kept coming out, making no sense——"

"Aphasia," Holly said. "A result of the stroke."

Henry nodded. "Once, hooked up to all those machines, I tried to tell him what I'd known for almost thirteen years—that he wasn't a killer and that I'd been cruel to him." New tears flooded his eyes. "But when it came out, it wasn't right at all, not what I meant, and he misunderstood it, thought I'd *called* him a murderer and was afraid of him. He left, and now's the first I've seen him since. More than four years."

Jim sat with his head bowed.

Hands fisted.

What had he remembered of that night in the mill, the part that no one but him could know?

Holly got up from the bench, unable to endure the wait for Jim's reaction. She stood there, with no idea where to go. At last she sat down again. She put her hand over his fist, as before.

She looked up,

More birds. Maybe thirty of them now.

"I'm afraid," Jim said, but that was all.

"After that night," Henry said, "he never went into the mill again, never mentioned The Friend or the Willott book. And at first I thought it was good he turned away from that obsession . . . he seemed less strange. But later I've wondered . . . maybe he lost the one comfort he had."

"I'm afraid to remember," Jim said.

She knew what he meant: only one last long-hidden memory waited to be revealed. Whether his grandmother had died by accident. Or whether The Enemy had killed her. Whether *he*, as The Enemy, had killed her.

Unable to stare at Jim's bowed head a moment longer, unable to bear Henry Ironheart's wretched look of guilt and fragile hope, Holly glanced up at the birds again—and saw them coming. More than thirty of them now, dark knives slicing down through the somber sky, still high up but coming straight toward the courtyard.

"Jim, no!"

Henry looked up.

Jim lifted his face, too, but not to see what was coming. He *knew* what was coming. He raised his face as if to offer his eyes to their sharp beaks and frenzied claws.

Holly leaped to her feet, making herself a more prominent target than he was. "Jim, face it, remember it, for Christ's sake!"

She could hear the shrieks of the swift-descending birds.

"Even if The Enemy did it," she said, pulling Jim's upturned face to her breast, shielding him, "you can get past that somehow, you can go on."

Henry Ironheart cried out in shock, and the birds burst over Holly, flapping and squirming against her, swooping away, then more of them fluttering and scraping, trying to get past her and at Jim's face, at his eyes.

They didn't tear at her with either their beaks or talons, but she did not know how long they would spare her. They were The Enemy, after all, manifesting itself in a whole new way, and The Enemy hated her as much as it hated Jim.

The birds swirled out of the courtyard, back into the sky, gone like so many leaves in a violent updraft.

Henry Ironheart was frightened but unhurt. "Move away," she told him.

"No," he said. He reached helplessly for Jim, who would not reach for him.

When Holly dared look up, she knew that the birds were not finished. They had only soared to the fringe of the bearded gray clouds, where another score of them had collected. Fifty or sixty now, churning and dark, Hungry and quick.

She was aware of people at the windows and sliding glass doors that opened onto the courtyard. Two nurses came through the same slider that she had used when wheeling Henry out to meet Jim.

"Stay back!" she shouted at them, not sure how much danger they might be in.

Jim's rage, while directed at himself and perhaps at God for the very fact of death's existence, might nevertheless spill over and spend itself on the innocent. Her shouted warning must have frightened the nurses, for they retreated and stood in the doorway.

She raised her eyes again. The larger flock was coming.

"Jim," she said urgently, holding his face in both hands, peering into his beautiful blue eyes, icy now with a cold fire of self-hatred, "only one more step, only one more thing to remember." Though their eyes were only a few inches apart, she did not believe that he saw her; he seemed to be looking through her as he had earlier in Tivoli Gardens when the burrowing creature had been racing at them.

The descending flock squealed demonically.

"Jim, damn you, what happened to Lena might not be *worth* suicide!"

The rustle-roar of wings filled the day. She pulled Jim's face against her body, and as before he did not struggle when she shielded him, which gave her hope. She bent her head and closed her eyes as tightly as she could.

They came: silken feathers; smooth cold beaks ticking, prying, searching; claws scrabbling gently, then not so gently, but still not drawing blood;

swarming around her almost as if they were hungry rats, swirling, darting, fluttering, squirming along her back and legs, between her thighs, up along her torso, trying to get between his face and her bosom, where they could tear and gouge; batting against her head; and always the shrieking, as shrill as the cries of madwomen in a psychopathic fury, screaming in her ears, wordless demands for blood, blood, blood, and then she felt a sharp pain in her arm as one of the flock ripped open her sleeve and pinched skin with it.

"No!"

They rose and departed again. Holly did not realize they were gone, because her own beating heart and fluttering breath continued to sound like thunderous wings to her. Then she raised her head, opened her eyes, and saw they were spiraling back into the leaden sky to join a storm cloud of other birds, a mass of dark bodies and wings, perhaps two hundred of them high overhead.

She glanced at Henry Ironheart. The birds had drawn blood from one of his hands. Having huddled back into his chair during the attack, he now leaned forward again, reached out with one hand, and called Jim's name pleadingly.

Holly looked down into Jim's eyes as he sat on the bench in front of her, and still he was not there. He was in the mill, most likely, on the night of the storm, looking at his grandmother just one second before the fall, frozen at that moment in time, unable to advance the memory-film one more frame.

The birds were coming.

They were still far away, just under the cloud cover, but there were so many of them now that the thunder of their wings carried a greater distance. Their shrieks were like the voices of the damned.

"Jim, you can take the path that Larry Kakonis took, you can kill yourself. I can't stop you. But if The Enemy doesn't want me any more, if it wants only you, don't think I'm spared. If you die, Jim, I'm dead, too, as good as dead, I'll do what Larry Kakonis did, I'll kill myself, and I'll rot in hell with you if I can't have you anywhere else!"

The Enemy of countless parts fell upon her as she pulled Jim's face against her a third time. She didn't hide her own face or close her eyes as before, but stood in that maelstrom of wings and beaks and talons. She looked back into scores of small, glistening, pure-black eyes that circled her unblinking, each as wet and deep as the night reflected on the face of the sea, each as merciless and cruel as the universe itself and as anything in the heart of humankind. She knew that, staring into those eyes, she was staring into a part of Jim, his most secret and darkest part, which she could not reach otherwise, and she said his name. She did not shout, did not scream, did not beg or plead, did not vent her anger or fear, but said his name softly, again and again, with all the tenderness that she felt for him, with all the love she had. They battered against her so hard that pinions snapped, opened their hooked beaks and shrieked in her face, plucked threateningly at her clothes and hair, tugging but not ripping, giving her one last chance to flee. They tried to intimidate her with their eyes, the cold and uncaring eyes of beasts of prey, but she was not intimidated, she just kept repeating his name, then the promise that she loved him, over and over until—

—they were gone.

They didn't whirl up into the sky, as before. They vanished. One moment the air was filled with them and their fierce cries—but the next moment they were gone as if they had never been.

Holly held Jim against her for a moment then let him go. He still looked through her more than at her and seemed to be in a trance.

"Jim," Henry Ironheart said beseechingly, still reaching out toward his grandson.

After a hesitation, Jim slid off the bench, onto his knees in front of the old man. He took the withered hand and kissed it.

Without looking up at either Holly or Henry, Jim said, "Grandma saw The Enemy coming out of the wall. First time it happened, first time I saw it, too." His voice sounded faraway, as if a part of him were still back in the past, reliving that dreaded moment, grateful that there had not been as much reason to dread it as he had thought. "She saw it, and it frightened her, and she stumbled back into the stairs, tripped, fell . . ." He pressed his grandfather's hand to his cheek and said, "I didn't kill her."

"I know you didn't, Jim," Henry Ironheart said. "My God, I know you didn't."

The old man looked up at Holly with a thousand questions about birds and enemies and things in walls. But she knew he would have to wait for answers until another day, as she had waited—as Jim had waited, too.

3 During the drive over the mountains and down into Santa Barbara, Jim slumped in his seat, eyes closed. He seemed to have fallen into a deep sleep. She supposed he needed sleep as desperately as any man could need it, for he'd enjoyed almost no real rest in twenty-five years.

She was no longer afraid to let him sleep. She was certain that The Enemy was gone, with The Friend, and that only one personality inhabited his body now. Dreams were no longer doorways.

For the time being, she did not want to return to the mill, even though they had left some gear there. She'd had enough of Svenborg, too, and all it represented in Jim's life. She wanted to hole up in a new place, where neither of them had been, where new beginnings might be forged with no taint of the past.

As she drove through that parched land under the ashen sky, she put the pieces together and studied the resulting picture:

...AN ENORMOUSLY GIFTED boy, far more gifted than even he knows, lives through the slaughter in the Dixie Duck, but comes out of the holocaust with a shattered soul. In his desperation to feel good about himself again, he borrows Arthur Willott's fantasy, using his special power to create The Friend, an embodiment of his most noble aspirations, and The Friend tells him he has a mission in life.

But the boy is so full of despair and rage that The Friend alone is not enough to heal him. He needs a third personality, something into which he can shove all his negative feelings, all the darkness in himself that frightens him. So he creates The Enemy, embellishing Willott's story structure. Alone in the windmill, he has exhilarating conversations with The Friend—and works out his rage through the materialization of The Enemy.

Until, one night, Lena Ironheart walks in at the wrong moment. Frightened, she falls backward. . . .

In shock because of what The Enemy has done, merely by its presence, Jim forces himself to forget the fantasy, both The Friend and Enemy, just as Jim Jamison forgot his alien encounter after saving the life of the future president of the United States. For twenty-five years, he struggles to keep a lid firmly on those fragmented personalities, suppressing both his very best and his very worst qualities, leading a relatively quiet and colorless life because he dares not tap his stronger feelings.

He finds purpose in teaching, which to some extent redeems him—until Larry Kakonis commits suicide. Without purpose any more, feeling that he has failed Kakonis as he failed his parents and, even more profoundly, his grandmother, he subconsciously longs to live out Jim Jamison's courageous and redeeming adventure, which means freeing The Friend.

But when he frees The Friend, he frees The Enemy as well. And after all these years of being bottled inside him, his rage has only intensified, become blacker and more bitter, utterly inhuman in its intensity. The Enemy is something even more evil now than it was twenty-five years ago, a creature of singularly murderous appearance and temperament. . . .

SO JIM WAS like any victim of multiple-personality syndrome. Except for one thing. One little thing. He created nonhuman entities to embody aspects of himself, not other human identities—and had the power to give them flesh of their own. He hadn't been like Sally Field playing Sybil, sixteen people in one body. He had been three beings in three bodies, and one of them had been a killer.

Holly turned on the car heater. Though it must have been seventy degrees outside, she was chilled. The heat from the dashboard vents did nothing to warm her.

THE CLOCK BEHIND the registration desk showed 1:11 P.M. when Holly checked them into a Quality motor lodge in Santa Barbara. While she filled out the form and provided her credit card to the clerk, Jim continued to sleep in the Ford.

When she returned with their key, she was able to rouse him enough to get him out of the car and into their room. He was in a stupor and went directly to the bed, where he curled up and once more fell instantly into a deep sleep.

She got diet sodas, ice, and candy bars from the vending-machine center near the pool.

In the room again, she closed the drapes. She switched on one lamp and arranged a towel over the shade to soften the light.

She pulled a chair near the bed and sat down. She drank diet soda and ate candy while she watched him sleep.

The worst was over. The fantasy had been burned away, and he had plunged completely into cold reality.

But she did not know what the aftermath would bring. She had never known him without his delusions, and she didn't know what he would be like when he had none. She didn't know if he would be a more optimistic man—or a darker one. She didn't know if he would still have the same degree of superhuman powers that he'd had before. He had summoned those powers from within himself only because he had needed them to sustain his fantasy and cling to his precarious sanity; perhaps, now, he would be only as gifted as he had been before his parents had died—able to levitate a pie pan, flip a coin with his mind, nothing more. Worst of all, she didn't know if he would still love her.

By dinnertime he was still asleep.

She went out and got more candy bars. Another binge. She *would* end up as plump as her mother if she didn't get control of herself.

He was still asleep at ten o'clock. Eleven. Midnight.

She considered waking him. But she realized that he was in a chrysalis, waiting to be born from his old life into a new one. A caterpillar needed time to turn itself into a butterfly. That was her hope, anyway.

Sometime between midnight and one o'clock in the morning, Holly fell asleep in her chair. She did not dream.

He woke her.

She looked up into his beautiful eyes, which were not cold in the dim light of the towel-draped lamp, but which were still mysterious.

He was leaning over her chair, shaking her gently. "Holly, come on. We've got to go."

Instantly casting off sleep, she sat up. "Go where?"

"Scranton, Pennsylvania."

"Why?"

Grabbing up one of her uneaten candy bars, peeling off the wrapper, biting into it, he said, "Tomorrow afternoon, three-thirty, a reckless school-bus driver is going to try to beat a train at a crossing. Twenty-six kids are going to die if we're not there first."

Rising from her chair, she said, "You know all that, the whole thing, not just a part of it?"

"Of course," he said around a mouthful of candy bar. He grinned. "I know these things, Holly. I'm psychic, for God's sake."

She grinned right back at him.

"We're going to be something, Holly," he said enthusiastically. "Superman? Why the hell did he waste so much time holding down a job on a newspaper when he could've been doing good?"

In a voice that cracked with relief and with love for him, Holly said, "I always wondered about that."

Jim gave her a chocolaty kiss. "The world hasn't seen anything like us, kid. Of course, you're going to have to learn martial arts, how to handle a gun, a few other things. But you're gonna be good at it, I know you are."

She threw her arms around him and hugged him fiercely, with unadulterated joy.

Purpose.

The Key to Midnight

This better version
is for Gerda.
I can go back and improve
the earlier pen-name books
—but I'm afraid I don't
have enough energy to make
all the desperately needed
improvements in myself!

A sound of something;
The scarecrow
   Has fallen down of itself.

        —Boncho, 1670–1714

   ❭ ❭ ❭

Part One

Joanna

1 In the dark, Joanna Rand went to the window. Naked, trembling, she peered between the wooden slats of the blind.

Wind from the distant mountains pressed coldly against the glass and rattled a loose pane.

At four o'clock in the morning, the city of Kyoto was quiet, even in Gion, the entertainment quarter crowded with nightclubs and geisha houses. Kyoto, the spiritual heart of Japan, was a thousand years old yet as new as a fresh idea: a fascinating hodgepodge of neon signs and ancient temples, plastic gimcrackery and beautifully hand-carved stone, the worst of modern architecture thrusting up next to palaces and ornate shrines that were weathered by centuries of hot, damp summers and cold, damp winters. By a mysterious combination of tradition and popular culture, the metropolis renewed her sense of humanity's permanence and purpose, refreshed her sometimes shaky belief in the importance of the individual.

The earth revolves around the sun; society continuously changes; the city grows; new generations come forth . . . and I'll go on just as they do.

That was always a comforting thought when she was in darkness, alone, unable to sleep, morbidly energized by the powerful yet indefinable fear that came to her every night.

Calmed somewhat but not anxious to go to bed, Joanna dressed in a red silk robe and slippers. Her slender hands were still shaking, but the tremors were not as severe as they had been.

She felt violated, used, and discarded—as though the hateful creature in her nightmare had assumed a real physical form and had repeatedly, brutally raped her while she'd slept.

The man with the steel fingers reaches for the hypodermic syringe. . . .

That single image was all that she retained from the nightmare. It had been so vivid that she could recall it at will, in unsettling detail: the smooth texture of those metal fingers, the clicking and whirring of gears working in them, the gleam of light off the robotic knuckles.

She switched on the bedside lamp and studied the familiar room. Nothing was out of place. The air contained only familiar scents. Yet she wondered if she truly *had* been alone all night.

She shivered.

2   Joanna stepped out of the narrow stairwell into her ground-floor office. She switched on the light and studied the room as she had inspected those upstairs, half expecting the fearsome phantom of her dream to be waiting somewhere in the real world. The soft glow from the porcelain lamp didn't reach every corner. Purple shadows draped the bookshelves, the rosewood furniture, and the rice-paper scroll paintings. Potted palms cast complex, lacy shadows across one wall. Everything was in order.

Unfinished paperwork littered the desk, but she wasn't in a bookkeeping frame of mind. She needed a drink.

The outer door of the office opened on the carpeted area that encircled the long cocktail bar at one end of the Moonglow Lounge. The club wasn't completely dark: Two low-wattage security lights glowed above the smoky blue mirrors behind the bar and made the beveled edges of the glass gleam like the blades of well-stropped knives. An eerie green bulb marked each of the four exits. Beyond the bar stools, in the main room, two hundred chairs at sixty tables faced a small stage. The nightclub was silent, deserted.

Joanna went behind the bar, took a glass from the rack, and poured a double shot of Dry Sack over ice. She sipped the sherry, sighed—and became aware of movement near the open door to her office.

Mariko Inamura, the assistant manager, had come downstairs from the apartment that she occupied on the third floor, above Joanna's quarters. As modest as always, Mariko wore a bulky green bathrobe that hung to the floor and was two sizes too large for her; lost in all that quilted fabric, she seemed less a woman than a waif. Her black hair, usually held up by ivory pins, now spilled to her shoulders. She went to the bar and sat on one of the stools.

"Like a drink?" Joanna asked.

Mariko smiled. "Water would be nice, thank you."

"Have something stronger."

"No, thank you. Just water, please."

"Trying to make me feel like a lush?"

"You aren't a lush."

"Thanks for the vote of confidence," Joanna said. "But I wonder. I seem to wind up here at the bar more nights than not, around this time." She put a glass of ice water on the counter.

Mariko turned the glass slowly in her small hands, but she didn't drink from it.

Joanna admired the woman's natural grace, which transformed every ordinary act into a moment of theater. Mariko was thirty, two years younger than Joanna, with big, dark eyes and delicate features. She seemed to be unaware of her exceptional good looks, and her humility enhanced her beauty.

Mariko had come to work at the Moonglow Lounge one week after opening night. She'd wanted the job as much for the opportunity to practice her English with Joanna as for the salary. She'd made it clear that she intended to leave after a year or two, to obtain a position as an executive secretary with one of the larger American companies with a branch office in Tokyo. But six years later, she no longer found Tokyo appealing, at least not by comparison with the life she now enjoyed.

The Moonglow had worked its spell on Mariko too. It was the main interest in her life as surely as it was the *only* interest in Joanna's.

Strangely, the insular world of the club was in some ways as sheltering and safe as a Zen monastery high in a remote mountain pass. Nightly, the place was crowded with customers, yet the outside world did not intrude to any significant extent. When the employees went home and the doors closed, the lounge—with its blue lights, mirrored walls, silver-and-black art deco appointments, and appealing air of mystery—might have been in any country, in any decade since the 1930s. It might even have been a place in a dream. Both Joanna and Mariko seemed to need that peculiar sanctuary.

Besides, an unexpected sisterly affection and concern had developed between them. Neither made friends easily. Mariko was warm and charming— but still surprisingly shy for a woman who worked in a Gion nightclub. In part she was like the retiring, soft-spoken, self-effacing Japanese women of another and less democratic age. By contrast, Joanna was vivacious, out-going—yet she also found it difficult to permit that extra degree of closeness that allowed an acquaintance to become a friend. Therefore, she'd made a special effort to keep Mariko at the Moonglow, regularly increasing her responsibilities and her salary; Mariko had reciprocated by working hard and diligently. Without once discussing their quiet friendship, they had decided that separation was neither desirable nor necessary.

Now, not for the first time, Joanna wondered, *Why Mariko?*

Of all the people whom Joanna might have chosen for a friend, Mariko was not the obvious first choice—except that she had an unusually strong sense of privacy and considerable discretion even by Japanese standards. She would never press for details from a friend's past, never indulge in that gossipy, inquisitive, and revelatory chatter that so many people assumed was an essential part of friendship.

There's never a danger that she'll try to find out too much about me.

That thought surprised Joanna. She didn't understand herself. After all, she had no secrets, no past of which to be ashamed.

With the glass of dry sherry in her hand, Joanna came out from behind the bar and sat on a stool.

"You had a nightmare again," Mariko said.

"Just a dream."

"A nightmare," Mariko quietly insisted. "The same one you've had on a thousand other nights."

"Not a thousand," Joanna demurred.

"Two thousand? Three?"

"Did I wake you?"

"It sounded worse than ever," Mariko said.

"Just the usual."

"Thought I'd left the TV on."

"Oh?"

"Thought I was hearing some old Godzilla movie," Mariko said.

Joanna smiled. "All that screaming, huh?"

"Like Tokyo being smashed flat again, mobs running for their lives."

"All right, it was a nightmare, not just a dream. And worse than usual."

"I worry about you," Mariko said.

"No need to worry. I'm a tough girl."

"You saw him again . . . the man with the steel fingers?"

"I never see his face," Joanna said wearily. "I've never seen anything at all but his hand, those god-awful metal fingers. Or at least that's all I remember seeing. I guess there's more to the nightmare than that, but the rest of it never stays with me after I wake up." She shuddered and sipped some sherry.

Mariko put a hand on Joanna's shoulder, squeezed gently. "I have an uncle who is—"

"A hypnotist."

"Psychiatrist," Mariko said. "A doctor. He uses hypnotism only to—"

"Yes, Mariko-san, you've told me about him before. I'm really not interested."

"He could help you remember the entire dream. He might even be able to help you learn the cause of it."

Joanna stared at her own reflection in the blue bar mirror and finally said, "I don't think I ever *want* to know the cause of it."

They were silent for a while.

Eventually Mariko said, "I didn't like it when they made him into a hero."

Joanna frowned. "Who?"

"Godzilla. Those later movies, when he battles other monsters to protect Japan. So silly. We need our monsters to be scary. They don't do us any good if they don't frighten us."

"Am I about to get hit with some philosophy of the mysterious East? I didn't hear the Zen warning siren."

"Sometimes we need to be frightened," Mariko said.

Joanna softly imitated a submarine diving alarm: *"Whoop-whoop-whoop-whoop."*

"Sometimes fear purges us, Joanna-san."

"We're deep in the unfathomable waters of the Japanese mind," Joanna whispered theatrically.

Mariko continued unfazed: "But when we confront our demons—"

"Deeper and deeper in the Japanese mind, tremendous pressure building up—"

"—and rid ourselves of those demons—"

"—deeper and deeper—"

"—we don't need the fear any more—"

"—the weight of sudden enlightenment will crush me as though I'm just a bug—"

"—don't need it to purge us—"

"—I tremble on the edge of revelation—"

"—and we are then freed."

"I'm surrounded by the light of reason," Joanna said.

"Yes, you are, but you're blind to it," said Mariko. "You are too in love with your fear to see the truth."

"That's me. A victim of phobophilia," Joanna said, and drank the rest of her sherry in one long swallow.

"And you call us Japanese inscrutable."

"Who does?" Joanna said with mock innocence.

"I hope Godzilla comes to Kyoto," Mariko said.

"Does he have a new movie to promote?"

"And if he does come, he'll be the patriotic Godzilla, seeking out new threats to the Japanese people."

"Good for him."

"When he sees all that long blond hair of yours, he'll go right for you."

"I think you've got him confused with King Kong."

"Squash you flat in the middle of the street, while the grateful citizens of Kyoto cheer wildly."

Joanna said, "You'll miss me."

"On the contrary. It'll be messy, hosing all that blood and guts off the street. But the lounge should reopen in a day or two, and then it'll be *my* place."

"Yeah? Who's going to sing when I'm gone?"

"The customers."

"Good God, you'd turn it into a karaoke bar!"

"All I need are a stack of old Engelbert Humperdinck tapes."

Joanna said, "You're scarier than Godzilla *ever* was."

They smiled at each other in the blue mirror behind the bar.

3 If his employees back in the States could have seen Alex Hunter at dinner in the Moonglow Lounge, they would have been astonished by his relaxed demeanor. To them, he was a demanding boss who expected perfection and quickly dismissed employees who couldn't deliver to his standards, a man who was at all times fair but who was given to sharp and accurate criticism. They knew him to be more often silent than not, and they rarely saw him smile. In Chicago, his hometown, he was widely envied and respected, but he was well liked only by a handful of friends. His office staff and field investigators would gape in disbelief if they could see him now, because he was chatting amiably with the waiters and smiling nearly continuously.

He did not appear capable of killing anyone, but he was. A few years ago he had pumped five bullets into a man named Ross Baglio. On another occasion, he had stabbed a man in the throat with the wickedly splintered end of a broken broomstick. Both times he had acted in self-defense. Now he appeared to be nothing more than a well-dressed business executive enjoying a night on the town.

This society, this comparatively depressurized culture, which was so different from the American way, had a great deal to do with his high spirits. The relentlessly pleasant and polite Japanese inspired a smile. Alex had been in their country just ten days, on vacation, but he could not recall another period of his life during which he had felt even half as relaxed and at peace with himself as he did at that moment.

Of course, the food contributed to his excellent spirits. The Moonglow Lounge maintained a first-rate kitchen. Japanese cuisine changed with the seasons more than any style of cooking with which Alex was familiar, and late autumn provided special treats. It was also important that each item of food complement the item next to it, and that everything be served on china that—both in pattern and color—was in harmony with the food that it carried. He was enjoying a dinner perfectly suited to the cool November evening. A delicate wooden tray held a bone-white china pot that was filled with thick slices of *daikon* radish, reddish sections of octopus—and *konnyaku*, a jellylike food made from devil's tongue. A fluted green bowl contained a fragrant hot mustard in which each delicacy could be anointed. On a large gray platter stood two black-and-red bowls: One contained *akadashi* soup with mushrooms, and the other was filled with rice. An oblong plate offered sea bream and three garnishes, plus a cup of finely grated *daikon* for seasoning. It was a hearty autumn meal, of the proper somber colors.

When he finished the last morsel of bream, Alex admitted to himself that it was neither the hospitable Japanese nor the quality of the food that made him feel so fine. His good humor resulted primarily from the fact that Joanna Rand would soon appear on the small stage.

Promptly at eight o'clock, the house lights dimmed, the silvery stage curtains drew back, and the Moonglow band opened with a great rendition of "A String of Pearls." Their playing wasn't the equal of any of the famous orchestras, not a match for Goodman or Miller or either of the Dorsey brothers, but surprisingly good for house musicians who had been born, raised, and trained many thousands of miles and a few decades from the origin of the music. At the end of the number, as the audience applauded enthusiastically, the band swung into "Moonglow," and Joanna Rand entered from stage right.

Alex's heartbeat quickened.

Joanna was slim, graceful, striking, though not beautiful in any classic sense. Her chin was feminine but too strong—and her nose neither narrow enough nor straight enough—to be seen in any ancient Grecian sculpture. Her cheekbones weren't high enough to satisfy the arbiters of beauty at *Vogue*, and her startlingly blue eyes were shades darker than the washed-out blue of the ennui-drenched models currently in demand for magazine covers and television commercials. She was a vibrant, golden vision, with light amber skin and cascades of platinum-blond hair. She looked thirty, not sixteen, but her beauty was inexpressibly enhanced by every mark of experience and line of character.

She *belonged* on a stage, not merely to be seen but to be heard. Her voice was first-rate. She sang with a tremulous clarity that pierced the stuffy air and seemed to reverberate within Alex. Though the lounge was crowded and everyone had been drinking, there was none of the expected nightclub chatter when Joanna Rand performed. The audience was attentive, rapt.

He knew her from another place and time, although he could not recall where or when they'd met. Her face was hauntingly familiar, especially her eyes. In fact, he felt that he hadn't just met her once before but had known her well, even intimately.

Ridiculous. He wouldn't have forgotten a woman as striking as this one. Surely, had they met before, he would be able to remember every smallest detail of their encounter.

He watched. He listened. He wanted to hold her.

4 When Joanna finished her last song and the applause finally faded, the band swung into a lively number. Couples crowded onto the dance floor. Conversation picked up again, and the lounge filled with sporadic laughter and the clatter of dinnerware.

As she did every night, Joanna briefly surveyed her domain from the edge of the stage, allowing herself a moment of pride. She ran a damn good place.

In addition to being a restaurateur, she was a practical social politician. At the end of her first of two hour-long performances, she didn't disappear behind the curtains until the ten o'clock show. Instead, she stepped down from the stage in a soft swish of pleated silk and moved slowly among the tables, acknowledging compliments, bowing and being bowed to, stopping to inquire if dinner had been enjoyable, greeting new faces and chatting at length with regular, honored customers. Good food, a romantic atmosphere, and high quality entertainment were sufficient to establish a profitable nightclub, but more than that was required for the Moonglow to become legendary. She wanted that extra degree of success. People were flattered to receive personal attention from the owner, and the forty minutes that she spent in the lounge between acts was worth uncountable yen in repeat business.

The handsome American with the neatly trimmed mustache was present for the third evening in a row. The previous two nights, they had exchanged no more than a dozen words, but Joanna had sensed that they wouldn't remain strangers. At each performance, he sat at a small table near the stage and watched her so intently that she had to avoid looking at him for fear that she would become distracted and forget the words to a song. After each show, as she mingled with the customers, she knew without looking at him that he was watching her every move. She imagined that she could feel the pressure of his gaze. Although being scrutinized by him was vaguely disturbing, it was also surprisingly pleasant.

When she reached his table, he stood and smiled. Tall, broad-shouldered, he had a European elegance in spite of his daunting size. He wore a three-piece, charcoal-gray Savile Row suit, what appeared to be a hand-tailored Egyptian-cotton shirt, and a pearl-gray tie.

He said, "When you sing 'These Foolish Things' or 'You Turned the Tables on Me,' I'm reminded of Helen Ward when she sang with Benny Goodman."

"That's fifty years ago," Joanna said. "You're not old enough to remember Helen Ward."

"Never saw her perform. But I have all her records, and you're better than she was."

"You flatter me too much. You're a jazz buff?"

"Mostly swing music."

"So we like the same corner of jazz."

Looking around at the crowd, he said, "Apparently, so do the Japanese. I was told the Moonglow was *the* nightclub for transplanted Americans. But ninety percent of your customers are Japanese."

"It surprises me, but they love the music—even though it comes from an era they otherwise prefer to forget."

"Swing is the only music I've developed a lasting enthusiasm for." He hesitated. "I'd offer you a cognac, but since you own the place, I don't suppose I can do that."

"I'll buy you one," she said.

He pulled out a chair for her, and she sat.

A white-jacketed waiter approached and bowed to them.

Joanna said, "Yamada-san, *burande wo ima omegai, shimasu.* Rémy Martin."

"Hai, hai," Yamada said. *"Sugu."* He hurried toward the bar at the back of the big room.

The American had not taken his eyes off her. "You really do have an extraordinary voice, you know. Better than Martha Tilton, Margaret Mc-Crae, Betty Van—"

"Ella Fitzgerald?"

He appeared to consider the comparison, then said, "Well, she's really not someone you should be compared to."

"Oh?"

"I mean, her style is utterly different from yours. It'd be like comparing oranges to apples."

Joanna laughed at his diplomacy. "So I'm not better than Ella Fitzgerald."

He smiled. "Hell, no."

"Good. I'm glad you said that. I was beginning to think you had no standards at all."

"I have very high standards," he said quietly.

His dark eyes were instruments of power. His unwavering stare seemed to establish an electrical current between them, sending an extended series of pleasant tremors through her. She felt not only as though he had undressed her with his eyes—men had done as much every night that she'd stepped onto the stage—but as though he had stripped her mind bare as well and had discovered, in one minute, everything worth knowing about her, every private fold of flesh and thought. She'd never before met a man who concentrated on a woman with such intensity, as if everyone else on earth had ceased to exist. Again she felt that peculiar combination of uneasiness and pleasure at being the focus of his undivided attention.

When the two snifters of Rémy Martin were served, she used the interruption as an excuse to glance away from him. She closed her eyes and sipped the cognac as if to savor it without distraction. In that self-imposed darkness, she realized that while he had been staring into her eyes, he had transmitted some of his own intensity to her. She had lost all awareness of the noisy club around her: the clinking of glasses, the laughter and buzz of conversation, even the music. Now all that clamor returned to her with the gradualness of silence reasserting itself in the wake of a tremendous explosion.

Finally she opened her eyes. "I'm at a disadvantage. I don't know your name."

"You're sure you don't? I've felt . . . perhaps we've met before."

She frowned. "I'm sure not."

"Maybe it's just that I *wish* we'd met sooner. I'm Alex Hunter. From Chicago."

"You work for an American company here?"

"No. I'm on vacation for a month. I landed in Tokyo eight days ago. I planned on spending two days in Kyoto, but I've already been here longer than that. I've got three weeks left. Maybe I'll spend them all in Kyoto and cancel the rest of my schedule. *Anata no machi wa hijo ni kyomi ga arimatsu.*"

"Yes," she said, "it is an interesting city, the most beautiful in Japan. But the entire country is fascinating, Mr. Hunter."

"Call me Alex."

"There's much to see in these islands, Alex."

"Maybe I should come back next year and take in all those other places. Right now, everything I could want to see in Japan is here."

She stared at him, braving those insistent dark eyes, not certain what to think of him. He was quite the male animal, making his intentions known.

Joanna prided herself on her strength, not merely in business but in her emotional life. She seldom wept and never lost her temper. She valued self-control, and she was almost obsessively self-reliant. Always, she preferred to be the dominant partner in her relations with men, to choose when and how a friendship with a man would develop, to be the one who decided when—and if—they would become more than friends. She had her own ideas about the proper, desirable pace of a romance. Ordinarily she wouldn't have liked a man as direct as Alex Hunter, so she was surprised that she found his stylishly aggressive approach to be appealing.

Nevertheless, she pretended not to see that he was more than casually interested in her. She glanced around as if checking on the waiters and gauging the happiness of her customers, sipped the cognac, and said, "You speak Japanese so well."

He bowed his head an inch or two. *"Arigato."*

"Do itashimashite."

"Languages are a hobby of mine," he said. "Like swing music. And good restaurants. Speaking of which, since the Moonglow is open only evenings, do you know a place that serves lunch?"

"In the next block. A lovely little restaurant built around a garden with a fountain. It's called Mizutani."

"That sounds perfect. Shall we meet at Mizutani for lunch tomorrow?"

Joanna was startled by the question but even more surprised to hear herself answer without hesitation. "Yes. That would be nice."

"Noon?"

"Yes. Noon."

She sensed that whatever happened between her and this unusual man, whether good or bad, would be entirely different from anything she'd experienced before.

5 *The man with the steel fingers reaches for the hypodermic syringe. . . .*
Joanna sat straight up in bed, soaked in perspiration, gasping for breath, clawing at the unyielding darkness before she regained control of herself and switched on the nightstand lamp.

She was alone.

She pushed back the covers and got out of bed with an urgency sparked by some deep-seated anxiety that she could not understand. She walked unsteadily to the center of the room and stood there, trembling in fear and confusion.

The air was cool and somehow *wrong*. She smelled a combination of strong antiseptics that hadn't been used in that room: ammonia, Lysol, alcohol, a pungent brew of germicidal substances unpleasant enough to make her eyes water. She drew a long breath, then another, but the vapors faded as she attempted to pinpoint their source.

When the stink was gone altogether, she reluctantly admitted that the odors hadn't actually existed. They were left over from the dream, figments of her imagination.

Or perhaps they were fragments of memory.

Although she had no recollection of ever having been seriously ill or injured, she half believed that once she must have been in a hospital room that had reeked with an abnormally powerful odor of antiseptics. A hospital . . . in which something terrible had happened to her, something that was the cause of the repeating nightmare about the man with steel fingers.

Silly. But the dream always left her rattled and irrational.

She went into the bathroom and drew a glass of water from the tap. She returned to the bed, sat on the edge of it, drank the water, and then slipped under the covers once more. After a brief hesitation, she switched off the lamp.

Outside, in the predawn stillness, a bird cried. A large bird, a piercing cry. The flutter of wings. Past the window. Feathers brushing the glass. Then the bird sailed off into the night, its thin screams growing thinner, fainter.

6 Suddenly, as he sat in bed reading, Alex recalled where and when he'd previously seen the woman. Joanna Rand wasn't her real name.

He had awakened at six-thirty Wednesday morning in his suite at the Kyoto Hotel. Whether vacationing or working, he was always up early and to bed late, requiring never more than five hours of rest to feel alert and refreshed.

He was grateful for his uncommon metabolism, because he knew that by spending fewer hours in bed, he was at an advantage in any dealings with people who were greater slaves to the mattress than he was. To Alex, who was an overachiever by choice as well as by nature, sleep was a detestable form of slavery, insidious. Each night was a temporary death to be endured but never enjoyed. Time spent in sleep was time wasted, surrendered, stolen By saving three hours a night, he was gaining eleven hundred hours of waking life each year, *eleven hundred hours* in which to read books and watch films and make love, more than forty-five "found" days in which to study, observe, learn—and make money.

It was a cliché but also true that time was money. And in Alex Hunter's philosophy, money was the only sure way to obtain the two most important things in life: independence and dignity, either of which meant immeasurably more to him than did love, sex, friendship, praise, or anything else.

He had been born poor, raised by a pair of hopeless alcoholics to whom the word "dignity" was as empty of meaning as the word "responsibility." As a child, he had resolved to discover the secret of obtaining wealth, and he'd found it before he had turned twenty: *time*. The secret of wealth was time. Having learned that lesson, he applied it with fervor. In more than twenty years of judiciously managed time, his net worth had increased from a thousand dollars to more than twelve million. His habit of being late to bed and early to rise, while half at odds with Ben Franklin's immortal advice, was a major factor in his phenomenal success.

Ordinarily he would begin the day by showering, shaving, and dressing precisely within twenty minutes of waking, but this morning he allowed himself the routine-shattering luxury of reading in bed. He was on vacation, after all.

Now, as he sat propped up by pillows, with a book in his lap, he realized who Joanna Rand really was. While he read, his subconscious mind, loath to squander time, apparently remained occupied with the mystery of Joanna, for although he hadn't been consciously thinking of her, he suddenly made the connection between her and an important face out of his past.

"Lisa," he whispered.

He put the book aside.

Lisa. She was twelve years older. A different hairstyle. All the baby fat of a twenty-year-old girl was gone from her face, and she was a mature woman now. But she was still Lisa.

Agitated, he got up, showered, and shaved.

Staring into his own eyes in the bathroom mirror, he said, "Slow down. Maybe the resemblance isn't as remarkable as you think."

He hadn't seen a photograph of Lisa Chelgrin in at least ten years. When he got his hands on a picture, he might discover that Joanna looked like Lisa only to the extent that a robin resembled a bluejay.

He dressed, sat at the writing desk in the suite's sparsely furnished living room, and tried to convince himself that everyone in the world had a doppelgänger, an unrelated twin. Even if Joanna *was* a dead ringer for Lisa, the resemblance might be pure chance.

For a while he stared at the telephone on the desk, and finally he said aloud, "Yeah. Only thing is, I never did believe in chance."

He'd built one of the largest security and private-investigation firms in the United States, and experience had taught him that every apparent coincidence was likely to be the visible tip on an iceberg of truth, with much more below the waterline than above.

He pulled the telephone closer and placed an overseas call through the hotel switchboard. By eight-thirty in the morning, Kyoto time (four-thirty in the afternoon, Chicago time), he got hold of Ted Blankenship, his top man in the home office. "Ted, I want you to go personally to the dead-file room and pull everything we've got on Lisa Chelgrin. I want that file in Kyoto as soon as possible. Don't trust it to an air courier service. Keep it inside the company. Give it to one of our junior field ops who doesn't have anything better to do, and put him on the first available flight."

Blankenship chose his words carefully, slowly. "Alex . . . does this mean the case . . . is being . . . reactivated?"

"I'm not sure."

"Is there a chance you've found her after all this time?"

"I'm probably chasing shadows. Most likely, nothing will come of it. So don't talk about this, not even with your wife."

"Of course."

"Go to the dead files yourself. Don't send a secretary. I don't want any rumors getting started."

"I understand."

"And the field operative who brings it shouldn't know what he's carrying."

"I'll keep him in the dark. But, Alex . . . if you've found her . . . it's very big news."

"Very big," Alex agreed. "Call me back after you've arranged things, and let me know when I can expect the file."

"Will do."

Alex put down the telephone and went to one of the living-room windows, from which he watched the bicyclists and motorists in the crowded street below. They were in a hurry, as though they clearly comprehended the value of time. As he watched, one cyclist made an error in judgment, tried to pass between two cars where there wasn't sufficient space. A white Honda bumped the bike, and the cyclist went down in a skidding-rolling-bouncing tangle of skinned legs, bent bicycle wheels, broken arms, and twisted handlebars. Brakes squealed, traffic halted, and people rushed toward the injured man.

Although Alex was not superstitious, he had the eerie feeling that the sudden violence in the street below was an omen and that he himself was rushing headlong toward an ugly crash of his own.

7 At noon Alex met Joanna at Mizutani for lunch.

When he saw her again, he realized that the mental picture of her that he carried with him captured her beauty no more accurately than a snapshot of Niagara Falls could convey the beauty of wildly tumbling water. She was more golden, more vibrant and *alive*—her eyes a far deeper and more electrifying blue—than he remembered.

He kissed her hand. He was not accustomed to European manners; he just needed an excuse to touch his lips to her warm skin.

Mizutani was an *o-zashiki* restaurant, divided by rice-paper partitions into many private dining rooms where meals were served strictly Japanese style. The ceiling wasn't high, less than eighteen inches above Alex's head, and the floor was of brilliantly polished pine that seemed transparent and as unplumbable as a sea. In the vestibule, Alex and Joanna exchanged their street shoes for soft slippers. They followed a petite young hostess to a small room where they sat on the floor, side by side on thin but comfortable cushions, in front of a low table.

They faced a six-foot-square window, beyond which lay a walled garden. That late in the year, no flowers brightened the view, but there were several varieties of well-tended evergreens, and a carpet of moss had not yet turned brown for the winter. In the center of the garden, water fountained from a seven-foot-high pyramid of rocks and spilled down the stones to a shallow, trembling pool.

They ate *mizutaki*, the white meat of a chicken stewed in an earthenware pot and flavored with scallions, icicle radish, and many herbs. This was accompanied by several tiny cups of steaming sake, delicious when piping hot but like a spoiled sauterne when cool.

Throughout lunch they talked about music, Japanese customs, art, and books. Alex wanted to mention the magic name—Lisa Chelgrin—because at times he had an almost psychic ability to read guilt or innocence in the reactions of a suspect, in fleeting expressions at the instant that accusations were made, in the nuances of a voice. But he wasn't eager to discuss the Chelgrin disappearance with Joanna until he heard where she'd been born and raised, where she'd learned to sing, and why she'd come to Japan. Her biography might have enough substance to convince him that she was who she claimed to be, that her resemblance to the long-missing Chelgrin woman was coincidental, in which case he wouldn't raise the subject. It was essential that he induce her to talk unselfconsciously about herself, but she resisted— evidently not out of any sinister motive but out of sheer modesty. Ordinarily Alex was also reluctant to talk about himself, even with close friends; curiously, in Joanna's company, those inhibitions dissolved. While trying unsuccessfully to probe into her past, he told her a great deal about his own.

"Are you really a private detective?" she asked. "It's hard to believe. Where's your trench coat?"

"At the cleaners. They're removing the unsightly bloodstains."

"You aren't wearing a shoulder holster."

"It chafes my shoulder."

"Aren't you carrying a gun at all?"

"There's a miniature derringer in my left nostril."

"Come on. I'm serious."

"I'm not here on business, and the Japanese government tends to frown on pistol-packing American tourists."

"I'd expect a private detective to be . . . well, slightly seedy."

"Oh, thank you very much."

"Tough, squint-eyed, sentimental but at the same time cynical."

"Sam Spade played by Humphrey Bogart. The business isn't like that any more," Alex said. "If it ever was. Mostly mundane work, seldom anything dangerous. Divorce investigations. Skip tracing. Gathering evidence for defense attorneys in criminal cases. Providing bodyguards for the rich and famous, security guards for department stores. Not half as romantic or glamorous as Bogart, I'm afraid."

"Well, it's more romantic than being an accountant." She savored a tender piece of chicken, eating as daintily as did the Japanese, but with a healthy and decidedly erotic appetite.

Alex watched her surreptitiously: the clenching of her jaw muscles, the sinuous movement of her throat as she swallowed, and the exquisite line of her lips as she sipped the hot sake.

She put down the cup. "How'd you get into such an unusual line of work?"

"As a kid, I decided not to live my life on the edge of poverty, like my parents, and I thought every attorney on earth was filthy rich. So with a few scholarships and a long string of night jobs, I got through college and law school."

"Summa cum laude?"

Surprised, he said, "How'd you know that?"

"You're obsessive-compulsive."

"Am I? You should be a private detective."

"Samantha Spade. What happened after graduation?"

"I spent a year with a major Chicago firm that specialized in corporate law. Hated it."

"But that's an easier road to riches than being a P.I."

"The average income for an attorney these days is around maybe eighty thousand. Less back then. As a kid, it looked like riches, because what does a kid know. But after taxes, it would never be enough to put me behind the wheel of a Rolls-Royce."

"And is that what you wanted—a Rolls-Royce lifestyle?"

"Why not? I had the opposite as a child. There's nothing ennobling about poverty. Anyway, after a couple of months of writing briefs and doing legal research, I knew the really enormous money was only for senior partners of the big firms. By the time I could have worked my way to the top, I'd have been in my fifties."

When he was twenty-five, confident that the private security field would be a major growth industry for several decades, Alex had left the law firm to work for the fifty-man Bonner Agency, where he intended to learn the business from the inside. By the time he was thirty, he arranged a bank loan to buy the agency from Martin Bonner. Under his guidance, the company moved aggressively into all areas of the industry, including installation and maintenance of electronic security systems. Now Bonner-Hunter Security had offices in eleven cities and employed two thousand people.

"You have your Rolls-Royce?" Joanna asked.

"Two."

"Is life better for having two?"

"Sounds like a Zen question."

"And *that* sounds like an evasion."

"Money's neither dirty nor noble. It's a neutral substance, an inevitable part of civilization. But your voice, your talent—that's a gift from God."

For a long moment she regarded him in silence, and he knew she was judging him. She put down her chopsticks and patted her mouth with a napkin. "Most men who started out with nothing and piled up a fortune by the age of forty would be insufferable egomaniacs."

"Not at all. There's nothing special about me. I know quite a few wealthy, self-made men and women, and most of them have every bit as much humility as any office clerk. Maybe more."

Their waitress, a pleasant round-faced woman dressed in a white *yukata* and short maroon jacket, brought dessert: peeled mandarin orange slices coated with finely shredded almonds and coconut.

"Now we've talked too much about me," Alex said. "What about you? How did you get to Japan, to the Moonglow? I want to hear all about you."

"There's not a lot to hear."

"Nonsense."

"My life seems boring compared to yours."

She was either secretive about her past or genuinely intimidated by him. He couldn't decide which, but he continued to encourage her until she finally opened up.

"I was born in New York City," she said, "but I don't remember it well. My father was an executive with one of those hydra-headed conglomerates.

When I was ten, he was promoted to a top management position in a British subsidiary, so then I grew up in London and attended university there."

"What did you study?"

"Music for a while . . . then Asian languages. I became interested in the Orient because of a brief, intense infatuation with a Japanese exchange student. He and I shared an apartment for a year. Our affair didn't last, but my interest in the Orient grew."

"When did you come to Japan?"

"Almost twelve years ago."

Coincidental with the disappearance of Lisa Chelgrin, he thought. But he said nothing.

With her chopsticks, Joanna picked up another slice of orange, ate it with visible delight, and licked away a paper-thin curl of coconut that clung to the corner of her mouth.

To Alex, she resembled a tawny cat: sleek-muscled, full of kinetic energy.

As though she had heard his thought, she turned her head with feline fluidity to gaze at him. Her eyes had that catlike quality of harmoniously blended opposites: sleepiness combined with total awareness, watchfulness mixed with cool indifference, and a proud isolation that coexisted with a longing for affection.

She said, "My parents were killed in an auto accident while they were on vacation in Brighton. I had no relatives in the States, no great desire to return there. And England seemed terribly dreary all of a sudden, full of bad memories. When my dad's life insurance was paid and the estate was settled, I took the money and came to Japan."

"Looking for that exchange student?"

"Oh, no. That was over. I came because I thought I'd like it here. And I did. I spent a few months playing tourist. Then I put together an act and got a gig singing Japanese and American pop music in a Yokohama nightclub. I've always had a good voice but not always much stage presence. I was dreadful at the start, but I learned."

"How'd you get to Kyoto?"

"There was a stopover in Tokyo, a better job than the one in Yokohama. A big club called Ongaku, Ongaku."

"Music, Music," Alex translated. "I know the place. I was there only five days ago!"

"The club had a reasonably good house band back then, and they were willing to take chances. Some of them were familiar with jazz, and I taught them what I knew. The management was skeptical at first, but the customers loved the Big Band sound. A Japanese audience is usually more reserved than a Western audience, but the people at Ongaku really let down their hair when they heard us."

That first triumph was, Alex saw, a sweet recollection for Joanna. Smiling faintly, she stared at the garden without seeing it, eyes glazed, looking back along the curve of time.

"It was a crazy place for a while. It really jumped. I surprised even myself.

I was the main attraction for two years. If I'd wanted to stay, I'd still be there. But I realized I'd do better with my own club."

"Ongaku, Ongaku is changed, not like you describe it," Alex said. "It must've lost a lot when you left. It doesn't jump these days. It doesn't even twitch."

Joanna laughed and tossed her head to get a long wave of hair out of her face. With that gesture, she looked like a schoolgirl, fresh, innocent—and more than ever like Lisa Chelgrin. Indeed, for a moment, she was not merely a Chelgrin look-alike: She was a dead ringer for the missing woman.

"I came to Kyoto for a vacation in July, more than six years ago," she said. "It was during the annual Gion Matsuri."

"Matsuri . . . a festival."

"It's Kyoto's most elaborate celebration. Parties, exhibits, art shows. The beautiful old houses on Muromachi were open to the public with displays of family treasures and heirlooms, and there was a parade of the most enormous ornate floats you ever saw. Absolutely enchanting. I stayed an extra week and fell in love with Kyoto even when it wasn't in the midst of a festival. Used a lot of my savings to buy the building that's now the Moonglow. The rest is history. I warned you it was dull compared to your life. Not a single murder mystery or Rolls-Royce in the entire tale."

"I didn't yawn once."

"I try to make the Moonglow a little like the Café Americain, in *Casablanca*, but the dangerous, romantic stuff that happened to Bogart doesn't happen to me and never will. I'm a lightning rod for the *ordinary* forces in life. The last major crisis I can recall was when the dishwasher broke down for two days."

Alex wasn't certain that everything Joanna had told him was true, but he was favorably impressed. Her capsule biography was generally convincing, as much for the manner in which it was delivered as for its detail. Although she'd been reluctant to talk about herself, there had been no hesitation in her voice once she'd begun, not the slightest hint of a liar's discomfort. Her history as a nightclub singer in Yokohama and Tokyo was undoubtedly true. If she'd needed to invent a story to cover those years, she wouldn't have created one that was so easy to investigate and disprove. The part about England and the parents who'd been killed while on holiday in Brighton . . . well, he wasn't sure what to make of that. As a device for totally sealing off her life prior to Japan, it was effective but far too pat. Furthermore, at a few points, her biography intersected with that of Lisa Chelgrin, which seemed to be piling coincidence on coincidence.

Joanna turned on her cushion to face him directly. Her knee pressed against his leg, sending a pleasant shiver through him. "Do you have any plans for the afternoon?" she asked. "If you'd like to do some sightseeing, I'll be your guide for a few hours."

"Thanks for the offer, but you must have business to attend to."

"Mariko can handle things at the club until it opens. I don't have to put in an appearance until at least six o'clock."

"Mariko?"

"Mariko Inamura. My assistant manager. The best thing that's happened to me since I came to Japan. She's smart, trustworthy, and works like a demon."

Alex repeated the name to himself until he was sure that he would remember it. If he had a chance to talk with Mariko, she might inadvertently reveal more about her boss than he could learn from Joanna herself.

"Well," he said, "if you're sure you have the time, I'd like nothing better than a tour."

He had expected to make up his mind about her during lunch, but he had reached no conclusions.

Her uncommonly dark blue eyes seemed to grow darker still. He stared into them, entranced.

Joanna Rand or Lisa Chelgrin?

He couldn't decide which.

8

At Joanna's request, the hostess at Mizutani telephoned the Sogo Taxi Company. The cab arrived in less than five minutes, a black car with red lettering.

Joanna was delighted with the driver. No one could have been better suited than he was for the little tour that she had in mind. He was a wrinkled, white-haired old man with an appealing smile that lacked one tooth. He sensed romance between her and Alex, so he interrupted their conversation only to make certain that they didn't miss special scenery here and there, using his rearview mirror to glance furtively at them, always with bright-eyed approval.

For more than an hour, at the driver's discretion, they cruised the ancient city. Joanna drew Alex's attention to interesting houses and temples, and she kept up a stream of patter about Japanese history and architecture. He smiled, laughed frequently, and asked questions about what he was seeing. But he looked at her as much as at the city, and again she felt the incredible power of his dark eyes and direct stare.

They were stopped at a traffic light near the National Museum when he said, "Your accent intrigues me."

She blinked. "What accent?"

"It isn't New York, is it?"

"I wasn't aware I *had* an accent."

"No, it's certainly not New York. Boston?"

"I've never been to Boston."

"It's not Boston, anyway. Difficult to pin down. Maybe there's a slight trace of British English in it. Maybe that's it."

"I hope not," Joanna said. "I've always disliked Americans who assume an English accent after living a few years there. So phony."

"It's not English." He studied her while he pondered the problem, and as the cab started up again, he said, "I know what it sounds like! Chicago."

"You're from Chicago, and I don't sound like you."

"Oh, but you do. Just a little. A very little."

"Not at all. And I've never been to Chicago, either."

"You must have lived somewhere in Illinois," he insisted.

Suddenly his smile seemed to be false, maintained only with considerable effort.

"No," she said, "I've never been to Illinois."

He shrugged. "Then I'm wrong." He pointed to a building ahead, on the left. "That's an odd-looking place. What is it?"

Joanna resumed her role as his guide, although with the uneasy feeling that the questions about her accent had not been casual. That sudden turn in the conversation had a purpose that eluded her.

A shiver passed through Joanna, and it felt like an echo of the chills that she endured every night, when waking from the nightmare.

9 At Nijo Castle, they paid the cab fare and continued sightseeing on foot. Turning away from the small Sogo taxi as it roared off into traffic, they followed three other tourists toward the palace's huge iron-plated East Gate.

Joanna glanced at Alex and saw that he was impressed. "It's something, huh?"

"Now *this* is my idea of a castle!" Then he shook his head. "But it looks too . . . garish for Japan."

Joanna sighed. "I'm glad you said that. If you admired Nijo Castle too much, then how could I ever like you?"

"You mean I'm supposed to find it garish?"

"Most sensitive people do . . . if they understand Japanese style, that is."

"I thought it was a landmark."

"It is, historically. But it's an attraction with more appeal for tourists than for the Japanese."

They entered through the main gate and passed a second gate, the *Kara-mon*, which was richly ornamented with metalwork and elaborate wood carvings. Ahead lay a wide courtyard and then the palace itself.

As they crossed the courtyard, Joanna said, "Most Westerners expect ancient palaces to be massive, lavish. They're disappointed to find so few imposing monuments here—but they like Nijo Castle. Its rococo grandeur is something they can relate to. But Nijo doesn't actually represent the fundamental qualities of Japanese life and philosophy."

She was beginning to babble, but she couldn't stop. Over lunch and in the taxi, she had grown aware of a building sexual tension between them.

She welcomed it, yet at the same time was frightened of the commitment that she might have to make. For more than ten months, she'd had no lover, and her loneliness had become as heavy as cast-iron shackles. Now she wanted Alex, wanted the pleasure of being with him, giving and taking, sharing that special tenderness, animal closeness. But if she opened herself to joy, she would only have to endure another painful separation, and that prospect made her nervous.

Separation was inevitable—and not because he would go back to Chicago. She ended every love affair the same way: badly. She harbored a strong, inexplicable, destructive urge—no, a *need*—to demolish anything good and right that developed between her and any man. All of her adult life, she had wanted a permanent relationship and had sought it with quiet desperation. Yet she rebelled against marriage when it was proposed, fled from affection when it threatened to ripen into love. She worried that any would-be fiancé might have more curiosity about her when he was her husband than he'd exhibited when he was her lover; she worried that he'd probe too deeply into her past and learn the truth. *The truth.* The worry always swelled into fear, and the fear swiftly became debilitating, unbearable. But why? *Why?* She had nothing to hide. Her life story *was* singularly lacking in momentous events and dark secrets, just as she had told Alex. Nevertheless, she knew that if she had an affair with him, and if he began to feel that they had a future together, she would reject and alienate him with a suddenness and viciousness that would leave him stunned. And when he was gone, when she was alone, she would be crushed by the loss and unable to understand why she had treated him so cruelly. Her fear was irrational, but she knew by now that she would never conquer it.

With Alex, she sensed the potential for a deeper relationship than she had ever known, which meant that she was walking the edge of an emotional precipice, foolishly testing her balance. Consequently, as they crossed the courtyard of Nijo Castle, she talked incessantly and filled all possible silences with trivial chatter that left no room for anything of a personal nature. She didn't think she could bear the pain of loving him and then driving him away.

"Westerners," she told him pedantically, "seek constant action and excitement from morning to night, then complain about the awful pressures that deform their lives. Life here is the opposite—calm and sane. The key words of the Japanese experience, at least for most of its philosophical history, are 'serenity' and 'simplicity.' "

Alex grinned winningly. "No offense meant . . . but judging by the hyperactive state you've been in since we left the restaurant, you're still more American than Japanese."

"Sorry. It's just that I love Kyoto and Japan so much that I tend to run on. I'm so anxious for you to like it too."

They stopped at the main entrance to the largest of the castle's five connected buildings. "Joanna, are you worried about something?"

"Me? No. Nothing."

She was unsettled by his perception. Again, she sensed that she could hide nothing from him.

"Are you certain you have the time for this today?"

"Really, I'm enjoying myself. I have all the time in the world."

He stared thoughtfully at her. With two pinched fingers, he tugged at one point of his neatly trimmed mustache.

"Come along," she said brightly, trying to cover her uneasiness. "There's so much to see here."

They followed a group of tourists through the ornate chambers, and Joanna shared with him the colorful history of Nijo Castle. The place was a trove of priceless art, even if a large measure of it tended to gaudiness. The first buildings had been erected in 1603, to serve as the Kyoto residence of the first shogun of the honorable Tokugawa family, and later enlarged with sections of Hideyoshi's dismantled Fushimi Castle. In spite of its moat and turrets and magnificent iron gate, the castle had been constructed by a man who had no doubts about his safety; with its low walls and broad gardens, it never could have withstood a determined enemy. Although the palace was not representative of Japanese style, it was quite successful as the meant-to-be impressive home of a rich and powerful military dictator who commanded absolute obedience and could afford to live as well as the emperor himself.

In the middle of the tour, when the other visitors had drifted far ahead, as Joanna was explaining the meaning and the value of a beautiful and complex mural, Alex said, "Nijo Castle is wonderful, but I'm more impressed with you than with it."

"How so?"

"If you came to Chicago, I wouldn't be able to do anything like this. I don't know a damn thing about the history of my own hometown. I couldn't even tell you the year that the great fire burned it all to the ground. Yet here you are, an American in a strange country, and you know everything."

"It amazes me too," she said quietly. "I know Kyoto better than most of the people who were born here. Japanese history has been a hobby ever since I moved here from England. More than hobby, I guess. Almost an avocation. Sometimes . . . an obsession."

His eyes narrowed slightly and seemed to shine with professional curiosity. "Obsession? That's an odd way of putting it."

Again the conversation had ceased to be casual. He was leading her, probing gently but insistently, motivated by more than friendly interest. What did this man want from her? Sometimes he made her feel as though she was concealing a dreadful crime. She wished that she could change the subject before another word was said, but she couldn't see any polite way to do so.

"I read a lot of books on Japanese history," she said, "and I attend lectures in history. Spend most of my holidays poking around ancient shrines, museums. It's almost as if I . . ."

"As if you what?" Alex prompted.

She looked at the mural again. "It's as if I'm obsessed with Japanese history because I've no real roots of my own. Born in the U.S., raised in England, parents dead for nearly twelve years now, Yokohama to Tokyo to Kyoto, no living relatives . . ."

"Is that true?"

"Is what true?"

"That you have no relatives."

"None living."

"Not any grandparents or—"

"Like I said."

"Not even an aunt or uncle?"

"Not a one."

"Not even a cousin—"

"No."

"How odd."

"It happens."

"Not often."

She turned to face him, and she couldn't be sure whether his handsome face was lined with sympathy or calculation, concern for her or suspicion. "I came to Japan because there was nowhere else for me to go, no one I could turn to."

He frowned. "Almost anyone your age can claim at least one relative kicking around somewhere . . . maybe not someone you know well or really care about, but a bona fide relative nonetheless."

Joanna shrugged, wishing he'd drop the subject. "Well, if I do have any folks out there, I don't know about them."

His response was quick. "I could help you search for them. After all, investigations are my trade."

"I couldn't afford your rates."

"Oh, I'm very reasonable."

"Yeah? You *do* buy Rolls-Royces with your fees."

"Just for you, I'd do it for the cost of a bicycle."

"A very large and ornate bicycle, I'll bet."

"I'll do it for a smile, Joanna."

She smiled. "That's generous of you, but I couldn't accept."

"I'd charge it to overhead. The cost would be a tax write-off."

Although she couldn't imagine his reasons, he was eager to dig into her past. This time, she wasn't suffering from her usual, irrational paranoia: He really *was* too curious.

Nevertheless, she wanted to talk to him and be with him. There was good chemistry between them. He was a medicine for loneliness.

"No," she said. "Forget it, Alex. Even if I've got folks out there someplace, they're strangers. I mean nothing to them. That's why it's important to me to get a solid grip on the history of Kyoto and Japan. This is my hometown now. It's my past and present and future. They've accepted me here."

"Which is rather odd, isn't it? The Japanese are pretty insular. They rarely accept immigrants who aren't at least half Japanese."

Ignoring his question, she said, "I don't have roots like other people do. Mine have been dug up and burned. So maybe I can *create* new roots for myself, grow them right here, and maybe they'll be as strong and meaningful as the roots that were destroyed. In fact, it's something I *have* to do. I don't have any choice. I need to belong, not just as a successful immigrant but as an integral part of this lovely country. Belonging . . . being securely and deeply connected to it all, like a fiber in the cloth . . . that's what counts. I need to lose myself in Japan. A lot of days there's a terrible emptiness in me. Not all the time. Now and then. But when it comes, it's almost too much to bear. And I think . . . I *know* that if I melt completely into this society, then I won't have to suffer that emptiness any longer."

She amazed herself, because with Alex Hunter, she was allowing an unusual intimacy. She was telling him things that she had never told anyone before.

He spoke so quietly that she could barely hear. " 'Emptiness.' That's another odd word choice."

"I guess it is."

"What do you mean by it?"

Joanna groped for words that could convey the hollowness, the cold feeling of being different from all other people, the cancerous alienation that sometimes crept over her, usually when she least expected it. Periodically she fell victim to a brutal, disabling loneliness that bordered on despair. Bleak, unremitting loneliness, yet more than that, worse than that. *Aloneness.* That was a better term for it. Without apparent reason, she sometimes felt certain that she was separate, hideously unique. *Aloneness.* The depression that accompanied one of these inexplicable moods was a black pit out of which she could claw only with fierce determination.

Haltingly she said, "The emptiness is like . . . well, it's like I'm nobody."

"You mean . . . you're bothered that you have no one."

"No. That's not it. I feel that I *am* no one."

"I still don't understand."

"It's as if I'm not Joanna Rand . . . not anybody at all . . . just a shell . . . a cipher . . . hollow . . . not the same as other people . . . not even human. And when I'm like that, I wonder why I'm alive . . . what purpose I have. My connections seem so tenuous. . . ."

He was silent for a while, but she was aware that he was staring at her while she gazed blindly at the mural. At last he said, "How can you live with this attitude, this emptiness, and still be . . . the way you are?"

"The way I am?"

"Generally so outgoing, cheerful."

"Oh," Joanna said quickly, "I don't feel alienated all the time. The mood comes over me only now and then, and never for longer than a day or two. I fight it off."

He touched her cheek with his fingertips.

Abruptly Joanna was aware of how intently he was staring, and she saw a trace of pity mixed with the compassion in his eyes. The reality of Nijo Castle and the actuality of the limited relationship that they shared now flooded back to her, and she was surprised— even shocked—by how much she had said and by how far she had opened herself to him. Why had she cast aside the armor of her privacy in front of this man rather than at the feet of someone before him? Why was she willing to reveal herself to Alex Hunter in a way and to a degree that she had never allowed Mariko Inamura to know her? She wondered if her hunger for companionship and love was much greater than she had ever realized until this disturbing moment.

She blushed. "Enough of this soul baring. How'd you get me to do that? You aren't a psychoanalyst, are you?"

"Every private detective has to be a bit of a psychiatrist . . . just like any popular bartender."

"Well, I don't know what in the world got me started on that."

"I don't mind listening."

"You're sweet."

"I mean it."

"Maybe you don't mind listening," she said, "but I mind talking about it."

"Why?"

"It's private. And silly."

"Didn't sound silly to me. It's probably good for you to talk about it."

"Probably," she admitted. "But it's not like me to babble on about myself to a perfect stranger."

"Hey, I'm not a perfect stranger."

"Well, almost."

"Oh, I see," he said. "I understand. You mean I'm perfect but not a stranger. I can live with that."

Joanna smiled. She wanted to touch him, but she didn't. "Well, anyway, we're here to show you the palace, not to have long boring Freudian discussions. There are a thousand things to see, and every one of them is more interesting than my psyche."

"You underestimate yourself."

Another group of chattering tourists rounded the corner and approached from behind Joanna. She turned toward them, using them as an excuse to avoid Alex's eyes for the few seconds required to regain her composure, but what she saw made her gasp.

A man with no right hand.

Twenty feet away.

Walking toward her.

A. Man. With. No. Right. Hand.

He was at the front of the group: a smiling, grandfatherly Korean gentleman with a softly creased face and iron-gray hair. He wore sharply pressed slacks, a white shirt, a blue tie, and a light blue sweater with the right sleeve rolled up a few inches. His arm was deformed at the wrist: There was nothing but a smooth, knobby, pinkish stub where the hand should have been.

"Are you all right?" Alex asked, apparently sensing the sudden tension in her.

She wasn't able to speak.

The one-handed man drew closer.

Fifteen feet away now.

She could smell antiseptics. Alcohol. Lysol. Lye soap.

That was ridiculous. She couldn't *really* smell antiseptics. Imagination. Nothing to fear. Nothing to fear in Nijo Castle.

Lysol.

Alcohol.

No. Nothing to fear. The one-handed Korean was a stranger, a kindly little *ojii-san* who couldn't possibly hurt anyone. She had to get a grip on herself.

Lysol.

Alcohol.

"Joanna? What's happening? What's wrong?" Alex asked, touching her shoulder.

The elderly Korean seemed to advance with the slow-motion single-mindedness of a monster in a horror film or in a nightmare. Joanna felt trapped in the unearthly, oppressive gravity of her dream, in that same syrupy flow of time.

Her tongue was thick. A bad taste filled her mouth, the coppery flavor of blood, which was no doubt as imaginary as the miasma of antiseptics, although it was as sickening as if it had been real. Her throat was constricted. She felt as if she might begin to gag. She heard herself straining for air.

Lysol.

Alcohol.

She blinked, and the flutter of her eyelids magically altered reality even further, so the Korean's pinkish stump now ended in a mechanical hand. Incredibly, she could hear the compact servo-mechanisms purring with power, the oiled push-pull rods sliding in their tracks, and the gears *click-click-clicking* as the fingers opened from a clenched fist.

No. That was imagination too.

"Joanna?"

When the Korean was less than three yards from her, he raised his twisted limb and pointed with the mechanical hand that wasn't really there. Intellectually Joanna knew that he was interested only in the mural that she and Alex had been studying, but on a more primitive and affecting emotional level, she reacted with the certainty that he was pointing at *her*, reaching for *her* with unmistakably malevolent purpose.

"Joanna."

It was Alex speaking her name, but she could almost believe that it had been the Korean.

From the deepest reaches of memory came a frightening sound: a gravelly, jagged, icy voice seething with hatred and bitterness. A familiar voice, synonymous with pain and terror. She wanted to scream. Although the man in her nightmare, the faceless bastard with steel fingers, had never spoken to her in sleep, she knew this was his voice. With a jolt, she realized that while she had never heard him speak in the nightmare, she *had* heard him when she was awake, a long time ago . . . somehow, somewhere. The words he spoke to her now were not imagined or dredged up from her worst dreams, but recollected. The voice was a cold, dark effervescence bubbling up from a long-forgotten place and time: *"Once more the needle, my lovely little lady. Once more the needle."* It grew louder, reverberating in her mind, a voice to which the rest of the world was deaf—*"Once more the needle, once more the needle, once more the needle"*—booming with firecracker repetitiveness, until she thought her head would explode.

The Korean stopped two feet from her.

Lysol.

Alcohol.

Once more the needle, my lovely little lady . . .

Joanna ran. She cried out like a wounded animal and turned away from the startled Korean, pushed at Alex without fully realizing who he was, pushed so hard that she almost knocked him down, and darted past him, her heels tapping noisily on the hardwood floor. She hurried into the next chamber, trying to scream but unable to find her voice, ran without looking back, convinced that the Korean was pursuing her, ran past the dazzling seventeenth-century artworks of the master Kano Tan'yu and his students, fled between strikingly beautiful wood sculptures, and all the while she struggled to draw a breath, but the air was like a thick dust that clogged her lungs. She ran past richly carved transoms, past intricate scenes painted on sliding doors, footsteps echoing off the coffered ceilings, ran past a surprised guard who called to her, dashed through an exit into cool November air, started across the big courtyard, heard a familiar voice calling her name, *not* the cold voice of the man with the steel hand, so she finally stopped, stunned, in the center of the Nijo garden, shaking, shaking.

10 Alex led her to a garden bench and sat beside her in the brisk autumn breeze. Her eyes were unnaturally wide, and her face was as pale and fragile as bridal lace. He held her hand. Her fingers were cold and chalky white, and she squeezed his hand so hard that her manicured nails bit into his skin.

"Should I get you to a doctor?"

"No. It's over. I'll be all right. I just . . . I need to sit here for a while."

She still appeared to be ill, but a trace of color slowly began to return to her cheeks.

"What happened, Joanna?"

Her lower lip quivered like a suspended bead of water about to surrender to the insistent pull of gravity. Bright tears glistened in the corners of her eyes.

"Hey. Hey now," he said softly.

"Alex, I'm so sorry."

"About what?"

"I made such a fool of myself."

"Nonsense."

"Embarrassed you," she said.

"Not a chance."

Her eyes brimmed with tears.

"It's okay," he told her.

"I was just . . . scared."

"Of what?"

"The Korean."

"What Korean?"

"The man with one hand."

"Was he Korean? Do you know him?"

"Never saw him before."

"Then what? Did he say something?"

She shook her head. "No. He . . . he reminded me of something awful . . . and I panicked." Her hand tightened on his.

"Reminded you of what?"

She was silent, biting her lower lip.

He said, "It might help to talk about it."

For a long moment she gazed up into the lowering sky, as if reading enigmatic messages into the patterns of the swift-moving clouds. Finally she told him about the nightmare.

"You have it *every* night?" he asked.

"For as far back as I can remember."

"When you were a child?"

"I guess . . . no . . . not then."

"Exactly how far back?"

"Seven or eight years. Maybe ten."

"Maybe twelve?"

Through her shimmering tears she regarded him curiously. "What do you mean?"

Rather than answer, he said, "The odd thing about it is the frequency. *Every night.* That must be unbearable. It must drain you. The dream itself isn't particularly strange. I've had worse. But the endless repetition—"

"Everyone's had worse," Joanna said. "When I try to describe the nightmare, it doesn't sound all that terrifying or threatening. But at night . . . I feel as if I'm dying. There aren't words for what I go through, what it does to me."

Alex felt her stiffen as though steeling herself against the recollected impact of the nightly ordeal. She bit her lip and for a while said nothing, merely stared at the funereal gray-black clouds that moved in an endless cortege from east to west across the city.

When at last she looked at him again, her eyes were haunted. "Years ago, I'd wake up from the dream and be so damned scared I'd throw up. Physically ill with fear, hysterical. These days, it's not so acute . . . though more often than not, I can't get back to sleep. Not right away. The mechanical hand, the needle . . . it makes me feel so . . . slimy . . . sick in my soul."

Alex held her hand in both of his hands, cupping her frigid fingers in his warmth. "Have you ever talked to anyone about this dream?"

"Just Mariko . . . and now you."

"I was thinking of a doctor."

"Psychiatrist?"

"It might help."

"He'd try to free me of the dream by discovering the cause of it," she said tensely.

"What's wrong with that?"

She huddled on the bench, silent, the image of despair.

"Joanna?"

"I don't want to know the cause."

"If it'll help cure—"

"I don't want to know," she said firmly.

"All right. But why not?"

She didn't answer.

"Joanna?"

"Knowing would destroy me."

Frowning, he said, "Destroy? How?"

"I can't explain . . . but I feel it."

"It's *not* knowing that's tearing you apart."

She was silent again. She withdrew her hand from his, rummaged in her purse for a handkerchief, and blew her nose.

After a while he said, "Okay, forget the psychiatrist. What do *you* suppose is the cause of the nightmare?"

She shrugged.

"You must have given it a lot of thought over the years."

"Thousands of hours," Joanna said bleakly.

"And? Not even one idea?"

"Alex, I'm tired. And still embarrassed. Can we just . . . not talk about it any more?"

"All right."

She cocked her head. "You'll really drop it that easily?"

"What right do I have to pry?"

She smiled thinly. It was her first smile since they had sat down, and it looked unnatural. "Shouldn't a private detective be pushy at a time like this, inquisitive, absolutely relentless?"

Although her question was meant to sound casual, flippant, Alex saw that she was genuinely afraid of him probing too far. "I'm not a private detective here. I'm not investigating you. I'm just a friend who's offering a shoulder if you feel like crying on one." As he spoke, a pang of guilt pierced him, because he actually *was* investigating her.

"Can we get a taxi?" she asked. "I'm not up to any more sightseeing."

"Sure."

She clung to his arm as they crossed the palace garden toward the *Kara-mon*, the ornate inner gate.

Overhead, a pair of crows wheeled against the somber sky, cawing as they dived and soared. With a dry flutter of wings, they settled into the exquisitely sculptured branches of a large bonsai pine.

Wanting to pursue the conversation but resigned to Joanna's silence, Alex was surprised when she suddenly began to talk about the nightmare again. Evidently, on some level and in spite of what she'd said, she *wanted* him to be an aggressive inquisitor, so she would have an excuse to tell him more.

"For a long time," she continued as they walked, "I've thought it's a symbolic dream, totally Freudian. I figured the mechanical hand and hypodermic syringe weren't what they seemed. You know? That they represented other things. I thought maybe the nightmare was symbolic of some real-life trauma that I couldn't face up to even when I was asleep. But . . ." She faltered. Her voice grew shaky on the last few words and then faded altogether.

"Go on," he said softly.

"A few minutes ago in the palace, when I saw that man with one hand . . . what scared me so much was . . . for the first time I realized the dream isn't symbolic at all. It's a memory. A memory that comes to me in sleep. It really happened."

"When?"

"I don't know."

"Where?"

"I don't know."

They passed the *Kara-mon*. No other tourists were in sight. Alex stopped Joanna in the space between the inner and outer gates of the castle. Even the nippy autumn breeze hadn't restored significant color to her cheeks. She was as white-faced as any powdered geisha.

"So somewhere in your past . . . there actually *was* a man with a mechanical hand?"

She nodded.

"And for reasons you don't understand, he used a hypodermic needle on you?"

"Yeah. And when I saw the Korean, something . . . snapped in me. I remembered the voice of the man in the dream. He just kept saying, 'Once more the needle, once more the needle,' over and over again."

"But you don't know who he was?"

"Or where or when or why. But I swear to God it happened. I'm not crazy. Something happened to me . . . was done to me . . . something I can't remember."

"Something you don't *want* to remember. That's what you said before."

She spoke in a whisper, as if afraid that the beast in her nightmare might hear her. "That man hurt me . . . did something to me that was . . . a sort of death. Worse than death."

Each whispered sibilant in her voice was like the hissing of an electrical current leaping in a bright blue arc across the tiny gap between two wires. Alex shivered.

Instinctively he opened his arms. She moved against him, and he held her.

A gust of wind passed through the trees with a sound like scarecrows on the march.

"I know it sounds . . . so bizarre," she said miserably. "A man with a mechanical hand, like a villain out of a comic book. But I swear, Alex—"

"I believe you."

Still in his embrace, she looked up. "You do?"

He watched her closely as he said, "Yes, I really do—Lisa."

She blinked. "What?"

"Lisa Chelgrin."

Puzzled, she slipped out of his arms, stepped back from him.

He waited, watched.

"Who's Lisa Chelgrin?" she asked.

He studied her.

"Alex?"

"I think maybe you honestly don't know."

"I don't."

"*You* are Lisa Chelgrin," he said.

He was intent upon catching any fleeting expression that might betray her, a brief glimpse of hidden knowledge, the look of the hunted in her eyes, or perhaps guilt expressed in briefly visible lines of tension at the corners of her mouth. She seemed genuinely perplexed. If Joanna Rand and the long-lost Lisa Chelgrin were one and the same—and Alex was certain now that she could be no one else—then all memory of her true identity had been scrubbed from her either by accident or by intent.

"Lisa Chelgrin?" She seemed dazed. "I don't get it."

"Neither do I."

"Who is she? What's the joke?"

"No joke. But it's a long story. Too long for me to tell it while we're standing here in the cold."

11 During the return trip to the Moonglow Lounge, Joanna huddled in one corner of the rear seat of the taxi while Alex told her who he thought she was. Her face remained blank. Her dark-blue eyes were guarded, and she would not look at him directly. He was unable to determine how his words were affecting her.

The driver didn't speak English. He hummed along softly with the music on a Sony Discman.

"Thomas Moore Chelgrin," Alex told Joanna. "Ring a bell?"

"No."

"Never heard of him?"

She shook her head.

"He's been a United States Senator from Illinois for almost fourteen years. Before that, he served two terms in the House of Representatives—a liberal on social issues, to the right on defense and foreign policy. He's well liked in Washington, primarily because he's a team player. And he throws some of the best shindigs in the capital, which makes him popular too. They're a bunch of partying fools in Washington. They appreciate a man who knows how to set a table and pour whiskey. Apparently Tom Chelgrin satisfies his constituents too, because they keep returning him to office with ever larger vote totals. I've never seen a more clever politician, and I hope I never do. He knows how to manipulate the voters—white, brown, black, Catholics and Protestants and Jews and atheists, young and old, right and left. Out of six times at bat, he's lost only one election, and that was his first. He's an imposing man—tall, lean, with the trained voice of an actor. His hair turned silver when he was in his early thirties, and his opponents attribute his success to the fact that he *looks* like a senator. That's damned cynical, and it's a simplification, but there's some truth in it."

When Alex paused, waiting for her reaction, she only said, "Go on."

"Can you place him yet?"

"I never met him."

"I think you know him as well as anyone."

"Not me."

The cabdriver tried to speed through a changing traffic signal, decided not to risk it after all, and tramped on the brakes. When the car stopped rocking, he glanced at Alex in the rearview mirror, grinned disarmingly, and apologized: *"Gomen-nasai, jokyaku-san."*

Alex inclined his head respectfully and said, *"Yoroshii desu. Karedomo . . . untenshu-san yukkuri."*

The driver nodded vigorously in agreement. *"Hai."* Henceforth he would go slowly, as requested.

Alex turned to Joanna. "When Tom Chelgrin was thirteen, his father died. The family already had been on the edge of poverty, and now they plunged all the way in. Tom worked through high school and college, earned a degree in business. In his early twenties, he was drafted into the army, wound up in Vietnam. While on a search-and-destroy mission, he was taken prisoner by the Viet Cong. Do you know anything about what happened to our POWs during that war?"

"Not much. Not really."

"During World Wars One and Two, nearly all our POWs had been stubborn in captivity, difficult to contain. They conspired against their keepers, resisted, engineered elaborate escapes. Starting with the Korean War, all that changed. With brutal physical torture and sophisticated brainwashing, by applying continuous psychological stress, the Communists broke their spirit. Not many attempted to escape, and those who actually got away can just about be counted on my fingers. It was the same in Vietnam. If anything, the torture our POWs were subjected to was worse than in Korea. But Chelgrin was one of the few who refused to be passive, cooperative. After fourteen months in captivity, he escaped, made it back to friendly territory. *Time* devoted a cover story to him, and he wrote a successful book about his adventures. He ran for office a few years later, and he milked his service record for every vote it was worth."

"I've never heard of him," Joanna insisted.

As the taxi moved through the heavy traffic on Horikawa Street, Alex said, "When Tom Chelgrin got out of the army, he met a girl, got married, and fathered a child. His mother had died while he was in that North Vietnamese prison camp, and he'd inherited seventy-five or eighty thousand dollars after taxes, which was a good chunk in those pre-inflation days. He put that money with his book earnings and whatever he could borrow, and he purchased a Honda dealership. Soon it seemed like half the people in the country were driving Japanese cars, especially Hondas. Tom added three more dealerships, got into other businesses, and became a rich man. He did a lot of charity work, earned a reputation as a humanitarian in his community, and finally campaigned for a congressional seat. He lost the first time, but came back two years later and won. Won again. And then moved on to the U.S. Senate, where he's been since—"

Joanna interrupted him. "What about the name you used, what you called me?"

"Lisa Chelgrin."

"How's she fit in?"

"She was Thomas Chelgrin's only child."

Joanna's eyes widened. Again, Alex was unable to detect any deception in her response. With genuine surprise, she said, "You think I'm this man's *daughter?*"

"I believe there's a chance you might be."

"Are you crazy?"

"Am I?"

"I'm beginning to wonder," she said.

"Considering the—"

"I *know* whose daughter I am, for God's sake."

"Do you?"

"Of course. Robert and Elizabeth Rand were my parents."

"And they died in an accident near Brighton," he said.

"Yes. A long time ago."

"And you've no living relatives."

"So?"

"Convenient, don't you think?"

"Why would I lie to you?" she asked, not just baffled by his peculiar conviction that she was living under a false identity but increasingly angered by it. "I'm not a liar."

The driver clearly sensed the antagonism in her voice. He glanced at them in the rearview mirror, and then he looked straight ahead, humming a bit louder than the music on the Sony Discman, too polite to eavesdrop even when he didn't understand the language that they were speaking.

"I'm not calling you a liar," Alex said quietly.

"That's sure what I'm hearing."

"You're overreacting."

"The hell I am. This is weird."

"I agree. It is weird. Your repeating nightmare, your reaction to the Korean with one hand, your resemblance to Lisa Chelgrin. It's definitely weird."

She didn't reply, just glared at him.

"Maybe you're afraid of what I'm leading up to."

"I'm not afraid of you," she said curtly.

"Then what *are* you afraid of?"

"What are you accusing me of?"

"Joanna, I'm not accusing you of anything. I'm only—"

"I feel like you *are* accusing me, and I don't like it. I don't understand it, and I don't like it. All right?"

She looked away from him and out the side window at the cars and cyclists on Shijo Street.

For a moment Alex was silent, but then he continued as if her outburst had never occurred. "One night in July, more than twelve years ago, the summer after Lisa Chelgrin's junior year at Georgetown University, she vanished from her father's vacation villa in Jamaica. Someone got into her bedroom through an unlocked window. Although there were signs of a struggle, even a few smears of her blood on the bedclothes and one windowsill, no one in the house heard her scream. Clearly, she'd been kidnapped, but no ransom demand was received. The police believed she'd been abducted and murdered. A sex maniac, they said. On the other hand, they weren't able to find her body, so they couldn't just assume she was dead. At least not right away, not until they went through the motions of an exhaustive search. After three weeks, Chelgrin lost all confidence in the island police—which he should have done the second day he had to deal with them. Because he was from the Chicago area, because a friend of his had used my company and recommended me, Chelgrin asked me to fly to Jamaica to look for Lisa—even though Bonner-Hunter was still a relatively small company back then and I was just turning thirty. My people worked on the case for ten months before Tom Chelgrin gave up. We used eight damned good men full time and hired as many Jamaicans to do a lot of footwork. It was an expensive deal for the senator, but he didn't care. Still . . . it wouldn't have mattered if we'd had ten thousand men on the case. It was a perfect crime. It's one of only two major investigations that we've failed to wrap up successfully since I took over the business."

The taxi swung around another corner. The Moonglow Lounge stood half a block ahead.

Joanna finally spoke again, although she still wouldn't look at him. "But why do you think I'm Lisa Chelgrin?"

"Lots of reasons. For one thing, you're the same age she'd be if she were still alive. More important, you're a dead ringer for her, just twelve years older."

Frowning, she looked at him at last. "Do you have a photograph of her?"

"Not on me. But I'll get one."

The taxi slowed, pulled to the curb, and stopped in front of the Moonglow Lounge. The driver switched off the meter, opened his door, and got out.

"When you have a photo," Joanna said, "I'd like to see it." She shook hands with him as if they'd experienced nothing more together than a pleasant business lunch. "Thanks for lunch. Sorry I spoiled the sightseeing."

Alex realized that she was dismissing him. "Can't we have a drink and—"

"I don't feel well," she said.

The cabdriver opened her door, and she started to get out.

Alex held on to her hand, forcing her to look at him again. "Joanna, we have a lot to talk about. We—"

"Maybe later."

"Aren't you still curious, for God's sake?"

"Not nearly as curious as I am ill. Queasy stomach, headache. It must be something I ate. Or maybe all the excitement."

"Do you want a doctor?"

"I just need to lie down a while."

"When *can* we talk." He sensed a widening gulf between them that had not existed a few minutes ago. "Tonight? Between shows?"

"Yes. We can chat then."

"Promise?"

"Really, Alex, the poor driver will catch pneumonia if he stands there holding the door for me any longer. It's gotten fifteen degrees colder since lunch."

Reluctantly he let go of her.

As she got out of the taxi, a blast of frigid air rushed past her and struck Alex in the face.

12

Joanna felt threatened.

She was overcome by the unshakable conviction that her every move was being watched and recorded.

She locked the door of her apartment. She went into the bedroom and latched that door as well.

For a minute she stood in the center of the room, listening. Then she poured a double brandy from a crystal decanter, drank it quickly, poured another shot, and put the snifter on the nightstand.

The room was too warm.

Stifling. Tropical.

She was sweating.

Each breath seemed to scorch her lungs.

She opened a window two inches to let in a cold draft, took off her clothes, and stretched out nude atop the silk bedspread.

Nevertheless, she still felt that she was smothering. Her pulse raced. She was dizzy. The room began to move around her as if the bed had become a slowly revolving carousel. She experienced a series of mild hallucinations too, none new to her, images that had been a part of other days and moods like the one that now gripped her. The ceiling appeared to descend between the walls, like the ceiling of an execution chamber in one of those corny old Tarzan movie serials. And the mattress, which she'd chosen for its firmness, suddenly softened to her touch, not in reality but in her mind: It became marshmallowy, gradually closing around her, relentlessly engulfing her, as though it were a living, amoeboid creature.

Imagination. Nothing to fear.

Gritting her teeth, fisting her hands, she strained to suppress all sensations that she knew to be false. But they were beyond her control.

She shut her eyes—but then opened them at once, suffocated and terrified by the brief self-imposed darkness.

She was dismayingly familiar with that peculiar state of mind, those emotions, that unfocused dread. She suffered the same terrors every time that she allowed a friendship to develop into more than a casual relationship, every time that she traveled beyond mere desire and approached the special intimacy of love. The panic attacks had just begun sooner this time, much sooner than usual. She desired Alex Hunter, but she didn't love him. Not yet. She hadn't known him long enough to feel more than strong affection. A bond was forming between them, however, and she sensed that their relationship would be special, that it would evolve far faster than usual—which was sufficient to trigger the anguish that had washed like a dark tide over her. And now events, people, inanimate objects, and the very air itself seemed to acquire evil purpose that was focused upon her. She felt a malevolent pressure, squeezing her from all sides, like a vast weight of water, as though she had sunk to the bottom of a deep sea. Already it was unbearable. The pressure would not relent until she turned forever from Alex Hunter and put behind her any danger of emotional intimacy. Intense fear lay dormant in her at all times; now it had been translated into a physical power that squeezed all hope out of her. She knew how it would have to end. She needed to break off the relationship that sparked her claustrophobia; only then would she obtain relief from the crushing, closed-in, listened-to, watched-over feeling that made her heart pound painfully against her ribs.

She would never see Alex Hunter again.

He would come to the Moonglow, of course. Tonight. Maybe other nights. He would sit through both performances.

Until the man left Kyoto, however, Joanna would not mingle with the audience between shows.

He'd telephone. She'd hang up.

If he came around to visit in the afternoon, she would be unavailable.

If he wrote to her, she would throw his letters in the trash without reading them.

Joanna could be cruel. She'd had plenty of experience with other men when simple attraction had threatened to develop into something deeper . . . and more dangerous.

The decision to freeze Alex out of her life had a markedly beneficial effect on her. Almost imperceptibly at first, but then more rapidly, the immobilizing fear diminished. The bedroom grew steadily cooler, and the sweat began to dry on her naked body. The humid air became less oppressive, breathable. The ceiling rose to its proper height, and the mattress beneath her grew firm once more.

13 The Kyoto Hotel, the largest first-class hotel in the city, was Western style in most regards, and the telephones in Alex's suite featured beeping-flashing message indicators, which were signaling him when he returned from the eventful afternoon with Joanna Rand. He called the operator for messages, certain that Joanna had phoned during his trip from the Moonglow to the hotel.

But it wasn't Joanna. The front desk was holding a fax for him. At his request a bellhop brought it to the suite.

Alex exchanged polite greetings and bows with the man, accepted the cable, tipped him, and went through the bowing again. When he was alone, he sat at the drawing-room desk and tore open the flimsy envelope. The message was from Ted Blankenship in Chicago, on Bonner-Hunter letterhead:

Courier arrives at your hotel noon Thursday, your time.

By noon tomorrow Alex would have the complete Chelgrin file, which had been closed for more than ten years but which definitely had now been reopened. In addition to hundreds of field-agent reports and meticulously transcribed interviews, the file contained several excellent photographs of Lisa that had been taken just days before she disappeared. Perhaps those pictures would shock Joanna out of her eerie detachment.

Alex thought of her as she had been when she'd gotten out of the taxi a short while ago, and he wondered why she'd so suddenly turned cold toward him. If she was Lisa Chelgrin, she didn't seem to know it. Yet she acted like a woman with dangerous secrets and a sordid past to hide.

He suspected that amnesia was the explanation for her situation—perhaps the result of a head injury or even psychological trauma. Of course, amnesia didn't explain where and why she had come up with an alternate past history.

He looked at his watch: 4:30.

At six-thirty he would take his nightly stroll through the bustling Gion district to the Moonglow Lounge for drinks and dinner—and for that important conversation with Joanna. He had time for a leisurely soak in the tub, and he looked forward to balancing the steamy heat with sips of cold beer.

After fetching an ice-cold bottle of Asahi from the softly humming bar refrigerator, he left the drawing room and went halfway across the bedroom before he stopped dead, aware that something was wrong. He surveyed his surroundings, tense, baffled. The chambermaid had straightened the pile of paperbacks, magazines, and newspapers on the dresser, and she'd remade the bed while he'd been gone. The drapes were open; he preferred to keep them drawn. What else? He couldn't see anything out of the ordinary—and certainly nothing sinister. But something was wrong. Call it intuition: He'd experienced it before, and usually he'd found it worth heeding.

Alex set the bottle of Asahi on the vanity bench and approached the bathroom with caution. He put his left hand against the heavy swinging door, listened, heard nothing, hesitated, then pushed the door inward and stepped quickly across the threshold.

The late-afternoon sun pierced a frosted window high in one wall, and the bathroom glowed with golden light. He was alone.

This time his sixth sense had misled him. A false alarm. He felt slightly foolish.

He was jumpy. And no wonder. Although lunch with Joanna had been immensely enjoyable, the rest of the day had been a grinding emery wheel that had put a sharp edge on his nerves: her irrational flight from the Korean at Nijo Castle; her description of the oft-repeated nightmare; and his growing belief that the unexplained disappearance of Lisa Jean Chelgrin had been an event with powerful causes and effects, with layers of complex and mysterious meaning that went far deeper than anything that he had uncovered or even imagined at the time it had happened. He had a right to be jumpy.

Alex stripped off his shirt and put it in the laundry bag. He brought a magazine and the bottle of beer from the other room and put them on a low utility table that he had moved next to the bath. He bent down at the tub, turned on the water, adjusted the temperature.

In the bedroom again, he went to the walk-in closet to choose a suit for the evening. The door was ajar. As Alex pulled it open, a man leapt at him from the darkness beyond. *Dorobo*. A burglar. The guy was Japanese, short, stocky, muscular, very quick. He swung a fistful of wire shirt hangers. The bristling cluster of hooked ends struck Alex in the face, could have blinded him, and he cried out, but the hangers spared his sight, stung one cheek, and rained around him in a burst of dissonant music.

Counting on the element of surprise, the stranger tried to push past Alex to the bedroom door, but Alex clutched the guy's jacket and spun him around. Unbalanced, they fell against the side of the bed, then to the floor, with the intruder on top.

Alex took a punch in the ribs, another, and a punch in the face. He wasn't in a good position to use his own fists, but he heaved hard enough to pitch off his assailant.

The stranger rolled into the vanity bench and knocked it over. Cursing continuously in Japanese, he scrambled to his feet.

Still on the floor, dazed only for an instant, Alex seized the intruder's ankle. The stocky man toppled to the floor, kicking as he fell. Alex howled as a kick caught his left elbow. Sharp pain crackled the length of his arm and brought a stinging flood of tears to his eyes.

The Japanese was on his feet again, moving through the open doorway, into the drawing room, toward the suite's entrance foyer.

Blinking away the involuntary tears that blurred his vision, Alex got up, staggered to the doorway. In the drawing room, when he saw that he couldn't reach the intruder in time to prevent him from getting to the hotel corridor, he plucked a vase from a decorative pedestal and threw it with anger and accuracy. The heavy ceramic exploded against the back of the *dorobo's* skull, instantly dropping him to his knees, and Alex slipped past him to block the only exit.

They were breathing like long-distance runners.

Shaking his head, flicking shards of the vase from his broad shoulders, the *dorobo* got up. He glared at Alex and motioned for him to move away from the door. "Don't be a hero," he said in heavily accented English.

"What're you doing here?" Alex demanded.

"Get out of my way."

"What are you doing here? A *dorobo*? No. You're more than just a cheap burglar, aren't you?"

The stranger said nothing.

"It's the Chelgrin case, isn't it?"

"Move."

"Who's your boss?" Alex asked.

The intruder balled his chunky hands into formidable fists and advanced a single threatening step.

Alex refused to stand aside.

The *dorobo* withdrew a bone-handled switchblade from a jacket pocket. He touched a button on the handle, and faster than the eye could follow, a seven-inch blade popped into sight. "Move."

Alex licked his lips. His mouth was dry. While he considered his alternatives—none appealing—he divided his attention between the man's hard black eyes and the point of the blade.

Thinking he sensed fear and imminent surrender, the stranger waved the knife and smiled.

"It's not going to be that easy," Alex said.

"I can break you."

At first glance, the intruder seemed soft, out of shape. On closer inspection, however, Alex realized that the guy was iron hard beneath the masking layer of fat. A sumo wrestler had the same look in the early days of training, before attaining his gross physique.

Brandishing the switchblade again, the intruder said, "Move."

"Are you familiar with the English expression 'Fuck you'?"

The stranger moved faster than any man Alex had ever seen, as fluid as a dancer in spite of his bulk. Alex clutched the thick wrist of the knife hand, but with the amazing dexterity of a magician, the *dorobo* tossed the weapon from one hand to the other—and struck. The cold blade sliced smoothly, lightly along the underside of Alex's left arm, which still tingled from being kicked.

The stocky intruder stepped back as abruptly as he had attacked. "Gave you just a scratch, Mr. Hunter."

The blade had skipped across the flesh: Two wounds glistened, thin and scarlet, the first about three inches long, the other marginally longer. Alex stared at the shallow cuts as if they had opened utterly without cause, miraculous stigmata. Blood oozed down his arm, trickled into his hand, dripped from his fingertips, but it didn't spurt; no major artery or vein was violated, and the flow was stanchable.

He was badly shaken by the lightning-swift attack. It had happened so fast that he still hadn't begun to feel any pain.

"Won't require stitches," the stranger said. "But if you make me cut again . . . no promises next time."

"There won't be a next time," Alex said. He found it difficult to admit defeat, but he wasn't a fool. "You're too good."

The intruder smiled like a malevolent Buddha. "Go across the room. Sit on the couch."

Alex did as instructed, cradling his bloodied arm and thinking furiously, hoping to come up with a wonderful trick that would turn defeat into triumph. But he wasn't a sorcerer. There was nothing he could do.

The burglar remained in the foyer until Alex was seated. Then he left, slamming the door behind him.

The instant he was alone, Alex sprinted to the telephone on the desk. He punched the single number for hotel security. He changed his mind, however, and hung up before anyone answered.

Hotel security would call in the police. He didn't want the cops involved. Not yet. Maybe never.

He went to the door and locked the deadbolt. He also braced the door shut by jamming the straight-backed desk chair at an angle under the knob.

Hugging himself with his injured arm so the blood would soak into his undershirt instead of dripping on the carpet, he went into the bathroom. He shut off the taps just as the water was about to overflow the tub, and he opened the drain.

The bastard hadn't been a burglar. No way. He was someone—or worked for someone—who was worried that Alex would uncover the truth about Joanna, someone who wanted the suite searched for evidence that Alex had already made the link between the singer and the long-lost girl.

The knife wounds were beginning to burn and throb. He hugged himself harder, attempting to stop or slow the bleeding by applying direct pressure to the cuts. The entire front and side of his undershirt were crimson.

He sat on the edge of the tub.

Perspiration seeped into the corners of his eyes, making him blink. He wiped his forehead with a washcloth. He was thirsty. He picked up the bottle of Asahi beer and chugged a third of it.

The knife man was working for people with good connections. International connections. They might even have a man planted in the Chicago office. How else had they managed to put someone on his ass so soon after he had spoken on the phone with Blankenship?

The tub was half empty. He turned on the cold water.

More likely than a plant in Chicago: His hotel phone must be tapped. He had probably been followed since he'd arrived in Kyoto.

Gingerly he moved his arm, held it away from his chest. Although the wounds continued to bleed freely, they weren't serious enough to require a doctor's attention. He hadn't any desire to explain the injury to anyone other than Joanna.

The burning-stinging had grown worse, intolerable. He plunged his arm under the cold water that foamed out of the faucet. Relief was instantaneous, and he sat for a couple of minutes, just thinking.

The first time he'd seen Joanna Rand at the Moonglow, when he'd first suspected that she might be Lisa Chelgrin, he'd figured that she must have engineered her own kidnapping in Jamaica, twelve years ago. He couldn't imagine *why* she would have done such a thing, but his years as a detective had taught him that people committed drastic acts for the thinnest and strangest reasons. Sometimes they hurtled off the rails in a simple quest for freedom or new thrills or self-destruction. They sought change for the sake of change, for better or worse.

After talking to Joanna, however, he'd known she wasn't one of those reckless types. Besides, it was ludicrous to suppose that she could have planned her own abduction and confused Bonner-Hunter's best investigators, especially when, at that time, she had been an inexperienced college girl.

He considered amnesia again, but that was as unsatisfying as the other explanations. As an amnesiac, she might have forgotten every detail of her previous life, but she would not have fabricated and come to believe a completely false set of memories in order to fill the gap, which was precisely what Joanna seemed to have done.

Okay, she was not consciously deceiving anyone, and she was not an amnesiac, at least not in the classic sense. What possibilities were left?

He withdrew his arm from the cold water. The flow of blood had been reduced. He wrapped the arm tightly in a towel. Eventually blood would seep through, but as a temporary bandage, the towel was adequate.

He returned to the drawing room and telephoned the bell captain in the hotel lobby. He asked for a bottle of rubbing alcohol, a bottle of Mercurochrome, a box of gauze pads, a roll of gauze, and adhesive tape. "If the man who brings it is fast, there'll be an especially generous tip for him."

The bell captain said, "If there's been an accident, we have a house doctor who—"

"Only a minor accident. No need for a doctor, thank you. Just those items I requested."

While he waited for the bandages and antiseptics, Alex made himself presentable. In the bathroom, he stripped out of his blood-drenched undershirt, scrubbed his chest with the washcloth, and combed his hair.

The worst of the stinging pain in the wounds had subsided to a pounding but tolerable ache. The arm was stiff, as if undergoing a medusan metamorphosis: flesh into stone.

In the drawing room, he picked up most of the shattered vase and dropped the pieces in the wastebasket. He took the straight-backed chair from under the doorknob and returned it to the desk.

Blood was beginning to work through the layers of the towel that was wrapped around his arm.

He sat at the desk to wait for the bellhop, and the room seemed to move slowly around him.

If he ruled out deception and classic amnesia, he was left with only one credible explanation for Joanna's condition: brainwashing.

"Crazy," he said aloud.

With drugs, hypnosis, and subliminal reeducation, they could have wiped her mind clean. Absolutely spotless. Actually, he was not a hundred percent certain that such a thing was possible, but he thought it was a good bet. The modern menu of psychological-conditioning and brainwashing techniques was far more extensive than it had been in the Korean or Vietnam wars. In the past ten years there had been truly amazing advances in those areas of research—psychopharmacology, biochemistry, psychosurgery, clinical psychology—that directly and indirectly contributed to the less reputable but nonetheless hotly pursued science of mind control.

He hoped that something far less severe had been done to Lisa. If the complete eradication of a life-set of memories still eluded modern science, then the girl's kidnappers might have been able to do no more than repress her original personality. In which case, Lisa might still be buried deep beneath the Joanna cover, missing but not gone forever. She might still be reached, resurrected, and helped to remember the circumstances of her premature burial.

In either case, the kidnappers had stuffed her full of fake memories. They had provided her with phony identification and turned her loose in Japan with a substantial bankroll that had supposedly come from the settlement of her make-believe father's estate.

But for God's sake, *why?*

Alex got to his feet and paced nervously. His legs felt more rubbery with every step.

Who could have done it to her? Why? And why were they still interested in her?

He had no idea what the stakes of the game might be. If they thought it was important enough to keep Joanna's true identity a secret, they might kill him if he was on the verge of proving who she really was. Indeed, if he managed to convince Joanna of the truth, they might even kill *her* to keep the whole story from being revealed.

Regardless of the risk, he was determined to have the answers that he wanted. His rooms had been searched, and he had been cut. He owed these people a measure of humiliation and pain.

14

West of Kyoto, the last light of day gradually faded like the glow in a bank of dying embers. The city smoldered into evening under an ash-colored sky.

The streets of the Gion district were crowded. In the bars, clubs, restaurants, and geisha houses, another night of escape from reality had begun.

On his way to the Moonglow Lounge, immaculately dressed in a charcoal-gray suit, matching vest, pale-gray shirt, and green tie, with a gray topcoat thrown capelike across his shoulders, Alex walked at a tourist's pace. Although he pretended to be engrossed by the passing scene, he paid scant attention to the whirl of color and activity on all sides. Instead, he was trying to learn if the opposition had put a tail on him. In the busy throng that hurried over the washed-stone pavement, Alex had difficulty detecting any one person who might have been following him. Every time he turned a corner or stopped at a crosswalk, he glanced casually behind, as if taking a second look at some landmark of the Gion, and without appearing to do so, he studied the people in his wake.

Eventually he grew suspicious of three men, each walking alone, each caught watching him at one point or another, each remaining behind him block after block. The first was a fat man with deeply set eyes, enormous jowls, and a wispy chin beard. His size made him the least likely of the three candidates, because he was highly visible; this was a line of work that favored nondescript men. The second suspect was slender, in his forties, with a narrow, bony face. The third was young, perhaps twenty-five, dressed in blue jeans and a yellow nylon windbreaker; as he walked, he puffed nervously on a cigarette. By the time Alex reached the Moonglow Lounge, he still hadn't decided which of the three men was tailing him, but he had committed every detail of their faces to memory for future reference.

Just inside the front door of Moonglow, an easel supported a yard-square posterboard sign. The red-and-black announcement was neatly handprinted, first in Japanese characters and then in English.

DUE TO ILLNESS
JOANNA RAND
WILL NOT PERFORM TONIGHT

THE MOONGLOW ORCHESTRA
WILL PROVIDE MUSIC FOR DANCING

Alex left his topcoat with the hat-check girl and went to the bar for a drink. The restaurant was doing a lot of business, but only six customers were in the lounge. He sat alone at the curved end of the bar and ordered Old Suntory. When the bartender brought the whiskey, Alex said, "I hope Miss Rand's illness isn't serious."

"Not serious," the bartender assured him in heavily accented English. "Only sore throat."

"Would you please call upstairs and tell her that Alex Hunter is here?"

"Too sick see anyone," the man said, nodding and smiling.

"I'm a friend."

"Much too sick."

"She'll talk to me."

"Sore throat."

"We have an appointment."

"So sorry."

They went around and around for a while, until the bartender finally surrendered and picked up a phone beside the cash register. As he spoke with Joanna, he glanced repeatedly at Alex. When he hung up and returned to Alex, he said, "Sorry. She say can't see you."

"You must be mistaken. Call her again, please."

The bartender was clearly embarrassed for him. "She say don't know anyone name Alex Hunter."

"But she does."

The bartender said nothing.

"We had lunch together," Alex said.

The man shrugged.

"Just this afternoon."

A pained smile. And: "So sorry."

A customer asked for service at the far end of the bar, and the bartender hurried away with obvious relief.

Alex stared at his reflection in the bluish bar mirror. He sipped the Old Suntory.

Softly he said, "What the hell's going on here?"

15

When Alex asked for Mariko Inamura, the bartender was at first no more inclined to cooperate than when he'd been asked to put in a call to Joanna. At last, however, he relented and summoned Mariko on the house phone.

A few minutes later she entered the lounge through a door marked PRIVATE. She was Joanna's age and quite lovely. Her thick black hair was held up with ivory pins.

Alex stood and bowed to her.

After she returned the bow, they introduced themselves, and she sat on the stool next to his.

As he sat again, he said, "Mariko-san, I've heard many good things about you."

"Likewise, Mr. Hunter." Her English was flawless. She didn't have the slightest difficulty pronouncing the L sound, which had no equivalent in her native tongue.

"How's Joanna?"

"She has a sore throat."

He sipped his whiskey. "Excuse me if I act like a stereotypical American. I don't mean to be blunt and boorish, but I wonder if that is really the truth—that story about a sore throat."

Mariko was silent. She looked away from him, down at her hands.

Alex said, "Joanna told the bartender she didn't know anyone named Alex Hunter."

Mariko sighed.

"What's wrong here, Mariko-san?"

"She spoke so well of you. She was like a young girl. I began to hope it would be different this time."

"What's wrong with her?"

Mariko continued to stare at the polished bartop in front of her and said nothing. The Japanese had a highly developed sense of propriety, a complex system of social graces, and a very rigid set of standards concerning the conduct of personal relationships. She was reluctant to talk about her friend, for in doing so, she would not be conducting herself according to those standards.

"I already know about the bad dream she has every night," Alex prodded gently.

Mariko was clearly surprised. "Joanna's never told anyone about that—except me."

"And now me."

She glanced at Alex, and he saw a greater warmth in her coal-colored eyes than he'd seen a minute ago. Nevertheless, to stall, she signaled the bartender and ordered Old Suntory over ice.

Alex sensed that Mariko was basically conservative and old-fashioned. She couldn't easily overcome the traditional Japanese respect for other people's privacy.

When her drink came, she sipped it slowly, rattled the ice in the glass, and at last said, "If Joanna's told you about her nightmare, then she's probably told you as much about herself as she ever tells anyone."

"She's secretive?"

"Not that, exactly."

"Modest?"

"That's part of it. But only part. It's also as if . . . as if she's afraid to talk about herself too much."

He watched Mariko closely. "Afraid? What do you mean?"

"I can't explain it . . ."

He waited, aware that she had capitulated. She needed a moment to decide where to begin.

After another sip of Old Suntory, she said, "What Joanna did to you tonight . . . pretending not to know you . . . this isn't the first time she's behaved that way."

"It doesn't seem to be her style."

"Every time she does it, I'm shocked. It's out of character. She's really the sweetest, kindest person. Yet, whenever she begins to feel close to a man, when she begins perhaps to fall in love with him—or he with her—she kills the romance. And she's never nice about it. A different woman. Almost . . . mean. Cold."

"But I don't see how that applies to me. We've only had one date, an innocent lunch together."

Mariko nodded solemnly. "But she's fallen for you. Fast."

"No. You're wrong about that."

"Just before you came on the scene, she was deeply depressed."

"She didn't seem that way to me."

"That's what I mean. You had an instant effect on her. She's always in bad shape for a few weeks or even months after she drops someone she cares for, but recently she'd reached new lows. She felt so alone, lost. You lifted her spirits overnight."

"If she's really so lonely . . . why does she keep destroying every relationship?"

"She never wants to. But she seems compelled to shatter every hope of companionship."

"Has she tried therapy?"

Mariko frowned. "My uncle's a fine psychologist. I've urged her to see him about this and the nightmare, but she refuses. I worry about her all the time. At its deepest and blackest, her depression is contagious. It infects me at times, a little. If she didn't need me and if I didn't care for her so much, like my own sister, I'd have left long ago. She needs to share her life with friends, a partner. The last few months she's pushed people away harder than usual, even me to some extent. In fact, it's been so bad I'd just about decided to get out no matter what—and then you came along. Her immediate reaction to you was . . . Well, this time it seemed as if she might overcome her fear and form something permanent."

Alex shifted on the bar stool. "Mariko-san, you're making me uneasy. You're seeing a lot more in this relationship than there really is. She doesn't love me, for heaven's sake. Love doesn't happen this fast."

"Don't you believe in love at first sight?"

"That's a poet's conceit."

"I think it can happen," she demurred.

"Good luck. Fact is, I don't think I believe in love at all, much less in love at first sight."

She regarded him with amazement. "Not believe in love? Then what do you call it when a man and woman—"

"I call it lust—"

"Not just that."

"—and affection, mutual dependence, sometimes even temporary insanity."

"That's all you've ever felt? I don't believe it."

He shrugged. "It's true."

"Love is the only thing we can depend on in this world. To deny that it exists—"

"Love is the *last* thing we can depend on. People say they're in love. But it never lasts. The only constants are death and taxes."

"Some men don't work," Mariko said, "therefore, they pay no taxes. And there are many wise men who believe in life everlasting."

He opened his mouth to argue but grinned instead. "I have a hunch you're a natural-born debater. I'd better stop while I'm only slightly behind."

"What about Joanna?" she asked. "Don't you care for her?"

"Yes, of course, I do."

"But you don't believe in love."

"I *like* Joanna enormously. But as for love—"

Mariko raised one hand to silence him. "I'm sorry. This is rude of me. You've no reason to reveal so much of yourself."

"If I didn't want to talk, you couldn't pry a word out of me."

"I just wanted you to know that regardless of what you feel for her, Joanna is drawn to you. Strongly. Perhaps it's even love. That's why she rejected you so bluntly—because she's afraid of such a deep commitment."

As Mariko drank the last of her whiskey and got up to leave, Alex said, "Wait. I've got to see her."

"Why?"

"Because . . . I've got to."

"Lust, I suppose."

"Maybe."

"Not love, of course."

He said nothing.

"Because you don't believe in love," she said.

He nodded.

Mariko smiled knowingly.

Alex didn't want to explain about Lisa Chelgrin, so he let Mariko think that, after all, he felt more for Joanna than he was willing to admit. "It's important, Mariko-san."

"Come back tomorrow night. Joanna can't take off work forever."

"Won't you just go upstairs now and persuade her to see me?"

"It wouldn't help. She's at her worst just after she's broken off with someone. When she's in this mood, she won't listen to me or anyone."

"I'll be back tomorrow."

"She'll be cold to you."

He smiled weakly. "I'll charm her."

"Other good men have given up."

"I won't."

Mariko put one hand on his arm. "Pursue her, Alex-san. I think you need her every bit as much as she needs you."

She walked away from him and disappeared through the door marked PRIVATE.

For a while after she left, Alex stared at himself in the blue mirror behind the bar.

The Moonglow orchestra played dance music. A Glenn Miller tune. The legendary Miller was long dead. Lost in a mysterious plane crash in World War II. His body had never been found.

Sometimes people vanish. The world goes on.

16

Alex was surprised by his reaction to Joanna's rejection. He had the irrational urge to punch someone, anyone, and to pitch his whiskey glass at the bar mirror.

He restrained himself but only because surrender to the urge would be an admission of how powerfully this woman affected him. He'd always thought that he was immune to the sickness of romance. Now he was uneasy about his response to her—and as yet unwilling to think seriously about it.

He ate a light dinner at the Moonglow and left before the orchestra had finished its first set of the evening. The brassy, bouncy music—"A String of Pearls"—followed him into the street.

The sun had abandoned Kyoto. The city gave forth its own cold, electric illumination. With the arrival of darkness, the temperature had plummeted below freezing. Fat snowflakes circled lazily through the light from windows, open doors, neon signs, and passing cars, but they melted upon contact with the pavement, where the same lights were reflected in a skin of icy water.

Instead of putting on his topcoat, Alex draped it capelike over his shoulders. He could foresee several circumstances in which he might wish to be quickly free of such a bulky, encumbering garment.

Standing outside the Moonglow Lounge, he looked around as if deciding where to go next. In seconds, he spotted one of the three men who had appeared to be following him earlier in the evening.

The gaunt, middle-aged Japanese with a narrow face and prominent cheekbones waited thirty yards away, in front of a neon-emblazoned nightclub called Serene Dragon. Coat collar turned up, shoulders hunched against the wintry wind, he tried to blend with the pleasure-seekers streaming through the Gion, but his furtive manner made him conspicuous.

Smiling, pretending to be unaware of being watched, Alex considered the possibilities. He could take an uneventful stroll to the Kyoto Hotel, return to his suite, and go to bed for the night—still buzzing with energy, tied in knots of frustration, and none the wiser about the people behind the Chelgrin kidnapping. Or he could have some fun with the man who had him under surveillance.

The choice was easy.

Whistling happily, Alex walked deeper into the glittering Gion. After five minutes, having changed streets twice, he glanced behind and saw the operative following at a discreet distance.

In spite of the rising wind and shatters of snowflakes, the streets were still busy. Sometimes the nightlife in Kyoto seemed too frantic for Japan—perhaps because it was squeezed into fewer hours than in Tokyo and most Western cities. The nightclubs opened in late afternoon and usually closed by eleven-thirty. The two million residents of Kyoto had the provincial habit of going to bed before midnight. Already, by their schedule, half the night was gone, and they were in a rush to enjoy themselves.

Alex was fascinated by the Gion: a complex maze of streets, alleys, winding passages, and covered footpaths, all crowded with nightclubs, bars, craft shops, short-time hotels, sedate inns, restaurants, public baths, temples, movie theaters, shrines, snack shops, geisha houses. The larger streets were noisy, exciting, garish, ablaze with rainbow neon that was reflected and refracted in acres of glass, polished steel, and plastic. Here, the wholesale adoption of the worst elements of Western style proved that not *all* of the Japanese possessed the good taste and highly refined sense of design for which the country was noted. In many alleyways and cobbled lanes, however, a more appealing Gion flourished. Off major thoroughfares, pockets of traditional architecture survived: houses that still served as homes, as well as old-style houses that had been transformed into expensive spas, restaurants, bars, or intimate cabarets; and all shared the time-honored construction of satiny, weather-smoothed woods and polished stones and heavy bronze or ironwork.

Alex walked the backstreets, thinking furiously, searching for an opportunity to play turnabout with the man who was tailing him.

The tail also assumed the role of a tourist. He did his phony window-shopping half a block behind Alex and, amusingly, in perfect harmony with him.

Of course, the guy might be more than merely a hired shadow. If Joanna was really Senator Tom Chelgrin's daughter, the stakes in this mysterious game were likely to be so high that the rules might allow murder.

Finally, seeking respite from the chill wind, Alex went into a bar and ordered sake. He drank several small cups of the hot brew, and when he went outside again, the gaunt man was waiting, a shadow among shadows, twenty yards away.

Fewer people were on the street than when Alex had gone into the bar, but the Gion was still far too busy for the stranger to risk an assault—if, in fact, his mission was to do anything more than conduct surveillance. The Japanese people were generally not as apathetic about crime as were most Americans. They respected tradition, stability, order, and the law. Most would attempt to apprehend a man who committed a crime in public.

Alex went into a beverage shop and bought a bottle of Awamori, an Okinawa sweet-potato brandy that was smooth and delicious to the Japanese palate but coarse and acrid by Western standards. He wasn't concerned about the taste, because he didn't intend to drink it.

When Alex came out of the shop, the gaunt man was standing fifty or sixty feet to the north, at a jewelry-store window. He didn't look up, but when Alex headed south, the hired shadow drifted after him.

Alex turned right at the first crossroads and ventured into a lane that was only open to pedestrians. The beauty of the old buildings was tainted by only a small amount of neon: Fewer than a dozen signs shone in the snowy night, and all were much smaller than the flashing monstrosities elsewhere in the Gion. Spirals of snow spun around half-century-old, globe-type street lamps. He passed a shrine that was flanked by cocktail lounges and bathed in dim yellow light, where worshipers practiced ancient central Asian temple dances to the accompaniment of finger bells and eerie string music. People were walking in that block too; though considerably fewer than in the lane that he'd just left, they were still numerous enough to discourage murder or even assault.

With the stranger tagging along, Alex tried other branches of the maze. He progressed from commercial blocks to areas that were half residential. The gaunt man became increasingly conspicuous in the thinning crowd and fell back more than thirty yards.

Eventually Alex found a quiet, deserted lane that fronted single-family homes and apartments. The only lights were those above the doors of the houses: accordionlike paper lanterns, waterproofed with oil and suspended on electric cords. The lanterns swung in the wind, and macabre shadows capered demonically across the snow-wet cobblestones.

The next alleyway was precisely what he needed: a six-foot-wide, brick-paved serviceway. On both sides, the backs of houses faced the passage. The first block featured three lights, one at each end and one in the middle. Among shadows that pooled between the alleyway lamps, there were groups of trash barrels and a few bicycles tethered to fences, but no people were anywhere to be seen.

Alex hurried into the alley, pulling off his topcoat as he went. Holding the coat, and with the bottle of Awamori gripped firmly in his right hand, he broke into a run. His shoes slipped on the damp bricks, but he didn't fall. His heart pounded as he sprinted out of the light into the first long patch of darkness, ran under the midpoint lamp, and dashed into another stretch of deep gloom. His breath exploded in bursts of steam, and his injured arm bumped painfully against his side. When he reached the well-illuminated circle of brick pavement beneath the third and final street lamp, he stopped and turned and looked back.

The gaunt man was not yet in sight.

Alex dropped his topcoat in the center of the puddle of light. He hurried back the way he had come, but only ten or fifteen feet, until he was out of the reach of the street lamp and in the embrace of darkness once more.

He was still alone.

He quickly slipped behind a row of five enormous trash barrels and hunkered down. From the space between the barrels and the back wall of the house, he had an unobstructed view of the intersection where the gaunt man would soon appear.

Footsteps. Sound carried well in the cold air.

Alex strove to quiet his own ragged breathing.

The stranger entered the far end of the serviceway and stopped abruptly, surprised by the disappearance of his prey.

In spite of the apprehension that had pulled him as taut as a drumhead, Alex smiled.

The stranger stood without moving, without making a sound.

Come on, you bastard.

Finally the man approached along the serviceway. Warier than he had been a minute ago, he moved as lightly as a cat, making no noise to betray himself.

Alex cupped one hand over his mouth, directing the crystallized plumes of his breath toward the ground, hoping they would dissipate before they could rise like ghosts in the darkness and possibly betray his position.

As the stranger approached, he cautiously checked behind the trash cans on both sides of the alley. He moved in a half crouch. His right hand was jammed in his coat pocket.

Holding a gun?

The gaunt man walked out of the first circle of light and into darkness, visible only as a silhouette.

Although the night was cold and Alex was without a coat, he began to perspire.

The stranger reached the midpoint light. Methodically he continued to inspect every object and shadow behind which—or in which—a man might hide.

Beside Alex, the garbage cans exuded the nauseating odor of spoiled fish and rancid cooking oil. He'd been aware of the stench from the moment he'd hidden behind the barrels, and second by second, it grew riper, more disgusting. He imagined that he could taste as well as smell the fish. He resisted the urge to gag, to clear his throat, and to spit out the offending substance.

The gaunt man was almost out of the light at the halfway point, about to step into the second stretch of darkness, when again he stopped and stood as if quick-frozen.

He had seen the topcoat. Perhaps he was thinking that the coat had slipped off Alex's shoulder and that, in a panic, Alex had not stopped to retrieve it.

The stranger moved again—not slowly, as before, and not with caution either. He strode purposefully toward the third streetlight and the discarded topcoat. The hard echoes of his footsteps bounced back and forth between the houses that bracketed him, and he didn't look closely at any more of the trash barrels.

Alex held his breath.

The stranger was twenty feet away.

Ten feet.

Five.

As soon as the guy passed by, literally close enough to touch, Alex rose in the shadows.

The stranger's attention was fixed on the coat.

Alex slipped soundlessly into the passageway behind his adversary. What little noise he made was masked by the other man's footsteps.

The stranger stopped in the circle of light, bent down, and picked up the topcoat.

Because it fell behind, Alex's shadow did not betray him as he moved into the light, but the stranger sensed the danger. He gasped and began to turn.

Alex swung the Awamori with all his strength. The bottle exploded against the side of the stranger's head, and a rain of glass rang down on the brick pavement. The night was filled with the aroma of sweet-potato brandy.

The stranger staggered, dropped the coat, put one hand to his head, reached feebly for Alex with the other hand, and then fell as if his flesh had been transformed into lead by some perverse alchemy.

Glancing left and right along the alleyway, Alex expected people to come out of the houses to see what was happening. The pop of the bottle as it broke and the clink of glass had seemed loud. He stood with the neck of the bottle still clamped in his right hand, ready to flee at the first sign of response, but after half a minute he realized that he hadn't been heard.

17 The flurries of snow had grown into a squall. Dense sheets of fat white flakes swirled through the passageway.

The gaunt man was unconscious but not seriously hurt. His heart was beating strongly, and his breathing was shallow but steady. The ugly red precursor of a bruise marked the spot where the bottle had shattered against his temple, but the superficial cuts in his face had already begun to clot.

Alex searched the stranger's pockets. He found coins, a wad of paper money, a book of matches that bore no advertising, a packet of facial tissues, breath mints, and a comb. He didn't find a wallet, credit cards, a driver's license, or any other identification, and the absence of ID told him almost as much as he could hope to learn: He was dealing with a cautious professional.

The guy was carrying a gun: a Japanese-made 9mm automatic with a sound suppressor. It was in his right overcoat pocket, which was much deeper than the left pocket. Evidently he carried the pistol so routinely that he had modified his wardrobe to accommodate it. He also had a spare magazine of ammunition.

Alex propped him against a wall on one side of the alleyway. The gunman sat where he was placed, hands at his sides, palms turned up. His chin rested on his chest.

After retrieving his soiled topcoat, Alex slipped it on, not just cape style this time. The knife wounds flared with pain as he eased his bandaged left arm into the coat sleeve.

By now a thin, icy lace of snow covered the unconscious man's hair. In his battered condition, with the snowflake mantilla, he looked like a pathetic yet determinedly jaunty drunk who was trying to get laughs by wearing a doily on his head.

Alex stooped beside him and slapped his face a couple of times to bring him around.

The gunman stirred, opened his eyes, and blinked stupidly. Comprehension came gradually to him.

Alex pointed the pistol at the guy's heart. When he was sure that his captive was no longer disoriented, he said, "I have a few questions."

"Go to hell," the guy said in Japanese.

Alex spoke in the same language. "Why were you following me?"

"I wasn't."

"You think I'm a fool?"

"Yes."

Alex poked him hard in the stomach with the gun, then again.

Wincing, the stranger said, "I was going to rob you."

"No. Nothing that simple. Someone ordered you to watch me."

The man said nothing.

"Who's your boss?" Alex asked.

"I'm my own boss."

"Don't lie." Alex poked him hard with the gun once more.

The stranger gasped in pain, glared at him, but didn't respond.

Although Alex was incapable of using physical abuse to extract information, he was willing to engage in light psychological torture. He put the cold muzzle of the weapon against the man's left eye.

With his right eye, the stranger stared back unwaveringly. He didn't appear to be intimidated.

"Who's your boss?" Alex asked.

No response.

"One round, through the brain."

The stranger remained silent.

"I'll do it," Alex said quietly.

"You're not a killer."

"Is that what they told you?" Alex pressed the muzzle against the guy's left eye just hard enough to hurt him.

The wind fluted through the clusters of trash barrels, playing them as though they were organ pipes, producing a crude, hollow, ululant, unearthly music.

Finally Alex sighed and rose to his feet. Staring down at the stranger, still training the gun on him, he said, "Tell your bosses I'll get to the truth one way or another. If they want to save me time, if they want to cooperate, maybe I'll keep my mouth shut when I know what this is all about."

The gaunt man virtually spat out his response: "You're dead."

"We're all dead sooner or later."

"In your case, sooner."

"I'm not going to drop this case. I'm going to be a bulldog. Tell them that," Alex said. "You people don't scare me."

"We haven't tried yet."

Still holding the pistol, Alex backed off. When he and the stranger were separated by twenty yards of pavement, he turned and walked away.

At the end of the alley, when Alex glanced back, the gaunt man had vanished into the gloom and the snow.

Alex rounded the corner and walked swiftly through the Gion maze toward more major thoroughfares.

The blackness above the city seemed to be something other than an ordinary night sky, something worse, an astronomical oddity that bled all the heat from the world below, that sucked away the light as well, until even the dazzling spectacle of the Gion dimmed to a somber glow, until every bright-yellow bulb began to radiate a thin and sour aura, until red neon darkened to the muddy maroon of cold, coagulating blood.

The late-autumn chill pierced him and scraped like a steel scalpel along his bones.

It was not a night for sleeping alone, but the bed that awaited him would be empty, the sheets as crisp and cool as morgue shrouds.

18

In the lightless room, in bed, staring at the shadowy ceiling, Joanna startled herself by saying aloud: "Alex." That involuntary word seemed to have been spoken by someone else, and it sounded like a soft cry for help.

The name reverberated in her mind while she contemplated all the meanings that it had for her.

Misery was her only companion. She was being forced yet again to choose between a man and her obsessive need for an extraordinary degree of privacy. This time, however, either choice would destroy her. She was teetering on the brink of mental collapse.

Her joy in life—and therefore her strength—had been drained by years of compulsive solitude.

Nevertheless, if she dared to pursue Alex, the world would close like a vise around her, as it had done more than once before. In a waking nightmare, the ceiling, the walls, and the floor would appear to draw together from all sides, tighter, tighter, until she was reduced by claustrophobia to unreasoning animal panic. Huddled. Shaking. Unable to breathe. Gripped by an unshakable sense of doom.

On the other hand, if she didn't pursue him, she would finally have to accept that she would always be alone. Forever. He was her last chance. Resigning herself to unending loneliness was a heavier weight than she could carry.

Either way, whether she reached out to Alex or shunned him, she would be unable to endure the consequences. She was so tired of the struggle of living.

She longed for sleep. Her head ached. Her eyes burned. She felt as though innumerable lead weights encumbered her limbs. In sleep she would be briefly free.

She raised herself from the sheets and sat on the edge of the bed. Without switching on the lamp, she opened the nightstand drawer and located the small bottle of the prescription drug on which she depended more nights than not. Although she'd taken one sedative an hour ago, she wasn't even drowsy. One more couldn't do any harm.

But then she thought, *Why just one more? Why not five, ten, an entire bottleful?*

Her exhaustion, her fear, and her depression at the prospect of perpetual loneliness were so grave that she didn't reject the idea immediately, as she would have done only a day ago.

In the darkness, like a penitent reverently fingering rosary beads, Joanna counted pills.

Twenty.

That was surely enough for a long sleep.

No. She must not call it sleep. No euphemisms. She would hold on to at least some self-respect. She must be honest with herself, if nothing else. Call it by its true name. Suicide.

She wasn't frightened, repelled, or embarrassed by the word, and she realized that her weary acceptance represented a terrible loss of will. For as long as she could remember, she had been tough enough to face anything, but she had no resources left. She was so tired.

Twenty pills.

No more loneliness. No longer would she have to yearn for intimacy that she could never allow herself to accept. No more alienation. No more doubts. No more pain. No more nightmares, visions of syringes, and grasping mechanical hands. No more.

She no longer had to choose between Alex Hunter and her sick compulsion to smash love when and where it arose. Now the choice was much simpler yet far more profound. For the moment she had to decide only whether to take one more pill—or all twenty.

She held them in her cupped hands.

They were as smooth and cool as tiny pebbles fished from a mountain stream.

19

Alex was accustomed to sleeping as little as possible. If time was money, then every minute spent in sleep was an act of financial irresponsibility. This night, however, he was not going to get even the few hours of rest that he usually required. His mind raced, and he couldn't downshift it.

Finally he got a bottle of beer from the refrigerator in the suite's wet bar and sat in an armchair in the drawing room. The only light was that which came through the windows—the pale, ghostly radiance of predawn Kyoto.

He was not worried about the people who had sent the *dorobo* to his hotel room and had him followed in the Gion. The single cause of his insomnia was Joanna. A torrent of images cascaded through his mind: Joanna in the pantsuit that she'd worn to lunch at Mizutani; Joanna on the stage of the Moonglow Lounge, moving sinuously in a clinging, red silk dress; Joanna laughing; Joanna so vibrant and *alive* in the Kyoto sun; Joanna frightened and huddled in the shade of the trees in the garden at Nijo Castle.

He was filled with an almost painful desire, but more surprising was the tenderness that he felt toward her, something deeper than affection, deeper even than friendship.

Not love.

He didn't believe in love.

His parents had proved to him that love was a word that had no meaning. Love was a sham, a hoax. It was a drug with which people deluded themselves, repressing their true feelings and all awareness of the primitive jungle reality of existence. Occasionally, and always with apparent sincerity, his mother and father had told him that they loved him. Sometimes, when the mood seized them—usually after their morning hangovers abated but before the new day's intake of whiskey had awakened the dragons in them—they hugged him and wept and loudly despised themselves for what they had done the night before, for the latest black eye or bruise or burn or cut that they had administered. When they felt especially guilty, they bought lots of inexpensive gifts for him—comic books, small toys, candy, ice cream—as if a war had ended and reparations were required. They called it love, but it never lasted. In hours it faded, and it vanished altogether by nightfall. Eventually Alex had learned to dread his parents' slobbering, boozy displays of "love," because when love waned, as it always did, their anger and brutality seemed worse by comparison with the preceding brief moment of peace. At its best, love was just a seasoning like pepper and salt, enhancing the bitter flavor of loneliness, hatred, and pain.

Therefore, he had not, would not, *could* not fall in love with Joanna Rand. His feelings for her were strong, more than lust, more than affection. Something new. And strange. If he was not falling in love, then he was at least sailing in uncharted waters, and the guide that he most needed was caution.

He drank two bottles of beer and returned to bed. He couldn't get comfortable. He lay in every position permitted by his injured left arm, yet sleep eluded him. The injury wasn't the problem: Joanna was. He tried to banish all thoughts of her by picturing the hypnotic motion of the sea, the gracefully rolling masses of water, endless chains of waves surging through the night. After a time, he did grow drowsy, although even the primordial rhythms and mesmeric power of the sea couldn't bar Joanna from his mind: She was the only swimmer in the currents of his dreams.

He was awakened by the phone.

According to the luminous number on the travel clock, it was four-thirty in the morning. He had been asleep less than an hour.

He picked up the handset and recognized Mariko's voice. "Alex-san, Joanna asked me to call you. Can you come here right away? A very bad thing has happened."

He sat up in bed, shuddering and suddenly nauseous. "What have they done to her?"

"She's done it to herself, Alex-san." Mariko's voice broke. "She tried to commit suicide."

20 The sky was still spitting snow, but the accumulation on the streets was no more than a quarter of an inch by the time that the taxi dropped Alex at the Moonglow Lounge.

Black hair cascading over her shoulders, ivory pins forgotten, Mariko was waiting for him at the front door of the club. "Joanna's upstairs. The doctor's with her."

"Will she be okay?"

"He says she will."

"Is he a good doctor?"

"Dr. Mifuni has been treating her for years."

"But is he any *good?*" he demanded, surprised by the vehemence in his voice.

"Yes, Alex-san. He's a good doctor."

He followed Mariko past the bar with the blue mirror into an elegantly decorated office and up a set of stairs to Joanna's apartment.

The living room was furnished with cane, rattan, and rosewood. There were half a dozen excellent watercolors on scrolls, and numerous potted plants.

"She's in the bedroom with Dr. Mifuni. We'll wait here," said Mariko, indicating a couch.

Sitting beside her, Alex said, "Was it . . . a gun?"

"Oh, no. No. Thank God. Sleeping tablets."

"Who found her?"

"She found me. I have a three-room apartment on the floor above this one. I was asleep . . . and she came to my room, woke me." Mariko's voice faltered. "She said, 'Mariko-san, I'm afraid I'm making a goddamned silly fool of myself, as usual.' "

"Dear God."

"There were twenty pills in the bottle. She'd taken eighteen before she'd realized that suicide wasn't the answer. I called an ambulance."

"Why isn't she in a hospital?"

"The paramedics came, made her swallow a tube . . . pumped out her stomach right here." She closed her eyes and grimaced at the memory.

"I've seen it done," Alex said. "It isn't pleasant."

"I held her hand. By the time they were finished, Dr. Mifuni arrived. He didn't think a hospital was necessary."

Alex glanced at the bedroom door. The silence behind it seemed ominous, and he had to resist an impulse to cross the living room and yank the door open to see if Joanna was all right.

Looking at Mariko again, he said, "Is this the first time she tried to kill herself?"

"Of course!"

"Do you think she actually intended to go through with it?"

"Yes, at first."

"What changed her mind?"

"She realized it was wrong."

"Some people only pretend suicide. They're looking for sympathy, or maybe for—"

She interrupted him. Her voice was as cold as the vapor rising from a block of dry ice. "If you think Joanna would stoop to such a thing, then you don't know her at all." Mariko was stiff with anger. Her small hands were fisted on her lap.

After a while he nodded. "You're right. She's not that mixed up . . . or that selfish."

Gradually the stiffness left Mariko.

He said, "But I wouldn't think she's the type to seriously consider suicide, either."

"She was so depressed before she met you. Then after she . . . rejected you . . . it got worse. At one moment she was so far down that death seemed the only way out. But she's strong. Even stronger than my mama-san, who is an iron lady."

The bedroom door opened, and Dr. Mifuni entered the living room. He was a short man with a round face and thick black hair. When meeting someone new, the Japanese were usually quick to smile, but Mifuni was somber.

Alex was sure that something had gone wrong, that Joanna had taken a turn for the worse. His mouth went as dry as talcum.

Even under these less than ideal circumstances, Mariko took the time to introduce the two men formally, with a good word said about the qualities of each. Now there were bows and smiles all around.

The introductory ritual almost shattered Alex's brittle nerves. He nearly pushed past the physician and into the bedroom. But he controlled himself and said, "Isha-san *dozo yoroshiku.*"

Mufini bowed too. "I am honored to make your acquaintance, Mr. Hunter."

"Is Joanna feeling better?" Mariko asked.

"I've given her something to calm her. But there's still time for Mr. Hunter to talk with her before the sedative takes effect." He smiled at Alex again. "In fact, she insists on seeing you."

Unnerved by the emotional turmoil that gripped him, Alex went into the bedroom and closed the door behind him.

21 Joanna was sitting in bed, propped against pillows, wearing blue silk pajamas. Although her hair was damp and lank, although she was so pale that her skin seemed translucent, although vague dark smudges of weariness encircled her eyes, she was still beautiful to him. The suffering showed only in her amethyst-blue eyes; that evidence of her pain and fear made Alex weak as he sat on the edge of the bed.

"Hi," she said softly.

"Hi."

"After they pumped all the sleeping pills out of me, I've been given a sedative. Isn't that ironic?"

He could think of nothing to say.

"Before I fall asleep," she said, "I want to know . . . do you still think I'm really . . . not who I think I am?"

"Lisa Chelgrin? Yes. I do."

"How can you be so positive?"

"There've been developments since we had lunch. I'm being followed everywhere I go."

"By whom?"

"I need time to explain."

"I'm not going anywhere," she said.

"But your eyes are beginning to droop."

She blinked rapidly. "I reached the breaking point tonight. Almost did a stupid thing."

"Hush. It's over."

"I wanted to die. If I don't have the courage to die . . . then I've got to find out why I behave the way I do."

He held her hand and said nothing.

"There's something wrong with me, Alex. I've always felt so hollow, empty . . . detached. Something happened to me a long time ago, something to make me the way I am. I'm not just . . . not just making excuses for myself."

"I realize that. God knows what they did to you—or why."

"I have to find out what it was."

"You will."

"I've got to know his name."

"Whose name?" he asked.

"The man with the mechanical hand."

"We'll find him."

"He's dangerous," she said sleepily.

"So am I."

Joanna slid down on the bed until she was flat on her back. "Damn it, I don't want to go to sleep yet."

He took one of the two pillows from beneath her head and drew the covers to her chin.

Her voice was growing thick. "There was a room . . . a room that stank of antiseptics . . . maybe a hospital somewhere."

"We'll find it."

"I want to hire you to help me."

"I've already been hired. Senator Chelgrin paid me a small fortune to find his daughter. It's about time I gave him something for his money."

"You'll come back tomorrow?"

"Yes. Whenever you want."

"One o'clock."

"I'll be here."

Her eyes fluttered, closed. "What if I'm not . . . not awake by then?"

"I'll wait."

She was silent so long that he was sure she had fallen asleep. Then she said, "I was so scared."

"Everything will be fine. It's okay."

"I'm glad you're here, Alex."

"So am I."

She turned on her side.

She slept.

The only sound was the faint hum of the electric clock. *Neither of us used the word "love,"* Alex thought. After a while he kissed her forehead and left the room.

22

Mariko was sitting on the living-room couch. Mifuni had gone.

"The sedative worked," Alex said.

"The doctor said she'll sleep five or six hours. He'll be back this afternoon."

"You'll stay here with her?"

"Of course." She rose from the couch and straightened the collar of her shapeless brown robe. "Would you like tea?"

"Thank you. That would be nice."

While they sat at the small kitchen table, sipping hot tea and nibbling almond wafers, Alex told Mariko Inamura about the Chelgrin case, about the burglar he had encountered in his hotel suite, and about the man who had followed him in the Gion a few hours ago.

"Incredible," she said. "But *why?* Why would they change the girl's name . . . *change her complete set of memories* . . . and bring her here to Kyoto?"

"I haven't any idea. But I'll find out. Listen, Mariko, I've told you all this so you'll understand there are dangerous people manipulating Joanna. I don't know what they're trying to cover up, but it's obvious that the stakes are high. Tonight when you opened the door for me downstairs, you didn't ask who was there. You've got to be more careful."

"But I was expecting you."

"From now on, always expect the worst. Do you have a gun?"

Frowning, she said, "We can't protect her every minute. What about when she appears on stage? She's a perfect target then."

"If I have anything to say about it, she won't perform again until this is settled."

"But in spite of everything they've done to her, they've never hurt her physically."

"If they know she's investigating her past and might learn enough to expose them, God knows what they'll do."

She stared into her tea for a long moment, as if she had the power to read the future in that brew. "All right, Alex-san. I'll be more careful."

"Good."

He finished his tea while she telephoned the taxi company.

At the downstairs door, as he stepped into the street, Mariko said, "Alex-san, you won't be sorry that you helped her."

"I didn't expect to be."

"You'll find what you've been looking for in life."

He raised his eyebrows. "I thought I'd found it already."

"Men are the same."

"As what?"

"Men of all cultures, societies, races are equally capable of being such fools."

"We pride ourselves in our dependability," he said with a small smile.

"You need Joanna as much as she needs you."

"You've told me that before."

"Have I?"

"You know you have."

She smiled mischievously, bowed to him, and assumed an air of Asian wisdom that was partly a joke and partly serious. "Honorable detective should know that repetition of a truth does not make it any less true, and resistance to the truth can never be more than a brief folly."

She closed the door, and Alex didn't move until he heard the lock bolt slide into place.

The black taxi was waiting for him in the snow-skinned street. A few snowflakes still spiraled out of the morning sky.

A red Toyota followed his cab all the way to the hotel.

23 Exhaustion overcame insomnia. Alex slept four hours and got out of bed at twenty past eleven, Thursday morning.

He shaved, showered, and quickly changed the bandage on his arm, concerned that he wouldn't be ready to meet the courier from Chicago if the man arrived on time.

As he was dressing, the telephone rang. He snatched up the handset on the nightstand.

"Mr. Hunter?"

The voice was familiar, and Alex said, "Yes?"

"We met last night."

"Dr. Mifuni?"

"No, Mr. Hunter. You have my pistol." It was the gaunt-faced man from the alleyway. "You'll be receiving a message soon."

"What message?"

"You'll see," the man said, and he hung up.

After Alex hurriedly finished dressing, he removed the silencer from the 9mm automatic. He put the sound suppressor in an inside pocket of his suit coat and tucked the gun itself under his belt. He was sure that it was no more legal to carry a concealed handgun without a permit in Japan than it was in the U.S., but he preferred risking arrest to being defenseless.

At six minutes past noon, just as he buttoned his suit coat over the pistol, a sharp knock came at the door.

He went into the foyer. "Who's there?" he asked in Japanese.

"Bellhop, Mr. Hunter."

The view through the fish-eye lens revealed the bellman who had brought his luggage upstairs when he had checked into the hotel. The man was clearly distressed, fidgeting.

When Alex opened the door, the bellman bowed and said, "I'm so sorry to disturb you, sir, but do you know a Mr. Wayne Kennedy?"

"Yes, of course. He works for me."

"There's been an accident. Almost fifteen minutes ago," the bellman said anxiously. "A car, this pedestrian, very terrible, right here in front of the hotel."

Although Blankenship hadn't mentioned the courier in the fax that he had sent yesterday, Kennedy was no doubt the man.

The bellman said, "The ambulance crew wants to take Mr. Kennedy to the hospital, but every time they get close to him, he kicks and punches and tries to bite them."

Because they were speaking Japanese and because the bellman was speaking very fast, Alex thought he had misunderstood. "Kicking and punching, you said?"

"Yes, sir. He refuses to let anyone touch him or take him away until he talks to you. The police don't want to handle him because they're afraid of aggravating his injuries."

They hurried to the elevator alcove. Another bellman was holding open the doors at one of the elevators.

On the way down, Alex said, "Did you see it happen?"

"Yes, sir," said the first bellman. "Mr. Kennedy got out of the taxi, and a car angled through the traffic, jumped the curb, hit him."

"Do they have the driver?"

"He got away."

"Didn't stop?"

"No, sir," the bellman said, clearly embarrassed that any Japanese citizen could behave so lawlessly.

"What's Mr. Kennedy's condition?"

"It's his leg," said the bellman uneasily.

"Broken?" Alex asked.

"There's a lot of blood."

The hotel lobby was nearly deserted. Everyone except the desk clerks was at the scene of the accident in the street.

Alex pushed through the crowd and saw Wayne Kennedy sitting on the sidewalk with his back against the building, flanked by two blood-smeared and badly battered suitcases. The wide-eyed onlookers kept a respectful distance on three sides of him, as if he were a wild animal that no one dared approach. He was shouting furiously at a uniformed ambulance attendant who had ventured within six or seven feet of him.

Kennedy was an impressive sight: a handsome black man, about thirty years old, six foot five, two hundred forty pounds, with fierce dark eyes. Cursing at the top of his voice, shaking one huge fist at the paramedics, he looked as if he might be constructed of concrete, iron, two-by-fours, and railroad ties, and in spite of his incapacity, he didn't seem to be an ordinary mortal man.

When Alex glimpsed the courier's injuries, he was stunned and doubly impressed by all the shrieking, fist-shaking bravado. The leg wasn't merely broken: It was crushed. Splinters of bone had pierced the flesh and the blood-soaked trousers.

"Thank God you're here," Kennedy said as Alex knelt beside him.

The courier slumped against the wall as if someone had cut a set of supporting wires. He seemed to grow smaller, and the maniacal energy that had sustained him suddenly vanished. He was streaming sweat, shivering violently, in tremendous pain. It was amazing that he had summoned sufficient strength to hold everyone off for nearly a quarter of an hour.

"Have you really punched at the medics?" Alex asked.

"The bastards don't speak English!" Kennedy said, as if Chicagoans faced with an injured tourist from Kyoto would have held forth in fluent Japanese. "Jesus, what I had to go through to find someone . . . who could understand me. I couldn't let them cart me off until I'd delivered . . . the file." He indicated one of the suitcases at his side.

"Good God, man, the file isn't *that* important."

"It must be," Kennedy said shakily. "Someone tried . . . to kill me for it. This wasn't an accident."

"How do you know that?"

"Saw the stinking sonofabitch coming." Kennedy grimaced with pain. "A red Toyota."

Alex remembered the car that had followed his taxi from the Moonglow Lounge earlier that same morning.

"I stepped . . . out of the way . . . but he turned straight toward me."

When Alex signaled the waiting paramedics, two men rushed in with a stretcher.

"Two guys . . . in the Toyota," Kennedy said.

"Save your strength. You can tell me about it later."

"I'd rather . . . talk now," Kennedy said as the paramedics cut open his pants leg to examine his injury and to stabilize the broken bones with an inflatable splint before moving him. "Takes my mind off . . . the pain. The Toyota hit me . . . knocked me into the wall . . . ass over teakettle . . . pinned me there . . . then backed off. The guy on the passenger side got out . . . grabbed for the suitcase. We played . . . tug of war. Then I bit his hand . . . hard. He gave up."

Alex had been warned to expect a message. This was it.

With considerable effort—and a little lingering wariness—the paramedics lifted Wayne Kennedy onto the wheeled stretcher.

The courier howled as he was moved. Tears of pain streamed down his face.

The wheeled legs of the gurney folded under it as it was shoved into the van-style ambulance.

Alex picked up both suitcases and followed Kennedy. No one tried to stop him. In the van, he sat on the suitcases.

The rear doors slammed shut. One of the paramedics remained with Kennedy and began to prepare a bottle of plasma for intravenous transfusion.

The ambulance began to move, and the siren wailed.

Without raising his head from the stretcher, Wayne Kennedy said, "You still there, boss?"

"Right here," Alex assured him.

Kennedy's voice was twisted with pain, but he wouldn't be quiet. "You think I'm an idiot?"

Alex stared at the hideously crumpled leg. "Wayne, for God's sake, you were sitting there bleeding to death."

"If you'd been in my shoes . . . you'd have done the same."

"Not in a million years."

"Oh, yeah. You would've. I know you," Kennedy insisted. "You hate to lose."

The paramedic cut away the coat and shirt sleeves on Kennedy's left arm. He swabbed the ebony skin with an alcohol-damp sterile pad, then quickly placed the needle in the vein.

Kennedy's bad leg twitched. He groaned and said, "I've got something to say . . . Mr. Hunter. But maybe I shouldn't."

"Say it before you choke on it," Alex told him. "Then please shut the hell up before you talk yourself to death."

The ambulance turned the corner so sharply that Alex had to grab at the safety railing beside him to keep from sliding off the pair of suitcases.

Kennedy said, "You and me . . . we're an awful lot alike in some ways. I mean . . . like you started out with nothing . . . and so did I. You were damned determined to make it . . . to the top . . . and you did. *I'm* determined . . . to make it . . . and I will. We're both smooth on the surface and street fighters underneath."

Alex wondered if the courier was delirious. "I know all that, Wayne. Why do you think I hired you? I knew you'd be the same kind of field op that I was when I started."

Grinding the words out between clenched teeth, Kennedy said, "So I'd like to suggest . . . when you get back to the States . . . you've got to make a decision about filling Bob Feldman's job. Don't forget me."

Bob Feldman was in charge of the company's entire force of field operatives, and he was retiring in two months.

"I get things done," Kennedy said. "I'm right . . . for the job . . . Mr. Hunter."

Alex shook his head in amazement. "I can almost believe you traveled around the world and *arranged* to be hit by that car just to trap me in here for this sales pitch."

"Bob Feldman . . . retiring . . . keep me in mind," Kennedy said, his speech beginning to slur.

"I'll do better than that. I'll give you the job."

Kennedy tried to raise his head but couldn't manage to do so. "You . . . mean it?"

"I said it, didn't I?"

"Every cloud," Kennedy said, "has a silver lining," and at last he relinquished his tenuous grip on consciousness.

24 After Wayne Kennedy was taken into surgery, Alex used a hospital pay phone to call Joanna.

Mariko answered. "She's still asleep, Alex-san."

He told her what had happened. "So I'm going to stay here until Wayne comes out of surgery and the doctors can tell me whether the leg stays or goes."

"It's that bad?"

"Yes. So I won't be able to get there by one o'clock, like I promised Joanna."

"You belong with your friend. She'll understand."

"I don't want her to think I'm backing out."

"She knows you better than that."

"Does Joanna have a spare bedroom?"

"For your Mr. Kennedy?"

"No. He'll be staying here. The room would be for me. Neither you nor Joanna should be alone until this is finished. Besides, it's better strategy to work out of one place. Saves time. I'd like to check out of the hotel and move in there—if it won't ruin anyone's reputation."

"I'll prepare the spare room, Alex-san."

"I'll be there as soon as I can. Keep the doors locked. And Mariko . . . we aren't quitting until we know what was done to Joanna and why."

"Good," Mariko said.

"We're going to nail these bastards to the barn wall."

"Nail them to a barn wall? Whatever that means exactly, I think it will be most excellent," Mariko agreed.

Alex was far more energized than he'd been in years. Until this moment, he hadn't fully realized that all his financial success had to some degree dampened the fire in him. His fortune, his twenty-two-room estate, and his pair of Rolls-Royces had mellowed him. But now, once again, he was a driven man.

The hanging bridge
Creeping vines
Entwine our life.

—BASHO, 1664-1694

▶ ▶ ▶

Part Two

Clues

25 At six o'clock the chief surgeon, Dr. Ito, came to the hospital waiting room where Alex was pacing. The doctor was a thin, elegant man in his fifties. He had been working on Wayne Kennedy for five hours. He looked tired, but he smiled because he had good news: Amputation would not be necessary. Kennedy was not entirely out of danger; all manner of complications could yet arise. More likely than not, even without complications, he would have a pronounced limp for the rest of his life, but at least he'd walk on his own two legs.

Dr. Ito was leaving the lounge when Mariko Inamura arrived to take over the vigil from Alex and free him to move his belongings from the hotel to the spare bedroom above the Moonglow Lounge. When Wayne Kennedy came out of anesthesia, he would need to see a friendly face other than those of the nurses and physicians, and he would want someone close by who spoke fluent English. Dr. Mifuni was staying with Joanna until Alex could get to the Moonglow.

Alex led Mariko to a corner of the waiting room. They sat on a yellow leatherette couch and spoke in whispers.

"The police will want to talk to Wayne," Alex told her.

"Tonight? The way he is?"

"Probably not until tomorrow when he's got his wits about him. So when he wakes up and you're certain he understands what you're saying, tell him that I want him to cooperate with the police—"

"Of course."

"—but only to a point."

Mariko frowned.

"He should give them a description of the car and the men in it," Alex said, "but he shouldn't tell them about the file he was carrying from Chicago. He'll have to pretend he's just an ordinary tourist. He hasn't any idea why they were trying to steal his suitcase. Nothing in it but shirts and underwear. Got that?"

Mariko's traditional Japanese upbringing had instilled in her a respect for authority that was as much a part of her as grain is a part of wood. "But wouldn't it be better to tell the police everything and have them working for us? They have the facilities, the manpower—"

"If Joanna is really Lisa Chelgrin, do you think her forged passport and phony identification are so convincing that no one's ever doubted them? Not for a minute? No one?"

"Well, I don't know, but—"

"Japan is insular. It doesn't welcome non-Japanese immigrants with open arms. Yet the authorities have allowed this woman to take up residence and open a business, evidently with no serious check of her background."

"You're saying this is some big international conspiracy? That the Japanese government might be involved? Alex-san, excuse me, but isn't this paranoid?"

"Joanna . . . *Lisa* isn't just an ordinary missing person. This is a damned strange situation. We're dealing with the daughter of a United States Senator. We don't know what political forces and interests are at work in this."

"In Japan the police are—"

"Do you want to take chances with Joanna's life?"

"No. But . . ."

"Trust me."

She hesitated. "All right."

Alex got to his feet. "I've arranged a private room for Wayne. You'd better go up there now. They'll be transferring him from the recovery room in a few minutes."

"Is it safe for you to leave here alone?" Mariko asked.

He picked up the suitcase that contained the Chelgrin file, having left the other bag in Wayne's room. "They think they've scared me off. For a while they'll be lying low, just watching."

Outside the hospital, the night was cold, but the snow flurries had long ago stopped. Backlighted by the moon, fast-moving trains of clouds tracked west to east.

Alex took a taxicab to the hotel, packed his bags, and checked out of his suite. From the hospital to the hotel, then from the hotel to the Moonglow Lounge, he was followed by two men in a white Honda.

By seven-thirty at Joanna's place, he had unpacked. The spare bedroom was cozy, with a low, slanted ceiling and a pair of dormer windows.

Shortly before Dr. Mifuni left, Joanna went into the kitchen to check on dinner, and the physician took advantage of her absence to draw Alex aside and speak with him. "Once or twice a night, you should look in on her to be certain she's only sleeping."

"You don't think she'd try it again?"

"No, no," Mifuni said. "There's virtually no chance. What she did last night was strictly impulsive, and she's not really impulsive by nature. Nevertheless . . ."

"I'll watch over her," Alex said softly.

"Good," Mifuni said. "I've known her since she came to Kyoto. A singer who performs more evenings than not is bound to have throat problems once in a while. But she's more than a patient. She's a friend too."

"Right now she needs all the friends she can get."

"But she's an amazingly resilient woman. She's got that going for her. Last night's experience appears to have left only minor psychological scars. And physically, she doesn't seem marked at all. Untouched. It almost seems a month has passed, not just one day."

Joanna returned from the kitchen to say good-bye to the doctor, and indeed she did look splendid. Even in faded jeans and a midnight-blue sweater worn to a smooth shine at the elbows and frayed at the cuffs, she was a vision, the golden girl once more.

"*Arigato, Isha-san.*"

"*Do itashimashita.*"

"*Konbanwa.*"

"*Konbanwa.*"

Suddenly, as Alex watched Joanna and Mifuni bowing to each other at the apartment door, he was caught in a powerful wave of desire that swept him into a strange state of mind. He seemed to be looking back and down at himself, somewhere between a condition of heightened consciousness and an out-of-body experience. He saw the familiar Alex Hunter, the carefully crafted persona that he put on view to the world—the quiet, self-assured, self-contained, determined, no-nonsense businessman—but he was also aware of an aspect of himself that had never before been visible to him. Within the cool and analytical detective was an insecure, lonely, desperately seeking, hungry creature driven by emotional need. Regarding this heretofore hidden aspect of himself, he understood that the power to see deeper into himself came from his desire for Joanna, from his need to share a life with her.

For the first time in his experience, Alex was overwhelmed by a desire that couldn't be satisfied solely through hard work and the application of his intellect. He was filled with a longing for something more abstract and spiritual than the drive for success, money, and status that had always motivated him. Joanna. He wanted Joanna. He wanted to touch her. He wanted to hold her, make love to her, be as close to her as one human being could ever get to another. But he required far more than mere physical intimacy. He sought from her a number of things that he couldn't entirely understand: a kind of peace that he could not describe; satisfactions he had never known; feelings for which he had no words. After a lifetime shaped by his unwavering denial of love's existence, he wanted love from Joanna Rand.

Old convictions and reliable psychic crutches were not easily cast aside. He couldn't yet accept the reality of love, but a part of him desperately *wanted* to believe.

The prospect of belief, however, scared the hell out of him.

26

Joanna wanted the dinner to be perfect. She needed to prove to herself, as much as to Alex, that she was coping again, that life was going on, that the event of the past night was an aberration.

She served at the low table in her Japanese-style dining room, using royal-blue placemats, several shades of gray dinnerware, and dark red napkins. Six fresh white carnations were spread in a fan on one end of the table.

The food was hearty but not heavy. *Igaguri*: thorny shrimp balls filled with sweet chestnuts. *Sumashi wan*: clear soup with soybean curd and shrimp. *Tatsuta age*: sliced beef garnished with red peppers and radish. *Yuan zuke*: grilled fish in a soy-and-sake marinade. *Umani*: chicken and vegetables simmered in a richly seasoned broth. And of course they also had steamed rice—a staple of the Japanese menu—and they accompanied everything with cups of hot tea.

The dinner was a success, and Joanna felt better than she had in months. In a curious way, the suicide attempt was beneficial. Having sunk to the depths of ultimate despair, having reached even a brief moment during which she'd had no reason to go on living, she could now face anything that might come. Even by acting halfheartedly on her death wish, she seemed to have been purged of it. For the first time, she felt that she would be able to overcome the periodic paranoia and the strange claustrophobia that had destroyed so many opportunities for happiness in the past.

Immediately after they had eaten, Joanna had a chance to test her new-found strength. She and Alex moved into the living room, sat together on the sofa, and began to look through the Chelgrin file, which filled the large suitcase—and which, according to Alex, held the true story of the first two decades of her life. There were thick stacks of field investigators' reports in the gray-and-green folders of the Bonner-Hunter Security Corporation, Alex's company, scores of transcriptions of interviews with potential witnesses as well as with friends and relatives of Lisa Chelgrin, plus copies of the Jamaican police records and other official documents. The sight of all that evidence had a negative effect on Joanna, and for the first time all day, she felt threatened. The familiar strains of paranoia were a distant, ominous music in her mind—but growing louder.

More than anything else in the suitcase, the photographs disturbed her. Here was Lisa Chelgrin in blue jeans and a T-shirt, standing in front of a Cadillac convertible, smiling and waving at the camera. Here was Lisa Chelgrin in a bikini, posed at the foot of an enormous palm tree. Several close-ups, in all of which she was smiling. A dozen photos in all. All were snapshots except for the professional portrait taken for the high-school yearbook when she had been a senior. The settings in which Lisa posed and the people with whom she was photographed meant nothing whatsoever to Joanna. Nevertheless, the young girl herself—blond, with a full but lithe figure—was as familiar as the image in any mirror. As Joanna stared in disbelief at the face of the missing woman, a chill crept along her spine.

Finally she got up and retrieved half a dozen photographs of her own from a box in the bedroom closet. These shots had been taken the first year she'd lived in Japan, when she'd been working in Yokohama. She spread them on the coffee table, next to the old photos from the Chelgrin file. As she studied the resemblance between Lisa's face and her own as she had looked more than a decade ago, a dynamic but formless fear stirred in her.

"It's a remarkable likeness, isn't it?" Alex asked.

"Identical," she said weakly.

"You can see why I was convinced almost from the moment I saw you in the Moonglow."

Suddenly the air seemed too thick to breathe comfortably. The room was warm. Hot. She stood, intending to open a window to get a breath of fresh air, but she sat down again at once, too dizzy to remain on her feet. The walls moved in and out like living membranes, and the ceiling was descending, coming down, slowly but relentlessly down. Although she knew the shrinkage of the room was occurring only in her imagination, she was nevertheless terrified of being crushed to death.

"Joanna?"

She closed her eyes.

"Is something wrong?" he asked.

She was overcome by an irrational urge to tell him to pack up his pictures and his reports, and get out. His presence now seemed to be a terrible intrusion into her life, an unconscionable intimacy, and a flutter of nausea went through her at the thought that he might touch her. *He's dangerous*, she thought.

"Joanna?"

Restraining herself from lashing out at him, she said in a whisper: "The walls are closing in again."

"Walls?" Alex looked around, perplexed.

To her, the room appeared to be only a third of its former size.

The air was so hot and dry that it scorched her lungs, parched her lips.

"And the ceiling," she said. "Coming lower."

She broke into a sweat. Dissolving in the heat. Melting. As if made of wax. Unable to breathe. The heat was going to kill her.

"Is that really what you see?" he asked. "Walls closing in?"

"Y-yes."

She stared at the walls, trying to make them roll back, willing the room to return to its former proportions. She was determined not to let fear get the better of her this time.

"You're hallucinating," Alex said.

"I know. Because of you. Because of feeling . . . too close to you. This is always what happens. I've never told anyone . . . not even Mariko. I've never told anyone about the spells of paranoia either. Sometimes I think the whole world's against me, out to get me. Seems like nothing's real, all just a clever stage setting. When I start thinking like that, I want to run off and hide where no one can find me, hurt me." She was speaking rapidly, in part because she was afraid that she would lose the courage she needed to reveal these things, and in part because she hoped that talking would distract her from the advancing walls and the steadily lowering ceiling. "I've never told anyone about it because I've been afraid people will think I'm crazy. But I'm not nuts. If I were crazy, I'd accept paranoia as a perfectly normal state of mind. I wouldn't even realize I was *having* spells of paranoia."

The hallucinations grew worse. Although she was sitting, the ceiling appeared to be no more than ten or twelve inches above her head. The walls were only a few feet away on every side, rolling closer on well-oiled tracks. The atmosphere was being compressed within this space, molecules jamming against molecules, until the air ceased to be a gas and became a liquid, first as dense as water, then syrup. When she breathed, she was convinced against all reason that her throat and lungs were filling with fluid. She heard herself whimpering, and she despised her weakness, but she couldn't silence herself.

Alex took her hand. "None of it's real. You can turn it off if you try."

The air became so thick that she choked on it. She bent forward, coughed, gagged.

Alex tried to guide her through the seizure. "You've been brainwashed, Joanna. That's got to be it. The answer. Somehow. All the memories of your true past have been eradicated, replaced with totally false recollections."

She understood, but that understanding didn't stop the ceiling from descending farther.

"After they did that to you," Alex said, holding fast to her hand as she tried to pull away from him, "they must have implanted a couple of post-hypnotic suggestions that have twisted your life ever since. One of those suggestions is affecting you right this minute. Every time you meet someone who's interested in your past, anyone who might uncover the deception, then you suffer attacks of paranoia and claustrophobia *because the people who brainwashed you told you this would happen.*"

To Joanna's ear, at least, his voice boomed and echoed within the shrinking room. He was loud, demanding, as fearsome as the relentless advance of the viselike walls.

"And each time you reject the person with whom you've become close," he continued, "the claustrophobia goes away, the paranoid fear declines—*because they told you it would.* That's a damn effective method for keeping inquisitive people out of your life. You're programmed to be a loner, Joanna. *Programmed.*"

He was so plausible, so earnest—but he was not a friend. He was one of *Them.* He was one of the people who had been trying to kill her, part of the conspiracy. He couldn't be trusted. He was the worst of them all, a conniving and despicable—

As if reading her mind, he said, "No, Joanna. I'm with you. I'm here for you. I'm the best friend and the best hope you have."

She jerked reflexively as the ceiling shuddered and dropped closer to her, and she wrenched her hand out of his. She slid down on the couch.

The air had been compressed to such a degree that she could feel it against her skin. Insistent. Heavy. Metallic. All around her. Like a suit of armor. A suit of armor that was constantly growing tighter, smaller, more confining. Inside that defensive garment, she was drenched with perspiration. Her flesh was bruised by the steel embrace of her armor, and the bones ached in every torturously compressed joint.

"Fight it," Alex said.

"The walls, the walls," she keened, because the room began to close around her more quickly. No previous attack of claustrophobia had been as fierce as this one. She gasped. Her lungs were clogged. She tasted blood and realized that she had bitten her tongue. The room was rapidly shrinking to the size of a coffin, and she foresaw the conditions of the grave so clearly that she could actually *feel* the cold, damp embrace of eternity.

"Close your eyes," Alex said urgently.

"No!" That would be intolerable. If she closed her eyes, she would be surrendering to the grave. She would never be able to open her eyes again. The darkness would seize her and drag her down, the cold and the dampness, the silence, down into the bottomless black maw of forever. "Oh, my *God*," she groaned miserably.

"Close your eyes," Alex insisted.

He put one hand on her shoulder, and she tried to pull away, but his grip tightened.

"Let me alone. Get away," she demanded.

"Trust me."

"I know what you are."

"I'm your best hope."

She found the strength to draw herself into a sitting position from which she could confront him. For the moment she was able to bear up under the colossal weight of the descending ceiling. The most important thing was to get rid of him. "Get out."

"No, Joanna."

"Now. I mean it. Get out."

"No."

"I don't want you here. I don't need you. *Get out!*"

"No."

"This is *my* place, you sonofabitch. I *hate* you, get out, get out, damn you!"

"It's not your place. It's Joanna's place. Right now you aren't Joanna. You don't act like her at all."

She knew that what he said was true. She was behaving like a woman possessed. In her heart, she didn't want to argue with him or drive him away, but she could not stop herself. She struck at his face, and he blocked the blow, so she tried to claw at his eyes, but he seized her wrist.

"You creep, you sick sonofabitch!"

They struggled on the couch. She was atop him, trying to hurt him, so badly *needing* to hurt him, but he was holding her off, and the longer that he prevented her from drawing his blood the more enraged she became.

"I know what you are," she shrieked, "I know *exactly* what you are, oh, yes, you *rotten* bastard."

Her heart was thudding with terror that she couldn't understand. Her vision blurred with a fierce anger that wasn't real, for she had nothing to be angry *about*, yet her fury was so powerful that it was shaking her to pieces.

"You're one of *Them!*" she cried, and she had no idea what she meant by that.

"Who?"

"Them!"

"Who?"

"I hate your guts," she said, trying to jam her knee into his crotch and break his hold on her.

"Listen, listen to me," he demanded, holding both her wrists, struggling against her determined assault. "Listen, damn it!"

But she dared not listen, because if she listened, the walls would complete their inward journey, and she would be crushed. Listening to him was what had gotten her into this trouble in the first place.

"Stop it, Joanna!"

She rolled off the couch, pulling him with her, kicking at him, twisting in his grasp. She tore loose and scrambled to her feet. "Get out! I'll call the police. Get the hell out of my house," she shouted, and she could feel that her face was wrenched into a mask of blind fury.

It was an inexplicable rage—except somehow she knew that she would be all right if she could force him to leave. When he was gone, when she was alone, the walls would roll back. The air would no longer be so thick, so difficult to breathe. The terror would subside when at last he went away, and thereafter she would find peace again.

"You don't really want me to go," he said, getting to his own feet, calmly challenging her.

She slapped his face so hard that her hand stung as if an electrical current had blasted through it.

He didn't move.

She slapped him again, harder, leaving the imprint of her hand on his cheek.

With no anger in his face, with an infuriating compassion in his eyes, he reached out to touch her.

She shrank back.

"Give me your hand," he pleaded.

"Get away."

"I'm going to lead you through this."

"Get out of my life."

"Give me your hand."

She backed into one corner of the living room. Nowhere to go. He stood in front of her. Trapped.

She was shaking violently with fear. Her heart was knocking in her breast. She couldn't get her breath; each inhalation was shaken out of her before she could draw it all the way into her lungs.

He took her hand before she realized what he'd done. She no longer had the strength to wrench away from him.

"I'm going to stay here until you close your eyes and cooperate with me," he said quietly. "Or until the walls crush you or the ceiling presses you into the floor. Which will it be?"

She slumped against the wall.

"Close your eyes," he said.

Tears blurred her vision so completely that she couldn't see his face. He might have been anyone.

"Close your eyes."

Weeping, she slid down the wall, her back in the corner, until she was sitting on the floor.

He dropped to his knees in front of her. Now he was holding both of her hands. "Close your eyes, Joanna. Please. Trust me."

Sobbing uncontrollably, Joanna closed her eyes, and immediately she felt that she was in a coffin, one of those hulking bronze models with a lead lining, and the lid was bolted down just inches above her face. Such a narrow space, shallow and dark, as black as the heart of a moonless midnight, so utterly lightless that the darkness might have been a living thing, an amorphous entity that flowed all around her and molded to her shape, sucking the heat of life out of her.

Nevertheless, cornered and in an extreme state of helplessness, she could do nothing but keep her eyes closed and listen to Alex. His voice was a beacon that marked the way to release, to freedom.

"Keep your eyes closed. No need to look," Alex said softly. "I'll be your eyes. I'll tell you what's happening."

She couldn't stop sobbing.

"The walls aren't closing in as fast as they were. Barely creeping inward now. Barely creeping . . . and now . . . now they've stopped altogether. The ceiling too . . . not descending any more. Everything's stopped. Stable. Do you hear me, Joanna?"

"Y-yes."

"No, don't open your eyes yet. Squeeze them tight shut. Just visualize what I'm telling you. See the world through me."

She nodded.

The air wasn't normal, but it was thinner than it had been since the seizure had stricken her. Breathable. Sweet.

"Eyes closed . . . closed . . . but see what's happening," Alex said as softly and lullingly as a hypnotist. "The ceiling is starting to withdraw . . . moving up where it belongs. The walls too . . . pulling back from you, back from us, away . . . slowly away. You understand? The room is getting larger . . . a lot of space now. Do you feel the room gradually getting bigger, Joanna?"

"Yes," she said, and though hot tears were still streaming from her eyes, she was no longer sobbing.

Alex spoke to her in that fashion for several minutes, and Joanna listened closely to each word and visualized each statement. Eventually the air pressure returned to normal; she was no longer suffocating.

When her tears had dried and when her breathing had become rhythmic, relaxed, almost normal, he said, "Okay, open your eyes."

She opened them, although reluctantly. The living room was as it should be.

"You made it all go away," she said wonderingly. "You made it right again."

He was still holding her hands. He gently squeezed them, smiled, and said, "Not just me. We did it together. And from now on, I'm pretty sure you'll be able to do it alone."

"Oh, no. Never by myself."

"Yes, you will. Because this phobia isn't a natural part of your psychological makeup. I'd bet everything I own that it's just posthypnotic suggestion. You don't need psychoanalysis to get rid of it. From now on, when a seizure hits you, just close your eyes and picture everything opening up and moving away from you."

"But I've tried that before. It never worked . . . until now, until you . . ."

"Just once, you needed someone to hold your hand and force you to face up to the fear, someone who wouldn't be driven away. Until tonight, you thought it was an interior problem, an embarrassing mental illness. Now you know it's an *exterior* problem, not your fault, like a curse someone placed on you."

Joanna looked at the ceiling, daring it to descend.

Alex said, "Subsequent attacks ought to be less and less fierce—until they finally stop altogether. Neither the paranoia nor the claustrophobia has any genuine roots in you. They were both grafted onto you by the bastards who transformed you from Lisa into Joanna. You've been programmed. Now you have the power to *reprogram* yourself to be like other people."

To be like other people . . .

For the first time in more than a decade, Joanna felt that she had at least some control of her life. She could at last deal with the malignant forces that had made a loner of her. From this day forward, if she wanted an intimate relationship with Alex or with anyone else, nothing within her could prevent her from having what she wanted. The only obstacles remaining were external. That thought was exhilarating, like a rejuvenation drug, water from the fountain of youth. The years dropped from her. Time ran backward. She felt as though she were a girl again. She would never hereafter cringe in fear as the ceiling descended and the walls closed in on her, nor would spells of irrational paranoia keep her from the succor and sanctuary of her friends.

To be like other people . . .

The cage door had been opened. She was free.

27

The photographs no longer disturbed Joanna. She studied them in the same spirit of awe that people must have known when gazing into the first mirrors many centuries ago—with a superstitious fascination but not with fear.

Alex sat beside her on the sofa, reading aloud from some of the reports in the massive Chelgrin file. They discussed what he read, trying to see the information from every angle, searching for a perspective that might have been overlooked at the time of the investigation.

As the evening wore on, Joanna made a list of the ways in which she and Lisa Chelgrin were alike. Intellectually, she was more than half convinced that Alex was right, that she was indeed the missing daughter of the senator. But emotionally, she lacked conviction. Could it really be possible that the mother and father she remembered so well—Elizabeth and Robert Rand—were merely phantoms, that they had never existed except in her mind? And the apartment in London—was it conceivable that she had never actually lived in that place? She needed to see the evidence in black and white, a list of reasons why she should seriously consider such outrageous concepts.

LISA	ME
1) She looks like me.	1) Therefore, I look like her.
2) She is five foot six.	2) Same height.
3) She weighed 115 pounds.	3) So do I, give or take.
4) She studied music.	4) Likewise.
5) She had a fine voice.	5) So do I.
6) Her mother died when she was ten.	6) My mother is dead too.
7) Wherever she is, she's separated from her father.	7) My father is dead.
8) She had appendicitis surgery when she was nine.	8) I have an appendix scar.
9) She had a brown birthmark as big as a dime on her right hip.	9) So do I.

As Joanna was reading the list yet again, Alex pulled another report from the file, glanced at it, and said, "Here's something damned curious. I'd forgotten all about it."

"What?"

"It's an interview with Mr. and Mrs. Morimoto."

"Who're they?"

"Lovely people," Alex said. "Domestic servants. They've been employed by Tom Chelgrin since Lisa . . . since you were five years old."

"The senator brought a couple from Japan to work in his home?"

"No, no. They're both second-generation Japanese Americans. From San Francisco, I think."

"Still, like you said, it's curious. Now there's a Japanese link between me and Lisa."

"You haven't heard the half of it."

Frowning, she said, "You think the Morimotos had something to do with my . . . with Lisa's disappearance?"

"Not at all. They're good people. Not a drop of larceny in them. Besides, they weren't in Jamaica when Lisa disappeared. They were at the senator's house in Virginia, near Washington."

"So what is it exactly that you find so curious about them?"

Paging through the transcript of the Morimoto interview, he said, "Well . . . the Morimotos were around the house all day, every day when Lisa was growing up. Fumi was the cook. She did a little light housekeeping too. Her husband, Koji, was a combination house manager and butler. They both were Lisa's baby-sitters when she was growing up, and she adored them. She picked up a lot of Japanese from them. The senator was all in favor of that. He thought it was a good idea to teach languages to children when they were very young and had fewer mental blocks against learning. He sent Lisa to an elementary school where she was taught French beginning in the first grade—"

"I speak French."

"—and where she was taught German starting in the third grade."

"I speak German too," Joanna said.

She added those items to her list of similarities. The pen trembled slightly in her fingers.

"So what I'm leading up to," Alex said, "is that Tom Chelgrin used the Morimotos to tutor Lisa in Japanese. She spoke it fluently. Better than she spoke either French or German."

Joanna looked up from the list that she was making. She felt dizzy. "My God."

"Yeah. Too incredible to be coincidence."

"But I learned Japanese in England," she insisted.

"Did you?"

"At the university—and from my boyfriend."

"Did you?"

They stared at each other.

For Joanna, the impossible now seemed probable.

28 Joanna found the letters in her bedroom closet, at the bottom of a box of snapshots and other mementos. They were in one thin bundle, tied together with faded yellow ribbon. She brought them back to the living room and gave them to Alex. "I don't really know why I've held on to them all these years."

"You probably kept them because you were *told* to keep them."

"Told—by whom?"

"By the people who kidnapped Lisa. By the people who tinkered with your mind. Letters like these are superficial proof of your Joanna Rand identity."

"Only superficial?"

"We'll see."

The packet contained five letters, three of which were from J. Compton Woolrich, a London solicitor and the executor of the Robert and Elizabeth Rand estate. The final letter from Woolrich mentioned the enclosure of an after-tax, estate-settlement check in excess of three hundred thousand dollars.

As far as Joanna could see, that money from Woolrich blasted an enormous hole in Alex's conspiracy theory.

"You actually received that check?" he asked.

"Yes."

"And it cleared? You got the money?"

"Every dime. And if there was such a large estate, then my father and mother—Robert and Elizabeth—must have been real people."

"Maybe," Alex said doubtfully. "Real people. But even if they did exist, that doesn't mean you were their daughter."

"How else could I inherit from them?"

Instead of responding, he read the last two of the five letters, both of which were from the claims office of the United British-Continental Insurance Association, Limited. Upon its receipt of the medical examiner's official certification of the death of Robert and Elizabeth (née Henderson) Rand, British-Continental had honored Robert's life insurance policy and had paid the full death benefits to Joanna, the sole surviving heir. The sum received—which was in addition to the three hundred thousand dollars that had been realized from the liquidation of the estate—was a hundred thousand pounds Sterling, minus the applicable taxes.

"A hundred thousand pounds. More than another hundred and fifty thousand bucks. And you received this too?" Alex asked.

"Yes."

"Quite a lot of money."

"It was," Joanna agreed. "But I needed virtually all of it to purchase this building and renovate it. The place needed a lot of work. Then I had to use most of what was left to operate the Moonglow until it became profitable—which, thank God, wasn't all that long."

Alex shuffled the letters, stopped when he found the last one from the London solicitor, and said, "This Woolrich guy—did you do all of your business with him by mail and on the phone?"

"Of course not."

"You met him face-to-face?"

"Sure. Lots of times."

"When? Where?"

"He was my father's . . . He was Robert Rand's personal attorney. They were also friends. He was a dinner guest at our apartment in London at least three or four times a year."

"What was he like?"

"Very kind, gentle," Joanna said. "After my parents were killed in the accident near Brighton—well, if they *were* my parents—Mr. Woolrich came to see me a number of times. And not just when he needed my approval or my signature to proceed with the settlement of the estate. He paid me frequent visits. I was horribly depressed. He worried about keeping my spirits up. I don't know how I'd have gotten through without him. He loved jokes. He always had a couple of new jokes to tell me every time he came by. Usually quite funny jokes too. Always trying to get a little laugh out of me. He was extraordinarily considerate. He never made me go to his office on business. He always came to me. He never put me out in the least. He was warm and considerate. He was a nice man. I liked him."

Alex studied her with narrowed eyes, very much the detective again. "Did you listen to yourself just now?"

"What?"

"The way you sounded."

"How did I sound?"

Rather than answer, he got up from the couch and began to pace. "Tell me one of his jokes."

"Jokes?"

"Yes. Tell me one."

"You can't be serious. I don't remember any. Not after all these years."

"His jokes were usually quite funny. You stressed that. Seems reasonable to assume you might remember at least one."

She was puzzled by his interest. "Well, I don't. Sorry. Why does it matter anyway?"

He stopped pacing and stared down at her.

Those eyes. Once again she was aware of their power. They opened her with a glance and left her defenseless. She had thought she was armored against their effect, but she wasn't. Paranoia surged in her, the stark terror of having no secrets and no place to hide. She fought off that brief madness and retained her composure.

"If you could recall one of his jokes," Alex said, "you'd provide some much needed detail. You'd be adding verisimilitude to what are now, frankly, very thin recollections of him."

"I'm not trying to hide anything. I'm giving you all the details I can."

"I know. That's what bothers me." Alex sat beside her again. "Didn't you notice anything odd about the way you summed up Woolrich a moment ago?"

"Odd?"

"Your voice changed. In fact, your whole manner changed. Subtly. But I noticed it. As soon as you started talking about this Woolrich, you spoke in ... almost a monotone, choppy sentences ... as if you were reciting something you'd memorized."

"Really now, Alex. You make me sound like a zombie. You were imagining it."

"My business is observation, not imagination. Tell me more about Woolrich. What does he look like?"

"Does it really matter?"

Alex was quick to press the point. "Don't you remember that either?"

She sighed. "He was in his forties when my parents died. A slender man. Five foot ten. Maybe a hundred forty or a hundred fifty pounds. Very nervous. Talked rather fast. Energetic. He had a pinched face. Pale. Thin lips. Brown eyes. Brown, thinning hair. He wore heavy tortoiseshell glasses, and he—"

Joanna stopped in midsentence, because suddenly she could hear what Alex had heard before. She sounded as if she were standing at attention in front of a class of schoolchildren, reciting an assigned poem. It was eerie, and she shivered.

"Do you correspond with Woolrich?" Alex asked.

"Write letters to him? Why should I?"

"He was your father's friend."

"They were casual friends, not best buddies."

"But he was your friend too."

"Yes, well, in a way he was."

"And after all he did for you when you were feeling so low—"

"Maybe I should have kept in touch with him."

"That would have been more in character, don't you think? You aren't a thoughtless person."

"You know how it is. Friends drift apart."

"Not always."

"Well, they generally do when you put twelve thousand miles between them." She frowned. "You're making me feel guilty."

Alex shook his head. "You're missing my point. Look, if Woolrich was really a friend of your father's and if he actually was extraordinarily helpful to you after the accident in Brighton, you would have maintained contact with him at least for a couple of years. That would be like you. From what I know of you, it's entirely out of character for you to forget a friend so quickly and easily."

Joanna smiled ruefully. "You have an idealized image of me."

"No. I'm aware of your faults. But ingratitude isn't one of them. I think this J. Compton Woolrich never existed—which is why you couldn't possibly have kept in touch with him."

"But I remember him!" Joanna said exasperatedly.

"As I said, you may have been made to remember a lot of things that never happened."

"Programmed," she said sarcastically.

"I'm close to the truth," he said confidently. "Do you realize how tense it's made you to have to listen to me?"

She realized that she was leaning forward, shoulders drawn up, hunched as if in anticipation of a blow to the back of the neck. She was even biting her fingernails. She sat back on the couch and tried to relax.

"I heard the change in my voice when I was telling you what Woolrich looked like. A monotone. It's spooky. And when I try to expand on those few memories of him . . . I can't recall anything new. There's no color, no detail. It all seems . . . flat. Like photographs or a painting. But I *did* receive those letters from him."

"That's another thing that bothers me. You said that after the accident, Woolrich came to visit you frequently."

"Yes, that's right."

"So why would he write to you at all?"

"Well, of course, he had to be careful. . . ." Joanna frowned. "I'll be damned. I don't know. I hadn't thought about that."

Alex shook the thin packet of correspondence as if he hoped a secret would drop out of it. "There isn't anything in these three letters that requires a written notice to you. He could have conducted all this business in person. He didn't even have to deliver the settlement check by mail." Alex tossed the letters on the coffee table. "The only reason that these were sent to you was so you'd have superficial proof of your phony background."

"If Mr. Woolrich never existed . . . and if Robert and Elizabeth Rand never existed . . . then who the hell sent me that three hundred thousand dollars?"

"Maybe it came from the people who kidnapped you when you were Lisa Chelgrin. For some reason, they wanted to set you up well in your new identity."

Amazed, she said, "You've got it all backward. Kidnappers are out to get money, not to give it away."

"These weren't ordinary kidnappers. They never sent a ransom demand to the senator. Their motives apparently were unique."

"Yeah? So who were they?"

"Maybe we can find out." He pointed to the telephone that stood on a rosewood desk in one corner of the living room. "As a start, maybe you should make a call to J. Compton Woolrich."

"I thought you'd decided he doesn't exist."

"There's a telephone number on his stationery. We're obliged to try it, even if it won't get us anywhere. And it won't. After that, we'll make a call to the United British-Continental Insurance Association."

"Will that get us anywhere?"

"No. But I want you to make the call for the same reason that a curious little boy might poke a stick into a hornet's nest: to see what will happen."

29
Joanna sat at the small rosewood desk on which stood the telephone. Alex pulled up a chair beside her and sat close enough to hear the other end of the conversation when she turned the receiver half away from her ear.

Midnight Kyoto time was two o'clock in the afternoon in London, and the insurance company's switchboard operator answered on the second ring. She had a sweet, girlish voice. "May I help you?"

Joanna said, "Is this British-Continental Insurance?"

After a pause the operator said, "Yes."

"I need to speak to someone in your claims department."

"Do you know the name of the claims officer you want?"

"No," Joanna said. "Anyone will do."

"What sort of policy does the claim involve?"

"Life insurance."

"One moment, please."

For a while the line carried nothing but background static: a steady hissing, intermittent sputtering.

The man in the claims department finally came on the line. He clipped his words with crisp efficiency as sharp as any scissors. "Phillips speaking. Something I can help you with?"

Joanna told him the story that she and Alex had concocted: After all these years, the Japanese tax authorities wanted to be certain that the funds with which she had started life in Japan had not, in fact, been earned there either by her or someone else. She needed to prove the provenance of her original capital in order to avoid paying back taxes. Unfortunately, she had thrown away the cover letter that had come with the insurance company's check.

She felt that she was convincing. Even Alex seemed to think so, for he nodded at her several times to indicate that she was doing a good job.

"Now I was wondering, Mr. Phillips, if you can possibly send me a copy of that letter, so I can satisfy the tax authorities here."

Phillips said, "When did you receive our check?"

Joanna gave him the date.

"Oh, then I can't help. Our records don't go back that far."

"What happened to them?"

"Threw them out. We're always short of file space. We're legally obligated to store them only seven years. In fact, I'm surprised it's still a worry to you. Don't they have a statute of limitations in Japan?"

"Not in tax matters," Joanna said. She hadn't the slightest idea whether that was true. "With everything on computer these days, I would think nothing ever gets thrown out."

"Well, I'm sorry, but they're gone."

She thought for a moment and then said, "Mr. Phillips, were you working for British-Continental when my claim was paid?"

"No. I've been here only eight years."

"What about other people in your department? Weren't some of them working there twelve years ago?"

"Oh, yes. Quite a few."

"Do you think one of them might remember?"

"Remember back twelve years to the payoff on an ordinary life policy?" Phillips asked, incredulous. "Highly unlikely."

"Just the same, would you ask around for me?"

"You don't mean now, while you hold long distance from Japan?"

"Oh, no. If you'd just make inquiries when you've got the time, I'd appreciate it. And if anyone does remember anything, please write me immediately."

"A memory isn't a legal record," Phillips said doubtfully. "I'm not sure what good someone's recollections would be to you."

"Can't do any harm," she said.

"I suppose not. All right. I'll ask."

Joanna gave Phillips her address, thanked him, and hung up.

"Threw out all the records. Convenient," Alex said sourly.

"But it doesn't prove anything."

"Exactly. It doesn't prove anything—one way or the other."

At twenty minutes past midnight, Kyoto time, Joanna reached the number that they had found on J. Compton Woolrich's impressively heavy vellum stationery.

The woman who answered the phone in London had never heard of a solicitor named Woolrich. She was the owner and manager of an antique shop on Jermyn Street. The number had belonged to her for more than eight years. She didn't know to whom it might have been assigned prior to the opening of her shop.

Another blank wall.

30 The Moonglow Lounge had closed early, at eleven-thirty, nearly an hour ago, and the staff had gone home by the time Joanna concluded the second call to London. Music no longer drifted up through the floor, and without a background melody, the winter night seemed preternaturally quiet, impossibly dark at the windows.

Joanna switched on the CD player. Bach.

She sat beside Alex on the sofa, and they continued to leaf through the gray-and-green Bonner-Hunter Security Corporation file folders that were stacked on the coffee table.

Suddenly Alex said, "I'll be damned!" He took a pair of eight-by-ten, black-and-white glossies from one of the folders. "Look at this. Photographic enlargements of Lisa Chelgrin's thumbprints. We got one from her driver's license application and lifted the other from the clock radio in her bedroom. I'd forgotten about them."

"Hard proof," Joanna said softly, half wishing that the prints did not exist.

"We'll need an ink pad. And paper with a soft finish . . . but nothing too absorbent. We want a clear print, not a meaningless blot. And we've got to have a magnifying glass."

"The paper I have," she said. "And the ink pad. But not the magnifying glass . . . unless. There's a paperweight that might do."

She led him out of the living room, down the narrow stairs, and into her first-floor office.

The paperweight was a clear, two-inch-thick lens, four inches in diameter. It had no frame or handle, and it wasn't optically flawless. But when Alex held it above the open accounts ledger that was filled with Joanna's neat handwriting, the letters and figures appeared three to five times larger than they did to the unassisted eye.

"It'll do," he said.

Joanna got the ink and paper from the center drawer of her desk. After several tries, she managed to make two smudge-free thumbprints.

Alex placed them beside the photographs. While Joanna scrubbed her inky fingers with paper tissues and spit, he used the lens to compare the prints.

When Joanna had cleaned up as best she could without soap and hot water, Alex passed the magnifying glass to her.

"I don't know what to look for," she said.

"Here. I'll show you."

"Can we cut to the chase?" she asked impatiently.

"Sure." He hesitated. "Your prints and Lisa's are identical."

31 When at last Mariko returned to the Moonglow Lounge from the hospital where she had been at the bedside of Wayne Kennedy, Joanna and Alex were waiting for her at the table in the kitchen. They had made hot tea and a stack of small sandwiches.

Mariko was exhausted, having slept less than three hours in the past thirty-six. Her face felt grimy, and her eyes burned. Her feet and legs were as leaden and swollen as those of an old woman.

Joanna and Alex wanted a report on Wayne Kennedy, but Mariko had little to tell, other than that she was impressed by his strength and vitality. Kennedy had come out of anesthesia at six forty-five, but he had not been fully coherent until nine o'clock, when he had complained about a dry mouth and gnawing hunger. The nurses gave him chips of ice to suck, but his dinner came from an intravenous-drip bottle even though he demanded eggs and bacon.

"Is he in a lot of pain?" Alex asked.

"A little. But drugs mask most of it."

When Wayne had been told by Dr. Ito that he would be in the hospital for a month and might need additional surgery, he had not been depressed in the least but had predicted that he'd be out in a week and back at work in two. Mariko had been prepared for the hard job of cheering him up, but he had been in good spirits and, before he had finally fallen asleep, had told her a lot of funny stories about his work with the security agency in Chicago.

"Have the police questioned him?" Alex asked.

"Not yet," Mariko said. "In the morning. I don't envy them if they hope to get more out of Wayne than you told him to give, Alex-san. Even in a sickbed, with one leg in traction, he'll be more than a match for them."

As she'd told them about Wayne, Mariko had been content to sip tea. Now she was ravenous. She devoured her share of the sandwiches while Joanna and Alex told her about the Chelgrin file, the two calls to London, and the thumbprints.

Although their stunning revelations made Mariko forget her weariness, she was as intrigued by their demeanor as by what they told her. They were relaxed with each other. Joanna regarded Alex with obvious affection, trust—and a certain proprietary concern. For once, he was without his omnipresent jacket and tie, and his shirtsleeves were rolled up. He had even kicked off his shoes, although Joanna didn't maintain the traditional shoeless Japanese house. Mariko didn't think they'd been to bed together. Not yet.

But soon. In their eyes and voices, she could see and hear that special, sweet anticipation.

She wondered how much longer Alex would argue that love did not actually exist.

She smiled, sipped her tea. "Now that you've matched the thumbprints, what will you do? Call the senator and tell him?"

"No. Not yet," Alex said.

"Why not?"

"I have a hunch . . . he's somehow part of this whole thing."

This was evidently a thought that he had not previously shared with Joanna, because she seemed surprised.

Alex said, "I think the senator knows you're here in Kyoto, Joanna. I think he's always known who kidnapped his daughter—and maybe even arranged the whole thing himself."

"But for God's sake, why?"

He took hold of Joanna's hand, and Mariko smiled again.

"It's just a hunch," he said, "but it explains a few things. Like where you got all that money to start a new life. We know now it didn't come from the Rand estate or Robert Rand's life insurance."

Mariko put down her teacup and patted her lips with a napkin. "Let me get this straight. The senator had his own daughter kidnapped from the vacation house in Jamaica, brainwashed her, then arranged for her to be set up in a new life with an entirely new identity?"

Alex nodded. "I don't pretend to know *why*. But where else would all the money come from—if not from Tom Chelgrin?"

Perplexed, Mariko said, "How could any father send his daughter away? How could he ever be happy if he could not see her any more?"

"Here in Japan," Alex said, "you're aware of the continuity of generations, you have a strong sense of family. It isn't always like that where I come from. My own parents were alcoholics. They nearly destroyed me—emotionally and physically."

"We have a few like that. Human animals."

"Fewer than we do."

"Even one is too many. But this thing you say Joanna's father did . . . it's still beyond my comprehension."

Alex smiled so beautifully that for an instant Mariko wished that she had found him first, before Joanna had ever seen him and before he had seen Joanna.

He said, "It's beyond your comprehension because you're so exquisitely civilized, Mariko."

She blushed and acknowledged the compliment with a slow bow of her head.

"There's something you haven't accounted for," Joanna told Alex. "The senator hired you to find his daughter, spent a small fortune on the search. Why would he do that if he knew where she was?"

Pouring more tea for himself, Alex said, "Misdirection. He was playing the stricken father who'd stop at nothing, spend anything, to get his child back. Who could suspect him of involvement? And he could afford to play expensive games."

Joanna was grim. "What he did to me—*if* he did it to me—was not a game. Since you first mentioned Tom Chelgrin on Wednesday, in the taxi, you've made it clear you don't like him or trust him. But why not?"

"He manipulates people."

"Don't all politicians?"

"I don't have to like them for it. And Chelgrin is smoother than most politicians. He's oily." Alex picked up another sandwich, hesitated, and put it down again without taking a bite. He seemed to have lost his appetite. "I was around Chelgrin a lot, and I finally figured he had only four facial expressions he put on for the public: a somber, attentive look when he pretended to be listening to the views of a constituent; a fatherly smile that crinkled his whole face but was maybe one micron deep; a stern frown when he wanted to be perceived as a hard-nosed negotiator; and grief for when his wife died, for when his daughter disappeared, for occasions when American soldiers were killed in one far place or another. Masks. He has all these masks. I think he enjoys manipulating people even more than the average politician. For him it's almost a form of masturbation."

"*Whew!*" Joanna said.

"Sorry if I come on a bit strong about him," Alex said. "But this is the first time I've had an opportunity to tell anyone what I really think of the man. He was an important client, so I always hid my true feelings. But in spite of the money he spent to find Lisa and all his weeping about his lost little girl, I never believed he was as devastated about her disappearance as everyone thought. He seemed . . . hollow. There was a coldness, a deep emptiness about him."

"Then maybe we should just stop right here."

"That's not an option."

Joanna frowned. "But if the senator is the kind of man you say, if he's capable of anything . . . we might all be better off if we forget him. At least now I know a little bit about why I've made a loner of myself. Programmed. I don't really have to know any more. I can live without knowing how it was done or who did it or why."

Mariko glanced at Alex. He met her eyes, and he was clearly as dismayed as she herself was. "Joanna-san, maybe right now you feel that you can live without knowing, but later you'll change your mind. You'll be curious. It'll eat at you like an acid. Everyone needs to know who he is, where he's come from. Ignorance isn't bliss."

"Besides," Alex said, taking a less philosophical approach, "it's too late for us to walk away from this. They won't let us. We've learned too much."

Joanna looked skeptical. "You think they might try to kill us?"

"Or worse."

"What's worse?"

Alex got up, went to the small window, and stood with his back to them, staring at the Gion and the dark city beyond. "Maybe one day we'll all wake up in other parts of the world with new names, new pasts, new sets of memories, troubled by nightmares but unaware that we were once Joanna Rand, Mariko Inamura, and Alex Hunter."

Mariko saw Joanna turn sickly white, as if pale moonlight had pierced the window and lit nothing in the room but her face.

"Would they really do it again?" Mariko asked.

Alex turned from the window. "Why not? It's an effective way of silencing us—without leaving behind any dead bodies to excite the police."

"No," Joanna said, and she looked haunted. "Everything that's happened to me in Japan, everything I am and want to become—all of it wiped out of my mind? No."

Mariko shuddered at the thought of being erased, remade, so utterly *controlled.*

"But *why?*" Joanna demanded. In frustration she slammed one fist onto the table, rattling the teacups and saucers. "Why did all of this happen? It's insane. It makes no sense."

"It makes perfect sense to the people who did it." Alex said.

"And it would make sense to us too, if we knew what they know," Mariko added.

Alex nodded. "Right. And we won't be safe until we *do* know what they know. As soon as we understand what motivated the Lisa-Joanna switch, we can go public, make headlines. When all the secrets are out in the open, the people behind this won't have any reason either to kill us or brainwash us."

"No reason except revenge," Joanna said.

"There's that," he admitted. "But maybe it won't matter to them once the game is over."

"All right. Then what's next?" Joanna asked.

Alex said, "Mariko-san, you have an uncle who's a psychiatrist. Sometimes does he use hypnotic regression to help his patients?"

"Yes." For years Mariko had tried to persuade Joanna to see Uncle Omi, but always without success.

To Joanna, Alex said, "He can pry open the memory block and help you recall things we need to know."

Joanna was skeptical. "Yeah? Like what?"

"Like the name of the man with the mechanical hand."

Joanna bit her lip, scowled. "Him? But what's it matter. He's just a man in a nightmare."

"Oh? Don't you remember what you said about him on Wednesday?"

Joanna shifted uneasily in her chair, glanced at Mariko, looked down at the table, and focused on her own pale, interlocked hands.

"At Nijo Castle?" Alex prompted.

"I was hysterical."

"You said that you suddenly realized the man in your nightmare was someone you'd actually known, not just a figment of a dream."

Reluctantly she said, "Yes. All right. But I'm not sure I want to find him."

"Until you find him and know what he did to you and understand why, the dreams aren't going to go away," Alex said.

Joanna continued to stare at her hands, which were clasped so tightly that the knuckles were sharp and bone-white.

"When you meet this man with the mechanical hand," Mariko said, "when you confront him face-to-face, you'll discover he isn't half as frightening in reality as he is in the nightmare."

"I wish I could believe that," Joanna said.

"The known," Mariko said, "is never as terrifying as the unknown. Damn it, Joanna, you *must* talk to Uncle Omi."

Joanna was clearly surprised to hear Mariko swear.

Mariko was a little surprised as well. She pressed on. "I'll call him in the morning."

Joanna hesitated, then nodded. "All right. But, Alex, you've got to go with me."

"A psychiatrist might not want me looking over his shoulder."

"If you can't go with me, I won't go."

Mariko said, "I'm sure Uncle Omi won't mind. After all, this is a very special case."

Relieved, Joanna leaned back in her chair.

"It won't be so bad, Joanna-san. My Uncle Omi isn't as scary as Godzilla. No radioactive breath. No giant tail to knock over skyscrapers."

Joanna found a smile. "You're a good friend, Mariko-san."

"Patients *are* sometimes spooked by his mechanical hand," Mariko said, and she was rewarded with Joanna's laughter like the music of silver bells, which reverberated in the windowpane that separated them from the cold, watchful face of the night.

32 Ignacio Carrera's breathing was violent but metronomical, as if he was exercising to Prussian martial music that no one else could hear. The barbells with which he struggled were heavier than he was, and judging by his cries of agony, which echoed through the private gym, the weight was too difficult for him. Nevertheless, he continued without pause. If the task had been nearer possibility, it wouldn't have been worthwhile. His strenuous efforts distilled alcohol-clear drops of sweat from him; perspiration streamed down his slick flesh, dripped off his earlobes, nose, chin, elbows, and fingertips. He wore only a pair of royal-blue workout shorts, and his strikingly powerful body glistened like every boy's dream of brute masculine strength. The sound of tortured tissues being torn down and stronger muscle fibers growing in their place was almost audible.

On Mondays, Wednesdays, and Fridays, without exception, Ignacio Carrera worked diligently on his calves, thighs, buttocks, hips, waist, lower back, and stomach. He had a prodigious set of stomach muscles. His belly was hard and concave, like a sheet of corrugated steel. On Tuesdays, Thursdays, and Saturdays, he labored to improve his chest, upper back, neck, shoulders, biceps, triceps, and forearms. On the seventh day he rested, although inactivity made him nervous.

Ignacio yearned for the transmutation of his flesh—every ounce, every cell. For relaxation, he read science fiction, and he longed to have the body of the perfect robot that occasionally appeared in those books—flexible yet invulnerable, precise in its movements and capable of grace yet charged with crude power.

He was only thirty-eight years old, but he looked much younger than his true age. His hair was coarse, thick, and black, and while he exercised, he wore a bright yellow ribbon around his head to keep the hair out of his face. With his strong features, prominent nose, dark and deeply set eyes, dusky complexion, and headband, he could have passed for an American Indian.

He did not claim to be an Indian, American or otherwise. He told people that he was a Brazilian. That was a lie.

In more genteel times, the gymnasium on the first floor of the Carrera house had been a music room in which guests in formal attire had frequently attended evenings of chamber music. At one end of the room was a circular dais on which a piano had stood. Now the enormous space—thirty by thirty feet—was carpeted solely with scattered vinyl mats and furnished largely with exercise machines. The high ceiling featured richly carved moldings, painted white with accents of gold leaf, and the plaster was pale blue.

Carrera was on the dais, imitating a machine, grimly working through yet another set of two-arm, standing presses. His obsessive-compulsive behavior in his private gym was similar to his approach to everything in life. He would almost rather die than lose, even when his only competition was himself. He pressed the great weight up, up, up again, through a haze of pain that, like a fog, engulfed him. He was determined to make it through the set of ten repetitions, just as he had endured tens of thousands of other sets over the years.

Antonio Paz, another bodybuilder who served as bodyguard and exercise partner to Carrera, stood slightly behind and to one side of his boss, counting aloud as each repetition was concluded. Paz was forty years old, but he also appeared to be younger than he was. At six-two, Paz was three inches taller than Carrera and twenty-five pounds heavier. He had none of his employer's good looks: His face was broad, flat, with a low brow. He also claimed to be Brazilian, but he was not.

Paz said, "Three." Seven repetitions remained in the set.

The telephone rang. Carrera could barely hear it above his own labored breathing. Through a veil of sweat and tears of pain, he watched Paz cross the room to answer the call.

All the way up with the barbell. Hold it at any cost. Four. Bring it down. Rest. Take it up. Hold. Five. Lungs burning. Bring it down. Machinelike.

Paz spoke rapidly into the phone, but Carrera could not hear what he was saying. The only sounds were his own breathing and the fierce thudding of his heart.

Up again. Hold. Arms quivering. Back spasming. Neck bulging. The pain! *Glorious.* Bring it down.

Paz left the telephone handset off the hook and returned to the dais. He resumed his former position and waited.

Carrera did four more presses, and when at last he dropped the barbell at the end of the set, he felt as though quarts of adrenaline were pumping through him. He was soaring, lighter than air. Pumping iron never left him tired. On the contrary, he was filled with an effervescent feeling of freedom.

In fact, the only other act that gave him as much of a rush was killing. Carrera loved to kill. Men. Women. Children. He didn't care about the sex or age of the prey.

He didn't often get the chance to kill, of course. Certainly not as frequently as he lifted weights and not as often as he would have liked.

Paz picked up a towel from a chair at the edge of the dais. He handed it to Carrera. "Marlowe is on the line from London."

"What does he want?"

"He wouldn't say. Except that it's urgent."

Both men spoke English as if they had learned the language at an upperclass school in England, but neither had ever attended any such institution.

Carrera stepped off the platform and went to the telephone to deal with Marlowe. He didn't move with the heavy, purposeful steps of his bodyguard but with such lightness and grace that he appeared to know the secret of levitation.

The telephone was on a table by one of the tall, mullioned windows. The tapestry drapes were drawn aside, but most of the light in the room came from the huge chandelier that hung above the dais; its hundreds of crystal beads and finely cut pendants shimmered with rainbow beauty. Now, in the late afternoon, the winter sunlight was thin, tinted gray by curdled masses of snow clouds; it seemed barely able to pierce the panes of the windows. Beyond the leaded glass lay Zurich, Switzerland: the clear blue lake, the crystalline Limmat River, the massive churches, the discreet banks, the solidly built houses, the glass office buildings, the ancient guildhalls, the twelfthcentury Grossmunster Cathedral, the smokeless factories—a fascinating mix of oppressive Gothic somberness and alpine charm, modern and medieval. The city shelved down the hills and spread along the shores of the lake, and the Carrera house stood above it all. The view was spectacular, and the telephone table seemed to be perched on top of the world.

Carrera picked up the receiver. "Marlowe?"

"Good afternoon, Ignacio."

Rolling his shoulders and stretching as he spoke, Carrera said, "What's wrong?"

He could be direct with Marlowe, because both his phone and the one in London were equipped with state-of-the-art scrambler devices, which made it nearly impossible for anyone to eavesdrop.

Marlowe said, "A couple hours ago Joanna Rand called British-Continental to ask about the payoff on her father's life insurance."

"You spoke to her?"

"Someone else. And a few minutes ago I was finally told about it, as if it wasn't terribly important. We have some idiots here."

"What did your idiot say to her?"

"He told her we hadn't any files that old. He used the Phillips name, of course. Now what do we do?"

"Nothing yet," Carrera said.

"I should think time is of the essence."

"It's not actually necessary that you think."

"Obviously the whole charade is crumbling."

"Perhaps."

"You're damned cool. What am I to do if she comes calling?"

"She won't," Carrera said confidently.

"If she's beginning to question her entire past, what's to keep her from popping up here in London for a closer inspection?"

"For one thing," Carrera said, "she carries a posthypnotic suggestion that makes it impossible for her to leave Japan. When she attempts to board a plane—or a ship, for that matter—she'll be overwhelmed by fear. She'll become violently ill. She'll need a doctor, and she'll miss her flight."

"Oh." Marlowe considered that information for a moment. "But maybe a posthypnotic suggestion won't have much force after all these years. What if she finds a way around it?"

"She might. But I'm getting daily reports from Kyoto. If she gets out of Japan, I'll know within an hour. You'll be warned."

"Nevertheless, I simply can't have her nosing around here. Far too much is at stake."

"If she gets to England," Carrera said, "she won't stay long."

"She can cause irreparable damage in just a day or two."

"If she gets to London, she'll be seeking an unraveled thread of the conspiracy. We'll provide several she can't overlook, and all of them will lead to Zurich. She'll decide this is where the mystery can be solved, and she'll come here. Then I'll deal with her."

"Look here, if she *does* slip past your people in Kyoto and out of the country, if she *does* show up in London by surprise, I'll make my own decisions about how to handle her. I'll have to move fast."

"That wouldn't be wise," Carrera said with a softness that was more ominous than any shouted threat could have been.

"I'm not just part of your game, you know. In fact, it's little more than a sideline to me. I've got a lot of things going on, a lot of interests to protect.

If the woman comes knocking at my door without warning, and if I feel she's endangering my entire operation, then I'll have her terminated. I'll have no choice. Is that clear?"

"She won't arrive without notice," Carrera said. "And if you harm her without permission, she won't be the only termination."

"Are you threatening me?"

"I'm merely explaining the consequences."

"I don't like to be threatened."

"I haven't the authority to whack you," Carrera said. "You know that. I'm just telling you what others will surely decide to do with you if you make a wrong move with this woman."

"Oh? And who would pull the trigger on me?" Marlowe asked.

Carrera named a singularly powerful and ruthless man.

The name had the desired effect. Marlowe hesitated and then said, "Are you serious?"

"I'll arrange for you to receive a phone call from him."

"For God's sake, Ignacio, why would a man of his position be so intently interested in one of these relocations?"

"Because it's not simply another relocation. She's special."

"What makes her different from the others? Who is she?"

"I can't tell you that."

"You can, but you won't."

"That's right."

"I've never seen her," Marlowe said. "She's liable to show up on my doorstep, and I wouldn't even recognize her."

"If the need arises, you'll be shown a photograph," Carrera said impatiently, eager to end the conversation and return to his exercises.

A moment ago Marlowe had been securely wrapped in that false but unshakable sense of superiority that came from pride in lineage, from years at Eton and then Oxford, and from the upper-crust, old-boy circles in which he moved. Now he was worried about being relegated to a secondary role in a major operation. To a man like Marlowe, who felt that he had been born to special privilege, any indication that he was *not* regarded as an insider was not merely a blow to his sense of job security but to his entire self-image. Carrera could hear a burgeoning anxiety in the Brit's voice, and it amused him.

Marlowe said, "You must be exaggerating the need for security. After all, I'm on your side. Surely a description of this woman can't hurt anything."

"I can't give you even a description. Not yet."

"What's her name?"

"Joanna Rand."

"I know *that* name. I mean, what's her real name?"

"You shouldn't even ask," Carrera said, and he hung up.

A strong gust of wind pressed suddenly and insistently against the window. A few specks of powdery snow spun through the ash-gray afternoon light. A storm was coming.

33

Shortly after six o'clock in the morning, Alex was awakened by Joanna's cries for help.

He was sleeping in the room next to hers, lying atop the covers in pants and T-shirt. His shoes were beside the bed, and he stepped into them as he plucked the pistol off the nightstand.

When he burst into Joanna's room and switched on the lights, she sat up in bed, blinking, dazed. She had been asleep and calling for help in a nightmare.

"The man with the mechanical hand?" he asked as he sat on the edge of her bed.

"Yeah."

"Want to tell me about it?"

"I already have. It's always the same."

Her face was pale. Her mouth was soft and slack from sleep, and her golden hair was damp with perspiration, yet she was a vision in yellow silk pajamas.

She leaned against him, wanting to be held—and they were kissing before he realized the depth of comfort that both of them needed. He slid his hands down her silk-sheathed back, up along her sides, to her breasts, and she whispered "yes," between kisses. He was overcome not merely by desire but by a great tenderness unlike anything he had ever felt before, by something that for a moment he couldn't name. But then he *did* have a name for it—love. He wanted her, needed her, but he also loved her, and in that moment he half believed in love even though he still struggled to resist its pull. The very thought of that freighted word brought to mind his parents' faces, their voices, their protestations of affection always followed swiftly by anger, shouts, curses, blows, pain. He must have become tense, because the quality of their kiss changed. Joanna felt it too, and when she pulled away, Alex didn't try to hold her.

"What's wrong?" she asked.

"I'm confused."

"Don't you want me?"

"More than anything."

"Then what're you confused about?"

"About what we can have together. Beyond tonight."

She touched his face. "Let the future take care of itself."

"I can't. I've got to know what you expect . . . what you think we can have together."

"Everything. If we want it."

"I don't want to disappoint you, Joanna."

"You won't."

"You don't know me. In some ways, commitment hasn't been any easier for me than it's been for you. I'm . . . an emotional cripple." He was amazed that he had admitted it even to himself, let alone to her. "A part of me is . . . missing."

"There's nothing wrong with you that I can see," she said.

"I've never said, 'I love you.' "

"But I've known it."

"I mean . . . I've never said it to *anyone*."

"Good. Then I'm the first."

"You still don't understand. I've never believed love exists. I don't know if I can say it . . . and *mean* it. Not even to you."

She was the first person to whom he had ever revealed anything of what had happened to him, and he talked for an hour, dredging up both familiar and long-repressed details of his nightmare childhood. The beatings. The bruises, the split lips, the blackened eyes, the broken bones. Scalded once with a pan of hot water that his mother threw at him. The scar was still between his shoulders. He'd turned from her just in time. Otherwise, his face would have borne the scar, and he might have been blinded. He recalled the psychological torture that filled every potential empty space between the physical assaults, like mortar in a stone wall. The insults, vicious teasing. The shouting, cursing. The unrelenting denigration and humiliation. Periodically they had locked him in a closet, sometimes for a few hours, sometimes for two or three days. No light. Food and water only if they remembered to provide it. . . .

At first, as he journeyed through his troubled past, his voice was supercharged with hatred, but gradually hatred gave way to hurt, and he found that he was grieving for the child he might have been and for the man into which that child might have grown. That was another Alex Hunter, lost forever, who perhaps would have been a better—certainly a happier—person than the Alex who had survived. As he talked, the memory sludge gushed from him in much the way that guilt might flow from a devout Catholic in a confessional, and when at last he stopped, he felt mercifully cleaner and freer than ever before in his life.

She kissed his eyes.

"Sorry," he said, ashamed of the pent-up tears that blurred his vision and that he was barely able to hold back.

"What for?"

"I never cry."

"That's part of your problem."

"I never wanted them to have the satisfaction of seeing me cry, so I learned to keep everything inside." He forced a smile. "This is the man you're relying on. Still have any confidence in him?"

"More confidence than ever. You seem human now."

More than ever, she wanted to make love, and so did he. But he needed to exercise the iron will and self-control that his monstrous parents had unwittingly taught him. "With you, Joanna, it's got to be right. Special. With you I want to wait until I *can* say those three little words and mean them. For the rest of my life, I'll carry with me every detail of the first time we make love, and from now on I don't intend to lug around anything but *good* memories."

"And neither do I. We'll wait."

She turned out the lights, and they lay together on the bed.

Shadows pooled around them. They were beyond the direct reach of the thin streams of morning sun that drizzled through the narrow gaps in the draperies.

Holding each other, kissing chastely, they were neither lovers nor would-be lovers. Rather, they were like animals in a burrow, pressing against each other for reassurance, warmth, and protection from the mysterious forces of a hostile universe.

Eventually he dozed off. When he woke, he was alone on the bed. At first he thought that he heard rain beating on the windows, but then he realized it was the sound of the shower, coming through the half-open door from the adjacent bathroom.

In a peculiar but comfortably domestic mood, he returned to the guest room, showered, and changed the bandage on his left arm. The shallow knife wounds were healing well.

By the time he dressed and got to the kitchen, Joanna was preparing a light breakfast: *shiro dashi*, white *miso*-flavored soup. Floating in each bowl was a neat tie of *kanpyo*, paper-thin gourd shavings, topped by a dab of hot mustard. The soup was properly served in a red dish with a gold rim, in keeping with the Japanese belief that a man "eats with his eyes as well as his mouth."

In this instance, however, Alex was at odds with traditional Japanese wisdom. He couldn't look away from Joanna long enough to appreciate the presentation of the *shiro dashi*.

Outside, a chill wind stripped dead leaves from a nearby mulberry tree and blew them against the kitchen window, startling him. It was a scarecrow sound, dry and brittle—and somehow more ominous than it should have been.

Streaked with rust-maroon the same shade as dried blood, the crisp brown leaves spun against the glass, and for a moment he half thought that they were about to coalesce into a monstrous face. Instead, the capricious wind suddenly carried them up and out of sight into the dead sky.

For a long time Joanna stared at the mulberry tree. Her mood, like his, had inexplicably changed.

After breakfast, Alex called Ted Blankenship's home number in Chicago. He wanted Ted to use Bonner-Hunter contacts in England, respected colleagues in the private security trade, to dig up all available information on the United British-Continental Insurance Association and on the solicitor J. Compton Woolrich.

He and Joanna passed the remainder of the morning with the Chelgrin file, searching for new clues. They didn't find any.

Mariko joined them for lunch at a restaurant two blocks from the Moon-glow, and then Joanna drove them directly to the hospital to see Wayne Kennedy. The police had already been there. Wayne had told them only what Alex wanted him to reveal, and they'd seemed satisfied—or at least not terribly suspicious. Wayne was just as Mariko had described him the previous night: brimming with energy in spite of his condition, joking with everyone, demanding to know when he would be permitted to walk, "because if I lay here much longer, my legs will atrophy." One of the nurses spoke English, and Wayne tried to convince her that he'd come to Japan to enter a tap-dancing contest and was determined to participate on crutches if necessary. The nurse was amused, but Wayne's best audience was Mariko. Alex had never seen her so animated and cheerful as she was in that small, clean, but decidedly dreary hospital room.

At three o'clock he and Joanna left to keep an appointment with Dr. Omi Inamura, but Mariko remained at the hospital.

The leaden sky had darkened and descended since they'd arrived at the hospital, as if a solar eclipse was in progress behind the vault of clouds.

In Joanna's Lexus, as she drove across the busy city, Alex said, "From now on, Mariko's going to put her matchmaking energy to work for herself."

"What do you mean?"

"You didn't notice the attraction between them?"

"Who? Mariko and Wayne?"

"It was obvious to me."

On the sidewalks, pedestrians hurried stoop-shouldered through a cold, brisk wind that flapped their coattails.

"I don't doubt Mariko and Wayne are attracted to each other, but nothing'll come of it," Joanna predicted. "Sad to say, but there's a strong cultural bias here against interracial relationships. If you aren't Japanese, then you're regarded as one degree of barbarian or another. It's almost not something you can become angry about when you encounter their prejudice, because they're so unfailingly polite about it, and they do treat everyone with great respect. It's just been a part of their worldview so long that it's in their bones."

Alex frowned. "Mariko doesn't think of *you* as a barbarian."

"Not entirely. She's a modern woman, but in some deep recess of her Japanese soul, the attitude is still present. On a subconscious level maybe, but it's there. And she's definitely not modern enough . . . for Wayne."

"I suspect you're wrong about that. She believes in love at first sight, you know."

"Mariko?"

"She told me."

"She was talking about Wayne?"

"About you and me. But she believes in it for herself too. Love at first sight."

"Is he good enough for her?" Joanna asked.

"He's first-rate, I think."

"Well, then, I hope she's even more of a modern woman than I think she is."

Joanna parked half a block from Omi Inamura's office but did not switch off the engine. Staring at his building through the windshield, she said, "Maybe this is a mistake."

"Why?"

"I'm scared."

"I'll be with you."

"What if Inamura *can* help me remember the face and name of the man with the mechanical hand? Then we'll have to go looking for him, won't we?"

"Yes."

"And when we find him . . ."

"Don't worry. It's like Mariko said last night. When you finally find him, he won't be as frightening as he is in your nightmares."

"No. Not as frightening. Maybe worse."

"Think positive," he said.

He reached out and took her hand. It was cold and moist.

A piercing wail rose in the distance. Traffic pulled aside to allow an ambulance to pass. The shrieking siren filled the world for a moment. In the gray-on-gray day, the fierce red light from the revolving emergency beacons seemed to have preternatural substance: It splashed like blood across the street, washed through the car in an intangible tide, and briefly transformed Joanna's face into a mask that might have been the universal face of any spattered victim, blue eyes wide but sightless and darkened by a glimpse of Death's own cold face in the penultimate moment.

Alex shivered.

"I'm ready," she said. She let go of his hand and switched off the car engine.

The siren had dwindled beyond hearing. The splashing red light was gone. Once again, the day was dead gray.

34 Bowing not from the waist but with a discreet inclination of his head and a rounding of his shoulders, not with any disrespect but with a sense that he understood the need for the old traditions while being personally somewhat above them, Dr. Omi Inamura welcomed Joanna and Alex into his inner office. He was in his early fifties, an inch shorter than Joanna, with slightly crinkled, papery skin and brown eyes as warm as his quick smile. In black slacks, suspenders, white shirt, baggy gray cardigan, and half-lens reading glasses, he seemed more like a literature professor than a psychiatrist.

The inner office, where Inamura treated his patients, was reassuringly cozy. One wall featured floor-to-ceiling shelves crammed with books, and another was covered by a tapestry depicting a wooded mountainside, a foaming waterfall and a river where accordion-sail boats were running with the wind toward a small village just below the caracts. Instead of a traditional analyst's couch, four dark-green armchairs were arranged around a low coffee table. The pine-slat blinds closed out the ashen daylight, and the electric lighting was indirect, soft, relaxing. A sweet, elusive fragrance threaded the air: perhaps lemon incense.

In one corner, a large birdcage hung from a brass stand. On a perch in the cage was a coal-black myna with eyes that were simultaneously bright and dark, like little drops of oil glistening in moonlight. From Mariko, they had learned that its name was Freud.

They sat in the armchairs, and Alex told Omi Inamura about Lisa Chelgrin's inexplicable metamorphosis into Joanna Rand. Mariko had prepared her uncle to expect a strange case, so the doctor was neither greatly surprised nor disbelieving. He was even cautiously optimistic about the chances of conducting a successful program of hypnotic regression therapy.

"However," Omi Inamura said, "ordinarily, I wouldn't employ hypnosis until I'd done extensive groundwork with you, Miss Rand. I find that it's always wise to begin with certain standard tests, a series of casual conversations, another series of investigative dialogues. I progress slowly, and I thoroughly explore the patient's problems until trust has been established. *Then* I use hypnosis only if it is indicated. This takes time. Weeks. Months."

"I appreciate your concern for the patient," Joanna said, "but we don't have months. Or even weeks."

Alex said, "What these people did to Wayne Kennedy was meant to be a warning. They'll give us a day or two to learn from it. When they see we aren't scared off, they'll try something . . . more violent."

The doctor frowned, still unconvinced that standard procedure should be set aside under even these circumstances.

"Isha-san," Joanna said, "all your other patients suffer from neuroses that they developed subtly and unconsciously over a period of many years. Am I correct?"

"Not entirely. Essentially—yes."

"But, you see, everything that I suffer from was *implanted* in me twelve years ago, in that room in my nightmare, by the man with the mechanical hand. With your other patients, of course, you must do a lot of groundwork to discover the sources of their illnesses. But in my case, we know the source. We just don't know *why* or *who*. So couldn't you just this once set aside your customary procedures?"

Alex was impressed by the vigor with which Joanna made her argument. He knew that she dreaded what she might discover when she was regressed, but she was not afraid to make that journey.

Omi Inamura was careful and conscientious. For a quarter of an hour they discussed the situation, studied it from various points of view, before he finally agreed to begin the regression therapy.

"But you must realize," he said, "that we very likely won't finish today. Indeed, it would be amazing if we did."

"How long?" Joanna asked.

The doctor shook his head. "I can't say. Therapy creates its own pace, which is different for each patient. But I understand how urgent this is, and I'll see you for at least an hour or two every day until we've learned what you need to know."

"That's kind of you, *Isha-san*, but I don't want you to interfere with your regularly scheduled appointments just because I'm a friend of Mariko's."

Dr. Inamura waved one slender hand dismissively and insisted that she was not causing him any trouble. "In Japan a psychiatrist is in somewhat the same position as that proverbial salesman who tries to sell refrigerators to the Eskimos. Because they live in a society that values tradition, teaches meditation, and encourages a code of etiquette and mutual respect, my people are generally at peace with themselves." With typical Japanese modesty, Inamura said, "While some colleagues might be so kind as to say I am moderately successful in my profession, I nevertheless have open appointments every day. Believe me, Miss Rand, you are not an inconvenience. Quite the opposite. It is an honor to provide treatment for you."

She inclined her head toward the doctor. "It is a privilege to be your patient, *Isha-san*."

"You regard me too highly, Joanna-san."

"As you do me."

"Shall we begin now?"

"Yes, please." She tried to appear calm, but a tremor in her voice betrayed her fear.

Alex put his hand on her arm. "It'll be okay."

After picking up a remote control from the coffee table, the doctor rose from his chair and came around the table, soundless on the thick carpet. He stood by Joanna's chair. "Lean back, please. Relax. Put your hands in your lap with the palms up. Very good."

He pointed the remote control at the tapestry, and the room lights, although not bright to begin with, slowly dimmed. Like cautious predators, shadows crept out of the corners.

"Ahhhhh," Freud said softly and appreciatively from his brass cage. "Ahhhhh."

The vanes of the highly lacquered pine shutters had previously glimmered with a liquid amber luminescence, but now they faded into gloom. Only the tapestry remained clearly revealed—and in the altered light it was transformed. It appeared to be mysteriously illuminated from within, and in spite of the stylized and idealized nature of the scene, it acquired such a strong aspect of reality that it almost seemed to be a view from a window.

"Look straight ahead," Inamura told Joanna. "Do you see the lovely tapestry on the wall?"

"Yes."

"Do you see the river in the tapestry?"

"Yes."

"Do you see the small boats?"

"I see them."

The tapestry light was subtly cycling up and down on a rheostat, within a narrow range of brightness: a hypnotic pulse.

"Concentrate on those boats, Joanna. Look closely at those little boats. Imagine yourself on one of them. You are standing on the deck. Water is lapping at the hull. Lapping gently at the hull. The water makes a soothing, rhythmic sound. The boat sways in the current. Gently. Gently. The boat sways gently in the water. Can you feel it swaying?"

"Yes," Joanna said.

Alex looked away from the tapestry and blinked rapidly. Omi Inamura's voice was so remarkably mellow and entrancing that Alex actually had felt the sway of the boat and had heard the faintest lapping of water.

Joanna continued to stare straight ahead.

"The boat is like a baby's cradle." Inamura's voice grew even softer and more intimate than it had been at the start. "It rocks gently, gently like a cradle. Gently like a cradle, rocking, rocking. Putting the baby to sleep. If you feel your eyes getting heavy now, you may close them."

Joanna closed her eyes.

The tapestry light stopped pulsing.

"Now I'm going to tilt your chair back slightly," Inamura said. "To help you relax."

Pointing the remote control at her, he touched another button, and her armchair changed positions until it was halfway between being a chair and a couch.

"Now I want you to think of your forehead, Joanna. You are frowning. Your forehead is lined. It should be smooth. As smooth as glass. You will relax. I will touch you, and those lines will vanish."

He placed his fingertips on her forehead, on her eyelids. The lines in her brow did, indeed, vanish.

"Joanna, you're clenching your teeth. I want you to relax the muscles in your face."

He lightly pressed his fingertips to her left temple, her right temple, her cheekbones, her chin. His touch was magical, smoothing away all visible signs of her anxiety.

"And now your neck . . . relax your neck muscles . . . now your left shoulder . . . very relaxed . . . your right shoulder . . . both arms . . . so very relaxed . . . deeper . . . deeper . . . your abdomen and your hips . . . limp . . . no tension . . . relaxed . . . and now your legs, your feet . . . even into your toes, all relaxed, totally and wonderfully relaxed. You feel as if you are floating on a vast body of water . . . floating on blue water under blue sky . . . drowsy . . . drowsy . . . drowsier . . . until you are now in a deep and natural sleep."

Joanna's breathing had become slow and regular, but Inamura continued:

"I am taking hold of your right hand, Joanna. I'm lifting your right arm. And now your arm is becoming stiff . . . rigid . . . cannot be moved . . . cannot be lowered. It is impossible for you to lower your arm. It is rigid and will stay where I have put it. I'm going to count down from three, and when I say 'one,' you will be unable to put your arm down. Three . . . you are sleeping deeply . . . two . . . deeper and deeper into a relaxed, natural sleep . . . one . . . your arm is rigid. Rigid. But try to prove me wrong, Joanna. Try to move your arm."

She tried, but the arm trembled, and she could not lower it.

Inamura nodded with satisfaction. "You may now lower your arm, Joanna. I am now *allowing* you to lower it. Indeed, your arm is now so limp that you cannot possibly hold it up."

Her arm dropped into her lap.

"And now you are in a deep, deep, very relaxed sleep, and you will answer a number of questions for me. You will enjoy answering them. Do you understand?"

"Yes," she murmured.

"Speak more clearly, please."

"Yes."

Inamura returned to his chair. He put the remote control on the coffee table.

"Fly away," said the myna in the cage. A wistfulness colored those two words, as if the bird actually understood their meaning.

Joanna was limp, but now Alex was tense. He slid to the edge of his chair and turned to his right, so he could look directly at her.

To Alex, Inamura said, "She's an excellent subject for hypnosis. Usually, there's a little resistance, but not with her."

"Perhaps she's had a lot of practice."

"Quite a lot of it, I think," said Inamura.

Joanna waited.

The doctor leaned back in his chair, every bit as relaxed as his patient. His face was half in shadow. One eye was dark, the other gilded by a soft golden light, a reflection off the brass birdcage. He thought for a moment, then said, "Joanna, what is your full name?"

"Joanna Louise Rand," she said.

"Is that truly your name?"

"Yes."

"Recently you learned that Joanna Rand is a false name and that you were once called something else. Is that true?"

"No."

"You don't remember making that discovery?"

"My name is Joanna Louise Rand."

"Have you heard the name 'Lisa Chelgrin'?"

"No."

"Think about it before answering."

Silence. Then: "I've never heard the name."

"Do you know a man named Alex Hunter?"

"Of course. He's here."

"Did he mention Lisa Chelgrin to you?"

"I've never heard that name."

"Joanna, you can't lie to me. Understand?"

"Yes."

"You must always tell me the truth."

"Always."

"It is utterly impossible for you to lie to me."

"Impossible. I understand."

"Have you ever heard the name 'Lisa Chelgrin'?"

"No."

Alex glanced at the doctor. "What's happening?"

Inamura stared at Joanna for a while, tilting his head just far enough so the reflected spot of golden light shifted from his right eye to his cheek, where it shimmered like a strange stigmata. Finally he said, "She might have been programmed with this response to this particular question."

"Then how do we get around the program?" Alex asked.

"Patience."

"I haven't much of that at the moment."

Inamura said, "Joanna, we will now do something amazing. Something you might think impossible. But it is not impossible and is not even difficult. It is simple, easy. We are going to make time run backward. You are going to get younger. It is beginning to happen already. You can't resist it. You don't want to resist it. It is a lovely, sweet, flowing feeling . . . getting younger . . . and younger. The hands of the clock are turning backward . . . and you feel yourself floating in time . . . getting younger . . . rapidly younger . . . and now you are thirty-one years old, not thirty-two any more . . . and now thirty . . . and now twenty-nine . . . floating back through time." He continued in that fashion until he had regressed Joanna to her twentieth year, where he stopped her. "You are in London, Joanna. The apartment in London. You are sitting in . . . let's make it the kitchen. You are sitting at the kitchen table. Your mother is cooking something. It smells delicious. Makes your mouth water. What is your mother cooking, Joanna?"

Silence.

"What is your mother cooking, Joanna?"

"Nothing."

"She is not cooking?"

"No."

"Then what smells so delicious?"

"Nothing. There's no smell."

"What is your mother doing if not cooking?"

"Nothing."

"Are you in the kitchen?"

"Yes."

"What's happening?"

"Nothing."

"All right then. What is your mother's name?"

"My mother's name is Elizabeth Rand."

"What does she look like?"

"She has blond hair like mine."

"What color are her eyes?"

"Blue. Like mine."

"Is she pretty?"

"Yes."

"Heavy or thin."

"Slender."

"How tall is she, Joanna?"

Silence.

"How tall is your mother?"

"I don't know."

"Is she tall, short, or of medium height?"

"I don't know."

"Okay. All right. But you are there in the kitchen."

"Yes."

"Now . . . does your mother *like* to cook, Joanna?"

"I don't know."

"What is her favorite food?"

Silence.

"What is your mother's favorite food, Joanna?"

"I don't know."

"She must like to eat certain things in particular."

"I suppose so."

"What kind of meals does she prepare for you?"

"Regular meals."

"All right . . . what about beef? Does she favor beef dishes?"

After a hesitation Joanna sighed and said, "My mother's name is Elizabeth Rand."

Frowning, Inamura said, "Answer my question, Joanna. Does your mother prepare beef for you?"

"I don't remember."

"Yes, you do," he said gently, encouragingly. "You're in the kitchen. What is your mother cooking for you, Joanna?"

She said nothing.

Inamura was silent, pondering her blank face. He changed the subject. "Joanna, does your mother like to go to the movies?"

Joanna shifted uneasily in the armchair but kept her eyes shut.

Inamura said, "Does your mother like the theater, perhaps?"

"I guess she does."

"Does she like the movies too?"

"I guess she does."

"Don't you know for sure?"

Joanna made no response.

"Does your mother like to read?"

Silence.

"Does your mother enjoy books, Joanna?"

"I . . . I don't know."

"Does it seem strange to you that you know so little about your own mother?"

Joanna squirmed in her chair.

Inamura said, "What's your mother's name, Joanna?"

"My mother's name is Elizabeth Rand."

"Tell me everything you know about her."

"She has blond hair and blue eyes like mine."

"Tell me more."

"She's slender and pretty."

"More, Joanna. Tell me more."

Silence.

"Surely you know more, Joanna."

"She's very pretty."

"And?"

"Slender."

"And?"

"I can't remember, damn it!" Her face contorted. "Leave me alone!"

"Relax, Joanna," Inamura said. "You will relax."

Joanna's hands were no longer in her lap. She was fiercely gripping the arms of the chair, digging her fingernails into the upholstery. Under her closed lids, her eyes moved rapidly, like those of a sleeper caught in a bad dream.

Alex wanted to touch and comfort her, but he was afraid that he might break the spell that the doctor had cast.

"Relax and be calm," Inamura instructed. "You are very relaxed and calm. In deep sleep . . . deep natural sleep . . . yes . . . yes, that's better . . . deep relaxation. Joanna, perhaps you can't remember these things because you never knew them. And perhaps you never knew them . . . because Elizabeth Rand never existed."

"My mother's name is Elizabeth Rand," Joanna said woodenly.

"And perhaps Robert Rand never existed either."

"My father's name is Robert Rand."

"And perhaps you cannot picture the activity in that kitchen," Inamura pressed on, "because it never existed. Nor the apartment in London. So I want you to float freely in time . . . drift . . . just drift in time . . . backward . . . backward in time. You are looking for a special place, a unique and important place in your life . . . a place that reeks strongly of antiseptics, disinfectants. You know the place I mean. You dream of it repeatedly. Now you're searching for it . . . drifting toward it . . . drifting toward that special place and time . . . settling into it . . . and now . . . *there* . . . you are there in that room."

"Yes," she whispered.

"Are you sitting or standing?"

A tremor passed through her.

"Easy, relax. You're safe, Joanna. Answer all my questions, and you will be perfectly safe. Are you sitting or standing in that room?"

"Lying down."

"On the floor or on a bed?"

"Yes. I'm . . ."

"What?"

"I'm . . ."

"You're what, Joanna?"

"I'm n-naked."

"You seem frightened. Are you frightened?"

"Yes. S-scared."

"What are you frightened of?"

"I'm . . . s-strapped down."

"Restrained?"

"Oh, God."

"Relax, Joanna."

"Oh, God. My ankles, my wrists."

"Fly away," said the myna bird. "Fly away."

Inamura said, "Who did this to you, Joanna?"

"The straps are so tight."

"Who did this to you?"

"They hurt."

"Who strapped you to this bed, Joanna? You must answer me."

"I smell ammonia. Strong. Makes me sick."

"Look around the room, Joanna."

She grimaced at the stench of ammonia.

"Look around the room," Inamura repeated.

She lifted her head from the chair in which she reclined, opened her eyes, and looked obediently from left to right. She didn't see Alex or the office. She now existed in another day and place. In her haunted eyes, a veil of weeks and months and years seemed to shimmer like a sheet of tears.

"What do you see?" Inamura asked.

Joanna lowered her head. Closed her eyes.

"What do you see in that room?" Inamura persisted.

A strange, guttural sound issued from her.

Inamura repeated the question.

Joanna made the peculiar noise again, then louder: an ugly, asthmatic wheezing. Suddenly her eyes popped open and rolled up until only the whites were visible. She tried to lift her hands from the arms of the chair, but apparently she believed they were strapped down, and her wheezing grew worse.

Alex rose to his feet in alarm. "She can't breathe."

Joanna began to jerk and twitch violently, as if great jolts of electricity were slamming through her.

"She's choking to death!"

"Don't touch her," Inamura said.

Although the psychiatrist hadn't raised his voice, his tone halted Alex.

Inamura's left eye gleamed from deep in the shadows that fell across that side of his face, and the reflection of gold light was over his right eye again, a bright cataract that gave him an eerie aspect. He seemed to have no concern about Joanna's apparent agony.

As Alex watched, Joanna's blank white eyes bulged. Her face flushed, darkened. Flecks of spittle glistened on her lips. Her wheezing grew louder, louder.

"For God's sake, help her!" Alex demanded.

Inamura said, "Joanna, you will be calm and relaxed. Let your throat muscles relax. You will do as I say. You *must* do as I say. Relax . . . tension draining out of you . . . breath coming easier . . . easier. Breathe slowly . . . slowly and deeply . . . deeply . . . evenly . . . very relaxed. You are in a deep and natural sleep . . . perfectly safe . . . in a deep and peaceful sleep. . . ."

Joanna gradually grew quiet. Her eyes, which had been rolled back in her head, came down where they belonged. She closed them. She was breathing normally again.

"What the hell was that all about?" Alex asked, badly shaken.

Inamura waved him back into his chair, and Alex sat reluctantly.

The doctor said, "Do you hear me, Joanna?"

"Yes."

"I never lie to you, Joanna. I tell you only the truth. I'm here only to help you. Do you understand that?"

"Yes."

"Now, I'm going to tell you why you had that little respiratory problem. And when you understand, you will not allow such a thing to happen ever again."

"I can't control it," she said.

"Yes, you can. I'm telling you the truth now, and you are well aware of that truth. You had difficulty breathing only because *they* told you that you'd be unable to breathe, that you'd suffocate, that you'd spiral down into uncontrollable panic if you were questioned thoroughly under the influence of drugs or hypnosis. They implanted a posthypnotic suggestion that caused this attack when I probed too deeply, evidently with the hope your seizure would terminate this interrogation."

Joanna scowled. "That's the same thing that caused my claustrophobia."

"Precisely," Inamura said. "And now that you're aware of it, you won't allow it to happen again."

"I hate them," she said bitterly.

"Will you allow it to happen again, Joanna?"

"No."

"Good," Inamura said.

Even in the dimly lighted room, Joanna looked so pale that Alex said, "Maybe we shouldn't continue with this."

"It's perfectly safe," the doctor said.

"I'm not so sure."

Inamura said, "Joanna, are you still in the room, that special room, the place that reeks of ammonia?"

"Ammonia . . . alcohol . . . other things," she said. "Sickening. It's so strong I can smell it and *taste* it."

"You are unclothed—"

"—naked—"

"—and strapped to the bed."

"The straps are too tight. I can't move. Can't get up. I've got to get up and out of here."

"Relax," Inamura said. "Easy. Easy."

Alex watched her anxiously.

"Be calm," Inamura said. "You will remember all of it, but you will do so quietly. You will be calm and relaxed, and you will not be afraid."

"At least the room's warm," she said.

"That's the spirit. Now, I want you to look around and tell me what you see."

"Not much."

"Is it a large place?"

"No. Small."

"Any furniture other than the bed?"

She didn't reply. He repeated the question, and she said, "I don't know if you'd call it furniture."

"All right. But what is it? Can you describe what's in the room with you?"

"Beside my bed . . . it's . . . I guess it's one of those cardiac monitors . . . you know . . . like in an intensive-care ward or hospital operating theater."

"An electrocardiograph."

"Yes. And beside it . . . maybe . . . a brainwave machine."

"An electroencephalograph. Are you in a hospital?"

"No. I don't think so."

"Are you hooked up to the machines now?"

"Sometimes. Not now. No beeping. No wiggly lines of light. Machines are . . . shut off."

"Is there anything else in the room?"

"A chair. And a cabinet . . . with a glass door."

"What's in the cabinet, Joanna?"

"Lots of small bottles . . . vials . . . ampules . . ."

"Drugs?"

"Yes. And hypodermic syringes wrapped in plastic."

"Are those drugs used on you?"

"Yes. I hate . . ." Her hands closed into fists, opened, closed. "I hate . . ."

"Go on."

"I hate the needle." She twitched at the word "needle."

"What else do you see?"

"Nothing."

"Does the room have a window?"

"Yes. One."

"Good. Does it have a blind or drapes?"

"A blind."

"Is the blind open or shut?"

"Open."

"What do you see through the window, Joanna?"

She was silent again.

"What do you see through the window?"

Her voice suddenly changed. It was so hard, flat, and cold that it might have been the voice of an altogether different person. "Tension, apprehension, and dissension have begun."

Omi Inamura gazed at her, captured by a silence of his own. At last he repeated the question. "What do you see beyond the window?"

She chanted—not woodenly but with a strange, cold anger. "Tension, apprehension, and dissension have begun."

"You are relaxed and calm. You are not tense or apprehensive. You are completely safe, utterly relaxed, calm, in a deep and natural sleep."

"Tension, apprehension, and dissension have begun."

Alex put one hand to the nape of his neck where a chill crept across his skin.

Inamura said, "What do you mean by that, Joanna?"

She was rigid in her reclining chair. Her hands were fisted against her abdomen. "Tension, apprehension, and dissension have begun."

A dry scratching noise rose from the shadows across the room. Freud was scraping his talons against his wooden perch.

"Tension, apprehension, and dissension have begun," Joanna repeated.

"Very well," Inamura said. "Forget about the window for the time being. Let's talk about the people who came to see you when you were kept in that room. Were there many of them?"

Shaking with what seemed to be anger but which Alex now realized might be the physical evidence of a fierce internal struggle to break free of the implanted psychological bonds that imprisoned her memory, she repeated, "Tension, apprehension, and dissension have begun."

"Now what?" Alex asked.

Omi Inamura was silent for so long that Alex thought he hadn't heard the question. Then: "The posthypnotic suggestion that triggered her breathing difficulties was their first line of defense. This is their second. I suspect this one is going to be harder to crack."

35

"Tension, apprehension, and dissension have begun."

"Do you hear me, Joanna?" the psychiatrist asked.

"Tension, apprehension, and dissension have begun."

Alex closed his eyes, silently repeating her chant along with her. He was teased by a vague sense of familiarity, as though he had heard it somewhere before.

Inamura said, "At the moment, Joanna, I'm not trying to pry any of your secrets out of you. I just want to know if you are listening, if you can hear my voice."

"Yes," she said.

"That sentence you keep repeating is a memory block. It must have been implanted posthypnotically. You will not use that sentence—'Tension, apprehension, and dissension have begun'—when you talk with me. You neither need nor want to avoid my questions. You came here to learn the truth. So just relax. Be calm. You are in a deep and natural sleep, safe in a deep sleep, and you will answer all my questions. I want you to *see* that memory block. It's lying in your mind, rather like a fallen tree lying across a highway, preventing you from going deeper into your memories. Visualize it, Joanna. A fallen tree. Or a boulder. Lying across the highway of memory. You can see it now . . . and you can even put your hands on it. You're getting a grip on it . . . such a powerful grip . . . and you feel a sudden rush of superhuman strength . . . so very strong, you are, so powerful . . . straining . . . lifting . . . lifting the boulder . . . casting it aside . . . out of the way. It's gone. The highway is open. No obstacle any more. Now you will remember. You will cooperate. Is that clear?"

"Yes," she said.

"Good. Very good. Now, Joanna, you are still in that room. You smell the alcohol . . . ammonia. Such a stench that you can even taste it. You're strapped to the bed . . . and the straps are biting into you. The blind is open at the window. Look at the window, Joanna. What do you see beyond the window?"

"Tension, apprehension, and dissension have begun."

"As I expected," Inamura said. "A difficult barrier."

Alex opened his eyes. "I've heard that chant before."

Inamura blinked and leaned forward in his chair. "You have? Where? When?"

"I can't recall. But it's strangely familiar."

"If you can remember, it would be enormously helpful," Inamura said. "I've got several tools with which I might be able to reach her, but I wouldn't be surprised if none of them worked. She's been programmed by clever and capable people, and more likely than not, they've anticipated most methods of treatment. I suspect there are only two ways I might be able to break through the memory block. And under the circumstances, with time so short, the first method—years of intensive therapy—isn't really acceptable."

"Not really," Alex agreed. "What's the second way?"

"An answering sentence."

"Answering sentence?"

Inamura nodded. "She might be requesting a password, you see. It's unlikely. But possible. Once she gives me the first line—'Tension, apprehension, and dissension have begun'—she might be waiting for me to respond with the appropriate second line. A sort of code. If that's the case, she won't answer my questions until I've given her the correct answering sentence."

Alex was impressed by the doctor's insight and imagination. "A two-piece puzzle. She's got the first piece, and we've got to find the second before we can proceed."

"Perhaps."

"I'll be damned."

"If we knew the source of the line she uses, we might be able to come up with the answering sentence. For instance, perhaps she's giving us the first line of a couplet of poetry."

"I believe it's from a book," Alex said. He rose to his feet, stepped out of the circle of chairs, and began to pace around the shadow-shrouded room, because pacing sometimes helped him think. "Something I read once a long time ago."

"While you think," said Omi Inamura, "I'll see what I can do with her."

For thirty minutes the doctor strove to break down the memory block. He cajoled and argued and reasoned with Joanna; he used humor and discipline and logic; he demanded, asked, pleaded; he pried and probed and thrust and picked at her resistance.

Nothing worked. She continued to answer with those same six words, grating them out in a tone of barely contained rage: "Tension, apprehension, and dissension have begun."

For a while Alex stood at the cage, eye to eye with the myna. It was a small bird, but its stare was fierce. Most of the time, the myna worked its orange beak without producing any sound, but once it said, "Nevermore," as though it were perched on a plaster bust above a study door, lamenting Poe's lost Lenore.

Alex wondered why the myna spoke in English rather than in Japanese. Omi Inamura spoke English well, but with most of his patients, he would converse in his native language.

"Freud," said the myna. "Freud. Fly away."

The creature's speech was simple mimicry, of course; it didn't understand anything it said. Still, Alex was intrigued by the quick intelligence in its eyes, and he wondered what thoughts went through the mind of a bird. Somewhere he'd read that birds were descended from flying reptiles. Although the myna was cute and appealing, its basically reptilian view of the world was most likely cold, strange, and utterly alien. If he'd been able to read its mind, no doubt he'd have recoiled in horror and disgust from—

Read its mind.

Mind reading.

Telepathy.

Tension, apprehension, and dissension have begun.

"I've got it," he said, turning away from the bird and hurrying back to the circle of armchairs. "The line. It's from a science fiction novel." He sat down on the edge of his chair. "I read it years and years ago."

"What's the title?" Inamura asked.

"The Demolished Man."

"You're certain?"

"Absolutely. It's a classic of the genre. When I was young, I read a lot of science fiction. It was the perfect escape from . . . well, from everything."

"Do you remember the author?"

"Alfred Bester."

"And the line Joanna keeps repeating? What's the significance of it?"

Alex closed his eyes and cast his mind back into his childhood, when the covers of books had been doors through which he escaped to far places where there had been no monsters as terrible as drunken and abusive parents. He could see the futuristic artwork on the paperback almost as clearly as if he'd held it in his hands only a week ago.

"The novel's set a few hundred years in the future, during a time when the police use telepathy to enforce the law. They're mind readers. It's impossible for anyone to commit murder and get away with it in the society Bester envisions, but there's one character who's determined to kill someone and escape punishment. He finds a way to conceal his incriminating innermost thoughts. To prevent the telepathic detectives from reading his guilt in his own mind, he mentally recites a cleverly constructed, infectious jingle while retaining the ability to concentrate on other things at the same time. The monotonous repetition of the jingle acts like a shield to deflect the snooping telepaths."

Inamura said, "And one of the lines he recites is 'Tension, apprehension, and dissension have begun.' "

"Yeah."

"Then if there *is* an answering sentence that will dispose of Joanna's memory block, it's almost certainly another line of that jingle. Do you remember the rest of it?"

"No," Alex said. "We'll have to get the book. I'll call my office in Chicago and have someone track down a copy. We—"

"That might not be necessary," Dr. Inamura said. "If the novel is a classic in its field, there's a good chance it's been translated into Japanese. I'll be able to obtain it from a bookstore here or from a man I know who deals in rare and out-of-print titles."

That put an end to their first session. There was no point in continuing until Inamura had a copy of *The Demolished Man.* Once more the doctor turned his attention to Joanna. He told her that upon waking she'd remem-

ber all that had transpired between them—and would be more easily hyp-
notized the next time that he treated her.

"In fact," Inamura told her, "in the future you will slip into a deep trance
upon hearing me speak just two words: 'dancing butterflies.' "

"Dancing butterflies," Joanna repeated, at his request.

The psychiatrist brought her slowly back from the past to the present,
used the remote control to tilt her chair into the full upright position, and
then woke her.

Outside, when Alex and Joanna left Inamura's building, the day had
grown colder. The huffing wind seemed like a living presence, pulling and
shoving with malicious intent.

As they walked toward Joanna's Lexus, a large black-and-yellow cat scurried along the gutter. It jumped the curb to the sidewalk, directly into their
path, glanced warily at them, and then dashed down a set of shadow-filled
basement steps. Alex was glad for the touch of yellow in its coat.

"Dancing butterflies," Joanna said.

"You find that curious?"

"I find it very Japanese. Dancing butterflies. Such a lovely, delicate image
to be associated with a grim business like this."

The afternoon was giving way to evening. The low clouds were as dark
as slate, and the sky looked too hard to be the home of any but malevolent
gods.

36 Twenty-four hours later. Saturday afternoon.
The myna climbed the curved walls of its cage, and from
time to time its talons plucked a reverberant note from the
brass, which to Alex sounded like a piano wire snapping under too much tension.

"Dancing butterflies," said Omi Inamura.

Joanna's eyes fluttered and closed. Her breathing changed. She went limp
in the big reclining chair.

With great skill, the psychiatrist took her back through the years until she
was once again deep in the past, in the room that stank of antiseptics and
disinfectants.

"There is a window in that room, isn't there, Joanna?" Inamura asked.

"Yes. One."

"Is the blind open?"

"Yes."

The doctor hesitated, then asked, "What do you see beyond that window?"

"Tension, apprehension, and dissension have begun."

Inamura opened a copy of the Japanese edition of *The Demolished Man*, one page of which he had marked with a blue silk ribbon. Joanna had recited the last line of the jingle that was an integral part of Bester's story. Inamura read aloud the next to last line, hoping that it would prove to be the answering sentence—if there was such a thing. " 'Tenser, said the Tensor.' "

Although the doctor had not asked a question, Joanna responded. "Tension, apprehension, and dissension have begun."

" 'Tenser, said the Tensor.' "

Joanna did not respond this time.

Inamura leaned forward in his armchair. "You are in the room that smells of alcohol . . . ammonia. You're strapped to the bed."

"Yes."

"There is a window. An open window. What do you see beyond the window, Joanna?"

"The roof of a house," she said without hesitation. "It's a mansard roof. Black slate. No windows in it. I can see two brick chimneys."

"By God, it worked!" Alex said.

"I got the Bester novel last evening," Inamura said, "and read it in a single sitting. It's engrossing science fiction. Do you remember what happens to the killer at the end of the novel?"

"He's caught by the telepathic police," Alex said.

"Yes. Caught in spite of all his cleverness. And after they apprehend him, rather than imprison or execute him, they 'demolish' the man. They tear down his psyche, wipe out his memory. They remove every twist and quirk that made it possible for him to commit murder. Then they reconstruct him as a model citizen. *They make an entirely new person out of him.*"

"So in some ways it's similar to Joanna's experience. Except that she's an innocent victim."

"Some things that were science fiction thirty years ago are fact today. For better or worse."

"I've never doubted that modern brainwashing techniques could produce a total identity change," Alex said. "I just want to know why the hell it was done to Joanna."

"Perhaps we'll find the answer today," the psychiatrist said. He faced his patient again. "What else do you see beyond the window, Joanna?"

"Just the sky."

"Do you know what city you're in?"

"No."

"What country?"

"No."

"Let's talk about the people who visit you in that room. Are there many of them?"

"A nurse. Heavyset. Gray hair. I don't like her. She has a . . . strange smile."

"Do you know her name?"

"I can't remember."

"Take your time."

Her face clouded with puzzlement as she struggled to recall the nurse's name. At last: "No. It's gone."

"Who else visits you?"

"A woman with brown hair, brown eyes. Sharp features. She's very brisk, businesslike. She's a doctor."

"How do you know that?"

"I . . . I guess maybe she told me. And she does things . . . doctor things."

"Such as?"

"She takes my blood pressure and gives me injections and runs all kinds of tests on me."

"What's her name?"

"I don't know."

"Have you just forgotten—or did she never tell you her name?"

"I don't think she ever told me."

"Is there anyone else who comes to see you in that room?"

Joanna shuddered. Although she didn't reply, she crossed her arms protectively across her breasts, and a shadow of fear fell across her face.

"There is someone," said Inamura. "Who, Joanna? Who else comes to see you?"

She chewed on her lower lip. Her hands were fisted. Her voice faded to a tremulous whisper: "Oh, God, no. No. No."

"Relax. Be calm," Inamura instructed.

Alex fidgeted in his chair. He wanted to take her in his arms and hold her, let her know that she was safe.

Inamura persisted: "Who else comes to see you, Joanna?"

"The Hand," she said thinly.

"The Hand? Do you mean the man with the prosthetic device, the mechanical hand?"

"Him."

"Is he a doctor too?"

"Yes."

"How do you know that?"

"The woman doctor and the nurse call him 'Herr Doktor.' "

"Did you say *Herr*, the German form of address?"

"Yes."

"Are the women German?"

"I don't know."

"Is the man German?"

"The . . . The Hand? I don't know."

"Do they speak German?"

"Not to me. Only English to me."

"What language do they speak among themselves?"

"Sometimes English."

"And at other times?"

"Something else."

"Might it be German?"

"I guess. Maybe."

"When they're speaking in English, do they have German accents?"

"I . . . I'm not sure. Accents. All of them have accents. But not necessarily German."

"Do you think this room could be somewhere in Germany?"

"No. Maybe. Well . . . I don't know where it is."

"The doctor, this man who—"

"Do we have to talk about him?" she asked plaintively.

"Yes, Joanna. We must talk about him. Just relax. He can't hurt you now. Tell me—what does he look like?"

"Brown hair. He's going bald."

"What color eyes?"

"Light brown. Pale. Almost yellow."

"Tall or short? Thin or fat?"

"Tall and thin."

"What does he do to you in that room?"

She rolled her head slowly from side to side on the chair, declining to answer.

"What does he do to you?"

The myna was suddenly frantic, rapidly circling the walls of its cage, plucking at the brass bars with its talons and beak.

"What does he do to you, Joanna?"

The *plink-plonk-plink* of brass was a cold, flat music, as though a draft out of Hell were stirring the music of damnation from a set of wind chimes.

Inamura was insistent. "What does he do to you, Joanna?"

At last she said shakily: "Treatments."

"What sort of treatments?"

Her lashes fluttered, and from her closed eyes came slow tears.

Alex reached out for her from his chair.

"No," the doctor said almost sotto voce but forcefully.

"But she needs—"

"She needs to remember."

Alex said, "But I can't—"

"Trust me, Mr. Hunter."

Anguished, Alex drew back from Joanna.

"What sort of treatments?" Inamura asked again.

"I'm dying." She shuddered. She pressed her arms even tighter across her chest, shrank back defensively into the chair. "Each time I d-d-die just a little more. Why not kill me all at once? Why not get it over with?" She was crying openly now. "Please, just get it over with."

"You aren't dying," Inamura assured her. "You're safe. I am protecting you, Joanna. Just tell me about these treatments. What are they like?"

She could not speak.

"All right," the psychiatrist said gently. "Relax. Be calm. You are calm and relaxed . . . relaxed . . . safe and at peace and relaxed . . . sleeping deeply . . . such sweet tranquillity."

Her shaking subsided. Her tears stopped flowing. But she kept her arms crossed defensively.

"You are still in that room," Inamura said when Joanna was ready to go on. "Alone in that room, on the bed, strapped down."

"Naked," she said. "Under a sheet."

"You haven't yet had your daily treatment. Herr Doktor will be here in a moment, and you will describe what happens after he arrives. You will describe it calmly, serenely. Begin."

Joanna swallowed hard. "The woman doctor . . . comes into the room and pulls the sheet down to my waist. She makes me feel so helpless, utterly defenseless. She hooks me up to the machines."

"To the electrocardiograph and electroencephalograph?"

"Yes. She tapes electrodes to me. Cold against my skin. The machine keeps beeping . . . beeping . . . beeping. It drives me crazy. She slips a board under my arm. Tapes it in place. Hooks me up to the bottle."

"Do you mean that you're being fed intravenously?"

"That's always how the treatment starts." Gradually Joanna's speech became slower and thicker than normal. "And she covers my breasts with the sheet . . . watches me . . . watches me . . . takes my blood pressure . . . and after a while . . . I begin to float . . . light, so light, like a feather . . . but aware of everything . . . too aware, painfully aware . . . a sharp, terrible awareness . . . but all the time floating . . . floating."

"Joanna, why is your speech slurring?"

"Floating . . . numb . . . drifting . . ."

"Does the IV bottle contain a drug in addition to glucose?"

"Don't know. Maybe. Up, up, up like a balloon."

"It must be a drug," Alex said.

Inamura nodded. "Joanna, I don't want you to speak in that thick, sluggish manner. Speak normally. The drug is still being administered to you, but it won't affect your speech. You'll continue to experience this treatment, and you will tell me about it in your usual, unaffected voice."

"All right."

"Good. Continue."

"The woman leaves. I'm alone again. Still floating. But I don't feel high or happy. Never do. Just scared. Then . . ."

"What happens then?" Inamura encouraged.

"Then . . . then . . . the door opens and he enters. The Hand."

"Herr Doktor?"

"Him, him."

"What's he doing?"

"I want out of here."

"What is the doctor doing, Joanna?"

"Please. Please let me out."

"Be calm. You are in no danger. What is he doing?"

She continued reluctantly: "Pushing the cart."

"What cart is he pushing?"

"It's covered with medical instruments."

"Go on."

"He comes to the bed. His hand . . ."

"What about his hand, Joanna?"

"He . . . he . . . he . . . he holds his hand in front of my face."

"Yes?"

"Opens and closes his steel fingers."

"Does he say anything?"

"No. Just the s-sound of his fingers. Clicking."

"How long does this go on?"

"Until I'm crying."

"Is that what he wants—to see you cry?"

She was shivering.

The room seemed cold to Alex too.

"He wants to scare me," she said. "He enjoys it."

"How do you know he enjoys it?" asked Inamura.

"I know him. The Hand. I know him so well by now. I hate him. Standing over me. Looking down. The clicking fingers. He grins."

"So he makes you cry. He likes watching you cry. But then what does he do?"

"No," she said miserably. She turned onto her side in the big reclining chair, facing Alex, eyes still closed, arms still tucked against her breast. She drew her knees up slightly, into the fetal position. "No . . . please."

"Relax, Joanna," Inamura said. "You are there but detached from the experience now, insulated from the feelings this time. You are there only as an observer."

"No . . . no." But her protests were merely weak denials of the horror of those memories, not a refusal to proceed with the session.

Alex was suffering with her, because the helplessness that she had felt while strapped to that bed was akin to the sense of helplessness that had informed his entire childhood.

"What is Herr Doktor doing now?" Inamura asked.

"The needle."

"The IV?"

"No. Another. Oh, God."

"A hypodermic?"

"It'll kill me this time," she said with pathetic conviction.

"Rest easy. Be calm. You're safe now. What's so special about this needle?"

"It's so big. Huge. It's filled with fire."

"You're afraid the needle will sting?"

"Burn. Burn like acid. Squirting acid into me."

"Not this time," Inamura assured her. "No pain this time."

Beyond the closed pine shutters, a sudden gust of wind shrieked at the windows, and the glass thrummed.

Alex almost felt as if the man with the mechanical hand was in Omi Inamura's office. He could feel an evil presence, a sudden and chilling change in the air.

"Let's continue," the psychiatrist said. "The doctor uses this needle, gives you an injection, and then—"

"No. Not my neck. Not my neck. Jesus, *no!*"

She thrashed on the reclining chair, wrenching herself out of the fetal position almost as if racked by an extreme epileptic spasm, flopping onto her back, rigid, shaking, tossing her head from side to side.

Inamura said, "What's wrong with your neck, Joanna?"

"The needle!"

"He puts the needle in your neck?"

Alex felt ill. He touched his own neck.

Mentally, emotionally, spiritually, Joanna was not in Inamura's office. She was deep in the past, living through hell once more. And though the doctor had told her that she would remain emotionally detached from the memory and would report upon it in an objective fashion, she was unable to maintain the distance he demanded of her. She was convulsed by the memory of pain as if she were suffering the real agony at that very moment.

"It hurts, everything hurts, my veins are on fire, blood's boiling, bubbling, oh, God, Jesus, God, it's eating me up, eating me up, like acid, lye, turning me black inside. *Somebody, please, please help me!*"

Her eyes were squeezed tightly shut, as if she could not bear what she would see if she opened them. The arteries throbbed at her temples, and the muscles in her neck were taut. She writhed and cried out wordlessly, and her back raised up from the reclining chair in such an extreme arch that only her feet, her shoulders, and the back of her head were touching the upholstery.

Dr. Inamura spoke comfortingly to her, trying to talk her down from the ledge of hysteria on which she was precariously balanced.

Joanna responded to him but not as quickly as she had done earlier. She slowly relaxed—although not as completely as before. Still in a trance, she rested for a few minutes, though she never quite stopped trembling. Now and then her hands fluttered up from the arms of her chair and described meaningless patterns in the air before settling down again.

Dr. Inamura and Alex waited silently for her to be calm enough to go on with the session.

The wind huffed at the shuttered windows again, harder than before, and then keened shrilly, as if in disappointment, when it was unable to get inside.

At last Inamura said, "Joanna, you are in the room that smells of antiseptics, disinfectants. The odor is so heavy that you can taste it. You are strapped to the bed, and the treatment has begun. Now dispassionately, quietly, I want you to tell me what they do to you, what the treatment is like."

"Floating. Floating and burning at the same time."

"What does Herr Doktor do?"

"I'm not sure."

"What do you see?"

"Brilliant colors. Whirling, pulsing colors."

"What else do you see?"

"Nothing else. Just the colors."

"What do you hear?"

"The Hand. He's talking. Very distant."

"What's he saying?"

"Too distant. I can't make out the words."

"Is he talking to you?"

"Yes. And sometimes I answer him."

"What do you say to him?"

"My voice is as distant as his. I can barely hear myself. I'm so far away, high above, high up and floating in the fire, in the pain, lost in the pain."

"If you try now, you'll be able to hear yourself. Just listen to your voice, and you will hear it clearly."

"No. Can't make it out. I'm flying a thousand miles above myself, too high to hear."

"Joanna, he's talking to your subconscious. Your conscious awareness is being suppressed by drugs, and your subconscious is wide open to him."

"High, high above myself," she insisted.

"It's only your conscious mind that's floating up there. On a conscious level, perhaps you can't hear him, but your subconscious hears him clearly, every word, every nuance. I want you to let your subconscious speak. What is Herr Doktor saying?"

Joanna fell into silence and became deathly still.

"What does he say to you?"

"I don't know, but I'm scared."

"What are you scared of, Joanna?"

"Losing things."

"What things?"

"Everything."

"Please be more specific."

"Pieces of myself."

"You're afraid of losing pieces of yourself?"

"Pieces are falling away. I'm like a leper."

"Pieces of memory?" Alex guessed.

"I'm crumbling," Joanna said. "High above, I'm floating and burning, but down here I'm crumbling."

"Is it memory you're losing?" Inamura pressed.

"I don't know. But I feel it going."

"What does he say to you to make you forget?"

"Can't quite hear."

"Strain for it. You can remember."

"No. He took that away from me too."

Inamura followed that line of questioning until he was convinced that he would learn nothing more from it.

"You've done well, Joanna. Very well, indeed. And now the treatment is finished. The needle has been removed from your neck. The other needle has been removed from your arm. You are gradually settling down, down."

"No. I'm still floating. Not burning any more, not being eaten up inside any more, but floating. I keep floating for a long time afterward. For at least an hour. Longer."

"All right. You're floating, but the needles are out of you. What happens now?"

She covered her face with her hands.

"Joanna," Inamura said, "what's happening to you?"

"I'm ashamed," she said miserably.

"There's no need to be ashamed."

"You don't know," she said from behind her hands. "You can't ever know."

"Nothing to be ashamed of at all. Put your hands down, Joanna. Put them down. It's okay. That's right. You haven't done anything wrong. You're a good person. You have a good heart. You're the victim here, not the criminal."

She could not speak. She tried and failed.

The wind at the windows.

The bird in the cage. Talons on the brass.

She struggled to tell Inamura what he wanted to know, and it was clear by her tortured expression that she needed to spill those secrets and be rid of them. But her mouth worked without producing a sound.

Alex could hardly bear to watch her as she lay torn between shame and the need to confess, between fear and freedom. Yet he couldn't look away from her.

Finally she said, "If only . . . I could die."

"You don't really want to die," Inamura assured her.

"More than anything."

"No."

"It's the only way to stop him . . . what he does to me."

"It's already stopped. Years ago. You're only plagued by the memory now, because you haven't been able to face it. Confront it and be freed, Joanna. Tell me the rest of it and be free."

Her voice was so faint that Alex had to lean forward in his chair to catch what she said: "Hear it? Hear it?"

"What do you hear?" Inamura asked.

"The clicking."

"Clicking?"

"Click, click, click," she said softly.

"What is this clicking?"

"The gears."

"Ah. In his hand?"

"Soft at first. Then louder. Then as loud as gunshots. The gears in his fingers."

She shuddered and made a pitiful sound that weighed like a stone on Alex's heart.

Inamura said, "Where is Herr Doktor now?"

In her still small voice, she said, "Beside the bed. He strokes my face. With those steel fingers. Click, click, click."

"Go on."

Her hands moved from her face to her throat.

"He massages my throat," she said. "I try to pry his hand away. I really do try. But I can't. It's steel. So powerful. Hear the little motors purring in it?"

She opened her eyes, staring at the ceiling. Tears shimmered.

"Go on," said Inamura.

"He grins," she said. "I'm floating very high, but I can see his grin. I'm way up high, but I can feel what he's doing. I ask God to stop him, just to stop him, that's all, because I'm too weak, I need God's help, but it . . . never . . . it never comes."

"Don't bottle this up," the psychiatrist said gently. "Don't continue to make a secret of it. Tell me everything, Joanna. Free yourself of it."

Her hands were trembling. She lowered them from her throat to her breasts.

"The clicking," she said. "It's so loud I can't hear anything else. It fills the room. Deafening."

"What does he do?"

"He pulls the sheet away. He draws it to the bottom of the bed. Uncovers me. I'm naked."

Her cheeks were wet with tears again, but she was not sobbing.

"Go on," Inamura said.

"He stands there. Grinning. Takes the electrodes off me. Touches me. He has no right to touch me like that, not like that, but I can't do anything. I'm flying high and weak."

"Where is he touching you?"

"My breasts. Stroking, squeezing with those steel fingers. Hurting me. He knows he's hurting me. He likes to hurt me. Then he touches me with the other hand too, the real hand. It's sweaty. He's rough with that hand too . . . rough . . . demanding . . . using me. . . ."

Joanna's voice faded word by word, until she couldn't speak any more. Her face was wrenched into the most devastating expression of anguish that Alex had ever seen, yet she made only the softest sounds, as though her shame and sense of violation were so heavy that her voice was crushed beneath them.

The sight of her in such excruciating emotional pain struck Alex with the force of a thunderbolt. In the past few days he had learned to feel things he'd never felt before. In himself, he'd discovered possibilities of which he'd been ignorant all his life. Joanna had sensitized him. But everything that he had experienced since meeting her was only as powerful as a spring breeze compared to the emotional storm that shook him now. He couldn't bear to see her like this. The horror of her experiences with the man she called "The Hand" affected Alex more profoundly than if her suffering had been his own. If he had incurred the wound himself, he could grit his teeth and stitch it up with the stoicism he had long cultivated, but because it was her wound, he could do little to influence the healing of it. He was shattered by the full and unwelcome realization of his helplessness.

For a few minutes Dr. Inamura patiently reassured her, until at last she regained her composure. When she was still and no longer crying, he urged her to pick up her story where she had left it. "What is Herr Doktor doing now, Joanna?"

Alex interrupted. "Surely, *Isha-san*, you don't have to pursue this thing any further."

"But I must," Inamura disagreed.

"I think we know all too well what he did to her."

"Yes, of course, we know. And I understand how you feel," the psychiatrist said sympathetically. "But it's essential that she say it. She's got to reveal everything, not for your benefit or mine but for her own. If I allow her to stop now, the ugly details will remain in her forever, festering like filthy splinters."

"But it's so hard on her."

"Finding the truth is never easy."

"She's suffering such—"

"She'll suffer even more if I let her stop now, prematurely."

"Maybe we should give her a rest and pick up here tomorrow."

"Tomorrow we have other tasks," said Inamura. "I need only a few minutes to finish this line of questioning."

Without enthusiasm, Alex admitted the superiority of Inamura's argument.

The doctor said, "Joanna, where are Herr Doktor's hands now?"

"On me. On my breasts," she said.

There was a new, peculiar, and disturbing flatness in her voice, as though a part of her had died and was speaking from a dark, frigid place on the other side of life.

"What does he do next?" Inamura asked.

"The steel hand moves down my body."

"Go on."

"Down to my thighs," she said flatly.

"And then?"

"Everything's taken."

"What is taken?" Inamura asked.

"Hope. All gone. Nothing left to cling to."

"No, Joanna. Hope can never be taken away forever. It's the one thing in us that's always renewed. He took your hope away only for a short while. He can't win in the long run unless you allow him to win. What does he do now? Please tell me, Joanna."

"He touches me there."

"Where does he touch you?"

"Between my legs."

"And then?"

"He's grinning."

"And then?"

"Click, click, click."

"Go on."

She was silent.

"Joanna?"

She said, "I need . . ."

"Yes?"

". . . a minute."

"Take your time," Inamura said. He glanced at Alex, and his eyes revealed an infinite sadness.

Alex looked down at his hands. They were fisted on his knees. He wanted to beat Herr Doktor until his knuckles were scraped and raw, until every bone in his hands was broken, until his arms were so weary that he could no longer lift them from his sides.

On its perch in the cage, the myna erupted in a brief rage, flapping its wings frenziedly before abruptly going as still as though it had spotted a predator.

In that drab voice borrowed from someone dead, as though she were channeling a despairing spirit that was trapped in Hell, she said, "Touching me between the legs. Cold steel. Clicking so loud. Like explosions."

"And then?"

"He opens me."

"And then?"

"Puts one."

"Does what?"

"Puts one of his steel fingers."

"Puts it where?"

"Inside me."

"Be more specific."

"Isn't that enough—what I said?"

"No. You mustn't be afraid to say it clearly."

"Into . . . my vagina."

"You're doing well. You were used terribly. But in order to forget, you must first remember. Go on."

Her hands were still clasped protectively over her breasts. "The clicking noise fills me, fills me inside, so loud, echoing through me."

"And then?"

"I'm afraid he'll hurt me."

"Does he hurt you?"

"He threatens me."

"What does he threaten to do?"

"He says he'll . . . tear me apart."

37

At six o'clock Sunday morning, Joanna was awakened by thirst. Her lips were chapped, and her throat was dry. She felt dehydrated. The previous night, after the exhausting session in Inamura's office, they had eaten a large dinner: thick steaks, Kobe beef, the finest meat in the world, from cattle that had been hand-massaged daily and fed nothing but rice, beans, and plenty of beer. With the steaks, they had finished two bottles of fine French wine, a rare and expensive luxury in Japan. Now the alcohol had leached moisture from her and had left a sour taste.

She went into the bathroom and greedily drank two glasses of water. It tasted almost as good as wine.

Returning to bed, she realized that for the first time in twelve years, her sleep had not been interrupted by the familiar nightmare. She had not dreamed about the man with the mechanical hand.

She was free at last, and she stood very still for a moment, stunned. Then she laughed aloud.

Free!

In bed, wrapped in a newfound sense of security as well as in blankets and sheets, she sought sleep again and found it quickly after her head touched the pillow.

She woke naturally, three hours later, at nine o'clock. Though her sleep had been dreamless, she was less enthusiastic about her new freedom than she had been in the middle of the night. She wasn't certain why her attitude had changed; but whatever the reason, the mood of innocent optimism was gone. She was wary, cautious, tempered by an intuition that told her more—and worse—trouble was coming.

Curious about the weather, she went to the nearest window and drew back the drapes. A storm had passed through during the night. The sky was clear, but Kyoto lay under six or seven inches of fresh, dry snow. The streets held little traffic.

In addition to the snow, something else had arrived in the night. Across the street, on the second floor of a popular geisha house, a man stood at a window. He was watching her apartment through a pair of binoculars.

He saw her at the same moment that she saw him. He lowered the glasses and stepped back, out of sight.

That was why her mood had changed. Subconsciously she had been expecting something like the man with the binoculars. They were out there.

Waiting. Watching. Biding their time. Platoons of them, for all she knew. Until she and Alex could discover who they were and why they had stolen her past, she was neither safe nor free. In spite of the fact that the bad dream no longer had the power to disrupt her sleep, the sense of security that she enjoyed during the night was false. Although she'd lived through several kinds of hell, the worst of them all might be ahead of her.

In the morning sun, the snow was bright. The Gion looked pure. In the distance, a temple bell rang.

38

That morning, at eleven o'clock Kyoto time, Ted Blankenship called from Chicago. He had received detailed reports from the company's associates in London, in answer to the questions that Alex had asked two days ago.

According to the investigators in England, the solicitor who had acted as the executor of the Rand estate, J. Compton Woolrich, was a phantom. There was no record that he had ever existed. No birth certificate. No passport in that name. No driver's license. No file under that name with the tax authorities at Inland Revenue. No work or identity card of any sort. Nothing. No one named J. Compton Woolrich had been licensed to practice law at any time in this century. Nor had anyone with that name possessed a telephone number in greater London since 1946. As Joanna had discovered on Friday, Woolrich's telephone was actually that of an antique shop on Jermyn Street. Likewise, the return address on Compton's stationery was neither a home nor a law office; it was actually that of a library that had been established prior to the Second World War.

"What about British-Continental Insurance?" Alex asked.

"Another phony," Blankenship said. "There's no such firm registered or paying taxes in England."

"And though by some fluke they might have escaped registration, no one there escapes taxes."

"Exactly."

"But we talked to Phillips at British-Continental."

"Not his real name. A deception."

"Yes, I suppose so. What about the address on their stationery?"

"Oh, that's real enough," Blankenship said. "But it sure as hell isn't the headquarters for a major corporation. Our British friends say it's just a grimy, three-story office building in Soho."

"And there's not even a branch office of an insurance company in the place?"

"No. About a dozen other businesses operate there, all more or less cubbyhole outfits, nothing particularly successful—at least not on the surface of it. Importers. Exporters. A mail-forwarding service. A couple of talent bookers who service the cheapest clubs in the city. But no British-Continental."

"What about the telephone number?"

"It's listed to one of the importers at that address. Fielding Athison, Limited. They deal in furniture, clothes, dinnerware, crafts, jewelry, and a lot of other stuff that's made in South Korea, Taiwan, Indonesia, Hong Kong, Singapore, and Thailand."

"And they don't have a Mr. Phillips at that number?"

"That's what they say."

"They're playing games."

"I wish you'd tell me what kind of games," Blankenship said. "And how does this tie in with Tom Chelgrin and his missing daughter? I have to tell you, curiosity's got me nearly as bad shape as the proverbial cat."

"It's not a good idea for me to talk too much about my plans," Alex said. "At least not on this phone."

"Tapped?"

"I suspect it's been transformed into a regular party line."

"In that case, should we be talking at all?" Blankenship asked worriedly.

"It doesn't matter if they hear what you're going to tell me," Alex said. "None of it's news to them. What else have you got on this Fielding Athison company?"

"Well, it's a profitable business, but only by a hair. In fact, they're so overstaffed it's a miracle they manage to stay afloat."

"What does that suggest to you?"

"Other important companies of similar size make do with ten or twelve employees. Fielding Athison has twenty-seven, the majority of them in sales. There just doesn't appear to be enough work to keep them all busy."

"So the importing business is a front," Alex said.

"In the diplomatic phrasing of our English friends, 'The distinct possibility exists that the employees of Fielding Athison engage in some sort of unpublicized work in addition to the importation of Asian goods."

"A front for what? For whom?"

"If you want to find out," Blankenship said, "it's going to cost us dearly. And it's not the sort of thing that can be rung up quickly—if at all. I'd bet a thousand to one that the people using Fielding Athison are breaking a serious law or two. But they've been in business for fourteen years, and no one's tumbled to them yet, so they're good at keeping secrets. Do you want me to tell London to try to dig deeper?"

"No," Alex said. "Not right now. I'll see what develops here in the next couple of days. If it's necessary to put the Englishmen on the job again, I'll call you back."

"How's Wayne?" Blankenship asked.

"Better. He'll keep the leg."

"Thank God. Look, Alex, do you want me to send help?"

"I'm all right."

"I've got a few good men free at the moment."

"If they came, they'd only be targets. Like Wayne."

"Aren't you a target?"

"Yeah. But the fewer the better."

"A little protection—"

"I don't need protection."

"Wayne needed protection. But I guess you know best."

"What I need," Alex said, "is divine guidance."

"If a voice comes to me from a burning bush anytime soon, I'll let you know right away what it says."

"Seriously, Ted, I want you to keep a lid on this. I don't want to attack the problem with an army. I'd like to find the answers I'm after without, in the process, filling up Japanese hospitals with my employees."

"It's still an odd way to handle it—alone."

"I realize that," Alex said. "But I've thought about it . . . and it seems to me that these people, whoever they might be, have given me quite a lot of slack already. There's something odd about the fact that they haven't just blown my head off by now."

"You think they're playing two sides of some game? Using you?"

"Maybe. And maybe if I bring in a platoon from Chicago, they won't cut me any more slack. Maybe they want to keep the game quiet, with a limited number of players."

"Why?"

"If I knew that, then there wouldn't be any need for the game, would there?"

39

Five o'clock Sunday afternoon. Dr. Inamura's office. Pastel lighting. Lemon incense. The watchful bird in the brass cage.

The pine shutters were open, and purple twilight pressed at the windows.

"Dancing butterflies," said the psychiatrist.

In the final session with Omi Inamura, Joanna recalled the exact wording of the three posthypnotic suggestions that had been deeply implanted by the man with the mechanical hand. The first involved the memory block—"Tension, apprehension, and dissension have begun"—with which they had already dealt. The second concerned the devastating attacks of claustrophobia and paranoia that she suffered when anyone became more than casually interested in her. Inamura finished administering the cure that Alex had begun several days ago, patiently convincing Joanna that the words of Herr Doktor no longer had any power over her and that her fears were not valid. They never had been valid. Not surprisingly, the third of Herr Doktor's directives was that she would never leave Japan; and if she *did* attempt to get out of the country, if she *did* board a ship or an aircraft that was bound for any port beyond Japan's borders, she would become nauseous and extremely disoriented. Any attempt to escape from the prison to which she was assigned would end in an attack of blind terror and hysteria. Her faceless

masters had boxed her up every way that they could: emotionally, intellectually, psychologically, chronologically, and now even geographically. Omi
Inamura relieved her of that last restriction.

Alex was impressed by the cleverness with which Herr Doktor had programmed Joanna. Whoever and whatever else he might be, the man was a
genius in his field.

When Inamura was positive that Joanna could not remember any more
about what Herr Doktor had done to her, he took the session in a new
direction. He urged her to move further into her past.

She squirmed in the chair. "But there's nowhere to go."

"Of course there is. You weren't born in that room, Joanna."

"Nowhere to go."

"Listen carefully," Inamura said. "You're strapped in that bed. There's
one window. Outside there's a mansard roof against a blue sky. Are you
there?"

"Yes," she said, more relaxed in this trance than she had been in any of
the previous sessions. "Big black birds are sitting on the chimneys. A dozen
big black birds."

"You're approximately twenty years old," Inamura said. "But now you're
growing younger. Minute by minute, you're growing younger. You have not
been in that room for a long time. In fact you've just come there, and you
haven't yet even met the man with the mechanical hand. You haven't yet
undergone a treatment. You're drifting back, back in time. You have just
come awake in that room. And now time is running backward even faster
. . . back beyond the moment you were brought into that room . . . hours
slipping away . . . faster, faster . . . now days instead of hours . . . backward
in time, flowing like a great river . . . carrying you back, back, back . . .
Where are you now, Joanna?"

She didn't respond.

Inamura repeated the question.

"Nowhere," she said hollowly.

"Look around you."

"Nothing."

"What is your name?"

She didn't reply.

"Are you Joanna Rand?"

"Who?" she asked.

"Are you Lisa Chelgrin?"

"Who's she? Do I know her?"

"What's your name?"

"I . . . I don't have a name."

"Who are you?"

"Nobody."

"You must be somebody."

"I'm waiting to become."

"To become Joanna Rand?"

"I'm waiting," she said simply.

"Concentrate for me."

"I'm so cold. Freezing."

"Where are you?"

"Nowhere."

"What do you see?"

"Nothing," she insisted.

"What do you feel?"

"Dead."

Alex said, "Jesus."

Inamura stared thoughtfully at her. After a while he said, "I'll tell you where you are, Joanna."

"Okay."

"You are standing in front of a door. An iron door. Very imposing. Like the door to a fortress. Do you see it?"

"No."

"Try to visualize it," Inamura said. "Look closely. You really cannot miss it. The door is huge, absolutely massive. Solid iron. If you could see through to the far side of it, you would find four large hinges, each as thick as your wrist. The iron is pitted and spotted with rust, but the door nevertheless appears impregnable. It's five feet wide, nine feet high, rounded at the top, set in an arch in the middle of a great stone wall."

What the devil's he doing? Alex wondered.

"You see the door now, I'm sure," Inamura said.

"Yes," Joanna agreed.

"Touch it."

Lying in her chair but obviously believing herself to be in front of the door, Joanna raised one hand and tested the empty air.

"What does the door feel like?" Inamura asked.

"Cold and rough," she said.

"Rap your knuckles on it."

She rapped silently on nothing.

"What do you hear, Joanna?"

"A dull ringing sound. It's a very thick door."

"Yes, it is," Inamura said. "And it's locked."

Resting in the reclining chair but simultaneously existing in another time and place, Joanna tried the door that only she could see. "Yeah. Locked."

"But you've got to open it," Inamura said.

"Why?"

"Because beyond it lies twenty years of your life. The first twenty years. That's why you can't remember any of it. They've put it behind the door. They've locked it away from you."

"Oh. Yes. I see."

"Luckily, I've found the key that will unlock the door," said Inamura. "I have it right here."

Alex smiled, pleased with the doctor's creative approach to the problem.

"It's a large iron key," Inamura said. "A large iron key attached to an iron ring. I'll shake it. There. Do you hear it rattling, Joanna?"

"I hear it," she said.

Inamura was so skillful that Alex almost heard it too.

"I'm putting the key in your hand," Inamura told her, even though he didn't move from his armchair. "There. You have it now."

"I've got it," Joanna said, closing her right hand around the imaginary key.

"Now put the key in the door and give it a full turn. That's right. Just like that. Fine. You've unlocked it."

"What happens next?" Joanna asked apprehensively.

"Push the door open," the doctor said.

"It's so heavy."

"Yes, but it's coming open just the same. Hear the hinges creaking? It's been closed a long time. A long, long time. But it's coming open . . . open . . . open all the way. There. You've done it. Now step across the threshold."

"All right."

"Are you across?"

"Yes."

"Good. What do you see?"

Silence.

At the windows, twilight had given way to night. No wind pressed at the glass. Even the bird was still and attentive in its cage.

"What do you see?" Inamura repeated.

"No stars," Joanna said.

Frowning, Inamura said, "What do you mean?"

She fell silent again.

"Take another step," Inamura instructed.

"Whatever you say."

"And another. Five steps in all."

She counted them off: ". . . three . . . four . . . five."

"Now stop and look around, Joanna."

"I'm looking."

"Where are you?"

"I don't know."

"What do you see?"

"No stars, no moon."

"Joanna, what do you see?"

"Midnight."

"Be more specific, please."

"Just midnight," she said.

"Explain, please."

Joanna took a deep breath. "I see midnight. The most perfect midnight imaginable. Silky. Almost liquid. A fluid midnight sky runs all the way to the earth on all sides, sealing everything up tight, melting like tar over the whole world, over everything that comes before, over everywhere I've been and everything I've done and everything I've seen. No stars at all. Flawless blackness. Not a speck of light. And not a sound either. No wind. No odors. The earth itself is black. All darkness on all sides. Blackness is the only thing, and it goes on forever."

"No," Inamura said. "That's not true. Twenty years of your life will begin to unfold around you. It's starting to happen even as I speak. You see it now, a world coming to life all around you."

"Nothing."

"Look closer, Joanna. It may not be easy to see at first, but it's all there. I've given you the key to your past."

"You've only given me the key to midnight," Joanna said. A new despair echoed in her voice.

"The key to the past," Inamura insisted.

"To midnight," she said miserably. "A key to darkness and hopelessness. I am nobody. I am nowhere. I'm alone. All alone. I don't like it here."

40 By the time they left the psychiatrist's office, night had claimed Kyoto. From the north came a great wind that drove the bitter air through clothes and skin and flesh all the way to the bone. The light of the street lamps cast stark shadows on the wet pavement, on the dirty slush in the gutters, and on the piled-up snow that had fallen during the previous night.

Saying nothing, going nowhere, Alex and Joanna sat in her Lexus, shivering, steaming the windshield with their breath, waiting to get warm. The exhaust vapors plumed up from the tailpipe and rushed forward past the windows, like multitudes of ghosts hurrying to some otherworldly event.

"Omi Inamura can't do anything more for me," Joanna said.

Alex reluctantly agreed. The doctor had brought to the surface every existing scrap of memory involving the man with the mechanical hand, but he hadn't been able to help her recall enough to provide new leads. Thanks to the genius of those who had tampered with her memory, the specifics of the horrors perpetrated in that strange room had been scattered like the ashes of a long-extinguished fire; and the two thirds of her life spent as Lisa Chelgrin had been thoroughly, painstakingly eradicated beyond recall.

The dashboard fans pushed warm air through the vents, and the patches of condensation on the windshield shrank steadily.

Finally Joanna said, "I can accept that I've forgotten . . . Lisa. They stole my other life, but Joanna Rand is a good person to be."

"And to be with," he added.

"I can accept the loss. I can live without a past if I have to. I'm strong enough."

"I've no doubt about that."

She faced him. "But I can't just pick up and go on without knowing *why?*" she said angrily.

"We'll find out why."

"How? There's no more in me for Inamura to pull out."

"And I don't believe there's anything more to be discovered here in Kyoto. Not anything important."

"What about the man who followed you into that alleyway—or the man in your hotel room, the one who cut you?"

"Small fish. Minnows."

"Where are the big fish?" she asked. "In Jamaica—where Lisa disappeared?"

"More likely Chicago. That's Senator Tom's stomping grounds. Or in London."

"London? But you proved I never lived there. That entire background's fake."

"But Fielding Athison is there, the place that fronts on the phone as United British-Continental Insurance. I'm pretty sure they aren't just small fish."

"Will you put your British contacts on the case again?"

"No. At least not by long distance. I'd prefer to deal with these Fielding Athison people myself."

"Go to London? When?"

"As soon as possible. Tomorrow or the day after. I'll take the train to Tokyo and fly from there."

"*We'll* fly from there."

"You might be safer here. I'll bring in protection from the agency in Chicago."

"You're the only protection I can trust," she said. "I'm going to London with you."

41 Senator Thomas Chelgrin stood at a window in his second-floor study, watching the sparse traffic on the street below, waiting for the telephone to ring.

Monday night, December first, Washington, D.C., lay under a heavy blanket of cool, humid air. Occasionally people hurried from houses to parked cars or from cars to welcoming doorways, their shoulders hunched and heads tucked down and hands jammed in pockets. It wasn't quite cold enough for snow. Weather reports called for icy rain before morning.

Though he was in a warm room, Chelgrin felt as cold as any of the scurrying pedestrians who from time to time passed below.

His chill arose from the cold hand of guilt on his heart, the same guilt that always touched him on the first day of every month.

During most of the year, when the upper house of the United States Congress was in session or when other government business waited to be done, the senator made his home in a twenty-five-room house on a tree-lined street in Georgetown. He lived in Illinois less than one month of every year.

Although he hadn't remarried after the death of his wife, and although his only child had been kidnapped twelve years ago and had never been found, the enormous house was not too large for him. Tom Chelgrin wanted the best of everything, and he had the money to buy it all. His extensive collections, which ranged from rare coins to the finest antique Chippendale furniture, required a great deal of space. He was not driven merely by an investor's or a collector's passion; his need to acquire valuable and beautiful things was no less than an obsession. He had more than five thousand first editions of American novels and collections of poetry—Walt Whitman, Herman Melville, Edgar Allan Poe, Nathaniel Hawthorne, James Fenimore Cooper, Stephen Vincent Benet, Thoreau, Emerson, Dreiser, Henry James, Robert Frost. Hundreds of fine antique porcelains were displayed throughout his rooms, from the simplicity of Chinese pieces of the Han and Sung dynasties to elaborate Satsuma vases from Japan. His stamp collection was worth five million dollars. The walls of his house were hung with the world's largest collection of paintings by Childe Harold. He collected Chinese tapestries and screens, antique Persian carpets, Paul Storr silver, Tiffany lamps, Dore bronzes, Chinese export porcelain, French marquetry furniture from the nineteenth century, and much more—in fact, so much that he owned a small warehouse to store the overflow.

He didn't share the house only with inanimate objects. A butler, cook, two maids, and a chauffeur all lived in, and he entertained frequently. He didn't like to be alone, because solitude gave him too much time to think about certain terrible decisions he had made over the years, certain dark roads taken.

The telephone rang. The back line, a number known only to two or three people.

Chelgrin rushed to his desk and snatched up the receiver. "Hello."

"Senator, what a lovely night for it," said Peterson.

"Miserable night," Chelgrin disagreed.

"It's going to rain," Peterson said. "I like rain. It washes the world clean, and we need that now and then. It's a damned dirty world we live in. Enough?"

Chelgrin hesitated.

"Looks clean to me," said Peterson.

Chelgrin was studying the video display of an electronic device to which the phone was connected. It would reveal the presence of any tap on the line. "Okay," Chelgrin said at last.

"Good. We've got this month's report."

Chelgrin could hear his own pounding heartbeat. "Where do you want to meet?"

"We haven't used the market for a while."

"When?"

"Thirty minutes."

"I'll be there."

"Of course you will, dear Tom," Peterson said with amusement. "I know you wouldn't miss it for the world."

"I'm not a dog on a leash," Chelgrin said. "Don't think you can jerk me around."

"Dear Tom, don't get yourself in a snit."

Chelgrin hung up. His hands were shaking.

He went to the wet bar in one corner of the study and poured two ounces of scotch. He drank it in two long swallows without benefit of ice or water.

"God help me," he said softly.

42

Chelgrin had given the servants the day off, so he drove himself to the market in his dark-gray Cadillac. He could have driven any of three Rolls-Royces, a Mercedes sports coup, an Excalibur, or one of the other cars in his collection. He chose the Cadillac because it was the least conspicuous of the group.

He arrived at the rendezvous five minutes early. The supermarket was the cornerstone of a small shopping center, and even at eight o'clock on a blustery winter night, the place was busy. He parked at the end of a row of cars, sixty or seventy yards from the market entrance. After waiting a couple of minutes, he got out, locked the doors, and stood self-consciously near the rear bumper.

He turned up the collar of his gray Bally jacket, pulled down his leather cap, and kept his distinctive face away from the light. He was trying to appear casual, but he feared that he looked like a man playing at spies.

If he didn't take precautions, however, he would be recognized. He wasn't merely a United States Senator from Illinois: He aspired to the office of the presidency, and he spent a lot of hours in front of television cameras and in the poor company of obnoxious but powerful reporters laying the foundation for a campaign in either two or six years, depending on the fate of the new man who'd won the White House just two years ago. (Considering the sanctimonious and self-righteous lecturing, the numerous episodes of undisguised political duplicity, and the incredible bungling that marked the new man's first twenty-two months at the helm, Chelgrin was confident that his chance would come in two years rather than six.) If someone recognized him, the meeting with Peterson would have to be rescheduled for another night.

Two rows away, the lights of a Chevrolet snapped on, and the car pulled from its parking slip. It came down one aisle, around another, and stopped directly beside the senator's Cadillac.

Chelgrin opened the front passenger door, bent down, and looked inside. He knew the driver from other nights—a short, stout fellow with a prim mouth and thick glasses—but he didn't know his name. He had never asked. Now he got in and buckled his seat belt.

"Anybody on your tail?" the driver asked.

"If there were, I wouldn't be here."

"We'll play it safe just the same."

For ten minutes they traveled a maze of residential streets. The driver watched the rearview mirror as much as the road ahead.

Finally, when it was clear that they were not being followed, they went to a roadhouse seven miles from the supermarket. The place was called Smooth Joe's, and on the roof it boasted a pair of ten-foot-tall neon cowboy dancers.

Business was good for so early in the week: sixty or seventy cars surrounded the building. One was a chocolate-brown Mercedes with Maryland plates, and the stout man pulled in beside it.

Without another word to the driver, Chelgrin got out of the Chevrolet. The night air was vibrating with a thunderous rendition of Garth Brooks's "Friends in Low Places." He got quickly into the rear seat of the Mercedes, where Anson Peterson was waiting.

The instant the senator slammed the door, Peterson said, "Let's roll, Harry."

The driver was big, broad-shouldered, and totally bald. He held the steering wheel almost at arm's length, and he drove well. They headed from the suburbs into the Virginia countryside.

The interior of the car smelled of butter-rum Life Savers. They were an addiction of Peterson's.

"You're looking very well, Tom."

"And you."

In fact, Anson Peterson did not look well at all. Although he was only five feet nine, he weighed considerably in excess of three hundred pounds. His suit pants strained to encompass his enormous thighs. The buttons on his shirt met, but he had no hope of buttoning his jacket. As always, he wore a hand-knotted bow tie—this time white polka dots on a field of deep blue, to match his blue suit—which emphasized the extraordinary circumference of his neck. His face was a great, round pudding paler than vanilla— but within it shone two tar-black eyes that were bright with a fierce intelligence.

Offering the roll of candy, Peterson said, "Would you like one?"

"No, thank you."

Peterson took a circlet of butter-rum for himself and, with a girlish daintiness, popped it into his mouth. He carefully folded shut the end of the roll, as if it must be done just so to please a stern nanny, and put it in one of his jacket pockets. From another pocket he withdrew a clean white handkerchief; he shook it out and scrubbed vigorously at his fingertips.

In spite of his great size—or perhaps because of it—he was compulsively neat. His clothes were always immaculate, never a spot on shirt or tie. His hands were pink, the nails manicured and highly polished. He always looked as if he had just come from the barber: Not a hair was out of place on his round head. Occasionally Chelgrin had eaten dinner with the fat man, and Peterson had finished double servings without leaving a solitary crumb or drop of sauce on the tablecloth. The senator, hardly a sloppy man, always felt like a pig when, after dinner, he compared his place with Peterson's absolutely virginal expanse of linen.

Now they cruised along wide streets with half-acre estates and large houses, heading out to hunt country. Their monthly meetings were always conducted on the move, because a car could be checked for electronic listening devices and stripped of them more easily than could a room in any building. Furthermore, a moving car with a well-trained and observant chauffeur was almost proof against an eavesdropping directional microphone focused on them from a distance.

Of course it wasn't likely that Peterson would ever become the target of electronic surveillance. His cover as a successful real-estate entrepreneur was faultless. His secret work, done in addition to the real-estate dealing, was punishable by life imprisonment or even death if he were caught, so he was motivated to be methodical, circumspect, and security conscious.

As they sped toward the countryside, the fat man talked around his candy. "If I didn't know better, I'd think you engineered the election of this man in the White House. He seems to be determined to set himself up so precisely that you can knock him down with a single puff of breath."

"I'm not here to talk politics," Chelgrin said shortly. "May I see the report?"

"Dear Tom, since we must work together, we should try our best to be friendly. It really takes so little time to be sociable."

"The report."

Peterson sighed. "As you wish."

Chelgrin held out one hand for the file folder.

Peterson made no move to give it to him. Instead, he said, "There's nothing in writing this month. Just a *spoken* report."

Chelgrin stared at him in disbelief. "That's unacceptable."

Peterson crunched what remained of his Life Saver and swallowed. When he spoke, he expelled butter-rum fumes. "That's the way it is, I'm afraid."

The senator strove to control his temper, for to lose it would be to give the fat man an advantage. "These reports are important to me, Anson. Very personal, very private."

Peterson smiled. "You know perfectly well that they're read by at least a dozen other people. Including me."

"Yes, but then I always get to read them too. If you just summarize them instead . . . then suddenly you become an interpreter. It's not as private that way. I wouldn't feel as close to her."

Everything he knew about his daughter's current activities was third-hand information. In twelve years not one spoken word had passed between him and Lisa; therefore, he jealously guarded these few minutes of reading, the first of every month.

"That day in Jamaica," he said, "you promised I'd get written reports of her progress, her life. Always written. You hand it to me, I read it by a flashlight in a moving car, then I give it back to you, and you destroy it. That's how it works. I haven't agreed to any changes in the routine, and I never will."

"Calm down, dear Tom."

"Don't call me that, you bastard."

Peterson said, "I'll take no offense. You're distraught."

They rode in silence until Chelgrin said, "Do you have photos?"

"Oh, yes. We have photos, as we do every month. Though these are exceptionally interesting."

"Let me see them."

"They need a bit of explanation."

The senator's mouth went dry. He closed his eyes. All anger had been chased out by fear. "Is she . . . is she hurt? Dead?"

"Oh, no. Nothing like that, Tom. If it was anything like that, I wouldn't break the news this way. I'm not an insensitive man."

Relief brought anger back with it. Chelgrin opened his eyes. "Then what the hell is this all about?"

As the driver slowed the Mercedes, turned left onto a narrow lane, and accelerated again, Peterson picked up his attaché case and put it on his lap. From it, he withdrew a white envelope of the type that usually contained photographs of Lisa.

Chelgrin reached for it.

Peterson wasn't ready to relinquish the prize. As he undid the clasp and opened the flap, he said, "The report is spoken this time only because it's too complex and important to be committed to paper. We have a crisis of sorts."

The fat man took several eight-by-ten glossies from the white envelope, and Chelgrin accepted them with trepidation.

A flashlight lay on the seat between them. Chelgrin picked it up and switched it on.

In the first photograph, Lisa and a man were sitting on a bench in a tree-shaded plaza.

"Who's she with?" the senator asked.

"You know him."

Chelgrin held the flashlight at an angle to avoid casting glare on the photograph. "Something familiar . . ."

"You'll have to go back in time. Before he had the mustache. Go back at least ten years to the last time you might've seen him."

"My God, it's the detective. Hunter."

"He's become bored with his business and with Chicago," Peterson said. "So he's been taking a couple of month-long vacations every year. Last spring he went to Brazil. Two weeks ago—Japan."

Chelgrin couldn't look away from the photograph, which ceased to be merely a picture and became an omen of disaster. "But Hunter turning up in the Moonglow Lounge, that place of all places—the odds must be a million to one."

"Easily."

"She's changed over the years. Maybe he—"

"He recognized her at once. He's compared her fingerprints to Lisa's. Encouraged her to call London. Took her to a psychiatrist for hypnotic regression therapy. We had the office bugged."

As Chelgrin listened to what Dr. Omi Inamura had achieved with Joanna, the motion of the car began to make him nauseous.

"But why was this allowed to happen?" he demanded.

"We didn't expect this Inamura to be successful. By the time we realized that he was achieving a breakthrough with her, it seemed pointless to threaten or kill him."

Jagged lightning stepped down the dark sky, gouging the thick cloud cover with its spurred heels.

"And why hasn't Hunter contacted me?" the senator wondered. "I was his client. I paid him a hell of a lot of money to find her."

"He hasn't contacted you because he suspects you're part of the conspiracy that put her in Japan. He now thinks you hired him in the first place just to make yourself look good, playing the concerned father for political purposes. Which is true, of course."

Another flash of lightning illuminated the countryside beyond the car, briefly outlining clusters of leafless black trees.

Fat droplets of rain snapped against the windshield. The driver slowed the Mercedes and switched on the wipers.

"What's he going to do?" Chelgrin asked. "Go to the media?"

"Not yet," Peterson assured him. "He figures that if we wanted to remove the girl permanently, we could've killed her a long time ago. He realizes that after we've gone to all the trouble of giving her a new identity, we intend to keep her alive at nearly any cost. So he assumes she's safe in pushing this thing, at least up to a point. He figures we're most likely to turn nasty and try to kill them only when they go public. Therefore, he wants to be absolutely certain he's got most of the story before he dares to speak out."

Chelgrin frowned. "I don't like all this talk about killing."

"Dear Tom, I didn't mean we'd actually kill Lisa! Of course, that's not an option. Besides, good heavens, I feel almost as close to her as if she were my own daughter. A darling girl. No one would lift a finger against her. But Hunter's another matter altogether. He'll have to be taken out at the proper time. Soon."

"You should have killed him the moment he showed up in Kyoto. You screwed up."

Peterson was not disturbed by the accusation. "We didn't know he was going until he was there. We weren't watching him. No reason to. It's a long time since he investigated Lisa's disappearance."

"So after he's been eliminated, what will we do with her?" the senator worried.

Peterson shifted his great bulk, and the springs in the car seat protested. "She can't live as Joanna Rand any longer. She's finished with that life. We think the best thing is to send her home now."

"Back to Illinois?" Chelgrin asked, baffled by that impractical suggestion.

"No, no. That's not her real home. Neither is Jamaica nor even Washington."

Chelgrin's heart pounded faster, but he tried not to let the fat man see how alarmed he was. He stared at the photograph and then out at the rain-, swept night. "Where you want to send her . . . that's your home and mine, but it's not hers."

"Neither was Japan."

Chelgrin said nothing.

"We'll send her home," Peterson said.

"No."

"She'll be well taken care of. She'll be happy there."

Chelgrin took a couple of deep breaths before responding. "This is the same argument we had in Jamaica all those years ago. I won't let you send her home. Period. End of discussion."

"Why are you so set against it?" Peterson asked, clearly amused by the senator's distress. "And why is it that we even need to hold your daughter hostage in order to ensure your continued cooperation?"

"You don't have to do any such thing," Chelgrin said, but he could hear the lack of conviction in his voice.

"But we do," said Peterson. "That's clear to us. And why? Aren't we on the same side? Aren't we working toward the same goal?"

Chelgrin switched off the flashlight and gazed out the window at the dark land rushing past. He wished the interior of the car were even darker than it was, so the fat man couldn't see his face at all.

"Aren't we on the same side?" Peterson persisted.

Chelgrin cleared his throat. "It's just that . . . sending her home . . . Well, that's an entirely alien way of life to her. She was born and raised in America. She's used to certain . . . freedoms."

"She'd have freedom at home. It's all the rage now—freedom."

"And you'll change that if you get a chance."

"Restore order, yes, if we get a chance. But even then she would move in the very highest circles, with special privileges."

"None of which would equal what she could have here or what she has now in Japan."

"Listen, Tom, the likelihood is that we'll never be able to restore the old order at home. This freedom is a virulent disease. We're working hard to disrupt the economy, to keep the bureaucracy intact. And thanks to you and other politicians, the U.S. is helping us. But the disease is hard to eradicate. Freedom will most likely grow, not diminish."

"No," Chelgrin said adamantly. "She wouldn't be able to adapt. We'll have to put her somewhere else. That's final."

Peterson was delighted with Chelgrin's bravado—perhaps because he knew that it was hollow, merely the tremulous defiance of a child crossing a graveyard at night—and he giggled almost girlishly. The giggle swiftly became a full-fledged laugh. He gripped the senator's leg just above the knee and squeezed affectionately. Edgy, Chelgrin misinterpreted the action, detected a threat where none existed, and jerked away. The overreaction tickled the fat man. Peterson laughed and chortled and cackled, spraying spittle and expelling clouds of butter-rum fumes, until he had to gasp for breath.

"I wish I knew what was so funny," Chelgrin said.

At last Peterson got control of himself. He mopped his big moon face with his handkerchief.

"Dear Tom, why don't you just admit it? You don't want Lisa to go home to Mother Russia because you don't believe in what either of the major power blocs wants to do there. You lost faith in Marx and communism a long time ago, while we still ruled. And you don't like the crowd of socialists and thugs who're contesting for power these days. You still work for us because you have no choice, but you hate yourself for it. The good life here diverted you, dear Tom. Diverted, subverted, and thoroughly converted you. If you could get away with it, you'd make a clean break with us, cast us out of your life after all we've done for you. But you can't do that, because we've acted like wise capitalists in the way we've handled you over the years. We repossessed your daughter. We have a mortgage on your political career. Your fortune is built on credit we've extended to you. And we have a substantial—actually, *enormous*—lien against your soul."

Though Peterson now appeared willing to accept a relationship without pretense, Chelgrin remained wary about admitting to his true convictions. "I don't know where you get these ideas. I'm committed to the proletarian revolution and the people's state every bit as much as I was thirty years ago."

That statement elicited another spate of giggling from the fat man. "Dear Tom, be frank with me. We've known about the changes in you for twenty years, maybe even before you yourself were aware of them. We know the capitalist facade isn't just a facade any longer. But it doesn't matter. We aren't going to give you the axe merely because you've had a change of heart. There'll be no garroting, no bullets in the night, no poison in the wine, dear Tom. You're still an extremely valuable property. You help us enormously—though in a different way and for much different reasons now than when we all started on this little adventure."

For many years, as a congressman and then a senator, Chelgrin had passed military secrets to the Soviet regime. Since the fall of the Soviet, he'd been instrumental in arranging for tens of billions of dollars in loans to the new elected government of Russia, aware that none of it would ever be repaid. A large portion of those loans were misappropriated by the still Byzantine bureaucracy, going not to help the Russian people but to line the pockets of the same thugs who had ruled under the Soviet banner and to maintain a war chest for their indefatigable campaign to return to the pinnacle of power.

"All right. Honesty," said Chelgrin. "Every day of my life, I pray to God that the help I give you will never be enough to ensure your success, never enough to harm this big, bustling, freewheeling, wonderful country. I want you all to fail and rot in Hell."

"Good. Very good," said Peterson. "Refreshing to be open and direct for a change, isn't it?"

"All I care about now is my daughter."

"Would you like to see the other photographs?" Peterson asked.

Chelgrin switched on the flashlight and took the stack of eight-by-ten glossies from the fat man.

Rain drummed relentlessly on the roof of the car. The spinning tires sang sibilantly on the wet macadam.

After a while the senator said, "What'll happen to Lisa?"

"We didn't actually expect you to be enthusiastic about sending her home," Peterson acknowledged. "So we've worked out something else. We'll turn her over to Dr. Rotenhausen—"

"The one-armed wonder."

"—and he'll treat her at the clinic again."

"He gives me the creeps," Chelgrin said.

"Rotenhausen will erase all the Joanna Rand memories and give her yet another identity. When he's finished, we'll provide forged papers and set her up in a new life in Germany."

"Why Germany?"

"Why not? We knew you'd insist on a capitalist country with the so-called 'freedoms' you cherish."

"I thought perhaps she could . . . come back."

"Back here?" Peterson asked incredulously. "Impossible."

"I don't mean to Illinois or Washington."

"There's not a safe place in the States."

"But surely if we gave her a solid new identity and stuck her in a small town in Utah or rural Colorado or maybe Wyoming—"

"Too chancy."

"You won't even consider it?"

"Dear Tom, this trouble with Alex Hunter should make it obvious why I *can't* consider it. And I can't resist reminding you that she could've been here in the States all along, instead of Japan, if you had only agreed to plastic surgery along with the memory tampering."

"I won't even discuss the possibility."

"Your ego leaves no room for common sense. You see elements of your face in hers, and you can't bear to have them altered."

"I said I won't discuss it. I'll never let a surgeon touch her face. She won't be changed in any way."

"Stupid, dear Tom. Very stupid. If the surgery had been done immediately after the screw-up in Jamaica, Alex Hunter wouldn't have recognized her last week. We wouldn't be in trouble now."

"She's a beautiful woman. She'll stay that way."

"The point of the surgery wouldn't be to make her ugly! She'd still be beautiful. It would just be a different beauty."

"Any difference would make her less than she is now," Chelgrin insisted. "I won't allow her to be carved into someone else."

Outside, the storm grew more violent by the minute. Rain fell in dense cataracts. The driver slowed the Mercedes to a crawl.

Peterson smiled and shook his head. "You amaze me, Tom. It's so strange that you'll fight to the death to preserve her face—in which you can so readily see yourself—yet you don't feel any remorse for letting us carve away at her *mind*."

"There's nothing strange about it," Chelgrin said defensively.

"I suspect you didn't care about the brainwashing because she wasn't intellectually or emotionally your disciple. Her beliefs, her goals, her dreams, her hopes, were different from yours. So it didn't matter to you if we erased all that. Preservation of the physical Lisa—the color of her hair, the shape of her nose and jaw and lips, the proportions of her body—was enormously important to your ego, but the preservation of the actual *person* called Lisa—those special patterns of the mind, that unique creature of wants and needs and attitudes so different from your own—was none of your concern."

"So you're calling me an egotistical bastard," Chelgrin said. "So what? What am I supposed to do? Try to change your opinion of me? Promise to be a better person? What do you want from me?"

"Dear Tom, let me put it this way—"

"Put it any way you like."

"I don't think it was a loss to our side when you were won over to their philosophy," the fat man said. "And I'd bet that the average capitalist wouldn't look at you as much of a prize either."

"If this is meant to wear me down somehow and make me agree to plastic surgery for her, you're just wasting your time."

Peterson laughed softly. "You've got thick armor, Tom. It's impossible to insult you."

Chelgrin hated him.

For a while they rode in silence.

They passed through woodlands and open fields between suburbs. Thin patches of fog drifted across the road, and when lightning flashed, the ground mist briefly glowed as if it might be an unearthly, incandescent gas.

Finally the fat man said, "There's some danger involved if we tamper with the girl's memory a second time."

"Danger?"

"The good Dr. Rotenhausen has never worked his magic twice on the same patient. He has doubts. This time the treatment might not take. It might even end badly."

"What do you mean? What could happen?"

"Madness perhaps. Or she might wind up in a catatonic state. You know—just sitting, staring into space, a vegetable, unable to talk or feed herself. She might even die."

Chelgrin stared at Peterson, trying to read his round, smiling, inscrutable face. "I don't believe it. You're making this up so I'll be afraid to send her to Rotenhausen. Then my only choice would be to let you take her home. Forget it."

"I'm being honest with you, Tom. Rotenhausen says her chances of coming through a second time are poor, less than fifty-fifty."

"You're lying. But even if you were telling the truth, I'd rather send her to Rotenhausen. I refuse to have her taken to Russia. I'd rather see her dead."

"You might," said Peterson.

Rain was falling with such force and in such tremendous quantity that the driver had to pull off the road. Visibility was no more than twenty to thirty feet. They parked in a roadside rest area, near trash barrels and picnic tables.

Peterson slipped another butter-rum circlet between his pursed lips, scrubbed his fingers with his handkerchief, and made a small wordless sound of delight as the candy began to melt on his tongue.

The roar of the rain was so loud that Chelgrin raised his voice. "Moving her secretly from Jamaica to Switzerland was a nightmare."

"I remember it all too well."

"How will you get her out of Japan, all the way to Rotenhausen?"

"She's making it easy for us. She and Hunter are going to England to look into the British-Continental Insurance scam."

"When?"

"The day after tomorrow. We've got a scenario planned for them. We'll drop clues they can't miss, steer them away from London and straight to Switzerland. We'll put them on to Rotenhausen, and when they go after him, we'll let the trap fall shut."

"You sound so confident."

"By Friday or Saturday, Hunter will be dead, and your lovely daughter will be back in Rotenhausen's clinic."

43

Wednesday afternoon, when the time came for Joanna to leave the Moonglow with Alex and take a taxi to the train depot, she didn't want to leave. Each step out of the second-floor apartment, down the narrow stairs, and across the lounge was difficult. She seemed to be walking through deep water. She stopped several times on one pretense or another—a forgotten passport; a last-minute decision to wear a different pair of traveling shoes; a sudden desire to say good-bye to the head chef, who was even then preparing the sauces and soups for that evening's customers—but eventually Alex insisted that she hurry lest they miss their train.

Her delaying tactics resulted not from worry about what would happen to the business in her absence. She trusted Mariko to manage the club efficiently and profitably.

Instead, her reluctance to depart was the result of a surprising homesickness that seized her even before she left home. She had come to this country under queer circumstances, a stranger in a strange land, and she had prospered. She loved Japan and Kyoto and the Gion district and the Moonglow Lounge. She loved the musical quality of the language, the extravagant politeness of the people, the merry ringing of finger bells at worship services, the beauty of the temple dancers, the scattered ancient structures that had survived both war and the encroachment of Westernstyle architecture. She loved the taste of sake and tempura, the delicious fragrance of hot brown *kamo yorshino-ni*. She felt a part of this ancient yet ever blossoming culture. This was her world now, the only place to which she had ever truly belonged, and she dreaded leaving it even temporarily.

Nevertheless, she was determined not to let Alex go to England alone.

While Alex went outside to be sure the taxi waited, Joanna and Mariko stood just inside the front door, hugging one last time.

"I'll miss you, Mariko-san."

"I'm scared for you," Mariko said.

"I have Alex. But you're at risk too. Someone may decide that you know too much."

"Me and Uncle Omi and my whole family know too much. Too many of us know too much. There's safety in numbers. Besides, we don't actually have proof of anything. Just your fingerprints—and you're taking those with you. I think these people are less of a danger to me than old Godzilla."

"I just realized—we'll be staying overnight in Tokyo. His favorite stomping grounds."

"I don't know why they keep rebuilding the city when they know he's just going to come back and knock it down again."

Joanna smiled. "Maybe they figure one day he'll learn the error of his ways. The Japanese are infinitely patient."

Mariko inclined her head. "Thank you for not saying 'stubborn,' Joanna-san."

"One more thing, Mariko-san . . . Is it true what Alex says about you and Wayne? That a certain attraction exists?"

Mariko blushed fiercely. "He's in the hospital. I've only sat at his bedside a few times to keep him company."

"And?"

Lowering her eyes, Mariko said, "He is an interesting man."

"But?"

"These things don't happen, Joanna-san. You know how it is."

"Wayne is different, and there will be many people you love who will be unhappy with you. You don't want them to feel that you've dishonored them. Yes, I know how it is. But life is short. A chance for great happiness doesn't come along all that often."

Mariko said nothing.

"When the bright-winged bird sees a fallen cherry on the ground beneath a tree," Joanna said, "it seizes the fruit and flies, full of joy, and deals with the pit later."

Amused, Mariko met her eyes. "I didn't hear the Zen warning siren."

Hugging her friend again, Joanna whispered: *"Whoop-whoop-whooop."*

"Too late," said Mariko. "I think I might already have been enlightened."

The front door opened, and Alex leaned inside. "We're going to miss that train if we don't hurry."

As they drove away in the black-and-red taxi, Joanna looked back at the Moonglow Lounge and at Mariko in the open door. "It can all evaporate like a dream."

"What can?" Alex asked.

"Happiness. Places. People. Everything."

He took her hand.

The taxi turned a corner.

The Moonglow Lounge was gone. Mariko too.

THE SUPEREXPRESS TO Tokyo was a luxurious train with a buffet car, plush seats, and, considering the great speed it attained, surprisingly little rail noise and lateral motion. She wanted Alex to sit by the window for the four-hour trip, but he insisted that she have that privilege, and the porter was amused by their argument.

At the Western-style hotel in Tokyo, a two-bedroom suite was reserved for them. The employees at the front desk were unable to conceal their amazement at this brassy behavior. A man and woman with different last names, using the same suite and making no effort to conceal their association, were considered decadent, regardless of the number of bedrooms at their disposal. Alex didn't notice the raised eyebrows, but Joanna nudged him until he realized everyone was watching them surreptitiously. She was amused, and her unrepressed smile, interpreted as an expression of lascivious anticipation, only made matters worse. The registration clerk wouldn't look at her directly. But they were not turned away. That would have been unthinkably impolite. Besides, in any hotel catering to Westerners, the employees knew that almost any boldness could be expected of Americans.

Two shy young bellmen escorted her and Alex to the top floor, efficiently distributed their luggage between the bedrooms, adjusted the thermostat in the drawing room, opened the heavy drapes, and then refused tips until Alex assured them that he offered the gratuities only out of respect for their fine service and impeccable manners. Tipping had not yet taken hold in most of Japan, but Alex was so long accustomed to American expectations that he felt guilty if he didn't provide anything.

The accommodations looked pretty much like any good two-bedroom suite in Los Angeles or Dallas or Chicago or Boston. Only the view from the windows firmly established the Japanese setting.

When they were alone, she moved into his arms. They stood by the window, all of Tokyo below them, and just held each other for a while.

He kissed her once. Then again. They were lovely kisses, but the moment was not right for more than that. As he had said, their first time together must be special, because it was a commitment that would change both their lives forever.

"What about sushi for dinner?" she asked.

"Sounds good."

"At the Ozasa?"

"You know Tokyo better than I do. Wherever you say."

Beyond the window, in the rapidly deepening twilight, the great city began to put on dazzling ornamental kimonos of neon.

THE RESTAURANT, OZASA, was in the Ginza district, around the corner from the Central Geisha Exchange. It was upstairs, cramped, and noisy, but it was one of the finest sushi shops in all of Japan. A scrubbed wooden counter ran the length of the place, and behind it were chefs dressed all in white, their hands red from continual washing.

When Alex and Joanna entered, the chefs shouted the traditional greeting: *"Irasshai!"*

The room was awash in wonderful aromas: omelets sizzling in vegetable oil, soy sauce, various spicy mustards, vinegared rice, horseradish, mushrooms that had been cooked in aromatic broth, and more. Not the slightest whiff of fish tainted the air, however, though raw seafood of many varieties was the primary ingredient in every dish in the house. The only fish fresher than Ozasa's were those that still swam in the deeps.

Joanna knew one of the chefs, Toshio, from her days as a Tokyo performer. She made introductions, and there was much bowing all around.

She and Alex sat at the counter, and Toshio put large mugs of tea in front of them. They each received an *oshibori*, with which they wiped their hands while examining the selection of fish that filled a long refrigerated glass case behind the counter.

The unique and exquisitely tortuous tension between Alex and Joanna transformed even the simple act of eating dinner into a rare experience charged with erotic energy. He ordered *tataki*—little chunks of raw bonito that had been singed in wet straw; each would come wrapped in a bright yellow strip of omelet. Joanna began with an order of *toro sushi*, which was served first. Toshio had trained and practiced for years before he was permitted to serve his first customer; now his long apprenticeship was evident in the swift grace of his culinary art. He removed the *toro*—fatty, marbled tuna—from the glass case, and his hands moved as quickly and surely as those of a master magician. With a huge knife, he smoothly sliced off two pieces of tuna. From a large tub beside him, he grabbed a handful of vinegared rice and deftly kneaded it into two tiny loaves spiced with a dash of *wasabi*. Toshio pressed the bits of fish to the tops of the loaves, and with a proud flourish he placed the twin morsels before Joanna. The entire preparation required less than thirty seconds from the moment that he had slid open the door of the refrigerated case. The brief ceremony, which ended with Toshio washing his hands before creating the *tataki*, reminded Alex of the posthypnotic code words that Omi Inamura had used with Joanna: Toshio's hands were like dancing butterflies. Sushi could be a messy dish, especially for a novice, but Joanna was no novice, and while consuming the *toro*, she managed to be both prissily neat and sensuous. She picked up one piece, dipped the rice portion in a saucer of *shoyu*, turned it over to keep it from dripping, and placed the entire morsel on her tongue. She closed her eyes and chewed slowly. The sight of her enjoying the *toro* increased the pleasure that Alex took in his own food. She ate with that peculiar combination of dainty grace and avid hunger that one saw in cats. Her slow pink tongue licked left and right at the corners of her mouth; she smiled as she opened her eyes and picked up the second piece of *toro*.

Alex said, "Joanna, I . . ."

"Yes?"

He hesitated. "You're beautiful."

That wasn't everything he had intended to tell her, and it was surely not as much as she wanted to hear, but her smile seemed to say that she could not possibly have been happier.

They drank tea and ordered other kinds of sushi—dark-red lean tuna, snow-white squid, blood-red *akagai* clams, octopus tentacles, pale shrimp, caviar, and abalone—and between servings they cleared their palates with sliced ginger.

Each order of sushi contained two pieces, but they ate slowly, heartily, sampling every variety, then returned to their favorites. In Japan, Joanna explained, the complex system of etiquette, the rigid code of manners, and the tradition of excessive politeness ensured a special sensitivity to the sometimes multiple meanings of language, and the two-piece-and-only-two-piece servings of sushi was an example of that sensitivity. Nothing that was sliced could ever be served singly or in threes, for the Japanese words for "one slice" were *hito kire*, which also meant *kill myself*. Therefore, if sliced food were presented in either of those quantities, it would be an insult to the customer as well as a tasteless reminder of an unpleasant subject.

So they ate sushi two pieces at a time, and Alex thought about how desperately he wanted Joanna. They drank tea, and Alex wanted her more with each sip that he watched her take. They talked, they joked with Toshio, and when they weren't eating they turned slightly toward each other so their knees rubbed together, and they chewed bits of ginger, and Alex wanted her. He was sweating slightly and not merely because of the fiercely hot *wasabi* in the sushi loaves.

His inner heat was almost acute enough to be painful. That pain was the risk of commitment. But nothing worth having could be had without risk.

More things than sushi came best in twos. A man and a woman. Love and hope.

WHITE FACES. BRIGHT lips. Eyes heavily outlined in black mascara. Eerie. Erotic.

Ornate kimonos. The men in dark colors. Other men dressed as women in brilliant hues, bewigged, mincing, coy.

And the knife.

The lights dimmed. Suddenly a spotlight bored through the gloom.

The knife appeared in the bright shaft, trembled in a pale fist, then plunged down.

Light exploded again, illuminating all.

The killer and victim were attached by the blade, an umbilical of death.

The killer twisted the knife once, twice, three times, with gleeful ferocity, playing the midwife of the grave.

The onlookers watched in silence and awe.

The victim shrieked, staggered backward. He spoke a line and then another: last words. Then the immense stage resounded with his mortal fall.

Joanna and Alex stood in darkness at the back of the auditorium.

Ordinarily, advance reservations were required by every kabuki theater in Tokyo, but Joanna knew the manager of this place.

The program had begun at eleven o'clock that morning and would not end until ten o'clock that night. Like the other patrons, Joanna and Alex had stopped in for just one act.

Kabuki was the essence of dramatic art: The acting was highly stylized, all emotions exaggerated; and the stage effects were elaborate, dazzling. In 1600, a woman named O-kuni, who was in the service of a shrine, organized a troupe of dancers and presented a show on the banks of the Kano River, in Kyoto, and thus began kabuki. In 1630, in an attempt to control so-called immoral practices, the government prohibited women from appearing on stage. Consequently, there arose the *Oyama*, specialized and highly accomplished male actors who took the roles of female characters in the kabuki plays. Eventually women were permitted to appear on stage again, but the newer tradition of all-male kabuki was by then firmly established and inviolate. In spite of the archaic language—which few members of the audience understood—and in spite of the artistic restrictions imposed by transvestism, the popularity of kabuki never waned, partly because of the gorgeous spectacle but largely because of the themes it explored—comedy and tragedy, love and hate, forgiveness and revenge—which were all made bigger and brighter than life by the ancient playwrights.

As he watched, Alex realized that the basic emotions varied not at all from city to city, country to country, year to year, and century to century. The stimuli to which the heart responded might change slightly as people grew older: The child, the adolescent, the adult, and the elder didn't respond to exactly the same causes of joy and sorrow. Nevertheless, the *feelings* were identical in all of them, for feelings were woven together to form the one true fabric of life, which was always and without exception a fabric with but one master pattern.

Through the medium of kabuki, Alex achieved two sudden insights that, in a moment, changed him forever. First, if emotions were universal, then in one sense he was not alone, never had been alone, and never could be alone. As a child cowering under the harsh hands of his drunken parents, he had existed in despair, because he'd thought of himself as isolated and lost. But every night that Alex's father had beaten him, other children in every corner of the world had suffered with him, victims of their own sick parents or of strangers, and *together* they had all endured. They were a family of sorts, united by suffering. No pain or happiness was unique. All humanity drank from the same river of emotion; and by drinking, every race, religion, and nationality became one indivisible species. Therefore, no matter what protective emotional distance he tried to put between himself and his friends, between himself and his lovers, perfect isolation would forever elude him. Whether he liked it or not, life meant emotional involvement, and involvement meant taking risks.

He also realized that if emotions were universal and timeless, they represented the greatest truths known to humankind. If billions of people in scores of cultures had arrived independently at the same concept of love, then the reality of love could not be denied.

The loud, dramatic music that had accompanied the murder now began to subside.

On the huge stage, one of the "women" stepped forward to address the audience.

The music fluttered and was extinguished by the *Oyama*'s first words.

Joanna glanced at Alex. "Like it?"

He was speechless. He merely nodded. His heart pounded, and with each hard beat, he came more awake to life.

THEY WENT TO a bar where the owner greeted them in English with three words: "Japanese only, please."

Joanna spoke rapidly in Japanese, assuring him that they were natives in mind and heart if not by birth. Won over, he smilingly admitted them.

They had sake, and Joanna said, "Don't drink it like that, dear."

Alex frowned. "What am I doing wrong?"

"You shouldn't hold the cup in your right hand."

"Why not?"

"Because that's considered to be the sign of a gross impatient drunkard."

"Maybe I *am* a gross, impatient drunkard."

"Ah, but do you wish everyone to know it, Alex-san?"

"So I hold the cup in my left hand?"

"That's right."

"Like this?"

"That's right."

"I feel like I've been such a barbarian."

She blew on her sake to cool it slightly. "Later, when the time is right, you can use both hands on me."

THEY WENT TO the Nichiegeki Music Hall for a one-hour show that smacked of vaudeville and burlesque. Comedians told low jokes, many of them very amusing, but Alex was cheered more by the sight of Joanna laughing than he was by anything that the funnymen had to say. Between the variety acts, gorgeous young women in revealing costumes danced rather poorly but with unfaltering enthusiasm and energy. Most of the chorines were breathtaking beauties, but in Alex's eyes, at least, none of them was a match for Joanna.

BACK IN THE hotel suite, Joanna called room service and ordered a bottle of champagne. She also requested appropriate pastries, treats that were not too sweet, and these were delivered in a pretty red lacquered wood box.

At her suggestion, Alex opened the drapes, and they pulled the drawing-room sofa in front of the low windows. Sitting side by side they studied the Tokyo skyline while they drank champagne and nibbled almond crusts and walnut crescents.

Shortly after midnight, some of the neon lights in the Ginza began to wink out.

"Japanese nightlife can be frantic," Joanna said, "but they start to roll up the sidewalks early by Western standards."

"Shall we roll up our own sidewalks?"

"I'm not sleepy," she said.

He wanted her but felt as awkward as an inexperienced boy. "We have to be up at six o'clock."

"No, we don't."

"We do if we want to catch the plane."

"We don't have to get up at six if we never go to sleep in the first place," she said. "We can sleep on the plane tomorrow."

She slid against him and put her lips to his throat. It wasn't exactly a kiss. She seemed to be feeling the passion in the artery that throbbed in his neck.

As he turned to her, she rose to him, and her soft mouth opened under his. She tasted like almonds and champagne.

He carried her into his room and put her on the bed. Slowly, lovingly, he undressed her.

The only light was that which came from the drawing room, through the open door. Pale as moonglow, it fell across the bed, and she lay naked in the ghostly glow, too beautiful to be real.

When he settled down beside her, the bedsprings sang in the cathedral silence, and then a prayerlike hush settled once again through the shadows.

He explored and worshiped her with kisses.

On their last night in Japan, they didn't sleep at all. They wrapped the hours of the night around them, as though time were a brightly shining thread and they were a wildly spinning spool.

44
In Zurich, in the magnificent house above the lake, Ignacio Carrera was working diligently on his calves, thighs, buttocks, hips, waist, lower back, and abdominal muscles. He'd been lifting weights for two hours, with little time off to rest. After all, when he rested there was no pain, and he wanted the pain because it tested him and because it was an indication of muscle-tissue growth.

Seeking pain at the limits of his endurance, he began his last exercise of the day: one more set of Jefferson lifts. He straddled the barbell, keeping his feet twenty-four inches apart. He squatted, grasped the bar with his right hand in front of him and his left hand behind, and inhaled deeply. Exhaling, he rose to a standing position, bringing the bar up to his crotch. His calves and thighs throbbed painfully.

"One," said Antonio Paz.

Carrera squatted, hesitated only a second, and rose with the bar again. His legs seemed to be on fire. He was gasping. His pumped-up muscles bulged like thick steel cables. While Paz counted, Carrera squatted, rose, squatted, and rose again, and the pain was at first a flame and then a roaring blaze.

Other men lifted weights to improve their health. Some did it just to have their pick of the women who pursued bodybuilders. Some did it to gain improved strength for martial arts, some merely to prove their perseverance, some as a game, some as a sport.

To Ignacio Carrera, those were all secondary reasons.

"Seven," said Paz.

Carrera groaned, striving to ignore the pain.

"Eight," said Paz.

Carrera endured the torture because he was obsessed with power. He enjoyed holding power of every kind over other people: financial, political, psychological, and physical power. His wealth would have meant nothing to him if he had been physically weak. He was able to break his enemies with his bare hands as well as with his money, and he enjoyed having that range of options.

"Ten," said Paz.

Carrera put down the barbells and wiped his hands on a towel.

"Excellent," Paz told him.

"No."

Carrera stepped in front of a full-length mirror and posed for himself, studying every visible muscle in his body, searching for improvement.

"Superb," Paz said.

"The older I get, the harder it becomes to build. In fact, I don't think I'm growing at all. Only thirty-eight, yet these days it's a battle just to stay even."

"Nonsense," said Paz. "You're in wonderful shape."

"Not good enough."

"Getting better and better."

"Never good enough."

"Madame Dumont is waiting in the front room," said Paz.

"She can continue to wait."

Carrera left Paz and went upstairs to the master suite on the third floor.

The ceiling was high, white, richly carved, with gold-leafed moldings. The fabric wallpaper was a two-tone gold stripe, and the wainscoting had been painted with a gray wash. The Louis XVI bed had a high headboard and a high footboard, and against the wall directly opposite the bed stood a matched pair of Louis XVI mahogany cabinets with painted tole plaques on the drawers and doors. One corner was occupied by an enormous eighteenth-century harp that was intricately carved, gold-leafed, and in perfect playing condition.

Carrera sometimes joked that he was going to take harp lessons in order to be ready for Heaven when he was called, but he was aware that in his elegant bedroom he looked like an ape that had lumbered into the middle of a lady's tea party. The contrast between himself and his refined surroundings emphasized his wild, animal power—and he liked that.

He stripped out of his sweat-damp shorts, went into the huge master bath, and spent ten minutes baking in the attached sauna. He thought about Madame Marie Dumont, who was surely tapping her foot impatiently downstairs, and he smiled. For another half an hour, he soaked in the big tub.

Then he suffered through a brief icy shower to tone his skin, staying warm by picturing Marie down in the reception room.

He toweled himself vigorously, put on a robe, and walked into the bedroom just as the telephone sounded. Paz answered it downstairs but rang through a moment later. "London calling on line one."

"Marlowe?" Carrera asked.

"No. Peterson."

"The fat man's in London? Put him through. And make sure that Madame Dumont doesn't get a chance to pick up an extension."

"Yes, sir," said Paz.

A scrambler was attached to the incoming line, and it could be activated from any phone. Carrera switched it on.

Peterson said, "Ignacio? Safe to talk?"

"As safe as it ever gets. What're you doing in London?"

"Hunter and the girl will arrive here tonight."

Carrera was surprised. "Dr. Rotenhausen swore she'd never be able to leave Japan."

"He was wrong. Can you move fast? I want you to go to the good doctor in Saint Moritz."

"I'll leave this evening," said Carrera.

"We'll try to put Hunter on Rotenhausen's trail, as planned."

"Are you directing the show in London now?"

"Not all of it. Just this business with Hunter and the girl."

"Good enough. Marlowe isn't fit to handle that. It's made him hypertense."

"I've noticed."

"He broke some rules. For one thing, he tried to pry her name out of me."

"Out of me too," Peterson said.

"He made some silly threats. I've recommended his removal."

"So have I," Peterson said.

"If approval comes through, I'll take care of him myself."

"Don't worry. No one's going to deny you your fun."

"See you in Moritz?" Carrera asked.

"Certainly," said the fat man. "I think I'll take a few skiing lessons."

Carrera laughed. "That would be an unforgettable sight."

"Wouldn't it?" Peterson laughed at his own expense and hung up.

The telephone doubled as an intercom, and Carrera buzzed the front room downstairs.

Paz answered, "Yes, sir."

"Madame Dumont may come up now. And you should pack a suitcase for yourself. We'll be going to Saint Moritz in a few hours."

Carrera put down the receiver and went to a wall panel that concealed a fully equipped bar. It slid aside at the touch of a button, and he began to mix drinks: orange juice and a couple of raw eggs for himself, vodka and tonic for Marie Dumont.

She arrived before he finished preparing her vodka, and she slammed the bedroom door behind her. She strode directly to him, in one of her best confrontational moods.

"Hello, Marie."

"Who the *hell* do you think you are?" she demanded.

"I think I'm Ignacio Carrera."

"You bastard."

"I've made vodka and tonic for you."

"You can't keep *me* waiting like that," she said furiously.

"Oh? I thought I just did."

"I hope you get rectal cancer and die."

"Such a sweet-talking young lady."

"Stuff it."

She was uncommonly beautiful, and she knew it. She was only twenty-six, wise and sophisticated beyond her years—though not nearly as wise as she thought. Her dark eyes revealed strange hungers and an intensely burning pain deep in her soul. Her fine features and the elegant carriage that she'd learned in expensive boarding schools gave her a haughty air.

She was dressed beautifully too: Her well-tailored, two-piece suit was a five-thousand-dollar Paris original, brightened with a turquoise blouse and minimal jewelry. Her perfume was so subtle that it must have cost upward of a thousand dollars an ounce.

"I expect an apology," she announced.

"There's your drink on the bar."

"You can't treat me like this. No one treats me like this."

She had been spoiled all her life. Her father was a wealthy Belgian merchant, and her much older husband was an even wealthier French industrialist. She had been denied nothing—even though her demands were never less than excessive.

"Apologize," she insisted.

"You wouldn't like it if I did."

"Like it? I demand it, damn you."

"You're a snotty kid."

"Apologize, damn you."

"But a beautiful snotty kid."

"Listen, you greasy ape, if you don't apologize—"

He slapped her face just hard enough to sting.

"There's your drink," he repeated, indicating the bar.

"If you ever touch me again, I'll have you killed," she said.

He slapped her so hard that she staggered, almost fell, and had to grip the edge of the bar to keep her balance. Punishment was what she wanted. It was why she had come.

"Pick up your drink," he said ominously. "I made it for you."

"You make me sick."

"Then why do you come?"

"Slumming."

"Pick up your drink," he said sternly.

She spat in his face.

This time he *did* knock her down. She sat on the floor, stunned. Carrera quickly pulled her to her feet. With one big hand on her throat, he pinned her against the wall.

She was crying, but her eyes shone with perverse desire.

"You're sick," he told her. "You're a sick, twisted little rich girl. You have your white Rolls-Royce and your little Mercedes. You live in a mansion. You've got servants who do everything but crap for you. You spend money as if every day is the last day of your life, but you can't buy what you want. You want someone to say 'no' to you. You've been pampered all your life, and now you want someone to push you around and hurt you. You feel guilty about all that money, and you'd probably be happiest if someone took it away from you. But that won't happen. And you can't give it away, because so much of it is tied up in trusts. So you settle for being slapped and humiliated and debased. I understand, girl, I think you're crazy, but I understand. You're too shallow to realize what great good fortune you've had in life, too shallow to enjoy it, too shallow to find some way to use your money for a meaningful purpose. So you come to me. *You come to me.* Keep that in mind. You're in my house, and you will do what I say. Right now, you'll shut up and drink your vodka and tonic."

She had worked up saliva while he'd been talking, and again she spat in his face.

He pressed her against the wall with his left hand, and with his right hand he grabbed the drink that he had fixed for her. He held the glass to her lips, but she kept her mouth tightly shut.

"Take it," Carrera insisted.

She refused.

Finally he forced her head back and tried to pour the vodka into her nose. She tossed her head as best she could in his fierce grip, but at last she opened her mouth to avoid drowning. She snorted and gasped and choked, spraying vodka from her nostrils. He poured the rest of the drink between her lips and let her go as she spluttered and gagged.

Carrera turned away from her and picked up the mixture of orange juice and raw eggs that he had made for himself. He drank it in a few swallows.

When he had finished his drink, Marie was still not recovered from having been force-fed hers. She was doubled over, coughing, trying to clear her throat and get her breath.

Carrera seized her by the arm, dragged her to the bed and pushed her facedown against the mattress. He pushed up her skirt, tore at her undergarments, shucked off his own robe, and fell upon her savagely.

"You're hurting me," she said weakly.

He knew that was true. But he also knew that she liked it this way more than any other. Besides, this was the only way he liked it.

The power to inflict pain was the ultimate power.

Sexual power over women was as important to him as financial, psychological, and sheer physical power. Before he finished with Marie Dumont, he would hurt her badly, degrade and humiliate her, demand things that would disgust her and leave her feeling totally worthless, because that would make *him* feel godlike.

As Marie wept and struggled beneath him, he thought of Lisa-Joanna. He wondered if he would have the chance to do to her all that he was now doing to Marie. The very thought of it made him drive even more ferociously into his current willing victim.

When he had first seen the Chelgrin girl twelve years ago, she had been the most beautiful and desirable creature he'd ever encountered, but because of who she was, he had not been able to touch her. Judging by the photos taken in Kyoto, time had only improved her.

Carrera ardently wished that Dr. Rotenhausen's treatment would fail this time, and that Lisa-Joanna would then be passed to him for disposal. There was a risk that a second mindwipe would leave her with the mental capacity of a four-year-old, and the thought of a four-year-old's mind in that lush body appealed to Carrera as nothing else ever had. If she ended up that way, he would tell them that he had killed her and buried her, but he would keep her alive for his own use. If he possessed her in such a retarded state, he would be able to dominate her and use her to an extent that he had never been able to dominate or use anyone, including Marie Dumont. She would be his little animal, and he would train her to perform some amazing tricks.

Under him, Madame Dumont was screaming. He was hurting her too much. She had her limits. He didn't care about her limits. He pushed her face against the mattress, muffling her cries.

In his possession, the Chelgrin girl would learn the limits of joy, and she would be thrust beyond the limits of pain in order to learn total, unquestioning obedience. She would know extreme terror, and from terror she would learn to be eager to please. He would use her until he had explored every permutation of lust, and then he would share her with Paz. Finally, when there was nothing left to demand of her, when she had endured every degradation, Carrera would beat her to death with his hands. He would take at least an entire day to murder her; in her prolonged agony, he would find a pleasure so intense that bearing up under it would be as challenging as bearing up under any weight he had ever put on his barbells.

Borne away by his fantasy of absolute domination, he almost killed Marie Dumont. He realized that he was jamming her face so hard into the pillows that she couldn't breathe. He let her up just enough to allow her to gasp for air.

He happily would have killed her, but at the moment, disposing of her body would have been a serious inconvenience. He would soon have to leave for Saint Moritz.

That was where his true destiny lay. In Saint Moritz. With the Chelgrin girl.

The winter tempest
Blows small stones
Onto the temple bell.

—Buson, 1716–1783

▶ ▶ ▶

Part Three

A Puzzle in a Puzzle

45 After getting no sleep in Tokyo, Alex and Joanna also slept little and poorly on the flight to London. They were tense, excited about their new relationship, and worried about what might await them in England. To make matters worse, the plane encountered heavy turbulence, and they lolled in their seats as miserably as seasick cruisers on their first ocean voyage.

When they landed at Heathrow, Alex's long legs were cramped, swollen, and leaden; sharp pains shot through his calves and thighs with every step. His back ached all the way from the base of his spine to his neck. His eyes were bloodshot, grainy, and sore.

From the look of her, Joanna had the same list of complaints. She promised to get down on her knees and kiss the earth—just as soon as she was certain that she had enough strength to get up again.

Alex found it difficult to believe that less than twenty-four hours ago, he'd experienced the greatest ecstasy of his life.

At the hotel they unpacked none of his suitcases and only part of one of hers. The rest could wait until morning.

She had brought two handheld hair dryers. One was a lightweight plastic model, and the other was a big old-fashioned blower with a metal casing and a ten-inch metal snout. A small screwdriver was in the same suitcase, and Alex used it to dismantle the bulkier of the two hair dryers. Before leaving Kyoto, he had stripped the insides from the machine and carefully fitted a gun into the hollow shell: the silencer-equipped 9mm automatic that he had taken off the man in the alleyway more than a week ago. It had passed through X rays and customs inspection without being detected.

He took a large tin of body powder from the same suitcase. In the bathroom, he stooped beside the commode, put up the lid and the seat, and sifted the talc out of the can, through his fingers. Two magazines of extra ammunition had been concealed in the powder.

"You'd make a great criminal," Joanna observed from the doorway.

"Yeah. But I've done better being honest than I'd ever have done on the other side of the law."

"We could rob banks."

"Why don't we just buy control of one?"

"You're a regular stick-in-the-mud."

"Dull," he agreed. "That's me."

They ate a room-service dinner in the suite, and at ten o'clock London time, they crawled under the covers of the same bed. This time, however, before they slept, they were too exhausted to share more than a single chaste goodnight kiss.

Alex had a strange dream. He was lying in a soft bed in a white room, and three surgeons—all in white gowns, white face masks—stood over him. The first surgeon said, "Where does he think he is?" The second surgeon said, "South America. Rio." And the third said, "So what happens if this doesn't work?" The first surgeon said, "Then he'll probably get himself killed without solving our problem." Alex grew bored with their conversation, and he raised one hand to touch the nearest doctor, hoping to silence him, but his fingers suddenly changed into tiny replicas of buildings, five tiny buildings at the end of his hand, which then became five *tall* buildings seen at a distance, and then the buildings grew larger, became skyscrapers, and they drew nearer, and a city grew across the palm of his hand and up his arm, and the faces of the surgeons were replaced by clear blue sky, and the city wasn't on his hand and arm any more but below him, the city of Rio below him, the fantastic bay and the sea beyond, and then the plane landed, and he got out. He was in Rio. A Spanish guitar played mournful music. He was on vacation and having a good time, having a very good time, a memorable and good, good time.

At seven o'clock in the morning, he was awakened by a loud pounding. At first he thought the sound was inside his head, but it was real.

Joanna sat up in bed beside him, clutching the covers. "What's that?"

Alex strove to shake off the last shroud of sleep. He cocked his head, listened for a moment, and said, "Someone's at the door to the hall, out in the drawing room."

"Sounds like they're breaking it down."

He picked up the loaded pistol from the nightstand.

"Stay here," he said, getting out of bed.

"No way."

In the drawing room, dim gray daylight seeped in at the edges of the closed drapes. The writing desk, chairs, and sofa might have been sleeping animals in the gloom.

Alex felt for the light switch, found it. He squinted in the sudden glare and held the gun in front of him.

"There's no one here," Joanna said.

In the foyer, they found a blue envelope on the carpet. It had been slipped under the door.

As Alex picked it up, Joanna said, "What's that?"

"A note from the senator."

"How do you know that?"

He blinked at her. Even after nine hours of sleep, he was still fuzzy-minded.

"How?" she persisted.

The envelope was unmarked by typewriter or pen, and it was sealed.

"I don't know," he said. "Instinct, I guess."

46

London was rainy and cold. The bleak December sky was so low and heavy that the city seemed to huddle beneath it in expectation of being crushed. The tops of the tallest buildings disappeared into gray mist.

The taxi driver who picked up Alex and Joanna in front of their hotel was a burly man with a neatly trimmed white beard. He wore a rumpled hat and a heavy green cardigan. He smelled of peppermint and rain-dampened wool. "Where can I take you this morning?"

"Eventually," Alex said, "we want to go to the British Museum. But first you'll have to lose the people who'll be following us. Can you do that?"

The driver stared at him as if unsure he had heard correctly.

"He's perfectly serious," Joanna said.

"He seems to be," said the driver.

"And he's sober," she said.

"He seems to be."

"And he isn't crazy."

"That remains to be seen," said the driver.

Alex counted out thirty pounds to the man. "I'll have more for you at the other end, plus the fare. Will you help us?"

"Well, sir, they tell you to humor madmen if you meet one. And it seems especially wise to humor one with money. The only thing that bothers me— is it coppers watching you?"

"No," Alex said.

"Is it coppers, young lady?"

"No," Joanna said. "They're not good men at all."

"Sometimes neither are the coppers." He grinned, tucked the bills into his shirt pocket, stroked his white beard with one hand, and said, "Name's Nicholas. At your service. What should I be looking for? What sort of car might they be using?"

"I don't know," Alex said. "But they'll stay close behind us. If we keep an eye open, we'll spot them."

The morning traffic was heavy. Nicholas turned right at the first corner, left at the second, then right, left, left, right.

Alex watched out the back window. "Brown Jaguar. Lose it."

Nicholas wasn't a master of evasive driving. He weaved from lane to lane, slipping around cars and buses, trying to put traffic between them and their tail—but at such a sedate pace that his passengers might have been a couple of frail centenarians on their way to their hundred and first birthday party. His maneuvers were not sufficiently dangerous to discourage pursuit. He turned corners without signaling his intent, but never at even a high enough speed to splash pedestrians standing at the curb, and never from the wrong lane, which made it easy for the Jaguar to stay with him.

"Your daring doesn't take my breath away," Alex said.

"Be fair, sir. It's London traffic. Rather difficult to put the pedal to the metal, as you Americans say."

"Still, there's room for a bit more risk than this," Alex said impatiently.

Joanna put one hand on his arm. "Remember the story of the tortoise and the hare."

"Yeah. But I want to lose these people quickly. At the rate we're going, we'll only lose them after eight or ten hours—when they're too tired to bother with us any more."

A London taxi was not permitted to operate if it bore any mark of a collision—even a small dent or scrape. Obviously Nicholas was acutely aware of that regulation. The insurance company would pay for repairs, but the car might be in the garage for a week, which would be lost work time.

Nevertheless, even at his stately—not to say snail's—pace, he managed to put three cars between them and the Jaguar. "We're going to lose them," he said happily.

"Maybe. As long as they play fair and stop for lunch at the same time we do," Alex said.

"You have a funny man here, miss," Nicholas told Joanna. "Quite a sense of humor."

To Alex, it appeared that Nicholas was being *allowed* to lose the tail. The driver of the Jaguar wasn't handling his car as well as he had at the start.

A surveillance unit only willingly detached itself from a target when it was confident that the target's ultimate destination was known. It was almost as if the men in the Jaguar knew that Alex and Joanna were going to the British Museum to meet the senator and were tailing them only so they could gradually fall back and ultimately appear to have been shaken off.

They came to an intersection where the traffic signal had just gone from green to red, but Nicholas screwed up enough courage to round the corner illegally. The tires even squealed. A little.

The cars behind them stopped, and the Jaguar was boxed in. It wouldn't be able to move again until the light changed.

They were on a narrow street flanked by exclusive shops and theaters, amid fewer cars than there'd been on the main avenue. Nicholas drove to the middle of the block and swung into an alley before the Jaguar had a chance to round the corner after them. They went to another alley, then onto a main street once more.

As they continued to wind slowly from avenue to avenue through the slanting gray rain, Nicholas glanced repeatedly at the rearview mirror. Gradually he broke into a smile, and at last he said, "I did it. I actually lost them. Just like in those American police shows on the telly."

"You were marvelous," Joanna said.

"You really think so?"

"Simply terrific," she said.

"I guess I was. I quite *liked* that. Not good for the heart on a regular basis, mind you, but an invigorating experience."

Alex stared out the back window.

At the British Museum, Joanna got out of the cab and ran for the shelter of the main entrance.

As Alex paid the fare, Nicholas said, "Her husband, I suppose."

"Excuse me?"

"Well, if it wasn't coppers—"

"Oh, no, not her husband."

The driver stroked his beard. "You aren't going to let me hang like this?"

"Indeed I am." Alex got out of the cab and slammed the door.

For a moment Nicholas stared at him curiously through the rain-streaked window, but then he drove away.

Alex stood in the cold drizzle, shoulders hunched, hands in his coat pockets. He looked both ways along the street, studying the traffic, but he saw nothing suspicious.

When he joined Joanna in the doorway, out of the rain, she said, "You're soaked. What were you looking for?"

"I don't know," he said. He was still reluctant to go inside. He surveyed the street.

"Alex, what's wrong?"

"Getting rid of the Jaguar was too easy. Nothing's been this easy so far. Why this?"

"Isn't it time our luck changed?"

"I don't believe in luck."

Finally he turned away from the street and followed her into the museum.

47 They were standing in front of an impressive array of Assyrian antiquities, to which Chelgrin's note had directed them, when they were finally contacted. The senator's representative was a small, wiry man in a peacoat and dark-brown cap. He had a hard face with eyes squinted in perpetual suspicion, and his mouth appeared to have been surgically sewn into a permanent sneer. He stood beside Alex, pretending to appreciate a piece of Assyrian weaponry, and then said, "Yer 'unter, ain't yer?"

The stranger's Cockney accent was nearly impenetrable, but Alex understood him: *You're Hunter, aren't you?*

Occasionally Alex's interest in languages extended to especially colorful dialects. Richer in slang, more distorted in pronunciation than any other regional usage of the English tongue, Cockney was nothing if not colorful. The dialect had evolved in the East End of London, but it had spread to many parts of England. Originally it had been a means by which East End neighbors could talk to one another without making sense to the law or to outsiders.

The stranger squinted at Alex and then at Joanna. "Yer butchers like yer pitchers. Both of yer."

Alex translated: *You look like your pictures. Both of you.* The word "butchers" meant "look" by virtue of Cockney rhyming slang. A "butcher's hook" rhymed with "look"; therefore, by the logic of the code, "butchers" meant "look" when used in the proper context.

"And yer butchers bent ter me," Alex said. "Wot yer want?" *And you look like a less than honest man to me. What do you want?*

The stranger blinked, astonished to hear an American speaking the East End dialect with such confidence. "Yer s'pposed ter be a Yank."

" 'At's wot I am."

"Yer rabbit right good." *You talk very well.*

"Tar," said Alex. *Thanks.*

Joanna said, "I'm not following this."

"I'll explain later," Alex promised.

"Yer rabbit so doddle . . . 'ell, nofink surprise me no more," said the stranger.

Sensing that the Cockney didn't much *like* the idea of a Yank talking to him as though they were mates, Alex dropped the dialect. "What do you want?"

"Got a message from a right pound-note geezer."

Alex translated: *from a man who speaks real fancy*, which usually meant a man with a la-de-da Oxford accent, though not always.

"That doesn't tell me much," Alex said.

"Geezer wif a double of white barnet." *A man with a lot of white hair*.

Barnet Fair was a famous carnival outside London. Since Barnet Fair rhymed with hair, the single word "barnet" meant "hair."

"What does this geezer call himself?" Alex asked.

"Tom. He gimme a poney ter bring yer a message. Seems 'ee's stayin' at the Churchill in Portman Square, and wants to see yer."

It was Senator Thomas Chelgrin who was waiting in a room at the Churchill Hotel. It could be no one else.

"What else?" Alex asked.

" 'At's all der was, mate." The little man started to turn away, then stopped, looked back, licked his lips, and said, "One fink. Be careful of 'im, 'ee's dodgey, that one. Maybe worse an dodgey—'ee's shnide."

Dodgey. *No good.*

Shnide. *Slimy.*

"I'll be careful," Alex said. "Thanks."

The stranger pulled on his cap. "It was me, I wouldn't touch him less 'ee was wearin' a durex from 'ead ter foot of 'imself."

Alex translated and laughed. *I wouldn't touch him unless he was wearing a condom from head to foot.* He shared the Cockney's opinion of the senator from Illinois.

48 From a public telephone at the museum, Alex called the Churchill Hotel in Portman Square.

Joanna fidgeted beside him. She was frightened. The prospect of meeting her duplicitous father couldn't be expected to fill her with joy.

Alex asked the hotel operator for Mr. Chelgrin's room, and the senator answered on the first ring. "Hello?"

"It's me," Alex said. "I recognize your voice, so I figure you recognize mine."

"Is . . . she with you?"

"Of course."

"I can't wait to see her. Come on up."

"We're not in the hotel. Still at the museum. I think we should have a nice long chat by phone before we get together."

"That's not possible. The situation is too urgent. I don't know how much time I have."

"We need to know a few things. Like what happened in Jamaica. And why Lisa became Joanna."

"It's too important to discuss on the phone," Chelgrin said. "Much more important than you can have guessed."

Alex hesitated, glanced at Joanna. "All right. Let's meet just inside the entrance to the National Gallery in half an hour."

"No. That's impossible," Chelgrin said. "It has to be here in my room at the Churchill."

"I don't like that. Too risky for us."

"I'm not here to harm you. I want to help."

"I'd prefer to meet on neutral ground."

"I don't dare go out," Chelgrin said, and the uncharacteristic tension in his voice wound tighter. "I've taken every precaution to conceal this trip. My office is telling everyone that I've gone home to Illinois. I didn't fly out of Washington because I could be traced too easily." He spoke faster, running the words together. "Drove to New York, flew from there to Toronto in a chartered jet, then in another charter to Montreal, and in a third from Montreal to London. I'm wiped out. Exhausted. I'm staying at the Churchill because it's not my usual hotel. I usually stay at Claridge's. But if they discover I've come to London, they'll know I've changed sides, and they'll kill me."

"Who is they?"

Chelgrin hesitated. Then: "The Russians."

"You need a better story, Senator. The Cold War's over."

"Nothing's ever over. Listen, Hunter, all I want is a chance to make up for what I've done, for the past. I want to help you and my daughter . . . that is . . . if she'll allow me to call her my daughter, after what I've done. Together we can expose this whole dirty thing. But you've got to come to me. I can't risk showing my face. And you've got to make *damned* sure you aren't being followed."

Alex thought about it.

"Hunter? Are you still there? My room number's four-sixteen. Hunter?"

"Yeah."

"You have to come."

"We don't *have* to do anything."

The senator was silent for a while. Then he sighed. "All right. Trust your instincts. I don't blame you."

"We'll come," Alex said.

49

They took a taxi to Harrod's. Even that early in the day, the huge, world-famous store was aswarm with shoppers.

Harrod's Telex address had long been "Everything, London." In two hundred departments, the legendary store carried everything from specialty foods to sporting goods, chewing gum to Chinese art, from rare books to rubber boots, faddish clothes to fine antiques, nail polish to expensive oriental rugs—a million and one delights.

Alex and Joanna ignored all the exotic merchandise as well as most of the mundane stuff. They purchased only two sturdy umbrellas and a set of plain but well-made steel cutlery.

In the privacy of a stall in the ladies' room, Joanna unwrapped the package of cutlery. She examined each piece and chose a wickedly sharp butcher's knife that she concealed in her coat pocket. She left the other knives behind when she departed.

Now both she and Alex were armed. Carrying concealed weapons was a more serious offense in London than it would have been almost anywhere else in the world, but they weren't concerned about spending time in jail. Walking *unarmed* into Tom Chelgrin's hotel room would have been by far the most dangerous course they could have taken.

Outside Harrod's they hailed another cab and followed a winding, random course through rain-slicked streets, until Alex was certain that they were not being followed. They got out of the cab three blocks from the Churchill.

Using the umbrellas to hide their faces as much as to shield them from the rain, they approached the hotel from its least public aspect. Rather than barge through the front entrance and across the Regency-style lobby, where they were most likely to be spotted by a lookout, they used an unlocked rear door meant for hotel deliveries, and they quickly found a service stairwell.

"Better leave your bumbershoot here," Alex said. "We'll want our hands free when we get there."

She stood her umbrella beside his, in the corner at the bottom of the stairs.

"Scared?" he asked.

"Yeah."

"Want to back out?"

"Can't," she said.

Though they were whispering, their voices echoed in the cold stairwell.

He unbuttoned his coat and withdrew the 9mm pistol that had been jammed under his belt. He put it in an overcoat pocket and kept his hand on the grip.

She put her hand on the butcher's knife in her pocket.

They climbed the stairs to the fourth floor.

The corridor was brightly lighted, deserted—and too quiet.

They hurried along the hallway, glancing at room numbers. In spite of the elegant decor, Alex couldn't shake the feeling that he was in a carnival funhouse and that a monster was going to spring at them suddenly from a door or out of the ceiling.

Just before they reached 416, Alex was stopped abruptly by a vivid premonition: an intense vision like the brief but commanding burst of a camera's electronic flash. In his mind's eye, he saw Tom Chelgrin spattered with blood. Never before had anything like that happened to him, and he was shaken both by the weirdness of it and by the wet, red *vividness* of the image.

Joanna stopped beside him, gripped his arm. "What's wrong?"

"He's dead."

"What? The senator? How do you know?"

"I just . . . I do. I'm sure of it."

He took the pistol from his coat pocket and continued along the corridor. The door to 416 was ajar.

"Stand behind me," he said.

She shuddered. "Let's call the police."

"We can't. Not yet."

"We have enough proof now."

"We don't have anything more than we had yesterday."

"If he's dead—that's proof of something."

"We don't *know* he's dead," Alex said, though he knew. "Besides, even if he is—that's not proof of anything."

"Let's get out of here."

"We don't have anywhere to go."

He used the pistol to push the door all the way open.

Stillness.

The lights were on in the suite.

"Senator?" he said softly.

When no one answered, Alex stepped across the threshold, and Joanna followed him.

Thomas Chelgrin was facedown on the drawing-room floor.

50 Tom Chelgrin was unquestionably dead. The quantity of blood alone was sufficient to eliminate any doubt.

The senator was wearing a blue bathrobe that had soaked up a great deal of blood. The back of the garment was marred by three bloody holes. He had been shot once at the base of the spine, once in the middle of the back, and once between the shoulders. His left arm was extended in front of him, fingers hooked into the carpet, and his right arm was folded under his chest. His head was turned to one side. Only half his face remained visible, and that was obscured by smears of blood and by a thick shock of white hair that had fallen across his eye.

Alex closed the door to the hall and cautiously inspected the rest of the small suite, but the killers were not to be found. He had known they would be gone.

When he returned to the drawing room, Joanna was kneeling beside the corpse. Alarmed, he said, "Don't touch him!"

She looked puzzled. "Why not?"

"It won't be easy to walk out of here and into our hotel if you're covered with bloodstains."

"I'll be careful."

"You've already got blood on the hem of your coat."

She glanced down. "Damn!"

He pulled her to her feet and away from the corpse. With his handkerchief, he rubbed at the stain on her coat. "It doesn't look good, but it'll have to pass."

"Shouldn't we check him over? Maybe he's alive."

"Alive? Look at those wounds. They used a weapon with a hell of a punch. All this blood. He's dead as a man can be."

"How did you know he'd be here like this? Out there in the hall, how did you know what we'd find?"

"Hard to explain," he said uneasily. "I'd call it a premonition if that didn't sound too crazy. But it does sound crazy, and I'm no clairvoyant."

"So it wasn't just a hunch, professional instinct, like you've said before?"

He recalled the alarmingly vivid mental image of the blood-spattered corpse, and although the position and condition of the real body did not perfectly match the details of the vision, the differences were not substantial.

"Weird," he said.

She stared at the cadaver and shook her head sadly. "I don't feel a thing. No grief."

"Why should you?"

"He *was* my father."

"No. He surrendered all those rights and privileges a long time ago. He didn't mourn for Lisa. He let them do . . . all they did to you. You don't owe him any tears."

"But *why?*" she wondered.

"We'll find out."

"I don't think so. I think maybe we're in some sort of gigantic Chinese puzzle. We'll keep climbing into smaller and smaller boxes forever, and there won't be answers in any of them."

Alex wondered if she might go to pieces on him after all. He wouldn't blame her if she did. She was right: This was her father, after all. She appeared to be calm, but she might be suppressing her feelings.

Realizing that he was worried about her, Joanna conjured a ghost of a smile. "I'll be okay. Like I told you—I don't feel a thing. I wish I did. I wish I could. But he's a stranger to me. They took away all memory of him." She turned away from the body. "Come on, let's get out of here."

"Not yet."

"But what if they come back—"

"They won't be back. If they'd known Chelgrin had made contact with us, and if they'd wanted to kill us, they would've waited right here. They think they got to him before he got to us. Come on. We have to search the place."

She grimaced. "Search for what?"

"For anything. For everything. For whatever little scrap might help us solve this puzzle."

"If the maid walks in—"

"The housekeeper's already been here this morning. The bed's freshly made."

Joanna took a deep breath. "All right, let's finish this as fast as we can."

"You follow me," Alex said. "Double-check me, make sure I don't overlook something. But don't touch anything."

In the bedroom, Chelgrin's two calfskin suitcases were on a pair of folding luggage racks. One case was open. Alex pawed through the clothes until he found a pair of the senator's black socks. He pulled them over his hands: makeshift gloves.

Chelgrin's billfold and credit-card wallet were on the dresser. Alex went through them, with Joanna watching closely, but neither the billfold nor the wallet contained anything unusual.

The closet held two suits and a topcoat. The pockets were empty.

Two pairs of freshly shined shoes were on the closet floor. Alex slipped the shoe trees out of them and searched inside. Nothing.

A shaving kit stood beside the sink in the bathroom: an electric razor, shaving powder, cologne, a comb, a can of hair spray.

Alex returned to the open suitcase. It also proved to contain nothing of interest.

The second suitcase wasn't locked. He opened it and tossed the clothes onto the floor, piece by piece, until he found a nine-by-twelve-inch manila envelope.

He took off the makeshift gloves and emptied the contents of the envelope onto the dresser: several age-yellowed clippings from *The New York Times* and *The Washington Post* an unfinished letter, apparently in the senator's handwriting addressed to Joanna. Alex didn't take time to read either the letter or the newspaper pieces, but from a quick scan of the clippings, he saw that they were all fourteen or fifteen years old and dealt with a German doctor named Franz Rotenhausen. One of the articles featured a photograph of the man: thin face, sharp features, balding, eyes so pale that they appeared to be all but colorless.

Joanna flinched as if she had been bee-stung. "Oh, God. It's him. The man in my nightmare. The Hand."

"His name's Rotenhausen."

"I've never heard it before." She was shaking badly. "I . . . I never thought I'd s-see him again."

"This is what we wanted—a name."

She looked toward the open door between the bedroom and the drawing room, as if Rotenhausen might walk through it at any moment. "Please, Alex, let's get out of here."

The face in the grainy photograph was hard, bony, vampiric. The pale eyes seemed to be staring into a dimension that other men couldn't see.

Alex felt the hairs bristling on the back of his neck. Perhaps it was time to leave.

"We'll read these later," he said, stuffing the clippings and the unfinished letter back into the envelope.

In the drawing room, the dead senator still lay where they had last seen him. Alex had half expected the corpse to be missing. Or standing up, swaying, grinning at them. After recent developments, anything seemed possible.

51 Alex and Joanna ate lunch in a busy café near Piccadilly Circus. Heavy rain sluiced down the windows, blurring modern London until only the ancient lines of the city were visible. The inclement weather was a time machine, washing away the years.

Over thick sandwiches and too many cups of tea, they read the old clippings from *The New York Times* and *The Washington Post*.

Franz Rotenhausen was a genius in more than one field. He had degrees in biology, chemistry, medicine and psychology. He'd written many widely recognized and important papers in all those disciplines. When he was twenty-four, he lost his hand in an automobile accident. Unimpressed with the prostheses available at that time he invented a new device, a mechanical hand nearly as functional as flesh and bone, controlled by nerve impulses from the stump and powered by a battery pack. Later, he'd spent eighteen years as a lecturer and research scientist at a major West German university. He was mainly interested in brain function and dysfunction, and especially in the electrical and chemical nature of thoughts and memory.

"Why would they let anyone work on this?" Joanna asked angrily. "It's George Orwell time. It's *1984*, for God's sake."

"It's also the route to ultimate power," Alex said. "And that's what all politicians are after. So of course they funded his work."

Fifteen years ago, at the peak of a brilliant career, Franz Rotenhausen had made a terrible mistake. He'd written a book about the human brain with an emphasis on recent developments in behavioral engineering, contending that even the most drastic of techniques—including brainwashing—should be used by "responsible" governments to create a dissension-free, crime-free, worry-free Utopian society. His greatest error was not the writing of the book but his subsequent failure to be contrite after it became controversial. The scientific and political communities can forgive any stupidity, indiscretion, or gross miscalculation as long as public apologies come loud and long; humble contrition doesn't even have to be sincere to earn a pardon from the establishment; it must only *appear* genuine, so the citizenry can be allowed to settle back into its usual stupor. As controversy grew in the wake of the publication, however, Rotenhausen had no second thoughts. He responded to critics with increasing irritation. He showed the world a sneer instead of the remorse it wanted to see. His public statements were given an unusually threatening edge by his harsh voice and his unfortunate habit of making violent gestures with his steel hand. European newspapers were quick to give him nicknames—Dr. Strangelove and Dr. Frankenstein—but those soon gave way to another that stuck: Dr. Zombie. He was accused of wanting to create a world of mindless obedient automatons. The furor increased. He complained that reporters and photographers were hounding him, and he was intemperate enough to suggest that they would be his first choice for behavior modification if he were in charge. He steadfastly refused to back down from his position, and thus he was unable to take the pressure off himself.

"I can usually sympathize with victims of press harassment," Alex said. "But not this time."

"He'd like to do to everyone what he did to me."

"Or worse."

The waitress brought more tea and small cakes for dessert.

The lunch crowd was thinning out.

Beyond the windows, the rain was coming down with such force that London had been blurred back into the eighteenth century.

Alex and Joanna continued to read about Rotenhausen:

In Bonn, back in that time before reunification, the West German government was exceedingly sensitive to world opinion. Rotenhausen was widely viewed as Hitler's spiritual descendant. The brilliant doctor ceased to be a national treasure (not so much because of his work but because he'd been unable to keep his mouth shut about it), ceased to be even a national asset, and became a distinct liability to the German state. Pressure was brought to bear on the university that gave him a research home, and eventually he was dismissed on a morals charge involving a student. He denied all wrongdoing and accused the university and the girl of conspiring against him. Nevertheless, he was weary of wasting time on politics when so much research awaited. He departed gracelessly but without challenging the powers that had gone after him with such success, and eventually the morals charge was dropped.

"He might not have been guilty of molesting that girl, but he was probably guilty of molesting others. I know him well. Too well."

Unable to endure the haunted expression in her eyes, Alex stared for a moment at the half-eaten cake on the plate in front of him, and then he took another yellowed clipping from the stack.

Six months after Dr. Zombie was forced out of the university, he liquidated his holdings in West Germany and moved to Saint Moritz, Switzerland. The Swiss granted him permanent residency for two reasons. First, Switzerland was a country with a long and admirable tradition of providing asylum for prominent—though seldom ordinary—outcasts from other countries. Second, Rotenhausen was a millionaire many times over, having inherited a fortune and later having earned substantially more from his dozens of medical and chemical patents. He reached an agreement with the Swiss tax authorities, and each year he paid a tithe that was meager to him but that covered a substantial percentage of the government's expenses in the canton where he lived. It was believed that he continued to do research in his private laboratory in Saint Moritz, but because he never wrote another word for publication and never spoke to newsmen, that suspicion couldn't be verified.

"With time he's been forgotten," Joanna said.

"Too many new monsters to excite the media every day. No time to keep track of the old ones."

Finished with the clippings, they turned to the unfinished, unsigned, handwritten letter from Chelgrin to his daughter. It was two pages of half-baked apologia: an ineffective, self-justifying whine. It provided no new information, not even a single fresh clue.

"How does Rotenhausen connect with the senator and with whatever happened in Jamaica?" Joanna wondered.

"I don't know, but we'll find out."

"You said the senator mentioned Russians when you spoke to him on the phone."

"Yeah, but I don't know what he meant. It seems ridiculous. The Cold War was still on in those days, but it's over now."

"What would Rotenhausen have been doing in a deal with the Soviets, anyway? He sounds more like a Nazi than a communist."

"Nazis and communists have a lot in common," Alex said. "They want the same thing—absolute control, unqualified power. A man like Franz Rotenhausen can find sympathy in both camps."

"Now what?" she asked.

"Now we go to Switzerland."

52 As a hard wind blew shatters of rain against the café windows and as London seemed to dissolve toward prehistoric rock formations, Joanna leaned across the table. "No, Alex. Please, let's not do that. Not Switzerland. Not into . . . into his lair. We can turn this whole thing over to the police now."

"We still don't have enough proof."

She shook her head adamantly. "I disagree. We've got all these clippings, this letter, a dead body at the Churchill Hotel, and the fact that my fingerprints match Lisa's."

Alex reached across the table and put his hand over hers. "I understand your fear. But what police should we go to? The Jamaican police? The Americans? Chicago police? The FBI, the CIA? Japanese police? The British? Scotland Yard? Or maybe the Swiss police?"

She frowned. "It's not so simple, is it?"

"If we go to *any* cops now, we'll be dead by morning. These people, whoever they are, have been hiding something big for a long time. Now the cover-up isn't working any more. The whole thing's falling apart. And they know it. That's why they killed the senator—they've finally decided to clean up the mess before anyone notices it. Right now they're probably looking for us. Whatever immunity you might have had is gone—gone with your father. If we go public with the case now, we'll just be targets. Until we've got the entire story, until we understand the why of it, until we can blow them out of the water, we'll stay alive only as long as we stay out of sight."

Joanna seized on that. "But we'll be extremely visible if we go hunting Rotenhausen in Switzerland."

"We won't blunder straight over there. We'll be discreet."

She wasn't impressed. "The senator tried to sneak into London. It didn't work for him."

"It'll work for us. It has to."

"But even if it does—what'll we do after we get to Saint Moritz?"

He sipped his tea and thought about her question. Finally he said, "I'll find Rotenhausen's place, look it over. If it isn't too heavily guarded, I'll get in, find his file room. If he's the careful, methodical man of science he seems to be maybe he'll have a record of what he did to you, how he did it, and why."

"What about British-Continental Insurance?"

"What about it?"

"If we follow up on that lead, maybe we won't have to go to Saint Moritz."

"Now that we know where they put you through this 'treatment,' we don't have to pry into British-Continental. Besides, that would be just as dangerous as going to Switzerland, but we wouldn't be likely to find as much there as at Rotenhausen's place."

She slumped back in her chair, resigned to the trip. "When do we leave London?"

"As soon as possible. Within the hour, if we can manage it."

53 When Alex and Joanna returned to the hotel for their passports and luggage, they didn't go to their suite alone. They stopped at the front desk, ordered a rental car, told the clerk that they were checking out sooner than originally anticipated, and took two bellmen upstairs with them.

Although the bellmen served as unwitting guards, and though the senator's killers were not likely to strike in front of witnesses, Alex paced nervously in the drawing room and watched the door, alert for the silent turning of the knob, while Joanna got their bags ready to go. Fortunately, when they had arrived the previous night from Tokyo, they had been too tired to unpack more than essentials; and this morning, awakened by Tom Chelgrin's noisy messenger, they'd had no time to hang up their clothes and transfer their things from the suitcases to the dresser drawers, so repacking only required a couple of minutes.

On the way downstairs, the elevator stopped to take aboard more people at the tenth floor. As the doors slid open, Alex unhooked one button on his overcoat, reached inside, and put his hand on the butt of the pistol tucked under the waistband of his trousers. He was half convinced that the people waiting in the corridor were not merely other hotel guests, that they would have submachine guns and would spray the elevator with bullets. The doors rolled open. An elderly couple entered the cab, conducting an animated discussion in rapid-fire Spanish, hardly aware of their fellow passengers.

Joanna smiled grimly at Alex. She knew what he'd been thinking.

He took his hand off the 9mm automatic and buttoned his coat.

They had to wait in the lobby fifteen minutes for the rental car to arrive, but by a quarter past three, they drove away into rain so silver that it appeared to be sleet. Gray mist as thick as smoke settled lower with the waning of the day, engulfing the tops of the tallest buildings, and in the strange pewter light, London seemed medieval even where the buildings were all of glass and steel and modern angles.

For a while they weaved through a Byzantine complexity of rain-lashed streets that branched off from one another with no discernible logic. They were lost but didn't care, because until they identified their tail and lost it, they had no specific destination.

Turned in her seat, staring out the back window, Joanna said at last, "Another Jaguar. A yellow one this time."

"All these bastards seem to travel in style."

"Well, they knew the senator," Joanna said sarcastically, facing forward and engaging her seat belt, "and the senator always moved in the very best circles, didn't he?"

Alex swerved right, in front of a bus and into thinner traffic. The tires squealed, the car shot forward, and he whipped from lane to lane, as if trying to make a car do what an Olympic skier could accomplish in a giant slalom. Motorists braked in surprise as the rental car swerved around and flashed past them, a truck driver blew his horn angrily, and pedestrians stopped and pointed. But the clog of London traffic didn't permit a protracted car chase like those in the movies, and the lanes ahead quickly began to jam up. Alex hung a hard left at the first corner and darted in front of a taxi with only centimeters to spare. At midblock he swung the wrong way into a one-way backstreet and stomped the accelerator. Building walls flashed past in a stony blur, two feet away on either side. The small car bounced and shimmied on the rough cobblestones, severely testing Alex's grip on the steering wheel. If anyone entered the alleyway ahead of them, a head-on crash couldn't be averted; but luck was with them, and they exploded out of the cramped street onto a main thoroughfare, fishtailing across the wet pavement in front of oncoming traffic and into a cacophony of squealing brakes and blaring horns. Alex turned right and sped through a red traffic light as it changed from yellow.

The Jaguar was no longer in sight.

"Terrific!" Joanna said.

"Not so terrific." He kept glancing worriedly at the rearview mirror. "We shouldn't have lost them. Not that easily."

"Easily? You think that was easy? We nearly wrecked half a dozen times!"

"They kill like professionals, so they ought to be able to run a tail like professionals. Should've kept on top of us every minute. They had a better car than this one. And they must be a lot more familiar with these streets than we are. It's just like this morning with the other Jaguar. It's as if they *wanted* to let us get away—so we'd feel safe."

"But why would they be playing a game like that?"

He scowled. "I don't know. I feel like we're being manipulated, and I sure don't like the feeling. It scares me."

"Maybe they don't have to take exceptional risks to keep us in view," she said, "because they've got this car bugged. A concealed transmitter. Or am I being paranoid?"

"These days," Alex said, "only the paranoid survive."

SOMEWHERE IN THE suburban sprawl, as the storm diluted the last light of dusk and washed it into a deep ocean of night, they stopped in the loneliest end of a shopping-center parking lot. Joanna stayed in the car and kept watch while Alex removed the license plates from their rental car and put them on a nearby Toyota. He didn't put the Toyota plates on the rental but kept them for later use.

A few miles farther on, they stopped at a busy roadside supper club. Over rolling thunder and the incessant roar of the rain, big-band music and laughter drifted through the drenched night.

Alex checked parked cars for unlocked doors, then looked inside each accessible vehicle in hope of finding keys in the ignition. In a silver-gray Ford, he discovered what he was looking for under the driver's seat.

Alex drove away in the stolen vehicle. Joanna stayed close behind him in the rental car. As far as he could tell, no one followed them.

In an apartment-complex parking lot, they quickly transferred their bags to the Ford. They abandoned the rental, sans license plates, and went in search of a quiet residential neighborhood.

Ten minutes later, they parked on a street lined with relatively new, identical, single-family brick houses with shallow front lawns and bare-limbed trees, where Alex removed the Ford's license plates and replaced them with the set he had taken from the Toyota in the shopping center. He dropped the Ford's tags into a drainage grate at the curb, and they splashed into the dark water below.

The owner of the Toyota was unlikely to notice immediately that his plates had been replaced with those from the rental car. And when the Ford was reported stolen back at the supper club, police would be looking for a car with the plates that were now lost in the storm drain.

By the time they were on the move again, Alex and Joanna were soaked and shivering, but they felt safer. He turned up the heater to its maximum setting. It was going to take a while to chase away the chill, because he was cold all the way into his bones.

54

Joanna fiddled with the car radio until she located a station playing Beethoven. The beautiful music relieved her tension.

Using complimentary road maps provided by the car-rental agency, they got lost only three times before they were headed south on the correct highway. They were going to Brighton, on the coast, where Alex intended to spend the night.

For years Joanna had thought that the highway they now traveled was the same on which Robert and Elizabeth Rand had lost their lives. But both London and this outlying landscape were new and strange to her. Hard as it was to accept, she now knew that she had never spent her childhood and adolescence in London, as she had believed for so long; this was her first visit to England. Robert and Elizabeth Rand had existed only in a handful of phony documents—and, of course, in her mind.

As the windshield wipers thumped like a heartbeat, she thought of her real father, Thomas Chelgrin, lying dead on that hotel-room floor, and she wished that the image of the bloodied senator could reduce her to tears. Feeling grief would be better than feeling nothing at all. But her heart was closed to him.

She put one hand on Alex's shoulder, just to reassure herself that he was real and that she was not alone.

He glanced at her, evidently sensed her mood, and winked.

The storm continued without surcease. On the black highway, the headlights shimmered like the lambent glow of the moon reflecting off the glassy surface of a swift-flowing river.

"Just west of Brighton," Alex said, "on the way to Worthing, there's a quaint little inn called The Bell and The Dragon. It's a couple hundred years old but beautifully kept, and the food's quite good."

"Won't we need a reservation?"

"Not this late in the year. The tourist season is long past. They ought to have a few nice rooms available."

When they arrived at The Bell and The Dragon a short while later, the only sign announcing it was a large wooden billboard hung from a crossbar between two posts near the highway—no neon, no well-lighted announcement panel advertising an early-bird dinner special or a piano bar. The inn was tucked in a stand of ancient oaks, and the parking lot was nearly as dark as it must have been in the days when the guests arrived in horse-drawn coaches. It was a rambling structure, pleasing to the eye, half brick and half plaster with a crosswork of rugged, exposed beams. The front doors were fashioned from oak timbers and featured hand-carved plaques indicating that beds, food, and drink were offered inside. In the lobby and public rooms, soft electric lights hidden in converted gas lamps imparted a marvelous luster to the polished, richly inlaid paneling.

Alex and Joanna were given spacious quarters on the second floor. White plaster walls. Darkly stained beams. A pegged oak floor protected by plush area carpets.

Joanna examined the griffin-head water spouts in the bathroom, was pleased to find that the stone fireplace in the bedroom would actually work if they chose to use it, and finally threw herself on the four-poster bed. "It's absolutely delightful."

"It belongs to another age—one more hospitable than ours."

"It's charming. I love it. How often have you stayed here?"

The question appeared to surprise him. He stared at her but didn't speak. She sat up on the bed. "What's wrong?"

He turned slowly in a full circle, studying the room. At last he said, "I've never stayed here before."

"Who told you about it?"

"I haven't the slightest idea. I've never been to Brighton before, can't remember ever talking to anyone about it—except to you, of course. This is the third time today."

"The third time what?" Joanna asked.

He went to the nearest window and gazed into the rainy darkness beyond. "It's the third time I've known about something I shouldn't know about. Have no way of knowing about. Creepy. Before I opened that note this morning, I knew it was from the senator."

"That was just a good guess," Joanna said.

"And before we ever got to his hotel room, before I saw that his door was ajar, I knew Tom Chelgrin was dead."

"Intuition."

Alex turned away from the window, shaking his head. "No. This place is more than a hunch. I knew the name—The Bell and The Dragon. I knew exactly how it would look, as if I'd seen it before."

"Maybe someone told you about it, but you just don't recall. Or you read about it in a travel article—one with photographs."

"No. I'd remember," he insisted.

"Not if it was a few years ago. Not if it was casual reading. Maybe a magazine in a doctor's office. Something you skimmed and pretty much forgot, except this place stuck in your subconscious."

"Maybe," he said, though he was obviously unconvinced. He turned to the window again, put his face close to the glass, and stared into the night, as if certain that people were there staring back at him.

55

With the descent of night in London, the temperature had dropped ten degrees. It now hovered at the freezing point. The wind had grown stronger, and the rain had become sleet.

On his way home from the Fielding Athison offices in Soho, Marlowe—previously in charge of all Soviet operations that had used the importing company as a front, now working for post-Soviet forces that still dreamed of a Russian Marxist Utopia—drove slowly and cursed the weather. He kept his head tucked down and his shoulders drawn up in anticipation of a collision. Everywhere he looked, cars slid on the icy pavement, and as far as he could tell, he was the only motorist in all of Greater London who wasn't driving like a suicidal maniac.

In a line of work that demanded caution, Marlowe was one of the most cautious men he knew. He had committed himself to a life of treason, which was, thank you very much, more than enough risk for any man. Having made that one dangerous decision, he tried thereafter to ensure that espionage would be as thoroughly safe and serene an occupation as floral arrangement or managing a tobacco shop. He abhorred taking any action without first thinking through all the ramifications, and he was always markedly slower to act than any of his associates. He kept four stashes of false passports and getaway cash at various places in England, as well as secret bank accounts in Switzerland *and* Grand Cayman.

His aversion to risk extended beyond his working world into his private life. He participated in no leisure sports that were likely to result in broken bones or torn ligaments. He didn't hunt, because occasionally one saw stories in the press about hunting accidents, chaps shooting themselves or one another, either out of carelessness or because they'd mistaken one another for game. He had acquaintances who enjoyed hot-air ballooning, which he considered no safer than bungee jumping off high bridges, so he refused to join them on their mad weekend flights. He faithfully followed a low-fat, low-salt diet. He never drank alcoholic beverages or any beverage containing caffeine. He ate only trace amounts of refined sugar, always bundled up well and wore a hat in cold weather, underwent a complete physical examination twice a year, never had sex without a condom, and drove as sedately as an octogenarian vicar.

On the roadway ahead, another driver stood on the brakes, and the car fishtailed wildly on the ice-sheathed pavement.

Marlowe tamped his brakes judiciously and congratulated himself on having left enough room to stop short of a collision.

Behind him, the brakes of another vehicle squealed horribly.

Marlowe winced, gritted his teeth, and counted the seconds until impact.

Miraculously, no crash ensued.

"Morons," Marlowe said.

He cherished life. He intended to die no sooner than his one hundredth birthday—and then in bed with a young woman. A very young woman. *Two* very young women.

At the moment his anxiety was exacerbated by his inability to concentrate on his driving to the degree he would have liked. In spite of the constant fear that some lunatic would plow into him, he couldn't prevent his mind from wandering. The past few days had been filled with signs and portents, bad omens—and he couldn't stop mulling them over, trying to decide what they meant.

First, he had come out of the confrontation with Ignacio Carrera less well than expected. When he'd tried to learn Joanna Rand's real name, he had been operating on his long-held conviction that he and Carrera were equals in the eyes of the masters whom they served. Instead, he'd been slapped down. Hard. Then word had come from Moscow that Marlowe was to back off the Rand situation, obey Carrera, and leave the mysterious woman unharmed even if she blundered into the offices of Fielding Athison and threatened to disrupt the entire operation.

Marlowe was still smarting from that loss of face when the grotesque Anson Peterson swept in from America and began issuing commands with royal arrogance. Marlowe wasn't permitted to see the Rand woman, not even a photograph of her. He was told not to speak to her if she should call British-Continental again. He was not even supposed to *think* about her any more. Peterson was in charge of the operation, and Marlowe was instructed to go about his other work as if he knew nothing whatsoever about the crisis.

But Marlowe was reluctant to surrender even a single minor prerogative of his position. He jealously guarded his authority and privileges; it was dangerous to relinquish even a small amount of hard-won power. One backward step on the ladder could turn into a long, bone-crunching fall to the bottom, because everywhere there were schemers who envied their betters and were willing to give them a killing push over the brink at the first sign of weakness.

Marlowe was jolted out of his reverie by the mighty blast of an air horn. A big lorry loaded with frozen poultry skidded and nearly sideswiped him. He glanced at the rearview mirror, saw that no one was close behind, and jammed his foot down on the brake pedal harder than he should have. The car began to slide, but he let the wheel spin as it wished, and a moment later he was in control again. The lorry slid past him, swayed as if it would topple, then regained its equilibrium, and sped on.

Taking heart from the way he handled the car, he told himself that he would manage the current crisis at work with equal skill, once he'd had time to think out all courses of action open to him.

Marlowe lived on the entire top floor of a large three-story, eighteen-room townhouse that had been converted into apartments. When he parked at the curb in front of the building and switched off the car engine, he sighed with relief.

As he carefully negotiated the icy sidewalk to the front door, he was pelted furiously by sleet, but it couldn't get under his coat collar because he'd wound a scarf around his neck and then buttoned the collar securely over it.

At the third floor, Marlowe unlocked his apartment door and felt for the light switch as he stepped across the threshold. He smelled the natural gas even as his fingers touched the switch. But in the fraction of a second that his mind raced frantically through all the ramifications of the situation in search of the safest action, his right index finger recklessly completed its small arc and flicked the switch. Marlowe was blown to Hell with a flash of remorse at all the potato chips never eaten, the beers never drunk, and the women never experienced without the desensitizing barrier of a latex sheath.

ACROSS THE STREET from the apartment house, Peterson sat alone in a parked car, watching as the third-floor windows blew out, the wall exploded, and Marlowe arced out into the rainy night as though he were a clown shot from a cannon. Briefly the dead man appeared to be able to fly as well as any bird—but then he plummeted to the pavement and did less damage to it than it did to him.

A man and a woman ran from the front entrance of the building. No one was at home on the second floor, so Peterson figured these two were ground-floor residents. They rushed to Marlowe's crumpled body—but they hastily drew back, sickened, when they got a close look at him.

The fat man popped a butter-rum Life Saver into his mouth. He released the parking brake, put the car in gear, and drove away from that sorry place.

Peterson hadn't received permission to eliminate Marlowe. In fact, he had never expected to receive it, so he hadn't even bothered to ask for it. Marlowe's transgressions had been far too minor to generate a kill order from the directorate in Moscow.

Nevertheless, Marlowe had to die. He was the first of six primary targets on the hit list. Peterson had made promises to an extremely powerful group, and if he failed to keep those promises, his own life would end as quickly and brutally as Marlowe's.

He had worked for an hour to set up the gas explosion so it would appear to have been an accident. The bosses in Moscow, who demanded absolute obedience from Anson Peterson, might be suspicious about an "accident" that killed one of their major London operatives, but they would blame the other side rather than one of their own best agents.

And the other men, those to whom Anson Peterson had made so many commitments, would be satisfied. The first of his promises had been kept. One man was dead. The first of many.

56

Alex and Joanna ate dinner in the cozy, oak-paneled dining room at The Bell and The Dragon. The food was excellent, but Alex was unable to get a full measure of enjoyment from it. While he ate, he surreptitiously watched the other customers, trying to determine if any of them might be watching him.

Later, in bed in the dark, he and Joanna made love. This time it was slow and tender, and they finished like a pair of spoons in a drawer. He fell asleep pressed against her warm back.

The peculiar dream came to him again. The soft bed. The white room. The three surgeons in white gowns and masks, staring down at him. The first surgeon asked the same question he'd asked before—"Where does he think he is?"—and the same conversation ensued among the three men. Alex lifted one hand to touch the nearest doctor, but as before his fingers were transformed magically into tiny replicas of buildings. He stared at them, amazed, and then his fingers ceased to be merely replicas and became five tall buildings seen at a great distance, and the buildings grew larger, larger, and he drew nearer to them, dropping down from the sky, and a city grew across the palm of his hand and up his arm. The looming faces of the surgeons were replaced by blue sky. Below him was Rio, the fantastic bay and the ocean beyond. Then his plane landed, and he got out, and he was *in* Rio. The mournful but beautiful music of a Spanish guitar filled the Brazilian air.

He mumbled and turned over in his sleep.

And he turned into a new dream. He was in a cool dark crypt. Candles flickered dimly. He walked to a black coffin that rested on a stone bier, grasped the massive bronze handles, and lifted the lid. Thomas Chelgrin lay inside: bloodsmeared, gray-skinned, as dead as the stone on which his casket rested. Heart pounding, overcome with dread, Alex gazed at the senator, and then as he started to lower the lid, the eyes of the corpse opened. Chelgrin grinned malevolently, exposing blood-caked teeth. He grabbed Alex's wrist in his strong, gray, cold hands and tried to drag him down into the coffin.

Alex sat straight up in bed, an unvoiced scream trapped in his throat.

Joanna was asleep.

He remained very still for a while, suspicious of the deep shadows in the corners. He had left the bathroom door ajar, with the light burning beyond it. Nevertheless, most of the room was shrouded in gloom. Gradually his eyes adjusted, and he could see that there were no intruders, either real or supernatural.

He got out of bed and went to the nearest window.

Their room offered a view of the sea. Alex could see nothing, however, except a vast black emptiness marked by the vague lights of a ship behind curtains of rain. He shifted his gaze to something closer at hand: the slate-shingled roof that slanted low over the window, creating a deep eave. Still closer: The windows had diamond-shaped panes of leaded glass, and each pane was beveled at the edges. Closer: In the surface of the glass, he saw himself—his drawn face, his troubled eyes, his mouth set in a tight grim line.

The case had begun with Joanna's repeating nightmare. Now he had a recurring dream of his own. He didn't believe in coincidence. He was certain that his dream of Rio harbored a message that he must interpret if they were to survive. His subconscious was trying to tell him something desperately important.

But for God's sake, what?

He had been to Rio for a month the previous spring, but he hadn't been hospitalized while there. He hadn't met any doctors. The trip had been per-fectly ordinary—just one in a series of brief escapes from a job that had begun to bore him.

He shifted his attention from his own reflection and stared into the dis-tance again.

We're puppets, he thought. *Joanna and me. Puppets. And the puppet-master is out there. Somewhere. Who? Where? And what does he want?*

Lightning slashed the soft flesh of the night.

57

Rain was no longer falling. The morning air was piercingly clear. Judging by the window glass to which Joanna touched her fingertips, the day was also fearfully cold.

She felt refreshed and more at ease than she'd been in a long time. She could see, however, that Alex had not benefited from the night at the inn. His eyes were bloodshot and ringed by dark circles of slack skin.

He returned the 9mm pistol to its hiding place in the hollowed-out hair dryer and packed the dryer in Joanna's largest suitcase.

They checked out of The Bell and The Dragon at nine o'clock. The clerk wished them a swift, safe trip.

They went to an apothecary and purchased a tin of body powder to re-place the one that Alex had emptied into the toilet in London. In the car again, he slipped the extra magazines of ammunition into the talc. Joanna put the resealed can in her suitcase.

They drove from the outskirts of Brighton to Southampton. No one fol-lowed them.

At the Southampton airport, they abandoned the stolen Ford in the park-ing lot.

Aurigny Airlines hadn't yet sold out the Saturday morning flight to Cherbourg. Alex and Joanna sat behind the starboard wing, and she had the window seat. The flight was uneventful, with such an utter lack of turbulence that it almost seemed as though they hadn't left the ground.

The French customs officials thoroughly inspected the luggage, but they neither opened the can of body powder nor took a close look at the hair dryer.

On the express turbotrain from Cherbourg to Paris, Alex's mood brightened somewhat, apparently because Paris was his favorite city. He usually stayed at the Hotel George V; indeed, he was so well known by the staff that he might have gotten a room without a reservation. They stayed elsewhere, however, in less grand quarters, precisely because they didn't want to go where Alex was well known.

From their hotel, he telephoned another hotel in Saint Moritz. Speaking fluent French and using the name Maurice Demuth, he inquired about reserving a room for one full week, beginning Sunday, two days hence. Fortunately, a recent cancellation had made a room available, and currently there was no waiting list for week-long accommodations.

When Alex put down the phone, Joanna said, "Why Maurice Demuth?"

"So if anyone connected with Rotenhausen should go around Saint Moritz checking advance bookings at the hotels, he won't find us."

"I mean, why Maurice Demuth instead of some other name?"

"Well . . . I don't know. It's just a good French name."

"I thought maybe you knew someone with that name."

"No. I just plucked it out of the air."

"You lied so smoothly. I better start taking everything you say with a grain of salt." She moved into his arms.

"Like when you tell me I'm pretty—how can I be sure you mean it?"

"You're more than pretty. You're beautiful," he said.

"You sound so sincere."

"No one has ever done to me what you do."

"So sincere . . . and yet . . ."

"Easy to prove I'm not lying."

"How?"

He took her to bed.

Later, they ate dinner at a small restaurant overlooking the Seine, which was speckled with the lights of small boats and the reflected amber wedges of the windows in the buildings that stood along its banks.

As she nibbled flawless *oie rotie aux pruneaux* and listened to Alex's stories about Paris, she knew that she could never allow anyone or anything to separate her from him. She would rather die.

58

In Saint Moritz, Peterson had a gray Mercedes at his disposal. He drove himself, continuously peeling a roll of Life Savers and popping a series of butter-rum morsels into his mouth.

Low over the towering mountains, the sky appeared to be nine months gone, bulging with gray-black storm clouds that were about to deliver torrents of fine dry snow.

During the afternoon Peterson played tourist. He drove from one viewing point to another, enchanted by the scenery.

The resort of Saint Moritz is in three parts: Saint Moritz-Dorf, which is on a mountain terrace more than two hundred feet above the lake; Saint Moritz-Bad, which is a charming place at the end of the lake; and Champfer-Suvretta. Until the end of the nineteenth century, Saint Moritz-Bad was *the* spa, but thereafter it lost ground to Saint Moritz-Dorf, which is perhaps the most dazzling water playground in the world. Recently, Moritz-Bad had been making a concerted effort to recapture its lost position, but its ambitious recovery program had led to a most unlovely building boom.

An hour after nightfall, Peterson kept an appointment in Saint Moritz-Bad. He left the Mercedes with a valet at one of the newer and uglier hotels. Inside, he crossed the lobby to the lakefront cocktail lounge. The room was crowded and noisy.

The hotel's day-registration clerk, Rudolph Uberman, had gone off duty fifteen minutes ago and was waiting at a corner table: a thin man with long, slim hands that were seldom still.

Peterson shrugged out of his overcoat, hung it across the back of a chair, and sat facing Uberman. The clerk was nearly finished with a brandy and wanted another, and Peterson ordered the same.

After they were served, Peterson said, "Any word?"

Uberman was nervous. "Monsieur Maurice Demuth telephoned four hours ago."

"Excellent."

"He will arrive Sunday with his wife."

Peterson withdrew an envelope from an inside coat pocket and passed it to Uberman. "That's your second payment. If all goes well on Sunday, you'll receive a third envelope."

The clerk glanced left and right before quickly tucking the payoff out of sight—as if anyone who witnessed the exchange would immediately know that it was dirty business. In fact, none of the other customers was the least bit interested in them.

"I would like some assurance," Uberman said.

Peterson scowled. "Assurance?"

"I would like a guarantee that no one . . ."

"Yes? Go on."

"That no one will be killed."

"Oh, of course, dear man, you have my word on that."

Uberman studied him. "If anyone were killed in the hotel, I'd have no choice but to tell the authorities what I know."

Peterson kept his voice low, but he spoke sharply. "That would be foolish. You're an accomplice, sir. The authorities wouldn't deal lightly with you. And neither would I."

Uberman tossed back his brandy as though it were water. "Perhaps I should return the money."

"I wouldn't accept it. A deal is a deal."

"I guess I'm in over my head."

"Relax, sir. You've a tendency to melodramatize. It will all go very smoothly, and no one will ever know it happened."

"What do you want with them anyway?"

"You wouldn't care to know that. Just think of all those Swiss francs in the envelope and the rest to come, and forget the source of it all. Forgetting is always best. Forgetting is safe. Now, tell me, is the restaurant here any good?"

"The food is terrible," Uberman said.

"I suspected as much."

"Try Chesa Veglia."

"I'll do that."

"Or perhaps Corviglia at the top of the funicular."

Peterson put enough money on the table to cover the bill. As he stood and struggled into his overcoat, he said, "I'm a heeder of my own advice. I've already forgotten your name."

"I never knew yours," Uberman noted.

"Did someone speak?" Peterson asked, looking around as though he couldn't even see Uberman.

Smiling at his own joke, he left the hotel for dinner at Chesa Veglia.

59 On Saturday they flew from Paris to Zurich. Their hotel, Baur Au Lac, stood in its own lakeside park at the end of Bahnhofstrasse.

In their room, Alex dismantled the hair dryer yet again and put the pistol under his belt. He took the spare clips of ammunition from the talcum powder.

"I wish you didn't have to carry that," Joanna said.

"So do I. But we're getting too close to Rotenhausen to risk going without it."

They made love again. Twice. He could not get enough of her—but he wasn't seeking sex as much as closeness.

That night he had the dream again.

He woke shortly before three o'clock, gasping in panic, but he regained control of himself before he woke Joanna. He couldn't go back to sleep. He sat in a chair beside the bed, the pistol in his lap, until the wake-up call came at six o'clock.

He was grateful for his peculiar metabolism, which allowed him to function well on little sleep.

Monday morning they boarded a train at Zurich's Haupbahnhof, and they headed east.

As the train pulled out of the station, Joanna said, "We're sure going roundabout. No one'll be able to track us down easily."

"Maybe they don't need to track us down," Alex said. "Maybe they knew our route before we did."

"What do you mean?"

"I'm not sure. But sometimes I feel . . . manipulated . . . programmed. Like a robot."

"I don't understand."

"Neither do I," he said wearily. "Forget it. I'm just edgy. Let's enjoy the scenery."

At Chur they changed trains to follow the fertile Rhine Valley downstream. In summer the land would be green with vineyards, wheat fields, and orchards, but now it lay dormant under a blanket of snow. The train chugged into the towering Rhaetian Alps, passed through the dramatic Landquart Gorge, and followed a new river upstream. After a long, winding, but for the most part gentle ascent, past a handful of resort villages, they came to Klosters, which was nearly as famous as Saint Moritz.

They debarked at Klosters and left their luggage at the station while they outfitted themselves in ski clothes. During the trip from Zurich, they had realized that nothing they'd packed was adequate for high-altitude December weather. Besides, dressed in the usual winter clothes of city dwellers, they were conspicuous, which was precisely what they did not want to be. They changed in the dressing rooms at the ski shop and threw away the clothes they had been wearing which amazed the clerk.

After lunch they boarded a train to Davos. It was crowded with a large party of French skiers bound for Saint Moritz. The French were happy, noisy, drinking wine from bottles that were concealed in plain paper sacks.

A fine snow began to fall. The wind was but a breeze.

The Rhaetian Railway crossed the Landquart River high on a terrifyingly lofty bridge, climbed through magnificent pine forests, and chugged past a ski center called Wolfgang. Eventually the tracks dropped down again to Davosersee and the town of Davos, which was composed of Davos-Dorf and Davos-Platz.

Snow fell fast and hard now. The wind had gained power.

From the train window, Alex could see that the storm concealed the upper regions of Weissfluh, the mountain that most dominated the town. Up there in the mists, behind a heavy drape of falling snow, skiers began the descent along the Parsenn run, from Weissfluhjoch—at the 9,000-foot level—down to the town at 5,500 feet.

In spite of the charming village beyond the train window, a sense of absolute isolation was unavoidable. That was one of the qualities that had attracted people to this place for more than a century. Sir Arthur Conan Doyle often had come to escape London and perhaps to think about Sherlock Holmes. In 1881, Robert Louis Stevenson had sought the solitude and the healthful air of Davos in which to finish his masterpiece, *Treasure Island*.

"The top of the world," Alex said.

"I get the strange feeling that the rest of the earth was destroyed," Joanna said, "all of it gone in a nuclear war or some other great cataclysm. This might be all that's left. It's so separate . . . so remote."

And if we disappeared in this vastness, Alex thought uneasily, *no one would ever find us.*

From Davos the train went to Susch and Scuol. The French were singing reasonably well, and no one complained. In early darkness, the train moved up the Engadine Valley, past the lake, and into Saint Moritz.

They were in the middle of a blizzard. The wind was coming off the mountains at thirty—gusting to fifty—kilometers an hour. The preternaturally dense snowfall reduced visibility to a single block.

At the hotel when Alex and Joanna checked in, they were required to present their passports and, therefore, used their real names; but he asked that the Maurice Demuth nom de guerre be the only name kept in the registration file. In a town that was accustomed to playing host to privacy-conscious movie stars, dukes, duchesses, counts, countesses, and wealthy industrialists from all corners of the world, such a request was not unusual, and it was honored.

They had a small but comfortable suite on the fifth floor. When the bellmen left, Alex tested the two locks and double-bolted the door. He went into the bedroom to help Joanna with the unpacking.

"I'm exhausted," she said.

"Me too." He took the pistol out of the waistband of his slacks and put it on the nightstand.

"I'm too tired to stand up," she said, "but still . . . I'm afraid to sleep."

"We'll be safe tonight."

"Do you still have that feeling? That somehow we're being manipulated?"

"Maybe I was just wired too tight," he said.

"What will we do tomorrow?"

"Scout around. Find out where Rotenhausen lives, if we can."

"And then?"

Alex heard a noise behind them. He turned and saw a tall, husky man standing in the open doorway between the bedroom and the living room.

So soon! Alex thought.

Joanna saw the intruder and cried out.

The intruder was holding an odd-looking gun and wearing a gas mask.

Alex lunged for the pistol that he had left on the nightstand.

The man in the mask fired the gas-pellet gun. Soft, waxy bullets struck Alex and disintegrated on impact, expelling clouds of sweet fumes.

He picked up the 9mm pistol, but before he could use it, the world dissolved in whirling white clouds, as though the blizzard beyond the windows had swept inside.

60

In the front room of the suite, Ignacio Carrera and Antonio Paz loaded the luggage into the bottoms of two large hotel laundry carts. Then they placed Alex Hunter and Joanna Rand into the carts, on top of the suitcases.

To Carrera, the woman was even more beautiful than she appeared in photographs. If the gas could have been counted upon to keep her unconscious more than just another half hour, he would have undressed her and raped her here, now. Helplessly asleep, she would be warm and exquisitely pliant. But he didn't have time for fun just yet.

Carrera had brought two pieces of Hermes leather luggage with him. They belonged to the fat man. He put them in the bedroom.

Tomorrow, the day clerk would secretly alter the registration card. It would appear that Anson Peterson had checked in on Sunday. There would be no record of Hunter and the woman: They would simply have ceased to exist.

Paz covered the unconscious couple with towels and rumpled bed linens.

They wheeled the carts to the service elevator and rode down to ground level without encountering anyone.

61

When Alex regained consciousness, he wished he hadn't. He tasted bile. His vision was blurry and tinted red, as if his eyes were full of blood. A demon donkey was inside his head, kicking to get out.

At least he was alive. Which was inexplicable. They had no use for him—only for Joanna—and should have wasted him by now.

He was lying on his left side on a white-and-black tile floor. A kitchen. A light glowed above the stove.

His back was against a row of cabinets, and his hands were tied behind him. Good, heavy cord. His feet were also bound together.

Joanna wasn't with him. He called her name softly but received no reply.

He despised himself for letting them take her so easily. In his own defense, he could only argue that no one could have expected such a bold assault in a busy hotel and only minutes after their arrival.

He listened for movement or voices in another room. Nothing. Silence.

Knowing that the restraints wouldn't break or come loose easily, nevertheless hoping for a bit of luck, he tried to jerk his wrists apart. Incredibly, impossibly, the rope snapped on the third try.

Stunned, he lay motionless, listening and wondering.

Deep silence.

Fear sharpened his senses, and he was able to smell items that were shut away in the cupboards: cloves of garlic, soap, a pungent cheese.

Finally he brought his hands out from behind his back. The broken rope was loosely draped around his wrists. He pulled it off.

He scooted around on the shiny tile floor until he was sitting with his back to the cabinets. He untied the rope at his ankles, threw it aside, and got to his feet.

His skull seemed to be cracking under the punishing hooves of that indefatigable donkey. His vision dimmed-brightened-dimmed in a dependable rhythm, but gradually the red tint was fading.

He picked up the length of rope that had been around his hands and took it to the stove. Examining it under the small fluorescent light, he saw why he'd been able to snap it with so little effort: While he'd been unconscious, someone had cut most of the way through the line, leaving only a fraction of the diameter intact.

Manipulated. Programmed.

He had the uncanny conviction that everything that was going to happen during the next few hours had been planned a long time ago.

But by whom? And why?

He wondered if he and Joanna would be the winners or the losers of the game.

62   Joanna woke with a vile taste, swimming vision, and a fierce headache. When she began to be able to see, she discovered that she was in a hospital bed in a white room with a high window: the familiar setting of her nightmare. An electroencephalograph, an electrocardiograph, and other machines stood nearby, but she wasn't connected to them. The air reeked of a mélange of disinfectants.

Initially she thought that she was dreaming, but the full horror of her situation quickly became apparent. Her hammering heart pounded a cold sweat out of her.

Broad leather straps with Velcro fasteners restrained her wrists and ankles. She wrenched at them, but she was well secured.

"Ah," a woman said behind Joanna, "the patient's awake at last."

She had thought that the head of the bed was against the wall and that she was alone, but she was in the center of the room. She twisted her neck, trying to see the person who had spoken, but the straps and the inclined mattress foiled her.

After a taunting moment, a woman in a white smock walked around to the side of the bed where she could be seen. Brown hair. Brown eyes. Sharp features. Unsmiling. Rotenhausen's assistant. Joanna remembered the pinched face and hard eyes from one of the regression-therapy sessions in Omi Inamura's office.

"Where's Alex?" Joanna asked.

Without answering, the woman picked up a sphygmomanometer from a tray of medical instruments and wrapped the pressure pad around Joanna's arm.

She tried to struggle, but the straps rendered her helpless. "Where's Alex?" she repeated.

The physician took her blood pressure. "Excellent." She unwound the pad and put it aside.

"Unbuckle these straps," Joanna demanded, trying to quell her terror by focusing on her rage.

"It's over," the woman said, tying a rubber tube around Joanna's arm, forcing a vein to bulge. She swabbed the skin with alcohol.

"I'll fight you," Joanna promised.

"If it makes you happy."

The woman had an accent, as Joanna had recalled in regression therapy. It wasn't German or Scandinavian. A Slavic accent of some kind. Russian? The senator had said something about Russians when he'd telephoned Alex in London.

The woman tore open a plastic packet that contained a hypodermic syringe.

Joanna's heart was already slamming. The sight of the syringe made it throb painfully harder than before.

The physician thrust the needle through the sterile seal on the end of a small bottle that contained a colorless drug. She drew some of the fluid into the syringe.

When the woman took hold of her arm, Joanna twisted and jerked in the restraining straps just enough to make the vein a difficult target. "No. No way. Get away from me."

The doctor backhanded her across the face, and in the instant that Joanna needed to recover from the shock and pain, the needle slipped into her.

With tears running down her face, she said, "Bitch."

"You'll feel better in a minute."

"You rotten, stinking bitch," Joanna said bitterly.

"I'll give you a name to hate," the physician said with a small smile. "Ursula Zaitsev."

"That's you? I'll remember. I'll remember your name, and I'll destroy you."

Ursula Zaitsev's economical smile grew broader by a millimeter or two. "No, you're quite wrong. You won't remember it—or anything else."

63

Alex slowly pushed open the swinging door from the kitchen. The dimly lighted hallway was deserted, and he eased into it.

Five other doors opened off the corridor before it reached the head of the stairs. Three were closed. Past the two open doors were dark rooms.

He stepped to the closed door across the hall, hesitated, opened it, and peered into a bedroom with exquisite contemporary furnishings in lacewood and bird's-eye maple, which somehow didn't seem at odds with the considerable age of the house. The lamp on the nightstand cast warm light on a deeply sculpted, predominantly green carpet. He checked the adjacent master bath but found no one.

Beside the bed were half a dozen books. Five dealt with new discoveries in the behavioral sciences. The sixth was a heavily illustrated, privately printed collection of pornography: The subject was sadism; the beautiful, vulnerable-looking women in the pictures appeared to be suffering in earnest. The blood appeared to be real. It turned Alex's stomach.

In one of the bureau drawers were two pairs of fine leather gloves. No. Not pairs. When he looked closer, he saw that the four gloves were all for the same hand.

Unquestionably, this was Franz Rotenhausen's house.

In the corridor again, Alex went to one of the open doors. He found the light switch, flipped it on, and immediately snapped it off again when he saw that it was a deserted dining room.

The second open door led to a living room with more low modern furniture and what might have been two Picasso originals. The big casement windows framed a dramatic view of Saint Moritz at night, aswirl with snow, revealing that the house was slightly above the town and at the edge of the forest.

The fourth door led to a large guest bedroom with its own bath. It had not been used in a long time and had an unpleasant musty odor.

The house remained unnaturally quiet. The walls were so thick and the bronze windows so well made that even the howling of the storm wind was a distant threnody.

Alex was impressed with the size of the building. Evidently, Rotenhausen lived in this sprawling top-floor apartment, which left an enormous amount of space below for unknown purposes.

The final door opened on a library furnished in a traditional style more in keeping with the house itself: mahogany paneling and bookshelves, a magnificent antique desk with an intricate marquetry top, a few wing-backed chairs upholstered in well-aged red leather. A Tiffany desk lamp with twelve trumpet-flower shades cast a light so golden that it seemed palpable.

Alex stopped just over the threshold, overwhelmed by déjà vu, frightened almost to the point of immobility. Although he had never been in the house on any prior occasion, he had seen this library before. Even the smaller objects were eerily familiar: a carousel-style pipe rack on the desk, a huge globe softly lighted from within, a sterling-silver magnifying glass with a long ornate handle, a two-bottle brandy chest . . .

He had broken his paralysis and walked around behind the desk before he even realized that he was moving—as if half in a trance.

He opened a desk drawer and then another. In the second drawer he found the 9mm pistol that he had taken off the man in the alleyway in Kyoto several days ago.

The instant he saw the pistol, he realized that he had known it would be there.

64 After she administered the injection, Ursula Zaitsev left Joanna alone in the white-walled room.

The winter storm huffed at the high window that Joanna had recalled in one of her regression-therapy sessions with Dr. Inamura, but it also whined and whispered at another window behind her, which she could not see.

She strained against the straps once more, but she was so well secured that any attempt to pull free was useless. She finally fell back against the mattress, gasping for breath.

A minute passed. Two. Three. Five.

Joanna expected the drug to take hold of her, because Ursula Zaitsev had implied that it was a sedative or a depressant. She ought to be getting drowsy—but, instead, she was thinking faster and more clearly by the minute.

She figured she was on an adrenaline rush. It would fade in a minute or two, and the drug would begin to affect her.

But she was still clearheaded when Rotenhausen entered the room. He closed the door after himself. Locked it.

65 Sitting at the library desk, Alex thoroughly examined the gun. He was suspicious. They could have disabled the weapon.

The pistol appeared to be in perfect working order. Unless the ammunition had been replaced with blanks.

He assumed that he was being set up somehow. Suckered into a trap. But the nature of that trap seemed more incomprehensible the longer that he tried to puzzle out what it might be.

Though he was reluctant to be manipulated any further he could not simply sit there all night. He had to find Joanna and get her out of the house.

He rose from the desk chair, pointed the silencer-equipped pistol at a row of books on the far side of the room, and squeezed the trigger.

Whump!

One of the books jumped on the shelf, and the spine cracked with a sound louder than the noise made by the gun itself.

The pistol wasn't loaded with blanks.

He left the library and went to the head of the stairs.

66

The Hand.

He looked much the same as he had in her nightmares: tall and thin, clothes hanging loosely on him, balder than he had been twelve years ago but still without gray in his hair. His eyes were pale brown, almost yellow, and in them shone a controlled madness as cold as Arctic sun flickering on strange configurations of ice. The shiny, chitinous, gear-jointed fingers of his steel hand reminded her of the grasping legs of certain carnivorous insects.

Mariko had assured her that she'd find this man less frightening in reality than he was in her nightmares, but the opposite was true: She was weak with terror.

As he approached the bed, he said, "Sleepy, little lady?"

Though it was clear that he expected her to be in a stupor or on the edge of one, her mind wasn't in the least clouded. She wondered if Zaitsev had made a mistake and given her the wrong drug.

"Hmmm?" he said. "Sleepy?"

Fate—or someone in its employ—had given her a last, desperate chance, though it was as thin as an atheist's hope.

"Let me go," she said, slurring her voice as though sinking under the influence of the medication. Through her half-closed eyes, she thought that he was suddenly suspicious, and she said, "Wake up. Gotta . . . wake up."

"You think you're already asleep?" he asked, amusement replacing any suspicion that he might have had. "You think getting rid of me will be as easy as waking up? Not this time."

She closed her eyes and didn't answer him at once, pretending to slip away for a moment. Then she opened her eyes but squinted as if having difficulty focusing on him. "I . . . hate you . . . hate. . . . you," she said with no edge of true anger, but in a dreamy voice, as though the drug had disconnected her mind from her emotions.

"Good," he said. "I like it when there's hatred."

The steel fingers clicked as he reached for her.

67

The house was solidly built. Not one step creaked.

Alex paused at the second-floor landing. The deserted hallway was hung with shadows, illumined only by a weak amber mist of light that drifted into it from the stairwell. The air was redolent of disinfectants and medicinal odors, indicating that Joanna might have been imprisoned twelve years ago in one of these second-floor rooms.

He was about to investigate the first of the closed doors when he heard voices. He crouched, prepared to run or open fire, but then he realized that he was hearing a conversation in progress downstairs and that no one was approaching. Deciding to explore the second floor later, he descended toward the ground floor.

In the dimly lighted lower hallway, he edged close to a door from behind which the voices arose. It was ajar an inch, and as he reached it, he heard someone say Joanna's name and then his.

He risked looking through the crack between the door and the jamb. Beyond was a conference room. Three men sat at a large oval table that could have accommodated a dozen, and a fourth man stood at the tall windows with his back to the others.

The nearest man was extremely obese. He was opening the end of a roll of Life Savers.

Anson Peterson.

Alex heard the name as if someone had whispered it to him, but he was still alone in the hall. He had never seen the fat man before, yet he knew his name. He was intrigued and still frightened by the sense of being caught up in events as preordained as the course of a bobsled in a luge chute, but he was not surprised. He didn't think anything could surprise him after he'd found his gun in the library desk where he'd somehow known that it would be.

The next man at the table was unusually large but not obese. Even sitting down he appeared to be tall. Bull neck. Massive shoulders. His face was broad and flat beneath a low brow.

Again, an inner voice spoke the name: *Antonio Paz.*

The third man at the table had coarse black hair, a prominent nose, and deeply set dark eyes. He was shorter than Paz but even more powerfully built.

Ignacio Carrera.

The fourth man turned away from the windows and the cascading snow beyond them.

Alex was capable of surprise after all. The fourth man was Senator Thomas Chelgrin.

68

With his mechanical hand, Rotenhausen grasped the sheet, pulled it off Joanna, and tossed it to the floor.

She was wearing only a thin hospital gown tied in back, but she was so cold inside that the cool air didn't chill her.

Faking the effects of the drug as she imagined they would have been, she let her eyes swim out of focus and murmured wordlessly to herself.

"Pretty," he said, looming.

She required all the courage that she could summon to continue to feign a drugged indifference.

The steel fingers gripped the neckline of her gown and tore the garment from her.

She almost gasped, but kept a grip on herself because she knew that he was watching her closely.

The steel hand touched her breasts.

69

Peterson popped a butter-rum Life Saver into his mouth, savored it, and then said to Carrera, "So it's decided. You'll kill Hunter tonight, strip him, and dump his body into the lake, under the ice."

"I'll cut off the tips of his fingers so the police won't be able to print the body, smash out his teeth to prevent dental-record identification."

"Isn't that excessive? By the time the lake thaws and they find him next summer, perhaps even the summer *after* next—if they ever *do* find him—the fish will have left nothing but bare bones."

"Can't be too careful," Carrera disagreed. "I'll also disfigure his face so he can't be identified from a photograph."

And you'll enjoy every minute of it, Peterson thought.

Chelgrin hadn't said much during the past half hour, but now he walked to the table and faced Peterson. "You told me I'd be allowed to see my daughter as soon as they brought her here."

"Yes, Tom. But Rotenhausen must examine her first."

"Why?"

"I don't know. But he felt it was necessary, and he's the boss in this place."

"Not when you're around," Chelgrin said sourly. "Wherever you are, you're the boss. It's in your genes. You'll be in charge of Hell an hour after you get there."

"How very kind of you to say so," Peterson replied.

"Damn it, I want to see Lisa. I want—"

Carrera interrupted: "And there you have another problem. The girl. What do we do about the girl if she comes through the second treatment with a lot of mental damage?"

"That won't happen," Chelgrin said firmly, as though he could determine her fate by fiat.

"Fifty-fifty chance," Carrera said.

Refusing to confront that dreadful possibility, Chelgrin turned from Carrera, started toward the hallway door, but then halted and backed up a step. "Someone's there, listening."

70

The instant that he knew he had been seen, Alex pushed the door all the way open and stepped into the room, thrusting the pistol in front of him.

"Ah, hello," said the fat man with curious aplomb. "How're you feeling?"

Ignoring him, Alex stared at Chelgrin. "You're dead."

The senator didn't respond.

Sickened and infuriated by a profound and growing sense of violation, by having been so totally manipulated, Alex said, *"Why aren't you dead?"*

"Faked," Chelgrin said, nervously focusing on the muzzle of the gun. "We just wanted you to find the clipping about Rotenhausen."

"And the unfinished letter to Lisa—?"

"Nice touch, wasn't it?" Peterson asked.

Confused, Alex said, "Now that I think about it . . . at the time, I should've checked you for a pulse. Why didn't I check you?"

"The bullet wounds, the rabbit blood," Chelgrin said, "the hair over my eyes so you wouldn't notice any involuntary eye-muscle spasms—it was all very convincing. And I wore only the robe and left my wallet on the dresser so you wouldn't have any reason to search me."

Alex glanced at each of the men, then at Chelgrin again. "No. Doesn't wash. I made Joanna stay away from you too. As if I'd been programmed to keep us at a distance from you. Programmed not to shatter the illusion. Isn't that right?"

Chelgrin blinked. "Programmed?"

"Don't lie to me," Alex said, raising the gun a few inches until the muzzle was lined up with the senator's heart.

Chelgrin seemed genuinely baffled. "What're you talking about?"

Turning to the fat man, Alex said, "It's true, isn't it? I've been running around like a damn robot, programmed like a machine."

Peterson smiled. He knew the truth, even if Chelgrin didn't.

Alex thrust the pistol at him. "Last spring, when I went to Rio for a vacation—what in the name of God happened to me there?"

Before Peterson could answer, Antonio Paz reached under his jacket for a gun. Alex caught the movement from the corner of his eye, swung away from Peterson, and fired twice. Both shots ripped into Paz's face. Like perfume from an atomizer, a mist of blood puffed into the air. Paz and his chair crashed over backward.

Even as Paz went down, Carrera sprang to his feet.

That mysterious inner voice whispered to Alex again, *Kill him.* Before he could think about what he was doing, he obeyed, squeezing the trigger twice more.

One of the rounds hit Carrera, and he fell.

Shocked, wide-eyed, terrified, the senator backed away. He held his hands out in front of him, palms toward Alex, fingers spread, as if he thought he might be able to ward off the bullets meant for him.

Kill him.

Alex heard the interior voice again, icy and insistent, but he hesitated. Bewildered. Shaking.

He tried to think through to another, less violent solution: Paz and Carrera had been dangerous men, but they were dead, no longer any threat, and the senator wasn't a threat either, just a broken man, a pitiful specimen, begging for his life, so there was no need to waste him, no justification for it.

Kill him, kill him, kill him, killhim, killhim.

Alex couldn't resist that inner voice, and again he squeezed the trigger twice.

Hit once in the chest, Chelgrin fell backward into the window. His head struck the glass, and one of the thick panes cracked. He dropped to the floor and was as still as stone.

"Oh, God," Alex said, and stared at the hand in which he held the gun, as if he couldn't quite believe that it was his own hand. He was out of control, acting before thinking. "What am I doing? *What am I doing?*"

The fat man was still in his chair on the far side of the table. "The terrible angel of vengeance," he said with a smile. He appeared to be delighted.

Bloody but not mortally wounded after all, Carrera launched up from the floor, seized a chair, and threw it.

Alex fired, missed.

The chair struck him as he tried to dodge it. Pain speared through his right arm. The pistol flew out of his hand and across the room, clattered off the wall. He staggered backward, collided with the door, and Carrera charged him.

71

Gleaming, cold, humming, clicking, the steel hand caressed her. Squeezed her. Patted, stroked, pinched her.

Click, click, click.

She was impressed by her own courage. She didn't flinch. She endured Rotenhausen's obscene explorations and pretended to be doped. She mumbled, murmured, sometimes feigned a dreamy pleasure at his touch, occasionally warned him off as if she had briefly surfaced from her delirium, but then drifted away again.

She'd just about decided that he was never going to stop petting her with that monstrous hand, when he finally reached across her and disengaged the strap on her right wrist. He freed her left hand as well, and then he moved to the foot of the bed to release her ankles. She was unbound.

He returned to the head of the bed.

She still did not make a break for freedom.

Taking off his white smock and draping it across the cart that held the syringes and other instruments, he said, "I remember you so well. I remember . . . how you felt." He took off his shirt.

Through half-closed eyes, Joanna studied the mechanical hand. A flexible steel-ring cable trailed up from the metal wrist and terminated in a pair of male jacks that were plugged into a battery pack. The pack was strapped to his biceps.

"This will be better even than before," he said. "With your father just downstairs."

Joanna seized the cable and tore the jacks out of the battery pack. The steel fingers froze. She rolled away from Rotenhausen. Naked, she dropped off the other side of the bed and ran for the door.

He caught her with his real hand as she touched the dead-bolt lock. Clenching a handful of her hair, he spun her around to face him, and his pale eyes were full of inhuman menace.

Screaming in pain and fear, she flailed at him, and her fists landed with satisfyingly hard, flat sounds.

Rotenhausen cursed her, dragged her from the door, and shoved her away.

She collided with the bed. Unbalanced, she grabbed the footrail to avoid falling.

Standing between her and the door, he plugged the jacks into the battery again. The hand purred. The steel fingers moved. *Click, click, click.*

72

Carrera came low and fast, like a human locomotive.

Without the pistol, Alex had no chance to get the best of the powerful bodybuilder. He had some knowledge of martial arts, but no doubt Carrera was even better trained.

He stumbled backward through the door, pulled it shut after him, and ran along the ground-floor hallway. The last room on the right was dark. He plunged across the threshold, slammed the door, fumbled frantically for a latch. He found a privacy-lock button in the center of the knob.

An instant later Carrera reached the other side, tried to get in, discovered that he had been locked out, and immediately threw himself against the door, determined to break it down.

Alex located the light switch. The overhead bulb revealed an empty storeroom that offered nothing he could use as a weapon.

He was loath to leave the house with Joanna held somewhere in it, but he would be no good to her if he got himself killed.

As Carrera battered the door, Alex crossed to the storeroom window and put up the blind. A fierce gust of wind fired a barrage of fine white granules against the glass.

Carrera hit the door again, again, and wood splintered.

With trembling hands, Alex unlatched the casement window and pushed the halves outward. Arctic wind exploded into the room.

Carrera rammed into the door. In the lock, tortured metal shrieked against metal.

Even wounded, the man was a bull.

Alex clambered over the window ledge and stepped into a foot of fresh snow. Wind howled along the valley wall, clocking at least seventy or eighty kilometers an hour; it bit his face, wrung tears from his eyes, and flash-numbed his hands. He was thankful for the insulated ski clothes that they had bought in Klosters.

In the room that he'd just left, the door went down with a thunderous boom.

Alex hurried away into the bitter darkness, kicking up clouds of snow as he went.

73

By the time Peterson reached the storeroom, Carrera was climbing through the window in pursuit of Hunter. Peterson started after him, but then he changed his mind and crossed the hall to Ursula Zaitsev's private quarters.

She refused to answer when he knocked.

"Ursula, it's me. Anson. Hurry."

The door cracked open on a security chain, and she peered at him fearfully. "What's all the noise? What's gone wrong?"

"Everything. We have to get out of here now, right away, before the police arrive."

"Go?" She was a strange, self-involved woman even in the best of times, but in her bewilderment she had the wild-eyed look of an asylum inmate. "Go where?"

"Damn it, Ursula, *hurry!* Do you want to go home—or spend the rest of your life in a Swiss jail?"

She had left Russia twenty years ago and had been Rotenhausen's assistant—and watchdog—for fifteen, from the day that his funding had been provided exclusively by Moscow. Since she'd been away from home, the old order had fallen, and judging by her expression, the home to which she would be going was one that she either found unappealing or could not quite comprehend.

"*Ursula,*" Peterson hissed with red-faced urgency. "The police—do you hear me?—the *police!*"

In a panic, she undid the security chain and opened her door.

Peterson drew the silencer-equipped pistol from the shoulder holster under his jacket, and he shot her three times.

For such a severe-looking, even mannish woman, Ursula died gracefully, almost prettily. The bullets spun her around as if she were twirling to show a new skirt to a boyfriend. There wasn't much mess, perhaps because she was too thin and dry to contain any substantial quantity of blood. She sagged against the wall, gazed at Peterson without seeing him, allowed a delicate thread of blood to escape one corner of her mouth, let go of her icy expression for the first time since he had known her, and slid down into death.

Four of the six people on Anson Peterson's hit list had been eliminated. Marlowe. Paz. Chelgrin. Ursula Zaitsev. Only two others awaited disposal.

He sprinted across the hall and into the storeroom with that peculiar grace that certain very fat men could summon on occasion. He climbed through the open casement window and groaned when the bitter night air slapped his face. The only thing he disliked more than exertion and an unsatisfied appetite was physical discomfort.

He was having a very bad evening.

The wind was busily scouring the footprints from the newly fallen snow, but he was still able to follow Hunter and Carrera.

74 Shouting and a series of muffled noises arose in a distant part of the house. At first, Joanna hoped it was Alex coming for her—or someone from outside coming for both of them. But Rotenhausen ignored the uproar, either because he was so focused on her that he didn't hear it or because there were other people to deal with whatever was happening; and when quiet quickly returned, she knew that she was finished.

He backed her into a corner, pinned her there with his body, spread his steel fingers, and gripped her throat. He placed his real hand over the battery pack to prevent her from pulling out the jacks.

She couldn't look away from his extraordinary eyes: They now seemed as yellow as those of a cat.

He cocked his head and watched her quizzically while he squeezed her throat, as though he were observing a laboratory animal through the walls of its cage. His expression was not bland; on the contrary, in his face was a cold passion that defied description and, most likely, understanding.

When she began to choke, and when she saw that her choking only elicited a smile from him, she struggled fiercely to break free—twisted, thrashed, kicked ineffectually with her bare feet. She was too tightly pinned to be able to go for his eyes, but she clawed at his arms and flanks, drawing blood.

Until now, she'd held fast to the hope of being saved from both Rotenhausen and his treatments, but his unexpected reaction to her counterattack stole all hope from her. He flinched and hissed each time that she drew his blood—but each pain that she inflicted seemed only to arouse him further. Crushing her against the wall, he said excitedly, "That's it, yes, fight for your life, girl, fight me, yes, fight me with everything you've got," and she knew then that each wound she inflicted would have no effect other than to give him even greater pleasure later, when he subjected her to various tortures on the bed.

The steel hand tightened inexorably around her throat, and black spots glided like dozens of ink-dark moths across her vision.

75 Great surging rivers of snow poured out of the Swiss mountains, and Alex seemed to be carried through the deep night by the powerful currents of the storm almost as he would have been swept away by a real river. With the buoying wind at his back, he crossed a hundred yards of open land before he reached the shelter of the forest. The mammoth pines grew close together, providing relief from the wind, but a considerable amount of snow still found its way through the evergreen canopy.

He was on a narrow but well-established trail that might have been made by deer. The heavy white crusts that bent the pine boughs and the white winter mantle on the forest floor provided what meager light there was: He navigated the woods by the eerie phosphorescence of the snow, able to distinguish shapes but no details, afraid of catching a tree branch in the face and blinding himself.

He stumbled over rocks hidden by the snow, hit the ground hard, but scrambled up at once. He was certain that Carrera was close behind.

As he came to his feet, he realized that he had one of the loose rocks in his hand. A weapon. It was the size of an orange, not as good as a gun but better than nothing. It felt like a ball of ice, and he was concerned that he wouldn't be able to keep a grip on it as his fingers rapidly continued to stiffen.

He hurried deeper into the woods, and thirty feet from the spot where he had fallen, the trail bent sharply to the right and curved around an especially dense stand of shoulder-high brush. He skidded to a halt and quickly considered the potential for an ambush.

Squinting at the trail, he could barely discern the disturbance that his own feet had made in the smooth skin of softly radiant white powder. He weighed the rock in his hand, backed against the wall of brush until it poked him painfully, and hunched down, becoming a shadow among shadows.

Overhead, wind raged through the pine and fir boughs, howling as incessantly as the devil's own pack of hell hounds, but even above that shrieking, Alex immediately heard Carrera approaching. Fearless of his quarry, the bodybuilder made no effort to be quiet, crashing along the trail as though he were a drunk in transit between two taverns.

Alex tensed, keeping his eyes on the bend in the trail just four feet away. The subzero air had so numbed his hand that he couldn't feel the rock any more. He squeezed hard, hoping that the weapon was still in his grip, but for all he knew, he might have dropped it and might be curling his half-frozen fingers around empty air.

Carrera appeared, moving fast, bent forward, intent on the vague footprints that he was following.

Alex swung his arm high and brought the rock down with all his strength, and it caught Carrera in the face. The big man dropped to his knees as if he'd been hit by a sledgehammer, toppled forward, and knocked Alex off his feet. They rolled along the sloping trail, through the snow, and came to a stop side by side, facedown.

Gasping air so bitterly cold that it made his lungs ache, Alex pushed onto his knees and then to his feet again.

Carrera remained on the ground: a dark, huddled, vaguely human shape in the bed of snow.

In spite of his still desperate circumstances and even though Joanna remained captive in the house, Alex felt a thrill of triumph, the dark animal exhilaration of having gone up against a predator and beaten him.

He looked up the trail, back through the woods, but he'd come too far to be able to see the house any more. Considering Carrera's size and ferocity, the other men wouldn't give Alex much chance of getting out of the woods alive, so his quick return would take them by surprise and might give him just the advantage he needed.

He started to go back for Joanna, but Carrera grabbed his ankle.

76

Joanna rammed her knee into Rotenhausen's crotch. He sensed it coming and deflected most of the impact with his thigh. The blow made him cry out in pain, however, and he bent forward reflexively, protectively.

His mechanical hand slid down her throat as his cold, clicking fingers loosened their grip on her.

She slipped out of his grasp, from between him and the wall, but he was after her at once. His pain forced him to hobble like a troll, but he wasn't disabled nearly enough to let her get away.

Unable to reach the door in time to throw the lock and get out, she put the wheeled cart between them instead. In addition to an array of syringes, a bottle of glucose for the IV tree, a packet of tongue depressors, a penlight, a device for examining eyes, and many small bottles of various drugs, the instrument tray on the cart held a pair of surgical scissors. Joanna snatched them up and brandished them at Rotenhausen.

He glared at her, red-faced and furious.

"I won't let you do it to me again," she said. "I won't let you tamper with my mind. You'll either have to let me go or kill me."

With his mechanical hand, he reached across the cart, seized the scissors, wrenched them away from her, and squeezed them in his steel fingers until the blades snapped.

"I could do the same to you," he said.

He threw the broken scissors aside.

Joanna's heartbeat exploded, and the governor on the engine of time seemed to burn out. Suddenly everything happened very fast.

She plucked the glucose from the tray, thankful it wasn't in one of the plastic bags so widely used these days, but the robotic hand arced down, smashing the bottle before she could throw it. Glass and glucose showered across the floor, leaving her with only the neck of the bottle in her grip. He shoved the cart out of the way, toppling it, scattering the instruments and the small bottles of drugs, and he rushed her, pale eyes bright with murderous intent. Desperately she turned. Scanning the floor. The litter. A weapon. Something. Anything. He grabbed her by the hair. She already *had* the weapon. In her hand. The bottle. The broken neck of the bottle. He yanked her around to face him. She thrust. Jagged glass. Deep into his throat. Blood spurting. Oh, God. Pale eyes wide. Yellow and wide. The robotic fingers released her hair, plucked at the glass in his throat—*click, click, click*—but only succeeded in bringing forth more blood. He gagged, slipped on the glucose-wet floor, fell to his knees, reached for her with his steel hand, working the fingers uselessly in the air, fell onto his side, twitched, kicked, made a terrible raspy effort to breathe, spasmed as if an electrical current had crackled through him, spasmed again, and was still.

77

Alex fell, jerked free of Carrera, rolled back down the trail, and sprang to his feet, acutely aware that he was not likely to get up again if he gave the big man a chance to get atop him.

The bodybuilder was badly enough hurt that he wasn't able to reach his feet as quickly as Alex. He was still on all fours in the middle of the path, shaking his head as if to clear his mind.

Seizing the advantage, Alex rushed forward and kicked Carrera squarely under the chin.

The thug's head snapped back, and he fell onto his side.

Alex was sure the kick had broken his adversary's neck, crushed his windpipe, but Carrera struggled onto his hands and knees again.

The bastard doesn't quit.

Alex took another kick at Carrera's head.

The bodybuilder saw it coming, grabbed Alex's boot, toppled him, and clambered atop him, growling like a bear. He swung one huge fist.

Alex wasn't able to duck it. The punch landed in his face, split his lips, loosened some teeth, and filled his mouth with blood.

He was no match for Carrera in hand-to-hand combat. He had to regain his feet and be able to maneuver.

As Carrera threw another punch, Alex thrashed and bucked. The fist missed him, drove into the trail beside his head, and Carrera howled in pain.

Heaving harder than before, Alex threw Carrera off, crawled up the slope, clutched a tree for support, and pulled himself erect.

Carrera was also struggling to his feet.

Alex kicked him squarely in the stomach, which gave no more than a board fence.

Carrera skidded in the snow, windmilled his arms, and went down on his hands and knees again.

Cursing, Alex kicked him in the face.

Carrera sprawled on his back in the snow, arms extended like wings. He didn't move. Didn't move. Still didn't move. Didn't move.

Cautiously, as though he were Dr. Von Helsing approaching a coffin in which Dracula slept, Alex crept up on Carrera. He knelt at the bodybuilder's side. Even in that dim and eerily phosphorescent light, he could see that the man's eyes were open wide but blind to any sight in this world. He didn't need to fetch a wooden stake or a crucifix or a necklace of garlic, because this time the monster was definitely dead.

He got up, turned away from Carrera, and ascended the trail, heading back toward the house.

Anson Peterson was waiting for him in the open field just beyond the forest. The fat man was holding a gun.

78

Rotenhausen was dead.

Joanna felt no remorse for having killed him, but she didn't experience much in the way of triumph either. She was too worried about Alex to feel anything more than fear.

Stepping carefully to avoid the broken glass scattered across the floor, she found her ski clothes in a closet.

As she was hurriedly dressing, she heard the steel fingers—click-click-click-click—and she looked up in terror, frozen by the hateful sound. It must have been a reflex action, a postmortem nerve spasm sending a last meaningless instruction to the mechanical hand, because Rotenhausen was stone-cold dead.

Nevertheless, for a minute she stared at the hand. Her heart was knocking so loudly that she could hear nothing else, not even her own breathing or the wind beyond the windows. Gradually, as the hand made no new move, the fierce drumming in her chest subsided somewhat.

When she finished dressing, as she knelt on her left knee to lace up the boot on her right foot, she spotted the small bottle from which Ursula Zaitsev had filled the syringe. It was among the litter on the floor, but it had not broken.

She laced both boots, then picked up the bottle and pulled the seal from it. She shook a couple of drops of the drug onto the palm of her hand, sniffed, hesitated, then tasted it. She was pretty sure that it was nothing but water and that someone had switched bottles on Zaitsev.

But who? And why?

Puppets. They were all puppets—as Alex had said.

Cautiously she unlocked the door and peered into the hall. No one in sight. But for the background noise of the storm, muffled by the thick walls, the house was silent.

Room by room, she inspected the rest of that level but found no one. For almost a minute she stood on the second-floor landing, looking alternately up and down the steps, listening intently, and at last descended to the ground floor.

A corpse lay in the hallway. Even in the poor light and from a distance, Joanna could see that it was Ursula Zaitsev.

Several doors led off the hall. She didn't want to open any of them, but she would have to search the place if she had any hope of finding Alex.

The nearest door was ajar. She eased it open, hesitated, crossed the threshold—and her father stepped in front of her.

Tom Chelgrin was ashen. His hair was streaked with blood, and his face was spotted with it. His left hand was pressed over what must have been a bullet wound in his chest, for his shirt was soaked with blood as dark as burgundy. He swayed, almost fell, took one step toward her, and put his bloody hand on her shoulder.

79

On the snow-swept slope, less than a hundred yards from the house, above the storm-dimmed lights of Saint Moritz, Alex and Peterson stared at each other for a long, uncertain moment.

Alex couldn't speak clearly or without pain, because his mouth was swollen and sore from the punch he'd taken, but he had questions and he wanted answers. "Why didn't I kill you when I killed Paz and Chelgrin?"

"You weren't supposed to," said the fat man. "Where's Carrera?"

"Dead."

"But you didn't have a gun," Peterson said incredulously.

"No gun," Alex agreed. He was weary. His eyes watered from the stinging cold. The fat man shimmered like a mirage in the night.

"It's hard to believe you could kill that mean bastard without a gun."

Alex spat blood onto the snow. "I didn't say it was easy."

Peterson let out a short bray of laughter.

"All right," Alex said, "all right, get it over with. I killed him, now you kill me."

"Oh, heavens, no! No, no," Peterson said. "You've got it all wrong, all backward, dear boy. You and I—we're on the same team."

80

Chelgrin had been dead in London. Dead on a hotel-room floor. Now he was here in Switzerland, dying again.

The sight of the blood-smeared specter immobilized Joanna. She stood in shock, every muscle locked, while the senator clung to her shoulder.

"I'm weak," he said shakily. "Can't stand up any more. Don't let me . . . fall. Please. Help me . . . down easy. Let's go down easy."

Joanna put one hand on the doorjamb to brace herself. She dropped slowly to her knees, and the senator used her for support. At last he was sitting with his back against the wall, pressing his left hand against the chest wound, and she was kneeling at his side.

"Daughter," he said, gazing at her wonderingly. "My baby."

She couldn't accept him as her father. She thought of the long years of programmed loneliness, the attacks of claustrophobia when she'd dared to consider building a life with someone, the nightmares, the fear that might have been defeated if it could have been defined. She thought of how Rotenhausen had repeatedly raped her during her first stay in this place—and how he had tried to use her again this very night. Worse: If Alex was dead, Tom Chelgrin had directly or indirectly pulled the trigger. She had no room in her heart for this man. Maybe it was unfair of her to freeze him out before she knew his reasons for doing what he'd done; perhaps her inability to forgive her own father was itself unforgivable. Nevertheless, she felt no guilt whatsoever and knew that she never would. She despised him.

"My little girl," he said, but his voice seemed colored more by self-pitying sentimentality than by genuine love or remorse.

"No," she said, denying him.

"You are. You're my daughter."

"No."

"Lisa."

"Joanna. My name's Joanna Rand."

He wheezed and cleared his throat. His speech was slurred. "You hate me . . . don't you?"

"Yes."

"But you don't understand."

"I understand enough."

"No. No, you don't. You've got to listen to me."

"Nothing you have to say could make me want to be your daughter. Lisa Chelgrin is dead. Forever."

The senator closed his eyes. A fierce wave of pain swept through him. He grimaced and bent forward.

She made no move to comfort him.

When the attack passed, he sat up straight again and opened his eyes. "I've got to tell you about it. You've got to give me a chance to explain. You have to listen to me."

"I'm listening," she assured him, "but not because I have to."

His breath rattled in his throat. "Everyone thinks I was a war hero. They think I escaped from that Viet Cong prison camp and made my way back to friendly lines. I built my entire political career on that story, but it's all a lie. I didn't spend weeks in the jungle, inching my way out of enemy territory. I never escaped from a prison camp because . . . I was never in one to begin with. Tom Chelgrin was a prisoner of war, all right, but not me."

"Not you? But *you're* Tom Chelgrin," she said, wondering if his pain and the loss of blood had clouded his mind.

"No. My real name is Ilya Lyshenko. I'm a Russian."

Haltingly, pausing often to wheeze or to spit dark blood, he told her how Ilya Lyshenko had become the Honorable United States Senator from the great state of Illinois, the well-known and widely respected potential candidate for the presidency, Thomas Chelgrin. He was convincing—although Joanna supposed that every dying man's confession was convincing.

She listened, amazed and fascinated.

81

At the height of the Vietnam War in the late 1960s, in every Viet Cong labor camp, commandants were looking for certain special American prisoners of war: soldiers who shared a list of physical characteristics with a dozen young Russian intelligence officers who had volunteered for a project code-named "Mirror." None of the Vietnamese assisting in the search knew the name of the project or what the Russians hoped to achieve with it, but they did not allow themselves to be in the least curious because they understood that curiosity killed more than cats.

When Tom Chelgrin was brought in chains to a camp outside Hanoi, the commandant saw at once that he somewhat resembled a member of the Russian Mirror group. Chelgrin and the Russian were the same height and build, had the same color hair and eyes. Their basic facial-bone structures were similar. Upon his arrival at the camp, Chelgrin was segregated from the other prisoners, and for the rest of his life he spent mornings and afternoons with interrogators, evenings and nights in solitary confinement. A Vietnamese photographer took more than two hundred shots of Chelgrin's entire body, but mostly of his face from every possible angle, in every light: close-ups, medium shots, long shots to show how he stood and how he held his shoulders. The undeveloped negatives were sent to Moscow by special courier, where KGB directors in charge of the Mirror group anxiously awaited them.

Military physicians in Moscow studied the photographs of Thomas Chelgrin for three days before reporting that he appeared to be a reasonably good match for Ilya Lyshenko, a Mirror volunteer. One week later, Ilya underwent the first of many surgeries to transform him into Chelgrin's double. His hairline was too low, so cosmetic surgeons destroyed some hair follicles and moved the line back three quarters of an inch. His eyelids drooped slightly, thanks to the genetic heritage of a Mongolian great-great-grandfather; they lifted the lids to make them look more Western. His nose was pared down, and a bump was removed from the bridge. His earlobes were too large, so they were reduced as well. His mouth was shaped quite like Tom Chelgrin's mouth, but his teeth required major dental work to match Chelgrin's. Lyshenko's chin was round, which was no good for this masquerade, so it was made square. Finally, the surgeons circumcised Lyshenko and pronounced him a fit dopplegänger.

While Lyshenko was enduring seven months of plastic surgery, Thomas Chelgrin was sweating out a seemingly endless series of brutal inquisitions at the camp outside Hanoi. He was in the hands of the Viet Cong's best interrogators—who were being assisted by two Soviet advisers. They employed drugs, threats, promises, hypnosis, beatings, and torture to learn everything they needed to know about him. They compiled an immense dossier: the foods he liked least; the foods he liked most; his favorite brands of beer, cigarettes; his public and private religious beliefs; the names of his friends, descriptions of them, and lists of their likes, dislikes, quirks, foibles, habits, virtues, weaknesses; his political convictions; his favorite sports, movies; his racial prejudices; his fears; his hopes; his sexual preferences and techniques; and thousands upon thousands of other things. They squeezed him as though he were an orange, and they didn't intend to leave one drop of juice in him.

Once a week, lengthy transcripts of the sessions with Chelgrin were flown to Moscow, where they were edited down to lists of data. Ilya Lyshenko studied them while convalescing between surgeries. He was required to commit to memory literally tens of thousands of bits of information, and it was the most difficult job that he had ever undertaken.

He was treated by two psychologists who specialized in memory research under the auspices of the KGB. They used both drugs and hypnosis to assist him in the retention of the information he needed to *become* Thomas Chelgrin, and while he slept, recordings of the lists played softly in his room, conveying the information directly to his subconscious.

After fourteen years of English studies, which had begun when he was eight years old, Lyshenko had learned to speak the language without a Russian accent. In fact, he had the clear but colorless diction of local television newsmen in the Middle Atlantic States. Now he listened to recordings of Chelgrin's voice and attempted to imprint a Midwest accent over the bland English that he already spoke. By the time the final surgeries had been performed, he sounded as though he had been born and raised on an Illinois farm.

When Lyshenko was halfway through his metamorphosis, the men in charge of Mirror began to worry about Tom Chelgrin's mother. They were confident that Lyshenko would be able to deceive Chelgrin's friends and acquaintances, even most of his relatives, but they were worried that anyone especially close to him—such as his mother, father, or wife—would notice changes in him or lapses of memory. Fortunately Chelgrin had never been married or even terribly serious about any one girl. He was handsome and popular, and he played the field. Equally fortunate: His father had died when Tom was a child. As far as the KGB was concerned, that left Tom's mother as the only serious threat to the success of the masquerade. That problem was easily remedied, for in those flush days when the Soviet economy had been largely militarized, the KGB had a long arm and deep pockets for operations on foreign soil. Orders were sent to an agent in New York, and ten days later, Tom's mother died in an automobile accident on her way home from a bridge party. The night was dark and the narrow road was icy; it was a tragedy that could have befallen anyone.

In late 1968, eight months after Tom Chelgrin had been captured, Ilya Lyshenko arrived by night at the labor camp outside Hanoi. He was in the company of Emil Gotrov, the KGB director who had conceived of the scheme, found funding for it, and overseen its implementation. He waited with Gotrov in the camp commandant's private quarters while Chelgrin was brought from his isolation cell.

When the American walked into the room and saw Lyshenko, he knew immediately that he was not destined to live. The fear in his haggard face and the despair in his eyes were, of course, a testimony to the work of the Soviet surgeons—but the doomed man's anguished expression had haunted Ilya Lyshenko across three decades.

"Mirror," Gotrov had said, astounded. "A mirror image."

That night the real Thomas Chelgrin was taken out of the prison camp, shot in the back of the head, tumbled into a deep grave, soaked with gasoline, burned, and then buried.

Within a week, the new Thomas Chelgrin "escaped" from the camp outside Hanoi and, against impossible odds and over the period of a few weeks, made his way back to friendly territory and eventually connected with his own division. He was sent home to Illinois, where he wrote a best-selling book about his amazing experiences—actually, it was ghost-written by a world-famous American writer who had long been sympathetic to the Soviet cause—and he became a war hero.

Tom Chelgrin's mother hadn't been a wealthy woman, but she had managed to pay premiums on a life insurance policy that named her son—and only child—as the sole beneficiary. That money came into his hands when he returned from the war. He used it and the earnings from his book to purchase a Honda dealership just before Americans fell in love with Japanese cars. The business flourished beyond his wildest expectations, and he put the profits into other investments that also did well.

His orders from the men behind Mirror had been simple. He was expected to become a business entrepreneur. He was expected to prosper, and if he could not turn a large buck on his own, KGB money would be funneled into his enterprises by various subtle means and an array of third parties. In his thirties, when his community knew him to be a respectable citizen and a successful businessman, he would run for a major public office, and the KGB would indirectly contribute substantial funds to his campaign.

He followed the plan—but with one important change. By the time he was prepared to seek elective office, he had become hugely wealthy on his own, without KGB help. And by the time he sought a seat in the United States House of Representatives, he was able to obtain all the legitimate financial backing he needed to complement his own money, and the KGB didn't have to open its purse.

In Moscow the highest hope was that he would become a member of the lower house of Congress and win reelection for three or four terms. During those eight or ten years, he would be able to pass along incredible quantities of vital military information.

He lost his first election by a narrow margin, primarily because he had never remarried after the loss of his first wife, who had died in childbirth. At that time, the American public had a prejudice against bachelors in politics. Two years later, when he tried again, he used his adorable young daughter, Lisa Jean, to win the hearts of voters. Thereafter, he swiftly rose from the lower house of Congress to the upper—until he developed into a prime presidential candidate.

His success had been a thousandfold greater than Moscow had ever hoped, and even after the collapse of the Soviet Union, the surviving Marxist element in the new government of Russia held a tight rein on Tom Chelgrin. He was more valuable than diamond mines. Where once he had labored to obtain and pass along highly sensitive military information, he now worked somewhat more openly to transfer billions of U.S. dollars in loans and foreign aid into the grasping hands of his masters, who had lost the Cold War but still prospered.

Eventually his success became the central problem of his life. Even while the Cold War had still been under way, Thomas Chelgrin—who had once been Ilya Lyshenko—had lost all faith in the principles of communism. As a United States Congressman and then as a Senator, with his soul secretly in hock to the KGB, he was called upon to betray the country that he had learned to love. By then he didn't want to pass along the information they sought, but he could find no way to refuse. The KGB owned him. He was trapped.

82

"But why was my past taken from me?" Joanna demanded. "Stolen from me. Why did you send me to Rotenhausen?"

"Had to." The senator bent forward, racked by a vicious twist of pain. His breath bubbled wetly, hideously in his throat. When he found the strength to sit up straight again, he said, "Jamaica. You and I were . . . going to spend a whole week down there . . . at the vacation house in Jamaica."

"You and Lisa," she corrected.

"I was going to fly down from Washington on a Thursday night. You were at school in New York. Columbia. A senior. Summer term. There was a project you had to finish. You couldn't . . . get away until Friday."

He closed his eyes and didn't speak for so long that she thought he had lost consciousness, even though his breathing was still ragged and labored. Finally he continued:

"You changed plans without telling me. You flew to Jamaica . . . on Thursday morning . . . got there hours ahead of me. When I arrived that evening, I thought the house was deserted . . . but you were in your bed upstairs . . . napping."

His voice grew fainter. He was striving mightily to stay alive long enough to explain himself in hope of gaining her absolution.

"I had arranged to meet some men . . . Soviet agents . . . in the last years of the Soviet Union, though none of us realized it then. I was handing over a suitcase of reports . . . important stuff related to the strategic defense initiative. You woke up . . . heard us downstairs . . . came down . . . overheard just enough to know I was a . . . a traitor. You barged into the middle of it . . . shocked and indignant . . . angry as hell. You tried to leave. You were so naive, thinking you could just leave. Of course they couldn't let you go. The KGB gave me a simple choice. Either you . . . had to be killed . . . or sent off to Rotenhausen . . . for the treatments."

His account of the events in Jamaica did not stir even the shadow of a memory in her, although she knew he must be telling the truth. "But why did Lisa's entire life have to be eradicated? Why couldn't Rotenhausen just remove all memories about what she . . . about what I overheard . . . and leave the rest untouched?"

Chelgrin spat blood again, more and darker than previously. "It's comparatively easy . . . for Rotenhausen to scour away . . . large blocks of memory. Far more difficult . . . to reach into a mind . . . and pinch off just a few . . . selected pieces. He refused to guarantee the results . . . unless he was permitted to erase all of Lisa . . . and create an entirely new person. You were put in Japan . . . because you knew the language . . . and because they felt it was unlikely . . . that anyone there would spot you and realize you were Lisa."

"Dear God," Joanna said shakily.

"I had no choice."

"You could have refused. You could have broken with them."

"They would've killed you."

"Would you have worked for them after they killed me?"

"No!"

"Then they would never have touched me," she said. "They wouldn't have had anything to gain."

"But I couldn't . . . couldn't go up against them," Chelgrin said weakly, miserably. "The only way I could've gotten free . . . was go to the FBI . . . expose myself. I'd have been jailed . . . treated like a spy. I would've lost everything . . . my businesses, investments, all the houses . . . the cars . . . everything . . . everything."

"Not everything," Joanna said.

He blinked at her, uncomprehending.

"You wouldn't have lost your daughter," she said.

"You're not . . . not even . . . trying to understand." He sighed as if in frustration, and the sigh ended in a wet rattle.

"I understand too well," she said. "You went from one extreme to the other. There wasn't room for humanity in either position."

He didn't reply.

He was dead. For real this time.

She stared at him, thinking about what might have been. Perhaps there never could have been anything between them. Perhaps the only Tom Chelgrin who could have been a decent father was the one who had never left Vietnam, the one whose charred bones were still buried in a deep, unmarked grave.

At last she got up from beside the dead senator and returned to the ground-floor hallway.

Alex was there, coming toward her. He called her name, and she ran to him.

83 As if the bodies littering the house were of little concern, Peterson insisted on a cognac. He led Alex and Joanna to the third floor, into the library where Alex had found the pistol. They sat in the red leather chairs while the fat man poured double measures of Rémy Martin from a crystal decanter. He sat in a chair opposite them, nearly overflowing it, and clasped the brandy snifter in both thick hands, warming the Rémy with his body heat.

"A little toast," Peterson said. He lifted his glass. "Here's to living."

Alex and Joanna didn't bother to raise their glasses. They just drank the cognac—fast. Alex hissed in pain as the Rémy stung his cut lips, but he still took a second swallow.

Peterson savored the Rémy and smiled contentedly.

"Who are you?" Joanna asked.

"I'm from Maryland, dear. I'm in real estate there."

"If you're trying to be funny—"

"It's true," said Peterson. "But of course I'm more than just a Realtor."

"Of course."

"I'm also a Russian."

"Isn't everyone?"

"My name was once Anton Broskov. Oh, you should have seen me in those days of my youth. Very dashing. I was so thin and fit, my dear. Positively svelte. I started getting fat the day that I was sent to the States from Vietnam, the day I began impersonating Anson Peterson in front of his friends and relatives. Eating became my way of coping with the terrible pressures."

Joanna finished her cognac. "The senator told me about the Mirror group before he died. You're one of them?"

"There were twelve of us," Peterson said. "They made us into mirror images of American prisoners of war, Alex. Sent us home in their place. They transformed us—not unlike the way in which this dear lady was transformed."

"Bullshit," Alex said angrily. "You didn't endure pain like she endured. You weren't raped. You always knew who you really were and where you came from, but Joanna lived in the dark."

She reached out and touched Alex's arm. "The worst is past. You're here. It's okay now."

Peterson sighed. "The idea was that all twelve of us would go to the States, get rich with the help of the KGB. Some of us needed that help, some didn't. We all made it to the top—except the two who died young, one in an accident, the other of cancer. Moscow figured that the perfect cover for an agent was wealth. Who'd ever suspect a self-made multimillionaire of plotting to overthrow the very system that made him a success?"

"But you said you're on our team," Alex reminded him.

"I am. I've gone over to the other side. Did it a long time ago. I'm not the only one. It was a possibility that the fanatics behind Mirror didn't consider carefully enough. If you let a man make his mark in a capitalistic society, if you let him achieve all that he wants in that society, then after a while he feels grateful toward that system, toward his neighbors. Four of the others have switched. Dear Tom would have come over too, if he could have gotten past his fear of having his millions stripped from him."

"The other side," Joanna said thoughtfully. "So you're working for the United States?"

"The CIA, yes," Peterson said. "Years and years ago, I told them all about Tom and the others. They hoped Tom would turn double like I did, of his own free will. But he didn't. And rather than try to turn him, they decided to use him without his knowledge. All these years, they fed subtly twisted information to dear old Tom, and he dutifully passed it on to Moscow. We've been quietly misleading first the communists, then the hash of ideologues who replaced them. In fact, we had a lot to do with the fall of the Soviet. Too bad it couldn't continue with Tom."

"Why couldn't it?"

"Dear Tom was going too far in politics. Much, much too far. He had a better than even chance of becoming the next President of the United States. Think of that! With him in the Oval Office, we couldn't hope to continue to deceive *any* faction in the Russian government."

"Wouldn't it be even easier to deceive them?"

"You see, when intelligence analysts in the Kremlin occasionally discovered a mistake in the information passed on to them by *Senator* Chelgrin, they figured it was because he wasn't in a sufficiently high position to acquire the entire unvarnished story. But they never lost faith in him. They continued to trust him. However, if he rose to the presidency, and if they discovered errors in the information passed to them by *President* Chelgrin, they would know something was rotten. They'd go back and painstakingly reexamine everything that he'd ever given them, and in time they'd realize that it was all doctored data, that they'd been played for fools."

Joanna shook her head, perplexed. "But why does it matter any more whether they find out or not? The Soviet Union is gone. The new people in charge are all our friends."

"Some of them are friends. Some of the old thugs are still around, however, still riddling the bureaucracy, still in some key positions in the military—just waiting for an opportunity to come storming back."

"No one really believes they'll get into power again."

Peterson swirled the remaining cognac in his crystal snifter. "You're perceptive, dear lady. Let's just say . . . we didn't merely feed them false information. For years, we engaged in a masterful charade that deceived them into a reckless expenditure of their national wealth on unnecessary military projects, leading to poverty and unrest in the civilian population. Furthermore, we played upon their systemic paranoia, giving them reason to believe they needed to make greater use of the Gulag, and the more people they dragged away to prison in the dead of night, the more their fragile system cracked under the strain of the people's fear, resentment, and anger."

"You *encouraged* them to put more people in concentration camps?" she asked, disbelieving.

"We didn't encourage it so much as provide them with information that led them to believe it was necessary for their survival."

"Are you saying you fingered people as enemies of the state who actually weren't spies or provocateurs? You provided phony evidence against them, condemned innocent Russians to suffering just to cause more internal turmoil?"

Peterson smiled. "Don't get moralistic, dear lady. It *was* a war, even if cold, and the Soviets were a formidable enemy. In a war, some sacrifices must be made."

"Sacrifices of innocent people."

He shrugged his big round shoulders. "Sometimes."

"Dear God."

"But you can see why we wouldn't want to have light thrown on the whole operation. Some pretty nasty stuff happened here. Let's just say . . . it would taint the victory we so well deserved and won. So when Tom began to seem not merely like a credible candidate for the presidency but like an inevitable successor to the current bumbler, he had to be removed."

"Why not just kill him in a staged accident?" Joanna asked.

"For one thing, the other side would have been alarmed and highly suspicious. In this line of work, we tend not to believe that there are *ever* any genuine accidents."

"But why did *I* have to do the removing?" Alex asked.

Peterson finished his cognac and, incredibly, took a roll of butter-rum Life Savers from his pocket. He offered them to Alex and Joanna, then popped one into his mouth. "The CIA determined that maximum propaganda value should be gotten from the senator's death. They decided that his status as a former Soviet—and now Russian—intelligence operative should be revealed to the world—but in such a way that the Russians would think the Mirror network of deep-cover agents had not been uncovered, just Tom. The Cold

War is over, yes, and we're all chums with the Russians now, skipping hand in hand toward the carefree and glorious dawn of the millennium, but we still spy on them and they still spy on us, and thus will it always be among powerful nations with big nuclear arsenals. We don't want to damage my position or that of the other turncoat Mirror agents in the States. If the CIA itself tore the mask off Tom Chelgrin, the Russians would be convinced that he had been made to tell everything about Mirror. But if a civilian—such as you, Alex—stumbled across Chelgrin's double identity through a chance encounter with his long-lost daughter, and if Chelgrin were killed before the CIA could have a chance to interrogate him, the Russians might think that Mirror was still safe."

"But the senator told me all about it," Joanna said, "and now it isn't a secret any more."

"You'll merely pretend that he didn't tell you a thing," the fat man advised. "In a few minutes, I'll leave. What we would like you to do is wait for half an hour, giving me time to make myself scarce, and then call the Swiss police."

"We'll be arrested for murder," Alex objected, "in case you've forgotten the carnage downstairs."

"No, you won't be arrested when the whole story comes out. You see . . . you'll tell them how you tracked backward through Joanna's life to London and then to here, how you discovered that Lisa was made into Joanna because of what she heard in Jamaica all those years ago, and how you shot these people in self-defense." He smiled at Joanna. "You'll tell the press that your father was a Soviet agent, that he told you his pathetic story as he lay dying. But you'll make no mention of Mirror or of the other doppelgängers like him. You must pretend to believe that he *was* Tom Chelgrin, the *real* Tom Chelgrin, who just fell into a secret love of Marxism after Vietnam."

"And what if I *do* mention Mirror and the other doubles?" she asked.

Peterson looked distressed. "Most unwise. You'd destroy the most spectacular counterintelligence operation in history. There are people who wouldn't take that lightly."

"The CIA," Alex said.

"Among others," Peterson said.

"You're saying they'd kill me if I told it all?" Joanna asked.

"Dear lady, they would certainly regret having to do it."

Alex said, "Don't threaten her."

"I didn't make a threat," Peterson said placatingly. "I merely stated an incontrovertible truth."

Putting down his empty brandy snifter, tenderly blotting his hand against his bloody lips, Alex said, "What happened to me in Rio?"

"We stole a week of your vacation. Like the KGB, the Agency has long sponsored a few behavioral psychologists and biochemists who have been expanding upon Rotenhausen's research. We used some of Franz's techniques to implant a program in you."

"That's why I went to Japan on vacation."

"Yes. You were programmed to go."

"That's why I stopped in Kyoto."

"Yes."

"And went to the Moonglow Lounge."

"We implanted that and a lot of other things, and I must say you performed perfectly."

Joanna slid forward on her chair, filled with a new fear. "How detailed was the program?"

"How detailed?" the fat man asked.

"I mean . . . was Alex . . . ?" She bit her lip and then took a deep breath. "Was he programmed to fall in love with me?"

Peterson smiled. "No, I assure you that he wasn't. But by God, I wish I'd thought of it! That would've been a surefire guarantee that he'd follow the rest of the program."

Alex got up from his chair, went to the bar, and poured more of the Rémy Martin into his glass. "Moscow will wonder why you weren't killed too."

"You'll tell the press and police there was a fat man who got away. That's the only description you'll be able to give. You'll say I shot at you, and you returned my fire. When I ran out of ammunition, you chased me, but I had quite a lead, and I got away in the darkness."

"How do I explain Ursula Zaitsev?" Alex asked bitterly. "She wasn't armed, was she? Don't the Swiss frown on killing unarmed women?"

"We'll put the 9mm pistol in her hand. Believe me, Alex, you won't wind up in jail. The CIA has friends here. It'll use them on your behalf if necessary. But that won't even be called for. All of this killing was strictly in self-defense."

They spent the next fifteen minutes constructing and memorizing a story that would explain everything that had transpired without mentioning Mirror or the fat man's true role in Chelgrin's downfall.

Finally Peterson stood up and stretched. "I'd better get out of here. Just remember . . . give me half an hour before you call the police."

84

They stood at the open door of Rotenhausen's house and watched the fat man drive out of sight in his gray Mercedes, down toward the lights of Saint Moritz.

When Alex closed the door, he looked at Joanna and said, "Well?"

"I guess we have to do what he wants. If we talk about Mirror, if we spoil their fun and games, they'll kill us. I don't doubt that. You know they will."

"They'll kill us anyway," Alex said. "They'll kill us even if we do exactly what they want. We'll call the Swiss police, tell them our story. They won't believe us at first, but in a day or two or three, they'll match your fingerprints to Lisa's. And other things will fall into place, so then they'll accept what we've told them. They'll let us go. We'll tell the same story to the press, just the way Peterson wants it told, with no mention of Mirror or Lyshenko. Newspapers all over the world will front-page it. War hero, Senator Tom Chelgrin, was a Russian agent through the two decades of the Cold War. Big news. The former members of the KGB will gloat and preen about how clever they were, and the current government of Russia will pretend to be embarrassed and distressed that such a thing could have been done by their predecessors. In time everything will quiet down. We'll start to lead normal lives again. Then someone in the CIA will begin to worry about us, about a couple of civilians walking around with this big secret. They'll send someone after us, sure as hell."

"But what can we do?"

He had been considering their options while Peterson had been helping them create a slightly altered version of the truth for the police. "It's a cliché, but it'll work. It's the only thing we *can* do. We won't call the cops. We're going to walk out of here, go to Zurich tonight or in the morning, hole up in a hotel, and write a complete account of this, all of it, including Mirror and everything Peterson just told us. We'll make a hundred copies of it and spread them among a hundred attorneys and bank trust departments in ten or twenty countries. With each sealed copy, we'll leave instructions that it be sent to a major newspaper, each copy to a *different* major newspaper in the event that we're killed—or in the event that we simply disappear. Then we'll send a copy to Peterson at his real-estate office in Maryland and another to the Director of the CIA, along with notes explaining what we've done."

"Will it work?"

"It better."

For twenty minutes they moved rapidly through the house, wiping everything that they might have touched.

In the garage they found the van in which they'd been brought unconscious from the hotel. Their luggage was still in the back.

Exactly half an hour after Peterson left, they drove away from Rotenhausen's clinic. The windshield wipers thumped metronomically, as if counting cadence for the dead; snow caked on the blades and turned to ice.

"We can't drive through these mountains tonight," Joanna said. "The roads won't be passable. Where will we go?"

"To the depot," he said. "Maybe there's another train out."

"To where?"

"Anywhere."

"Whose life will we live?"

"Our own," he said without hesitation. "No disguises. No running. In our own ways, we've been running for a long, long time. Neither of us can do that any more."

"I know. I just meant—your life in Chicago or mine in Kyoto?"

"Kyoto," he said. "You can't be asked to start over yet again. And there's nothing for me in Chicago if you're not there. Besides, I really do like big-band music. It's not a taste they programmed into me. And on a winter night, I like the way that snow falls like powdered starlight on the Gion. I like the pure notes of temple bells and oiled-paper lanterns that make shadows dance in a breeze."

Within the hour, they were sitting in a nearly empty passenger car, holding hands, as the last train out clattered toward midnight and then, finally, beyond.

Afterword

The Key to Midnight was the first novel that I wrote under the pen name Leigh Nichols, which I now no longer use. The other Nichols novels included *Shadowfires, The Servants of Twilight, The House of Thunder,* and *The Eyes of Darkness.*

Like all my pen names, Leigh met a tragic end. (Please see the Afterword to *The Funhouse* for the story of the death of "Owen West," who also wrote *The Mask*.) I used to tell people that while taking a tour for research purposes, Leigh had been killed in an explosion at a jalapeño-processing plant. Later, I insisted that Leigh died in a catastrophic rickshaw pile-up in Hong Kong. The truth, of course, is uglier. After drinking too much champagne one evening on a Caribbean cruise ship, Leigh Nichols was decapitated in a freak limbo accident.

This first Nichols book was meant to be my stab at an action-suspense-romance novel with a background of international intrigue, because I like to read stories of that kind when they are well done. Before giving Berkley Books the go-ahead to reprint *Key*, I reread it. Although many readers who discovered this novel through the years wrote to say that they enjoyed it, I decided that I hadn't succeeded with the original version as well as I'd thought at the time. Furthermore, it needed to be updated to reflect world events since its initial publication.

I am my own worst critic and a full-blown obsessive-compulsive, which is a bad combination in a line of work that requires me to meet deadlines. I swore that I would only lightly revise *Key*, but as is often the case, I was lying to myself. After all these years, one might think that I would no longer trust myself, but I continue to be a sucker for my own lies. I have this wide-eyed, puppy-dog look that I give myself in the mirror, when I'm lying, and I'm always fooled by it. I could sell myself the Brooklyn Bridge. In fact, I have. And I've no idea what I did with the money that I swindled from myself. I hope I had fun with it. Anyway, by the time I'd finished revising *The Key to Midnight*, I'd cut 30,000 words from it, added about 5,000 new words, and reworked it nearly line by line.

Nevertheless, I resisted the demonic urge to write an entirely new version of the story—even though the satanically induced desire to do so was so strong that at one point my head was spinning around 360 degrees on my shoulders. In spite of all these changes, *Key* is still largely the novel that it was on first publication. The plot and the characters have not been changed materially, and I have not altered the style in which it was written, but I believe and hope that the story is much more smoothly told and more fun to read than it was in its previous incarnation.

None of my other books is in the genre or the style of *The Key to Midnight*, but lurking in these pages is the Dean Koontz you know. I can't repress a love of twist-and-turn storytelling, and a certain characteristic eeriness creeps in, as with the scenes involving Omi Inamura, in spite of the intentionally spare (essentially Japanese) tone. I hope you enjoyed this change of pace. And remember, when you drink, don't limbo.

Hideaway

To Gerda.
Forever.

Part One

Just Seconds from a Clean Getaway

One

An entire world hummed and bustled beyond the dark ramparts of the mountains, yet to Lindsey Harrison the night seemed empty, as hollow as the vacant chambers of a cold, dead heart. Shivering, she slumped deeper in the passenger seat of the Honda.

Serried ranks of ancient evergreens receded up the slopes that flanked the highway, parting occasionally to accommodate sparse stands of winter-stripped maples and birches that poked at the sky with jagged black branches. However, that vast forest and the formidable rock formations to which it clung did not reduce the emptiness of the bitter March night. As the Honda descended the winding blacktop, the trees and stony outcroppings seemed to float past as if they were only dream images without real substance.

Harried by fierce wind, fine dry snow

slanted through the headlight beams. But the storm could not fill the void, either.

The emptiness that Lindsey perceived was internal, not external. The night was brimming, as ever, with the chaos of creation. Her own soul was the only hollow thing.

She glanced at Hatch. He was leaning forward, hunched slightly over the steering wheel, peering ahead with an expression which might be flat and inscrutable to anyone else but which, after twelve years of marriage, Lindsey could easily read. An excellent driver, Hatch was not daunted by poor road conditions. His thoughts, like hers, were no doubt on the long weekend they had just spent at Big Bear Lake.

Yet again they had tried to recapture the easiness with each other that they had once known. And again they had failed.

The chains of the past still bound them.

The death of a five-year-old son had incalculable emotional weight. It pressed on the mind, quickly deflating every moment of buoyancy, crushing each new blossom of joy. Jimmy had been dead for more than four and a half years, nearly as long as he had lived, yet his death weighed as heavily on them now as on the day they had lost him, like some colossal moon looming in a low orbit overhead.

Squinting through the smeared windshield, past snow-caked wiper blades that stuttered across the glass, Hatch sighed softly. He glanced at Lindsey and smiled. It was a pale smile, just a ghost of the real thing, barren of amusement, tired and melancholy. He seemed about to say something, changed his mind, and returned his attention to the highway.

The three lanes of blacktop—one descending, two ascending—were disappearing under a shifting shroud of snow. The road slipped to the bottom of the slope and entered a short straightaway leading into a wide, blind curve. In spite of that flat stretch of pavement, they were not out of the San Bernardino Mountains yet. The state route eventually would turn steeply downward once more.

As they followed the curve, the land changed around them: the slope to their right angled upward more sharply than before, while on the far side of the road, a black ravine yawned. White metal guardrails marked that precipice, but they were barely visible in the sheeting snow.

A second or two before they came out of the curve, Lindsey had a premonition of danger. She said, "Hatch . . ."

Perhaps Hatch sensed trouble, too, for even as Lindsey spoke, he gently applied the brakes, cutting their speed slightly.

A downgrade straightaway lay beyond the bend, and a beer distributor's large truck was halted at an angle across two lanes, just fifty or sixty feet in front of them.

Lindsey tried to say, *oh God,* but her voice was locked within her.

While making a delivery to one of the area ski resorts, the trucker evidently had been surprised by the blizzard, which had set in only a short while ago but half a day ahead of the forecasters' predictions. Without benefit of snow chains, the big truck tires churned ineffectively on the icy pavement as the driver struggled desperately to bring his rig around and get it moving again.

Cursing under his breath but otherwise as controlled as ever, Hatch eased his foot down on the brake pedal. He dared not jam it to the floor and risk sending the Honda into a deadly spin.

In response to the glare of the car headlights, the trucker looked through his side window. Across the rapidly closing gap of night and snow, Lindsey saw nothing of the man's face but a pallid oval and twin charry holes where the eyes should have been, a ghostly countenance, as if some malign spirit was at the wheel of that vehicle. Or Death himself.

Hatch was heading for the outermost of the two ascending lanes, the only part of the highway not blocked.

Lindsey wondered if other traffic was coming uphill, hidden from them by the truck. Even at reduced speed, if they collided head-on, they would not survive.

In spite of Hatch's best efforts, the Honda began to slide. The tail end came around to the left, and Lindsey found herself swinging away from the stranded truck. The smooth, greasy, out-of-control motion was like the transition between scenes in a bad dream. Her stomach twisted with nausea, and although she was restrained by a safety harness, she instinctively pressed her right hand against the door and her left against the dashboard, bracing herself.

"Hang on," Hatch said, turning the wheel where the car wanted to go, which was his only hope of regaining control.

But the slide became a sickening spin, and the Honda rotated three hundred and sixty degrees, as if it were a carousel without calliope: around . . . around . . . until the truck began to come into view again. For an instant, as they glided downhill, still turning, Lindsey was certain the car would slip safely past the other vehicle. She could see beyond the big rig now, and the road below was free of traffic.

Then the front bumper on Hatch's side caught the back of the truck. Tortured metal shrieked.

The Honda shuddered and seemed to *explode* away from the point of collision, slamming backward into the guardrail. Lindsey's teeth clacked together hard enough to ignite sparks of pain in her jaws, all the way into her temples, and the hand braced against the dashboard bent painfully at the wrist. Simultaneously, the strap of the shoulder harness, which stretched diagonally across her chest from right shoulder to left hip, abruptly cinched so tight that her breath burst from her.

The car rebounded from the guardrail, not with sufficient momentum to reconnect with the truck but with so much torque that it pivoted three hundred and sixty degrees again. As they spun-glided past the truck, Hatch fought for control, but the steering wheel jerked erratically back and forth, tearing through his hands so violently that he cried out as his palms were abraded.

Suddenly the moderate gradient appeared precipitously steep, like the wa-ter-greased spillway of an amusement-park flume ride. Lindsey would have screamed if she could have drawn breath. But although the safety strap had loosened, a diagonal line of pain still cut across her chest, making it impos-sible to inhale. Then she was rattled by a vision of the Honda skating in a long glissade to the next bend in the road, crashing through the guardrail, tumbling out into the void—and the image was so horrifying that it was like a blow, knocking breath back *into* her.

As the Honda came out of the second rotation, the entire driver's side slammed into the guardrail, and they slid thirty or forty feet without losing contact. To the accompaniment of a grinding-screeching-scraping of metal against metal, showers of yellow sparks plumed up, mingling with the falling snow, like swarms of summer fireflies that had flown through a time warp into the wrong season.

The car shuddered to a halt, canted up slightly at the front left corner, evidently hooked on a guard post. For an instant the resultant silence was so deep that Lindsey was half stunned by it; she shattered it with an explosive exhalation.

She had never before experienced such an overwhelming sense of relief.

Then the car moved again.

It began to tilt to the left. The guardrail was giving way, perhaps weak-ened by corrosion or by the erosion of the highway shoulder beneath it.

"Out!" Hatch shouted, frantically fumbling with the release on his safety harness.

Lindsey didn't even have time to pop loose of her own harness or grab the door handle before the railing cracked apart and the Honda slipped into the ravine. Even as it was happening, she couldn't believe it. The brain ac-knowledged the approach of death, while the heart stubbornly insisted on immortality. In almost five years she had not adjusted to Jimmy's death, so she was not easily going to accept the imminence of her own demise.

In a jangle of detached posts and railings, the Honda slid sideways along the ice-crusted slope, then flipped over as the embankment grew steeper. Gasping for breath, heart pounding, wrenched painfully from side to side in her harness, Lindsey hoped for a tree, a rock outcropping, anything that would halt their fall, but the embankment seemed clear. She was not sure how often the car rolled—maybe only twice—because up and down and left and right lost all meaning. Her head banged into the ceiling almost hard enough to knock her out. She didn't know if she'd been thrown upward or if the roof had caved in to meet her, so she tried to slump in her seat, afraid the roof might crumple further on the next roll and crush her skull. The headlights slashed at the night, and from the wounds spouted torrents of snow. Then the windshield burst, showering her with minutely fragmented safety glass, and abruptly she was plunged into total darkness. Apparently the headlights blinked off, and the dashboard lights, reflected in Hatch's sweat-slicked face. The car rolled onto its roof again and stayed there. In that inverted posture it sledded farther into the seemingly bottomless ravine, with the thunderous noise of a thousand tons of coal pouring down a steel chute.

The gloom was utterly tenebrous, seamless, as if she and Hatch were not outdoors but in some windowless funhouse, rocketing down a roller-coaster track. Even the snow, which usually had a natural phosphorescence, was suddenly invisible. Cold flakes stung her face as the freezing wind drove them through the empty windshield frame, but she could not see them even as they frosted her lashes. Struggling to quell a rising panic, she wondered if she had been blinded by the imploding glass.

Blindness.

That was her special fear. She was an artist. Her talent took inspiration from what her eyes observed, and her wonderfully dexterous hands rendered inspiration into art with the critical judgment of those eyes to guide them. What did a blind painter paint? What could she hope to create if suddenly deprived of the sense that she relied upon the most?

Just as she started to scream, the car hit bottom and rolled back onto its wheels, landing upright with less impact than she had anticipated. It came to a halt almost gently, as if on an immense pillow.

"Hatch?" Her voice was hoarse.

After the cacophonous roar of their plunge down the ravine wall, she felt half deaf, not sure if the preternatural silence around her was real or only perceived.

"Hatch?"

She looked to her left, where he ought to have been, but she could not see him—or anything else.

She *was* blind.

"Oh, God, no. Please."

She was dizzy, too. The car seemed to be turning, wallowing like an airborne kite dipping and rising in the thermal currents of a summer sky.

"Hatch!"

No response.

Her lightheadedness increased. The car rocked and wallowed worse than ever. Lindsey was afraid she would faint. If Hatch was injured, he might bleed to death while she was unconscious and unable to help him.

She reached out blindly and found him crumpled in the driver's seat. His head was bent toward her, resting against his own shoulder. She touched his face, and he did not move. Something warm and sticky covered his right cheek and temple. Blood. From a head injury. With trembling fingers, she touched his mouth and sobbed with relief when she felt the hot exhalation of his breath between his slightly parted lips.

He was unconscious, not dead.

Fumbling in frustration with the release mechanism on her safety harness, Lindsey heard new sounds that she could not identify. A soft slapping. Hungry licking. An eerie, liquid chuckling. For a moment she froze, straining to identify the source of those unnerving noises.

Without warning the Honda tipped forward, admitting a cascade of icy water through the broken windshield onto Lindsey's lap. She gasped in surprise as the arctic bath chilled her to the marrow, and realized she was not lightheaded after all. The car *was* moving. It was afloat. They had landed in a lake or river. Probably a river. The placid surface of a lake would not have been so active.

The shock of the cold water briefly paralyzed her and made her wince with pain, but when she opened her eyes, she could see again. The Honda's headlights were, indeed, extinguished, but the dials and gauges in the dashboard still glowed. She must have been suffering from hysterical blindness rather than genuine physical damage.

She couldn't see much, but there was not much to see at the bottom of the night-draped ravine. Splinters of dimly glimmering glass rimmed the broken-out windshield. Outside, the oily water was revealed only by a sinuous, silvery phosphorescence that highlighted its purling surface and imparted a dark obsidian sparkle to the jewels of ice that floated in tangled necklaces atop it. The riverbanks would have been lost in absolute blackness but for the ghostly raiments of snow that cloaked the otherwise naked rocks, earth, and brush. The Honda appeared to be motoring through the river: water poured halfway up its hood before parting in a "V" and streaming away to either side as it might from the prow of a ship, lapping at the sills of the side windows. They were being swept downstream, where eventually the currents were certain to turn more turbulent, bringing them to rapids or rocks or worse. At a glance, Lindsey grasped the extremity of their situation, but she was still so relieved by the remission of her blindness that she was grateful for the sight of anything, even of trouble this serious.

Shivering, she freed herself from the entangling straps of the safety harness, and touched Hatch again. His face was ghastly in the queer backsplash of the instrument lights: sunken eyes, waxen skin, colorless lips, blood oozing—but, thank God, not spurting—from the gash on the right side of his head. She shook him gently, then a little harder, calling his name.

They wouldn't be able to get out of the car easily, if at all, while it was being borne down the river—especially as it now began to move faster. But at least they had to be prepared to scramble out if it came up against a rock or caught for a moment against one of the banks. The opportunity to escape might be short-lived.

Hatch could not be awakened.

Without warning the car dipped sharply forward. Again icy water gushed in through the shattered windshield, so cold that it had some of the effect of an electrical shock, halting Lindsey's heart for a beat or two and locking the breath in her lungs.

The front of the car did not rise in the currents, as it had done previously. It was settling deeper than before, so there was less river under it to provide lift. The water continued to pour in, quickly rising past Lindsey's ankles to mid-calf. They were sinking.

"Hatch!" She was shouting now, shaking him hard, heedless of his injuries.

The river gushed inside, rising to seat level, churning up foam that refracted the amber light from the instrument panel and looked like garlands of golden Christmas tinsel.

Lindsey pulled her feet out of the water, knelt on her seat, and splashed Hatch's face, desperately hoping to bring him around. But he was sunk in deeper levels of unconsciousness than mere concussive sleep, perhaps in a coma as plumbless as a mid-ocean trench.

Swirling water rose to the bottom of the steering wheel.

Frantically Lindsey ripped at Hatch's safety harness, trying to strip it away from him, only half aware of the hot flashes of pain when she tore a couple of fingernails.

"Hatch, damn it!"

The water was halfway up the steering wheel, and the Honda all but ceased its forward movement. It was too heavy now to be budged by the persistent pressure of the river behind it.

Hatch was five-feet-ten, a hundred and sixty pounds, only average in size, but he might as well have been a giant. As dead weight, resistant to her every effort, he was virtually immovable. Tugging, shoving, wrenching, clawing, Lindsey struggled to free him, and by the time she finally managed to disentangle him from the straps, the water had risen over the top of the dashboard, more than halfway up her chest. It was even higher on Hatch, just under his chin, because he was slumped in his seat.

The river was unbelievably icy, and Lindsey felt the warmth pumping out of her body as if it were blood gushing from a severed artery. As body heat bled from her, the cold bled in, and her muscles began to ache.

Nevertheless, she welcomed the rising flood because it would make Hatch buoyant and therefore easier to maneuver out from under the wheel and through the shattered windshield. That was her theory, anyway, but when she tugged on him, he seemed heavier than ever, and now the water was at his lips.

"Come on, come on," she said furiously, "you're gonna drown, damn it!"

2

Finally pulling his beer truck off the road, Bill Cooper broadcast a Mayday on his CB radio. Another trucker responded and, equipped with a cellular telephone as well as a CB, promised to call the authorities in nearby Big Bear.

Bill hung up the citizen's-band handset, took a long-handled six-battery flashlight from under the driver's seat, and stepped out into the storm. The frigid wind cut through even his fleece-lined denim jacket, but the bitterness of the winter night was not half as icy as his stomach, which had turned sour and cold as he had watched the Honda spin its luckless occupants down the highway and over the brink of the chasm.

He hurried across the slippery pavement and along the shoulder to the missing section of guardrail. He hoped to see the Honda close below, caught up against the trunk of a tree. But there were no trees on that slope—just a smooth mantle of snow from previous storms, scarred by the passage of the car, disappearing beyond the reach of his flashlight beam.

An almost disabling pang of guilt stabbed through him. He'd been drinking again. Not much. A few shots out of the flask he carried. He had been certain he was sober when he'd started up the mountain. Now he wasn't so sure. He felt . . . fuzzy. And suddenly it seemed stupid to have tried to make a delivery with the weather turning ugly so fast.

Below him, the abyss appeared supernaturally bottomless, and the apparent extreme depth engendered in Bill the feeling that he was gazing into the damnation to which he'd be delivered when his own life ended. He was paralyzed by that sense of futility that sometimes overcame even the best of men—though usually when they were alone in a bedroom, staring at the meaningless patterns of shadows on the ceiling at three o'clock in the morning.

Then the curtains of snow parted for a moment, and he saw the floor of the ravine about a hundred or a hundred and fifty feet below, not as deep as he had feared. He stepped through the gap in the guardrail, intending to crab down the treacherous hillside and assist the survivors if there were any. Instead he hesitated on the narrow shelf of flat earth at the brink of the slope because he was whiskey-dizzy but also because he could not see where the car had come to rest.

A serpentine black band, like satin ribbon, curved through the snow down there, intersecting the tracks the car had made. Bill blinked at it uncomprehendingly, as if staring at an abstract painting, until he remembered that a river lay below.

The car had gone into that ebony ribbon of water.

Following a winter of freakishly heavy snow, the weather had turned warmer a couple of weeks ago, triggering a premature spring melt. The runoff continued, for winter had returned too recently to have locked the river in ice again. The temperature of the water would be only a few degrees above freezing. Any occupant of the car, having survived both the wreck and death by drowning, would perish swiftly from exposure.

If I'd been sober, he thought, I would've turned back in this weather. I'm a pathetic joke, a tanked-up beer deliveryman who didn't even have enough loyalty to get plastered on beer. Christ.

A joke, but people were dying because of him. He tasted vomit in the back of his throat, choked it down.

Frantically he surveyed the murky ravine until he spotted an eerie radiance, like an otherworldly presence, drifting spectrally with the river to the right of him. Soft amber, it faded in and out through the falling snow. He figured it must be the interior lights of the Honda, which was being borne downriver.

Hunched for protection against the biting wind, holding on to the guard-rail in case he slipped and fell over the edge, Bill scuttled along the top of the slope, in the same direction as the waterswept car below, trying to keep it in sight. The Honda drifted swiftly at first, then slower, slower. Finally it came to a complete halt, perhaps stopped by rocks in the watercourse or by a projection of the riverbank.

The light was slowly fading, as if the car's battery was running out of juice.

3 Though Hatch was freed from the safety harness, Lindsey could not budge him, maybe because his clothes were caught on something she could not see, maybe because his foot was wedged under the brake pedal or bent back and trapped under his own seat.

The water rose over Hatch's nose. Lindsey could not hold his head any higher. He was breathing the river now.

She let go of him because she hoped that the loss of his air supply would finally bring him around, coughing and spluttering and splashing up from his seat, but also because she did not have the energy to continue struggling with him. The intense cold of the water sapped her strength. With frightening rapidity, her extremities were growing numb. Her exhaled breath seemed just as cold as every inhalation, as if her body had no heat left to impart to the used air.

The car had stopped moving. It was resting on the bottom of the river, completely filled and weighed down with water, except for a bubble of air under the shallow dome of the roof. Into that space she pressed her face, gasping for breath.

She was making horrid little sounds of terror, like the bleats of an animal. She tried to silence herself but could not.

The queer, water-filtered light from the instrument panel began to fade from amber to muddy yellow.

A dark part of her wanted to give up, let go of this world, and move on to someplace better. It had a small quiet voice of its own: *Don't fight, there's nothing left to live for anyway, Jimmy has been dead for so long, so very long, now Hatch is dead or dying, just let go, surrender, maybe you'll wake up in Heaven with them* . . . The voice possessed a lulling, hypnotic appeal.

The remaining air could last only a few minutes, if that long, and she would die in the car if she did not escape immediately.

Hatch is dead, lungs full of water, only waiting to be fish food, so let go, surrender, what's the point, Hatch is dead . . .

She gulped air that was swiftly acquiring a tart, metallic taste. She was able to draw only small breaths, as if her lungs had shriveled.

If any body heat was left in her, she was not aware of it. In reaction to the cold, her stomach knotted with nausea, and even the vomit that kept rising into her throat was icy; each time she choked it down, she felt as if she had swallowed a vile slush of dirty snow.

Hatch is dead, Hatch is dead . . .

"No," she said in a harsh, angry whisper. "No. No."

Denial raged through her with the fury of a storm: Hatch could not be dead. Unthinkable. Not Hatch, who never forgot a birthday or an anniversary, who bought her flowers for no reason at all, who never lost his temper and rarely raised his voice. Not Hatch, who always had time to listen to the troubles of others and sympathize with them, who never failed to have an open wallet for a friend in need, whose greatest fault was that he was too damn much of a soft touch. He could not be, must not be, *would* not be dead. He ran five miles a day, ate a low-fat diet with plenty of fruits and vegetables, avoided caffeine *and* decaffeinated beverages. Didn't that count for something, damn it? He lathered on sunscreen in the summer, did not smoke, never drank more than two beers or two glasses of wine in a single evening, and was too easy-going ever to develop heart disease due to stress. Didn't self-denial and self-control count for anything? Was creation so screwed up that there was *no* justice any more? Okay, all right, they said the good died young, which sure had been true of Jimmy, and Hatch was not yet forty, young by any standard, okay, agreed, but they also said that virtue was its own reward, and there was plenty of virtue here, damn it, a whole shitload of virtue, which ought to count for something, unless God wasn't listening, unless He didn't care, unless the world was an even crueler place than she had believed.

She refused to accept it.

Hatch. Was. Not. Dead.

She drew as deep a breath as she could manage. Just as the last of the light faded, plunging her into blindness again, she sank into the water, pushed across the dashboard, and went through the missing windshield onto the hood of the car.

Now she was not merely blind but deprived of virtually all five senses. She could hear nothing but the wild thumping of her own heart, for the water effectively muffled sound. She could smell and speak only at the penalty of death by drowning. The anesthetizing effect of the glacial river left her with a fraction of her sense of touch, so she felt as if she were a disembodied spirit suspended in whatever medium composed Purgatory, awaiting final judgment.

Assuming that the river was not much deeper than the car and that she would not need to hold her breath long before she reached the surface, she made another attempt to free Hatch. Lying on the hood of the car, holding fast to the edge of the windshield frame with one numb hand, straining against her body's natural buoyancy, she reached back inside, groped in the blackness until she located the steering wheel and then her husband.

Heat rose in her again, at last, but it was not a sustaining warmth. Her lungs were beginning to burn with the need for air.

Gripping a fistful of Hatch's jacket, she pulled with all her might—and to her surprise he floated out of his seat, no longer immovable, suddenly buoyant and unfettered. He caught on the steering wheel, but only briefly, then bobbled out through the windshield as Lindsey slid backward across the hood to make way for him.

A hot, pulsing pain filled her chest. The urge to breathe grew over-powering, but she resisted it.

When Hatch was out of the car, Lindsey embraced him and kicked for the surface. He was surely drowned, and she was clinging to a corpse, but she was not repulsed by that macabre thought. If she could get him ashore, she would be able to administer artificial respiration. Although the chance of reviving him was slim, at least some hope remained. He was not truly dead, not really a corpse, until all hope had been exhausted.

She burst through the surface into a howling wind that made the marrow-freezing water seem almost warm by comparison. When that air hit her burning lungs, her heart stuttered, her chest clenched with pain, and the second breath was harder to draw than the first.

Treading water, holding tight to Hatch, Lindsey swallowed mouthfuls of the river as it splashed her face. Cursing, she spat it out. Nature seemed alive, like a great hostile beast, and she found herself irrationally angry with the river and the storm, as if they were conscious entities willfully aligned against her.

She tried to orient herself, but it was not easy in the darkness and shriek-ing wind, without solid ground beneath her. When she saw the riverbank, vaguely luminous in its coat of snow, she attempted a one-arm sidestroke toward it with Hatch in tow, but the current was too strong to be resisted, even if she'd been able to swim with both arms. She and Hatch were swept downstream, repeatedly dragged beneath the surface by an undertow, re-peatedly thrust back into the wintry air, battered by fragments of tree branches and chunks of ice that were also caught up in the current, moving helplessly and inexorably toward whatever sudden fall or deadly phalanx of rapids marked the river's descent from the mountains.

4 He had started drinking when Myra left him. He never could handle being womanless. Yeah, and wouldn't God Almighty treat that ex-cuse with contempt when it came time for judgment?

Still holding the guardrail, Bill Cooper crouched indecisively on the brink of the slope and stared intently down at the river. Beyond the screen of falling snow, the lights of the Honda had gone out.

He didn't dare take his eyes off the obscured scene below to check the highway for the ambulance. He was afraid that when he looked back into the ravine again, he would misremember the exact spot where the light had disappeared and would send the rescuers to the wrong point along the riverbank. The dim black-and-white world below offered few prominent land-marks.

"Come on, hurry up," he muttered.

The wind—which stung his face, made his eyes water, and pasted snow in his mustache—was keening so loudly that it masked the approaching sirens of the emergency vehicles until they rounded the bend uphill, enliv-ening the night with their headlights and red flashers. Bill rose, waving his arms to draw their attention, but he still did not look away from the river.

Behind him, they pulled to the side of the road. Because one of their sirens wound down to silence faster than the other, he knew there were two ve-hicles, probably an ambulance and a police cruiser.

They would smell the whiskey on his breath. No, maybe not in all that wind and cold. He felt that he deserved to die for what he'd done—but if he wasn't going to die, then he didn't think he deserved to lose his job. These were hard times. A recession. Good jobs weren't easy to find.

Reflections of the revolving emergency beacons lent a stroboscopic quality to the night. Real life had become a choppy and technically inept piece of stop-motion animation, with the scarlet snow like a spray of blood falling haltingly from the wounded sky.

5   Sooner than Lindsey could have hoped, the surging river shoved her and Hatch against a formation of water-smoothed rocks that rose like a series of worn teeth in the middle of its course, wedging them into a gap sufficiently narrow to prevent them from being swept farther downstream. Water foamed and gurgled around them, but with the rocks behind her, she was able to stop struggling against the deadly undertow.

She felt limp, every muscle soft and unresponsive. She could barely man-age to keep Hatch's head from tipping forward into the water, though doing so should have been a simple task now that she no longer needed to fight the river.

Though she was incapable of letting go of him, keeping his head above water was a pointless task: he had drowned. She could not kid herself that he was still alive. And minute by minute he was less likely to be revived with artificial respiration. But she would not give up. Would not. She was aston-ished by her fierce refusal to relinquish hope, though just before the accident she had thought she was devoid of hope forever.

The chill of the water had thoroughly penetrated Lindsey, numbing mind as well as flesh. When she tried to concentrate on forming a plan that would get her from the middle of the river to the shore, she could not bring her thoughts into focus. She felt drugged. She knew that drowsiness was a com-panion of hypothermia, that dozing off would invite deeper unconsciousness and ultimately death. She was determined to keep awake and alert at all costs—but suddenly she realized that she had closed her eyes, giving in to the temptation of sleep.

Fear twisted through her. Renewed strength coiled in her muscles.

Blinking feverishly, eyelashes frosted with snow that no longer melted from her body heat, she peered around Hatch and along the line of water-polished boulders. The safety of the bank was only fifteen feet away. If the rocks were close to one another, she might be able to tow Hatch to shore without being sucked through a gap and carried downriver.

Her vision had adapted sufficiently to the gloom, however, for her to see that centuries of patient currents had carved a five-foot-wide hole in the middle of the granite span against which she was wedged. It was halfway between her and the river's edge. Dimly glistening under a lacework shawl of ice, the ebony water quickened as it was funneled toward the gap; no doubt it exploded out the other side with tremendous force.

Lindsey knew she was too weak to propel herself across that powerful affluxion. She and Hatch would be swept through the breach and, at last, to certain death.

Just when surrender to an endless sleep began, again, to look more appealing than continued pointless struggle against nature's hostile power, she saw strange lights at the top of the ravine, a couple of hundred yards upriver. She was so disoriented and her mind so anesthetized by the cold that for a while the pulsing crimson glow seemed eerie, mysterious, supernatural, as if she were staring upward at the wondrous radiance of a hovering, divine presence.

Gradually she realized that she was seeing the throb of police or ambulance beacons on the highway far above, and then she spotted the flashlight beams nearer at hand, like silver swords slashing the darkness. Rescuers had descended the ravine wall. They were maybe a hundred yards upriver, where the car had sunk.

She called to them. Her shout issued as a whisper. She tried again, with greater success, but they must not have heard her above the keening wind, for the flashlights continued to sweep back and forth over the same section of riverbank and turbulent water.

Suddenly she realized that Hatch was slipping out of her grasp again. His face was underwater.

With the abruptness of a switch being thrown, Lindsey's terror became anger again. She was angry with the truck driver for being caught in the mountains during a snowstorm, angry with herself for being so weak, angry with Hatch for reasons she could not define, angry with the cold and insistent river, and *enraged* at God for the violence and injustice of His universe.

Lindsey found greater strength in anger than in terror. She flexed her half-frozen hands, got a better grip on Hatch, pulled his head out of the water again, and let out a cry for help that was louder than the banshee voice of the wind. Upstream, the flashlight beams, as one, swung searchingly in her direction.

6 The stranded couple looked dead already. Targeted by the flashlights, their faces floated on the dark water, as white as apparitions—translucent, unreal, lost.

Lee Reedman, a San Bernardino County Deputy Sheriff with emergency rescue training, waded into the water to haul them ashore, bracing himself against a rampart of boulders that extended out to midstream. He was on a half-inch, hawser-laid nylon line with a breaking strength of four thousand pounds, secured to the trunk of a sturdy pine and belayed by two other deputies.

He had taken off his parka but not his uniform or boots. In those fierce currents, swimming was impossible anyway, so he did not have to worry about being hampered by clothes. And even sodden garments would protect him from the worst bite of the frigid water, reducing the rate at which body heat was sucked out of him.

Within a minute of entering the river, however, when he was only halfway toward the stranded couple, Lee felt as if a refrigerant had been injected into his bloodstream. He couldn't believe that he would have been any colder had he dived naked into those icy currents.

He would have preferred to wait for the Winter Rescue Team that was on its way, men who had experience pulling skiers out of avalanches and retrieving careless skaters who had fallen through thin ice. They would have insulated wetsuits and all the necessary gear. But the situation was too desperate to delay; the people in the river would not last until the specialists arrived.

He came to a five-foot-wide gap in the rocks, where the river gushed through as if being drawn forward by a huge suction pump. He was knocked off his feet, but the men on the bank kept the line taut, paying it out precisely at the rate he was moving, so he was not swept into the breach. He flailed forward through the surging river, swallowing a mouthful of water so bitterly cold that it made his teeth ache, but he got a grip on the rock at the far side of the gap and pulled himself across.

A minute later, gasping for breath and shivering violently, Lee reached the couple. The man was unconscious, but the woman was alert. Their faces bobbled in and out of the overlapping flashlight beams directed from shore, and they both looked in terrible shape. The woman's flesh seemed to have both shriveled and blanched of all color, so the natural phosphorescence of bone shone like a light within, revealing the skull beneath her skin. Her lips were as white as her teeth; other than her sodden black hair, only her eyes were dark, as sunken as the eyes of a corpse and bleak with the pain of dying. Under the circumstances he could not guess her age within fifteen years and could not tell if she was ugly or attractive, but he could see, at once, that she was at the limit of her resources, holding on to life by will-power alone.

"Take my husband first," she said, pushing the unconscious man into Lee's arms. Her shrill voice cracked repeatedly. "He's got a head injury, needs help, hurry up, go on, go on, damn you!"

Her anger didn't offend Lee. He knew it was not directed against him, really, and that it gave her the strength to endure.

"Hold on, and we'll all go together." He raised his voice above the roar of the wind and the racing river. "Don't fight it, don't try to grab on to the rocks or keep your feet on the bottom. They'll have an easier time reeling us in if we let the water buoy us."

She seemed to understand.

Lee glanced back toward shore. A light focused on his face, and he shouted, "Ready! Now!"

The team on the riverbank began to reel him in, with the unconscious man and the exhausted woman in tow.

7

After Lindsey was hauled out of the water, she drifted in and out of consciousness. For a while life seemed to be a videotape being fast-forwarded from one randomly chosen scene to another, with gray-white static in between.

As she lay gasping on the ground at the river's edge, a young paramedic with a snow-caked beard knelt at her side and directed a penlight at her eyes, checking her pupils for uneven dilation. He said, "Can you hear me?"

"Of course. Where's Hatch?"

"Do you know your name?"

"Where's my husband? He needs . . . CPR."

"We're taking care of him. Now, do you know your name?"

"Lindsey."

"Good. Are you cold?"

That seemed like a stupid question, but then she realized she was no longer freezing. In fact, a mildly unpleasant heat had arisen in her extremi-ties. It was not the sharp, painful heat of flames. Instead, she felt as if her feet and hands had been dipped in a caustic fluid that was gradually dis-solving her skin and leaving raw nerve ends exposed. She knew, without having to be told, that her inability to feel the bitter night air was an indi-cation of physical deterioration.

Fast forward . . .

She was being moved on a stretcher. They were heading along the river-bank. With her head toward the front of the litter, she could look back at the man who was carrying the rear of it. The snow-covered ground reflected the flashlight beams, but that soft eerie glow was only bright enough to reveal the basic contours of the stranger's face and add a disquieting glimmer to his iron-hard eyes.

As colorless as a charcoal drawing, strangely silent, full of dreamlike motion and mystery, that place and moment had the quality of a nightmare. She felt her heartbeat accelerate as she squinted back and up at the almost faceless man. The illogic of a dream shaped her fear, and suddenly she was certain that she was dead and that the shadowy men carrying her stretcher were not men at all but carrion-bearers delivering her to the boat that would convey her across the Styx to the land of the dead and damned.

Fast forward . . .

Lashed to the stretcher now, tilted almost into a standing position, she was being pulled along the snow-covered slope of the ravine wall by unseen men reeling in a pair of ropes from above. Two other men accompanied her, one on each side of the stretcher, struggling up through the knee-deep drifts, guiding her and making sure she didn't flip over.

She was ascending into the red glow of the emergency beacons. As that crimson radiance completely surrounded her, she began to hear the urgent voices of the rescuers above and the crackle of police-band radios. When she could smell the pungent exhaust fumes of their vehicles, she knew that she was going to survive.

Just seconds from a clean getaway, she thought.

Though in the grip of a delirium born of exhaustion, confused and fuzzy-minded, Lindsey was alert enough to be unnerved by that thought and the subconscious longing it represented. Just seconds from a clean getaway? The only thing she had been seconds away from was death. Was she still so depressed from the loss of Jimmy that, even after five years, her own death was an acceptable release from the burden of her grief?

Then why didn't I surrender to the river? she wondered. Why not just let go?

Hatch, of course. Hatch had needed her. She'd been ready to step out of this world in hope of setting foot into a better one. But she had not been able to make that decision for Hatch, and to surrender her own life under those circumstances would have meant forfeiting his as well.

With a clatter and a jolt, the stretcher was pulled over the brink of the ravine and lowered flat onto the shoulder of the mountain highway beside an ambulance. Red snow swirled into her face.

A paramedic with a weather-beaten face and beautiful blue eyes leaned over her. "You're going to be all right."

"I didn't want to die," she said.

She was not really speaking to the man. She was arguing with herself, trying to deny that her despair over the loss of her son had become such a chronic emotional infection that she had been secretly longing to join him in death. Her self-image did not include the word "suicidal," and she was shocked and repulsed to discover, under extreme stress, that such an impulse might be a part of her.

Just seconds from a clean getaway . . .

She said, "Did I want to die?"

"You aren't going to die," the paramedic assured her as he and another man untied the ropes from the handles of the litter, preparatory to loading her into the ambulance. "The worst is over now. The worst is over."

Two

Half a dozen police and emergency vehicles were parked across two lanes of the mountain highway. Uphill and downhill traffic shared the third lane, regulated by uniformed deputies. Lindsey was aware of people gawking at her from a Jeep Wagoneer, but they vanished beyond shatters of snow and heavy plumes of crystallized exhaust fumes.

The ambulance van could accommodate two patients. They loaded Lindsey onto a wheeled gurney that was fixed to the left wall by two spring clamps to prevent it from rolling while the vehicle was in motion. They put Hatch on another identical gurney along the right wall.

Two paramedics crowded into the rear of the ambulance and pulled the wide door shut behind them. As they moved, their white, insulated nylon pants and jackets produced continuous frictional sounds, a series of soft whistles that seemed to be electronically amplified in those close quarters.

With a short burst of its siren, the ambulance started to move. The paramedics swayed easily with the rocking motion. Experience had made them surefooted.

Side by side in the narrow aisle between the gurneys, both men turned to Lindsey. Their names were stitched on the breast pockets of their jackets: David O'Malley and Jerry Epstein. With a curious combination of professional detachment and concerned attentiveness, they began to work on her, exchanging medical information with each other in crisp emotionless voices but speaking to her in soft, sympathetic, encouraging tones.

That dichotomy in their behavior alarmed rather than soothed Lindsey, but she was too weak and disoriented to express her fear. She felt infuriatingly delicate. Shaky. She was reminded of a surrealistic painting titled *This World and the Next,* which she had done last year, because the central figure in that piece had been a wire-walking circus acrobat plagued by uncertainty. Right now consciousness was a high wire on which she was precariously perched. Any effort to speak to the paramedics, if sustained for more than a word or two, might unbalance her and send her into a long, dark fall.

Although her mind was too clouded to find any sense in most of what the two men were saying, she understood enough to know that she was suffering from hypothermia, possibly frostbite, and that they were worried about her. Blood pressure too low. Heartbeat slow and irregular. Slow and shallow respiration.

Maybe that clean getaway was still possible.

If she really wanted it.

She was ambivalent. If she actually had hungered for death on a subconscious level since Jimmy's funeral, she had no special appetite for it now—though neither did she find it particularly unappealing. Whatever happened to her would happen, and in her current condition, with her emotions as numb as her five senses, she did not much care about her fate. Hypothermia switched off the survival instinct with a narcotizing pall as effective as that produced by an alcoholic binge.

Then, between the two muttering paramedics, she caught a glimpse of Hatch lying on the other gurney, and abruptly she was jolted out of her half-trance by her concern for him. He looked so pale. But not just white. Another, less healthy shade of pale with a lot of gray in it. His face—turned toward her, eyes closed, mouth open slightly—looked as if a flash fire had swept through it, leaving nothing between bone and skin except the ashes of flesh consumed.

"Please," she said, "my husband." She was surprised that her voice was just a low, rough croak.

"You first," O'Malley said.

"No. Hatch. Hatch . . . needs . . . help."

"You first," O'Malley repeated.

His insistence reassured her somewhat. As bad as Hatch looked, he must be all right, must have responded to CPR, must be in better shape than she was, or otherwise they would have tended to him first. Wouldn't they?

Her thoughts grew fuzzy again. The sense of urgency that had gripped her now abated. She closed her eyes.

2 Later . . .

In Lindsey's hypothermic torpor, the murmuring voices above her seemed as rhythmic, if not as melodic, as a lullaby. But she was kept awake by the increasingly painful stinging sensation in her extremities and by the rough handling of the medics, who were packing small pillowlike objects against her sides. Whatever the things were—electric or chemical heating pads, she supposed—they radiated a soothing warmth far different from the fire burning within her feet and hands.

"Hatch needs warmed up, too," she said thickly.

"He's fine, don't you worry about him," Epstein said. His breath puffed out in small white clouds as he spoke.

"But he's cold."

"That's what he needs to be. That's just how we want him."

O'Malley said, "But not too cold, Jerry. Nyebern doesn't want a Popsicle. Ice crystals form in the tissue, there'll be brain damage."

Epstein turned to the small half-open window that separated the rear of the ambulance from the forward compartment. He called loudly to the driver: "Mike, turn on a little heat maybe."

Lindsey wondered who Nyebern might be, and she was alarmed by the words "brain damage." But she was too weary to concentrate and make sense of what they said.

Her mind drifted to recollections from childhood, but they were so distorted and strange that she must have slipped across the border of consciousness into a half-sleep where her subconscious could work nightmarish tricks on her memories.

... she saw herself, five years of age, at play in a meadow behind her house. The sloped field was familiar in its contours, but some hateful influence had crept into her mind and meddled with the details, wickedly recoloring the grass a spider-belly black. The petals of all the flowers were blacker still, with crimson stamens that glistened like fat drops of blood. ...

... she saw herself, at seven, on the school playground at twilight, but alone as she had never been in real life. Around her stood the usual array of swings and seesaws and jungle gyms and slides, casting crisp shadows in the peculiar orange light of day's end. Those machineries of joy seemed curiously ominous now. They loomed malevolently, as if they might begin to move at any second, with much creaking and clanking, blue St. Elmo's fire glowing on their flanks and limbs, seeking blood for a lubricant, robotic vampires of aluminum and steel. ...

3 Periodically Lindsey heard a strange and distant cry, the mournful bleat of some great, mysterious beast. Eventually, even in her semi-delirious condition, she realized that the sound did not originate either in her imagination or in the distance but directly overhead. It was no beast, just the ambulance siren, which was needed only in short bursts to clear what little traffic had ventured onto the snowswept highways.

The ambulance came to a stop sooner than she had expected, but that might be only because her sense of time was as out of whack as her other perceptions. Epstein threw the rear door open while O'Malley released the spring clamps that fixed Lindsey's gurney in place.

When they lifted her out of the van, she was surprised to see that she was not at a hospital in San Bernardino, as she expected to be, but in a parking lot in front of a small shopping center. At that late hour the lot was deserted except for the ambulance and, astonishingly, a large helicopter on the side of which was emblazoned a red cross in a white circle and the words AIR AMBULANCE SERVICE.

The night was still cold, and wind hooted across the blacktop. They were now below the snow line, although just at the base of the mountains and still far from San Bernardino. The ground was bare, and the wheels of the gurney creaked as Epstein and O'Malley rushed Lindsey into the care of the two men waiting beside the chopper.

The engine of the air ambulance was idling. The rotors turned sluggishly.

The mere presence of the craft—and the sense of extreme urgency that it represented—was like a flare of sunlight that burned off some of the dense fog in Lindsey's mind. She realized that either she or Hatch was in worse shape than she had thought, for only a critical case could justify such an unconventional and expensive method of conveyance. And they obviously were going farther than to a hospital in San Bernardino, perhaps to a treatment center specializing in state-of-the-art trauma medicine of one kind or another. Even as that light of understanding came to her, she wished that it could be extinguished, and she despairingly sought the comfort of that mental fog again.

As the chopper medics took charge of her and lifted her into the aircraft, one of them shouted above the engine noise, "But she's alive."

"She's in bad shape," Epstein said.

"Yeah, okay, she looks like shit," the chopper medic said, "but she's still alive. Nyebern's expecting a stiff."

O'Malley said, "It's the other one."

"The husband," Epstein said.

"We'll bring him over," O'Malley said.

Lindsey was aware that a monumental piece of information had been revealed in those few brief exchanges, but she was not clearheaded enough to understand what it was. Or maybe she simply did not want to understand.

As they moved her into the spacious rear compartment of the helicopter, transferred her onto one of their own litters, and strapped her to the vinyl-covered mattress, she sank back into frighteningly corrupted memories of childhood:

. . . *she was nine years old, playing fetch with her dog, Boo, but when the frisky labrador brought the red rubber ball back to her and dropped it at her feet, it was not a ball any longer. It was a throbbing heart, trailing torn arteries and veins. It was pulsing not because it was alive but because a mass of worms and sarcophagus beetles churned within its rotting chambers . . .*

4

The helicopter was airborne. Its movement, perhaps because of the winter wind, was less reminiscent of an aircraft than of a boat tumbling in a bad tide. Nausea uncoiled in Lindsey's stomach.

A medic bent over her, his face masked in shadows, applying a stethoscope to her breast.

Across the cabin, another medic was shouting into a radio headset as he bent over Hatch, talking not to the pilot in the forward compartment but perhaps to a receiving physician at whatever hospital awaited them. His words were sliced into a series of thin sounds by the air-carving rotors overhead, so his voice fluttered like that of a nervous adolescent.

"... minor head injury ... no mortal wounds ... apparent cause of death ... seems to be ... drowning ..."

On the far side of the chopper, near the foot of Hatch's litter, the sliding door was open a few inches, and Lindsey realized the door on her side was not fully closed, either, creating an arctic cross-draught. That also explained why the roar of the wind outside and the clatter of the rotors was so deafening.

Why did they want it so cold?

The medic attending to Hatch was still shouting into his headset: "... mouth-to-mouth ... mechanical resuscitator ... O-2 and CO-2 without results ... epinephrine was ineffective ..."

The real world had become too real, even viewed through her delirium. She didn't like it. Her twisted dreamscapes, in all their mutant horror, were more appealing than the inside of the air ambulance, perhaps because on a subconscious level she was able to exert at least *some* control on her nightmares but none at all on real events.

... she was at her senior prom, dancing in the arms of Joey Delvecchio, the boy with whom she had been going steady in those days. They were under a vast canopy of crepe-paper streamers. She was speckled with sequins of blue and white and yellow light cast off by the revolving crystal-and-mirror chandelier above the dance floor. It was the music of a better age, before rock-'n'-roll started to lose its soul, before disco and New Age and hip-hop, back when Elton John and the Eagles were at their peak, when the Isley Brothers were still recording, the Doobie Brothers, Stevie Wonder, Neil Sedaka making a major comeback, the music still alive, everything and everyone so alive, the world filled with hope and possibilities now long since lost. They were slow-dancing to a Freddy Fender tune reasonably well rendered by a local band, and she was suffused with happiness and a sense of well-being—until she lifted her head from Joey's shoulder and looked up and saw not Joey's face but the rotting countenance of a cadaver, yellow teeth exposed between shriveled black lips, flesh pocked and blistered and oozing, bloodshot eyes bulging and weeping vile fluid from lesions of decay. She tried to scream and pull away from him, but she could only continue to dance, listening to the overly sweet romantic strains of "Before the Next Teardrop Falls," aware that she was seeing Joey as he would be in a few years, after he had died in the Marine-barracks explosion in Lebanon. She felt death leeching from his cold flesh into hers. She knew she had to tear herself from his embrace before that mortal tide filled her. But when she looked desperately around for someone who might help her, she saw that Joey was not the only dead dancer. Sally Ontkeen, who in eight years would succumb to cocaine poisoning, glided by in an advanced stage of decomposition, in the arms of her boyfriend who smiled down on her as if unaware of the corruption of her flesh. Jack Winslow, the school football star who would be killed in a drunken driving accident in less than a year, spun his date past them; his face was swollen, purple tinged with green, and his skull was crushed along the left side as it would be after the wreck. He spoke to

Lindsey and Joey in a raspy voice that didn't belong to Jack Winslow but to a creature on holiday from a graveyard, vocal cords withered into dry strings: "What a night! Man, what a night!"

Lindsey shuddered, but not solely because of the frigid wind that howled through the partly open chopper doors.

The medic, his face still in shadows, was taking her blood pressure. Her left arm was no longer under the blanket. The sleeves of her sweater and blouse had been cut away, exposing her bare skin. The cuff of the sphygmomanometer was wound tightly around her biceps and secured by Velcro strips.

Her shudders were so pronounced that they evidently looked, to the paramedic, as if they might be the muscle spasms that accompanied convulsions. He plucked a small rubber wedge from a nearby supply tray and started to insert it in her mouth to prevent her from biting or swallowing her tongue.

She pushed his hand away. "I'm going to die."

Relieved that she was not having convulsions, he said, "No, you're not that bad, you're okay, you're going to be fine."

He didn't understand what she meant. Impatiently, she said, "We're *all* going to die."

That was the meaning of her dream-distorted memories. Death had been with her from the day she'd been born, always at her side, constant companion, which she had not understood until Jimmy's death five years ago, and which she had not *accepted* until tonight when death took Hatch from her.

Her heart seemed to clutch up like a fist within her breast. A new pain filled her, separate from all the other agonies and more profound. In spite of terror and delirium and exhaustion, all of which she had used as shields against the awful insistence of reality, truth came to her at last, and she was helpless to do anything but accept it.

Hatch had drowned.

Hatch was dead. CPR had not worked.

Hatch was gone forever.

. . . she was twenty-five years old, propped against bed pillows in the maternity ward at St. Joseph's Hospital. The nurse was bringing her a small blanket-wrapped bundle, her baby, her son, James Eugene Harrison, whom she had carried for nine months but had not met, whom she loved with all her heart but had not seen. The smiling nurse gently conveyed the bundle into Lindsey's arms, and Lindsey tenderly lifted aside the satin-trimmed edge of the blue cotton blanket. She saw that she cradled a tiny skeleton with hollow eye sockets, the small bones of its fingers curled in the wanting-needing gesture of an infant. Jimmy had been born with death in him, as everyone was, and in less than five years cancer would claim him. The small, bony mouth of the skeleton-child eased open in a long, slow, silent cry . . .

5 Lindsey could hear the chopper blades carving the night air, but she was no longer inside the craft. She was being wheeled across a parking lot toward a large building with many lighted windows. She thought she ought to know what it was, but she couldn't think clearly, and in fact she didn't care what it was or where she was going or why.

Ahead, a pair of double doors flew open, revealing a space warmed by yellow light, peopled by several silhouettes of men and women. Then Lindsey was rushed into the light and among the silhouettes . . . a long hallway . . . a room that smelled of alcohol and other disinfectants . . . the silhouettes becoming people with faces, then more faces appearing . . . soft but urgent voices . . . hands gripping her, lifting . . . off the gurney, onto a bed . . . tipped back a little, her head below the level of her body . . . rhythmic beeps and clicks issuing from electronic equipment of some kind. . . .

She wished they would just all go away and leave her alone, in peace. Just go away. Turn off the lights as they went. Leave her in darkness. She longed for silence, stillness, peace.

A vile odor with an edge of ammonia assaulted her. It burned her nasal passages, made her eyes pop open and water.

A man in a white coat was holding something under her nose and peering intently into her eyes. As she began to choke and gag on the stench, he took the object away and handed it to a brunette in a white uniform. The pungent odor quickly faded.

Lindsey was aware of movement around her, faces coming and going. She knew that she was the center of attention, an object of urgent inquiry, but she did not—could not manage to—care. It was all more like a dream than her actual dreams had been. A soft tide of voices rose and fell around her, swelling rhythmically like gentle breakers whispering on a sandy shore:

". . . marked paleness of the skin . . . cyanosis of lips, nails, fingertips, lobes of the ears . . ."

". . . weak pulse, very rapid . . . respiration quick and shallow . . ."

". . . blood pressure's so damned low I can't get a reading . . ."

"Didn't those assholes treat her for shock?"

"Sure, all the way in."

"Oxygen, CO-2 mix. And make it fast!"

"Epinephrine?"

"Yeah, prepare it."

"Epinephrine? But what if she has internal injuries? You can't see a hemorrhage if one's there."

"Hell, I gotta take a chance."

Someone put a hand over her face, as if trying to smother her. Lindsey felt something plugging up her nostrils, and for a moment she could not breathe. The curious thing was that she didn't care. Then cool dry air hissed into her nose and seemed to force an expansion of her lungs.

A young blonde, dressed all in white, leaned close, adjusted the inhalator, and smiled winningly. "There you go, honey. Are you getting that?"

The woman was beautiful, ethereal, with a singularly musical voice, back-lit by a golden glow.

A heavenly apparition. An angel.

Wheezing, Lindsey said, "My husband is dead."

"It'll be okay, honey. Just relax, breathe as deeply as you can, everything will be all right."

"No, he's dead," Lindsey said. "Dead and gone, gone forever. Don't you lie to me, angels aren't allowed to lie."

On the other side of the bed, a man in white was swabbing the inside of Lindsey's left elbow with an alcohol-soaked pad. It was icy cold.

To the angel, Lindsey said, "Dead and gone."

Sadly, the angel nodded. Her blue eyes were filled with love, as an angel's eyes should be. "He's gone, honey. But maybe this time that isn't the end of it."

Death was always the end. How could death not be the end?

A needle stung Lindsey's left arm.

"This time," the angel said softly, "there's still a chance. We've got a special program here, a real—"

Another woman burst into the room and interrupted excitedly: "Nye-bern's in the hospital!"

A communal sigh of relief, almost a quiet cheer, swept those gathered in the room.

"He was at dinner in Marina Del Rey when they reached him. He must've driven like a bat out of Hell to get back here this fast."

"You see, dear?" the angel said to Lindsey. "There's a chance. There's still a chance. We'll be praying."

So what? Lindsey thought bitterly. Praying never works for me. Expect no miracles. The dead stay dead, and the living only wait to join them.

Three

1
Guided by procedures outlined by Dr. Jonas Nyebern and kept on file in the Resuscitation Medicine Project office, the Orange County General Hospital emergency staff had prepared an operating room to receive the body of Hatchford Benjamin Harrison. They had gone into action the moment the on-site paramedics in the San Bernardino Mountains had reported, by police-band radio, that the victim had drowned in near-freezing water but had suffered only minor injuries in the accident itself, which made him a perfect subject for Nyebern. By the time the air ambulance was touching down in the hospital parking lot, the usual array of operating-room instruments and devices had been augmented

with a bypass machine and other equipment required by the resuscitation team.

Treatment would not take place in the regular emergency room. Those facilities offered insufficient space to deal with Harrison in addition to the usual influx of patients. Though Jonas Nyebern was a cardiovascular surgeon and the project team was rich with surgical skills, resuscitation procedures seldom involved surgery. Only the discovery of a severe internal injury would require them to cut Harrison, and their use of an operating room was more a matter of convenience than necessity.

When Jonas entered from the surgical hallway after preparing himself at the scrub sinks, his project team was waiting for him. Because fate had deprived him of his wife, daughter, and son, leaving him without family, and because an innate shyness had always inhibited him from making friends beyond the boundaries of his profession, these were not merely his colleagues but the only people in the world with whom he felt entirely comfortable and about whom he cared deeply.

Helga Dorner stood by the instrument cabinets to Jonas's left, in the penumbra of the light that fell from the array of halogen bulbs over the operating table. She was a superb circulating nurse with a broad face and sturdy body reminiscent of any of countless steroid-saturated female Soviet track stars, but her eyes and hands were those of the gentlest Raphaelite Madonna. Patients initially feared her, soon respected her, eventually adored her.

With solemnity that was characteristic in moments like this, Helga did not smile but gave Jonas a thumbs-up sign.

Near the bypass machine stood Gina Delilo, a thirty-year-old RN and surgical technician who chose, for whatever reasons, to conceal her extraordinary competence and sense of responsibility behind a pert, cute, ponytailed exterior that made her seem to be an escapee from one of those old Gidget or beach-party movies that had been popular decades ago. Like the others, Gina was dressed in hospital greens and a string-tied cotton cap that concealed her blond hair, but bright-pink ankle socks sprouted above the elastic-edged cloth boots that covered her shoes.

Flanking the operating table were Dr. Ken Nakamura and Dr. Kari Dovell, two hospital-staff physicians with successful local private practices. Ken was a rare double threat, holding advanced degrees in internal medicine and neurology. Daily experience with the fragility of human physiology drove some doctors to drink and caused others to harden their hearts until they were emotionally isolated from their patients; Ken's healthier defense was a sense of humor that was sometimes twisted but always psychologically healing. Kari, a first-rate specialist in pediatric medicine, was four inches taller than Ken's five-feet-seven, reed-thin where he was slightly pudgy, but she was as quick to laugh as the internist. Sometimes, though, a profound sadness in her eyes troubled Jonas and led him to believe that a cyst of loneliness lay so deep within her that friendship could never provide a scalpel long or sharp enough to excise it.

Jonas looked at each of his four colleagues in turn, but none of them spoke. The windowless room was eerily quiet.

For the most part the team had a curiously passive air, as if disinterested in what was about to happen. But their eyes gave them away, for they were the eyes of astronauts who were standing in the exit bay of an orbiting shuttle on the brink of a space walk: aglow with excitement, wonder, a sense of adventure—and a little fear.

Other hospitals had emergency-room staffs skilled enough at resuscitation medicine to give a patient a fighting chance at recovery, but Orange County General was one of only three centers in all of southern California that could boast a separately funded, cutting-edge project aimed at maximizing the success of reanimation procedures. Harrison was the project's forty-fifth patient in the fourteen months since it had been established, but the manner of his death made him the most interesting. Drowning. Followed by rapidly induced hypothermia. Drowning meant relatively little physical damage, and the chill factor dramatically slowed the rate at which postmortem cell deterioration took place.

More often than not, Jonas and his team had treated victims of catastrophic stroke, cardiac arrest, asphyxiation due to tracheal obstruction, or drug overdose. Those patients usually had suffered at least some irreversible brain damage prior to or at the moment of death, before coming under the care of the Resuscitation Project, compromising their chances of being brought back in perfect condition. And of those who had died from violent trauma of one kind or another, some had been too severely injured to be saved even after being resuscitated. Others had been resuscitated and stabilized, only to succumb to secondary infections that swiftly developed into toxic shock. Three had been dead so long that, once resuscitated, brain damage was either too severe to allow them to regain consciousness or, if they were conscious, too extensive to allow them to lead anything like a normal life.

With sudden anguish and a twinge of guilt, Jonas thought of his failures, of life incompletely restored, of patients in whose eyes he had seen the tortured awareness of their own pathetic condition. . . .

"This time will be different." Kari Dovell's voice was soft, only a whisper, but it shattered Jonas's reverie.

Jonas nodded. He felt considerable affection for these people. For their sake more than his own, he wanted the team to have a major, unqualified success.

"Let's do it," he said.

Even as he spoke, the double doors to the operating room crashed open, and two surgical orderlies rushed in with the dead man on a gurney. Swiftly and skillfully, they transferred the body onto the slightly tilted operating table, treating it with more care and respect than they might have shown a corpse in other circumstances, and then exited.

The team went to work even as the orderlies were heading out of the room. With speed and economy of movement, they scissored the remaining clothes off the dead man, leaving him naked on his back, and attached to him the leads of an electrocardiograph, an electroencephalograph, and a skin-patch digital-readout thermometer.

Seconds were golden. Minutes were beyond price. The longer the man remained dead, the less chance they had of bringing him back with any degree of success whatsoever.

Kari Dovell adjusted the controls of the EKG, sharpening the contrast. For the benefit of the tape recording that was being made of the entire procedure, she repeated what all of them could see: "Flat line. No heartbeat."

"No alpha, no beta," Ken Nakamura added, confirming the absence of all electrical activity in the patient's brain.

Having wrapped the pressure cuff of a sphygmomanometer around the patient's right arm, Helga reported the reading they expected: "No measurable blood pressure."

Gina stood beside Jonas, monitoring the digital-readout thermometer. "Body temperature's forty-six degrees."

"So low!" Kari said, her green eyes widening with surprise as she stared down at the cadaver. "And he must've warmed up at least ten degrees since they pulled him out of that stream. We keep it cool in here, but not *that* cool."

The thermostat was set at sixty-four degrees to balance the comfort of the resuscitation team against the need to prevent the victim from warming too fast.

Looking up from the dead man to Jonas, Kari said, "Cold is good, okay, we want him cold, but not too damned cold. What if his tissues froze and he sustained massive cerebral-cell damage?"

Examining the dead man's toes and then his fingers, Jonas was almost embarrassed to hear himself say, "There's no indication of vesicles—"

"That doesn't prove anything," Kari said.

Jonas knew that what she said was true. They all knew it. There would not have been time for vesicles to form in the dead flesh of frost-bitten fingertips and toes before the man, himself, had died. But, damn it, Jonas did not want to give up before they had even started.

He said, "Still, there's no sign of necrotic tissue—"

"Because the entire patient is necrotic," Kari said, unwilling to let go of it. Sometimes she seemed as ungainly as a spindly-legged bird that, although a master of the air, was out of its element on the land. But at other times, like now, she used her height to advantage, casting an intimidating shadow, looking down at an adversary with a hard gaze that seemed to say better-listen-to-me-or-I-might-peck-your-eyes-out-mister. Jonas was two inches taller than Kari, so she couldn't actually look down at him, but few women were that close to being able to give him even a level-eyed stare, and the effect was the same as if he had been five-feet-two.

Jonas looked at Ken, seeking support.

The neurologist was having none of it. "In fact the body temperature could have fallen below freezing *after* death, then warmed up on the trip here, and there'd be no way for us to tell. You know that, Jonas. The only thing we can say for sure about this guy is that he's deader than Elvis has ever been."

"If he's only forty-six degrees *now . . . ,*" Kari said.

Every cell in the human body is composed primarily of water. The percentage of water differs from blood cells to bone cells, from skin cells to liver cells, but there is always more water than anything else. And when water freezes, it expands. Put a bottle of soda in the freezer to quick-chill it, leave it too long, and you're left with just the exploded contents bristling with shattered glass. Frozen water bursts the walls of brain cells—all body cells—in a similar fashion.

No one on the team wanted to revive Harrison from death if they were assured of bringing back something dramatically less than a whole person. No good physician, regardless of his passion to heal, wanted to battle and defeat death only to wind up with a conscious patient suffering from massive brain damage or one who could be sustained "alive" only in a deep coma with the aid of machines.

Jonas knew that his own greatest weakness as a physician was the extremity of his hatred for death. It was an anger he carried at all times. At moments like this the anger could swell into a quiet fury that affected his judgment. Every patient's death was a personal affront to him. He tended to err on the side of optimism, proceeding with a resuscitation that could have more tragic consequences if it succeeded than if it failed.

The other four members of the team understood his weakness, too. They watched him expectantly.

If the operating room had been tomb-still before, it was now as silent as the vacuum of any lonely place between the stars where God, if He existed, passed judgment on His helpless creations.

Jonas was acutely aware of the precious seconds ticking past.

The patient had been in the operating room less than two minutes. But two minutes could make all the difference.

On the table, Harrison was as dead as any man had ever been. His skin was an unhealthy shade of gray, lips and fingernails and toenails a cyanotic blue, lips slightly parted in an eternal exhalation. His flesh was utterly devoid of the tension of life.

However, aside from the two-inch-long shallow gash on the right side of his forehead, an abrasion on his left jaw, and abrasions on the palms of his hands, he was apparently uninjured. He had been in excellent physical condition for a man of thirty-eight, carrying no more than five extra pounds, with straight bones and well-defined musculature. No matter what might have happened to his brain cells, he *looked* like a perfect candidate for resuscitation.

A decade ago, a physician in Jonas's position would have been guided by the Five-Minute Limit, which then had been acknowledged as the maximum length of time the human brain could go without blood-borne oxygen and suffer no diminution of mental faculties. During the past decade, however, as resuscitation medicine had become an exciting new field, the Five-Minute Limit had been exceeded so often that it was eventually disregarded. With new drugs that acted as free-radical scavengers, machines that could cool and heat blood, massive doses of epinephrine, and other tools, doctors could step well past the Five-Minute Limit and snatch some patients back from deeper regions of death. And hypothermia—extreme cooling of the brain which blocked the swift and ruinous chemical changes in cells following death—could extend the length of time a patient might lie dead yet be successfully revived. Twenty minutes was common. Thirty was not hopeless. Cases of triumphant resuscitation at forty and fifty minutes were on record. In 1988, a two-year-old girl in Utah, plucked from an icy river, was brought back to life without any apparent brain damage after being dead at least sixty-six minutes, and only last year a twenty-year-old woman in Pennsylvania had been revived with all faculties intact seventy minutes after death.

The other four members of the team were still staring at Jonas.

Death, he told himself, is just another pathological state.

Most pathological states could be reversed with treatment.

Dead was one thing. But *cold* and dead was another.

To Gina, he said, "How long's he been dead?"

Part of Gina's job was to serve as liaison, by radio, with the on-site paramedics and make a record of the information most vital to the resuscitation team at this moment of decision. She looked at her watch—a Rolex on an incongruous pink leather band to match her socks—and did not even have to pause to calculate: "Sixty minutes, but they're only guessing how long he was dead in the water before they found him. Could be longer."

"Or shorter," Jonas said.

While Jonas made his decision, Helga rounded the table to Gina's side and, together, they began to study the flesh on the cadaver's left arm, searching for the major vein, just in case Jonas decided to resuscitate. Locating blood vessels in the slack flesh of a corpse was not always easy, since applying a rubber tourniquet would not increase systemic pressure. There *was* no pressure in the system.

"Okay, I'm going to call it," Jonas said.

He looked around at Ken, Kari, Helga, and Gina, giving them one last chance to challenge him. Then he checked his own Timex wristwatch and said, "It's nine-twelve P.M., Monday night, March fourth. The patient, Hatchford Benjamin Harrison, is dead . . . but retrievable."

To their credit, whatever their doubts might have been, no one on the team hesitated once the call had been made. They had the right—and the duty—to advise Jonas as he was making the decision, but once it was made, they put all of their knowledge, skill, and training to work to insure that the "retrievable" part of his call proved correct.

Dear God, Jonas thought, I hope I've done the right thing.

Already Gina had inserted an exsanguination needle into the vein that she and Helga had located. Together they switched on and adjusted the bypass machine, which would draw the blood out of Harrison's body and gradually warm it to one hundred degrees. Once warmed, the blood would be pumped back into the still-blue patient through another tube feeding a needle inserted in a thigh vein.

With the process begun, more urgent work awaited than time to do it. Harrison's vital signs, currently nonexistent, had to be monitored for the first indications of response to therapy. The treatment already provided by the paramedics needed to be reviewed to determine if a previously administered dose of epinephrine—a heart-stimulating hormone—was so large as to rule out giving more of it to Harrison at this time. Meanwhile Jonas pulled up a wheeled cart of medications, prepared by Helga before the body had arrived, and began to calculate the variety and quantity of ingredients for a chemical cocktail of free-radical scavengers designed to retard tissue damage.

"Sixty-one minutes," Gina said, updating them on the estimated length of time that the patient had been dead. "Wow! That's a long time talking to the angels. Getting this one back isn't going to be a weenie roast, boys and girls."

"Forty-eight degrees," Helga reported solemnly, noting the cadaver's body temperature as it slowly rose toward the temperature of the room around it.

Death is just an ordinary pathological state, Jonas reminded himself. Pathological states can usually be reversed.

With her incongruously slender, long-fingered hands, Helga folded a cotton surgical towel over the patient's genitals, and Jonas recognized that she was not merely making a concession to modesty but was performing an act of kindness that expressed an important new attitude toward Harrison. A dead man had no interest in modesty. A dead man did not require kindness. Helga's consideration was a way of saying that she believed this man would once more be one of the living, welcomed back to the brotherhood and sisterhood of humanity, and that he should be treated henceforth with tenderness and compassion and not just as an interesting and challenging prospect for reanimation.

2
The weeds and grass were as high as his knees, lush from an unusually rainy winter. A cool breeze whispered through the meadow. Occasionally bats and night birds passed overhead or swooped low off to one side, briefly drawn to him as if they recognized a fellow predator but immediately repelled when they sensed the terrible difference between him and them.

He stood defiantly, gazing up at the stars shining between the steadily thickening clouds that moved eastward across the late-winter sky. He believed that the universe was a kingdom of death, where life was so rare as to be freakish, a place filled with countless barren planets, a testament not to the creative powers of God but to the sterility of His imagination and the triumph of the forces of darkness aligned against Him. Of the two realities that coexisted in this universe—life and death—life was the smaller and less consequential. As a citizen in the land of the living, your existence was limited to years, months, weeks, days, hours. But as a citizen in the kingdom of the dead, you were immortal.

He lived in the borderland.

He hated the world of the living, into which he had been born. He loathed the pretense to meaning and manners and morals and virtue that the living embraced. The hypocrisy of human interaction, wherein selflessness was publicly championed and selfishness privately pursued, both amused and disgusted him. Every act of kindness seemed, to him, to be performed only with an eye to the payback that might one day be extracted from the recipient.

His greatest scorn—and sometimes fury—was reserved for those who spoke of love and made claims to feeling such a thing. Love, he knew, was like all the other high-minded virtues that family, teachers, and priests blathered about. It didn't exist. It was a sham, a way to control others, a con.

He cherished, instead, the darkness and strange anti-life of the world of the dead in which he belonged but to which he could not yet return. His rightful place was with the damned. He felt at home among those who despised love, who knew that the pursuit of pleasure was the sole purpose of existence. Self was primary. There were no such things as "wrong" and "sin."

The longer he stared at the stars between the clouds, the brighter they appeared, until each pinpoint of light in the void seemed to prick his eyes. Tears of discomfort blurred his vision, and he lowered his gaze to the earth at his feet. Even at night, the land of the living was too bright for the likes of him. He didn't need light to see. His vision had adapted to the perfect blackness of death, to the catacombs of Hell. Light was not merely superfluous to eyes like his; it was a nuisance and, at times, an abomination.

Ignoring the heavens, he walked out of the field, returning to the cracked pavement. His footsteps echoed hollowly through this place that had once been filled with the voices and laughter of multitudes. If he had wanted, he could have moved with the silence of a stalking cat.

The clouds parted and the lunar lamp beamed down, making him wince. On all sides, the decaying structures of his hideaway cast stark and jagged shadows in moonlight that would have seemed wan to anyone else but that, to him, shimmered on the pavement as if it were luminous paint.

He took a pair of sunglasses from an inside pocket of his leather jacket and put them on. That was better.

For a moment he hesitated, not sure what he wanted to do with the rest of the night. He had two basic choices, really: spend the remaining pre-dawn hours with the living or with the dead. This time it was even an easier choice than usual, for in his current mood, he much preferred the dead.

He stepped out of a moon-shadow that resembled a giant, canted, broken wheel, and he headed toward the moldering structure where he kept the dead. His collection.

3 "Sixty-four minutes," Gina said, consulting her Rolex with the pink leather band. "This one could get messy."

Jonas couldn't believe how fast time was passing, just speeding by, surely faster than usual, as if there had been some freak acceleration of the continuum. But it was always the same in situations like this, when the difference between life and death was measured in minutes and seconds.

He glanced at the blood, more blue than red, moving through the clear-plastic exsanguination tube into the purring bypass machine. The average human body contained five liters of blood. Before the resuscitation team was done with Harrison, his five liters would have been repeatedly recycled, heated, and filtered.

Ken Nakamura was at a light board, studying head and chest X rays and body-sonograms that had been taken in the air ambulance during its hundred-eighty-mile-per-hour journey from the base of the San Bernardinos to the hospital in Newport Beach. Kari was bent close to the patient's face, examining his eyes through an ophthalmoscope, checking for indications of dangerous cranial pressure from a buildup of fluid on the brain.

With Helga's assistance, Jonas had filled a series of syringes with large doses of various free-radical neutralizers. Vitamins E and C were effective scavengers and had the advantage of being natural substances, but he also intended to administer a lazeroid—tirilazad mesylate—and phenyl tertiary butyl nitrone.

Free radicals were fast-moving, unstable molecules that ricocheted through the body, causing chemical reactions that damaged most cells with which they came into contact. Current theory held that they were the primary cause of human aging, which explained why natural scavengers like vitamins E and C boosted the immune system and, in long-term users, promoted a more youthful appearance and higher energy levels. Free radicals were a by-product of ordinary metabolic processes and were always present in the system. But when the body was deprived of oxygenated blood for an extended period, even with the protection of hypothermia, huge pools of free radicals were created in excess of anything the body had to deal with normally. When the heart was started again, renewed circulation swept those destructive molecules through the brain, where their impact was devastating.

The vitamin and chemical scavengers would deal with the free radicals before they could cause any irreversible damage. At least that was the hope.

Jonas inserted the three syringes in different ports that fed the main intravenous line in the patient's thigh, but he did not yet inject the contents.

"Sixty-five minutes," Gina said.

A long time dead, Jonas thought.

It was very near the record for a successful reanimation.

In spite of the cool air, Jonas felt sweat breaking out on his scalp, under his thinning hair. He always got too involved, emotional. Some of his colleagues disapproved of his excessive empathy; they believed a judicious perspective was insured by the maintenance of a professional distance between the doctor and those he treated. But no patient was *just* a patient. Every one of them was loved and needed by someone. Jonas was acutely aware that if he failed a patient, he was failing more than one person, bringing pain and suffering to a wide network of relatives and friends. Even when he was treating someone like Harrison, of whom Jonas knew virtually nothing, he began to *imagine* the lives interlinking with that of the patient, and he felt responsible to them as much as he would have if he had known them intimately.

"The guy looks clean," Ken said, turning away from the X rays and sonograms. "No broken bones. No internal injuries."

"But those sonograms were taken after he was dead," Jonas noted, "so they don't show *functioning* organs."

"Right. We'll snap some pictures again when he's reanimated, make sure nothing's ruptured, but it looks good so far."

Straightening up from her examination of the dead man's eyes, Kari Dovell said, "There might be concussion to deal with. Hard to say from what I can see."

"Sixty-six minutes."

"Seconds count here. Be ready, people," Jonas said, although he knew they were ready.

The cool air couldn't reach his head because of his surgical cap, but the sweat on his scalp felt icy. Shivers cascaded through him.

Blood, heated to one hundred degrees, began to move through the clear plastic IV line and into the body through a thigh vein, surging rhythmically to the artificial pulse of the bypass machine.

Jonas depressed the plungers halfway on each of the three syringes, introducing heavy doses of the free-radical scavengers into the first blood passing through the line. He waited less than a minute, then swiftly depressed the plungers all the way.

Helga had already prepared three more syringes according to his instructions. He removed the depleted ones from the IV ports and introduced the full syringes without injecting any of their contents.

Ken had moved the portable defibrillation machine next to the patient. Subsequent to reanimation, if Harrison's heart began to beat erratically or chaotically—fibrillation—it might be coerced into a normal rhythm by the application of an electric shock. That was a last-hope strategy, however, for violent defibrillation could also have a serious adverse effect on a patient who, having been recently brought back from the dead, was in an exceptionally fragile state.

Consulting the digital thermometer, Kari said, "His body temperature's up to only fifty-six degrees."

"Sixty-seven minutes," Gina said.

"Too slow," Jonas said.

"External heat?"

Jonas hesitated.

"Let's go for it," Ken advised.

"Fifty-seven degrees," Kari said.

"At this rate," Helga said worriedly, "we're going to be past eighty minutes before he's anywhere near warm enough for the heart to kick in."

Heating pads had been placed under the operating-table sheet before the patient had been brought into the room. They extended the length of his spine.

"Okay," Jonas said.

Kari clicked the switch on the heating pads.

"But easy," Jonas advised.

Kari adjusted the temperature controls.

They needed to warm the body, but potential problems could arise from a too-rapid reheating. Every resuscitation was a tightrope walk.

Jonas tended to the syringes in the IV ports, administering additional doses of vitamins E and C, tirilazad mesylate, and phenyl tertiary butyl nitrone.

The patient was motionless, pale. He reminded Jonas of a figure in a life-size tableau in some old cathedral: the supine body of Christ sculpted from white marble, rendered by the artist in the position of entombment as He would have rested just prior to the most successful resurrection of all time.

Because Kari Dovell had peeled back Harrison's eyelids for the ophthalmoscopic examination, his eyes were open, staring sightlessly at the ceiling, and Gina was putting artificial tears in them with a dropper to insure that the lenses did not dry out. She hummed "Little Surfer Girl" as she worked. She was a Beach Boys fan.

No shock or fear was visible in the cadaver's eyes, as one might have expected. Instead, they held an expression that was almost peaceful, almost touched by wonder. Harrison looked as if he had seen something, in the moment of death, to lift his heart.

Finishing with the eyedrops, Gina checked her watch. "Sixty-eight minutes."

Jonas had the crazy urge to tell her to shut up, as though time would halt as long as she was not calling it out, minute by minute.

Blood pumped in and out of the bypass machine.

"Sixty-two degrees." Helga spoke so sternly that she might have been chastising the dead man for the laggardly pace of his reheating.

Flat lines on the EKG.

Flat lines on the EEG.

"Come on," Jonas urged. "Come on, come on."

4 He entered the museum of the dead not through one of its upper doors but through the waterless lagoon. In that shallow depression, three gondolas still lay on the cracked concrete. They were ten-passenger models that had long ago been tipped off the heavy chain-drive track along which they'd once carried their happy passengers. Even at night, wearing sunglasses, he could see they did not have the swan-neck prows of real gondolas in Venice, but sported leering gargoyles as figureheads, hand-carved from wood, garishly painted, perhaps fearsome at one time but now cracked, weathered, and peeling. The lagoon doors, which in better days had swung smoothly out of the way at the approach of each gondola, were no longer motorized. One of them was frozen open; the other was closed, but it was hanging from only two of its four corroded hinges. He walked through the open door into a passageway that was far blacker than the night behind him.

He took off the sunglasses. He didn't need them in that gloom.

Neither did he require a flashlight. Where an ordinary man would have been blind, he could see.

The concrete sluiceway, along which the gondolas had once moved, was three feet deep and eight feet wide. A much narrower channel in the sluiceway floor contained the rusted chain-drive mechanism—a long series of blunt, curved, six-inch-high hooks that had pulled the boats forward by engaging the steel loops on the bottoms of their hulls. When the ride had been in operation, those hooks had been concealed by water, contributing to the illusion that the gondolas were actually adrift. Now, dwindling into the dreary realm ahead, they looked like a row of stubby spines on the back of an immense prehistoric reptile.

The world of the living, he thought, is always fraught with deception. Beneath the placid surface, ugly mechanisms grind away at secret tasks.

He walked deeper into the building. The gradual downward slope of the sluiceway was at first barely perceptible, but he was aware of it because he had passed that way many times before.

Above him, to either side of the channel, were concrete service walks, about four feet wide. Beyond them were the tunnel walls, which had been painted black to serve as a non-reflective backdrop for the moments of half-baked theater performed in front of them.

The walkways widened occasionally to form niches, in some places even whole rooms. When the ride had been in operation, the niches had been filled with tableaus meant to amuse or horrify or both: ghosts and goblins, ghouls and monsters, ax-wielding madmen standing over the prostrate bodies of their beheaded victims. In one of the room-sized areas, there had been an elaborate graveyard filled with stalking zombies; in another, a large and convincing flying saucer had disgorged blood-thirsty aliens with a shark's profusion of teeth in their huge heads. The robotic figures had moved, grimaced, reared up, and threatened all passersby with tape-recorded voices, eternally repeating the same brief programmed dramas with the same menacing words and snarls.

No, not eternally. They were gone now, carted away by the official salvagers, by agents of the creditors, or by scavengers.

Nothing was eternal.

Except death.

A hundred feet beyond the entrance doors, he reached the end of the first section of the chain-drive. The tunnel floor, which had been sloping imperceptibly, now tilted down sharply, at about a thirty-five-degree angle, falling away into flawless blackness. Here, the gondolas had slipped free of the blunt hooks in the channel floor and, with a stomach-wrenching lurch, sailed down a hundred-and-fifty-foot incline, knifing into the pool below with a colossal splash that drenched the passengers up front, much to the delight of those fortunate—or smart—enough to get a seat in the back.

Because he was not like ordinary men and possessed certain special powers, he could see part of the way down the incline, even in that utterly lightless environment, although his perception did not extend to the very bottom. His catlike night vision was limited: within a radius of ten or fifteen feet, he could see as clearly as if he stood in daylight; thereafter, objects grew blurry, steadily less distinct, shadowy, until darkness swallowed everything at a distance of perhaps forty or fifty feet.

Leaning backward to retain his balance on the steep slope, he headed down into the bowels of the abandoned funhouse. He was not afraid of what might wait below. Nothing could frighten him any more. After all, he was deadlier and more savage than anything with which this world could threaten him.

Before he descended half the distance to the lower chamber, he detected the odor of death. It rose to him on currents of cool dry air. The stench excited him. No perfume, regardless of how exquisite, even if applied to the tender throat of a lovely woman, could ever thrill him as profoundly as the singular, sweet fragrance of corrupted flesh.

5 Under the halogen lamps, the stainless-steel and white-enameled surfaces of the operating room were a little hard on the eyes, like the geometric configurations of an arctic landscape polished by the glare of a winter sun. The room seemed to have gotten chillier, as if the heat flowing into the dead man was pushing the cold out of him, thereby lowering the air temperature. Jonas Nyebern shivered.

Helga checked the digital thermometer that was patched to Harrison. "Body temperature's up to seventy degrees."

"Seventy-two minutes," Gina said.

"We're going for the brass ring now," Ken said. "Medical history, the *Guinness Book of World Records,* TV appearances, books, movies, T-shirts with our faces on 'em, novelty hats, plastic lawn ornaments in our images."

"Some dogs have been brought back after ninety minutes," Kari reminded him.

"Yeah," Ken said, "but they were *dogs.* Besides, they were so screwed up, they chased bones and buried cars."

Gina and Kari laughed softly, and the joke seemed to break the tension for everyone except Jonas. He could never relax for a moment in the process of a resuscitation, although he knew that it was possible for a physician to get so tightly wound that he was no longer performing at his peak. Ken's ability to vent a little nervous energy was admirable, and in the service of the patient; however, Jonas was incapable of doing likewise in the midst of a battle.

"Seventy-two degrees, seventy-three."

It *was* a battle. Death was the adversary: clever, mighty, and relentless. To Jonas, death was not *just* a pathological state, not merely the inevitable fate of all living things, but actually an entity that walked the world, perhaps not always the robed figure of myth with its skeletal face hidden in the shadows of a cowl, but a very real presence nonetheless, Death with a capital D.

"Seventy-four degrees," Helga said.

Gina said, "Seventy-three minutes."

Jonas introduced more free-radical scavengers into the blood that surged through the IV line.

He supposed that his belief in Death as a supernatural force with a will and consciousness of its own, his certainty that it sometimes walked the earth in an embodied form, his awareness of its presence right now in this room in a cloak of invisibility, would seem like silly superstition to his colleagues. It might even be regarded as a sign of mental imbalance or incipient madness. But Jonas was confident of his sanity. After all, his belief in Death was based on empirical evidence. He had *seen* the hated enemy when he was only seven years old, had heard it speak, had looked into its eyes and smelled its fetid breath and felt its icy touch upon his face.

"Seventy-five degrees."

"Get ready," Jonas said.

The patient's body temperature was nearing a threshold beyond which reanimation might begin at any moment. Kari finished filling a hypodermic syringe with epinephrine, and Ken activated the defibrillation machine to let it build up a charge. Gina opened the flow valve on a tank containing an oxygen–carbon dioxide mixture that had been formulated to the special considerations of resuscitation procedures, and picked up the mask of the pulmonary machine to make sure it was functioning.

"Seventy-six degrees," Helga said, "seventy-seven."

Gina checked her watch. "Coming up on . . . seventy-four minutes."

6 At the bottom of the long incline, he entered a cavernous room as large as an airplane hangar. Hell had once been re-created there, according to the unimaginative vision of an amusement-park designer, complete with gas-jet fires lapping at formed-concrete rocks around the perimeter.

The gas had been turned off long ago. Hell was tar-black now. But not to him, of course.

He moved slowly across the concrete floor, which was bisected by a serpentine channel housing another chain-drive. There, the gondolas had moved through a lake of water made to look like a lake of fire by clever lighting and bubbling air hoses that simulated boiling oil. As he walked, he savored the stench of decay, which grew more exquisitely pungent by the second.

A dozen mechanical demons had once stood on higher formations, spreading immense bat wings, peering down with glowing eyes that periodically raked the passing gondolas with harmless crimson laser beams. Eleven of the demons had been hauled away, peddled to some competing park or sold for scrap. For unknown reasons, one devil remained—a silent and unmoving agglomeration of rusted metal, moth-eaten fabric, torn plastic, and grease-caked hydraulic mechanisms. It was still perched on a rocky spire two-thirds of the way toward the high ceiling, pathetic rather than frightening.

As he passed beneath that sorry funhouse figure, he thought, *I am the only real demon this place has ever known or ever will,* and that pleased him.

Months ago he stopped thinking of himself by his Christian name. He adopted the name of a fiend that he had read about in a book on Satanism. Vassago. One of the three most powerful demon princes of Hell, who answered only to His Satanic Majesty. Vassago. He liked the sound of it. When he said it aloud, the name rolled from his tongue so easily that it seemed as if he'd never answered to anything else.

"Vassago."

In the heavy subterranean silence, it echoed back to him from the concrete rocks: *"Vassago."*

7 "Eighty degrees."

"It should be happening," Ken said.

Surveying the monitors, Kari said, "Flat lines, just flat lines."

Her long, swanlike neck was so slender that Jonas could see her pulse pounding rapidly in her carotid artery.

He looked down at the dead man's neck. No pulse there.

"Seventy-five minutes," Gina announced.

"If he comes around, it's officially a record now," Ken said. "We'll be obligated to celebrate, get drunk, puke on our shoes, and make fools of ourselves."

"Eighty-one degrees."

Jonas was so frustrated that he could not speak—for fear of uttering an obscenity or a low, savage snarl of anger. They had made all the right moves, but they were losing. He hated losing. He hated Death. He hated the limitations of modern medicine, all circumscriptions of human knowledge, and his own inadequacies.

"Eighty-two degrees."

Suddenly the dead man gasped.

Jonas twitched and looked at the monitors.

The EKG showed spastic movement in the patient's heart.

"Here we go," Kari said.

8 The robotic figures of the damned, more than a hundred in Hell's heyday, were gone with eleven of the twelve demons; gone, as well, were the wails of agony and the lamentations that had been broadcast through their speaker-grille mouths. The desolate chamber, however, was not without lost souls. But now it housed something more appropriate than robots, more like the real thing: Vassago's collection.

At the center of the room, Satan waited in all his majesty, fierce and colossal. A circular pit in the floor, sixteen to eighteen feet in diameter, housed a massive statue of the Prince of Darkness himself. He was not shown from the waist down; but from his navel to the tips of his segmented horns, he measured thirty feet. When the funhouse had been in operation, the monstrous sculpture waited in a thirty-five-foot pit, hidden beneath the lake, then periodically surged up out of its lair, water cascading from it, huge eyes afire, monstrous jaws working, sharp teeth gnashing, forked tongue flickering, thundering a warning—"Abandon hope all ye who enter here!"—and then laughing malevolently.

Vassago had ridden the gondolas several times as a boy, when he had been one of the wholly alive, before he had become a citizen of the borderland, and in those days he had been spooked by the handcrafted devil, affected especially by its hideous laugh. If the machinery had overcome years of corrosion and suddenly brought the cackling monster to life again, Vassago would not have been impressed, for he was now old enough and sufficiently experienced to know that Satan was incapable of laughter.

He halted near the base of the towering Lucifer and studied it with a mixture of scorn and admiration. It was corny, yes, a funhouse fake meant to test the bladders of small children and give teenage girls a reason to squeal and cuddle for protection in the arms of their smirking boyfriends. But he had to admit that it was also an inspired creation, because the designer had not opted for the traditional image of Satan as a lean-faced, sharp-nosed, thin-lipped Lothario of troubled souls, hair slicked back from a widow's peak, goatee sprouting absurdly from a pointed chin. Instead, this was a Beast worthy of the title: part reptile, part insect, part humanoid, repulsive enough to command respect, just familiar enough to seem real, alien enough to be awesome. Several years of dust, moisture, and mold had contributed a patina that softened the garish carnival colors and lent it the authority of one of those gigantic stone statues of Egyptian gods found in ancient sand-covered temples, far beneath the desert dunes.

Although he didn't know what Lucifer actually looked like, and though he assumed that the Father of Lies would be far more heart-chilling and formidable than this funhouse version, Vassago found the plastic and poly-foam behemoth sufficiently impressive to make it the center of the secret existence that he led within his hideaway. At the base of it, on the dry concrete floor of the drained lake, he had arranged his collection partly for his own pleasure and amusement but also as an offering to the god of terror and pain.

The naked and decaying bodies of seven women and three men were displayed to their best advantage, as if they were ten exquisite sculptures by some perverse Michelangelo in a museum of death.

9 A single shallow gasp, one brief spasm of the heart muscles, and an involuntary nerve reaction that made his right arm twitch and his fingers open and close like the curling legs of a dying spider—those were the only signs of life the patient exhibited before settling once more into the still and silent posture of the dead.

"Eighty-three degrees," Helga said.

Ken Nakamura wondered: "Defibrillation?"

Jonas shook his head. "His heart's not in fibrillation. It's not beating at all. Just wait."

Kari was holding a syringe. "More epinephrine?"

Jonas stared intently at the monitors. "Wait. We don't want to bring him back only to overmedicate him and precipitate a heart attack."

"Seventy-six minutes," Gina said, her voice as youthful and breathless and perkily excited as if she were announcing the score in a game of beach volleyball.

"Eighty-four degrees."

Harrison gasped again. His heart stuttered, sending a series of spikes across the screen of the electrocardiograph. His whole body shuddered. Then he went flatline again.

Grabbing the handles on the positive and negative pads of the defibrillation machine, Ken looked expectantly at Jonas.

"Eighty-five degrees," Helga announced. "He's in the right thermal territory, and he wants to come back."

Jonas felt a bead of sweat trickle with centipede swiftness down his right temple and along his jaw line. The hardest part was waiting, giving the patient a chance to kick-start himself before risking more punishing techniques of forced reanimation.

A third spasm of heart activity registered as a shorter burst of spikes than the previous one, and it was not accompanied by a pulmonary response as before. No muscle contractions were visible, either. Harrison lay slack and cold.

"He's not able to make the leap," Kari Dovell said.

Ken agreed. "We're gonna lose him."

"Seventy-seven minutes," Gina said.

Not four days in the tomb, like Lazarus, before Jesus had called him forth, Jonas thought, but a long time dead nevertheless.

"Epinephrine," Jonas said.

Kari handed the hypodermic syringe to Jonas, and he quickly administered the dosage through one of the same IV ports that he had used earlier to inject free-radical scavengers into the patient's blood.

Ken lifted the negative and positive pads of the defibrillation machine, and positioned himself over the patient, ready to give him a jolt if it came to that.

Then the massive charge of epinephrine, a powerful hormone extracted from the adrenal glands of sheep and cattle and referred to by some resuscitation specialists as "reanimator juice," hit Harrison as hard as any electrical shock that Ken Nakamura was prepared to give him. The stale breath of the grave exploded from him, he gasped air as if he were still drowning in that icy river, he shuddered violently, and his heart began to beat like that of a rabbit with a fox close on its tail.

10

Vassago had arranged each piece in his macabre collection with more than casual contemplation. They were not simply ten corpses dumped unceremoniously on the concrete. He not only respected death but loved it with an ardor akin to Beethoven's passion for music or Rembrandt's fervent devotion to art. Death, after all, was the gift that Satan had brought to the inhabitants of the Garden, a gift disguised as something prettier; he was the Giver of Death, and his was the kingdom of death everlasting. Any flesh that death had touched was to be regarded with all the reverence that a devout Catholic might reserve for the Eucharist. Just as their god was said to live within that thin wafer of unleavened bread, so the face of Vassago's unforgiving god could be seen everywhere in the patterns of decay and dissolution.

The first body at the base of the thirty-foot Satan was that of Jenny Purcell, a twenty-two-year-old waitress who had worked the evening shift in a re-creation of a 1950s diner, where the jukebox played Elvis Presley and Chuck Berry, Lloyd Price and the Platters, Buddy Holly and Connie Francis and the Everly Brothers. When Vassago had gone in for a burger and a beer, Jenny thought he looked cool in his black clothes, wearing sunglasses indoors at night and making no move to take them off. With his baby-faced good looks given interest by a contrastingly firm set to his jaw and a slight cruel twist to his mouth, and with thick black hair falling across his forehead, he looked a little like a young Elvis. *What's your name,* she asked, and he said, *Vassago,* and she said, *What's your first name,* so he said, *That's it, the whole thing, first and last,* which must have intrigued her, got her imagination going, because she said, *What, you mean like Cher only has one name or Madonna or Sting?* He stared hard at her from behind his heavily tinted sunglasses and said, *Yeah—you have a problem with that?* She didn't have a problem. In fact she was attracted to him. She said he was "different," but only later did she discover just *how* different he really was.

Everything about Jenny marked her as a slut in his eyes, so after killing her with an eight-inch stiletto that he drove under her rib cage and into her heart, he arranged her in a posture suitable for a sexually profligate woman. Once he had stripped her naked, he braced her in a sitting position with her thighs spread wide and knees drawn up. He bound her slender wrists to her shins to keep her upright. Then he used strong lengths of cord to pull her head forward and down farther than she could have managed to do while alive, brutally compressing her midriff; he anchored the cords around her thighs, so she was left eternally looking up the cleft between her legs, contemplating her sins.

Jenny had been the first piece in his collection. Dead for about nine months, trussed up like a ham in a curing barn, she was withered now, a mummified husk, no longer of interest to worms or other agents of decomposition. She did not stink as she had once stunk.

Indeed, in her peculiar posture, having contracted into a ball as she had decayed and dried out, she resembled a human being so little that it was difficult to think of her as ever having been a living person, therefore equally difficult to think of her as a dead person. Consequently, death seemed no longer to reside in her remains. To Vassago, she had ceased to be a corpse and had become merely a curious object, an impersonal thing that might always have been inanimate. As a result, although she was the start of his collection, she was now of minimal interest to him.

He was fascinated solely with death and the dead. The living were of interest to him only insofar as they carried the ripe promise of death within them.

11 The patient's heart oscillated between mild and severe tachycardia, from a hundred and twenty to over two hundred and thirty beats per minute, a transient condition resulting from the epinephrine and hypothermia. Except it wasn't acting like a transient condition. Each time the pulse rate declined, it did not subside as far as it had previously, and with each new acceleration, the EKG showed escalating arrhythmia that could lead only to cardiac arrest.

No longer sweating, calmer now that the decision to fight Death had been made and was being acted upon, Jonas said, "Better hit him with it."

No one doubted to whom he was speaking, and Ken Nakamura pressed the cold pads of the defibrillation machine to Harrison's chest, bracketing his heart. The electrical discharge caused the patient to bounce violently against the table, and a sound like an iron mallet striking a leather sofa— *wham!*—slammed through the room.

Jonas looked at the electrocardiograph just as Kari read the meaning of the spikes of light moving across the display: "Still two hundred a minute but the rhythm's there now . . . steady . . . steady."

Similarly, the electroencephalograph showed alpha and beta brain waves within normal parameters for an unconscious man.

"There's self-sustained pulmonary activity," Ken said.

"Okay," Jonas decided, "let's respirate him and make sure he's getting enough oxygen in those brain cells."

Gina immediately put the oxygen mask on Harrison's face.

"Body temperature's at ninety degrees," Helga reported.

The patient's lips were still somewhat blue, but that same deathly hue had faded from under his fingernails.

Likewise, his muscle tone was partially restored. His flesh no longer had the flaccidity of the dead. As feeling returned to Harrison's deep-chilled extremities, his punished nerve endings excited a host of tics and twitches.

His eyes rolled and jiggled under his closed lids, a sure sign of REM sleep. He was dreaming.

"One hundred and twenty beats a minute," Kari said, "and declining . . . completely rhythmic now . . . very steady."

Gina consulted her watch and let her breath out in a *whoosh* of amazement. "Eighty minutes."

"Sonofabitch," Ken said wonderingly, "that beats the record by ten."

Jonas hesitated only a brief moment before checking the wall clock and making the formal announcement for the benefit of the tape recorder: "Patient successfully resuscitated as of nine-thirty-two Monday evening, March fourth."

A murmur of mutual congratulations accompanied by smiles of relief was as close as they would get to a triumphant cheer of the sort that might have been heard on a real battleground. They were not restrained by modesty but by a keen awareness of Harrison's tenuous condition. They had won the battle with Death, but their patient had not yet regained consciousness. Until he was awake and his mental performance could be tested and evaluated, there was a chance that he had been reanimated only to live out a life of anguish and frustration, his potential tragically circumscribed by irreparable brain damage.

12

Enraptured by the spicy perfume of death, at home in the subterranean bleakness, Vassago walked admiringly past his collection. It encircled one-third of the colossal Lucifer.

Of the male specimens, one had been taken while changing a flat tire on a lonely section of the Ortega Highway at night. Another had been asleep in his car in a public-beach parking lot. The third had tried to pick up Vassago at a bar in Dana Point. The dive hadn't even been a gay hangout; the guy had just been drunk, desperate, lonely—and careless.

Nothing enraged Vassago more than the sexual needs and excitement of others. He had no interest in sex any more, and he never raped any of the women he killed. But his disgust and anger, engendered by the mere perception of sexuality in others, were not a result of jealousy, and did not spring from any sense that his impotency was a curse or even an unfair burden. No, he was glad to be free of lust and longing. Since becoming a citizen of the borderland and accepting the promise of the grave, he did not regret the loss of desire. Though he was not entirely sure *why* the very thought of sex could sometimes throw him into a rage, why a flirtatious wink or a short skirt or a sweater stretched across a full bosom could incite him to torture and homicide, he suspected that it was because sex and life were inextricably entwined. Next to self-preservation, the sex drive was, they said, the most powerful human motivator. Through sex, life was created. Because he hated life in all its gaudy variety, hated it with such intensity, it was only natural that he would hate sex as well.

He preferred to kill women because society encouraged them, more than men, to flaunt their sexuality, which they did with the assistance of makeup, lipstick, alluring scents, revealing clothes, and coquettish behavior. Besides, from a woman's womb came new life, and Vassago was sworn to destroy life wherever he could. From women came the very thing he loathed in himself: the spark of life that still sputtered in him and prevented him from moving on to the land of the dead, where he belonged.

Of the remaining six female specimens in his collection, two had been housewives, one a young attorney, one a medical secretary, and two college students. Though he had arranged each corpse in a manner fitting the personality, spirit, and weaknesses of the person who had once inhabited it, and though he had considerable talent for cadaver art, making especially clever use of a variety of props, he was far more pleased by the effect he had achieved with one of the students than with all of the others combined.

He stopped walking when he reached her.

He regarded her in the darkness, pleased by his work. . . .

MARGARET . . .

He first saw her during one of his restless late-night rambles, in a dimly lighted bar near the university campus, where she was sipping diet cola, either because she was not old enough to be served beer along with her friends or because she was not a drinker. He suspected the latter.

She looked singularly wholesome and uncomfortable in the smoke and din of the tavern. Even from halfway across the room, judging by her reactions to her friends and her body language, Vassago could see that she was a shy girl struggling hard to fit in with the crowd, even though in her heart she knew that she would never entirely belong. The roar of liquor-amplified conversation, the clink and clatter of glasses, the thunderous juke-box music of Madonna and Michael Jackson and Michael Bolton, the stink of cigarettes and stale beer, the moist heat of college boys on the make—none of that touched her. She sat in the bar but existed apart from it, unstained by it, filled with more secret energy than that entire roomful of young men and women combined.

She was so vital, she seemed to glow. Vassago found it hard to believe that the ordinary, sluggish blood of humanity moved through her veins. Surely, instead, her heart pumped the distilled essence of life itself.

Her vitality drew him. It would be enormously satisfying to snuff such a brightly burning flame of life.

To learn where she lived, he followed her home from the bar. For the next two days, he stalked the campus, gathering information about her as diligently as a real student might have researched a term paper.

Her name was Margaret Ann Campion. She was a senior, twenty years old, majoring in music. She could play the piano, flute, clarinet, guitar, and almost any other instrument she took a fancy to learn. Perhaps the best-known and most-admired student in the music program, she was also widely considered to possess an exceptional talent for composition. An essentially shy person, she made a point of forcing herself out of her shell, so music was not her only interest. She was on the track team, the second-fastest woman in their lineup, a spirited competitor; she wrote about music and movies for the student paper; and she was active in the Baptist church.

Her astonishing vitality was evident not merely in the joy with which she wrote and played music, not just in the almost spiritual aura that Vassago had seen in the bar, but also in her physical appearance. She was incomparably beautiful, with the body of a silver-screen sex goddess and the face of a saint. Clear skin. Perfect cheekbones. Full lips, a generous mouth, a beatific smile. Limpid blue eyes. She dressed modestly in an attempt to conceal the sweet fullness of her breasts, the contrasting narrowness of her waist, the firmness of her buttocks, and the long supple lines of her legs. But he was certain that when he stripped her, she would be revealed for what he had known her to be when he had first glimpsed her: a prodigious breeder, a hot furnace of life in which eventually other life of unparalleled brightness would be conceived and shaped.

He wanted her dead.

He wanted to stop her heart and then hold her for hours, feeling the heat of life radiate out of her, until she was cold.

This one murder, it seemed to him, might at last earn him passage out of the borderland in which he lived and into the land of the dead and damned, where he belonged, where he longed to be.

Margaret made the mistake of going alone to a laundry room in her apartment complex at eleven o'clock at night. Many of the units were leased to financially comfortable senior citizens and, because they were near the University of California at Irvine, to pairs and trios of students who shared the rent. Maybe the tenant mix, the fact that it was a safe and friendly neighborhood, and the abundance of landscape and walkway lighting all combined to give her a false sense of security.

When Vassago entered the laundry room, Margaret had just begun to put her dirty clothes into one of the washing machines. She looked at him with a smile of surprise but with no apparent concern, though he was dressed all in black and wearing sunglasses at night.

She probably thought he was just another university student who favored an eccentric look as a way of proclaiming his rebellious spirit and intellectual superiority. Every campus had a slew of the type, since it was easier to *dress* as a rebellious intellectual than *be* one.

"Oh, I'm sorry, Miss," he said, "I didn't realize anyone was in here."

"That's okay. I'm only using just one washer," she said. "There're two others."

"No, I already did my laundry, then back at the apartment when I took it out of the basket, I was missing one sock, so I figure it's got to be in one of the washers or dryers. But I didn't mean to get in your way. Sorry about that."

She smiled a little broader, maybe because she thought it funny that a would-be James Dean, black-clad rebel without a cause, would choose to be so polite—or would do his own laundry and chase down lost socks.

By then he was beside her. He hit her in the face—two hard, sharp punches that knocked her unconscious. She crumpled onto the vinyl-tile floor as if she were a pile of laundry.

Later, in the dismantled Hell under the moldering funhouse, when she regained consciousness and found herself naked on the concrete floor and effectively blind in those lightless confines, tied hand and foot, she did not attempt to bargain for her life as some of the others had done. She didn't offer her body to him, didn't pretend to be turned on by his savagery or the power that he wielded over her. She didn't offer him money, or claim to understand and sympathize with him in a pathetic attempt to convert him from nemesis to friend. Neither did she scream nor weep nor wail nor curse. She was different from the others, for she found hope and comfort in a quiet, dignified, unending chain of whispered prayers. But she never prayed to be delivered from her tormentor and returned to the world out of which she had been torn—as if she knew that death was inevitable. Instead, she prayed that her family would be given the strength to cope with the loss of her, that God would take care of her two younger sisters, and even that her murderer would receive divine grace and mercy.

Vassago swiftly came to loathe her. He knew that love and mercy were nonexistent, just empty words. *He* had never felt love, neither during his time in the borderland nor when he had been one of the living. Often, however, he had pretended to love someone—father, mother, a girl—to get what he wanted, and they had always been deceived. Being deceived into believing that love existed in others, when it didn't exist in you, was a sign of fatal weakness. Human interaction was nothing but a game, after all, and the ability to see through deception was what separated the good players from the inept.

To show her that he could not be deceived and that her god was powerless, Vassago rewarded her quiet prayers with a long and painful death. At last she *did* scream. But her screams were not satisfying, for they were only the sounds of physical agony; they did not reverberate with terror, rage, or despair.

He thought he would like her better when she was dead, but even then he still hated her. For a few minutes he held her body against him, feeling the heat drain from it. But the chilly advance of death through her flesh was not as thrilling as it should have been. Because she had died with an unbroken faith in life everlasting, she had cheated Vassago of the satisfaction of seeing the awareness of death in her eyes. He pushed her limp body aside in disgust.

NOW, TWO WEEKS after Vassago had finished with her, Margaret Campion knelt in perpetual prayer on the floor of that dismantled Hell, the most recent addition to his collection. She remained upright because she was lashed to a length of steel rebar which he had inserted into a hole he had drilled in the concrete. Naked, she faced away from the giant, funhouse devil. Though she had been Baptist, a crucifix was clasped in her dead hands because Vassago liked the image of the crucifix better than a simple cross; it was turned upside down, with Christ's thorn-prickled head toward the floor. Margaret's own head had been cut off then resewn to her neck with obsessive care. Even though her body was turned away from Satan, she faced toward him in denial of the crucifix held irreverently in her hands. Her posture was symbolic of hypocrisy, mocking her pretense to faith, love, and life everlasting.

Although Vassago hadn't received nearly as much pleasure from murdering Margaret as from what he had done to her after she was dead, he was still pleased to have made her acquaintance. Her stubbornness, stupidity, and self-deception had made her death less satisfying for him than it should have been, but at least the aura he had seen around her in the bar was quenched. Her irritating vitality was drained away. The only energy her body harbored was that of the multitudinous carrion-eaters that teemed within her, consuming her flesh and bent on reducing her to a dry husk like Jenny, the waitress, who rested at the other end of the collection.

As he studied Margaret, a familiar need arose in him. Finally the need became a compulsion. He turned away from his collection, retracing his path across the huge room, heading for the ramp that led up to the entrance tunnel. Ordinarily, selecting another acquisition, killing it, and arranging it in the most aesthetically satisfying pose would have left him quiescent and sated for as much as a month. But after less than two weeks, he was compelled to find another worthy sacrifice.

Regretfully, he ascended the ramp, out of the purifying scent of death, into air tainted with the odors of life, like a vampire driven to hunt the living though preferring the company of the dead.

13 At ten-thirty, almost an hour after Harrison was resuscitated, he remained unconscious. His body temperature was normal. His vital signs were good. And though the patterns of alpha and beta brain waves were those of a man in a profound sleep, they were not obviously indicative of anything as deep as a coma.

When Jonas finally declared the patient out of immediate danger and ordered him moved to a private room on the fifth floor, Ken Nakamura and Kari Dovell elected to go home. Leaving Helga and Gina with the patient, Jonas accompanied the neurologist and the pediatrician to the scrub sinks, and eventually as far as the door to the staff parking lot. They discussed Harrison and what procedures might have to be performed on him in the morning, but for the most part they shared inconsequential small talk about hospital politics and gossip involving mutual acquaintances, as if they had not just participated in a miracle that should have made such banalities impossible.

Beyond the glass door, the night looked cold and inhospitable. Rain had begun to fall. Puddles were filling every depression in the pavement, and in the reflected glow of the parking-lot lamps, they looked like shattered mirrors, collections of sharp silvery shards.

Kari leaned against Jonas, kissed his cheek, clung to him for a moment. She seemed to want to say something but was unable to find the words. Then she pulled back, turned up the collar of her coat, and went out into the wind-driven rain.

Lingering after Kari's departure, Ken Nakamura said, "I hope you realize she's a perfect match for you."

Through the rain-streaked glass door, Jonas watched the woman as she hurried toward her car. He would have been lying if he had said that he never looked at Kari as a woman. Though tall, rangy, and a formidable presence, she was also feminine. Sometimes he marveled at the delicacy of her wrists, at her swanlike neck that seemed too gracefully thin to support her head. Intellectually and emotionally she was stronger than she looked. Otherwise she couldn't have dealt with the obstacles and challenges that surely had blocked her advance in the medical profession, which was still dominated by men for whom—in some cases—chauvinism was less a character trait than an article of faith.

Ken said, "All you'd have to do is ask her, Jonas."

"I'm not free to do that," Jonas said.

"You can't mourn Marion forever."

"It's only been two years."

"Yeah, but you have to step back into life sometime."

"Not yet."

"Ever?"

"I don't know."

Outside, halfway across the parking lot, Kari Dovell had gotten into her car.

"She won't wait forever," Ken said.

"Goodnight, Ken."

"I can take a hint."

"Good," Jonas said.

Smiling ruefully, Ken pulled open the door, letting in a gust of wind that spat jewel-clear drops of rain on the gray tile floor. He hurried out into the night.

Jonas turned away from the door and followed a series of hallways to the elevators. He went up to the fifth floor.

He hadn't needed to tell Ken and Kari that he would spend the night in the hospital. They knew he always stayed after an apparently successful reanimation. To them, resuscitation medicine was a fascinating new field, an interesting sideline to their primary work, a way to expand their professional knowledge and keep their minds flexible; every success was deeply satisfying, a reminder of why they had become physicians in the first place—to heal. But it was more than that to Jonas. Each reanimation was a battle won in an endless war with Death, not just a healing act but an act of defiance, an angry fist raised in the face of fate. Resuscitation medicine was his love, his passion, his definition of himself, his only reason for arising in the morning and getting on with life in a world that had otherwise become too colorless and purposeless to endure.

He had submitted applications and proposals to half a dozen universities, seeking to teach in their medical schools in return for the establishment of a resuscitation-medicine research facility under his supervision, for which he felt able to raise a sizable part of the financing. He was well-known and widely respected both as a cardiovascular surgeon and a reanimation specialist, and he was confident that he would soon obtain the position he wanted. But he was impatient. He was no longer satisfied with supervising reanimations. He wanted to study the effects of short-term death on human cells, explore the mechanisms of free-radicals and free-radical scavengers, test his own theories, and find new ways to evict Death from those in whom it had already taken up tenancy.

On the fifth floor, at the nurses' station, he learned that Harrison had been taken to 518. It was a semi-private room, but an abundance of empty beds in the hospital insured that it would be effectively maintained as a private unit as long as Harrison was likely to need it.

When Jonas entered 518, Helga and Gina were finishing with the patient, who was in the bed farthest from the door and nearest the rain-spotted window. They had gotten him into a hospital gown and hooked him to another electrocardiograph with a telemetry function that would reproduce his heart rhythms on a monitor at the nurses' station. A bottle of clear fluid hung from a rack beside the bed, feeding an IV line into the patient's left arm, which was already beginning to bruise from other intravenous injections administered by the paramedics earlier in the evening; the clear fluid was glucose enriched with an antibiotic to prevent dehydration and to guard against one of the many infections that could undo everything that had been achieved in the resuscitation room. Helga had smoothed Harrison's hair with a comb that she was now tucking away in the nightstand drawer. Gina was delicately applying a lubricant to his eyelids to prevent them from sticking together, a danger with comatose patients who spent long periods of time without opening their eyes or even blinking and who sometimes suffered from diminished lachrymal-gland secretion.

"Heart's still steady as a metronome," Gina said when she saw Jonas. "I have a hunch, before the end of the week, this one's going to be out playing golf, dancing, doing whatever he wants." She brushed at her bangs, which were an inch too long and hanging in her eyes. "He's a lucky man."

"One hour at a time," Jonas cautioned, knowing too well how Death liked to tease them by pretending to retreat, then returning in a rush to snatch away their victory.

When Gina and Helga left for the night, Jonas turned off all the lights. Illuminated only by the faint fluorescent wash from the corridor and the green glow of the cardiac monitor, room 518 was replete with shadows.

It was silent, too. The audio signal on the EKG had been turned off, leaving only the rhythmically bouncing light endlessly making its way across the screen. The only sounds were the soft moans of the wind at the window and the occasional faint tapping of rain against the glass.

Jonas stood at the foot of the bed, looking at Harrison for a moment. Though he had saved the man's life, he knew little about him. Thirty-eight years old. Five-ten, a hundred and sixty pounds. Brown hair, brown eyes. Excellent physical condition.

But what of the inner person? Was Hatchford Benjamin Harrison a good man? Honest? Trustworthy? Faithful to his wife? Was he reasonably free of envy and greed, capable of mercy, aware of the difference between right and wrong?

Did he have a kind heart?

Did he love?

In the heat of a resuscitation procedure, when seconds counted and there was too much to be done in too short a time, Jonas never dared to think about the central ethical dilemma facing any doctor who assumed the role of reanimator, for to think of it then might have inhibited him to the patient's disadvantage. Afterward, there was time to doubt, to wonder.... Although a physician was morally committed and professionally obligated to saving lives wherever he could, were all lives worth saving? When Death took an evil man, wasn't it wiser—and more ethically correct—to let him stay dead?

If Harrison was a bad man, the evil that he committed upon resuming his life after leaving the hospital would in part be the responsibility of Jonas Nyebern. The pain Harrison caused others would to some extent stain Jonas's soul, as well.

Fortunately, this time the dilemma seemed moot. Harrison appeared to be an upstanding citizen—a respected antique dealer, they said—married to an artist of some reputation, whose name Jonas recognized. A good artist had to be sensitive, perceptive, able to see the world more clearly than most people saw it. Didn't she? If she was married to a bad man, she would know it, and she wouldn't remain married to him. This time there was every reason to believe that a life had been saved that *should* have been saved.

Jonas only wished his actions had always been so correct.

He turned away from the bed and took two steps to the window. Five stories below, the nearly deserted parking lot lay under hooded pole lamps. The falling rain churned the puddles, so they appeared to be boiling, as if a subterranean fire consumed the blacktop from underneath.

He could pick out the spot where Kari Dovell's car had been parked, and he stared at it for a long time. He admired Kari enormously. He also found her attractive. Sometimes he dreamed of being with her, and it was a surprisingly comforting dream. He could admit to wanting her at times, as well, and to being pleased by the thought that she might also want him. But he did not *need* her. He needed nothing but his work, the satisfaction of occasionally beating Death, and the—

"Something's . . . out . . . there . . ."

The first word interrupted Jonas's thoughts, but the voice was so thin and soft that he didn't immediately perceive the source of it. He turned around, looking toward the open door, assuming the voice had come from the corridor, and only by the third word did he realize that the speaker was Harrison.

The patient's head was turned toward Jonas, but his eyes were focused on the window.

Moving quickly to the side of the bed, Jonas glanced at the electrocardiograph and saw that Harrison's heart was beating fast but, thank God, rhythmically.

"Something's . . . out there," Harrison repeated.

His eyes were not, after all, focused on the window itself, on nothing so close as that, but on some distant point in the stormy night.

"Just rain," Jonas assured him.

"No."

"Just a little winter rain."

"Something bad," Harrison whispered.

Hurried footsteps echoed in the corridor, and a young nurse burst through the open door, into the nearly dark room. Her name was Ramona Perez, and Jonas knew her to be competent and concerned.

"Oh, Doctor Nyebern, good, you're here. The telemetry unit, his heartbeat—"

"Accelerated, yes, I know. He just woke up."

Ramona came to the bed and switched on the lamp above it, revealing the patient more clearly.

Harrison was still staring beyond the rain-spotted window, as if oblivious of Jonas and the nurse. In a voice even softer than before, heavy with weariness, he repeated: "Something's out there." Then his eyes fluttered sleepily, and fell shut.

"Mr. Harrison, can you hear me?" Jonas asked.

The patient did not answer.

The EKG showed a quickly de-accelerating heartbeat: from one-forty to one-twenty to one hundred beats a minute.

"Mr. Harrison?"

Ninety per minute. Eighty.

"He's asleep again," Ramona said.

"Appears to be."

"Just sleeping, though," she said. "No question of it being a coma now."

"Not a coma," Jonas agreed.

"And he was speaking. Did he make sense?"

"Sort of. But hard to tell," Jonas said, leaning over the bed railing to study the man's eyelids, which fluttered with the rapid movement of the eyes under them. REM sleep. Harrison was dreaming again.

Outside, the rain suddenly began to fall harder than before. The wind picked up, too, and keened at the window.

Ramona said, "The words I heard were clear, not slurred."

"No. Not slurred. And he spoke some complete sentences."

"Then he's not aphasic," she said. "That's terrific."

Aphasia, the complete inability to speak or understand spoken or written language, was one of the most devastating forms of brain damage resulting from disease or injury. Thus affected, a patient was reduced to using gestures to communicate, and the inadequacy of pantomime soon cast him into deep depression, from which there was sometimes no coming back.

Harrison was evidently free of that curse. If he was also free of paralysis, and if there were not *too* many holes in his memory, he had a good chance of eventually getting out of bed and leading a normal life.

"Let's not jump to conclusions," Jonas said. "Let's not build up any false hopes. He still has a long way to go. But you can enter on his record that he regained consciousness for the first time at eleven-thirty, two hours after resuscitation."

Harrison was murmuring in his sleep.

Jonas leaned over the bed and put his ear close to the patient's lips, which were barely moving. The words were faint, carried on his shallow exhalations. It was like a spectral voice heard on an open radio channel, broadcast from a station halfway around the world, bounced off a freak inversion layer high in the atmosphere and filtered through so much space and bad weather that it sounded mysterious and prophetic in spite of being less than half-intelligible.

"What's he saying?" Ramona asked.

With the howl of the storm rising outside, Jonas was unable to catch enough of Harrison's words to be sure, but he thought the man was repeating what he'd said before: "Something's . . . out there. . . ."

Abruptly the wind shrieked, and rain drummed against the window so hard that it seemed certain to shatter the glass.

14 Vassago liked the rain. The storm clouds had plated over the sky, leaving no holes through which the too-bright moon could gaze. The downpour also veiled the glow of streetlamps and the headlights of oncoming cars, moderated the dazzle of neon signs, and in general softened the Orange County night, making it possible for him to drive with more comfort than could be provided by his sunglasses alone.

He had traveled west from his hideaway, then north along the coast, in search of a bar where the lights might be low and a woman or two available for consideration. A lot of places were closed Mondays, and others didn't appear too active that late at night, between the half-hour and the witching hour.

At last he found a lounge in Newport Beach, along the Pacific Coast Highway. It was a tony joint with a canopy to the street, rows of miniature white lights defining the roof line, and a sign advertising DANCING WED THRU SAT/JOHNNY WILTON'S BIG BAND. Newport was the most affluent city in the county, with the world's largest private yacht harbor, so almost any establishment that pretended to a monied clientele most likely had one. Beginning mid-week, valet parking was probably provided, which would not have been good for his purposes, since a valet was a potential witness, but on a rainy Monday no valet was in sight.

He parked in the lot beside the club, and as he switched off the engine, the seizure hit him. He felt as if he'd received a mild but sustained electrical shock. His eyes rolled back in his head, and for a moment he thought he was having convulsions, because he was unable to breathe or swallow. An involuntary moan escaped him. The attack lasted only ten or fifteen seconds, and ended with three words that seemed to have been spoken *inside* his head: *Something's . . . out . . . there . . .* It was not just a random thought sparked by some short-circuiting synapse in his brain, for it came to him in a distinct *voice*, with the timbre and inflection of spoken words as distinguished from thoughts. Not his own voice, either, but that of a stranger. He had an overpowering sense of another presence in the car, as well, as if a spirit had passed through some curtain between worlds to visit with him, an alien presence that was real in spite of being invisible. Then the episode ended as abruptly as it had begun.

He sat for a while, waiting for a reoccurrence.

Rain hammered on the roof.

The car ticked and pinged as the engine cooled down.

Whatever had happened, it was over now.

He tried to understand the experience. Had those words—*Something's out there*—been a warning, a psychic premonition? A threat? To what did it refer?

Beyond the car, there seemed to be nothing special about the night. Just rain. Blessed darkness. The distorted reflections of electric lights and signs shimmered on the wet pavement, in puddles, and in the torrents pouring along the overflowing gutters. Sparse traffic passed on Pacific Coast Highway, but as far as he could see, no one was on foot—and he could see as well as any cat.

After a while he decided that he would understand the episode when he was *meant* to understand it. Nothing was to be gained by brooding over it. If it was a threat, from whatever source, it did not trouble him. He was incapable of fear. That was the best thing about having left the world of the living, even if he was temporarily stuck in the borderland this side of death: nothing in existence held any terror for him.

Nevertheless, that inner voice had been one of the strangest things he had ever experienced. And he was not exactly without a store of strange experiences with which to compare it.

He got out of his silver Camaro, slammed the door, and walked to the club entrance. The rain was cold. In the blustering wind, the fronds of the palm trees rattled like old bones.

15 Lindsey Harrison was also on the fifth floor, at the far end of the main corridor from her husband. Little of the room was revealed when Jonas entered and approached the side of the bed, for there was not even the green light from a cardiac monitor. The woman was barely visible.

He wondered if he should try to wake her, and was surprised when she spoke:

"Who're you?"

He said, "I thought you were asleep."

"Can't sleep."

"Didn't they give you something?"

"It didn't help."

As in her husband's room, the rain drove against the window with sullen fury. Jonas could hear torrents cascading through the confines of a nearby aluminum downspout.

"How do you feel?" he asked.

"How the hell do you think I feel?" She tried to infuse the words with anger, but she was too exhausted and too depressed to manage it.

He put down the bed railing, sat on the edge of the mattress, and held out one hand, assuming that her eyes were better adapted to the gloom than his were. "Give me your hand."

"Why?"

"I'm Jonas Nyebern. I'm a doctor. I want to tell you about your husband, and somehow I think it'll be better if you'll just let me hold your hand."

She was silent.

"Humor me," he said.

Although the woman believed her husband to be dead, Jonas did not mean to torment her by withholding his report of the resuscitation. From experience, he knew that good news of this sort could be as shocking to the recipient as bad news; it had to be delivered with care and sensitivity. She had been mildly delirious upon admission to the hospital, largely as a result of exposure and shock, but that condition had been swiftly remedied with the administration of heat and medication. She had been in possession of all her faculties for a few hours now, long enough to absorb her husband's death and to begin to find her way toward a tentative accommodation of her loss. Though deep in grief and far from adjusted to her widowhood, she had by now found a ledge on the emotional cliff down which she had plunged, a narrow perch, a precarious stability—from which he was about to knock her loose.

Still, he might have been more direct with her if he'd been able to bring her unalloyed good news. Unfortunately, he could not promise that her husband was going to be entirely his former self, unmarked by his experience, able to reenter his old life without a hitch. They would need hours, perhaps days, in which to examine and evaluate Harrison before they could hazard a prediction as to the likelihood of a full recovery. Thereafter, weeks or months of physical and occupational therapy might lie ahead for him, with no guarantee of effectiveness.

Jonas was still waiting for her hand. At last she offered it diffidently.

In his best bedside manner, he quickly outlined the basics of resuscitation medicine. When she began to realize why he thought she needed to know about such an esoteric subject, her grip on his hand suddenly grew tight.

16 In room 518, Hatch foundered in a sea of bad dreams that were nothing but disassociated images melding into one another without even the illogical narrative flow that usually shaped nightmares. Wind-whipped snow. A huge Ferris wheel sometimes bedecked with festive lights, sometimes dark and broken and ominous in a night seething with rain. Groves of scarecrow trees, gnarled and coaly, stripped leafless by winter. A beer truck angled across a snowswept highway. A tunnel with a concrete floor that sloped down into perfect blackness, into something unknown that filled him with heart-bursting dread. His lost son, Jimmy, lying sallow-skinned against hospital sheets, dying of cancer. Water, cold and deep, impenetrable as ink, stretching to all horizons, with no possible escape. A naked woman, her head on backwards, hands clasping a crucifix . . .

Frequently he was aware of a faceless and mysterious figure at the perimeter of the dreamscapes, dressed in black like some grim reaper, moving in such fluid harmony with the shadows that he might have been only a shadow himself. At other times, the reaper was not part of the scene but seemed to be the viewpoint through which it was observed, as if Hatch was looking out through the eyes of another—eyes that beheld the world with all the compassionless, hungry, calculating practicality of a graveyard rat.

For a time, the dream took on more of a narrative quality, wherein Hatch found himself running along a train-station platform, trying to catch up with a passenger car that was slowly pulling away on the outbound track. Through one of the train windows, he saw Jimmy, gaunt and hollow-eyed in the grip of his disease, dressed only in a hospital gown, peering sadly at Hatch, one small hand raised as he waved goodbye, goodbye, goodbye. Hatch reached desperately for the vertical railing beside the boarding steps at the end of Jimmy's car, but the train picked up speed; Hatch lost ground; the steps slipped away. Jimmy's pale, small face lost definition and finally vanished as the speeding passenger car dwindled into the terrible nothingness beyond the station platform, a lightless void of which Hatch only now became aware. Then another passenger car began to glide past him (*clackety-*

clack, clackety-clack), and he was startled to see Lindsey seated at one of the windows, looking out at the platform, a lost expression on her face. Hatch called to her—"Lindsey!"—but she did not hear or see him, she seemed to be in a trance, so he began to run again, trying to board her car *(clackety-clack, clackety-clack),* which drew away from him as Jimmy's had done. "Lindsey!" His hand was inches from the railing beside the boarding stairs. . . . Suddenly the railing and stairs vanished, and the train was not a train any more. With the eerie fluidity of all changes in all dreams, it became a roller coaster in an amusement park, heading out on the start of a thrill ride. (*Clackety-clack.*) Hatch came to the end of the platform without being able to board Lindsey's car, and she rocketed away from him, up the first steep hill of the long and undulant track. Then the last car in the caravan passed him, close behind Lindsey's. It held a single passenger. The figure in black—around whom shadows clustered like ravens on a cemetery fence—sat in front of the car, head bowed, his face concealed by thick hair that fell forward in the fashion of a monk's hood. (*Clackety-clack!*) Hatch shouted at Lindsey, warning her to look back and be aware of what rode in the car behind her, pleading with her to be careful and hold on tight, for God's sake, *hold on tight!* The caterpillar procession of linked cars reached the crest of the hill, hung there for a moment as if time had been suspended, then disappeared in a scream-filled plummet down the far side.

RAMONA PEREZ, THE night nurse assigned to the fifth-floor wing that included room 518, stood beside the bed, watching her patient. She was worried about him, but she was not sure that she should go looking for Dr. Nyebern yet.

According to the heart monitor, Harrison's pulse was in a highly fluctuant state. Generally it ranged between a reassuring seventy to eighty beats per minute. Periodically, however, it raced as high as a hundred and forty. On the positive side, she observed no indications of serious arrhythmia.

His blood pressure was affected by his accelerated heartbeat, but he was in no apparent danger of stroke or cerebral hemorrhage related to spiking hypertension, because his systolic reading was never dangerously high.

He was sweating profusely, and the circles around his eyes were so dark, they appeared to have been applied with actors' greasepaint. He was shivering in spite of the blankets piled on him. The fingers of his left hand—exposed because of the intravenous feed—spasmed occasionally, though not forcefully enough to disturb the needle inserted just below the crook of his elbow.

In a whisper he repeated his wife's name, sometimes with considerable urgency: "Lindsey . . . Lindsey . . . *Lindsey, no!*"

Harrison was dreaming, obviously, and events in a nightmare could elicit physiological responses every bit as much as waking experiences.

Finally Ramona decided that the accelerated heartbeat was solely the result of the poor man's bad dreams, not an indication of genuine cardiovascular destabilization. He was in no danger. Nevertheless, she remained at his bedside, watching over him.

17

Vassago sat at a window table overlooking the harbor. He had been in the lounge only five minutes, and already he suspected it was not good hunting grounds. The atmosphere was all wrong. He wished he had not ordered a drink.

No dance music was provided on Monday nights, but a pianist was at work in one corner. He played neither gutless renditions of '30s and '40s songs nor the studiedly bland arrangements of easy-listening rock-'n'-roll that rotted the brains of regular lounge patrons. But he spun out the equally noxious repetitive melodies of New Age numbers composed for those who found elevator music too complex and intellectually taxing.

Vassago preferred music with a hard beat, fast and driving, something that put his teeth on edge. Since becoming a citizen of the borderland, he could not take pleasure in most music, for its orderly structures irritated him. He could tolerate only music that was atonal, harsh, unmelodious. He responded to jarring key changes, thunderously crashing chords, and squealing guitar riffs that abraded the nerves. He enjoyed discord and broken patterns of rhythm. He was excited by music that filled his mind with images of blood and violence.

To Vassago, the scene beyond the big windows, because of its beauty, was as displeasing as the lounge music. Sailboats and motor yachts crowded one another at the private docks along the harbor. They were tied up, sails furled, engines silent, wallowing only slightly because the harbor was well protected and the storm was not particularly ferocious. Few of the wealthy owners actually lived aboard, regardless of the size of the craft or amenities, so lights glowed at only a few of the portholes. Rain, here and there transmuted into quicksilver by the dock lights, hammered the boats, beaded on their brightwork, drizzled like molten metal down their masts and across their decks and out of their scuppers. He had no tolerance for prettiness, for postcard scenes of harmonious composition, because they seemed false, a lie about what the world was really like. He was drawn, instead, to visual discord, jagged shapes, malignant and festering forms.

With its plush chairs and low amber lighting, the lounge was too soft for a hunter like him. It dulled his killing instincts.

He surveyed the patrons, hoping to spot an object of the quality suitable for his collection. If he saw something truly superb that excited his acquisitional fever, even the stultifying atmosphere would not be able to sap his energy.

A few men sat at the bar, but they were of no interest to him. The three men in his collection had been his second, fourth, and fifth acquisitions, taken because they had been vulnerable and in lonely circumstances that allowed him to overpower them and take them away without being seen. He had no aversion to killing men, but preferred women. Young women. He liked to get them before they could breed more life.

The only really young people among the customers were four women in their twenties who were seated by the windows, three tables away from him. They were tipsy and a little giddy, hunched over as if sharing gossip, talking intently, periodically bursting into gales of laughter.

One of them was lovely enough to engage Vassago's hatred of beautiful things. She had enormous chocolate-brown eyes, and an animal grace that reminded him of a doe. He dubbed her "Bambi." Her raven hair was cut into short wings, exposing the lower halves of her ears.

They were exceptional ears, large but delicately formed. He thought he might be able to do something interesting with them, and he continued to watch her, trying to decide if she was up to his standards.

Bambi talked more than her friends, and she was the loudest of the group. Her laugh was the loudest, as well, a jackass braying. She *was* exceptionally attractive, but her incessant chatter and annoying laughter spoiled the package. Clearly, she loved the sound of her own voice.

She'd be vastly improved, he thought, if she were to be stricken deaf and mute.

Inspiration seized him, and he sat up straighter in his chair. By removing her ears, tucking them into her dead mouth, and sewing her lips shut, he would be neatly symbolizing the fatal flaw in her beauty. It was a vision of such simplicity, yet such power, that—

"One rum and Coke," the waitress said, putting a glass and paper cocktail napkin on the table in front of Vassago. "You want to run a tab?"

He looked up at her, blinking in confusion. She was a stout middle-aged woman with auburn hair. He could see her quite clearly through his sunglasses, but in his fever of creative excitement, he had difficulty placing her.

Finally he said, "Tab? Uh, no. Cash, thank you, ma'am."

When he took out his wallet, it didn't feel like a wallet at all but like one of Bambi's ears might feel. When he slid his thumb back and forth across the smooth leather, he felt not what was there but what might soon be available for his caress: delicately shaped ridges of cartilage forming the auricula and pinna, the graceful curves of the channels that focused sound waves inward toward the tympanic membrane. . . .

He realized the waitress had spoken to him again, stating the price of his drink, and then he realized that it was the second time she had done so. He had been fingering his wallet for long, delicious seconds, daydreaming of death and disfigurement.

He fished out a crisp bill without looking at it, and handed it to her.

"This is a hundred," she said. "Don't you have anything smaller?"

"No, ma'am, sorry," he said, impatient now to be rid of her, "that's it."

"I'll have to go back to the bar to get this much change."

"Okay, yeah, whatever. Thank you, ma'am."

As she started away from his table, he returned his attention to the four young women—only to discover that they were leaving. They were nearing the door, pulling on their coats as they went.

He started to rise, intending to follow them, but he froze when he heard himself say, "Lindsey."

He didn't call out the name. No one in the bar heard him say it. He was the only one who reacted, and his reaction was one of total surprise.

For a moment he hesitated with one hand on the table, one on the arm of his chair, halfway to his feet. While he was paralyzed in that posture of indecisiveness, the four young women left the lounge. Bambi became of less interest to him than the mysterious name—"Lindsey"—so he sat down.

He did not know anyone named Lindsey.

He had *never* known anyone named Lindsey.

It made no sense that he would suddenly speak the name aloud.

He looked out the window at the harbor. Hundreds of millions of dollars of ego-gratification rose and fell and wallowed side to side on the rolling water. The sunless sky was another sea above, as cold and merciless as the one below. The air was full of rain like millions of gray and silver threads, as if nature was trying to sew the ocean to the heavens and thereby obliterate the narrow space between, where life was possible. Having been one of the living, one of the dead, and now one of the living dead, he had seen himself as the ultimate sophisticate, as experienced as any man born of woman could ever hope to be. He had assumed that the world held nothing new for him, had nothing to teach him. Now this. First the seizure in the car: *Something's out there!* And now Lindsey. The two experiences were different, because he heard no voice in his head the second time, and when he spoke it was with his own familiar voice and not that of a stranger. But both events were so peculiar that he knew they were linked. As he gazed at the moored boats, the harbor, and the dark world beyond, it began to seem more mysterious to him than it had in ages.

He picked up his rum and Coke. He took a long swallow of it.

As he was putting the drink down, he said, "Lindsey."

The glass rattled against the table, and he almost knocked it over, because the name surprised him again. He hadn't spoken it aloud to ponder the meaning of it. Rather, it had burst from him as before, a bit more breathlessly this time and somewhat louder.

Interesting.

The lounge seemed to be a magical place for him.

He decided to settle down for a while and wait to see what might happen next.

When the waitress arrived with his change, he said, "I'd like another drink, ma'am." He handed her a twenty. "This'll take care of it, and please keep the change."

Happy with the tip, she hurried back to the bar.

Vassago turned to the window again, but this time he looked at his own reflection in the glass instead of at the harbor beyond. The dim lights of the lounge threw insufficient glare on the pane to provide him with a detailed image. In that murky mirror, his sunglasses did not register well. His face appeared to have two gaping eye sockets like those of a fleshless skull. The illusion pleased him.

In a husky whisper not loud enough to draw the attention of anyone else in the lounge, but with more urgency than before, he said, "Lindsey, no!"

He had not anticipated that outburst any more than the previous two, but it did not rattle him. He had quickly adapted to the fact of these mysterious events, and had begun to try to understand them. Nothing could surprise him for long. After all, he had been to Hell and back, both to the real Hell and the one beneath the funhouse, so the intrusion of the fantastic into real life did not frighten or awe him.

He drank a third rum and Coke. When more than an hour passed without further developments, and when the bartender announced the last round of the night, Vassago left.

The need was still with him, the need to murder and create. It was a fierce heat in his gut that had nothing to do with the rum, such a steely tension in his chest that his heart might have been a clockwork mechanism with its spring wound to the breaking point. He wished that he had gone after the doe-eyed woman whom he had named Bambi.

Would he have removed her ears when she was dead at last—or while she was still alive?

Would she have been capable of understanding the artistic statement he was making as he sewed her lips shut over her full mouth? Probably not. None of the others had the wit or insight to appreciate his singular talent.

In the nearly deserted parking lot, he stood in the rain for a while, letting it soak him and extinguish some of the fire of his obsession. It was nearly two in the morning. Not enough time remained, before dawn, to do any hunting. He would have to return to his hideaway without an addition to his collection. If he were to get any sleep during the coming day and be prepared to hunt with the next nightfall, he had to dampen his blazing creative drive.

Eventually he began to shiver. The heat within him gave way to a relentless chill. He raised one hand, touched his cheek. His face felt cold, but his fingers were colder, like the marble hand of a statue of David that he'd admired in a memorial garden at Forest Lawn Cemetery when he had still been one of the living.

That was better.

As he opened the car door, he looked around once more at the rain-riven night. This time of his own volition, he said, "Lindsey?"

No answer.

Whoever she might be, she was not yet destined to cross his path.

He would have to be patient. He was mystified, therefore fascinated and curious. But whatever was happening would happen at its own pace. One of the virtues of the dead was patience, and though he was still half-alive, he knew he could find within himself the strength to match the forbearance of the deceased.

18 Early Tuesday morning, an hour after dawn, Lindsey could sleep no more. She ached in every muscle and joint, and what sleep she'd gotten had not lessened her exhaustion by any noticeable degree. She did not want sedatives. Unable to bear any further delay, she insisted they take her to Hatch's room. The charge nurse cleared it with Jonas Nyebern, who was still in the hospital, then wheeled Lindsey down the hall to 518.

Nyebern was there, red-eyed and rumpled. The sheets on the bed nearest the door were not turned back, but they were wrinkled, as if the doctor had stretched out to rest at least once during the night.

By now Lindsey had learned enough about Nyebern—some of it from him, much of it from the nurses—to know that he was a local legend. He had been a busy cardiovascular surgeon, but over the past two years, after losing his wife and two children in some kind of horrible accident, he had devoted steadily less time to surgery and more to resuscitation medicine. His commitment to his work was too strong to be called mere dedication. It was more of an obsession. In a society that was struggling to emerge from three decades of self-indulgence and me-firstism, it was easy to admire a man as selflessly committed as Nyebern, and everyone did seem to admire him.

Lindsey, for one, admired the hell out of him. After all, he had saved Hatch's life.

His weariness betrayed only by his bloodshot eyes and the rumpled condition of his clothes, Nyebern moved swiftly to pull back the privacy curtain that surrounded the bed nearest the window. He took the handles of Lindsey's wheelchair and rolled her to her husband's bedside.

The storm had passed during the night. Morning sun slanted through the slats of the Levolor blinds, striping the sheets and blankets with shadow and golden light.

Hatch lay beneath that faux tiger skin, only one arm and his face exposed. Although his skin was painted with the same jungle-cat camouflage as the bedding, his extreme pallor was evident. Seated in the wheelchair, regarding Hatch at an odd angle through the bed railing, Lindsey grew queasy at the sight of an ugly bruise that spread from the stitched gash on his forehead. But for the proof of the cardiac monitor and the barely perceptible rise-and-fall of Hatch's chest as he breathed, she would have assumed he was dead.

But he was alive, *alive*, and she felt a tightness in her chest and throat that presaged tears as surely as lightning was a sign of oncoming thunder. The prospect of tears surprised her, quickening her breath.

From the moment their Honda had gone over the brink and into the ravine, through the entire physical and emotional ordeal of the night just passed, Lindsey had never cried. She didn't pride herself on stoicism; it was just the way she was.

No, strike that.

It was just the way she had to become during Jimmy's bout with cancer. From the day of diagnosis until the end, her boy had taken nine months to die, as long as she had taken to lovingly shape him within her womb. Every day of that dying, Lindsey had wanted nothing more than to curl up in bed with the covers over her head and cry, just let the tears pour forth until all the moisture in her body was gone, until she dried up and crumbled into dust and ceased to exist. She *had* wept, at first. But her tears frightened Jimmy, and she realized that any expression of her inner turmoil was an unconscionable self-indulgence. Even when she cried in private, Jimmy knew it later; he had always been perceptive and sensitive beyond his years, and his disease seemed to make him more acutely aware of everything. Current theory of immunology gave considerable weight to the importance of a positive attitude, laughter, and confidence as weapons in the battle against life-threatening illness. So she had learned to suppress her terror at the prospect of losing him. She had given him laughter, love, confidence, courage—and never a reason to doubt her conviction that he would beat the malignancy.

By the time Jimmy died, Lindsey had become so successful at repressing her tears that she could not simply turn them on again. Denied the release that easy tears might have given her, she spiraled down into a lost time of despair. She dropped weight—ten pounds, fifteen, twenty—until she was emaciated. She could not be bothered to wash her hair or look after her complexion or press her clothes. Convinced that she had failed Jimmy, that she had encouraged him to rely on her but then had not been special enough to help him reject his disease, she did not believe she deserved to take pleasure from food, from her appearance, a book, a movie, music, from anything. Eventually, with much patience and kindness, Hatch helped her see that her insistence on taking responsibility for an act of blind fate was, in its way, as much a disease as Jimmy's cancer had been.

Though she had still not been able to cry, she had climbed out of the psychological hole she'd dug for herself. Ever since, however, she had lived on the rim of it, her balance precarious.

Now, her first tears in a long, long time were surprising, unsettling. Her eyes stung, became hot. Her vision blurred. Disbelieving, she raised one shaky hand to touch the warm tracks on her cheeks.

Nyebern plucked a Kleenex from a box on the nightstand and gave it to her.

That small kindness affected her far out of proportion to the consideration behind it, and a soft sob escaped her.

"Lindsey . . ."

Because his throat was raw from his ordeal, his voice was hoarse, barely more than a whisper. But she knew at once who had spoken to her, and that it was not Nyebern.

She wiped hastily at her eyes with the Kleenex and leaned forward in the wheelchair until her forehead touched the cold bed railing. Hatch's head was turned toward her. His eyes were open, and they looked clear, alert.

"Lindsey . . ."

He had found the strength to push his right hand out from under the blankets, stretching it toward her.

She reached between the railings. She took his hand in hers.

His skin was dry. A thin bandage was taped over his abraded palm. He was too weak to give her hand more than the faintest squeeze, but he was warm, blessedly warm, and alive.

"You're crying," Hatch said.

She was, too, harder than ever, a storm of tears, but she was smiling through them. Grief had not been able to free her first tears in five terrible years but joy *had* at last unleashed them. She was crying for joy, which seemed right, seemed healing. She felt a loosening of long-sustained tensions in her heart, as if the knotted adhesions of old wounds were dissolving, all because Hatch was alive, had been dead but was now alive.

If a miracle couldn't lift the heart, what could?

Hatch said, "I love you."

The storm of tears became a flood, oh God, an ocean, and she heard herself blubber "I love you" back at him, then she felt Nyebern put a hand on her shoulder comfortingly, another small kindness that seemed huge, which only made her cry harder. But she was laughing even as she was weeping, and she saw that Hatch was smiling, too.

"It's okay," Hatch said hoarsely. "The worst . . . is over. The worst is . . . behind us now. . . ."

19

During the daylight hours, when he stayed beyond the reach of the sun, Vassago parked the Camaro in an underground garage that had once been filled with electric trams, carts, and lorries used by the park-maintenance crew. All of those vehicles were long gone, reclaimed by creditors. The Camaro stood alone in the center of that dank, windowless space.

From the garage, Vassago descended wide stairs—the elevators had not operated in years—to an even deeper subterranean level. The entire park was built on a basement that had once contained the security headquarters with scores of video monitors able to reveal every niche of the grounds, a ride-control center that had been an even more complex high-tech nest of computers and monitors, carpentry and electrical shops, a staff cafeteria, lockers and changing rooms for the hundreds of costumed employees working each shift, an emergency infirmary, business offices, and much more.

Vassago passed the door to that level without hesitating and continued down to the sub-basement at the very bottom of the complex. Even in the dry sands of southern California, the concrete walls exuded a damp lime smell at that depth.

No rats fled before him, as he had expected during his first descent into those realms many months ago. He had seen no rats at all, anywhere, in all the weeks he had roamed the tenebrous corridors and silent rooms of that vast structure, though he would not have been averse to sharing space with them. He liked rats. They were carrion-eaters, revelers in decay, scurrying janitors that cleaned up in the wake of death. Maybe they had never invaded the cellars of the park because, after its closure, the place had been pretty much stripped bare. It was all concrete, plastic, and metal, nothing biodegradable for rats to feed on, a little dusty, yes, with some crumpled paper here and there, but otherwise as sterile as an orbiting space station and of no interest to rodents.

Eventually rats might find his collection in Hell at the bottom of the funhouse and, having fed, spread out from there. Then he would have some suitable company in the bright hours when he could not venture out in comfort.

At the bottom of the fourth and last flight of stairs, two levels below the underground garage, Vassago passed through a doorway. The door was missing, as were virtually all the doors in the complex, hauled off by the salvagers and resold for a few bucks apiece.

Beyond was an eighteen-foot-wide tunnel. The floor was flat with a yellow stripe painted down the center, as if it were a highway—which it had been, of sorts. Concrete walls curved up to meet and form the ceiling.

Part of that lowest level was comprised of storerooms that had once held huge quantities of supplies. Styrofoam cups and burger packages, cardboard popcorn boxes and french-fry holders, paper napkins and little foil packets of ketchup and mustard for the many snack stands scattered over the grounds. Business forms for the offices. Packages of fertilizer and cans of insecticide for the landscape crew. All of that—and everything else a small city might need—had been removed long ago. The rooms were empty.

A network of tunnels connected the storage chambers to elevators that led upward into all the main attractions and restaurants. Goods could be delivered—or repairmen conveyed—throughout the park without disturbing the paying customers and shattering the fantasy they had paid to experience. Numbers were painted on the walls every hundred feet, to mark routes, and at intersections there were even signs with arrows to provide better directions:

◄HAUNTED HOUSE
◄ALPINE CHALET RESTAURANT
COSMIC WHEEL ►
BIG FOOT MOUNTAIN ►

Vassago turned right at the next intersection, left at the one after that, then right again. Even if his extraordinary vision had not permitted him to see in those obscure byways, he would have been able to follow the route he desired, for by now he knew the desiccated arteries of the dead park as well as he knew the contours of his own body.

Eventually he came to a sign—FUNHOUSE MACHINERY—beside an elevator. The doors of the elevator were gone, as were the cab and the lift mechanism, sold for reuse or for scrap. But the shaft remained, dropping about four feet below the floor of the tunnel, and leading up through five stories of darkness to the level that housed security and ride-control and park offices, on to the lowest level of the funhouse where he kept his collection, then to the second and third floors of that attraction.

He slipped over the edge, into the bottom of the elevator shaft. He sat on the old mattress he had brought in to make his hideaway more comfortable.

When he tilted his head back, he could see only a couple of floors into the unlighted shaft. The rusted steel bars of a service ladder dwindled up into the gloom.

If he climbed the ladder to the lowest level of the funhouse, he would come out in a service room behind the walls of Hell, from which the machinery operating the gondola chain-drive had been accessed and repaired—before it had been carted away forever.

A door from that chamber, disguised on the far side as a concrete boulder, opened into the now-dry lake of Hades, from which Lucifer towered.

He was at the deepest point of his hideaway, four feet more than two stories below Hell. There, he felt at home as much as it was possible for him to feel at home anywhere. Out in the world of the living, he moved with the confidence of a secret master of the universe, but he never felt as if he belonged there. Though he was not actually afraid of anything any more, a trace current of anxiety buzzed through him every minute that he spent beyond the stark, black corridors and sepulchral chambers of his hideaway.

After a while he opened the lid of a sturdy plastic cooler with a Styrofoam lining, in which he kept cans of root beer. He had always liked root beer. It was too much trouble to keep ice in the cooler, so he just drank the soda warm. He didn't mind.

He also kept snack foods in the cooler: Mars bars, Reese's peanut butter cups, Clark Bars, a bag of potato chips, packages of peanut-butter-and-cheese crackers, Mallomars, and Oreo cookies. When he had crossed into the borderland, something had happened to his metabolism; he seemed to be able to eat anything he wanted and burn it off without gaining weight or turning soft. And what he wanted to eat, for some reason he didn't understand, was what he had liked when he'd been a kid.

He opened a root beer and took a long, warm swallow.

He withdrew a single cookie from the bag of Oreos. He carefully separated the two chocolate wafers without damaging them. The circle of white icing stuck entirely to the wafer in his left hand. That meant he was going to be rich and famous when he grew up. If it had stuck to the one in his right hand, it would have meant that he was going to be famous but not necessarily rich, which could mean just about anything from being a rock-'n'-roll star to an assassin who would take out the President of the United States. If some of the icing stuck to both wafers, that meant you had to eat another cookie or risk having no future at all.

As he licked the sweet icing, letting it dissolve slowly on his tongue, he stared up the empty elevator shaft, thinking about how interesting it was that he had chosen the abandoned amusement park for his hideaway when the world offered so many dark and lonely places from which to choose. He had been there a few times as a boy, when the park was still in operation, most recently eight years ago, when he had been twelve, little more than a year before the operation closed down. On that most special evening of his childhood, he had committed his first murder there, beginning his long romance with death. Now he was back.

He licked away the last of the icing.

He ate the first chocolate wafer. He ate the second.

He took another cookie out of the bag.

He sipped the warm root beer.

He wished he were dead. Fully dead. It was the only way to begin his existence on the Other Side.

"If wishes were cows," he said, "we'd eat steak every day, wouldn't we?"

He ate the second cookie, finished the root beer, then stretched out on his back to sleep.

Sleeping, he dreamed. They were peculiar dreams of people he had never seen, places he had never been, events that he had never witnessed. Water all around him, chunks of floating ice, snow sheeting through a hard wind. A woman in a wheelchair, laughing and weeping at the same time. A hospital bed, banded by shadows and stripes of golden sunlight. The woman in the wheelchair, laughing and weeping. The woman in the wheelchair, laughing. The woman in the wheelchair. The woman.

In the fields of life, a harvest
sometimes comes far out of season,
when we thought the earth was old
and could see no earthly reason
to rise for work at break of dawn,
and put our muscles to the test.
With winter here and autumn gone,
it just seems best to rest, to rest.
But under winter fields so cold,
wait the dormant seeds of seasons
unborn, and so the heart does hold
hope that heals all bitter lesions.
In the fields of life, a harvest.

—THE BOOK OF COUNTED SORROWS

▶ ▶ ▶

Part Two

Alive Again

Four

1 Hatch felt as if time had slipped backward to the fourteenth century, as if he were an accused infidel on trial for his life during the Inquisition.

Two priests were present in the attorney's office. Although only of average height, Father Jiminez was as imposing as any man a foot taller, with jet-black hair and eyes even darker, in a black clerical suit with a Roman collar. He stood with his back to the windows. The gently swaying palm trees and blue skies of Newport Beach behind him did not lighten the atmosphere in the mahogany-paneled, antique-filled office where they were gathered, and in silhouette Jiminez was an ominous figure. Father Duran, still in his twenties and perhaps twenty-five years younger than Father Jiminez, was thin, with ascetic features and a pallid complexion. The young priest appeared to be enthralled by a collection of Meiji Period Satsuma vases, incensers, and bowls in a large display case at the far end of the office, but Hatch could not escape the feeling that Duran was faking interest in the Japanese porcelains and was actually furtively observing him and Lindsey where they sat side by side on a Louis XVI sofa.

Two nuns were present, as well, and they seemed, to Hatch, more threatening than the priests. They were of an order that favored the voluminous, old-fashioned habits not seen so often these days. They wore starched wimples, their faces framed in ovals of white linen that made them look especially severe. Sister Immaculata, who was in charge of St. Thomas's Home for Children, looked like a great black bird of prey perched on the armchair to the right of the sofa, and Hatch would not have been surprised if she had suddenly let out a screaky cry, leapt into flight with a great flap of her robes, swooped around the room, and dive-bombed him with the intention of pecking off his nose. Her executive assistant was a somewhat younger, intense nun who paced ceaselessly and had a stare more penetrating than a steel-cutting laser beam. Hatch had temporarily forgotten her name and thought of her as The Nun with No Name, because she reminded him of Clint Eastwood playing The *Man* with No Name in those old spaghetti Westerns.

He was being unfair, more than unfair, a little irrational due to a world-class case of nerves. Everyone in the attorney's office was there to help him and Lindsey. Father Jiminez, the rector of St. Thomas's Church, who raised much of the annual budget of the orphanage headed by Sister Immaculata, was really no more ominous than the priest in *Going My Way,* a Latino Bing Crosby, and Father Duran seemed sweet-tempered and shy. In reality, Sister Immaculata looked no more like a bird of prey than she did a stripper, and The Nun with No Name had a genuine and almost constant smile that more than compensated for whatever negative emotions one might choose to read into her piercing stare. The priests and nuns tried to keep a light conversation going; Hatch and Lindsey were, in fact, the ones who were too tense to be as sociable as the situation required.

So much was at stake. That was what made Hatch jumpy, which was unusual, because he was ordinarily the most mellow man to be found outside of the third hour of a beer-drinking contest. He wanted the meeting to go well because his and Lindsey's happiness, their future, the success of their new life depended on it.

Well, that was not true, either. That was overstating the case again.

He couldn't help it.

Since he had been resuscitated more than seven weeks ago, he and Lindsey had undergone an emotional sea change together. The long, smothering tide of despair, which had rolled over them upon Jimmy's death, abruptly abated. They realized they were still together only by virtue of a medical miracle. Not to be thankful for that reprieve, not to fully enjoy the borrowed time they had been given, would have made them ungrateful to both God and their physicians. More than that—it would have been stupid. They had been right to mourn Jimmy, but somewhere along the way, they had allowed grief to degenerate into self-pity and chronic depression, which had not been right at all.

They had needed Hatch's death, reanimation, and Lindsey's near death to jolt them out of their deplorable habit of gloom, which told him that they were more stubborn than he had thought. The important thing was that they *had* been jolted and were determined to get on with their lives at last.

To both of them, getting on with life meant having a child in the house again. The desire for a child was not a sentimental attempt to recapture the mood of the past, and it wasn't a neurotic need to replace Jimmy in order to finish getting over his death. They were just good with kids; they liked kids; and giving of themselves to a child was enormously satisfying.

They had to adopt. That was the hitch. Lindsey's pregnancy had been troubled, and her labor had been unusually long and painful. Jimmy's birth was a near thing, and when at last he made it into the world, the doctors informed Lindsey that she would not be capable of having any more children.

The Nun with No Name stopped pacing, pulled up the voluminous sleeve of her habit, and looked at her wristwatch. "Maybe I should go see what's keeping her."

"Give the child a little more time," Sister Immaculata said quietly. With one plump white hand, she smoothed the folds of her habit. "If you go to check on her, she'll feel you don't trust her to be able to take care of herself. There's nothing in the ladies' restroom that she can't deal with herself. I doubt she even had the need to use it. She probably just wanted to be alone a few minutes before the meeting, to settle her nerves."

To Lindsey and Hatch, Father Jiminez said, "Sorry about the delay."

"That's okay," Hatch said, fidgeting on the sofa. "We understand. We're a little nervous ourselves."

Initial inquiries made it clear that a lot—a veritable *army*—of couples were waiting for children to become available for adoption. Some had been kept in suspense for two years. After being childless for five years already, Hatch and Lindsey didn't have the patience to go on the bottom of anyone's waiting list.

They were left with only two options, the first of which was to attempt to adopt a child of another race, black or Asian or Hispanic. Most would-be adoptive parents were white and were waiting for a white baby that might conceivably pass for their own, while countless orphans of various minority groups were destined for institutions and unfulfilled dreams of being part of a family. Skin color meant nothing to either Hatch or Lindsey. They would have been happy with any child regardless of its heritage. But in recent years, misguided do-goodism in the name of civil rights had led to the imposition of an array of new rules and regulations designed to inhibit interracial adoption, and vast government bureaucracies enforced them with mind-numbing exactitude. The theory was that no child could be truly happy if raised outside of its ethnic group, which was the kind of elitist nonsense—and reverse racism—that sociologists and academics formulated without consulting the lonely kids they purported to protect.

The second option was to adopt a disabled child. There were far fewer disabled than minority orphans—even including technical orphans whose parents were alive somewhere but who'd been abandoned to the care of the church or state because of their differentness. On the other hand, though fewer in number, they were in even less demand than minority kids. They had the tremendous advantage of being currently beyond the interest of any pressure group eager to apply politically correct standards to their care and handling. Sooner or later, no doubt, a marching moron army would secure the passage of laws forbidding adoption of a green-eyed, blond, deaf child by anyone but green-eyed, blond, deaf parents, but Hatch and Lindsey had the good fortune to have submitted an application before the forces of chaos had descended.

Sometimes, when he thought about the troublesome bureaucrats they had dealt with six weeks ago, when they had first decided to adopt, he wanted to go back to those agencies and throttle the social workers who had thwarted them, just choke a little common sense into them. And wouldn't the expression of *that* desire make the good nuns and priests of St. Thomas's Home eager to commend one of their charges to his care!

"You're still feeling well, no lasting effects from your ordeal, eating well, sleeping well?" Father Jiminez inquired, obviously just to pass the time while they waited for the subject of the meeting to arrive, not meaning to impugn Hatch's claim to a full recovery and good health.

Lindsey—by nature more nervous than Hatch, and usually more prone to overreaction than he was—leaned forward on the sofa. Just a touch sharply, she said, "Hatch is at the top of the recovery curve for people who've been resuscitated. Dr. Nyebern's ecstatic about him, given him a clean bill of health, totally clean. It was all in our application."

Trying to soften Lindsey's reaction lest the priests and nuns start to wonder if she was protesting too much, Hatch said, "I'm terrific, really. I'd recommend a brief death to everyone. It relaxes you, gives you a calmer perspective on life."

Everyone laughed politely.

In truth, Hatch *was* in excellent health. During the four days following reanimation, he had suffered weakness, dizziness, nausea, lethargy, and some memory lapses. But his strength, memory, and intellectual functions returned one hundred percent. He had been back to normal for almost seven weeks.

Jiminez's casual reference to sleeping habits had rattled Hatch a little, which was probably what had also put Lindsey on edge. He had not been fully honest when he had implied he was sleeping well, but his strange dreams and the curious emotional effects they had on him were not serious, hardly worth mentioning, so he did not feel that he had actually lied to the priest.

They were so close to getting their new life started that he did not want to say the wrong thing and cause any delays. Though Catholic adoption services took considerable care in the placement of children, they were not pointlessly slow and obstructive, as were public agencies, especially when the would-be adopters were solid members of the community like Hatch and Lindsey, and when the adoptee was a disabled child with no option except continued institutionalization. The future could begin for them this week, as long as they gave the folks from St. Thomas's, who were already on their side, no reason to reconsider.

Hatch was a little surprised by the piquancy of his desire to be a father again. He felt as if he had been only half-alive, at best, during the past five years. Now suddenly all the unused energies of that half-decade flooded into him, overcharging him, making colors more vibrant and sounds more melodious and feelings more intense, filling him with a passion to go, do, see, *live*. And be somebody's dad again.

"I was wondering if I could ask you something," Father Duran said to Hatch, turning away from the Satsuma collection. His wan complexion and sharp features were enlivened by owlish eyes, full of warmth and intelligence, enlarged by thick glasses. "It's a little personal, which is why I hesitate."

"Oh, sure, anything," Hatch said.

The young priest said, "Some people who've been clinically dead for short periods of time, a minute or two, report . . . well . . . a certain similar experience. . . ."

"A sense of rushing through a tunnel with an awesome light at the far end," Hatch said, "a feeling of great peace, of going home at last?"

"Yes," Duran said, his pale face brightening. "That's what I meant exactly."

Father Jiminez and the nuns were looking at Hatch with new interest, and he wished he could tell them what they wanted to hear. He glanced at Lindsey on the sofa beside him, then around at the assemblage, and said, "I'm sorry, but I didn't have the experience so many people have reported."

Father Duran's thin shoulders sagged a little. "Then what *did* you experience?"

Hatch shook his head. "Nothing. I wish I had. It would be . . . comforting, wouldn't it? But in that sense, I guess I had a boring death. I don't remember anything whatsoever from the time I was knocked out when the car rolled over until I woke up hours later in a hospital bed, looking at rain beating on a windowpane—"

He was interrupted by the arrival of Salvatore Gujilio in whose office they were waiting. Gujilio, a huge man, heavy *and* tall, swung the door wide and entered as he always did—taking big strides instead of ordinary steps, closing the door behind him in a grand sweeping gesture. With the unstoppable determination of a force of nature—rather like a disciplined tornado—he swept around the room, greeting them one by one. Hatch would not have been surprised to see furniture spun aloft and artwork flung off walls as the attorney passed, for he seemed to radiate enough energy to levitate anything within his immediate sphere of influence.

Keeping up a continuous line of patter, Gujilio gave Jiminez a bear hug, shook hands vigorously with Duran, and bowed to each of the nuns with the sincerity of a passionate monarchist greeting members of the royal family. Gujilio bonded with people as quickly as one piece of pottery to another under the influence of super glue, and by their second meeting he'd greeted and said goodbye to Lindsey with a hug. She liked the man and didn't mind the hugging, but as she had told Hatch, she felt like a very small child embracing a sumo wrestler. "He lifts me off my feet, for God's sake," she'd said. Now she stayed on the sofa instead of rising, and merely shook hands with the attorney.

Hatch rose and extended his right hand, prepared to see it engulfed as if it were a speck of food in a culture dish filled with hungry amoebas, which is exactly what happened. Gujilio, as always, took Hatch's hand in both of his, and since each of his mitts was half-again the size of any ordinary man's, it wasn't so much a matter of shaking as being shaken.

"What a wonderful day," Gujilio said, "a special day. I hope for everyone's sake it goes as smooth as glass."

The attorney donated a certain number of hours a week to St. Thomas's Church and the orphanage. He appeared to take great satisfaction in connecting adoptive parents with disabled kids.

"Regina's on her way from the ladies," Gujilio told them. "She stopped to chat a moment with my receptionist, that's all. She's nervous, I think, trying to delay a little longer until she has her courage screwed up as far as it'll go. She'll be here in a moment."

Hatch looked at Lindsey. She smiled nervously and took his hand.

"Now, you understand," Salvatore Gujilio said, looming over them like one of those giant balloons in a Macy's Thanksgiving Day parade, "that the point of this meeting is for you to get to know Regina and for her to get to know you. Nobody makes a decision right here, today. You go away, think about it, and let us know tomorrow or the day after whether this is the one. The same goes for Regina. She has a day to think about it."

"It's a big step," Father Jiminez said.

"An enormous step," Sister Immaculata concurred.

Squeezing Hatch's hand, Lindsey said, "We understand."

The Nun with No Name went to the door, opened it, and peered down the hallway. Evidently Regina was not in sight.

Rounding his desk, Gujilio said, "She's coming, I'm sure."

The attorney settled his considerable bulk into the executive office chair beside his desk, but because he was six-feet-five, he seemed almost as tall seated as standing. The office was furnished entirely with antiques, and the desk was actually a Napoleon III table so fine that Hatch wished he had something like it in the front window of his shop. Banded by ormolu, the exotic woods of the marquetry top depicted a central cartouche with a detailed musical trophy over a conforming frieze of stylized foliage. The whole was raised on circular legs with acanthus-leaf ormolu joined by a voluted X stretcher centered with an ormolu urn finial, on toupie feet. At every meeting, Gujilio's size and dangerous levels of kinetic energy initially made the desk—and all the antiques—seem fragile, in imminent jeopardy of being knocked over or smashed to smithereens. But after a few minutes, he and the room seemed in such perfect harmony, you had the eerie feeling that he had recreated a decor he had lived with in another—thinner—life.

A soft, distant, but peculiar *thud* drew Hatch's attention away from the attorney and the desk.

The Nun with No Name turned from the door and hurried back into the room, saying, "Here she comes," as if she didn't want Regina to think she had been looking for her.

The sound came again. Then again. And again.

It was rhythmic and getting louder.

Thud. Thud.

Lindsey's hand tightened on Hatch's.

Thud. Thud!

Someone seemed to be keeping time to an unheard tune by rapping a lead pipe against the hardwood floor of the hallway beyond the door.

Puzzled, Hatch looked at Father Jiminez, who was staring at the floor, shaking his head, his state of mind not easy to read. As the sound grew louder and closer, Father Duran stared at the half-open hall door with astonishment, as did The Nun with No Name. Salvatore Gujilio rose from his chair, looking alarmed. Sister Immaculata's pleasantly ruddy cheeks were now as white as the linen band that framed her face.

Hatch became aware of a softer scraping between each of the hard sounds.

Thud! Sccccuuuurrrr . . . Thud! Sccccuuuurrrr . . .

As the sounds grew nearer, their effect rapidly increased, until Hatch's mind was filled with images from a hundred old horror films: the-thing-from-out-of-the-lagoon hitching crablike toward its prey; the-thing-from-out-of-the-crypt shuffling along a graveyard path under a gibbous moon; the-thing-from-another-world propelling itself on God-knows-what sort of arachnoid-reptilian-horned feet.

THUD!

The windows seemed to rattle.

Or was that his imagination?

Sccccuuuurrrr . . .

A shiver went up his spine.

THUD!

He looked around at the alarmed attorney, the head-shaking priest, the wide-eyed younger priest, the two pale nuns, then quickly back at the half-open door, wondering just exactly what sort of disability this child had been born with, half expecting a startlingly tall and twisted figure to appear with a surprising resemblance to Charles Laughton in *The Hunchback of Notre Dame* and a grin full of fangs, whereupon Sister Immaculata would turn to

him and say, *You see, Mr. Harrison, Regina came under the care of the good
sisters at Saint Thomas's not from ordinary parents but from a laboratory
where the scientists are doing some really interesting genetic research. . . .*

A shadow tilted across the threshold.

Hatch realized that Lindsey's grip on his hand had become downright
painful. And his palm was damp with sweat.

The weird sounds stopped. A hush of expectation had fallen over the
room.

Slowly the door to the hall was pushed all the way open.

Regina took a single step inside. She dragged her right leg as if it were a
dead weight: *sccccuuuurrrr.* Then she slammed it down: *THUD!*

She stopped to look around at everyone. Challengingly.

Hatch found it difficult to believe that she had been the source of all that
ominous noise. She was small for a ten-year-old girl, a bit shorter and more
slender than the average kid her age. Her freckles, pert nose, and beautiful
deep-auburn hair thoroughly disqualified her for the role of the-thing-from-
the-lagoon or any other shudder-making creature, although there was something in her solemn gray eyes that Hatch did not expect to see in the eyes
of a child. An adult awareness. A heightened perceptivity. But for those eyes
and an aura of iron determination, the girl seemed fragile, almost frighteningly delicate and vulnerable.

Hatch was reminded of an exquisite 18th-century Mandarin-pattern Chi-
nese-export porcelain bowl currently for sale in his Laguna Beach shop. It
rang as sweetly as any bell when pinged with one finger, raising the expectation that it would shatter into thousands of pieces if struck hard or
dropped. But when you studied the bowl as it stood on an acrylic display
base, the hand-painted temple and garden scenes portrayed on its sides and
the floral designs on its inner rim were of such high quality and possessed
such power that you became acutely aware of the piece's age, the weight of
the history behind it. And you were soon convinced, in spite of its appearance, that it would bounce when dropped, cracking whatever surface it
struck but sustaining not even a small chip itself.

Aware that the moment was hers and hers alone, Regina hitched toward
the sofa where Hatch and Lindsey waited, making less noise as she limped
off the hardwood floor onto the antique Persian carpet. She was wearing a
white blouse, a Kelly-green skirt that fell two inches above her knees, green
kneesocks, black shoes—and on her right leg a metal brace that extended
from the ankle to above the knee and looked like a medieval torture device.
Her limp was so pronounced that she rocked from side to side at the hips
with each step, as if in danger of toppling over.

Sister Immaculata rose from her armchair, scowling at Regina in disapproval. "Exactly what is the reason for these theatrics, young lady?"

Ignoring the true meaning of the nun's question, the girl said, "I'm sorry
I'm so late, Sister. But some days it's harder for me than others." Before the
nun could respond, the girl turned to Hatch and Lindsey, who had stopped
holding hands and had risen from the sofa. "Hi, I'm Regina. I'm a cripple."

She reached out in greeting. Hatch reached out, too, before he realized that her right arm and hand were not well formed. The arm was almost normal, just a little thinner than her left, until it got to the wrist, where the bones took an odd twist. Instead of a full hand, she possessed just two fingers and the stub of a thumb that all seemed to have limited flexibility. Shaking hands with the girl felt strange—distinctly strange—but not unpleasant.

Her gray eyes were fixed intently on his eyes. Trying to read his reaction. He knew at once that it would be impossible ever to conceal true feelings from her, and he was relieved that he had not been in the least repelled by her deformity.

"I'm so happy to meet you, Regina," he said. "I'm Hatch Harrison, and this is my wife, Lindsey."

The girl turned to Lindsey and shook hands with her, as well, saying, "Well, I know I'm a disappointment. You child-starved women usually prefer babies young enough to cuddle—"

The Nun with No Name gasped in shock. "Regina, really!"

Sister Immaculata looked too apoplectic to speak, like a penguin that had frozen solid, mouth agape and eyes bulging in protest, hit by an arctic chill too cold even for Antarctic birds to survive.

Approaching from the windows, Father Jiminez said, "Mr. and Mrs. Harrison, I apologize for—"

"No need to apologize for anything," Lindsey said quickly, evidently sensing, as Hatch did, that the girl was testing them and that to have any hope of passing the test, they must not let themselves be co-opted into an adults-against-the-kid division of sympathies.

Regina hopped-squirmed-wriggled into the second armchair, and Hatch was fairly certain she was making herself appear a lot more awkward than she really was.

The Nun with No Name gently touched Sister Immaculata on the shoulder, and the older nun eased back into her chair, still with the frozen-penguin look. The two priests brought the client chairs from in front of the attorney's desk, and the younger nun pulled up a side chair from a corner, so they could all join the group. Hatch realized he was the only one still standing. He sat on the sofa beside Lindsey again.

Now that everyone had arrived, Salvatore Gujilio insisted on serving refreshments—Pepsi, ginger ale, or Perrier—which he did without calling for the assistance of his secretary, fetching everything from a wet bar discreetly tucked into one mahogany-paneled corner of the genteel office. As the attorney bustled about, quiet and quick in spite of his immensity, never crashing into a piece of furniture or knocking over a vase, never coming even close to obliterating one of the two Tiffany lamps with hand-blown trumpet-flower shades, Hatch realized that the big man was no longer an overpowering figure, no longer the inevitable center of attention: he could not compete with the girl, who was probably less than one-fourth his size.

"Well," Regina said to Hatch and Lindsey, as she accepted a glass of Pepsi from Gujilio, holding it in her left hand, the good one, "you came here to learn all about me, so I guess I should tell you about myself. First thing, of course, is that I'm a cripple." She tilted her head and looked at them quizzically. "Did you know I was a cripple?"

"We do now," Lindsey said.

"But I mean before you came."

"We knew you had—some sort of problem," Hatch said.

"Mutant genes," Regina said.

Father Jiminez let out a heavy sigh.

Sister Immaculata seemed about to say something, glanced at Hatch and Lindsey, then decided to remain silent.

"My parents were dope fiends," the girl said.

"Regina!" The Nun with No Name protested. "You don't know that for sure, you don't know any such a thing."

"Well, but it figures," the girl said. "For at least twenty years now, illegal drugs have been the cause of most birth defects. Did you know that? I read it in a book. I read a lot. I'm book crazy. I don't want to say I'm a book-worm. That sounds icky—don't you think? But if I were a worm, I'd rather be curled up in a book than in any apple. It's good for a cripple kid to like books, because *they* won't let you do the things ordinary people do, even if you're pretty sure you can do them, so books are like having a whole other life. I like adventure stories where they go to the north pole or Mars or New York or somewhere. I like good mysteries, too, most anything by Agatha Christie, but I especially like stories about animals, and most especially about talking animals like in *The Wind in the Willows*. I had a talking animal once. It was just a goldfish, and of course it was really me not the fish who talked, because I read this book on ventriloquism and learned to throw my voice, which is neat. So I'd sit across the room and throw my voice into the goldfish bowl." She began to talk squeakily, without moving her lips, and the voice seemed to come out of The Nun with No Name: *"Hi, my name's Binky the Fish, and if you try to put me in a sandwich and eat me, I'll shit on the mayonnaise."* She returned to her normal voice and talked right over the flurry of reactions from the religiosities around her. "There you have another problem with cripples like me. We tend to be smart-mouthed some-times because we know nobody has the guts to whack us on the ass."

Sister Immaculata looked as if *she* might have the guts, but in fact all she did was mumble something about no TV privileges for a week.

Hatch, who had found the nun as frightening as a pterodactyl when he'd first met her, was not impressed by her glower now, even though it was so intense that he registered it with his peripheral vision. He could not take his eyes off the girl.

Regina went blithely on without pause: "Besides being smart-mouthed sometimes, what you should know about me is, I'm so clumsy, hitching around like Long John Silver—now *there* was a good book—that I'll prob-ably break everything of value in your house. Never meaning to, of course. It'll be a regular destruction derby. Do you have the patience for that? I'd hate to be beaten senseless and locked in the attic just because I'm a poor crippled girl who can't always control herself. This leg doesn't look so bad, really, and if I keep exercising it, I think it's going to turn out pretty enough, but I don't really have much strength in it, and I don't feel too damned much in it, either." She balled up her deformed right hand and smacked it so hard against the thigh of her right leg that she startled Gujilio, who was trying to convey a ginger ale into the hand of the younger priest, who was staring at the girl as if mesmerized. She smacked herself again, so hard that Hatch winced, and she said, "You see? Dead meat. Speaking of meat, I'm also a fussy eater. I simply can't stomach dead meat. Oh, I don't mean I eat live animals. What I am is, I'm a vegetarian, which makes things harder for you, even supposing you didn't mind that I'm not a cuddly baby you can dress up cute. My only virtue is that I'm very bright, practically a genius. But even that's a drawback as far as some people are concerned. I'm smart beyond my years, so I don't act much like a child—"

"You're certainly acting like one now," Sister Immaculata said, and seemed pleased at getting in that zinger.

But Regina ignored it: "—and what you want, after all, is a child, a precious and ignorant blob, so you can show her the world, have the fun of watching her learn and blossom, whereas I have already done a lot of my blossoming. Intellectual blossoming, that is. I still don't have boobs. I'm also bored by TV, which means I wouldn't be able to join in a jolly family evening around the tube, and I'm allergic to cats in case you've got one, and I'm opinionated, which some people find infuriating in a ten-year-old girl." She paused, sipped her Pepsi, and smiled at them. "There. I think that pretty much covers it."

"She's never like this," Father Jiminez mumbled, more to himself or to God than to Hatch and Lindsey. He tossed back half of his Perrier as if chugging hard liquor.

Hatch turned to Lindsey. Her eyes were a little glazed. She didn't seem to know what to say, so he returned his attention to the girl. "I suppose it's only fair if I tell you something about us."

Putting aside her drink and starting to get up, Sister Immaculata said, "Really, Mr. Harrison, you don't have to put yourself through—"

Politely waving the nun back into her seat, Hatch said, "No, no. It's all right. Regina's a little nervous—"

"Not particularly," Regina said.

"Of course, you are," Hatch said.

"No, I'm not."

"A little nervous," Hatch insisted, "just as Lindsey and I are. It's okay." He smiled at the girl as winningly as he could. "Well, let's see . . . I've had a lifelong interest in antiques, an affection for things that endure and have real character about them, and I have my own antique shop with two employees. That's how I earn my living. I don't like television much myself or—"

"What kind of a name is Hatch?" the girl interrupted. She giggled as if to imply that it was too funny to be the name of anyone except, perhaps, a talking goldfish.

"My full first name is Hatchford."

"It's still funny."

"Blame my mother," Hatch said. "She always thought my dad was going to make a lot of money and move us up in society, and she thought Hatchford sounded like a really upper-crust name: Hatchford Benjamin Harrison. The only thing that would've made it a better name in her mind was if it was Hatchford Benjamin Rockefeller."

"Did he?" the girl asked.

"Who he, did what?"

"Did your father make a lot of money?"

Hatch winked broadly at Lindsey and said, "Looks like we have a gold digger on our hands."

"If you were rich," the girl said, "of course, that would be a consideration."

Sister Immaculata let a hiss of air escape between her teeth, and The Nun with No Name leaned back in her chair and closed her eyes with an expression of resignation. Father Jiminez got up and, waving Gujilio away, went to the wet bar to get something stronger than Perrier, Pepsi, or ginger ale. Because neither Hatch nor Lindsey seemed obviously offended by the girl's behavior, none of the others felt authorized to terminate the interview or even further reprimand the child.

"I'm afraid we're not rich," Hatch told her. "Comfortable, yes. We don't want for anything. But we don't drive a Rolls-Royce, and we don't wear caviar pajamas."

A flicker of genuine amusement crossed the girl's face, but she quickly suppressed it. She looked at Lindsey and said, "What about you?"

Lindsey blinked. She cleared her throat. "Uh, well, I'm an artist. A painter."

"Like Picasso?"

"Not that style, no, but an artist like him, yes."

"I saw a picture once of a bunch of dogs playing poker," the girl said. "Did you paint that?"

Lindsey said, "No, I'm afraid I didn't."

"Good. It was stupid. I saw a picture once of a bull and a bullfighter, it was on velvet, very bright colors. Do you paint in very bright colors on velvet?"

"No," Lindsey said. "But if you like that sort of thing, I could paint any scene you wanted on velvet for your room."

Regina crinkled up her face. "Puh-leeese. I'd rather put a dead cat on the wall."

Nothing surprised the folks from St. Thomas's any more. The younger priest actually smiled, and Sister Immaculata murmured "dead cat," not in exasperation but as if agreeing that such a bit of macabre decoration would, indeed, be preferable to a painting on velvet.

"My style," Lindsey said, eager to rescue her reputation after offering to paint something so tacky, "is generally described as a blending of neoclassicism and surrealism. I know that's quite a big mouthful—"

"Well, it's not my favorite sort of thing," Regina said, as if she had a hoot-owl's idea in hell what those styles were like and what a blend of them might resemble. "If I came to live with you, and if I had a room of my own, you wouldn't make me hang a lot of *your* paintings on my walls, would you?" The "your" was emphasized in such a way as to imply that she still preferred a dead cat even if velvet was not involved.

"Not a one," Lindsey assured her.

"Good."

"Do you think you might like living with us?" Lindsey asked, and Hatch wondered whether that prospect excited or terrified her.

Abruptly the girl struggled up from the chair, wobbling as she reached her feet, as if she might topple headfirst into the coffee table. Hatch rose, ready to grab her, even though he suspected it was all part of the act.

When she regained her balance, she put down her glass, from which she'd drunk all the Pepsi, and she said, "I've got to go pee, I've got a weak bladder. Part of my mutant genes. I can never hold myself. Half the time I feel like I'm going to burst in the most embarrassing places, like right here in Mr. Gujilio's office, which is another thing you should probably consider before taking me into your home. You probably have a lot of nice things, being in the antiques and art business, nice things you wouldn't want messed up, and here I am lurching into everything and breaking it or, worse, I get a bursting bladder attack all over something priceless. Then you'd ship me back to the orphanage, and I'd be so emotional about it, I'd clump up to the roof and throw myself off, a most tragic suicide, which none of us really would want to see happen. Nice meeting you."

She turned and wrenched herself across the Persian carpet and out of the room in that most unlikely gait—*sccccuuuurrrr . . . THUD!*—which no doubt sprang from the same well of talent out of which she had drawn her goldfish ventriloquism. Her deep-auburn hair swayed and glinted like fire.

They all stood in silence, listening to the girl's slowly fading footsteps. At one point, she bumped against the wall with a solid *thunk!* that must have hurt, then bravely scrape-thudded onward.

"She does *not* have a weak bladder," Father Jiminez said, taking a swallow from a glassful of amber liquid. He seemed to be drinking bourbon now. "That is *not* part of her disability."

"She's not really like that," Father Duran said, blinking his owlish eyes as if smoke had gotten in them. "She's a delightful child. I know that's hard for you to believe right now—"

"And she can walk much better than that, immeasurably better," said The Nun with No Name. "I don't know what's gotten into her."

"I do," Sister Immaculata said. She wiped one hand wearily down her face. Her eyes were sad. "Two years ago, when she was eight, we managed to place her with adoptive parents. A couple in their thirties who were told they could never have children of their own. They convinced themselves that a disabled child would be a special blessing. Then, two weeks after Regina went to live with them, while they were in the pre-adoption trial phase, the woman became pregnant. Suddenly they were going to have their own child, after all, and the adoption didn't seem so wise."

"And they just brought Regina back?" Lindsey asked. "Just dumped her at the orphanage? How terrible."

"I can't judge them," Sister Immaculata said. "They may have felt they didn't have enough love for a child of their own and poor Regina, too, in which case they did the right thing. Regina doesn't deserve to be raised in a home where every minute of every day she knows she's second best, second in love, something of an outsider. Anyway, she was broken up by the rejection. She took a long time to get her self-confidence back. And now I think she doesn't want to take another risk."

They stood in silence.

The sun was very bright beyond the windows. The palm trees swayed lazily. Between the trees lay glimpses of Fashion Island, the Newport Beach shopping center and business complex at the perimeter of which Gujilio's office was located.

"Sometimes, with the sensitive ones, a bad experience ruins any chance for them. They refuse to try again. I'm afraid our Regina is one of those. She came in here determined to alienate you and wreck the interview, and she succeeded in singular style."

"It's like somebody who's been in prison all his life," said Father Jiminez, "gets paroled, is all excited at first, then finds he can't make it on the outside. So he commits a crime just to get back in. The institution might be limiting, unsatisfying—but it's known, it's safe."

Salvatore Gujilio bustled around, relieving people of their empty glasses. He was still an enormous man by any standard, but even with Regina gone from the room, Gujilio no longer dominated it as he had done before. He had been forever diminished by that single comparison with the delicate, pert-nosed, gray-eyed child.

"I'm so sorry," Sister Immaculata said, putting a consoling hand on Lindsey's shoulder. "We'll try again, my dear. We'll go back to square one and match you up with another child, the perfect child this time."

2 Lindsey and Hatch left Salvatore Gujilio's office at ten past three that Thursday afternoon. They had agreed not to talk about the interview until dinner, giving themselves time to contemplate the encounter and examine their reactions to it. Neither wanted to make a decision based on emotion, or influence the other to act on initial impressions—then live to regret it.

Of course, they had never expected the meeting to progress remotely along the lines it had gone. Lindsey was eager to talk about it. She assumed that their decision was already made, had been made for them by the girl, and that there was no point in further contemplation. But they had agreed to wait, and Hatch did not seem disposed to violate that agreement, so she kept her mouth shut as well.

She drove their new sporty-red Mitsubishi. Hatch sat in the passenger seat with his shades on, one arm out his open window, tapping time against the side of the car as he listened to golden oldie rock-'n'-roll on the radio. "Please Mister Postman" by the Marvelettes.

She passed the last of the giant date palms along Newport Center Drive and turned left onto Pacific Coast Highway, past vine-covered walls, and headed south. The late-April day was warm but not hot, with one of those intensely blue skies that, toward sunset, would acquire an electric luminescence reminiscent of skies in Maxfield Parrish paintings. Traffic was light on the Coast Highway, and the ocean glimmered like a great swatch of silver-and gold-sequined cloth.

A quiet exuberance flowed through Lindsey, as it had done for seven weeks. It was exhilaration over just being alive, which was in every child but which most adults lost during the process of growing up. She'd lost it, too, without realizing. A close encounter with death was just the thing to give you back the *joie de vivre* of extreme youth.

MORE THAN TWO floors below Hell, naked beneath a blanket on his stained and sagging mattress, Vassago passed the daylight hours in sleep. His slumber was usually filled with dreams of violated flesh and shattered bone, blood and bile, vistas of human skulls. Sometimes he dreamed of dying multitudes writhing in agony on barren ground beneath a black sky, and he walked among them as a prince of Hell among the common rabble of the damned.

The dreams that occupied him on that day, however, were strange and remarkable for their ordinariness. A dark-haired, dark-eyed woman in a cherry-red car, viewed from the perspective of an unseen man in the passenger seat beside her. Palm trees. Red bougainvillea. The ocean spangled with light.

HARRISON'S ANTIQUES WAS at the south end of Laguna Beach, on Pacific Coast Highway. It was in a stylish two-story Art Deco building that contrasted interestingly with the 18th- and 19th-century merchandise in the big display windows.

Glenda Dockridge, Hatch's assistant and the store manager, was helping Lew Booner, their general handyman, with the dusting. In a large antique store, dusting was akin to the painting of the Golden Gate Bridge: once you reached the far end, it was time to come back to the beginning and start all over again. Glenda was in a great mood because she had sold a Napoleon III ormolu-mounted black-lacquered cabinet with Japanned panels *and,* to the same customer, a 19th-century Italian polygonal, tilt-top table with elaborate marquetry inlay. They were excellent sales—especially considering that she worked on salary against a commission.

While Hatch looked through the day's mail, attended to some correspondence, and examined a pair of 18th-century rosewood palace pedestals with inlaid jade dragons that had arrived from a scout in Hong Kong, Lindsey helped Glenda and Lew with the dusting. In her new frame of mind, even that chore was a pleasure. It gave her a chance to appreciate the details of the antiques—the turn of a finial on a bronze lamp, the carving on a table leg, the delicately pierced and hand-finished rims on a set of 18th-century English porcelains. Contemplating the history and cultural meaning of each piece as she happily dusted it, she realized that her new attitude had a distinctly Zen quality.

AT TWILIGHT, SENSING the approach of night, Vassago woke and sat up in the approximation of a grave that was his home. He was filled with a hunger for death and a need to kill.

The last image he remembered from his dream was of the woman from the red car. She was not in the car any more, but in a chamber he could not quite see, standing in front of a Chinese screen, wiping it with a white cloth. She turned, as if he had spoken to her, and she smiled.

Her smile was so radiant, so full of life, that Vassago wanted to smash her face in with a hammer, break out her teeth, shatter her jaw bones, make it impossible for her to smile ever again.

He had dreamed of her two or three times over the past several weeks. The first time she had been in a wheelchair, weeping and laughing simultaneously.

Again, he searched his memory, but he could not recall her face among those he had ever seen outside of dreams. He wondered who she was and why she visited him when he slept.

Outside, night fell. He sensed it coming down. A great black drape that gave the world a preview of death at the end of every bright and shining day.

He dressed and left his hideaway.

BY SEVEN O'CLOCK that early-spring night, Lindsey and Hatch were at Zov's, a small but busy restaurant in Tustin. The decor was mainly black and white, with lots of big windows and mirrors. The staff, unfailingly friendly and efficient, were dressed in black and white to complement the long room. The food they served was such a perfect sensual experience that the monochromatic bistro seemed ablaze with color.

The noise level was congenial rather than annoying. They did not have to raise their voices to hear each other, and felt as if the background buzz provided a screen of privacy from nearby tables. Through the first two courses—calamari; black-bean soup—they spoke of trivial things. But when the main course was served—swordfish for both of them—Lindsey could no longer contain herself.

She said, "Okay, all right, we've had all day to brood about it. We haven't colored each other's opinions. So what do you think of Regina?"

"What do *you* think of Regina?"

"You first."

"Why me?"

Lindsey said, "Why not?"

He took a deep breath, hesitated. "I'm crazy about the kid."

Lindsey felt like leaping up and doing a little dance, the way a cartoon character might express uncontainable delight, because her joy and excitement were brighter and bolder than things were supposed to be in real life. She had hoped for just that reaction from him, but she hadn't known what he would say, really hadn't had a clue, because the meeting had been . . . well, one apt word would be "daunting."

"Oh, God, I love her," Lindsey said. "She's so sweet."

"She's a tough cookie."

"That's an act."

"She was putting on an act for us, yeah, but she's tough just the same. She's had to be tough. Life didn't give her a choice."

"But it's a good tough."

"It's a great tough," he agreed. "I'm not saying it put me off. I admired it, I loved her."

"She's so bright."

"Struggling so hard to make herself unappealing," Hatch said, "and that only made her *more* appealing."

"The poor kid. Afraid of being rejected again, so she took the offensive."

"When I heard her coming down the hall, I thought it was—"

"Godzilla!" Lindsey said.

"At least. And how'd you like Binky the talking goldfish?"

"Shit on the mayonnaise!" Lindsey said.

They both laughed, and people around them turned to look, either because of their laughter or because some of what Lindsey said was overheard, which only made them laugh harder.

"She's going to be a handful," Hatch said.

"She'll be a dream."

"Nothing's that easy."

"*She* will be."

"One problem."

"What's that?"

He hesitated. "What if she doesn't want to come with us?"

Lindsey's smile froze. "She will. She'll come."

"Maybe not."

"Don't be negative."

"I'm only saying we've got to be prepared for disappointment."

Lindsey shook her head adamantly. "No. It's going to work out. It has to. We've had more than our share of bad luck, bad times. We deserve better. The wheel has turned. We're going to put a family together again. Life is going to be good, it's going to be so fine. The worst is behind us now."

3 That Thursday night, Vassago enjoyed the conveniences of a motel room.

Usually he used one of the fields behind the abandoned amusement park as a toilet. He also washed each evening with bottled water and liquid soap. He shaved with a straight razor, an aerosol can of lather, and a piece of a broken mirror that he had found in a corner of the park.

When rain fell at night, he liked to bathe in the open, letting the downpour sluice over him. If lightning accompanied the storm, he sought the highest point on the paved midway, hoping that he was about to receive the grace of Satan and be recalled to the land of the dead by one scintillant bolt of electricity. But the rainy season in southern California was over now, and most likely would not come around again until December. If he earned his way back into the fold of the dead and damned before then, the means of his deliverance from the hateful world of the living would be some other force than lightning.

Once a week, sometimes twice, he rented a motel room to use the shower and make a better job of grooming than he could in the primitive conditions of his hideaway, though not because hygiene was important to him. Filth had its powerful attractions. The air and water of Hades, to which he longed to return, were filth of infinite variety. But if he was to move among the living and prey upon them, building the collection that might win him readmission to the realm of the damned, there were certain conventions that had to be followed in order not to draw undue attention to himself. Among them was a certain degree of cleanliness.

Vassago always used the same motel, the Blue Skies, a seedy hole toward the southern end of Santa Ana, where the unshaven desk clerk accepted only cash, asked for no identification, and never looked guests in the eyes, as if afraid of what he might see in theirs or they in his. The area was a swamp of drug dealers and streetwalkers. Vassago was one of the few men who did not check in with a whore in tow. He stayed only an hour or two, however, which was in keeping with the duration of the average customer's use of the accommodations, and he was allowed the same anonymity as those who, grunting and sweating, noisily rocked the headboards of their beds against the walls in rooms adjoining his.

He could not have lived there full time, if only because his awareness of the frenzied coupling of the sluts and their johns filled him with anger, anxiety, and nausea at the urgent needs and frenetic rhythms of the living. The atmosphere made it difficult to think clearly and impossible to rest, even though the perversion and dementia of the place was the very thing in which he had reveled when he had been one of the fully alive.

No other motel or boarding house would have been safe. They would have wanted identification. Besides, he could pass among the living as one of them only as long as their contact with him was casual. Any motel clerk or landlord who took a deeper interest in his character and encountered him repeatedly would soon realize that he was different from them in some indefinable yet deeply disturbing way.

Anyway, to avoid drawing attention to himself, he preferred the amusement park as primary quarters. The authorities looking for him would be less likely to find him there than anywhere else. Most important, the park offered solitude, graveyard stillness, and regions of perfect darkness to which he could escape during daylight hours when his sensitive eyes could not tolerate the insistent brightness of the sun.

Motels were tolerable only between dusk and dawn.

That pleasantly warm Thursday night, when he came out of the Blue Skies Motel office with his room key, he noticed a familiar Pontiac parked in shadows at the back of the lot, beyond the end unit, not nose-in to the motel but facing the office. The car had been there on Sunday, the last time Vassago had used the Blue Skies. A man was slumped behind the wheel, as if sleeping or just passing time while he waited for someone to meet him. He had been there Sunday night, features veiled by the night and the haze of reflected light on his windshield.

Vassago drove the Camaro to unit six, about in the middle of the long arm of the L-shaped structure, parked in front, and let himself into his room. He carried only a change of clothes—all black like the clothes he was wearing.

Inside the room, he did not turn on the light. He never did.

For a while he stood with his back against the door, thinking about the

Pontiac and the man behind the steering wheel. He might have been just a drug dealer working out of his car. The number of dealers crawling the neighborhood was even greater than the number of cockroaches swarming inside the walls of that decaying motel. But where were his customers with their quick nervous eyes and greasy wads of money?

Vassago dropped his clothes on the bed, put his sunglasses in his jacket pocket, and went into the small bathroom. It smelled of hastily sloshed disinfectant that could not mask a mélange of vile biological odors.

A rectangle of pale light marked a window above the back wall of the shower. Sliding open the glass door, which made a scraping noise as it moved along the corroded track, he stepped into the stall. If the window had been fixed, or if it had been divided vertically into two panes, he would have been foiled. But it swung outward from the top on rusted hinges. He gripped the sill above his head, pulled himself through the window, and wriggled out into the service alley behind the motel.

He paused to put on his sunglasses again. A nearby sodium-vapor street-lamp cast a urine-yellow glare that scratched like windblown sand at his eyes. The glasses mellowed it to a muddy amber and clarified his vision.

He went right, all the way to the end of the block, turned right on the side street, then right again at the next corner, circling the motel. He slipped around the end of the short wing of the L-shaped building and moved along the covered walkway in front of the last units until he was behind the Pontiac.

At the moment that end of the motel was quiet. No one was coming or going from any of the rooms.

The man behind the wheel was sitting with one arm out of the open car window. If he had glanced at the side mirror, he might have seen Vassago coming up on him, but his attention was focused on room six in the other wing of the L.

Vassago jerked open the door, and the guy actually started to fall out because he'd been leaning against it. Vassago hit him hard in the face, using his elbow like a battering ram, which was better than a fist, except he didn't hit him squarely enough. The guy was rocked but not finished, so he pushed up and out of the Pontiac, trying to grapple with Vassago. He was overweight and slow. A knee driven hard into his crotch slowed him even more. The guy went into a prayer posture, gagging, and Vassago stepped back far enough to kick him. The stranger fell over onto his side, so Vassago kicked him again, in the head this time. The guy was out cold, as still as the pavement on which he was sprawled.

Hearing a startled intake of breath, Vassago turned and saw a frizzy-haired blond hooker in a miniskirt and a middle-aged guy in a cheap suit and a bad toupee. They were coming out of the nearest room. They gaped at the man on the ground. At Vassago. He stared back at them until they reentered their room and quietly pulled the door shut behind them.

The unconscious man was heavy, maybe two hundred pounds, but Vassago was more than strong enough to lift him. He carried the guy around to the passenger side and loaded him into the other front seat. Then he got behind the wheel, started the Pontiac, and departed the Blue Skies.

Several blocks away, he turned onto a street of tract homes built thirty years ago and aging badly. Ancient Indian laurels and coral trees flanked the canted sidewalks and lent a note of grace in spite of the neighborhood's decline. He pulled the Pontiac to the curb. He switched off the engine and the lights.

As no streetlamps were nearby, he removed his sunglasses to search the unconscious man. He found a loaded revolver in a shoulder holster under the guy's jacket. He took it for himself.

The stranger was carrying two wallets. The first, and thicker, contained three hundred dollars in cash, which Vassago confiscated. It also held credit cards, photographs of people he didn't know, a receipt from a dry cleaner, a buy-ten-get-one-free punch card from a frozen-yogurt shop, a driver's license that identified the man as Morton Redlow of Anaheim, and insignificant odds and ends. The second wallet was quite thin, and it proved to be not a real wallet at all but a leather ID holder. In it were Redlow's license to operate as a private investigator and another license to carry a concealed weapon.

In the glove compartment, Vassago found only candy bars and a paperback detective novel. In the console between seats, he found chewing gum, breath mints, another candy bar, and a bent Thomas Brothers map book of Orange County.

He studied the map book for a while, then started the car and pulled away from the curb. He headed for Anaheim and the address on Redlow's driver's license.

When they were more than halfway there, Redlow began to groan and twitch, as if he might come to his senses. Driving with one hand, Vassago picked up the revolver he had taken off the man and clubbed him alongside the head with it. Redlow was quiet again.

4

One of the five other kids who shared Regina's table in the dining hall was Carl Cavanaugh, who was eight years old and acted every bit of it. He was a paraplegic, confined to a wheelchair, which you would have thought was enough of a handicap, but he made his lot in life worse by being a complete nerd. Their plates had no sooner been put on the table than Carl said, "I really like Friday afternoons, and you know why?" He didn't give anyone a chance to express a lack of interest. "Because Thursday night we always have beans *and* pea soup, so by Friday afternoon you can really cut some ripe farts."

The other kids groaned in disgust. Regina just ignored him.

Nerd or not, Carl was right: Thursday dinner at St. Thomas's Home for Children was always split-pea soup, ham, green beans, potatoes in herb butter sauce, and a square of fruited Jell-O with a blob of fake whipped cream for dessert. Sometimes the nuns got into the sherry or just went wild from too many years in their suffocating habits, and if they lost control on a Thursday, you might get corn instead of green beans or, if they were really over the top, maybe a pair of vanilla cookies with the Jell-O.

That Thursday the menu held no surprises, but Regina would not have cared—and might not have noticed—if the fare had included filet mignon or, conversely, cow pies. Well, she probably would have noticed a cow pie on her plate, though she wouldn't have cared if it was substituted for the green beans because she didn't like green beans. She liked ham. She had lied when she'd told the Harrisons she was a vegetarian, figuring they would find dietary fussiness one more reason to reject her flat-out, at the start, instead of later when it would hurt more. But even as she ate, her attention was not on her food and not on the conversation of the other kids at her table, but on the meeting in Mr. Gujilio's office that afternoon.

She had screwed up.

They were going to have to build a Museum of Famous Screwups just to have a place for a statue of her, so people could come from all over the world, from France and Japan and Chile, just to see it. Schoolkids would come, whole classes at a time with their teachers, to study her so they could learn what *not* to do and how *not* to act. Parents would point at her statue and ominously warn their children, "Anytime you think you're so smart, just remember her and think how you might wind up like *that,* a figure of pity and ridicule, laughed at and reviled."

Two thirds of the way through the interview, she had realized the Harrisons were special people. They probably would never treat her as badly as she had been treated by the Infamous Dotterfields, the couple who accepted her and took her home and then rejected her in two weeks when they discovered they going to have a child of their own, Satan's child, no doubt, who would one day destroy the world and turn against even the Dotterfields, burning them alive with a flash of fire from his demonic little pig eyes. (Uh-oh. Wishing harm to another. The thought is as bad as the deed. Remember that for confession, Reg.) Anyway, the Harrisons were different, which she began to realize slowly—such a screwup—and which she knew for sure when Mr. Harrison made the crack about caviar pajamas and showed he had a sense of humor. But by then she was so *into* her act that somehow she couldn't stop being obnoxious—screwup that she was—couldn't find a way to retreat and start over. Now the Harrisons were probably getting drunk, celebrating their narrow escape, or maybe down on their knees in a church, weeping with relief and fervently saying the Rosary, thanking the Holy Mother for interceding to spare them the mistake of adopting that awful girl sight-unseen. Shit. (Oops. Vulgarity. But not as bad as taking the Lord's name in vain. Even worth mentioning in the confessional?)

In spite of having no appetite and in spite of Carl Cavanaugh and his crude humor, she ate all of her dinner, but only because God's policemen, the nuns, would not let her leave the table until she cleaned her plate. The fruit in the lime Jell-O was peaches, which made dessert an ordeal. She couldn't understand how anyone could think that lime and peaches went together. Okay, so nuns were not very worldly, but she wasn't asking them to learn which rare wine to serve with roast tenderloin of platypus, for God's sake. (Sorry, God.) Pineapple and lime Jell-O, certainly. Pears and lime Jell-O, okay. Even bananas and lime Jell-O. But putting peaches in lime Jell-O was, to her way of thinking, like leaving the raisins out of rice pudding and replacing them with chunks of watermelon, for God's sake. (Sorry, God.) She managed to eat the dessert by telling herself that it could have been worse; the nuns could have served dead mice dipped in chocolate—though why nuns, of all people, would want to do that, she had no idea. Still, imagining something worse than what she had to face was a trick that worked, a technique of self-persuasion that she had used many times before. Soon the hated Jell-O was gone, and she was free to leave the dining hall.

After dinner most kids went to the recreation room to play Monopoly and other games, or to the TV room to watch whatever slop was on the boob tube, but as usual she returned to her room. She spent most evenings reading. Not tonight, though. She planned to spend this evening feeling sorry for herself and contemplating her status as a world-class screwup (good thing stupidity isn't a sin), so she would never forget how dumb she had been and would remember never to make such a jackass of herself again.

Moving along the tile-floored hallways nearly as fast as a kid with two good legs, she remembered how she had clumped into the attorney's office, and she began to blush. In her room, which she shared with a blind girl named Winnie, as she jumped into bed and flopped on her back, she recalled the calculated clumsiness with which she had levered herself into the chair in front of Mr. and Mrs. Harrison. Her blush deepened, and she put both hands over her face.

"Reg," she said softly against the palms of her own hands, "you are the biggest asshole in the world." (One more item on the list for the next confession, besides lying and deceiving and taking God's name in vain: the repeated use of a vulgarity.) "Shit, shit, shit!" (Going to be a long confession.)

5

When Redlow regained consciousness, his assorted pains were so bad, they took one hundred percent of his attention. He had a violent headache to which he could have testified with such feeling in a television commercial that they would have been forced to open new aspirin factories to meet the consumer response. One eye was puffed half shut. His lips were split and swollen; they were numb and felt huge. His neck hurt, and his stomach was sore, and his testicles throbbed so fiercely from the knee he had taken in the crotch that the idea of getting up and walking sent a paroxysm of nausea through him.

Gradually he remembered what had happened to him, that the bastard had taken him by surprise. Then he realized he was not lying on the motel parking lot but sitting in a chair, and for the first time he was afraid.

He was not merely sitting in the chair. He was tied in it. Ropes bound him at chest and waist, and more ropes wound across his thighs, securing him to the seat. His arms were fixed to the arms of the chair just below his elbows and again at the wrists.

Pain had muddied his thought processes. Now fear clarified them.

Simultaneously squinting his good right eye and trying to widen his swollen left eye, he studied the darkness. For a moment he assumed he was in a room at the Blue Skies Motel, outside of which he had been running a surveillance in hope of spotting the kid. Then he recognized his own living room. He couldn't see much. No lights were on. But having lived in that house for eighteen years, he could identify the patterns of ambient nightglow at the windows, the dim shapes of the furniture, shadows among shadows of differing intensity, and the subtle but singular smell of home, which was as special and instantly identifiable to him as the odor of any particular lair to any particular wolf in the wild.

He did not feel much like a wolf tonight. He felt like a rabbit, shivering in recognition of its status as prey.

For a few seconds he thought he was alone, and he began to strain at the ropes. Then a shadow rose from other shadows and approached him.

He could see nothing more of his adversary than a silhouette. Even that seemed to melt into the silhouettes of inanimate objects, or to change as if the kid were a polymorphous creature that could assume a variety of forms. But he knew it was the kid because he sensed that difference, that *alienness* he had perceived the first time he had laid eyes on the bastard on Sunday, just four nights ago, at the Blue Skies.

"Comfortable, Mr. Redlow?"

Over the past three months, as he had searched for the creep, Redlow had developed a deep curiosity about him, trying to puzzle out what he wanted, what he needed, how he thought. After showing countless people the various photographs of the kid, and after spending more than a little of his own time in contemplation of them, he had been especially curious about what the voice would be like that went with that remarkably handsome yet forbidding face. It sounded nothing like he had imagined it would be, neither cold and steely like the voice of a machine designed to pass for human nor the guttural and savage snarling of a beast. Rather, it was soothing, honey-toned, with an appealing reverberant timbre.

"Mr. Redlow, sir, can you hear me?"

More than anything else, the kid's politeness and the natural formality of his speech disconcerted Redlow.

"I apologize for having been so rough with you, sir, but you really didn't give me much choice."

Nothing in the voice indicated that the kid was being snide or mocking. He was just a boy who had been raised to address his elders with consideration and respect, a habit he could not cast off even under circumstances such as these. The detective was gripped by a primitive, superstitious feeling that he was in the presence of an entity that could imitate humanity but had nothing whatsoever in common with the human species.

Speaking through split lips, his words somewhat slurred, Morton Redlow said, "Who are you, what the hell do you want?"

"You know who I am."

"I haven't a fucking clue. You blindsided me. I haven't seen your face. What—are you a bat or something? Why don't you turn on a light?"

Still only a black form, the kid moved closer, to within a few feet of the chair. "You were hired to find me."

"I was hired to run surveillance on a guy named Kirkaby. Leonard Kirkaby. Wife thinks he's cheating on her. And he is. Brings his secretary to the Blue Skies every Thursday for some in-and-out."

"Well, sir, that's a little hard for me to believe, you know? The Blue Skies is for low-life guys and cheap whores, not business executives and their secretaries."

"Maybe he gets off on the sleaziness of it, treating the girl like a whore. Who the hell knows, huh? Anyway, you sure aren't Kirkaby. I know his voice. He doesn't sound anything like you. Not as young as you, either. Besides, he's a piece of puff pastry. He couldn't have handled me the way you did."

The kid was quiet for a while. Just staring down at Redlow. Then he began to pace. In the dark. Unhesitating, never bumping into furniture. Like a restless cat, except his eyes didn't glow.

Finally he said, "So what're you saying, sir? That this is all just a big mistake?"

Redlow knew his only chance of staying alive was to convince the kid of the lie—that a guy named Kirkaby had a letch for his secretary, and a bitter wife seeking evidence for a divorce. He just didn't know what tone to take to sell the story. With most people, Redlow had an unerring sense of which approach would beguile them and make them accept even the wildest proposition as the truth. But the kid was different; he didn't think or react like ordinary people.

Redlow decided to play it tough. "Listen, asshole, I wish I did know who you are or at least what the hell you look like, 'cause once this was finished, I'd come after you and bash your fuckin' head in."

The kid was silent for a while, mulling it over.

Then he said, "All right, I believe you."

Redlow sagged with relief, but sagging made all of his pains worse, so he tensed his muscles and sat up straight again.

"Too bad, but you just aren't right for my collection," the kid said.

"Collection?"

"Not enough life in you."

"What're you talking about?" Redlow asked.

"Burnt out."

The conversation was taking a turn Redlow didn't understand, which made him uneasy.

"Excuse me, sir, no offense meant, but you're getting too old for this kind of work."

Don't I know it, Redlow thought. He realized that, aside from one initial tug, he had not again tested the ropes that bound him. Only a few years ago, he would have quietly but steadily strained against them, trying to stretch the knots. Now he was passive.

"You're a muscular man, but you've gone a little soft, you've got a gut on you, and you're slow. From your driver's license, I see you're fifty-four, you're getting up there. Why do you still do it, keep hanging in there?"

"It's all I've got," Redlow said, and he was alert enough to be surprised by his own answer. He had meant to say, *It's all I know.*

"Well, yessir, I can see that," the kid said, looming over him in the darkness. "You've been divorced twice, no kids, and no woman lives with you right now. Probably hasn't been one living with you for years. Sorry, but I was snooping around the house while you were out cold, even though I knew it wasn't really right of me. Sorry. But I just wanted to get a handle on you, try to understand what you get out of this."

Redlow said nothing because he couldn't understand where all of this was leading. He was afraid of saying the wrong thing, and setting the kid off like a bottle rocket. The son of a bitch was insane. You never knew what might light the fuse on a nutcase like him. The kid had been through some analysis of his own over the years, and now he seemed to want to analyze Redlow, for reasons even he probably could not have explained. Maybe it was best to just let him rattle on, get it out of his system.

"Is it money, Mr. Redlow?"

"You mean, do I make any?"

"That's what I mean, sir."

"I do okay."

"You don't drive a great car or wear expensive clothes."

"I'm not into flash," Redlow said.

"No offense, sir, but this house isn't much."

"Maybe not, but there's no mortgage on it."

The kid was right over him, slowly leaning farther in with each question, as if he could see Redlow in the lightless room and was intently studying facial tics and twitches as he questioned him. Weird. Even in the dark, Redlow could sense the kid bending closer, closer, closer.

"No mortgage on it," the kid said thoughtfully. "Is that your reason for working, for living? To be able to say you paid off a mortgage on a dump like this?"

Redlow wanted to tell him to go fuck himself, but suddenly he was not so sure that playing tough was a good idea, after all.

"Is that what life's all about, sir? Is that all it's about? Is that why you find it so precious, why you're so eager to hold on to it? Is that why you life-lovers struggle to go on living—just to acquire a pitiful pile of belongings, so you can go out of the game a winner? I'm sorry, sir, but I just don't understand that. I don't understand at all."

The detective's heart was pounding too hard. It slammed painfully against his bruised ribs. He hadn't treated his heart well over the years, too many hamburgers, too many cigarettes, too much beer and bourbon. What was the crazy kid trying to do—talk him to death, scare him to death?

"I'd imagine you have some clients who don't want it on record that they ever hired you, they pay in cash. Would that be a valid assumption, sir?"

Redlow cleared his throat and tried not to sound frightened. "Yeah. Sure. Some of them."

"And part of winning the game would be to keep as much of that money as you could, avoiding taxes on it, which would mean never putting it in a bank."

The kid was so close now that the detective could smell his breath. For some reason he had expected it to be sour, vile. But it smelled sweet, like chocolate, as if the kid had been eating candy in the dark.

"So I'd imagine you have a nice little stash here in the house somewhere. Is that right, sir?"

A warm quiver of hope caused a diminishment of the cold chills that had been chattering through Redlow for the past few minutes. If it was about money, he could deal with that. It made sense. He could understand the kid's motivation, and could see a way to get through the evening alive.

"Yeah," the detective said. "There's money. Take it. Take it and go. In the kitchen, there's a waste can with a plastic bag for a liner. Lift out the bag of trash, there's a brown paper bag full of cash under it, in the bottom of the can."

Something cold and rough touched the detective's right cheek, and he flinched from it.

"Pliers," the kid said, and the detective felt the jaws take a grip on his flesh.

"What're you doing?"

The kid twisted the pliers.

Redlow cried out in pain. "Wait, wait, stop it, shit, please, stop it, no!"

The kid stopped. He took the pliers away. He said, "I'm sorry, sir, but I just want you to understand that if there isn't any cash in the trash can, I won't be happy. I'll figure if you lied to me about this, you lied to me about everything."

"It's there," Redlow assured him hastily.

"It's not nice to lie, sir. It's not good. Good people don't lie. That's what they teach you, isn't it, sir?"

"Go, look, you'll see it's there," Redlow said desperately.

The kid went out of the living room, through the dining room archway. Soft footsteps echoed through the house from the tile floor of the kitchen. A clatter and rustle arose as the garbage bag was pulled out of the waste can.

Already damp with perspiration, Redlow began to gush sweat as he listened to the kid return through the pitch-black house. He appeared in the living room again, partly silhouetted against the pale-gray rectangle of a window.

"How can you see?" the detective asked, dismayed to hear a faint note of hysteria in his voice when he was struggling so hard to maintain control of himself. He *was* getting old. "What—are you wearing night-vision glasses or something, some military hardware? How in the hell would you get your hands on anything like that?"

Ignoring him, the kid said, "There isn't much I want or need, just food and changes of clothes. The only money I get is when I make an addition to my collection, whatever she happens to be carrying. Sometimes it's not much, only a few dollars. This is really a help. It really is. This much should last me as long as it takes for me to get back to where I belong. Do you know where I belong, Mr. Redlow?"

The detective did not answer. The kid had dropped down below the windows, out of sight. Redlow was squinting into the gloom, trying to detect movement and figure where he had gone.

"You know where I belong, Mr. Redlow?" the kid repeated.

Redlow heard a piece of furniture being shoved aside. Maybe an end table beside the sofa.

"I belong in Hell," the kid said. "I was there for a while. I want to go back. What kind of life have you led, Mr. Redlow? Do you think, when I go back to Hell, that maybe I'll see you over there?"

"What're you doing?" Redlow asked.

"Looking for an electrical outlet," the kid said as he shoved aside another piece of furniture. "Ah, here we go."

"Electrical outlet?" Redlow asked agitatedly. "Why?"

A frightening noise cut through the darkness: *zzzzrrrrrrrrrr.*

"What was that?" Redlow demanded.

"Just testing, sir."

"Testing what?"

"You've got all sorts of pots and pans and gourmet utensils out there in the kitchen, sir. I guess you're really into cooking, are you?" The kid rose up again, appearing against the backdrop of the dim ash-gray glow in the window glass. "The cooking—was that an interest before the second divorce, or more recent?"

"What were you testing?" Redlow asked again.

The kid approached the chair.

"There's more money," Redlow said frantically. He was soaked in sweat now. It was running down him in rivulets. "In the master bedroom." The kid loomed over him again, a mysterious and inhuman form. He seemed to be darker than anything around him, a black hole in the shape of a man, blacker than black. "In the c-closet. There's a w-w-wooden floor." The detective's bladder was suddenly full. It had blown up like a balloon all in an instant. Bursting. "Take out the shoes and crap. Lift up the back f-ffloorboards." He was going to piss himself. "There's a cash box. Thirty thousand dollars. Take it. Please. Take it and go."

"Thank you, sir, but I really don't need it. I've got enough, more than enough."

"Oh, Jesus, help me," Redlow said, and he was despairingly aware that this was the first time he had spoken to God—or even thought of Him—in decades.

"Let's talk about who you're *really* working for, sir."

"I told you—"

"But I lied when I said I believed you."

Zzzzrrrrrrrrrrrr.

"What *is* that?" Redlow asked.

"Testing."

"Testing what, damn it?"

"It works real nice."

"What, what is it, what've you got?"

"An electric carving knife," the kid said.

6 Hatch and Lindsey drove home from dinner without getting on a freeway, taking their time, using the coast road from Newport Beach south, listening to K-Earth 101.1 FM, and singing along with golden oldies like "New Orleans," "Whispering Bells," and "California Dreamin'." She couldn't remember when they had last harmonized with the radio, though in the old days they had done it all the time. When he'd been three, Jimmy had known all the words to "Pretty Woman." When he was four he could sing "Fifty Ways to Leave Your Lover" without missing a line. For the first time in five years, she could think of Jimmy and still feel like singing.

They lived in Laguna Niguel, south of Laguna Beach, on the eastern side of the coastal hills, without an ocean view but with the benefit of sea breezes that moderated summer heat and winter chill. Their neighborhood, like most south-county developments, was so meticulously laid out that at times it seemed as if the planners had come to community design with a military background. But the gracefully curving streets, iron streetlamps with an artificial green patina, just-so arrangements of palms and jacarandas and ficus benjaminas, and well-maintained greenbelts with beds of colorful flowers were so soothing to the eye and soul that the subliminal sense of regimentation was not stifling.

As an artist, Lindsey believed that the hands of men and women were as capable of creating great beauty as nature was, and that discipline was fundamental to the creation of real art because art was meant to reveal meaning in the chaos of life. Therefore, she understood the impulse of the planners who had labored countless hours to coordinate the design of the community all the way down to the configuration of the steel grilles in the street drains that were set in the gutters.

Their two-story house, where they had lived only since Jimmy's death, was an Italian-Mediterranean model—the whole community was Italian Mediterranean—with four bedrooms and den, in cream-colored stucco with a Mexican tile roof. Two large ficus trees flanked the front walk. Malibu lights revealed beds of impatiens and petunias in front of red-flowering azalea bushes. As they pulled into the garage, they finished the last bars of "You Send Me."

Between taking turns in the bathroom, Hatch started a gas-log fire in the family-room fireplace, and Lindsey poured Baileys Irish Cream on the rocks for both of them. They sat on the sofa in front of the fire, their feet on a large, matching ottoman.

All the upholstered furniture in the house was modern with soft lines and in light natural tones. It made a pleasing contrast with—and good backdrop for—the many antique pieces and Lindsey's paintings.

The sofa was also hugely comfortable, good for conversation and, as she discovered for the first time, a great spot to snuggle. To her surprise, snuggling turned into necking, and their necking escalated into petting, as if they were a couple of teenagers, for God's sake. Passion overwhelmed her as it had not done in years.

Their clothes came off slowly, as in a series of dissolves in a motion picture, until they were naked without quite knowing how they had gotten that way. Then they were just as mysteriously coupled, moving together in a silken rhythm, bathed in flickering firelight. The joyful naturalness of it, escalating from a dreamy motion to breathless urgency, was a radical departure from the stilted and dutiful lovemaking they had known during the past five years, and Lindsey could almost believe it really was a dream patterned on some remembered scrap of Hollywood eroticism. But as she slid her hands over the muscles of his arms and shoulders and back, as she rose to meet each of his thrusts, as she climaxed, then again, and as she felt him loose himself within her and dissolve from iron to molten flow, she was wonderfully, acutely aware that it was not a dream. In fact, she had opened her eyes at last from a long twilight sleep and was, with this release, only now fully awake for the first time in years. The true dream was real life during the past half-decade, a nightmare that had finally drawn to an end.

Leaving their clothes scattered on the floor and hearth behind them, they went upstairs to make love again, this time in the huge Chinese sleigh bed, with less urgency than before, more tenderness, to the accompaniment of murmured endearments that seemed almost to comprise the lyrics and melody of a quiet song. The less insistent rhythm allowed a keener awareness of the exquisite textures of skin, the marvelous flexibility of muscle, the firmness of bone, the pliancy of lips, and the syncopated beating of their hearts. When the tide of ecstasy crested and ebbed, in the stillness that followed, the words "I love you" were superfluous but nonetheless musical to the ear, and cherished.

That April day, from first awareness of the morning light until surrender to sleep, had been one of the best of their lives. Ironically, the night that followed was one of Hatch's worst, so frightening and so strange.

BY ELEVEN O'CLOCK Vassago had finished with Redlow and disposed of the body in a most satisfying fashion. He returned to the Blue Skies Motel in the detective's Pontiac, took the long hot shower that he had intended to take earlier in the night, changed into clean clothes, and left with the intention of never going there again. If Redlow had made the place, it was not safe any longer.

He drove the Camaro a few blocks and abandoned it on a street of decrepit industrial buildings where it might sit undisturbed for weeks before it was either stolen or hauled off by the police. He had been using it for a month, after taking it from one of the women whom he had added to his collection. He had changed license plates on it a few times, always stealing the replacements from parked cars in the early hours before dawn.

After walking back to the motel, he drove away in Redlow's Pontiac. It was not as sexy as the silver Camaro, but he figured it would serve him well enough for a couple of weeks.

He went to a neo-punk nightclub named Rip It, in Huntington Beach, where he parked at the darkest end of the lot. He found a pouch of tools in the trunk and used a screwdriver and pliers to remove the plates, which he swapped with those on a battered gray Ford parked beside him. Then he drove to the other end of the lot and reparked.

Fog, with the clammy feel of something dead, moved in from the sea. Palm trees and telephone poles disappeared as if dissolved by the acidity of the mist, and the streetlamps became ghost lights adrift in the murk.

Inside, the club was everything he liked. Loud, dirty, and dark. Reeking of smoke, spilled liquor, and sweat. The band hit the chords harder than any musicians he'd ever heard, rammed pure rage into each tune, twisting the melody into a squealing mutant voice, banging the numbingly repetitious rhythms home with savage fury, playing each number so loud that, with the help of huge amplifiers, they rattled the filthy windows and almost made his eyes bleed.

The crowd was energetic, high on drugs of every variety, some of them drunk, many of them dangerous. In clothing, the preferred color was black, so Vassago fit right in. And he was not the only one wearing sunglasses. Some of them, both men and women, were skinheads, and some wore their hair in short spikes, but none of them favored the frivolous flamboyancy of huge spikes and cock's combs and colorful dye jobs that had been a part of early punk. On the jammed dance floor, people seemed to be shoving each other and roughing each other up, maybe feeling each other up in some cases, but no one there had ever taken lessons at an Arthur Murray studio or watched "Soul Train."

At the scarred, stained, greasy bar, Vassago pointed to the Corona, one of six brands of beer lined up on a shelf. He paid and took the bottle from the bartender without the need to exchange a word. He stood there, drinking and scanning the crowd.

Only a few of the customers at the bar and tables, or those standing along the walls, were talking to one another. Most were sullen and silent, not because the pounding music made conversation difficult but because they were the new wave of alienated youth, estranged not only from society but from one another. They were convinced that nothing mattered except self-gratification, that nothing was worth talking about, that they were the last generation on a world headed for destruction, with no future.

He knew of other neo-punk bars, but this was one of only two in Orange and Los Angeles counties—the area that so many chamber of commerce types liked to call the Southland—that were the real thing. Many of the others catered to people who wanted to play at the lifestyle the same way some dentists and accountants liked to put on hand-tooled boots, faded jeans, checkered shirts, and ten-gallon hats to go to a country-and-western bar and pretend they were cowboys. At Rip It, there was no pretense in anyone's eyes, and everyone you encountered met you with a challenging stare, trying to decide whether they wanted sex or violence from you and whether you were likely to give them either. If it was an either-or situation, many of them would have chosen violence over sex.

A few were looking for something that transcended violence and sex, without a clear idea of what it might be. Vassago could have shown them precisely that for which they were searching.

The problem was, he did not at first see anyone who appealed to him sufficiently to consider an addition to his collection. He was not a crude killer, piling up bodies for the sake of piling them up. Quantity had no appeal to him; he was more interested in quality. A connoisseur of death. If he could earn his way back into Hell, he would have to do so with an exceptional offering, a collection that was superior in both its overall composition and in the character of each of its components.

He had made a previous acquisition at Rip It three months ago, a girl who insisted her name was Neon. In his car, when he tried to knock her unconscious, one blow didn't do the job, and she fought back with a ferocity that was exhilarating. Even later, in the bottom floor of the funhouse, when she regained consciousness, she resisted fiercely, though bound at wrists and ankles. She squirmed and thrashed, biting him until he repeatedly bashed her skull against the concrete floor.

Now, just as he finished his beer, he saw another woman who reminded him of Neon. Physically they were far different, but spiritually they were the same: hard cases, angry for reasons they didn't always understand themselves, worldly beyond their years, with all the potential violence of tigresses. Neon had been five-four, brunette, with a dusky complexion. This one was a blonde in her early twenties, about five-seven. Lean and rangy. Riveting eyes the same shade of blue as a pure gas flame, yet icy. She was wearing a ragged black denim jacket over a tight black sweater, a short black skirt, and boots.

In an age when attitude was admired more than intelligence, she knew how to carry herself for the maximum impact. She moved with her shoulders back and her head lifted almost haughtily. Her self-possession was as intimidating as spiked armor. Although every man in the room looked at her in a way that said he wanted her, none of them dared to come on to her, for she appeared to be able to emasculate with a single word or look.

Her powerful sexuality, however, was what made her of interest to Vassago. Men would always be drawn to her—he noticed that those flanking him at the bar were watching her even now—and some would not be intimidated. She possessed a savage vitality that made even Neon seem timid. When her defenses were penetrated, she would be lubricious and disgustingly fertile, soon fat with new life, a wild but fruitful brood mare.

He decided that she had two great weaknesses. The first was her clear conviction that she was superior to everyone she met and was, therefore, untouchable and safe, the same conviction that had made it possible for royalty, in more innocent times, to walk among commoners in complete confidence that everyone they passed would draw back respectfully or drop to their knees in awe. The second weakness was her extreme anger, which she stored in such quantity that Vassago seemed to be able to see it crackling off her smooth pale skin, like an overcharge of electricity.

He wondered how he might arrange her death to best symbolize her flaws. Soon he had a couple of good ideas.

She was with a group of about six men and four women, though she did not seem to be attached to any one of them. Vassago was trying to decide on an approach to her when, not entirely to his surprise, *she* approached *him.* He supposed their encounter was inevitable. They were, after all, the two most dangerous people at the dance.

Just as the band took a break and the decibel level fell to a point at which the interior of the club would no longer have been lethal to cats, the blonde came to the bar. She pushed between Vassago and another man, ordered and paid for a beer. She took the bottle from the bartender, turned sideways to face Vassago, and looked at him across the top of the open bottle, from which wisps of cold vapor rose like smoke.

She said, "You blind?"

"To some things, Miss."

She looked incredulous. "Miss?"

He shrugged.

"Why the sunglasses?" she asked.

"I've been to Hell."

"What's that supposed to mean?"

"Hell is cold, dark."

"That so? I still don't get the sunglasses."

"Over there, you learn to see in total darkness."

"This is an interesting line of bullshit."

"So now I'm sensitive to light."

"A real *different* line of bullshit."

He said nothing.

She drank some beer, but her eyes never left him.

He liked the way her throat muscles worked when she swallowed.

After a moment she said, "This your usual line of crap, or do you just make it up as you go?"

He shrugged again.

"You were watching me," she said.

"So?"

"You're right. Every asshole in here is watching me most of the time."

He was studying her intensely blue eyes. What he thought he might do was cut them out, then reinsert them backward, so she was looking into her own skull. A comment on her self-absorbtion.

IN THE DREAM Hatch was talking to a beautiful but incredibly cold-looking blonde. Her flawless skin was as white as porcelain, and her eyes were like polished ice reflecting a clear winter sky. They were standing at a bar in a strange establishment he had never seen before. She was looking at him across the top of a beer bottle that she held—and brought to her mouth—as she might have held a phallus. But the taunting way she drank from it and licked the glass rim seemed to be as much a threat as it was an erotic invitation. He could not hear a thing she said, and he could hear only a few words that he spoke himself: ". . . been to Hell . . . cold, dark . . . sensitive to light . . ." The blonde was looking at him, and it was surely he who was speaking to her, yet the words were not in his own voice. Suddenly he found himself focusing more intently on her arctic eyes, and before he knew what he was doing, he produced a switchblade knife and flicked it open. As if she felt no pain, as if in fact she was dead already, the blonde did not react when, with a swift whip of the knife, he took her left eye from its socket. He rolled it over on his fingertips, and replaced it with the blind end outward and the blue lens gazing inward—

Hatch sat up. Unable to breathe. Heart hammering. He swung his legs out of bed and stood, feeling as if he had to run away from something. But he just gasped for breath, not sure where to run to find shelter, safety.

They had fallen asleep with a bedside lamp on, a towel draped over the shade to soften the light while they made love. The room was well enough lit for him to see Lindsey lying on her side of the bed in a tangle of covers.

She was so still, he thought she was dead. He had the crazy feeling that he'd killed her. With a switchblade.

Then she stirred and mumbled in her sleep.

He shuddered. He looked at his hands. They were shaking.

VASSAGO WAS SO enamored of his artistic vision that he had the impulsive desire to reverse her eyes right there, in the bar, with everyone watching. He restrained himself.

"So what do you want?" she asked, after taking another swallow of beer.

He said, "Out of what—life?"

"Out of me."

"What do you think?"

"A few thrills," she said.

"More than that."

"Home and family?" she asked sarcastically.

He didn't answer right away. He wanted time to think. This one was not easy to play, a different sort of fish. He did not want to risk saying the wrong thing and letting her slip the hook. He got another beer, drank some of it.

Four members of a backup band approached the stage. They were going to play during the other musicians' break. Soon conversation would be impossible again. More important, when the crashing music began, the energy level of the club would rise, and it might exceed the energy level between him and the blonde. She might not be as susceptible to the suggestion that they leave together.

He finally answered her question, told her a lie about what he wanted to do with her: "You know anybody you wish was dead?"

"Who doesn't?"

"Who is it?"

"Half the people I've ever met."

"I mean, one person in particular."

She began to realize what he was suggesting. She took another sip of beer and lingered with her mouth and tongue against the rim of the bottle. "What—is this a game or something?"

"Only if you want it to be, Miss."

"You're weird."

"Isn't that what you like?"

"Maybe you're a cop."

"You really think so?"

She stared intently at his sunglasses, though she wouldn't have been able to see more than a dim suggestion of his eyes beyond the heavily tinted lenses. "No. Not a cop."

"Sex isn't a good way to start," he said.

"It isn't, huh?"

"Death is a better opener. Make a little death together, then make a little sex. You won't believe how intense it can get."

She said nothing.

The backup band was picking up the instruments on the stage.

He said, "This one in particular you'd like dead—it's a guy?"

"Yeah."

"He live within driving distance?"

"Twenty minutes from here."

"So let's do it."

The musicians began to tune up, though it seemed a pointless exercise, considering the type of music they were going to play. They had better play the right stuff, and they had better be good at it, because it was the kind of club where the customers wouldn't hesitate to trash the band if they didn't like it.

At last the blonde said, "I've got a little PCP. Want to do some with me?"

"Angel dust? It runs in my veins."

"You got a car?"

"Let's go."

On the way out he opened the door for her.

She laughed. "You're one weird son of a bitch."

ACCORDING TO THE digital clock on the nightstand, it was 1:28 in the morning. Although Hatch had been asleep only a couple of hours, he was wide awake and unwilling to lie down again.

Besides, his mouth was dry. He felt as if he had been eating sand. He needed a drink.

The towel-draped lamp provided enough light for him to make his way to the dresser and quietly open the correct drawer without waking Lindsey. Shivering, he took a sweatshirt from the drawer and pulled it on. He was wearing only pajama bottoms, but he knew that the addition of a thin pajama top would not quell his chills.

He opened the bedroom door and stepped into the upstairs hall. He glanced back at his slumbering wife. She looked beautiful there in the soft amber light, dark hair against the white pillow, her face relaxed, lips slightly parted, one hand tucked under her chin. The sight of her, more than the sweatshirt, warmed him. Then he thought about the years they had lost in their surrender to grief, and the residual fear from the nightmare was further diluted by a flood of regret. He pulled the door shut soundlessly behind him.

The second-floor hall was hung with shadows, but wan light rose along the stairwell from the foyer below. On their way from the family-room sofa to the sleigh bed, they had not paused to switch off lamps.

Like a couple of horny teenagers. He smiled at the thought.

On his way down the stairs, he remembered the nightmare, and his smile slipped away.

The blonde. The knife. The eye.

It had seemed so *real*.

At the foot of the stairs he stopped, listening. The silence in the house was unnatural. He rapped one knuckle against the newel post, just to hear a sound. The tap seemed softer than it should have been. The silence following it was deeper than before.

"Jesus, that dream really spooked you," he said aloud, and the sound of his own voice was reassuring.

His bare feet made an amusing slapping sound on the oak floor of the downstairs hall, and even more noise on the tile floor of the kitchen. His thirst growing more acute by the second, he took a can of Pepsi from the refrigerator, popped it open, tilted his head back, closed his eyes, and had a long drink.

It didn't taste like cola. It tasted like beer.

Frowning, he opened his eyes and looked at the can. It was not a can any more. It was a bottle of beer, the same brand as in the dream: Corona. Neither he nor Lindsey drank Corona. When they had a beer, which was rarely, it was a Heineken.

Fear went through him like vibrations through a wire.

Then he noticed that the tile floor of the kitchen was gone. He was standing barefoot on gravel. The stones cut into the balls of his feet.

As his heart began to race, he looked around the kitchen with a desperate need to reaffirm that he was in his own house, that the world had not just tilted into some bizarre new dimension. He let his gaze travel over the familiar white-washed birch cabinets, the dark granite countertops, the dishwasher, the gleaming face of the built-in microwave, and he willed the nightmare to recede. But the gravel floor remained. He was still holding a Corona in his right hand. He turned toward the sink, intent on splashing cold water in his face, but the sink was no longer there. One half of the kitchen had vanished, replaced by a roadside bar along which cars were parked in a row, and then—

—he was not in his kitchen at all. It was entirely gone. He was in the open air of the April night, where thick fog glowed with the reflection of red neon from a sign somewhere behind him. He was walking along a graveled parking lot, past the row of parked cars. He was not barefoot any more but wearing rubber-soled black Rockports.

He heard a woman say, "My name's Lisa. What's yours?"

He turned his head and saw the blonde. She was at his side, keeping pace with him across the parking lot.

Instead of answering her right away, he tipped the Corona to his mouth, sucked down the last couple of ounces, and dropped the empty bottle on the gravel. "My name—"

—he gasped as cold Pepsi foamed from the dropped can, and puddled around his bare feet. The gravel had disappeared. A spreading pool of cola glistened on the peach-colored Santa Fe tiles of his kitchen floor.

IN REDLOW'S PONTIAC, Lisa told Vassago to take the San Diego Freeway south. By the time he traveled eastward on fog-filled surface streets and eventually found a freeway entrance, she had extracted capsules of what she said was PCP from the pharmacopoeia in her purse, and they had washed them down with the rest of her beer.

PCP was an animal tranquilizer that often had the opposite of a tranquilizing effect on human beings, exciting them into destructive frenzies. It would be interesting to watch the impact of the drug on Lisa, who seemed to have the conscience of a snake, to whom the concept of morality was utterly alien, who viewed the world with unrelenting hatred and contempt, whose sense of personal power and superiority did not preclude a self-destructive streak, and who was already so full of tightly contained psychotic energy that she always seemed about to explode. He suspected that, with the aid of PCP, she'd be capable of highly entertaining extremes of violence, fierce storms of bloody destruction that he would find exhilarating to watch.

"Where are we going?" he asked as they cruised south on the freeway. The headlights drilled into a white mist that hid the world and made it seem as if they could invent any landscape and future they wished. Whatever they imagined might take substance from the fog and appear around them.

"El Toro," she said.

"That's where he lives?"

"Yeah."

"Who is he?"

"You need a name?"

"No, ma'am. Why do you want him dead?"

She studied him for a while. Gradually a smile spread across her face, as if it were a wound being carved by a slow-moving and invisible knife. Her small white teeth looked pointy. Piranha teeth. "You'll really do it, won't you?" she asked. "You'll just go in there and kill the guy to prove I oughta want you."

"To prove nothing," he said. "Just because it might be fun. Like I told you—"

"First make some death together, then make some sex," she finished for him.

Just to keep her talking and make her feel increasingly at ease with him, he said, "Does he live in an apartment or a house?"

"Why's it matter?"

"Lots more ways to get into a house, and neighbors aren't as close."

"It's a house," she said.

"Why do you want him dead?"

"He wanted me, I didn't want him, and he felt he could take what he wanted anyway."

"Couldn't have been easy taking anything from you."

Her eyes were colder than ever. "The bastard had to have stitches in his face when it was over."

"But he still got what he wanted?"

"He was bigger than me."

She turned away from him and gazed at the road ahead.

A breeze had risen from the west, and the fog no longer eddied lazily through the night. It churned across the highway like smoke billowing off a vast fire, as if the entire coastline was ablaze, whole cities incinerated and the ruins smouldering.

Vassago kept glancing at her profile, wishing that he could go with her to El Toro and see how deep in blood she would wade for vengeance. Then he would have liked to convince her to come with him to his hideaway and give herself, of her own free will, to his collection. Whether she knew it or not, she wanted death. She would be grateful for the sweet pain that would be her ticket to damnation. Pale skin almost luminescent against her black clothes, filled with hatred so intense that it made her darkly radiant, she would be an incomparable vision as she walked to her destiny among Vassago's collection and accepted the killing blow, a willing sacrifice for his repatriation to Hell.

He knew, however, that she would not accede to his fantasy and die for him even if death was what she wanted. She would die only for herself, when she eventually concluded that termination was her deepest desire.

The moment she began to realize what he really wanted from her, she would lash out at him. She would be harder to control—and would do more damage—than Neon. He preferred to take each new acquisition to his museum of death while she was still alive, extracting the life from her beneath the malevolent gaze of the funhouse Lucifer. But he knew that he did not have that luxury with Lisa. She would not be easy to subdue, even with a sudden unexpected blow. And once he had lost the advantage of surprise, she would be a fierce adversary.

He was not concerned about being hurt. Nothing, including the prospect of pain, could frighten him. Indeed, each blow she landed, each cut she opened in him, would be an exquisite thrill, pure pleasure.

The problem was, she might be strong enough to get away from him, and he could not risk her escape. He wasn't worried that she would report him to the cops. She existed in a subculture that was suspicious and scornful of the police, seething with hatred for them. If she slipped out of his grasp, however, he would lose the chance to add her to his collection. And he was convinced that her tremendous perverse energy would be the final offering that would win him readmission to Hell.

"You feeling anything yet?" she asked, still looking ahead at the fog, into which they barreled at a dangerous speed.

"A little," he said.

"I don't feel anything." She opened her purse again and began rummaging through it, taking stock of what other pills and capsules she possessed. "We need some kind of booster to help the crap kick in good."

While Lisa was distracted by her search for the right chemical to enhance the PCP, Vassago drove with his left hand and reached under his seat with his right to get the revolver that he had taken off Morton Redlow. She looked up just as he thrust the muzzle against her left side. If she knew what was happening, she showed no surprise. He fired two shots, killing her instantly.

HATCH CLEANED UP the spilled Pepsi with paper towels. By the time he stepped to the kitchen sink to wash his hands, he was still shaking but not as badly as he had been.

Terror, which had been briefly all-consuming, made some room for curiosity. He hesitantly touched the rim of the stainless-steel sink and then the faucet, as if they might dissolve beneath his hand. He struggled to understand how a dream could continue after he had awakened. The only explanation, which he could not accept, was insanity.

He turned on the water, adjusted hot and cold, pumped some liquid soap out of the container, began to lather his hands, and looked up at the window above the sink, which faced onto the rear yard. The yard was gone. A highway lay in its place. The kitchen window had become a windshield. Swaddled in fog and only partially revealed by two headlight beams, the pavement rolled toward him as if the house was racing over it at sixty miles an hour. He sensed a presence beside him where there should have been nothing but the double ovens. When he turned his head he saw the blonde clawing in her purse. He realized that something was in his hand, firmer than mere lather, and he looked down at a revolver—

—the kitchen snapped completely out of existence. He was in a car, rocketing along a foggy highway, pushing the muzzle of the revolver into the blonde's side. With horror, as she looked up at him, he felt his finger squeeze the trigger once, twice. She was punched sideways by the dual impact as the ear-shattering crash of the shots slammed through the car.

VASSAGO COULD NOT have anticipated what happened next.

The gun must have been loaded with magnum cartridges, for the two shots ripped through the blonde more violently than he expected and slammed her into the passenger door. Either her door was not properly shut or one of the rounds punched all the way through her, damaging the latch, because the door flew open. Wind rushed into the Pontiac, shrieking like a living beast, and Lisa was snatched out into the night.

He jammed on the brakes and looked at the rearview mirror. As the car began to fishtail, he saw the blonde's body tumbling along the pavement behind him.

He intended to stop, throw the car into reverse, and go back for her, but even at that dead hour of the morning, other traffic shared the freeway. He saw two sets of headlights maybe half a mile behind him, bright smudges in the mist but clarifying by the second. Those drivers would encounter the body before he could reach it and scoop it into the Pontiac.

Taking his foot off the brake and accelerating, he swung the car hard to the left, across two lanes, then whipped it back to the right, forcing the door to slam shut. It rattled in its frame but didn't pop open again. The latch must be at least partially effective.

Although visibility had declined to about a hundred feet, he put the Pontiac up to eighty, bulleting blindly into the churning fog. Two exits later, he left the freeway and rapidly slowed down. On surface streets he made his way out of the area as swiftly as possible, obeying speed limits because any cop who stopped him would surely notice the blood splashed across the upholstery and glass of the passenger door.

IN THE REARVIEW mirror, Hatch saw the body tumbling along the pavement, vanishing into the fog. Then for a brief moment he saw his own reflection from the bridge of his nose to his eyebrows. He was wearing sunglasses even though driving at night. No. *He* wasn't wearing them. The driver of the car was wearing them, and the reflection at which he stared was not his own. Although he seemed to be the driver, he realized that he was not, because even the dim glimpse he got of the eyes behind the tinted lenses was sufficient to convince him that they were peculiar, troubled, and utterly different from his own eyes. Then—

—he was standing at the kitchen sink again, breathing hard and making choking sounds of revulsion. Beyond the window lay only the backyard, blanketed by night and fog.

"Hatch?"

Startled, he turned.

Lindsey was standing in the doorway, in her bathrobe. "Is something wrong?"

Wiping his soapy hands on his sweatshirt, he tried to speak, but terror had rendered him mute.

She hurried to him. "Hatch?"

He held her tightly and was glad for her embrace, which at last squeezed the words from him. "I shot her, she flew out of the car, Jesus God Almighty, bounced along the highway like a rag doll!"

7 At Hatch's request, Lindsey brewed a pot of coffee. The familiarity of the delicious aroma was an antidote to the strangeness of the night. More than anything else, that smell restored a sense of normalcy that helped settle Hatch's nerves. They drank the coffee at the breakfast table at one end of the kitchen.

Hatch insisted on closing the Levolor blind over the nearby window. He said, "I have the feeling . . . something's out there . . . and I don't want it looking in at us." He could not explain what he meant by "something."

When Hatch had recounted everything that had happened to him since waking from the nightmare of the icy blonde, the switchblade, and the mutilated eye, Lindsey had only one explanation to offer. "No matter how it seemed at the time, you must not have been fully awake when you got out of bed. You were sleepwalking. You didn't really wake up until I stepped into the kitchen and called your name."

"I've never been a sleepwalker," he said.

She tried to make light of his objection. "Never too late to take up a new affliction."

"I don't buy it."

"Then what's your explanation?"

"I don't have one."

"So sleepwalking," she said.

He stared down into the white porcelain cup that he clasped in both hands, as if he were a Gypsy trying to foresee the future in the patterns of light on the surface of the black brew. "Have you ever dreamed you were someone else?"

"I suppose so," she said.

He looked hard at her. "No supposing. Have you ever seen a dream through the eyes of a stranger? A specific dream you can tell me about?"

"Well . . . no. But I'm sure I must've, at one time. I just don't remember. Dreams are smoke, after all. They fade so fast. Who remembers them for long?"

"I'll remember this one for the rest of my life," he said.

ALTHOUGH THEY RETURNED to bed, neither of them could get to sleep again. Maybe it was partly the coffee. She thought he had wanted the coffee precisely because he hoped that it would prevent sleep, sparing him a return to the nightmare. Well, it had worked.

They both were lying on their backs, staring at the ceiling.

At first he had been unwilling to turn off the bedside lamp, though he had revealed his reluctance only in the hesitancy with which he clicked the switch. He was almost like a child who was old enough to know real fears from false ones but not quite old enough to escape all of the latter, certain that some monster lurked under the bed but ashamed to say as much.

Now, with the lamp off and with only the indirect glow of distant streetlamps piercing the windows between the halves of the drapes, his anxiety had infected her. She found it easy to imagine that some shadows on the ceiling moved, bat-lizard-spider forms of singular stealth and malevolent purpose.

They talked softly, on and off, about nothing special. They both knew what they wanted to talk about, but they were afraid of it. Unlike the creepy-crawlies on the ceiling and things that lived under children's beds, it was a real fear. Brain damage.

Since waking up in the hospital, reanimated, Hatch had been having bad dreams of unnerving power. He didn't have them every night. His sleep might even be undisturbed for as long as three or four nights in a row. But he was having them more frequently, week by week, and the intensity was increasing.

They were not always the same dreams, as he described them, but they contained similar elements. Violence. Horrific images of naked, rotting bodies contorted into peculiar positions. Always, the dreams unfolded from the point of view of a stranger, the same mysterious figure, as if Hatch were a spirit in possession of the man but unable to control him, along for the ride. Routinely the nightmares began or ended—or began *and* ended—in the same setting: an assemblage of unusual buildings and other queer structures that resisted identification, all of it unlighted and seen most often as a series of baffling silhouettes against a night sky. He also saw cavernous rooms and mazes of concrete corridors that were somehow revealed in spite of having no windows or artificial lighting. The location was, he said, familiar to him, but recognition remained elusive, for he never saw enough to be able to identify it.

Until tonight, they had tried to convince themselves that his affliction would be short-lived. Hatch was full of positive thoughts, as usual. Bad dreams were not remarkable. Everyone had them. They were often caused by stress. Alleviate the stress, and the nightmares went away.

But they were not fading. And now they had taken a new and deeply disturbing turn: sleepwalking.

Or perhaps he was beginning, while awake, to hallucinate the same images that troubled his sleep.

Shortly before dawn, Hatch reached out for her beneath the sheets and took her hand, held it tight. "I'll be all right. It's nothing, really. Just a dream."

"First thing in the morning, you should call Nyebern," she said, her heart sinking like a stone in a pond. "We haven't been straight with him. He told you to let him know immediately if there were any symptoms—"

"This isn't really a symptom," he said, trying to put the best face on it.

"Physical *or* mental symptoms," she said, afraid for him—and for herself if something *was* wrong with him.

"I had all the tests, most of them twice. They gave me a clean bill of health. No brain damage."

"Then you've nothing to worry about, do you? No reason to delay seeing Nyebern."

"If there'd been brain damage, it would've showed up right away. It's not a residual thing, doesn't kick in on a delay."

They were silent for a while.

She could no longer imagine that creepy-crawlies moved through the shadows on the ceiling. False fears had evaporated the moment he had spoken the name of the biggest real fear that they faced.

At last she said, "What about Regina?"

He considered her question for a while. Then: "I think we should go ahead with it, fill out the papers—assuming she wants to come with us, of course."

"And if . . . you've got a problem? And it gets worse?"

"It'll take a few days to make the arrangements and be able to bring her home. By then we'll have the results of the physical, the tests. I'm sure I'll be fine."

"You're too relaxed about this."

"Stress kills."

"If Nyebern finds something seriously wrong . . . ?"

"Then we'll ask the orphanage for a postponement if we have to. The thing is, if we tell them I'm having problems that don't allow me to go ahead with the papers tomorrow, they might have second thoughts about our suitability. We might be rejected and never have a chance with Regina."

The day had been so perfect, from their meeting in Salvatore Gujilio's office to their lovemaking before the fire and again in the massive old Chinese sleigh bed. The future had looked so bright, the worst behind them. She was stunned at how suddenly they had taken another nasty plunge.

She said, "God, Hatch, I love you."

In the darkness he moved close to her and took her in his arms. Until long after dawn, they just held each other, saying nothing because, for the moment, everything had been said.

LATER, AFTER THEY showered and dressed, they went downstairs and had more coffee at the breakfast table. Mornings, they always listened to the radio, an all-news station. That was how they heard about Lisa Blaine, the blonde who had been shot twice and thrown from a moving car on the San Diego Freeway the previous night—at precisely the time that Hatch, standing in the kitchen, had a vision of the trigger being pulled and the body tumbling along the pavement in the wake of the car.

8 For reasons he could not understand, Hatch was compelled to see the section of the freeway where the dead woman had been found. "Maybe something will click," was all the explanation he could offer.

He drove their new red Mitsubishi. They went north on the coast highway, then east on a series of surface streets to the South Coast Plaza Shopping Mall, where they entered the San Diego Freeway heading south. He wanted to come upon the site of the murder from the same direction in which the killer had been traveling the previous night.

By nine-fifteen, rush-hour traffic should have abated, but all of the lanes were still clogged. They made halting progress southward in a haze of exhaust fumes, from which the car air-conditioning spared them.

The marine layer that surged in from the Pacific during the night had burned off. Trees stirred in a spring breeze, and birds swooped in giddy arcs across the cloudless, piercingly blue sky. The day did not seem like one in which anyone would have reason to think of death.

They passed the MacArthur Boulevard exit, then Jamboree, and with every turn of the wheels, Hatch felt the muscles growing tenser in his neck and shoulders. He was overcome by the uncanny feeling that he actually had followed this route last night, when fog had obscured the airport, hotels, office buildings, and the brown hills in the distance, though in fact he had been at home.

"They were going to El Toro," he said, which was a detail he had not remembered until now. Or perhaps he had only now perceived it by the grace of some sixth sense.

"Maybe that's where she lived—or where he lives."

Frowning, Hatch said, "I don't think so."

As they crept forward through the snarled traffic, he began to recall not just details of the dream but the *feeling* of it, the edgy atmosphere of pending violence.

His hands slipped on the steering wheel. They were clammy. He blotted them on his shirt.

"I think in some ways," he said, "the blonde was almost as dangerous as I . . . as he was. . . ."

"What do you mean?"

"I don't know. It's just the feeling I had then."

Sunshine glimmered on—and glinted off—the multitude of vehicles that churned both north and south in two great rivers of steel and chrome and glass. Outside, the temperature was hovering around eighty degrees. But Hatch was cold.

As a sign notified them of the upcoming Culver Boulevard exit, Hatch leaned forward slightly. He let go of the steering wheel with his right hand and reached under his seat. "It was here that he went for the gun . . . pulled it out . . . she was looking in her purse for something. . . ."

He would not have been too surprised if he had found a gun under his seat, for he still had a frighteningly clear recollection of how fluidly the dream and reality had mingled, separated, and mingled again last night. Why not now, even in daylight? He let out a hiss of relief when he found that the space beneath his seat was empty.

"Cops," Lindsey said.

Hatch was so caught up in the re-creation of the events in the nightmare that he didn't immediately realize what Lindsey was talking about. Then he saw black-and-whites and other police vehicles parked along the interstate.

Bent forward, intently studying the dusty ground before them, uniformed officers were walking the shoulder of the highway and picking through the dry grass beyond it. They were evidently conducting an expanded search for evidence to discover anything else that might have fallen out of the killer's car before, with, or after the blonde.

He noticed that every one of the cops was wearing sunglasses, as were he and Lindsey. The day was eye-stingingly bright.

But the killer had been wearing sunglasses, too, when he had looked in the rearview mirror. Why would he have been wearing them in the dark in dense fog, for God's sake?

Shades at night in bad weather was more than just affectation or eccentricity. It was weird.

Hatch still had the imaginary gun in his hand, withdrawn from under the seat. But because they were moving so much slower than the killer had been driving, they had not yet reached the spot at which the revolver had been fired.

Traffic was creeping bumper-to-bumper not because the rush hour was heavier than usual but because motorists were slowing to stare at the police. It was what the radio traffic reporters called "gawkers' block."

"He was really barreling along," Hatch said.

"In heavy fog."

"And sunglasses."

"Stupid," Lindsey said.

"No. This guy's smart."

"Sounds stupid to me."

"Fearless." Hatch tried to settle back into the skin of the man with whom he had shared a body in the nightmare. It wasn't easy. Something about the killer was totally alien and firmly resisted analysis. "He's extremely cold . . . cold and dark inside . . . he doesn't think like you or me. . . ." Hatch struggled to find words to convey what the killer had felt like. "Dirty." He shook his head. "I don't mean he was unwashed, nothing like that. It's more as if . . . well, as if he was contaminated." He sighed and gave up. "Anyway, he's utterly fearless. Nothing scares him. He believes that nothing can hurt him. But in his case that's not the same as recklessness. Because . . . somehow he's right."

"What're you saying—that he's invulnerable?"

"No. Not exactly. But nothing you could do to him . . . would matter to him."

Lindsey hugged herself. "You make him sound . . . inhuman."

At the moment the police search for evidence was concentrated in the quarter of a mile just south of the Culver Boulevard exit. When Hatch got past that activity, traffic began to move faster.

The imaginary gun in his right hand seemed to take on greater substance. He could almost feel the cold steel against his palm.

When he pointed the phantom revolver at Lindsey and glanced at her, she winced. He saw her clearly, but he could also see, in memory, the face of the blonde as she had looked up from her purse with too little reaction time even to show surprise.

"Here, right here, two shots, fast as I . . . as he could pull the trigger,"

Hatch said, shuddering because the memory of violence was far easier to recapture than were the mood and malign spirit of the gunman. "Big holes in her." He could see it so clearly. "Jesus, it was awful." He was really into it. "The way she tore open. And the sound like thunder, the end of the world." The bitter taste of stomach acid rose in his throat. "She was thrown back by the impact, against the door, instantly dead, but the door flew open. He wasn't expecting it to fly open. He wanted her, she was part of his collection now, but then she was gone, out into the night, gone, rolling like a piece of litter along the blacktop."

Caught up in the dream memory, he rammed his foot down on the brake pedal, as the killer had done.

"Hatch, no!"

A car, then another, then a third, swerved around them in flashes of chrome and sun-silvered glass, horns blaring, narrowly avoiding a collision.

Shaking himself out of the memory, Hatch accelerated again, back into the traffic flow. He was aware of people staring at him from other cars.

He didn't care about their scrutiny, for he had picked up the trail as if he were a bloodhound. It was not actually a scent that he followed. It was an indefinable something that led him on, maybe psychic vibrations, a disturbance in the ether made by the killer's passage just as a shark's fin would carve a trough in the surface of the sea, although the ether had not repaired itself with the alacrity of water.

"He considered going back for her, knew it was hopeless, so he drove on," Hatch said, aware that his voice had become low and slightly raspy, as if he were recounting secrets that were painful to reveal.

"Then I walked into the kitchen, and you were making an odd choking-gasping sound," Lindsey said. "Gripping the edge of the counter tight enough to crack the granite. I thought you were having a heart attack—"

"Drove very fast," Hatch said, accelerating only slightly himself, "seventy, eighty, even faster, anxious to get away before the traffic behind him encountered the body."

Realizing that he was not merely speculating on what the killer had done, Lindsey said, "You're remembering more than you dreamed, past the point when I came into the kitchen and woke you."

"Not remembering," he said huskily.

"Then what?"

"Sensing . . ."

"Now?"

"Yes."

"How?"

"Somehow." He simply could not explain it better than that. "Somehow," he whispered, and he followed the ribbon of pavement across that largely flat expanse of land, which seemed to darken in spite of the bright morning sun, as if the killer cast a shadow vastly larger than himself, a shadow that lingered behind him even hours after he had gone. "Eighty . . . eighty-five . . . almost ninety miles an hour . . . able to see only a hundred feet ahead."

If any traffic had been there in the fog, the killer would have crashed into it with cataclysmic force. "He didn't take the first exit, wanted to get farther away than that . . . kept going . . . going. . . ."

He almost didn't slow down in time to make the exit for State Route 133, which became the canyon road into Laguna Beach. At the last moment he hit the brakes too hard and whipped the wheel to the right. The Mitsubishi slid as they departed the interstate, but he decreased speed and immediately regained full control.

"He got off here?" Lindsey asked.

"Yes."

Hatch followed the new road to the right.

"Did he go into Laguna?"

"I . . . don't think so."

He braked to a complete halt at a crossroads marked by a stop sign. He pulled onto the shoulder. Open country lay ahead, hills dressed in crisp brown grass. If he went straight through the crossroads, he'd be heading into Laguna Canyon, where developers had not yet managed to raze the wilderness and erect more tract homes. Miles of brushland and scattered oaks flanked the canyon route all the way into Laguna Beach. The killer also might have turned left or right. Hatch looked in each direction, searching for . . . for whatever invisible signs had guided him that far.

After a moment, Lindsey said, "You don't know where he went from here?"

"Hideaway."

"Huh?"

Hatch blinked, not sure why he had chosen that word. "He went back to his hideaway . . . into the ground. . . ."

"Ground?" Lindsey asked. With puzzlement she surveyed the sere hills.

". . . into the darkness . . ."

"You mean he went underground somewhere?"

". . . cool, cool silence . . ."

Hatch sat for a while, staring at the crossroads as a few cars came and went. He had reached the end of the trail. The killer was not there; he knew that much, but he did not know where the man had gone. Nothing more came to him—except, strangely, the sweet chocolate taste of Oreo cookies, as intense as if he had just bitten into one.

9 At The Cottage in Laguna Beach, they had a late breakfast of homefries, eggs, bacon, and buttered toast. Since he had died and been resuscitated, Hatch didn't worry about things like his cholesterol count or the long-term effects of passive inhalation of other people's cigarette smoke. He supposed the day would come when little risks would seem big again, whereupon he would return to a diet high in fruits and vegetables, scowl at smokers who blew their filth his way, and open a bottle of fine wine with a mixture of delight and a grim awareness of the health consequences of consuming alcohol. At the moment he was appreciating life too much to worry unduly about losing it again—which was why he was determined not to let the dreams and the death of the blonde push him off the deep end.

Food had a natural tranquilizing effect. Each bite of egg yolk soothed his nerves.

"Okay," Lindsey said, going at her breakfast somewhat less heartily than Hatch did, "let's suppose there was brain damage of some sort, after all. But minor. So minor it never showed up on any of the tests. Not bad enough to cause paralysis or speech problems or anything like that. In fact, by an incredible stroke of luck, a one in a billion chance, this brain damage had a freak effect that was actually beneficial. It could've made a few new connections in the cerebral tissues, and left you psychic."

"Bull."

"Why?"

"I'm not psychic."

"Then what do you call it?"

"Even if I was psychic, I wouldn't say it was beneficial."

Because the breakfast rush had passed, the restaurant was not too busy. The nearest tables to theirs were vacant. They could discuss the morning's events without fear of being overheard, but Hatch kept glancing around self-consciously anyway.

Immediately following his reanimation, the media had swarmed to Orange County General Hospital, and in the days after Hatch's release, reporters had virtually camped on his doorstep at home. After all, he had been dead longer than any man alive, which made him eligible for considerably more than the fifteen minutes of fame that Andy Warhol had said would eventually be every person's fate in celebrity-obsessed America. He'd done nothing to earn his fame. He didn't want it. He hadn't fought his way out of death; Lindsey, Nyebern, and the resuscitation team had dragged him back. He was a private person, content with just the quiet respect of the better antique dealers who knew his shop and traded with him sometimes. In fact, if the only respect he had was Lindsey's, if he was famous only in her eyes and only for being a good husband, that would be enough for him. By steadfastly refusing to talk to the press, he had finally convinced them to leave him alone and chase after whatever newly born two-headed goat—or its equivalent—was available to fill newspaper space or a minute of the airwaves between deodorant commercials.

Now, if he revealed that he had come back from the dead with some strange power to connect with the mind of a psycho killer, swarms of newspeople would descend on him again. He could not tolerate even the prospect of it. He would find it easier to endure a plague of killer bees or a hive of Hare Krishna solicitors with collection cups and eyes glazed by spiritual transcendence.

"If it's not some psychic ability," Lindsey persisted, "then what *is* it?"

"I don't know."

"That's not good enough."

"It could pass, never happen again. It could be a fluke."

"You don't believe that."

"Well . . . I want to believe it."

"We have to deal with this."

"Why?"

"We have to try to understand it."

"Why?"

"Don't 'why' me like a five-year-old child."

"Why?"

"Be serious, Hatch. A woman's dead. She may not be the first. She may not be the last."

He put his fork on his half-empty plate, and swallowed some orange juice to wash down the homefries. "Okay, all right, it's like a psychic vision, yeah, just the way they show it in the movies. But it's more than that. Creepier."

He closed his eyes, trying to think of an analogy. When he had it, he opened his eyes and looked around the restaurant again to be sure no new diners had entered and sat near them.

He looked regretfully at his plate. His eggs were getting cold. He sighed.

"You know," he said, "how they say identical twins, separated at birth and raised a thousand miles apart by utterly different adopted families, will still grow up to live similar lives?"

"Sure, I've heard of that. So?"

"Even raised apart, with totally different backgrounds, they'll choose similar careers, achieve the same income levels, marry women who resemble each other, even give their kids the same names. It's uncanny. And even if they don't know they're twins, even if each of them was told he was an only child when he was adopted, they'll sense each other out there, across the miles, even if they don't know who or what they're sensing. They have a bond that no one can explain, not even geneticists."

"So how does this apply to you?"

He hesitated, then picked up his fork. He wanted to eat instead of talk. Eating was safe. But she wouldn't let him get away with that. His eggs were congealing. His tranquilizers. He put the fork down again.

"Sometimes," he said, "I see through this guy's eyes when I'm sleeping, and now sometimes I can even feel him out there when I'm awake, and it's like the psychic crap in movies, yeah. But I also feel this . . . this bond with him that I really *can't* explain or describe to you, no matter how much you prod me about it."

"You're not saying you think he's your twin or something?"

"No, not at all. I think he's a lot younger than me, maybe only twenty or twenty-one. And no blood relation. But it's that kind of bond, that mystical twin crap, as if this guy and I share something, have some fundamental quality in common."

"Like what?"

"I don't know. I wish I did." He paused. He decided to be entirely truthful. "Or maybe I don't."

LATER, AFTER THE waitress had cleared away their empty dishes and brought them strong black coffee, Hatch said, "There's no way I'm going to go to the cops and offer to help them, if that's what you're thinking."

"There is a duty here—"

"I don't know anything that could help them anyway."

She blew on her hot coffee. "You know he was driving a Pontiac."

"I don't even think it was his."

"Whose then?"

"Stolen, maybe."

"That was something else you sensed?"

"Yeah. But I don't know what he looks like, his name, where he lives, anything useful."

"What if something like that comes to you? What if you see something that could help the cops?"

"Then I'll call it in anonymously."

"They'll take the information more seriously if you give it to them in person."

He felt violated by the intrusion of this psychotic stranger into his life. That violation made him angry, and he feared his anger more than he feared the stranger, or the supernatural aspect of the situation, or the prospect of brain damage. He dreaded being driven by some extremity to discover that his father's hot temper was within him, too, waiting to be tapped.

"It's a homicide case," he said. "They take *every* tip seriously in a murder investigation, even if it's anonymous. I'm not going to let them make headlines out of me again."

FROM THE RESTAURANT they went across town to Harrison's Antiques, where Lindsey had an art studio on part of the top floor in addition to the one at home. When she painted, a regular change of environment contributed to fresher work.

In the car, with the sun-spangled ocean visible between some of the buildings to their right, Lindsey pressed the point that she had nagged him about over breakfast, because she knew that Hatch's only serious character flaw was a tendency to be too easy-going. Jimmy's death was the only bad thing in his life that he had never been able to rationalize, minimalize, and put out of mind. And even with that, he had tried to suppress it rather than face up to his grief, which is why his grief had a chance to grow. Given time, and not much of it, he'd begin to downplay the importance of what had just happened to him.

She said, "You've still got to see Nyebern."

"I suppose so."

"Definitely."

"If there's brain damage, if that's where this psychic stuff comes from, you said yourself it was *benevolent* brain damage."

"But maybe it's degenerative, maybe it'll get worse."

"I really don't think so," he said. "I feel fine otherwise."

"You're no doctor."

"All right," he said. He braked for the traffic light at the crossing to the public beach in the heart of town. "I'll call him. But we have to see Gujilio later this afternoon."

"You can still squeeze in Nyebern if he has time for you."

Hatch's father had been a tyrant, quick-tempered, sharp-tongued, with a penchant for subduing his wife and disciplining his son by the application of regular doses of verbal abuse in the form of nasty mockery, cutting sarcasm, or just plain threats. Anything at all could set Hatch's father off, or nothing at all, because secretly he cherished irritation and actively sought new sources of it. He was a man who believed he was not destined to be happy—and he insured that his destiny was fulfilled by making himself and everyone around him miserable.

Perhaps afraid that the potential for a murderously bad temper was within him, too, or only because he'd had enough tumult in his life, Hatch had consciously striven to make himself as mellow as his father was high-strung, as sweetly tolerant as his father was narrow-minded, as great-hearted as his father was unforgiving, as determined to roll with all of life's punches as his father was determined to punch back at even imaginary blows. As a result, he was the nicest man Lindsey had ever known, the nicest by light-years or by whatever measure niceness was calculated: bunches, bucketsful, gobs. Sometimes, however, Hatch turned away from an unpleasantness that had to be dealt with, rather than risk getting in touch with any negative emotion that was remotely reminiscent of his old man's paranoia and anger.

The light changed from red to green, but three young women in bikinis were in the crosswalk, laden with beach gear and heading for the ocean. Hatch didn't just wait for them. He watched them with a smile of appreciation for the way they filled out their suits.

"I take it back," Lindsey said.

"What?"

"I was just thinking what a nice guy you are, too nice, but obviously you're a piece of lecherous scum."

"Nice scum, though."

"*I'll* call Nyebern as soon as we get to the shop," Lindsey said.

He drove up the hill through the main part of town, past the old Laguna Hotel. "Okay. But I'm sure as hell not going to tell him I'm suddenly psychic. He's a good man, but he won't be able to sit on that kind of news. The next thing I know, my face'll be all over the cover of the *National Enquirer*. Besides, I'm not psychic, not exactly. I don't know what the hell I am— aside from lecherous scum."

"So what'll you tell him?"

"Just enough about the dreams so he'll realize how troubling they are and how strange, so he'll order whatever tests I ought to have. Good enough?"

"I guess it'll have to be."

IN THE TOMB-DEEP blackness of his hideaway, curled naked upon the stained and lumpy mattress, fast asleep, Vassago saw sunlight, sand, the sea, and three bikinied girls beyond the windshield of a red car.

He was dreaming and knew he dreamed, which was a peculiar sensation. He rolled with it.

He saw, as well, the dark-haired and dark-eyed woman about whom he had dreamed yesterday, when she had been behind the wheel of that same car. She had appeared in other dreams, once in a wheelchair, when she had been laughing and weeping at the same time.

He found her more interesting than the scantily clad beach bunnies because she was unusually vital. Radiant. Through the unknown man driving the car, Vassago somehow knew that the woman had once considered embracing death, had hesitated on the edge of either active or passive self-destruction, and had rejected an early grave—

. . . *water, he sensed a watery vault, cold and suffocating, narrowly escaped* . . .

—whereafter she had been more full of life, energetic, and vivid than ever before. She had cheated death. Denied the devil. Vassago hated her for that, because it was in the service of death that he had found meaning to his own existence.

He tried to reach out and touch her through the body of the man driving the car. Failed. It was only a dream. Dreams could not be controlled. If he could have touched her, he would have made her regret that she had turned away from the comparatively painless death by drowning that could have been hers.

Five

When she moved in with the Harrisons, Regina almost thought she had died and gone to Heaven, except she had her own bathroom, and she didn't believe anyone had his own bathroom up in Heaven because in Heaven no one needed a bathroom. They were not all permanently constipated in Heaven or anything like that, and they certainly didn't just do their business out in public, for God's sake (sorry, God), because no one in his right mind would want to go to Heaven if it was the kind of place where you had to watch where you stepped. It was just that in Heaven all the concerns of earthly existence passed away. You didn't even have a body in Heaven; you were probably just a sphere of mental energy, sort of like a balloon full of golden glowing gas, drifting around among the angels, singing the praises of God—which was pretty weird when you thought about it, all those glowing and singing balloons, but the most you'd ever have to do in the way of waste elimination was maybe vent a little gas now and then, which wouldn't even smell bad, probably like the sweet incense in church, or perfume.

That first day in the Harrisons' house, late Monday afternoon, the twenty-ninth of April, she would remember forever, because they were so nice. They didn't even mention the real reason why they gave her a choice between a bedroom on the second floor and a den on the first floor that could be converted into a bedroom.

"One thing in its favor," Mr. Harrison said about the den, "is the view. Better than the view from the upstairs room."

He led Regina to the big windows that looked out on a rose garden ringed by a border of huge ferns. The view *was* pretty.

Mrs. Harrison said, "And you'd have all these bookshelves, which you might want to fill up gradually with your own collection, since you're a book lover."

Actually, without ever hinting at it, their concern was that she might find the stairs troublesome. But she didn't mind stairs so much. In fact she liked stairs, she loved stairs, she ate stairs for breakfast. In the orphanage, they had put her on the first floor, until she was eight years old and realized she'd been given ground-level accommodations because of her clunky leg brace and deformed right hand, whereupon she immediately demanded to be moved to the third floor. The nuns would not hear of it, so she threw a tantrum, but the nuns knew how to deal with that, so she tried withering scorn, but the nuns could not be withered, so she went on a hunger strike, and finally the nuns surrendered to her demand on a trial basis. She'd lived on the third floor for more than two years, and she had never used the elevator. When she chose the second-floor bedroom in the Harrisons' house, without having seen it, neither of them tried to talk her out of it, or wondered aloud if she were "up" to it, or even blinked. She loved them for that.

The house was gorgeous—cream walls, white woodwork, modern furniture mixed with antiques, Chinese bowls and vases, everything just so. When they took her on a tour, Regina actually felt as dangerously clumsy as she had claimed to be in the meeting in Mr. Gujilio's office. She moved with exaggerated care, afraid that she would knock over one precious item and kick off a chain reaction that would spread across the entire room, then through a doorway into the next room and from there throughout the house, one beautiful treasure tipping into the next like dominoes in a world-championship toppling contest, two-hundred-year-old porcelains exploding, antique furniture reduced to match sticks, until they were left standing in mounds of worthless rubble, coated with the dust of what had been a *fortune* in interior design.

She was so absolutely certain it was going to happen that she wracked her mind urgently, room by room, for something winning to say when catastrophe struck, after the last exquisite crystal candy dish had crashed off the last disintegrating table that had once been the property of the First King of France. "Oops," did not seem appropriate, and neither did "Jesus Christ!" because they thought they had adopted a good Catholic girl not a foul-mouthed heathen (sorry, God), and neither did "somebody pushed me," because that was a lie, and lying bought you a ticket to Hell, though she suspected she was going to wind up in Hell anyway, considering how she couldn't stop thinking the Lord's name in vain and using vulgarities. No balloon full of glowing golden gas for her.

Throughout the house, the walls were adorned with art, and Regina noted that the most wonderful pieces all had the same signature at the bottom right corner: Lindsey Sparling. Even as much of a screwup as she was, she was smart enough to figure that the name Lindsey was no coincidence and that Sparling must be Mrs. Harrison's maiden name. They were the strangest and most beautiful paintings Regina had ever seen, some of them so bright and full of good feeling that you had to smile, some of them dark and brooding. She wanted to spend a long time in front of each of them, sort of soaking them up, but she was afraid Mr. and Mrs. Harrison would think she was a brownnosing phony, pretending interest as a way of apologizing for the wisecracks she had made in Mr. Gujilio's office about paintings on velvet.

Somehow she got through the entire house without destroying anything, and the last room was hers. It was bigger than any room at the orphanage, and she didn't have to share it with anyone. The windows were covered with white plantation shutters. Furnishings included a corner desk and chair, a bookcase, an armchair with footstool, nightstands with matching lamps— and an amazing bed.

"It's from about 1850," Mrs. Harrison said, as Regina let her hand glide slowly over the beautiful bed.

"English," Mr. Harrison said. "Mahogany with hand-painted decoration under several coats of lacquer."

On the footboard, side rails, and headboard, the dark-red and dark-yellow roses and emerald-green leaves seemed alive, not bright against the deeply colored wood but so lustrous and dewy-looking that she was sure she would be able to smell them if she put her nose to their petals.

Mrs. Harrison said, "It might seem a little *old* for a young girl, a little stuffy—"

"Yes, of course," Mr. Harrison said, "we can send it over to the store, sell it, let you choose something you'd like, something modern. This was just furnished as a guest room."

"No," Regina said hastily. "I like it, I really do. Could I keep it, I mean even though it's so expensive?"

"It's not that expensive," Mr. Harrison said, "and of course you can keep anything you want."

"Or get rid of anything you want," Mrs. Harrison said.

"Except us, of course," Mr. Harrison said.

"That's right," Mrs. Harrison said, "I'm afraid we come with the house."

Regina's heart was pounding so hard she could barely get her breath. Happiness. And fear. Everything was so wonderful—but surely it couldn't last. Nothing so good could last very long.

Sliding, mirrored doors covered one wall of the bedroom, and Mrs. Harrison showed Regina a closet behind the mirrors. The hugest closet in the world. Maybe you needed a closet that size if you were a movie star, or if you were one of those men she had read about, who liked to dress up in women's clothes sometimes, 'cause then you'd need both a girl's and boy's wardrobe. But it was much bigger than she needed; it would hold ten times the clothes that she possessed.

With some embarrassment, she looked at the two cardboard suitcases she had brought with her from St. Thomas's. They held everything she owned in the world. For the first time in her life, she realized she was poor. Which was peculiar, really, not to have understood her poverty before, since she was an orphan who had inherited nothing. Well, nothing other than a bum leg and a twisted right hand with two fingers missing.

As if reading Regina's mind, Mrs. Harrison said, "Let's go shopping."

They went to South Coast Plaza Mall. They bought her too many clothes, books, anything she wanted. Regina worried that they were overspending and would have to eat beans for a year to balance their budget—she didn't like beans—but they failed to pick up on her hints about the virtues of frugality. Finally she had to stop them by pretending that her weak leg was bothering her.

From the mall they went to dinner at an Italian restaurant. She had eaten out twice before, but only at a fast-food place, where the owner treated all the kids at the orphanage to burgers and fries. This was a *real* restaurant, and there was so much to absorb that she could hardly eat, keep up her end of the table conversation, *and* enjoy the place all at the same time. The chairs weren't made out of hard plastic, and neither were the knives and forks. The plates weren't either paper or Styrofoam, and drinks came in actual glasses, which must mean that the customers in real restaurants were not as clumsy as those in fast-food places and could be trusted with breakable things. The waitresses weren't teenagers, and they brought your food to you instead of handing it across a counter by the cash register. And they didn't make you pay for it until *after* you'd eaten it!

Later, back at the Harrison house, after Regina unpacked her things, brushed her teeth, put on pajamas, took off her leg brace, and got into bed, both the Harrisons came in to say goodnight. Mr. Harrison sat on the edge of her bed and told her that everything might seem strange at first, even unsettling, but that soon enough she would feel at home, then he kissed her on the forehead and said, "Sweet dreams, princess." Mrs. Harrison was next, and she sat on the edge of the bed, too. She talked for a while about all the things they would do together in the days ahead. Then she kissed Regina on the cheek, said, "Goodnight, honey," and turned off the overhead light as she went out the door into the hall.

Regina had never before been kissed goodnight, so she had not known how to respond. Some of the nuns were huggers; they liked to give you an affectionate squeeze now and then, but none of them was a smoocher. For as far back as Regina could remember, a flicker of the dorm lights was the signal to be in bed within fifteen minutes, and when the lights went out, each kid was responsible for getting tucked in himself. Now she had been tucked in twice and kissed goodnight twice, all in the same evening, and she had been too surprised to kiss either of them in return, which she now realized she should have done.

"You're such a screwup, Reg," she said aloud.

Lying in her magnificent bed, with the painted roses twining around her in the darkness, Regina could imagine the conversation they were having, right that minute, in their own bedroom:

Did she kiss you goodnight?

No, did she kiss you?

No. Maybe she's a cold fish.

Maybe she's a psycho demon child.

Yeah, like that kid in The Omen.

You know what I'm worried about?

She'll stab us to death in our sleep.

Let's hide all the kitchen knives.

Better hide the power tools, too.

You still have the gun in the nightstand?

Yeah, but a gun will never stop her.

Thank God, we have a crucifix.

We'll sleep in shifts.

Send her back to the orphanage tomorrow.

"Such a screwup," Regina said. "Shit." She sighed. "Sorry, God." Then she folded her hands in prayer and said softly, "Dear God, if you'll convince the Harrisons to give me one more chance, I'll never say 'shit' again, and I'll be a better person." That didn't seem like a good enough bargain from God's point of view, so she threw in other inducements: "I'll continue to keep an A average in school, I'll never again put Jell-O in the holy water font, and I'll give serious thought to becoming a nun." Still not good enough. "And I'll eat beans." That ought to do it. God was probably proud of beans. After all, He'd made all kinds of them. Her refusal to eat green or wax or Lima or navy or any other kind of beans had no doubt been noted in Heaven, where they had her down in the Big Book of Insults to God— *Regina, currently age ten, thinks God pulled a real boner when He created beans.* She yawned. She felt better now about her chances with the Harrisons and about her relationship with God, though she didn't feel better about the change in her diet. Anyway, she slept.

2 While Lindsey was washing her face, scrubbing her teeth, and brushing her hair in the master bathroom, Hatch sat in bed with the newspaper. He read the science page first, because it contained the real news these days. Then he skimmed the entertainment section and read his favorite comic strips before turning, at last, to the A section where the latest exploits of politicians were as terrifying and darkly amusing as usual. On page three he saw the story about Bill Cooper, the beer deliveryman whose truck they had found crosswise on the mountain road that fateful, snowy night in March.

Within a couple of days of being resuscitated, Hatch had heard that the trucker had been charged with driving under the influence and that the percentage of alcohol in his blood had been more than twice that required for a conviction under the law. George Glover, Hatch's personal attorney, had asked him if he wanted to press a civil suit against Cooper or the company for which he worked, but Hatch was not by nature litigious. Besides, he dreaded becoming bogged down in the dull and thorny world of lawyers and courtrooms. He was alive. That was all that mattered. A drunk-driving charge would be brought against the trucker without Hatch's involvement, and he was satisfied to let the system handle it.

He had received two pieces of correspondence from William Cooper, the first just four days after his reanimation. It was an apparently sincere, if long-winded and obsequious, apology seeking personal absolution, which was delivered to the hospital where Hatch was undergoing physical therapy. "Sue me if you want," Cooper wrote, "I deserve it. I'd give you everything if you wanted it, though I don't got much, I'm no rich man. But no matter whether you sue me or if not, I most sincerely hope you'll find it in your generous heart to forgive me one ways or another. Except for the genius of Dr. Nyebern and his wonderful people, you'd be dead for sure, and I'd carry it on my conscience all the rest of my days." He rambled on in that fashion for four pages of tightly spaced, cramped, and at times inscrutable handwriting.

Hatch had responded with a short note, assuring Cooper that he did not intend to sue him and that he harbored no animosity toward him. He also had urged the man to seek counseling for alcohol abuse if he had not already done so.

A few weeks later, when Hatch was living at home again and back at work, after the media storm had swept over him, a second letter had arrived from Cooper. Incredibly, he was seeking Hatch's help to get his truck-driving job back, from which he had been fired subsequent to the charges that the police had filed against him. "I been chased down for driving drunk twice before, it's true," Cooper wrote, "but both them times, I was in my car, not the truck, on my own time, not during work hours. Now my job is gone, plus they're fixing to take away my license, which'll make life hard. I mean, for one thing, how am I going to get a new job without a license? Now what I figure is, from your kind answer to my first letter, you proved yourself a fine Christian gentleman, so if you was to speak up on my behalf, it would be a big help. After all, you didn't wind up dead, and in fact you got a lot of publicity out of the whole thing, which must've helped your antique business a considerable amount."

Astonished and uncharacteristically furious, Hatch had filed the letter without answering it. In fact he quickly put it out of his mind, because he was scared by how angry he grew whenever he contemplated it.

Now, according to the brief story on page three of the paper, based on a single technical error in police procedures, Cooper's attorney had won a dismissal of all charges against him. The article included a three-sentence summary of the accident and a silly reference to Hatch as "holding the current record for being dead the longest time prior to a successful resuscitation," as if he had arranged the entire ordeal with the hope of winning a place in the next edition of the *Guinness Book of World Records*.

Other revelations in the piece made Hatch curse out loud and sit up straight in bed, culminating with the news that Cooper was going to sue his employer for wrongful termination and expected to get his old job back or, failing that, a substantial financial settlement. "I have suffered considerable humiliation at the hands of my former employer, subsequent to which I developed a serious stress-related health condition," Cooper had told reporters, obviously disgorging an attorney-written statement that he had memorized. "Yet even Mr. Harrison has written to tell me that he holds me blameless for the events of that night."

Anger propelled Hatch off the bed and onto his feet. His face felt flushed, and he was shaking uncontrollably.

Ludicrous. The drunken bastard was trying to get his job back by using Hatch's compassionate note as an endorsement, which required a complete misrepresentation of what Hatch had actually written. It was deceptive. It was unconscionable.

"Of all the fucking nerve!" Hatch said fiercely between clenched teeth.

Dropping most of the newspaper at his feet, crumpling the page with the story in his right hand, he hurried out of the bedroom and descended the stairs two at a time. In the den, he threw the paper on the desk, banged open a sliding closet door, and jerked out the top drawer on a three-drawer filing cabinet.

He had saved Cooper's handwritten letters, and although they were not on printed stationery, he knew the trucker had included not only a return address but a phone number on both pieces of correspondence. He was so disturbed, he flicked past the correct file folder—labeled MISCELLANEOUS BUSINESS—cursed softly but fluently when he couldn't find it, then searched backward and pulled it out. As he pawed through the contents, other letters slipped out of the folder and clattered to the floor at his feet.

Cooper's second letter had a telephone number carefully hand-printed at the top. Hatch put the disarranged file folder on the cabinet and hurried to the phone on the desk. His hand was shaking so badly that he couldn't read the number, so he put the letter on the blotter, in the cone of light from the brass desk lamp.

He punched William Cooper's number, intent on telling him off. The line was busy.

He jammed his thumb down on the disconnect button, got the dial tone, and tried again. Still busy.

"Sonofabitch!" He slammed down the receiver, but snatched it up again because there was nothing else he could do to let off steam. He tried the number a third time, using the redial button. It was still busy, of course, because no more than half a minute had passed since the first time he had tried it. He smashed the handset into the cradle so hard he might have broken the phone.

On one level he was startled by the savagery of the act, the childishness of it. But that part of him was not in control, and the mere awareness that he was over the top did not help him regain a grip on himself.

"Hatch?"

He looked up in surprise at the sound of his name and saw Lindsey, in her bathrobe, standing in the doorway between the den and the foyer.

Frowning, she said, "What's wrong?"

"What's wrong?" he asked, his fury growing irrationally, as if she were somehow in league with Cooper, as if she were only pretending to be unaware of this latest turn of events. "I'll tell you what's wrong. They let this Cooper bastard off the hook! The son of a bitch kills me, runs me off the goddamned road and *kills* me, then slips off the hook and has the nerve to try to use the letter I wrote him to get his job back!" He snatched up the crumpled newspaper and shook it at her, almost accusingly, as if she knew what was in it. "Get his job back—so he can run someone else off the fucking road and kill *them!*"

Looking worried and confused, Lindsey stepped into the den. "They let him off the hook? How?"

"A technicality. Isn't that cute? A cop misspells a word on the citation or something, and the guy walks!"

"Honey, calm down—"

"Calm down? Calm *down?*" He shook the crumpled newspaper again. "You know what else it says here? The jerk sold his story to that sleazy tabloid, the one that kept chasing after me, and I wouldn't have anything to do with them. So now this drunken son of a bitch sells them the story about"—he was spraying spittle he was so angry; he flattened out the newspaper, found the article, read from it—"about 'his emotional ordeal and his role in the rescue that saved Mr. Harrison's life.' What role did he have in my rescue? Except he used his CB to call for help after we went off the road, which we wouldn't have done if he hadn't been there in the first place! He's not only keeping his driver's license and probably going to get his job back, but he's making money off the whole damn thing! If I could get my hands on the bastard, I'd kill him, I swear I would!"

"You don't mean that," she said, looking shocked.

"You better believe I do! The irresponsible, greedy bastard. I'd like to kick him in the head a few times to knock some sense into him, pitch *him* into that freezing river—"

"Honey, lower your voice—"

"Why the hell should I lower my voice in my own—"

"You'll wake Regina."

It was not the mention of the girl that jolted him out of his blind rage, but the sight of himself in the mirrored closet door beside Lindsey. Actually, he didn't see himself at all. For an instant he saw a young man with thick black hair falling across his forehead, wearing sunglasses, dressed all in black. He knew he was looking at the killer, but the killer seemed to be *him*. At that moment they were one and the same. That aberrant thought—and the young man's image—passed in a second or two, leaving Hatch staring at his familiar reflection.

Stunned less by the hallucination than by that momentary confusion of identity, Hatch gazed into the mirror and was appalled as much by what he saw now as by the brief glimpse of the killer. He looked apoplectic. His hair was disarranged. His face was red and contorted with rage, and his eyes were . . . wild. He reminded himself of his father, which was unthinkable, intolerable.

He could not remember the last time he had been that angry. In fact he had *never* been in a comparable rage. Until now, he'd thought he was incapable of that kind of outburst or of the intense anger that could lead to it.

"I . . . I don't know what happened."

He dropped the crumpled page of the newspaper. It struck his desk and fell to the floor with a crisp rustling noise that wrought an inexplicably vivid picture in his mind—

dry brown leaves tumbling in a breeze along the cracked pavement in a crumbling, abandoned amusement park

—and for just a moment he was *there*, with weeds sprouting up around him from cracks in the blacktop, dead leaves whirling past, the moon glaring down through the elaborate open-beam supports of a roller-coaster track. Then he was in his office again, leaning weakly against his desk.

"Hatch?"

He blinked at her, unable to speak.

"What's wrong?" she asked, moving quickly to him. She touched his arm tentatively, as if she thought he might shatter from the contact—or perhaps as if she expected him to respond to her touch with a blow struck in anger.

He put his arms around her, and hugged her tightly. "Lindsey, I'm sorry. I don't know what happened, what got into me."

"It's all right."

"No, it isn't. I was so . . . so *furious.*"

"You were just angry, that's all."

"I'm sorry," he repeated miserably.

Even if it had appeared to her to be nothing but anger, he knew that it had been more than that, something strange, a terrible rage. White hot. Psychotic. He had felt an edge beneath him, as if he were teetering on the brink of a precipice, with only his heels planted on solid ground.

TO VASSAGO'S EYES, the monument of Lucifer cast a shadow even in absolute darkness, but he could still see and enjoy the cadavers in their postures of degradation. He was enraptured by the organic collage that he had created, by the sight of the humbled forms and the stench that arose from them. His hearing was not remotely as acute as his night vision, but he did not believe that he was entirely imagining the soft, wet sounds of decomposition to which he swayed as a music lover might sway to strains of Beethoven.

When he was suddenly overcome by anger, he was not sure why. It was a quiet sort of rage at first, curiously unfocused. He opened himself to it, enjoyed it, fed it to make it grow.

A vision of a newspaper flashed through his mind. He could not see it clearly, but something on the page was the cause of his anger. He squinted as if narrowing his eyes would help him see the words.

The vision passed, but the anger remained. He nurtured it the way a happy man might consciously force a laugh beyond its natural span just because the sound of laughter buoyed him. Words blurted from him, "Of all the fucking nerve!"

He had no idea where the exclamation had come from, just as he had no idea why he had said the name "Lindsey" out loud in that lounge in Newport Beach, several weeks ago, when these weird experiences had begun.

He was so abruptly energized by anger that he turned away from his collection and stalked across the enormous chamber, up the ramp down which the gargoyle gondolas had once plunged, and out into the night, where the moon forced him to put on his sunglasses again. He could not stand still. He had to move, move. He walked the abandoned midway, not sure who or what he was looking for, curious about what would happen next.

Disjointed images flashed through his mind, none remaining long enough to allow contemplation: the newspaper, a book-lined den, a filing cabinet, a hand-written letter, a telephone. . . . He walked faster and faster, pivoting suddenly onto new avenues or into narrower passageways between the decaying buildings, in a fruitless search for a connection that would link him more clearly with the source of the pictures that appeared and swiftly faded from his mind.

As he passed the roller coaster, cold moonlight fell through the maze of supporting crossbeams and glinted off the track in such a way as to make those twin ribbons of steel look like rails of ice. When he lifted his gaze to stare at the monolithic—and suddenly mysterious—structure, an angry exclamation burst from him: "Pitch *him* into that freezing river!"

A woman said, *Honey, lower your voice.*

Though he knew that her voice had arisen from within him, as an auditory adjunct to the fragmentary visions, Vassago turned in search of her anyway. She was *there*. In a bathrobe. Standing just this side of a doorway that had no right to be where it was, with no walls surrounding it. To the left of the doorway, to the right of it, and above it, there was only the night. The silent amusement park. But beyond the doorway, past the woman who stood in it, was what appeared to be the entrance foyer of a house, a small table with a vase of flowers, a staircase curving up to a second floor.

She was the woman he had thus far seen only in his dreams, first in a wheelchair and most recently in a red automobile on a sun-splashed highway. As he took a step toward her, she said, *You'll wake Regina.*

He halted, not because he was afraid of waking Regina, whoever the hell she was, and not because he still didn't want to get his hands on the woman, which he did—she was so *vital*—but because he became aware of a full-length mirror to the left of the Twilight-Zone door, a mirror floating impossibly in the night air. It was filled with his reflection, except that it was not him but a man he had never seen before, his size but maybe twice his age, lean and fit, his face contorted in rage.

The look of rage gave way to one of shock and disgust, and both Vassago and the man in the vision turned from the mirror to the woman in the doorway. "Lindsey, I'm sorry," Vassago said.

Lindsey. The name he had spoken three times at that lounge in Newport Beach.

Until now, he had not linked it to this woman who, nameless, had appeared so often in his recent dreams.

"Lindsey," Vassago repeated.

He was speaking of his own volition this time, not repeating what the man in the mirror was saying, and that seemed to shatter the vision. The mirror and the reflection in it flew apart in a billion shards, as did the doorway and the dark-eyed woman.

As the hushed and moon-washed park reclaimed the night, Vassago reached out with one hand toward the spot where the woman had stood. "Lindsey." He longed to touch her. So alive, she was. "Lindsey." He wanted to cut her open and enfold her beating heart in both hands, until its metronomic pumping slowed . . . slowed . . . slowed to a full stop. He wanted to be holding her heart when life retreated from it and death took possession.

AS SWIFTLY AS the flood of rage had poured into Hatch, it drained out of him. He balled up the pages of the newspaper and threw them in the waste can beside the desk, without glancing again at the story about the truck driver. Cooper was pathetic, a self-destructive loser who would bring his own punishment down upon himself sooner or later; and it would be worse than anything that Hatch would have done to him.

Lindsey gathered the letters that were scattered on the floor in front of the filing cabinet. She returned them to the file folder labeled MISCELLANEOUS BUSINESS.

The letter from Cooper was on the desk beside the telephone. When Hatch picked it up, he looked at the hand-written address at the top, above the telephone number, and a ghost of his anger returned. But it was a pale spirit of the real thing, and in a moment it vanished like a revenant. He took the letter to Lindsey and put it in the file folder, which she reinserted into the cabinet.

STANDING IN MOONGLARE and night breeze, in the shadow of the roller coaster, Vassago waited for additional visions.

He was intrigued by what had transpired, though not surprised. He had traveled Beyond. He knew another world existed, separated from this one by the flimsiest of curtains. Therefore, events of a supernatural nature did not astonish him.

Just when he began to think that the enigmatic episode had reached a conclusion, one more vision flickered through his mind. He saw a single page of a hand-written letter. White, lined paper. Blue ink. At the top was a name. William X. Cooper. And an address in the city of Tustin.

"Pitch *him* into that freezing river," Vassago muttered, and knew somehow that William Cooper was the object of the unfocused anger that had overcome him when he was with his collection in the funhouse, and which later seemed to link him with the man he had seen in the mirror. It was an anger he had embraced and amplified because he wanted to understand whose anger it was and why he could feel it, but also because anger was the yeast in the bread of violence, and violence was the staple of his diet.

From the roller coaster he went directly to the subterranean garage. Two cars waited there.

Morton Redlow's Pontiac was parked in the farthest corner, in the deepest shadows. Vassago had not used it since last Thursday night, when he had killed Redlow and later the blonde. Though he believed the fog had provided adequate cover, he was concerned that the Pontiac might have been glimpsed by witnesses who had seen the woman tumble from it on the freeway.

He longed to return to the land of endless night and eternal damnation, to be once more among his own kind, but he did not want to be gunned down by police until his collection was finished. If his offering was incomplete when he died, he believed that he would be deemed as yet unfit for Hell and would be pulled back into the world of the living to start another collection.

The second car was a pearl-gray Honda that had belonged to a woman named Renata Desseux, whom he had clubbed on the back of the head in a shopping-mall parking lot on Saturday night, two nights after the fiasco with the blonde. She, instead of the neo-punker named Lisa, had become the latest addition to his collection.

He had removed the license plates from the Honda, tossed them in the trunk, and later replaced them with plates stolen off an old Ford on the outskirts of Santa Ana. Besides, Hondas were so ubiquitous that he felt safe and anonymous in this one. He drove off the park grounds and out of the county's largely unpopulated eastern hills toward the panorama of golden light that filled the lowlands as far south and as far north as he could see, from the hills to the ocean.

Urban sprawl.

Civilization.

Hunting grounds.

The very immensity of southern California—thousands of square miles, tens of millions of people, even excluding Ventura County to the north and San Diego County to the south—was Vassago's ally in his determination to acquire the pieces of his collection without arousing the interest of the police. Three of his victims had been taken from different communities in Los Angeles County, two from Riverside, the rest from Orange County, spread over many months. Among the hundreds of missing persons reported during that time, his few acquisitions would not affect the statistics enough to alarm the public or alert the authorities.

He was also abetted by the fact that these last years of the century and the millennium were an age of inconstancy. Many people changed jobs, neighbors, friends, and marriages with little or no concern for continuity in life. As a result, there were fewer people to notice or care when any one person vanished, fewer to harass authorities into a meaningful response. And more often than not, those who disappeared were later discovered in changed circumstances of their own invention. A young executive might trade the grind of corporate life for a job as a blackjack dealer in Vegas or Reno, and a young mother—disillusioned with the demands of an infant and an infantile husband—might end up dealing cards or serving drinks or dancing topless in those same cities, leaving on the spur of the moment, blowing off their past lives as if a standard middle-class existence was as much a cause for shame as a criminal background. Others were found deep in the arms of various addictions, living in cheap rat-infested hotels that rented rooms by the week to the glassy-eyed legions of the counterculture. Because it was California, many missing persons eventually turned up in religious communes in Marin County or in Oregon, worshipping some new god or new manifestation of an old god or even just some shrewd-eyed man who said he *was* God.

It was a new age, disdaining tradition. It provided for whatever lifestyle one wished to pursue. Even one like Vassago's.

If he had left bodies behind, similarities in the victims and methods of murder would have linked them. The police would have realized that one perpetrator of unique strength and cunning was on the prowl, and they would have established a special task force to find him.

But the only bodies he had not taken to the Hell below the funhouse were those of the blonde and the private detective. No pattern would be deduced from just those two corpses, for they had died in radically different ways. Besides, Morton Redlow might not be found for weeks yet.

The only links between Redlow and the neo-punker were the detective's revolver, with which the woman had been shot, and his car, out of which she had fallen. The car was safely hidden in the farthest corner of the long-abandoned park garage. The gun was in the Styrofoam cooler with the Oreo cookies and other snacks, at the bottom of the elevator shaft more than two floors below the funhouse. He did not intend to use it again.

He was unarmed when, after driving far north into the county, he arrived at the address he had seen on the hand-written letter in the vision. William X. Cooper, whoever the hell he was and if he actually existed, lived in an attractive garden-apartment complex called Palm Court. The name of the place and the street number were carved in a decorative wooden sign, floodlit from the front and backed by the promised palms.

Vassago drove past Palm Court, turned right at the corner, and parked two blocks away. He didn't want anyone to remember the Honda sitting in front of the building. He didn't flat-out intend to kill this Cooper, just talk to him, ask him some questions, especially about the dark-haired, dark-eyed bitch named Lindsey. But he was walking into a situation he did not understand, and he needed to take every precaution. Besides, the truth was, these days he killed most of the people to whom he bothered to talk any length of time.

AFTER CLOSING THE file drawer and turning off the lamp in the den, Hatch and Lindsey stopped at Regina's room to make sure she was all right, moving quietly to the side of her bed. The hall light, falling through her door, revealed that the girl was sound asleep. The small knuckles of one fisted hand were against her chin. She was breathing evenly through slightly parted lips. If she dreamed, her dreams must have been pleasant.

Hatch felt his heart pinch as he looked at her, for she seemed so desperately young. He found it hard to believe that he had ever been as young as Regina was just then, for youth was innocence. Having been raised under the hateful and oppressive hand of his father, he had surrendered innocence at an early age in return for an intuitive grasp of aberrant psychology that had permitted him to survive in a home where anger and brutal "discipline" were the rewards for innocent mistakes and misunderstandings. He knew that Regina could not be as tender as she looked, for life had given her reasons of her own to develop thick skin and an armored heart.

Tough as they might be, however, they were both vulnerable, child and man. In fact, at that moment Hatch felt more vulnerable than the girl. If given a choice between her infirmities—the game leg, the twisted and incomplete hand—and whatever damage had been done to some deep region of his brain, he would have opted for her physical impairments without hesitation. After recent experiences, including the inexplicable escalation of his anger into blind rage, Hatch did not feel entirely in control of himself. And from the time he had been a small boy, with the terrifying example of his father to shape his fears, he had feared nothing half as much as being out of control.

I will not fail you, he promised the sleeping child.

He looked at Lindsey, to whom he owed his lives, both of them, before and after dying. Silently he made her the same promise: I will not fail you.

He wondered if they were promises he could keep.

Later, in their own room, with the lights out, as they lay on their separate halves of the bed, Lindsey said, "The rest of the test results should be back to Dr. Nyebern tomorrow."

Hatch had spent most of Saturday at the hospital, giving blood and urine samples, submitting to the prying of X-ray and sonogram machines. At one point he had been hooked up to more electrodes than the creature that Dr. Frankenstein, in those old movies, had energized from kites sent aloft in a lightning storm.

He said, "When I spoke to him today, he told me everything was looking good. I'm sure the rest of the tests will all come in negative, too. Whatever's happening to me, it has nothing to do with any mental or physical damage from the accident or from being . . . dead. I'm healthy, I'm okay."

"Oh, God, I hope so."

"I'm just fine."

"Do you really think so?"

"Yes, I really think so, I really do." He wondered how he could lie to her so smoothly. Maybe because the lie was not meant to hurt or harm, merely to soothe her so she could get some sleep.

"I love you," she said.

"I love you, too."

In a couple of minutes—shortly before midnight, according to the digital clock at bedside—she was asleep, snoring softly.

Hatch was unable to sleep, worrying about what he might learn of his future—or lack of it—tomorrow. He suspected that Dr. Nyebern would be gray-faced and grim, bearing somber news of some meaningful shadow detected in one lobe of Hatch's brain or another, a patch of dead cells, lesion, cyst, or tumor. Something deadly. Inoperable. And certain to get worse.

His confidence had been increasing slowly ever since he had gotten past the events of Thursday night and Friday morning, when he had dreamed of the blonde's murder and, later, had actually followed the trail of the killer to the Route 133 off-ramp from the San Diego Freeway. The weekend had been uneventful. The day just past, enlivened and uplifted by Regina's arrival, had been delightful. Then he had seen the newspaper piece about Cooper, and had lost control.

He hadn't told Lindsey about the stranger's reflection that he had seen in the den mirror. This time he was unable to pretend that he might have been sleepwalking, half awake, half dreaming. He had been wide awake, which meant the image in the mirror was an hallucination of one kind or another. A healthy, undamaged brain didn't hallucinate. He hadn't shared that terror with her because he knew, with the receipt of the test results tomorrow, there would be fear enough to go around.

Unable to sleep, he began to think about the newspaper story again, even though he didn't want to chew on it any more. He tried to direct his thoughts away from William Cooper, but he returned to the subject the way he might have obsessively probed at a sore tooth with his tongue. It almost seemed as if he were being *forced* to think about the truck driver, as if a giant mental magnet was pulling his attention inexorably in that direction. Soon, to his dismay, anger rose in him again. Worse, almost at once, the anger exploded into fury and a hunger for violence so intense that he had to fist his hands at his sides and clench his teeth and struggle to keep from letting loose a primal cry of rage.

FROM THE BANKS of mailboxes in the breezeway at the main entrance to the garden apartments, Vassago learned that William Cooper was in apartment twenty-eight. He followed the breezeway into the courtyard, which was filled with palms and ficuses and ferns and too many landscape lights to please him, and he climbed an exterior staircase to the covered balcony that served the second-floor units of the two-story complex.

No one was in sight. Palm Court was silent, peaceful.

Though it was a few minutes past midnight, lights were on in the Cooper apartment. Vassago could hear a television turned low.

The window to the right of the door was covered with Levolor blinds. The slats were not tightly closed. Vassago could see a kitchen illuminated only by the low-wattage bulb in the range hood.

To the left of the door a larger window looked onto the balcony and courtyard from the apartment living room. The drapes were not drawn all the way shut. Through the gap, a man could be seen slumped in a big recliner with his feet up in front of the television. His head was tilted to one side, his face toward the window, and he appeared to be asleep. A glass containing an inch of golden liquid stood beside a half-empty bottle of Jack Daniel's on a small table next to the recliner. A bag of cheese puffs had been knocked off the table, and some of the bright orange contents had scattered across the bile-green carpet.

Vassago scanned the balcony to the left, right, and on the other side of the courtyard. Still deserted.

He tried to slide open Cooper's living-room window, but it was either corroded or locked. He moved to the right again, toward the kitchen window, but he stopped at the door on the way and, without any real hope, tried it. The door was unlocked. He pushed it open, went inside—and locked it behind him.

The man in the recliner, probably Cooper, did not stir as Vassago quietly pulled the drapes all the way shut across the big living-room window. No one else, passing on the balcony, would be able to look inside.

Already assured that the kitchen, dining area, and living room were deserted, Vassago moved catlike through the bathroom and two bedrooms (one without furniture, used primarily for storage) that comprised the rest of the apartment. The man in the recliner was alone.

On the dresser in the bedroom, Vassago spotted a wallet and a ring of keys. In the wallet he found fifty-eight dollars, which he took, and a driver's license in the name of William X. Cooper. The photograph on the license was of the man in the living room, a few years younger and, of course, not in a drunken stupor.

He returned to the living room with the intention of waking Cooper and having an informative little chat with him. Who is Lindsey? Where does she live?

But as he approached the recliner, a current of anger shot through him, too sudden and causeless to be his own, as if he were a human radio that received other people's emotions. And what he was receiving was the same anger that had suddenly struck him while he had been with his collection in the funhouse hardly an hour ago. As before, he opened himself to it, amplified the current with his own singular rage, wondering if he would receive visions, as he had on that previous occasion. But this time, as he stood looking down on William Cooper, the anger flared too abruptly into insensate fury, and he lost control. From the table beside the recliner, he grabbed the Jack Daniel's by the neck of the bottle.

LYING RIGID IN his bed, hands fisted so tightly that even his blunt fingernails were gouging painfully into his palms, Hatch had the crazy feeling that his mind had been invaded. His flicker of anger had been like opening a door just a hairline crack but wide enough for something on the other side to get a grip and tear it off its hinges. He felt something unnameable storming into him, a force without form or features, defined only by its hatred and rage. Its fury was that of the hurricane, the typhoon, beyond mere human dimensions, and he knew that he was too small a vessel to contain all of the anger that was pumping into him. He felt as if he would explode, shatter as if he were not a man but a crystal figurine.

THE HALF-FULL bottle of Jack Daniel's whacked the side of the sleeping man's head with such impact that it was almost as loud as a shotgun blast. Whiskey and sharp fragments of glass showered up, rained down, splattered and clinked against the television set, the other furniture, and the walls. The air was filled with the velvety aroma of corn-mash bourbon, but underlying it was the scent of blood, for the gashed and battered side of Cooper's face was bleeding copiously.

The man was no longer merely sleeping. He had been hammered into a deeper level of unconsciousness.

Vassago was left with just the neck of the bottle in his hand. It terminated in three sharp spikes of glass that dripped bourbon and made him think of snake fangs glistening with venom. Shifting his grip, he raised the weapon above his head and brought it down, letting out a fierce hiss of rage, and the glass serpent bit deep into William Cooper's face.

THE VOLCANIC WRATH that erupted into Hatch was unlike anything he had ever experienced before, far beyond any rage that his father had ever achieved. Indeed, it was nothing he could have generated within himself for the same reason that one could not manufacture sulfuric acid in a paper cauldron: the vessel would be dissolved by the substance it was required to contain. A high-pressure lava flow of anger gushed into him, so hot that he wanted to scream, so white-hot that he had no time to scream. Consciousness was burned away, and he fell into a mercifully dreamless darkness where there was neither anger nor terror.

VASSAGO REALIZED THAT he was shouting with wordless, savage glee. After a dozen or twenty blows, the glass weapon had utterly disintegrated. He finally, reluctantly dropped the short fragment of the bottle neck still in his white-knuckled grip. Snarling, he threw himself against the Naugahyde recliner, tipping it over and rolling the dead man onto the bile-green carpet. He picked up the end table and pitched it into the television set, where Humphrey Bogart was sitting in a military courtroom, rolling a couple of ball bearings in his leathery hand, talking about strawberries. The screen imploded, and Bogart was transformed into a shower of yellow sparks, the sight of which ignited new fires of destructive frenzy in Vassago. He kicked over a coffee table, tore two K Mart prints off the walls and smashed the glass out of the frames, swept a collection of cheap ceramic knickknacks off the mantel. He would have liked nothing better than to have continued from one end of the apartment to the other, pulling all the dishes out of the kitchen cabinets and smashing them, reducing all the glassware to bright shards, seizing the food in the refrigerator and heaving it against the walls, hammering one piece of furniture against another until everything was broken and splintered, but he was halted by the sound of a siren, distant now, rapidly drawing nearer, the meaning of it penetrating even through the mist of blood frenzy that clouded his thoughts. He headed for the door, then swung away from it, realizing that people might have come out into the courtyard or might be watching from their windows. He ran out of the living room, back the short hall, to the window in the master bedroom, where he pulled aside the drapes and looked onto the roof over the building-long carport. An alleyway, bordered by a block wall, lay beyond. He twisted open the latch on the double-hung window, shoved up the bottom half, squeezed through, dropped onto the roof of the long carport, rolled to the edge, fell to the pavement, and landed on his feet as if he were a cat. He lost his sunglasses, scooped them up, put them on again. He sprinted left, toward the back of the property, with the siren louder now, much louder, very close. When he came to the next flank of the eight-foot-high concrete-block wall that ringed the property, he swiftly clambered over it with the agility of a spider skittering up any porous surface, and then he was over, into another alleyway serving carports along the back of another apartment complex, and so he ran from serviceway to serviceway, picking a route through the maze by sheer instinct, and came out on the street where he had parked, half a block from the pearl-gray Honda. He got in the car, started the engine, and drove away from there as sedately as he could manage, sweating and breathing so hard that he steamed up the windows. Reveling in the fragrant mélange of bourbon, blood, and perspiration, he was tremendously excited, so profoundly *satisfied* by the violence he had unleashed that he pounded the steering wheel and let out peals of laughter that had a shrieky edge.

For a while he drove randomly from one street to another with no idea where he was headed. After his laughter faded, when his heart stopped racing, he gradually oriented himself and struck out south and east, in the general direction of his hideaway.

If William Cooper could have provided any connection to the woman named Lindsey, that lead was now closed to Vassago forever. He wasn't worried. He didn't know what was happening to him, why Cooper or Lindsey or the man in the mirror had been brought to his attention by these supernatural means. But he knew that if he only trusted in his dark god, everything would eventually be made clear to him.

He was beginning to wonder if Hell had let him go willingly, returning him to the land of the living in order to use him to deal with certain people whom the god of darkness wanted dead. Perhaps he'd not been stolen from Hell, after all, but had been *sent* back to life on a mission of destruction that was only slowly becoming comprehensible. If that were the case, he was pleased to make himself the instrument of the dark and powerful divinity whose company he longed to rejoin, and he anxiously awaited whatever task he might be assigned next.

TOWARD DAWN, AFTER several hours in a deep slumber of almost deathlike perfection, Hatch woke and did not know where he was. For a moment he drifted in confusion, then washed up on the shore of memory: the bedroom, Lindsey breathing softly in her sleep beside him, the ash-gray first light of morning like a fine silver dust on the windowpanes.

When he recalled the inexplicable and inhuman fit of rage that had slammed through him with paralytic force, Hatch stiffened with fear. He tried to remember where that spiraling anger had led, in what act of violence it had culminated, but his mind was blank. It seemed to him that he had simply passed out, as if that unnaturally intense fury had overloaded the circuits in his brain and blown a fuse or two.

Passed out—or blacked out? There was a fateful difference between the two. Passed out, he might have been in bed all night, exhausted, as still as a stone on the floor of the sea. But if he *blacked* out, remaining conscious but unaware of what he was doing, in a psychotic fugue, God alone knew what he might have done.

Suddenly he sensed that Lindsey was in grave danger.

Heart hammering against the cage of his ribs, he sat up in bed and looked at her. The dawn light at the window was too soft to reveal her clearly. She was only a shadowy shape against the sheets.

He reached for the switch on the bedside lamp, but then hesitated. He was afraid of what he might see.

I would never hurt Lindsey, never, he thought desperately.

But he remembered all too well that, for a moment last night, he had not been entirely himself. His anger at Cooper had seemed to open a door within him, letting in a monster from some vast darkness beyond.

Trembling, he finally clicked the switch. In the lamplight he saw that Lindsey was untouched, as fair as ever, sleeping with a peaceful smile.

Greatly relieved, he switched off the lamp—and thought of Regina. The engine of anxiety revved up again.

Ridiculous. He would no sooner harm Regina than Lindsey. She was a defenseless child.

He could not stop shaking, wondering.

He slipped out of bed without disturbing his wife. He picked up his bath-robe from the back of the armchair, pulled it on, and quietly left the room.

Barefoot, he entered the hall, where a pair of skylights admitted large pieces of the morning, and followed it to Regina's room. He moved swiftly at first, then more slowly, weighed down by dread as heavy as a pair of iron boots.

He had a mental image of the flower-painted mahogany bed splashed with blood, the sheets sodden and red. For some reason, he had the crazy notion that he would find the child with fragments of glass in her ravaged face. The weird specificity of that image convinced him that he had, indeed, done something unthinkable after he had blacked out.

When he eased open the door and looked into the girl's room, she was sleeping as peacefully as Lindsey, in the same posture he had seen her in last night, when he and Lindsey had checked on her before going to bed. No blood. No broken glass.

Swallowing hard, he pulled the door shut and returned along the hall as far as the first skylight. He stood in the fall of dim morning light, looking up through the tinted glass at a sky of indeterminate hue, as if an explanation would suddenly be writ large across the heavens.

No explanation came to him. He remained confused and anxious.

At least Lindsey and Regina were fine, untouched by whatever presence he had connected with last night.

He was reminded of an old vampire movie he had once seen, in which a wizened priest had warned a young woman that the undead could enter her house only if she invited them—but that they were cunning and persuasive, capable of inducing even the wary to issue that mortal invitation.

Somehow a bond existed between Hatch and the psychotic who had killed the young blond punker named Lisa. By failing to repress his anger at William Cooper, he had strengthened that bond. His anger was the key that opened the door. When he indulged in anger, he was issuing an invitation just like the one against which the priest in that movie had warned the young woman. He could not explain how he knew this to be true, but he *did* know it, all right, knew it in his bones. He just wished to God he *understood* it.

He felt lost.

Small and powerless and afraid.

And although Lindsey and Regina had come through the night unharmed, he sensed more strongly than ever that they were in great danger. Growing greater by the day. By the hour.

3
Before dawn, the thirtieth of April, Vassago bathed outdoors with bottled water and liquid soap. By the first light of day, he was safely ensconced in the deepest part of his hideaway. Lying on his mattress, staring up the elevator shaft, he treated himself to Oreos and warm root beer, then to a couple of snack-size bags of Reese's Pieces.

Murder was always enormously satisfying. Tremendous internal pressures were released with the strike of a killing blow. More important, each murder was an act of rebellion against all things holy, against commandments and laws and rules and the irritatingly prissy systems of manners employed by human beings to support the fiction that life was precious and endowed with meaning. Life was cheap and pointless. Nothing mattered but sensation and the swift gratification of all desires, which only the strong and free really understood. After every killing, Vassago felt as liberated as the wind and mightier than any steel machine.

Until one special, glorious night in his twelfth year, he had been one of the enslaved masses, dumbly plodding through life according to the rules of so-called civilization, though they made no sense to him. He pretended to love his mother, father, sister, and a host of relatives, though he felt nothing more for them than he did for strangers encountered on the street. As a child, when he was old enough to begin thinking about such things, he wondered if something was wrong with him, a crucial element missing from his makeup. As he listened to himself playing the game of love, employing strategies of false affection and shameless flattery, he was amazed at how convincing others found him, for he could hear the insincerity in his voice, could feel the fraudulence in every gesture, and was acutely aware of the deceit behind his every loving smile. Then one day he suddenly heard the deception in their voices and saw it in their faces, and he realized that none of *them* had ever experienced love, either, or any of the nobler sentiments toward which a civilized person was supposed to aspire—selflessness, courage, piety, humility, and all the rest of that dreary catechism. *They* were all playing the game, too. Later he came to the conclusion that most of them, even the adults, had never enjoyed his degree of insight, and remained unaware that other people were exactly like them. Each person thought he was unique, that something was missing in him, and that he must play the game well or be uncovered and ostracized as something less than human. God had tried to create a world of love, had failed, and had commanded His creations to pretend to the perfection with which He had been unable to imbue them. Perceiving that stunning truth, Vassago had taken his first step toward freedom. Then one summer night when he was twelve, he finally understood that in order to be really free, totally free, he had to act upon his understanding, begin to live differently from the herd of humanity, with his own pleasure as the only consideration. He had to be willing to exercise the power over others which he possessed by virtue of his insight into the true nature of the world. That night he learned that the ability to kill without compunction was the purest form of power, and that the exercise of power was the greatest pleasure of them all . . .

IN THOSE DAYS, before he died and came back from the dead and chose the name of the demon prince Vassago, the name to which he had answered and under which he had lived was Jeremy. His best friend had been Tod Ledderbeck, the son of Dr. Sam Ledderbeck, a gynecologist whom Jeremy called the "crack quack" when he wanted to rag Tod.

In the morning of that early June day, Mrs. Ledderbeck had taken Jeremy and Tod to Fantasy World, the lavish amusement park that, against all expectations, had begun to give Disneyland a run for its money. It was in the hills, a few miles east of San Juan Capistrano, somewhat out of the way—just as Magic Mountain had been a bit isolated before the suburbs north of Los Angeles had spread around it, and just as Disneyland had seemed to be in the middle of nowhere when first constructed on farmland near the obscure town of Anaheim. It was built with Japanese money, which worried some people who believed the Japanese were going to own the whole country some day, and there were rumors of Mafia money being involved, which only made it more mysterious and appealing. But finally what mattered was that the atmosphere of the place was cool, the rides radical, and the junk food almost deliriously junky. Fantasy World was where Tod wanted to spend his twelfth birthday, in the company of his best friend, free of parental control from morning until ten o'clock at night, and Tod usually got what he wanted because he was a good kid; everyone liked him; he knew exactly how to play the game.

Mrs. Ledderbeck left them off at the front gate and shouted after them as they raced away from the car: "I'll pick you up right here at ten o'clock! Right here at ten o'clock sharp!"

After paying for their tickets and getting onto the grounds of the park, Tod said, "What do you wanna do first?"

"I don't know. What do you wanna do first?"

"Ride the Scorpion?"

"Yeah!"

"Yeah!"

Bang, they were off, hurrying toward the north end of the park where the track for the Scorpion—"The Roller Coaster with a Sting!" the TV ads all proclaimed—rose in sweet undulant terror against the clear blue sky. The park was not crowded yet, and they didn't need to snake between cow-slow herds of people. Their tennis shoes pounded noisily on the blacktop, and each slap of rubber against pavement was a shout of freedom. They rode the Scorpion, yelling and screaming as it plummeted and whipped and turned upside down and plummeted again, and when the ride ended, they ran directly to the boarding ramp and did it once more.

Then, as now, Jeremy had loved speed. The stomach-flopping sharp turns and plunges of amusement-park rides had been a childish substitute for the violence he had unknowingly craved. After two rides on the Scorpion, with so many speeding-swooping-looping-twisting delights ahead, Jeremy was in a terrific mood.

But Tod tainted the day as they were coming down the exit ramp from their second trip on the roller coaster. He threw one arm around Jeremy's shoulders and said, "Man, this is gonna be for sure the greatest birthday anybody's ever had, just you and me."

The camaraderie, like all camaraderie, was totally fake. Deception. Fraud. Jeremy hated all that phoney-baloney crap, but Tod was full of it. Best friends. Blood brothers. You and me against the world.

Jeremy wasn't sure what rubbed him the rawest: that Tod jived him all the time about being good buddies and seemed to think that Jeremy was taken in by the con—or that sometimes Tod seemed dumb enough to be suckered by his *own* con. Recently, Jeremy had begun to suspect that some people played the game of life so well, they didn't realize it was a game. They deceived even themselves with all their talk of friendship, love, and compassion. Tod was looking more and more like one of *those* hopeless jerks.

Being best friends was just a way to get a guy to do things for you that he wouldn't do for anyone else in a thousand years. Friendship was also a mutual defense arrangement, a way of joining forces against the mobs of your fellow citizens who would just as soon smash your face and take whatever they wanted from you. Everyone knew that's all friendship was, but no one ever talked truthfully about it, least of all Tod.

Later, on their way from the Haunted House to an attraction called Swamp Creature, they stopped at a stand selling blocks of ice cream dipped in chocolate and rolled in crushed nuts. They sat on plastic chairs at a plastic table, under a red umbrella, against a backdrop of acacias and manmade waterfalls, chomping down, and everything was fine at first, but then Tod had to spoil it.

"It's great coming to the park without grownups, isn't it?" Tod said with his mouth full. "You can eat ice cream before lunch, like this. Hell, you can eat it for lunch, too, if you want, and after lunch, and nobody's there to whine at you about spoiling your appetite or getting sick."

"It's great," Jeremy agreed.

"Let's sit here and eat ice cream till we puke."

"Sounds good to me. But let's not waste it."

"Huh?"

Jeremy said, "Let's be sure, when we puke, we just don't spew on the ground. Let's be sure we puke *on* somebody."

"Yeah!" Tod said, getting the drift right away, "on somebody who deserves it, who's really pukeworthy."

"Like those girls," Jeremy said, indicating a pair of pretty teenagers who were passing by. They wore white shorts and bright summery blouses, and they were so sure that they were cute, you wanted to puke on them even if you hadn't eaten anything and all you could manage was the dry heaves.

"Or those old farts," Tod said, pointing to an elderly couple buying ice cream nearby.

"No, not them," Jeremy said. "They already *look* like they've been puked on."

Tod thought that was so hilarious, he choked on his ice cream. In some ways Tod was all right.

"Funny about this ice cream," he said when he stopped choking.

Jeremy bit: "What's funny about it?"

"I know the ice cream is made from milk, which comes from cows. And they make chocolate out of cocoa beans. But whose nuts do they crush to sprinkle over it all?"

Yeah, for sure, old Tod was all right in some ways.

But just when they were laughing the loudest, feeling good, he leaned across the table, swatted Jeremy lightly alongside the head, and said, "You and me, Jer, we're gonna be *tight* forever, friends till they feed us to the worms. Right?"

He really believed it. He had conned himself. He was so stupidly sincere that he made Jeremy want to puke on *him*.

Instead, Jeremy said, "What're you gonna do next, try to kiss me on the lips?"

Grinning, not picking up on the impatience and hostility aimed at him, Tod said, "Up your grandma's ass."

"Up *your* grandma's ass."

"My grandma doesn't have an ass."

"Yeah? Then what's she sit on?"

"Your face."

They kept ragging each other all the way to Swamp Creature. The attraction was hokey, not well done, but good for a lot of jokes because of that. For a while, Tod was just wild and fun to be around.

Later, however, after they came out of Space Battle, Tod started referring to them as "the two best rocket jockeys in the universe," which half embarrassed Jeremy because it was so stupid and juvenile. It also irritated him because it was just another way of saying "we're buddies, blood brothers, pals." They'd get on the Scorpion, and just as it pulled out of the station, Tod would say, "This is nothing, this is just a Sunday drive to the two best rocket jockeys in the universe." Or they'd be on their way into World of the Giants, and Tod would throw his arm around Jeremy's shoulder and say, "The two best rocket jockeys in the universe can handle a fucking giant, can't we, bro?"

Jeremy wanted to say, *Look, you jerk, the only reason we're friends is because your old man and mine are sort of in the same kind of work, so we got thrown together. I hate this arm-around-the-shoulders shit, so just knock it off, let's have some laughs and be happy with that. Okay?*

But he did not say anything of the sort because, of course, good players in life never admitted that they knew it was all just a game. If you let the other players see you didn't care about the rules and regulations, they wouldn't let you play. Go to Jail. Go directly to Jail. Don't pass Go. Don't have any fun.

By seven o'clock that evening, after they had eaten enough junk food to produce radically interesting vomit if they really did decide to puke on anyone, Jeremy was so tired of the rocket jockey crap and so irritated by Tod's friendship rap, that he couldn't wait for ten o'clock to roll around and Mrs. Ledderbeck to pull up to the gate in her station wagon.

They were on the Millipede, blasting through one of the pitch-black sections of the ride, when Tod made one too many references to the two best rocket jockeys in the universe, and Jeremy decided to kill him. The instant the thought flashed through his mind, he knew he had to murder his "best friend." It felt so *right*. If life was a game with a zillion-page book of rules, it wasn't going to be a whole hell of a lot of fun—unless you found ways to break the rules and still be allowed to play. *Any* game was a bore if you played by the rules—Monopoly, 500 rummy, baseball. But if you stole bases, filched cards without getting caught, or changed the numbers on the dice when the other guy was distracted, a dull game could be a kick. And in the game of life, getting away with murder was the biggest kick of all.

When the Millipede shrieked to a halt at the debarkation platform, Jeremy said, "Let's do it again."

"Sure," Tod said.

They hurried along the exit corridor, in a rush to get outside and into line again. The park had filled up during the day, and the wait to board any ride was now at least twenty minutes.

When they came out of the Millipede pavillion, the sky was black in the east, deep blue overhead, and orange in the west. Twilight came sooner and lasted longer at Fantasy World than in the western part of the county, because between the park and the distant sea rose ranks of high, sun-swallowing hills. Those ridges were now black silhouettes against the orange heavens, like Halloween decorations out of season.

Fantasy World had taken on a new, manic quality with the approach of night. Christmas-style lights outlined the rides and buildings. White twinkle lights lent a festive sparkle to all the trees, while a pair of unsynchronized spotlights swooped back and forth across the snow-covered peak of the man-made Big Foot Mountain. On every side neon glowed in all the hues that neon offered, and out on Mars Island, bursts of brightly colored laser beams shot randomly into the darkening sky as if fending off a spaceship attack. Scented with popcorn and roasted peanuts, a warm breeze snapped garlands of pennants overhead. Music of every period and type leaked out of the pavilions, and rock-'n'-roll boomed from the open-air dance floor at the south end of the park, and from somewhere else came the bouncy strains of Big Band swing. People laughed and chattered excitedly, and on the thrill rides they were screaming, screaming.

"Daredevil this time," Jeremy said as he and Tod sprinted to the end of the Millipede boarding line.

"Yeah," Tod said, "daredevil!"

The Millipede was essentially an indoor roller coaster, like Space Mountain at Disneyland, except instead of shooting up and down and around one huge room, it whipped through a long series of tunnels, some lit and some not. The lap bar, meant to restrain the riders, was tight enough to be safe, but if a kid was slim and agile, he could contort himself in such way as to squeeze out from under it, scramble over it, and stand in the leg well. Then he could lean against the lap bar and grip it behind his back—or hook his arms around it—riding daredevil.

It was a stupid and dangerous thing to do, which Jeremy and Tod realized. But they had done it a couple of times anyway, not only on the Millipede but on other rides in other parks. Riding daredevil pumped up the excitement level at least a thousand percent, especially in pitch-dark tunnels where it was impossible to see what was coming next.

"Rocket jockeys!" Tod said when they were halfway through the line. He insisted on giving Jeremy a low five and then a high five, though they looked like a couple of asshole kids. "No rocket jockey is afraid of daredeviling the Millipede, right?"

"Right," Jeremy said as they inched through the main doors and entered the pavilion. Shrill screams echoed to them from the riders on the cars that shot away into the tunnel ahead.

According to legend (as kid-created legends went at every amusement park with a similar ride), a boy had been killed riding daredevil on the Millipede because he'd been too tall. The ceiling of the tunnel was high in all lighted stretches, but they said it dropped low at one spot in a darkened passage—maybe because air-conditioning pipes passed through at that point, maybe because the engineers made the contractor put in another support that hadn't been planned for, maybe because the architect was a no-brain. Anyway, this tall kid, standing up, smacked his head into the low part of the ceiling, never even saw it coming. It instantly pulverized his face, decapitated him. All the unsuspecting bozos riding behind him were splattered with blood and brains and broken teeth.

Jeremy didn't believe it for a minute. Fantasy World hadn't been built by guys with horse turds for brains. They had to have figured kids would find a way to get out from under the lap bars, because nothing was entirely kid-proof, and they would have kept the ceiling high all the way through. Legend also had it that the low overhang was still somewhere in one of the dark sections of the tunnel, with bloodstains and flecks of dried brains on it, which was total cow flop.

For anybody riding daredevil, standing up, the real danger was that he would fall out of the car when it whipped around a sharp turn or accelerated unexpectedly. Jeremy figured there were six or eight particularly radical curves on the Millipede course where Tod Ledderbeck might easily topple out of the car with only minimal assistance.

The line moved slowly forward.

Jeremy was not impatient or afraid. As they drew closer to the boarding gates, he became more excited but also more confident. His hands were not trembling. He had no butterflies in his belly. He just wanted to *do* it.

The boarding chamber for the ride was constructed to resemble a cavern with immense stalactites and stalagmites. Strange bright-eyed creatures swam in the murky depths of eerie pools, and albino mutant crabs prowled the shores, reaching up with huge wicked claws toward the people on the boarding platform, snapping at them but not quite long-armed enough to snare any dinner.

Each train had six cars, and each car carried two people. The cars were painted like segments of a Millipede; the first had a big insect head with moving jaws and multifaceted black eyes, not a cartoon but a really fierce monster face; the one at the back boasted a curved stinger that looked more like part of a scorpion than the ass-end of a Millipede. Two trains were boarding at any one time, the second behind the first, and they shot off into the tunnel with only a few seconds between them because the whole operation was computer-controlled, eliminating any danger that one train would crash into the back of another.

Jeremy and Tod were among the twelve customers that the attendant sent to the first train.

Tod wanted the front car, but they didn't get it. That was the best position from which to ride daredevil because everything would happen to them first: every plunge into darkness, every squirt of cold steam from the wall vents, every explosion through swinging doors into whirling lights. Besides, part of the fun of riding daredevil was showing off, and the front car provided a perfect platform for exhibitionism, with the occupants of the last five cars as a captive audience in the lighted stretches.

With the first car claimed, they raced for the sixth. Being the last to experience every plunge and twist of the track was next-best to being first, because the squeals of the riders ahead of you raised your adrenaline level and expectations. Something about being securely in the middle of the train just didn't go with daredevil riding.

The lap bars descended automatically when all twelve people were aboard. An attendant came along the platform, visually inspecting to be sure all of the restraints had locked into place.

Jeremy was relieved they had not gotten the front car, where they would have had ten witnesses behind them. In the tomb-dark confines of the unlit sections of tunnel, he wouldn't be able to see his own hand an inch in front of his face, so it wasn't likely that anyone would be able to see him push Tod out of the car. But this was a big-time violation of the rules, and he didn't want to take any chances. Now, potential witnesses were all safely in front of them, staring straight ahead; in fact they could not easily glance back, since every seat had a high back to prevent whiplash.

When the attendant finished checking the lap bars, he turned and signaled the operator, who was seated at an instrument panel on a rock formation to the right of the tunnel entrance.

"Here we go," Tod said.

"Here we go," Jeremy agreed.

"Rocket jockeys!" Tod shouted.

Jeremy gritted his teeth.

"Rocket jockeys!" Tod repeated.

What the hell. One more time wouldn't hurt. Jeremy yelled: "Rocket jockeys!"

The train did not pull away from the boarding station with the jerky uncertainty of most roller coasters. A tremendous blast of compressed air shot it forward at high speed, like a bullet out of a barrel, with a *whoosh!* that almost hurt the ears. They were pinned against their seats as they flashed past the operator and into the black mouth of the tunnel.

Total darkness.

He was only twelve then. He had not died. He had not been to Hell. He had not come back. He was as blind in darkness as anyone else, as Tod.

Then they slammed through swinging doors and up a long incline of well-lit track, moving fast at first but gradually slowing to a crawl. On both sides they were menaced by pale white slugs as big as men, which reared up and shrieked at them through round mouths full of teeth that whirled like the blades in a garbage disposal. The ascent was six or seven stories, at a steep angle, and other mechanical monsters gibbered, hooted, snarled, and squealed at the train; all of them were pale and slimy, with either glowing eyes or blind black eyes, the kind of critters you might think would live miles below the surface of the earth—if you didn't know *any* science at all.

That initial slope was where daredevils had to take their stand. Though a couple of other inclines marked the course of the Millipede, no other section of the track provided a sufficiently extended period of calm in which to execute a safe escape from the lap bar.

Jeremy contorted himself, wriggling up against the back of the seat, inching over the lap bar, but at first Tod did not move. "Come on, dickhead, you've gotta be in position before we get to the top."

Tod looked troubled. "If they catch us, they'll kick us out of the park."

"They won't catch us."

At the far end of the ride, the train would coast along a final stretch of dark tunnel, giving riders a chance to calm down. In those last few seconds, before they returned to the fake cavern from which they had started, it was just possible for a kid to scramble back over the lap bar and shoehorn himself into his seat. Jeremy knew he could do it; he was not worried about getting caught. Tod didn't have to worry about getting under the lap bar again, either, because by then Tod would be dead; he wouldn't have to worry about anything ever.

"I don't want to be kicked out for daredeviling," Tod said as the train approached the halfway point on the long, long initial incline. "It's been a neat day, and we still have a couple hours before Mom comes for us."

Mutant albino rats chattered at them from the fake rock ledges on both sides as Jeremy said, "Okay, so be a dorkless wonder." He continued to extricate himself from the lap bar.

"I'm no dorkless wonder," Tod said defensively.

"Sure, sure."

"I'm not."

"Maybe when school starts again in September, you'll be able to get into the Young Homemakers Club, learn how to cook, knit nice little doilies, do flower arranging."

"You're a jerkoff, you know that?"

"Ooooooooooo, you've broken my heart now," Jeremy said as he extracted both of his legs from the well under the lap bar and crouched on the seat. "You girls sure know how to hurt a guy's feelings."

"Creepazoid."

The train strained up the slope with the hard clicking and clattering so specific to roller coasters that the sound alone could make the heart pump faster and the stomach flutter.

Jeremy scrambled over the lap bar and stood in the well in front of it, facing forward. He looked over his shoulder at Tod, who sat scowling behind the restraint. He didn't care that much if Tod joined him or not. He had already decided to kill the boy, and if he didn't have a chance to do it at Fantasy World on Tod's twelfth birthday, he would do it somewhere else, sooner or later. Just thinking about doing it was a lot of fun. Like that song said in the television commercial where the Heinz ketchup was so thick it took what seemed like hours coming out of the bottle: *An-tic-i-paaa-aa-tion.* Having to wait a few days or even weeks to get another good chance to kill Tod would only make the killing that much more fun. So he didn't rag Tod any more, just looked at him scornfully. *An-tic-i-paaa-aa-tion.*

"I'm not afraid," Tod insisted.

"Yeah."

"I just don't want to spoil the day."

"Sure."

"Creepazoid," Tod said again.

Jeremy said, "Rocket jockey, my ass."

That insult had a powerful effect. Tod was so sold on his own friendship con that he could actually be stung by the implication that he didn't know how a real friend was supposed to behave. The expression on his broad and open face revealed not only a world of hurt but a surprising desperation that startled Jeremy. Maybe Tod *did* understand what life was all about, that it was nothing but a brutal game with every player concentrated on the purely selfish goal of coming out a winner, and maybe old Tod was rattled by that, scared by it, and was holding on to one last hope, to the idea of friendship. If the game could be played with a partner or two, if it was really everyone else in the world against your own little team, that was tolerable, better than everyone in the world against just *you*. Tod Ledderbeck and his good buddy Jeremy against the rest of humanity was even sort of romantic and adventurous, but Tod Ledderbeck alone obviously made his bowels quiver.

Sitting behind the lap bar, Tod first looked stricken, then resolute. Indecision gave way to action, and Tod moved fast, wriggling furiously against the restraint.

"Come on, come on," Jeremy urged. "We're almost to the top."

Tod eeled over the lap bar, into the leg well where Jeremy stood. He caught his foot in that restraining mechanism, and almost fell out of the car.

Jeremy grabbed him, hauled him back. *This* was not the place for Tod to take a fall. They weren't moving fast enough. At most he'd suffer a couple of bruises.

Then they were side by side, their feet planted wide on the floor of the car, leaning back against the restraint from under which they had escaped, arms behind them, hands locked on the lap bar, grinning at each other, as the train reached the top of the incline. It slammed through swinging doors into the next stretch of lightless tunnel. The track remained flat just long enough to crank up the riders' tension a couple of notches. *An-tic-i-paaa-aa-tion.* When Jeremy could not hold his breath any longer, the front car tipped over the brink, and the people up there screamed in the darkness. Then in rapid succession the second and third and fourth and fifth cars—

"Rocket jockeys!" Jeremy and Tod shouted in unison.

—and the final car of the train followed the others into a steep plunge, building speed by the second. Wind whooshed past them and whipped their hair out behind their heads. Then came a swooping turn to the right when it was least expected, a little upgrade to toss the stomach, another turn to the right, the track tilting so the cars were tipped onto their sides, faster, faster, then a straightaway and another incline, using their speed to go higher than ever, slowing toward the top, slowing, slowing. *An-tic-i-paaa-aa-tion.* They went over the edge and down, down, down, waaaaaaaaaaay down so hard and fast that Jeremy felt as if his stomach had fallen out of him, leaving a hole in the middle of his body. He knew what was coming, but he was left breathless by it nonetheless. The train did a loop-de-loop, turning upside down. He pressed his feet tight to the floor and gripped the lap bar behind him as if he were trying to fuse his flesh with the steel, because it felt as if he would fall out, straight down onto the section of the track that had led them into the loop, to crack his skull open on the rails below. He knew centripetal force would hold him in place even though he was standing up where he didn't belong, but what he knew was of no consequence: *what you felt always carried a lot more weight than what you* knew, *emotion mattered more than intellect.* Then they were out of the loop, banging through another pair of swinging doors onto a second lighted incline, using their tremendous speed to build height for the next series of plunges and sharp turns.

Jeremy looked at Tod.

The old rocket jockey was a little green.

"No more loops," Tod shouted above the clatter of the train wheels. "The worst is behind us."

Jeremy exploded with laughter. He thought: *The worst is still ahead for you, dickhead. And for me the best is yet to come. An-tic-i-paaa-aa-tion.*

Tod laughed, too, but certainly for different reasons.

At the top of the second incline, the rattling cars pushed through a third set of swinging doors, returning to a grave-dark world that thrilled Jeremy because he knew Tod Ledderbeck had just seen the last light of his life. The train snapped left and right, swooped up and plummeted down, rolled onto its side in a series of corkscrew turns.

Through it all Jeremy could feel Tod beside him. Their bare arms brushed together, and their shoulders bumped as they swayed with the movement of the train. Every contact sent a current of intense pleasure through Jeremy, made the hairs stand up on his arms and on the back of his neck, pebbled his skin with gooseflesh. He knew that he possessed the ultimate power over the other boy, the power of life and death, and he was different from the other gutless wonders of the world because he wasn't afraid to *use* the power.

He waited for a section of track near the end of the ride, where he knew the undulant motion would provide the greatest degree of instability for daredevil riders. By then Tod would be feeling confident—*the worst is behind us*—and easier to catch by surprise. The approach to the killing ground was announced by one of the most unusual tricks in the ride, a three-hundred-and-sixty-degree turn at high speed, with the cars on their sides all the way around. When they finished that circle and leveled out once more, they would immediately enter a series of six hills, all low but packed close together, so the train would move like an inchworm on drugs, pulling itself up-down-up-down-up-down-up-down toward the last set of swinging doors, which would admit them to the cavernous boarding and disembarkation chamber where they had begun.

The train began to tilt.

They entered the three-hundred-and-sixty-degree turn.

The train was on its side.

Tod tried to remain rigid, but he sagged a little against Jeremy, who was on the inside of the car when it curved to the right. The old rocket jockey was whooping like an air-raid siren, doing his best to hype himself and get the most out of the ride, now that the worst was behind them.

An-tic-i-paa-aa-tion.

Jeremy estimated they were a third of the way around the circle. . . . halfway around . . . two-thirds. . . .

The track leveled out. The train stopped fighting gravity.

With a suddenness that almost took Jeremy's breath away, the train hit the first of the six hills and shot upward.

He let go of the lap bar with his right hand, the one farthest from Tod.

The train swooped down.

He made a fist of his right hand.

And almost as soon as the train dropped, it swooped upward again toward the crown of the second hill.

Jeremy swung his fist in a roundhouse blow, trusting instinct to find Tod's face.

The train dropped.

His fist hit home, smashing Tod hard in the face, and he felt the boy's nose split.

The train shot upward again, with Tod screaming, though no one would hear anything special about it among the screams of all the other passengers.

Just for a split second, Tod would probably think he'd smacked into the overhang where, in legend, a boy had been decapitated. He would let go of the lap bar in panic. At least that was what Jeremy hoped, so as soon as he hit the old rocket jockey, when the train started to drop down the third hill, Jeremy let go of the lap bar, too, and threw himself against his best friend, grabbing him, lifting and shoving, hard as he could. He felt Tod trying to get a fistful of his hair, but he shook his head furiously and shoved harder, took a kick on the hip—

—the train shot up the fourth hill—

—Tod went over the edge, out into the darkness, away from the car, as if he had dropped into deep space. Jeremy started to topple with him, grabbed frantically for the lap bar in the seamless blackness, found it, held on—

—down, the train swooped down the fourth hill—

—Jeremy thought he heard one last scream from Tod and then a solid *thunk!* as he hit the tunnel wall and bounced back onto the tracks in the wake of the train, although it might have been imagination—

—up, the train shot up the fifth hill with a rollicking motion that made Jeremy want to whoop his cookies—

—Tod was either dead back there in the darkness or stunned, half-conscious, trying to get to his feet—

—down the fifth hill, and Jeremy was whipped back and forth, almost lost his grip on the bar, then was soaring again, up the sixth and final hill—

—and if he wasn't dead back there, Tod was maybe just beginning to realize that another train was coming—

—down, down the sixth hill and onto the last straightaway.

As soon as he knew he was on stable ground, Jeremy scrambled back across the restraint bar and wriggled under it, first his left leg, then his right leg.

The last set of doors was rushing toward them in the dark. Beyond would be light, the main cavern, and attendants who would see that he had been daredevil riding.

He squirmed frantically to pass his hips through the gap between the back of the seat and the lap bar. Not too difficult, really. It was easier to slip under the bar than it had been to get out from beneath its protective grip.

They hit the swinging doors—*wham!*—and coasted at a steadily declining speed toward the disembarkation platform, a hundred feet this side of the gates through which they had entered the roller coaster. People were jammed on the boarding platform, and a lot of them were looking back at the train as it came out of the tunnel mouth. For a moment Jeremy expected them to point at him and cry, "Murderer!"

Just as the train coasted up to the disembarkation gates and came to a full stop, red emergency lights blinked on all over the cavern, showing the way to the exits. A computerized alarm voice echoed through speakers set high in the fake rock formations: *"The Millipede has been brought to an emergency stop. All riders please remain in your seats—"*

As the lap bar released automatically at the end of the ride, Jeremy stood on the seat, grabbed a handrail, and pulled himself onto the disembarkation platform.

"—all riders please remain in your seats until attendants arrive to lead you out of the tunnels—"

The uniformed attendants on the platforms were looking to one another for guidance, wondering what had happened.

"—all riders remain in your seats—"

From the platform, Jeremy looked back toward the tunnel out of which his own train had just entered the cavern. He saw another train pushing through the swinging doors.

"—all other guests please proceed in an orderly fashion to the nearest exit—"

The oncoming train was no longer moving fast or smoothly. It shuddered and tried to jump the track.

With a jolt, Jeremy saw what was jamming the foremost wheels and forcing the front car to rise off the rails. Other people on the platform must have seen it, too, because suddenly they started to scream, not the we-sure-are-having-a-damned-fine-time screams that could be heard all over the carnival, but screams of horror and revulsion.

"—all riders remain in your seats—"

The train rocked and spasmed to a complete stop far short of the disembarkation platform. Something was dangling from the fierce mouth of the insect head that protruded from the front of the first car, snared in the jagged mandibles. It was the rest of the old rocket jockey, a nice bite-size piece for a monster bug the size of that one.

"—all other guests please proceed in an orderly fashion to the nearest exit—"

"Don't look, son," an attendant said compassionately, turning Jeremy away from the gruesome spectacle. "For God's sake, get out of here."

The shocked attendants had recovered enough to begin to direct the waiting crowd toward exit doors marked with glowing red signs. Realizing that he was bursting with excitement, grinning like a fool, and too overcome with joy to successfully play the bereaved best friend of the deceased, Jeremy joined the exodus, which was conducted in a panicky rush, with some pushing and shoving.

In the night air, where Christmasy lights continued to twinkle and the laser beams shot into the black sky and rainbows of neon rippled on every side, where thousands of customers continued their pursuit of pleasure without the slightest awareness that Death walked among them, Jeremy sprinted away from the Millipede. Dodging through the crowds, narrowly avoiding one collision after another, he had no idea where he was going. He just kept on the move until he was far from the torn body of Tod Ledderbeck.

He finally stopped at the manmade lake, across which a few Hovercraft buzzed with travelers bound to and from Mars Island. He felt as if he were on Mars himself, or some other alien planet where the gravity was less than that on earth. He was buoyant, ready to float up, up, and away.

He sat on a concrete bench to anchor himself, with his back to the lake, facing a flower-bordered promenade along which passed an endless parade of people, and he surrendered to the giddy laughter that insistently bubbled in him like Pepsi in a shaken bottle. It gushed out, such effervescent giggles in such long spouts that he had to hug himself and lean back on the bench to avoid falling off. People glanced at him, and one couple stopped to ask if he was lost. His laughter was so intense that he was choking with it, tears streaming down his face. They thought he was crying, a twelve-year-old ninny who had gotten separated from his family and was too much of a pussy to handle it. Their incomprehension only made him laugh harder.

When the laughter passed, he sat forward on the bench, staring at his sneakered feet, working on the line of crap he would give Mrs. Ledderbeck when she came to collect him and Tod at ten o'clock—assuming park officials didn't identify the body and get in touch with her before that. It was eight o'clock. "He wanted to ride daredevil," Jeremy mumbled to his sneakers, "and I tried to talk him out of it, but he wouldn't listen, he called me a dickhead when I wouldn't go with him. I'm sorry, Mrs. Ledderbeck, Doctor Ledderbeck, but he talked that way sometimes. He thought it made him sound cool." Good enough so far, but he needed more of a tremor in his voice: "I wouldn't ride daredevil, so he went on the Millipede by himself. I waited at the exit, and when all those people came running out, talking about a body all torn and bloody, I knew who it had to be and I . . . and I . . . just sort of, you know, snapped. I just snapped." The boarding attendants wouldn't remember whether Tod had gotten on the ride by himself or with another boy; they dealt with thousands of passengers a day, so they weren't going to recall who was alone or who was with whom. "I'm so sorry, Mrs. Ledderbeck, I should've been able to talk him out of it. I should've stayed with him and stopped him somehow. I feel so stupid, so . . . so helpless. How could I let him get on the Millipede? What kind of best friend am I?"

Not bad. It needed a little work, and he would have to be careful not to overdramatize it. Tears, a breaking voice. But no wild sobs, no thrashing around.

He was sure he could pull it off.

He was a Master of the Game now.

As soon as he felt confident about his story, he realized he was hungry. Starving. He was literally shaking with hunger. He went to a refreshment stand and bought a hot dog with the works—onions, relish, chili, mustard, ketchup—and wolfed it down. He chased it with Orange Crush. Still shaking. He had an ice cream sandwich made with chocolate-chip oatmeal cookies for the "bread."

His visible shaking stopped, but he still trembled inside. Not with fear. It was a delicious shiver, like the flutter in the belly that he'd experienced during the past year whenever he looked at a girl and thought of being with her, but indescribably better than that. And it was a little like the thrilling shiver that caressed his spine when he slipped past the safety railing and stood on the very edge of a sandy cliff in Laguna Beach Park, looking down at the waves crashing on the rocks and feeling the earth crumble slowly under the toes of his shoes, working its way back to mid-sole . . . waiting, waiting, wondering if the treacherous ground would abruptly give way and drop him to the rocks far below before he would have time to leap backward and grab the safety railing, but still waiting . . . waiting.

But this thrill was better than all of those combined. It was growing by the minute rather than diminishing, a sensuous inner heat which the murder of Tod had not quenched but fueled.

His dark desire became an urgent need.

He prowled the park, seeking satisfaction.

He was a little surprised that Fantasy World continued to turn as if nothing had happened in the Millipede. He had expected the whole operation to close down, not just that one ride. Now he realized money was more important than mourning one dead customer. And if those who'd seen Tod's battered body had spread the story to others, it was probably discounted as a rehash of the legend. The level of frivolity in the park had not noticeably declined.

Once he dared to pass the Millipede, although he stayed at a distance because he still did not trust himself to be able to conceal his excitement over his achievement and his delight in the new status that he had attained. Master of the Game. Chains were looped from stanchion to stanchion in front of the pavilion, to block anyone attempting to gain access. A CLOSED FOR REPAIRS sign was on the entrance door. Not for repairs to old Tod. The rocket jockey was beyond repair. No ambulance was in sight, which they might have *thought* they needed, and no hearse was anywhere to be seen. No police, either. Weird.

Then he remembered a TV story about the world under Fantasy World: catacombs of service tunnels, storage rooms, security and ride-computer control centers, just like at Disneyland. To avoid disturbing the paying customers and drawing the attention of the morbidly curious, they were probably using the tunnels now to bring in the cops and corpse-pokers from the coroner's office.

The shivers within Jeremy increased. The desire. The need.

He was a Master of the Game. No one could touch him.

Might as well give the cops and corpse-pokers more to do, keep them entertained.

He kept moving, seeking, alert for opportunity. He found it where he least expected it, when he stopped at a men's restroom to take a leak.

A guy, about thirty, was at one of the sinks, checking himself out in the mirror, combing his thick blond hair, which glistened with Vitalis. He had arranged an array of personal objects on the ledge under the mirror: wallet, car keys, a tiny aerosol bottle of Binaca breath freshener, a half-empty pack of Dentyne (this guy had a bad-breath fixation), and a cigarette lighter.

The lighter was what immediately caught Jeremy's attention. It was not just a plastic Bic butane disposable, but one of those steel models, shaped like a miniature slice of bread, with a hinged top that flipped back to reveal a striker wheel and a wick. The way the overhead fluorescent gleamed on the smooth curves of that lighter, it seemed to be a supernatural object, full of its own eerie radiance, a beacon for Jeremy's eyes alone.

He hesitated a moment, then went to one of the urinals. When he finished and zipped up, the blond guy was still at the sink, primping himself.

Jeremy always washed his hands after using a bathroom because that was what polite people did. It was one of the rules that a good player followed.

He went to the sink beside the primper. As he lathered his hands with liquid soap from the pump dispenser, he could not take his eyes off the lighter on the shelf inches away. He told himself he should avert his gaze. The guy would realize he was thinking about snatching the damn thing. But its sleek silvery contours held him rapt. Staring at it as he rinsed the lather from his hands, he imagined that he could hear the crisp crackle of all-consuming flames.

Returning his wallet to his hip pocket but leaving the other objects on the ledge, the guy turned away from the sink and went to one of the urinals. As Jeremy was about to reach for the lighter, a father and his teenage son entered. They could have screwed everything up, but they went into two of the stalls and closed the doors. Jeremy knew that was a sign. Do it, the sign said. Take it, go, do it, do it. Jeremy glanced at the man at the urinal, plucked the lighter off the shelf, turned and walked out without drying his hands. No one ran after him.

Clutching the lighter tightly in his right hand, he prowled the park, searching for the perfect kindling. The desire in him was so intense that his shivers spread outward from his crotch and belly and spine, appearing once more in his hands, and in his legs, too, which sometimes were rubbery with excitement.

Need . . .

FINISHING THE LAST of the Reese's Pieces, Vassago neatly rolled the empty bag into a tight tube, tied the tube in a knot to make the smallest possible object of it, and dropped it into a plastic garbage bag that was just to the left of the iceless Styrofoam cooler. Neatness was one of the rules in the world of the living.

He enjoyed losing himself in the memory of that special night, eight years ago, when he had been twelve and had changed forever, but he was tired now and wanted to sleep. Maybe he would dream of the woman named Lindsey. Maybe he would have another vision that would lead him to someone connected with her, for somehow she seemed to be part of his destiny; he was being drawn toward her by forces he could not entirely understand but which he respected. Next time, he would not make the mistake he had made with Cooper. He would not let the need overwhelm him. He would ask questions first. When he had received all the answers, and only then, he would free the beautiful blood and, with it, another soul to join the infinite throngs beyond this hateful world.

4 Tuesday morning, Lindsey stayed home to get some work done in her studio while Hatch took Regina to school on his way to a meeting with an executor of an estate in North Tustin who was seeking bids on a collection of antique Wedgwood urns and vases. After lunch he had an appointment with Dr. Nyebern to learn the results of the tests he had undergone on Saturday. By the time he picked up Regina and returned home late in the afternoon, Lindsey figured to have finished the canvas she had been working on for the past month.

That was the plan, anyway, but all the fates and evil elves—and her own psychology—conspired to prevent the fulfillment of it. First of all the coffee maker went on the fritz. Lindsey had to tinker with the machine for an hour to find and fix the problem. She was a good tinkerer, and fortunately the brewer was fixable. She could not face the day without a blast of caffeine to jump-start her heart. She knew coffee was bad for her, but so was battery acid and cyanide, and she didn't drink either one of those, which showed she had more than her share of self-control when it came to destructive dietary habits; hell, she was an absolute rock!

By the time she got up to her second-floor studio with a mug and a full thermos besides, the light coming through the north-facing windows was perfect for her purposes. She had everything she needed. She had her paints, brushes, and palette knives. She had her supply cabinet. She had her adjustable stool and her easel and her stereo system with stacks of Garth Brooks, Glenn Miller, and Van Halen CDs, which somehow seemed the right mix of background music for a painter whose style was a combination of neoclassicism and surrealism. The only things she didn't have were an interest in the work at hand and the ability to concentrate.

She was repeatedly diverted by a glossy black spider that was exploring the upper right-hand corner of the window nearest to her. She didn't like spiders, but she was loath to kill them anyway. Later, she would have to capture it in a jar to release it outside. It crept upside down across the window header to the left-hand corner, immediately lost interest in that territory, and returned to the right-hand corner, where it quivered and flexed its long legs and seemed to be taking pleasure from some quality of that particular niche that was apprehensible only to spiders.

Lindsey turned to her painting again. Nearly complete, it was one of her best, lacking only a few refining touches.

But she hesitated to open paints and pick up a brush because she was every bit as devoted a worrier as she was an artist. She was anxious about Hatch's health, of course—both his physical and mental health. She was apprehensive, too, about the strange man who had killed the blonde, and about the eerie connection between that savage predator and her Hatch.

The spider crept down the side of the window frame to the right-hand corner of the sill. After using whatever arachnid senses it possessed, it rejected that nook, as well, and returned once more to the *upper* right-hand corner.

Like most people Lindsey considered psychics to be good subjects for spooky movies but charlatans in real life. Yet she had been quick to suggest clairvoyance as an explanation for what had been happening to Hatch. She had pressed the theory more insistently when he had declared that he was not psychic.

Now, turning away from the spider and staring frustratedly at the unfinished canvas before her, she realized why she had become such an earnest advocate of the reality of psychic power in the car on Friday, when they had followed the killer's trail to the head of Laguna Canyon Road. If Hatch had become psychic, eventually he would begin to receive impressions from all sorts of people, and his link to this murderer would not be unique. But if he was *not* psychic, if the bond between him and this monster was more profound and infinitely stranger than random clairvoyant reception, as he insisted that it was, then they were hip-deep into the unknown. And the unknown was a hell of a lot scarier than something you could describe and define.

Besides, if the link between them was more mysterious and intimate than psychic reception, the consequences for Hatch might be psychologically disastrous. What mental trauma might result from being even briefly inside the mind of a ruthless killer? Was the link between them a source of contamination, as any such intimate *biological* link would have been? If so, perhaps the virus of madness could creep across the ether and infect Hatch.

No. Ridiculous. Not her husband. He was reliable, levelheaded, mellow, as sane a human being as any who walked the earth.

The spider had taken possession of the upper right-hand corner of the window. It began to spin a web.

Lindsey remembered Hatch's anger last night when he had seen the story about Cooper in the newspaper. The hardness of rage in his face. The unsettling fevered look in his eyes. She had never seen Hatch like that. His father, yes, but never him. Though she knew he worried that he might have some of his father in him, she had never seen evidence of it before. And maybe she had not seen evidence of it last night, either. What she had seen might be some of the rage of the killer leaking back into Hatch along the link that existed between them—

No. She had nothing to fear from Hatch. He was a good man, the best she had ever met. He was such a deep well of goodness that all the madness of the blond girl's killer could be dropped into him, and he would dilute it until it was without effect.

A glistening, silky filament spewed from the spider's abdomen as the arachnid industriously claimed the corner of the window for its lair. Lindsey opened a drawer in her equipment cabinet and took out a small magnifying glass, which she used to observe the spinner more closely. Its spindly legs were prickled with hundreds of fine hairs that could not be seen without the assistance of the lens. Its horrid, multifaceted eyes looked everywhere at once, and its ragged maw worked continuously as if in anticipation of the first living fly to become stuck in the trap that it was weaving.

Although she understood that it was a part of nature as surely as she was, and therefore not evil, the thing nevertheless revolted Lindsey. It was a part of nature that she preferred not to dwell upon: the part that had to do with hunting and killing, with things that fed eagerly on the living. She put the magnifying glass on the windowsill and went downstairs to get a jar from the kitchen pantry. She wanted to capture the spider and get it out of her house before it was any more securely settled.

Reaching the foot of the stairs, she glanced at the window beside the front door and saw the postman's car. She collected the mail from the box at the curb: a few bills, the usual minimum of two mail-order catalogues, and the latest issue of *Arts American.*

She was in the mood to seize any excuse not to work, which was unusual for her, because she loved her work. Quite forgetting that she had come downstairs in the first place for a jar in which to transport the spider, she took the mail back up to her studio and settled down in the old armchair in the corner with a fresh mug of coffee and *Arts American.*

She spotted the article about herself as soon as she glanced at the table of contents. She was surprised. The magazine had covered her work before, but she had always known in advance that articles were forthcoming. Usually the writer had at least a few questions for her, even if he was not doing a straight interview.

Then she saw the byline and winced. S. Steven Honell. She knew before reading the first word that she was the target of a hatchet job.

Honell was a well-reviewed writer of fiction who, from time to time, also wrote about art. He was in his sixties and had never married. A phlegmatic fellow, he had decided as a young man to forego the comforts of a wife and family in the interest of his writing. To write well, he said, one ought to possess a monk's preference for solitude. In isolation, one was forced to confront oneself more directly and honestly than possible in the hustle-bustle of the peopled world, and through oneself also confront the nature of every human heart. He had lived in splendid isolation first in northern California, then in New Mexico. Most recently he had settled at the eastern edge of the developed part of Orange County at the end of Silverado Canyon, which was part of a series of brush-covered hills and ravines spotted with numerous California live oaks and less numerous rustic cabins.

In September of the previous year, Lindsey and Hatch had gone to a restaurant at the civilized end of Silverado Canyon, which served strong drinks and good steaks. They had eaten at one of the tables in the taproom, which was paneled in knotty pine with limestone columns supporting the roof. An inebriated white-haired man, sitting at the bar, was holding forth on literature, art, and politics. His opinions were strongly held and expressed in caustic language. From the affectionate tolerance the curmudgeon received from the bartender and patrons on the other bar stools, Lindsey guessed he was a regular customer and a local character who told only half as many tales as were told about him.

Then Lindsey recognized him. S. Steven Honell. She had read and liked some of his writing. She'd admired his selfless devotion to his art; for she could not have sacrificed love, marriage, and children for her painting, even though the exploration of her creative talent was as important to her as having enough food to eat and water to drink. Listening to Honell, she wished that she and Hatch had gone somewhere else for dinner because she would never again be able to read the author's work without remembering some of the vicious statements he made about the writings and personalities of his contemporaries in letters. With each drink, he grew more bitter, more scathing, more indulgent of his own darkest instincts, and markedly more garrulous. Liquor revealed the gabby fool hidden inside the legend of taciturnity; anyone wanting to shut him up would have needed a horse veterinarian's hypodermic full of Demerol or a .357 Magnum. Lindsey ate faster, deciding to skip dessert and depart Honell's company as swiftly as possible.

Then he recognized her. He kept glancing over his shoulder at her, blinking his rheumy eyes. Finally he unsteadily approached their table. "Excuse me, are you Lindsey Sparling, the artist?" She had known that he sometimes wrote about American art, but she had not imagined he would know her work or her face. "Yes, I am," she said, hoping he would not say that he liked her work and that he would not tell her who he was. "I like your work very much," he said. "I won't bother you to say more." But just as she relaxed and thanked him, he told her his name, and she was obligated to say that she liked his work, too, which she did, though now she saw it in a light different from that in which it had previously appeared to her. He seemed less like a man who had sacrificed family love for his art than like a man incapable of giving that love. In isolation he might have found a greater power to create; but he had also found more time to admire himself and contemplate the infinite number of ways in which he was superior to the ruck of his fellow men. She tried not to let her distaste show, spoke only glowingly of his novels, but he seemed to sense her disapproval. He quickly terminated the encounter and returned to the bar.

He never looked her way again during the night. And he no longer held forth to the assembled drinkers about anything, his attention directed largely at the contents of his glass.

Now, sitting in the armchair in her studio, holding the copy of *Arts American*, and staring at Honell's byline, she felt her stomach curdle. She had seen the great man in his cups, when he had uncloaked more of his true self than it was his nature to reveal. Worse, she was a person of some accomplishment, who moved in circles that might bring her into contact with people Honell also knew. He saw her as a threat. One way of neutralizing her was to undertake a well-written, if unfair, article criticizing her body of work; thereafter, he could claim that any tales she told about him were motivated by spite, of questionable truthfulness. She knew what to expect from him in the *Arts American* piece, and Honell did not surprise her. Never before had she read criticism so vicious yet so cunningly crafted to spare the critic accusations of personal animosity.

When she finished, she closed the magazine and put it down gently on the small table beside her chair. She didn't want to pitch it across the room because she knew that reaction would have pleased Honell if he had been present to see it.

Then she said, "To hell with it," picked up the magazine, and threw it across the room with all the force she could muster. It slapped hard against the wall and clattered to the floor.

Her work was important to her. Intellect, emotion, talent, and craft went into it, and even on those occasions when a painting did not turn out as well as she had hoped, no creation ever came easily. Anguish always was a part of it. And more self-revelation than seemed prudent. Exhilaration and despair in equal measure. A critic had every right to dislike an artist if his judgment was based on thoughtful consideration and an understanding of what the artist was trying to achieve. But *this* was not genuine criticism. This was sick invective. Bile. Her work was important to her, and he had shit on it.

Filled with the energy of anger, she got up and paced. She knew that by surrendering to anger she was letting Honell win; this was the response he had hoped to extract from her with his dental-pliers criticism. But she couldn't help it.

She wished Hatch was there, so she could share her fury with him. He had a calming effect greater than a fifth of bourbon.

Her angry pacing brought her eventually to the window where by now the fat black spider had constructed an elaborate web in the upper right-hand corner. Realizing that she had forgotten to get a jar from the pantry, Lindsey picked up the magnifying glass and examined the silken filigree of the eight-legged fisherman's net, which glimmered with a pastel mother-of-pearl iridescence. The trap was so delicate, so alluring. But the living loom that spun it was the very essence of all predators, strong for its size and sleek and quick. Its bulbous body glistened like a drop of thick black blood, and its rending mandibles worked the air in anticipation of the flesh of prey not yet snared.

The spider and Steven Honell were of a kind, utterly alien to her and beyond understanding regardless of how long she observed them. Both spun their webs in silence and isolation. Both had brought their viciousness into her house uninvited, one through words in a magazine and the other through a tiny crack in a window frame or door jamb. Both were poisonous, vile.

She put down the magnifying glass. She could do nothing about Honell, but at least she could deal with the spider. She snatched two Kleenex from a box atop her supply cabinet, and in one swift movement she swept up the spinner and its web, crushing both.

She threw the wad of tissues in the waste can.

Though she usually captured a spider when possible and kindly returned it to the outdoors, she had no compunction about the way she had dealt with this one. Indeed, if Honell had been present at that moment, when his hateful attack was still so fresh in her mind, she might have been tempted to deal with him in some manner as quick and violent as the treatment she had accorded the spider.

She returned to her stool, regarded the unfinished canvas, and was suddenly certain what refinements it required. She opened tubes of paint and set out her brushes. That wasn't the first time she had been motivated by an unjust blow or a puerile insult, and she wondered how many artists of all kinds had produced their best work with the determination to rub it in the faces of the naysayers who had tried to undercut or belittle them.

When Lindsey had been at work on the painting for ten or fifteen minutes, she was stricken by an unsettling thought which brought her back to the worries that had preoccupied her before the arrival of the mail and *Arts American*. Honell and the spider were not the only creatures who had invaded her home uninvited. The unknown killer in sunglasses also had invaded it, in a way, by feedback through the mysterious link between him and Hatch. And what if he was as aware of Hatch as Hatch was of him? He might find a way to track Hatch down and invade their home for real, with the intention of doing far more harm than either the spider or Honell could ever accomplish.

5 Previously, Hatch had visited Jonas Nyebern in his office at Orange County General, but that Tuesday his appointment was at the medical building off Jamboree Road, where the physician operated his private practice.

The waiting room was remarkable, not for its short-nap gray carpet and standard-issue furniture, but for the artwork on its walls. Hatch was surprised and impressed by a collection of high-quality antique oil paintings portraying religious scenes of a Catholic nature: the passion of St. Jude, the Crucifixion, the Holy Mother, the Annunciation, the Resurrection, and much more.

The most curious thing was not that the collection was worth considerable money. After all, Nyebern was an extremely successful cardiovascular surgeon who came from a family of more than average resources. But it was odd that a member of the medical profession, which had taken an increasingly agnostic public posture throughout the last few decades, should choose religious art of any kind for his office walls, let alone such obvious denominational art that might offend non-Catholics or nonbelievers.

When the nurse escorted Hatch out of the waiting room, he discovered the collection continued along the hallways serving the entire suite. He found it peculiar to see a fine oil of Jesus' agony in Gethsemane hung to the left of a stainless-steel and white-enamel scale, and beside a chart listing ideal weight according to height, age, and sex.

After weighing in and having his blood pressure and pulse taken, he waited for Nyebern in a small private room, sitting on the end of an examination table that was covered by a continuous roll of sanitary paper. On one wall hung an eye chart and an exquisite depiction of the Ascension in which the artist's skill with light was so great that the scene became three-dimensional and the figures therein seemed almost alive.

Nyebern kept him waiting only a minute or two, and entered with a broad smile. As they shook hands, the physician said, "I won't draw out the suspense, Hatch. The tests all came in negative. You've got a clean bill of health."

Those words were not as welcome as they ought to have been. Hatch had been hoping for some finding that would point the way to an understanding of his nightmares and his mystical connection with the man who had killed the blond punker. But the verdict did not in the least surprise him. He had suspected that the answers he sought were not going to be that easy to find.

"So your nightmares are only that," Nyebern said, "and nothing more—just nightmares."

Hatch had not told him about the vision of the gunshot blonde who had later been found dead, for real, on the freeway. As he had made clear to Lindsey, he was not going to set himself up to become a headline again, at least not unless he saw enough of the killer to identify him to the police, more than he'd glimpsed in the mirror last night, in which case he would have no choice but to face the media spotlight.

"No cranial pressure," Nyebern said, "no chemicoelectrical imbalance, no sign of a shift in the location of the pineal gland—which can sometimes lead to severe nightmares and even waking hallucinations . . ." He went over the tests one by one, methodical as usual.

As he listened, Hatch realized that he always remembered the physician as being older than he actually was. Jonas Nyebern had a grayness about him, and a gravity, that left the impression of advanced age. Tall and lanky, he hunched his shoulders and stooped slightly to de-emphasize his height, resulting in a posture more like that of an elderly man than of someone his true age, which was fifty. At times there was about him, as well, an air of sadness, as if he had known great tragedy.

When he finished going over the tests, Nyebern looked up and smiled again. It was a warm smile, but that air of sadness clung to him in spite of it. "The problem isn't physical, Hatch."

"Is it possible you could have missed something?"

"Possible, I suppose, but very unlikely. We—"

"An extremely minor piece of brain damage, a few hundred cells, might not show up on your tests yet have a serious effect."

"As I said, very unlikely. I think we can safely assume that this is strictly an emotional problem, a perfectly understandable consequence of the trauma you've been through. Let's try a little standard therapy."

"Psychotherapy?"

"Do you have a problem with that?"

"No."

Except, Hatch thought, it won't work. This isn't an emotional problem. This is real.

"I know a good man, first-rate, you'll like him," Nyebern said, taking a pen from the breast pocket of his white smock and writing the name of the psychotherapist on the blank top sheet of a prescription pad. "I'll discuss your case with him and tell him you'll be calling. Is that all right?"

"Yeah. Sure. That's fine."

He wished he could tell Nyebern the whole story. But then he would *definitely* sound as if he needed therapy. Reluctantly he faced the realization that neither a medical doctor nor a psychotherapist could help him. His ailment was too strange to respond to standard treatments of any kind. Maybe what he needed was a witch doctor. Or an exorcist. He *did* almost feel as if the black-clad killer in sunglasses was a demon testing his defenses to determine whether to attempt possessing him.

They chatted a couple of minutes about things non-medical.

Then as Hatch was getting up to go, he pointed to the painting of the Ascension. "Beautiful piece."

"Thank you. It is exceptional, isn't it?"

"Italian."

"That's right."

"Early eighteenth century?"

"Right again," Nyebern said. "You know religious art?"

"Not all that well. But I think the whole collection is Italian from the same period."

"That it is. Another piece, maybe two, and I'll call it complete."

"Odd to see it here," Hatch said, stepping closer to the painting beside the eye chart.

"Yes, I know what you mean," Nybern said, "but I don't have enough wall space for all this at home. There, I'm putting together a collection of *modern* religious art."

"Is there any?"

"Not much. Religious subject matter isn't fashionable these days among the really talented artists. The bulk of it is done by hacks. But here and there . . . someone with genuine talent is seeking enlightenment along the old paths, painting these subjects with a contemporary eye. I'll move the modern collection here when I finish this one and dispose of it."

Hatch turned away from the painting and regarded the doctor with professional interest. "You're planning to sell?"

"Oh, no," the physician said, returning his pen to his breast pocket. His hand, with the long elegant fingers that one expected of a surgeon, lingered at the pocket, as if he were pledging the truth of what he was saying. "I'll donate it. This will be the sixth collection of religious art I've put together over the past twenty years, then given away."

Because he could roughly estimate the value of the artwork he had seen on the walls of the medical suite, Hatch was astonished by the degree of philanthropy indicated by Nyebern's simple statement. "Who's the fortunate recipient?"

"Well, usually a Catholic university, but on two occasions another Church institution," Nyebern said.

The surgeon was staring at the depiction of the Ascension, a distant gaze in his eyes, as if he were seeing something beyond the painting, beyond the wall on which it hung, and beyond the farthest horizon. His hand still lingered over his breast pocket.

"Very generous of you," Hatch said.

"It's not an act of generosity." Nyebern's faraway voice now matched the look in his eyes. "It's an act of atonement."

That statement begged for a question in response, although Hatch felt that asking it was an intrusion of the physician's privacy. "Atonement for what?"

Still staring at the painting, Nyebern said, "I never talk about it."

"I don't mean to pry. I just thought—"

"Maybe it would do me good to talk about it. Do you think it might?"

Hatch did not answer—partly because he didn't believe the doctor was actually listening to him anyway.

"Atonement," Nyebern said again. "At first . . . atonement for being the son of my father. Later . . . for being the father of my son."

Hatch didn't see how either thing could be a sin, but he waited, certain that the physician would explain. He was beginning to feel like that partygoer in the old Coleridge poem, waylaid by the distraught Ancient Mariner who had a tale of terror that he was driven to impart to others lest, by keeping it to himself, he lose what little sanity he still retained.

Gazing unblinking at the painting, Nyebern said, "When I was only seven, my father suffered a psychotic breakdown. He shot and killed my mother and my brother. He wounded my sister and me, left us for dead, then killed himself."

"Jesus, I'm sorry," Hatch said, and he thought of his own father's bottomless well of anger. "I'm very sorry, Doctor." But he still did not understand the failure or sin for which Nyebern felt the need to atone.

"Certain psychoses may sometimes have a genetic cause. When I saw signs of sociopathic behavior in my son, even at an early age, I should have known what was coming, should've prevented it somehow. But I couldn't face the truth. Too painful. Then two years ago, when he was eighteen, he stabbed his sister to death—"

Hatch shuddered.

"—then his mother," Nyebern said.

Hatch started to put a hand on the doctor's arm, then pulled back when he sensed that Nyebern's pain could never be eased and that his wound was beyond healing by any medication as simple as consolation. Although he was speaking of an intensely personal tragedy, the physician plainly was not seeking sympathy or the intimacy of friendship from Hatch. Suddenly he seemed almost frighteningly self-contained. He was talking about the tragedy because the time had come to take it out of his personal darkness to examine it again, and he would have spoken of it to anyone who had been in that place at that time instead of Hatch—or perhaps to the empty air itself if no one at all had been present.

"And when they were dead," Nyebern said, "Jeremy took the same knife into the garage, a butcher knife, secured it by the handle in the vise on my workbench, stood on a stool, and fell forward, impaling himself on the blade. He bled to death."

The physician's right hand was still at his breast pocket, but he no longer seemed like a man pledging the truth of what he said. Instead, he reminded Hatch of a painting of Christ with the Sacred Heart revealed, the slender hand of divine grace pointing to that symbol of sacrifice and promise of eternity.

At last Nyebern looked away from the Ascension and met Hatch's eyes. "Some say evil is just the consequences of our actions, no more than a result of our will. But I believe it's that—and much more. I believe evil is a very real force, an energy quite apart from us, a presence in the world. Is that what you believe, Hatch?"

"Yes," Hatch said at once, and somewhat to his surprise.

Nyebern looked down at the prescription pad in his left hand. He took his right hand away from his breast pocket, tore the top sheet off the pad, and gave it to Hatch. "His name's Foster. Dr. Gabriel Foster. I'm sure he'll be able to help you."

"Thanks," Hatch said numbly.

Nyebern opened the door of the examination room and gestured for Hatch to precede him.

In the hallway, the physician said, "Hatch?"

Hatch stopped and looked back at him.

"Sorry," Nyebern said.

"For what?"

"For explaining why I donate the paintings."

Hatch nodded. "Well, I asked, didn't I?"

"But I could have been much briefer."

"Oh?"

"I could have just said—maybe I think the only way for me to get into Heaven is to buy my way."

Outside, in the sun-splashed parking lot, Hatch sat in his car for a long time, watching a wasp that hovered over the red hood as if it thought it had found an enormous rose.

The conversation in Nyebern's office had seemed strangely like a dream, and Hatch felt as if he were still rising out of sleep. He sensed that the tragedy of Jonas Nyebern's death-haunted life had a direct bearing on his own current problems, but although he reached for the connection, he could not grasp it.

The wasp swayed to the left, to the right, but faced steadily toward the windshield as though it could see him in the car and was mysteriously drawn to him. Repeatedly, it darted at the glass, bounced off, and resumed its hovering. Tap, hover, tap, hover, tap-tap, hover. It was a very determined wasp. He wondered if it was one of those species that possessed a single stinger that broke off in the target, resulting in the subsequent death of the wasp. Tap, hover, tap, hover, tap-tap-tap. If it was one of those species, did it fully understand what reward it would earn by its persistence? Tap, hover, tap-tap-tap.

AFTER SEEING THE last patient of the day, a follow-up visit with an engaging thirty-year-old woman on whom he had performed an aortal graft last March, Jonas Nyebern entered his private office at the back of the medical suite and closed the door. He went behind the desk, sat down, and looked in his wallet for a slip of paper on which was written a telephone number that he chose not to include on his Rolodex. He found it, pulled the phone close, and punched in the seven numbers.

Following the third ring, an answering machine picked up as it had on his previous calls yesterday and earlier that morning: *"This is Morton Redlow. I'm not in the office right now. After the beep, please leave a message and a number where you can be reached, and I will get back to you as soon as possible."*

Jonas waited for the signal, then spoke softly. "Mr. Redlow, this is Dr. Nyebern. I know I've left other messages, but I was under the impression that I would receive a report from you last Friday. Certainly by the weekend at the latest. Please call me as soon as possible. Thank you."

He hung up.

He wondered if he had reason to worry.

He wondered if he had any reason *not* to worry.

6

Regina sat at her desk in Sister Mary Margaret's French class, weary of the smell of chalk dust and annoyed by the hardness of the plastic seat under her butt, learning how to say, *Hello, I am an American. Can you direct me to the nearest church where I might attend Sunday Mass?*

Très boring.

She was still a fifth-grade student at St. Thomas's Elementary School, because continued attendance was a strict condition of her adoption. (Trial adoption. Nothing final yet. Could blow up. The Harrisons could decide they preferred raising parakeets to children, give her back, get a bird. Please, God, make sure they realize that in Your divine wisdom You designed birds so they poop a lot. Make sure they know what a mess it'll be keeping the cage clean.) When she graduated from St. Thomas's Elementary, she would move on to St. Thomas's High School, because St. Thomas's had its fingers in everything. In addition to the children's care home and the two schools, it had a day-care center and a thrift shop. The parish was like a conglomerate, and Father Jiminez was sort of a big executive like Donald Trump, except Father Jiminez didn't run around with bimbos or own gambling casinos. The bingo parlor hardly counted. (Dear God, that stuff about birds pooping a lot—that was in no way meant as a criticism. I'm sure You had Your reasons for making birds poop a lot, all over everything, and like the mystery of the Holy Trinity, it's just one of those things we ordinary humans can't ever quite understand. No offense meant.) Anyway, she didn't mind going to St. Thomas's School, because both the nuns and the lay teachers pushed you hard, and you ended up learning a lot, and she loved to learn.

By the last class on that Tuesday afternoon, however, she was full up with learning, and if Sister Mary Margaret called on her to say anything in French, she would probably confuse the word for church with the word for sewer, which she had done once before, much to the delight of the other kids and to her own mortification. (Dear God, please remember that I made myself say the Rosary as penance for that boner, just to prove I didn't mean anything by it, it was only a mistake.) When the dismissal bell rang, she was the first out of her seat and the first out of the classroom door, even though most of the kids at St. Thomas's School did not come from St. Thomas's Home and were not disabled in any way.

All the way to her locker and all the way from her locker to the front exit, she wondered if Mr. Harrison would really be waiting for her, as he had promised. She imagined herself standing on the sidewalk with kids swarming around her, unable to spot his car, the crowd gradually diminishing until she stood alone, and still no sign of his car, and her waiting as the sun set and the moon rose and her wristwatch ticked toward midnight, and in the morning when the kids returned for another day of school, she'd just go back inside with them and not tell anyone the Harrisons didn't want her any more.

He was there. In the red car. In a line of cars driven by other kids' parents. He leaned across the seat to open the door for her as she approached.

When she got in with her book bag and closed the door, he said, "Hard day?"

"Yeah," she said, suddenly shy when shyness had never been one of her major problems. She was having trouble getting the hang of this family thing. She was afraid maybe she'd never get it.

He said, "Those nuns."

"Yeah," she agreed.

"They're tough."

"Tough."

"Tough as nails, those nuns."

"Nails," she said, nodding agreement, wondering if she would ever be able to speak more than one-word sentences again.

As he pulled away from the curb, he said, "I'll bet you could put any nun

in the ring with any heavyweight champion in the whole history of boxing—
I don't care if it was even Muhammad Ali—and she'd knock him out in the
first round."

Regina couldn't help grinning at him.

"Sure," he said. "Only Superman could survive a fight with a real hard-
case nun. Batman? Fooie! Even your *average* nun could mop up the floor
with Batman—or make soup out of the whole gang of Teenage Mutant
Ninja Turtles."

"They mean well," she said, which was three words, at least, but sounded
goofy. She might be better off not talking at all; she just didn't have any
experience at this father-kid stuff.

"Nuns?" he said. "Well, of course, they mean well. If they didn't mean
well, they wouldn't be nuns. They'd be maybe Mafia hitmen, international
terrorists, United States Congressmen."

He did not speed home like a busy man with lots to do, but like somebody
out for a leisurely drive. She had not been in a car with him enough to know
if that was how he always drove, but she suspected maybe he was loafing
along a little slower than he usually did, so they could have more time together, just the two of them. That was sweet. It made her throat a little tight
and her eyes watery. Oh, terrific. A pile of cow flop could've carried on a
better conversation than she was managing, so now she was going to burst
into tears, which would really cement the relationship. Surely every adoptive
parent desperately hoped to receive a mute, emotionally unstable girl with
physical problems—right? It was all the rage, don't you know. Well, if she
did cry, her treacherous sinuses would kick in, and the old snot-faucet would
start gushing, which would surely make her even *more* appealing. He'd give
up the idea of a leisurely drive, and head for home at such tremendous speed
that he'd have to stand on the brakes a mile from the house to avoid shooting
straight through the back of the garage. (Please, God, help me here. You'll
notice I thought "cow flop" not "cow shit," so I deserve a little mercy.)

They chatted about this and that. Actually, for a while he chatted and
she pretty much just grunted like she was a subhuman out on a pass from
the zoo. But eventually she realized, to her surprise, that she was talking in
complete sentences, had been doing so for a couple of miles, and was at ease
with him.

He asked her what she wanted to be when she grew up, and she just
about bent his ear clear off explaining that some people actually made a
living writing the kinds of books she liked to read and that she had been
composing her own stories for a year or two. Lame stuff, she admitted, but
she would get better at it. She was very bright for ten, older than her years,
but she couldn't expect actually to have a career going until she was eighteen,
maybe sixteen if she was lucky. When had Mr. Christopher Pike started
publishing? Seventeen? Eighteen? Maybe he'd been as old as twenty, but
certainly no older, so that's what she would shoot for—being the next Mr.
Christopher Pike by the time she was twenty. She had an entire notebook

full of story ideas. Quite a few of those ideas were good even when you crossed out the embarrassingly childish ones like the story about the intelligent pig from space that she had been so hot about for a while but now saw was hopelessly dumb. She was still talking about writing books when they pulled into the driveway of the house in Laguna Niguel, and he actually seemed interested.

She figured she might get the hang of this family thing yet.

VASSAGO DREAMED OF fire. The click of the cigarette-lighter cover being flipped open in the dark. The dry rasp of the striker wheel scraping against the flint. A spark. A young girl's white summer dress flowering into flames. The Haunted House ablaze. Screams as the calculatedly spooky darkness dissolved under licking tongues of orange light. Tod Ledderbeck was dead in the cavern of the Millipede, and now the house of plastic skeletons and rubber ghouls was abruptly filled with real terror and pungent death.

He had dreamed of that fire previously, countless times since the night of Tod's twelfth birthday. It always provided the most beautiful of all the chimeras and phantasms that passed behind his eyes in sleep.

But on this occasion, strange faces and images appeared in the flames. The red car again. A solemnly beautiful, auburn-haired child with large gray eyes that seemed too old for her face. A small hand, cruelly bent, with fingers missing. A name, which had come to him once before, echoed through the leaping flames and melting shadows in the Haunted House. *Regina . . . Regina . . . Regina.*

THE VISIT TO Dr. Nyebern's office had depressed Hatch, both because the tests had revealed nothing that shed any light on his strange experiences and because of the glimpse he had gotten into the physician's own troubled life. But Regina was a medicine for melancholy if ever there had been one. She had all the enthusiasm of a child her age; life had not beaten her down one inch.

On the way from the car to the front door of the house, she moved more swiftly and easily than when she had entered Salvatore Gujilio's office, but the leg brace did give her a measured and solemn gait. A bright yellow and blue butterfly accompanied her every step, fluttering gaily a few inches from her head, as if it knew that her spirit was very like itself, beautiful and buoyant.

She said solemnly, "Thank you for picking me up, Mr. Harrison."

"You're welcome, I'm sure," he said with equal gravity.

They would have to do something about this "Mr. Harrison" business before the day was out. He sensed that her formality was partly a fear of getting too close—and then being rejected as she had been during the trial phase of her first adoption. But it was also a fear of saying or doing the wrong thing and unwittingly destroying her own prospects for happiness.

At the front door, he said, "Either Lindsey or I will be at the school for you every day—unless you've got a driver's license and would just rather come and go on your own."

She looked up at Hatch. The butterfly was describing circles in the air above her head, as if it were a living crown or halo. She said, "You're teasing me, aren't you?"

"Well, yes, I'm afraid I am."

She blushed and looked away from him, as if she was not sure if being teased was a good or bad thing. He could almost hear her inner thoughts: *Is he teasing me because he thinks I'm cute or because he thinks I'm hopelessly stupid*, or something pretty close to that.

Throughout the drive home from school, Hatch had seen that Regina suffered from her share of self-doubt, which she thought she concealed but which, when it struck, was evident in her lovely, wonderfully expressive face. Each time he sensed a crack in the kid's self-confidence, he wanted to put his arms around her, hug her tight, and reassure her—which would be exactly the wrong thing to do because she would be appalled to realize that her moments of inner turmoil were so obvious to him. She prided herself on being tough, resilient, and self-sufficient. She projected that image as armor against the world.

"I hope you don't mind some teasing," he said as he inserted the key in the door. "That's the way I am. I could check myself into a Teasers Anonymous program, shake the habit, but it's a tough outfit. They beat you with rubber hoses and make you eat Lima beans."

When enough time passed, when she felt she was loved and part of a family, her self-confidence would be as unshakable as she wanted it to be now. In the meantime, the best thing he could do for her was pretend that he saw her exactly as she wished to be seen—and quietly, patiently help her finish becoming the poised and assured person she hoped to be.

As he opened the door and they went inside, Regina said, "I used to hate Lima beans, all kinds of beans, but I made a deal with God. If he gives me . . . something I 'specially want, I'll eat every kind of bean there is for the rest of my life without ever complaining."

In the foyer, closing the door behind them, Hatch said, "That's quite an offer. God ought to be impressed."

"I sure hope so," she said.

AND IN VASSAGO'S dream, Regina moved in sunlight, one leg embraced in steel, a butterfly attending her as it might a flower. A house flanked by palm trees. A door. She looked up at Vassago, and her eyes revealed a soul of tremendous vitality and a heart so vulnerable that the beat of his own was quickened even in sleep.

THEY FOUND LINDSEY upstairs, in the extra bedroom that served as her at-home studio. The easel was angled away from the door, so Hatch couldn't see the painting. Lindsey's blouse was half in and half out of her jeans, her hair was in disarray, a smear of rust-red paint marked her left cheek, and she had a look that Hatch knew from experience meant she was in the final fever of work on a piece that was turning out to be everything she had hoped.

"Hi, honey," Lindsey said to Regina. "How was school?"

Regina was flustered, as she always seemed to be, by any term of endearment. "Well, school is school, you know."

"Well, you must like it. I know you get good grades."

Regina shrugged off the compliment and looked embarrassed.

Repressing the urge to hug the kid, Hatch said to Lindsey, "She's going to be a writer when she grows up."

"Really?" Lindsey said. "That's exciting. I knew you loved books, but I didn't realize you wanted to write them."

"Neither did I," the girl said, and suddenly she was in gear and off, her initial awkwardness with Lindsey past, words pouring out of her as she crossed the room and went behind the easel to have a look at the work in progress, "until just last Christmas, when my gift under the tree at the home was six paperbacks. Not books for a ten-year-old, either, but the real stuff, because I read at a tenth-grade level, which is *fifteen* years old. I'm what they call precocious. Anyway, those books made the best gift ever, and I thought it'd be neat if someday a girl like me at the home got *my* books under the tree and felt the way I felt, not that I'll ever be as good a writer as Mr. Daniel Pinkwater or Mr. Christopher Pike. Jeez, I mean, they're right up there with Shakespeare and Judy Blume. But I've got good stories to tell, and they're not all that intelligent-pig-from-space crap. Sorry. I mean poop. I mean junk. Intelligent-pig-from-space junk. They're not all like that."

Lindsey never showed Hatch—or anyone else—a canvas in progress, withholding even a glimpse of it until the final brush stroke had been applied. Though she was evidently near completion of the current painting, she was still working on it, and Hatch was surprised that she didn't even twitch when Regina went around to the front of the easel to have a look. He decided that no kid, just because she had a cute nose and some freckles, was going to be accorded a privilege he was denied, so he also walked boldly around the easel to take a peek.

It was a stunning piece of work. The background was a field of stars, and superimposed over it was the transparent face of an ethereally beautiful young boy. Not just any boy. Their Jimmy. When he was alive she had painted him a few times, but never since his death—until now. It was an idealized Jimmy of such perfection that his face might have been that of an angel. His loving eyes were turned upward, toward a warm light that rained down upon him from beyond the top of the canvas, and his expression was more profound than joy. Rapture. In the foreground, as the focus of the work, floated a black rose, not transparent like the face, rendered in such sensuous detail that Hatch could almost feel the velvety texture of each plush petal. The green skin of the stem was moist with a cool dew, and the thorns were portrayed with such piercingly sharp points that he half believed they would prick like real thorns if touched. A single drop of blood glistened on one of the black petals. Somehow Lindsey had imbued the floating rose with an aura of preternatural power, so it drew the eye, demanded attention, almost mesmeric in its effect. Yet the boy did not look down at the rose; he gazed up at the radiant object only he could see, the implication being that, as powerful as the rose might be, it was of no interest whatsoever when compared to the source of the light above.

From the day of Jimmy's death until Hatch's resuscitation, Lindsey had refused to take solace from any god who would create a world with death in it. He recalled a priest suggesting prayer as a route to acceptance and psychological healing, and Lindsey's response had been cold and dismissive: *Prayer never works. Expect no miracles, Father. The dead stay dead, and the living only wait to join them.* Something had changed in her now. The black rose in the painting was death. Yet it had no power over Jimmy. He had gone beyond death, and it meant nothing to him. He was rising above it. And by being able to conceive of the painting and bring it off so flawlessly, Lindsey had found a way to say goodbye to the boy at last, goodbye without regrets, goodbye without bitterness, goodbye with love and with a startling new acceptance of the need for belief in something more than a life that ended always in a cold, black hole in the ground.

"It's so beautiful," Regina said with genuine awe. "Scary in a way, I don't know why . . . scary . . . but so beautiful."

Hatch looked up from the painting, met Lindsey's eyes, tried to say something, but could not speak. Since his resuscitation, there had been a rebirth of Lindsey's heart as well as his own, and they had confronted the mistake they had made by losing five years to grief. But on some fundamental level, they had not accepted that life could ever be as sweet as it had been before that one small death; they had not really let Jimmy go. Now, meeting Lindsey's eyes, he knew that she had finally embraced hope again without reservation. The full weight of his little boy's death fell upon Hatch as it had not in years, because if Lindsey could make peace with God, he must do so as well. He tried to speak again, could not, looked again at the painting, realized he was going to cry, and left the room.

He didn't know where he was going. Without quite remembering taking any step along the route, he went downstairs, into the den that they had offered to Regina as a bedroom, opened the French doors, and stepped into the rose garden at the side of the house.

In the warm, late-afternoon sun, the roses were red, white, yellow, pink, and the shade of peach skins, some only buds and some as big as saucers, but not one of them black. The air was full of their enchanting fragrance.

With the taste of salt in the corners of his mouth, he reached out with both hands toward the nearest rose-laden bush, intending to touch the flowers, but his hands stopped short of them. With his arms thus forming a cradle, he suddenly could feel a weight draped across them. In reality, nothing was in his arms, but the burden he felt was no mystery; he remembered, as if it had been an hour ago, how the body of his cancer-wasted son had felt.

In the final moments before death's hateful visitation, he had pulled the wires and tubes from Jim, had lifted him off the sweat-soaked hospital bed, and had sat in a chair by the window, holding him close and murmuring to him until the pale, parted lips drew no more breath. Until his own death, Hatch would remember precisely the weight of the wasted boy in his arms, the sharpness of bones with so little flesh left to pad them, the awful dry heat pouring off skin translucent with sickness, the heart-rending fragility.

He felt all that now, in his empty arms, there in the rose garden. When he looked up at the summer sky, he said, "Why?" as if there were Someone to answer. "He was so small," Hatch said. "He was so damned small."

As he spoke, the burden was heavier than it had ever been in that hospital room, a thousand tons in his empty arms, maybe because he still didn't want to free himself of it as much as he thought he did. But then a strange thing happened—the weight in his arms slowly diminished, and the invisible body of his son seemed to float out of his embrace, as if the flesh had been transmuted entirely to spirit at long last, as if Jim had no need of comforting or consolation any more.

Hatch lowered his arms.

Maybe from now on the bittersweet memory of a child lost would be only the sweet memory of a child loved. And maybe, henceforth, it would not be a memory so heavy that it oppressed the heart.

He stood among the roses.

The day was warm. The late-afternoon light was golden.

The sky was perfectly clear—and utterly mysterious.

REGINA ASKED IF she could have some of Lindsey's paintings in her room, and she sounded sincere. They chose three. Together they hammered in picture hooks and hung the paintings where she wanted them—along with a foot-tall crucifix she had brought from her room at the orphanage.

As they worked, Lindsey said, "How about dinner at a really super pizza parlor I know?"

"Yeah!" the girl said enthusiastically. "I love pizza."

"They make it with a nice thick crust, lots of cheese."

"Pepperoni?"

"Cut thin, but lots of it."

"Sausage?"

"Sure, why not. Though you're sure this isn't getting to be a pretty revolting pizza for a vegetarian like you?"

Regina blushed. "Oh, that. I was such a little shit that day. Oh, Jeez, sorry. I mean, such a smartass. I mean, such a jerk."

"That's okay," Lindsey said. "We all behave like jerks now and then."

"You don't. Mr. Harrison doesn't."

"Oh, just wait." Standing on a stepstool in front of the wall opposite the bed, Lindsey pounded in a nail for a picture hook. Regina was holding the painting for her. As she took it from the girl to hang it, Lindsey said, "Listen, will you do me a favor at dinner tonight?"

"Favor? Sure?"

"I know it's still awkward for you, this new arrangement. You don't really feel at home and probably won't for a long time—"

"Oh, it's very nice here," the girl protested.

Lindsey slipped the wire over the picture hook and adjusted the painting until it hung straight. Then she sat down on the stepstool, which just about brought her and the girl eye to eye. She took hold of both of Regina's hands, the normal one and the different one. "You're right—it's very nice here. But you and I both know that's not the same as *home*. I wasn't going to push you on this. I was going to let you take your time, but . . . Even if it seems a little premature to you, do you think tonight at dinner you could stop calling us Mr. and Mrs. Harrison? Especially Hatch. It would be very important to him, just now, if you could at least call him Hatch."

The girl lowered her eyes to their interlocked hands. "Well, I guess . . . sure . . . that would be okay."

"And you know what? I realize this is asking more than it's fair to ask yet, before you really know him that well. But do you know what would be the best thing in the world for him right now?"

The girl was still staring at their hands. "What?"

"If somehow you could find it in your heart to call him Dad. Don't say yes or no just now. Think about it. But it would be a wonderful thing for you to do for him, for reasons I don't have time to explain right here. And I promise you this, Regina—he is a good man. He will do anything for you, put his life on the line for you if it ever came to that, and never ask for anything. He'd be upset if he knew I was even asking you for this. But all I'm asking, really, is for you to think about it."

After a long silence, the girl looked up from their linked hands and nodded. "Okay. I'll think about it."

"Thank you, Regina." She got up from the stepstool. "Now let's hang that last painting."

Lindsey measured, penciled a spot on the wall, and nailed in a picture hook.

When Regina handed over the painting, she said, "It's just that all my life . . . there's never been anyone I called Mom or Dad. It's a very new thing."

Lindsey smiled. "I understand, honey. I really do. And so will Hatch if it takes time."

IN THE BLAZING Haunted House, as the cries for help and the screams of agony swelled louder, a strange object appeared in the firelight. A single rose. A black rose. It floated as if an unseen magician was levitating it. Vassago had never encountered anything more beautiful in the world of the living, in the world of the dead, or in the realm of dreams. It shimmered before him, its petals so smooth and soft that they seemed to have been cut from swatches of the night sky unspoiled by stars. The thorns were exquisitely sharp, needles of glass. The green stem had the oiled sheen of a serpent's skin. One petal held a single drop of blood.

The rose faded from his dream, but later it returned—and with it the woman named Lindsey and the auburn-haired girl with the soft-gray eyes. Vassago yearned to possess all three: the black rose, the woman, and the girl with the gray eyes.

AFTER HATCH FRESHENED up for dinner, while Lindsey finished getting ready in the bathroom, he sat alone on the edge of their bed and read the article by S. Steven Honell in *Arts American*. He could shrug off virtually any insult to himself, but if someone slammed Lindsey, he always reacted with anger. He couldn't even deal well with reviews of her work that *she* thought had made valid criticisms. Reading Honell's vicious, snide, and ultimately stupid diatribe dismissing her entire career as "wasted energy," Hatch grew angrier by the sentence.

As had happened the previous night, his anger erupted into fiery rage with volcanic abruptness. The muscles in his jaws clenched so hard, his teeth ached. The magazine began to shake because his hands were trembling with fury. His vision blurred slightly, as if he were looking at everything through shimmering waves of heat, and he had to blink and squint to make the fuzzy-edged words on the page resolve into readable print.

As when he had been lying in bed last night, he felt as if his anger opened a door and as if something entered him through it, a foul spirit that knew only rage and hate. Or maybe it had been with him all along but sleeping, and his anger had roused it. He was not alone inside his own head. He was aware of another presence, like a spider crawling through the narrow space between the inside of his skull and the surface of his brain.

He tried to put the magazine aside and calm down. But he kept reading because he was not in full possession of himself.

VASSAGO MOVED THROUGH the Haunted House, untroubled by the hungry fire, because he had planned an escape route. Sometimes he was twelve years old, and sometimes he was twenty. But always his path was lit by human torches, some of whom had collapsed into silent melting heaps upon the smoking floor, some of whom exploded into flames even as he passed them.

In the dream he was carrying a magazine, folded open to an article that angered him and seemed imperative he read. The edges of the pages curled in the heat and threatened to catch fire. Names leaped at him from the pages. Lindsey. Lindsey Sparling. Now he had a last name for her. He felt an urge to toss the magazine aside, slow his breathing, calm down. Instead he stoked his anger, let a sweet flood of rage overwhelm him, and told himself that he must know more. The edges of the magazine pages curled in the heat. Honell. Another name. Steven Honell. Bits of burning debris fell on the article. Steven S. Honell. No. The S first. S. Steven Honell. The paper caught fire. Honell. A writer. A barroom. Silverado Canyon. In his hands, the magazine burst into flames that flashed into his face—

He shed sleep like a fired bullet shedding its brass jacket, and sat up in his dark hideaway. Wide awake. Excited. He knew enough now to find the woman.

ONE MOMENT RAGE like a fire swept through Hatch, and the next moment it was extinguished. His jaws relaxed, his tense shoulders sagged, and his hands unclenched so suddenly that he dropped the magazine on the floor between his feet.

He continued to sit on the edge of the bed for a while, stunned and confused. He looked toward the bathroom door, relieved that Lindsey had not walked in on him while he had been . . . Been what? In his trance? Possessed?

He smelled something peculiar, out of place. Smoke.

He looked at the issue of *Arts American* on the floor between his feet. Hesitantly, he picked it up. It was still folded open to Honell's article about Lindsey. Although no visible vapors rose from the magazine, the paper exuded the heavy smell of smoke. The odors of burning wood, paper, tar, plastics . . . and something worse. The edges of the paper were yellow-brown and crisp, as if they had been exposed to almost enough heat to induce spontaneous combustion.

7

When the knock came at the door, Honell was sitting in a rocking chair by the fireplace. He was drinking Chivas Regal and reading one of his own novels, *Miss Culvert,* which he had written twenty-five years ago when he was only thirty.

He re-read each of his nine books once a year because he was in perpetual competition with himself, striving to improve as he grew old instead of settling quietly into senescence the way most writers did. Constant betterment was a formidable challenge because he had been *awfully* good at an early age. Every time he re-read himself, he was surprised to discover that his body of work was considerably more impressive than he remembered it.

Miss Culvert was a fictional treatment of his mother's self-absorbed life in the respectable upper-middle-class society of a downstate Illinois town, an indictment of the self-satisfied and stiflingly bland "culture" of the Midwest. He had really captured the essence of the bitch. Oh, how he had captured her. Reading *Miss Culvert,* he was reminded of the hurt and horror with which his mother had received the novel on first publication, and he decided that as soon as he had finished the book, he would take down the sequel, *Mrs. Towers,* which dealt with her marriage to his father, her widowhood, and her second marriage. He remained convinced that the sequel was what had killed her. Officially, it was a heart attack. But cardiac infarction had to be triggered by something, and the timing was satisfyingly concurrent with the release of *Mrs. Towers* and the media attention it received.

When the unexpected caller knocked, a pang of resentment shot through Honell. His face puckered sourly. He preferred the company of his own characters to that of anyone who might conceivably come visiting, uninvited. Or invited, for that matter. All of the people in his books were carefully refined, clarified, whereas people in real life were unfailingly . . . well, fuzzy, murky, pointlessly complex.

He glanced at the clock on the mantel. Ten past nine o'clock.

The knock sounded again. More insistent this time. It was probably a neighbor, which was a dismaying thought because his neighbors were all fools.

He considered not answering. But in these rural canyons, the locals thought of themselves as "neighborly," never as the pests they actually were, and if he didn't respond to the knocking, they would circle the house, peeping in windows, out of a country-folk concern for his welfare. God, he hated them. He tolerated them only because he hated the people in the cities even more, and *loathed* suburbanites.

He put down his Chivas and the book, pushed up from the rocking chair, and went to the door with the intention of giving a fierce dressing-down to whoever was out there on the porch. With his command of language, he could mortify anyone in about one minute flat, and have them running for cover in two minutes. The pleasure of meting out humiliation would almost compensate for the interruption.

When he pulled the curtain back from the glass panes in the front door, he was surprised to see that his visitor was not one of the neighbors—in fact, not anyone he recognized. The boy was no more than twenty, pale as the wings of the snowflake moths that batted against the porch light. He was dressed entirely in black and wore sunglasses.

Honell was unconcerned about the caller's intentions. The canyon was less than an hour from the most heavily populated parts of Orange County, but it was nonetheless remote by virtue of its forbidding geography and the poor condition of the roads. Crime was no problem, because criminals were generally attracted to more populous areas where the pickings were more plentiful. Besides, most of the people living in the cabins thereabouts had nothing worth stealing.

He found the pale young man intriguing.

"What do you want?" he asked without opening the door.

"Mr. Honell?"

"That's right."

"S. Steven Honell?"

"Are you going to make a torture of this?"

"Sir, excuse me, but are you the writer?"

College student. That's what he had to be.

A decade ago—well, nearly two—Honell had been besieged by college English majors who wanted to apprentice under him or just worship at his feet. They were an inconstant crowd, however, on the lookout for the latest trend, with no genuine appreciation for high literary art.

Hell, these days, most of them couldn't even read; they were college students in name only. The institutions through which they matriculated were little more than day-care centers for the terminally immature, and they were no more likely to study than to fly to Mars by flapping their arms.

"Yes, I'm the writer. What of it?"

"Sir, I'm a great admirer of your books."

"Listened to them on audiotape, have you?"

"Sir? No, I've read them, all of them."

The audiotapes, licensed by his publisher without his consent, were abridged by two-thirds. Travesties.

"Ah. Read them in comic-book format, have you?" Honell said sourly, though to the best of his knowledge the sacrilege of comic-book adaptation had not yet been perpetrated.

"Sir, I'm sorry to intrude like this. It really took a lot of time for me to work up the courage to come see you. Tonight I finally had the guts, and I knew if I delayed I'd never get up the nerve again. I am in awe of your writing, sir, and if you could spare me the time, just a little time, to answer a few questions, I'd be most grateful."

A little conversation with an intelligent young man might, in fact, have more charm than re-reading *Miss Culvert*. A long time had passed since the last such visitor, who had come to the eyrie in which Honell had then been living above Santa Fe. After only a brief hesitation, he opened the door.

"Come in, then, and we'll see if you really understand the complexities of what you've read."

The young man stepped across the threshold, and Honell turned away, heading back toward the rocking chair and the Chivas.

"This is very kind of you, sir," the visitor said as he closed the door.

"Kindness is a quality of the weak and stupid, young man. I've other motivations." As he reached his chair, he turned and said, "Take off those sunglasses. Sunglasses at night is the worst kind of Hollywood affectation, not the sign of a serious person."

"I'm sorry, sir, but they're not an affectation. It's just that this world is so much more painfully bright than Hell—which I'm sure you'll eventually discover."

HATCH HAD NO appetite for dinner. He only wanted to sit alone with the inexplicably heat-curled issue of *Arts American* and stare at it until, by God, he *forced* himself to understand exactly what was happening to him. He was a man of reason. He could not easily embrace supernatural explanations. He was not in the antiques business by accident; he had a need to surround himself with things that contributed to an atmosphere of order and stability.

But kids also hungered for stability, which included regular mealtimes, so they went to dinner at a pizza parlor, after which they caught a movie at the theater complex next door. It was a comedy. Though the film couldn't make Hatch forget the strange problems plaguing him, the frequent sound of Regina's musical giggle did somewhat soothe his abraded nerves.

Later, at home, after he had tucked the girl in bed, kissed her forehead, wished her sweet dreams, and turned off the light, she said, "Goodnight . . . Dad."

He was in her doorway, stepping into the hall, when the word "dad" stopped him. He turned and looked back at her.

"Goodnight," he said, deciding to receive her gift as casually as she had given it, for fear that if he made a big deal about it, she would call him Mr. Harrison forever. But his heart soared.

In the bedroom, where Lindsey was undressing, he said, "She called me Dad."

"Who did?"

"Be serious, who do you think?"

"How much did you pay her?"

"You're just jealous 'cause she hasn't called you Mom yet."

"She will. She's not so afraid any more."

"Of you?"

"Of taking a chance."

Before getting undressed for bed, Hatch went downstairs to check the telephone answering machine in the kitchen. Funny, after all that had happened to him and considering the problems he still had to sort out, the mere fact that the girl had called him Dad was enough to quicken his step and lift his spirits. He descended the stairs two at a time.

The answering machine was on the counter to the left of the refrigerator, below the cork memo board. He was hoping to have a response from the estate executor to whom he had given a bid for the Wedgwood collection that morning. The window on the machine showed three messages. The first was from Glenda Dockridge, his right hand at the antique shop. The second was from Simpson Smith, a friend and antique dealer on Melrose Place in Los Angeles. The third was from Janice Dimes, a friend of Lindsey's. All three were reporting the same news: *Hatch, Lindsey, Hatch and Lindsey, have you seen the paper, have you read the paper, have you heard the news about Cooper, about that guy who ran you off the road, about Bill Cooper, he's dead, he was killed, he was killed last night.*

Hatch felt as if a refrigerant, instead of blood, pumped through his veins.

Last evening he had raged about Cooper getting off scot-free, and had wished him dead. No, wait. He'd said he wanted to hurt him, make him pay, pitch *him* in that icy river, but he hadn't actually wanted Cooper dead. And so what if he *had* wanted him dead? He had not actually killed the man. He was not at fault for what had happened.

Punching the button to erase the messages, he thought: The cops will want to talk to me sooner or later.

Then he wondered why he was worried about the police. Maybe the murderer was already in custody, in which case no suspicion would fall upon him. But why should he come under suspicion anyway? He had done nothing. *Nothing.* Why was guilt creeping through him like the Millipede inching up a long tunnel?

Millipede?

The utterly enigmatic nature of that image chilled him. He couldn't reference the source of it. As if it wasn't his own thought but something he had . . . *received.*

He hurried upstairs.

Lindsey was lying on her back in bed, adjusting the covers around her.

The newspaper was on his nightstand, where she always put it. He snatched it up and quickly scanned the front page.

"Hatch?" she said. "What's wrong?"

"Cooper's dead."

"What?"

"The guy driving the beer truck. William Cooper. Murdered."

She threw back the covers and sat on the edge of the bed.

He found the story on page three. He sat beside Lindsey, and they read the article together.

According to the newspaper, police were interested in talking to a young man in his early twenties, with pale skin and dark hair. A neighbor had glimpsed him fleeing down the alleyway behind the Palm Court apartments. He might have been wearing sunglasses. At night.

"He's the same damned one who killed the blonde," Hatch said fearfully. "The sunglasses in the rearview mirror. And now he's picking up on my thoughts. He's acting out *my* anger, murdering people that I'd like to see punished."

"That doesn't make sense. It can't be."

"It is." He felt sick. He looked at his hands, as if he might actually find the truck driver's blood on them. "My God, I sent him after Cooper."

He was so appalled, so psychologically oppressed by a sense of responsibility for what had happened, that he wanted desperately to wash his hands, scrub them until they were raw. When he tried to get up, his legs were too weak to support him, and he had to sit right down again.

Lindsey was baffled and horrified, but she did not react to the news story as strongly as Hatch did.

Then he told her about the reflection of the black-clad young man in sunglasses, which he had seen in the mirrored door in place of his own image, last night in the den when he had been ranting about Cooper. He told her, as well, how he lay in bed after she was asleep, brooding about Cooper, and how his anger suddenly exploded into artery-popping rage. He spoke of the sense he'd had of being invaded and overwhelmed, ending in the blackout. And for a kicker, he recounted how his anger had escalated unreasonably as he had read the piece in *Arts American* earlier this evening, and he took the magazine out of his nightstand to show her the inexplicably scorched pages.

By the time Hatch finished, Lindsey's anxiety matched his, but dismay at his secretiveness seemed greater than anything else she was feeling. "Why'd you hide all of this from me?"

"I didn't want to worry you," he said, knowing how feeble it sounded.

"We've never hidden anything from each other before. We've always shared everything. Everything."

"I'm sorry, Lindsey. I just . . . it's just that . . . these last couple months . . . the nightmares of rotting bodies, violence, fire . . . and the last few days, all this *weirdness*. . . ."

"From now on," she said, "there'll be no secrets."

"I only wanted to spare you—"

"No secrets," she insisted.

"Okay. No secrets."

"And you're not responsible for what happened to Cooper. Even if there is some kind of link between you and this killer, and even if that's why Cooper became a target, it's not your fault. You didn't *know* that being angry at Cooper was equivalent to a death sentence. You couldn't have done anything to prevent it."

Hatch looked at the heat-seared magazine in her hands, and a shudder of dread passed through him. "But it'll be my fault if I don't try to save Honell."

Frowning, she said, "What do you mean?"

"If my anger somehow focused this guy on Cooper, why wouldn't it also focus him on Honell?"

HONELL WOKE TO a world of pain. The difference was, this time he was on the receiving end of it—and it was physical rather than emotional pain. His crotch ached from the kick he'd taken. A blow to his throat had left his esophagus feeling like broken glass. His headache was excruciating. His wrists and ankles burned, and at first he could not understand why; then he realized he was tied to the four posts of something, probably his bed, and the ropes were chafing his skin.

He could not see much, partly because his vision was blurred by tears but also because his contact lenses had been knocked out in the attack. He knew he had been assaulted, but for a moment he could not recall the identity of his assailant.

Then the young man's face loomed over him, blurred at first like the surface of the moon through an unadjusted telescope. The boy bent closer, closer, and his face came into focus, handsome and pale, framed by thick black hair. He was not smiling in the tradition of movie psychotics, as Honell expected he would be. He was not scowling, either, or even frowning. He was expressionless—except, perhaps, for a subtle hint of that solemn professional curiosity with which an entomologist might study some new mutant variation of a familiar species of insect.

"I'm sorry for this discourteous treatment, sir, after you were kind enough to welcome me into your home. But I'm rather in a hurry and couldn't take the time to discover what I need to know through ordinary conversation."

"Whatever you want," Honell said placatingly. He was shocked to hear how drastically his mellifluous voice, always a reliable tool for seduction and expressive instrument of scorn, had changed. It was raspy, marked by a wet gurgle, thoroughly disgusting.

"I would like to know who Lindsey Sparling is," the young man said dispassionately, "and where I can find her."

HATCH WAS SURPRISED to find Honell's number in the telephone book. Of course, the author's name was not as familiar to the average citizen as it had been during his brief glory years, when he had published *Miss Culvert* and *Mrs. Towers*. Honell didn't need to be worried about privacy these days; evidently the public gave him more of it than he desired.

While Hatch called the number, Lindsey paced the length of the bedroom and back. She had made her position clear: she didn't think Honell would interpret Hatch's warning as anything other than a cheap threat.

Hatch agreed with her. But he had to try.

He was spared the humiliation and frustration of listening to Honell's reaction, however, because no one answered the phone out there in the far canyons of the desert night. He let it ring twenty times.

He was about to hang up, when a series of images snapped through his mind with a sound like short-circuiting electrical wires: a disarranged bed quilt; a bleeding, rope-encircled wrist; a pair of frightened, bloodshot, myopic eyes . . . and in the eyes, the twin reflections of a dark face looming close, distinguished only by a pair of sunglasses.

Hatch slammed down the phone and backed away from it as if the receiver had turned into a rattlesnake in his hand. "It's happening now."

THE RINGING PHONE fell silent.

Vassago stared at it, but the ringing did not resume.

He returned his attention to the man who was tied spread-eagle to the brass posts of the bed. "So Lindsey Harrison is the married name?"

"Yes," the old guy croaked.

"Now what I most urgently need, sir, is an address."

THE PUBLIC TELEPHONE was outside of a convenience store in a shopping center just two miles from the Harrison house. It was protected from the elements by a Plexiglas hood and surrounded by a curved sound shield. Hatch would have preferred the greater privacy of a real booth, but those were hard to find these days, a luxury of less cost-conscious times.

He parked at the end of the center, at too great a distance for anyone in the glass-fronted convenience store to notice—and perhaps recall—his license number.

He walked through a cool, blustery wind to the telephone. The center's Indian laurels were infested with thrips, and drifts of dead, tightly curled leaves blew along the pavement at Hatch's feet. They made a dry, scuttling sound. In the urine-yellow glow of the parking-lot lights, they almost looked like hordes of insects, queerly mutated locusts perhaps, swarming toward their subterranean hive.

The convenience store was not busy, and everything else in the shopping center was closed. He hunched his shoulders and head into the pay phone sound shield, convinced he wouldn't be overheard.

He did not want to call the police from home, because he knew they had equipment that printed out every caller's number at their end. If they found Honell dead, Hatch didn't want to become their prime suspect. And if his concern for Honell's safety proved to be unfounded, he didn't want to be on record with the police as some kind of nutcase or hysteric.

Even as he punched in the number with one bent knuckle and held the handset with a Kleenex to avoid leaving prints, he was uncertain what to say. He knew what he could *not* say: *Hi, I was dead eighty minutes, then brought back to life, and now I have this crude but at times effective telepathic connection to a psychotic killer, and I think I should warn you he's about to strike again.* He could not imagine the authorities taking him any more seriously than they would take a guy who wore a pyramid-shaped aluminum-foil hat to protect his brain from sinister radiation and who bothered them with complaints about evil, mind-warping extraterrestrials next door.

He had decided to call the Orange County Sheriff's Department rather than any particular city's police agency, because the crimes committed by the man in sunglasses fell in several jurisdictions. When the sheriff's operator answered, Hatch talked fast, talked over her when she began to interrupt, because he knew they could trace him to a pay phone given enough time. "The man who killed the blonde and dumped her on the freeway last week is the same guy who killed William Cooper last night, and tonight he's going to murder Steven Honell, the writer, if you don't give him protection quick, and I mean right now. Honell lives in Silverado Canyon, I don't know the address, but he's probably in your jurisdiction, and he's a dead man if you don't move now."

He hung up, turned away from the phone, and headed for his car, jamming the Kleenex into his pants pocket. He felt less relieved than he had expected to, and more of a fool than seemed reasonable.

On his way back to the car, he was walking into the wind. All the laurel leaves, sucked dry by thrips, were now blown toward him instead of with him. They hissed against the blacktop and crunched under his shoes.

He knew that the trip had been a waste and that his effort to help Honell had been ineffective. The sheriff's department would probably treat it like just another crank call.

When he got home, he parked in the driveway, afraid that the clatter of the garage door would wake Regina. His scalp prickled when he got out of the car. He stood for a minute, surveying the shadows along the house, around the shrubbery, under the trees. Nothing.

Lindsey was pouring a cup of coffee for him when he walked into the kitchen.

He took it, sipped gratefully at the hot brew. Suddenly he was colder than he had been while standing out in the night chill.

"What do you think?" she asked worriedly. "Did they take you seriously?"

"Pissing in the wind," he said.

VASSAGO WAS STILL driving the pearl-gray Honda belonging to Renata Desseux, the woman he had overpowered in the mall parking lot on Saturday night and later added to his collection. It was a fine car and handled well on the twisting roads as he drove down the canyon from Honell's place, heading for more populated areas of Orange County.

As he rounded a particularly sharp curve, a patrol car from the sheriff's department swept past him, heading up the canyon. Its siren was not blaring, but its emergency beacons splashed red and blue light on the shale banks and on the gnarled branches of the overhanging trees.

He divided his attention between the winding road ahead and the dwindling taillights of the patrol car in his rearview mirror, until it rounded another bend upslope and vanished. He was sure the cop was speeding to Honell's. The unanswered, interminably ringing telephone, which had interrupted his interrogation of the author, was the trigger that had set the sheriff's department in motion, but he could not figure how or why.

Vassago did not drive faster. At the end of Silverado Canyon, he turned south on Santiago Canyon Road and maintained the legal speed limit as any good citizen was expected to do.

8

In bed in the dark, Hatch felt his world crumbling around him. He was going to be left with dust.

Happiness with Lindsey and Regina was within his grasp. Or was that an illusion? Were they infinitely beyond his reach?

He wished for an insight that would give him a new perspective on these apparently supernatural events. Until he could understand the nature of the evil that had entered his life, he could not fight it.

Dr. Nyebern's voice spoke softly in his mind: *I believe evil is a very real force, an energy quite apart from us, a presence in the world.*

He thought he could smell a lingering trace of smoke from the heat-browned pages of *Arts American*. He had put the magazine in the desk in the den downstairs, in the drawer with a lock. He had added the small key to the ring he carried.

He had never locked anything in the desk before. He was not sure why he had done so this time. Protecting evidence, he'd told himself. But evidence of what? The singed pages of the magazine proved nothing to anyone about anything.

No. That was not precisely true. The existence of the magazine proved, to him if to no one else, that he wasn't merely imagining and hallucinating everything that was happening to him. What he had locked away, for his own peace of mind, was indeed evidence. Evidence of his sanity.

Beside him, Lindsey was also awake, either uninterested in sleep or unable to find a way into it. She said, "What if this killer . . ."

Hatch waited. He didn't need to ask her to finish the thought, for he knew what she was going to say. After a moment she said just what he expected:

"What if this killer is aware of you as much as you're aware of him? What if he comes after you . . . us . . . Regina?"

"Tomorrow we're going to start taking precautions."

"What precautions?"

"Guns, for one thing."

"Maybe this isn't something we can handle ourselves."

"We don't have any choice."

"Maybe we need police protection."

"Somehow I don't think they'll commit a lot of manpower to protect a guy just because he claims to have a supernatural bond with a psychotic killer."

The wind that had harried laurel leaves across the shopping-center parking lot now found a loose brace on a section of rain gutter and worried it. Metal creaked softly against metal.

Hatch said, "I went somewhere when I died, right?"

"What do you mean?"

"Purgatory, Heaven, Hell—those are the basic possibilities for a Catholic, if what we say we believe turns out to be true."

"Well . . . you've always said you had no near-death experience."

"I didn't. I can't remember anything from . . . the Other Side. But that doesn't mean I wasn't there."

"What's your point?"

"Maybe this killer isn't an ordinary man."

"You're losing me, Hatch."

"Maybe I brought something back with me."

"Back with you?"

"From wherever I was while I was dead."

"Something?"

Darkness had its advantages. The superstitious primitive within could speak of things that would seem too foolish to voice in a well-lighted place.

He said, "A spirit. An entity."

She said nothing.

"My passage in and out of death might have opened a door somehow," he said, "and let something through."

"Something," she said again, but with no note of inquiry in her voice, as there had been before. He sensed that she knew what he meant—and did not like the theory.

"And now it's loose in the world. Which explains its link to me—and why it might kill people who anger me."

She was silent awhile. Then: "If something was brought back, it's evidently pure evil. What—are you saying that when you died, you went to Hell and this killer piggy-backed with you from there?"

"Maybe. I'm no saint, no matter what you think. After all, I've got at least Cooper's blood on my hands."

"That happened after you died and were brought back. Besides, you don't share in the guilt for that."

"It was my anger that targeted him, my anger—"

"Bullshit," Lindsey said sharply. "You're the best man I've ever known. If housing in the afterlife includes a Heaven and Hell, you've earned the apartment with a better view."

His thoughts were so dark, he was surprised that he could smile. He reached under the sheets, found her hand, and held it gratefully. "I love you, too."

"Think up another theory if you want to keep me awake and interested."

"Let's just make a little adjustment to the theory we already have. What if there's an afterlife, but it isn't ordered like anything theologians have ever described. It wouldn't have to be *either* Heaven or Hell that I came back from. Just another place, stranger than here, different, with unknown dangers."

"I don't like that much better."

"If I'm going to deal with this thing, I have to find a way to explain it. I can't fight back if I don't even know where to throw my punches."

"There's got to be a more logical explanation," she said.

"That's what I tell myself. But when I try to find it, I keep coming back to the illogical."

The rain gutter creaked. The wind soughed under the eaves and called down the flue of the master-bedroom fireplace.

He wondered if Honell was able to hear the wind wherever he was—and whether it was the wind of this world or the next.

VASSAGO PARKED DIRECTLY in front of Harrison's Antiques at the south end of Laguna Beach. The shop occupied an entire Art Deco building. The big display windows were unlighted as Tuesday passed through midnight, becoming Wednesday.

Steven Honell had been unable to tell him where the Harrisons lived, and a quick check of the telephone book turned up no listed number for them. The writer had known only the name of their business and its approximate location on Pacific Coast Highway.

Their home address was sure to be on file somewhere in the store's office. Getting it might be difficult. A decal on each of the big Plexiglas windows and another on the front door warned that the premises were fitted with a burglar alarm and protected by a security company.

He had come back from Hell with the ability to see in the dark, animal-quick reflexes, a lack of inhibitions that left him capable of any act or atrocity, and a fearlessness that made him every bit as formidable an adversary as a robot might have been. But he could not walk through walls, or transform himself from flesh into vapor into flesh again, or fly, or perform any of the other feats that were within the powers of a true demon. Until he had earned his way back into Hell either by acquiring a perfect collection in his museum of the dead or by killing those he had been sent here to destroy, he possessed only the minor powers of the demon demimonde, which were insufficient to defeat a burglar alarm.

He drove away from the store.

In the heart of town, he found a telephone booth beside a service station. Despite the hour, the station was still pumping gasoline, and the outdoor lighting was so bright that Vassago was forced to squint behind his sunglasses.

Swooping around the lamps, moths with inch-long wings cast shadows as large as ravens on the pavement.

The floor of the telephone booth was littered with cigarette butts. Ants teamed over the corpse of a beetle.

Someone had taped a hand-lettered OUT OF ORDER notice to the coin box, but Vassago didn't care because he didn't intend to call anyone. He was only interested in the phone book, which was secured to the frame of the booth by a sturdy chain.

He checked "Antiques" in the Yellow Pages. Laguna Beach had a lot of businesses under that heading; it was a regular shoppers' paradise. He studied their space ads. Some had institutional names like International Antiques, but others were named after their owners, as was Harrison's Antiques.

A few used both first *and* last names, and some of the space ads also included the full names of the proprietors because, in that business, personal reputation could be a drawing card. Robert O. Loffman Antiques in the Yellow Pages cross-referenced neatly with a Robert O. Loffman in the white pages, providing Vassago with a street address, which he committed to memory.

On his way back to the Honda, he saw a bat swoop out of the night. It arced down through the blue-white glare from the service-station lights, snatching a fat moth from the air in mid-flight, then vanished back up into the darkness from which it had come. Neither predator nor prey made a sound.

LOFFMAN WAS SEVENTY years old, but in his best dreams he was eighteen again, spry and limber, strong and happy. They were never sex dreams, no bosomy young women parting their smooth thighs in welcome. They weren't power dreams, either, no running or jumping or leaping off cliffs into wild adventures. The action was always mundane: a leisurely walk along a beach at twilight, barefoot, the feel of damp sand between his toes, the froth on the incoming waves sparkling with reflections of the dazzling purple-red sunset; or just sitting on the grass in the shadow of a date palm on a summer afternoon, watching a hummingbird sip nectar from the bright blooms in a bed of flowers. The mere fact that he was young again seemed miracle enough to sustain a dream and keep it interesting.

At the moment he was eighteen, lying on a big bench swing on the front porch of the Santa Ana house in which he had been born and raised. He was just swinging gently and peeling an apple that he intended to eat, nothing more, but it was a wonderful dream, rich with scents and textures, more erotic than if he had imagined himself in a harem of undressed beauties.

"Wake up, Mr. Loffman."

He tried to ignore the voice because he wanted to be alone on that porch. He kept his eyes on the curled length of peel that he was paring from the apple.

"Come on, you old sleepyhead."

He was trying to strip the apple in one continuous ribbon of peel.

"Did you take a sleeping pill or what?"

To Loffman's regret, the front porch, the swing, the apple and paring knife dissolved into darkness. His bedroom.

He struggled awake and realized an intruder was present. A barely visible, spectral figure stood beside the bed.

Although he'd never been the victim of a crime and lived in as safe a neighborhood as existed these days, age had saddled Loffman with feelings of vulnerability. He had started keeping a loaded pistol next to the lamp at his bedside. He reached for it now, his heart pounding hard as he groped along the cool marble surface of the 18th-century French ormolu chest that served as his nightstand. The gun was gone.

"I'm sorry, sir," the intruder said. "I didn't mean to scare you. Please calm down. If it's the pistol you're after, I saw it as soon as I came in. I have it now."

The stranger could not have seen the gun without turning on the light, and the light would have awakened Loffman sooner. He was sure of that, so he kept groping for the weapon.

From out of the darkness, something cold and blunt probed against his throat. He twitched away from it, but the coldness followed him, pressing insistently, as if the specter tormenting him could see him clearly in the gloom. He froze when he realized what the coldness was. The muzzle of the pistol. Against his Adam's apple. It slid slowly upward, under his chin.

"If I pulled the trigger, sir, your brains would be all over the headboard. But I do not need to hurt you, sir. Pain is quite unnecessary as long as you cooperate. I only want you to answer one important question for me."

If Robert Loffman actually had been eighteen, as in his best dreams, he could not have valued the remainder of his time on earth more highly than he did at seventy, in spite of having far less of it to lose now. He was prepared to hold onto life with all the tenacity of a burrowing tick. He would answer any question, perform any deed to save himself, regardless of the cost to his pride and dignity. He tried to convey all of that to the phantom who held the pistol under his chin, but it seemed to him that he produced a gabble of words and sounds that, in sum, had no meaning whatsoever.

"Yes, sir," the intruder said, "I understand, and I appreciate your attitude. Now correct me if I am wrong, but I suppose the antique business, being relatively small when compared to others, is a tight community here in Laguna. You all know each other, see each other socially, you're friends."

Antique business? Loffman was tempted to believe that he was still asleep and that his dream had become an absurd nightmare. Why would anyone break into his house in the dead of night to talk about the antique business at gunpoint?

"We know each other, some of us are good friends, of course, but some bastards in this business are thieves," Loffman said. He was babbling, unable to stop, hopeful that his obvious fear would testify to his truthfulness, whether this was nightmare or reality. "They're nothing more than crooks with cash registers, and you aren't friends with that kind if you have any self-respect at all."

"Do you know Mr. Harrison of Harrison's Antiques?"

"Oh, yes, very well, I know him quite well, he's a reputable dealer, totally trustworthy, a nice man."

"Have you been to his house?"

"His house? Yes, certainly, on three or four occasions, and he's been here to mine."

"Then you must have the answer to that important question I mentioned, sir. Can you give me Mr. Harrison's address and clear directions to it?"

Loffman sagged with relief upon realizing that he would be able to provide the intruder with the desired information. Only fleetingly, he considered that he might be putting Harrison in great jeopardy. But maybe it was a nightmare, after all, and revelation of the information would not matter. He repeated the address and directions several times, at the intruder's request.

"Thank you, sir. You've been most helpful. Like I said, causing you any pain is quite unnecessary. But I'm going to hurt you anyway, because I enjoy it so much."

So it *was* a nightmare after all.

VASSAGO DROVE PAST the Harrison house in Laguna Niguel. Then he circled the block and drove past it again.

The house was a powerful attractant, similar in style to all of the other houses on the street but so different from them in some indescribable but fundamental way that it might as well have been an isolated structure rising out of a featureless plain. Its windows were dark, and the landscape lighting had evidently been turned off by a timer, but it could not have been more of a beacon to Vassago if light had blazed from every window.

As he drove slowly past the house a second time, he felt its immense gravity pulling him. His immutable destiny involved this place and the vital woman who lived within.

Nothing he saw suggested a trap. A red car was parked in the driveway instead of in the garage, but he couldn't see anything ominous about that. Nevertheless, he decided to circle the block a third time to give the house another thorough looking over.

As he turned the corner, a lone silvery moth darted through his headlight beams, refracting them and briefly glowing like an ember from a great fire. He remembered the bat that had swooped into the service-station lights to snatch the hapless moth out of the air, eating it alive.

LONG AFTER MIDNIGHT, Hatch had finally dozed off. His sleep was a deep mine, where veins of dreams flowed like bright ribbons of minerals through the otherwise dark walls. None of the dreams was pleasant, but none of them was grotesque enough to wake him.

Currently he saw himself standing at the bottom of a ravine with ramparts so steep they could not be climbed. Even if the slopes had risen at an angle that allowed ascent, they would not have been scaleable because they were composed of a curious, loose white shale that crumbled and shifted treacherously. The shale radiated a soft calcimine glow, which was the only light, for the sky far above was black and moonless, deep but starless. Hatch moved restlessly from one end of the long narrow ravine to the other, then back again, filled with apprehension but unsure of the cause of it.

Then he realized two things that made the fine hairs tingle on the back of his neck. The white shale was not composed of rock and the shells of millions of ancient sea creatures; it was made of human skeletons, splintered and compacted but recognizable here and there, where the articulated bones of two fingers survived compression or where what seemed a small animal's burrow proved to be the empty eye socket in a skull. He became aware, as well, that the sky was not empty, that something circled in it, so black that it blended with the heavens, its leathery wings working silently. He could not see it, but he could feel its gaze, and he sensed a hunger in it that could never be satisfied.

In his troubled sleep, Hatch turned and murmured anxious, wordless sounds into his pillow.

VASSAGO CHECKED THE car clock. Even without its confirming numbers, he knew instinctively that dawn was less than an hour away.

He no longer could be sure he had enough time to get into the house, kill the husband, and take the woman back to his hideaway before sunrise. He could not risk getting caught in the open in daylight. Though he would not shrivel up and turn to dust like the living dead in the movies, nothing as dramatic as that, his eyes were so sensitive that his glasses would not provide adequate protection from full sunlight. Dawn would render him nearly blind, dramatically affecting his ability to drive and bringing him to the attention of any policeman who happened to spot his weaving, halting progress. In that debilitated condition, he might have difficulty dealing with the cop.

More important, he might lose the woman. After appearing so often in his dreams, she had become an object of intense desire. Before, he had seen acquisitions of such quality that he had been convinced they would complete his collection and earn him immediate readmission to the savage world of eternal darkness and hatred to which he belonged—and he had been wrong. But none of those others had appeared to him in dreams. *This* woman was the true jewel in the crown for which he had been seeking. He must avoid taking possession of her prematurely, only to lose her before he could draw the life from her at the base of the giant Lucifer and wrench her cooling corpse into whatever configuration seemed most symbolic of her sins and weaknesses.

As he cruised past the house for the third time, he considered leaving immediately for his hideaway and returning here as soon as the sun had set the following evening. But that plan had no appeal. Being so close to her excited him, and he was loath to be separated from her again. He felt the tidal pull of her in his blood.

He needed a place to hide that was near her. Perhaps a secret corner in her own house. A niche in which she was unlikely to look during the long, bright, hostile hours of the day.

He parked the Honda two blocks from their house and returned on foot along the tree-flanked sidewalk. The tall, green-patinated streetlamps had angled arms at the top that directed their light onto the roadway, and only a ghost of their glow reached past the sidewalk onto the front lawns of the silent houses. Confident that neighbors were still sleeping and unlikely to see him prowling through shadow-hung shrubbery around the perimeter of the house, he searched quietly for an unlocked door, an unlatched window. He had no luck until he came to the window on the back wall of the garage.

REGINA WAS AWAKENED by a scraping noise, a dull *thump-thump* and a soft protracted squeak. Still unaccustomed to her new home, she always woke in confusion, not sure where she was, certain only that she was not in her room at the orphanage. She fumbled for the bedside lamp, clicked it on, and squinted at the glare for a second before orienting herself and realizing the noises that had bumped her out of sleep had been *sneaky* sounds. They had stopped when she had snapped on the light. Which seemed even sneakier.

She clicked the light off and listened in the darkness, which was now filled with aureoles of color because the lamp had worked like a camera flashbulb on her eyes, temporarily stealing her night vision. Though the sounds did not resume, she believed they had come from the backyard.

Her bed was comfortable. The room almost seemed to be scented with the perfume of the painted flowers. Encircled by those roses, she felt safer than she had ever felt before.

Although she didn't want to get up, she was also aware that the Harrisons were having problems of some kind, and she wondered if these sneaky sounds in the middle of the night somehow might be related to that. Yesterday during the drive from school, as well as last night during dinner and after the movie, she had sensed a tension in them that they were trying to conceal from her. Even though she knew herself to be a screwup around whom anyone would have a right to feel nervous, she was sure that she was not the cause of their edginess. Before going to sleep, she had prayed that their troubles, if they had any, would prove to be minor and would be dealt with soon, and she had reminded God of her selfless pledge to eat beans of all varieties.

If there was any possibility the sneaky noises were related to the Harrisons' uneasy state of mind, Regina supposed she had an obligation to check it out. She looked up and back at the crucifix above her bed, and sighed. You couldn't rely on Jesus and Mary for everything. They were busy people. They had a universe to run. God helped those who helped themselves.

She slipped out from under the covers, stood, and made her way to the window, leaning against furniture and then the wall. She was not wearing her leg brace, and she needed the support.

The window looked onto the small backyard behind the garage, the area from which the suspicious noises had seemed to come. Night-shadows from the house, trees, and shrubs were unrelieved by moonlight. The longer Regina stared, the less she could make out, as if the darkness were a sponge soaking up her ability to see. It became easy to believe that *every* impenetrable pocket of gloom was alive and watchful.

THE GARAGE WINDOW had been unlocked but difficult to open. The hinges at the top were corroded, and the frame was paint-sealed to the jamb in places. Vassago made more noise than he intended, but he didn't think he had been loud enough to draw the attention of anyone in the house. Then just as the paint cracked and the hinges moved to grant him access, a light had appeared in another window on the second floor.

He had backed away from the garage at once, even though the light went off again even as he moved. He had taken cover in a stand of six-foot eugenia bushes near the property fence.

From there he saw her appear at the obsidian window, more visible to him, perhaps, than she would have been if she had left the lamp on. It was the girl he had seen in dreams a couple of times, most recently with Lindsey Harrison. They had faced each other across a levitated black rose with one drop of blood glistening on a velvet petal.

Regina.

He stared at her in disbelief, then with growing excitement. Earlier in the night, he had asked Steven Honell if the Harrisons had a daughter, but the author had told him that he knew only of a son who had died years ago.

Separated from Vassago by nothing but the night air and one pane of glass, the girl seemed to float above him as if she were a vision. In reality she was, if anything, lovelier than she had been in his dreams. She was so exceptionally vital, so full of life, that he would not have been surprised if she could walk the night as confidently as he did, though for a reason different from his; she seemed to have within her all the light she needed to illuminate her path through any darkness. He drew back farther into the eugenias, convinced that she possessed the power to see him as clearly as he saw her.

A trellis covered the wall immediately below her window. A lush trumpet vine with purple flowers grew up the sturdy lattice to the windowsill, and then around one side almost to the eaves. She was like some princess locked in a tower, pining for a prince to climb up the vine and rescue her. The tower that served as her prison was life itself, and the prince for whom she waited was Death, and that from which she longed to be rescued was the curse of existence.

Vassago said softly, "I am here for you," but he did not move from his hiding place.

After a couple of minutes, she turned away from the window. Vanished. A void lay behind the glass where she had stood.

He ached for her return, one more brief look at her.

Regina.

He waited five minutes, then another five. But she did not come to the window again.

At last, aware that dawn was closer than ever, he crept to the back of the garage once more. Because he had already freed it, the window swung out silently this time. The opening was tight, but he eeled through with only the softest scrape of clothes against wood.

LINDSEY DOZED IN half-hour and hour naps throughout the night, but her sleep was not restful. Each time she woke, she was sticky with perspiration, even though the house was cool. Beside her, Hatch issued murmured protests in his sleep.

Toward dawn she heard noise in the hall and rose up from her pillows to listen. After a moment she identified the sound of the toilet flushing in the guest bathroom. Regina.

She settled back on her pillows, oddly soothed by the fading sound of the toilet. It seemed like such a mundane—not to say ridiculous—thing from which to take solace. But a long time had passed without a child under her roof. It felt good and right to hear the girl engaged in ordinary domestic business; it made the night seem less hostile. In spite of their current problems, the promise of happiness might be more real than it had been in years.

IN BED AGAIN, Regina wondered why God had given people bowels and bladders. Was that really the best possible design, or was He a little bit of a comedian?

She remembered getting up at three o'clock in the morning at the orphanage, needing to pee, encountering a nun on the way to the bathroom down the hall, and asking the good sister that very question. The nun, Sister Sarafina, had not been startled at all. Regina had been too young then to know how to startle a nun; that took years of thinking and practice. Sister Sarafina had responded without pause, suggesting that perhaps God wanted to give people a reason to get up in the middle of the night so they would have another opportunity to think of Him and be grateful for the life He had granted them. Regina had smiled and nodded, but she had figured Sister Sarafina was either too tired to think straight or a little dim-witted. God had too much class to want His children thinking about Him all the time while they were sitting on the pot.

Satisfied from her visit to the bathroom, she snuggled down in the covers of her painted mahogany bed and tried to think of an explanation better than the one the nun had given her years ago. No more curious noises arose from the backyard, and even before the vague light of dawn touched the windowpanes, she was asleep again.

HIGH, DECORATIVE WINDOWS were set in the big sectional doors, admitting just enough light from the streetlamps out front to reveal to Vassago, without his sunglasses, that only one car, a black Chevy, was parked in the three-car garage. A quick inspection of that space did not reveal any hiding place where he might conceal himself from the Harrisons and be beyond the reach of sunlight until the next nightfall.

Then he saw the cord dangling from the ceiling over one of the empty parking stalls. He slipped his hand through the loop and pulled downward gently, less gently, then less gently still, but always steadily and smoothly, until the trapdoor swung open. It was well oiled and soundless.

When the door was all the way open, Vassago slowly unfolded the three sections of the wooden ladder that were fixed to the back of it. He took plenty of time, more concerned with silence than with speed.

He climbed into the garage attic. No doubt there were vents in the eaves, but at the moment the place appeared to be sealed tight.

With his sensitive eyes, he could see a finished floor, lots of cardboard boxes, and a few small items of furniture stored under dropcloths. No windows. Above him, the underside of rough roofing boards were visible between open rafters. At two points in the long rectangular chamber, light fixtures dangled from the peaked ceiling; he did not turn on either of them.

Cautiously, quietly, as if he were an actor in a slow-motion film, he stretched out on his belly on the attic floor, reached down through the hole, and pulled up the folding ladder, section by section. Slowly, silently, he secured it to the back of the trapdoor. He eased the door into place again with no sound but the soft *spang* of the big spring that held it shut, closing himself off from the three-car garage below.

He pulled a few of the dropcloths off the furniture. They were relatively dust free. He folded them to make a nest among the boxes and then settled down to await the passage of the day.

Regina. Lindsey. I am with you.

Six

Lindsey drove Regina to school Wednesday morning. When she got back to the house in Laguna Niguel, Hatch was at the kitchen table, cleaning and oiling the pair of Browning 9mm pistols that he had acquired for home security.

He had purchased the guns five years ago, shortly after Jimmy's cancer had been diagnosed as terminal. He had professed a sudden concern about the crime rate, though it never had been—and was not then—particularly high in their part of Orange County. Lindsey had known, but had never said, that he was not afraid of burglars but of the disease that was stealing his son from him; and because he was helpless to fight off the cancer, he secretly longed for an enemy who *could* be dispatched with a pistol.

The Brownings had never been used anywhere but on a firing range. He had insisted that Lindsey learn to shoot alongside him. But neither of them had even taken target practice in a year or two.

"Do you really think that's wise?" she asked, indicating the pistols.

He was tight-lipped. "Yes."

"Maybe we should call the police."

"We've already discussed why we can't."

"Still, it might be worth a try."

"They won't help us. Can't."

She knew he was right. They had no proof that they were in danger.

"Besides," he said, keeping his eyes on the pistol as he worked a tubular brush in and out of the barrel, "when I first started cleaning these, I turned on the TV to have some company. Morning news."

The small set, on a pull-out swivel shelf in the end-most of the kitchen cabinets, was off now.

Lindsey didn't ask him what had been on the news. She was afraid that she would be sorry to hear it—and was convinced that she already knew what he would tell her.

Finally looking up from the pistol, Hatch said, "They found Steven Honell last night. Tied to the four corners of his bed and beaten to death with a fireplace poker."

At first Lindsey was too shocked to move. Then she was too weak to continue standing. She pulled a chair out from the table and settled into it.

For a while yesterday, she had hated Steven Honell as much as she had ever hated anyone in her life. More. Now she felt no animosity for him whatsoever. Just pity. He had been an insecure man, concealing his insecurity from himself behind a pretense of contemptuous superiority. He had been petty and vicious, perhaps worse, but now he was dead; and death was too great a punishment for his faults.

She folded her arms on the table and put her head down on them. She could not cry for Honell, for she had liked nothing about him—except his talent. If the extinguishing of his talent was not enough to bring tears, it did at least cast a pall of despair over her.

"Sooner or later," Hatch said, "the son of a bitch is going to come after me."

Lindsey lifted her head even though it felt as if it weighed a thousand pounds. "But why?"

"I don't know. Maybe we'll never know why, never understand it. But somehow he and I are linked, and eventually he'll come."

"Let the cops handle him," she said, painfully aware that there was no help for them from the authorities but stubbornly unwilling to let go of that hope.

"Cops can't find him," Hatch said grimly. "He's smoke."

"He won't come," she said, willing it to be true.

"Maybe not tomorrow. Maybe not next week or even next month. But as sure as the sun rises every morning, he'll come. And we'll be ready for him."

"Will we?" she wondered.

"Very ready."

"Remember what you said last night."

He looked up from the pistol again and met her eyes. "What?"

"That maybe he's not just an ordinary man, that he might have hitchhiked back with you from . . . somewhere else."

"I thought you dismissed that theory."

"I did. I can't believe it. But do you? Really?"

Instead of answering, he resumed cleaning the Browning.

She said, "If you believe it, even half believe it, put any credence in it at all—then what good is a gun?"

He didn't reply.

"How can bullets stop an evil spirit?" she pressed, feeling as if her memory of waking up and taking Regina to school was just part of a continuing dream, as if she was not caught in a real-life dilemma but in a nightmare. "How can something from beyond the grave be stopped with just a gun?"

"It's all I have," he said.

LIKE MANY DOCTORS, Jonas Nyebern did not maintain office hours or perform surgery on Wednesday. However, he never spent the afternoon golfing, sailing, or playing cards at the country club. He used Wednesdays to catch up on paperwork, or to write research papers and case studies related to the Resuscitation Medicine Project at Orange County General.

That first Wednesday in May, he planned to spend eight or ten busy hours in the study of his house on Spyglass Hill, where he had lived for almost two years, since the loss of his family. He hoped to finish writing a paper that he was going to deliver at a conference in San Francisco on the eighth of May.

The big windows in the teak-paneled room looked out on Corona Del Mar and Newport Beach below. Across twenty-six miles of gray water veined with green and blue, the dark palisades of Santa Catalina Island rose against the sky, but they were unable to make the vast Pacific Ocean seem any less immense or less humbling than if they had not been there.

He did not bother to draw the drapes because the panorama never distracted him. He had bought the property because he had hoped that the luxuries of the house and the magnificence of the view would make life seem beautiful and worth living in spite of great tragedy. But only his work had managed to do that for him, and so he always went directly to it with no more than a glance out of the windows.

That morning, he could not concentrate on the white words against the blue background on his computer screen. His thoughts were not pulled toward Pacific vistas, however, but toward his son, Jeremy.

On that overcast spring day two years ago, when he had come home to find Marion and Stephanie stabbed so often and so brutally that they were beyond revival, when he had found an unconscious Jeremy impaled on the vise-held knife in the garage and rapidly bleeding to death, Jonas had not blamed an unknown madman or burglars caught by surprise in the act. He had known at once that the murderer was the teenage boy slumped against the workbench with his life drizzling onto the concrete floor. Something had been wrong with Jeremy—*missing* in him—all his life, a difference that had become more marked and frightening as the years passed, though Jonas had tried for so long to convince himself the boy's attitudes and actions were manifestations of ordinary rebelliousness. But the madness of Jonas's father, having skipped one generation, had appeared again in Jeremy's corrupted genes.

The boy survived the extraction of the knife and the frantic ambulance ride to Orange County General, which was only minutes away. But he died on the stretcher as they were wheeling him along a hospital corridor.

Jonas had recently convinced the hospital to establish a special resuscitation team. Instead of using the bypass machine to warm the dead boy's blood, they employed it to recirculate *cooled* blood into his body, hastening to lower his body temperature drastically to delay cell deterioration and brain damage until surgery could be performed. The air conditioner was set all the way down at fifty, bags of crushed ice were packed along the sides of the patient, and Jonas personally opened the knife wound to search for— and repair—the damage that would foil reanimation.

He might have known at the time why he wanted so desperately to save Jeremy, but afterwards he was never able to understand his motivations fully, clearly.

Because he was my son, Jonas sometimes thought, and was therefore my responsibility.

But what parental responsibility did he owe to the slaughterer of his daughter and wife?

I saved him to ask him *why*, to pry from him an explanation, Jonas told himself at other times.

But he knew there was no answer that would make sense. Neither philosophers nor psychologists—not even the murderers themselves—had ever, in all of history, been able to provide an adequate explanation for a single act of monstrous sociopathic violence.

The only cogent answer, really, was that the human species was imperfect, stained, and carried within itself the seeds of its own destruction. The Church would call it the legacy of the Serpent, dating back to the Garden and the Fall. Scientists would refer to the mysteries of genetics, biochemistry, the fundamental actions of nucleotides. Maybe they were both talking about the same stain, merely describing it in different terms. To Jonas it seemed that this answer, whether provided by scientists or theologians, was always unsatisfying in precisely the same way and to the same degree, for it suggested no solution, prescribed no preventative. Except faith in God or in the potential of science.

Regardless of his reasons for taking the action he did, Jonas had saved Jeremy. The boy had been dead for thirty-one minutes, not an absolute record even in those days, because the young girl in Utah had already been reanimated after being in the arms of Death for sixty-six minutes. But she'd been severely hypothermic, while Jeremy had died warm, which made the feat a record of one kind, anyway. Actually, revival after thirty-one minutes of warm death was as miraculous as revival after eighty minutes of cold death. His own son and Hatch Harrison were Jonas's most amazing successes to date—if the first one qualified as a success.

For ten months Jeremy lay in a coma, feeding intravenously but able to breathe on his own and otherwise in need of no life-support machines. Early in that period, he was moved from the hospital to a high-quality nursing home.

During those months, Jonas could have petitioned a court to have the boy removed from the intravenous feed. But Jeremy would have perished from starvation or dehydration, and sometimes even a comatose patient might suffer pain from such a cruel death, depending on the depth of his stupor. Jonas was not prepared to be the cause of that pain. More insidiously, on a level so deep that even he did not realize it until much later, he suffered from the egotistic notion that he still might extract from the boy—supposing the boy ever woke—an explanation of sociopathic behavior that had eluded all other seekers in the history of mankind. Perhaps he thought he would have greater insight owing to his unique experience with the madness of his father and his son, orphaned and wounded by the first, widowed by the second. In any event he paid the nursing-home bills. And every Sunday afternoon, he sat at his son's bedside, staring at the pale, placid face in which he could see so much of himself.

After ten months, Jeremy regained consciousness. Brain damage had left him aphasic, without the power to speak or read. He had not known his name or how he had gotten to be where he was. He reacted to his face in the mirror as if it were that of a stranger, and he did not recognize his father. When the police came to question him, he exhibited neither guilt nor comprehension. He had awakened as a dullard, his intellectual capacity severely reduced from what it had been, his attention span short, easily confused.

With gestures, he complained vigorously of severe eye pain and sensitivity to bright light. An ophthalmological examination revealed a curious—indeed, inexplicable—degeneration of the irises. The contractile membrane seemed to have been partially eaten away. The sphincter pupillae—the muscle causing the iris to contract, thereby shrinking the pupil and admitting less light to the eye—had all but atrophied. Also, the dilator pupillae had shrunk, pulling the iris wide open. And the connection between the dilator muscle and oculomotor nerve was fused, leaving the eye virtually no ability to reduce the amount of incoming light. The condition was without precedent and degenerative in nature, making surgical correction impossible. The boy was provided with heavily tinted, wraparound sunglasses. Even then he preferred to pass daylight hours only in rooms where metal blinds or heavy drapes could close off the windows.

Incredibly, Jeremy became a favorite of the staff at the rehabilitation hospital to which he was transferred a few days after awakening at the nursing home. They were inclined to feel sorry for him because of his eye affliction, and because he was such a good-looking boy who had fallen so low. In addition, he now had the sweet temperament of a shy child, a result of his IQ loss, and there was no sign whatsoever of his former arrogance, cool calculation, and smouldering hostility.

For over four months he walked the halls, helped the nurses with simple tasks, struggled with a speech therapist to little effect, stared out the windows at the night for hours at a time, ate well enough to put flesh on his bones, and exercised in the gym during the evening with most of the lights off. His wasted body was rebuilt, and his straw-dry hair regained its luster.

Almost ten months ago, when Jonas was beginning to wonder where Jeremy could be placed when he was no longer able to benefit from physical or occupational therapy, the boy had disappeared. Although he had shown no previous inclination to roam beyond the grounds of the rehabilitation hospital, he walked out unnoticed one night, and never came back.

Jonas had assumed the police would be quick to track the boy. But they had been interested in him only as a missing person, not as a suspected murderer. If he had regained all of his faculties, they would have considered him both a threat and a fugitive from justice, but his continued—and apparently permanent—mental disabilities were a kind of immunity. Jeremy was no longer the same person that he had been when the crimes were committed; with his diminished intellectual capacity, inability to speak, and beguilingly simple personality, no jury would ever convict.

A missing-person investigation was no investigation at all. Police manpower had to be directed against immediate and serious crimes.

Though the cops believed that the boy had probably wandered away, fallen into the hands of the wrong people, and already been exploited and killed, Jonas knew his son was alive. And in his heart he knew that what was loose in the world was not a smiling dullard but a cunning, dangerous, and exceedingly sick young man.

They had all been deceived.

He could not prove that Jeremy's retardation was an act, but in his heart he knew that he had allowed himself to be fooled. He had accepted the new Jeremy because, when it came right down to it, he could not bear the anguish of having to confront the Jeremy who had killed Marion and Stephanie. The most damning proof of his own complicity in Jeremy's fraud was the fact that he had not requested a CAT scan to determine the precise nature of the brain damage. At the time he told himself the fact of the damage was the only thing that mattered, not its precise etiology, an incredible reaction for any physician but not so incredible for a father who was unwilling to come face-to-face with the monster inside his son.

And now the monster was set free. He had no proof, but he knew. Jeremy was out there somewhere. The old Jeremy.

For ten months, through a series of three detective agencies, he had sought his son, because he shared in the moral, though not the legal, responsibility for any crimes the boy committed. The first two agencies had gotten nowhere, eventually concluding that their inability to pick up a trail meant no trail existed. The boy, they reported, was most likely dead.

The third, Morton Redlow, was a one-man shop. Though not as glitzy as the bigger agencies, Redlow possessed a bulldog determination that encouraged Jonas to believe progress would be made. And last week, Redlow had hinted that he was onto something, that he would have concrete news by the weekend.

The detective had not been heard from since. He had failed to respond to messages left on his phone machine.

Now, turning away from his computer and the conference paper he was unable to work on, Jonas picked up the telephone and tried the detective again. He got the recording. But he could no longer leave his name and number, because the incoming tape on Redlow's machine was already full of messages. It cut him off.

Jonas had a bad feeling about the detective.

He put down the phone, got up from the desk, and went to the window. His spirits were so low, he doubted they could be lifted any more by anything as simple as a magnificent view, but he was willing to try. Each new day was filled with so much more dread than the day before it, he needed all the help he could get just to be able to sleep at night and rise in the morning.

Reflections of the morning sun rippled in silver filaments through the incoming waves, as if the sea were a great piece of rippling blue-gray fabric with interwoven metallic threads.

He told himself that Redlow was only a few days late with his report, less than a week, nothing to be worried about. The failure to return answering-machine messages might only mean the detective was ill or preoccupied with a personal crisis.

But he knew. Redlow had found Jeremy and, in spite of every warning from Jonas, had underestimated the boy.

A yacht with white sails was making its way south along the coast. Large white birds kited in the sky behind the ship, diving into the sea and out again, no doubt snaring fish with each plunge. Graceful and free, the birds were a beautiful sight, though not to the fish, of course. Not to the fish.

LINDSEY WENT TO her studio between the master bedroom and the room beside Regina's. She moved her high stool from the easel to the drawing board, opened her sketch pad, and started to plan her next painting.

She felt that it was important to focus on her work, not only because the making of art could soothe the soul as surely as the appreciation of it, but because sticking to everyday routine was the only way she could try to push back the forces of irrationality that seemed to be surging like black floodwaters into their lives. Nothing could really go too far wrong—could it?—if she just kept painting, drinking her usual black coffee, eating three meals a day, washing dishes when they needed washed, brushing her teeth at night, showering and rolling on her deodorant in the morning. How could some homicidal creature from Beyond intrude into an *orderly* life? Surely ghouls and ghosts, goblins and monsters, had no power over those who were properly groomed, deodorized, fluoridated, dressed, fed, employed, and motivated.

That was what she wanted to believe. But when she tried to sketch, she couldn't quiet the tremors in her hands.

Honell was dead.

Cooper was dead.

She kept looking at the window, expecting to see that the spider had returned. But there was no scurrying black form or the lacework of a new web. Just glass. Treetops and blue sky beyond.

After a while Hatch stopped in. He hugged her from behind, and kissed her cheek.

But he was in a solemn rather than romantic mood. He had one of the Brownings with him. He put the pistol on the top of her supply cabinet. "Keep this with you if you leave the room. He's not going to come around during the day. I know that. I feel it. Like he's a vampire or something, for God's sake. But it still doesn't hurt to be careful, especially when you're here alone."

She was dubious, but she said, "All right."

"I'm going out for a while. Do a little shopping."

"For what?" She turned on her stool, facing him more directly.

"We don't have enough ammunition for the guns."

"Both have full clips."

"Besides, I want to get a shotgun."

"Hatch! Even if he comes, and he probably won't, it's not going to be a war. A man breaks into your house, it's a matter of a shot or two, not a pitched battle."

Standing before her, he was stone-faced and adamant. "The right shotgun is the best of all home-defensive weapons. You don't have to be a good shot. The spread gets him. I know just which one I want. It's a short-barreled, pistol-grip with—"

She put one hand flat against his chest in a "stop" gesture. "You're scaring the crap out of me."

"Good. If we're scared, we're likely to be more alert, less careless."

"If you really think there's danger, then we shouldn't have Regina here."

"We can't send her back to St. Thomas's," he said at once, as if he had already considered that.

"Only until this is resolved."

"No." He shook his head. "Regina's too sensitive, you know that, too fragile, too quick to interpret everything as rejection. We might not be able to make her understand—and then she might not give us a second chance."

"I'm sure she—"

"Besides, we'd have to tell the orphanage something. If we concocted some lie—and I can't imagine what it would be—they'd know we were flimflamming them. They'd wonder why. Pretty soon they'd start second-guessing their approval of us. And if we told them the truth, started jabbering about psychic visions and telepathic bonds with psycho killers, they'd write us off as a couple of nuts, never give her back to us."

He *had* thought it out.

Lindsey knew what he said was true.

He kissed her lightly again. "I'll be back in an hour. Two at most."

When he had gone, she stared at the gun for a while.

Then she turned angrily away from it and picked up her pencil. She tore off a page from the big drawing tablet. The new page was blank. White and clean. It stayed that way.

Nervously chewing her lip, she looked at the window. No web. No spider. Just the glass pane. Treetops and blue skies beyond.

She had never realized until now that a pristine blue sky could be ominous.

THE TWO SCREENED vents in the garage attic were provided for ventilation. The overhanging roof and the density of the screen mesh did not allow much penetration by the sun, but some wan light entered with the vague currents of cool morning air.

Vassago was untroubled by the light, in part because his nest was formed by piles of boxes and furniture that spared him a direct view of the vents. The air smelled of dry wood, aging cardboard.

He was having difficulty getting to sleep, so he tried to relax by imagining what a fine fire might be fueled by the contents of the garage attic. His rich imagination made it easy to envision sheets of red flames, spirals of orange and yellow, and the sharp pop of sap bubbles exploding in burning rafters. Cardboard and packing paper and combustible memorabilia disappeared in silent rising curtains of smoke, with a papery crackling like the manic applause of millions in some dark and distant theater. Though the conflagration was in his mind, he had to squint his eyes against the phantom light.

Yet the fantasy of fire did not entertain him—perhaps because the attic would be filled merely with burning *things*, mere lifeless objects. Where was the fun in that?

Eighteen had burned to death—or been trampled—in the Haunted House on the night that Tod Ledderbeck had perished in the cavern of the Millipede. *There* had been a fire.

He had escaped all suspicion in the rocket jockey's death and the disaster at the Haunted House, but he'd been shaken by the repercussions of his night of games. The deaths at Fantasy World were at the top of the news for at least two weeks, and were the primary topic of conversation around school for maybe a month. The park closed temporarily, reopened to poor business, closed again for refurbishing, reopened to continued low attendance, and eventually succumbed two years later to all of the bad publicity and to a welter of lawsuits. A few thousand people lost their jobs. And Mrs. Ledderbeck had a nervous breakdown, though Jeremy figured it was part of her act, pretending she had actually loved Tod, the same crappy hypocrisy he saw in everyone.

But other, more personal repercussions were what shook Jeremy. In the immediate aftermath, toward morning of the long sleepless night that followed his adventures at Fantasy World, he realized he had been out of control. Not when he killed Tod. He knew that was right and good, a Master of the Game proving his mastery. But from the moment he had tipped Tod out of the Millipede, he had been drunk on power, banging around the park in a state of mind similar to what he imagined he'd have been like after chugging a six-pack or two. He had been swacked, plastered, crocked, totally wasted, polluted, stinko with power, for he had taken unto himself the role of Death and become the one whom all men feared. The experience was not only inebriating: it was addictive; he wanted to repeat it the next day, and the day after that, and every day for the rest of his life. He wanted to set someone afire again, and he wanted to know what it felt like to take a life with a sharp blade, with a gun, with a hammer, with his bare hands. That night he had achieved an early puberty, erect with fantasies of death, orgasmic at the contemplation of murders yet to be committed. Shocked by that first sexual spasm and the fluid that escaped him, he finally understood, toward dawn, that a Master of the Game not only had to be able to kill without fear but had to *control* the powerful desire to kill again that was generated by killing once.

Getting away with murder proved his superiority to all the other players, but he could not continue to get away with it if he were out of control, berserk, like one of those guys you saw on the news who opened up with a semiautomatic weapon on a crowd at a shopping mall. That was not a Master. That was a fool and a loser. A Master must pick and choose, select his targets with great care, and eliminate them with style.

Now, lying in the garage attic on a pile of folded dropcloths, he thought that a Master must be like a spider. Choose his killing ground. Weave his web. Settle down, pull in his long legs, make a small and insignificant thing of himself . . . and wait.

Plenty of spiders shared the attic with him. Even in the gloom they were visible to his exquisitely sensitive eyes. Some of them were admirably industrious. Others were alive but as cunningly still as death. He felt an affinity for them. His little brothers.

THE GUN SHOP was a fortress. A sign near the front door warned that the premises were guarded by multi-system silent alarms and also, at night, by attack dogs. Steel bars were welded over the windows. Hatch noticed the door was at least three inches thick, wood but probably with a steel core, and that the three hinges on the inside appeared to have been designed for use on a bathysphere to withstand thousands of tons of pressure deep under the sea. Though much weapons-associated merchandise was on open shelves, the rifles, shotguns, and handguns were in locked glass cases or securely chained in open wall racks. Video cameras had been installed near the ceiling in each of the four corners of the long main room, all behind thick sheets of bulletproof glass.

The shop was better protected than a bank. Hatch wondered if he was living in a time when weaponry had more appeal to thieves than did money itself.

The four clerks were pleasant men with easy camaraderie among themselves and a folksy manner with customers. They wore straight-hemmed shirts outside their pants. Maybe they prized comfort. Or maybe each was carrying a handgun in a holster underneath his shirt, tucked into the small of his back.

Hatch bought a Mossberg short-barreled, pistol-grip, pump-action 12-gauge shotgun.

"The perfect weapon for home-defense," the clerk told him. "You have this, you don't really need anything else."

Hatch supposed that he should be grateful he was living in an age when the government promised to protect and defend its citizens from threats even so small as radon in the cellar and the ultimate environmental consequences of the extinction of the one-eyed, blue-tailed gnat. In a less civilized era—say the turn of the century—he no doubt would have required an armory containing hundreds of weapons, a ton of explosives, and a chain-mail vest to wear when answering the door.

He decided irony was a bitter form of humor and not to his taste. At least not in his current mood.

He filled out the requisite federal and state forms, paid with a credit card, and left with the Mossberg, a cleaning kit, and boxes of ammunition for the Brownings as well as the shotgun. Behind him, the shop door fell shut with a heavy thud, as if he were exiting a vault.

After putting his purchases in the trunk of the Mitsubishi, he got behind the wheel, started the engine—and froze with his hand on the gearshift. Beyond the windshield, the small parking lot had vanished. The gun shop was no longer there.

As if a mighty sorcerer had cast an evil spell, the sunny day had disappeared. Hatch was in a long, eerily lighted tunnel. He glanced out the side windows, turned to check the back, but the illusion or hallucination—whatever the hell it might be—enwrapped him, as realistic in its detail as the parking lot had been.

When he faced forward, he was confronted by a long slope in the center of which was a narrow-gauge railroad track. Suddenly the car began to move as if it were a train pulling up that hill.

Hatch jammed his foot down on the brake pedal. No effect.

He closed his eyes, counted to ten, listening to his heart pound harder by the second and unsuccessfully willing himself to relax. When he opened his eyes, the tunnel was still there.

He switched the car engine off. He heard it die. The car continued to move.

The silence that followed the cessation of the engine noise was brief. A new sound arose: *clackety-clack, clackety-clack, clackety-clack.*

An inhuman shriek erupted to the left, and from the corner of his eye, Hatch detected threatening movement. He snapped his head toward it. To his astonishment he saw an utterly alien figure, a pale white slug as big as a man. It reared up and shrieked at him through a round mouth full of teeth that whirled like the sharp blades in a garbage disposal. An identical beast shrieked from a niche in the tunnel wall to his right, and more of them ahead, and beyond them other monsters of other forms, gibbering, hooting, snarling, squealing as he passed them.

In spite of his disorientation and terror, he realized that the grotesqueries along the tunnel walls were mechanical beasts, not real. And as that understanding sank in, he finally recognized the familiar sound. *Clackety-clack, clackety-clack.* He was on an indoor roller coaster, yet in his car, moving with decreasing speed toward the high point, with a precipitous fall ahead.

He did not argue with himself that this couldn't be happening, did not try to shake himself awake or back to his senses. He was past denial. He understood that he did not have to *believe* in this experience to insure its continuation; it would progress whether he believed in it or not, so he might as well grit his teeth and get through it.

Being past denial didn't mean, however, that he was past fear. He was scared shitless.

Briefly he considered opening the car door and getting out. Maybe that would break the spell. But he didn't try it because he was afraid that when he stepped out he would not be in the parking lot in front of the gun shop but in the tunnel, and that the car would continue uphill without him. Losing contact with his little red Mitsubishi might be like slamming a door on reality, consigning himself forever to the vision, with no way out, no way back.

The car passed the last mechanical monster. It reached the crest of the inclined track. Pushed through a pair of swinging doors. Into darkness. The doors fell shut behind. The car crept forward. Forward. Forward. Abruptly it dropped as if into a bottomless pit.

Hatch cried out, and with his cry the darkness vanished. The sunny spring day made a welcome reappearance. The parking lot. The gun shop.

His hands were locked so tightly around the steering wheel that they ached.

THROUGHOUT THE MORNING, Vassago was awake more than asleep. But when he dozed, he was back in the Millipede again, on that night of glory.

In the days and weeks following the deaths at Fantasy World, he had without doubt proved himself a Master by exerting iron control over his compulsive desire to kill. Merely the memory of having killed was sufficient to release the periodic pressure that built in him. Hundreds of times, he relived the sensuous details of each death, temporarily quenching his hot need. And the knowledge that he would kill again, any time he could do so without arousing suspicion, was an additional restraint on self-indulgence.

He did not kill anyone else for two years. Then, when he was fourteen, he drowned another boy at summer camp. The kid was smaller and weaker, but he put up a good fight. When he was found floating facedown in the pond, it was the talk of the camp for the rest of that month. Water could be as thrilling as fire.

When he was sixteen and had a driver's license, he wasted two transients, both hitchhikers, one in October, the other a couple of days before Thanksgiving. The guy in November was just a college kid going home for the holiday. But the other one was something else, a predator who thought he had stumbled across a foolish and naive high-school boy who would provide him with some thrills of his own. Jeremy had used knives on both of them.

At seventeen, when he discovered Satanism, he couldn't read enough about it, surprised to find that his secret philosophy had been codified and embraced by clandestine cults. Oh, there were relatively benign forms, propagated by gutless wimps who were just looking for a way to play at wickedness, an excuse for hedonism. But real believers existed, as well, committed to the truth that God had failed to create people in His image, that the bulk of humanity was equivalent to a herd of cattle, that selfishness was admirable, that pleasure was the only worthwhile goal, and that the greatest pleasure was the brutal exercise of power over others.

The ultimate expression of power, one privately published volume had assured him, was to destroy those who had spawned you, thereby breaking the bonds of family "love." The book said that one must as violently as possible reject the whole hypocrisy of rules, laws, and noble sentiments by which other men pretended to live. Taking that advice to heart was what had earned him a place in Hell—from which his father had pulled him back.

But he would soon be there again. A few more deaths, two in particular, would earn him repatriation to the land of darkness and the damned.

The attic grew warmer as the day progressed.

A few fat flies buzzed back and forth through his shadowy retreat, and some of them settled down forever on one or another of the alluring but sticky webs that spanned the junctions of the rafters. *Then* the spiders moved.

In the warm, closed space, Vassago's dozing became a deeper sleep with more intense dreams. Fire and water, blade and bullet.

CROUCHING AT THE corner of the garage, Hatch reached between two azaleas and flipped open the cover on the landscape-lighting control box. He adjusted the timer to prevent the pathway and shrubbery lights from blinking off at midnight. Now they would stay on until sunrise.

He closed the metal box, stood, and looked around at the quiet, well-groomed street. All was harmony. Every house had a tile roof in shades of tan and sand and peach, not the more stark orange-red tiles of many older California homes. The stucco walls were cream-colored or within a narrow range of coordinated pastels specified by the "Covenants, Conventions & Restrictions" that came with the grant deed and mortgage. Lawns were green and recently mown, flower beds were well tended, and trees were neatly trimmed. It was difficult to believe that unspeakable violence could ever intrude from the outer world into such an orderly, upwardly mobile community, and *inconceivable* that anything supernatural could stalk those streets. The neighborhood's normalcy was so solid that it seemed like encircling stone ramparts crowned with battlements.

Not for the first time, he thought that Lindsey and Regina might be perfectly safe there—but for him. If madness had invaded this fortress of normalcy, he had opened the door to it. Maybe he was mad himself; maybe his weird experiences were nothing as grand as psychic visions, merely the hallucinations of an insane mind. He would bet everything he owned on his sanity—though he also could not dismiss the slim possibility that he would lose the bet. In any event, whether or not he was insane, he was the conduit for whatever violence might rain down on them, and perhaps they would be better off if they went away for the duration, put some distance between themselves and him until this crazy business was settled.

Sending them away seemed wise and responsible—except that a small voice deep inside him spoke against that option. He had a terrible hunch—or was it more than a hunch?—that the killer would not be coming after him but after Lindsey and Regina. If they went away somewhere, just Lindsey and the girl, that homicidal monster would follow them, leaving Hatch to wait alone for a showdown that would never happen.

All right, then they had to stick together. Like a family. Rise or fall as one.

Before leaving to pick Regina up at school, he slowly circled the house, looking for lapses in their defenses. The only one he found was an unlocked window at the back of the garage. The latch had been loose for a long time, and he had been meaning to fix it. He got some tools from one of the garage cabinets and worked on the mechanism until the bolt seated securely in the catch.

As he'd told Lindsey earlier, he didn't think the man in his visions would come as soon as tonight, probably not even this week, maybe not for a month or longer, but he *would* come eventually. Even if that unwelcome visit was days or weeks away, it felt good to be prepared.

2 Vassago woke.

Without opening his eyes, he knew that night was coming. He could feel the oppressive sun rolling off the world and slipping over the edge of the horizon. When he did open his eyes, the last fading light coming through the attic vents confirmed that the waters of the night were on the rise.

HATCH FOUND THAT it was not exactly easy to conduct a normal domestic life while waiting to be stricken by a terrifying, maybe even bloody, vision so powerful it would blank out reality for its duration. It was hard to sit in your pleasant dining room, smile, enjoy the pasta and Parmesan bread, make with the light banter, and tease a giggle from the young lady with the solemn gray eyes—when you kept thinking of the loaded shotgun secreted in the corner behind the Coromandel screen or the handgun in the adjacent kitchen atop the refrigerator, above the line of sight of a small girl's eyes.

He wondered how the man in black would enter when he came. At night, for one thing. He only came out at night. They didn't have to worry about him going after Regina at school. But would he boldly ring the bell or knock smartly on the door, while they were still up and around with all the lights on, hoping to catch them off-guard at a civilized hour when they might assume it was a neighbor come to call? Or would he wait until they were asleep, lights off, and try to slip through their defenses to take them unaware?

Hatch wished they had an alarm system, as they did at the store. When they sold the old house and moved into the new place following Jimmy's death, they should have called Brinks right away. Valuable antiques graced every room. But for the longest time after Jimmy had been taken from them, it hadn't seemed to matter if anything—or everything—else was taken as well.

Throughout dinner, Lindsey was a trooper. She ate a mound of rigatoni as if she had an appetite, which was something Hatch could not manage, and she filled his frequent worried silences with natural-sounding patter, doing her best to preserve the feeling of an ordinary night at home.

Regina was sufficiently observant to know something was wrong. And though she was tough enough to handle nearly anything, she was also infected with seemingly chronic self-doubt that would probably lead her to interpret their uneasiness as dissatisfaction with her.

Earlier Hatch and Lindsey had discussed what they might be able to tell the girl about the situation they faced, without alarming her more than was necessary. The answer seemed to be: nothing. She had been with them only two days. She didn't know them well enough to have this crazy stuff thrown at her. She'd hear about Hatch's bad dreams, his waking hallucinations, the heat-browned magazine, the murders, all of it, and figure she had been entrusted to a couple of lunatics.

Anyway the kid didn't really need to be warned at this stage. They could look out for her; it was what they were sworn to do.

Hatch found it difficult to believe that just three days ago the problem of his repetitive nightmares had not seemed significant enough to delay a trial adoption. But Honell and Cooper had not been dead then, and supernatural forces seemed only the material of popcorn movies and *National Enquirer* stories.

Halfway through dinner he heard a noise in the kitchen. A click and scrape. Lindsey and Regina were engaged in an intense conversation about whether Nancy Drew, girl detective of countless books, was a "dorkette," which was Regina's view, or whether she was a smart and savvy girl for her times but just old-fashioned when you looked at her from a more modern viewpoint. Either they were too engrossed in their debate to hear the noise in the kitchen—or there had been no noise, and he had imagined it.

"Excuse me," he said, getting up from the table, "I'll be right back."

He pushed through the swinging door into the large kitchen and looked around suspiciously. The only movement in the deserted room was a faint ribbon of steam still unraveling from the crack between the tilted lid and the pot of hot spaghetti sauce that stood on a ceramic pad on the counter beside the stove.

Something thumped softly in the L-shaped family room, which opened off the kitchen. He could see part of that room from where he stood but not all of it. He stepped silently across the kitchen and through the archway, taking the Browning 9mm off the top of the refrigerator as he went.

The family room was also deserted. But he was sure that he had not imagined that second noise. He stood for a moment, looking around in bafflement.

His skin prickled, and he whirled toward the short hallway that led from the family room to the foyer inside the front door. Nothing. He was alone. So why did he feel as if someone was holding an ice cube against the back of his neck?

He moved cautiously into the hallway until he came to the coat closet. The door was closed. Directly across the hall was the powder room. That door was also shut. He felt drawn toward the foyer, and his inclination was to trust his hunch and move on, but he didn't want to put either of those closed doors at his back.

When he jerked open the closet door, he saw at once that no one was in there. He felt stupid with the gun thrust out in front of him and pointing at nothing but a couple of coats on hangers, playing a movie cop or something. Better hope it wasn't the final reel. Sometimes, when the story required it, they killed off the good guy in the end.

He checked the powder room, found it also empty, and continued into the foyer. The uncanny feeling was still with him but not as strong as before. The foyer was deserted. He glanced at the stairs, but no one was on them.

He looked in the living room. No one. He could see a corner of the dining-room table through the archway at the end of the living room. Although he could hear Lindsey and Regina still discussing Nancy Drew, he couldn't see them.

He checked the den, which was also off the entrance foyer. And the closet in the den. And the kneehole space under the desk.

Back in the foyer, he tried the front door. It was locked, as it should have been.

No good. If he was this jumpy already, what in the name of God was he going to be like in another day or week? Lindsey would have to pry him off the ceiling just to give him his morning coffee each day.

Nevertheless, reversing the route he had just taken through the house, he stopped in the family room to try the sliding glass doors that served the patio and backyard. They were locked, with the burglar-foiling bar inserted properly in the floor track.

In the kitchen once more, he tried the door to the garage. It was unlocked, and again he felt as if spiders were crawling on his scalp.

He eased the door open. The garage was dark. He fumbled for the switch, clicked the lights on. Banks of big fluorescent tubes dropped a flood of harsh light straight down the width and breadth of the room, virtually eliminating shadows, revealing nothing out of the ordinary.

Stepping over the threshold, he let the door ease shut behind him. He cautiously walked the length of the room with the large roll-up sectional doors on his right, the backs of the two cars on his left. The middle stall was empty.

His rubber-soled Rockports made no sound. He expected to surprise someone crouched along the far side of one of the cars, but no one was sheltering behind either of them.

At the end of the garage, when he was past the Chevy, he abruptly dropped to the floor and looked under the car. He could see all the way across the room, beneath the Mitsubishi, as well. No one was hiding under either vehicle. As best as he could tell, considering that the tires provided blind spots, no one appeared to be circling the cars to keep out of his sight.

He got up and turned to a regular door in the end wall. It served the side yard and had a thumb-turn dead-bolt lock, which was engaged. No one could get in that way.

Returning to the kitchen door, he stayed to the back of the garage. He tried only the two storage cabinets that had tall doors and were large enough to provide a hiding place for a grown man. Neither was occupied.

He checked the window latch he had repaired earlier in the day. It was secure, the bolt seated snugly in the vertically mounted hasp.

Again, he felt foolish. Like a grown man engaged in a boy's game, fancying himself a movie hero.

How fast would he have reacted if someone *had* been hiding in one of those tall cabinets and had flung himself outward when the door opened? Or what if he had dropped to the floor to look under the Chevy, and *right there* had been the man in black, face-to-face with him, inches away?

He was glad he hadn't been required to learn the answer to either of those unnerving questions. But at least, having asked them, he no longer felt foolish, because indeed the man in black might have been there.

Sooner or later the bastard *would* be there. Hatch was no less certain than ever about the inevitability of a confrontation. Call it a hunch, call it a premonition, call it Christmas turkey if you liked, but he knew that he could trust the small warning voice within him.

As he was passing the front of the Mitsubishi, he saw what appeared to be a dent on the hood. He stopped, sure that it must be a trick of light, the shadow of the pull-cord that hung from the ceiling trap. It was directly over the hood. He swatted the dangling cord, but the mark on the car didn't leap and dance as it would have done if it had been just the cord shadow.

Leaning over the grille, he touched the smooth sheet metal and felt the depression, shallow but as big as his hand. He sighed heavily. The car was still new, and already it needed a session in the body shop. Take a brand new car to the mall, and an hour after it's out of the showroom, some damn fool would park beside it and slam open his door into yours. It never failed.

He hadn't noticed the dent either when he had come home this afternoon from the gun shop or when he'd brought Regina back from school. Maybe it wasn't as visible from inside the car, behind the steering wheel; maybe you had to be out in front, looking at it from the right angle. It sure seemed big enough to be seen from anywhere.

He was trying to figure how it could have happened—somebody must have been passing by and dropped something on the car—when he saw the footprint. It was in a gossamer coating of beige dust on the red paint, the sole and part of the heel of a walking shoe probably not much different from the ones he was wearing. Someone had stood on or walked across the hood of the Mitsubishi.

It must have happened outside St. Thomas's School, because it was the kind of thing a kid might do, showing off to friends. Having allowed too much time for bad traffic, Hatch had arrived at St. Tom's twenty minutes before classes let out. Rather than wait in the car, he'd gone for a walk to work off some excess nervous energy. Probably, some wiseass and his buddies from the adjacent high school—the footprint was too big to belong to a smaller kid—sneaked out a little ahead of the final bell, and were showing off for each other as they raced away from the school, maybe leaping and clambering over obstacles instead of going around them, as if they'd escaped from a prison with the bloodhounds close on their—

"Hatch?"

Startled out of his train of thought just when it seemed to be leading somewhere, he spun around toward the voice as if it did not sound familiar to him, which of course it did.

Lindsey stood in the doorway between the garage and kitchen. She looked at the gun in his hand, met his eyes. "What's wrong?"

"Thought I heard something."

"And?"

"Nothing." She had startled him so much that he had forgotten the footprint and dent on the car hood. As he followed her into the kitchen, he said, "This door was open. I locked it earlier."

"Oh, Regina left one of her books in the car when she came home from school. She went out just before dinner to get it."

"You should have made sure she locked up."

"It's only the door to the garage," Lindsey said, heading toward the dining room.

He put a hand on her shoulder to stop her, turned her around. "It's a point of vulnerability," he said with perhaps more anxiety than such a minor breach of security warranted.

"Aren't the outer garage doors locked?"

"Yes, and this one should be locked, too."

"But as many times as we go back and forth from the kitchen"—they had a second refrigerator in the garage—"it's just convenient to leave the door unlocked. We've always left it unlocked."

"We don't any more," he said firmly.

They were face-to-face, and she studied him worriedly. He knew she thought he was walking a fine line between prudent precautions and a sort of quiet hysteria, even treading the wrong way over that line sometimes. On the other hand, *she* hadn't had the benefit of his nightmares and visions.

Perhaps the same thought crossed Lindsey's mind, for she nodded and said, "Okay. I'm sorry. You're right."

He leaned back into the garage and turned off the lights. He closed the door, engaged the deadbolt—and felt no safer, really.

She had started toward the dining room again. She glanced back as he followed her, indicating the pistol in his hand. "Going to bring that to the table?"

Deciding he had come down a little heavy on her, he shook his head and bugged his eyes out, trying to make a Christopher Lloyd face and lighten the moment: "I think some of my rigatoni are still alive. I don't like to eat them till they're dead."

"Well, you've got the shotgun behind the Coromandel screen for that," she reminded him.

"You're right!" He put the pistol on top of the refrigerator again. "And if that doesn't work, I can always take them out in the driveway and run them over with the car!"

She pushed open the swinging door, and Hatch followed her into the dining room.

Regina looked up and said, "Your food's getting cold."

Still making like Christopher Lloyd, Hatch said, "Then we'll get some sweaters and mittens for them!"

Regina giggled. Hatch *adored* the way she giggled.

AFTER THE DINNER dishes were done, Regina went to her room to study. "Big history test tomorrow," she said.

Lindsey returned to her studio to try to get some work done. When she sat down at her drawing board, she saw the second Browning 9mm. It was still atop the low art-supply cabinet, where Hatch had put it earlier in the day.

She scowled at it. She didn't necessarily disapprove of guns themselves, but this one was more than merely a handgun. It was a symbol of their powerlessness in the face of the amorphous threat that hung over them. Keeping a gun ever within reach seemed an admission that they were desperate and couldn't control their own destiny. The sight of a snake coiled on the cabinet could not have carved a deeper scowl on her face.

She didn't want Regina walking in and seeing it.

She pulled open the first drawer of the cabinet and shoved aside some gum erasers and pencils to make room for the weapon. The Browning barely fit in that shallow space. Closing the drawer, she felt better.

During the long morning and afternoon, she had accomplished nothing. She had made lots of false starts with sketches that went nowhere. She was not even close to being ready to prepare a canvas.

Masonite, actually. She worked on Masonite, as did most artists these days, but she still thought of each rectangle as a canvas, as though she were the reincarnation of an artist from another age and could not shake her old way of thinking. Also, she painted in acrylics rather than oils. Masonite did not deteriorate over time the way canvas did, and acrylics retained their true colors far better than oil-based paints.

Of course if she didn't *do* something soon, it wouldn't matter if she used acrylics or cat's piss. She couldn't call herself an artist in the first place if she couldn't come up with an idea that excited her and a composition that did the idea justice. Picking up a thick charcoal pencil, she leaned over the sketch pad that was open on the drawing board in front of her. She tried to knock inspiration off its perch and get its lazy butt flying again.

After no more than a minute, her gaze floated off the page, up and up, until she was staring at the window. No interesting sight waited to distract her tonight, no treetops gracefully swaying in a breeze or even a patch of cerulean sky. The night beyond the pane was featureless.

The black backdrop transformed the window glass into a mirror in which she saw herself looking over the top of the drawing board. Because it was not a true mirror, her reflection was transparent, ghostly, as if she had died and come back to haunt the last place she had ever known on earth.

That was an unsettling thought, so she returned her attention to the blank page of the drawing tablet in front of her.

AFTER LINDSEY AND Regina went upstairs, Hatch walked from room to room on the ground floor, checking windows and doors to be sure they were secured. He had inspected the locks before. Doing it again was pointless. He did it anyway.

When he reached the pair of sliding glass doors in the family room, he switched on the outdoor patio lights to augment the low landscape lighting. The backyard was now bright enough for him to see most of it—although someone could have been crouched among the shrubs along the rear fence. He stood at the doors, waiting for one of the shadows along the perimeter of the property to shift.

Maybe he was wrong. Maybe the guy would never come after them. In which case, in a month or two or three, Hatch would most likely be certifiably mad from the tension of waiting. He almost thought it would be better if the creep came now and got it over with.

He moved on to the breakfast nook and examined those windows. They were still locked.

REGINA RETURNED TO her bedroom and prepared her corner desk for homework. She put her books to one side of the blotter, pens and felt-tip Hi-Liter to the other side, and her notebook in the middle, everything squared-up and neat.

As she got her desk set up, she worried about the Harrisons. Something was wrong with them.

Well, not wrong in the sense that they were thieves or enemy spies or counterfeiters or murderers or child-eating cannibals. For a while she'd had an idea for a novel in which this absolute screwup girl is adopted by a couple who *are* child-eating cannibals, and she finds a pile of child bones in the basement, and a recipe file in the kitchen with cards that say things like LITTLE GIRL KABOB and GIRL SOUP, with instructions like "INGREDIENTS: one tender young girl, unsalted; one onion, chopped; one pound carrots, diced. . . ." In the story the girl goes to the authorities, but they will not believe her because she's widely known as a screwup and a teller of tall tales. Well, that was fiction, and this was real life, and the Harrisons seemed perfectly happy eating pizza and pasta and hamburgers.

She clicked on the fluorescent desk lamp.

Though there was nothing wrong with the Harrisons themselves, they definitely had problems, because they were tense and trying hard to hide it. Maybe they weren't able to make their mortgage payments, and the bank was going to take the house, and all three of them would have to move back into her old room at the orphanage. Maybe they had discovered that Mrs. Harrison had a sister she'd never heard about before, an evil twin like all those people on television shows were always discovering they had. Or maybe they owed money to the Mafia and couldn't pay it and were going to get their legs broken.

Regina withdrew a dictionary from the bookshelves and put it on the desk.

If they had a bad problem, Regina hoped it was the Mafia thing, because she could handle that pretty well. The Harrisons' legs would get better eventually, and they'd learn an important lesson about not borrowing money from loansharks. Meanwhile, she could take care of them, make sure they got their medicine, check their temperatures now and then, bring them dishes of ice cream with a little animal cookie stuck in the top of each one, and even empty their bedpans (Gross!) if it came to that. She knew a lot about nursing, having been on the receiving end of so much of it at various times over the years. (Dear God, if their big problem is *me,* could I have a miracle here and get the problem changed to the Mafia, so they'll keep me and we'll be happy? In exchange for the miracle, I'd even be willing to have my legs broken, too. At least talk it over with the guys at the Mafia and see what they say.)

When the desk was fully prepared for homework, Regina decided that she needed to be dressed more comfortably in order to study. Having changed out of her parochial-school uniform when she had gotten home, she was wearing gray corduroy pants and a lime-green, long-sleeve cotton sweater. Pajamas and a robe were much better for studying. Besides, her leg brace was making her itch in a couple of places, and she wanted to take it off for the day.

When she slid open the mirrored closet door, she was face-to-face with a crouching man dressed all in black and wearing sunglasses.

3
On yet one more tour of the downstairs, Hatch decided to turn off the lamps and chandeliers as he went. With the landscape and exterior house lights all ablaze but the interior dark, he would be able to see a prowler without being seen himself.

He concluded the patrol in the unlighted den, which he had decided to make his primary guard station. Sitting at the big desk in the gloom, he could look through the double doors into the front foyer and cover the foot of the stairs to the second floor. If anyone tried to enter through a den window or the French doors to the rose garden, he would know at once. If the intruder breached their security in another room, Hatch would nail the guy when he tried to go upstairs, because the spill of second-floor hall light illuminated the steps. He couldn't be everywhere at once, and the den seemed to be the most strategic position.

He put both the shotgun and the handgun on top of the desk, within easy reach. He couldn't see them well without the lights on, but he could grab either of them in an instant if anything happened. He practiced a few times, sitting in his swivel chair and facing the foyer, then abruptly reaching out to grab the Browning, this time the Mossberg 12-gauge, Browning, Browning, Mossberg, Browning, Mossberg, Mossberg. Every time, maybe because his reactions were heightened by adrenaline, his right hand swooped through darkness and with precise accuracy came to rest upon the handgrip of the Browning or the stock of the Mossberg, whichever was wanted.

He took no satisfaction in his preparedness, because he knew he could not remain vigilant twenty-four hours a day, seven days a week. He had to sleep and eat. He had not gone to the shop today, and he could take off a few days more, but he couldn't leave everything to Glenda and Lew indefinitely; sooner or later he would have to go to work.

Realistically, even with breaks to eat and sleep, he would cease to be an effective watchman long before he needed to return to work. Sustaining a high degree of mental and physical alertness was a draining enterprise. In time he'd have to consider hiring a guard or two from a private security firm, and he didn't know how much that would cost. More important, he didn't know how reliable a hired guard would be.

He doubted he would ever have to make that decision, because the bastard was going to come soon, maybe tonight. On a primitive level, a vague impression of the man's intentions flowed to Hatch along whatever mystical bond they shared. It was like a child's words spoken into a tin can and conveyed along a string to another tin can, where they were reproduced as dim fuzzy sounds, most of the coherency lost due to the poor quality of the conductive material but the essential tone still perceptible. The current message on the psychic string could not be heard in any detail, but the primary meaning was clear: *Coming . . . I'm coming . . . I'm coming . . .*

Probably after midnight. Hatch sensed that their encounter would take place between that dead hour and dawn. It was now exactly 7:46 by his watch.

He withdrew his ring of car and house keys from his pocket, found the desk key that he had added earlier, opened the locked drawer, and took out the heat-darkened, smoke-scented issue of *Arts American,* letting the keys dangle in the lock. He held the magazine in both hands in the dark, hoping the feel of it would, like a talisman, amplify his magical vision and allow him to see precisely when, where, and how the killer would arrive.

Mingled odors of fire and destruction—some so bitterly pungent that they were nauseating, others merely ashy—rose from the crisp pages.

VASSAGO CLICKED OFF the fluorescent desk lamp. He crossed the girl's room to the door, where he also switched off the ceiling light.

He put his hand on the doorknob but hesitated, reluctant to leave the child behind him. She was so exquisite, so vital. He *knew* the moment he had pulled her into his arms that she was the caliber of acquisition that would complete his collection and win him the eternal reward he sought.

Stifling her cry and cutting off her breathing with one gloved hand, he had swept her into the closet and crushed her against him with his strong arms. He had held her so fiercely that she could barely squirm and couldn't kick against anything to draw attention to her plight.

When she had passed out in his arms, he had been almost in a swoon and had been overcome by the urge to kill her right there. In her closet. Among the soft piles of clothes that had fallen off the hangers above them. The scent of freshly laundered cotton and spray starch. The warm fragrance of wool. And girl. He wanted to wring her neck and feel her life energy pass through his powerful hands, into him, and through him to the land of the dead.

He had taken so long to shake off that overpowering desire that he almost *had* killed her. She fell silent and still. By the time he unclamped his hand from her nose and mouth, he thought he had smothered her. But when he put his ear to her parted lips, he could hear and feel faint exhalations. A hand against her chest rewarded him with the solid thud of her slow, strong heartbeat.

Now, looking back at the child, Vassago repressed the need to kill by promising himself that he would have satisfaction long before dawn. Meanwhile, he must be a Master. Exercise control.

Control.

He opened the door and studied the second-floor hallway beyond the girl's room. Deserted. A chandelier was aglow at the far end, at the head of the stairs, in front of the entrance to the master bedroom, producing too much light for his comfort if he had not had his sunglasses. He still needed to squint.

He must butcher neither the child nor the mother until he had both of them in the museum of the dead, where he had killed all the others who were part of his collection. He knew now why he had been drawn to Lindsey and Regina. Mother and daughter. Bitch and mini-bitch. To regain his place in Hell, he was expected to commit the same act that had won him damnation in the first place: the murder of a mother and her daughter. As his own mother and sister were not available to be killed again, Lindsey and Regina had been selected.

Standing in the open doorway, he listened to the house. It was silent.

He knew the artist was not the girl's birth mother. Earlier, when the Harrisons were in the dining room and he slipped into the house from the garage, he'd had time to poke around in Regina's room. He'd found mementoes with the orphanage name on them, for the most part cheaply printed drama programs handed out at holiday plays in which the girl had held minor roles. Nevertheless, he had been drawn to her and Lindsey, and his own master apparently judged them to be suitable sacrifices.

The house was so still that he would have to move as quietly as a cat. He could manage that.

He glanced back at the girl on the bed, able to see her better in the darkness than he could see most of the details of the too-bright hallway. She was still unconscious, one of her own scarves wadded in her mouth and another tied around her head to keep the gag in place. Strong lengths of cord, which he had untied from around storage boxes in the garage attic, tightly bound her wrists and ankles.

Control.

Leaving Regina's door open behind him, he eased along the hallway, staying close to the wall, where the plywood sub-flooring under the thick carpet was least likely to creak.

He knew the layout. He had cautiously explored the second floor while the Harrisons had been finishing dinner.

Beside the girl's room was a guest bedroom. It was dark now. He crept on toward Lindsey's studio.

Because the main hallway chandelier was directly ahead of him, his shadow fell in his wake, which was fortunate. Otherwise, if the woman happened to be looking toward the hall, she would have been warned of his approach.

He inched to the studio door and stopped.

Standing with his back flat to the wall, eyes straight ahead, he could see between the balusters under the handrail of the open staircase, to the foyer below. As far as he could tell, no lights were on downstairs.

He wondered where the husband had gone. The tall doors to the master bedroom were open, but no lights were on in there. He could hear small noises coming from within the woman's studio, so he figured she was at work. If the husband was with her, surely they would have exchanged a few words, at least, during the time Vassago had been making his way along the hall.

He hoped the husband had gone out on an errand. He had no particular need to kill the man. And any confrontation would be dangerous.

From his jacket pocket, he withdrew the supple leather sap, filled with lead shot, that he had appropriated last week from Morton Redlow, the detective. It was an extremely effective-looking blackjack. It felt good in his hand. In the pearl-gray Honda, two blocks away, a handgun was tucked under the driver's seat, and Vassago almost wished he had brought it. He had taken it from the antique dealer, Robert Loffman, in Laguna Beach a couple of hours before dawn that morning.

But he didn't want to shoot the woman and the girl. Even if he just wounded and disabled them, they might bleed to death before he got them back to his hideaway and down into the museum of death, to the altar where his offerings were arranged. And if he used a gun to remove the husband, he could risk only one shot, maybe two. Too much gunfire was bound to be heard by neighbors and the source located. In that quiet community, once gunfire was identified, cops would be crawling over the place in two minutes.

The sap was better. He hefted it in his right hand, getting the feel of it.

With great care, he leaned across the doorjamb. Tilted his head. Peeked into the studio.

She sat on the stool, her back to the door. He recognized her even from behind. His heart galloped almost as fast as when the girl had struggled and passed out in his arms. Lindsey was at the drawing board, charcoal pencil in her right hand. Busy, busy, busy. Pencil making a soft snaky hiss as it worked against the paper.

NO MATTER HOW determined she was to keep her attention firmly on the problem of the blank sheet of drawing paper, Lindsey looked up repeatedly at the window. Her creative block crumbled only when she surrendered and began to *draw* the window. The uncurtained frame. Darkness beyond the glass. Her face like the countenance of a ghost engaged in a haunting. When she added the spider web in the upper right-hand corner, the concept jelled, and suddenly she became excited. She thought she might title it *The Web of Life and Death,* and use a surreal series of symbolic items to knit the theme into every corner of the canvas. Not canvas, Masonite. In fact, just paper now, only a sketch, but worth pursuing.

She repositioned the drawing tablet on the board, setting it higher. Now she could just raise her eyes slightly from the page to look over the top of the board at the window, and didn't have to keep raising and lowering her head.

More elements than just her face, the window, and the web would be required to give the painting depth and interest. As she worked she considered and rejected a score of additional images.

Then an image appeared almost magically in the glass above her own reflection: the face that Hatch had described from nightmares. Pale. A shock of dark hair. The sunglasses.

For an instant she thought it was a supernatural event, an apparition in the glass. Even as her breath caught in her throat, however, she realized that she was seeing a reflection like her own and that the killer in Hatch's dreams was in their house, leaning around the doorway to look at her. She repressed an impulse to scream. As soon as he realized she had seen him, she would lose what little advantage she had, and he would be all over her, slashing at her, pounding on her, finishing her off before Hatch even got upstairs. Instead, she sighed loudly and shook her head as if displeased with what she was getting down on the drawing paper.

Hatch might already be dead.

She slowly put down her charcoal pencil, letting her fingers rest on it as if she might decide to pick it up again and go on.

If Hatch wasn't dead, how else could this bastard have gotten to the second floor? No. She couldn't think about Hatch being dead, or she would be dead herself, and then Regina. Dear God, Regina.

She reached toward the top drawer of the supply cabinet at her side, and a shiver went through her as she touched the cold chrome handle.

Reflecting the door behind her, the window showed the killer not just leaning around the jamb now, but stepping boldly into the open doorway. He paused arrogantly to stare at her, evidently relishing the moment. He was unnaturally quiet. If she had not seen his image in the glass, she would have had no awareness whatsoever of his presence.

She pulled open the drawer, felt the gun under her hand.

Behind her, he crossed the threshold.

She drew the pistol out of the drawer and swung around on her stool in one motion, bringing the heavy weapon up, clasping it in both hands, pointing it at him. She would not have been entirely surprised if he had not been there, and if her first impression of him only as an apparition in the windowpane had turned out to be correct. But he was there, all right, one step inside the door when she drew down on him with the Browning.

She said, "Don't move, you son of a bitch."

Whether he thought he saw weakness in her or whether he just didn't give a damn if she shot him or not, he backed out of the doorway and into the hall even as she swung toward him and told him not to move.

"Stop, damn it!"

He was gone. Lindsey would have shot him without hesitation, without moral compunction, but he moved so incredibly fast, like a cat springing for safety, that all she would have gotten was a piece of the doorjamb.

Shouting for Hatch, she was off the high stool and leaping for the door even as the last of the killer—a black shoe, his left foot—vanished out of the door frame. But she brought herself up short, realizing he might not have gone anywhere, might be waiting just to the side of the door, expecting her to come through in a panic, then step in behind her and pound her across the back of the head or push her into the stair railing and over and out and down onto the foyer floor. Regina. She couldn't delay. He might be going after Regina. A hesitation of only a second, then she crashed through her fear and through the open door, all this time shouting Hatch's name.

Looking to her right as she came into the hall, she saw the guy going for Regina's door, also open, at the far end. The room was dark beyond when there ought to have been lights, Regina studying. She didn't have time to stop and aim. Almost squeezed the trigger. Wanted to pump out bullets in the hope that one of them would nail the bastard. But Regina's room was so dark, and the girl could be anywhere. Lindsey was afraid that she would miss the killer and blow away the girl, bullets flying through the open door-way. So she held her fire and went after the guy, screaming Regina's name now instead of Hatch's.

He disappeared into the girl's room and threw the door shut behind him, a hell of a slam that shook the house. Lindsey hit that barrier a second later, bounced off it. Locked. She heard Hatch shouting her name—thank God, he was alive, he was alive—but she didn't stop or turn around to see where he was. She stepped back and kicked the door hard, then kicked it again. It was only a privacy latch, flimsy, it ought to pop open easily, but didn't.

She was going to kick it again, but the killer spoke to her through the door. His voice was raised but not a shout, menacing but cool, no panic in it, no fear, just businesslike and a little loud, terrifyingly smooth and calm: "Get away from the door, or I'll kill the little bitch."

JUST BEFORE LINDSEY began to shout his name, Hatch was sitting at the desk in the den, lights off, holding *Arts American* in both hands. A vision hit him with an electric sound, the crackle of a current jumping an arc, as if the magazine were a live power cable that he had gripped in his bare hands.

He saw Lindsey from behind, sitting on the high stool in her office, at the drawing board, working on a sketch. Then she was not Lindsey any more. Suddenly she was another woman, taller, also seen from behind but not on the stool, in an armchair in a different room in a strange house. She was knitting. A bright skein of yarn slowly unraveled from a retaining bowl on the small table beside her chair. Hatch thought of her as "mother," though she was nothing whatsoever like his mother. He looked down at his right hand, in which he held a knife, immense, already wet with blood. He approached her chair. She was unaware of him. As Hatch, he wanted to cry out and warn her. But as the user of the knife, through whose eyes he was seeing everything, he wanted only to savage her, tear the life out of her, and thereby complete the task that would free him. He stepped to the back of her armchair. She hadn't heard him yet. He raised the knife high. He struck. She screamed. He struck. She tried to get out of the chair. He moved around her, and from his point of view it was like a swooping shot in a movie meant to convey flight, the smooth glide of a bird or bat. He pushed her back into the chair, struck. She raised her hands to protect herself. He struck. He struck. And now, as if it was all a loop of film, he was behind her again, standing in the doorway, except she wasn't "mother" any more, she was Lindsey again, sitting at the drawing board in her upstairs studio, reaching to the top drawer of her supply cabinet and pulling it open. His gaze rose from her to the window. He saw himself—pale face, dark hair, sunglasses—and knew she had seen him. She spun around on the stool, a pistol coming up, the muzzle aimed straight at his chest—

"Hatch!"

His name, echoing through the house, shattered the link. He shot up from the desk chair, shuddering, and the magazine fell out of his hands.

"Hatch!"

Reaching out in the darkness, he unerringly found the handgrip of the Browning, and raced out of the den. As he crossed the foyer and climbed the stairs two at a time, looking up as he went, trying to see what was happening, he heard Lindsey stop shouting his name and start screaming "Regina!" Not the girl, Jesus, please, not the girl. Reaching the top of the stairs, he thought for an instant that the slamming door was a shot. But the sound was too distinct to be mistaken for gunfire, and as he looked back the hall he saw Lindsey bounce off the door to Regina's room with another crash. As he ran to join her, she kicked the door, kicked again, and then she stumbled back from it as he reached her.

"Lemme try," he said, pushing past her.

"No! He said back off or he'll kill her."

For a couple of seconds, Hatch stared at the door, literally shaking with frustration. Then he took hold of the knob, tried to turn it slowly. But it was locked, so he put the muzzle of the pistol against the base of the knob plate.

"Hatch," Lindsey said plaintively, "he'll kill her."

He thought of the young blonde taking two bullets in the chest, flying backward out of the car onto the freeway, tumbling, tumbling along the pavement into the fog. And the mother suffering the massive blade of the butcher knife as she dropped her knitting and struggled desperately for her life.

He said, "He'll kill her anyway, turn your face away," and he pulled the trigger.

Wood and thin metal dissolved into splinters. He grabbed the brass knob, it came off in his hand, and he threw it aside. When he shoved on the door, it creaked inward an inch but no farther. The cheap lock had disintegrated. But the shank on which the knob had been seated was still bristling from the wood, and something must have been wedged under the other knob on the inside. He pushed on the shank with the palm of his hand, but that didn't provide enough force to move it; whatever was wedged against the other side—most likely the girl's desk chair—was exerting upward pressure, thereby holding the shank in place.

Hatch gripped the Browning by its barrel and used the butt as a hammer. Cursing, he pounded the shank, driving it inch by inch back through the door.

Just as the shank flew free and clattered to the floor inside, a vivid series of images flooded through Hatch's mind, temporarily washing away the up-stairs hall. They were all from the killer's eyes: a weird angle, looking up at the side of a house, this house, the wall outside Regina's bedroom. The open window. Below the sill, a tangle of trumpet-vine runners. A hornlike flower in his face. Latticework under his hands, splinters digging into his skin. Clutching with one hand, searching with the other for a new place to grip, one foot dangling in space, a weight bearing down hard over his shoulder. Then a creaking, a splitting sound. A sudden sense of perilous looseness in the geometric web to which he clung—

Hatch was snapped back to reality by a brief, loud noise from beyond the door: clattering and splintering wood, nails popping loose with tortured screeches, scraping, a crash.

Then a new wave of psychic images and sensations flushed through him. Falling. Backward and out into the night. Not far, hitting the ground, a brief flash of pain. Rolling once on the grass. Beside him, a small huddled form, lying still. Scuttling to it, seeing the face. Regina. Eyes closed. A scarf tied across her mouth—

"Regina!" Lindsey cried.

When reality clicked into place once again, Hatch was already slamming his shoulder against the bedroom door. The brace on the other side fell away. The door shuddered open. He went inside, slapping the wall with one hand until he found the light switch. In the sudden glare, he stepped over the fallen desk chair and swung the Browning right, then left. The room was deserted, which he already knew from his vision.

At the open window he looked out at the collapsed trellis and tangled vines on the lawn below. There was no sign of the man in sunglasses or of Regina.

"Shit!" Hatch hurried back across the room, grabbing Lindsey, turning her around, pushing her through the door, into the hall, toward the head of the stairs. "You take the front, I'll take the back, he's got her, stop him, go, go." She didn't resist, picked up at once on what he was saying, and flew down the steps with him at her heels. "Shoot him, bring him down, aim for the legs, can't worry about hitting Regina, he's getting away!"

In the foyer Lindsey reached the front door even as Hatch was coming off the bottom step and turning toward the short hallway. He dashed into the family room, then into the kitchen, peering out the back windows of the house as he ran past them. The lawn and patios were well lighted, but he didn't see anyone out there.

He tore open the door between the kitchen and the garage, stepped through, switched on the lights. He raced across the three stalls, behind the cars, to the exterior door at the far end even before the last of the fluorescent tubes had stopped flickering and come all the way on.

He disengaged the dead-bolt lock, stepped out into the narrow side yard, and glanced to his right. No killer. No Regina. The front of the house lay in that direction, the street, more houses facing theirs from the other side. That was part of the territory Lindsey already was covering.

His heart knocked so hard, it seemed to drive each breath out of his lungs before he could get it all the way in.

She's only ten, only ten.

He turned left and ran along the side of the house, around the corner of the garage, into the backyard, where the fallen trellis and trumpet vines lay in a heap.

So small, a little thing. God, please.

Afraid of stepping on a nail and disabling himself, he skirted the debris and searched frantically along the perimeter of the property, plunging recklessly into the shrubbery, probing behind the tall eugenias.

No one was in the backyard.

He reached the side of the property farthest from the garage, almost slipped and fell as he skidded around the corner, but kept his balance. He thrust the Browning out in front of him with both hands, covering the walkway between the house and the fence. No one there, either.

He'd heard nothing from out front, certainly no gunfire, which meant Lindsey must be having no better luck than he was. If the killer had not gone that way, the only other thing he could have done was scale the fence on one side or another, escaping into someone else's property.

Turning away from the front of the house, Hatch surveyed the seven-foot-high fence that encircled the backyard, separating it from the abutting yards of the houses to the east, west, and south. Developers and Realtors called it a fence in southern California, although it was actually a wall, concrete blocks reinforced with steel and covered with stucco, capped with bricks, painted to match the houses. Most neighborhoods had them, guarantors of privacy at swimming pools or barbecues. Good fences make good neighbors, make strangers for neighbors—and make it damn easy for an intruder to scramble over a single barrier and vanish from one part of the maze into another.

Hatch was on an emotional wire-walk across a chasm of despair, his balance sustained only by the hope that the killer couldn't move fast with Regina in his arms or over his shoulder. He looked east, west, south, frozen by indecision.

Finally he started toward the back wall, which was on their southern flank. He halted, gasping and bending forward, when the mysterious connection between him and the man in sunglasses was re-established.

Again Hatch saw through the other man's eyes, and in spite of the sunglasses the night seemed more like late twilight. He was in a car, behind the steering wheel, leaning across the console to adjust the unconscious girl in the passenger seat as if she were a mannequin. Her wrists were lashed together in her lap, and she was held in place by the safety harness. After arranging her auburn hair to cover the scarf that crossed the back of her head, he pushed her against the door, so she slumped with her face turned away from the side window. People in passing cars would not be able to see the gag in her mouth. She appeared to be sleeping. Indeed she was so pale and still, he suddenly wondered if she was dead. No point in taking her to his hideaway if she was already dead. Might as well open the door and push her out, dump the little bitch right there. He put his hand against her cheek. Her skin was wonderfully smooth but seemed cool. Pressing his fingertips to her throat, he detected her heartbeat in a carotid artery, thumping strongly, so strongly. She was so *alive,* even more vital than she had seemed in the vision with the butterfly flitting around her head. He had never before made an acquisition of such value, and he was grateful to all the powers of Hell for giving her to him. He thrilled at the prospect of reaching deep within and clasping that strong young heart as it twitched and thudded into final stillness, all the while staring into her beautiful gray eyes to watch life pass out of her and death enter—

Hatch's cry of rage, anguish, and terror broke the psychic connection. He was in his backyard again, holding his right hand up in front of his face, staring at it in horror, as if Regina's blood already stained his trembling fingers.

He turned away from the back fence, and sprinted along the east side of the house, toward the front.

But for his own hard breathing, all was quiet. Evidently some of the neighbors weren't home. Others hadn't heard anything, or at least not enough to bring them outside.

The serenity of the community made him want to scream with frustration. Even as his own world was falling apart, however, he realized the appearance of normality was exactly that—merely an *appearance,* not a reality. God knew what might be happening behind the walls of some of those houses, horrors equal to the one that had overcome him and Lindsey and Regina, perpetrated not by an intruder but by one member of a family upon another. The human species possessed a knack for creating monsters, and the beasts themselves often had a talent for hiding away behind convincing masks of sanity.

When Hatch reached the front lawn, Lindsey was nowhere to be seen. He hurried to the walkway, through the open door—and discovered her in the den, where she was standing beside the desk, making a phone call.

"You find her?" she asked.

"No. What're you doing?"

"Calling the police."

Taking the receiver out of her hand, dropping it onto the phone, he said,

"By the time they get here, listen to our story, and start to *do* something, he'll be gone, he'll have Regina so far away they'll never find her—until they stumble across her body someday."

"But we need help—"

Snatching the shotgun off the desk and pushing it into her hands, he said, "We're going to follow the bastard. He's got her in a car. A Honda, I think."

"You have a license number?"

"No."

"Did you see if—"

"I didn't actually *see* anything," he said, jerking open the desk drawer, plucking out the box of 12-gauge ammunition, handing that to her as well, desperately aware of the seconds ticking away. "I'm connecting with him, it flickers in and out, but I think the link is good enough, strong enough." He pulled his ring of keys from the desk lock, in which he had left them dangling when he had taken the magazine from the drawer. "We can stay on his ass if we don't let him get too far ahead of us." Hurrying into the foyer, he said, "But we have to *move*."

"Hatch, wait!"

He stopped and swiveled to face her as she followed him out of the den.

She said, "You go, follow them if you think you can, and I'll stay here to talk to the cops, get them started—"

Shaking his head, he said, "No. I need you to drive. These . . . these visions are like being punched, I sort of black out, I'm disoriented while it's happening. There's no way I won't run the car right off the damn road. Put the shotgun and the shells in the Mitsubishi." Climbing the stairs two at a time, he shouted back to her: "And get flashlights."

"Why?"

"I don't know, but we'll need them."

He was lying. He had been somewhat surprised to hear himself ask for flashlights, but he knew his subconscious was driving him at the moment, and he had a hunch why flashlights were going to be essential. In his nightmares over the past couple of months, he had often moved through cavernous rooms and a maze of concrete corridors that were somehow revealed in spite of having no windows or artificial lighting. One tunnel in particular, sloping down into perfect blackness, into something unknown, filled him with such dread that his heart swelled and pounded as if it would burst. *That* was why they needed flashlights—because they were going where he had previously been only in dreams or in visions, into the heart of the nightmare.

He was all the way upstairs and entering Regina's room before he realized that he didn't know why he had gone there. Stopping just inside the threshold, he looked down at the broken doorknob and the overturned desk chair, then at the closet where clothes had fallen off the hangers and were lying in a pile, then at the open window where the night breeze had begun to stir the draperies.

Something . . . something important. Right here, right now, in this room, something he needed.

But what?

He switched the Browning to his left hand, wiped the damp palm of his right hand against his jeans. By now the son of a bitch in the sunglasses had started the car and was on his way out of the neighborhood with Regina, probably on Crown Valley Parkway already. Every second counted.

Although he was beginning to wonder if he had flown upstairs in a panic rather than because there was anything he really needed, Hatch decided to trust the compulsion a little further. He went to the corner desk and let his gaze travel over the books, pencils, and a notebook. The bookcase next to the desk. One of Lindsey's paintings on the wall beside it.

Come on, come on. Something he needed . . . needed as badly as the flashlights, as badly as the shotgun and the box of shells. Something.

He turned, saw the crucifix, and went straight for it. He scrambled onto Regina's bed and wrenched the cross from the wall behind it.

Off the bed and on the floor again, heading out of the room and along the hall toward the stairs, he gripped the icon tightly, fisted his right hand around it. He realized he was holding it as if it were not an object of religious symbolism and veneration but a weapon, a hatchet or cleaver.

By the time he got to the garage, the big sectional door was rolling up. Lindsey had started the car.

When Hatch got in the passenger's side, Lindsey looked at the crucifix. "What's that for?"

"We'll need it."

Backing out of the garage, she said, "Need it for what?"

"I don't know."

As the car rolled into the street, she looked at Hatch curiously. "A crucifix?"

"I don't know, but maybe it'll be useful. When I linked with him he was . . . he felt thankful to all the powers of Hell, that's how it went through his mind, thankful to all the powers of Hell for giving Regina to him." He pointed left. "That way."

Fear had aged Lindsey a few years in the past ten minutes. Now the lines in her face grew deeper still as she threw the car in gear and turned left. "Hatch, what are we dealing with here, one of those Satanists, those crazies, guys in these cults you read about in the paper, when they catch one of them, they find severed heads in the refrigerator, bones buried under the front porch?"

"Yeah, maybe, something like that." At the intersection he said, "Left here. Maybe something like that . . . but worse, I think."

"We can't handle this, Hatch."

"The hell we can't," he said sharply. "There's no time for anybody else to handle it. If we don't, Regina's dead."

They came to an intersection with Crown Valley Parkway, which was a wide four- to six-lane boulevard with a garden strip and trees planted down the center. The hour was not yet late, and the parkway was busy, though not crowded.

"Which way?" Lindsey asked.

Hatch put his Browning on the floor. He did not let go of the crucifix. He held it in both hands. He looked left and right, left and right, waiting for a feeling, a sign, something. The headlights of passing cars washed over them but brought no revelations.

"Hatch?" Lindsey said worriedly.

Left and right, left and right. Nothing. Jesus.

Hatch thought about Regina. Auburn hair. Gray eyes. Her right hand curled and twisted like a claw, a gift from God. No, not from God. Not this time. Can't blame them all on God. She might have been right: a gift from her parents, drug-users' legacy.

A car pulled up behind them, waiting to get out onto the main street.

The way she walked, determined to minimize the limp. The way she never concealed her deformed hand, neither ashamed nor proud of it, just accepting. Going to be a writer. Intelligent pigs from outer space.

The driver waiting behind them blew his horn.

"Hatch?"

Regina, so small under the weight of the world, yet always standing straight, her head never bowed. Made a deal with God. In return for something precious to her, a promise to eat beans. And Hatch knew what the precious thing was, though she had never said it, knew it was a family, a chance to escape the orphanage.

The other driver blew his horn again.

Lindsey was shaking. She started to cry.

A chance. Just a chance. All the girl wanted. Not to be alone any more. A chance to sleep in a bed painted with flowers. A chance to love, be loved, grow up. The small curled hand. The small sweet smile. *Goodnight . . . Dad.*

The driver behind them blew his horn insistently.

"Right," Hatch said abruptly. "Go right."

With a sob of relief, Lindsey turned right onto the parkway. She drove faster than she usually did, changing lanes as traffic required, crossing the south-county flatlands toward the distant foothills and the night-shrouded mountains in the east.

At first Hatch was not sure that he had done more than guess at what direction to take. But soon conviction came to him. The boulevard led east between endless tracts of houses that speckled the hills with lights as if they were thousands of memorial flames on the tiers of immense votive-candle racks, and with each mile he sensed more strongly that he and Lindsey were following in the wake of the beast.

Because he had agreed there would be no more secrets between them, because he thought she should know—and could handle—a full understanding of the extremity of Regina's circumstances, Hatch said, "What he wants to do is hold her beating heart in his bare hand for its last few beats, feel the life go out of it."

"Oh, God."

"She's still alive. She has a chance. There's hope."

He believed what he said was true, had to believe it or go mad. But he was troubled by the memory of having said those same things so often in the weeks before cancer had finally finished with Jimmy.

Death is no fearsome mystery.
He is well known to thee
and me.
He hath no secrets he can keep
to trouble any good
man's sleep.

Turn not thy face from
Death away.
Care not he takes our
breath away.
Fear him not, he's not
thy master,
rushing at thee faster, faster.
Not thy master but servant to
the Maker of thee, what
or Who
created Death, created thee
—and is the only mystery.

THE BOOK OF COUNTED SORROWS

❱ ❱ ❱

Part Three

Down among the Dead

Seven

1 Jonas Nyebern and Kari Dovell sat in armchairs before the big windows in the darkened living room of his house on Spyglass Hill, looking at the millions of lights that glimmered across Orange and Los Angeles counties. The night was relatively clear, and they could see as far as Long Beach Harbor to the north. Civilization sprawled like a luminescent fungus, devouring all.

A bottle of Robert Mondavi chenin blanc was in an ice bucket on the floor between their chairs. It was their second bottle. They had not eaten dinner yet. He was talking too much.

They had been seeing each other socially once or twice a week for more than a month. They had not gone to bed together, and he didn't think they ever would. She was still desirable, with that odd combination of grace and awkwardness that sometimes reminded him of an exotic long-legged crane, even if the side of her that was a serious and dedicated physician could never quite let the woman in her have full rein. However, he doubted she even expected physical intimacy. In any case, he didn't believe he was capable of it. He was a haunted man; too many ghosts waited to bedevil him if happiness came within his reach. What each of them got from the relationship was a friendly ear, patience, and genuine sympathy without maudlin excess.

That evening he talked about Jeremy, which was not a subject conducive to romance even if there had been any prospect of it. Mostly he worried over the signs of Jeremy's congenital madness that he'd failed to realize—or admit—were signs.

Even as a child Jeremy had been unusually quiet, invariably preferring solitude to anyone's company. That was explained away as simple shyness. From the earliest age he seemed to have no interest in toys, which was written off to his indisputably high intelligence and a too-serious nature. But now all those untouched model airplanes and games and balls and elaborate Erector sets were disquieting indications that his interior fantasy life had been richer than any entertainment that could be provided by Tonka, Mattel, or Lionel.

"He was never able to receive a hug without stiffening a little," Jonas remembered. "When he returned a kiss for a kiss, he always planted his lips on the air instead of your cheek."

"Lots of kids have difficulty being demonstrative," Kari insisted. She lifted the wine bottle from the ice, leaned out, and refilled the glass he held. "It would seem like just another aspect of his shyness. Shyness and self-effacement aren't faults, and you couldn't be expected to see them that way."

"But it wasn't self-effacement," he said miserably. "It was an inability to feel, to care."

"You can't keep beating yourself up like this, Jonas."

"What if Marion and Stephanie weren't even the first?"

"They must have been."

"But what if they weren't?"

"A teenage boy might be a killer, but he's not going to have the sophistication to get away with murder for any length of time."

"What if he's killed someone since he slipped away from the rehab hospital?"

"He's probably been victimized himself, Jonas."

"No. He's not the victim type."

"He's probably dead."

"He's out there somewhere. Because of me."

Jonas stared at the vast panorama of lights. Civilization lay in all its glimmering wonder, all its blazing glory, all its bright terror.

AS THEY APPROACHED the San Diego Freeway, Interstate 405, Hatch said, "South. He's gone south."

Lindsey flipped on the turn signal and caught the entrance ramp just in time.

At first she had glanced at Hatch whenever she could take her eyes off the road, expecting him to tell her what he was seeing or receiving from the man they were trailing. But after a while she focused on the highway whether she needed to or not, because he was sharing nothing with her. She suspected his silence simply meant he was seeing very little, that the link between him and the killer was either weak or flickering on and off. She didn't press him to include her, because she was afraid that if she distracted him, the bond might be broken altogether—and Regina lost.

Hatch continued to hold the crucifix. Even from the corner of her eye, Lindsey could see how the fingertips of his left hand ceaselessly traced the contours of the cast-metal figure suffering upon the faux dogwood cross. His gaze seemed to be turned inward, as if he were virtually unaware of the night and the car in which he traveled.

Lindsey realized that her life had become as surreal as any of her paintings. Supernatural experiences were juxtaposed with the familiar mundane world. Disparate elements filled the composition: crucifixes and guns, psychic visions and flashlights.

In her paintings, she used surrealism to elucidate a theme, provide insight. In real life, each intrusion of the surreal only further confused and mystified her.

Hatch shuddered and leaned forward as far as the safety harness would allow, as if he had seen something fantastic and frightening cross the highway, though she knew he was not actually looking at the blacktop ahead. He slumped back into his seat. "He's taken the Ortega Highway exit. East. The same exit's coming up for us in a couple of miles. East on the Ortega Highway."

SOMETIMES THE HEADLIGHTS of oncoming cars forced him to squint in spite of the protection provided by his heavily tinted glasses.

As he drove, Vassago periodically glanced at the unconscious girl in the seat beside him, facing him. Her chin rested on her breast. Though her head was tipped down and auburn hair hung over one side of her face, he could see her lips pulled back by the scarf that held in the gag, the tilt of her pixie nose, all of one closed eyelid and most of the other—such long lashes—and part of her smooth brow. His imagination played with all the possible ways he might disfigure her to produce the most effective offering.

She was perfect for his purposes. With her beauty compromised by her leg and deformed hand, she was already a symbol of God's fallibility. A trophy, indeed, for his collection.

He was disappointed that he had failed to get the mother, but he had not given up hope of acquiring her. He was toying with the idea of not killing the child tonight. If he kept her alive for only a few days, he might have an opportunity to make another bid for Lindsey. If he had them together, able to work on them at the same time, he could present their corpses as a mocking version of Michelangelo's *Pietà*, or dismember them and stitch them together in a highly imaginative obscene collage.

He was waiting for guidance, another vision, before deciding what to do.

As he took the Ortega Highway off-ramp and turned east, he recalled how Lindsey, at the drawing board in her studio, had reminded him of his mother at her knitting on the afternoon when he had killed her. Having disposed of his sister and mother with the same knife in the same hour, he had known in his heart that he had paved the way to Hell, had been so convinced that he had taken the final step and impaled himself.

A privately published book had described for him that route to damnation. Titled *The Hidden,* it was the work of a condemned murderer named Thomas Nicene who had killed his own mother and a brother, and then committed suicide. His carefully planned descent into the Pit had been foiled by a paramedic team with too much dedication and a little luck. Nicene was revived, healed, imprisoned, put on trial, convicted of murder, and sentenced to death. Rule-playing society had made it clear that the power of death, even the right to choose one's own, was not ever to be given to an individual.

While awaiting execution, Thomas Nicene had committed to paper the visions of Hell that he had experienced during the time that he had been on the edge of this life, before the paramedics denied him eternity. His writings had been smuggled out of prison to fellow believers who could print and distribute them. Nicene's book was filled with powerful, convincing images of darkness and cold, not the heat of classic hells, but visions of a kingdom of vast spaces, chilling emptiness. Peering through Death's door and the door of Hell beyond, Thomas had seen titanic powers at work on mysterious structures. Demons of colossal size and strength strode through night mists across lightless continents on unknown missions, each clothed in black with a flowing cape and upon its head a shining black helmet with a flared rim. He had seen dark seas crashing on black shores under starless and moonless skies that gave the feeling of a subterranean world. Enormous ships, windowless and mysterious, were driven through the tenebrous waves by powerful engines that produced a noise like the anguished screams of multitudes.

When he had read Nicene's words, Jeremy had known they were truer than any ever inked upon a page, and he had determined to follow the great man's example. Marion and Stephanie became his tickets to the exotic and enormously attractive netherworld where he belonged. He had punched those tickets with a butcher knife and delivered himself to that dark kingdom, encountering precisely what Nicene promised. He had never imagined that his own escape from the hateful world of the living would be undone not by paramedics but by his own father.

He would soon earn repatriation to the damned.

Glancing at the girl again, Vassago remembered how she had felt when she shuddered and collapsed limply in his fierce embrace. A shiver of delicious anticipation whidded through him.

He had considered killing his father to learn if that act would win him back his citizenship in Hades. But he was wary of his old man. Jonas Nyebern was a life-giver and seemed to shine with an inner light that Vassago found forbidding. His earliest memories of his father were wrapped up in images of Christ and angels and the Holy Mother and miracles, scenes from the paintings that Jonas collected and with which their home had always been decorated. And only two years ago, his father had resurrected him in the manner of Jesus raising cold Lazarus. Consequently, he thought of Jonas not merely as the enemy but as a figure of power, an embodiment of those bright forces that were opposed to the will of Hell. His father was no doubt protected, untouchable, living in the loathsome grace of that *other* deity.

His hopes, then, were pinned on the woman and the girl. One acquisition made, the other pending.

He drove east past endless tracts of houses that had sprung up in the six years since Fantasy World had been abandoned, and he was grateful that the spawning multitudes of life-loving hypocrites had not pressed to the very perimeter of his special hideaway, which still lay miles beyond the last of the new communities. As the peopled hills passed by, as the land grew steadily less hospitable though still inhabited, Vassago drove more slowly than he would have done any other night.

He was waiting for a vision that would tell him if he should kill the child upon arrival at the park or wait until the mother was his, as well.

Turning his head to look at her once more, he discovered she was watching him. Her eyes shone with the reflected light from the instrument panel. He could see that her fear was great.

"Poor baby," he said. "Don't be afraid. Okay? Don't be afraid. We're just going to an amusement park, that's all. You know, like Disneyland, like Magic Mountain?"

If he was unable to acquire the mother, perhaps he should look for another child about the same size as Regina, a particularly pretty one with four strong, healthy limbs. He could then remake this girl with the arm, hand, and leg of the other, as if to say that he, a mere twenty-year-old expatriate of Hell, could do a better job than the Creator. That would make a fine addition to his collection, a singular work of art.

He listened to the contained thunder of the engine. The hum of the tires on the pavement. The soft whistle of wind at the windows.

Waiting for an epiphany. Waiting for guidance. Waiting to be told what he should do. Waiting, waiting, a vision to behold.

EVEN BEFORE THEY reached the Ortega Highway off-ramp, Hatch received a flurry of images stranger than anything he had seen before. None lasted longer than a few seconds, as if he were watching a film with no narrative structure. Dark seas crashing on black shores under starless and moonless skies. Enormous ships, windowless and mysterious, driven through the ten-ebrous waves by powerful engines that produced a noise like the anguished screams of multitudes. Colossal demonic figures, a hundred feet tall, striding alien landscapes, black capes flowing behind them, heads encased in black helmets as shiny as glass. Titanic, half-glimpsed machines at work on mon-umental structures of such odd design that purpose and function could not even be guessed.

Sometimes Hatch saw that hideous landscape in chillingly vivid detail, but sometimes he saw only descriptions of it in words on the printed pages of a book. If it existed, it must be on some far world, for it was not of this earth. But he was never sure if he was receiving pictures of a real place or one that was merely imagined. At times it seemed as vividly depicted as any street in Laguna but at other times seemed tissue-paper thin.

JONAS RETURNED TO the living room with the box of items he had saved from Jeremy's room, and put it down beside his armchair. He withdrew from the box a small, shoddily printed volume titled *The Hidden* and gave it to Kari, who examined it as if he had handed her an object encrusted with filth.

"You're right to wrinkle your nose at it," he said, picking up his glass of wine and moving to the large window. "It's nonsense. Sick and twisted but nonsense. The author was a convicted killer who claimed to have seen Hell. His description isn't like anything in Dante, let me tell you. Oh, it possesses a certain romance, undeniable power. In fact, if you were a psychotic young man with delusions of grandeur and a bent for violence, with the unnaturally high testosterone levels that usually accompany a mental condition like that, then the Hell he describes would be your ultimate wet dream of power. You would swoon over it. You might not be able to get it out of your mind. You might *long* for it, do anything to be a part of it, achieve damnation."

Kari put the book down and wiped her fingertips on the sleeve of her blouse. "This author, Thomas Nicene—you said he killed his mother."

"Yes. Mother and brother. Set the example." Jonas knew he had already drunk too much. He took another long sip of his wine anyway. Turning from the night view, he said, "And you know what makes it all so absurd, pathetically absurd? If you read that damn book, which I did afterward, trying to understand, and if you're not psychotic and disposed to believe it, you'll see right away that Nicene isn't reporting what he saw in Hell. He's taking his inspiration from a source as stupidly obvious as it is stupidly ridiculous. Kari, his Hell is nothing more than the Evil Empire in the *Star Wars* movies, somewhat changed, expanded upon, filmed through the lens of religious myth, but still *Star Wars*." A bitter laugh escaped him. He chased it with more wine. "His demons are nothing more than hundred-foot-tall versions of Darth Vader, for God's sake. Read his description of Satan and then go look at whichever film Jabba the Hut was a part of. Old Jabba the Hut is a ringer for Satan, if you believe this lunatic." One more glass of Chenin Blanc, one more glass. "Marion and Stephanie died—" A sip. Too long a sip. Half the glass gone. "—died so Jeremy could get into Hell and have great, dark, antiheroic adventures in a fucking Darth Vader costume."

He had offended or unsettled her, probably both. That had not been his intention, and he regretted it. He wasn't sure what his intention had been. Maybe just to unburden himself. He had never done so before, and he didn't know why he'd chosen to do so tonight—except that Morton Redlow's disappearance had scared him more than anything since the day he had found the bodies of his wife and daughter.

Instead of pouring more wine for herself, Kari rose from her armchair. "I think we should get something to eat."

"Not hungry," he said, and heard the slur of the inebriate in his voice. "Well, maybe we should have something."

"We could go out somewhere," she said, taking the wine glass from his hand and putting it on the nearest end table. Her face was quite lovely in the ambient light that came through the view windows, the golden radiance from the web of cities below. "Or call for pizza."

"How about steaks? I've got some filets in the freezer."

"That'll take too long."

"Sure won't. Just thaw 'em out in the microwave, throw 'em on the grill. There's a big Gaggenau grill in the kitchen."

"Well, if that's what you'd like."

He met her eyes. Her gaze was as clear, penetrating, and forthright as ever, but Jonas saw a greater tenderness in her eyes than before. He supposed it was the same concern she had for her young patients, part of what made her a first-rate pediatrician. Maybe that tenderness had always been there for him, too, and he had just not seen it until now. Or perhaps this was the first time she realized how desperately he needed nurturing.

"Thank you, Kari."

"For what?"

"For being you," he said. He put his arm around her shoulders as he walked her to the kitchen.

MIXED WITH THE visions of gargantuan machines and dark seas and colossal demonic figures, Hatch received an array of images of other types. Choiring angels. The Holy Mother in prayer. Christ with the Apostles at the Last Supper, Christ in Gethsemane, Christ in agony upon the cross, Christ ascending.

He recognized them as paintings Jonas Nyebern might have collected at one time or another. They were different periods and styles from those he had seen in the physician's office, but in the same spirit. A connection was made, a braiding of wires in his subconscious, but he didn't understand what it meant yet.

And more visions: the Ortega Highway. Glimpses of the nightscapes unrolling on both sides of an eastward-bound car. Instruments on a dashboard. Oncoming headlights that sometimes made him squint. And suddenly Regina. Regina in the backsplash of yellow light from that same instrument panel. Eyes closed. Head tipped forward. Something wadded in her mouth and held in place by a scarf.

She opens her eyes.

Looking into Regina's terrified eyes, Hatch broke from the visions like an underwater swimmer breaking for air. "She's alive!"

He looked at Lindsey, who shifted her gaze from the highway to him. "But you never said she wasn't."

Until then he did not realize how little faith he'd had in the girl's continued existence.

Before he could take heart from the sight of her gray eyes gleaming in the yellow dashboard light of the killer's car, Hatch was hit by new clairvoyant visions that pummeled him as hard as a series of blows from real fists:

Contorted figures loomed out of murky shadows. Human forms in bizarre positions. He saw a woman as withered and dry as tumbleweed, another in a repugnant state of putrefaction, a mummified face of indeterminate sex, a bloated green-black hand raised in horrid supplication. The collection. His collection. He saw Regina's face again, eyes open, revealed in the dashboard lights. So many ways to disfigure, to mutilate, to mock God's work. Regina. *Poor baby. Don't be afraid. Okay? Don't be afraid. We're only going to an amusement park. You know, like Disneyland, like Magic Mountain?* How nicely will she fit in my collection. Corpses as performance art, held in place by wires, rebar, blocks of wood. He saw frozen screams, silent forever. Skeletal jaws held open in eternal cries for mercy. The precious collection. Regina, sweet baby, pretty baby, such an exquisite acquisition.

Hatch came out of his trance, clawing wildly at his safety harness, for it felt like binding wires, ropes, and cords. He tore at the straps as a panicked victim of premature burial might rip at his enwrapping shrouds. He realized that he was shouting, too, and sucking breath as if in fear of suffocation, letting it out at once in great explosive exhalations. He heard Lindsey saying his name, understood that he was terrifying her, but could not cease thrashing or crying out for long seconds, until he had found the release on the safety harness and cast it off.

With that, he was fully back in the Mitsubishi, contact with the madman broken for the moment, the horror of the collection diminished though not forgotten, not in the least forgotten. He turned to Lindsey, remembering her fortitude in the icy waters of that mountain river the night that she had saved him. She would need all of that strength and more tonight.

"Fantasy World," he said urgently, "where they had the fire years ago, abandoned now, that's where he's going. Jesus Christ, Lindsey, drive like you've never driven in your life, put the pedal to the floor, the son of a bitch, the crazy rotten son of a bitch is taking her down among the dead!''

And they were flying. Though she could have no idea what he meant, they were suddenly flying eastward faster than was safe on that highway, through the last clusters of closely spaced lights, out of civilization into ever darker realms.

WHILE KARI SEARCHED the refrigerator in the kitchen for the makings of a salad, Jonas went to the garage to liberate a couple of steaks from the chest-style freezer. The garage vents brought in the coolish night air, which he found refreshing. He stood for a moment just inside the door from the house, taking slow deep breaths to clear his head a little.

He had no appetite for anything except perhaps more wine, but he did not want Kari to see him drunk. Besides, though he had no surgery scheduled for the following day, he never knew what emergency might require the skills of the resuscitation team, and he felt a responsibility to those potential patients.

In his darkest hours, he sometimes considered leaving the field of resuscitation medicine to concentrate on cardiovascular surgery. When he saw a reanimated patient return to a useful life of work and family and service, he knew a reward sweeter than most other men could ever know. But in the moment of crisis, when the candidate for resuscitation lay on the table, Jonas rarely knew anything about him, which meant he might sometimes bring evil back into the world once the world had shed it. That was more than a moral dilemma to him; it was a crushing weight upon his conscience. Thus far, being a religious man—though with his share of doubts—he had trusted in God to guide him. He had decided that God had given him his brain and his skills to use, and it was not his place to out-guess God and withhold his services from any patient.

Jeremy, of course, was an unsettling new factor in the equation. If he had brought Jeremy back, and if Jeremy had killed innocent people . . . It did not bear thinking about.

The cool air no longer seemed refreshing. It seeped into the hollows of his spine.

Okay, dinner. Two steaks. Filet mignon. Lightly grilled, with a little Worcestershire sauce. Salads with no dressing but a squirt of lemon and a sprinkle of black pepper. Maybe he *did* have an appetite. He didn't eat much red meat; it was a rare treat. He was a heart surgeon, after all, and saw firsthand the gruesome effects of a high-fat diet.

He went to the freezer in the corner. He pushed the latch-release and put up the lid.

Within lay Morton Redlow, late of the Redlow Detective Agency, pale and gray as if carved from marble but not yet obscured by a layer of frost. A smear of blood had frozen into a brittle crust on his face, and there was a terrible vacancy where his nose had been. His eyes were open. Forever.

Jonas did not recoil. As a surgeon, he was equally familiar with the horrors and wonders of biology, and he was not easily repulsed. Something in him withered when he saw Redlow. Something in him died. His heart turned as cold as that of the detective before him. In some fundamental way, he knew that he was finished as a man. He didn't trust God any more. Not any more. What God? But he was not nauseated or forced to turn away in disgust.

He saw the folded note clutched in Redlow's stiff right hand. The dead man let go of it easily, for his fingers had contracted during the freezing process, shrinking away from the paper around which the killer had pressed them.

Numbly, he unfolded the letter and immediately recognized his son's neat penmanship. The post-coma aphasia had been faked. His retardation was an immensely clever ruse.

The note said, *Dear Daddy: For a proper burial, they'll need to know where to find his nose. Look up his back end. He stuck it in my business, so I stuck it in his. If he'd had any manners, I would have treated him better. I'm sorry, sir, if this behavior distresses you.*

LINDSEY DROVE WITH utmost urgency, pushing the Mitsubishi to its limits, finding every planning flaw in a highway not always designed for speed. There was little traffic as they moved deeper into the east, which stacked the odds in their favor when once she crossed the center line in the middle of a too-tight turn.

Having snapped on his safety harness again, Hatch used the car phone to get Jonas Nyebern's office number from information, then to call the number itself, which was answered at once by a physician's-service operator. She took his message, which baffled her. Although the operator seemed sincere in her promise to pass it on to the doctor, Hatch was not confident that his definition of "immediately" and hers were materially the same.

He saw all the connections so clearly now, but he knew he could not have seen them sooner. Jonas's question in the office on Monday took on a new significance: Did Hatch, he asked, believe that evil was only the result of the acts of men, or did he think that evil was a real force, a presence that walked the world? The story Jonas had told of losing wife and daughter to a homicidal, psychopathic son, and the son himself to suicide, connected now to the vision of the woman knitting. The father's collections. And the son's. The Satanic aspects to the visions were what one might expect from a bad son in mindless rebellion against a father to whom religion was a center post of life. And finally—he and Jeremy Nyebern shared one obvious link, miraculous resurrection at the hands of the same man.

"But how does that explain anything?" Lindsey demanded, when he told her only a little more than he had told the physician's-service operator.

"I don't know."

He couldn't think about anything except what he had seen in those last visions, less than half of which he understood. The part he *had* comprehended, the nature of Jeremy's collection, filled him with fear for Regina.

Without having seen the collection as Hatch had seen it, Lindsey was fixated, instead, on the mystery of the link, which was somewhat explained—yet not explained at all—by learning the identity of the killer in sunglasses. "What about the visions? How do they fit the damned composition?" she insisted, trying to make sense of the supernatural in perhaps not too different a way from that in which she made sense of the world by reducing it to ordered images on Masonite.

"I don't know," he said.

"The link that's letting you follow him—"

"I don't know."

She took a turn too wide. The car went off the pavement, onto the gravel shoulder. The back end slid, gravel spraying out from beneath the tires and rattling against the undercarriage. The guardrail flashed close, too close, and the car was shaken by the hard bang-bang-bang of sheet metal taking a beating. She seemed to bring it back under control by a sheer effort of will, biting her lower lip so hard it appeared as if she would draw blood.

Although Hatch was aware of Lindsey and the car and the reckless pace they were keeping along that sometimes dangerously curved highway, he could not turn his mind from the outrage he had seen in the vision. The longer he thought about Regina being added to that grisly collection, the more his fear was augmented by anger. It was the hot, uncontainable anger he had seen so often in his father, but directed now against something deserving of hatred, against a target worthy of such seething rage.

AS HE APPROACHED the entrance road to the abandoned park, Vassago glanced away from the now lonely highway, to the girl who was bound and gagged in the other seat. Even in that poor light he could see that she had been straining at her bonds. Her wrists were chafed and beginning to bleed. Little Regina had hopes of breaking free, striking out or escaping, though her situation was so clearly hopeless. Such vitality. She thrilled him.

The child was so special that he might not need the mother at all, if he could think of a way to place her in his collection that would result in a piece of art with all the power of the various mother-daughter tableaux that he had already conceived.

He had been unconcerned with speed. Now, after he turned off the highway onto the park's long approach road, he accelerated, eager to return to the museum of the dead with the hope that the atmosphere there would inspire him.

Years ago, the four-lane entrance had been bordered by lush flowers, shrubbery, and groupings of palms. The trees and larger shrubs had been dug up, potted, and hauled away ages ago by agents of the creditors. The flowers had died and turned to dust when the landscape watering system had been shut off.

Southern California was a desert, transformed by the hand of man, and when the hand of man moved on, the desert reclaimed its rightful territory. So much for the genius of humanity, God's imperfect creatures. The pavement had cracked and hoved from years of inattention, and in places it had begun to vanish under drifts of sandy soil. His headlights revealed tumbleweed and scraps of other desert brush, already brown hardly six weeks after the end of the rainy season, chased westward by a night wind that came out of the parched hills.

When he reached the tollbooths he slowed down. They stretched across all four lanes. They had been left standing as a barrier to easy exploration of the shuttered park, linked and closed off by chains so heavy that simple bolt cutters could not sever them. Now the bays, once overseen by attendants, were filled with tangled brush that the wind had put there and trash deposited by vandals. He pulled around the booths, bouncing over a low curb and traveling on the sun-hardened soil of the planting beds where lush tropical landscaping would once have blocked the way, then back to the pavement when he had bypassed the barrier.

At the end of the entrance road, he switched off his headlights. He didn't need them, and he was at last beyond the notice of any highway patrolmen who might pull him over for driving without lights. His eyes immediately felt more comfortable, and now if his pursuers drew too close, they would not be able to follow him by sight alone.

He angled across the immense and eerily empty parking lot. He was heading toward a service road at the southwest corner of the inner fence that circumscribed the grounds of the park proper.

As the Honda jolted over the pot-holed blacktop, Vassago ransacked his imagination, which was a busy abattoir of psychotic industry, seeking solutions for the artistic problems presented by the child. He conceived and rejected concept after concept. The image must stir him. Excite him. If it was really art, he would know it; he would be moved.

As Vassago lovingly envisioned tortures for Regina, he became aware of that other strange presence in the night and its singular rage. Suddenly he was plunged into another psychic vision, a flurry of familiar elements, with one crucial new addition: he got a glimpse of Lindsey behind the wheel of a car . . . a car phone in a man's trembling hand . . . and then the object that instantly resolved his artistic dilemma . . . a crucifix. The nailed and tortured body of Christ in its famous posture of noble self-sacrifice.

He blinked away that image, glanced at the petrified girl in the car with him, blinked her away as well, and in his imagination saw the two combined—girl and cruciform. He would use Regina to mock the Crucifixion. Yes, lovely, perfect. But not raised upon a cross of dogwood. Instead, she must be executed upon the segmented belly of the Serpent, under the bosom of the thirty-foot Lucifer in the deepest regions of the funhouse, crucified and her sacred heart revealed, as backdrop to the rest of his collection. Such a cruel and stunning use of her negated the need to include her mother, for in such a pose she would alone be his crowning achievement.

HATCH WAS FRANTICALLY trying to contact the Orange County Sheriff's Department on the cellular car phone, which was having transmission problems, when he felt the intrusion of another mind. He "saw" images of Regina disfigured in a multitude of ways, and he began to shake with rage. Then he was struck by a vision of a crucifixion; it was so powerful, vivid, and monstrous that it almost rendered him unconscious as effectively as a skull-cracking blow from a hard-swung hammer.

He urged Lindsey to drive faster, without explaining what he had seen. He couldn't speak of it.

The terror was amplified by Hatch's perfect understanding of the statement Jeremy intended to make by the perpetration of the outrage. Was God in error to have made His Only Begotten Child a man? Should Christ have been a woman? Were not women those who had suffered the most and therefore served as the greatest symbol of self-sacrifice, grace, and transcendence? God had granted women a special sensitivity, a talent for understanding and tenderness, for caring and nurturing—then had dumped them into a world of savage violence in which their singular qualities made them easy targets for the cruel and depraved.

Horror enough existed in that truth, but a greater horror, for Hatch, lay in the discovery that anyone as insane as Jeremy Nyebern could have such a complex insight. If a homicidal sociopath could perceive such a truth and grasp its theological implications, then creation itself must be an asylum. For surely, if the universe were a rational place, no madman would be able to understand any portion of it.

Lindsey reached the approach road to Fantasy World and took the turn so fast and sharp that the Mitsubishi slid sideways and felt, for a moment, as if it would roll. But it remained upright. She pulled hard on the wheel, brought it around, tramped on the accelerator.

Not Regina. No way was Jeremy going to be permitted to realize his decadent vision with that lamb of innocence. Hatch was prepared to die to prevent it.

Fear and fury flooded him in equal torrents. The plastic casing of the cellular-phone handset creaked in his right fist as though the pressure of his grip would crack it as easily as if it had been an eggshell.

Tollbooths appeared ahead. Lindsey braked indecisively, then seemed to notice the tire tracks through the drifting, sandy earth at the same time Hatch saw them. She whipped the car to the right, and it bounced over the concrete border of what had once been a flower bed.

He had to rein in his rage, not succumb to it as his father had always done, for if he didn't remain in control of himself, Regina was as good as dead. He tried to place the emergency 911 call again. Tried to hold fast to his reason. He must not descend to the level of the walking filth through whose eyes he had seen the bound wrists and frightened eyes of his child.

THE SURGE OF rage pouring back across the telepathic wire excited Vassago, pumped up his own hatred, and convinced him that he must not wait until both the woman and the child were within his grasp. Even the prospect of the single crucifixion brought him such a richness of loathing and revulsion that he knew his artistic concept was of sufficient power. Once realized through the flesh of the gray-eyed girl, his art would reopen the doors of Hell to him.

He had to stop the Honda at the entrance to the service road, which appeared to be blocked by a padlocked gate. He had broken the massive padlock long ago. It only hung through the hasp with the appearance of effectiveness. He got out of the car, opened the gate, drove through, got out again and closed it.

Behind the wheel once more, he decided not to leave the Honda in the underground garage or go to the museum of the dead through the cata- combs. No time. God's slow but persistent paladins were closing in on him. He had so much to do, so much, in so few precious minutes. It wasn't fair. He needed time. Every artist needed *time*. To save a few minutes, he was going to have to drive along the wide pedestrian walkways, between the rotting and empty pavilions, and park in front of the funhouse, take the girl across the dry lagoon and in by way of the gondola doors, through the tunnel with the chain-drive track still in the concrete floor and down into Hell by that more direct route.

WHILE HATCH WAS on the phone with the sheriff's department, Lindsey drove into the parking lot. The tall lamp poles shed no light. Vistas of empty blacktop faded away in every direction. Straight ahead a few hundred yards stood the once glittery but now dark and decaying castle through which the paying customers had entered Fantasy World. She saw no sign of Jeremy Nyebern's car, and not enough dust on the acres of unprotected, windswept pavement to track him by his tire prints.

She drove as close to the castle as she could get, halted by a long row of ticket booths and crowd-control stanchions of poured concrete. They looked like massive barricades erected on a heavily defended beach to prevent enemy tanks from being put ashore.

When Hatch slammed down the handset, Lindsey was not sure what to make of his end of the conversation, which had alternated between pleading and angry insistence. She didn't know whether the cops were coming or not, but her sense of urgency was so great, she didn't want to take time to ask him about it. She just wanted to move, move. She threw the car into park the moment it braked to a full stop, didn't even bother to switch off the engine or the headlights. She liked the headlights, a little something against the cloying night. She flung open her door, ready to go in on foot. But he shook his head, no, and picked up his Browning from the floor at his feet.

"What?" she demanded.

"He went in by car somehow, somewhere. I think I'll find the creep quicker if we stay on his trail, go in the way he went in, let myself open to this bond between us. Besides, the place is so damned huge, we'll get around it faster in a car."

She got behind the wheel again, popped the Mitsubishi into gear, and said, *"Where?"*

He hesitated only a second, perhaps a fraction of a second, but it seemed that any number of small helpless girls could have been slaughtered in that interlude before he said, "Left, go left, along the fence."

2   Vassago parked the car by the lagoon, cut the engine, got out, and went around to the girl's side. Opening her door, he said, "Here we are, angel. An amusement park, just like I promised you. Isn't it fun? Aren't you amused?"

He swung her around on her seat to bring her legs out of the car. He took his switchblade from his jacket pocket, snapped the well-honed knife out of the handle, and showed it to her.

Even with the thinnest crescent moon, and although her eyes were not as sensitive as his, she saw the blade. He saw her see it, and he was thrilled by the quickening of terror in her face and eyes.

"I'm going to free your legs so you can walk," he told her, turning the blade slowly, slowly, so a quicksilver glimmer trickled liquidly along the cutting edge. "If you're stupid enough to kick me, if you think you can catch my head maybe and knock me silly long enough to get away, then *you're* silly, angel. It won't work, and then I'll have to cut you to teach you a lesson. Do you hear me, precious? Do you understand?"

She emitted a muffled sound through the wadded scarf in her mouth, and the tone of it was an acknowledgement of his power.

"Good," he said. "Good girl. So wise. You'll make a fine Jesus, won't you? A really fine little Jesus."

He cut the cords binding her ankles, then helped her out of the car. She was unsteady, probably because her muscles had cramped during the trip, but he did not intend to let her dawdle. Seizing her by one arm, leaving her wrists bound in front of her and the gag in place, he pulled her around the front of the car to the retaining wall of the funhouse lagoon.

THE RETAINING WALL was two feet high on the outside, twice that on the inside where the water once had been. He helped Regina over it, onto the dry concrete floor of the broad lagoon. She hated to let him touch her, even though he still wore gloves, because she could feel his coldness through the gloves, or thought she could, his coldness and damp skin, which made her want to scream. She knew already that she couldn't scream, not with the gag filling her mouth. If she tried to scream she only choked on it and had trouble breathing, so she had to let him help her over the wall. Even when he didn't touch her bare hand with his gloved one, even when he gripped her arm and there was also her sweater between them, the contact made her belly quiver so badly that she thought she was going to vomit, but she fought that urge because, with the gag in her mouth, she would choke to death on her own regurgitation.

Through ten years of adversity, Regina had developed lots of tricks to get her through bad times. There was the think-of-something-worse trick, where she endured by imagining what more terrible circumstances might befall her than those in which she actually found herself. Like thinking of eating dead mice dipped in chocolate when she felt sorry for herself about having to eat lime Jell-O with peaches. Like thinking about being blind on top of her other disabilities. After the awful shock of being rejected during her first trial adoption with the Dotterfields, she had often spent hours with her eyes closed to show herself what she *might* have suffered if her eyes had been as faulty as her right arm. But the think-of-something-worse trick wasn't working now because she couldn't think of anything worse than being where she was, with this stranger dressed all in black and wearing sunglasses at night, calling her "baby" and "precious." None of her other tricks were working, either.

As he pulled her impatiently across the lagoon, she dragged her right leg as if she could not move fast. She needed to slow him down to gain time to think, to find some new trick.

But she was just a kid, and tricks didn't come that easy, not even to a smart kid like her, not even to a kid who had spent ten years devising so many clever tricks to make everyone think that she could take care of herself, that she was tough, that she would never cry. But her trick bag was finally empty, and she was more afraid than she had ever been.

He dragged her past big boats like the gondolas in Venice of which she had seen pictures, but these had dragon prows from Viking ships. With the stranger pulling impatiently on her arm, she limped past a fearful snarling serpent's head bigger than she was.

Dead leaves and moldering papers had blown down into the empty pool. In the nocturnal breeze, which occasionally gusted heartily, that trash eddied around them with the hiss-splash of a ghost sea.

"Come on, precious one," he said in his honey-smooth but unkind voice, "I want you to walk to your Golgotha just as He did. Don't you think that's fitting? Is that so much to ask? Hmmm? I'm not also insisting that you carry your own cross, am I? What do you say, precious, will you *move your ass?*"

She was scared, with no fine tricks left to hide the fact, no tricks left to hold back her tears, either. She began to shake and cry, and her right leg grew weak for real, so she could hardly remain standing let alone move as fast as he demanded.

In the past, she would have turned to God at a moment like this, would have talked to Him, talked and talked, because no one had talked to God more often or more bluntly than she had done from the time she was just little. But she had been talking to God in the car, and she had not heard Him listening. Over the years, all their conversations had been one-sided, yes, but she had always heard Him listening, at least, a hint of His great slow steady breathing. But now she knew He couldn't be listening because if He was there, hearing how desperate she was, He would not have failed to answer her this time. He was gone, and she didn't know where, and she was alone as she had never been.

When she was so overcome by tears and weakness that she could not walk at all, the stranger scooped her up. He was very strong. She was unable to resist, but she didn't hold on to him, either. She just curled her arms against her chest, made small fists of her hands, and pulled away within herself.

"Let me carry my little Jesus," he said, "my sweet little lamb, it will be my privilege to carry you." There was no warmth in his voice in spite of the way he was talking. Only hatred and scorn. She knew that tone, had heard it before. No matter how hard you tried to fit in and be everybody's friend, some kids hated you if you were too different, and in their voices you heard this same thing, and shrank from it.

He carried her through the open, broken, rotting doors into a darkness that made her feel so small.

LINDSEY DIDN'T EVEN bother getting out of the car to see if the gate could be opened. When Hatch pointed the way, she jammed the accelerator to the floor. The car bucked, shot forward. They crashed onto the grounds of the park, demolishing the gate and sustaining more damage to their already battered car, including one shattered headlight.

At Hatch's direction, she followed a service loop around half the park. On the left was a high fence covered with the gnarled and bristling remnants of a vine that once might have concealed the chainlink entirely but had died when the irrigation system had been shut off. On the right were the backs of rides that had been too permanently constructed to be dismantled easily. There were also buildings fronted by fantastic facades held up by angled supports that could be seen from behind.

Leaving the service road, they drove between two structures and onto what had once been a winding promenade along which crowds had moved throughout the park. The largest Ferris wheel she had ever seen, savaged by wind and sun and years of neglect, rose in the night like the bones of a leviathan picked clean by unknown carrion-eaters.

A car was parked beside what appeared to be a drained pool in front of an immense structure.

"The funhouse," Hatch said, for he had seen it before through other eyes.

It had a roof with multiple peaks like a three-ring circus tent, and disintegrating stucco walls. She could view only one narrow aspect of the structure at a time, as the headlights swept across it, but she did not like any part of what she saw. She was not by nature a superstitious person—although she was fast becoming one in response to recent experience—but she sensed an aura of death around the funhouse as surely as she could have felt cold air rising off a block of ice.

She parked behind the other car. A Honda. Its occupants had departed in such a hurry that both front doors were open, and the interior lights were on.

Snatching up her Browning and a flashlight, she got out of the Mitsubishi and ran to the Honda, looked inside. No sign of Regina.

She had discovered there was a point at which fear could grow no greater. Every nerve was raw. The brain could not process more input, so it merely sustained the peak of terror once achieved. Each new shock, each new terrible thought did not add to the burden of fear because the brain just dumped old data to make way for the new. She could hardly remember anything of what had happened at the house, or the surreal drive to the park; most of it was gone for now, only a few scraps of memory remaining, leaving her focused on the immediate moment.

On the ground at her feet, visible in the spill of light from the open car door and then in her flashlight beam, was a four-foot length of sturdy cord. She picked it up and saw that it had once been tied in a loop and later cut at the knot.

Hatch took the cord out of her hand. "It was around Regina's ankles. He wanted her to walk."

"Where are they now?"

He pointed with his flashlight across the drained lagoon, past the three large gray canted gondolas with prodigious mastheads, to a pair of wooden doors in the base of the funhouse. One sagged on broken hinges, and the other was open wide. The flashlight was a four-battery model, just strong enough to cast some dim light on those far doors but not to penetrate the terrible darkness beyond.

Lindsey took off around the car and scrambled over the lagoon wall. Though Hatch called out, "Lindsey, wait," she could not delay another moment—and how could he?—with the thought of Regina in the hands of Nyebern's resurrected, psychotic son.

As Lindsey crossed the lagoon, fear for Regina still far outweighed any concern she might have for her own safety. However, realizing that she, herself, must survive if the girl were to have any chance at all, she swept the flashlight beam side to side, side to side, wary of an attack from behind one of the huge gondolas.

Old leaves and paper trash danced in the wind, for the most part waltzing across the floor of the dry lagoon, but sometimes spinning up in columns and churning to a faster beat. Nothing else moved.

Hatch caught up with her by the time she reached the funhouse entrance. He had delayed only to use the cord she had found to bind his flashlight to the back of the crucifix. Now he could carry both in one hand, pointing the head of Christ at anything upon which he directed the light. That left his right hand free for the Browning 9mm. He had left the Mossberg behind. If he had tied the flashlight to the 12-gauge, he could have brought both the handgun and the shotgun. Evidently he felt that the crucifix was a better weapon than the Mossberg.

She didn't know why he had taken the icon from the wall of Regina's room. She didn't think he knew, either. They were wading hip deep in the big muddy river of the unknown, and in addition to the cross, she would have welcomed a necklace of garlic, a vial of holy water, a few silver bullets, and anything else that might have helped.

As an artist, she had always known that the world of the five senses, solid and secure, was not the *whole* of existence, and she had incorporated that understanding into her work. Now she was merely incorporating it into the rest of her life, surprised that she had not done so a long time ago.

With both flashlights carving through the darkness in front of them, they entered the funhouse.

ALL OF REGINA'S tricks for coping were not exhausted, after all. She invented one more.

She found a room deep inside her mind, where she could go and close the door and be safe, a place only she knew about, in which she could never be found. It was a pretty room with peach-colored walls, soft lighting, and a bed covered with painted flowers. Once she had entered, the door could only be opened again from her side. There were no windows. Once she was in that most secret of all retreats, it didn't matter what was done to the other her, the physical Regina in the hateful world outside. The *real* Regina was safe in her hideaway, beyond fear and pain, beyond tears and doubt and sadness. She could hear nothing beyond the room, most especially not the wickedly soft voice of the man in black. She could see nothing beyond the room, only the peach walls and her painted bed and soft light, never darkness. Nothing beyond the room could really touch her, certainly not his pale quick hands which had recently shed their gloves.

Most important, the only smell in her sanctuary was the scent of roses like those painted on the bed, a clean sweet fragrance. Never the stench of dead things. Never the awful choking odor of decomposition that could bring a sour gushing into the back of your throat and nearly strangle you when your mouth was full of crushed, saliva-damp scarf. Nothing like that, no, never, not in her secret room, her blessed room, her deep and sacred, safe and solitary haven.

SOMETHING HAD HAPPENED to the girl. The singular vitality that had made her so appealing was gone.

When he put her on the floor of Hell, with her back against the base of the towering Lucifer, he thought she'd passed out. But that wasn't it. For one thing, when he crouched in front of her and put his hand against her chest, he felt her heart leaping like a rabbit whose hindquarters were already in the jaws of the fox. No one could possibly be unconscious with a thundering heartbeat like that.

Besides, her eyes were open. They were staring blindly, as if she could find nothing upon which to fix her gaze. Of course, she could not see him in the dark as he could see her, couldn't see anything else for that matter, but that wasn't the reason she was staring through him. When he flicked the eyelash over her right eye with his fingertip, she did not flinch, did not even blink. Tears were drying on her cheeks, but no new tears welled up.

Catatonic. The little bitch had blanked out on him, closed her mind down, become a vegetable. That didn't suit his purposes at all. The value of the offering was in the vitality of the subject. Art was about energy, vibrancy, pain, and terror. What statement could he make with his little gray-eyed Christ if she could not experience and express her agony?

He was so angry with her, just so spitting angry, that he didn't want to play with her any more. Keeping one hand on her chest, above her rabbity heart, he took his switchblade from his jacket pocket and popped it open.

Control.

He would have opened her then, and had the intense pleasure of feeling her heart go still in his grip, except that he was a Master of the Game who knew the meaning and value of control. He could deny himself such transitory thrills in the pursuit of more meaningful and enduring rewards. He hesitated only a moment before putting the knife away.

He was better than that.

His lapse surprised him.

Perhaps she would come out of her trance by the time he was ready to incorporate her into his collection. If not, then he felt sure that the first driven nail would bring her to her senses and transform her into the radiant work of art that he knew she had the potential to be.

He turned from her to the tools that were piled at the point where the arc of his collection currently ended. He possessed hammers and screwdrivers, wrenches and pliers, saws and a miter box, a battery-powered drill with an array of bits, screws and nails, rope and wire, brackets of all kinds, and everything else a handyman might need, all of it purchased at Sears when he had realized that properly arranging and displaying each piece in his collection would require the construction of some clever supports and, in a couple of cases, thematic backdrops. His chosen medium was not as easy to work with as oil paints or watercolors or clay or sculptor's granite, for gravity tended to quickly distort each effect that he achieved.

He knew he was short on time, that on his heels were those who did not understand his art and would make the amusement park impossible for him by morning. But that would not matter if he made one more addition to the collection that rounded it out and earned him the approbation he sought.

Haste, then.

The first thing to do, before hauling the girl to her feet and bracing her in a standing position, was to see if the material that composed the segmented, reptilian belly and chest of the funhouse Lucifer would take a nail. It seemed to be a hard rubber, perhaps soft plastic. Depending on thickness, brittleness, and resiliency of the material, a nail would either drive into it as smoothly as into wood, bounce off, or bend. If the fake devil's hide proved too resistant, he'd have to use the battery-powered drill instead of the hammer, two-inch screws instead of nails, but it shouldn't detract from the artistic integrity of the piece to lend a modern touch to the reenactment of this ancient ritual.

He hefted the hammer. He placed the nail. The first blow drove it a quarter of the way into Lucifer's abdomen. The second blow slammed it halfway home.

So nails would work just fine.

He looked down at the girl, who still sat on the floor with her back against the base of the statue. She had not reacted to either of the hammer blows.

He was disappointed but not yet despairing.

Before lifting her into place, he quickly collected everything he would need. A couple of two-by-fours to serve as braces until the acquisition was firmly fixed in place. Two nails. Plus one longer and more wickedly pointed number that could fairly be called a spike. The hammer, of course. Hurry. Smaller nails, barely more than tacks, a score of which could be placed just-so in her brow to represent the crown of thorns. The switchblade, with which to recreate the spear wound attributed to the taunting Centurion. Anything else? Think. Quickly now. He had no vinegar or sponge to soak it in, therefore could not offer that traditional drink to the dying lips, but he didn't think the absence of that detail would in any way detract from the composition.

He was ready.

HATCH AND LINDSEY were deep in the gondola tunnel, proceeding as fast as they dared, but slowed by the need to shine flashlights into the deepest reaches of each niche and room-size display area that opened off the flanking walls. The moving beams caused black shadows to fly and dance off concrete stalactites and stalagmites and other manmade rock formations, but all of those dangerous spaces were empty.

Two solid thuds, like hammer blows, echoed to them from farther in the funhouse, one immediately after the other. Then silence.

"He's ahead of us somewhere," Lindsey whispered, "not real close. We can move faster."

Hatch agreed.

They proceeded along the tunnel without scanning all the deep recesses, which once had held clockwork monsters. Along the way, the bond between Hatch and Jeremy Nyebern was established again. He sensed the madman's excitement, an obscene and palpitating need. He received, as well, disconnected images: nails, a spike, a hammer, two lengths of two-by-four, a scattering of tacks, the slender steel blade of a knife popping out of its spring-loaded handle. . . .

His anger escalating with his fear, determined not to let the disorienting visions impede his advance, he reached the end of the horizontal tunnel and stumbled a few steps down the incline before he realized that the angle of the floor had changed radically under his feet.

The first of the odor hit him. Drifting upward on a natural draft. He gagged, heard Lindsey do the same, then tightened his throat and swallowed hard.

He knew what lay below. At least some of it. Glimpses of the collection had been among the visions that had pounded him when he had been in the car on the highway. If he didn't get an iron grip on himself and stifle his repulsion now, he would never make it all the way into the depths of this hellhole, and he had to go there in order to save Regina.

Apparently Lindsey understood, for she found the will to repress her retching, and she followed him down the steep slope.

THE FIRST THING to attract Vassago's attention was the glow of light high up toward one end of the cavern, far back in the tunnel that led to the spillway. The rapid rate at which the light grew brighter convinced him that he would not have time to add the girl to his collection before the intruders were upon him.

He knew who they were. He had seen them in visions as they, evidently, had seen him. Lindsey and her husband had followed him all the way from Laguna Niguel. He was just beginning to recognize that more forces were at work in this affair than had appeared to be the case at first.

He considered letting them descend the spillway into Hell, slipping behind them, killing the man, disabling the woman, and then proceeding with a *dual* crucifixion. But there was something about the husband that unsettled him. He couldn't put his finger on it.

But he realized now that, in spite of his bravado, he had been avoiding a confrontation with the husband. In their house earlier in the night, when the element of surprise had still been his, he should have circled behind the husband and disposed of him first, before going after either Regina or Lindsey. Had he done so, he might have been able to acquire both woman and child at that time. By now he might have been happily engrossed in their mutilation.

Far above, the pearly glow of light had resolved into a pair of flashlight beams at the brink of the spillway. After a brief hesitation, they started down. Because he had put his sunglasses in his shirt pocket, Vassago was forced to squint at the slashing swords of light.

As before, he decided not to move against the man, choosing instead to retreat with the child. This time, however, he wondered at his prudence.

A Master of the Game, he thought, must exhibit iron control and choose the right moments to prove his power and superiority.

True. But this time the thought struck him as spineless justification for avoiding confrontation.

Nonsense. He was afraid of nothing in this world.

The flashlights were still a considerable distance away, focused on the floor of the spillway, not yet to the midpoint of the long incline. He could hear their footsteps, which grew louder and developed an echo as the pair advanced into the huge chamber.

He seized the catatonic girl, lifted her as if she weighed no more than a pillow, slung her over his shoulder, and moved soundlessly across the floor of Hell toward those rock formations where he knew a door to a service room was hidden.

"OH, MY GOD. Don't look," he told Lindsey as he swept the beam of his flashlight across the macabre collection. "Don't look, Jesus, cover my back, make sure he's not coming around on us."

Gratefully, she did as he said, turning away from the array of posed cadavers in various stages of decomposition. She was certain that her sleep, even if she lived to be a hundred, would be haunted every night by those forms and faces. But who was she kidding—she would never make a hundred. She was beginning to think she wouldn't even make it through the night.

The very idea of breathing *that* air, reeking and impure, through her mouth was almost enough to make her violently ill. She did it anyway because it minimized the stink.

The darkness was so deep. The flashlight seemed barely able to penetrate. It was like syrup, flowing back into the brief channel that the beam stirred through it.

She could hear Hatch moving along the collection of bodies, and she knew what he had to be doing—taking a quick look at each of them, just to be sure that Jeremy Nyebern was not posed among them, one living monstrosity among those consumed by rot, waiting to spring at them the moment they passed him.

Where was Regina?

Ceaselessly, Lindsey swept her flashlight back and forth, back and forth, in a wide arc, never giving the murderous bastard a chance to sneak up on her before she brought the beam around again. But, oh, he was fast. She had seen how fast. Flying down the hallway into Regina's room, slamming the door behind him, fast as if he'd flown, had wings, bat wings. And agile. Down the trumpet-vine trellis with the girl over his shoulder, unfazed by the fall, up and off into the night with her.

Where was Regina?

She heard Hatch moving away, and she knew where he was going, not just following the line of bodies but circling the towering figure of Satan, to be sure Jeremy Nyebern wasn't on the other side of it. He was just doing what he had to do. She knew that, but she didn't like it anyway, not one little bit, because now she was alone with all of those dead people behind her. Some of them were withered and would make papery sounds if somehow they became animated and edged toward her, while others were in more horrendous stages of decomposition and sure to reveal their approach with thick, wet sounds. . . . And what crazy thoughts were these? They were all *dead*. Nothing to fear from them. The dead stayed dead. Except they didn't always, did they? No, not in her own personal experience, they didn't. But she kept sweeping her light back and forth, back and forth, resisting the urge to turn around and shine it on the festering cadavers behind her. She knew she should mourn them rather than fear them, be angry for the abuse and loss of dignity that they had suffered, but she only had room at the moment for fear. And now she heard Hatch coming closer, around the other side of the statue, completing his circumnavigation, thank God. But in the next breath, horribly metallic as it passed through her mouth, she wondered if it was Hatch or one of the bodies moving. Or Jeremy. She swung around, looking past the row of corpses rather than at them, and her light showed her that it was, indeed, Hatch coming back.

Where was Regina?

As if in answer, a distinctive creak sliced through the heavy air. Doors the world over made that identical sound when their hinges were corroded and unoiled.

She and Hatch swung their flashlights in the same direction. The overlapping terminuses of their beams showed they had both judged the origin of the sound to have come from a rock formation along the far shore of what would have been, with water, a lake larger than the lagoon outside.

She was moving before she realized it. Hatch whispered her name in an urgent tone that meant *move aside, let me, I'll go first*. But she could no more have held back than she could have turned coward and retreated up the spillway. Her Regina had been among the dead, perhaps spared the direct sight of them because of her strange keeper's aversion to light, but among them nevertheless and surely aware of them. Lindsey could not *bear* the thought of that innocent child held in this slaughterhouse one minute longer. Lindsey's own safety didn't matter, only Regina's.

As she reached the rocks and plunged in among them, stabbing here with her light, then there, then over there, shadows leaping, she heard the wail of distant sirens. Sheriff's men. Hatch's phone call had been taken seriously. But Regina was in the hands of Death. If the girl was still alive, she would not last as long as it would take the cops to find the funhouse and get down to the lair of Lucifer. So Lindsey pressed deeper into the rocks, the Browning in one hand, flashlight in the other, turning corners recklessly, taking chances, with Hatch close behind her.

She came upon the door abruptly. Metal, streaked with rust, operated by a push-bar rather than a knob. Ajar.

She shoved it open and went through without even the finesse that she should have learned from a lifetime of police movies and television shows. She exploded across the threshold as might a mother lion in pursuit of the predator that had dared to drag off her cub. Stupid, she knew that it was stupid, that she could get herself killed, but mother lions in a fever of matriarchal aggression were not notably creatures of reason. She was operating on instinct now, and instinct told her that they had the bastard on the run, had to keep him running to prevent him from dealing with the girl as he wanted, and should press him harder and harder until they had him in a corner.

Beyond the door in the rocks, behind the walls of Hell, was a twenty-foot-wide area that had once been crowded with machinery. It was now littered with the bolts and steel plates on which those machines had been mounted. Elaborate scaffolding, festooned with spider webs, rose forty or fifty feet; it provided access to other doors and crawlspaces and panels through which the complex lighting and effects equipment—cold-steam generators, lasers—had been serviced. That stuff was gone now, stripped out and carted away.

How long did he need to cut the girl open, seize her beating heart, and take his satisfaction from her death? One minute? Two? Perhaps no more than that. To keep her safe, they had to breathe down his goddamned neck.

Lindsey swept her flashlight beam across that spider-infested conglomeration of steel pipes and elbow joints and tread plates. She quickly decided their quarry had not ascended to any hiding place above.

Hatch was at her side and slightly behind her, staying close. They were breathing hard, not because they had exerted themselves but because their chests were tight with fear, constricting their lungs.

Turning left, Lindsey moved straight toward a dark opening in the concrete-block wall on the far side of that twenty-foot-wide chamber. She was drawn to it because it appeared to have been boarded over at one time, not solidly but with enough planks to prevent anyone entering the forbidden space beyond without effort. Some of the nails still prickled the block walls on both sides of the opening, but all of the planks had been torn away and shoved to one side on the floor.

Although Hatch whispered her name, warning her to hold back, she stepped straight to the brink of that room, shone her light into it, and discovered it was not a room at all but an elevator shaft. The doors, cab, cables, and mechanism had been salvaged, leaving a hole in the building as sure as an extracted tooth left a hole in the jaw.

She pointed her light up. The shaft rose three stories, having once conveyed mechanics and other repairmen to the top of the funhouse. She swung the beam slowly down the concrete wall from above, noticing the iron rungs of the service ladder.

Hatch stepped in beside her as the light found its way to the bottom of the shaft, just two floors below, where it revealed some litter, a Styrofoam ice chest, several empty cans of root beer, and a plastic garbage bag nearly full of trash, all arranged around a stained and battered mattress.

On the mattress, huddled in a corner of the shaft, was Jeremy Nyebern. Regina was in his lap, held against his chest, so she could shield him against gunfire. He was holding a pistol, and he squeezed off two shots even as Lindsey spotted him down there.

The first slug missed both her and Hatch, but the second round tore through her shoulder. She was knocked against the door frame. On the rebound, she bent forward involuntarily, lost her balance, and fell into the shaft, following her flashlight, which she had already dropped.

Going down, she didn't believe it was happening. Even when she hit bottom, landing on her left side, the whole thing seemed unreal, maybe because she was still too numb from the impact of the bullet to feel the damage it had done, and maybe because she fell mostly on the mattress, at the far end of it from Nyebern, knocking out what wind the slug had left in her but breaking no bones.

Her flashlight had also landed on the mattress, unharmed. It lit one gray wall.

As if in a dream, and though unable to get her breath quite yet, Lindsey brought her right hand slowly around to point her gun at him. But she had no gun. The Browning had spun from her grip in the fall.

During Lindsey's drop, Nyebern must have tracked her with his own weapon, for she was looking into it. The barrel was impossibly long, measuring exactly one eternity from firing chamber to muzzle.

Beyond the gun she saw Regina's face, which was as slack as her gray eyes were empty, and beyond that beloved countenance was the hateful one, pale as milk. His eyes, unshielded by glasses, were fierce and strange. She could see them even though the glow of the flashlight forced him to squint. Meeting his gaze she felt that she was face-to-face with something alien that was only passing as human, and not well.

Oh, wow, surreal, she thought, and knew that she was on the verge of passing out.

She hoped to faint before he squeezed the trigger. Though it didn't matter, really. She was so close to the gun that she wouldn't live to hear the shot that blew her face off.

HATCH'S HORROR, AS he watched Lindsey fall into the shaft, was exceeded by his surprise at what he did next.

When he saw Jeremy track her with the pistol until she hit the mattress, the muzzle three feet from her face, Hatch tossed his own Browning away, onto the pile of planks that once boarded off the shaft. He figured he wouldn't be able to get off a clear shot with Regina in the way. And he knew that no gun would properly dispatch the thing that Jeremy had become. He had no time to wonder at *that* curious thought, for as soon as he pitched away the Browning, he shifted the crucifix-flashlight from his left hand to his right, and leaped into the elevator shaft without any expectation that he was about to do so.

After that, everything got weird.

It seemed to him that he didn't crash down the shaft as he should have done, but glided in slow motion, as if he were only slightly heavier than air, taking as much as half a minute to reach bottom.

Perhaps his sense of time had merely been distorted by the profundity of his terror.

Jeremy saw him coming, shifted the pistol from Lindsey to Hatch, and fired all eight remaining rounds. Hatch was certain that he was hit at least three or four times, though he sustained no wounds. It seemed impossible that the killer could miss so often in such a confined space.

Perhaps the sloppy marksmanship was attributable to the gunman's panic and to the fact that Hatch was a moving target.

While he was still floating down like dandelion fluff, he experienced a reconnection of the peculiar bond between him and Nyebern, and for a moment he saw himself descending from the young killer's point of view. What he glimpsed, however, was not only himself but the image of some-one—or something—superimposed over him, as if he shared his body with another entity. He thought he saw white wings folded close against his sides. Under his own face was that of a stranger—the visage of a warrior if ever there had been one, yet not a face that frightened him.

Perhaps by then Nyebern was hallucinating, and what Hatch was receiving from him was not actually what he saw but only what he imagined that he saw. Perhaps.

Then Hatch was gazing down from his own eyes again, still in that slow glide, and he was sure that he saw something superimposed over Jeremy Nyebern, too, a form and face that were part reptilian and part insectile.

Perhaps it was a trick of light, the confusion of shadows and conflicting flashlight beams.

He could not explain away their final exchange, however, and he dwelt upon it often in the days that followed:

"Who are you?" Nyebern asked as Hatch landed catlike in spite of a thirty-foot descent.

"Uriel," Hatch replied, though that was not a name he had heard before.

"I am Vassago," Nyebern said.

"I know," Hatch said, though he was hearing that name for the first time, as well.

"Only you can send me back."

"And when you get sent back by such as me," Hatch said, wondering where the words came from, "you don't go back a prince. You'll be a slave below, just like the heartless and stupid boy with whom you hitched a ride."

Nyebern was afraid. It was the first time he had shown any capacity for fear. "And I thought *I* was the spider."

With strength, agility, and economy of motion that Hatch had not known he possessed, he grabbed Regina's belt in his left hand, pulled her away from Jeremy Nyebern, set her aside out of harm's way, and brought the crucifix down like a club upon the madman's head. The lens of the attached flashlight shattered, and the casing burst open, spilling batteries. He chopped the crucifix hard against the killer's skull a second time, and with the third blow he sent Nyebern to a grave that had been twice earned.

The anger Hatch felt was righteous anger. When he dropped the crucifix, when it was all over, he felt no guilt or shame. He was nothing at all like his father.

He had a strange awareness of a power leaving him, a presence he had not realized was there. He sensed a mission accomplished, balance restored. All things were now in their rightful places.

Regina was unresponsive when he spoke to her. Physically she seemed unharmed. Hatch was not worried about her, for somehow he knew that none of them would suffer unduly for having been caught up in . . . whatever they had been caught up in.

Lindsey was unconscious and bleeding. He examined her wound and felt it was not too serious.

Voices arose two floors above. They were calling his name. The authorities had arrived. Late as always. Well, not always. Sometimes . . . one of them was there just when you needed him.

3 The apocryphal story of the three blind men examining the elephant is widely known. The first blind man feels only the elephant's trunk and thereafter confidently describes the beast as a great snakelike creature, similar to a python. The second blind man feels only the elephant's ears and announces that it is a bird that can soar to great heights. The third blind man examines only the elephant's fringe-tipped, fly-chasing tail and "sees" an animal that is curiously like a bottle brush.

So it is with any experience that human beings share. Each participant perceives it in a different way and takes from it a different lesson than do his or her compatriots.

IN THE YEARS following the events at the abandoned amusement park, Jonas Nyebern lost interest in resuscitation medicine. Other men took over his work and did it well.

He sold at auction every piece of religious art in the two collections that he had not yet completed, and he put the money in savings instruments that would return the highest possible rate of interest.

Though he continued to practice cardiovascular surgery for a while, he no longer found any satisfaction in it. Eventually he retired young and looked for a new career in which to finish out the last decades of his life.

He stopped attending Mass. He no longer believed that evil was a force in itself, a real presence that walked the world. He had learned that humanity itself was a source of evil sufficient to explain everything that was wrong with the world. Obversely, he decided humanity was its own—and only—salvation.

He became a veterinarian. Every patient seemed deserving.

He never married again.

He was neither happy nor unhappy, and that suited him fine.

REGINA REMAINED WITHIN her inner room for a couple of days, and when she came out she was never quite the same. But then no one ever is quite the same for any length of time. Change is the only constant. It's called growing up.

She addressed them as Dad and Mom, because she wanted to, and because she meant it. Day by day, she gave them as much happiness as they gave her.

She never set off a chain reaction of destruction among their antiques. She never embarrassed them by getting inappropriately sentimental, bursting into tears, and thereby activating the old snot faucet; she unfailingly produced tears and snot only when they were called for. She never mortified them by accidentally flipping an entire plate of food into the air at a restaurant and over the head of the President of the United States at the next table. She never accidentally set the house on fire, never farted in polite company, and never scared the bejesus out of smaller neighborhood children with her leg brace and curious right hand. Better still, she stopped worrying about doing all those things (and more), and in time she did not even recall the tremendous energies that she once had wasted upon such unlikely concerns.

She kept writing. She got better at it. When she was just fourteen, she won a national writing competition for teenagers. The prize was a rather nice watch and a check for five hundred dollars. She used some of the money for a subscription to *Publishers Weekly* and a complete set of the novels of William Makepeace Thackeray. She no longer had an interest in writing about intelligent pigs from outer space, largely because she was learning that more curious characters could be found all around her, many of them native Californians.

She no longer talked to God. It seemed childish to chatter at Him. Besides, she no longer needed His constant attention. For a while she had thought He had gone away or had never existed, but she had decided that was foolish. She was aware of Him all the time, winking at her from the flowers, serenading her in the song of a bird, smiling at her from the furry face of a kitten, touching her with a soft summer breeze. She found a line in a book that she thought was apt, from Dave Tyson Gentry: "True friendship comes when silence between two people is comfortable." Well, who was your best friend, if not God, and what did you really need to say to Him or He to you when you both already knew the most—and only—important thing, which was that you would always be there for each other.

LINDSEY CAME THROUGH the events of those days less changed than she had expected. Her paintings improved somewhat, but not tremendously. She had never been dissatisfied with her work in the first place. She loved Hatch no less than ever, and could not possibly have loved him more.

One thing that made her cringe, which never had before, was hearing anyone say, "The worst is behind us now." She knew that the worst was never behind us. The worst came at the end. It *was* the end, the very fact of it. Nothing could be worse than that. But she had learned to live with the understanding that the worst was never behind her—and still find joy in the day at hand.

As for God—she didn't dwell on the issue. She raised Regina in the Catholic Church, attending Mass with her each week, for that was part of the promise she had made St. Thomas's when they had arranged the adoption. But she didn't do it solely out of duty. She figured that the Church was good for Regina—and that Regina might be good for the Church, too. Any institution that counted Regina a member was going to discover itself changed by her at least as much as she was changed—and to its everlasting benefit. She had once said that prayers were never answered, that the living lived only to die, but she had progressed beyond that attitude. She would wait and see.

HATCH CONTINUED TO deal successfully in antiques. Day by day his life went pretty much as he hoped it would. As before, he was an easy-going guy. He never got angry. But the difference was that he had no anger left in him to repress. The mellowness was genuine now.

From time to time, when the patterns of life seemed to have a grand meaning that just barely eluded him, and when he was therefore in a philosophical mood, he would go to his den and take two items from the locked drawer.

One was the heat-browned issue of *Arts American*.

The other was a slip of paper he had brought back from the library one day, after doing a bit of research. Two names were written on it, with an identifying line after each. "Vassago—according to mythology, one of the nine crown princes of Hell." Below that was the name he had once claimed was his own: "Uriel—according to mythology, one of the archangels serving as a personal attendant to God."

He stared at these things and considered them carefully, and always he reached no firm conclusions. Though he did decide, if you had to be dead for eighty minutes and come back with no memory of the Other Side, maybe it was because eighty minutes of that knowledge was more than just a glimpse of a tunnel with a light at the end, and therefore more than you could be expected to handle.

And if you had to bring something back with you from Beyond, and carry it within you until it had concluded its assignment on this side of the veil, an archangel wasn't too shabby.